T3-BHN-453

RULES OF SURVIVAL

Books by Kristine Smith

CODE OF CONDUCT
RULES OF CONFLICT
LAW OF SURVIVAl
CONTACT IMMINENT
ENDGAME

KRISTINE SMITH

RULES OF SURVIVAL

The Chronicles of Jani Killian

This is a work of fiction. All of the characters, organizations and events portrayed in this novel are either products of the author's imagination or are used fictitiously and are not to be construed as real. Any resemblance to actual events, locales, organizations, or persons, living or dead, is entirely coincidental.

Publication History: Avon Eos mass market paperback, November 1999

Publication History: Eos mass market paperback, September 2000

Publication History: Eos mass market paperback, October 2001

First SFBC Science Fiction Printing: October 2007

Published by arrangement with
Eos
An Imprint of HarperCollins *Publishers*
10 East 53rd Street
New York, NY 10022-5299

Visit The SFBC online at http://www.sfbc.com

ISBN 978-0-7394-8916-1

Printed in the United States of America.

Contents

CODE OF CONDUCT

Acknowledgments

A first book is usually the most difficult to write, firstly, because you're still trying to find your sea legs, and secondly, because you've no assurance whatsoever that what you've spent years producing will go anywhere other than a box in the cellar.

I've been lucky enough to have had help from many people in assisting me through the difficulties. In particular, I'd like to thank Katharine Eliska Kimbriel, who helped keep me on track, and my parents, Gordon and Charlotte Smith, whose love and support helped keep me going.

The visible aspects of the condition, it is believed, first manifested themselves during a stressful period in the patient's life. Therefore, the mild agitation that commonly precedes the acute phase, although evident, was easily ascribable to the patient's augmentation or other, more mundane, causes.

—Internal Communication, Neoclona/Seattle,
Shroud, J., Parini, V., concerning Patient S-1

CHAPTER 1

The frigid morning dampness seeped through Jani's weatherall as she hurried out of the charge lot. She jammed the notes from her crack-of-dawn meeting into the side pocket of her duffel; as she did, she quickly surveyed the scene behind her. Rain-slick skimmers hovered beside boxy charge stations. Trickle-charge lights glimmered like distant stars. A single streetlight bathed everything in a cold blue sheen. No movement in the ice-light. No sound.

Jani took a step. Stopped. She could feel eyes follow her, could sense their probing like a skin-crawl across her shoulders. She turned.

A few meters away, a feral cat regarded her from its perch atop a discarded shipping crate. It stared at her for a few moments, then poured to the ground and vanished into an alley. Seconds later, Jani heard the scatter of garbage, followed by a strangled squeak.

Sounds familiar. The poor mouse. It probably never knew what hit it. Jani could sympathize. Her meeting had gone much the same way.

It's like everyone's forgotten Whalen's Planet exists, girly. Commercial traffic at the docks is down sixty percent in the last two weeks. That's six-oh.

She trotted down a side street that led to the main thoroughfare. Her right knee locked as she turned the corner, and she stumbled against a pair of mutually supportive inebriates who had emerged from one of NorthPort's many bars.

One of the drunks shouted as Jani disentangled herself and hurried away. Something about how her limp made her ass wiggle. She looked over her shoulder, caught glimpses of brightly colored ship patches and a slack-jawed leer. She felt the heat creep up her neck and kept moving.

She entered the lobby of a hostel that catered to merchant-fleet officers, tossing a wave to the desk clerk as she hurried to the holoVee alcove. Several employees already sat on the floor in front of the display screen, their positions carefully gauged to allow them a clear view of the front desk.

On the lookout for the manager. Jani kept quiet until she entered within range of the holoVee's soundshielding. She knew an unauthorized break when she saw one. "Is this it?"

One of the cleaners nodded. "Hi, Cory," she said without looking up. "It's the CapNet broadcast. It's just getting started."

Jani did a quick mental roll call of the small group, counting faces, uniforms. She didn't know their names—she tried to avoid the complication of names whenever possible. "Where's the garage guy?"

"He's still out sick," the cleaner said. "Should be back tomorrow. He'll be mad he missed this." The young woman grinned. "I'll tell him you asked about him. He thinks you jam."

Jani responded with her "Cory" smile. Quiet. Closed. A smile whose owner would blush and keep walking. She leaned against a planter and surveyed with satisfaction the lack of fuss that greeted her arrival. Yes, Cory Sato, documents technician, had settled quite nicely in NorthPort over the last six months. Jani Kilian had never seemed farther away.

Until her morning meeting.

Business has dropped over the side these past two weeks, girly. NUVA-SCAN annex won't answer our calls. Even the Haárin are complaining. But you wouldn't know anything about that, would you?

An overwrought voice interrupted Jani's troubled meditation. "A great honor is being paid the Commonwealth," the CapNet reporter gushed, "opening a new and exciting chapter in human-idomeni relations!"

Spoken like someone who has no idea what she's talking about, Jani thought as she watched members of the Commonwealth Cabinet walk out onto the sheltered stage that had been erected in front of the Prime Minister's palatial Main House. Steam puffed from their mouths. A few of the coatless ministers shivered in their formal, color-coded uniforms. Chicago in winter looked even less hospitable than NorthPort, if that was possible.

Treasury Minister Abascal, ever-flushed face glowing in lurid contrast to his gold tunic, trundled to the podium "to say a few words."

"Where's the ambassador?" someone grumbled.

"He doesn't come out till later—you want the poor old bastard to freeze to death?"

"Never get to see him at this rate." One of the day-shift waiters checked his timepiece. "All fourteen ministers gonna talk—it'll be hours."

"Not all fourteen," said the restaurant hostess. "Van Reuter's not there."

Really? Jani studied the rows of faces, looking for the one she knew. Had known. Long ago. "Too bad," she said. "He's the best speaker of the bunch."

"You like him?" The waiter glanced at Jani over his shoulder and sneered. "He's a Family boy nance."

"He knows the idomeni," Jani replied. "That's more than you can say for the rest of them."

"You don't see him much since his wife died," the hostess said. "Poor man."

"You hear about him, though," the waiter muttered. "Nance."

On-screen, Abascal finished to scattered applause and gave way to Commerce Minister al-Muhammed. Jani leaned forward, straining to hear the commentary over the buzz of multiple conversations. Commerce controlled trade and transport schedules—maybe something al-Muhammed said would shed light on the slowdown around Whalen.

"Is al-Muhammed the 'A' in NUVA or the 'A' in SCAN?" someone piped, drowning out the minister's voice.

Oh blow! Jani shouldered her bag and walked through the middle of the huddle. "Al-Muhammed's the 'A' in SCAN," she said, bumping the speaker in the back of his head with her knee.

"He's another nance," griped the waiter.

"Cory, I thought you wanted to see this," someone called after her. "You'll miss the ambassador."

"I have to go. I'll catch it somewhere else." Somewhere quieter. She should have known better than to try to watch the program with others. Some things needed to be studied in private. Pondered. Mulled.

We've officially reopened relations with the idomeni. Jani rubbed her stomach, which had begun to ache. *Wonderful.* She walked past buildings of black-and-yellow thermal scan-brick toward NorthPort's Government Hall. The elegant twelve-story edifice loomed over all like a stern but forgiving patriarch, offering numerous types of guidance to his wayward children. Audit assistance from External Revenue Outreach. Documents counseling from the Commerce and Treasury Ministry annexes. By all appearances, family relations appeared very close.

Appearances, as the old saying went, could be deceiving.

Why you always hang about with the nances at Guv Hall, girly? What goes on there so interesting you need to see it every day?

She increased her pace as she headed out of the business district, monitoring her stride in shop windows and mirror-glazed brick. She had only become aware of the hitch in her walk over the past couple of months, and had attributed it to a combination of the NorthPort weather and a cheap mattress.

Among other things. Jani took a step. *Right foot down.* Another. *Left foot . . . down.* She had to assume that. She hadn't much sensation in her left leg. Or her left arm. The lack of feeling sometimes made quick movement an adventure, but she maneuvered pretty well for a half-animandroid patch job. *And my ass does not wiggle*—she glanced at her reflection—*not much, anyway.*

Block after block fell behind as she tried to walk off her growing apprehension. She passed warehouses, long-term skimmer charge lots, then a three-hundred-meter stretch of sand and scrub before coming to the houses.

The facades of the one- and two-story polystone homes would have appeared familiar to most humans, but a careful observer would have noticed the subtle alterations. Smaller, fewer windows. No doors opening out to the street. Blank walls facing the human side of town. *For humanish ways are strange ways, and godly idomeni avert their eyes.*

The low clouds opened. Cold rain splattered down. Jani yanked the hood of her weatherall up over her head, but not before looking around to see if she was being observed. She wouldn't be welcomed here. The made-sect Haárin, like their more disciplined born-sect counterparts, preferred that their humanish neighbors keep their distance.

Except when it comes to business. The Haárin were nonviolent criminals and other idomeni social anomalies, their manufactured sect the pit into which the born-sects dumped their misfits. Even though Jani understood the Haárin better than most, she still couldn't be sure whether they settled on human worlds because they enjoyed aggravating their governing Council or because they actually liked the neighborhood. They definitely enjoyed learning concepts like float-rebound accounting. They liked dealing, and possessed a disrespect for Commonwealth rules and regs that was almost colonial in its fervor.

They're probably all at the gathering hall, waiting for Tsecha's speech. The reopening of formal diplomatic relations between the Commonwealth and the Shèrá worldskein, and the subsequent reevaluation of trade and taxation laws, concerned them as much as it did Jani's bosses in the Merchants' Association.

I foresee busy times ahead for documents technicians. Jani squinted as the rain pelted harder and thick fog wended around homes and down the empty street. Then a shadowed movement in the murky distance caught her eye; her stomach clenched as it always did when she saw a NorthPort Haárin. Their born-sect forebears had been Vynshàrau and Pathen, and the strains had remained undiluted. The approaching Haárin was rope-muscled, slender, and two meters tall. His yellow-orange skin, which screamed *jaundice* to humans, in idomeni reality marked the races that originated in Shèrá's desert regions.

It's only Genta. Jani's anxiety subsided. The shuttle dealer walked toward her with long, loose-limbed strides. His dark green overrobe clung wetly to his matching belted shirt and trousers, the hem catching on the fasteners of his knee-high boots. Clothing drenched, fine brown hair plastered to his scalp, the Haárin appeared completely at ease. With his narrow shoulders, age-grooved jowls, and wide-spaced yellow eyes, he bore more than a passing resemblance to a bored cheetah.

"Nìa Chaw-ree." Genta crossed an arm over his chest in greeting. His right arm, palm facing inward. A sign of regard, if not respect. "You ar-re noth ath a holoVee, watching speeches? That is wher-re all idomeni ar-re, watching speeches." The English words tumbled from barely moving lips, all trilled r's and fuzzed hard consonants. "Insthead, you ar-re her-re in the rain."

"Yes, ní Genta—I don't like speeches," Jani replied as she returned Genta's greeting gesture. *And I have some nerves to walk off.* But a Haárin wouldn't know a nerve if it reared up and bit him in the ass, so no use mentioning that. "Why aren't you in the gathering hall? Tsecha's born Vynshàrau—they've always been friends of Haárin. You might like what he has to say."

Genta held a spindle-fingered hand to his face and brushed water from his hairless cheeks. His stare pierced Jani. She, of all people, should have been used to it by now, but the direct gaze of idomeni eyes, dark irises surrounded by more lightly colored sclera, could still disconcert. Looking strangers in the eye was taboo for all born-sect idomeni, but the NorthPort Haárin were adopting the custom as a matter of good business. The fact that it rattled the hell out of most humans had nothing to do with it. Of course not.

"I did not wait for Vynshàrau to tell me to live with humanish," Genta said, "and I do not need what Vynshàrau says now to work with humanish." Like all his fellow world-men, he became much more intelligible when he had a point to make. "NìRau Tsecha is not for Haárin. He is not for Vynshàrau, or even for idomeni. He is for something *here*"—he thumped the middle of his stomach, where most idomeni believed the soul resided— "and to fight for such does not extend GateWay rights or alter contract law." With a distracted gesture of departure, he started back down the street.

"It will be bad for business," he continued, his rumbling voice deadened by the fog. "Bad, as it was before. Even now it starts—where are all the ships these past weeks? No good can come from this. No good." With that, Genta disappeared into the swallowing mist, leaving Jani alone in the rain.

Eventually, she returned to the human side of town. She wandered from storefront to storefront, finally joining a small crowd that had gathered in front of a communications shop. Every holoVee screen in the window contained the image of Prime Minister Cao.

"And now, fellow ministers, distinguished guests, ladies and gentlemen," Cao paused, drawing out the moment, "it is my honor and my privilege to introduce His Excellency, ambassador of the Shèrá worldskein, of the Vynshàrau and of all idomeni peoples—"

"Sects," Jani muttered.

"—Ègri nìRau Tsecha." Cao looked off to the side and extended her arm. "Excellency!"

Jani sensed the tension around her as, on the screen, a familiar face came into view. Familiar not because of the Genta-like skin tone, the same gold eyes and long, straight nose, but because of something deeper, something older. She felt wet cold wind brush her face and imagined it drier, hotter. Instead of damp mingled with the acid bitterness of skimmer cells, the sweet odor of lamptree blooms filled the air. The crowd surrounding her towered above her, wore flowing overrobes, and spoke in lilting rises and falls.

Eighteen years ago, in the godly capital of Rauta Shèràa, when we both were known by the names we'd been born with—

"Dear-rest fr-riends—"

—I almost got you killed, didn't I, nìRau?

"—it has been too long."

The recorded audience exploded into applause as the ambassador raised his right hand above his head in a subservient greeting. The red stone in his ring of station flashed reflected daylight like a small warning light. As the clapping died, Tsecha bowed his head and continued his speech in High Vynshàrau.

Jani positioned herself so that the crowd blocked the subtitles. She watched Tsecha's posture and gestures, the sweep and flourish of the highly choreographed language, and intuited meaning the way a musician discerned note, tone, and tempo. It had taken her seven years to develop the skill; pride and respect for the language prevented her from playing ignorant and covering it up. The Haárin had noticed her ability soon after she'd arrived in NorthPort. Whenever their trade council experienced a communications breakdown with the Whalen's Planet Merchants' Association, they always contacted Cory Sato to help resolve it, a fact that only helped worsen her relationship with her bosses.

Jani flinched as the woman next to her pointed to the news-screen. "It's so beautiful! That language. Those gestures. Like a kind of dancing!"

A man in a dockworker's coverall shook his head firmly. "Don't trust them. None of them, not even the ones we got here." He gestured in the direction of the Haárin enclave. "Sneaky bastards. Don't see none of 'em here, do you? No, they gotta shut themselves away all private."

"Tsecha's the Pathen Haárin's religious as well as secular leader," the woman said. "They're required to gather together in their meeting hall to listen to him. Then afterwards, they'll pray."

Jani nodded in agreement. Genta had, in fact, committed a serious breach of order by not attending the program. But even the most humanish-behaving idomeni felt that acting one way while believing another was disorderly; Genta's cultural conditioning prevented him from hiding his displeasure with his ambassador. Likewise, his council's action against him would be very public, and very swift. *If his delivery contracts are canceled, the MA will explode.* And she would be dragged in to ladle oil over the whitecaps, sure as hell—

"Them and their prayers." The dockworker glared at Tsecha's image. "Everything's a damned prayer. Even their damned meals. Say it's their religion, but whoever heard of a religion where it's a sin to eat in public? With friends. Like normal."

The woman frowned at him. "Eating's different for them. They store food very carefully and keep records of where it comes from. They call their meals *sacraments* and their cooks *priests*. They eat by themselves and pray the whole time. Very ceremonial. Very precise." She nodded knowingly. "That's how they honor their gods."

"The Haárin honor money more than gods," another man said. "You can buy some of their blessed sacrament if you really want it." He grimaced. "Don't know why you would, though. They season their food like to blow the top of your head off. Even the sweet stuff."

"Sacraments." The dockworker snorted. "Bunch of creeps. Talk like they got marbles in their mouths, look at you like you're dirt." He walked away, his expression stony. "Didn't need any damned ambassadors for almost twenty years. Why now?"

Interesting question, sir—I've pondered it myself the past few weeks. Jani cast a last look toward the screen, taking note of the ministers sharing the stage with Tsecha. Every face wore a broad smile. Well, those expressions would be wiped out soon enough when they realized what they'd let themselves in for. At least this time she'd be far enough away to avoid shrapnel. For once in her screwed-up life, she'd stationed herself, as her mainline Service buddies used to say, well back of the front.

The rain had turned to mist. Time to head back to the Association tracking station she called home. Jani hurried in the direction of the lot where her skimmer sat charging, picking up her pace even though her back had begun to ache. Her bosses would soon be screaming for the official morning docking numbers. She couldn't afford to piss them off any more.

A shout sounded from behind. The pound of running feet. Jani's heart raced. Her breath caught in her throat. Then chill calm washed over her, like an old friend resting a hand on her shoulder. She reached into the inner pocket of her duffel. Her hand closed around the grip of her old Service shooter. She turned, only to see the desk clerk from the hostel racing toward her.

"Jeez, Cory, wake up!" The young man slowed to a gasping halt. "I need—to talk to you."

Jani withdrew her empty hand from the duffel and tried to smile.

"Boy, you look wrecked." The clerk's voice dropped to a whisper. "You get those old farts you work for through that audit ok?"

"As always," Jani replied.

"You know"—he leaned closer—"there's a doe here from SouthPort Consolidated. Jammin' blonde. She's looking for doc techs. Pass her exam, she's offering Registry-level jobs."

"So?"

The clerk rolled his eyes. "*You*, dummy! You're the talk of the Merchants', my manager says. All the paper you vet is so clean, it squeaks. Six months on the job, not one observation from Guv Hall. My manager calls it a miracle."

My bosses call it something else. Jani's smile faded. The word "verifier" hadn't been said aloud at this morning's meeting, but the mute accusation had hung heavy in the air. *Government spy. They think I'm a government spy.*

If they only knew.

Jani glanced down the street, where the crowd still gathered in front of the communications shop. "I'll think about it."

The clerk sighed. "Yeah, well, don't think too long. She's checking out tonight." He shook his head. "Registry-level jobs. Just think. Exterior Ministry on Amsun. Maybe even Earth!" He punched Jani's arm. "Registry—that's the top of the tree!"

I know all about the Registry, child—my name resides in a very prominent place in that epic tome. "Thanks for the word," Jani said. "I'll give it all due consideration." She left the clerk to argue with her retreating back and ducked into the alley she always used to reach the charge lot. Then her stomach grumbled, and she tried to recall what waited at home in her cooler. *Cold air—damn, I need to buy food.* And all the decent shops were in the opposite direction.

Jani hurried out of the alley, slid to a stop, and scurried back into the shelter of a doorway. The desk clerk was talking to an attractive blonde. His new contact from SouthPort Consolidated, Jani assumed. Try as she might, she couldn't recall ever seeing that company name on any shipping logs that had passed through her hands.

Jani studied the woman's neat hair and stylish clothes, both several GateWays removed from the best SouthPort had to offer. She watched as the desk clerk nodded, then pointed in the direction of the alley.

She backed down the passageway, her sore back protesting every stride. When she reached the other end, she looked up and down the street, ducking into the shadows as a passenger skimmer drifted by. She listened, until she heard only faraway street sounds and knew for certain that she was alone. Then she ran.

CHAPTER 2

Scrub and sand blurred past as Jani concentrated on the approaching tracking station. The squat building sat like an overturned bowl in the middle of the plain, its safety beacon shining gamely through the fog.

The steadying hand on her shoulder returned as the calmness reasserted itself. A survival checklist formed in her mind. What she had to do, how quickly, and how thoroughly. She hadn't always been that organized. The Service had literally drilled it into her head. Augmentation. The implants in her brain that had, at least officially, made her a soldier. Jani resented augie when she didn't need it, but gripped it like a life preserver now. As she neared the station, it kept her focused, compelled her to watch the shallow recesses in the dome, the dark shadows where someone could hide.

She circled the small dome twice before she edged the skimmer into its charge slot. Shooter at the ready, she carded through the station's two sets of doors and scanned the cell-like single room. Finding nothing out of place, she set the weapon on standby and tucked it into the belt of her coverall. Working with speed born of habit and dispassion born of chemistry, she packed her few clothes into her small duffel. Then she stripped the bed and bath area, feeding the flimsy sheets and towels into the trashzap. The volume of material overwhelmed the unit's filter, the odor of burnt cloth filled the room.

Jani rummaged through one of the side compartments of her duffel and carefully withdrew the small Naxin bomb. After the protein digester did its work, no trace of her presence, no hair, skin cell, or fingerprint, would remain. A second bomb nestled in her bag. She would use it on the skimmer after she reached the shuttleport.

Jani checked her timepiece. Shuttles to the NorthPort docks

departed every half hour, but with the slowdown, there was no guarantee they'd follow their normal schedule. She sat on the narrow bed, bomb in hand. If this all turned out to be nothing, there would be hell to pay. Naxin lingered like bad memories—the station would require a thorough decontamination. Expensive decontamination. *In other words, kiss this job good-bye.*

But who knew? Maybe the desk clerk's friend with the Registry job would come to her aid. Jani smiled sadly. Who could guess the offer of a Registry job would hold enough attraction to make her drop her carefully maintained guard?

Someone who knew her well.

And who knows you that well, Captain Kilian?

She broke the seal on the protein bomb, set it on the mattress, and hurried toward the door. Within seconds, the device's outer housing would split, releasing a steady yellow stream of digestive mist.

Just as the door swept open, the station's proximity alarm activated. "Skimmer approaching from north-northwest," the tinny voice entoned. "Speed sixty-five kilometers per hour. Single occupant. Estimated time of arrival two minutes."

Jani looked back at the bed. The protein bomb emitted a sound like cracking ice, releasing the first puffs of corrosive fog. Too late to hurl it out the door. A few good pulls of Naxin would turn her lungs to soup.

She let the station's inner door close behind her, backed against the narrow entryway wall, and forced the outer door to remain closed by pushing with her left foot against its raised metal frame. Then she reached up and shattered the casing of the overhead light with the grip of her shooter, plunging the small space into darkness. In the meantime, the barest whiff of Naxin had worked its way through the gaps in the inner door seal. Jani closed her eyes against the stinging mist and stifled a cough.

The alarm spoke again. "Approach is made."

She activated her shooter. After her visitor made a few attempts to force the door, she'd pull her foot away. Allow the door to open. Then wait for that first tentative step forward into the dark.

Oblique line of fire—aim for the head.

Jani heard the crunch of footsteps, a plastic click as someone inserted a card into the reader, silence as the jammed door forced the reader to deny access. Again, the click of the card. Once more, nothing.

"Damn her!"

That voice. Jani tensed as the outer door shook under the force of banging knocks.

"Jani! It's Evan! Please let me in!" A pause. "I'm alone." Softer. "Please."

Her calm cracked like the bomb housing. *Oh God! Not him!* She tightened her grip on her weapon. *They wouldn't let him come here alone.* Evan. Van Reuter. The Commonwealth Interior Minister. No security officer worth a damn would have allowed him to wander unescorted on any colony. His face had been plastered on the cover of every newssheet for weeks—even the most info-starved transport jockey would recognize him.

"Jani? Jani?" The banging resumed, louder, more insistent. The air in the tiny space shook with the noise. *"I know you're in there! Talk to me!"*

More Naxin had seeped into the enclosure, choking Jani's breath away as she tried to inhale. Her eyes burned. The skin of her face felt hot. She pulled her foot away from the door. It slid open, but she remained back in the shadows, letting the cold air pour over her.

At first, nothing. Then Evan van Reuter stepped forward. Almost twenty years had passed since Jani had seen that tall, slim form, that tilt of the head. Not as much of a stomach-clench as with the Haárin. Not quite. "Should I curtsy, Excellency?" she asked as she stepped out of the doorway, forcing him to backpedal.

"Jani?" He stared at her, broad brow furrowed in confusion. "Is that you?" Then his gaze fell on her shooter. Thin lips tensed in a tight line. Dark, hooded eyes narrowed. Jani could hear his thoughts as though he spoke them out loud. After so long, he was unsure of her. She almost felt flattered.

"It's really me, Evan." She disengaged the power pack and shoved her inactivated weapon into her duffel.

Evan thrust his hands into the pockets of his Interior field coat. The hem of the heavy black garment flapped around his knees as the wind howled. "I need to talk to you. It's important. But it's freezing out here! Can't we go inside?"

Jani shook her head. She felt the augmentation leach away, leaving vague edginess in its place. She held up her right hand and watched it shake. "Can't. Bombed it."

"Well, at least we can get out of this damned wind!" Evan grabbed her arm and pulled her after him behind the small building. There, a sleek black sedan hovered shadowlike beside her battered single-seater.

He yanked open the sedan's gullwing and pushed Jani into the passenger seat. The heavy door closed over her with a solid *thunk*. Black trueleather cushions, soft as butter, sensed her chill and grew warm.

Evan got in beside her and pulled his door closed. "God, how can you live here!" He dug under his seat, came up first with a large thermoflask, then two polished metal cups.

He thrust one of the cups into Jani's hand and filled it. The weighty aromas of chocolate and fresh coffee flooded the cabin. Despite her nerves, her mouth watered—she hadn't tasted truebean in years. She drained her cup with childlike greed.

"Jani? For cry—you want more?" Evan held out the thermoflask, then hesitated. "What's wrong with your face? It's all red."

She felt her cheek. Despite exposure to cold wind and rain, the skin felt dry and hot. "Naxin exposure. It's like sunburn. I'll be fine."

"I have to get you to a doctor—"

"I'll be *fine*."

Evan retreated slowly. "And to think I thought this would be the easy part, after what I went through to find you." He set his cup in a niche in the dash and dug through his coat pockets. "I had nothing to go on. Your file's been buried. All I had was your canceled lieutenant's ID, the one you gave me after your promotion to captain. I had copies made, sent out to my people."

"Like your blonde from SouthPort Consolidated?" Jani slumped in her seat and felt the ergoworks vibrate in their efforts to support her properly. "Why that hostel? Why the hell did I have to run into *that* hostel?"

"I had people all over NorthPort," Evan said as he searched. "SouthPort, too. The docks. I had no intention of letting you slip away." He pulled a tiny slipcase from the inside pocket of his coat. "My blonde came back and told me they had found a likely suspect. You, of course. Only problem was, you didn't look like the holo. But she did say the Haárin liked you, you were damned good at your job, and the people you worked for couldn't figure you out. That sounded familiar." He removed a card from the slipcase and handed it to Jani. "The crash changed things, I guess."

Jani avoided looking at the ID at first, then grim fascination got the better of her. She took the card from Evan and stared at the image that smirked back.

Her hair had been longer then. A stick-straight, collar-grazing pageboy, rather than the scalp-hugging cap of waves she now bore, framed a rounder, less angular face. Fringed bangs accentuated thicker eyebrows, an upward-curving nose.

Jani ran a finger along her current arched bridge. Her coloring hadn't changed, though. Hair thick and black, then as now. Skin still light brown. Eyes . . . still green.

Well, they are—I just don't show them to company. The black color filming she'd applied the previous day felt scratchy in the dry air of the skimmer cabin. She restrained the urge to rub her eyes and refocused on her image. Yellow lieutenant's bars imprinted with tiny silver *D*s shone from the sides of her steel blue banded collar. Sideline yellow. Sideline Service. Not the real thing, her mainline buddies had stressed to her repeatedly. Real lieutenants, *mainline* lieutenants, had red bars. She was a documents examiner. Ineligible for command school. Banned from combat training. Not a real soldier.

Let us sing a song of real soldiers. Jani tossed the ID back in Evan's lap. "Too little-girly, don't you think?"

Evan grabbed the card before it slid to the floor, polishing the places where his fingers had smudged the surface. "I always liked it," he muttered defensively as he tucked it gently back into the slipcase and returned it to his pocket.

A few fidgety moments passed. Jani toyed with her empty cup. "I didn't see you on the welcoming committee." She shrugged at Evan's puzzled frown. "That thing for Tsecha. They broadcast the holoVee show here today, but it happened over six weeks ago. Takes about that long to get here from Earth."

"Jani—"

"Even sooner, when you can clear the nav paths by invoking ministerial privilege. What are you doing here?"

Evan tapped a thumb against the skimmer's steering wheel. He'd worked off his coat, revealing the dress-down Interior uniform of loose-fitting black tunic tucked into dark grey trousers. His profile, backlit by the skimmer cabin's subdued lighting, now resembled his late father's in a way Jani would never have thought possible years before. *From Acton to Evan—the van Reuter hawk lives.* Closely clipped dark brown hair accentuated his cheekbone, the curve of his long jaw, the line of his neck. *What I used to do to that neck.*

Correction, what the girl in the ID used to do to that neck.

Evan sipped his coffee. "The reason I didn't attend the welcoming ceremony for the ambassador," he said quietly, "is because the PM requested I stay away."

"That makes no sense. You knew Tsecha when we were stationed in Rauta Shèràa. You're the only minister who can claim that. Doesn't Cao realize how valuable that experience is?"

Evan smiled grimly. "Thanks for the vote of confidence. I'll add you to my list of supporters. There's plenty of room—it's shrinking as we speak." He watched the storm rage outside. "How much have you heard out here about my wife's death?"

"We heard what we were told," Jani said. Every aspect picked over in sickening detail. Tsecha's welcoming was the first program she had watched in the four months since. "Lyssa died at the spa on Chira."

"An accident?"

"With mitigating circumstances. Hints she'd been ill." Jani hesitated. "Later, there were rumors she'd been drinking, doping. She tried to hop the road skimmer she was driving over a narrow gorge. Road skimmers don't hop. She lost control, flipped into a rock formation." She remembered the OC-Net cut-in, the crumpled skimmer, and the reporter running his hands over the rocks in question with the bright-eyed wonder of someone who had never seen a person die.

"Any—" Evan's voice cracked. He pulled the thermoflask from beneath the seat and refilled both their cups. "Any speculation that I could have been involved?"

Jani studied the side of Evan's face. Only the way his jaw muscle worked indicated the tension he otherwise managed to hide. "No. Why would there be?"

"There have been rumors, damning enough for the Cabinet to initiate a Court of Inquiry. That's why Cao asked me to stay away. Because things are so touchy. Our relations with the idomeni. Earth's relations with the colonies. Our colonies butting heads with the idomeni colonies. Does the term 'vicious circle' mean anything to you?" Evan's hand moved to his throat. "Cao's trying to use it like a noose around my neck. She and her old school friend, Exterior Minister Ulanova. I don't agree with the way they do business. They want me gone."

"You once told me the occasional purge is a fact of political life."

"I don't possess the edge I used to, Jan. My wife is dead. Our children died years ago. I stink of death. It drives people away. People I thought I could count on." The rain had intensified, sluicing down the windows as though they sat beneath a waterfall. "The knives are out for me this time. I can't fight alone."

Jani watched the rain. The statement that Evan was only forty-two, that he'd live to fight another day, remarry and father his own Cabinet if he so desired, didn't seem appropriate. Death altered that scenario. It raised imposing questions. Questions of coping, closure, setting the record straight. *And I know all about that, don't I?*

She heard Evan stir beside her.

"I believe Lyssa was murdered, too, you see," he said. "I think since we're on speaking terms with the idomeni again, someone wants me out of the picture. That's why I need a friend." He reached out to her, his hand hovering above hers without touching. "A friend who can find out what happened."

"You want to take me back to Earth with you?"

"I need your help, Jan. I need a friend who knows me, knows the idomeni, and knows where the bones are buried."

I buried some of those bones, Jani thought as she watched Evan's hand. It shook. Very slightly. Did she make him that nervous? Or was he in that much trouble?

"I know what we had didn't end well," he said as he let his hand rest on the seat near her knee. "Do you hold a grudge?"

"No."

"I didn't think so. You're not the type. You follow your own rules, your own code. You're tough, but you're fair."

"You haven't known me for a long time. I may have changed."

Evan continued as though she hadn't spoken. "For my part, I'd show how much I trust you by placing my career in your hands. All I ask is that, as events warrant, you proceed with caution."

"That would be a first for me, don't you think?" Jani studied her distorted reflection in her cup's polished surface. "You really want to take me back to Earth?"

"You have to go somewhere. My blonde mentioned I blew your situation here."

" 'Blew' doesn't begin to describe it. The Merchants' Association blames me for your traffic slowdown. They think *I'm* a verifier. I'm probably being watched. If I returned to NorthPort after being seen with you, I'd be dead by nightfall."

"So, you need to get out of here." Evan's voice sounded stronger, surer. That made sense. He was negotiating now. "Ok, I'll get you out of here. Where do you want to go?"

"I don't know."

"Then what's wrong with Earth?" He counted on his fingers. "Look, we pass through four GateWays on the way. Amsun, Padishah, Felix, and Mars. If you change your mind on the way, I'll give you whatever you need and let you go." He leaned toward her, his voice coldly eager.

"But if you had a chance to work at a job that utilized your training, realized you could live a different life, wouldn't it make sense to stick with me? Look around you, Jan." He gestured toward the storm-whipped scenery. "You don't belong here. You deserve a second chance. Officially, sure, the Service is still looking for you, but unofficially?" He shook his head. "They think you're dead. You can reinvent yourself any way you want, and I'm offering you the opportunity to do just that."

"If I work for you?"

"If you find out what happened to Lyssa. Call it working for me if you want. Call it anything."

"You could be the bait in a Service trap. Why should I trust you?"

"Well, if what you told me about your popularity in NorthPort is true, you'd better trust me at least as far as Amsun." He raised his cup to her in a toast. "What choice do you have?"

What choice, indeed? Jani stared into her cup. Then she drained it and handed it back to him. "You know, some old Service officer once said that if you fall back far enough, you'll just wind up at the front again." She pulled the second Naxin bomb from her duffel and punched a fingernail through the sealant coating. Popping up her door, she darted into the rain, pulled open the door of the single-seater, tossed the bomb inside, slammed the door, and closed herself back in the sedan before the first wisps of Naxin appeared in her old skimmer's windows.

Evan stared at her. "That was quick."

"The Service taught me things like that, remember?"

"Remind me never to pull up next to you." He glanced down at the floor near her feet. His smile flickered back to life. "Still carrying your bag of tricks, I see." He punched the sedan's charge-through. The vehicle activated with a low hum. "I'll send some people over to mop up. It'll be like you were never even here."

"They're going to need HazMat gear."

"People always need HazMat gear when they clean up after you. It's one of the constants of life." His eyes glistened with suppressed merriment. He reversed the skimmer out of its slot, then eased it forward. "Is there anyone you want to message before we leave? Anyone you need to notify?"

"No," Jani said. That was the advantage with avoiding names—it always made bugging out easier. She reached beneath Evan's seat for the thermoflask. "I didn't watch the entire welcome program. Were you the only minister Cao took exception to?"

Evan steered the skimmer into a wide, banking turn. "No, there were more. Gisela Detmers-Neumann, the Communications Minister. Fitzhugh and Ebben, the deputies from Commerce. Unser from Education."

Coffee sloshed into Jani's lap, running down her weatherall and spilling to the skimmer floor. "Why them?" she asked.

Evan looked at her, then at the beading puddle on the carpet. "Now, Jani, you of all people should know the answer to that." He reached into the glove box, pulled out a dispo, and handed it to her. "Don't get too nervous. This visit doesn't have to be all business. Who knows, you might run into Tsecha. You were his pet at the Academy. I'm sure he'd enjoy seeing you again."

"At this point," Jani said as she dabbed at the spilled coffee, "I think any running I'd do with regard to him would be in the opposite direction."

The faint glow of the shuttle pad glimmered in the distance. Evan pressed the accelerator. "By the way," he asked, "who was that old Service officer? You always used to mention him in Rauta Shèràa, too."

"Wasn't a 'him.' Was a 'her.' " Jani sighed. "It was me."

CHAPTER 3

Amsun Primary's VIP wing exuded the chilly luxury of a Family mausoleum. Jani hitched her duffel, eyed the sculptures lining the station's carpeted gangway, and kept pace a few meters behind Evan, who was busy dictating orders to a quartet of Amsun annex staffers. Each underling took their position at his shoulder, then backed off and let another take their place, just like lead changes during skim-bike races. It had been that way since they'd left Whalen two days ago. Every time Jani tried to question Evan about Lyssa, an advisor would turn up to drag him off.

Maybe I need a uniform and a title to get his attention. A possibility, but not one she wanted to consider. Even in her current circumstances, she wouldn't have traded places with Evan or any member of his escort. Voices snapped. No one smiled.

We're in Exterior country, my friends. Unlike every other Ministry, which located its main headquarters in Chicago and scattered its annexes throughout the colonies, Exterior had moved its Main House to the Outer Circle planet of Amsun and maintained only a token presence on Earth. That hadn't seemed wise when the late David Scriabin, Lyssa van Reuter's father, had set the transfer wheels in motion fifteen years before.

Smacks of genius now. Exterior burgundy formed the basis for every aspect of interior decoration in Amsun Primary, a constant reminder to all parties wearing Treasury gold, Commerce green, Interior black, and every other Cabinet hue in exactly whose sandbox they played.

Jani passed the portrait of a severe, dark-haired woman wearing a high-necked tunic in the ubiquitous *colour du monde.* Everyone thought Exterior Minister Anais Ulanova should have stood for Prime during the last election. When she didn't, the Earthbound news services professed shock. The colonial reaction, in contrast, had been blasé. *Why fight to be shepherd when you already own the sheep*?

As she came upon yet another holosilk study in red and orange, Jani rolled her eyes. It was partly artistic opinion, partly aggravation. Red was the color of blood and warning lights to her augie, the chromatic equivalent of a scream in the night. Unfortunately, the action caused an eyefilm to shift. She tried to blink it back into place, and it hung up on her eyelid. Tears brimmed, then spilled as the film edge curled and split. She cupped a hand over the damage and searched in vain for a sign indicating a restroom.

"Ms. Tyi?"

Tyi? Tyi? That was her name now. Risa Tyi. Josephan. Bad choice. She couldn't speak Josephani.

"Ms. Tyi!" Evan had pulled up short and stared back at her. "Is everything all right?" The look in Jani's visible eye must have set off alarms. "Folks, I'll get back with you." He left his puzzled entourage behind and hurried to her side. "I knew you shouldn't have flown so soon after the surgery." He gripped Jani by the elbow and pulled her toward the elevator bank. "I hope the incision glue held."

One of the underlings called out, "Your Excellency, if a physician is required—"

"No, no," Evan said as he pushed Jani ahead of him into the first open car. "We'll meet you at the *Arapaho* gate in a few minutes." The door hissed shut. "What happened!"

Jani sagged against the wall. "Film broke."

"Can you fix it?"

"Yeah." She shivered as the odor of berries filled the elevator. Her mouth watered. What the overdose of red started, the stress of the moment intensified. She breathed through her mouth in an effort to block out the smell of fruit.

"Are you all right? I know red used to get to you sometimes." Evan leaned close and blanched. "Oh shit." As the door opened, he held her back and looked up and down the hall. "Still red—cover up."

Jani pressed her hands over her eyes as she was herded, dragged, and prodded. Another door opened, then whispered closed. "Evan? What color are the walls now?"

"They're a very calming shade of blue."

Jani lowered her hands. The walls were indeed quite relaxing, but some of the fixtures appeared unusual. "Evan, we're in a men's toilet."

"It was the closest door to the elevator, ok? People were coming." He activated the lock. "There. That lights up the 'being cleaned—come back in ten minutes' sign."

"If the hall monitoring picked us up—"

"This is the *private* section. Anais does any scanning here, I'll have her ass." Evan's voice grew hushed. "That look you had in the eye I could see scared the hell out of me—like you were staring up from the bottom of a pit. Was that some kind of seizure?"

Jani walked to the mirror above the row of sinks. "No." A few fissures had formed along the film's black-and-white surface. "A combination of the stress and the environment. The nervousness of the moment. The augmentation kicked in."

"Augmentation." Evan gave each syllable a twist of disgust. "You were sideline Service, not mainline. How could you let them do that to you?"

"I was still Service, Ev. When they tell you to peel and bend over, you drop your drawers and think of the Commonwealth." Jani dug into her duffel. "Guess they thought we all needed it, with the way the Laumrau-Vynshà situation was heating up." She shrugged. "I have mixed feelings about it. It helps me think more clearly in emergencies—almost like a permanent tranquilizer implant. If I get hurt while it's active, it kicks on adrenal and thyroid boosters, and helps the wounds heal faster." She checked her clear face in the mirror. The peeling skin and rash caused by her brief exposure to the Naxin had healed in two days, instead of two weeks. "Dulls pain."

"Helped you survive the crash," Evan added with an encouraging smile.

"That's why I have mixed feelings." Jani freed the bottles of film former from the depths of her bag, then blended the memory film with its activator. "Sometimes I think justice would have been better served if I'd died with everyone else. Or if I'd died, and they'd lived." She looked up to find Evan's reflection staring at her in shocked surprise. "Don't worry. I won't go suicidal on you. Just a little objective over-analysis on my part."

"Really?" He studied her skeptically. "I know some people back home you could talk to about it."

"PTs?" Jani peeled the ruptured film from her eye. The tear-swollen black-and-white fragments smacked wetly into the sink. "Ev, if the psychotherapeuticians ever got me, they'd never let go." She activated the faucet, cupped tepid water in her hand, rinsed away the last specks of old film, and washed them down the drain. She didn't notice Evan's approach until he stood beside her.

"Jesus!"

Jani stared into the mirror at her eye. The iris was still the dark jade of her childhood. But the sclera, instead of white, shone a lighter, glassy green that took on a bluish cast in the harsh bathroom lighting. *Corroded copper coins—built-in pennies on my eyes.* At least the pupil hadn't changed in shape or size. And her sight had never seemed any better or worse than other people's.

Evan drew closer. "How the hell did that happen?"

"Contaminated starter tissue, the doctors said. No time to grow them over."

"The doctors?"

"*The* doctors. John Shroud, Valentin Parini, and Eamon DeVries." They had worked out of the Service hospital in Rauta Shèràa. They had rebuilt her after the crash, gave her strange eyes and numb limbs, and remained together after the war to form Neoclona. Now, they controlled all the hospitals in the Commonwealth that were worth a damn. Jani tilted her head back and counted out the drops of film. *One . . . four, five.* She held her lids open for ten seconds, then looked in the mirror. Her purple-black eye gazed back with teenage clarity.

Evan cleared his throat. "Don't you think you should do the other one?"

"I just did it three days ago. Barring incident, the stuff lasts seven to ten."

"I think you should make sure."

Jani watched Evan in the mirror until he turned away. After some hesitation, she peeled, poured, mixed, and counted. "Are you sure you want to go through with this?"

"That sounds hopeful." He turned back to her. "Does that mean you've decided to come at least as far as Padishah?"

"Amsun's too close to Whalen. I'd feel better a little farther out."

"How will I know when you feel you've gone far enough?"

"You won't." Jani dabbed away a drop of film former that had spilled down her cheek. "I'll just be gone."

"That sounds familiar." Evan hoisted himself on the counter next to her sink. "Sorry. Completely inappropriate."

"Yes, it was."

"What's past is past. I apologize." He fingered the soap dispenser. "So, how've you been?" He shrugged off Jani's incredulous look. "I've been weighed down with work the past two days. This is the first chance we've had to talk since I rescued you from that hellhole."

"I'm fine, Evan."

"Really?"

"Really." Jani's back twinged, and she leaned against a urinal for support. "You?"

"Fine."

"I'm sorry. About your wife." The words came haltingly. She'd never had a talent for saying the right thing; anything she thought of now seemed inappropriate. Death didn't just alter. It razed. Annihilated. "Your children, too. That was tragic."

"Yes. Thank you. Not a day goes by that I don't think of them." Evan looked at her and sighed. "You've wanted to ask me something delicate for days. I can tell. Go ahead."

There were no right words for this, either. "We heard gossip out here in the beyond. That you and Lyssa had problems."

"Yes, we did. For the most part, however, our marriage functioned."

"Sounds mechanical."

"Most Family marriages are." Evan's eyes glinted. Sapphires in snow. "I don't recall you as the type to be drawn in by rumor."

"Rumors blossom and seed all the time. They don't all result in the convention of a Court of Inquiry."

"I told you, Cao and Ulanova want me out."

"You must have really ticked them off."

"I don't quite have your talent for alienating the opposition, but I'm working on it."

"There's something you didn't tell me. Something you left out."

"And what could that be?"

Jani leaned more heavily against the urinal. She could feel the cold porcelain through her thin coverall. As cold as her right hand. As cold as the chill that gripped her.

"Is something wrong, Jan?"

"This concerns Knevçet Shèràa, doesn't it?"

"I don't know. But I bet you could find out."

"You bastard. You set me up."

"No, I gave you A and B and let you reach the logical C. The setup was all yours." Evan glanced at his timepiece. "We better get going." He pushed himself off the counter, then turned to wash his hands. "I'm sorry, Jan, but if I'd mentioned Knevçet Shèràa back on Whalen, you'd have bolted. I couldn't let you do that."

"What am I walking into?"

"Nothing that endangers you. I'm the one in trouble. You're assumed dead, remember?" Evan gripped the rim of the sink. "Jani, your own family wouldn't know you. That's how different you look. Hell, I didn't know you." He reached blindly for a dispo towel. "And I knew you better than anyone."

"Better not call me 'Jani' anymore. Stick to Risa." Jani tossed her bottles into her bag and gave her eyes one last check in the mirror. "I don't speak Josephani, you know."

"It's like High Dutch."

"Oh, that narrows it down. Thanks."

Evan unlatched the door. "We're going to walk past a lot of red between here and the shuttle. Will you make it?"

"Yes. I'll just get a bit wound-up. I'll be fine." Jani waited for him to raise the all clear, then followed him into the hall. "Well, that brought back memories."

Evan paused in mid-step, eyes widening as he remembered. "That play. At the Consulate Hall. *Becket.* Intermission. The ladies' was crowded, and you barged in and—"

"Told you to shut up and guard the door. That's how we met." She patted his arm. "You still guard doors pretty well."

They both laughed, a little too loudly and a little too long. Evan offered her his arm as they walked to the elevator bank, then bowed like a gallant as the door opened, gesturing for her to enter first. The other occupants smiled at them, as though the little show had brightened their day.

You set me up, Evan. Jani stepped to the rear of the half-filled elevator and tried not to flinch as he crowded beside her.

Knevçet Shèràa. *Not a day goes by that I don't think*—She leaned against the rear of the car, closed her filmed eyes, and clenched her numb left hand.

"I guess you could consider this a working vacation," Evan said. He nodded curtly to the steward who bustled past him, towing Jani's luggage in a hand-skimmer.

Correction—Risa's luggage. Jani shook her head in disbelief as the steward disappeared into her bedroom to stash the seven brown trueleather bags in her closet.

"I'll unpack while you're at dinner, ma'am," he said as he took his leave, all silver-blond hair and flashing smile. Jani returned the smile to the best of her ability, then turned back to Evan to find him glaring at her.

"But don't get carried away with the vacation part." He walked across the large sitting room and flopped into a lounge chair. "Of course, I don't think I have enough work to keep you occupied for five weeks, and what you do in your off time is your own . . . affair." He smoothed the front of his black uniform tunic and fixed his sights on the wall opposite.

"I'll try to keep the orgies to a minimum, sir," Jani replied quietly.

"That's not what I meant."

"I know exactly what Your Excellency meant. I think I should take this opportunity to remind Your Excellency that, considering certain situations in which I have found myself in the past, if I had been the type to think with my pussy, I'd have been dead years ago."

"Ja—" Evan stopped himself. He rose slowly. "Risa. How vividly put. My apologies. I should know better."

"I think with my head," Jani continued. "If *it* sees the way clear, that is of course a different story."

Evan gaped. He seemed to have trouble deciding what to do with his hands, finally shoving them into his pants pockets. The move caused his tunic to bunch unministerially over his hips. "Dinner," he finally said. "My private dining room. One hour after breakaway. We will have company." He eyed Jani's coverall, an overlarge, chalk brown item she'd liberated from the Whalen transport's lost lambs bin. "We should dress."

"Yes, sir." Jani returned Evan's cool smile and followed him to the door. "Label the forks, so I know which one to use when," she added as he stepped into the hall. The door closed before he could reply, but not before he had shown he hadn't lost his capacity to redden alarmingly.

Jani knocked against the door with her forehead. *Too late to bolt now.* The *Arapaho* was in prebreakaway lockdown—she'd have to trip a hazard alarm. *I've done that before.* But not on a Cabinet-class ship. They had Service crews aboard to put out their fires. She'd be up to her ass in steel blue before the klaxons stopped screaming.

I'm jumping ship at Padishah. She made a circuit of her cabin sitting room, a posh retreat in pale yellow and cream, scanning the shelves and cabinets for anything she could hock. She was examining the contents of an étagère with a pawnbroker's eye when she heard the door open.

"Ma'am." Her steward stood in the entry holding a bottle-filled tray. "Do you require any assistance before dinner?"

Jani straightened. "No. Thank you."

"I thought you might like something to drink."

"Fine." She nodded, larcenous hands locked behind her back.

"A jeune marie?"

"Fine." *What the hell's a "young mary"?*

The young man filled a small glass to the brim with a garnet-colored liquid and handed it to Jani. She raised the drink to her lips, hoping to get rid of him by downing it quickly, when the odor of berries filled her nose.

"Do you like it, ma'am?" His voice held stewardly anxiety. "It's new. From Serra."

"A 'jeune marie' is a kind of berry, isn't it?"

"Yes, ma'am. Is everything—"

"Everything's fine. Please go now. I need to get ready." She fought down a yell as he took his time gathering up his tray and waited for the door to close before sinking into the nearest chair. Her stomach burned. Her hand trembled, causing a stream of red beadlets to slosh over the glass's rim onto the carpet. She hurried to the bathroom, poured the reeking liqueur into the sink, and flushed it down until she could smell only water.

Evan's on his own—I'm jumping ship at Padishah. He didn't need her to get him through his crisis—he was far from vanquished politically. Or personally, for that matter. He had certainly dealt with his own deaths better than she had with hers.

Coping? You're kidding.

Closure? No, her wounds had gaped for eighteen years.

You'd have to execute one hell of an inside-out to set Knevçet Shèràa straight, Kilian. She wasn't that limber anymore.

Jani sat on the edge of the bathtub and unclasped her boots. *But Evan thinks I deserve a second chance.* Of course, since he felt his career was in jeopardy, he'd say anything to get her to help. Just as he'd withhold anything he thought might scare her away. *He thinks in terms of distance to goal and whether goal had been achieved or lost.* Always the pragmatist. Even as a young Consulate deputy, his first time away from home, with every opportunity to go off track, he always kept his eye on the ball.

So? Maybe Evan didn't mean what he'd said about second chances. It didn't follow that it wasn't true. All her records were in secured storage on Earth. Maybe there was something she could learn, something she could discover that would make it not hurt as much. Something she could use to help Evan, and, just possibly, herself.

I don't think like that anymore. Every time I try to help, I fuck up. I'm jumping ship at Padishah. She started undoing the fasteners of her coverall. Her hands stilled. *No, I'm not.* Evan had been right. After almost twenty years, her Family boy still knew her very well. She pondered that disquieting thought as she headed for the bedroom to mine something presentable from the depths of Risa's luggage.

In contrast to the interior of Jani's cabin, the *Arapaho* hallways were simple: undecorated walls of light grey composite, floors of dark grey, footstep-muffling lyno.

Jani hurried after her guide, a frazzled mainline Spacer First Class who had apparently been instructed to *bring Ms. Tyi to dinner without delay.* Her hip twinged with every step. The outfit she wore, a tight, one-shoulder, floor-length column dress in dark blue, had not been her first choice. Or her second. Or her eighth.

Seven damned bags of clothes, and none of them fit! Jani tugged at the dress again as she struggled to keep up with the sensibly booted SFC. Her own sensible boots were hiding beneath her bed—cowards that they were. Her current footwear—strappy, metallic-colored, and high-heeled—had been spared a one-way trip down the disposal chute solely because they were the only shoes in her possession that kept the dress from dragging on the floor.

She and Evan were going to have to discuss hazard pay.

The rough polycotton strap of Jani's duffel bit into the skin of her bare shoulder. Her choice of handbag might cause raised eyebrows among her dinner companions, but she didn't care. Some things, a woman kept with her at all times. *Like her shooter, for example.* She straightened as best she could in her impossible shoes. It had been a very long time since she'd had to look this polished.

"Here we are, ma'am." The SFC slid to a halt before a double wide set of sliders embossed with the Interior seal and knocked sharply. The doors opened immediately. She mumbled, "Good evening, sir," and bolted around the nearest corner just as Evan, resplendent in formal black, stepped out into the hall.

"Well, this *is* a change for the better!" His face lit up as he held out his arm. "I picked that dress," he added as he led her inside. "I must say, I have excellent taste."

Jani tugged at the gown's rear. "It's too tight." The back of her neck tingled as Evan lagged behind to take in the view.

"No, not a bit," he said. "Just confirms you still have a waist. Judging from your previous attire, I'd given it up for lost." As they walked through the sitting room, Jani heard Evan clear his throat. "Can't say I agree with that purse, though."

"Bugger," she said as she strode on ahead. The dark green and silver suite was furnished with a tasteful, expensive blend of ornate modern and stark antique. She swallowed a comment that it was larger than some homes in which she'd lived as the odors coming from the dining room made her mouth water. Her step quickened. *God, I'm starved!* Over the past few months, it seemed she could never get enough to eat.

She pulled up short as she entered the dining room. Evan's steadying hand gripped her numb left arm as two pairs of eyes stared in surprise. Jani managed a composed smile. She recognized her dinner companions from the postings in various Guv Halls. *Maybe this dress wasn't such a bad idea after all.*

Evan pushed past her. "Risa, I'd like to introduce two of the more important members of my staff." He nodded toward a tall, dark blond man dressed in a dandyish, pale lilac dinner suit. "This is Durian Ridgeway, my Documents chief."

Jani forced herself to extend her hand as Ridgeway pursed his lips and looked her slowly up and down. "Ms. Tyi." The soft cast of his boyish features was offset by the glitter of his blue eyes. "I've looked forward to meeting you." His accent was clipped and difficult to place.

Earth British, Jani decided. She'd thought New Manx, at first, but no self-respecting Manxman would have allowed himself to be seen wearing the curious wad of bright purple braiding Ridgeway had fashioned into a neckpiece. *Clotted octopus,* she thought. Maybe it indicated a sense of humor?

Ridgeway beckoned to a slight young woman who appeared lost amid the furniture. "This is my deputy, Angevin Wyle."

Angevin stepped forward. Her outfit, a fitted copper gauze gown with matching nosebleed heels, seemed to be giving her trouble as well. Jani studied her face. Wide-spaced mossy green eyes, carrot red curls shot through with gold, stubborn chin, all combined to uncover long-buried memories.

I attended school with your father. Hansen Wyle and I were going to change worlds, once. She accepted Angevin's subdued greeting. *Then it all fell apart.*

Evan herded them toward the dinner table, where a first course of glistening vegetable jellies coddled in crushed ice awaited. "I'm glad we could meet now," he said as he helped Jani with her chair. "I don't think we could afford to delay until we returned to Earth."

"Perhaps not, Ev," Ridgeway agreed grudgingly as he assisted Angevin with her chair. "I'm just hesitant to leave documents of this nature aboard an unsecured vessel." He nodded toward the sideboard, where an anodized metal documents case rested.

Jani noted the large case's double touchlocks and felt a pleasant shiver of anticipation. She hadn't had the opportunity to handle close-controlled paper since her Service days.

"If you consider the *Arapaho* unsecured, Durian, we *are* in trouble." Evan speared a tan star-shape with a narrow, two-pronged fork and ferried the wobbly morsel to his mouth. "But I prefer to believe that in this, as in so many things, you are erring on the side of caution."

"Perhaps." Ridgeway tried repeatedly to snag a quivering orange sphere, but the tidbit kept sliding off his fork. "These *méduse*," he said with a nervous chuckle. "I always have trouble eating these things."

"It's probably afraid of your neckpiece," Angevin Wyle said as she executed an expert forking. She chewed thoughtfully, expression placid, the look in her eyes as flinty as the documents case's finish.

Evan coughed and reached for his wineglass. "It is a bit much, Durian."

Ridgeway fingered his garish neckwear and smiled. Lips only. The sidelong glare he gave Angevin promised a stern lecture behind closed, soundproofed doors.

Thy father's daughter. Jani looked down at her plate to hide her grin. The *Arapaho* suddenly felt very homey.

CHAPTER 4

The balance of the meal passed uneventfully. Make that the imbalance. Embers of conversation sparked fitfully, only to die. Except for her single instance of fashion commentary, Angevin remained silent. Ridgeway was sociable, though guarded, while Evan alternated between expansiveness and distraction as the synergistic effects of lack of sleep and generous servings of five varieties of wine took hold. He had always enjoyed his liquor, but you'd think he'd have known better.

Now is not the time, Evan. After-dinner iced water in hand, Jani left the three behind to talk, or in Angevin's case, listen, shop. She examined the artwork in Evan's sitting room, then paused before an official portrait of the Interior Minister and his late wife. Evan looked thin and worn. His dress tunic hung on his slim frame like woven lead. Lyssa, also in black, appeared drawn and pale. Neither had made any attempt to smile.

"That was taken almost three years ago, a short time after the children died." Durian Ridgeway drew alongside. The tiny glass he held contained a bright pink, presumably lethal, liqueur. "Too soon, in my opinion. They both look ill. It's not the kind of image you want to see scattered throughout the Commonwealth."

Jani glanced into the dining room. Evan was holding forth and gesturing broadly as a seated Angevin Wyle stared and nodded like someone in a trance. *Bewitching, isn't he?* Even after all these years. *You'd think I'd have acquired immunity by now.* "Pity Evan and Lyssa couldn't time their tragedies better."

Ridgeway's eyebrows arched. "I'm sure I sound harsh, but that is part of my job. To observe, monitor, see things which perhaps His

Excellency would miss." He drew closer. Jani forced herself to stand still as he brushed against her bare shoulder. "Well, Ms. Tyi, this must all be a big change for you. From a little post on Hortensia to a Cabinet-class ship, all in a matter of weeks. But, you know what they say." He mumbled a few sentences, of which she recognized little and understood nothing.

Servir? Servirat? I'll bet that's Josephani. Her supposed native language, of which she knew zip. "I beg your pardon, Mr. Ridgeway?"

"Would you like me to repeat it, Ms. Tyi?"

"Judging from your accent, I don't think it would help."

He pressed closer. Jani felt his breath in her ear as his chest pushed against her left arm. The numb one. All she felt was the pressure. "If you couldn't understand that, understand this. The contents of the files I will be turning over to you, if revealed, could shake the Commonwealth to its foundations. If anything happens to that paper while it's registered to your control, I will not rest until I personally grind you to fine powder with my bare hands."

"No need to be melodramatic, Mr. Ridgeway."

"I have been with Evan for fifteen years. Since I left school, my primary duty has been to him. I will not stand by and watch everything he's built get blown to bloody fuck-all for the sake of one of his whims."

The fruity odor of Ridgeway's breath filled Jani's nose. Her full stomach gurgled in protest as she forced herself to look him in the face. His eyes watered—the liqueur was apparently as potent as she thought. "If you have anything to say to me, mister, you really should wait until you sober up."

Ridgeway's bleary glower sharpened. "You don't like me, Ms. Tyi. That's fine—I'm not mad for you, either. I don't believe your participation in what I consider should remain an in-House investigation is necessary." He took a step back.

"But we both follow orders, don't we? Live to serve? That's what I tried to tell you before, and so badly, too. I do apologize." He strolled from the portrait to a display case of ornaments, gesturing for Jani to follow. "But now, I think we understand one another. The idomeni have a term for our particular brand of impasse. Esteemed enemy. For now, let us consider ourselves esteemed enemies."

"We'd have to have a ceremony," Jani said, "to declare it properly. There are offertories to the gods, followed by the shedding of blood through ritual combat."

Ridgeway offered a sly smile. "Is that a challenge, Risa? Perhaps later. It sounds very . . . cross-cultural." He reached into the display case and fingered a polished shell. "What do you think of Ms. Wyle?"

She's like her father. "She's like most dexxies. Rough around the edges. Needs some social buffing."

Ridgeway scowled at Jani's use of the slang term for documents examiner. "Buffing," he said pointedly. "Not a day goes by when I don't stifle the urge to throttle her. But considering her background, I make allowances." He returned the shell to its niche. "You've heard of her father, of course?"

"Hansen?"

"Yes. One of only six humans to degree at the Academy in Rauta Shèràa. One of only six to study the paper system with the race that perfected it. What an honor." Jani could hear the envy in Ridgeway's voice. "Then that damned war started, and he had to stick his nose in. What a waste."

Jani struggled to keep her tone level. "From what I've heard, he knew the Laumrau leaders. He knew the Vynshà. I believe he did what he thought best, in order to help."

"And the shatterbox found the building he was in anyway, and the building collapsed on him anyway, and he died anyway, even though he was only trying to help." Ridgeway pushed the display case toward the center of the table. Jani winced as the metal supports screeched against the polished wood.

"Now the idomeni are back," she said, "and you have to work with them. How do you reconcile that?"

"I don't," Ridgeway replied too quickly. "But I do have the opportunity to help the daughter of the man I grew up wanting to emulate." The look in his eyes grew reverential. "Hansen was more than one of the six. He was One of Six. They were treated like idomeni, constantly being tested—the pressure was unending. But he always came out on top. He was the best." He sighed. "I'm afraid Angevin will have to emerge from under a fairly formidable shadow."

Jani worked her tensing shoulders. "I think," she said slowly, "part of the girl's problem, if she indeed has one, will be in having to deal with other people's expectations."

"True. True." Ridgeway nodded sagely, his sarcasm detector apparently flooded with ethanol. "All we can do is all we can. In the end it's up to her. No one can work magic with someone fundamentally unsuited to the task at hand." He gave Jani a superior smile, his sarcasm synthesizer apparently functioning just fine. "Speaking of which, why don't we get this transfer over with? You realize what I'm handing over to you?"

"Yes." Jani did a mental ten count. "You're giving me sensitive files pertinent to the investigation of Lyssa van Reuter's death, which contain details of His Excellency's life."

"Oh, they contain details, all right. Their contents may shock even a jaded soul like you, Ms. Tyi. We never realize what Mother Commonwealth knows about us until it's too late." Ridgeway offered her his arm. "Shall we?"

Angevin bounded to her feet as Jani and Ridgeway reentered the dining room. "His Excellency's been telling me the most ripping things! All about the idomeni!" Her enthusiasm withered as soon as her eyes met Ridgeway's. She walked over to the sideboard and rummaged through a large leather bag. From it, she removed a sheaf of papers and three pouches, two the size of a man's hand, one much larger.

In the meantime, Ridgeway collected the documents case and carried it to the dining room table. Evan, fresh from making young women's eyes shine, perched on the arm of a nearby chair and graced Jani with a tired grin.

The grin died when he saw what Ridgeway was doing.

We knew this was coming, Evan. Jani pulled her duffel from beneath her chair, cracked the fasteners, and removed her own small, scuffed pouch. *Besides, what can go wrong?* She knew the answer to that. She would just try not to think about it.

The world of close-controlled paper did get complicated at times, but an ownership transfer was one of the simpler procedures. As Angevin Wyle laid out the logs that they each would sign and date, Ridgeway prepared to reprogram the case's touchlocks to accept Jani's prints.

Of course, he'd have to scan her hands and retinas first, and run a comparison check against the various databases each Cabinet-class ship contained within its systems. Criminal. Service. Medical. A matter of procedure. Everyone understood that. Just another form to file away for future audits.

Ridgeway smirked as he removed his scanner from the largest of the three pouches and activated it.

Jani heard Evan fidget behind her. She smiled, which seemed to disappoint Ridgeway. He pouted when she stepped without hesitation into range of the boxlike scanner and held out her hands.

But my handprints aren't the same, are they? Or her retinas. The doctors who had reassembled her had been, after all, very forward-thinking. She watched as a bright yellow light throbbed beneath the scanner's surface. The device hummed, then the indicator display glowed bright, clear green.

"Happy, Durian?" Evan asked, injecting the distilled essence of generations of Familial ennui into his voice.

"Just following prescribed procedure, Ev," Ridgeway said as he stuffed the scanner back into its pouch. "Better safe than sorry." Using a UV stylus, he opened the switches in the document case's control panel, waited for Jani to place her palm against the sensor pad, then closed the switches, locking in her print as the key.

Just like the good old days. Jani glanced at Evan, who winked back. She removed her scanpack from its cracked plastic pouch. The oval device contained a mass of her farmed brain tissue, through which a network of nervelinks and data chips had been implanted. Working together to serve as guideposts on a roadway, the unit and its attachments stored the data necessary to enable its owner to navigate through the documents maze. Her brain-in-a-box, literally. How long had it been since she'd used it as it was meant to be used? In front of her peers, during a high-level documents transaction?

Jani brushed a few flecks of dirt from the scanpack's surface. Over twenty years of use meant that the hand-sized, five-centimeter-thick oval didn't look much better than its container. Scratches dulled its black polycoat finish. Some of the touchpad labeling had been worn away. She examined the nutrient insert slot along the side, then sniffed quickly. No fishy odor, which would have signaled a leak in the spent nutrient broth line, a sure sign of a poorly maintained 'pack. That had never been a problem for her, but accidents did happen. If Ridgeway even suspected she didn't maintain her equipment, she knew she'd never hear the end of it.

Ridgeway looked from his own immaculate tortoiseshell unit to Jani's. "Oh, Ms. Tyi, that *is* a confidence-builder."

Jani shrugged. "The problem with having nice things, Mr. Ridgeway, is that in some of the places I've lived, there are those who would wish to separate them from me. I try to avoid trouble." She turned on her device, waited for the display to activate, then gently slid it over the first of the three forms.

The sensors on the 'pack's underside evaluated the paper surface, analyzed the inks and metal foils decorating the ornate document, decoded the encryptions contained in the chips and prionics embedded in the parchment. *Everything but Luna's phase on the day it was made*—that's what the document would tell her scanpack, which then would compare that information to the data stored in its own chips and cells.

Bright green identification strings scrolled across the display. "It's a current-issue Interior Ministry ownership transfer log, all right,"

Jani said to Ridgeway. She ignored his glower, affixed her signature to the document, then moved on to the next as Angevin and Ridgeway completed their portion of the first. After all three forms were completed, they each took one copy. Jani stashed hers in her duffel, while Angevin returned hers and Ridgeway's to the leather bag.

"Are we finally finished?" Evan groaned. "I don't know how any business gets completed in a timely fashion these days." He sounded bored, but his face showed the drained relief of a man whose fever had finally broken.

"Yes, Ev, you can go to bed now," Ridgeway said as he jammed his 'pack back into its sheath. He followed up the snappish remark with a smile, but that did little to counter his bundled-underwear edginess. "We will be disembarking late day after tomorrow, at Padishah," he said to Jani. "If you need any assistance afterward, zip us a message through message central transmit. We'll do what we can." He eyed her scanpack again. "I'm sure the equipment you work with leaves something to be desired."

Angevin walked over to Jani, looking at her for the first time with something akin to a smile. "Looks used," she said, pointing to the scanpack's battered case.

Jani nodded. "It has been."

Angevin was about to say something else, but Ridgeway linked her arm through his and led her away.

"Till tomorrow, Ev," he said as they left. "And a good evening to you as well, Ms. Tyi. You will remember what we talked about?"

"What was that all about?" Evan asked after the sliders closed. "Don't tell me—Durian was being Durian." He eased into a lounge chair and ran a hand over his face. Even in the cabin's soft illumination, his skin looked dull. "Forgive him, Jan—he takes damned good care of me in the bargain. And he's worried about those docs."

"You're not?"

"I'm not sure what you'll think of me after reading some of them, but I have to take that chance. Besides, I trust you." He studied Jani for a few moments, his expression neutral. Then he motioned for her to take the seat across from him.

"Like Durian said, in two days we'll reach Padishah. He and Ange will be catching a Service courier that will get them home a week ahead of the *Arapaho*." He took a deep breath. "I need to go with them. Elyas is petitioning to reopen colonial secession talks. Along with the other Outer Circle worlds, they somehow dragged the Jewellers' Loop into the brawl, and that means lots of might and money flying around. The centrists want me home."

Jani said nothing. Instead, she watched Evan's hands, as she had learned to do during their time together. They rested easily on his knees. No nail-picking. No sleeve-tugging. Either he told the truth or he'd learned to hide his lies better.

"I'd been debating telling you for days. Thought if I mentioned it, I'd give you just another excuse to bolt. But I've no choice. Duty calls."

"You roust me out of my home, close off my escape routes, then tell me you're leaving me alone among strangers for five weeks?"

Evan wrinkled his nose. "Whalen was no home. And you don't need any escape routes." His eyes sparked. "Besides, I'm more concerned for the strangers than I am for you." His stare deepened and his features slackened until he wore the bewildered, slightly stunned expression Jani remembered from their first meeting. "I wish I could stay."

If you're going to look at me like that, maybe it's better you don't. Jani tugged as unobtrusively as she could at the bodice of her dress. A waste of time—the silky material snapped back into snug place like a second skin. "Well, I may be able to work better without you around." She snuck a peek at Evan beneath her lashes. He wore evening clothes as easily as other men wore ship coveralls; now, as he unfastened the stiff formal tunic, he looked very agreeably rumpled. *You're still the best-looking man I've ever known.* Yes, and he had very good reasons to go out of his way to make her feel cosseted and comfortable. If it so happened that keeping her cozy could get him laid, he wouldn't turn it down. Remember the pragmatist.

Not fair. Except for that single grumble in the Amsun station bathroom concerning their breakup, he had been silent on the matter of their past. *Sheep's eyes don't count.* Those could be chalked up to a heavy meal and too much alcohol. *Neither do wicked thoughts.* Lucky for her.

"The centrists," she said, "think the colonies will require a lengthy period of adjustment before full independence can be granted. I've heard numbers ranging from ten to one hundred years. Speaking as a colonial, I don't think we need babying."

If Evan noticed the abrupt cool-off, he hid it beneath a veneer of serious reflection. "The coalition pushing for these talks is led by a group being advised by Ulanova. They may know how to run businesses, but they don't know how to run governments. They'd need her help, and she'd give them just enough to keep their heads above water until they needed her again. That's not true independence."

"Maybe it's enough to get them started."

"You don't know Anais, Jan. Once she'd sunk her claws into that power base, she'd never let go. She wouldn't rest until she was PM of her own little Commonwealth."

"Funny she doesn't believe she can get what she wants with an Earthbound government," Jani said. "But then, you're fairly isolated with respect to GateWays. You've turned into a planet-sized office building over the years—you've got no substantial manufacturing or shipping anymore. The colonies are where the money is. By comparison, you're stagnant."

Evan scowled. "I wish you'd stop saying 'you.'" He sagged against the cushions and clasped his hands behind his head. "Are you angry with me? For holding out on you?"

Jani twitched a shoulder. It twitched back. "A little."

"I'll be waiting for you in Chicago. You will show up, won't you?"

"Yes."

He looked up at the ceiling and exhaled slowly. "Thank you. I'll sleep more easily tonight." He stifled a yawn. "It won't be horrible."

"It could be."

"I'll be there. I'll help you." He fell silent for a time. Then his eyes came to life again, and he laughed. "Before you arrived, Durian was filling my ear about Tsecha. Your old teacher's causing quite a stir, apparently. He took one of the embassy triple-lengths out for a spin a few weeks ago. Problem was, nobody knew he could drive. He got as far as Minneapolis before a Service-idomeni pursuit team caught up to him and herded him back to Chicago. They had a hell of a time hushing it up. That's all the anti-idomeni faction needs to hear is that the ambassador flits unguarded through the provinces."

Jani chuckled as well. "You're in for it now! Sounds like he hasn't changed. He used to like making himself up as a human in Rauta Shèràa. He even pulled down a job as a Consulate tour guide for a few days. Nobody could tell—his customers kept asking him what colony he was from."

"Oh shit, I'd forgotten about that. One more thing to worry about—what joy." Evan's expression grew wistful. "Seems odd, calling him *Tsecha.* We knew him as *Nema.* I still think of him by that name." He looked at Jani, his eyes narrowing. "He liked you."

"Yep."

"He thought you were special."

"Uh-huh."

"He had plans for you."

"Evan, if you have a point to make, please do so."

"No. No. Just rambling. Exhausted."

"Too much to drink."

"Hmm." Worry clouded his features for a moment. "How do you feel?"

"Fine."

"Are you sure? You look ill."

"Thanks." Jani rubbed her stomach. It had started to ache. "I just ate too much."

"We've had a few nasty new bugs crop up in the Outer Circle over the past few years. Maybe you should see a doctor."

"*No.*"

Evan held up his hands in surrender. "Ok, ok. Sorry I mentioned it." He struggled to his feet, then helped her gather her bag and case. "Cabin's to your liking, I hope? Your clothes?"

"Nothing fits, Evan."

"Really?" He circled her, studying her in a way not entirely objective. "I did my best. Took your measurements from your old ID and turned it over to my tailor. She seldom errs."

"She made up for lost time."

"I disagree. This dress is perfect." He chucked her under the chin. "Goes with the face." His hand lingered near her cheek. "I'm getting used to it. It fits you. Very 'Queen of the Nile.' " He hesitated, then leaned close and hugged her lightly, as though he feared she'd pull away. "We'll be fine. You'll see." His breath smelled of wine; his neck, of the haygrass-scented cologne he'd always favored. Jani broke the embrace before she wanted to and rushed out the door before he could say good night. She walked back to her cabin in the grip of the sensation that she'd just skimmed over a land mine.

I have to play this at arm's length. She hated to admit how good it felt to talk to Evan, to someone who knew the long-submerged Jani Kilian and, if outward signs could be believed, still cared about her as well. It wouldn't take long to become used to nice dinners and pleasant conversation again. *And anything else that might reasonably follow.* Soon, the roots would go so deep that when the time came to cut and run, she'd be fixed in place by indecision and fear of what she would lose. *I can't afford to relax.* Especially now, with Ridgeway watching her every move.

She turned the corner in time to see her steward emerge from her cabin.

"Ma'am?" He brushed a hank of hair from his sweaty brow. "There's a problem with the climate control on this deck. I've notified Environmental, but they may not be able to return it to full function until we stop at Padi."

"Oh please!" Jani sagged against the wall. She looked at the name tag on his left breast pocket. "Mister Ostern. Can't this wait until morning?"

Ostern thrust a small touchbox toward her. "Oh, everything's under control for now, ma'am. I've jury-rigged a bypass." His face glowed with pride. *Look what I made, Mommy!*

Jani accepted the small device with the hesitation of someone who'd learned long ago there was no such thing as "free." She looked again at Ostern, shifting from his blinding smile to his eyes. Dark brown, like chocolate. A warm color, normally. When brown eyes chilled, the cold came from within.

Her steward had cold brown eyes.

"I can show you how it works, if you like?" Ostern's voice, a pleasant tenor, still sounded boyish, but the examining look he gave the documents case aged him several stony decades.

"No, Mister Ostern, it's all right." Jani hoisted the case and, smiling sweetly, pushed past him and palmed her way into her cabin.

"Are you sure, ma'am? I—"

"It's all *right*," she said as the door slid closed. "I think I can figure things out." She paused in the entryway and sniffed the air. It did smell vaguely metallic and dusty, as though various things had gone *plonk* in the depths of the ventilation system.

She removed her shoes. Blessedly barefoot, she knelt in the middle of the sitting room and positioned Ostern's little box on the carpet in front of her. Using one of the spindly heels like a hammer, she smashed the device to bits.

After she tossed the fragments down the trash chute, Jani rooted through her duffel. She pushed aside her magnispecs, assorted scanpack parts twined through a holder of braided red cloth, broken UV styluses, and cracked touchpads, until she reached the scanproof false bottom, beneath which lay her shooter and her devices.

Her sensor looked like a UV stylus, except that the light at its pointed end blinked yellow instead of blue, and it had cost more than such things did when purchased through the usual channels. *One does what one has to.* As long as she'd never hurt anyone but herself, what difference did it make?

She flicked the device on. Holding it before her like a glow stick, she took a turn about the sitting room. *If I were an insect, where would I hide?*

It took the better part of an hour to locate the bug, lodged in the bedroom temperature control panel. Bold of Ostern to set it up so she would activate it herself with his cunning control box. She wrapped the tiny plastic cylinder in a strip of antistatic cloth and buried it in the depths of her duffel. A simple listening device, rather than a full sight-and-sound recorder. In that respect, Ostern had disappointed her. She would have expected more from someone with such cold eyes.

Jani ferreted through her cabin a second time. Reasonably certain she had done all she could to ensure her privacy for the shipnight, she undressed. Her stomach ached in earnest now. Her skin felt clammy. She opted for a hot shower in an effort to warm up, and to wash the food odors from her hair. She stood under the water stream until the utilities monitor squealed an imminent cutoff. Then she toweled slowly, all the while thinking about the garage guy. He'd had stomach problems, too. Nausea. Sweats.

Last thing I need is personal experience with the latest colonial epidemic. They'd become more and more common in the last few years—planet-specific infections which, in all the cases Jani heard about, led to long hospital stays and vague medical mumblings about mutating viruses. Well, she'd had enough doctoring to last a lifetime. Anything she had, she'd fight off herself.

She trudged into her bedroom and dug one of her Service tee shirts out of the warren of drawers. The white polycotton still looked new, even after twenty years. *I remember when I got you.* She pulled the use-softened shirt over her head. *I'd just graduated OCS, surprising one and all.* She smiled. Some memories, at least, were pleasant.

One of Six for tongue of gold, Two for eyes and ears.

"It had nothing to do with brains or rank, Ridgeway—we were all on the ball back then," Jani explained to her furniture. "And we needed our little games, to keep us sane."

Three and Four for hands of light, Five and Six for Earthly might. They each had their own special method for keeping the Laumrau Academy administrators off-balance. Senna and Tsai possessed their "hands of light," their talents as musicians, which ranked them quite highly as far as the born-sect idomeni were concerned. Aryton's and Nawar's "Earthly might" derived from their Family connections.

"But Hansen was the *Ambassador*," Jani said, stressing the point for the benefit of her bedclothes. True red hair was extremely rare among the idomeni's major sects. Red in all its variations being a holy color to them, they were inclined to believe any human gifted with such to be possessed of talents in many areas. When trouble brewed in Rauta Shèràa's human enclave, Hansen was always called in to help lift the pot off the boil.

"And I always went with him." Kilian, with her knack for understanding idomeni languages and mannerisms, and her ability to fade into the background. *I'll talk*, Hansen had always told her, *you just watch.*

"You get used to watching." She crawled into bed, duffel and documents case in hand. She unlocked the case and pulled out black-jacketed, confidential Interior files, arranging them in a semicircle on the blanket.

Then she activated her scanpack, her original, unadorned, idomeni-made unit, awarded to her personally upon her graduation by the being who now called himself Tsecha. Then, as now, he served as chief propitiator, the religious leader of his sect. Thus empowered, he had compelled his order-loving, xenophobic people to accept his dictum that humanish be allowed to school with them. Work with them. Even live with them, if isolation in an enclave two kilometers from the farthest outskirts of Rauta Shèràa could be called "living with."

Scores of humans had studied various subjects at the rigorous Academy. But the Six had been favored, and Jani Kilian and Hansen Wyle had been the most favored of all.

Not that she recalled any envy. If anything, her fellow documents trainees had been happy to allow her and Hansen the bulk of Nema's attention. And of his plotting. *Grim Death with a Deal for You*, Jani had dubbed him, much to Hansen's delight. But he had been theirs to laugh at. After all he'd put them through, they'd felt entitled.

And now he's back. And still causing trouble, according to Evan. *If all you think he's interested in is the occasional joyride, have I got news for you.*

She cracked a file seal and glanced down the table of contents of an Interior budget report, then scanned the file. Her 'pack worked without a hitch, as it had since the day she'd received it. "Anytime you want to compare equipment, Mr. Ridgeway, you just say the word." With that, Two of Six, the Eyes and Ears, set to work.

By the time the patient arrived on Earth, she had already entered the acute phase of the condition. This phase, which is characterized by physical malaise and extreme neurochemical imbalances, played itself out over the seventy-two-hour period predicted during lab trials.

—Internal Communication, Neoclona/Seattle,
Shroud J., Parini, V., concerning Patient S-1

The First Day

CHAPTER 5

"Do you have anything to declare, madam?"

Jani edged away from the half-opened door, which led to the Customs check-in booths reserved for "personal interviews," and left the young Commerce staffer and her husband, both sweaty and shaken, to their fates. *They know you're smuggling something, dears—may as well give it up.* Once a Customs inspector began addressing you formally, all bets were off.

My guess is collectibles or jewelry. Jani had followed the couple since they'd docked at Luna. Well dressed and parcel-laden, they had shunned the bullet cars that would have taken them to the shuttle docks' VIP section in minutes, preferring instead the hike through two kilometers of walkways.

Jani had followed them, curiosity egging her on even as fatigue set in, aggravating her limp. She watched them shift packages and whisper frantically, and waited out their frequent restroom stops, stifling the urge to sneak up behind them and shout, *"Boo!"* Instead, she'd trailed them into the deceptively comforting confines of the lounge, and waited.

Within minutes, a Treasury Customs official, dark gold uniform making him look like a tarnished elf, interrupted the pair's exploration of the buffet and led them away.

The restroom stops tipped Customs off. Scancams lined the public walkways of shuttle stations, but they were unobtrusive and easily ignored by fatigued travelers now a mere five-hour hop from home. Amateurs. Like any game, smuggling had its rules. You followed them, or you paid the penalty.

She cut down the short hallway and entered the spacious lounge.

Collecting a cup of tea and a sandwich from the extravagant buffet, she searched for a seat near the wall-spanning window. In the distance, the Lunar shipyards gleamed in the unfiltered sunlight with molten force, drawing the attention of most of the waiting passengers as construction sites always did.

Jani settled into a recently vacated chair, the documents case between her feet, duffel in her lap. Residual stranger-warmth soaked into her lower back. She took a bite of her sandwich, some sort of smoked fish with herbed mayonnaise. *Good, but Lucien could have done better.*

Lucien. Pascal. Her excellent steward's real name. After several more failed attempts to bug Jani's cabin, followed by futile efforts to gain access to her duffel and documents case, he had proposed a truce, which she had accepted. Life aboard the *Arapaho* became more conventional after that, though no less interesting. Watching Lucien operate within the strict hierarchy of the Cabinet ship's Service crew had proven educational. He never broke rules. He never bucked authority. But things got done his way, usually by people who should have known better.

He had even finagled her some Interiorwear that actually fit, like the grey-and-white wrapshirt and trousers she wore. A courtesy, he had told her, from one professional to another.

I almost preferred it when he was trying to gig me—it took my mind off my work. Evan's files. She understood why he had been so reluctant to let her see them. There had been some dealings with a junior member of the Justice Ministry that wouldn't have borne the weight of a public inquiry, as well as personal financial hopscotch of the sort that implied tax evasion. It had taken her almost two weeks just to sort out the intricacies of the accounting involved. The NorthPort Haárin could have learned something from Evan's financial advisor.

But even so, she'd seen worse. Certainly nothing to merit a death. There had already been too many. First, Evan's and Lyssa's children, drowned during their efforts to sail an antique boat during a summer holiday. Two boys and a girl—ages fourteen, twelve, and ten. Martin, Jerrold, and Serena.

Then came Lyssa. Official record confirmed the gossip. The woman's behavior had become increasingly erratic over the past two years. Unexplained disappearances. Rumors of drug abuse. Hushed-up accidents.

But all the documents scanned within normal variation. Nothing to suggest tampering. Nothing to merit a murder. *Have I proved your fears unfounded already, Evan?* As things now stood, Lyssa died a broken woman's death, driven by past tragedy.

Jani watched construction workers flit along a future commercial transport's spindly framework, one beat ahead of the immense robot ganglion that did the actual hoisting, joining, and fastening. No matter how well-programmed the 'bot, however fuzzified the thinking, human supervision was still required. No robot was capable of seeing the overall picture. Ultimately, it only knew what it was told.

Jani watched a moon-suited human dodge and weave about one of the arms like an armored gnat . . .

I sense an effort to lead me by the nose.

. . . ensuring that the arm moved in the correct direction and hit the chosen target.

His initials are Durian Ridgeway.

Jani finished her sandwich. She hoped she hadn't wasted almost five weeks working with half the data, but she knew that hope was misplaced. She had slipped an urgent meeting request, coded to Evan's attention, into the queue of scrambled messages transmitted to Chicago every half hour. But she doubted she would receive a reply before her shuttle left in—she checked her timepiece—forty-five minutes.

"Do you have anything to declare?"

Jani turned toward the voice. On the far side of the lounge, Customs clerks moved among the waiting passengers, logging colonial purchases, calculating tariffs, handing out receipts. She exhaled with a shudder. Augie notwithstanding, she hadn't been breathing very easily the past few minutes. But she could relax now. The sending-out-of-the-clerks meant all those who merited more personal attention from Customs had already been winnowed.

I wonder how my young couple is doing? Had the body cavity scans begun? Attorneys been contacted?

"Do you have anything to declare?" Chipper voices grew closer. Paper rustled. Recording boards chirped. "Anything at all?"

If you only knew.

"Nothing?"

Not an issue, now. You had your shot and missed. Go away.

"Are you quite sure?"

Yes. My secrets remain mine. I am Jani Moragh Kilian. Captain. United Services. C-number S-one-two-dash-four-seven-dash-one-seven-nine-D. Sideline Service, assigned to Rauta Shèràa Base, First Documents and Documentation Division. Not a real soldier.

"Anything else?"

Eighteen years ago, in a place called Knevçet Shèràa, during the height of the idomeni civil war, I killed my commanding officer in self-defense. His name was Rikart Neumann—Colonel—Gisela Detmers-Neumann's uncle. She and others would perhaps take exception to the self-defense argument, but since they're aware of the events that precipitated the shoot-out, they may not dare voice such.

"Do you have anything to declare?"

The Laumrau panicked when they learned of Neumann's death. First they lobbed "pink"; the microbe infested and disabled all the weapons, environmental, and communication arrays. Then came the shatterboxes. *The Laumrau had secrets to bury, which are none of your concern. All you need know is that, in the process, they buried my corporal. She died when a wall collapsed on her. Corporal Yolan Cray, Mainline Service, Twelfth Rover Corps, C-number M-four-seven-dash-five-six-dash-two-eight-six-R.*

"I'm ready, miss—please continue."

One idomeni day later, I killed twenty-six Laumrau in an effort to save my remaining troops. The deaths were not "clean" as far as the Laumrau were concerned. No human had ever become involved in one of their skirmishes before—the resulting disorder upset them. Since I had violated the Bilateral Accord, the Service would have turned me over to the idomeni for trial followed by inevitable execution, but—

"I'm sorry, miss, could you speak up, please?"

—but the transport carrying me and my troops from Knevçet Shèràa to Rauta Shèràa exploded on takeoff. Lift-array failure. Everyone gone. All her real soldiers. *I know their C-numbers, too.* All fourteen of them. *Do you want to hear them, too?*

"That's not necessary, ma'am. Please continue."

I, however, did not die. Not medically, anyway. *Three doctors salvaged me from the wreckage, for reasons that would shock you to your core. They pieced me together and hid me in a hospital basement in Rauta Shèràa's human enclave. As I healed, the tide of civil war turned, and the Laumrau lost to the Vynshà.* Laumrau descended to Laum, and Vynshà ascended to Vynshàrau. No one fights to avenge the deaths of the losers, not even the well-ordered idomeni.

But they remembered. They called her *kièrshia*, she'd learned later. Toxin. *You don't want to allow me within your perimeter—everything I touch dies.*

"Do you have anything to declare?"

The pennies on my eyes.

"Do you have anything to declare?" The smiling Customs clerk stationed himself beside Jani's chair, recording board in hand, beaming in a way that reminded her of Lucien.

"Just these." Jani removed some pieces of truesilver jewelry, purchased in a hurried swoop through a pricey Felix Station shop, from the side pocket of her duffel. With cheerful efficiency, the clerk scanned the information from the still-attached price tags into his board's data bank and totaled the tariff. Jani just as cheerfully rattled off the Interior account to which the tariff could be billed.

Rule One: Always have something hefty to declare to throw them off. Transaction completed, receipt tucked away, Jani settled back and watched the construction workers hover and dart like metallic bees around a skeletal hive. *Take it from an old smuggler.* She sipped the tea, winced at its bitterness, and waited for her boarding call.

"Admit it, Jani. You'd never seen anything like it in your life. All those old skyscrapers! All that history!" Evan bustled her out onto the glass-walled balcony that adjoined his office and pointed out his view, which included both the Chicago skyline and the nearby lake. "I hope you got a chance to see the memorial to the Greatest War on the way in."

Jani took in the curious array of oddly shaped buildings, all obscured by wind-whipped snow. "You mean 'The War of Family Aggression,' don't you?"

"There were no Families back then, Jani," Evan said patiently.

"No. They came later."

"I seem to recall us having this discussion before." Evan sighed. "Politics aside, it's worth a visit. It's a liquiprism obelisk that changes color on the hour. Really quite striking."

"Evan, I don't know if you've noticed, but it's not sight-seeing weather." Jani looked out at the lake, which had taken on a churning, milky grey life of its own. "If this balcony wasn't enclosed and well heated, we'd be icicles within seconds."

"Yes, but it's home."

"Not for me." She turned her back on his fallen face. "Sorry—didn't mean to rain on your birthday." She hesitated at the office entry. *Why do I feel like I just kicked a puppy?* "I'm sure it must be very nice. In the spring."

"Oh, it is." Evan hurried to her side. "The parks. The arboretums. You'd love it here in the spring." He escorted her back into his retreat's soothing blue-and-green depths. "I gathered your ride here from O'Hare was more exciting than you may have liked."

"That's an understatement." Jani sank into a chair across from Evan's desk. "Nothing like a collision with split batteries to disrupt the flow of traffic on a twelve-lane skimway. Then the HazMat unit came. Then this storm. At least it held off until after I landed." She shuddered. "I think my driver has a death wish. I'd yank her license."

Evan perched on the edge of his desk. "Quite an indictment, coming from you. I blamed my first grey hairs on our sojourns through Rauta Shèràa." That little *bon mot* launched, he eased behind his desk and kicked back. "Chicago is the Commonwealth capital, Jani. Over seventeen million people live within the metroplex limits. I can't tell you the exact square kilometers offhand, but the number borders on the ridiculous." His look turned concerned. "I hadn't considered culture shock. Are you?"

"Shocked by the wonder of it all? I'll live." Jani massaged the hard knot in the back of her neck where augie had planted his foot. She had coped with the throbbing red lights on the emergency vehicles well enough, but the sirens had gotten to her. She held out her hands. The right one had finally stopped shaking. The left one had never started. *Half-sane, at least, but which half?* "Does this place have a gym? Exercise helps."

"Five. I'll get you a pass for the one I use—it has the best equipment." He picked absently at his fingernails. "We have a decent medical staff, as well," he added carefully. "All Neoclona-trained."

"*No*, thank you."

"Oh, for crying out loud, stop acting like an idomeni!" Evan's voice rasped with irritation. "What, I'm not your physician-priest, so you can't talk to me? When was the last time you had your augmentation evaluated? Any augmented vet who works for Interior has to be checked out every six months and have at least one precautionary take-down per year."

"Forget it. Look, I received enough doctoring after the crash to last a lifetime. Half my limbs and most of my insides were grown in a tank. I'm sick of the smell of antiseptic, poking and prodding, and white sheets, not necessarily in that order. And forget any damned take-down. No one's going to stick a blinking box in my face and short out my brain for my own good. I've had it. And speaking of 'had it.' " She gave Evan a brief rundown of her thoughts with regard to his files. His headshaking grew more and more pronounced each time Jani alluded to the possibility that Durian Ridgeway had purposely withheld information.

"I can't accept that!" Evan's feet hit the carpeted floor with a muffled *thud*. "Durian knows how important this is. Hell, he has as much to lose as I do if things fall to pieces. He's been cleaning up after me for so long, his nickname around here is *the janitor*. Everyone knows if I show up, he's never far behind. We're joined at the hip—if I go, he goes."

Oh goodie—I've come between a dog and his man. And between both of them and what? Jani stared at Evan until he broke eye contact and began pushing his pen stand back and forth. "You're still holding out on me." She worked her hands over the brocaded upholstery that covered the arms of her chair. Only her right could detect the changes in texture.

"Jani—"

"Have you forgotten what *I* have to lose if things fall to pieces?"

"*No one could possibly—*"

"I'm wanted by the Service for mutinous murder and desertion. No dust has ever settled on that warrant. It's reposted every six Common months without fail in every colonial Government Hall. Wherever I happened to be, I'd stop by, keep myself company."

"I know it must—"

"Funny how oddly comforting I found it at times. Like a touchstone—"

"Will you shut up!" Evan's face had taken on a hunted look. "I didn't want to tell you this. Knowing how you may react, I'm still not sure I should." The pen stand jerked and shook. "Exterior's looking for you, Jan. I arrived on Whalen only twelve hours ahead of a cruiser carrying members of Ulanova's executive staff. I heard rumors of a Service ship trolling the area as well, but I couldn't confirm them."

Jani crossed her legs to ease the pressure on her lower back. *You'd think a Cabinet House would have better chairs.* "Why now, I wonder?"

Evan's brow furrowed. "You don't seem surprised."

Jani shook her head. "My record states, 'missing, assumed dead.' The gulf between that and 'declared dead' is very wide." She poked her numb left arm. "No remains were ever found. No indestructible Service ID chip was recovered from the wreckage and canceled out. The Admiral-General doesn't know for sure I'm dead; therefore, I am alive. That's why the outstanding warrant. That's why a rep gets sent out to follow up every rumor of my existence. I killed my CO. Then I violated the Bilateral Accord by interfering in idomeni affairs. Those are two biggies, Ev. You may think they've given up on me, but you're wrong. They're not going to rest until they nail me to the wall."

Evan's expression grew confused. "What I don't understand is how Shroud and his buddies managed to keep you hidden? What did they think they played at?"

I remember them standing outside my door, when they thought I couldn't hear. Laughing, calling one another Dr. Frankenstein. No, she took that back. John never laughed. "I don't know how they did it. I think it was all a game to them; an escape from the boredom. Most of the humans had been evac'd by that time. They had nothing to do. So they built themselves a friend." She walked over to the bar and poured herself a glass of water. She gulped the cold liquid, felt it cool her from within. It took her some time to realize Evan had remained silent. She turned to find him staring at her.

"What do you mean by 'friend'? Tell me what I'm thinking didn't happen. Please tell me they didn't—"

"They didn't, Evan. Parini's homosexual and DeVries only likes blondes with big tits."

"What about Shroud? I knew him back then, you know. From his visits to the Consulate. He was strange then, and he hasn't improved with time."

"I knew him, too. A little." If encounters in the entryway of Nema's house counted as "knowing." *He'd mumble, "Hello," and stare at the floor.* Poor John. Funny the things she remembered. How hands that performed the most delicate medical procedures could turn so clumsy when working under a different sort of pressure. "It's over. Why worry about it? What am I going to do, sue for malpractice?" She returned to the bar and poured herself more water, this time adding ice.

"I guess I understand your medical phobia now," Evan said. "I'm surprised they let you escape."

"They didn't. I slipped away during the final blitz." Jani leaned against a bookcase. The odor of the leather binding seemed especially sharp, almost meaty. "Remember?"

Evan nodded slowly. "The Night of the Blade. The Vynshà sent the Haárin into Rauta Shèràa first. Debriding the wound, they called it."

Jani picked up the thread. "They had set up observation points in the hills. I could see the halolamps flashing signals to the Haárin in the city center."

Evan gaped. "They let you walk the streets!"

"I wasn't walking. More like limping double time." She tried to smile. "They didn't want humanish at that point, anyway. They had other concerns." She looked at Evan, sitting hunched over his desk. "Where were you?"

"The sub-basement of the Consulate. We'd been down there for eleven idomeni days. Almost two weeks. The Service got us out at dawn, as the Vynshà entered the city proper. They'd just declared themselves 'rau,' and set fire to the ring the Haárin had erected around Rauta Shèràa's perimeter. We could see the flames from the transport windows." He swallowed. "There were bodies in that ring."

"Not all of them were dead, either." Jani walked away from the bookcase. The odor of the books was making her sick to her stomach. "The ring of souls released by cleansing fire. Supposed to guarantee peace and protection until the next imbalance of power." She looked out the balcony window. The wind still whipped, blowing so much snow that the view looked like a malfunctioning holoVee screen. A roaring gust rattled the panes.

It was Evan's turn to visit the bar. He ignored the water pitcher and reached for the bourbon. "That convergence on Whalen may not mean anything. The way things have been going lately, a display of any type of proficiency with things idomeni would have been enough to attract attention. Ulanova may just be looking for translators." He poured himself a single shot, downed it, then paused to catch his breath. "I slipped a decoy into NorthPort—one of my own people—to distract them." He frowned. "She was one of my best Vynshà-watchers. I'm going to miss her. Probably take us months to get her back."

"Sorry for the inconvenience."

Evan smiled. He hefted the bourbon decanter as though testing its weight, then set it back in its place in the bottle rack. "I think I know what Durian removed from the files. And I know where to find it. You'll have it by tonight."

"Are you going to confront him?"

"No. Not yet. He's not here now, anyway. He and Ange are flying in later today from London. A visit to his family, I believe." He flinched as another gust shook the balcony panes.

That was Hansen Wyle exploding out of his grave. "A visit to *chez* Ridgeway? *Really*?"

"Durian's relationship with Angevin is completely professional," Evan huffed defensively. "You just don't like him."

"He doesn't like me either. He tried to trip me up on the *Arapaho*. He threw some Josephani at me. I pretended I couldn't understand his accent."

"Did you have a chance to study those language discs I slipped into your documents portfolio?"

"That's not the point!"

"No. No, you're right. I'll have a talk with him." He leaned against the bar. "Jani, nobody here knows you except me. In any case, no one who knew you eighteen years ago could place you now. Your face is completely different, your hair. You've lost weight—hell, you even look *taller*." His aimless stare came to rest on her and sharpened. "You're safe. I'll keep you safe."

Jani raised her glass in a mock toast, took a last sip, and headed for the door. "I need to walk off my Chicago driving adventure. I'll see you later."

"Jani?"

She turned to find Evan had opted for the second bourbon after all.

"You really killed Riky Neumann?"

"Yes."

"But he drew first? It was self-defense?"

"His hand went to his holster. I wasn't going to wait to discover whether he was serious or just bluffing. Considering I'd just threatened to declare anarchy rules, relieve him of command, and place him under arrest, I don't think he was simply trying to gauge my reaction."

"Anarchy rules? *You* were going to take over command?"

"The integrity of the documents in my care was threatened. I saw no other alternative. I was within my rights."

Evan downed his second shot. His face flushed. "You killed him over a paper issue?"

"You're upset because he was a Family member?"

"He was my father's best friend. I grew up calling him Uncle Rik."

"And I served under him. Apparently he made a better uncle than commanding officer." Jani rifled through her pockets for her key card. Her duffel and documents case waited outside in a locked desk. "I'll see you tonight. In the meantime, I think I'll explore." She left without looking back. She knew what she'd see if she did. Evan, with his puzzled expression, liquor-fueled curiosity, and unspoken question. *Why, Jani?*

Because when the first patient died, Neumann lied when I asked how it happened, and when the second patient mutilated himself, he told me the truth and expected me to go along. Jani recovered her bags from the desk, took comfort in their weight and shape. But it didn't last. Her mind had set off down another trail, one she tried to avoid but never could for long.

Human patients. At the idomeni hospital. At Knevçet Shèràa. She leaned against the anteroom doorway until the arrival of a flock of staffers forced her to brace up. Then she struck out in search of someone who could tell her where her room was.

CHAPTER 6

Jani sat in the living room of her suite, which occupied a substantial portion of the second floor rear, Interior House Private, and listened to the blizzard's relentless assault against her windows.

After requesting assistance from the occupants of an office down the hall from Evan's, she had soon found herself being passed like a human baton from one black-clad staffer to another. Interior House Main, the Ministry headquarters, was a twelve-story-high, two-kilometer-long city-in-miniature, and Jani felt sure she had been ferried through every centimeter of hallway, lift shaft, and underground skimway before being deposited within the confines of her latest home.

I could stop here for a while. Lots of green, icy on the walls, dark and patterned for rugs and curtains. Flooring and furniture in blond truewood; lamps and accent pieces in black, burnished copper, and emerald. The artwork, realistic seascapes and white curves of Channel School sculpture, were either originals or damned good reproductions.

Makes a difference when you enter through the front door, doesn't it? Figuratively speaking. Judging from the sounds filtering through the sealed windows, Jani didn't expect to see a Chicago front door for at least four months.

If I'm here that long. She sagged farther into her chair. The prospect of getting up seemed as daunting as that of leaving Chicago, post-augie jitters having given way to travel lag. She closed her eyes and tried to nap, but nosiness began sending "let's explore" jolts through her system. She answered the call and started opening doors and checking drawers.

Her bags had already been unpacked, the contents distributed among chests, armoires, and a walk-in closet the size of the NorthPort tracking station. A door she thought led to the bathroom actually opened to a fully applianced kitchenette. Jani checked the cooler and found it stocked with the fruit drinks and snack foods she vaguely recalled mentioning to one of the staffers as her favorites. She cracked the seal on a dispo of helgeth and took a tentative sip. The frothy purple juice tasted crisp and slightly astringent. She polished off that container and half of another before resuming her search. She hadn't realized how thirsty she was.

Another door, palm lock in place but not yet activated, led into a small office. The room contained a desk, also lockable, on which sat a workstation with a secured Cabinet link, the newest model parchment imprinter, and a vase of fresh flowers. Jani stashed the documents case in the desk, tested the chair, then drew aside the curtain and looked out at the storm-whipped lake. *An office with windows—you've skipped up a few grades, Captain.*

She wandered into the bathroom to wash her hands, took one look at the multijet shower, and soon stood beneath pounding streams of hot water. Thus refreshed, she rooted through drawers for clean clothes, and pounced on a set of charcoal grey ship coveralls Lucien had scrounged for her. She dug out a matching tee shirt emblazoned across the front with the legend CSS *ARAPAHO* and freed her scuffed, black, steel-toed boots from the civilized confines of one of the armoires. Working a towel through her damp hair, she collected her duffel and returned to her office.

She activated all her locks using a UV stylus she had liberated from the *Arapaho* inventory. That task completed, she tried to return the stylus to its scanproof pocket in her duffel, but something stiff and sharp-edged slipped into the space and dug into her hand, blocking her.

Jani eased out the holocard, taking special care to avoid bending it. As she tilted the card back and forth, the two holographed sailracers swooped and soared like fighting birds. The brilliant purple-and-blue sails reflected the light like colored mirrors, while the racers' multihued wetsuits shimmered with pearly iridescence.

So, Risa, what's your real name? I've told you mine—it's only fair you tell me yours.

Lucien, I'll tell you mine when you tell me who you're working for.

Jani turned the card over and studied the blank writing surface. Lucien hadn't signed his farewell to her, but then, one could hardly have expected him to leave a traceable signature. For her part, Jani had bug-scanned the card immediately. Twice. A show of respect. From one professional to another.

She propped the card against the vase, tilting it until the two racers were displayed to their best advantage. Then she shouldered her bag, locked her office, and set out to explore.

Jani paused in a sunroomlike walkway which, according to the large display in the center of the tiled floor, joined the Colonial Affairs Offices with Employee Services Section Two, the area she had just left. She stared at the network of connected mazes glowing in yellow and green on the display screen, groaning when she realized she was looking at the ground-floor map only. She touched a pad on the side of the display frame. The mazes shimmered and altered to form the second floor.

She touched the pad ten more times.

I'm not lost—I'm buried. Outside, snow sheeted against glass walls and tornadoed into curves and crevices, reinforcing the illusion. Jani again flipped through floor plans, this time with a better idea of what she wanted.

Five hours later, she emerged from the Library the proud possessor of the passcard and linkcodes necessary to access confidential Cabinet references from her office workstation. She had also arranged for the delivery of several Earth-based and colonial newssheets, and impressed the head documents librarian sufficiently to ensure preferential treatment whenever she submitted a special request.

She'd also stolen a magazine.

I'll give it back. Jani's duffel banged against her hip accusingly, its sides bulging with the addition of an expensive, paper-bound gossip holozine, the slick cover of which bore the brutally unretouched image of a glassy-eyed, disheveled Lyssa van Reuter. *I'm surprised Evan allowed this on-site.* But librarians were a notoriously independent-minded lot, and the public's morbid curiosity regarding the hard life and violent death of one of the more hologenic Family members apparently extended to those who should have known better.

The holozine's title had struck her as particularly ludicrous. "Lyssa—A Life Tragically Cut Short." As if a life could be cheerfully cut short. Maybe they'd explain that novel concept in next month's issue. Jani hugged her duffel close as she boarded the first elevator she came to. She felt a common thief, but she didn't want Evan to know what she read. She'd bet her 'pack he'd asked the Library to inform him of what she checked out. Even independent minds had to follow direct orders from Cabinet Ministers.

The elevator started down. Jani checked her timepiece and wondered at the possibility of hitching a ride into the city. Just to look around, get her bearings. It could prove interesting, now the blizzard had finally stopped.

But first, she needed food. She pressed the second-floor pad again. There was a cafeteria on that floor, as well as an Interior-subsidized grocery store. Her stomach rumbled in anticipation of a very late lunch.

Her absent gaze fell on the car's indicator. It had flickered when she touched it, but the display above the door showed she had bypassed the second floor and was continuing down. Jani punched floor pads, then tried to activate the override, but her efforts to halt the car's descent failed. She tried to push through the ceiling access panel. No go.

The indicator continued to flash. ONE. GROUND. BASE-ONE.

She was heading for the sub-basements. According to the touchpad display, Interior Main stretched five floors below ground level.

BASE-TWO.

Sub-basements were extremely well-secured. They were designed, after all, to serve as disaster shelters.

BASE-THREE.

"You should have taken the stairs, idiot." She dug for her shooter, then tried to crack the seals on the car's ceiling lights with the grip. The thick safety plastic resisted—only two of the four lights succumbed. The car didn't plunge into darkness—more a cloudy dusk. It would serve.

BASE-FOUR.

Jani disengaged her weapon's safety, then braced against the car's rear wall. Feet shoulder width apart. Both hands on the grip. Maybe they wouldn't expect her to stand out in the open. Maybe they wouldn't expect her to shoot.

Direct line of fire—aim for the chest.

BASE-FIVE.

The door swept open. Durian Ridgeway, windblown and agitated, squinted into the car. "Who the—*oh*. Good afternoon, Ms. Tyi. This *is* a restricted-use lift, in case no one informed you."

"Sorry," Jani replied as she secreted her shooter in her coverall pocket

He glared at the car ceiling. "What in bloody hell happened to the lights?"

Angevin Wyle bustled in behind him, weighed down with shopping bags. "Hello, Risa." She joined Jani in the rear of the car. "Why's it so frickin' dark in here?"

"Angevin." Ridgeway thumped the touchpad in the vicinity of the fourth floor. "Language." He didn't bother to ask Jani which floor she wanted. The door closed like a judgment, and they ascended in silence.

The door opened to reveal a mob. Jani found herself surrounded by aggressively helpful staffers who first sought to separate her from her duffel and, when that failed, tried to usher her down the hall toward a large conference room. At the sight of the reporters, holocam operators, and Security guards milling at the room's entrance, she executed a sloppy but successful *excuse me* ricochet spin-off. The move propelled her away from the conference room and past Angevin, who was engaged in heated conversation with a sulky young man who appeared determined to confiscate her shopping bags.

Jani skirted around a corner and down an empty hall as images from the display map paged past her mind's eye. She wandered up and down halls, avoiding guards, searching for a stairwell or secondary elevator that wasn't alarmed.

Close-controlled floors have one and only one nonemergency entry—slash—exit which means if I want to get out of here without lighting up the whole damn complex, I have to walk by the cams and have my face transmitted to every damn colony—shit!

"Ms. Tyi!"

Jani turned to find Durian Ridgeway rushing toward her.

"Have you seen Angevin? She's disappeared!" His ruddy face flushed as he palmed into several of the offices, searching for his wayward aide. "The meeting begins in five minutes, and she has all my notes. The Deputy Prime Minister is here. Angevin needs this exposure, damn it, but every time she gets a chance to put herself forward, she's nowhere to be found!"

What Angevin needs more than anything are six months' pay and an hour's head start. Jani leaned against the wall and watched Ridgeway pace. "Sounds important."

He nodded. "Emergency session. Called by Langley." His mouth twisted around the Deputy's name. " 'We'll meet as soon as you get back,' he said. 'Nothing important,' he said. Then we pull into the main parking garage to find vans from every major news service parked there. We had to flee down to the subs to avoid being blitzed. *Bastard*." His voice took on a desperate edge. "If you could help me find Angevin, Ms. Tyi, I would be very grateful."

Jani gave him a halfhearted salute, hurrying away before he felt compelled to say, "please." She picked a hall where most of the doors lacked palm locks. She tapped lightly on a couple, then pushed open one labeled, FURNITURE. The room lights had already been activated, brought to life, no doubt, by the furious motion taking place atop one of the desks. Angevin, her long skirt bunched up over her hips, had her bare legs wrapped around the arching back of the young man with whom Jani had seen her arguing a few minutes before. He wasn't sulking now.

Jani kicked at a nearby trashzap, sending the metal bucket clattering across the floor. "Durian!" she hissed before forcing the door closed. She took off down the hall, rounded the corner, and barreled into an agitated Ridgeway.

"What was that noise, Risa?" he asked as he tried to dart around her.

"Just me being clumsy," Jani said as she gripped his arm and spun him around. "Angevin's down on the third floor. The parts bins." That seemed reasonable. Documents examiners always fretted over their scanpack functions, especially before important meetings and transactions. "She'll be on her way back up within a few minutes. I ran into someone who saw her go down. There."

"I hope she doesn't show up stinking of broth. Who told you she was there?"

"One of the Security guards." *Please don't ask which one.* "Angevin gave him a message to give to you. I intercepted." Jani heaved an inward sigh as she felt Ridgeway's arm relax.

"Well, nice to know she hasn't lost all sense of responsibility." He eased out of Jani's grasp and smoothed the sleeve of his jacket. "Back to work, then. Thank you, Ms. Tyi." With a curt nod, he walked off in the direction of the conference room bustle.

Jani waited until she felt sure he wouldn't return. Then she hurried back around the corner and tapped on the storage-room door. "He's gone."

The door cracked open. The young man slipped out first. He glowered at Jani, looked past her down the hall, then whispered over his shoulder, " 'S ok."

Angevin crept out, jacket in hand. "Please don't tell Durian," she rasped as she struggled into the snug-fitting topper. "He'll kill us if he finds—"

"Don't *fookin'* beg!" The young man's Channel World accent could have blunted complexed steel. "We airn't done nothin' wrong!"

"You both shut up." Jani leaned close to Angevin. Her frazzled appearance could be written off as travel lag, but no one could mistake the smashed berry stains surrounding her swollen lips. "Collect your gear, splash some cold water on your face, and get your ass to that meeting."

Angevin rushed back into the storage room, reemerging with her documents bag in hand. "Please don't tell—"

Jani waved her quiet. "You told a *male* Security guard to tell Ridgeway you had gone to the parts bins. I ran into the guard and told him I'd deliver the message. Got that?" Angevin nodded wide-eyed as Jani pushed her down the hall. She watched her disappear around the corner, then sagged against the wall. Her neck seized up as she tried to flex it.

"We airn't done nothin' wrong."

Jani turned slowly to find the young man still scowling. He'd pulled a flat copper case from the inside pocket of his tunic and removed a nicstick. "Airn't seen each other for over three bloody months." He stuck the gold-and-white candy-striped cylinder in his mouth without cracking the ignition tip, shoved his hands in his trouser pockets, and started pacing.

Upon close examination, he proved good-looking, in a pouty, dissolute choirboy sort of way. Thick, straight auburn hair covered his ears and collar and flopped over his forehead. His skin had an office pallor, his uniform black boots needed polishing, and he slouched. *Boy, I bet Ridgeway hated you on sight.* "You Channel Worlder?" Jani asked.

He wheeled. "Yeah!" He stepped close, until his nose was only centimeters from hers and she could smell the spiced odor of his unignited nicstick. "So the fook what?"

Jani looked into his eyes, the same mossy green as Angevin's. More bloodshot, though. "What's your name?" she countered softly.

The question, or the manner in which it was asked, seemed to throw the young man. His jaw worked. "Steve. Forell."

"Jersey? Guernsey? Man?"

"Guernsey." He took a deep breath. "Helier."

Jani smiled. "I've been to Helier. A beautiful city." *If you were born with antifreeze in your veins.* "And what do you do here at Interior, Mr. Forell?"

The smile began in the depths of the narrowed eyes and quickly worked down. Steve Forell shook his shaggy head to help it along. Relaxed and grinning, he looked all of twelve years old. A gamy, street-wise twelve, but twelve all the same.

"Screw that—you're trying to redirect me attentions." He worked his nicstick like a toothpick. "I'm a dexxie, like Ange. Xenopolitical branch. Work with the idomeni. Schooled at Oxbridge Combined."

He tugged at his hair. "The xenos came looking for redheads and scooped me up."

"Colony boy at an Earthbound school. You must be good."

"I am." The grin flickered as Steve glanced down the hall in the direction Angevin had gone. "Not good enough, though, according to some." Then his smile vanished and instead of looking street-wise and twelve, he looked lonely, scared, and five and a half.

See what happens when you learn names. You get involved. Jani leaned harder into the wall. *I do not have the time.* Her back ached now, and the elevator episode coming so soon after the traffic adventure hadn't done her post-augie nerves any favors.

"What's the matter with you?" Steve asked. "You look fit to pass out."

Jani massaged her tightened scalp. "Can you get me out of here?" She forced a smile, and felt her travel-dry skin crinkle under the stress. "I'm not cleared for the close-controlled floors. The elevator won't listen to me."

"Surprised Durian didn't have you tossed out a window." Steve pushed his way back into the storage room, emerging with Angevin's shopping bags. "Here." He shoved two of the slick plastic sacks into Jani's arms and gripped the remaining bags with looped thumbs and forefingers only. "He even picks out her clothes," he grumbled as he glanced at the bags' contents. "We'll leave them with the door guard. Meeting'll go on for hours, anyway."

They walked back to the elevators. The area had been cleared of cams and reporters; a pair of guards stood sentry by the closed conference-room doors. They eyed Jani warily, but relaxed when Steve walked over and handed them the bags.

"What now?" he asked as he rejoined her. He flipped open a panel beside the elevator and punched in a code sequence.

"I haven't eaten since the Luna shuttle. That was over ten hours ago. Just point me toward the food."

"You need dinner?" Steve brightened. "I could do with some dinner. The cafeteria on Two is the best one. That's where all the nobbies eat." The doors closed, and he blinked in surprise. "What the hell happened to the lights?"

CHAPTER 7

"Your government takes issue with the bidding, nìRau?"

Tsecha remained very still in his low bench seat, conscious of the sidelong glances of the others at the table and the more direct, fear-filled stare of the man who had spoken. Humanish eyes. He should have grown used to them by now. *But so much white—like death-glaze.*

He crossed his left arm over his chest and lowered his chin. "The bidding, we are most content with, and truly, Mister Ridgeway." His voice rumbled, even in both tone and pitch and, he felt, unaccented. He was most proud of his English. "My Oligarch wonders only of the lapse in security. He fears it happening again."

Ridgeway shook his head in a show of impatience, obvious for even a humanish. "NìRau," he said, "Morden nìRau Ceèl has our word it won't happen again."

Tsecha remained calm as the other humanish at the table shifted in their chairs. Some exhaled loudly. He stared openly down the large wooden oval at Durian Ridgeway, but felt no pleasure as he watched the man's tired face flood with color. It had always been too easy with that one. "Yes, Mister Ridgeway," he replied, "but you also gave your word last year. And your office gave its word last month in your name. You pledged your word to research this company's documents, and you failed. What value is your word, Mister Ridgeway? I ask you that."

The room itself seemed to sigh in response. Then the man at the table's head, Deputy Prime Minister Langley, spoke. "In Durian's defense, Staffel Mitteilungen took us all by surprise, nìRau. They purposely delayed obtaining their start-up registration until the end of the fiscal year. Many of our new businesses do this for the tax advantage. StafMit did it in hope that, in the flood of applications, the screening committee Durian chaired would miss the fact that via a blind trust, Gisela Detmers-Neumann held a significant financial stake in the company."

Tsecha looked directly into the Deputy PM's eyes. *Dark Langley, as the night is dark.* If they were as idomeni, Langley's eyes would look as two black pits. He sat rigidly, his seat, like the seats of all the humanish, elevated above Tsecha's. The positioning of the chairs, the humans' stiff, formal posture, were meant to display respect. But he had never detected either the gentleness of friend or the wary regard of esteemed enemy in any of those in the room. What could he sense? Fear? Definitely. Dislike? Perhaps. *They do not want me here.* That was indeed unfortunate for them. Here, he was. Here, he would stay.

"Tax advantage, Mister Langley?" Tsecha placed his hands palms down on the tabletop. Red bands trimmed the broad cuffs of his sand white overrobe, making it appear as though blood flowed from his wrists. His ring of station glimmered on his finger, the jasperite also reminding him of blood.

"Yes, nìRau." Langley's thick, black eyebrows arched with some vague emotion, but he offered no accompanying gesture or change in posture to indicate which it was. Puzzlement? Surprise? Or perhaps the man felt embarrassment concerning the question? Who could tell with these government humanish? Their faces were as blocks of wood, their gestures, when they bothered to gesture, meaningless flailing. "Taxes," Langley repeated. "The saving of money."

"Ah." Tsecha spread his fingers. Wrinkled. Age-spotted. He touched a thread-fine scar near the base of his left thumb, the remains of a blade fight with an esteemed enemy, now long dead.

à lèrine—the ritual combat that declared to all idomeni the hatred between two. So many such bouts had he fought in defense of his beliefs—the scars etched his arms, his chest and shoulders. They had thinned and faded over time, as he had. He had grown so old, waiting. "Yes," he said, with a nod he hoped Langley comprehended. "I know humanish have great interest in money, and truly. That interest has been displayed to idomeni in times past."

The room sighed again, for those reasons all humanish knew, yet would not speak. In an effort to placate, Tsecha bared his teeth to the Deputy PM. Smiling, to humanish an expression of most benign regard. Why then did the man squirm so?

"We've been through all this, nìRau," Langley said. Indeed, he seemed most displeased. His jaw worked. He gripped the arms of his chair.

"Yes, Mister Langley, we have."

"Our purpose today is to discuss the Vynshàrau's reluctance to allow StafMit the opportunity to bid for contracts to install communications equipment in the Haárin settlement outside Tsing Tao."

"Yes, Mister Langley, it is."

"Since Mister Ridgeway's committee approved StafMit's preliminary registration, thus bringing them to the Haárin trade council's attention, I asked him here to—"

"To *trap* him, Mister Langley." Tsecha dropped his words slowly, carefully, like stones into still water. "And to embarrass Mister van Reuter."

Plink! Ridgeway stared at him openly, unsure whether to be grateful or to fear what could follow.

Plink! Langley exhaled with a shudder, his anger a solid thing that one could hold in the hand.

Plink! The other humanish at the table stared at their hands, in the air over each other's heads, anywhere but at one another.

Tsecha pressed his lips together to avoid baring his teeth. He most enjoyed telling humanish the obvious truths they so feared. It shocked them so.

"NìRau, I would have thought this neither the time nor the place, but perhaps—"

Tsecha shut out Langley's drone. He had heard the arguments before at too many meetings, could recite them as he did his prayers. It would have surprised the humanish to know if the choice had been his alone, Tsecha would have allowed Detmers-Neumann and her fellow outcasts to welcome him to this damned cold city, to sit and watch him speak to the shivering crowds. *But when her first openness failed, she tried to worm, to sneak, to . . . to . . .* Tsecha's command of English failed him. He only knew that blood had asserted itself as it always did. Gisela proved she shared skein with Rikart, and truly. So, just as truly, would he never acknowledge her.

His gaze flitted from one tense face to another, finally coming to rest on the female sitting next to Ridgeway. Blood asserted itself, or did it? He tried to will the red-haired youngish to look at him, but she kept her eyes fixed on her lap. Angevin. What did such a name mean? *Not-of-Hansen?* How much Tsecha missed her father, as well as the one who worked with him. His green-eyed Captain.

If they were here, what meetings we would have! But Hansen,

Tsecha's brilliant Wyle of the godly hair, was dead, and the man's daughter could not compare.

And Kilian . . .

Tsecha looked down at his mottled hands. He thought so much of age lately. Death. All these meetings brought such thoughts. All this talk with as-dead humanish was enough to drain the hope from any living thing. And he had had such hopes once, had seen the future in two faces. But one was dead and the other, according to the increasingly impatient word of all his experts, had to be as well.

But they never found the body. Though his Temple rejoiced in their belief that Jani Kilian had died in fire, Tsecha had nursed the slight doubt he had sensed in the humanish soldiers who had told him of the crash, grasped it like a handhold in a wall of sand. Had fire destroyed his toxin? He hoped not, with each progress report he received with shaking hands. He prayed not, over each of his six daily sacraments. With each bite of sacred food, he begged the gods to answer him. *Send me my kièrshia, please*, he wove his entreaty around Langley's continuing thrum, *before they bury me.*

And when his Captain had returned to him . . . ah, then, would there be meetings!

CHAPTER 8

Jani followed Steve into the dining hall and waited as he tried to figure out where to sit. In past lives, this hadn't posed a problem for her. *When alone, one-seat table, dark corner, facing the door.* The dictum had been drilled into her head by frustrated mainline Service instructors unprepared to deal with a documents examiner who felt it her primary duty to plant herself within view of the cashbox and watch the way the staff handled the money.

But then, for eighteen years, the scorned procedure had become second nature, an acknowledgment of a threat that, if not always acute, had staked a permanent claim in Jani's mind.

Well, now was the time for something new. Unlike the long, bench-seated tables she had always encountered in cheap public eating areas, the tables here were small and round or small and square, each covered with silver cloth, decorated with a vase of real flowers and surrounded by no more than eight flexframe chairs. The room itself, an expansive arrangement of tiered, skylit ceilings and windowed exterior walls, would easily hold a thousand. It appeared about half-full now, the mealtime din dampened by soundshielding.

"How's this, then?" Steve asked as he claimed a window table. The outside view of the House gardens was stunning, but he showed where his priorities lay as he turned his back on it and pointed out a nearby table filled with upper-management types. "Sit here long enough, whole world goes by."

Her growling stomach urging her to *please eat now*, Jani settled next to Steve and shoveled in a few steaming forkfuls. Then the tastes of the salmon steak and steamed fresh vegetables hit her, and she slowed down. A meal like this deserved some respect—this wasn't a pickup from the *tamè* stand across the street from NorthPort's Guv Hall.

"Good stuff, eh?" Steve asked after a few minutes.

"Hmm." Jani swallowed, then pointed toward the sea of diners with her fork. "So, which are the nobbies?"

In quick succession, she received capsule descriptions of several department and division heads, the general tone of which led Jani to conclude the gossip rag in her duffel had lost a giant when Steven Forell opted for the documents corps.

"Shut up!" She coughed into her napkin as he regaled her with a tale of the novel use to which the head of the Farms Bureau had once put his diplomatic courier service.

" 'S true." Steve's broad grin reflected a raconteur's joy in an appreciative audience. "You could hear 'em all up and down the hall. Some limp-dick from the Ag Ministry came here and threatened to have him classified as an animal-research facility if he didn't knock it off." He pushed away his empty plate and maneuvered the chair across from him so he could use it as a footstool. Then he picked up his nicstick from its perch on the edge of his tray and crunched the ignition tip between his teeth. "Thanks for covering for me and Ange," he said, his face obscured by spicy smoke. " 'Preciate it."

Jani pushed away her own cleaned plate and sat back to observe the passing parade. "Wasn't the smartest move, considering all the people milling around."

"Weren't my idea, either." Steve's shoulders hunched defensively, his good humor dissipating with the smoke. "Always supposed to be the randy young buck's idea, innit? Havin' it off on desks." He sneered. "I had dinner reservations at Gaetan's tonight. Treasury Minister eats there." He took a pull on his nicstick. Jani watched the thin dose line move halfway up the unit's shaft. "I know how to behave. Be nice if some people gave me a chance to prove it."

Jani watched a cluster of well-dressed manager-types scud past. "Is it that important to you? To pretend you're one of them, act like they do?" Unpleasant scenes from her Service past flashed in her memory. "Do you think you need to do it to keep your job?"

Steve bristled. "I don't act! Why should I pretend, anyway? I'm just as good as any of them."

"Not to them." Jani began tearing her dispo napkin into tiny bits. Talking about Earthbound–colony relations always made her shred things. "You don't sound like them, and you don't act like them. You're branded on the tongue and in every other way you can think of. Our great-great-etceteras lost the Greatest War, remember? That's why we got kicked out in the first place. We're the problem children. Forever and for always." She picked up a sprig of herb from her plate and stuck it in her mouth.

Steve edged straighter in his seat. "You sound like a secessionist," he mumbled, eyes locked on a pair of high-level staffers walking by the table.

"More a realist than anything. The day we get them to take notice won't come until we can bleed them semiconscious for using our GateWays and importing our goods. And for reeling in our best brains, convincing them they have to come here if they want to be somebody."

"They've started jailing secessionists, you know." Steve had, Jani noted with bemusement, toned down his accent considerably.

"There are a hell of a lot more of us than there are of them," she said. "How many jails they got?"

Steve exhaled with a shaky rumble. "Witch. Mam warned me about girls like you." He tossed his spent nicstick onto his plate. "I'm changing the subject. Not real comfortable talking politics. Always get that swimming-in-shit feeling after a while. Ange told me your name. Can't place your accent. Where you from, Risa?"

Jani hesitated. "Tyi's a Josephani name." *J'suise Acadienne, en actual.* The name of her home world sounded strange to her. Over the past eighteen years, she'd called herself everything *but* Acadian.

"Never been to Josephan," Steve said. "Heard it's nice. Bit off, rebel like you doing for the Minister. Everyone knows you're one of his spooks."

Oh, they did, did they? Jani surveyed the dining hall. About three-quarters full now, and no one, she noticed to her chagrin, wearing anything remotely resembling ship coveralls. Like it or not, she'd have to start dressing properly to avoid attracting attention. "Spook's a general term. The work I do is more specialized."

"Oh yeah? Do tell."

"Investigations of particular interest."

"As opposed to general butting-in?" Steve pushed his tray back and forth. "And what interesting bit of biz are you investigating at the moment?"

"You're the gossip expert. What have you heard?"

"That you're looking into Lyssa van Reuter's death." Steve ignited another 'stick. "Thought that were an accident."

"Might still be."

"But you don't know yet?"

"Not until I have a chance to see all the data."

"Data? You make it sound like an experiment."

"It could have been, to someone." Jani watched the side of Steve's face as she spoke. He appeared relaxed enough, if solemn. But then, he had a lot on his mind.

"She had problems," he said. "Or rather, you knew she had problems, but she never let on."

Jani thought of the bleary-eyed face on the holozine cover. "Except when the holographers were around?"

"Timing." Steve waved weakly to someone at another table. "I'm afraid if the Lady had problems, they were with timing."

"You sound as though you liked her."

He hesitated. "I never worked with her."

"But you must have friends who did. How did they feel?"

"She were Family. No brothers or sisters. Used to being the center of it all, if you know what I mean."

"Difficult to work with?" Jani knew it would be best for the investigation to remain neutral regarding Lyssa, but being Anais Ulanova's niece could have had the expected nasty influence. "Spoiled? Demanding?"

Steve ignored the question. "So, madam," he said, pushing his chair away from the table, "shall we go?"

They left the cafeteria to find a small crowd had gathered in the glass-sided walkway. Steve elbowed a path to the paned wall, frowning as he checked his timepiece. "He's leaving early. Wonder what happened?"

Jani looked over his shoulder toward the white-robed figure crossing the secured skimway oval two stories below. Whispers of "It's him! It's him!" buzzed about her. Her heart thumped.

"He doesn't look real happy." Steve shook his head. "You can tell by the set of his shoulders, how slouchy he is."

Jani's own spine straightened in self-defense. Nothing activated her urge to confess to everything and brace for the worst like the slumping amble of a pissed-off Vynshàrau. *No, this is Nema.* Jani watched the ambassador slip into the rear seat of an off-white, triple-length skimmer. *Chief propitiators do not get pissed; they become enraged.*

"I hope Ange is all right." Steve pulled on his tunic hem. "When things don't go well, Durian takes it out on her."

"What was the ambassador doing here?" Jani wedged beside him and watched the idomeni vehicle drift away like a land-hugging cloud. "You'd think there'd have been notices or something." She thought how close she had come to being shoved into that damned conference room. *Evan, why the hell didn't you warn me!*

"Langley were responsible for that. He says Interior has the best layout for meeting with Tsecha—the secured conference rooms are furthest away from any and all eating areas and food-storage facilities." Steve recited the policy with bland formality. " 'Course, doesn't mean our man should be allowed to attend these meetings, seeing as the flies are settling on the bloated corpse of his career and all."

"*Steve.*" Jani pressed a hand to her aching stomach. She'd definitely overeaten.

"Langley's one ham-handed wanker, 's all I can say. Likes twisting his little knife." Steve gestured toward the spot where the idomeni skimmer had been parked. "I wonder what he thinks of all this. Thought about asking him a couple times, figured I'd be gigged for bleedin' cheek."

"You've met him?"

"Nothing one-on-one. Sat in on some document-transfer protocols. Harmonizing paper systems. That'll be the bloody day—they run rings around us." He tugged at his bangs. "He stared at my hair, like they expected. Gave me a nod. I feel sorry for the old codge."

"Why?"

Steve gave an uncertain shrug. "Because he's so out of place here. I mean, he's the only member of his delegation who even tries to communicate directly with us. The rest of his crew just passes everything directly to the translator corps. But . . ."

"But?"

"He talks about the time before the war a lot. What went on at the Academy. What he tried to teach his students."

Oh hell. "Such as?"

Steve forced a laugh. "He thinks we're all going to be the same someday. Us and the idomeni. That living together will cause us to blend."

"Blend into what?" As if she didn't know.

"A hybrid race. Rauta Haárin, Tsecha called it." Steve tried his best, but he garbled the Haárin *r*, coughing it up from the back of his throat rather than trilling it. "A brand-new sect."

"You can't blend beings together like ingredients in a bowl," Jani said as she did her best to avoid looking at the reflection of her filmed eyes. "It doesn't work that way."

"You might be right," Steve said. "I ran it by a friend of mine. Genetics therapeutician. She thinks it's a joke." He frowned and toyed with a fastener on his tunic. He tried to appear sure of himself, but Jani could sense his confusion. How would the word of a human rate against that of an alien ambassador, one who possessed a most unique brand of charm?

Like a tsunami with legs. Oh, yes, she remembered it well.

"He makes a strange kind of sense, though," Steve said. "He says that idomeni and humanish both think they control their environments, while in reality, the environments control us. Our environments want order, and order means everything the same. He thinks our worlds will force change upon us, set it up so we'll have no choice but to hybridize." His stare grew dreamy, as though he focused on something far away.

Jani tried to laugh, but it caught in her throat. "You have let him get into your head, haven't you?" She had to wave a hand in front of Steve's face to get his attention. "Look, he's a religious leader. Charismatic and persuasive and sure he speaks the truth. Sincerity doesn't make him right."

"He's good though, Ris. 'We shall change or we shall die, and truly.' That's what he said. He really believes it. You can tell the way his eyes light up." Steve shook his head. "Maybe it is all about politics. Maybe he's just looking for humans who could lobby for his policies."

"He does know his way around a Council chamber." Jani looked at the place where Nema's skimmer had been parked. She could sense his presence, like a ghost forever seeking the thing that would allow it to rest. Humans had names for behavior like that. Fervid, when they felt kind. Fanatic, when they tired of mopping up the blood. But if you denied that part of Nema, you denied the charm as well. And felt the loss, as though you'd disappointed your champion. "Humans don't have the maturity to deal with Tsecha. We took an incredible risk allowing him here."

"What do you know about him?" Steve turned to her, eyes shining. "Have you ever met him?"

Shit. "No. I've just heard things. I know he changed his name after the last war."

Steve shrugged off that piece of old news. "Avrèl nìRau Nema, it used to be. They told us about that in the prep courses. Didn't tell us why, though, exactly." They were the only two left in the walkway now. He took the opportunity to ignite a nicstick. "Said it had something to do with the war. New government, new name."

Something to do with the Temple authorities pressuring him to sever every link to a past they found disordered. How had they felt when their chief priest informed them of his new name? Tsecha. Sìah Haárin for fool. *Depending on the accompanying gestures, of course.*

Jani could imagine him announcing his new skein and sect names, arms at his sides, hands obscured by the folds of his overrobe. Palms open, thumbs extended. The Vynshàrau equivalent of crossing his fingers behind his back.

"He's probably the most knowledgeable Vynshàrau where we're concerned," she said. Experience in dealing with humanish—that had to be the reason the idomeni risked sending him. Even now, the Council must be training his replacement.

"Yeah, he tries to be as human as he can. Always just misses, though." Steve bared his teeth in an apelike grimace. "I mean, he comes at you with that smile, holding his hand out for you to shake, and it's like—"

"Grim Death with a Deal for You," Jani said. And what deals he offered.

Someday, nìa, you will be Rauta Haárin. Then you will replace me. As chief propitiator, you will ensure the blending continues. You will guide souls along the Way to the Star. Tsecha had sounded so sure of himself, as always. He knew the gods were on his side. Fervor. Fanaticism.

They had stood on the Academy veranda after the graduation ceremony had been completed. Nema had awarded Jani a ring, as he had each of his Six. A lovely thing, crimson jasperite set in cagework gold, an exact duplicate of his ring of station. Everyone else's had fit, but hers had been too small. So he had explained what needed to happen in order for hers to fit.

He had been genuinely surprised when Jani handed the ring back to him. Confused. But he thought he could compel her. She told him she didn't liked being forced to play pawn in someone else's game.

This is not a game, nìa. This is life as it must be.

The sound of Steve's chuckling brought her back to the present. "Grim Death. That's great!" He flipped his spent 'stick into a trashzap and paced up and down the walkway.

Outside, the dusk-darkened sky was laced with orange and purple. In the distance, charge lot lights had activated. Jani looked at the wall clock in surprise. "It's still afternoon. It's getting dark already?"

Steve stopped in his tracks. "Yeah. Bloody winter. Nothin' to look forward to but nothin'." He looked at her expectantly. "You got plans?"

"Work, for a while. I'm lagged as hell. Probably be asleep before long." She made a show of stretching. "You never answered my question about Lyssa."

"Hmm." Steve strolled down the walkway. "Where you going now?"

"Executive offices." She fell into step beside him. "I need to pick up some docs."

"Anything planned for tomorrow?"

"Not sure. Why?"

Steve looked at her with the sort of grin that drove Earthbound girls to desktops. "You know that saying about one good turn," he said, disappearing into an unmarked stairwell.

CHAPTER 9

Jani found Evan waiting for her in the Interior executive wing.

"Get settled all right?" He ushered her down the painting-trimmed hallway and into his office. "How's your room?" He had changed into civvies. His blue pullover matched his eyes. Unfortunately, the color also accented the hollows beneath. "Hope you've found everything to your liking."

Jani watched him close in on the bar. She refused his offer of a drink, noticing glumly that he still opted for straight bourbon. "Why didn't you tell me about Nema?" she asked, following with a quick rundown of her near miss. "I was an eyelash away from being pushed into that room. The physical changes wouldn't have thrown him at all—he would have known me instantly."

Evan dragged another chair over to the visitor's side of his desk. He sighed and motioned for Jani to sit.

"It caught me by surprise, too." He lowered his lean frame into his chair as though he feared the cushions had teeth. "Langley doesn't bother to inform me of his visits anymore. I must allow him access to that portion of the Main House whenever he requires it. He seems to require it whenever it causes the most inconvenience." He scowled and sipped his drink. "What a coincidence."

"You could have told me."

"I tried! I called your suite. You didn't answer. Knowing the kind of day you'd had, I assumed you were taking a nap. You always slept like a rock." He offered a faint, knowing smile. "I'd been in meetings all afternoon—I had no idea you'd come back here. How did you get into the secured section anyway? I hadn't arranged for your clearance yet."

"The elevator let me ride, but it wouldn't let me steer." Jani pressed her fingers to her temples. Her scalp felt two sizes too small.

"Somebody must have overridden the security controls in order to get people up from the subs more quickly. At least we'll know to be on our guard for next time. Langley usually times these little invasions every six to ten days. My staff didn't expect him until early next week. I guess it was just Cao's way of saying, 'Welcome home.'" Evan rocked his glass back and forth, clinking nonexistent ice. "Do you need me for anything tonight—"

"No—"

"—because I'm busy. Social commitment. A dinner I don't want to eat hosted by people I despise. Welcome to the glamorous world of top-level government." He set down his drink. "I have what you came here for." He rose and walked back to his desk. "Don't want to waste your time."

"You're not." Jani watched Evan's shoulders work beneath his sweater. He had never been exactly strapping, but he looked bonier than she remembered. "Have you eaten anything today?"

"I had lunch," he replied vaguely as he opened a drawer and withdrew a thick, scuffed binder. "I found these in the parts bins, locked away in a drawer." He silenced Jani's protest with a look. "I know as a nondoc, I shouldn't be allowed in there. Don't ask me how I gained access—you don't want to know." He set the files on the table between them.

Jani hefted the binder into her lap and examined the black cover. She flipped the cover open. Her palms felt damp. *Call me Pandora.*

"Please don't read it now." Evan advanced on the bar again. "Take it out of here."

"Evan—"

"You don't understand how much it sickens me to know you're going to read that. But you have to, don't you? It's your job. It's what I asked you here to do." His voice had taken on a formal tone. Very van Reuter. "So you had better go do it."

Jani tucked the binder under her arm and headed for the door. "Enjoy your dinner." She paused in the doorway and looked back at him. "Bicarb lozenges are great for masking liquor breath, by the way."

Evan reached into his pants pocket and pulled out a half-empty foil-wrapped cylinder. "I've been buying them by the case for years," he said, raising his glass to her. Jani closed the door before she had to watch him drain it.

Against all logic, her stomach started growling as she mounted the Private House's sweeping main stairway and wended through the second-floor hallways toward her room. Her appetite had increased markedly over the past few months. *Must be the cold weather.* She was considering the possibilities her cooler offered when the faint smell of fresh coffee brought her to full alert.

On the table outside her door, she found a tray laden with what apparently constituted the House's version of an evening snack. Next to the swan-necked silver ewer containing the coffee rested a plate of sliced fresh fruit, a keep-warm basket filled with sweetened bread, and a three-tiered dish containing colorful miniature cakelets and cookies.

Jani wrestled through the door with her duffel, the file binder, and the tray, determined to shovel everything into the room at once even though she knew it would go much more smoothly if she'd just put something down. She staggered back-bowed and lopsided to the bed, depositing her burden just before straps slid and binders freed themselves and whomped onto trays.

She popped an anise cookie into her mouth as reward for a job well done, then activated the suite's music system, pressing the pad beside her bed until she found something appropriately calming. Mussorgska, she guessed, as strings swelled and faded. Not the current fashion, but comforting. Judging from Evan's behavior when he turned over the binder to her, she would need some comfort soon.

She pulled off her boots, carried the tray into the kitchenette, and poured and arranged. Soon, she was ensconced in her office, steaming mug in hand, feet on desk, binder in lap, scanpack within easy reach. She'd closed the curtains to block out the night, but left her office door wide open. She wanted to feel cozy, not trapped.

She opened the binder, glanced over the stripped-down table of contents, then paused to read more carefully as familiar terms caught her eye. *Initial Hopgood Analysis—Page Four. Insertion and Activation—Page Nine.* She set down her coffee and read further. *Dobriej Parameters. Physical Markers. Final Scans—Page Twenty-One.*

Jani thumbed through the hefty binder. "There are a hell of a lot more than twenty-one pages here!" She browsed psych evals, handwritten notes, Neoclona emergency calls, and wound up staring at the Commonwealth Police report of an accident that occurred at the van Reuter summer compound north of Chicago. A boating accident in which three children died.

A blast of woodwinds jerked Jani upright. She hurried into the bedroom and killed the music, then fixed herself a drink. Water. With lots of ice. To quell the burning in her stomach.

She returned to her office. From the recesses of well-stocked drawers, she removed a pad of paper and several colored pens. On the first sheet of the pad, Jani roughed out a three-column grid, then wrote, "Initial Hopgood" and "Insert and Act." in the first, "Dob," "PM," and "Finals" in the second.

The third column, she left blank.

Four hours later, the third column remained blank. Jani stared at the empty space, debated going through the binder one more time, then shook her head. She hadn't found what she sought because it wasn't there to find.

She walked to the window and drew aside the curtain. The night sky was clear, the glitter of city illumination reflecting sharp silver-gold off the lake surface. She cracked the weather seal and let frigid air wash over her. When her face felt the way her left arm always did, she closed the window and massaged the blood back into her cheeks.

After a few minutes, she returned to her desk and wrote, "Augmentation of Martin van Reuter" across the top of the grid. Every report needed a title, even the ones you couldn't finish.

During her postcrash recovery, she had learned more about her augmentation than she ever wanted to know. The physical reactions it induced had sped her recovery in some ways and hampered it in others, and John Shroud had been adamant she learn its idiosyncrasies along with him. *I can't believe you waited this long,* he had said. *Willful ignorance will only harm you in the long run.* So she forced herself to read the files he purloined for her, memorized the terms, the sequences, the whys and wherefores.

The evaluations had begun during her first month in OCS. She'd been a borderline case. Hopgood analysis confirmed her tendency toward vivid dreams. One Service physician had expressed grave concern over the activity seen in certain regions of her thalamus during Dobriej sensory-input testing.

But when the war came, the Service augmented Jani for the same reason they did all their eligible personnel—as a precaution. The enclave should have bugged out as soon as the fighting began. *But we had a GateWay station to protect, commercial interests to oversee.* Besides, the opportunity to observe the orderly idomeni at war proved too great a temptation. *To walk ignored past battles like figurines in bell jars. To be protected by the simple fact it wasn't our war.*

Of course, it couldn't last. *We watched with our faces pressed against the glass. Before we could stop ourselves, we'd broken through.* Learned names. Become involved.

Jani escaped to her sitting room. Desperate for voices, she activated her holoVee, flipping through the channels until she found a broadcast of a soccer match. The Gold Round of the last Commonwealth Cup. She watched bright blue Serran and red-and-gold-striped Phillipan jerseys dash up and down the field as the crowd roiled and roared.

I shouldn't have been augmented, but at least I was old enough to adapt. She sat on the couch, watched the colors flicker, listened to the ebb and flow of noise. She ate a balanced diet. Kept hydrated. Avoided conflict whenever possible. *I haven't had a precautionary take-down in almost twenty years.* And she'd never need one. *I know the difference between right and wrong—no altered neurochemical cascade is going to push me over the edge.*

Someone like her was supposed to be the worst-case scenario, the absolute limit to which a dodgy technology could be pushed.

So, whose decision was it to test a prototype personality augment on a three-year-old boy?

What did they think they were doing? When they enhanced what they believed to be Martin's authoritative tendencies, were they surprised when he fought with playmates and flew into tantrums when his wishes were thwarted? Were they astonished when he attacked his father with a lazor at the age of six, or when he pushed his little brother down stairs at eight. Repeatedly tried to force himself on his mother, then his sister, beginning at age eleven?

When they did everything they could to enhance Martin's feeling that he, and only he, was the van Reuter heir, were they shocked that he planned the murders of his brother and sister?

But the storm got you before your parents could. Given the justifications for Martin's behavior she found in the psych evals, it would have been interesting to see how *la famille* van Reuter would have worked out from under that one. And they would have. The pattern had been set.

Jani pondered Martin's blank third column. She had constructed the same sort of chart during her hospital stay, filling her own third column with the terms for post-augie analysis and counseling. In her case, they led to the conclusion that a mistake had been made, but that Captain Kilian, an Academy-trained documents examiner in whom the Service had invested so much, would just have to be taught how to adjust.

Poor Marty—they just turned you loose on an unsuspecting world. Then buried the evidence and prevented the unsuspecting world from figuring out what the hell had happened. *Evan didn't even allow an autopsy.* The miniscule masses, buried next to Martin's amygdala, would have shown up during the examination of his brain. They had formed from the components injected into his ventricular system, produced all those neurotransmitter analogues whose names Jani had managed to forget. Tried to forget. Would forget, eventually.

She worked a finger beneath her hair at the place where skull met spine, and felt the tiny, raised, round scar. The secondary depositions near her thyroid and adrenal glands had been minor discomforts compared to the insertion of the primary augmentation. Having her head immobilized in the stereotaxic restraint had shaken her up, and she'd been a grown woman. How would that damned skull-cage have affected a toddler?

And the headache afterward . . .

She fixed her attention upon the soccer match. Phillipi's star right wing had just scored what would prove to be the winning goal. The screen filled with the raucous tumble of a red-and-gold pile-on.

Jani switched channels, flicking past serials, documentaries, and travelogues before coming to rest on a real-time news transmit. *Live—from the palazzo of Treasury Main*! She watched the florid-faced Treasury Minister, the stark Exterior Minister, and several tightly wrapped colonial governors approach the eager throng of reporters like hikers nearing the edge of a cliff. The governors kept their replies short, while Treasury Minister Abascal entoned the anti-secession line in which Prime Minister Cao believed so firmly.

But Exterior Minister Ulanova held sway as always. As soon as she approached the Veephones, the governors fell silent and Abascal's mouth contorted in a dyspeptic smile. No, the PM's views on colonial autonomy did not alarm Exterior, Ulanova said in her warm alto, nor did Cao's unwillingness to entertain opposing views mean all talks on the subject would cease.

Then Ulanova relinquished the spotlight, and Evan sauntered to the fore, his clear eyes and healthy color a testament to the liberal ingestion of both black coffee and dehydro boosters. He ignored a question concerning Lyssa's death and launched into a point-by-point disassembly of Ulanova's views.

"Oh, Evan." Jani listened as he reaffirmed every point he'd made on the *Arapaho*. He left out his beliefs concerning Ulanova's ambitions, of course, but the intimation was there if you knew what to listen for. "I don't think that's what Anais had in mind." She watched the Exterior Minister's visage grow stonier as each verbal missile Evan launched made target. "You spiked her, Evan. This was your chance to play nice, and you bit your playmates and kicked sand."

A flash of silver-blond captured Jani's attention. She watched Lucien Pascal lean over Exterior Minister Ulanova's shoulder and whisper in her ear. The woman nodded sharply; Lucien responded with the smile Jani knew so well after five weeks on the *Arapaho*.

"*Roc cui'jaune*," she whispered to the smug face on the screen. "That means 'stones of brass,' you son of a bitch." Lucien bent forward again, allowing her a clear view of the red lieutenant's bars adorning his Service tunic collar. "A mainline spine." She squinted to see if she could pick up the tiny gold letter in the center of the bar.

"I spy with my little eye a letter *I*. Intelligence. Wonderful." Jani switched off the holoVee and stared into the blank screen. "What the hell have I walked into?" She slumped against the soft cushions and studied the ceiling. Then she went into the kitchenette and applied herself to the still-warm bread, washing it down with another healthy dose of coffee. Afterward, she cleaned her dishes, zapped her trash, stored the uneaten food, and scrubbed until everything shone and even her old drill instructor could not have found fault.

Then she returned to her office and studied her columns. After a while, she flipped to a clean page, and wrote, "Lyssa's death—Martin's augie" along the top. When Lucien's sailracers distracted her, she slammed them facedown on the desktop. When she grew too exhausted to hold her head up, she stretched out on her office floor, duffel by her side, and slept.

CHAPTER 10

"His troops would follow him anywhere, but only for the entertainment value."

Tsecha stared at the sentence until his eyes felt desert-dry. Finally, he admitted surrender with a rumbling sigh and reactivated his handheld. The small unit had long since gone dormant; he had to rock and jostle it before the blue activator pad glowed and the display lightened.

You are as me, grown most old. Tsecha entered codes and file keys both by voice and input pad, pausing frequently to allow the readout time to catch up. He practiced his English counting as the time passed.

Then, one after another, the words scrolled across the display, the looping curves and complex crosshatches of High Vynshàrau. Tsecha savored each nuance, every shading. Even after so long, he found his self-made dictionary most educating.

Entertainment. He read the line again. *This officer's troops intend to watch from a distance, as though he walks a stage.* That implied they did not trust him. A poor thing, such mistrust. A threat to order. Why then did the Service maintain the officer?

Why did humanish do so many foolish things?

"*Aháret.*" Tsecha spoke aloud the Pathen Haárin word. *Why*? An unseemly question in the Pathen tongue. It implied the gods did not know what they did. He stared for a time at the bare, sand-colored walls of his room. Sand—such a comforting hue.

How I miss heat, and truly. Heat, bright sun, and the bloom-laden trees of home. Relasetha and ìrel, fierce yellow and blessed red. The images he held in his memory seemed so much richer than the paper and paint ones that rested within niches in his walls.

I came to this damned cold place for a reason. Why now did that reason seem as hard to grasp as Service English?

Tsecha toyed with his handheld. So much easier to grasp. And so much did it contain. Notes, translations, and definitions of his three most favored humanish tongues, English, French, and Mandarin. He ran a finger along the unit's scuffed, gouged black case. *So much we have been through—peace and war, the death of that which I was and the birth of that which I became.* He looked at the handheld's screen. It flickered. The display fragmented. Half the words lost all meaning, while some took on meanings quite strange. He bared his teeth. *I say you tell me jokes to ease my mind. But my suborns call you broken.*

Once he had, with great reluctance, allowed one of his communications suborns to attempt to transfer the knowledge in his aged device to one of the new bracketed-neuron models much valued by Vynshàrau intelligence. Tsecha had almost screamed himself when his unit whistled and screeched as the young female attached the interphases and initiated connections. He had torn it out of the transfer array just in time, she admitted later. Any longer, and his old friend would have . . . would have . . .

The connections had aged, the suborn said. The neural sheaths contained too much plaque, there had been too much cell death. A transfer was not possible. *At this time, nìRau.*

At any time.

We have aged together. He stroked the plastic case, which felt warm and smooth as flesh beneath his fingers. *Perhaps together, we were meant to die.*

"Ah, you think of death again!" Tsecha rebuked himself aloud, in English. The language worked quite well for such. Its sharp, throaty sounds, aided by so much tongue and tooth, forced one to pay attention.

"So pay attention to this." He paged through the copy of the Service Officer Fitness Assessment, combing for more sentences that would challenge his knowledge and his repository. "The humanish think these words funny, and truly. Why?" It crossed Tsecha's mind that his hosts would be surprised to find an idomeni studying the personnel files of active officers in their military, but he felt it a point to be ignored. He wished to perfect his English, and Hansen Wyle had told him much of the language's meaning could be found in such humanish government files as this, in places "between the lines."

So shall I search. Between lines.

Tsecha put down the file he held and opened another, paging

through sheet after sheet until he came to the entry with the latest date.

"This officer should go far. I'll drive."

Tsecha stared and studied. This statement, he felt he understood. *Another incompetent—with so many, how do the humanish survive?* He closed the assessment and set it on the table beside his chair. He would have to remember to ask of his intelligence suborns where exactly they had obtained these files. They had insisted most strongly that their infiltration of humanish systems was not suspected. *But the humanish enjoy laughter so much.* A game, perhaps? Tsecha bared his teeth. Such, he understood most well.

He rose slowly from his rigid metal-and-wood seat, wincing at the popping sounds his aged joints made. He twisted and stretched his spine, worked blood and feeling back into his limbs. Humanish complained of uncomfortable idomeni furniture, but pain kept one sharp. Such did all believe. All idomeni, that is. Humanish were different. They could not accept the mind-focusing ability of pain.

He padded across the bare tiled floor, the same soft color as his walls. He opened a large wooden cupboard and stored his files in one of the touchlocked compartments of which his suborns knew. Then he pushed aside carved panels and etched veneers and opened a touchbox that contained things of which they knew not. Inside rested a ring, twin to his own ring of station, and a much thinner sheaf of documents.

Tsecha picked up the ring, held it under the light, savored its glisten. Then he returned it to its resting place and removed the documents. *Moragh*, he thought as he opened the file. *I must find a humanish to tell me what means,* Moragh. He had already sought the meanings of his Captain's other two names and had come away from each quest still wanting. Perhaps the key was in *Moragh*. There had to be some hint, some foretelling, somewhere. Surely his Captain could not have faded away without leaving some type of trail. Some type of sign for him, who believed.

I fought the Laumrau for you. You are all that is order to me. Tsecha returned to his chair and paged through the pale blue Service parchment. Long ago, some of the sheets had been stained by smoke, then by flame-retardant foam. Their surfaces shone greasy grey and mottled in his room's sunlike illumination.

I paid much to the Haárin to recover these from your Service base. His debriders, dispatched to search the cleansing flames of Rauta Shèràa for any paper they could find. *But all they found was this small amount*—Tsecha riffled the few stiff pages—*because even your own wished you erased.*

Even though he knew the words as he knew his born-sect and skein, Tsecha read Jani Kilian's Officer Assessment.

Insubordinate. Typical dexxie know-it-all. Stiff-necked colonial. Doesn't belong in a uniform. As ever, he could find no humor in Kilian's file.

A muffled, metallic sound stole his attention. Softly, at first, then more loudly, the cloth-wrapped bell that signaled the cook-priest's visitation rang its dull, late-evening song. Tsecha continued to comb the papers. Soon would come last sacrament, then sleep. He had not much time.

Where are you, my future? He read the passages which dealt with the Service's search for their officer, their condemnation of her disorder, their fear she would be found first by the Vynshàrau. *Mutiny . . . murder . . . conspiracy . . . forgery . . . assumed dead . . . body disappeared . . . door-to-door search . . . no sign.* Acadian, she was, but later, they searched for her there and found nothing. Rebellious, she was, but they continued their searches to this day on their colony planets and found nothing.

Words as written, ink on paper, Tsecha read and ignored, continuing his own search for the sign from his gods, his own quest for his Captain. In his own nothing. Between the lines.

The Second Day

CHAPTER 11

The "thank-you" Jani's back gave her for spending the night on her office floor was countered by the opinion expressed by her right hip and thigh. She limped into the bathroom, shedding clothes along the way.

Another hot shower—two in less than a day. A giddy surfeit of hydrodynamic riches. All wasted, unfortunately. Afterward, she only felt battered and slightly feverish. Never had so much hot water done so little for so few.

Travel lag. Had to be. *Over a month of artificial gee—it's never the same, no matter what they say.* She dug through drawers and shelves, searching for an outfit that didn't make her look like graveyard shift in the engine room, finally settling on a dark blue trouser suit. The color made her appear ill, but the cloth and cut of the outfit whispered "expensive" with an Earthbound accent. She could wander Interior halls at will in a getup like that. Besides, the trouser legs were cut wide enough to fit over her boots.

Jani buttoned the roomy jacket, flexing her shoulders as she checked herself in the full-length mirror. Keeping her hands in her pockets hid the fact that the sleeves were uneven in length, with the right one too short. She glumly examined the crooked breaks in her trouser cuffs. She looked all right. Businesslike. Unconcerned with fashion, as though—

"As though I'd been hurled from a speeding skimmer." She tamped down her damp curls, vowed to check out the cosmetics selection in the Interior stores, and gave the contents of her duffel a last check.

Just before she left, Jani glanced toward the comport light on the end table by the bed. No blink, which meant no message from Evan. She thought of Martin's files, locked in her desk. *Yeah, I probably wouldn't be eager to talk to me, either.* Her stomach rumbled, and she tried to recall the quickest route to Interior House Main. She'd take her meals there today. However averse Evan was to seeing her, the feeling was mutual.

Jani had found the second-floor dining hall extremely attractive the previous afternoon, which was why she avoided it now. Nobbies were to be avoided at all costs. Ridgeway. Angevin. Even Steve.

She rode elevators and scaled stairs until the signs meant nothing. DISPOSITION AND WAREHOUSING—FIELD ASSESSMENTS—CODES AND STATUTES. She ducked into the first breakroom she came to, and was treated to a view of skimmer charge lots and maintenance sheds through the single grimy window. She grabbed a tray, loaded it with single-serve dispos from the glass-fronted cooler and headed for the darkest corner of the deserted eating area.

Don't forget to face the door. Jani sat down, looking up just in time to see Durian Ridgeway enter.

"Good morning, Ms. Tyi." He strode toward her, not seeming at all surprised to find her in such a remote region of Interior Main. "Getting to know the layout of the place, I see." He was dressed in a black day suit and white shirt that had the same effect on his complexion that Jani's outfit had on hers. He sat down across from her and started toying with the spice dispenser.

"You've been following me," Jani said.

"Strictly speaking, no. I just had people keeping an eye out for you." He frowned as she continued eating. "You certainly don't seem the worse for wear, considering."

"Considering what?"

"You read Martin's file, didn't you? Evan gave it to you, didn't he?"

"Yes, and yes, again."

Ridgeway's ears reddened. "It's too early in the morning for flippancy, Ms. Tyi."

"On the contrary, Mr. Ridgeway, I am most serious."

"Then you agree with my estimation of the negative impact the release of that information could have on his career?"

"Oh, yes."

Ridgeway sat back with the edgy posture of one who knew there had to be another shoe teetering on the brink somewhere. "Evan would like to see you. After you finish your breakfast, of course."

Jani reached across the table and took the spice dispenser from his hand. "He can kiss my ass." She slid the spout around to the white-pepper compartment and sprinkled some on her melon. "I'm not interested in his explanations."

"He's your Minister, Ms. Tyi. When he says, 'jump,' it's your job to ask, 'how high.' "

"And yours to hold the measuring tape, Mr. Ridgeway. What a valuable man you are."

Ridgeway stared at her. Then his gaze flicked to her tray. "Would you mind telling me why you just put pepper on your fruit?"

"Because that's the way I choose to eat it."

"You know, Ms. Tyi, I don't think you're quite well."

Jani shook the spice dispenser over her bowl until the melon looked sand-dipped. "You can kiss my ass, too."

"Spit and show me where, Risa dear," Ridgeway replied coolly. He turned toward the breakroom entrance. "Colonel Doyle. Could you come in here please?"

Three guards dressed in mainline winter polywools filled the doorway like a steel blue eclipse in triplicate. A tall, rangy, dark-skinned woman with a shaved head stepped forward, her eyes on Jani, one hand on her shooter holster. "Sir?"

Ridgeway stood up. "It's always been up to me to clean up Evan's little errors in judgment, Ms. Tyi. Perhaps you should keep that in the back of what passes for your mind." He tugged on his jacket cuffs. "Shall we go?"

Jani looked from Ridgeway, to the guards, then back again. She knew she could get past them all and out of the room before any of them knew what had hit them. Augie was telling her how. She would sustain damage, of course, but she'd been damaged before. She wouldn't die. She'd never die. She'd tried it once. It didn't take. *I could let them have it for you, Marty. Show them what an augie can really do.* In the body of an adult who knew the drill.

A sour burning rose in her throat as she stood. "You've left me no choice, Mr. Ridgeway," she said, ignoring his smug smile. As he turned his back to her, her eyes locked on the place where his thin neck met his undeveloped shoulder. *Perhaps later, Marty.* Who knew what could happen later?

Outside, Jani excused herself and hurried to the nearby lavatory, Ridgeway's order to "hurry the hell up" ringing in her ears. She reached the toilet just in time, losing her breakfast in a few rapid heaves.

When she finished, she pressed her sweat-damp face against cold ceramic, closed her eyes, and tried not to think how a thwarted augie would take out his displeasure on a three-year-old boy. Or how the three-year-old boy would react. It never paid to think along those lines. A person could go crazy if she dwelled on things like that.

She cleaned up quickly, then rejoined her escort. Two of the guards bookended her, while Doyle brought up the rear. Ridgeway, of course, led the procession. Jani kept her eyes on the spot between his shoulder blades. The point bobbed up and down—he had an annoyingly bouncy gait.

She slowly relaxed. She'd encountered her share of Ridgeways in Rauta Shèràa, walked in more than one promenade to the principal's office. She shoved her hands in her pockets and swallowed down the last hint of bile. She needed freedom and access to do the job asked of her. Despite what Ridgeway wanted, Evan could only afford to bust her so far.

Evan waited for them in his office anteroom. Jani had to allow him some credit—the look he gave Ridgeway and the guards would have stopped a howling mob in its tracks. *It's a gift—comes with the nose.*

Ridgeway held up a hand. "Evan, let me explain." Pedantic tone. Mistake.

"An armed escort," Evan replied, very quietly. "Of my guest. In my house." Small "h." Easily discerned. He'd chosen to take it personally. He looked at Jani. "And what crime was committed?"

Ridgeway floundered. "She was insubordinate!" he finally sputtered.

Evan shrugged. "Of course she was, Durian. It's part of her charm." He stepped past Ridgeway, who watched him with mouth agape and walked over to Colonel Doyle, who seemed preoccupied with the pattern of the carpet. "Virginia."

"Sir." Doyle cast a sidelong glance at Jani and winced.

"Ms. Tyi is to be allowed free access to all parts of the House." Capital "H," this time. "I was remiss in handling that. I'm taking care of it now. You'll help me see to it, won't you?"

"Yes, sir."

"She is a professional, as are we all. Despite what you may have been told, you have nothing to fear where she is concerned."

"Yes, sir." Doyle looked at Jani again. In contrast to her dark skin, her eyes were surprisingly light, a pale gold-brown. "If Ms. Tyi will come by and see me afterward," she said flatly, "I'll see she's taken care of."

"Of course." Evan smiled. The temperature of the room rose above subarctic. "Now, Risa and Durian and I need to talk." He nodded toward Colonel Doyle, who shot Jani a last, reappraising look as she herded her two subordinates out of the anteroom.

Ridgeway erupted as soon as the door closed. "How bloody dare you! You made me look a fool!"

"You never needed any help from me in that regard!" Evan's voice shook. "We're all three of us on one level from this point on. In it up to our necks!" He spun on his heel. "We'll talk in my office, where it's secure."

Jani tried for a seat on the opposite side of the room from Evan's desk, but he blocked that move with a glare and gestured to a chair near his own. Next to Ridgeway's. Jani settled in and looked around. At least the bar was closed up.

"Well?" Evan planted his elbows on his desk. He wore the same sort of severely cut suit as did Ridgeway, but black was his color. It enlivened his complexion, gave his slim frame a solidity it didn't possess on its own, and invested his anger with the authority of worlds.

Not a great way to start the day.

"You already know my feelings." Ridgeway jerked his head toward Jani. "You'll be sorry you brought her into this. Mark my words."

"So you still decline to consider my side of things." Evan waved off Ridgeway's protest and turned to Jani. "And are you, Ms. Tyi, sorry you were brought into this?" A soft light filled his eyes. "You don't look pleased."

Jani teased at her right cuff. Try as she might, she couldn't pull it past her wrist. "Whose idea was it?"

Evan didn't need to ask which idea. "Does it matter? I was his father. It was my responsibility."

Ridgeway chuffed in disgust. "Go ahead—play the martyr. If you still think you can afford it." He looked at Jani. It took an effort—she could almost hear his spine crack from the tension. "It was Acton. He'd been kicked out as king, so he tried for kingmaker. He'd heard about some personality-enhancement work being done by researchers who'd broken off from Neoclona. Similar to combat augmentation, though with a different focus."

Evan cut in. "The secessionists were making noise even then. Nawar had just scrabbled his way back into power, won the interim election by a landslide. The feeling at the time was that he'd be Prime Minister for life. I'd taken the wrong side in a domestic appropriations dustup, so I was in the political doghouse. Dad ran scared. He didn't think he'd ever see a van Reuter in the Cabinet again."

Jani gave up on her jacket cuff and began tugging on her pants. "Any Neoclona hack and slash will tell you augmentation is exactly that, an enhancement of what's already been formed. Whoever told your father they could shape the personality of a three-year-old was a lying butcher, and he was a fool to believe them." A cold-blooded, megalomaniacal fool. But she herself had been gouged more than once by the Old Hawk's beak. "Did Lyssa know the details?"

"We believe so." Ridgeway and Evan answered simultaneously, then Ridgeway picked up the ball. "She was a physician, after all. Not a Neoclona affiliate but still well regarded. I'm sure she only suspected some type of standard behavioral dysfunction at first, but when the true nature of Martin's problem became known, she plunged into denial as readily as the rest of us. It began slowly. We thought it a phase, a bid for attention, especially after Jerrold and Serena were born. We thought he'd grow out of it."

Jani yanked on her right trouser leg—a high-pitched rip sounded as lining gave way. "You—" She tried to count to ten, but lost track after *three*. "You took an infant who had no true grasp of right or wrong, no firm moral foundation, and engineered him to automatically, at all times, put his own survival first above all things—"

Ridgeway's face flared. "I had nothing to do with it—"

"—and you thought he'd grow out of it!"

"*You're out of line, Tyi!*"

Jani stormed out of her chair, her stomach on fire. "*Kiss my ass, you son of a bitch!*"

Evan rushed around his desk and thrust an arm between them. "*Quiet!*" He leaned hard against Jani, pushing her back into her chair. "I don't give a damn how you two feel about each other. When you are under this roof, you will treat one another in a civil manner. You will not use any of my departments like little toy armies in your vendettas," he continued, catching Ridgeway's eye, "and, like it or not, you will work together. I need you both. If I have to grind you both into one meaty lump and drag in Neoclona to make a sensible person out of the mess, I will."

Jani fixed her eyes on the floor. She could hear Ridgeway's hard breathing slow.

Evan took his time returning to his seat. When he finally spoke, Jani heard the smile in his voice. "I won't ask you to shake hands. I'm no physicist, but I understand the concept of fission." His chair creaked. The silence stretched.

After what seemed hours, Jani looked up to find Ridgeway staring at Evan, naked pleading paling his ruddy face.

"Tell her, Durian."

"Oh, Christ, Ev—none of that can matter."

Evan looked at Jani, the shine in his eyes almost feverish. Dying for a drink, probably, but he wouldn't take one while she and Ridgeway were there. "The fact is, Risa, my late wife was suborned by her unfortunately not-late aunt to serve as an in-House verifier. How Ulanova managed to work around Lyssa's swan dives off the sobriety shuttle is anyone's guess, but Colonel Doyle and Durian uncovered evidence that, for the past several years, my loving spouse kept Exterior well informed of the goings-on here."

Jani pondered that kernel of information. *He kept that from me because he knew if he told me, I wouldn't have come.* "How much of worth could Lyssa have revealed? You didn't use her as counsel, did you?"

"Not per se. But I underestimated her influence, her access, her—"

"Her hatred." Ridgeway's voice tremored. "She hated us all. Blamed us all. Lyssa became expert at pointing fingers and slathering on guilt with a trowel."

Evan pressed his thumb and forefinger to the bridge of his nose. "Durian."

"It's true, Evan. No use denying it. She turned this House into a civil-war-in-a-jar. God, the lies she told, the people she sucked in. We had to purge entire divisions—we had Exterior-trained operatives running our departments! To tell you the truth, Ms. Tyi, we still don't know if we got everyone." His metal stare raked her. "We don't know who could still be out there, lurking."

Jani's stomach rumbled. She pressed a hand to it to quiet it. "I don't recall any of this in the files you gave me, Mr. Ridgeway."

"I gave you what I was told to give you. Information about Evan."

"Which was incomplete, as well."

"Yes." He didn't bother to explain or apologize. Those points worked in his favor, since Jani would have believed neither. "But now, it appears, the House is to be your oyster. Pry with care, Ms. Tyi. That's all I ask." He rose. "I'll earmark the files we've deemed most noteworthy, although you'll want to see them all, I'm sure. Have you ever investigated a death?"

"No." *Not officially.* "I've stuck with paper crimes." The memories of her Service work nestled under Jani's ribs, a bundle of warmth. Or maybe it was heartburn? "Just show me the paper—I'll take it from there. And if I need your help, Mr. Ridgeway—"

"You will have it, of course. Make an appointment to meet with me this afternoon," he said as he swept out.

Evan's groan rattled as the door closed. "It's going to take me days to settle him down. But it will have been worth it. He doesn't like you, but he will work with you."

Jani stared at the closed door. "He thinks I'm an Exterior plant. Any slip I make, he's going to magnify tenfold."

"Who's he going to bitch to? I'll take it all with a transport-load of salt. Virginia and the other execs will take their lead from me." Evan grinned. The years fell away. "He's just jealous, anyway. Do you know what he told me? He suspects you're my mistress, on top of everything else. Thinks I've been keeping you under wraps for years."

"Why would he think that?"

"Because I look so 'contented,' as he put it. That makes him nervous. He likes hungry leaders. In case of a feeding frenzy, he's guaranteed a pile of scraps." His smile wavered. "He saved my life, Jani. When all this hit the fan, I knew I could count on him. I know what he is, what he wants. But there were times when he could've hopped the fence with the others who followed Lyssa, and he didn't. Durian's thrown in with me for better or worse. That's more than anyone else has ever done." He looked at her. "Of course, you would have stuck, if I'd given you the chance. But I listened to *him*." Acton van Reuter's name, unspoken, hung heavy between them. "He chose Lyssa for me. Shows what he knew."

Jani looked toward the balcony. The sun battered through the glass—even from where she sat, she could feel the heat. She'd wanted to throttle Evan only minutes before. Now a part of her just wanted to sit with him, look out at the sunshine, listen to his assurances.

And fight back the other part of her that didn't believe a word of it. *Steve didn't like Lyssa.* He hadn't admitted it at dinner, but the assumption made sense considering his evasion of Jani's repeated questions. Had Lyssa asked him to assist her in her illegal fact gathering? Had he turned her down?

Had he?

Evan sat up with a start. "I'm actually at loose ends tonight. How about dinner, back at Private? I'll have cook do something colonial." He looked at her hopefully. "About seven?"

"Won't that upset Durian?" Jani stood and tried to readjust her ill-fitting jacket

"Screw him—I'm entitled." He rose and walked around his desk.

"I think I can make it." Jani tensed as Evan closed in and slipped his arm around her waist. *Like it never left.* "Saw your speech last night. I'm surprised Ulanova let you make it home alive."

"She tried to buy me off. If I threw in with her publicly on the secession-rights issue, she'd disband the Court. Problem is, I didn't trust her to keep her word. I also believe she's wrong." Evan opened the door for her, looking out to see whether his staff had arrived. "Seven o'clock, then." He pulled his arm away as voices drifted toward them. "Considering what else you've learned, I'm happy you're still talking to me."

"I didn't think I would be," Jani admitted. "The fact your father was involved explained a lot, though."

"Explained my rolling over and playing dead, you mean." He eyed her guiltily. "What Lyssa did doesn't seem to bother you as much."

"Vengeful behavior, I'm more familiar with. I understand her feelings. With her training, she could guess what Martin went through."

"Anything like what you've gone through?" Evan asked softly.

"Not the same thing, Ev. I could adjust." She gave her duffel an absent pat, as though it were an overlarge worry bead. "When did you know?"

"Looking back, I'd say the signs were there from the start. I just didn't want to face it. I think I even know the day it happened. Dad dropped by out of the blue and took Martin out for ice cream. I've never been able to track where the actual implantation was done, though." Evan slipped back into his office and waved to a pair of uniformed clerks who entered the anteroom. "Dad said Martin needed help. Right away, too, before things got out of hand. My son had shown signs of taking after me, you see. Dad always felt I lacked a sense of purpose, just because it wasn't the same as his." He gave Jani a last, sad smile. "Seven o'clock," he mouthed as he closed the door.

CHAPTER 12

Doyle handed over the House access codes with the eggshell grace of someone who didn't like being on the wrong end of the favor stick. Jani accepted them with a quick nod and a minimum of small talk, excusing herself when Doyle's questions drifted toward matters such as "which colony, exactly" had she come from?

She'd also deflected an invitation to brunch.

Not on my bones, you don't. Jani rushed through the Security section, knowing her every move was being monitored. She stifled the impulse to stick out her tongue at a wall-mounted scancam as the front-desk guard coded her departure.

I bet Evan would love for me to find proof Ulanova had something to do with Lyssa's death. That would give him the tool he needed to pry her and the PM off his back for good. Not to mention win Jani some breathing room. In the resulting scandal, who would care about her?

But that doesn't explain what Lyssa's death had to do with Knevçet Shèràa. Unless Evan only steered her to that conclusion to get her to come to Chicago. *Remember the pragmatist—even if he does look great in black.* She used some of her new codes to slip into the controlled Finance section. The division cafeteria was small and, at this between-meals hour, sparsely populated. She loaded a tray and wedged into an odd-shaped corner table with a view of the hallway as well as the door. She was in no mood to be caught twice. She ate quickly, then sat quietly for a few minutes. Only when she felt certain her stomach wouldn't reject her latest offering did she set out on her next project.

Arrange my appointment with Ridgeway. She dreaded the prospect, but the outcry would be tremendous if she didn't show. She coded into the controlled-access lift, noting with relief that the floor indicator stayed lit.

Fixed the lights, I see. Jani grinned at the bright illumination flooding her from above. She stepped into the same fourth-floor lobby she had visited the previous day. This time, the space was empty of both reporters and idomeni ambassadors. She headed down the widest hallway, looking for the largest offices with the best views.

Durian Ridgeway's, of course, proved to be the biggest of all, a commanding corner with views of both the Main House grounds and the lake. Jani made her appointment with a jumpy assistant, restraining an urge to pat the young man's hand when he made an incorrect schedule entry and wouldn't stop apologizing for what apparently constituted a Class X Commonwealth felony in domain Durian.

That task completed, Jani wandered. She checked names on doorplates, sneaked around empty offices, and brushed off curious guards and documents staffers by waving her access cards and sounding indignant—the time-honored way to get into places where one had no business being.

She was debating a visit to the third-floor parts bins when an unmarked door flew open and she found herself staring into Angevin Wyle's tear-stained face. She wore a rumpled Interior trouser suit. No makeup. Even her copper curls appeared tarnished and lifeless. *Bet I know your problem,* Jani thought as she reached into her duffel for more tissues. *A human chimney named Steve.*

Angevin snuffled and straightened her shoulders. "Hullo."

At first, Jani felt tempted to make sympathetic noises and offer womanly advice. But her own love life had never been anything to brag about. Besides, if the well-bred Miss Wyle had displayed the Earthbound behavior Steve hinted at, she deserved to shed a few tears. "If Durian sees you like this, he'll have a fit."

Angevin's chin jutted. "Durian can go drown himself."

She hasn't gone completely over to the enemy, Hansen—there's still hope. Jani looked up and down the hall. "Where's a breakroom—you could use one. I want to talk to you."

"Don't wanna talk."

"Yes, you do. Besides, you need to pull yourself together. You look like hell."

"Fuck you."

"See." Jani thumped Angevin on the back just hard enough to set her in motion. "You're feeling better already."

They bypassed the crowded department cafeteria. Instead, Angevin led Jani down a dead-end hall and into a converted office furnished with mismatched castoffs. In one corner, a bandy-legged table held an ancient brewer, supplies of cream and sugar in cracked plastic containers, and a tiny cooler decorated with a scrawled snack schedule.

"Does Ridgeway ever come here?" Jani asked as she looked around.

Angevin shook her head. "Nah, he hates this place. Thinks it's a pit. He's been trying to have it closed down for months, tells us the regular cafeteria is good enough for everybody. But we block him. Durian can lord it over civilians as much as he wants, but try telling the head of Interior Tax Form Compliance that she can't have her coffee and doughnut wherever she pleases and you're going to have a fight on your hands."

A few scattered souls already occupied the room, talking, perusing newssheets, rustling through paperwork. Angevin exchanged greetings as she led Jani to an unpopulated corner.

Jani sank into a semicollapsed lounge chair. "How far back does this room date? Since the Lyssa purge?"

"Yeah." Angevin gave her a startled look. "It got to the point that the cafeteria . . . sometimes there just isn't a room big enough, you know?" She sighed. "They don't teach you how to deal with things like that in school."

"Are the ones who come here still under a cloud?"

Angevin snorted softly. "If there was even a hint of an intimation of a possibility, Security met you at your desk and you were gone." She sat back in her squeaky chair. "The ones who come here—it's just our way of giving notice that we disagree with how things were done. It didn't have to be the way it was. Whatever happened to due process?"

"That only applies to official criminal charges."

"Then whatever happened to letting people explain? Most of them thought they were doing official Interior work—that's how she set things up to look!" Heads turned in Angevin's direction. She blushed and fell silent.

"You're Ridgeway's right hand," Jani said, "but you're accepted here."

"I'm Hansen Wyle's daughter. That means something, from what I understand." Angevin looked around the room. "Maybe if I hang here long enough, someone will tell me what that something is."

"Considering how closely Ridgeway controls you, I'm surprised he lets you come here."

Before Angevin could answer, the door opened and Steve Forell entered with a young woman in tow. As soon as she saw them,

Angevin's eyes filled. "Excuse me," she mumbled. Hands jammed in pockets, she exited just as Steve and his friend worked their way over to Jani's corner.

"Good morning, Ms. Tyi," Steve said as he claimed Angevin's chair. "I hope we didn't interrupt anything important." His look of wide-eyed innocence disappeared when he noticed his companion still standing shifty-footed beside him. "Crike, sit down," he said, pushing the girl into the empty seat next to Jani. She was as tall as Steve, with straight ash blond hair hacked at chin length. She had overwhelmed her pointed features with heavy makeup. A sweeping dark blue skirt and matching jacket hung on her thin frame.

"I'm glad we caught you up," Steve said. "I left you a message on your House line, but this works much better." He tossed an exasperated look at the young woman, who sat rigid, eyes locked on his face. "This is Betha Concannon—she's Guernsey, too. She were also Lyssa van Reuter's personal documents examiner. I thought you might be interested."

"It weren't official! She just used to have me check things for her. Travel docs—stuff like that."

In the friendly confines of Jani's Private House suite, Betha recovered both her voice and her ability to move. She paced, activated lights, pawed bric-a-brac. However long the nervous energy had been building, it was all dissipating now. Jani hid the sculptures and other breakables and stayed out of her way.

Steve, meanwhile, prodded cushions, examined furniture, and stared at the Channel World artwork as Jani stashed it. When the poshness became too much to bear, he pulled out a nicstick. She could hear the crack of the ignition tip across the room.

Betha slowed until she fell onto one of the sofas. "It's not like she had me forge IDs or anything. She just used to have me check things, fill out forms."

"What types of things, exactly?" Jani asked. "You mentioned travel docs. Were they hers?"

"For the most part. But a few of the things were old. Ten, fifteen, twenty years." Betha cradled a pillow in her lap. Every so often, she gave it a squeeze.

"Colonial travel?" Jani asked. "Earth vicinity? Where?"

"All over the place. She went everywhere. Elyas. Amaryllis. Kim Chun. Most of the trips were to Nueva Madrid, though. Can't think why the hell anyone would want to go there. All that's there is a Service hospital."

"Well, she was a physician," Jani said. "One could have all sorts of reasons for visiting a prestigious medical facility. How often did Lyssa visit Nueva Madrid? Were the trips quarterly? Six months? Twelve?"

"Every five to six," Betha replied.

"Over what time span?"

"Almost two years."

"How was she before these trips? Excited? Depressed? Apprehensive? Did they involve business? Research?"

"Well, the papers stated she were acting as some type of envoy. Trying to help smooth relations between Neoclona doctors and the nonaffiliated med groups." The rate of pillow-squeezing increased.

"Did that make sense to you?"

Betha shot Jani a surprised look. "Never really thought about it. I were just a drone in the Doc pool—thrilled to get the work."

"Was His Excellency ever present when you put the packets together? To give his wife advice, go over the itinerary?"

"N-no. *No*. But they weren't getting on, you know—"

"Did you sit in on the planning meetings? Trips like these must have involved a great deal of strategizing."

Betha glanced sideways at Steve. "Yes. A couple."

Out of the corner of her eye, Jani could see Steve shift in his seat. "Well, that's a good place to start." She put an enthusiastic kick in her voice. "We'll have agendas, lists of people Lyssa would be talking to, ship crew lists." She waited, her level gaze never leaving Betha's face. "I'm getting together with Durian Ridgeway this afternoon. If you can give me the dates of the meetings to which you went, I can have him get me copies of the minutes."

Steve emitted a strangled groan. Betha kept kneading the pillow.

"No one knew about you and Lyssa," Jani finally said. The sound of tearing interrupted her. "Months and months go by, coworkers all around you getting the hook," she continued, as Betha surveyed the ripped pillow in mute dismay. "Yet you manage to scoot through the barrage unscathed. Pretty good maneuvering for a drone, considering anybody with any sense would have swept you out at first pass."

"So Betha weren't the Lady's *official* dexxie." Steve, who no longer appeared quite so smug, sat up straight. "He were shipped out to a colonial post during the height of the troubles. No one's heard from him since." He pointed to Betha. "What did you expect her to do—turn herself in?"

"None of the paper you did for Lyssa went through Durian's office, did it?" Jani asked the sick-looking Betha. "At first, it was just a few small favors. She was, after all, the Lady. Maybe your ticket out of the Doc pool. Then, finally, after the favors began piling up, getting more and more complicated, more and more risky, you asked her what the hell was going on?"

"*Hey*," Steve shouted, "I brought her here as a favor—!"

"Be quiet." Jani turned back to Betha, who still clutched the ripped pillow. "That's when she threatened you. Told you what she'd do to you if you didn't keep your mouth shut?"

After a long silence, Betha spoke. "If you already know so much, why ask me? If you already know what happened, what chance do I have?"

More of one than I did, when Riky Neumann cornered me. "You filled out the travel docs for Nueva Madrid?"

"Yes."

"You didn't register them or obtain Durian's approval?"

"No. She asked me not to. She said she'd handle it."

Steve buried his head in his hands.

"In the meantime," Jani said, "Lyssa went through her regular dexxie for another set of travels docs, the ones her husband and her staff knew about. *Those* were the envoy papers. Same times, same location, different purpose."

"Yes," Betha said. "She said if I told anyone, she'd make sure I got deregistered. At the very least."

Steve cleared his throat. "You think the Lady were sick? Getting some type of medical treatment she didn't want the Minister to know about?"

Jani jerked her head in Betha's direction. "She vetted the return-trip papers, I assume. I think you should ask her."

"I don't think it could have been anything serious." Betha started picking out the pillow stuffing and worked the feathery foam between her fingers. "I don't have much experience in medical records—just my school courses—but I never saw any patient copies of referral documents, or codes for consultation summaries." She shrugged weakly. "Besides, she never seemed nervous or anything. Once, she even said she were taking a vacation. 'Going surfing, Betha' she told me. 'Going to learn how to surf.' "

Jani felt the clammy grip of nausea that had nothing to do with food. She might not yet know who killed Lyssa or why. But she knew how. "How many times did she mention surfing?"

"Two, three times."

Steve ignited another nicstick. "Does that mean something?"

"Maybe." Jani paused. "How much room do we have to maneuver? Any audits coming up in the foreseeable future?"

Steve moaned as Betha worked to her feet. "The general audit starts next week," she said.

"Next week!" Jani smothered a groan herself. "Seven days until your paper house gets blown down by the big bad wolf." She worked her neck, listened to the bones crackle. When general auditors fired, they seldom missed. She'd have to move pretty quickly if she wanted to help those two morons remain in the Registry. And out of prison. "That leaves us with lots of ground to cover in a very short time." She rose as quickly as her aching back would allow. "Leave me alone to think. I'll track you down when I need you."

"No reason why we should help you," Steve huffed, hands in pockets, slouch in full, sagging bloom.

"Felony documents fraud," Jani said, pointing to Betha, "and accessory after the fact," she added as she gripped his sleeve and pulled him toward the door. "Besides, you'd rather have to do for me than anyone else you've ever known." She met Betha's *not again* look head-on. "Well, if you had said no in the first place, you wouldn't be in this mess."

Betha fingered the worn edge of her jacket cuff. "How? She were the Lady. I'm just . . ." She pulled a thread from the frayed edge. Her shoulders slumped. "How could I say no?"

Same way I did. No, Colonel Neumann, sir, I will not sign off on your faked medical files. No, Colonel Neumann, sir, I will not fill out the transfer justification for your faked files.

No. No. It did get through, eventually. One way or another. Jani escorted the somber duo to the lift and smiled at them as they boarded the car. Steve looked away, while Betha stared at her like a trapped animal.

The stare jarred Jani. She remained in the hall as the lift doors closed, trying to punch holes in memories that insisted on forcing their way to the surface. Gawky, sloppy Betha. *Take away the bad makeup and trim the hair into a Service burr, you've got Yolan.* Corporal Yolan Cray, who would have been—Jani did a quick mental calculation—thirty-seven Common years old now.

She returned to her suite. After clearing away pillow remnants, she closed herself in her office, righted Lucien's card, and stared at it. *Were you trying to tell me something, Lieutenant?* Sailracing. Before the self-propelled sailboards had been perfected, the racers had to rely on Mother Nature. Windsurfing, they had called it then. *So Lady Lyssa learned to surf.* Learned to ride what Jani and her fellow augies had called, in grandiosity born of fear, the solar wind. Learned to smell berries the year 'round, hear colors, see sound, feel the blood flow in your veins. Learned that no matter what, dying was for others, but never for you.

She freed the gossip holozine from its hiding place in her duffel. Along with the childhood pictures, wedding portraits, and images of the great lady in decline, some ambitious soul had constructed a timetable of the last few years of Lyssa van Reuter's life. Jani studied the timeline. Public battles with Evan and other minor embarrassments filled in the gaps between the major blowups. Skimmer accidents, disappearances, extended visits to sanitariums run by unaffiliated meds. But never a Neoclona or Service facility. Never someplace where they could tell.

Every few months, another crash. Another disconnect with reality. It happened sometimes, with those who had been augmented when they shouldn't have been. *So she started taking herself to Nueva twice a year to have her brain reset.* Had the flashing lights shoved in her face and went bye-bye. Jani had hated take-down—a minute of fast-forward hallucinations followed by a week of "what's my name" logi-ness. *No more for me.* Not ever.

Any augmented vet who worked for Interior had to be checked out every six months, with at least one precautionary take-down per year. Evan had said so himself. He was aware of the pattern—you'd think the timing of Lyssa's trips would have sounded a chord with him. Then again, maybe not. Lyssa wasn't Service—any rumor that she had been augmented would have been laughed off the newssheets.

Oh my Lady. Why? To understand what Martin went through, why he did the things he did? Or was it to torture herself, punish herself for allowing it to happen? Jani poked absently at her numb left hand, ran a live finger over dead flesh and bone. *I wish I could have met you first, Lyssa.* She could have told her it wouldn't help. Nothing did.

CHAPTER 13

"NìRau?"

Tsecha suppressed a fatigued sigh as he lowered into his chair. Since before sunrise he had stood, still and straight, praying before the embassy's dominant altar. Now he could see the sun through one of the room's narrow windows, risen three-quarters to prime, its reflection off the lake a painful jolt to his long-closed eyes.

"NìRau? It is the Exterior Minister. Ulanova." Head held high in respect, Sànalàn, Tsecha's religious suborn, stepped into his sight line, a needle of light against the black stone of the altar wall. "She has been scheduled, nìRau, but we may send her away, as before—"

"No, nìa." Tsecha used the gentlest refusal his tongue and posture would allow, but the young female's reaction showed that even so she resented the interruption. Her shoulders rounded, her head tilted forward. Even then, she stood taller than he, fine-boned as a marsh bird, her skin the sand gold of her body mother, a central plains-dwelling Sìah. "This day, I must see her, I think." Tsecha continued to watch as his suborn's shoulders slumped farther. "You do not like her, nìa?"

"She is as a wall." Sànalàn now straightened, raising her cupped right hand chest high in question. "How can one promote order who withholds so much?"

"Such withholding is much admired by humanish."

"Ah." The narrow shoulders relaxed, the arm dropped to the side. "Humanish admire odd things." Sànalàn turned to lead Tsecha out of the altar room. "Which explains much, and truly."

Tsecha held back argument and followed his suborn. She wore a floor-grazing overrobe of bronze metalcloth; the material shone as a mirror. The altar room's bloodstone columns, black altar, sand-hued walls, the humanish sun and lake themselves, curved across Sànalàn's back as she walked, as though the world itself clothed her.

Tsecha bared his teeth in satisfaction. *Humanish grow most still when they see my nìa.* Sànalàn's hair, which matched her skin in hue and her robe in shine, had been drawn back into the tight, braided knot of an unbred Vynshàrau. Her eyes, Tsecha recalled from her embassy identity badge, were large and green.

They call her a walking Chinese porcelain, he remembered, thinking back to the humanish holo of the embassy staff's arrival ceremonies which he had watched. It pleased him greatly that humanish compared his nìa to something of Mandarin, for such promoted connection between alien and idomeni, a sense of order most greatly to be wished.

A sense of order which, Tsecha prayed, remained after his meeting with Ulanova.

Sànalàn led him to the entry of one of his less favored meeting rooms, but declined to open the door. "She will speak to you of Amsun GateWay tariff issues."

"To be expected, nìa."

"Then there are the humanish sicknesses. She will ask if we are, too, affected."

Ah, but that even I do not know, nìa. The Council I represent will not tell me, even when I demand. They believe if they do not speak of such sicknesses, those sicknesses will disappear. They have become most humanish in that regard.

The suborn placed her left hand over her stomach, as protection for her soul. "She has no right to ask of such things. As always, she will give nothing, and expect everything."

Tsecha gestured in affirmation. "The humanish are afraid, nìa. They do not yet understand the truth of what happens. So very few are ill now, but—"

"If humanish took their honor in preserving order, they would not so fear the death of the body." The suborn straightened and began to stroke patterns in the air, invocations against demons. So shaken was she that she did not offer apology for her interruption. "Their fear of death will destroy us all this time, and truly. They will strike at anything to save their lives. It is a most ungodly thing."

Tsecha reached out and gripped Sànalàn's hands, stilling them. "You speak of things you do not understand, nìa. You were not born when we first learned of the fear." He longed to look his suborn in her green eyes, but that would jar her to the roots of her soul, and such he could not afford to do.

"It is you who do not understand, nìRau." Sànalàn spoke slowly, boldly, as she tried to work free of his restraint. "So say the Temple. So say the Council. You took in humanish, not knowing their fear. Trained them in our ways, not understanding their fear. Paid almost with your life, for not destroying that fear when the gods allowed you the chance. You understand nothing! So say the Temple! So say the Council!"

"And what do you say, nìa?"

"Their words are mine." The uncertain tremor in Sànalàn's voice betrayed her, but she was of Sìah, and Sìah were most stubborn. "You understand nothing."

Slowly, Tsecha relaxed his hold on his suborn's wrists. "But that is why I speak to Ulanova, nìa. Because I who understand nothing understand her best." He spoke as humanish, with no gesture or change in stance, his tone flat, allowing his meaning to hide itself between the lines. Then he left his suborn to uncover that meaning as best she could and entered the meeting room.

Inside the sparsely furnished space, Exterior Minister Anais Ulanova met him as any suborn Vynshàrau would have: in the center of the room, posture most straight, chin high, eyes closed. Tsecha had himself just spent many humanish hours in that most uncomfortable position. He wondered how long Ulanova had been standing such, or whether she had been sitting until she heard his discussion with Sànalàn end.

Most humanish of me, to think in this way. Cynical, Hansen had called it. But the door to the meeting room was not soundproofed. To the best of Tsecha's knowledge, supplemented by the work of his Intelligence skein, the Exterior Minister possessed no strong devotion to any deity and little regard for the other ministers. *So what means this respect of hers?*

Tsecha bared his teeth, extended his hand as Hansen had taught him long ago, and summoned forth his best English. "Glories of the day to you, Minister Ulanova!"

The Exterior Minister's eyes snapped open, widening even more as Tsecha drew nearer. She tottered, took a step backwards to regain her balance, then held out her hand as well. Her lips curved, but she did not bare her teeth. "Glories of the day to you as well, nìRau," she said, her low voice pleasing to Tsecha's ear, though not precisely respectful. "I am so glad we could meet together at last." The skin of her hand felt cool and dry, her grip loose.

Cucumbers. The harsh humanish sound pleased Tsecha's internal ear as Ulanova's voice did the external, but why the peculiar word should enter his mind now . . . ? *My handheld.* It remained behind in his rooms—it could not help him now. *I am alone with the wall.*

Ulanova began the discussion, as was fitting. "Please extend my thanks to your suborn for her assistance in arranging this meeting, nìRau. I realize the notice was most short, and truly." She led Tsecha toward two metalframe seats placed in one corner of the room. "But we have received news of an alarming nature from our Outer Circle agents. I felt you should be informed." The Exterior Minister worked onto her tall seat with difficulty, appearing almost as a scuttling insect in the dark brown uniform she wore for her embassy visits. She was only of average height for a humanish female, which made her shorter than an adult Vynshàrau by half an arm's length. "This news may affect us both greatly, nìRau," she finally said as she edged upright.

Tsecha found himself focusing on Ulanova's feet, as always. *So far above the ground . . .* "Yes, Minister. Sànalàn mentioned your concerns of the Amsun GateWay."

"I lied to your suborn, nìRau."

Lied. Tsecha tore his attention from Ulanova's dangling feet and looked into her face. "Lied," he repeated aloud, as darkest brown eyes looked at him in turn.

"She's alive, nìRau."

"She?" He felt a tightening in his soul and took deep breaths to calm himself. "Of whom do you speak?"

"Of Jani Kilian, of course, nìRau. She was seen on an Outer Circle colony by the name of Whalen's Planet. It has one major population center in its northern hemisphere, a town called NorthPort."

"NorthPort, that is—"

"Yes, nìRau, the site of one of the major Haárin settlements." Ulanova's tone implied no apology for the interruption, as was usual. "She was, in fact, on quite good terms with several of the Pathen Haárin high dominants, especially a shuttle broker named Genta Res. It was he who told my agent of the Captain's existence."

Tsecha tugged at the sleeves of his overrobe. The loyalty of Haárin—*tidal*, Hansen had called it. And yet . . . "I suspect, Anais, that ní Genta was threatened perhaps with cancellation of business permits before he felt the need to inform your agent of the existence of the Captain. Allow me to save both our staffs much time by lodging my protest of such with you now."

"She is a criminal in your government's eyes as well as mine, nìRau. I thought this news would please you." Ulanova's tone grew harsh. "I have known for some time that your search for her has spanned years."

"*My* search, Anais. Not my government's."

"Is there a difference, nìRau?"

Tsecha smoothed the folds of his white overrobe, the red trim of his cuffs providing the only true color in the drab surround. "I was chosen to succeed Xinfa nìRau Ceèl as chief propitiator of my sect eighty-five of your years ago, as a most young one. The Laum had just claimed power from Sìahrau, and none believed Vynshà would ever rule over idomeni. Thus was I chief propitiator when we were only of Vynshà. If we become only of Vynshà again, chief propitiator I will still be."

"NìRau, I didn't mean—"

"To be in government serves only a purpose. For you as well as for me, I believe, Anais, and truly." Tsecha maintained an even, humanish tone throughout his speech, ending by baring his teeth and sighing. An advantage, perhaps, to being as a wall. If he had ever given this type of speech in Temple or before Council, embellished with the full range of Vynshàrau gesture and posture, so that every emotion and feeling of his was revealed . . . *I would again be fleeing from mixed-sect mobs demanding my life. Of that I am most sure.* He breathed in deeply in an effort to slow his pounding heart. *My Captain lives.*

Anais sat in silence. She had decorated her small hands, narrow as Vynshàrau but lifeless white, with several large-stoned rings, which she toyed with in turn. "We tracked Captain Kilian to a small Transport Ministry hostel located in what one might generously refer to as NorthPort's business district, but one of Interior's people beat us to the goal. My best man was able to catch up with her and work on her for over a month. He is positive we were put on the wrong scent, but I have been at this game longer than he." Stones flickered in the light. "Very soon, I expect to be proven correct. We will have her, nìRau."

Tsecha suppressed the urge to bare his teeth. Anais thought herself so subtle. When she grew angry, she spoke in ways she felt idomeni would not understand. *But I had my Hansen, and I knew my Kilian.* His living Kilian. Quick, yes, and suspicious, as she was always. *Are you quite sure you will have her, Anais? You have not the skill to read between her lines.*

The Exterior Minister continued. "Later, my agents hooked a red herring in NorthPort. She turned out to be an Interior staffer on holiday. On holiday—in bloody NorthPort! Studying the Haárin, she claimed. Sent there by Evan to cross me up, no doubt. Although I suppose it may have been true—she is one of his Vynshà-watchers."

Ulanova's mouth curved. "Vynshàrau, nìRau, of course. Stupid of me. No offense meant."

But your very life is an offense, Anais, Tsecha thought as he nodded his acceptance of her apology. "So you suspect van Reuter protects Captain Kilian now?" he asked. "Is that a surprise?" *It is not, to me.*

"Considering their linked pasts, yes and no." She pounded her thigh with a jeweled fist. "If I only knew where he'd stashed her! That man has allies all over the city, though with all those unanswered questions concerning his wife's death, perhaps not as many as he used to."

"Yes." Tsecha nodded. He had read accounts of the death of the Interior Minister's dominant, in fact only, wife. *Such a disordered life.* But there was blessed order in death, at least. "I rejoice in the Lady's death, for it has brought her peace, and truly. May Minister van Reuter find such order as well." He felt Anais's eyes on him again, their glitter hard as the stones on her fingers. Did she believe he wished van Reuter's death as a convenience for her? The thought angered him. "Thank you for the word of the Captain, Anais. What else must we speak of? My time for first prime sacrament draws most close, I believe." He wished to be at peace when he took sacrament, as well as later, when he planned. *So much planning—so many meetings!*

The Exterior Minister again worked her rings, studying him through narrowed eyes. "There has been the first death, nìRau. On Elyas, in the town of Zell, near the Haárin settlement. An older man, a shopkeeper. His family was able to get him to the Neoclona facility on Amsun before he died. The doctors there believe some type of environmental toxin is to blame, but no one can determine what this man ate or drank or touched which could account for his illness."

"This is the first and only death?"

"But not the first *sickness*, nìRau. There were two more in Zell, a husband and wife, and a young man in NorthPort. The symptoms were the same. Digestive problems and body aches, followed by mood disturbances, psychotic episodes, rapid wasting. In the case of the young man, his liver needed to be replaced."

Ulanova's shining gaze moved about the bare room, focusing on nothing. "We will, in deference to your sensibilities, refrain from asking you to question your physician-priest skeins as to whether any idomeni have likewise taken ill these past months. But we do need to know what types of soil and water treatment the Haárin have in place in Zell and NorthPort, nìRau. We need to know what sort of untaxed trade is taking place between your people and mine. Specifically, are your Haárin selling food to my colonists? Food that is proving to be more than an exotic delicacy, but that is poisoning them? I realize your religions and cultures all dictate care and secrecy with regard to the production of your foods, as they do with your treatment of illness, but we need that information. You must comply with our requests. An order is required. Through your Council, and coming from you."

"You know what the answer will be, Anais."

"Then we will expel the Haárin from the Outer Circle."

"And we will expel humanish from Samvasta and Nèae, and all will go as before."

"We need that information, nìRau."

"You know it already, Exterior Minister. Do not come to me for confirmation you have obtained from your own. Your doctors keep you well informed, this I know, and truly."

"No, nìRau—"

Tsecha bared his teeth quite broadly. "Ever since their first work in Rauta Shèràa, your Neoclona doctors have worked as they pleased, Anais. DeVries, and Parini, and your most excellent Shroud. You keep their secrets from idomeni. Why should idomeni behave as different?"

Ulanova looked Tsecha in the eye, her stare most steady. "Because idomeni, I think, want what we in the Commonwealth want. A well-ordered future." She stepped down from her high seat. When she stood most straight, she seemed not as short as Tsecha knew her to be. "This is what I assume, nìRau. To the best of my knowledge, your government does not share your vision of the future." Her gaze probed like a physician's instruments. "They know what you believe, and still they sent you here."

Tsecha bared his teeth. He welcomed the opportunity for open discussion, the chance to speak as idomeni. "Yes, Minister. All on Shèrá know my beliefs."

"That if we share worlds long enough, eat the same foods, drink the same water, we will begin to change? The idomeni will become more human and the human will become more idomeni."

"Until, in the end, we will be as one people, Minister. Such is order, greatly to be wished. All the same, in the end."

"Hybridization." Ulanova's eyes dulled. "John Shroud testified before the Cabinet last month on just that subject, nìRau. He believes the idea laughable."

"Does he, Minister? That is most interesting. When he labored in his basement in Rauta Shèràa's humanish enclave, he believed quite differently. So often would he visit me at the Academy, to argue the beliefs he does not believe in anymore." Tsecha remembered warm breezes, the sweet odor of lamptree, the raised voices. "Even then, his research told him the benefits of combining. Of hybridization. 'Humans could live two hundred years, nìRau,' he would tell me. How pink his face grew as he spoke. Even now, I remember the pinkness."

Ulanova stood very straight and crossed her arms. "But his research led nowhere, nìRau."

"Indeed, Minister?" Tsecha gestured in disregard. "This is why he and DeVries and Parini govern their hospitals as Oligarchs, watch over the Commonwealth as propitiators? Because John's research has led nowhere?" His hands trembled. Such joy to be had, in open disputation. "But he still thinks his new humans could be changed as he wills, and remain most as human. He thinks he can take the advantages of combining and give nothing in return. So little he understands of order. So little he has always understood." An even more joyous thought occurred to him. "Did you ever ask John Shroud, Minister, whether *he* knew where Jani Kilian is?"

Ulanova closed her eyes and began to massage her forehead. "Doctor Shroud assured me—"

"Did he, Minister!" Such joy Tsecha felt, he interrupted without apology. "So well John assures. He assured my Hansen, just before my Hansen died. And he assured me, just before the Haárin entered Rauta Shèràa and the sect dominants demanded my death. 'I do not have her, nìRau,' he said. 'She died in that transport crash. Nothing left but ashes.' Thus did John Shroud assure, while in his basement, his new human healed."

Ulanova's eyes snapped open. "If my hunch proves true, nìRau, and your Captain turns up, I will first use her to destroy Evan van Reuter. Then, she will face court-martial, and if I have any say in the matter, she will be executed for the murder of Rikart Neumann." Her lip curled. A humanish smile. The smile of a wall. "Ironic, if that augmentation which helped her survive the crash only served to keep her alive for me."

Tsecha bared his teeth. "My Captain was augmented for one reason only, Minister. So she would be alive when I needed her. So she would live until her time had come. Her time to succeed me. Her time to take my place as chief propitiator of the Vynshàrau."

Something shimmered in Ulanova's eyes. Was it fear? "In your own way, nìRau, you are as fanatical as our most radical religious leaders." Her tone hardened. "What you believe can never come to pass."

"Such is as it will be, Minister. Whether *you* believe or not is of no importance. You will come to accept or be left behind. As the Laum were left behind, and as all will be left behind who do not accept order. Order must proceed, Minister. Order is all."

"It is good I understand you, nìRau," Ulanova said softly as she looked down at him. "Now, with regard to your refusal to supply information concerning illegal Haárin trade, please allow me to save both our staffs much time by lodging my protest of your behavior with you now."

"Your protest is noted, Anais." Tsecha remained seated, his hands twisted through his overrobe to stop their shaking. *But my Captain lives, as I prayed, so lodge your protests where you will.* Double meaning, he knew, in those words. Between the lines. Hansen would have been proud.

CHAPTER 14

Jani sat at her desk, office door closed, curtains drawn against the distractions of sun, calm lake, and cloudless sky. Her workstation screen flashed in silence, its conversation input option shut down, alarms muted. Feet propped on her desk, touchboard cradled in her lap, she leaned forward to advance the shifting screen images with a stylus.

Then she hit the wrong section of the touchboard and dumped herself out of a sensitive region of Commonwealth systems. Exasperated, she leaned toward the screen too quickly and almost dumped herself out of her chair.

Voice would go faster. Jani berated herself as a series of Lyssa's files disappeared in a rainbow flash. Then she rehacked her way through the document tangle, once more by touch.

She had known dexxies for whom workstations provided the bulk of daily verbal exchange. For some, it had been a conscious choice; for others, it had just worked out that way.

Could have worked out that way for me. It's easy, and safe, and I could win all the arguments. There were plenty of jobs out there for a paper-savvy fugitive with an antisocial streak. She could have lain lower over the years.

But she needed to hear real voices. Or, more to the point, voices she knew to be real. Perhaps the difference was subtle, one for philosophers. But she'd seen more than one augmented colleague done in by that difference during her time on Shèrá.

Hearing things is a bad sign. Seeing things was worse. That meant all those neurochems whose names she kept trying to forget were building up in her head in vain search of release, a condition more properly known as augie psychosis. Sometimes reversible, if you excised the implants in time, but most times, not. Shroud had begged her to keep watch for the signs of impending problems, to come to him when she felt she needed medical help.

Of course, her dear doctor had begged for a lot of things.

What a couple we made—at the time, we added up to one normal person. Anyone's guess who contributed the bulk of the normalcy. Jani watched documents flick across the screen. She tried to avoid thinking of her medical history, which seemed equal parts tragedy and farce. There had been some good science in there as well, of course—it just got overshadowed. *I'm a walking tribute to some amazing minds, I suppose.* Galatea to three Pygmalions. *No, one Pygmalion, and two Frankensteins.*

A nested display sharded into prismatic chaos. With a groan, Jani flicked the workstation into standby mode. She walked to the window, swept the curtain aside, then gasped as the molten glare of sun on snow blasted through the glass and shocked her roomlight-adapted eyes. She buried her face in the curtain, patted away the tears, then eased her lids apart and tested the filming for the looseness that signaled stress fissures.

She blinked, waited, then looked out the window again. As well as the lake and city skyline, her view included the Private House grounds; snow-coated terrain banked and rolled around season-stripped native trees and shrubbery, forming a landscape of white sugar and dark chocolate. *You need to get out more,* Jani persuaded herself as she headed for the door.

"Cabin fever, huh?" The Interior staffer who helped Jani into the *one-size-adjusts-for-all-yeah-right* snowsuit nodded in commiseration. "Bites us all after a few days." He led her to the house's rear entry, cocked an eyebrow at her refusal of a skimmer for a trip into the city, and shrugged at her determination to "just take a walk."

"January in Chicago—it ain't for sissies," he said as he closed the door behind her.

Neither's taking a walk in some of the places I've lived, mister. Jani lowered the light transmittance of her goggles until her eyes stopped watering. Each stride cracked like stuttershot as her boots broke through the snow's crusty white surface. Within minutes, she'd cut across a flat, well-trampled expanse that would be a billiard table-like lawn come spring, and entered a less-traveled area of sparse woodland and ravine.

Even when inhaled through her humidifier mask, the air possessed a peppermint clarity. With every breath she drew, Jani felt her head grow clearer. After weeks of recycled ship and station air, she grappled with the urge to strip off her constrictive headgear and feel real wind in her face again. Then she checked the weather sensor on her right sleeve. *Windchill—forty-nine below. Cancel the blow for freedom.* Even after years of adjusting to their quirks, she didn't trust her revamped nerve endings' ability to warn her of impending frostbite.

The landscape glittered with fairy-tale desolation. She bounded over fallen trees and ambled down the ghosts of trails. When a squirrel darted into her path, then stopped short, tail twitching, she rummaged through the pockets of her community snowsuit in case someone had left something edible behind.

"Hang on," she said to the creature, which responded by launching itself across the path toward the remains of a storm-shattered tree. Jani watched it disappear just as her gloved hand closed over something crunchy. "Success—you should have waited," she called after the departed creature as she examined the smashed packet of crackers. With the grace of a beneficent monarch, she tore the packet open and sprinkled the crumbs near the base of the tree.

Her good deed for the day accomplished, Jani continued down the path. Every ten meters or so, she'd glance up at the treetops and wonder where Evan's Security force had stashed the buggery. If her sense of Colonel Doyle was as spot-on as she believed, someone was monitoring her heart rate and blood pressure at this very moment.

The distant shooter-crack of snapping branches didn't alarm her at first. She assumed a large animal, some type of ruminant. Or perhaps a member of the Interior grounds crew, who could fall into that category as well. *Not nice—everyone here has been very good to you.* With the exception of Ridgeway, of course. No one could mistake him for a cud-chewer. *Although the cloven-hoofed part—*

In the middle distance, hidden by trees, a high-powered skimmer shut down with an insect whine. Jani executed an about-face and started back toward Interior Private. She could just glimpse the house's roof between the trees.

My shooter is in my duffel, and my duffel is in my office. Good place for it. She ground her teeth and focused on the red brick chimneys, poking up through the slate roof like feathered badges. A beautiful house, really. Too bad she hadn't stayed behind to take a better look at it. Designed to appear hundreds of years old when it was really no more than twenty or thirty—

Branches fractured again. Jani dived off the path and behind a fallen tree.

If that skimmer turns out to belong to grounds crew clearing trails after the storm, I am going to feel mighty stupid. Not to mention look stupid. *Getting an eyeful, Ginny? Think Evan's guest is a loon yet?* She glanced around at the bare trees. No cover. No place to run. Not that she could make any time through the knee-deep snow, anyway. *Anytime, Colonel. Come collect the idiot.*

She gloved through the snow for anything that could serve as a weapon, but could uncover only brittle kindling. She waited for augie to kick in with the familiar calming cascade, but felt only the dry mouth and roiling stomach of growing panic. The air she gulped through her mask tasted only of bracing sharpness. And through it all, the broken thought worked through her racing mind, like subtle static, barely detectable . . . *I'm not right—this isn't right—it's not working right.*

Her berries didn't seem to be in season now. Who'd have thought in the end even augie would have let her down.

A short distance away, snow crunched. Jani nestled closer to the log, grateful for the shadowy color of her snowsuit.

The footsteps stopped. "Risa?"

Jani, hands working under the log, paused in mid-grope. She'd managed to half-bury herself in snow, uncovering a couple of small rocks as a bonus.

"Risa? I know you're here. I saw you take a header." Twigs snapped. "You're wasting time."

Jani looked up just as Lucien Pascal, dressed in full Service winter camouflage, leaned over the log. "You have a lot of nerve, coming here," she said as she sat up, rocks clasped in still-buried hands. She jerked her head toward the house. "You know you've been seen."

"Depends who's watching." Lucien's breath fogged the clear humidifier mask. He smiled, which she'd learned on the *Arapaho* wasn't necessarily a good sign, and held out a mottled white arm. "Could you come with me, please?"

"I'd rather not."

Lucien's arm hung in midair. What did his eyes, obscured by darkened goggles, look like now? Jani knew she'd see more warmth in the rocks she held. "I wish I could say you had a choice," he said, his voice muffled by the mask. "But I'm afraid you don't."

He was probably right. Without augie stoking her, Jani knew she didn't stand a chance in a hand-to-hand with him. She curled her legs beneath her in a semicrouch and considered her options. *He's got a full head, fifteen years, and at least twenty kilos on me, he's armed, and he has a vehicle hidden nearby that he could use to chase me down.* Add to that the fact that Exterior infiltration apparently extended to Private House as well as Main. *They must have contacted him as soon as I stepped outside.* Which meant he must have been waiting for an opportunity to get to her since she'd arrived. *And he's probably not alone—must be a backup out there somewhere—*

"So?" A hint of self-satisfaction flavored Lucien's voice. "Are you going to come quietly?"

In reply, Jani hunched her shoulders and shot forward at a forty-five-degree angle, cannoning into his midriff and pounding her rock-loaded fists into his solar plexus.

Lucien emitted a gratifying "oomph" as he stumbled backwards, but his jacket, well-padded and lined with impact absorbers, took the brunt of Jani's blows and cushioned his fall. He grabbed her by the shoulders before she could straddle him, rolled her, and rammed her to the ground.

Something hard, large, and pointed impacted Jani's upper back. Her "oomph" came much louder than Lucien's since her civilian snowsuit didn't come equipped with bumpers. Gold lights novaed and died before her eyes. Seeing stars—amazing how damned literal that term was.

"What the hell—" Lucien struggled to his feet and backed away "—were you trying to pull?"

The sound of his labored breathing wended through Jani's pained daze. *Took 'im by surprise on my own—augie, who needs you?* She tried to raise up on her elbows, but slumped back as some invisible giant planted his foot squarely in the middle of her chest. Then jumped up and down. *Me, that's who.* She attempted to draw breath through the suffocating mask, then to tear the clear shield away, but an upper-back cramp stopped her short. Vanquished, she closed her eyes, pulled in the occasional pained gasp, and waited for the fire in her lungs to go out.

Lucien made no move to assist her. He brushed snow and dead-leaf confetti from his suit, freeing his shooter from an inside holster in the process. "You aren't going to try to jump me again, are you?" He approached her gingerly, free hand extended. "Rolling around in the snow with you might have its attractions, but it's too damned cold right now."

"Sweet-talker." Jani waved him back and rose as best she could on her own. "Bet you say that to all the prisoners." She turned and kicked weakly at some dark ridging poking up through the snow, revealing the embedded rock that had knocked the wind out of her. "Lead on, Lieutenant."

Lucien stilled at the mention of his rank. Then he motioned with his shooter for Jani to walk on ahead.

Progress proved slow. The trail sloped and rose; Jani's back cramped with every jolting step, every strained breath. For a time, the only words spoken were Lucien's terse directions as he told her which way to turn. Then, as they approached the clearing in which he had stashed his skimmer, he drew alongside. Jani noted he had holstered his weapon. "You were going to brain me with a rock," he said, sounding genuinely upset. "I stole underwear for you."

"I wouldn't have hit you hard. Just enough to slow you down." She swallowed a moan as her back seized. "Honest."

Lucien cut in front of her and popped the skimmer passenger door. The vehicle was a newer sport model: satin-finish silver exterior, black-leather interior, and *very* low-slung. This time, when he offered Jani his arm, she took it. "Anything broken?" he asked, as she inserted herself into the cockpit.

Jani shook her head, slowly at first, then more vigorously as the pain in her upper back receded to a duller, more manageable ache. Augie to the rescue. *Now you show up.* "I'm too old for this crap."

"That's what you get for jumping poor unsuspecting lieutenants." Lucien slammed the gullwing shut and hurried around to the driver's side.

Take your time. Jani stared at the vehicle's dash, which resembled a GateWay-certified transport control array. *Not like I could skimjack this thing anytime soon.* She lifted her arms as high as she could, pulled off her goggles and mask, pushed back her hood, and worked a hand through her matted hair.

Lucien fell into his seat and yanked his door closed. Security seals whunked and hissed; the changing cockpit pressure made Jani's ears pop. "Fancy skim for a looie," she said, as he freed himself from his own headgear and gloves. His mussed hair gleamed in contrast to the cabin's dark decor. "Surprised someone from the A-G's office hasn't rapped your knuckles."

Lucien jabbed at the vehicle charge-through three times before he hit it. "I have permission."

"I know. Saw you and your permission on the 'Vee last night. You make quite a couple." She mouthed an "ow" as the skimmer rose with a jerk and banked sharply, causing her to ram against her unapologetic driver. "I finally got the meaning of your little card," she said as they flutter-glided down a slope. "Your sailracers. Off to surf the solar wind. You're trying to tell me a certain someone was augmented." Lucien jerked the wheel again, and she banged into her door. *And if you think I'm going to tell you who it is, you can go wrap yourself around a tree.* Hopefully, *after* she had disembarked. "I've never been kidnapped before. Are you taking me to Exterior Main? A stronghold outside Chicago? The next province?"

Lucien cocked his head. That was the only reply Jani received as they hopped over a low fence that marked Interior's boundary. Not once during the transit did she see any Interior vehicles or staffers. Anywhere. *Evan, we must talk when I get back.* When she got back—keep the happy thought.

Lucien's wariness lessened as soon as they ramped onto the Boul, the twelve-lane thoroughfare that had welcomed Jani so roughly the day before. He drove fairly well. The skimmer's proximity alarms didn't yelp that often, and he only passed on the right twice. After a few minutes, they ramped down, leaving the pressing traffic behind. The snow had fallen on this quiet world as well, but Jani could see from the bare sidewalks and roofs that staff had already seen to the cleaning up.

Lucien, too, eyed the facades of cream and light brown brick and stone, tiny patches of manicured hybrid greenery filling the narrow spaces between house and sidewalk. "This is the Parkway," he said softly. "I suppose you could call it a stronghold."

Jani recalled Minister Ulanova's stern portrait in the Amsun Station gangway. *I can't say how much I'm looking forward to this.*

They stopped in front of one of the buttercream manors. In the center panel of the double-wide front door, Jani spotted the gold-enameled oval centered with the black double-headed eagle of the Ulanovs. As a uniformed Exterior staffer hurried out to take the skimmer, she and Lucien disembarked and made their way up the narrow walk.

The doors flew open. A dark-haired young woman rushed out onto the landing.

"*Lucien!*" She wedged between him and Jani, imprisoning his arm in hers. "Where have you been? Milady has been calling for you every five minutes—the hell of it!" She pushed Lucien ahead of her through the entry, then tried to close it on Jani. "You go around the back," she snapped.

"*No*, Claire, she comes in the front." Lucien shook himself free of his petulant escort and ushered Jani into the mirror-lined entry hall. "Now go tell Her Excellency we're here." His not-so-gentle shove propelled Claire halfway down the hall. "*Bâtard*," she spit as she disappeared through an open doorway, her kittenish face aged to cat by a nasty glare.

"My thoughts exactly," Jani said as she turned to Lucien, who had developed an interest in the gilt frame of a mirror. "Stoking fires upstairs and down. You're asking for trouble." The dig elicited only a bored shrug. "What does Ulanova want from me?"

"You'll know soon enough." Lucien's eyes held the dull cast of ice left too long in the cooler. The *Arapaho* seemed a long time ago. A very long time.

CHAPTER 15

A still-pouting Claire poked her head into the hallway and motioned for Jani to follow. They passed through a series of sitting rooms, each larger and more ornately furnished than the last, ending up in a *salon grande* with crimson fabric-covered walls and museum-quality furnishings. Jani looked at the muraled ceiling and berugged floor. *Everything's freaking red—I dub thee the Bloodshot Room.*

"You wait here," Claire said as she departed, whipping her waist-length hair like an animal repelling flies.

Jani shrugged off her snowsuit jacket, gave up on the pants, then flexed her neck and worked her stiff shoulders. An odd languor had settled over her, an unsettling contrast to her usual post-augie jitters. *At least I won't go bouncing off these goddamn walls.* She listened for approaching footsteps, then stared blearily at the fragile glass and porcelain contents of the cabinets.

When that palled, she switched her attention to the wall decor. She contemplated several holos, their colors calibrated to resemble the mutedness of old oils, before stopping in front of the portrait of a young man. He wore a plain tunic in Exterior burgundy; his clipped hair shone white-blond. Full-lipped, his professional smile held a hint of dry humor. Jani couldn't see the color of his slanted eyes, but a long-forgotten fragment of Commonwealth gossip told her they'd be brown.

"That was my late brother-in-law, David Scriabin, at the age of twenty-five."

Jani twisted around. Her upper back cramped. She hadn't even heard the door open.

"He had just been elected First Deputy to Exterior Minister al-Muhammed." Anais Ulanova stood in the doorway, eyeing Jani with cool cordiality. Unlike many public figures, she was just as imposing in private. Medium height, very thin, she wore a long-sleeved, floor-length black gown of stark design. Weighty gold hoops hung from her ears. Her short, dark brown hair glistened in the room's soft light, its swept-back style accentuating her aquiline nose and wide-set eyes. Lyssa van Reuter, thirty annealing years on.

"Your Excellency," Jani said, with a shallow bow that was as much as her balky back and colonial sensibility would allow.

Ulanova's dark gaze shifted to the portrait, and softened. "He became Minister himself only five years later, the youngest Cabinet member in Commonwealth history. That was the year my sister and he married." She waved languidly toward two nearby chairs set at opposite ends of a long, low table, on which rested a silver beverage service. "You'd like a refreshment? Coffee, perhaps?"

Jani sat down, her stomach grumbling as the rich aroma of truebean reached her. "With all due respect, ma'am, if our positions were reversed, I doubt you'd drink anything I offered."

"Be rude if you wish, Ms. Tyi," Ulanova said as she poured. "But it is a cold winter's afternoon, and I need my coffee." She sat back, cup and saucer in hand, her posture impeccable. "Lieutenant Pascal will be joining us shortly." A smile flirted with the corners of her thin-lipped mouth. "Off seeing to things he could just as well leave to his staff. He really is the most . . . thorough young man."

Jani waited until Ulanova raised her cup to drink. "He's fucking Claire, too, you know. He's snaking you with her just like David Scriabin did with your sister."

Coffee sloshed, spattering Ulanova's dress. Fifty years in the public arena served her well—the pain that flashed across her face disappeared instantly. "I never would have suspected you a wallower in common gossip," she said slowly as she dabbed at her skirt with a linen napkin.

"Oh, I understand the situation was rather uncommon, even by Family standards. You and Scriabin had set the date and picked out the silver, next thing you know, you're a sister-in-law." Jani tilted her head in the direction of the Scriabin portrait. "The resemblance to Lieutenant Pascal is startling. Are they related, or do you breed David look-alikes on a farm somewhere?"

"If this is the way you intend to play, Ms. Tyi, please be advised I earned my letter in the sport before you were born."

"I intend to disclose fully to Minister van Reuter this conversation as soon as I return to Interior House, ma'am."

"My *ex*-nephew-in-law is an incompetent drunkard who has, in the grand tradition of his family, surrounded himself with a staff comprised of children and counter-jumpers. If you think your informing him of our meeting will help you in any way, you are doomed to disappointment."

"Your concern is duly noted, ma'am. Thank you."

"Why did he bring you to Earth?"

"A long-overdue vacation, ma'am."

"Lieutenant Pascal believes otherwise. He was quite taken with you, Ms. Tyi. I can't recall when anyone impressed him more."

"My thanks to the lieutenant for the vote of confidence." Jani rubbed her cheek and smothered a yawn. *She ordered Lucien to jump me. She knows I'm augmented, or made a damned good guess. She wanted me post-augie. She wanted me off my game.*

"Are you sure you won't have coffee, Captain? Or perhaps you'd prefer something stronger? You appear drawn."

Jani caught the tip of her tongue between her teeth, then shook her head. "Captain? I don't have a rank. I'm not Service." She forced a conciliatory smile. "I've only just come off a long-haul, ma'am. I don't recover from those as quickly as I used to."

Some emotion flared in Ulanova's eyes, the last flickers of a dying fire. Then, with a complete lack of fuss, she filled a cup from the coffee ewer and thrust it at Jani.

After a pointed pause, Jani accepted the coffee. The cup's holopattern caught the light as she drew it near; minuscule iridescent snowflakes seemed to tumble down the smooth white sides. She took a healthy swallow of the black, foamy brew. Strong. Sugared. Bracing. Lovely.

Ulanova's measured voice slithered past her strange torpor. "I can be a powerful ally, Ms. Tyi. The reverse also holds true."

"With all due respect, ma'am, why tell me?"

"Evan brought you here to perform an investigation. All I ask is that you inform me of your findings as you do him."

"You're asking me to betray my Minister's confidence, ma'am. What am I worth if I do that?"

"I've never been one to begrudge practicality." Ulanova raised the lid of one of a trio of small dishes and removed a tiny, multicolored cakelet. "And coming over to the winning side before the last decisive battle seems to me the height of practicality." The stiff icing crunched like frozen snow as she bit down.

"I wasn't aware we were at war, ma'am." Jani finished her coffee down to the bitter, grainy dregs.

"Trust me, Ms. Tyi, when I tell you we have a situation developing of even greater concern than the secessionist threat." Ulanova refilled her cup and pushed the cake server toward her side of the table. "Have you ever heard the name *Jani Kilian*?"

Only a few thousand times. "No, ma'am, it doesn't sound familiar."

"Knevçet Shèràa?"

Poor pronunciation—too much buzz in the "c." "Is that an idomeni phrase?"

"Rikart Neumann?"

"Everyone's heard of the Neumanns, ma'am."

"Acton van Reuter," Ulanova said, a shade too loudly.

"My minister's late father." Jani popped a cakelet into her mouth. "The Old Hawk. Died about four years ago. Age of sixty-seven. David Scriabin was only sixty-four. NUVA-SCAN patriarchs don't seem to live very long these days, do they, ma'am?"

Ulanova arched a stenciled eyebrow. "Perhaps the word *treason* may serve to fix your attention, Ms. Tyi. Treason, and premeditated murder."

Jani's jaw stalled in mid-chew. *I had my reasons.* "Ma'am?"

Before Ulanova could explain further, Lucien entered. He covered the distance to their table in a few rapid strides. "Your Excellency," he said, handing her a sheet of parchment.

As Ulanova studied the document, her expression grew more and more somber.

"Do you recall our recent discussion of Commonwealth kidnapping laws, ma'am?" Lucien asked as he dragged a chair tableside.

Parchment crackled as Ulanova's grip tightened. "Thank you, Lieutenant."

"We've wasted this lady's time," Lucien said, gesturing toward Jani, "and entered tricky legal territory in the process." He served himself coffee, then dug into the cakes, popping them into his mouth one after the other. "Kilian's dead. No one could have lived through that explosion." He had combed his hair and shed the snowgear. He now wore a snug turtleneck the color of rubies and Service winter-weight trousers striped down the side in the same rich hue.

Mainline stripe. Jani swirled her cup. *Mine was sideline white.* She checked his footwear. Sensible boots, like hers, though in better shape. Black. Mirror-polished and steel-toed.

Ulanova handed the paper back to Lucien. "The woman's ID chip was never found," she said. "Her death is assumption only."

Lucien staged another assault on the cakes. "Analysis of the wreckage showed that a pulse bomb had been placed directly over the transport's main battery, beneath the front of the passenger compartment."

He glanced at Jani. "Anyone sitting in the front of the craft was vaporized. The ID chips the recovery crew did find were as badly damaged as any they'd ever seen. It was their opinion Kilian's was obliterated."

Ulanova snorted. "That has never happened!"

"There's a first time for everything," Lucien replied.

Maybe, if I'd been sitting in the front. The memory of the transport cabin air's ozone tang burned Jani's throat. *But I was way in the back.* Jammed between the rearmost seat and the bulkhead, wrists bound to ankles, head between her knees. She could almost feel the rumble of the directionals shuddering through her dainty salon chair—

Pulse bomb?

"Ms. Tyi is just what she says she is, an Interior field agent," Lucien said. "Kilian's dead. Murdered along with the rest of the Twelfth Rovers."

Jani leaned forward slowly and set her cup on the table.

Ulanova grew thoughtful. "Some would maintain Kilian's death was an execution. My friend Gisela Detmers-Neumann, for one. You've heard of *her*, I assume, Ms. Tyi?" Her gaze sharpened as she shouldered on. "But innocent people died in that explosion, as well. Rescuers and rescued—loyal Spacers all. A great scandal, one to shake the foundations of the Commonwealth, the trust between those who administer and those who defend."

The explosion wasn't an accident. It had been planned, by someone who couldn't allow the events that transpired at Knevçet Shèràa to become known.

"I've been trying to connect Acton van Reuter to that transport explosion for nine years," Ulanova said. "He died before justice could be served directly. But I will accept his son in his stead, Ms. Tyi. Someone who could bring me proof Evan knew of his father's guilt and covered it up would earn the Commonwealth's gratitude as well as mine."

Jani grooved her right thumbnail into the lifeline of her numb left palm. *She called you a loyal Spacer, Borgie.* Rose pink carrier bled through the abraded synthon, forming a string of tiny, liquid pearls. *Isn't that nice of her?* "I'm sorry, ma'am," she said as she massaged away the sticky liquid. "I don't mean to appear thick, but I don't understand what you and Lieutenant Pascal are talking about."

Lucien stared straight ahead. Ulanova regarded Jani for a long moment, then pushed back the lids of the other two servers. "We also have fruit tarts and biscotti, Ms. Tyi," she said. "Unfortunately, the lieutenant has been greedy enough to eat all the cake." Her sidelong look at Lucien held murder. "No surprise there, it seems." She rose. "We have apparently detained you unnecessarily. Allow me to extend my most heartfelt apologies. The lieutenant will see to any compensation you feel is merited." She swept out of the room in a swirl of black.

Jani stared after the departed minister, her stomach gurgling its own farewell. Then the sound of muffled laughter claimed her attention. She turned to the chuckling Lucien.

He gave her a thumbs-up. "Good job," he offered around a mouthful of fruit tart. "The quieter she gets, the madder she is." His shoulders shook. "She's really pissed!"

"You can both—" Jani stopped as her stomach gurgled again, this time more urgently. Cramps rippled through her abdomen. Cold sweat bloomed and beaded. "Where's—" She clamped a hand over her mouth as the saliva flooded.

"Oh shit!" Lucien grabbed her by the shoulders and herded her toward the door. "Not on the rugs—not on the rugs!" He pushed her out into the hall. "Second door on the right!"

Jani stumbled into the bathroom, reaching the sink just in time. She kept her eyes closed as she vomited. She groped for the faucet and cranked it open, washing away the rancid stench, replacing it with the clean smell of flowing water.

Heavy footsteps closed in from behind. "Are you all right?" Jani jerked as an icy lump touched the back of her neck. "Steady on—it's just a coldpack." As the chill soaked through her shirt, her knees gave way. She sagged to the tiled floor, Lucien providing just enough support to keep her from cracking her head against the plumbing. Her emptied stomach gave a last trembling lurch. She moaned and rested her cheek on the cold floor.

"Do you need a doctor?"

Jani opened one eye. *What is it about me and men and bathrooms?* Lucien sat atop the marble vanity, legs swinging from the knee. Back—forth—back—forth. The motion nauseated her anew. "No." She closed her eye and tried to feel whether her filming had fissured. "What the hell was it, and where?"

Silence. A sigh. "Ascertane. Glazed inside your coffee cup." The sound of a fastener being worked, a bottle seal being cracked. "I don't understand your reaction. Ascertane's a mild anti-inhibitory—you're not supposed to know you've been drugged. You're just supposed to feel happy. Trusting." The slide of cloth against counter. Footsteps. "Here. Drink this."

Jani opened both eyes. Lucien and his identical twin slowly merged into a single, blurry-edged figure holding a small dispo filled with yellow liquid. "Stick it in your ear."

"It's for nausea."

"I already have that. Thank you."

"Look." Lucien gulped the tiny draft. "Same bottle. Same damned cup!" He refilled the dispo, swallowed that as well, refilled it again, then placed it on the floor in front of Jani. "Suit yourself," he said as he returned to his perch. "I'm just trying to help." He shoved the bottle into a Service-issue toiletry kit and yanked the fastener closed.

"Yeah, you're a real humanitarian." Jani worked into a sitting position, pausing every so often to give her stomach time to catch up. Then she picked up the tiny cup and sniffed the bright yellow syrup. The harsh lemon odor made her cough.

Lucien glared at her. "It's the same stuff we drank by the barrel during flight training."

"I didn't have flight training, did I?" Jani drained the dispo, gagging as the thick liquid burned her throat.

"I don't understand." Lucien linked his hands around his knee. "I've administered Ascertane a hundred times—all it does is make you blab." He rocked back. "That nausea stuff works fast. Feel better?"

Jani swallowed. Her stomach remained steady. "I think so." She rested her head against the wall and watched Lucien watch her. "I told her about Claire. Just to see her reaction."

His rocking continued without a hitch. "Which was?"

"Surprise. I think I actually caught her unawares."

"So she'll send Claire away. Won't be the first time she's sent someone away." His eyes slitted as he smirked, slanting upward at the corners. "Or the last."

Jani compared Lucien's face to David Scriabin's. His was longer, his cheekbones not as high. Close enough in the dark, though. "You know, David Scriabin and Anais Ulanova were quite the item until he lost his nerve and eloped with her younger, prettier, less ambitious sister. He and Anais never quite called it quits, however. A typical Family mess." She sat up straighter. The antinausea brew had functioned as promised. "So, you aren't her first twenty-five-year-old towhead." She tossed the coldpack back to Lucien. "Or her last."

Lucien caught the pack with one hand. Without a word, he slid off the vanity, placed the toiletry kit on the rim of the sink, and left.

Jani took a few "get-ready" breaths and eased to her feet, using the wall as a support. She rummaged through the kit, liberating a single-use toothbrush and a pouch of oral rinse. "The man's a born looker-after of old ladies." Jani removed the wrapper from the toothbrush. "Of course, if you took him home to meet mother, she'd fight you for him."

Lucien was waiting for Jani in the hall, her jacket in hand. Instead of his Service winter camou, he had opted for the standard-issue snowsuit in an alarming shade of bright blue. The glaring color made him look like an overgrown little boy.

Except around the eyes. Jani looked into the familiar chilly brown stare. She allowed him to help her with her jacket, then followed him silently. Just before leaving the house, she turned. The kittenish Claire watched them from the end of the hall, arms folded, face in the shadows.

Neither Jani nor Lucien donned their facegear before going outside. Instead, in psychic agreement, they made a bareheaded dash for the waiting skimmer, piling into seats and pulling shut gullwings, causing the vehicle to rock as though wind-buffeted. Jani's backache had lessened to stiffness; the short exposure to the frigid air slapped away the last of her sick haze. By the time Lucien ramped onto the Boul, she felt human again.

Near death makes you appreciate the simple things. She studied the Chicago skyline with heightened interest. *Near murder gives them that extra glow.* She savored the buildings of new stone and old glass, their angled, diamond-shaped summits and swirling scrollery. This time around, she even took note of the Greatest War Memorial, its molecular clock coating glowing crimson in the stark winter sun. "Did it take you two long to rehearse?" she asked as the capital zipped by. "My questioning."

"It wasn't my idea." Lucien eased behind a ponderous people-mover and backed off the accelerator. Their zip slowed to an easy glide. "She flipped as soon as she discovered van Reuter had gone to Whalen himself to collect you. That nailed it. As far as she was concerned, you were Jani Kilian."

"But you didn't think so?"

"On the *Arapaho*?" Lucien shrugged. "You acted like someone with something to hide. But then, don't we all?" He bypassed the ramp that would have returned them to the Interior access skimway. "Besides, I scanned you in this skimmer—it's off now—and compared the reading to the ID we'd lifted from Kilian's Service record. She had it all planned. Confrontation, forced confession, deal. But the scans didn't match, and she couldn't proceed without paper proof." He slowed the skimmer further, until other vehicles actually began passing them. "Aren't you even a little curious why this Kilian is so important?"

Jani watched a distant shuttle descend like a pulse-powered beetle. *Means to an end. Ulanova wants Evan's head on any platter she can find.* "I don't even know when all this was supposed to have happened."

"Eighteen years ago—the last idomeni civil war." Lucien snatched glances at her as he maneuvered off the Boul and into a crowded commercial district. "Laumrau versus Vynshà, winner take all. The Laumrau were winning until this thing with Kilian happened. All sorts of mess bubbled to the surface after she died. Some Family members, led by Rikart Neumann and Acton van Reuter, had apparently agreed to throw their support behind the Laum in exchange for augmentation technology."

It's for the home world, Kilian. Who cares about a few xenogeologists from a colonial consortium no one's ever fucking heard of! Neumann had stood nose to nose with her. His breath, scented from ever-present throat lozenges, had wafted around her in cinnamon-tinged puffs. *Work with me now, you come to Earth with me when it's over. Cross me, and I'll snap your spine.*

"Problem was, the idomeni had never had another race involved in their wars before. Everything had always been very ordered, in as much as a war can be ordered. Organized. Very . . . well, idomeni." Lucien steered into an underground lot and edged the skimmer into a narrow charge station. "The fact that the Laum had actually courted disorder by dealing with humans staggered all the idomeni. The Vynshà had been getting ripped up to that point, but they were able to publicize what happened and turn it to their advantage. They took the dominant capital of Rauta Shèràa less than four months later."

Jani followed Lucien out of the garage and onto a moving sidewalk. Pushed along by a swelling crowd, they entered a glass-enclosed mall with a large skating rink in its center.

Lucien tugged on her sleeve. "Do you feel up to anything?" He flashed a dark red plastic card that proved, at second glance, to be an Exterior Ministry expense voucher. "It's on her." They wandered over to a snack kiosk that, if the posted prices were any indication, did most of its business with Cabinet expense accounts.

In deference to her iffy stomach, Jani opted for an iced fruit drink. Lucien protested he had an image to maintain with Exterior Contractor Accounts and ordered enough overpriced food to feed them both for the day. They carried laden trays to a rinkside table, doffed their coats, and settled in. Jani's drink turned out to be grapefruit-flavored. Very tart; it stripped the last of the minty oral rinse from her tongue.

Then the assorted aromas from Lucien's side of the table reached her. Fried onion. Grilled beef. Melted butter. "What kind of technology did Neumann and van Reuter get from the Laum?" Jani asked as she tipped back her chair and started breathing through her mouth.

"Hints on how to upgrade augmentation technology, in a way that could be better adapted to personality alteration." Lucien dug into his food like a starved teenager. "I don't think it ever worked out, though. Idomeni brain chemistry is different from ours, and they've got that culture of theirs as an external force to keep their antisocial personalities in line. The humans they tried the augie upgrade on flipped. Twelve sheets to the wind. The research petered out years ago."

But not before Acton sacrificed his firstborn grandson on the R and D altar. Jani crunched ice. "Who did they test the new augie on?"

"Volunteers, I assume. Research subject stipends can be pretty substantial."

So you don't know everything. Some secrets still lay buried beneath the sands of Knevçet Shèràa. "And what does Kilian have to do with all this?"

Lucien dredged a forkful of fried potatoes through a dollop of mayonnaise. Jani looked away while he chewed. "She was a sideline captain," he said. "Documents examiner. Academy grad, of all things. Reported to Neumann." His tone grew thoughtful. "Anais thinks some kind of double cross occurred. Either they argued over division of the spoils, or Neumann tried to push Kilian out of the deal altogether. All she's certain of is that Kilian murdered Neumann, along with a few Laum who got in the way. What no one realized was, Acton was keeping tabs. He knew he faced prison if any details of his collusion with the Laum got out, so he arranged for the elimination of the one person who could put him there."

But I didn't know. Neither had any of her real soldiers. Jani took tiny sips of her drink, applying it like salve to her tender stomach. *By the way, Ev, you know my little investigation—your daddy is involved. Do you want me to stop now?* Dull pain radiated across her abdomen. She set her glass down with a clatter.

Lucien flinched. "What's the matter?" He tried to smile. "Aren't you having fun? I am."

"You have an odd idea of fun, Lieutenant." Jani turned her attention toward the rink skaters. Most were average at best, but one pair struck her as particularly good. "So, you and Anais are pretty close?" she asked, as the man flipped his partner into the air.

Lucien donned the look of innocence he'd employed to perfection on the *Arapaho*. "Look, I'm sorry if that bothers you, but it's none of your—"

"She ever bring work home?" Jani joined other shoppers in applause as the partner landed cleanly on one edge and spun immediately into a quad-triple combination. The attention she paid to the skating display seemed to bother Lucien. He tapped his fork against the rim of his plate, remaining silent until she looked at him.

"Sometimes," he said.

"She chairs the Cabinet Court Board of Inquiry?"

"Uh-huh."

"Think you could get me a copy of the Court Summary of Investigation of Evan van Reuter?"

"Why?"

Because Acton van Reuter tried to kill me to prevent his dealings in illegal idomeni technology from being known. He used that technology on his grandson. His grandson died. Then Lyssa had herself augmented. How much more deeply had she explored what happened to Martin, and why? Who had she spooked? *This didn't die with Acton van Reuter.* Which meant someone else was involved in what had happened at Knevçet Shèràa.

And that someone had murdered Lyssa.

"Because," Jani replied, "the Court Summary contains the documents references for all the evidence examined. Once you have a doc reference, you can track it down in systems."

"You can't do that without Court-level passwor—"

"That's why you're going to supply me with those, too."

Lucien segued from innocence to indignation. "I'm an Intelligence officer in the mainline Service. I signed the Commonwealth Secrets Act."

"Despite those obvious shortcomings, I still think you capable of carrying out simple theft."

"It's illeg—"

"So is kidnapping, as you were so kind to point out. But you don't see me belaboring the point. Not yet, anyway." *Acton van Reuter tried to murder me.* And slaughtered her real soldiers in the process. *Who else knew the story?* Who had Lyssa flushed from the undergrowth before she went on that final bender?

"The Summary hasn't been issued yet. It's still in draft, no final Court seal. Not as grave a sin." Suddenly, Lucien grinned. If you ignored his eyes, you'd think it was your lucky day. "If I get it for you, what do I get in exchange?"

"The Commonwealth's gratitude."

"Not yours?" He cupped his chin in his hand and leered politely. Jani reached across the table and brushed a finger along his arm.

"Considering your penchant for gadgets, do you by any chance have something that could secure a workstation?"

"I'm sure someone at your level in Interior would have secured—"

"I want to make sure."

Lucien's smile tightened. "Will you please stop interrupting me."

"It needs to be a portable jig, something I can move from machine to machine."

"I don't take orders from you."

"No, but you'll do it, if for no other reason than that someday you'll be able to tell Anais all about it."

Dead eyes widened. To call the look "surprised" would have been overstating the case. But awareness would do, appreciation that she knew Lucien better than he thought, that he didn't fool all the people all the time.

"I'll see what I can do," he said after a while. "Will there be anything else, General?"

"No, I think that should do it for now." Jani finished her drink. "Thanks for the snack. I'll be in touch"

"Where are you going?" Lucien scrambled for his coat. "I thought we'd spend the afternoon together." Judging from his flustered behavior, rejection was an unfamiliar experience. "Like we did on the *Arapaho*, remember?"

"I have things to do."

"How will I contact you?"

"Not directly. I'll send a runner for the paper and the jig. I don't think we should be seen together anymore."

"Just squeeze me dry and cast me aside, huh?"

"You got it." Jani patted his cheek in farewell. Then she darted into the midst of the milling shoppers. She heard Lucien call, "Damn it, Risa!" but she didn't look back, and she didn't slow down. She knew how to lose herself in a crowd.

CHAPTER 16

In response to the repeated inquiries of your staff, I regret to inform you, nìRau . . .

The note had been written on Ulanova's personal stationery, Tsecha noted. Thick, stone-colored parchment nearly idomeni in quality, edged in black and topped with a bird possessing two heads. The minister's family symbol. *Two heads. Two faces.* He bared his teeth. He was becoming quite good with double meanings, and truly. Perhaps the day would come when his old handheld would no longer be needed.

. . . that the matter we discussed earlier today has, unfortunately, not been resolved. After further inquiry, it has been determined that my initial conclusions were in error.

"She fooled you, Anais." Tsecha walked slowly to his favored chair and sat carefully to prevent the angled frame from poking him. "But she fooled all you humanish. Until that last evening at Knevçet Shèràa, your kind thought you knew Captain Kilian most well."

This avenue of exploration, regrettably, appears closed at this time. Rest assured, nìRau, and truly, that I will keep you apprised of any new developments. a lète ona vèste, Nemarau. Anais Ulanova.

Glories of the day to you, Nema. Tsecha reread the letter once, then again, his gaze drawn repeatedly to the final line, the curves and slashes of his born language. Quite adequate High Vynshàrau—the proper accents, the appropriate phrasing for his skein and standing. He could find no fault with it. Some Exterior suborn must have labored most diligently to produce the deceivingly simple phrase. And yet . . .

You did not know me in the time before, Anais. You have no right to call me by my born name. He would answer to few idomeni who referred to him as Nema. Not even from his less-favored chosen humans, Tsai and Senna, Aryton and Nawar, would he tolerate such.

My born name is for the very few. Esteemed enemies, some. Most favored, others. Hansen Wyle, if he had lived, would know him only as Nema. *And my toxin.* His excellent Captain, whom Ulanova had apparently misplaced.

Tsecha settled back against his unforgiving cushions and set the Exterior Minister's letter on the chairside table. Such careful wording, on unofficial paper. *She would not seem so tall now, I think.* Ulanova had stumbled, and badly.

Yet that morning, she had been so sure.

Humanish like my Anais do not state themselves strongly without reason. So between the morning and the afternoon, she had been thwarted, but how? *To whom may I speak of this?*

Tsecha looked across his room. His newly acquired comport, a bulky hybrid hastily adapted by his dominant Communications suborn to function within Commonwealth systems, rested on his inscribing table.

His newly acquired, *unmonitored*, comport.

He had had a most difficult time convincing his Security of his need for such. But he had, in the end, persuaded. He had, after all, once convinced a mixed-sect mob that, whatever they may truly have wished, dismembering him with long blades and adding him to the soul circle burning around Rauta Shèràa was not part of it. Thus had he sidestepped death. And if so death, why not Embassy Security?

Tsecha approached his comport as though it were a piece of engine wreckage which could explode. He had not yet used it, and the instruction provided by the Communications suborn had lacked detail. He touched the activation pad, feeling a tingle of accomplishment as the display shimmered.

He released the touchlock of one of the drawers and withdrew a folded sheet of parchment. True idomeni paper, smooth as metalcloth, its color the soft pink of the inside of a cavashell. Tsecha unfolded it, laid it on the desktop, and watched the creases lessen, straighten, then disappear completely until only the handwritten series of humanish numbers and letters marred its surface.

The code had been carefully acquired, requested with many others so that Tsecha's agents would not suspect its worth. He tapped it into the comport touchpad, then pulled his favored chair tableside as a series of low, ringing tones told him the connection had been made.

Moments later, rainbow light splayed across the display, assembling to form a most familiar face. "Glories of the day to you, Physician DeVries," Tsecha said.

Watery dark eyes, downturned at the corners, squinted, then widened. "*Nema!*" The sagged face, too much pale skin on too little bone, quivered. "How in hell did you get this number?"

"I bought it, DeVries."

"From whom?"

"As you said to me once, long ago, ah, sir, that would be telling."

"Son of a—" Eamon DeVries's jaw clamped, cutting off the balance of the insult. *Something of my lineage,* Tsecha thought, *of that I am most sure.* Although the most unseemly of the three doctors who had founded Neoclona, the man had always been, in a fashion almost as idomeni, comfortably predictable.

He bared his teeth, but not very much. "I could only obtain your satellite office code, unfortunately, Physician DeVries. Physician Parini's, I could not—"

"He's out of town."

"—nor could I Physician Shroud's. Most unfortunate, in that case, because he is the one to whom I must speak."

DeVries sat back and folded his arms across his chest. "I would rather," he said slowly, "be strung up by my nuts over a bonfire than tell John *you* want to talk to him."

"Find him, Eamon. Tell him."

"I can't disturb him." Flaps of skin shook back and forth. "He's in the lab."

"In the lab!" Tsecha folded his arms as DeVries had. "Still? After so much time? Is it true what is said, that he sleeps within, eats within, never leaves?"

"He works, Nema. You remember how he works."

"And I remember as well what he works on. Who does he hide in his basement now?" Tsecha revealed his teeth more as DeVries's face ceased its movement. "Physician DeVries, if you possess any sense, you will tell John Shroud I wish to speak to him."

DeVries muttered of "ruined days" and "hell to pay," and disappeared.

Tsecha stared at the blank display. *Perhaps I pushed too greatly?*

And now Eamon DeVries would alter his code. He resigned himself to planning yet another subterfuge. Fortunately, his Security could probably find DeVries's new code as they had this one. From a humanish female who sold. Hansen had been the first to discover that with Physician DeVries, there could always be found a female who sold.

The display flickered again. Tsecha stiffened as the face formed. Just as familiar, this face, but some humanish compelled more attention than others. He nodded toward the display. "John."

Eyes, pale blue as ice, glinted. "My God, it really is you. I thought Eamon had been dipping into the drug bins again." Long-fingered hands combed through lazored hair which shone as a young one's. White hands. White hair. Rimed eyes the only color in a white face. A body wrapped in death-glaze.

John Shroud is an . . . albino. Yes, that was the word, and truly. Tsecha forced himself to look the man in the face. Still so sharp the bones, like Vynshàrau, skin taut as paint over muscle and bone. "Yes, John, it really is me."

John bared his teeth. They glistened even more than his hair. "It figures you'd get hold of *Eamon's* code. The idiot scribbles it on everything short of restroom walls." And the voice. *A back-of-the-cave voice*, Hansen had called it, *the word from the bottom of the well.* When an idomeni possessed such a voice, it was said to come from the center of the soul, but whether one could say such in John's case, Tsecha did not know. Allowing the man possession of a soul seemed, as again Hansen would have said, a stretch.

"Well, points to you, Nema." John tilted his head well to his left, until he looked at Tsecha sideways. Unseemly familiarity in that, but such was his way. "Imagine seeing you again after all these years. Such a pleasure, I can't begin to say. I have to get back to work now. See you in the news-sheets." He drew up straight. A hand flicked toward a touch-pad, to end the connection.

"*John!*" Tsecha gripped the sides of his display as though doing such could trap the man within. "If I wanted to find her, how could I?"

John's hand stilled. Pale eyes stared. Such a color. So cold. And artificial, the result of filming. His born eyes were pink. *Lab rat, they called him, in youth.* That knowledge always seemed to give Hansen such pleasure.

The bone white hand lowered. "Who are you talking about, Nema?"

"Her, John. *Her.* I believe she is alive."

John's face deadened even more. "You believe? You don't know?"

"That is why I ask you. Her paper is yours. Her history. How would you search for her? How would *you* confirm she lives?"

John sat back, hands to his mouth, fingertips pressed together. The movement allowed Tsecha a glimpse of the short-sleeved, collarless white shirt he wore. The trousers, Tsecha knew, would be white as well. *Medwhites*, humanish called them. John's favored clothing. During his time in Rauta Shèràa, he seldom wore anything else.

"Assuming I care," John said, "why should I tell you?"

Oh, you care, John. "Ulanova wants her . . . arrested, I believe is the word." Tsecha released his display, sat back, paused. Periods of silence seemed as important in humanish speech as in some idomeni. *We like to let things sink in*, Hansen had taught him. "She believes it is the wish of the idomeni for that arrest, as well. But I possess no such wish."

"Are you sure your people feel the same, Nema? I seem to recall a few riots concerning that very wish. Demands for your own arrest. Oh, for the good old days." John struggled to bare his teeth but failed. "Why does Anais want to arrest her?"

"The Exterior Minister requires her as a tool only, I believe. To destroy Evan van Reuter."

John's barely visible eyebrows arched. "Evan? Is that secession issue heating up again? I remember Anais thinking her van Reuter problems would end when Acton died. Guess not." Bony fingers tapped against cheekbone. Tsecha almost expected to hear the click. "Unless the rumors about old Ev being responsible for Lyssa's death are true. But even then, would Anais care? She and Lyssa despised one another because of that scandal over Lyssa's father." He frowned. "Unfortunately, Val's my muck and sludge specialist, and he's unavailable."

Tsecha bared his teeth with enthusiasm. "Please allow my glories of the day to the most excellent Physician Parini when he returns from his vacation."

John's frown grew. "You always liked him, didn't you?"

"I found him always most seemly, yes."

"But you hate him as well?"

"Yes to that also, John. As a most esteemed enemy, how else could he be regarded by me?"

"Hmm." John worked his hands together as though he held something he wished to mold. "Sh-she . . . always tried to explain that to me. I didn't understand then, and it still makes no sense."

Tsecha eased against his lumpy cushions. "But you never possessed the wish to learn of idomeni. You only possessed the wish to take from idomeni. Most disordered, John. Balance must always be maintained."

"So says the priest." John's face turned most as a wall. His hands ceased movement. "You're no stranger to taking, Nema. If you'd been allowed your way, if that bloody war and your bloody Temple hadn't stopped you, how much would you have taken from them? From Wyle? From—especially from—" His jaw continued to work, but no sound emerged.

Tsecha looked into John Shroud's ungodly eyes. "I do not take, John. I possess no wish to possess. I only allow what must become to become. As a propitiator, I can do nothing else."

"The future as you see it? A race of human-idomeni hybrids with you as its spiritual leader?" John laughed quietly. "Hundreds of years ago, a human who said things like that would have been burned at the stake. Your people had the right idea, Nema. Maybe we are more alike than we realize."

Tsecha sat heavy in his chair. "Why must I always explain as to young ones? We must merge together. In the end, all will be as one. All the same. So it must be, John, for the journey to the Star to be complete."

"Your journey! To your Star! We don't believe in your Star!"

"But yet you began the journey yourself, John. The first span in the bridge was built by you. You are as responsible as I for what she will become. What we will all become." Tsecha's heart pounded hard and slow in his chest. Not since he had worked to persuade the Council to name him ambassador had he felt so alive. "I always felt you reasoned as a physician, of course, in your experimentation. You wished to heal her, to improve her. Hansen believed, though, something most different. 'He just wants another freak to keep him company,' is what he said."

Shroud's hands drew apart slowly as he sat forward in his chair. "Hansen Wyle," he said through his teeth, "was as crazy as you are."

"My Hansen was most sane, as I am. We tried so to find her, but you hid her well. And now, you who hid her should know how to find her. How would I know her? For her good, for yours, for us all, do you not think I should find her first?" Tsecha inscribed shapes in the air to ward off demons. He could not be as humanish, now. "My Captain. My suborn. She who will follow me. Your Jani. How will I know her?"

John stared at him. Even his hate could not warm his eyes. "She's dead." His hand flashed white motion, and his face fragmented.

Before the man's image faded completely, Tsecha reentered the code. Several times. But after each attempt, the display only flickered as the comport audio emitted a series of low beeps. *So quickly you work to thwart me, John.* He berated himself for revealing his soul so to the humanish, but it could not be helped. They merely spoke of what was already well-known—why did saying truth aloud matter so to humanish?

If they do not speak of it, it does not exist. If they do not think of it, it goes away. Illuminating thoughts, perhaps. Explanations of humanish behavior. But not logical. Tsecha relaxed into his chair, allowing the framing to stab him where it would and thus focus his mind. *They are not as idomeni.* But in some future time, they would be. *And idomeni will be as they.* Rather sooner, that inevitability, if his Council's behavior with regard to the idomeni sicknesses was indication. The thought made him hesitate. *John and I as one.*

From far away, the tones announcing his late-afternoon sacrament sounded. Tsecha rose as quickly as his bent, inflexible seat allowed, but not before resetting the comport for internal communication and notifying Security of his wish for a conference.

John and I as one.

Tsecha pressed his open left palm against his stomach, a gesture of supplication. Perhaps, for one of his standing, to understand fully was not to be, but the gift of some intimation struck him as most seemly—

John and I as one?

—and greatly to be wished.

CHAPTER 17

A jovial "Come in, Risa" sounded through the door just as Jani raised her hand to knock. The panel swung open in a whispery combination of mechanics and the brush of door edge over expensive carpet. She stepped onto the dark grey pile and experienced the fleeting sensation of the ground giving way beneath her as her boots sank in to just below the ankle.

Original artwork she recognized from holozines decorated the light grey walls. As she crossed the room toward Ridgeway, ensconced behind his desk, she was treated to a wall-spanning backdrop of the lake, tastefully muted through glare-filtering scanglass. *Large body of water as office accessory—very nice.*

Ridgeway made no effort to rise until Jani reached his desk. Only then did he execute a quick half-up-and-be-seated. His smile held the same consideration. "Nice of you to be so prompt," he muttered breathlessly as he gestured for her to sit. "It's been a hell of a day." An errant lock of hair provided emphasis by flopping over his forehead.

Hope I helped. Jani smiled wanly and held her tongue.

"I do try to promote an environment which is conducive to cooperation, Risa—"

I doubt that.

"—and Lord knows I'm no micromanager—"

I'd have guessed pico-.

"—but is it too much to expect a reasoned approach to tasks at hand? Circumspection? Forethought? Is it too much to ask of people that they think things through?"

As though on cue, the door opened, and Ridgeway's aide entered.

He still looked like the enemy artillery barrage had stretched into the third day with no end in sight. Jani shot a "take heart" grin at him, but he avoided her eye as he placed a black-edged file folder on the desk in front of Ridgeway.

"Thank you, Greer." Ridgeway's smile curdled as he opened the folder, positioning it so Jani couldn't see what it contained, and paged through it while Greer exited silently. Then, eyes bright and predatory, he leaned across the desk and splayed the folder's contents over the bare, polished bloodwood in front of her. "A rendezvous in the snow," he said, triumph causing his voice to quaver. "How romantic."

Jani surveyed what lay before her. Sceneshots—one short sequence per panel. Snippets of action, intercutting middle distance and zoom, replayed themselves every few seconds in a rolling series. The holographer had been selective. The first display showed her diving behind the log, but not her scrabble for rocks. The angle and replay speed of the second sequence made her attempted flattening of Lucien look like a playful shove. The third scene stopped just as Lucien flipped her on her back. The overall impression given was, to say the least, incriminating.

Just some playful precoital wrestling. Never mind the windchill—lust conquers all. Jani pulled in a slow, painful breath. She'd checked the condition of her stiff upper back in a rest-room mirror upon her return to Interior Main. The dinner-plate-sized bruise had bloomed nicely, thank you, Lucien.

The fourth scene showed her and the lieutenant making their way down the forest path, the angle of the shot hiding the shooter trained on her back.

"Circumspection." Ridgeway clucked softly. "Forethought. You aren't the first slimy little traitor to lack either of those vital qualities." His gloating smile threatened to split his face in two. "Your ass is mine now, Tyi. Evan won't let you get away with this."

Jani looked from Ridgeway to the sceneshots with a lack of concern that bothered her in an abstract way. It was as though she watched the missteps of a character in a play. Augie picked the damnedest times to overstay his welcome. Ridgeway apparently wondered at her reaction as well. His smile wavered.

"Interesting," she managed, eliciting sounds of choking from across the desk. On another level, her mind raced. A frame, but by whom? *Ulanova?* She seemed petty enough, jealous of what she perceived to be Lucien's attachment. *But you'd think she'd try to wring something out of me before hanging me out to dry.*

"Ms. Tyi, you are in a great deal of trouble, you know. I've been informed the man in these sceneshots is mainline Service. An Exterior Ministry Security officer."

Could be the PM. Keeping tabs on her prodigal van Reuter, trolling for tidbits. *Or any of the other ministers, for that matter—they wouldn't even have to be anti-Evan, necessarily.* Hell, anyone who could adapt a holoremote to get past sensescan could have taken those shots. Newssheets. Gossip rags. Lucien, the gadget expert, for the hell of it.

Bâtard, indeed.

Ridgeway cocked his head. "Are you listening to me, Ms. Tyi?"

Jani sat back. Her chair was designed to make the occupant feel off-balance—spindly, hard of seat, and tilted forward slightly. It didn't work. For visitor intimidation, Ridgeway should have tried idomeni furniture. Jani had, on countless occasions, sat through hours-long Academy exams in chairs that had treated her back in much the same way Lucien had.

"I doubt you did this," she said to Ridgeway, indicating the panels. "If you had, I don't believe you'd have bothered to show them to me first. You would have gone directly to His Excellency." She gripped her armrests as a helium bubble expanded in the depths of her skull. "And here you probably felt like Christmas made a second pass." She took a deep breath in an effort to dispel her lightheadedness. "Sorry to disappoint."

Ridgeway leaned so far forward he was in danger of pitching out of his chair. "You are a traitor—"

"Speaking of traitors," Jani interrupted, "I've come upon something interesting." The calmness of her voice fascinated her. She'd never been adept at extemporaneous self-defense—the results reflected in her Service record. Augie never bothered to kick in at those lower stress levels. So why was he being so helpful now? "His Excellency's father apparently made hash of the Bilateral Accord some years ago. He colluded with the Laumrau during the idomeni civil war and managed to have some of their augmentation technology smuggled back to Earth. Martin, it seems, paid the bulk of the fine for that particular violation."

"Careful how you speculate," Ridgeway said. His eyes still shone, but his voice had weakened.

"The technology came from a research hospital, a place called Knevçet Shèràa." Jani bit out the *c* as Ulanova had, gave "Shèràa" the two-syllable treatment instead of entoning the double-*a* upturn at the end, and sat on her hands to avoid gesturing. God, she hated sounding like an Earthbound hick. "Rumor has it that in order to eliminate possible witnesses, he ordered the deaths of the Service troops stationed there. Just imagine, multiple counts of premeditated murder. Oh, and let's not forget the treason." She smiled. "Nice to have something in common with a man of Acton van Reuter's standing, I suppose."

Ridgeway licked his lips. "Acton's dead," he said. From his tone, he didn't seem altogether sure.

"Yes, but the sins of the father, Durian. They matter to idomeni, and they make humans sit up as well. The shrapnel from this bombshell just might take out our boss." She looked into Ridgeway's eyes. *Don't tell me you didn't know.* Oh, he knew—knowing went a long way toward explaining his lack of cooperation in providing her Evan's documents.

Ridgeway fingered his chin. "Risa—"

Oh, it's "Risa" again, is it?

"—I don't know what to say." He appeared genuinely thoughtful. "Lieutenant Pascal told you this?"

So, no one traced me to the Parkway—sloppy. That implied a stationary cam, perhaps in the Private House. Well, it saved a lot of explaining, although it did make Jani wonder how secure her office really was. "The information was there for the taking." No reason to disclose who offered it.

Ridgeway's manner became very clipped. Perhaps he associated that with professionalism. "Did Pascal attempt to interfere with you in any way while he served as your steward on the *Arapaho*?"

Now it was Jani's turn to sound surprised. "So you knew about that?" Ridgeway's stare offered no reply. "Nothing I couldn't handle." She thought back to her lunches with Lucien. They had spent most of the time laughing over whatever human weakness he had exploited that particular ship-day. "I think he'd grown used to manipulating through his looks and charm. I saw no reason to disabuse him of his notion."

Ridgeway nodded sagely. "Brave of you."

Jani shrugged. "Solo older woman coming in from a long-term colony assignment. He probably figured me for an easy target." She looked away from Ridgeway's developing smirk. *I'll be sorry I said that.* Big mouth returns. Looked like augie had finally folded his tent.

Ridgeway swung his feet onto his desk. He'd changed clothes since their morning altercation. His pale green socks peeked through the gap between his black half boots and coal grey trousers. They matched his loosened neckpiece, which in turn contrasted nicely with his medium grey shirt. *Occupant as office accessory—very nice.*

The look he bestowed on Jani wouldn't have qualified as friendly. More like superior, but without the gloat. "Will you continue to see this man?" He wasn't quite able to control the lively curiosity in his voice. The idea of operating as a pimp for the House seemed to appeal to him.

"I'll play it for as long as it runs," Jani replied blandly.

"It bothers me that Ulanova has zeroed in on Acton again." Ridgeway pursed his lips. "She'd gone after him once before, of course, but that was before his death. Oh, dear Anais had her claws out for him—make no mistake. Back in the Dark Ages, he alternated between undercutting Scriabin business concerns and aiming Anais's younger sister at David Scriabin. Unfortunately, David was engaged to Anais at the time. The scandal when David and Milla eloped was horrendous. Poor Anais never really recovered from the humiliation." He glanced at Jani and smiled coolly. "I appreciate your help, Risa, really I do. I understand what it must have taken out of you. Do you suppose any of this may tie in with Lyssa's death?"

Jani stifled a yawn. Her head felt heavy—a nap sounded tempting. But she wanted to visit the Library. Then she needed to get ready for dinner with Evan. "It was implied to me that several Families were involved in the importation of the augmentation technology. If you believe Lyssa had discovered what had been done to her son and was trying to figure out who was responsible at the time of her death . . ." She let the sentence peter out, punctuating the silence with a raised eyebrow.

"Good God!" Ridgeway became positively buoyant, no doubt envisioning how many of Evan's rivals he could scuttle by linking them to a murder plot. "I'm going to have to meet with Colonel Doyle as soon as possible." He sat up straight and tightened his neckpiece. "Well, you've blown my evening all to hell, Risa, but I think the results may well prove worth the inconvenience." He hesitated noticeably. "You're welcome to sit in, of course."

"You—" Jani stopped her personal commentary in time. "You are too kind, Durian, but I'll be dining with His Excellency this evening." She ignored his arch look. "By the way, those files we discussed this morning. Could I have them, please?"

"Of course." Ridgeway grinned. Grin, hell, he bubbled. In a week, he'd be telling people hiring Risa Tyi was his idea. "In fact," he said, "let's get some drudgery out of the way now."

A few intercommed orders to the frazzled Greer later, Jani found herself in possession of a Class A Interior expense voucher (no manager approval necessary unless she tried to buy something substantial, like Chicago), parts bin and repair chits, and other pieces of paper and plastic designed to make the favored Interior employee's life easier. The promised files, however, were held up in document limbo. Jani would have to wait for those until tomorrow. Ridgeway apologized profusely as he walked her all the way to the outer-office door, adding they would have to have dinner "very soon."

Can't wait. Jani trudged down the hall, wondering what exactly she had opened herself up to. True, she'd gotten Ridgeway off her back, but it crossed her mind he might attempt to reap some of the benefits he thought her to be bestowing on Lucien and Evan. She wandered down the wrong hallway, backtracked, then found herself standing before the doorway leading to the alternate breakroom. *What would I do?* Probably whatever he wanted. Ridgeway, Jani sensed, was the sort of man who thought staking a claim in a woman's vagina locked up the rest of her as well. A risky assumption, but fortunately, not a rare one. On more than one occasion, her continued good health had depended upon her working that assumption to its limits.

Sometimes, it's whatever gets you from here to there. She was glad to find the breakroom empty. She spent a few minutes straightening the snack table, then cleaned and reloaded the brewer. Soon the aroma of fresh coffee filled the room and her stomach, having recovered from its bout with Ascertane, responded by growling each time she inhaled. She rummaged around for a cup, then settled into a battered corner seat.

Ridgeway let me off easy. He could have bounced me off three walls and the ceiling besides, and he caved as soon as I brought up Acton.

Nimble little counter-jumper, Anais Ulanova would have said. *Knows how to keep his feet under him.* One option, if Ridgeway felt Jani had uncovered knowledge he wished to keep buried, would be to shower her with bounty. She reached into her shirt pocket for the expense voucher. Silver, in contrast to Lucien's red, with a discreet scripted *a* in the lower left hand corner that she hadn't recalled seeing on the lieutenant's card. *Anything within reason, and maybe a thing or two without,* Ridgeway had said when he handed it to her. *Just be discreet.*

"But diddle an account once, and I'm all his." Jani re-pocketed the thin plastic card. "He thinks." If she put her mind to it, she could divert half of Interior's liquid assets into a float-rebound maze before the Comptroller's office had a chance to reconcile her first transaction. Working with the Haárin had been an education in more ways than one. She wouldn't think of doing it, of course. But it was nice to know she could.

When I'm good, I'm very, very good. When she was bad, she could make Lucien look like a stiff. Still, the ease with which she had gotten around Ridgeway nagged her. But then, her idea of what constituted "difficult" differed from most peoples'.

My Academy final exams were oral. In High Laumrau. Not one idomeni on the examining board, not even Nema, looked her in the face. Instead, they watched her posture, her hands, the way she moved. Listened to her tones, lilts, phrasings.

Pauses after her replies stretched for ten minutes or more, then suddenly questions would pile on questions, with no chance of a request for clarification being honored, or even acknowledged. The exam lasted for nine humanish hours, with Jani knowing every step of the way that only one other being in the room wanted her to succeed. And also knowing for that very reason, he dare not make a move to help her in any way.

I learned as idomeni. Which had made it damned difficult to slip back into the humanish way of doing things. Back to the world of subtext. Hidden meanings. Things left unsaid, glossed over. *The world between the lines,* Hansen had called it. He'd been able to move between idomeni and humanish without breaking a sweat, but there had been a very good reason for keeping Jani off to one side. *A typical socially backward paper pusher—I gabbled, and I blurted, and I explained too much.* To go from a culture where everything you say is understood instantly to one where you could talk for hours and not say a goddamned thing had rattled her. She had fit with the idomeni so well, she thought.

"Until I proved myself most human." She sipped her coffee, grown cold in the cup. *Too easy.* The coffee tasted greasy and harsh. Jani flushed it down the sink and set out for the Library.

It proved a happy accident that she ran into Angevin Wyle in the journal reading room. She had been trying to figure out how to contact her without using the Houseline or risking another encounter with Ridgeway.

"Hullo." Angevin leafed without interest through a documents journal. "What's up?"

"I have some info for you." Jani beckoned her toward a pair of chairs in an isolated corner of the room. "About those sailracing lessons we talked about. It'll give you a chance to get out of here for an hour or so."

"Sailracing? I never—" Angevin lowered herself to the edge of her seat. A flicker of life animated her pinched features. "What's going on?"

"I need you to contact someone outside Interior. You have to do it from a public comport in the city. He'll meet you to arrange the transfer of some things he's obtaining for me."

"Why don't you use the courier service?"

Because I don't trust the courier service. Jani debated the best handle by which to grip Angevin for this detail. "The Doc Control administers the courier service, and I don't want Durian to find out I had contact with this guy. He works for Exterior."

"Durian. Phfft!" Angevin cradled her chin in her hand. "Is this guy good-looking?"

"Oh yes."

"Even better." The young woman fluffed her mashed curls. "Any particular place I should contact him from?"

"The only spot I know in the city is the mall with the skating rink."

Angevin wrinkled her nose. "That tacky place." She rummaged through her small shoulder bag, liberating a colorstick and a mirror. "I'll call him from the Galleria," she said as she applied bright copper to her lips with a few deft strokes. "What's his name?"

"Lucien Pascal. He's in Exterior Security."

"*Lucien.*" Angevin waggled her eyebrows. "Oo la la."

"Blond. Brown eyes. Your age. As tall as Minister van Reuter. Make sure to mention the sailracing—then he'll know you came from me." Jani hid a smile behind her hand as Angevin applied the colorstick to her cheeks as well. "I appreciate this."

"Yeah, well, I need a break. Supper meeting coming up. Then I get to confer with Durian again." Angevin crossed her eyes. "Speaking of Durian," she said nonchalantly as she continued to apply her makeup, "what are you getting from this Lucien that might upset him?"

Jani leaned back in her seat. Her battered shoulders cramped. "Job-related things," she replied through clenched teeth. "Just stuff."

Angevin dabbed at the corners of her mouth. "Things. Just stuff. For the sake of my Registry standing, I don't want to know the details, do I?" She studied Jani over the top of her mirror. "Durian doesn't like you. He thinks you're trouble. He told me, and I quote, 'His Excellency has taken in a stray who will turn on him,' unquote. Durian tends to be melodramatic, but he didn't get where he is by being wrong a lot." She tossed the mirror and colorstick back in her bag. "Does this involve Lyssa van Reuter's death?"

"I thought that had been ruled an accident," Jani said.

"Oh, we're going to be that way, are we? Maybe I should beg off and let you arrange your own damned transfer."

Please don't. If Angevin didn't agree to help, Jani knew she'd have a difficult time finding another runner. Steve and Betha certainly wouldn't oblige, which meant she'd have to pick a suitable stranger and bribe him or her with nontraceable cash chits. And you could not get a dummy chit from a Cabinet House bank booth, no matter how many *a*'s you had on your expense voucher.

Assuming Lucien comes through with something worth paying for. Assuming he had anything to come through with. Courts of Inquiry weren't exactly known as fountains of useful information. Anything good had a tendency to be kept in the Family. "Why do people wonder about Lyssa's death?"

Angevin wandered to the window behind Jani's seat and stared into the winter darkness beyond the glass. "There were rumors."

"That her death wasn't an accident?"

Angevin nodded. "That it was murder. The big one for about a month was that His Excellency finally got so fed up with her that he arranged a mishap. When that led nowhere, everyone whispered about how much Anais Ulanova and Lyssa's mother hated one another over the mess with Lyssa's father, and that Anais waited until he died to murder Lyssa in revenge."

"That hypothesis sounds bizarre enough to be popular," Jani said with a dry laugh. "Doesn't jibe with the fact Lyssa worked for Auntie, though."

"How about the rumor Lyssa was really Anais's daughter by Scriabin." Angevin's lip curled. "Durian laughed till he cried when that one started circulating."

"Sounds like one he'd start himself."

"Doesn't it, though?" The young woman's tense face relaxed in a grin. "Nice to know we have the same opinion of my boss."

"So why work for him?"

Angevin shrugged. "Means to an end. Building the old Cabinet pedigree." She grew serious. "Last thing my dad would have done, according to all who knew him. When that's the case, sign me up."

Oh Hansen—maybe she doesn't mean it. Jani looked up at Angevin's somber face. *Oops.* Maybe she did, at that.

"What type of man," Angevin continued, "would leave his wife and child behind in order to school in a place that didn't want him and meddle in things that didn't concern him? That's my mom's slightly biased viewpoint."

"What's yours?"

"Every time someone who knew him sees me, they tell me how much I look like him. Then they stand back with this shit-eating grin on their face and wait for me to do my Hansen Wyle imitation." Angevin tugged at a flattened curl. "I don't know what they want me to say. I don't know what they want me to do. I never knew him. I don't remember him. To me, he's a few holos and a name in the first page of the Registry." She looked down at Jani. "You're about the age he'd be now. You've lived out for years. Did you ever meet him?"

Jani swallowed hard. "No."

"I wonder if he'd have ever met anyone in secret to arrange an iffy transfer?" Angevin shouldered her bag and moved away from the window. "I have to go to my office and get my coat. Then I'll be off."

Jani made an effort to elevate her dampened mood. "If I see Steve," she said, "do you want me to mention you're going off to see another man?"

"Steve can go to hell and take Betha Concannon with him," Angevin replied flatly as she strode out of the reading room.

Is that a yes *or a* no? Jani lacked recent experience in the Rules of War as they applied to battling lovers. *Maybe I'd better mind my own business.* She wandered around the reading room, paged through several journals, and arranged to have copies of technical updates sent to her suite workstation.

"Well, that used up a half hour." She debated conducting a search through Interior stacks, but doubted she'd uncover anything worthwhile in any legally accessible areas. She needed to get her hands on locked-down paper, documents that had been removed from public access. She didn't dare try that without Lucien's jig. If she tried and failed to bull into a controlled Cabinet system, the alarm would be raised. And if Ulanova discovered the burrowing attempt originated from Interior . . .

"We'll wait for Angevin." Jani limped along the convolve of short halls and aisles leading from the reading room to the main body of the Library. The technical dissertation section always proved the least visited area of every bibliodrome she'd ever visited; Interior proved no exception. She wandered down aisle after aisle of leather-bound dexxie theses, encountering no one, checking the quality of the couches and chairs along the way. "Do what you can when you can," she said with a yawn as she stretched out in a particularly comfortable lounge chair, "including nothing." She worked her duffel beneath her head to serve as a pillow and closed her eyes.

CHAPTER 18

It seemed only seconds had passed when Jani felt a sharp poke in her rib cage. Her hand shot out and closed around a wrist—a startled yelp filled her ears. She opened her eyes to find a gape-mouthed Angevin standing over her.

"Sorry," Jani said as she released her. "You surprised me." She sat up slowly. Her stiff back complained anyway. "How did you find me?"

"I work here, remember?" Angevin eyed Jani warily. "You want to ditch a meeting, you hide in the dissertation section." She massaged her wrist. "Damn it, that hurt!"

"I said I was sorry." Jani felt her cheeks burn. *You're in civilization now, remember? No one's going to arrest you in your sleep.* That was Evan's promise, anyway. "Want some friendly advice?"

"What?"

"Don't surprise people who do sneaky work in the Commonwealth's name. We tend to overreact."

"Now you tell me." Angevin dragged over a chair and sat down. She had already draped her coat over a nearby planter and set an assortment of bags on the floor near Jani's lounge. "Oh well, I'm sorry I sneaked up on you," she said hurriedly. "Never happen again, that's for sure." She remained quiet for a time, her hands folded in her lap. "I've brought that *stuff* from Lucien," she finally said.

"He had it ready!" Jani struggled to her feet, trying to decide which sack to root through first. "He gave you all these?" she asked as she reached for the nearest bag.

"No! That's mine." Angevin slid to the floor and wrested the bag from Jani's grasp. "These are mine, too," she added, indicating the others. Then she removed a battered yellow sack from the hidden depths of the melange and handed it to Jani. "This one is yours."

Jani stared from her single parcel to the impressive array spread out before her. "You went shopping?"

"Well, after I called Lucien I had to wait for him, didn't I? Then when he showed up, he said there was something he needed to buy, too. We worked fast." Angevin held up a pullover and eyed it skeptically. "I thought you said he was good-looking."

"You don't think so?"

"No. Good-looking for men equals average. Lucien is not average. Lucien is gorgeous." Angevin tugged at her rumpled shirt. "You could have warned me—I'd have changed. Not that it would have mattered. All he did was ask about you."

"Really?" Jani peeked into her bag and opened the plastic pouch containing the jig. The device's beige case shone back. "What did he want to know?"

"The usual. 'What's Risa doing tonight? How's she feeling? What did she tell you about me?' " Angevin had draped the pullover across her chair, and was now examining the seams on a pair of trousers. "I thought I was in prep school again. Introduction to the Lovelorn."

"Sorry." Jani stuck her finger in a shallow depression in the jig's side. It squealed in response, and she shut the bag hastily. "I thought it would be fun for you."

"Oh, he hit on me. Asked me out to dinner. But I could tell his heart wasn't in it." Angevin cast dubious glances at the bag in Jani's lap as she continued to fuss over her purchases. "All your *stuff* in good shape? Nothing missing?"

"Everything's fine," Jani said as she gathered her duffel and bag and rose to her feet. "Where are the workstation carrels?"

"I'll show you." Angevin assembled her booty. "Follow me," she said as she jostled down the aisle.

"You can tell me the way—I'll find them."

"I don't mind." Angevin led the way through the Library, fielding greetings from other patrons and offering comments on the state of her day.

Jani, for her part, avoided making eye contact with anyone. A disturbingly large number of people seemed interested in the reason for her presence in the Library. One young man, thwarted in his attempts to engage her in conversation, cursed her under his breath, calling her van Reuter's hatchet.

"You've become the topic of the day," Angevin said. "Some folks think you've been brought in to do the final post-troubles cleanup."

"That's ridiculous," Jani muttered. The workstation carrels, she was relieved to see, were located in a quiet area of the Library. She followed Angevin into one of the small rooms and immediately closed the door.

"Sorry about the gauntlet," Angevin said. "Like I told you, the place has become a rumor mill."

Jani sat down in front of the workstation display. "I just didn't think I'd be caught in the grinders." She set her bags on the desk, then looked over at Angevin. "Thanks for your help," she said. "I don't want to keep you from your meeting."

Angevin made no move to leave. She set her parcels on the floor, then massaged her palms where the handles had bitten. "Can I ask you a question?" She waited for Jani's nod. "You carry a 'pack."

"Yes."

"You're in Registry. I looked you up this afternoon."

Good job, Evan. "Your point?"

"You don't act like a documents examiner. You keep popping up all over the complex. Asking questions. You act like a verifier. You worry people."

"I don't mean to," Jani said. "Look, I'm working under His Excellency's mandate. Anything I ask someone to do is completely legal. You have nothing to be concerned about."

"I'm sorry, but friends of mine who swallowed that line before found themselves suspended. Or deregistered. Or worse." Angevin folded her arms and ground her heels into the thick carpet. "What are you doing here?"

"You took part in the documents transfer on the *Arapaho,* Angevin. I think you have a pretty good idea."

"You're supposed to be looking into Lyssa van Reuter's death," Angevin said. "Outside eyes, according to Durian, on the lookout for things that could hurt His Excellency. Is that really the whole story?"

"Like you said, Durian didn't get where he is by making mistakes."

"You know, I helped you. The least you could do is level with me."

"What makes you think I'm not?"

Angevin gathered her bags, her cheeks flaming. "Next time you need *stuff* picked up, you can get it yourself," she said as she hustled out of the carrel.

Jani sat still for a time, staring at nothing. *What the hell is going on here?* She should have been able to disappear within the hugeness of Interior, but the people she encountered were stretched tight emotionally, sensitive to every intrusion. *And the only buffer I have is Evan.* Evan, who didn't communicate with his staff. Evan the drunkard. Evan the target. Evan, who people thought capable of murdering his wife.

But that's a discounted rumor.

Why had it been a rumor at all?

Jani pulled the yellow bag into her lap. First, she removed the jig, then a thick documents pouch adorned with the crimson Exterior seal. The seal had been tampered with—the color had blotched and the Ministry emboss had puckered.

Lucien must have worked in a hurry. Jani cracked the ruined seal and removed the weighty sheaf of Cabinet parchment. TOP SECRET had been stamped in the margin of the first page. COURT OF INQUIRY adorned each header. The word *draft* was nowhere to be seen.

Lucien had stolen Ulanova's copy of the Court's final report.

"You don't mess about, do you, Lieutenant?" It crossed Jani's mind the sort of distraction Lucien must be providing to keep Anais Ulanova from discovering his crime; stomach churning, she hurriedly activated her scanpack and began a confirmation check of the report. Knowing the lieutenant, she realized that he relished the danger he'd put himself in. But the line between worthwhile risk and recklessness was hair-thin. If she had to walk the report through the snow herself, she'd make sure Lucien had it back in his hands in the morning. Even if he distracted Anais to the point of mutual exhaustion, the minister would have to look for the document eventually.

"All green," she breathed as she scanned the final page. Not a dummy report assembled to throw off an office mole, but the real thing. She quickly leafed through to the appendix and studied the ID strings of the evidence used in the compilation. *SRS-1* jumped out at her again and again. Service papers, issued by First D-Doc, Rauta Shèràa Base.

"I probably imprimateured some of those." Jani removed the jig from its bag, then gave it a once-over with her debugging stylus. *It's not that I don't trust you, Lucien—I just have a healthy respect for your sense of whimsy.* She stared at the doughnut-sized device's featureless case, trying to figure out how to attach it to the workstation. Finally, she touched it to the rear of the display, staring in wonder as it remained in place. After a few seconds, it emitted a barely audible squeak. Then a soft green light glimmered from its depths.

Jani took a deep breath and activated the workstation.

"Passwords, Lucien," she said as she worked her way from Interior House systems into general access Exterior. "I need passwords."

She scrabbled once more through the bag, but found it contained only a small box wrapped in silver paper.

"Damn it!" One of Angevin's purchases, no doubt, accidentally dumped in the wrong sack. Jani was ready to stuff it back in the bag when she stopped and took a better look.

This is posh Galleria gift wrapping, huh? Wrinkled paper. Crooked seams. Curled corners where the sealant had been sloppily applied.

Jani ran a thumbnail beneath the paper seaming, unwrapped the box, and smoothed the gift wrap. Scrawled passwords filled the white underside of the paper. Random strings of letters and numbers. Proper names. Places. The occasional foul word.

"You don't believe in keeping it simple either, do you?" She set the sheet of passwords beside the display. Then, with some trepidation, she opened the box.

. . . he said there was something he needed to buy, too.

The toy soldier was small, six or seven centimeters tall. Exquisitely crafted. Every button had been brushed with silver, each microscopic medal glazed with colored enamels. He wore modern dress blue-greys: steel blue crossover tunic and grey knife-creased trousers cut along the sides with the requisite mainline red stripe. The hair visible beneath his brimmed lid glimmered pale blond; his right arm was bent in a permanent salute.

"Are you trying to tell me something?" Jani examined the figure for any sign Lucien had inserted something untoward in the tiny body. She scrabbled again for her sensor and scanned the figure as she had the jig.

"Disease-free," she said, placing her new mascot beside the touchboard. Then she flexed her fingers like a musician warming up, keyed in the first of the purloined passwords, and began mining history. As she cut through the protective barriers of bomb shelters and mazes, she could almost imagine herself in the small office in the hospital, digging through the patient records Neumann hadn't managed to hide. For an instant, the burnt-leather tang of shooter gloves stung her nose. She sensed Borgie standing behind her, reading the screens over her shoulder as he had then. She twisted around in her seat, heart pounding, but of course no one was there.

Of course. Jani checked the carrel door to make sure Angevin had closed it. Only then did she return to work.

If the curious had found Jani unresponsive before her disappearance into the workstation carrel, they found her damned near aphasic when she emerged, an hour and a half later.

I'm sorry. Very sorry. She offered silent apology to the librarian she brushed past, the young man who smiled and offered, "Hello." Yes, they had their own reasons for wanting to talk to her, but she had the experience to work around their concern. She could have calmed their groundless fears with a few well-considered words, convinced them it was safe to let her fade into the background where she belonged. The problem was that she didn't trust herself to speak. No telling what she'd say. That always happened when she was very, very angry.

You're a lying bastard, Evan van Reuter. You don't give a damn how Lyssa died—you dragged me here to help save your father's reputation.

She rode the lift down to the third floor, keyed through the triple sets of doors, then let her nose guide her to the scanpack parts bins. The residents of the floor had no doubt grown used to the characteristic odor of spent nutrient broth, but the undercurrent of rotted fish managed to have its nasty way with Jani's temper-churned gut. She leaned against the doorway leading to the bins, one hand over her mouth, as nauseated as any first-year intern. It would only get worse once she went inside; she knew from experience the only odor-killing ionizers on the floor would be positioned at the exit. A dexxie was allowed to clean up for the civilians, but when in the land of your ancestors, you sucked it in and proved yourself worthy.

Cursing softly, Jani pushed through the door. The idomeni, with their food issues and general delicacy, handled it so much more intelligently. Ionizers everywhere—the air in the Academy parts bins had smelled boiled.

Place looked better, too. The term *bin* proved an apt description for this area, which resembled an overfilled tool kit. No windows. Low ceilings. Narrow aisles lined with open work shelving. Repair carrels ran along one side of the enormous room; on the other side, the check-in desk and order-entry booths competed for space.

Jani tried to duck into one of the booths. She accidentally caught the eye of one of the clerks, however, and soon found herself the focus of several pairs of helping hands. Good news traveled fast.

"Are you sure this is the part you want, ma'am?" one of the clerks asked as he read her scribbled order.

"Yes." Jani tightened her grip on her duffel, shaking off yet another eager soul's offer to stash it behind the check-in desk. "Is there a problem?"

"Mr. Ridgeway's orders, ma'am. We need to inform him when someone checks out an old-time chip."

"Oh, really?" Jani circled to the clerk's side of the desk and waited for him to key Ridgeway's code into his comport. Chimes sounded—the man's face filled the display. "Durian," she said, "I'm checking out a revised GB-Delta twenty-year chip. I understand that's a problem."

Ridgeway stared at her pointedly, the seconds ticking away. "Good evening, Ms. Tyi," he said at last, smiling stiffly. Then he took a look at his timepiece. "Shouldn't you be getting ready for dinner? His Excellency hates to be kept waiting."

The words *His Excellency* elicited shocked whispers from the clerks. Jani gritted her teeth. "If we can settle this quickly, I'll be spot on time."

"Yes." Ridgeway glanced off to one side and shrugged quickly at someone. "I'm in the middle of something myself." His smile disappeared. "Must you do this now?"

Ginny Doyle chose that moment to move in beside Ridgeway and stick her head in the display range. "Hello, Ms. Tyi."

"Colonel."

"Digging into the archives, are we?"

"Trying to, if Grandma here will give me the sign-off." Jani looked into Ridgeway's narrowed eyes. "You aren't going to force me to resort to shoplifting, are you?"

One of the clerks gasped. Another snickered.

On the display, Doyle's grin twitched. "You know," she said, resting a hand on Ridgeway's shoulder, "I wouldn't put it past her."

"We'd nab her at the exit."

"Perhaps, but we are due for a systems drill this week. Let's give her a shot."

"We don't have time for that crap now, Virginia." Ridgeway looked down at his desk, his fingers drumming on the shiny wood. "Simon."

The clerk who'd been waiting on Jani stepped into display range. "Sir?"

"Give her the goddamned thing." Durian's image shrank to a pinpoint of light.

Foot-shuffling silence reigned for a time. Then Jani brought her fist down on the desk. "Well, you heard Grandma," she said to the startled faces surrounding her. "Give me the goddamned thing!"

The transaction was sorted out in record time. Smiles turned from polite to genuine. *Durian, Durian, how thee are loved,* Jani thought as one of the clerks appointed herself her guide to the repair carrels. *I should have tried this in the Library.*

The young woman led her down the hall. "Is the smell getting to you?" she asked. "You looked a little green back there."

"It's been a while since I've visited a bin this size," Jani conceded.

"These help," the clerk said, handing her a small plastic-wrapped package. "We keep them for the civvies, but the smell gets to everyone once in a while."

Jani examined the small packet. Nose plugs, menthol-infused. "Thanks," she said as she inserted them.

The clerk stopped in front of one of the carrels and handed Jani the key card. "It's the only one open. Nobody else wants it." She jerked a thumb toward the door next to Jani's. "Your neighbor smokes up a storm. It seeps into the shared vent. People swear it screws up their 'packs, but there's no proof—"

"Smokes?" Jani stopped in front of her neighbor's door. "Is this Steve Forell's carrel?"

"Oh God, you know him?" The clerk shook her head. "Just yell if you need help. Make sure you open the door, first—these rooms are soundproofed." She flashed a smile. "If Grandma calls, we'll let you know," she said as she left.

Jani waited until the clerk was out of sight before she knocked on Steve's door. "Open up. It's Risa." She waited. Knocked louder. "Steve. Come on."

The door slid open. Steve blocked the entry. "What the hell do you want?" Behind him, Betha sat at a small table, a nicstick dangling from her lips. They both looked exhausted.

"You two been busy?" Jani stepped past Steve into the carrel. Her nostrils tingled as the clove stink of the nicsticks worked past the menthol. "Smells like you've been busy. I'm not surprised. They'll yank both your 'packs as soon as those fake documents surface unless you can hand them something bigger."

"Yeah, well." Steve flipped his spent nicstick into the trashzap. "We've only got your word for that, don't we?"

"That's why you're both huddled in here smoking your brains out, because you only have my word."

"She's right, Steve," Betha said. "I looked it up." Her voice lowered. "The shortest sentence I could find were ten years in Lowell Correctional. That were for only one violation. I jazzed the Lady's docs—" Shaking fingers ticked off the total. She sagged into her chair when she ran out of digits.

Steve slumped against the carrel wall and slid to the floor. "Yeah, well if it goes to hell, we can just blow off, can't we? Hide out in the colonies, with our own. Doing for our own." He nodded firmly. "Pushing paper on the home world—how bad could that be?"

"How bad do you want it to be?" Jani pulled the other chair up to the table and set her bags down on the floor. "From that point on, all your work would be non-Registry. You could never use your 'pack again. You could never sign your real name to anything. And you wouldn't be doing for your own. You won't even be able to *see* your own, because any contact with them would be traced." She sat down carefully. Her stomach ached. Her back hurt. Her anger had ebbed. She felt old.

It had been fourteen years since she'd last tried to contact her parents. No one had been home, so she'd been transferred to a staffer from CitéMessage. That had struck Jani as odd, since her parents had always subscribed to the standard account with autoservice. She disconnected in the middle of the staffer's insistent request for her name.

The Service cruiser bearing the Admiral-General's seal had docked at Chenonceaux Station eight days later. Jani, who had decided to wait it out at the station before trying another call, had huddled behind a vending machine and watched the uniforms stream into the shuttle bound for her hometown of Ville Acadie. "You will," she paused to allow the tightening in her chest to ease, "never be able to go home."

A year passed before Jani worked up the nerve to touch down at Chenonceaux and try again. She had tapped out the code with a sweaty hand, disconnecting as soon as she heard her father's voice sing out, "*C'est Declan*!"

"If you're smart," she continued, "you'll stay away from paper altogether. But that's hard to do when it's all you know. If you're lucky, you'll find work in some high-turnover post, like shipping tech. You'll fill out manifests, track transports. Monitor warehouse inventory." The words caught in Jani's throat. She *hated* warehouse inventory. "If you're not lucky, which is most of the time, you'll be at the mercy of every cheap crook who susses out the fact you're in trouble. So you'll do what they want, when they want, for whatever they choose to pay you, if anything. Because you'll both know one anonymous call to any Cabinet annex is all that stands between you and a prison cell. Have I made myself clear?"

Betha stared at her, round-eyed and blanched. Steve freed another nicstick from his pocket, wrinkled his nose, and shoved it into his mouth without igniting it.

"So." Jani paused to pat her eyelids. Her films had absorbed the clove smoke and her eyes felt grainy. She pressed lightly, until the tears came. "I'd like to ask you some questions, if you're agreeable." She waited. "Betha?"

The young woman sighed. "What?"

"Can you still access the paper Lyssa had you work on? Not the Nueva trips—the other stuff. You mentioned older documents." She knew all she needed concerning the details of Lyssa's visits to Nueva. They were indeed scheduled take-downs. *Surmise confirmed—aren't we the genius?* Ulanova had had her niece followed on her excursions. According to the Court report, Lucien had been quite the busy bee for eighteen months prior to Lyssa's death. So now she had the means and the opportunity nailed. *But I still need the damned motive*. And motive meant paper. Jani looked at Steve. "How about you?"

"I don't have them anymore, and they're probably beyond his security clearance," Betha said softly. "I don't think he can help you."

"You don't know what my clearance is!" Steve shot back.

Betha fingered a skirt pleat. "It would have to be at least Orange, possibly even Blue. Only Ridgeway's immediate staff rates Blue." She never looked at Steve. "Sepulveda. Zalestek. Wyle. They all rate Blue."

"I take meetings with the idomeni ambassador!" Steve shouted. "Anything I need to find, I'll find. If I care to," he added hastily.

Jani looked at Betha, who regarded her in turn, her expression blank except for a faint quivering around the eyes. It could have been a guarded attempt at a wink. Or just a tic.

"I'm also looking for Consulate papers from our Rauta Shèràa days," Jani continued, "dating from just before the war to expulsion." The section of the report dealing with Acton had covered a respectable span of time, but Jani had still found significant gaps. "Duty logs would be good. Communication logs. Anything indicating who talked to whom and when." She pulled her scanpack from her duffel and set it on the table along with the recently purchased chip. "Think we can meet tomorrow?"

"We're not demanding, are we?" Steve worked to his feet. "We can meet here at fourteen-thirty. I'll be upgrading." He stretched. "So why can't you just pull this paper yourself?" he asked. "Why step up the flame under our arses?"

"Fewer questions this way," Jani replied as she rose and walked to the carrel's environmental control panel. "You both have reasons to go where you'll be going. I make people nervous, apparently, and I don't have time to muck about laying groundwork." She touched the lightpad; everything in the room took on a bluish glow as the antiseptic lighting kicked in.

"What are you doing?" Steve asked.

Jani increased the ventilation setting—the carrel grew noticeably cooler. "Surgery."

"You can't do that in here till the air flushes out!" Steve stuffed his hands in his pockets and pouted. "People bitch about the smoke."

"Hell of a lot cleaner than some places I've worked." Jani returned to the table, pulled her tool kit out of her duffel, and set out instruments. Then she cracked her container of nerve solder and poured a few drops of the thick brown liquid into a heat cup. "Scanpacks are hardier than you think." *Trust me.*

Betha stationed herself at Jani's shoulder. Steve sat down at the table, fascinated in spite of the circumstances. "What are you loading?"

"Something that can read what you're going to find for me." Jani pressed her hands flat against the sides of her scanpack and squeezed. The cover ID'd her prints and sprang open. "A new chip's been added to those docs over the years. I needed new hardware." Nestled in its case, the fist-sized mass of brain tissue shuddered beneath its protective pink dura mater.

"What kind of chip?" Betha asked.

"Family mark. The kind used in private papers." Jani felt beneath the scanpack for the master touchswitch. She set the switch to CHILL, then shut down the battery that pumped nutrient through the brain like a miniature heart. The healthy pink color of the dura mater remained, but the brain's trembling slowed to an occasional shudder.

"Whose?" Steve asked.

"Won't know until I can read the paper." *But I can make a damned good guess, Evan.* "What's the call on that chip?"

Steve held up the chip's antistatic pouch and squinted. "Five-eighths, nine to two, bleeds to death, flash activate."

Jani clamped the oxy feed lines to the fifth octant region of the brain, then closed the nutrient web. The shuddering ceased. Using microforceps, she peeled back the dura mater and anchored it to one side with a butterfly clamp, revealing a raised freckled line of chips and nerve bundles. She activated her laser knife, cut away the old two-nerve chip, and drew a thread of nerve solder from the ninth nerve lead to the second, forming an eight-nerve circuit that would drive the newer, more powerful chip.

"Family chip, eh? You be diggin' where you shouldn't, Ris?" Steve asked, his stare fixed on the table.

"Wouldn't think of it," Jani replied. The fried-meat smell of nerve solder worked past the nose plugs. Tiny puffs of smoke streamed upward as she picked single pinholes in the tissue. Using her forceps,

Jani set the chip in place. The hair-thin anchors fit perfectly into the pattern of holes she had cut. She attached the ends of the solder thread to the chip, baking them into place with touches of the knife.

"Not bad," Betha said.

"Don't know why in hell they make an edition chip a 'bleeds to death.' Every time a new version comes out, you risk killing your 'pack on fire-up." Jani reactivated the battery, then touched the knife to the chip, breaking the seal. The chip activated with an emerald flash, then faded to the pink-tinged grey of the surrounding tissue. Slowly, Jani reopened the oxy lines, then set the master touchswitch back to NORMAL. The octant revived with a rippling shiver.

Betha exhaled slowly and massaged the back of her neck. "You think there's something in this House got to do with the Lady's death?"

"I know there is," Jani replied.

"Not an accident?"

"No."

"You think she were augmented." Betha smiled at Jani's look of surprise. "I remember your reaction when I told you about her 'surfin'.' Asked an ex-Service friend what it meant. He told me. You think all her trips to Nueva Madrid had something to do with the augmentation, that she died because something happened to it." She grew serious. "Because somebody did something to it."

"It's possible," Jani finally said.

Betha walked to the door. "You mean yes. Why don't you say what you mean." She turned to Steve. "See you later."

"Where you going?" he asked.

"Work. I'll be in one of the spare offices if you need to talk." Betha smiled weakly. " 'Bye."

"She's smarter than she looks," Jani said as the door closed.

Steve drew close. "Weirdo 'pack you've got there," he said. "Dull-lookin', like a lump of mud. Tsecha's got somethin' looks just like it. His thing's like a dictionary. Got a couple human languages in it."

"Coincidence," Jani said as she swept her gear back into her duffel.

"Don't tell me that! I seen it! I've sat in meetings with him. Watched him tap at the damned thing."

Jani stuffed the yellow sack containing the Court of Inquiry report into her duffel. "Have you talked to Angevin today?"

Steve's eyes widened. He stood up, rocked uncertainly from one foot to the other. "Nah," he finally muttered. "Don't have time for her crap. It's all over. It's done."

Jani rose, then closed in on Steve until she stood toe to toe with him. "You don't want her linked with you in case you get arrested."

Steve tensed. "Won't get arrested. Be gone long before then." He chewed his unactivated 'stick. "That story. That were just a story, weren't it? 'Bout what it's like. I mean, you're just a posh little Cabinet cracker—what do you know about rough?" He offered her a hide'n'seek smile—now you see it, now you don't. "Were just a story, weren't it?"

"Oh yes." Jani focused on the floor. "You found me out. Blatant exaggeration, just to scare you." She walked to the door. "Tomorrow," she said. She glanced at her timepiece as she headed for the lift. She'd be late for dinner with Evan. After he heard what she had to say, he'd wish she'd stood him up.

CHAPTER 19

Jani ignored a staffer's efforts to announce her arrival and brushed past him into the Private House dining room. Evan, who had been sitting with his back to the door, stood up unsteadily as she cut across the room to the portable bar.

"Jesus, you do bang around, don't you?" He smiled tentatively, swirling the contents of his glass. "There was no need for you to rush. First chance I've had to be by myself all day. Gave me a chance to catch my breath."

Jani poured herself a glass of water and watched Evan sample his drink. She had always known him as a steady drinker. The official term was *maintenance alcoholic,* according to the Court of Inquiry report. He was on a regimen of alcohol dehydrogenase boosters and nutritional supplements and had a replacement liver waiting for him in Neoclona-Chicago's organ storage bank. Every year, he had a battery of tests to monitor for signs of incipient alcoholic psychoses. He was on record as saying he had no intention of curbing his drinking. He would do as he pleased; it was up to his cadre of highly paid physicians to keep him functional.

He looked Jani up and down. His grin dimmed. "I thought you'd dress like you did on the *Arapaho*. I was looking forward to it." He had certainly gone the full formal route. Black evening suit. Gleaming white shirt with onyx fasteners. The only thing missing was the red rose in his crossover lapel.

"You don't give a damn what happened to Lyssa. For the last two years of her life, you and she barely spoke." Jani walked over to a serving cart. Too much time had passed since her last meal. Her stomach ached as though she'd been punched. "You found out the

Court had initiated an investigation of your father's conduct during the idomeni civil war. The van Reuter reputation was at stake. You needed someone with experience in Rauta Shèràa paper to do a minesweep, help you bury incriminating Service documents Acton recoded as private paper. Enter yours truly." She snagged a warm roll from one of the baskets and bit into it. "You thought I'd help you cover for him to save my ass. Need I remind you that your Uncle Rik made the same mistake?"

"Who have you been talking to?" Evan shrugged off Jani's answering glare. "Anais has tried to engineer my father's ruin many times. She's always come out looking the fool."

"My transport crash was no crash at all. Anais has proof Acton arranged to have a bomb placed on board. He was involved with Neumann in the illegal acquisition of augmentation technology from the Laum at Knevçet Shèràa. They tried to pull me into the mix. I said no. When Rikart pushed, I pushed back harder." Jani closed her eyes. She could smell it again, the singed-leather stink of shooter gloves. "Acton pushed back hardest of all."

"Wishful thinking on Anais's part."

"I was there, Evan, remember?"

"My father was many things. But he believed in Lady Commonwealth. He would never have slaughtered her soldiers."

"Knowing what happened to Martin, how can you stand there and say that to me?"

"Knowing what happened to Martin gives me every right. The van Reuter men were always ripe for sacrifice, Jan. That's our job—it's an honor reserved for us alone. Dad would never have deigned to share the glory." He walked to the bar and refilled his glass. Four fingers of bourbon—no water or ice. "I'm not denying what happened to you. I certainly can't deny Rikart's involvement. But nothing my father did is anyone's concern but mine. He did not become aware of the Laum technology until after the war. Martin paid the first installment on that bargain. Serena and Jerrold paid the second, Lyssa, the third. I'm responsible for the balance, to be repaid in my own currency." He took a large swallow. "Anais has come up empty with this search of hers for years. Now, all of a sudden, she thinks she's gotten lucky."

Jani perched on the edge of a dining-room chair. Took a bite of bread. A gulp of water. She'd eaten this way too many times. Mechanical, tasteless refueling, choked down just prior to getting the hell out of town. "Yes, but this time she had Lyssa acting as Interior mole. Your wife had good reason to hate Acton. She wanted the entire Commonwealth to know what he'd done to Martin."

"It never occurred to her that she could damage her own reputation in the process. People would ask how she could have allowed it to happen. I tried to explain that to her, but she wouldn't listen to reason. I'm a magnet for women who refuse to listen to reason." Evan walked slowly toward Jani, stopping when he came within arm's reach. "Durian told me about your forced excursion this afternoon. Don't you see what Anais is trying to do? She's trying to drive a wedge between us, convince you it's safe to throw in with her."

"She may have a point." Jani brushed crumbs from her fingers. The bread rested like ballast in her stomach. "The Court will be releasing its findings one week from today. The final summation contains a demand for your resignation."

"How do you know that?"

"I read the report."

A host of emotions played across Evan's face as Jani's words sank in. Surprise. Elation. Anger. Fear. "Aren't you the enterprising one," he finally said, his words strung out like beads on a wire. "How did you manage to obtain it?"

"Never mind." Jani picked out another roll. "Besides, I don't have it anymore." Technically, that was true. She had stashed it in the women's locker room next to Interior's main gymnasium. "You don't sound surprised."

"I had my own artfully acquired copy delivered into my hands earlier today. Neatest piece of fiction I've read in years. I noted several gaps in the evidence. They seemed to coincide with every point the Court needs to make its case." Evan sighted Jani with the cobalt stare that had swayed voters for two decades. "Did Anais provide you with your copy of the report, by any chance?"

"Why would she do that?"

"She'll use you, Jan. She'll take what she can, then lock you up and throw away the code."

"And you're offering me so much more, aren't you?"

"I can offer you anything you want." He sat in the chair next to hers, still taking care to keep his distance, not to allow anything he did to seem threatening. "I never stopped caring for you. I never stopped wishing things had worked out differently. My life with you in Rauta Shèràa was the best time of my life. I want that life back."

"Evan, don't lie to me. You brought me here to salvage that old bastard's reputation."

"I brought you here to take care of you!" His fingers tightened around his glass, the knuckles whitening. "To make it up to you, for everything you went through. I had a house in the city picked out for you. A job, if you wanted to work. I had it all planned."

"I don't need anyone to take care of me. I can take care of myself."

"I've seen your idea of taking care of yourself. I've seen what it's done to you. Leave the thinking to someone else."

But thought is all I have. Planning. Outwitting. The art of seeming to give in when actually giving nothing. She'd read her Service file in the library carrel, through shrewder, more discerning eyes. *I'm what I've always been, only more so.* "I don't like to be beholden, Evan. I prefer to pay my own way." Jani stared at him until the arrogant gleam in his eyes degraded to uncertainty. "In my own currency."

Evan sank back in his chair. The skin on his face was greyed, the hollows beneath his eyes, deepened. "Has Anais identified you? Does she know you're Jani Kilian?"

"No. She had me scanned. The current pattern doesn't match my Service ID."

"Well then, what can she do to you? How can she threaten you? Don't let her scare you—she has nothing!" He touched her at last, resting his hand on her knee. "Just keep your mouth shut and wait her out. Follow my lead—I've brazened my way through more than one full frontal assault in my time." Taking her silence for agreement, he pressed a touchpad alongside his place setting. Uniformed staffers entered by way of a narrow access door and began serving the first course.

"So what did you do today?" he asked when they were again alone. "Besides getting yourself kidnapped and purloining top secret Cabinet documents."

"Just mucked about." Jani fished a mushroom slice out of her soup. Fungi, she had learned over the past few months, were *not* an option. "Visited the Library."

"You seem to have made some interesting friends." Evan filled his wineglass to the brim. "Durian told me you've been seen with Steven Forell. Durian has a great deal to say about Mr. Forell, none of it complimentary."

"Durian wants to wrap his slimy paws around Angevin Wyle. He blames Steve for keeping that from happening. If he knew how Angevin really felt about him, he'd spin in his well-appointed seat for a week." Jani ate what she could of the soup, then tested the green salad. When she looked up, she found Evan studying her, chin cradled in hand. "What?"

"How long have you been here?" he asked.

He's so close. He wants me to reach out and touch—Jani felt the heat rise in her face; she looked down at her plate. "Little over a day." The salad contained chopped apple. She reached for the pepper mill instead.

"So much news acquired in a little over a day. Tell me, are there any other love affairs affecting members of my executive staff that you think I should know about?"

Jani regarded the mill in her hand. It had a decidedly suggestive shape. "Well, the head of your Farms Bureau used to holo himself screwing assorted animal life in his office. He's not doing it anymore, though. AgMin shut him down."

Evan's eyes widened. He sat back and clamped a hand over his mouth.

"I hope we're not having lamb or chicken tonight," she added peevishly.

His shoulders shook. Gently, at first, then more and more violently. He'd always been a remarkably quiet laugher. He'd turn red and choke before he'd make a sound.

Jani continued eating. After a minute or so, she reached over and thumped Evan between his shoulder blades. He inhaled with a wheezing gasp.

"I don't remember—the last time—oh shit, Jan, don't ever do that to me again." He wiped his tearing eyes with his napkin, then sat quietly, his hands over his face. "I remember the night—they threw us out—of the Consulate bar—oh hell." He started up again, though much more weakly. "You'll stay here, won't you?" he asked when he'd finally summoned the strength to talk in complete sentences. "If they can't ID you, why leave?"

Jani examined the spice dispenser. Something called *ground habañero* had a lightning bolt beside the name. She sprinkled it liberally on her salad. "What if you're forced to resign?"

"Then I'll resign. Move back to the house in the Bluffs, play the gentleman of leisure. Answer my question, Jan."

"Gentleman of leisure. You'll go crazy." She coughed. The habañero wasn't bad.

"I won't go crazy if I know you're nearby. I'd sleep easier tonight if I knew I could count on you. Can I?"

"Why would you think you couldn't?"

Evan pressed a hand to his temple. "You're deflecting me. One eye on the exit, just like always. I could afford your evasions in Rauta Shèràa. I can't afford them now. Can I count on your support or not?"

Always the pressure to give and give . . . in exchange for what? She wasn't the only one who hadn't changed with time. "Blind loyalty's a quality I can't afford, Evan. Tell me what to expect."

"These situations tend to follow a pattern. No one will officially acknowledge my existence for about six months, although my real friends will send notes and such, just to make sure I'm keeping body and soul together. Then I'll start getting visits. Old allies asking for advice. Old adversaries checking my pulse. Within a year to eighteen months, I'll be ready to make a run at a deputy Cabinet seat. Next thing you know, it'll be like I never left."

"Sounds formulaic."

"It happened to Dad. It's happened to me before." Evan stirred his soup, which he'd barely touched. "It's just politics." He watched her eat, his brow wrinkling. "You used to tell me how spicy your mother's cooking was." He pointed to her salad plate. "I never thought that was what you meant. Lacks subtlety, at least from where I'm sitting. What's going on?"

Jani looked down at her salad. "I don't know what you mean."

"The chef aboard the *Arapaho* had some interesting things to say concerning your culinary requests."

"You had crew reporting on me?"

"No. Durian did."

"Durian did?"

"I'll admit he may not have had the purest motives, but when I spoke with him a few hours ago, he seemed genuinely concerned." Evan propped his elbows on the table and tented his hands. "He suggested I ask you a few questions. For example, are you drinking a lot of water—"

Jani set down her refilled glass. The third. No, the fourth—

"—and are foods that you'd once been able to eat with no reaction making you sick now?" Evan jerked his chin in the direction of Jani's salad. "Have your tastes changed, become what most of us might consider odd? Have you been experiencing body aches, abdominal distress—"

"You sound like John Shroud." Jani tried to laugh. "Interrogations every third day, same hour of the morning, same crummy therapy room." If she closed her eyes, she could visualize the bare, dark tan walls, the restraint-bedecked myostimulator squatting in one corner like the hulking torture device it was.

Evan disrupted her grim vision. "Jani, one colonist has recently died from a condition which began with the symptoms I described. The symptoms you're evidencing. I wish you'd see a doctor."

Jani examined her hands. Her right one shook a bit, but that was only because she was angry. *The garage guy's stomach always hurt.* Well, hers did, too. *He threw up a lot*. Ok. *He tried to kill his grandmother with a lazor*. Except his grandmother had been dead for twenty years; he exhausted himself annihilating a pillow. Hepatic dementia, the doctors had called it. They had a name for everything.

I have never tried to kill any dead female relatives. Hah—had them there. Besides, everyone in NorthPort knew the garage guy became sick from eating Haárin food. Lots of people on Whalen tried Haárin foodstuffs at least once. Jani had been eating it for years—it wasn't her problem. She attacked her water again. "Well, I wish you'd do something about your drinking," she said as she came up for air. "We can't have everything, can we?"

On cosmic cue, two staffers entered. They cleared and carved silently, but with many covert glances toward the table.

"Here's a deal for you," Evan said after they left. "I'll face my little problem when you face yours." He cut into his roast beef. A smile flickered. "Not lamb or chicken," he said.

"I'm not sick." Jani drove the point home by adding habañero to her meat as well. "I'm sorry if my colonial taste offends your Earthbound sensibilities, but don't compound your prejudice by calling it a disease."

"Have it your own way, Jan," Evan replied. "For now." They finished eating in silence, then adjourned to the adjacent sitting room for dessert and coffee. He carried his cup to the bar and, with a pointed look at Jani, added a generous splash of brandy. "Do you want to talk about Lyssa? I'm sure, since you read the report, you have questions."

Jani swallowed a belch. It felt as though a hot coal had lodged beneath her sternum. "I had already guessed she was augmented. The Court report research confirmed it. I think she had it done in order to feel what Martin had gone through. But she didn't have the right brain chemistry to withstand the stress. It was all pretty easy to figure, if you knew what to look for." She explained about the gossip magazine's crisis timeline. "Someone saw their chance and took advantage. It didn't take much to make her death look like an accident."

Evan leaned against the bar. "You'd think it would have helped her, don't you?" he said, his voice dead. "The Service uses it to build better soldiers—you'd think it would've helped her cope."

"Lyssa should never have been augied. Her mental state was already precarious, and it only got worse. Even frequent take-downs weren't leveling her out—she was headed for augie psychosis. If she'd been Service, she'd never have made it past the initials. She'd have been typed as a likely burnout and kicked out of the program."

Evan smiled grimly. "Augie burnout. I used to hear that phrase in meetings." He looked at Jani. "Burnouts hallucinate to a greater degree than regular augies. Borderlines, too. Like you?"

"Depends what you mean by hallucinate. My problems are with smell, mostly. I catch a noseful of berries whenever I get aggravated. Never heard voices, thank God. Never saw spiders crawling out of the walls."

Evan approached her with the slow step and unfocused eye of a man on the way to his own execution. As he lowered himself into the chair next to her, he exuded the same beaten-down wariness she had felt toward the myostimulator. *This needs to be worked through. This needs to be done. But that doesn't mean we have to like it.*

"A year after the children died, I visited Lyssa's suite without calling first. We had reached the point where we called first. She was sitting alone on her bed. She looked so happy—I thought she'd drugged herself. Being a doctor, she had access to the staff infirmary." His spiked coffee rested on his knee, its surface rippling.

"She was talking. To them. She saw me eventually, or at least *sensed* me. Didn't Martin look nice in his school uniform, she asked? He'd just told her he wanted to be a doctor like his mum. I slipped out as quickly as I could." He hoisted his cup. "My drinking, to that point, hadn't been too bad, but it did pick up from then on."

Jani sipped her coffee. "You didn't know?"

"About the augment?" He shook his head. "Not until I read the report today. Like I said, I thought she'd been drugging."

"You'd been exposed to it so much in your day-to-day, I'm surprised nothing clicked."

Evan leaned back in his chair. "I blocked it out, I guess. Didn't feel I had the right to inquire. I figured by that time, Lyssa and I were each entitled to the pit of our choosing. I didn't even ok an autopsy—that's what set Cao on the warpath. But I felt she deserved that . . . privacy. A last kind gesture from me, to make up for all the others." He looked at Jani, his eyes reflecting the depths of his own abyss. "This may sound horrible, but I think whoever killed her did her a favor. Every once in a while, I wish they'd show me the same consideration." He refilled his cup from the ewer.

Jani shifted in her chair. She was angry. Her back ached. Her stomach had begun to rumble ominously. She didn't think she could deal with a drunken Evan as well.

"Don't worry," he said, reading her mind. "Just coffee, until you leave. I promise." He shook a finger at her. "But I must insist you allow me my pit. I've earned it. These past few months, it's become a second home." He gestured toward the curtained wall opposite them. "Here's something you might like." He pressed a touchpad near the tray. The drapes swept aside. "Isn't it pretty?"

A spun-sugar world filled the window. Lit by rainbow lights, with the night as a backdrop, two banked tiers of snow-frosted hybrid shrubs glittered. Some of the dwarf evergreens had been clipped into spires and coils, while others had been shaped into stylized buildings. In the center, a line of graceful, needled shrubs had been trimmed into a suspension bridge, joining the two tiers. "It's pretty," Jani said, but all it looked was cold. She rubbed her aching gut and shivered. She didn't feel very art-appreciative just then.

Evan picked through the dessert tray. "I had it made for Nema; we were supposed to have a reception in the main ballroom after his welcoming ceremony. A bridge for the chief bridge-builder. Obvious, perhaps, but I felt it appropriate." He chewed reflectively. "Cao and Ulanova blocked me, of course. They felt he'd be insulted. As if they'd fucking know. So I had it moved here. Next time those two come for dinner, if there ever is a next time, it'll be waiting. Hell, if the weather's good, maybe I'll have the tables set up under the damned bridge." He touched her arm to get her attention.

"How did you manage? After the children . . . I almost cashed in. How did you keep going?" His hand lingered. It was Jani's left arm. All she felt was the pressure. "What went through your mind? After Knevçet Shèràa. During your recovery. When, you knew you'd lost it all. How did you live?"

Jani pressed down on her aching stomach. "I told myself—" She stalled. That was the point, wasn't it? She'd told *herself*, never anyone else. "I told myself that I was the last one. If I died, there wouldn't be anyone left to remember Knevçet Shèràa." This time she pronounced it properly, adding the right-handed gesture that mimicked the sweep of the sand dunes.

Evan's hand tightened on her arm. "You're remembered, Jan, if it's any consolation. I've seen the files. They fill a two-meter-long shelf in the Judge Advocate's office."

"That's not the remembrance I mean." Jani grew still; even her stomach quieted. "I remember the heat. The blowing sand. The sense of dread when I walked into Eva Yatni's room." She had been the first patient to die. She'd plucked out her eyes and plunged her thumbs into her brain. Neumann called it suicide.

"I remember another patient named Simyan Baru. I watched him peel the skin from his cheek like it was a piece of fruit. I couldn't get in the room to stop him—it was locked. So I went to see Neumann to get the code. He wouldn't give it to me. We had a talk. You know what happened next."

"I remember when Baru and two other patients escaped. We tried to treat them as best we could, but they were too far gone. Hallucinating. They thought we were Laum, come to kill them. They jumped Felicio and Stanleigh and stole our people mover. The only transport we had. We had nothing to knock it down with, no way to repair it if we did. I watched it disappear over the rise. I saw the flash after the Laum chased it down.

"I remember the whine of the shatterboxes. My corporal's death. The last night, ordering Sergeant Burgoyne to take everyone into the basement. I said it was because of the threat of further bombing, but I looked at him and he looked at me and I *needed* that look he gave me." That last flame lick of hope, driving her forward.

"Jani?" Evan's voice rasped. "You don't have to tell me this if you don't want."

What does want have to do with it? "I left them behind, and I went outside. I checked my shooter. I said a prayer. *à Yestha raùn.* Preserve my soul. I cut my left arm from wrist to elbow, sopped up the blood with a rag, staked the rag near the front door of the hospital. *Chäusen tha sè rau.* Shelter my soul—keep it safe." The stiff red braid rested in her duffel now—somehow, it had found its way onto the transport, surviving both the explosion and the crash. John Shroud had recovered it from the wreckage and returned it to her. "It was so still. So quiet. I knew Knevçet Shèràa was important to the Laumrau. They needed to take it back from us, reclaim it from humanish contamination. That meant it was a Night of Conjunction—sacrament and prayer before a decisive battle. Even the guards were sequestered in their tents. I remember the silence as I walked over the rise and into their camp."

"Jani—"

"I remember . . . twenty-six expressions of surprise on twenty-six faces when I entered twenty-six tents and fired my shooter twenty-six times." Shredded the Bilateral Accord and every tenet of idomeni behavior. Slaughtered them one by one in a way no fellow idomeni had ever dared. She remembered how the shooter grip overheated and cooked the palm of her hand. *I became one with my weapon that night.* A real soldier. "But most of all, I remember, I *have* to remember, why. Because it loses something when you write it down." She had to remember the fear she'd seen in her real soldiers' eyes as

Borgie herded them down the stairs. Remember that only she possessed the knowledge that would guarantee they'd remain alive to walk back up. "I have to remember, because everyone else seems to want to forget."

She turned to find Evan hunched forward, his face buried in his hands. "Trust me when I tell you, Jan," he said, his voice muffled, "they can't." He rose and straightlined for the bar. "About that promise I made—I take it back." He filled a water glass halfway with bourbon, looked at her, and poured a second. "I never thought I'd say this to anyone," he said as he pressed the glass into her hands, "but you look like you need this more than I do."

Jani swirled the dark caramel liquid. Her films absorbed the ethanol vapors, stinging her eyes. The tears spilled. She tipped back the glass and drank. The bourbon burned down her throat. Desert heat.

"Attagirl." Evan raised his glass in a toast, then followed suit. He drank more than she did, and it seemed to have no effect whatsoever on his eyes. "What do you think would happen," he asked over the top of his glass, "if they found out you were you?"

Jani took another swallow. A sip, really. Her mouth had gone numb. "Court-martial. Execution, probably, unless the idomeni pushed for extradition. They'd probably want to kill me, too. Hell, the line forms in the rear—if they got inventive, they could have a Neoclona team standing by to revive me after every barrage. They could keep it going for years." Poor John—he'd probably offer to fire the first shot. She smiled bleakly. The expression froze as her stomach cramped.

"I won't let that happen." Evan reached out to stroke her arm. Then he pointed to the glazed garden. "Don't you wish you could just press a pad and make everything else disappear. The past. Whatever's outside the door. Just the two of us, and to hell with everyone else."

Jani tried to nod, but the movement started a trail of heat burning up from her stomach. She dropped her glass and bounded out of her chair, leaving Evan behind to stagger to his feet and call after her.

She made it to her bathroom. Barely. Her body let her know bourbon was never, *ever*, to be considered an option again. *Let us sing a song of real soldiers . . . first verse*. She slumped against the toilet as the room spun. *All dead, so you're stuck with me.* Then she lost what balance she had. Her skull impacted tile with a vibrating *crack*.

CHAPTER 20

"Here is your seat, sir. Would you like a program?"

Tsecha accepted the small booklet the young female handed him. He fingered a page and frowned. Paper-plastic interweave. Sturdy, perhaps, but no more so than mid-grade parchment. He looked over the polished gold railing and down at the banked rows of seats. *So much red.* Every chair had been covered in material like blood in color, even the less honored ones in the rows above the level of his head, which he had to squint to see in the half-light.

Behind him, doors opened and closed. "The bar is fully stocked," the female continued, "as is the cooler." An expectant silence followed. Tsecha turned to find her standing beside an open food repository which had been set into the back wall of the small space. "There's a seasonal fruit tray," she said, pointing to a multicolored pile, "and cold hors d'oeuvres. There's a touchpad by your seat that will connect you to our service area. In addition, a member of our staff will stop by throughout the course of the evening. If you prefer hot food, or if the bar lacks something, just ask, please."

Tsecha stared at the fruit tray. Such large pieces. All so mixed. Together. After so long, with all he had come to accept, still it shocked him. And just resting there, for anyone to look at, to touch. *And stored with meat and grain.* The words of his esteemed enemies in Temple sang in his mind. *They do not know their food.* A killing insult to any idomeni, even Haárin, but one which meant nothing to humanish.

"Will there be anything else, Mister Hansen?"

Tsecha blinked. His films, the darkest brown he could find, squeezed his eyes, drying them as the winds that blew through Rauta

Shèràa. "No," he said, "thank you." He smoothed his humanish neckpiece, black as his evening suit, and curved his mouth without baring his teeth. "I am quite fine."

He did not sit until the female left him. So unseemly, to remain standing in the suborn's presence. The anxiety that plagued him during these excursions coursed through him with his blood. *Not a good idea*, his Hansen of the godly hair had told him the first time Tsecha tried to impersonate humanish. The words *sore thumb* had also been used, although when Tsecha had sought to divine their meaning from his handheld, the definitions made no sense.

Despite Hansen Wyle's misgivings, Tsecha's first sojourn had gone well. One of Eamon DeVries's females had helped with makeup. John Shroud himself had applied the eyefilms. His Jani, who was still a lieutenant then, arrived later to brief him on things a colonial humanish should know. *You'd never pass as Earthbound in a thousand years, nìRau,* she had told him, so somber in her stiff uniform. *Don't even try*. She had been more concerned about his excursion than Hansen. Her doubt, more than anything, had driven Tsecha forward.

He had served as a tour guide to a group of the humanish Consulate's high-ranking visitors. He had been commended for his expertise as he escorted officials through the city of his life. In the process, he learned more of humanish behavior than he ever could have from his handheld or his discs.

"I was even given tips." Tsecha bared his teeth as he recalled the pile of chits and the look on Hansen's face as he counted them. *Only you could turn a profit from acting like a jackass,* his godly hair had said. Those words also made no sense. He had not acted as an animal, but most assuredly as humanish. One of the officials had even asked him if he was Phillipan. That had made him feel most proud.

He looked again over the railing. Humanish streamed in through many doors, then wound down aisles and up and down steps to their seats. Some had guides, dressed in dark blue tunics and trousers as his female had been. Others found their own way. A few could not, however, and wandered as though lost. Once or twice, voices rose as small groups waved their arms and pointed to seats. Tsecha bared his teeth. *The number on the ticket is to match the number on the chair*. That, he had learned on his own, only a short time ago, and by himself. Only humanish could turn such a simplicity into confusion.

He stroked the arms of his seat. The cloth that covered them felt as close-clipped fur, pleasing to his touch. *My nìa Sànalàn has told all I am at high prayer*. A series of pleas to each of the Vynshàrau's eight dominant gods, the holiest rite for a chief propitiator. Not even the head of Temple or the secular Oligarch could disturb him at such. *Nor my nìa*. For such did she believe as well. That he lied to his suborn at all did not disturb him as much as that he did so so easily. The change had embraced him already, perhaps, leaving none of its physical signs. *I am one with my kìershia, my Captain. I am toxin.*

Tsecha directed his attention to the front of the huge room. A large drapery, shiny as metalcloth and dark gold in color, separated the audience from the place where the performance would occur. A holodrama, to be performed by images of humanish actors, both living and dead.

He studied his program, which had been printed in the dominant humanish languages, decoding his way between blocky English script and more logical Mandarin. *Tales of Arthur*. An ancient dominant. *A king*. There would be battles on horseback and tragic love. Witches. Dragons. *And a dancing goat*. Tsecha made a gesture that would have shocked his suborns and made Hansen Wyle laugh. He longed for his handheld, if only to inform him what exactly a goat was.

Loud voices and laughter drew his attention. Other compartments like his ran along the curved sides of the immense room. The noise emanated from the third compartment to his right. The curve of the wall was such that he could see quite clearly the owners of the voices. Which meant, of course, they could see him as well.

Anais Ulanova expected to see no idomeni this night. The gown she wore glowed red as molten metal, revealing her body in the way many humanish females preferred. Five others joined her, three males and two females. Tsecha recognized Treasury Minister Abascal and his solitary wife, as well as Deputy Prime Minister Langley and a very young female he had once heard some humanish refer to as flavor of the month. Only this female was most dark, while the one he had seen at his welcome ceremony had been most light. A seemly elevation for all involved, he felt sure. Most as idomeni. *Why then did the humanish laugh so?*

Tsecha looked at the third male, who stood behind Anais's chair. He wore the uniform of a Service officer. Most young, he seemed; only the flavor appeared younger. *His hair is almost as John Shroud's*. Tsecha grew conscious of the fact the male studied him as well. He responded with the slight nod Hansen Wyle had told him was suitable for such meetings.

The male did not nod back, but continued to stare openly until Anais claimed his attention by turning in her seat and gripping his hand. Only then did he smile, baring his teeth almost as widely as Vynshàrau as he leaned toward his dominant. Quite a seemly pairing, perhaps, if one looked only at faces.

But Tsecha studied the man as idomeni. The stiffness of his neck. The angle of his head as he sought to turn away from the Exterior Minister without seeming to. How his left hand, hidden behind his back, clenched and worked. Almost as simple as idomeni, these walls, at times. *Anais's warrior is not a willing suborn.* Then what held him there, as spikes to the floor?

With signal flickers, the illumins died. Voices faded. Once more, Tsecha felt the male's gaze upon him, piercing through the half-night as a weapons sight. At last, the blessed curtain rose. The humanish clapped their hands, and the booming, wheezing disorder that constituted their music began. Even as the noise buffeted him, Tsecha felt his fear leave. With such as Anais's unwilling warrior near, he felt more comfortable in the dark.

If my Temple knew me to be here, I would be made Haárin, and truly.

The hologram actors, clothes aglow with too-vivid color, voices more measured and clear of tone than any humanish speech Tsecha had ever heard, displayed the story of the king. The Vynshàrau worked against the aggravating comfort of his chair. If only there were some humanish he could trust, who could explain this king to him!

Why is he dominant, this Arthur, when he has no more sense than a young one? His dominant wife had agreed to elevate a suborn male, who had chosen her freely. Such was a most seemly occurrence, greatly to be wished; yet the king looked upon it as betrayal, a threat to order. Then there was a skein member, a nephew, who sang of injustice and plotted murder even though he was true suborn and had no right to rule. And suborns who wore clothes of clanking metal and rode off on meaningless quests, for objects, leaving their own skein members behind, confused and grieving.

The tragedy is the disorder! An illumin shone on the pad near Tsecha's chair. He slapped it dark. Let his blue-clad female take her offerings elsewhere. He thought of the food repository behind him as, onstage, the actors sat down to a banquet. How they ate and drank and shouted as the humanish audience laughed and cheered.

He watched food pass from hand to hand, from one plate into many mouths, and felt an ache in his soul. Two actors dressed in scraps of dull cloth scuttled across the stage after a chunk of meat discarded by a dominant, tearing at it as animals. Just then, the hot, spicy odor of broiling drifted into Tsecha's compartment from another. His stomach lurched. He forced himself to stare at the carpet at his feet as his eyes watered and his throat tightened.

He barely staunched a cry as behind him, a soft tapping sounded. "Compliments of the theater, Mister Hansen," a voice muttered through the thin door. "If you pad me in, I can set it up for you."

Tsecha lowered to his hands and knees and crawled across his own floor as the beggars had across theirs. He pressed his face against the door, breathing through his mouth to shut out the stench of food not his own. "Go away," he rasped. "I want nothing."

"Compliments of the theater, Mister Hansen," the voice persisted, like the yammer of demons. "A signature is required, even if you turn it down. Procedure, sir."

A signature. To breathe, the humanish needed signatures. *But if I open the door, I can leave*. Escape the small compartment. Flee into the cold, cleansing night. Tsecha stood, scrabbled with the latch, flung the door wide and stilled as he looked into the face of Anais's warrior.

"*NìRau ti nìRau*." The moonlight head glinted as it tilted very slightly to Tsecha's right. An angle indicating true respect, but with no implied intimacy of friend or enemy. "Is this performance boring you as much as it is me?" He crossed his right arm in front of his chest, palm outward.

Tsecha glanced at the designators on the man's collar. Red bars. Mainline lieutenant. Yes, this officer had greeted him in quite the correct way, and truly. *a lète ona vèste, Nemarau*—his Anais's source for High Vynshàrau had, with no doubt, come from a place much closer than an office within Exterior Main.

"I could see you, even in the dim light." The lieutenant led Tsecha from an upper-level theater exit and into a glass-covered walkway suspended above the street. "You began fidgeting during that scene in the stables, where Lancelot fed his horse as he sang about Guinevere. After that, I waited fifteen minutes, then came by to pay my respects." He turned, hands linked behind his back. Even in the dark, his hair shimmered. "Actually, nìRau, I'm surprised you lasted as long as you did. Makes me wonder what you were trying to prove."

"Prove?" Tsecha slowed, stepping around the man as though avoiding a hazard in the street. "I am curious only, Lieutenant"—he edged just close enough to read the man's name designator—"Pascal. I wish only to learn of those with whom I have been charged to deal."

"Well, in the dark, you appear humanish enough. And your English is exceptional, nìRau."

"It is not a complicated language, Lieutenant." How easily he lied. But what could Pascal know of his handheld, or of his quest to read between lines?

"You consider Mandarin Chinese much more respectable, for its structure and order." Pascal proceeded down the walkway, beckoning Tsecha to follow. Beneath them, skimmers darted in the night like huge waterflicks, following the phosphor trail of the well-illumined roadway and bright buildings. "And French, for its sound." His pace quickened as he stepped off the walkway and down a narrow flight of stairs. Then came a series of winding indoor hallways.

We are in a building now—and I am most lost. Tsecha hurried after Pascal as they passed through door-lined halls and lobbies much as those in Interior Main, though smaller in scale. The other humanish he saw were male. Some stood in the halls and talked; others emerged from rooms in pairs or groups. At times, curious glances came to rest on Tsecha, but most seemed directed at Pascal. He ignored the attention, the occasional reaching hand or calling of his name. Instead, he walked on as though alone until he stopped before one of the identical doors, removed a key card from his tunic pocket, and coded his way inside.

The room contained only a bed, a frame chair, and, in a tiny alcove, a humanish sanitary room. "No food," Tsecha said. "I am most glad."

"People don't come here to eat, nìRau." Pascal unbuttoned his tunic and massaged the grooves the collar had pressed into his neck. His undershirt, to Tsecha's surprise, matched the red stripe running down the sides of his trousers.

"Has your Service altered its uniform code, Jeremy? I thought only white shirts were allowed."

The lieutenant sat down on the bed. "A small freedom. One of the benefits of a Cabinet posting." He looked at Tsecha with narrowed eyes. "Why did you call me *Jeremy*?"

Tsecha sat in the frame chair. The seat proved nicely rigid, but he wondered the purpose for the buckled fasteners on the chair's arms. "One of the men outside called to you in that way. Is that not your name?"

"Sometimes." Pascal's lips curved in the way Eamon's did when he felt he had been clever. "It's handy to have access to a place like this. At times, you need to talk to someone, but neither of you wants the true nature of your discussion known. So, you come here. Much better than a cabinet interrogation room. Rather like hiding in plain sight." He looked over at Tsecha. "My real name is Lucien, by the way, though I'd prefer you didn't use it here."

"But your name is on your tunic, most easy to see. How difficult would it be for someone to learn your true identity?" It would have taken Hansen no time. Of that, Tsecha felt most sure.

"I know. It's just the principle of the thing, nìRau."

I am between lines. "It is disorderly."

Lucien bared his teeth and laughed. "Actually, *disorderly* is a more appropriate term than you'll ever know, nìRau."

"Indeed." Tsecha looked out the room's tiny window, but there was nothing of interest to see, only the filtered illumins of buildings he did not know. "Anais will notice you are gone?"

"I told her I had a call. She's learned to accept my devotion to duty." Lucien continued to massage his neck. "Speaking of devotion to duty, nìRau, have you had any success with your search?"

Tsecha shifted in his seat. He valued the focusing ability of discomfort, but he would not try wearing close-fitting humanish trousers again soon. "My search?" He touched his eyelids. They had begun to itch.

"For Jani Kilian."

"Kilian? Who is—"

"Anais has been looking for her for months. She thought, for a time, that she had her." Lucien rose and walked to the window. "Maybe she did."

Tsecha rubbed his eyes again. He shivered—it had grown very cold as well. He clapped his hands together to warm them. "Who is this Kilian of whom you speak, Jeremy? Are you sure of your names? You possess so many. They must be easily confused, and truly."

Lucien turned. For the shortest time, his face held no emotion. Then his teeth flashed and he raised his right hand in a Haárin gesture of irreverence. "*Touché*, nìRau." He refastened his tunic, wincing as he clasped the collar. "Well, we never had her, and you didn't want her if we did. Nothing lost."

Tsecha again pressed his fingers to his eyelids. The films had begun to prickle, but at least that made his eyes water. He would have to find a heavier jacket for these humanish evenings, one that protected him from the icy Chicago air. *The inset read,* WINTER WOOL. Would he have to learn to read between the lines of clothing labels as well?

Between the lines.

Ah.

"Well, I'm sorry to have wasted your time, nìRau," Lucien said.

"But if we're lucky, that damned play might be over by the time we get back to the theater."

Tsecha remained seated. The chair proved quiet focusing. He had even developed a tolerance for the trousers. "Lucien, if you found this Kilian, what would you do with her?"

"Bring her here," the man answered after some time, "just to see the look on her face." Under Tsecha's steady stare, he hesitated. "I wouldn't hurt her." He stepped into the sanitary area and removed a comb from his pocket. "It's all theory, of course, isn't it, nìRau?" he said as he arranged his hair. "Seeing she's dead."

I understand this Lucien now. Could Hansen even have done so well? "How humanish talk. When they wish something not to exist, they execute it by not speaking of it. And when they want something more than their own life, they invent it from nothing by speaking of it at all times." Tsecha bared his teeth as Lucien turned to him, again expressionless. "But we have more than nothing here, do we not? She hides in plain sight. Where is she?"

"She's dead."

"Where is she!"

Lucien continued to comb his hair. "Safe, for now. In plain sight." The hands stopped. "Could you shelter her, nìRau, if necessary?"

"No." Tsecha again scratched the skin on his hands, then stifled a sneeze as his face started to itch as well. "But I know one who could."

"One who could. Does that mean you still talk to your friend, John Shroud?"

Tsecha shook his head. As an esteemed enemy, yes, but as a friend. . . . He shivered again, this time not from the cold. "I do not speak to Physician Shroud as a friend."

The lieutenant thrust his comb back into his pocket. "Well, the next time you don't talk to him, don't forget not to ask him about that illegal trial he never performed three years ago. The one where he studied the effects of Ascertane on some of the chev Haárin living on Elyas."

Don't forget . . . not . . . never. Tsecha took a deep breath. His head cleared even as the inside of his nose tingled, forcing him to fight back another sneeze. *So the rumors were true, John—yet how you denied*. "Trial? Ascertane?"

"A mild truth drug, nìRau. The Haárin can't tolerate it. Doesn't do a damn thing to get them to talk, and makes them violently ill besides. Tell him—" Lucien stopped, then gasped out another breath. He seemed surprised he could see the puff of air. He groped in his trouser pocket and pulled out a tiny black box, touching it so the red illumins on its surface dimmed.

"Is that a recording device?" Tsecha asked, most carefully.

"No, nìRau, an override. They're a specialty of mine. This one lets me take over a room's climate control. I can cool a room down." Lucien coughed. "Dry it out."

Tsecha gently prodded his eyelids. "Do you so value disorder, Lucien?"

"In myself, no." White teeth shone. "But I enjoy inspiring it in others." He opened the door, leaving the room before Tsecha, as was most proper. "Some advice, Mister Hansen," he said, as they stepped into the hall. "As much as I admire your daring, you shouldn't try a stunt like this again."

"My disguise is not good?"

"You're too distinctive-looking. Your posture. Your attitude. I wouldn't advise a repeat performance." Lucien led Tsecha down the hall, ignoring once more efforts made by other males to claim his attention. "But I can find you quite good makeup. And I can coach you. Escort you around Chicago. Show you the ropes, so to speak." He smiled. "Our first conspiracy. The first of many, I hope."

Tsecha studied Anais's unwilling warrior, now his own most willing guide. Another Hansen had found him, another teacher of humanish ways. *What can you teach me, Lucien?* He nodded to the young man, who smiled in a way Hansen had once warned him of. So bright. So wide. *Butter wouldn't melt in his mouth.* Interesting. *He tells me I do not look humanish. I, who have passed for Phillipan. He lies to me already, and keeps me from my Captain.* Oh yes, he could learn much from watching Lucien, and truly.

They left the building by a different walkway. Tsecha looked up into the night sky, picking out the brighter stars through the city glare and filtering glass.

"How did you get here, nìRau?" Lucien asked. "Just out of curiosity."

"I drove, Lieutenant."

"*Again!*" Lucien skidded to a halt. "Where did you park?"

"In the theater charge lot." Tsecha rummaged through his pockets, removing a chip of brown plastic. "I have a stub."

"Yes. Well." Lucien took the plastic piece away from him, then removed a small comunit from his pocket and keyed in a code. "I'll see you and your vehicle get back to the embassy. Separately." After a few hurried words, he repocketed the device. "How did you get out of the embassy in the first place?"

"I told all I would be at prayer. Thus would I be left alone. I knew when the guards would be at early-evening sacrament. I knew which exits were not fully scanned." Tsecha felt his inside jacket pocket, where his own black box rested. "I knew what to do when they were."

"And your clothes?"

"Hidden in the Exterior Security outpost which shares our property border. If such were found in my quarters, I would be made Haárin, and truly. But if such are found in a humanish place . . . ?" Tsecha hunched his shoulders in a most humanish shrug.

Lucien smiled. Differently, this time. Often had Hansen smiled at him in that way, when they spoke of changes to come. "You're quite different than I imagined, nìRau."

"Have you ever been in a war, Lucien?" Tsecha guessed the answer, but waited for the man to shake his head. "One learns the most alarming things in a war. You think you forget them, but you do not. They wait in your memory. They never leave." *This I know, as does my hidden Captain.*

Lucien stared at him in question. But before Tsecha could explain further, the skimmer the lieutenant had summoned glided up to the curb. Tsecha eased into the well-cushioned backseat, which, if not as demanding as a Vynshàrau chair, compensated by being as comfortable as a Vynshàrau bed. As the vehicle drifted down the street, Tsecha closed his eyes. The next thing he knew, the humanish was calling him awake, telling him they had reached the embassy.

The Third Day

CHAPTER 21

What do you think, Eamon?

Still the ugliest girl in the bar, John. DeVries's *r*s rolled like pebbles down a hillside. Jani felt his breath abrade her newly grown cheek as he leaned closer. *Not enough booze in the Commonwealth to make me take that home.*

She can hear you, Eamon. John's voice rumbled, the warning growl of a watchdog.

I know. Jani could hear the smile in DeVries's voice. *So what?* Brutal chill washed over the fresh skin of her torso as he yanked down her sheet. *I still think we should have given her bigger tits.*

No words after that. Sounds of a scuffle. DeVries's startled yelp. The whine of a door mechanism being forced open, then closed.

Footsteps.

Don't listen to him. John pulled up the thermal sheet and tucked it under her chin. *You're beautiful. Val made sure.* Then came silence. The hum of a skimgurney. Another trip to another lab. Another immersion tank. More jostling, jostling, jostling. . . .

"God damn you, Risa!" The mild rocking ramped to a Level Ten landquake. "Wake up! *Now*!"

Jani's head pounded. She forced open one eye. Saw red. Hair. Glowing in too-bright light. "Where's John?"

"Who the hell is John?" Fingers worked into Jani's hair, tilted her head up.

White white ceiling ceiling oh shit—! Her stomach shuddered. She closed her eye.

"Oh no. Don't you dare pass out on me." Skittering footsteps like fingernails on glass. Running water. "Stay awake this time, damn you!"

Cold. Wet. On her face, her neck, her hands. She opened both eyes this time as she licked away the droplets that had fallen on her lips.

"Are you thirsty?" Angevin's face lightened. "Good. Thirsty, I can handle." She stared at the soggy washcloth as though it had appeared by magic, then folded it and laid it across Jani's forehead. "Be right back."

Jani blinked, testing her films. The cloth slid down her face and settled in a drippy wad in the middle of her chest. Cold water soaked through her shirt, darkening the blue to black. She shivered.

"Where the hell is—" Angevin's voice bounced into the tiled bathroom from the kitchenette. "Oh, I found it—never mind." Sounds of running. "Is this ok?"

Jani turned her head. Carefully.

Angevin stood in the doorway holding a filled glass. "It's helgeth. Is that ok? I saw all the dispos in the front of the cooler—figured it was your favorite."

Jani nodded. Worked her stiff jaw. "Ye—yes. Thanks." She struggled into a sitting position and wrapped her shaky hands around the glass. The first swallow stripped the film from her mouth and some of the haze from her brain. "What time is it?"

"Two in the morning. At least it was when I—" Angevin glanced at her timepiece. "It's two-twenty now. I found you here on the floor. You came to a couple times, but you kept drifting out again. You've got an awful knock on your forehead. Scared me. I thought you had a concussion. What the hell happened to you?"

Out for almost six hours, eh? Jani forced herself to sip the juice. What went down in a hurry had a nasty habit of coming up the same way. "How did you get in here?"

"Housekeeping let me in." Angevin squatted on the tiled floor. She wasn't dressed for an early-morning call. In her green-velvet evening suit and pearl jewelry, she looked like an upper-class cricket. "I said you had some papers Durian needed, but that you weren't answering your comport. Everybody knows Durian—they let me in out of sympathy."

"You found me unconscious on my bathroom floor and didn't call a doctor?"

"No." Angevin wavered under Jani's hard stare. "I kept thinking about Lucien, about what I picked up for you. If anything happened to you, Durian would have found an excuse to search your suite." Worry dulled her eyes to brown. "I didn't want to get you into trouble."

"Thanks." Jani took a larger swallow of juice. "What's going on?"

"All our staff meetings have been canceled until further notice. Durian's been bumping all his appointments, but no one knows why."

"He saw me this afternoon." Jani hesitated. "Make that yesterday afternoon."

Angevin sat down on the floor and plucked the washcloth from its damp resting spot in Jani's lap. "He's been making lots of calls to other Cabinet Houses. No one's returning them. We were supposed to have a working dinner with the head of Commerce Doc Control tonight, but they canceled with about an hour's notice. Durian ordered me to stay put in my office, but he won't tell me anything." She twisted the cloth, sending more water dripping to the tile.

Jani drained her glass, then flexed her neck and shoulders. She could almost feel the sugar flood her bloodstream. "He met with Colonel Doyle."

Angevin shook her head. "He saw her, but not for long. Ginny teaches an advanced judo class three nights a week. A friend of mine takes it. Ginny was there tonight, same as always." Her eyes lightened to mossy ice. "What's going on?"

"What do you mean?"

"This involves Steve, doesn't it? He's in it up to his ears, isn't he?"

Jani rubbed a smudge on her glass. "I have no way of—"

"Don't give me that crap!" Angevin threw the cloth to the floor and bounded to her feet. Her green demiheels clicked on the glassy floor like finger cymbals. "He's been pulling some scam with that bonehead Guernsey buddy of his. Betha. I tried to warn him about her, but would he listen? Hell, no. I mean, what am I, anyway? Just a 'posh little anti-colonial Earthbounder' who doesn't understand what it means to have to work my way up!"

"That's what it sounded like to me," Jani muttered.

Angevin crouched down and grabbed a handful of Jani's collar. "Well that just shows you don't know everything either. So he's colony—it bothers him a hell of a lot more than it bothers me!" She released her, then started patting the rumpled material back into shape. "So," she said, her eyes on her task, "how bad is it?"

Jani took a steadying breath. "He could go to jail for a very long time. Betha jazzed paper for Lyssa. Steve helped her cover it up."

"Fuck. And the general audit's next week." Angevin sagged to the floor. "Why?"

"Loyalty to another Guernsey kid. The need to show up a system he hates and wants to join at the same time."

"Yeah." Angevin picked up the discarded cloth and twisted it into knots. "So how did you find out so much? Did Steve tell you?" She gave the cloth a particularly strong yank.

Jani gave a quick rundown of Lyssa's possible discovery of Acton van Reuter's dealings with the Laumrau. "If we can prove Lyssa was killed because of what she knew, I think we hand the Cabinet Court a much bigger problem than two low-level dexxies jazzing docs. They won't get off scot-free, but since they were involved in bringing a much greater crime to light, they won't sit in jail until they're eighty, either."

"And you trust Betha to see this through?"

"What else can she do? If she goes to any of her superiors with things as they now stand, she's screwed. I also tried to impress upon her the fact that, if she flees, her life on the run would be hell."

"Might work." Angevin made a sour face. "I have my doubts." She stared at the floor for a moment. When she looked up, her eyes were glistening. "Why did he shut me out? Why didn't he tell me?"

"In case it went to hell, he didn't want you involved."

Angevin's anxious expression did a slow melt into despair. She buried her face in her hands. "He puts his ass on the line for that cow, but he can't trust me enough to see him through!"

"Accessory after the fact."

"Bonehead." Angevin sniffled into her hands. "Is it too late to volunteer for save-the-idiot duty? I can't just sit around and wait for the ax to fall—I have to do something."

Jani maneuvered into a crouch, stopping every so often to let the private star show between her ears wink out. Her right knee popped as she rose. "You know, he may be doing you a favor."

"Yeah." Angevin straightened without any joints cracking. "But I'm going where he's going." She smiled sadly. "Believe it or not, I actually feel better. I thought Steve dumped me because he started sleeping with Betha."

Jani bit her lip before *extreme stress has made people do stranger things* slipped out. She checked herself in the mirror, dabbed cold water on her bruise, then toweled her face in an effort to rub some life into her ashen cheeks.

"Of course," Angevin continued with brittle gaiety, "if they are having it off, they won't have to worry about jail, will they?" She cracked her knuckles, the sound amplified by the tile into a rapid-fire of gravel crunches. "Let's go," she said as she clicked out of the bathroom.

"Coming, Your Excellency." Jani gave her face one last swipe and tossed the towel into the sink.

Jani wanted to work off the last of her muddle, and Angevin was pumping enough adrenaline to stock Neoclona for a month, so they walked the underground route to Interior Main. It was well populated for that hour of the morning. They passed grocery-laden skimtrollies, laundry and supply skiffs, and other vehicles that inhabited the world beneath the buildings.

All calm on the surface, but down here we have the business end of the duck. Jani walked quietly for a few minutes, her duffel bouncing comfortably against her left hip, when an unpleasantly familiar sound claimed her attention. She pulled up short as an overloaded skiff eased past them, the whine of its lift array pitched dangerously high. She took off after the vehicle, waving off Angevin's protest.

"You're too heavy!" She pointed to the skiff's cargo of a huge, chocolate-hued truewood desk, topped with a bookcase for sauce and a serving table as the tottering cherry. "Break that load down!"

"What?" The driver blinked at Jani as though coming out of a daze. "I'm not going to haul this stuff all the way back to Private."

"No, you're not. You're going to unload that bookcase and table right here."

"Yeah, right," the driver said. "In your dreams, lady."

"Don't. Move." Jani stared at the side of the driver's face, could almost hear the scrape of her grinding teeth. "You've had safety training, I assume?"

The woman's glance flicked down at the vehicle's dash, where the load gauge must have been thumping red like an overworked heart. She hesitated. "Yeah, but—"

"You know the damage that can occur when a mag shield fails in an enclosed space? To systems? To nearby human brains? Yours and those of all the poor innocents who just happen to be walking by?"

"Yea—*yes*, but—"

"Not to mention what could happen if the hyperacid fumes from blown battery cells ooze along for the ride?"

"Yes, *ma'am*, but—"

"Break that load down. Now." Jani bit back the *Spacer* just in time. Although it would have fit. The woman, close-cropped hair greyed at the temples, coverall sleeves and pants legs knife-creased, had suddenly developed the wild-eyed look of a person who had thought her order-taking days long over. She stepped off the skiff, grapplers in hand, and started unloading the table. The task began in grudging silence, although the words, *thought I left this behind at fuckin' Fort Sheridan* drifted down to Jani as she and Angevin continued on their way to Main.

"What the hell—?" Angevin glanced back at the muttering driver. "You really did whack your head, didn't you?"

"What do you mean?" Jani asked. The last traces of nausea had passed, taking with it the fuzzy-headedness and trembling in her thighs.

"Were you in the Service? Jeez, she almost saluted you."

"No, she didn't."

"I saw her arm tense. She wanted to." Angevin shook her head. "*I* wanted to." She gave Jani a worried look. "Or maybe she just wanted to belt you. But she didn't. What are you? I mean, really?"

I don't think I know, anymore. Fingering through her sense of calm, Jani sensed an unwelcome edginess, the feeling of being *au point.* She sensed the business end of her own duck paddling furiously, quacking for her to wake up. *Something is wrong with me.* Something more than travel lag, a stomach unsettled by stress and years of strange foods, a back wrenched by too many cheap mattresses. "I'm just an Interior staffer on special assignment," she answered hastily, as she recalled again how the garage guy had behaved in the days before his collapse.

"Yeah, ok. Whatever you say." Angevin fell silent for a time, then piped, "Wish you could bottle that voice—I'd buy it and use it on Durian."

Muscles aches. Disorientation.

"He'd shit himself. Twice."

Mood swings? She'd been so tightly wrapped for so long, how could she judge? *Chronic indigestion? Oh, hell.*

"Then I'd use it on Steve. He'd never cut me out again."

Am I really sick? Jani shivered, even though the tunnel air felt comfortably warm. *Dying?* She heard Angevin mutter something about stupid shoes, and followed her to a vacant two-seater parked at a mini-charge. Without thinking, Jani got in on the passenger side. Angevin could drive. She didn't feel up to it.

CHAPTER 22

Angevin's office, at the opposite end of the wing from Durian Ridgeway's, at first looked like a smaller version of her boss's grey aerie.

It was only upon closer inspection that the differences became obvious. Instead of Durian's great art, Angevin had hung holos of family and friends on her walls. From a well-lit place overlooking the sitting area, Hansen Wyle's face, young enough for the uninformed to think him Angevin's twin brother, smiled down.

She's doing ok, Jani thought at the portrait. *She's got your mouth and your temper, and your knack for sussing people out. It's going to take some effort for her to shake off Ridgeway, but she's got a colony boy to help her. You'd like him, I think. Too bad you're not here to wipe the Earth glitter from his eyes.*

"Tell me what you're looking for." Angevin sat down at her desk and activated her workstation. "I've got top-level clearance—I can find you anything you need."

"Can you get into Cabinet Court evidence files?" Jani dragged a chair around to Angevin's side of the desk.

"Oh, you don't ask for much, do you?" Angevin fingered her way through one color-coded screen after another. "This is going to be a one-shot, you know. As soon as systems sense me in there, they'll shut down and trace back."

Jani dug into her duffel for Lucien's jig. "This should help," she said as she attached the device to Angevin's workstation. "I've got passwords, too."

Angevin accepted the piece of wrapping paper with held breath. "That goddamn toy soldier," she said as she read the list of words. "I am not going to ask—I do not want to know." She uttered the first few passwords, then paused. "Where are we going?"

"Rauta Shèràa," Jani said. "Both Base and Consulate. SRS-1 designates."

"This is what you were doing in the Library, wasn't it?"

"Yes. I had to quit before I could finish."

"What do you think you'll find there?" Angevin looked directly at her display, uttered a few passwords in Hortensian German, then turned back to Jani as she waited for the codes to clear. "A signed letter from Acton van Reuter confessing to everything?"

Jani rubbed her face, then looked around for a source of something cold to drink. "A few communication logs with the right dates and names could serve the same function." She couldn't spot any ewers or coolers and made do with a trip to the bathroom sink. "I know when his Excellency was putting in his time at the Consulate, his father checked up on him on a fairly regular basis." *Boy, did I know.* She filled a large dispo from the tap, drained it, and filled it again. "Acton must have had a source or two there. It was a well-known fact he didn't approve of his son working so far from home."

Angevin nodded. "Yeah, I heard he was a real stick. Durian calls him The Old Hawk. Like he was some kind of god."

"If you were an Earth-firster who believed in keeping the colonies on a short leash, he was." Jani returned to her seat, dispo in hand. "Prime Minister Cao was a disciple of his, whether she'll admit it now or not. Her first major seat was on Acton's Back Door Cabinet—that interim election he won after Nawar was forced to resign, right after the idomeni kicked us out. Cao served as Deputy Finance Minister, I think."

Angevin toyed with her touchboard. "Maybe she just played up to him to get her foot in the big door. Wouldn't be the first time an old blowhard got sucked down his own pipe."

Jani pretended not to hear Angevin's tacit admission with regard to Durian Ridgeway. "Cao tries to sound more moderate now," she continued, "but she's coming down pretty hard on Ulanova's efforts to expand the concept of colonial semiautonomy. Not that I think the Exterior Minister's motives are pure."

Angevin folded her arms, her eyes fixed on her flickering screen. "Durian thinks she wants to be some kind of empress. Of course, he's just repeating His Excellency's opinion. If he had to choose between Empress Ulanova and political oblivion, though, he'd crown her himself."

Jani hid her grin at Angevin's assessment of her superior. *What does Nema think when he looks at you? Does he look for a copy of Hansen and come away disappointed?* He never grasped how different it could be for humanish, especially a pretty humanish female laboring under her legendary father's shadow. But Hansen the iconoclast appreciated the rebel. Would he have understood that his daughter was being as daring in her way as he had been in his?

But you know how she really feels—she's got your face on her wall where she can see it at all times.

"We're in the index." Angevin's fingers drummed against the arms of her chair. "There are executive staff comlogs and junior up-and-comer comlogs. Affiliated Service staff. Security." Her eyes widened. "There was even a kitchen comlog. Had to be, I guess. We must have had a hell of a time shipping food into Rauta Shèràa."

Doe, you just said a mouthful and a half. Jani had been involved in negotiating the supply shipments. That was due in part to her training and education, but also to the fact that the Laumrau had seemed afraid of her even then.

I was Nema's, and the first skirmishes had already taken place in the Vynshà strongholds in the south. The Laumrau felt sure the chief propitiator's Eyes and Ears would deliberately botch a shipment schedule, sending the wrong type of humanish food into Rauta Shèràa at the wrong time. That would have brought severe dishonor upon their blessed dominant city, providing the Vynshà with a compelling reason to force the Laumrau to relinquish their power. *Maybe I should have screwed up. I could have saved us all a great deal of trouble.*

"Try the executive staff logs first," she said to Angevin. "The Old Hawk was status-conscious, even when it came to snitches."

"Strong words, Risa. Almost as though you speak from personal experience." Angevin keyed in Jani's directive, then tossed her an inquisitive look. "Durian said you've spent your entire career 'working out.' Did you ever cross paths with our minister's late daddy?"

Paths, words, swords. Jani weighed her words. "The occasional order trickled down. I was pretty low-level back then. Didn't suffer many direct hits."

"Were you ever on Shèrá? My dad spent eight years there, with school and his work as Laumrau liaison. That's why it surprises me that Durian admires him so much. He and Acton van Reuter were constantly at each other's throats. It wasn't until I was at university that my mom finally told me about some of the battles they'd had. Maybe she thought it would scare me, keep me from studying paper. She told me van Reuter actually threatened my dad with a treason charge if he didn't cease and desist in his efforts to improve idomeni-human relations."

Jani dredged her memories, trying to separate the things she could have heard through the intelligence grapevine from those only a deep insider could know. It wasn't easy—like trying to cleave a single person and keep both halves alive.

"Acton had Laumrau support in that, actually," she finally said. "Everyone at the top of the tree gets scared when the ground beneath starts shaking. Parallels what's going on now. The Vynshàrau are having a hell of a time bringing the Haárin to heel, even though Haárin have been Vynshàrau hounds for the past several generations. And of course, we have the colonial problem."

"On the macro and micro level." Angevin made a wry face as she entered a series of rapid keyings. "This isn't working."

Jani strained for a better view of the display. "What's wrong?"

"Don't look at it!" Angevin gave Jani a one-armed shove that propelled her back into her chair. "My retinal lock's activated. If the display senses you looking at it, it'll shut my workstation down, and I'll need to get Ginny Doyle here in person to get it back up." She exhaled with a shudder. "Ginny gets very 'Colonel-ly' when she's rousted out of bed at three in the morning." She barked a few more commands at her screen, then slumped back in defeat. "It won't let me in. I'm using all the words you gave me, and it won't let me in."

Jani edged forward as much as she dared. "What's the reason code?"

"PM-seven eighty."

"Lock-down by the Prime Minister?"

"More than that. An examiner's lien. They're not even letting the members of the Court look at it now." Angevin's voice dropped to a whisper. "They know we're here."

"Not if that jig's working like it's supposed to." Unless Lucien had set her up. Jani took another gulp of water. What she had consumed so far sloshed in her stomach like an internal sea, whitecaps, undertow, and all. "I've got Ulanova's passwords. She's driving the Court—if she can't get in, nobody can. Back out and try again." She watched Angevin work. As the minutes passed, she grew conscious of a distinctive aroma. "I think we have company," she whispered.

"What?" Angevin scowled as she picked up the scent. "That jerk." She turned toward her door. It was just barely ajar, the crack scarcely visible.

"Don't you arm a proximity alarm when you work late?" Jani asked.

"Why bother? Who the hell can get up here?" Angevin punched her touchboard, activating too many pads at once and eliciting a squeal from the helpless electronic array. Then, faint as the clove scent in the air, a smile of triumph flicked to life. "You may as well come in, Steve," she called out. "We know you're there."

The seconds ticked by. Then the door eased open and Steve stepped inside. He still wore the clothes he'd had on when Jani had last seen him, but the overall effect had now degraded to distinctly-rumpled-and-needs-a-shave-to-boot. Portrait of a young man who had bought dinner from a machine and slept in his office.

"I were just walking by," he began lamely, the telltale nicstick smoking weakly in his hand. "Saw lights. Wondered what were up." His eyes chilled as he looked at Angevin. "My my, aren't we dressed fancy for the office." He sneered. "Oh. Right. Stupid of me. You had a *dinner* tonight."

"It was canceled."

"Oh. That's too bad." He smiled too brightly at Jani. "Well, Risa, you're looking well!"

Jani eyed Angevin, who looked quite pinched around the mouth. "Thanks, but I don't see how that's possible. Angevin found me on my bathroom floor. Too much to drink at dinner." She fingered the tender bruise on her forehead. "I doubt I look any better than you do." Steve winced at that, while Angevin stiffened. *Good—piss them both off.*

Silence filled every available space. Angevin sat with her arms crossed, eyes fixed on her bare desktop. Steve rocked slowly from one foot to the other.

"She told me." Angevin jerked her chin toward Jani. "I had to hear it from a stranger. You couldn't tell me."

Steve stepped toward the desk, one foot in front of the other, like a man on a balance beam. "Didn't want it to rub off on you." He flicked the nicstick into the trashzap. "Didn't want you to go through what the others did during the purge."

"So you hooked up with *her*? Talked about it all with *her*? And left me to wonder what the hell happened?"

"Betha needs a friend." Steve toed the carpet. "Needs support. You're different. You're a *Wyle*. You don't need anybody."

Angevin closed her eyes and covered her mouth with her hand.

"Well, we both need you now," Jani said. "We're trying to code into Court of Inquiry evidence files and systems won't let us in."

"Oh, *phfft*, you're not getting any of that," Steve said, "it all got seven-eightied about an hour ago. Expectin' an examiner's lien from Cao's head dex any minute now. They're shuttin' us down."

Angevin spun her chair to face him. "How do you know!"

He shrugged. "Everyone's talking about it down the hall. Third shift's in a tizz. Figured it would happen, though. Cao never were happy with all that House paper we shipped her last month. She claimed we were withholding from an Official Inquiry. Her complaint got bumped to your boss for reply." He eyed Angevin suspiciously. "Airn't heard nothing of it since. Till tonight."

"This is the first I've heard of any of this." Angevin glared at Steve. "Just one more thing you couldn't tell me!"

"Don't look at me like that. We were *sworn*!" Steve pulled at his pockets and freed a fresh 'stick. "Doyle stood at the door while we got all the paper together, watched us like a bloody vulture. Ever see her when she's on? All she needs are spurs and a whip." He dragged a chair in the vicinity of the desk, closer to Jani than to Angevin, and sat down with a heavy sigh. "I saw her in my sleep for a week after, bald head shinin'."

"That's exactly the paper I asked you to look for." Jani looked at Steve until he began leaning in Angevin's direction. "I would have appreciated it if you'd have told me you couldn't get it."

Steve cracked the 'stick's ignition tip. "Didn't say that, did I? All I said were you wouldn't be able to access the fiche through Ange's station." He studied Jani through his smoky veil. "I can get the originals."

"You held back Consulate paper from a Court of Inquiry, too!" Jani's temples started to throb.

"I'm sure he had a good—I'm sure he had a reason." Angevin's eyes were now as stormy as Jani's stomach. "Which he will explain to us now."

Steve scooted his chair away from the desk. "The originals we've got here were from His Excellency's private library. Willed to him by his father. Justice is supposed to decide soon whether private papers can be claimed by the PM under a blanket subpoena. Cao wouldn't tell us why exactly she wanted them, so van Reuter told her to blow. Betha and me split 'em up—the Lady had given them to her for safekeeping."

"Lyssa?" Jani nodded. That made sense. A great deal concerning old Acton must reside in those papers. "I want both sets. Where's Betha?" She stood up. "Home?"

Steve shook his head. "Vacant office down the hall. I saw her a few hours ago. She told me she'd probably be here most of the night, but that she'd have her papers in the morning. I'd bring mine from where I stashed them in my flat. We'd give them to you together." He blinked. "Teamwork, you know."

Angevin growled. "Teamwork, my ass! I'll show her teamwork." She swatted her workstation into standby, then ran from the room. Steve and Jani looked at one another, then pelted after her.

The vacant office was dark. Its trashzap had been recharged.

"What time do the cleaners come through?" Jani asked an extremely subdued Steve.

"Eleven," he replied. "She said she'd be here till morning." He pulled open a drawer, pushed it closed. "She wouldn't have run out on me." He leaned against the desk. "She wouldn't have left me behind." He pushed a hand through his hair, his eyes wide and lost. Angevin reached out to him, hesitated, then muttered, "Screw this," and threw herself into his arms.

"She probably went home," Jani said after a time. "I'll try to get in touch with her from here. You two try her place, then get some sleep. We'll meet in Angevin's office at oh-eight. Don't forget your half of the docs. Steve?" She waited in the doorway for some response from the enmeshed pair, finally detecting a hint of a nod from Steve. "Oh-eight," she repeated, closing the door softly.

The grumble in her stomach sounded animal. She stopped at a vend cooler in Doc Control's deserted cafeteria and bought juice and a sandwich. Then she dragged a chair over to the Houseline array in the corner of the room. In between mouthfuls, she made calls. House Security, the desk clerk at the Interior employee hostel, every third-shift manager she could find. The Doc pool. The parts bins. The Library. Every cafeteria in the complex. No one recalled seeing Betha, although the parts-bins clerk remembered her afternoon visit.

Personnel refused to give Jani Betha's homecode. When she dropped Evan's name, they told her she needed Ridgeway's sign-off to get the number.

She left the cafeteria and roamed the Doc Control halls, checking every vacant office and conference room. The rest rooms, men's and women's. The alternate breakroom. Janitor's closets, storage rooms, stairwells. She stopped short of pushing up ceiling tiles and checking crawl spaces. Harder to cram a body in a space like that. Messier. She didn't want to risk destroying evidence.

You've got death on the brain. Betha's home in bed. Take the hint. Jani trudged to the elevators and rode down to the restricted-access charge lots. On her way to the Main-Private tunnel, a Security guard tried to stop her, but when he looked her in the face he hesitated. Then he stepped aside and let her pass.

CHAPTER 23

The skimmer shuddered as it skirted the border between Exterior and Shèrá property and ran afoul of both sets of tracking arrays. Tsecha countered by applying the barest twitch to the vehicle's controls, redirecting it back within the Exterior domain. The skimmer's agitation, brought on by the confounding signals of two different systems, ceased immediately.

Tsecha's trembling, however, continued for some time. *This godless cold.* Rolling whiteness stretched about him in every direction save the east, where the lake-defining blackness stopped it short.

He searched the approaching darkness for the flicker of Security vehicle illumins. Ulanova's. His own. It made no difference—both would be as enemy to him. He felt for the Haárin-made shooter, a souvenir of his war, nestled in the chest pocket of his coat. *However, I cannot shoot at them.* Such would constitute an incident.

"So long, since I have taken part in an incident." Tsecha bared his teeth fully in the dimness of the skimmer cabin, then almost lost control of his vehicle as the expression degenerated into a jaw-flexing yawn. He had done much since his return from the play, little of which would have received sanction from either his Temple or his Oligarch.

He slowed as he approached the Exterior outpost, activating his black box at the same time. The device, also of Haárin origin, blocked the automated concrete booth's scanning equipment and prevented its outside alarms from activating. It also took the extra step of misleading the scanners, assuring them they were not being interfered with at all.

The only drawback to the ingenious device lay in the fact the designers believed they understood humanish systems much better than they actually did. The resulting errors in the interference program meant Tsecha had only a very short time to do that which he came to do.

Three humanish minutes, in fact, beginning from the time he first activated the unit.

On average.

So cold! He half jumped, half slid from the skimmer cockpit to the thermacrete slab on which the outpost rested, grunting in relief as his boots struck dry deck. The thermacrete had apparently done its job in preventing any snow from building up around the outpost, but Tsecha still stepped carefully in the pitch-darkness. Heat cells did occasionally fail. Failure here meant ice patches. Padding and shock absorption worked well for youngish, perhaps, but he did not trust them to protect his old bones.

Besides, if he did fall, who would rescue him? *Cats and police*, his Hansen had said, *only come when you don't want them.* Tsecha tapped the toe of his boot against the thermacrete, planting his foot only when he felt certain he would not slip. *Tap, step, tap, step*—like the odd, rapid gait of a shorebird, and truly. But he could not fall. He had come too far to risk any mistake.

The door slid partially open. Illumins activated to the dimmest setting. Once inside the windowless concrete booth, Tsecha hurried to the small, plastic-covered bench that served as the supplies bin, cracking the lock with a soundkey that also had been made by Haárin. *What would Vynshàrau have done without our most excellent Haárin*? He pulled the large tool pouch containing his humanish clothes from the recesses of his oversize coat, but before he laid his bundled disguise to rest, he rummaged through the cluttered bin.

Ah! It lay beneath the first layer of half-empty parts kits and battered all-weather gear. Most easy to find if you knew to look for it, knew from repeated visits the position of every object in the bin. A crumpled note. Tattered stone-colored parchment trimmed in dark Exterior red. *My Lieutenant. My new friend.* Tsecha stuffed the note inside his coat, worked his tool pouch to the bottom of the bin, relocked the lid, and hurried outside.

The outpost's proximity alarm illumins fluttered to half-life just as Tsecha threw himself into his skimmer, dying to dark as soon as he jerked the vehicle back within its boundary. He flitted along the border, hopped a pile of construction debris, then banked around a broad stand of winter-bare trees. The embassy appeared, its lakeside face, sheltered from the sight of godless humanish habits, enhanced by large windows, balconies, and enclosed patios.

Tsecha could see no idomeni in any of the windows, but that, of course, did not mean they could not see his skimmer. Not that they would take special notice if they did. The vehicle, after all, belonged to Exterior, and traveled along Ulanova's side of the border.

Tsecha eased back on the accelerator as he approached the Exterior maintenance shed located so conveniently close to his embassy. He coaxed the skimmer into its charge slot with finesse acquired through repetition, then fled across the border at the place his black box told him he could pass unnoticed.

Tsecha returned to his rooms by way of back stairways and little-used passages, Lucien's note resting like something burning against his chest. Not since the war had he felt so. Then, every communication held life and death between its lines. For himself. For his valued friends. And even for a few esteemed enemies, without whose presence everyday life would have become a desolation indeed.

My Lucien thinks I play at a game, I think. Tsecha sneaked into his front room and immediately began peeling away his protective clothing. Then he hurried to his favored chair, the crumpled paper clasped in his hand. On the way, he hesitated, detoured to his worktable, and recovered his handheld from its recess. What if, as Hansen before him, Lucien took it as his godly duty to instruct an idomeni in the nuances of English?

I will need to study this note as I do my files. Tsecha unfolded the Exterior parchment, and stared. What had he expected? An offer of an excursion? A suggestion of how to better pass himself off as humanish? A simple greeting?

He saw nothing like that.

Instead, Tsecha read his language. *His* language, in all its complexity, High Vynshàrau as his Sànalàn might compose if she were male and member of a military skein.

And the words. The phrases. The fear in the lines. Only during the war had he read such, when his sect-sharers had watched Rauta Shèràa from the hills above and Hansen pleaded with him that their time to act had grown most short.

. . . get her out . . . am meeting with her "captors" tomorrow evening . . . I can only get her so far . . . am depending on you . . .

Tsecha's grip on the note weakened and it fluttered to the bare floor. Such familiar words. So did Hansen plan his meeting with John

Shroud. *But my Hansen died,* on the morning of his meeting day. Most sorry were the Haárin, to have bombed a building containing humanish. But then, the humanish had left their untouchable enclave of their own free will, choosing to interfere in idomeni affairs. Thus they were no longer blameless in any of this, were they? The chief propitiator's Eyes and Ears had herself set the precedent. That being the case, where lay the disorder, or the blame?

But the Haárin, with their love of disorder, would feel that way, would they not? The members of the Vynshà Temple, positioning themselves for their ascension to *rau,* felt quite differently. They had seen how the godless events of Knevçet Shèràa had demoralized the Laumrau. While they had most willingly taken advantage of their foes' disorientation, such did not mean they wished to chance the same happening to them.

Tsecha felt a tightening in his soul. *They told me Hansen's death rediscovered order, Kilian's death resuscitated order, while my death*—he bent to pick up the fallen note—*my death would confirm order had truly returned.* But he had talked them out of killing him, just as he had earlier talked them into allowing humanish into their cities and schools. The gods had gifted him with the power to persuade. They had allowed him the wit to know when to take action and how.

And they had provided him patience, so he could wait so long for his Captain to return to him and not go mad.

Tsecha glanced at the timepiece on his worktable. *What do you do now, John?* The city where the man worked—Seattle—was located far west. That meant it was darker there, the middle of night. *Do you sleep, John, or do you work?* He walked across the room to his comport and keyed in a code any humanish with a Chicago city directory could find.

The face of a young, dark-haired male filled the display. "Neoclona Chicago. May I help—" His eyes widened as he realized whose face filled his display. Tsecha bared his teeth to alleviate his alarm, but the action only seemed to heighten his agitation. "May—m-may—oh shit!" The stricken face dissolved from the screen, leaving Tsecha to stare at nothing.

Humanish see bared teeth as reassurance. Hansen said so. Tsecha tried to key in the code of another Neoclona department, but the idiot youngish had activated some sort of lock which made such impossible. Too much time passed as Tsecha tried every code combination of which he could think to break the connection. *I cannot ask the communications skein for help—then all will know to whom I spoke.* He made ready to remove the unit's cover and disconnect its power source in an effort to reset the system. It could damage his unit beyond repair; if his Security had their way, he would not soon receive another. The risk was considerable, but he didn't know what else to do.

Just as he prepared to unclip the display screen from its support, it returned to life with a flash. This male as well, he had never seen. Pleasantly dark, with the facial hair many humanish males grew so easily, clipped to a sharp point at the end of the chin. "NìRau," the man said in a pleasant voice, "John warned me you might call."

"I must speak with him," Tsecha said. "Whoever you are, tell him he is to talk with me!"

"My name is Calvin Montoya, nìRau, and I'm a physician, like John. He has given me some instructions, which he recently gave the heads of all the major Neoclona facilities on Earth." He fingered the hair on his chin. "If you try to contact him through us, we are to tell you to go to hell. If you have any doubts as to what we are saying, John has told us to tell you to, and this is a direct quote, 'Use your goddamn handheld.' That is the message I am supposed to give you, nìRau. I am then supposed to end the call and report the attempted contact to John immediately."

Tsecha sat back in his chair, nodding as the man spoke. Quite a clear communication. Most as idomeni, and most unlike Physician Shroud. "Albino John may have given you meaning," he said to the face on the screen, "but Val Parini, I believe and truly, has given you the words. Physician Parini always enjoyed speaking as idomeni. He thought himself most shocking to other humanish as he did so. I am to guess from this he has been called back from vacation? Please greet him for me when next you report to him." Then, to ensure all would be taken well, Tsecha ended by baring his teeth.

Unlike the youngish, Physician Montoya maintained his composure, and even bared his teeth in return. "Alb—John warned me about you, nìRau. Something along the lines of, 'Don't let him get a goddamn foot in the door, or he'll walk out with half the goddamn facility.' I believe I understand his concern." He pushed a hand through his hair. "Now I am supposed to end this call, or John will be angry."

"John is a stern dominant, Calvin?" Tsecha always sought to call humanish by their primary names as soon as he learned them. Such a simple act, but it seemed to make them so happy. And cooperative.

"Yes, nìRau, and I do like my job."

Yes, but you do not wish to end this call, because you are curious.

"And what did Physician DeVries suggest you should do if I contacted you, Calvin?"

The physician's brows arched. He laughed. "Ooh boy—John warned us about the charm, too." He jerked his shoulders, a gesture that could have meant anything, and thus helped Tsecha not at all. "Actually, nìRau, what Eamon suggested involved tracking your comport signal to its source, then dropping shatterboxes until only a rubble-filled crater remained." Calvin's smile disappeared. "I believe he was joking."

Left hand clenched, Tsecha gestured in the extreme negative. "And I know he was not. Your John and your Val, I believe, accepted Eamon into their skein for his technical expertise, not his social."

Calvin coughed. "I really have to disconnect now, nìRau."

"You must tell John—you *must* tell him I am most concerned!"

Calvin grew very still. At first, Tsecha thought the display had malfunctioned. "Your concerns are noted, nìRau. And they are being explored. Now, I must go." He disconnected before Tsecha could again speak. Most wise, actually. Given more time, bearded Calvin would surely have told him everything he wanted to know.

It is how primary names affect these walls. So desperate are they for order, they interpret such as understanding. Tsecha slumped back in his chair. *But I understand so little.* Throughout his wing of the embassy, the tonal series that signaled time for early-morning sacrament sounded. He rose and listened for the preparatory scrapes and clattering which indicated the presence of his cook-priest and her suborn in his altar room. Tsecha waited until the blessed red illumin flickered above the altar-room door, meaning the room was fit for him to enter.

The meal did not go well. Tsecha ate his grains and fruits in the wrong order, forgot to spice his meats, lost track of his prayers. *Your concerns are being explored.* Hansen had often told him how humanish explored one another's concerns. *The more they claim they do, the less they truly do. It is a well-established fact with our species.*

But he tells me my concerns are being explored, Hansen. Tsecha withdrew from his altar room and headed to his favored enclosed patio. It viewed the lake, as did they all, but if one squinted, one could also catch a glimpse of the Interior compound far down the shore. He had often done so, in days past, when he considered the soul of Acton van Reuter and where it might currently reside.

But now Tsecha stood in his enclosure, watched the illumins far down the beach, and considered Acton's son. *He and my Captain—a most seemly pairing.* Or so it had appeared at the time. *But the father forbade it, and now the father is dead.* His Lucien's words returned to him. *She hides in plain sight, nìRau.* And his Calvin's words. *Your concerns are being explored.*

"Plain sight!" Tsecha hurried from the patio to the comport booths located within the documents repository. No reason to obscure the fact of this call. This call was indeed most seemly.

Tsecha entered the code for Interior House. The young female whose face appeared on the display also maintained her composure—she had spoken with him before.

"Angevin Wyle, please, Sandra."

The female bared her teeth, as Tsecha knew she would, and directed her attention to her House console. Her expression waned. "Ms. Wyle is unavailable, nìRau."

"Do not summon her in her office—she is not there yet."

"No, nìRau, I buzzed her residence. She's not home."

"Where is she?"

"She's left no forwarding code, nìRau." Sandra shrugged. Humanish, in Tsecha's opinion, shrugged too much. "I can leave her a message, if you wish?"

"No. No." He could not wait for messages. Another humanish came to mind. Male, this one. Slumped as the Oligarch. Red hair, though not as godly as Hansen's daughter's. "Steve!" he shouted.

"Mr. Forell in Xeno?" Sandra applied herself to her console. "I know he won't be in at this hour." The female's eyebrows rose. "His private code is blocked, nìRau."

"Blocked?"

"Blocked, nìRau." Yet another strange expression crossed the female's face. Something as a smile, and yet . . . "It means he's home, but doesn't wish to be disturbed."

"Ah."

"I can message them both, nìRau." Sandra's brow now lowered. That meant confusion. Sometimes. "Are you sure you don't want to speak to the head of Xeno? Perhaps His Excellency himself?"

"No, Sandra. Message Angevin Wyle please." He ended the call and returned to his rooms to dress for his appointments. *Today I see the Prime Minister, who will complain of my treatment of Detmers-Neumann, and a delegation from the Xhà Pathen, who will complain of my favoritism toward their brethren the laes.*

Both complaints held truth, of course. *I treat Detmers-Neumann as she deserves and the Xhà as they deserve, and for much the same reason.* Tsecha secured the privacy locks to his sanitary room. *I do not trust them.* He removed the overrobe and trousers he had donned for his excursion to the maintenance shed and prepared to lave. His scars glistened pale in the overhead illumination—he stared at them in his reflection and felt every blade slice him anew. His meal rested as a weight in his stomach, his knees ached from the leap he had made onto the thermacrete, and if John Shroud had, by some godish whimsy, appeared before him at that moment, he would with great joy have snapped the man's neck.

My Lucien knew where she was and did not tell me. His odd Lucien, who enjoyed disorder. Tsecha plunged his arms to his elbows in hot water, felt its steam condense upon and trickle down his face. *I must save her.* His Captain. With his odd Lucien's aid. And he would bury all who tried to stop him, as the Haárin had buried his Hansen.

CHAPTER 24

Jani punched her pillow and turned over. Again. Again. *I will not look at the clock.* She looked. Oh-six-thirty. She'd have to get up soon. The thought wouldn't have seemed so daunting if she had managed to fall asleep in the first place.

She rolled on her back and stared at the ceiling. Her real limbs sagged into the mattress like stalks of lead, while the fake ones felt the way they always did. She kicked off her covers, then rose in stages. One leg over the side. The other. *Sit up. Wait for the room to stop throbbing. Stand. Walk.*

Showering proved a challenge. Her upper back, a skinscape of green and purple centered by a fist-sized swelling, allowed movement, but drew the line at assault by pounding streams of water. Jani faced the main showerhead as she washed her hair and got cleanser in her eyes, thus scuttling her films. By the time she emerged, eyes stinging and back muscles twitching, her stomach had begun to ache. *Can I go back to bed?* She checked the clock again. Oh-seven-thirty. *Nope.* She re-filmed, threw on another expensive but ill-fitting trouser suit, and was halfway out the door before she noticed her comport's blinking message light.

Evan had recorded the message well after their aborted dinner. Dressed in pajamas, he sat hunched at the edge of his bed like a condemned prisoner on his bunk. "Jan? I'm asking you, no, I'm *ordering* you to stop. Just stop. Meet me for breakfast, and we'll talk over the reasons. But right now, as your minister, I'm ordering you to cease your investigation." He rubbed his face, pressed his fingers to his forehead.

"Durian showed me some sceneshots, Jan. You and some punk

from Exterior. I don't believe the things he told me about the two of you, but judging from the lengths to which he's gone already, I don't think it's a good idea to cross him right now. He'll do what he thinks he has to. That's his job. I'll let him. That's mine." He held a supplicating hand out to her. "I love you. I want to take care of you. Isn't that enough?" The message ended in a twinkling fade, like a dream.

Jani sat on her rumpled bed, duffel cradled in her lap. "No, Evan. It's not." She hit the touchpad and called up the time he had recorded the message. A little after one.

"Having second thoughts about bringing me here, are you?" With equal parts alcohol and Durian Ridgeway fertilizing the seeds of doubt. She hurried to the elevator, then rode down with her finger poised in front of the STOP OVERRIDE pad, ready to block anyone else from coming aboard. She didn't want to share the car with anyone. Especially someone who wanted to take care of her.

Jani entered Angevin's office to find her and Steve sitting at the desk, drinking coffee and talking in low tones. Both wore slacks and pullovers in shades of pale tan which, combined with their hair, made them look like a couple of lit matches.

Jani allowed herself a small feeling of satisfaction. *Nice to see the kids together again.* But an undercurrent of edginess and the thick haze of multiple nicsticks prevented her from thinking all was well.

Angevin confirmed the prevailing mood. "The idomeni ambassador tried to reach me early this morning. The House operator added the notation that he asked for Steve as well."

Steve waved Jani a vague greeting, then busied himself pouring her coffee from a disposable reservoir. "What do you think it means, Ris? Think he's upset we're digging into his old paper?"

Jani accepted the coffee with a grateful nod and eased into a deskside chair. "If he was, he wouldn't call you directly. He'd lodge his complaint using proper channels. First thing you'd hear of it would be when the Xeno liaison called you into the office and tore you a new orifice." She winced as she drank. The coffee tasted as though it had been filtered through a sock. "The ambassador was close to Angevin's father, I believe?" She looked to Angevin for confirmation she didn't need. "Maybe it had something to do with that?"

Angevin scowled. "God, I'd hoped that had stopped." She gave Jani a tired look and shook her head. "He tried to hook up with me as soon as he arrived. I don't know what he expected. I told him, 'I'm not my father, nìRau.' He said, 'I know, nìa—Hansen is most dead.' He's so damned literal."

Steve rocked back in his chair. "That's how their minds work. I told you, if you don't want to talk with him, I will. Knowing how blunt he is, he'll come right out and tell me what's the problem. And we'll proceed from there. I were thinkin' of callin' him after the midmorning sacrament. 'Round ten." He glanced at Jani. "Like to be there with me, Ris?"

"No." Jani choked down another swallow of coffee. "Thank you. I doubt I'd do any good." She ignored Steve's stare, leaving it to blister the side of her face. "We need to get to work. Let's see your paper."

Angevin crumpled a dispo and bounced it lightly off Steve's chest. "Tell her." Her voice tightened. "Or I will."

Steve stood, stretched, and walked to the curtained window. "Mind if I open this? Sun's a bloody bitch this early, but I need to see some light." He swept back the drape, revealing the shimmering lake, clear sky, and the sun hanging in the midst of it all like a self-suspending light set on high. "Not that bad, is it, with the filters in the glass?" He took his time pushing the drape into its niche.

"*Steve*." Angevin reached for another dispo.

Steve thumped the pane with his fist. Once. Again. "Betha's gone, ok! No one's seen her since last night. She never returned to her flat. Her half of the papers are gone, too. I checked her locker. I checked her cubicle. The office she used last night. So that's it. No one's seen her since last night, and the docs are gone. What else do you want me to say!"

Oh shit. "It's not your fault, Steve," Jani said. "We were both sure she would stick." Considering the scenarios running through her mind, Betha's merely running off would be a relief. "Where's your half?"

"My office. Locked in my desk." Steve flinched at Jani's glower. "Didn't want to be seen carrying them. Not with the lien and all."

"Let's go get them."

They had to pass the Doc Control cafeteria on the way to Steve's office. The noise made them pause; the crowd drew them inside. As they pushed their way to the front, sharp voices cut through the swell.

"*Son of a bitch—where the hell is he!*"

"Oh God." Angevin gripped Steve's arm. "That's Durian."

People turned toward them. A few pointed. The sound level dropped as though someone had flicked a switch.

"What the hell's on, Barry?" Steve called out to the stricken young man over whom Ridgeway loomed. "Someone forget to sign a req for toilet roll?"

A red-faced Durian Ridgeway pushed past bystanders. "Where the hell is Betha Concannon, Forell!" Coffee sloshed and work clothes were spattered, but no one made outraged noises. Everyone was too busy staring at Steve. Behind Ridgeway, two fully loaded Security officers shadowed into view, long-barreled shooters gripped in their glove-protected hands.

"Oh fuck." Steve took a step backward, his eyes fixed on the weapons.

"Don't run." Jani made a grab for him, but he dodged with a quick sidestep. "Whatever you do, don't—"

Steve shook off Angevin's scrabbling hands and cut for the door like a sprinter out of the blocks.

"—run." *Right.* Jani spun back around, let her bag slide to the ground, and took a step toward the nearer guard, who had raised her weapon. She gripped the barrel with both hands, tilted it to the ceiling, twisted it ninety degrees, jerked out and in. Gristly crunches cut the air, silencing onlookers' startled cries. The guard uttered a strangled half sob and sagged to her knees, her nose smashed and streaming blood, her fingers twisted.

Back muscles screaming, Jani swung the heavy weapon to her shoulder and aimed it at Ridgeway. Lousy weapon-handling on her part, but his stricken expression was worth a few broken rules.

Angevin waved and pointed toward the doorway. "Behind you. Trouble."

Jani shifted her stance to find Colonel Doyle sauntering toward her. Behind the Security chief, onlookers scattered. "Your friend won't get far, Ms. Tyi. The elevators and stairwells are already locked down." She reached out. "Hand over that weapon—it is not a crowd-control device."

"No," Jani said, "it's not. It's a V-40 Long-Range. Combat weapon. Enough power to punch you into the hallway and me through the wall if I fire. Stupid choice for indoors." She pretended to take aim at a planter. As she hoped, people scurried, ducking under tables and behind chairs.

"If you back around one more table, you're clear to the door," Angevin said. "Do you want me to get the other one?"

"*No*!" Jani shouted. One V-40 was enough. Thing had a kick like a skimmer head-on—it needed a strut support, damn it!

Just stand sideways like you're doin', and bend your back knee a tad. It'll brace you, Captain. You'll be fine.

"Thank you, Sergeant," Jani whispered. She aimed the weapon in Ridgeway's direction again. "Now, we're going to go somewhere and talk about this."

"Like hell we'll talk!" Ridgeway pointed to the door. "That bastard buggered paper with Betha Concannon. Now she's missing. The time for talk is over. I'm ranking documents examiner on-site, and I have cause. I'm declaring anarchy rules now!" He turned to Doyle. "Order a door-to-door! If the little cunt tries to bolt, shoot to kill!"

"Stop. Telling. Me. My. Job." Doyle pointed an accusing finger at Ridgeway. "*You* said the other Cabinet Doc offices were in a panic. *You* said a threat to the Commonwealth existed. Now you've scared off the only person in this building who could confirm either condition, and, mister, until you have confirmation, you do *not* have cause, and you do *not* give me orders!"

Oh good—dissension in the ranks. Does that mean I can hand this disaster-on-a-stick off to someone? Jani lowered the V-40; the other guard's shoulders sagged. She gave him a barely perceptible nod, which he returned. "I will safety the weapon and hand it to Colonel Doyle," she said. "Then we will go to a nice quiet place, and talk."

"You will be under arrest!" Ridgeway sputtered, his face purpling. "You threatened—"

"I just prevented a massacre by your order, Durian." Jani keyed the adjustment diverting the weapon's prep charge. The stock warmed as the heat dissipated. "The pulse packet from this thing could have blitzed half this room. Packets can be unpredictable, you know. I've seen them circle their targets and boomerang back on their source when conditions were right." The conditions involved magnetic interference caused by the lift-array rupture of a troop transport, but no reason to mention minor details when things were going so well.

Jani's words had the desired effect. Around her, outraged mutters rose dangerously high as a roomful of aggravated paper pushers shifted their attention to Ridgeway. She smiled at the nervous man, then handed the V-40, stock first, to Ginny Doyle. "Let's talk." Her eyes met Doyle's, and the colonel's glare turned even stonier. Jani recovered her bag and gave Angevin a smile she hoped appeared reassuring.

Jani, Angevin, and Ridgeway waited in brittle silence outside the cafeteria for Doyle to return from escorting her injured subordinate to the infirmary; they then adjourned to Ridgeway's office. He barked an order that they not be disturbed to Greer, who had witnessed the episode. The young man stood gaping at them until his boss shut the door in his face. "Probably be selling bloody tickets in a minute," Ridgeway muttered as he engaged the lock.

It was obvious he couldn't decide whom to play to. He pointedly ignored Jani as he walked to his desk, instead bestowing a look of professional neutrality upon Doyle. The colonel's narrow-eyed response was far from neutral, and could only be considered professional if you thought of occupations such as assassin. Ridgeway pulled in an unsteady breath as he sat and offered Angevin a wary half smile.

She beamed in return. "I'm thinking of finally taking your advice, Durian," she said in a sprightly tone.

Doyle glanced at Jani and cocked an eyebrow. Jani responded with a *beats me* shrug.

"Oh?" Ridgeway settled back in his chair.

"I'm going to look up those dexxies who went to the Academy with my father." Angevin paced in front of his desk and counted off on her fingers. "Senna and Tsai. Aryton and Nawar. The Big Four. The Hands and Feet and Left Armpit and whatever the hell other assorted body parts they comprise." She planted her hands on the desk's edge. "If anything happens to Steve, I will sic them on you like a pack of dogs. Mom always said I had Dad's mouth. Good a time as any to try it out, don't you think?"

During Angevin's speech, Ridgeway's expression altered from surprised anger to stern disapproval. "You've backed the wrong horse, my dear. That unfortunate young man has a long history of knocking over fences. Your championing him could do your own career irreparable harm. He's a common thug."

Doyle dragged a couple of chairs over to Ridgeway's desk. "Let's reserve judgment until we talk to the boy, Durian. My people should corral him anytime now." She sat, then motioned for Jani to do the same. "I need proof. All I see now is oversolicitous mentoring." She stared at Ridgeway, who scowled and tugged at his neckpiece.

Angevin, oblivious to Doyle's allusion, smacked a fist against her open palm. "He doesn't like Steve because he's colony." She fell into a chair and folded her arms across her chest.

Ridgeway rolled his eyes. "It's gone well beyond that, Angevin. Only an hour ago, I spoke to a friend of Ms. Concannon's. The man is ex-Service. He said she sought him out yesterday afternoon and asked him some rather peculiar questions concerning augmentation. He told me that the nature of the questions, along with Ms. Concannon's obvious distress, alarmed him. He tried all night to get back in touch with her. He even visited her flat. When he couldn't find her, he contacted me."

Doyle tapped a blunt-nailed thumb against her thigh. "It is not uncommon for young people to spend nights in apartments not their own."

Ridgeway shook his head. "It was for Betha, apparently. The poor young woman didn't have much of a social life, according to the man. So easy, to take advantage of someone like that. Lead her on."

"What are you getting at, Durian?" Doyle asked.

"Something unfortunate came to my attention a few days ago," Ridgeway said. "It appears our Betha had worked rather closely with our late Lady. The same crap we've been dealing with for the past few months, Virginia. You know the shape we're in. It's taken all my powers of persuasion thus far to keep Justice from shutting down our Doc Control and assigning an overseer. This examiner's lien Cao's doc chief has issued against us means we now have a visit from a Court-appointed auditor to look forward to. Considering the position our Minister is in already—"

Doyle ran a hand over her glistening scalp. "The unemployment line forms to the right. And Steven Forell, like many of us, is very fond of his job." She fixed the sullen Angevin with a level stare that worked on the young woman like a slap. "I understand Mr. Forell spent a portion of the evening with you, Ms. Wyle. Could you tell us about it, please?"

Angevin shot Jani a pleading look. "What do you want to know?"

My guess is Doyle knows it all already. Jani pressed a hand to her grumbling stomach. *She just wants to see where you especially feel the need to lie.*

Doyle's smile was deceptively reassuring. "Just start at the beginning. What time last night did you first encounter Mr. Forell?"

"About three. Maybe a little after."

"That late?"

"I was with Risa—we were busy."

Doyle gave Jani a look of mild curiosity, then turned back to Angevin. "How did Mr. Forell appear to you?"

"Fine. Normal. For him. A little pissed." Angevin's eyes goggled when she realized what she had said. "At *me*. Pissed at *me*. We'd been fighting."

"But you made up." Doyle smiled again. "This morning at a little after three."

Angevin exhaled shakily. "Yes."

"Then you and he left the compound together, visited Betha Concannon's flat, spent the balance of the night at his apartment, and returned here at seven-ten?"

"You've been monitoring Steve's and Angevin's movements?" Jani asked.

"Ms. Tyi, we'll discuss your late-afternoon encounter with Forell and Concannon after I finish with Ms. Wyle."

"Are you questioning me in connection with a crime, Colonel?"

"Not at this time, Ms. Tyi. Merely—"

"Fishing? If the issue is documents fraud, ma'am, you are neither qualified nor authorized to question me. Only a Registry mediator can do that, and since we are, last time I checked, in a peacetime, nonemergency situation—"

"Nonemergency!" Ridgeway yanked at his neckpiece again. "We're on the verge of being shut down, Risa—I'd shudder to think what you deem important!"

"No one's life is at stake," Jani replied. "No one has died." *We hope.* "We're only dealing with reputations, which may be ruined at our leisure." Gradually she became aware of Doyle, who pounded her chair arm like a uniformed metronome.

"Who in hell," she bit out, "are you to question my authority?"

"Who in hell do I have to be? Steve bolted from the cafeteria only moments before you showed up. You must have seen him, yet you made no move to pursue him."

"My people are searching for him now, Tyi—the sector-wide lock-down has him bottled."

"Lock-downs can be evaded surprisingly easily by someone who knows the area. It's amazing how many people seem to know this area. Yesterday, one of the Exterior Minister's goons kidnapped me in full view of Private House. Do you even know of this?"

Doyle's shocked expression answered that question. "What goon?"

"Stop it! Stop it!" Angevin pounded her thighs with her fists. "What has this got to do with Steve! What has this got to do with Nueva Madrid and all that other crap!"

At the mention of Nueva Madrid, Ridgeway took on the strangled appearance of someone who had just swallowed his tongue.

"Angevin," Jani said, "don't open your mouth again until you've spoken to a Registry mediator."

"But I—"

"Keep your mouth shut."

Angevin rose. "This is bullshit! Steve's in trouble and you're all fighting about rules!" She dashed past Doyle and ran from the office.

"Where the hell is she going!" Ridgeway shouted, as he, Doyle, and Jani hurried into the hall.

Doyle paced halfway down the passage. "She knows where her

boyfriend is, I'll bet." She spun on her heel toward Ridgeway. "You said his scanpack needed maintenance, that he'd need to be desperate to bolt without it." She motioned to two guards standing nearby. "Which repair carrel is his?"

The lock-down was tighter than Jani suspected. Or hoped. As they tried to enter the third-floor parts bins, the system balked at accepting even Doyle's palm and key card.

The stink of nutrient broth sent Ridgeway to the front desk for nose plugs. Jani trailed Doyle, Ridgeway, and the green-faced guards past the line of carrels. Only one door stood open. Angevin leaned against the jamb, a hand cupped over her mouth. "He didn't do it," she muttered as Doyle brushed past her into the tiny room. "He didn't do it."

Doyle muttered a heartfelt, "Oh shit," and turned back to Ridgeway. "Notify ComPol. Tell them we need an ambulance. And the medical examiner." As Ridgeway left to find a comport, Doyle whispered some orders to the guards, then gently maneuvered a shaken Angevin into the hall.

"He didn't do it," Angevin repeated like a desperate prayer. "He didn't do it."

Jani remained in the doorway. She could see Betha. On the floor. Far corner. No need to approach. No need to confirm. She had seen more than her share of corpses over the years.

Strange the way a body seemed to crumple in on itself after death.

Jani heard the *clack* of a charge-through being engaged. She turned to see Borgie draw alongside her, his T-40 humming its standby song. He wiped a grimy hand over his mouth. His brown eyes had that hollowed-out look, matched by his pale, sunken cheeks. "She dead, Captain?" he asked, his voice shaky.

"Yeah." Jani nodded, waiting for the next question. She knew what it was, but she waited anyway. *Do you think she felt—*

"Do you think she felt anything, ma'am?"

Jani looked at Betha. Outflung arms. Twisted neck. Her hair dragged around to the far side of her face, making her look close-cropped. Just like Yolan. "No, I don't think so, Sergeant. Looked quick to me." As if she could tell. As if she could find her way out of a goddamn closet.

"We aren't going to leave her like that, are we, ma'am?"

"No, Sergeant, we're not. I'll take care of it."

"Ms. Tyi, who are you talking to?"

Jani turned to see Doyle, surrounded by wary subordinates,

regarding her with a puzzled frown. “No one,” she replied, “just thinking out loud.” When she turned back, Borgie had gone. But he’d left her a gift—the burnt-leather stench of his T-40 scorched gloves. The acrid stink filled Jani’s nose. Her eyes watered. “No one at all.”

CHAPTER 25

Ridgeway joined Jani inside the parts-bin vending alcove; they took turns draining the water cooler. Jani downed dispo after dispo in an effort to assuage her relentless thirst, but Ridgeway just needed something to wash down the multicolored tablets he tossed into his mouth like candy.

"I recall your saying something about an emergency requiring a body." He popped a tiny yellow ovaloid Jani recognized as a black-market tranquilizer. "Check that point off your list, Risa—requirement met."

"Forell didn't do it."

"You've known him less than three days. I've dealt with him for over a year." Ridgeway made a vain attempt to brush his hair out of his eyes. "Allow the fact I know my people, however little you think of my ability to handle them."

Stick it. Jani looked down the hall. One of the Commonwealth Police officers had set up a dyetape barrier in front of the carrel door. Two others had entered the small room carrying scanscreens and evidence cases. A skimgurney hovered against the wall, its body bag zipped open, waiting to be filled. "Steve's feelings for Betha seemed almost paternal," she said. "I can't accept that he'd turn on her."

Ridgeway gave a tired shrug. "It wouldn't be the first time a mentor turned on his charge, Risa."

"True, but for a relationship like that to turn bad, it needs an edge. The edge just wasn't there. Substitute Angevin for Betha and you for Steve—there's a murder I could accept."

Ridgeway scowled. "Dear, dear Angevin." The black-and-grey shades of his daysuit, combined with his pallor and mood, made him look like an animated pencil sketch. "She chose her bed. Let her lie in it." He reinserted his nose plugs and stepped out of the alcove to take a look at the scene down the hall. "Tell me, my esteemed enemy, would you really have shot me?" The plugs made him sound nasal.

"No. Not with that weapon, not in an enclosed space." Jani considered stopping there, but with an esteemed enemy, one never held back certain truths. "I would have clouted you alongside the head with the butt end, though. But only if you became violent."

"Thank you, Risa," Ridgeway replied. "That makes me feel so much better." They walked down the aisle toward the dyetape barrier. "Are you going to tell me what you were working on with those two? Besides the fact it involved Lyssa."

"Ruining a reputation."

"Oh." Ridgeway stepped close to the barrier, taking care to avoid the trespass sensors and the splattering of marker dye that would follow. "Anyone I know? Or should I say, knew?" He clasped his hands behind his back and lifted his chin. All he needed was a blindfold and a nicstick to complete the effect. "You're going after Acton. The connection with Neumann. What he did to Martin."

"Oh, yes."

"Oh, hell!" One of the ComPol officers stationed outside the carrel entrance turned to stare at them, and Ridgeway lowered his voice. "Forget the scandal. Forget the political hay Ulanova would make of it. How can you think of piling something like that on your Minister, atop all he's been through already?" Anger returned the familiar flush to his face. "Your definition of loyalty appears as novel as your one for emergency. He'd have to resign. In disgrace."

"Have you looked at him lately! He's killing himself, Durian. It may be in a socially acceptable manner, but it's suicide all the same." Jani watched the flickers of multicolored light reflect off the surface of the open carrel door. That meant the forensic techs had set up their screens and were scangraphing the body and the area around it. "Forced retirement could save his life."

"Or end it." The fluttering light had drawn Ridgeway's attention as well. A muscle in his cheek twitched. "I saw him this morning. He told me he asked you to quit your investigation."

"Yes."

"So what are you doing here?"

"I was brought in to do a job."

"And now you've been asked to quit."

"Tell me why I should."

Before Ridgeway could respond, Colonel Doyle emerged from

the carrel. Dyetape deactivator wand in hand, she poked and pushed toward them, her expression grim.

"Damn, damn, damn." She massaged the back of her neck, but rejected Ridgeway's offer to share his tablet collection.

"So?" he asked.

"Manual strangulation. ME thinks she died around midnight." Doyle glanced at the cup in Jani's hand. "I could use some water, Ms. Tyi. Could you show me where it is, please?"

As soon as they reached the alcove, Doyle sagged against the wall, sliding down until she crouched on the floor. "Her neck. You could hear it crunch when the ME touched her chin. Then her head just flopped over. There were hemorrhages under her eyelids. Lots of them. Whoever killed her tightened down, then eased up and let her come to."

Jani filled a dispo with cold water. Doyle stared past her when she held out the cup, and she set it on the floor in front of her. "Torture strangulation. Whoever killed her was desperate for something she knew. Or had."

"You don't seem very surprised by this."

"No, not completely."

"Do you think Forell did it?"

"No."

"Then who?"

Jani moved to the other side of the alcove and sat on the floor. "Both she and Steve were working to keep themselves out of jail under my direction. Of the two, Betha seemed the more scared. I think she'd confided in someone else without Steve's knowledge. That person killed her."

Doyle covered her face with her hands. She stared at Jani through a cage of fingers. "Could you please back up to the 'keep themselves out of jail' part, and explain what you mean by 'direction'?"

Jani wavered. Because the murder occurred on Cabinet property, the ComPol had to work with House Security. If Steve turned up during the search, Doyle would handle his transfer into their eager hands. "Deal?"

"What kind?"

"Stall the ComPol. Don't tell them about Steve. If he turns up, hang on to him."

"How! It's a murder, Ms. Tyi. ComPol is setting up a command center in my office as we speak!"

"He didn't do it."

"According to Durian, Forell had means, motive, and opportunity."

"You'd listen to that jackass?"

"Murder makes me open-minded. Besides, if Forell is innocent, he could be in danger as well. Jail may be the safest place for him."

Jani tried to shake her head, but the rocking motion made her sick to her stomach. "I need him here," she said. "He has special knowledge of past events I'm investigating for His Excellency. Besides, imprisonment for any reason means a mandatory hearing. Unless Steve's able to build a good defense, he faces immediate deletion from the Registry."

"You goddamn dexxies are all alike, you know that! Self-centered morons! Betha Concannon is *dead*. She died horribly. Steven Forell can bundle his botched career with his scanpack and shove them both up his ass!"

"I'm perfectly aware of how Betha died, Colonel. Do you want the real murderer to go unpunished? What happened to your open mind?"

Doyle's jaw worked. She picked up the dispo of water and took a cautious sip. "What do you want?"

"Keep the ComPol away from Steve Forell. Give me two days." Jani waited for Doyle's grudging nod before continuing. "Betha buggered paper for Lyssa."

"Durian mentioned that already. That angered Steve because one bad colony kid ruins it for the others."

"No. Steve was trying to help Betha get out from under. He knew what she'd done. We were digging into why Lyssa wanted the work done in the first place." Jani straightened slowly and moved to Doyle's side of the alcove so she could talk more softly. "Eighteen years ago, during the last idomeni civil war, several ranking Family members made a deal with the Laumrau. Protection and support in exchange for research involving personality augmentation. Acton van Reuter used what he learned to have his grandson, Martin, augied at the age of three."

Doyle's jaw dropped. "That's what was wrong with that kid? Oh God! You don't augment someone that young—you create a monster." Her expression grew pained. "Five years ago. I had just begun working here. There were several episodes we needed to hush up. One with his sister—" Her look sharpened. "Did His Excellency and the Lady know?"

"I think Lyssa figured it out. I believe she had herself augmented, perhaps so she could better understand what Martin went through." She thought back to Evan's after-dinner confession. "Or perhaps, because of her particular brain chemistry, she knew it would cause her to hallucinate under stress. I think she saw what she wanted to see during those episodes."

Doyle winced. "Her kids?" She sighed when Jani nodded. "But there have been rumors about Acton van Reuter's dealings for years. He prospered in spite of them."

"Rumors are one thing. Betha had paper proof." Jani hesitated. "I'm pretty sure she had paper proof. Private documents from the van Reuter library. The stuff Cao's been trying to get her hands on for months."

Doyle nodded. "I oversaw one transfer. A tense time was had by all."

"Well, the private paper is untouchable until Justice makes a ruling, but if Nawar decides they're actionable—"

"That's the end of the *V* in NUVA-SCAN." Doyle crumpled the cup and tossed it into the trashzap, where it ignited with a soft *pop*. "And Stevie knows what these papers consist of?" She smiled coldly at Jani's affirmative. "Then let's go find Stevie." She stood, then rubbed her knees gingerly. "I remember my old CO telling me what a posh job House Security was. If I ever run into her again, she's in for one heavy-duty bout of reeducation."

Jani tried to stand, but her sore back balked. She held out a hand to Doyle, who pulled her easily to her feet.

"If what you say about Steve is true, Ms. Tyi, you've just done me out of my prime suspect. Maybe I should add your name to the list, just on general principles."

"Yours as well, Colonel. Anyone with a vested interest in the status quo."

"Good," Doyle said as she stepped into the hall. "That narrows down the list to mere thousands."

Two assistants from the ME's office had just maneuvered the skimgurney bearing Betha's body into the hall. The colonel's eyes locked on the dull green body bag as it floated down the aisle and toward the elevators. Ridgeway stood off to the side, conversing intently with a ComPol detective lieutenant holding a recorder. Angevin, however, was nowhere to be seen. Jani nudged Doyle. "Where's Angevin?"

"Infirmary. Shock combined with the stench in this place. First she was royally sick, then she fainted." The gurney disappeared around a corner, and Doyle turned back to Jani. "Were Steve and Betha having an affair? I did hear rumors. Ms. Wyle's temper is a minor legend around here."

"You've seen Angevin's hands. You saw Betha's neck. Did they match?"

"No." Doyle frowned. "The ME said it had to have been a man, or a very physically fit woman." Her grimace altered to a cool smile. "Like you, Risa."

Jani smiled in return. "Or you, Virginia."

They regarded one another until Doyle broke the impasse. "I hate to sound petty, but this could not have come at a worse time. My Exterior counterpart, Colonel Tanz, and his executive staff are coming over this evening. Informal monthly meeting. My turn to pour tea and pass cookies."

Jani's mind raced. Exterior. *The Court of Inquiry report.* Would Lucien be a member of the executive staff? Could she pass off the report to him under Doyle's beady eye?

"I've tried to cancel it these past two days, but Tanz wouldn't let me." Doyle started down the hall. " 'Things we need to discuss,' he said, the son of a bitch. Knowing how quickly good news travels in this town, I'm anticipating a lovely evening." She offered Jani a tired wave before disappearing around the corner.

Ridgeway, his interview over, brushed past Jani without a word. Then she felt a tap on her shoulder and turned to find herself fixed by the dubious eye of a detective sergeant who just wanted to "ask a few questions, please, ma'am."

Jani managed to escape with her pretenses intact. *Lying to police—piece of cake—do it all the time.* The thought of cake made Jani realize how starved she was. She ducked back into the alcove and built a late breakfast from the offerings of the various machines.

If one assumes Ridgeway lit a fire under ComPol's collective ass concerning Steve, Ginny's going to have a hell of a time holding them off. Jani chewed thoughtfully. Two days of stonewalling could prove impossible—one day could be pushing it. *Steve, where the hell are you?*

She watched food wrappers flash to powder in the trashzap and wondered if she'd soon be doing the same. *I saw Borgie clear as day. Heard his voice.* It felt good to see him, in spite of the circumstances and the intimation her health was deteriorating. Lyssa must have felt that way, as well. Any contact, however fleeting, would serve in the never-ending quest to ease the guilt-ridden ache.

By the time Jani left the alcove, ComPol had finished searching carrels. One lucky detective captain was donning a cartridge-filter mask in preparation for searching the aquariums, where damaged scanpack innards went to be rehabbed.

Well, the aquariums were technically the most visitor-friendly area of the bins. No static barriers to discharge. No nitrogen-blanketing to recharge. *Just the open-top tanks with their little baby brains.* The aquariums made the rest of the bin area smell like a flower garden. Someone who chose to hide there did so in the hope no one would look for them there. So, of course, ComPol would look there first.

Good luck, Captain—I give that mask twenty minutes, tops. Jani tried her Interior ID in the stairwell card reader. *Bet you burn your uniform, too.* The access light blinked; the door swept aside. Either Doyle had lowered the status of the lock-down, or Risa Tyi's status was loftier than Jani thought. She mounted the stairs, alert for movement of any kind. *Stevie, where the hell are you?* Doyle certainly seemed concerned about finding him, but she would have had him by now if she'd kept her eyes open outside the cafeteria.

If I were Ulanova, I'd want someone like Doyle in charge of my enemy's security. Jani paused to consider the concept, then took the steps two at a time until her cramping right hip told her to knock it off. The fourth-floor door opened for her as had the third. She flashed her ID at a trio of somber Security guards and studied wall maps until she found the corridor that led to the infirmary.

CHAPTER 26

Tsecha shifted against the rigid metal frame of his uncushioned chair and watched the Xhà Pathen representative state her skein's case against the laes. Xhà did not possess the fluidity of Vynshàrau, or even of Laum. The female jerked rather than gestured; her voice sounded as though she spoke in a metal box. Tsecha looked away from her twitching form, focusing instead on a favored sculpture. But even smooth riverstone failed to please him. His back ached. His head throbbed. He had lost patience with the mind-focusing ability of pain.

When the female finished, Tsecha nodded in acknowledgment of her statement of position, then gestured for her to go, neglecting the customary benediction. She hesitated, waiting for the blessing, but he slashed the air again with his right hand. More roughly, this time. An insult.

I will hear of this from the Oligarch, he thought glumly as the Xhà Pathen left him. Pathen-descended Haárin controlled much of the trade with Outer Circle humanish. They also claimed strong loyalty to their former born-sect. Tsecha sensed an upcoming trade slowdown. Perhaps even a strike.

A strike. How humanish of Haárin. *So well do they blend, even now.* Most as hybrid, even without the outward physical signs. The signs he and John Shroud had spoken of such a long time past as they sat on the Academy veranda, warmed by the sun and a blessedly hot breeze, and argued the possibilities of change.

But the reality of change is most different, and truly. The agent of change, his toxin, resided as prisoner within the bounds of Interior and needed to be freed. Did she even know herself to be imprisoned?

Tsecha hoped not. Kilian's reactions under such conditions had, after all, proven unpredictable, even by her own kind.

My odd Lucien is to liberate her this night. The thought made him uneasy. He did not fully trust his new guide. His dead Hansen had desired order of a sort, but Lucien seemed most content when all around him were confused. The Tsecha who had fought in a war rose from his cursed chair and massaged his numb thighs. *Confusion* and *rescue mission*, he felt most sure, were not a desirable combination.

His meeting with the Prime Minister had been put off until afternoon, so Tsecha retired to the quiet of his rooms. He studied the space, which appeared much larger than it truly was owing to the sparseness of its furnishings. *My Captain could hide here.* He bared his teeth at the disorder of the thought. *She could sleep under my bed.* During the day, she could labor at his workstation, deal with his tiresome duties, explain to him what he must do to survive humanish meetings.

But what would she eat? The prospect of sharing food bothered him, but if such was what the gods demanded, he would allow his Captain his food. What she could eat of it. *She could grow ill.* He lowered himself into his favored chair and pulled at his red-trimmed sleeves. *She could die.* John had warned of such. The nutritional requirements of a hybrid would change constantly as its body altered. A food that once nourished could act as poison a short time later. A wretched, wasting death, which would bring an end to the future as well as his Captain's life.

No. Tsecha settled back in his chair and contemplated a curve of polished sandwood in a niche across the room. *She cannot stay here.*

A sharp series of tones rang out, jolting him from his reverie. *A call to sacrament?* He glanced at the timeform at his workplace. *No, it is too early.*

The tones sounded once more. Tsecha slowly approached his comport. Across the surface of the device's input pad, illumins flashed and fluttered. "Someone has called me?" But the unit did not allow incoming messages, and no other possessed his code.

This lacks order. Tsecha activated the device's audio. *Thus do I know who calls.*

"NìRau?"

Ah. "Lieutenant Pascal, this comport does not accept incoming."

A pause. "It does now."

Tsecha bared his teeth and waited.

"NìRau?" His lieutenant sounded youngish now. Plaintive. Then, like the turning of a page, the tone changed, becoming harsh. "I won't be selling it to the newssheets, if that's what you're worried about."

I detect anger. Good to know his disorderly guide could be vexed. He dragged his chair by the comport table and sat.

"NìRau, would you please activate your video?"

"Yes, Lucien." Tsecha fingered the input pad. A side view of his guide's face filled the display. "I am most surprised to hear from you."

"Obviously." Lucien kept his head turned. Below the level of the display, his hands worked.

Tsecha saw a flash of white. Another. "Lieutenant?"

"My apologies, nìRau—I'm experiencing a technical difficulty." He at last held up a folded square of cloth and pressed it to the side of his face that Tsecha couldn't see.

"Lucien?"

"Yes, nìRau."

"Lower the cloth."

"No, it's—"

"Lower it!"

Slowly, Lucien did as he was told.

Tsecha touched his own face when he saw the four ragged, seeping gouges that ran from the middle of Lucien's cheek to the edge of his high Service collar. He recalled the humanish custom of sharing their homes with animals. "You were scratched by a pet, Lucien?"

Lucien's lips curved. "You could say that, nìRau." The expression altered to a grimace and he again pressed the cloth to his wounds. "I've had a lousy day so far."

"It will soon become worse."

"Thank you. I wouldn't have known that without you telling me."

"Then it is good we speak now, so I can remind you."

"What would I do without you, nìRau?" Lucien lifted the cloth from his face and stared at the crosshatches of blood. "There's been a murder, nìRau. A young woman. A documents examiner. Kilian knew her."

Tsecha felt a tightening in his soul. "Did my Captain kill her?"

"Why would you think that, nìRau?"

"The past—"

"Is the past." Lucien shook his head. "Kilian wasn't in the Main House at the time of the murder."

"And how do you know this, Lucien?"

"I have a source."

"Ah, a spy."

"Yes."

"Ah." Tsecha looked at his lieutenant, who had now become most as a wall. "This killing worries you."

"Kilian was working with the dead girl, nìRau. They were investigating Lyssa van Reuter's death and its connection to what happened at Knevçet Shèràa." The bright redness of Lucien's wounds made his skin seem most pale. "But we all know the connection. Acton van Reuter and Rikart Neumann were friends. After Kilian killed Neumann, van Reuter arranged the transport explosion. He did it for self-protection and to avenge Neumann's death. But there must be something else."

"Something else?"

"Another connection we're all missing."

"All will be connected in the end, Lucien. Such is the root of order."

"NìRau, I can't use philosophy now—I need facts."

Tsecha slumped against hard cushions. How often had he and Hansen argued of this? *There has to be something else, Nema!* His guide had stalked his rooms at Temple like a hunting animal. *How the hell did the order to blow up the transport get to the depot outside Knevçet Shèràa?*

"Does it matter?" Tsecha spoke as much to his dead friend as to the face on the display. "All we do affects all we know. A deed performed by one is a deed performed by all."

"The sins of the fathers, nìRau?"

"Sins are sins, Lucien—they taint the sect as a whole. That is why those who sin most greatly are made Haárin, to excise them from the whole and save the souls of their brethren."

"Ok then," Lucien sighed, "who in Interior House would you make Haárin?"

Tsecha bared his teeth. "My Captain, Lucien."

Lucien emitted a guttural, Haárin-like sound. "That's not the answer I'm looking for, nìRau, and you know it."

"But that is the answer you will receive from me. She must be excised from the rest of humanish. She does not belong with you any longer. She must be allowed to become what she must."

"Which is?"

"She is toxin. The agent of change. She is change's spy." He felt a tremor of satisfaction. *I thought of such without my handheld.* He was finally becoming used to this English.

"That's very poetic, nìRau." Lucien touched his cheek and moaned softly. "I plan to excuse myself from my meeting tonight and track her down within Main." For the first time, he looked Tsecha in the eye. "Eight o'clock, nìRau. One-half hour after the finish of midevening sacrament. You must be at your outpost with your Exterior skimmer, charged up and ready."

So he knows of that as well? Tsecha studied Lucien's face in return. Through the display, it did not seem such an intrusion. *Most as Haárin, my odd one's eyes.* From a sheltered corner of his memory, he heard the tensile song of blades being pulled from sheaths. "Yes, Lucien. For her to live is necessary for us both. You have chosen her as your dominant; thus you owe her your knife."

"My dominant? Yes, I suppose you're right." Lucien cocked his head. The gesture was not as idomeni. He looked as a humanish who contemplated the lines of a sculpture, or an object in a niche. "And you've chosen her for something else. Does she know what you plan for her?"

He knows! How much as Hansen he was, after all. "You know of the blending?" Tsecha asked. "The hybridization? You know of what is to be?"

"I've read your prewar essays, nìRau." Lucien wadded his bloody bandage and flung it out of range of the display. "I can't say I accept your conclusions."

Ah.

"But you want her to live, and I can't save her by myself."

"I will be there, Lucien." Tsecha watched his lieutenant carefully. "With my stolen skimmer." At that, Lucien's mouth curved upward, as he had hoped. Before he could say more, a more familiar series of chords echoed through the rooms. "I must go now," he said as the last series rang. "Midmorning sacrament. I will offer prayers for our success tonight." He waited for Lucien to nod before disconnecting. The screen blanked. He meditated upon the greyness.

No, not as Hansen. Something quite different, I believe, and truly. He smoothed a hand over the front of his overrobe, then reached for his handheld and picked at the touchpad. But the meanings he plumbed from the device's depths failed to help him. *He chose my Captain.* This young lieutenant whose eyes, whose soul, seemed wrapped in a death-glaze that could not be seen. The clatter of dishes and utensils reached Tsecha through the closed door. He felt a small rush of comfort at the sounds.

He chose me. The summoning illumin shone. He rose. His soul felt heavy. *This strange, dead humanish.* He could not keep his mind focused upon his prayers; he pleaded with his gods for understanding.

CHAPTER 27

Jani entered the infirmary to find Angevin in the midst of an animated discussion with the duty nurse. "How many times do I have to tell you"—she struck the check-in counter—"I'm not sick anymore. I'm fine!" The nurse, tall and heavily built, folded his arms and seemed ready to dig in for the duration.

"How about if she agrees to come back every couple of hours?" Jani leaned against the counter and gave the nurse a commiserating smile. "I know she's supposed to be in shock, but does she look shocky to you? I mean, she has her color back." She leaned close to Angevin, who glared at her. "Her pupils look ok. I can't speak for confused behavior, but two out of three isn't bad."

"I should have kicked you," Angevin grumbled as they departed a few minutes later. Security guards were stationed near the elevators and stairwell doors; every so often, one would pop his head around a corner like a treechuck. "And why do I have to check in? It's so stupid—I feel fine!"

"It's a good idea," Jani countered. "Doyle wouldn't have sent you up here if she didn't think you looked shaky." The thought also crossed her mind that the colonel would want Angevin closeted in a well-guarded place as long as Steve remained at large, but she kept it to herself.

"Doyle just sent me here to get me out of the way. I fainted, ok. It was my first dead body." Angevin snorted in disgust. "Doyle didn't take it so well, either. Saw her swallow hard a few times."

"She's a human being, Angevin. The day she stops swallowing hard is the day she better change professions."

"You didn't even blink! Just stood in the doorway and took it all in." Angevin keyed into her office. The look she shot Jani held envy, but something else as well. As in, *I wish I could do that. I think.* "Did you spot any clues?" She made a show of checking her paper message box. "Anything that could clear Steve?"

Jani thought back to the scene in the carrel. *I spied with my warped little eye* . . . something she'd rather not say. Betha had looked so much like Yolan, and in looking like Yolan, she had brought Borgie back for a little while. Jani flexed her shoulders. Her back felt loose. Her hip worked smoothly. Her stomach had even stopped aching. *You ghoul—a young woman is dead and you react by feeling better than you have in weeks.*

"Where the hell could he be hiding?" Angevin locked the door, then headed for her comport. "He couldn't have had enough time to get off the compound." She activated the unit and checked her voicebox. Message after message bit the trashbin after only a few words. "Where the hell is he!"

"Well, I should hope he wouldn't be dumb enough to leave you a message." Jani dragged a chair deskside. "He'd have to know Doyle would check."

"She wouldn't dare!"

"There's been a murder, Angevin. She can, she would, and more than likely she already has."

"She wouldn't have deleted it, would she?"

"No, she'd let you hear it. Then she'd hope Steve would give himself away to you and you'd lead her to him."

"Fuck." Angevin dropped into her chair. "Risa, he didn't do it." She pulled at the hem of her baggy pullover. "But why did he run away like that?"

"Durian had two V-40s pointed in his direction. The gut reaction of anyone with one working neuron would be to run."

"You didn't." That look, again. "You took it out of the guard's hands."

"I got lucky—she didn't know how to handle it."

"But you did." Angevin's gaze was steady and decidedly non-shocky. "Don't you have a guess where Steve could be?"

Jani rummaged through her duffel. She pulled out a squat brushed-metal cylinder, twisted the top, and set it on the desk. "This should buy us a few minutes."

Angevin eyed the device skeptically. "What is it?"

"Insecticide."

"She's bugged my office!"

"The court order was probably fiched over here while you were on your way to the infirmary. Just audio, probably. Holofield, they reserve for real crooks." *Like us after today—who knows?* Jani adjusted the cylinder until it rested in a direct line between the two of them. "But don't be surprised if someone from Systems shows up soon waving a repair order you don't remember requesting. The interference pattern this thing emits reads a lot like a transmission from a blown workstation card."

"How do you get hold of something like that?" Angevin's voice held the greedy wonder of someone ready to pull out a recorder and take notes.

"Oh, you can get hold of anything. All depends how much you're willing to give in return." Jani stroked the device with a fingertip. "With regard to Steve, there are a few places I can check—"

Angevin shot to her feet. "Let's go."

"Not so fast." She waved the young woman back into her seat. "*You* stay here."

"Bullshit!"

"Doyle has her eye on me sort of. You, she's watching like a hawk. The best thing you can do for Steve is stay here. Work. Make lots of calls. Walk the wing from end to end and talk to everyone you see. Check in at the infirmary every two hours."

Angevin's expression slowly lightened. "You want me to draw attention away from you while you hunt around?"

"It can't hurt." Jani raised a finger to her lips, then swept her device off the desk and back into her bag. "Keep a good thought," she said as she headed for the door. "I'm going to head back to Private for a while." Angevin offered Jani a thumbs-up, then turned back to her comport with a determined glare.

Where are you, Steven, you little jerk? Jani stuck her head in the alternate breakroom and encountered two guards playing cards at one of the battered tables. No one else was in the room; judging from the surprise on the guards' faces, dexxies had been avoiding the place the entire morning.

Every elevator and stairway Jani passed was monitored by at least one guard. She stopped on the second floor and entered the women's locker room next to the main gymnasium. She checked the ceiling directly overhead. *They wouldn't have video in here, would they?*

She dug into her trouser pocket for the tiny key card she had stolen earlier from the gymnasium office and slid the uncomplicated plastic sliver into its lockslot. For the benefit of any viewing device, she rummaged through a stack of washcloths and towels. When she came to the towel in which she'd wrapped the Court of Inquiry report, she rolled it into a loose cylinder and stuffed it into her duffel. She followed with a washcloth and some soap.

She stopped at the sink to wash her hands. *Always have a reason to be where you are.* The soap was black, with the throaty scent of a humid summer night. *I came here to try this soap—I overheard people in the hallway talking about this soap—this soap is legend.* She wrapped the wet bar in the washcloth and stuffed it into her bag.

Only a few employees walked the hall outside the locker room. Jani paused to study the message board outside the gym. Then she stopped at one of the glass panels set at regular intervals along the wide hall and spent a few minutes watching a man and a woman play handball. She felt calm. The rest of the world seemed to be moving just a bit more slowly than she.

She entered a lounge area filled with uniformed and plainclothes employees, sat at one of the small tables, and paged through the newssheet the previous occupant had left behind. When the noise level of the room dipped, she looked up. A pair of guards had wandered in and were perusing the contents of a vend cooler. Around her, she could hear the murmurs. "Murder . . . girl . . . the parts bins." She checked her timepiece. One and a half hours since they had found Betha's body. Well, if Doyle wanted to alarm the entire House and waste manpower in the process, she was certainly doing a good job. Jani watched the guards until they departed. Then she left as well.

Where are you hiding, Steven? Jani shuffled down the hall toward the elevators. She didn't bother to eavesdrop on any of the groups clustered in corners and near doorways. It didn't take a genius to figure out what they talked about.

Fear not, citizens—your friends in Security have it all under control. She rode down to the lowest parking level; once in the tunnel, she hitched a ride to Private on a grocery skim. She rode the elevator to her door and keyed herself inside. The housekeepers had been through, apparently. Her bed had been made and the air possessed the eye-watering scent of cleansing agents. Jani sniffed again and wrinkled her nose. Odd smell for a cleanser. Sharp. Spicy. Familiar.

Oh no!

Out of the corner of her eye, she detected movement.

"Risa?" Steve walked into the sitting room, his cupped hand hiding his smoking 'stick. "Don't yell. I can explain."

CHAPTER 28

"How the hell did you get in here?"

Steve backed away, stumbled, and wound up straddling a footstool. "I said, don't yell—"

"I'm not yelling," Jani said, just a touch louder than necessary. "Start at the beginning. What happened after you ran out of the cafeteria?"

Steve's nicstick puffed feebly. On the nearby coffee table, a small dish contained the remains of several others. "Scarpered down the hall. My office. Grabbed my shit and made for the stairs."

"Did you pass Ginny Doyle on the way?"

"Hell no." He looked horrified at the prospect. "Wouldn't be here if I had, would I?"

Don't be too sure. "The stairway lock let you through?"

"Yeah. Everything worked until I got to the first floor. Heard running. Ducked into a doorway. Saw guards running in all directions. Waited till they'd gone, then tried the stairway door again. Locked. I knew the main exits would be sealed before I could reach them, so I made for the delivery bays in the rear of the House."

"They were still open?"

"Yeah. Food deliveries today. Skimvans inside, filling the bays—skimvans outside lined up ten abreast, waiting to unload. In this weather, they don't shut down for anything. One of the supers saw me and started cussing me out. Told me to get my ass into some coldgear and start unloading. So I did."

"So you got all muffled up and unrecognizable in a snowsuit and nailed yourself a skiff."

Steve grinned. "Lucky, huh? I spent about a half hour unloading.

Worked my way through Oxbridge at the school docks, so I'm pretty good at it. Super watched me for a few minutes, then left to squawk at somebody else. Guards came through every once in a while. One stared right at me, but I looked like I knew what I were doing. No one expects a nance dexxie to know how to handle a loading skiff, do they?" His lip curled. "A few minutes later, I steered the skiff outside, made like the battery were low, and drifted it to a maintenance shed. Changed it for a grounds-crew skiff and floated down the access road to here."

Jani found herself listening with respectful interest. Then she thought of Betha, and her mood soured.

"Made for the tradesman's entrance," Steve continued. "Housekeeper leaves coffee and snacks for the Private crews in a little back room. I know because I stop by some days to check for blueberry tart. Outer door's always unlocked. Had to wait until someone came out to refresh the pot—ducked in through the inner door while her back were turned. Up the lift. Snuck in with the cleaners. Here I am." He looked at Jani in surprise. "You know, it really were easy to get in here."

"Doyle will love to hear it."

"Do you have to keep bringing her up?" Steve dug in his trouser pocket and pulled out another 'stick, which he shoved into his mouth without igniting. "How's Ange?"

"About what you'd expect."

"Pissed as hell. Doyle giving her fits?"

"I'm sure she has her under surveillance. I hope you haven't tried to call her." Steve shook his head. "Keep it that way. You both may go crazy in the interim, but if you try to hook up, you're screwed." Jani waited for his affirmative sigh. "So, you went straight from fourth floor to first? Never got off on the third floor? Didn't visit the repair carrels?"

Steve gave her a puzzled look. "Nah. Didn't have no bloody time, Ris."

"When was the last time you were down there?"

"Last night. I stayed a while after you left. Had to turn in my parts req." His expression grew guarded. "Why?"

A thin band of tension stretched from Jani's scalp and down her neck. "Betha's dead. We found her body in your repair carrel about two hours ago. She'd been strangled. The medical examiner put the time of death at around midnight."

Steve tried to shake his head, but all he could manage was a palsied tremor. "Why—why would someone want to hurt her?"

"I think she went behind your back and tried to work a deal with someone."

"Aw, no—"

"That someone killed her. The way she died suggested the killer wanted something from her." Jani sat on the arm of a chair and watched the light play over her boot as she swung her leg to and fro. *Now I feel better. It comes and goes in waves.* She looked up from her mesmerizing footwear and into Steve's frightened eyes.

"What do you mean, 'way she died'? What do you mean, 'wanted something'?"

"I mean it took a while for whoever killed her to kill her. They were trying to extract information from her."

"Did they get it?"

"I don't know."

"Well, maybe I can give 'em some of what they need," Steve said as he ran from the room.

"Steve!" Jani rushed after him, reaching him as he disappeared into the bathroom. "Where do you think you're going?"

Steve had already pulled on one leg of a pair of snowpants. Behind him, the lube-stained jacket lay in a heap on the floor. "Back to Main," he said as he shoved in the other leg, then yanked the thick grey pants up to his waist. "I'm going to find whoever did this."

Jani leaned against the doorway, positioning herself to throw a block if things needed to get physical. "I wouldn't do that if I were you."

"Yeah? Why not?" Steve finished fastening his pants and pulled the jacket over his head.

"Because a lot of people back at Main think you did it. Because Ridgeway tried to declare anarchy rules and order you killed if you tried to escape from the compound, and while Doyle countermanded the 'rules' part, I'm not a hundred percent sure about the 'kill' part."

The furious movement beneath the jacket slowly subsided.

"It's become more than doc-jazzing, Steve. You're wanted for questioning in a murder."

The jacket sagged to the tiled floor. "Does *Ange* think—?

"No." Jani moved out of her "brace" position. Steve didn't appear too eager to leave anymore. "The first thing she said was, 'He didn't do it.' "

"But that were the first thing she *thought*." He moaned softly. "She saw Betha?" He winced at Jani's affirmative. "Is she ok?"

"She got sick. Doyle sent her to the infirmary. Personally, I think she just wanted Angevin locked up as long as you still ran loose." Jani waited for Steve to reply, but he just stared over her shoulder. "That's why you have to stay here. Someone has committed murder and framed you for it. The case is all circumstantial, but as the old saying goes, 'Enough coincidence will surely hang a man.'" Steve's eyes finally moved to meet hers. They held the dumb misery of a wounded animal, waiting for the killing blow. "Let's go into the other room, where we can talk."

Jani returned to the sitting room while Steve removed his snowsuit. She sat carefully. Her back had begun to ache again. *The wave comes in. The wave goes out.*

"Now, after you bolted you went to the office to get your 'pack and the papers," she said, as Steve flopped into the chair across from her.

He nodded. "Yeah, I had—I usually wear my 'pack on me, but Ange and me, we got in sort of early, and after she parked in the garage, we just stayed put and sat and talked and then—" A blush crept up his neck. "You know."

Jani forced a smile. "Yeah, I know."

"And when we got into the building, I realized I left my belt and packpouch in her skimmer. Then we were running late, tryin' to track down Betha, so I locked my 'pack in my desk with the papers. Couldn't carry 'em around in my hand like my orb and bloody scepter, could I? Not with that fookin' lien."

"Where are the papers?"

Steve's face brightened a bit more. "They're in the jacket." He bounded to his feet and headed back to the bathroom, returning with the battered jacket. "I zipped it all in here. Thing's got more pockets than a snooker tournament." He unzipped and rummaged; soon, the coffee table between them held a scanpack in a scuffed case, an emergency 'pack tool kit, and a file pouch bursting with handwritten notes, general-purpose paper, and—

"Some of this stuff has the Prime Minister's seal." Jani fingered a creamy white page. The familiar silky smoothness of government parchment sent a shiver up her arm. "You've got original docs here. From another damn House! From *the* damn House!"

Steve stilled. "I know."

"Eyes-only docs."

"I know."

"The Prime Minister's eyes!"

"Yeah, well. She didn't seem to want to use them the way they should've been." Steve grimaced in disgust. "They followed her, you know. The Lady. They knew something were wrong with her, and they just followed her with scans and watched it unfold. She grew up with them, went to school with them. Treated some of their kids. She were one of them, and they just watched while she flamed out." He shoved the doc pouch across the table. "Here."

Jani flipped open the pouch. "Who compiled this?"

"Betha. The Lady helped with the personal stuff, but Betha did more than you think." Steve's expression darkened further. "She had ways of getting hold of stuff. She'd visit friends in other Houses and just go wandering on her own. She said the things people left out on their desks would scare you."

Jani held up one of the PM's documents. "Are you telling me she just walked into Li Cao's office, and said, 'Excuse me, Your Excellency, do you mind?' "

"I don't know how she got that." Steve fussed with a jacket zipper. A plastic rasp cut the air. "She wouldn't tell me. Just said she had connections."

She had connections, all right. "Well, maybe she did you a favor by not telling you," Jani said as she flipped through a few more cream white sheets. "We could have found you on the floor next to her." The image stalled Steve in mid-zip. He pushed the jacket to one side, mumbled something about needing a drink, and escaped to the kitchenette.

Jani continued paging through the pile. The PM documents contained information she already knew from the Court report. All of Lyssa's public missteps, and a few private ones, all neatly cataloged and cross-referenced with her trips to Nueva Madrid. *So, Betha didn't reach her own brilliant conclusions—she stole them from an entire team of Prime analysts.* She set the docs aside and rooted through the miscellaneous scraps.

Paper from Interior Grounds and Facilities, listing Lyssa's vehicular mishaps. Liquor bills. A listing of wrecked furniture. *Probably blasphemy coming from a paper pusher, but some things shouldn't be written down.* Physician, wife, mother—all forgotten amid the damning slips of paper. Jani brushed a stack of sheets aside, sending several of them fluttering to the floor.

Hold on! Jani picked up one of the fallen documents. A different sort of shiver moved up her arm. *Consulate paper.* From Rauta Shèràa. She checked the date code in the upper left corner. *I was still at Knevçet Shèràa then.* Yolan was dead, but the rest of them were alive, battered and weaponless, waiting for their Captain to keep her promise and see them safely home.

Jani touched the paper's snow-white body, ran a finger along the bright blue trim. A log excerpt, judging from its margins and formatting, but without a Consulate cipher glossary, it would be impossible to break the code. *They used semi-Rime iterations then.* With her 'pack and a workstation, Jani could crack it eventually. *Could take a day, or a couple thousand years.* She heard Steve clatter out of the kitchenette and folded the document into the inside pocket of her jacket.

"Find anything useful?" Steve asked as he twisted the cap off a bottle of New Indiesian beer.

Jani shrugged. "Nothing we don't already know. I was searching for Consulate paper from eighteen years ago."

Steve shook his head. "That's that blue-and-white stuff? I looked for that. There's none in there. Betha said she had it in her half of the files. Did anyone find it in the carrel?"

"Not that I know of," Jani said. "They could have been wedged beneath her body, or hidden in one of the desk drawers." But the desk had been more a table; none of its drawers could have contained a file pouch the size of the one she held. *And the one I'm holding didn't have any Consulate paper in it when Steve looked through it last night.* "Did you sleep in your office last night?"

Steve colored. "Yeah. Few hours. Didn't want to go home. Don't like sleeping alone."

"What time did you fall asleep?"

"Tennish. I remember because my 'zap's recharge light were blinking, and it weren't when I woke."

"And the cleaning crews come through about eleven?"

"At my end of the floor, more like ten-thirty."

Jani plopped the doc pouch on the couch beside her and sat back. *You had another visitor besides the cleaner.* She could imagine Betha sneaking into Steve's office, finding him asleep, and slipping the most important piece of paper Lyssa had given her into his share of the info tangle. *What were you up to, Betha?* Did she plan to withhold the most vital piece of information from her other co-conspirator? *Of course.* But her plan backfired. Her co-conspirator knew what to look for, knew what was missing. *I need that cipher glossary.* "I have to go."

Steve stood. "I don't suppose I can go with?"

"Not a chance." She pointed to a stack of paper that had been growing steadily since her arrival. "There's a three-day backlog of newssheets. Please keep your hands off my workstation. I've typed it to me, but I'm sure it's monitored for intrusions. In fact, the whole damn suite could be under monitoring. I try to check it a couple times a day, but it's their playpen. They know tricks I haven't heard of."

"They airn't gonna bug His Excellency's guest!"

"They're not that considerate." Jani walked over to the holoVee and patted the top of the console. "Keep away from this. Don't use the comport, either. We don't want signals coming out of this suite when they know I'm not here to make them. Understand?"

Steve sat down and dug out another 'stick. "Yes, Mother."

"And if you're going to keep smoking, do it in the bathroom." Jani cracked open her office door. "Stash the snowsuit in here. If someone tries to get in here, you may have to dress *tout de suite* and go out the window."

"We're on the second floor, Ris."

"There's over two meters of snow on the ground. It'll break your fall."

"Says you. They're not your bloody ankles, are they?" Steve sighed heavily. "Would they really shoot me?"

At this point, they're so damned spooked they'd take out the entire Cabinet. Jani pulled her shooter out of her duffel. "Do you know how to use one of these," she asked as she handed it to Steve.

"Y-yeah." His mouth gaped as he examined the bulky grip and dated styling. "Crike, my dad has one of these. Thing's a relic!"

"Thanks."

His look sharpened. "He got his in the Service." But his heart wasn't in this particular attempt to badger Jani about her past. He slumped back in his chair. "Would they really, really shoot me?"

Jani left Steve's pained question unanswered and hurried to the bathroom. *A quick splash of cold water on your face can take the place of a nap.* Sure it could. She checked her films in the mirror, then examined her face. *I look tired.* But the garage guy had looked sick. Sallow, clammy skin. Bones jutting. And the delirium. Seeing Borgie as she had didn't qualify as delirium. Hearing him. That was stress. Augie. The sight of combat weapons and dead bodies. She'd be fine as soon as she could manage some sleep. She finished washing up. When she reentered the sitting room, Steve still sat with the shooter cradled in his hands.

"Ris?"

Jani shouldered her duffel. The Consulate paper crackled against her chest as she moved. "Yeah?"

"Are you sure you don't want to keep this?" He held the weapon out to her, taking care to keep the barrel pointed at the floor. "Betha's murderer may have wanted her and me out of the way for starters, but you're helping us. They might go after you now, too."

"I'll be fine," she said as she locked the door on the worried young man. *Nobody can kill me—I'm never going to die.*

Everybody dies, Captain.

Not me. I tried it once, remember—it didn't take.

She hurried to the elevator. Her touchy stomach shuddered as the car moved down, but the sensation soon passed. She hugged her duffel, imagining the empty slot that usually held her shooter. She felt no regrets over her decision to leave the weapon with Steve. Better he should have it.

The wave goes out . . . the wave comes in.

She wouldn't need it anyway.

CHAPTER 29

Jani keyed into Doc Control's Archive wing. As she studied the nameplates on the doors lining the narrow hall, she rehearsed the reasons she hoped would compel the code-room supervisor to let her see the cipher glossary.

It's an ancient code—no one's used it since the war. Nope, too limp. *I'm cross-checking some old Service disability claims.* Now that sounded asinine enough to be true.

She stopped in front of a plain metal slider guarded only by a simple palm reader. *Bet it lets everyone in.* Getting out, however, could prove tricky if your scan didn't clear. A ready-made cell—no choice but to sit tight and wait for the cavalry to come. She wiped her right palm on her trouser leg and prepared to press it against the reader surface, but before she could, the door slid open of its own accord.

Whoops—la cavalerie c'est ici.

At the far end of the room, Ginny Doyle rose from behind the supervisor's desk. The supervisor, a slender, dark-haired young man wearing sweat-blotched grey civvies, stood nearer the door, in front of a tilt-top worktable. He glowered at Jani, then resumed inserting small data discs into a storage booklet. The iridescent circles glittered in their slots like an overgrown coin collection.

The cipher glossary. But why was Doyle interested in it?

"Ms. Tyi." The colonel's mouth turned up at the ends. Calling the expression a smile would have been charitable. "I was just going to call you." She turned to the supervisor. "I'll send someone for those discs in fifteen minutes. They'd better be ready."

"Bring me Ridgeway's sign-off, and they will be." The supervisor inserted the last disc in its slot, then closed the booklet with as much emphasis as he could without risking damage to the contents. "No sign-off, no discs."

"We've been over this, mister."

"And I've got a lien hanging over my head, Colonel. Nothing leaves this office without the ranking's ok."

Jani cleared her throat and waited for the supervisor to direct his stiff-necked scowl at her. *No, I don't think the disability-claims approach would have worked with this one.* She pulled her scanpack from her duffel, making sure he saw it. "Rauta Shèràa Consulate, civil war stratum? The cipher glossary for comlogs?"

"You need it, too?" The supervisor looked down at Jani's scanpack. "You're His Excellency's hired shooter, here to clean up after the troubles. Why do you need to see it?"

"My thought exactly," said Doyle, who had perched on the desk's edge. One leather-booted leg swung freely, a glistening play of polished black and silvery reflection. Jani forced herself to look away as the light patterning set off a series of buzzes and cracklings in her head.

"It's for Betha," she said, loudly enough to block out the noise. "It'll help us find out who killed Betha."

The supervisor's dark eyes misted. He jerked a thumb at Doyle. "You're working with her?"

Jani looked at the colonel, who stared back blandly. "If necessary." After a long silence, Doyle responded with a slow nod. Light danced across her dark brown scalp.

The supervisor sighed. "This glossary's directly related to van Reuter family records, so it's covered by the lien. I can only release it on the ranking's signature, and Ridgeway's not available."

"If I supply you with a valid reason and promise not to leave the compound, you can sign it out to me. If Ridgeway told you otherwise, he's wrong."

"Look." The supervisor tugged at his damp shirt. "I can't give you the whole damn glossary."

"How about a single disc?"

"To do that, I need a page code. Do you have a page code?"

Jani removed the sheet of Consulate paper from her inside shirt pocket and handed it to the supervisor.

"You *folded* it," he said, in a tone one might reserve for a slaughterer of baby animals. "Don't you know better than that?" He held the sheet between thumbs and forefingers and unfolded it slowly, as though a quick movement might injure it further. Then he set it down on the worktable and slid restraint bars along the top and bottom to fix it in place.

"Where did you get that, Ms. Tyi?" Doyle stood up and ambled toward the table, her hands locked behind her back. "It matches the description of the paper the PM's been looking for."

"Later, Colonel."

"Ms. Tyi—"

"*Later*, Colonel."

"I hope you didn't catch the code inset chip in the fold," the supervisor interrupted. "That would necessitate surgical repair before I could attempt a full scan. Something this old could take days to heal."

"Codes for that series of sheets were set in the lower left quadrant" Jani said, "just right of quadrant center. I took great care to leave that area smooth."

The supervisor's head shot up. "How do you know that?" He focused his attention on the document, smoothing his scanpack over the surface in the area she had described. "Well, well," was all he said as he took note of the page number on his display and checked it against the index inside the glossary binder. He removed the appropriate disc from its slot and slipped it into an antistatic pouch, then freed the Consulate document from its weighting and rolled it into a loose scroll. "Three hours," he said as he handed them to Jani. "Any longer, and I'll have no choice but to notify Ridgeway."

Jani slipped the items into her duffel. "Shall we go, Colonel?"

When they reached Security, Doyle turned down the executive wing, then stopped. "Wrong way," she muttered under her breath as she spun on her heel and led Jani in the opposite direction. Still grumbling, she palmed them into a small conference room that had been fitted out as a temporary office.

Doyle closed the door just as two ComPol officers bustled past. "They've taken over my office until further notice," she said. "They've seconded members of my staff until further notice. It wouldn't be so bad if they treated my people like fellow professionals, but it seems to be ComPol opinion that this murder is an indication of their incompetence."

Jani lowered herself into the first chair she came to. Her right hand felt weak, her fingers, stiff. Muscles twitched throughout her arm and up to her shoulder. "I bet the first thing they asked was why you didn't have visiscan set up in the parts bins."

Doyle sat down behind an old metal desk. The sides of the desk were dented, the dull brown electrostat paint worn away in patches.

"Please! The first thing I asked them was how closely they monitored *their* dexxies. They changed the subject so fast I almost got whiplash." She leaned back, chair creaking in protest. "No offense meant, but everyone knows dexxies are crazy. You try to keep them from getting overexcited and pray they stay away from sharp objects and the personnel files."

"Unfair, Colonel." Jani forced a smile. "Payroll is where you have the most fun."

Doyle's eyes glittered. "When I see Lieutenant Pascal this evening, I'll have to let him know you referred to him as a 'goon.' Lucien's many things to many people, but that, I believe, may take him by surprise. I doubt he'd enjoy being thought of as quite so common." She swung her feet up on her desk. "After we left the parts bins, Durian took great pains to fill me in on what he believes happened between you and Lucien yesterday. Such nice sceneshots." She smiled. "Do you work for Exterior, Ms. Tyi?"

"Funny, Colonel, I've been meaning to ask you the same question."

Doyle's smile froze, but she recovered quickly. "Please, call me Ginny." She stifled a yawn. "You certainly worked dexxie magic with that code-room supervisor. He's never given me the time of day. I love it when a bright boy gets set back on his heels by one of us old girls." The glint in her eyes softened, as though she recalled a bright boy of her own. "Why do you believe Angevin Wyle took the trouble to pay a visit to your Private suite at two o'clock in the morning?" She was good—the tone of her voice never changed. Neither did her expression of goodwill.

Jani flexed her hands again. The right one began to twitch. "I thought we'd decided she had nothing to do with Betha's death."

"But why seek you out at such an odd hour? To discuss her concern for Mr. Forell, perhaps? Her worry over what she'd suspected he'd done? Something she witnessed?" As the colonel's eyes followed the movements of Jani's hands, she frowned. "Then an odd thought occurred to me. Just let me say the term 'hired shooter' could prove more appropriate in the end than our supervisor friend could ever have imagined."

What! Jani hoped the surprise she felt didn't show. She didn't want Doyle to know she'd managed to rattle her. "You believe I murdered Betha? At my minister's request?"

"Lyssa, too. It explains the special trip to Whalen just to retrieve you. Taxi service from His Excellency himself as reward for a job well-done. I understand you and he had dinner for two at Private House last night."

Thank you, Durian. "And why would His Excellency have ordered it done?"

"To make sure the dead remained buried." Doyle's expression grew grim. "You have no idea what it's been like in this House the past few years. Believe me, Risa, as soon as we heard Lyssa had died, a half dozen scenarios passed through this floor like a bout of food poisoning, and every one of them began with the assumption Evan van Reuter *wanted* his wife dead."

"I never got that impression from him when we spoke of the matter."

"With all due respect, I only have your word for that and I'm not sure what that's worth." Doyle's voice grew eager. The hound on the scent. If she'd howled, Jani wouldn't have been too surprised. "If I could dig up any evidence whatsoever that you buggered Private security and made your way back here around the time Betha Concannon was killed, I'd walk you down to the ComPol command center myself. You had motive and means, Risa. Anyone who saw you in the cafeteria this morning knows you could make the opportunity."

"And you have a remarkably vivid imagination. Ginny." Jani's stomach grumbled in agreement. "I'm guessing I murdered Betha because she uncovered proof I murdered Lyssa. Very neat. I understand the appeal. I'm a stranger. No one likes me or trusts me. I can see where pinning it all on me would make everyone else feel much better. Pardon me if I decline to cooperate. I've killed no one." *At least, not lately.* "Your problems began here, you'll find your answers here, and I doubt they'll be as neat as you hope."

Doyle chewed on her lower lip. "You've bothered me since you arrived," she said. "Durian told me our dear lieutenant served as your steward during your journey here. Disgracefully bold of my favorite blond, but knowing Lucien as I do, not a surprise. The fact he's taken to you concerns me. He has a long history, Risa. Being his friend is no recommendation."

Jani remained silent. *They think I killed Lyssa. Evan says he brought me here to take care of me, but did he really plan to turn me over for his wife's murder?* Evan's career teetered on the brink—what steps would he take to save it?

Apprehending his wife's murderer, to start?

I'm the outsider here.

"Is everything all right, Risa?"

"Everything's fine."

"Hmm. I don't suppose you'd like to tell me where you got that piece of Consulate paper?"

"No, not at this time."

"You said in the code room that it was some sort of communications log?"

"Yeah. Ingoing and outgoing Consulate calls covering a three-day period. Idomeni days. They're a little longer than ours."

Doyle frowned. "I know that, Risa. Funny that so many calls could fit on a single page."

"Well, every department had its own log. I'm hoping this page came from the one used by executive staff." Jani removed the document from her bag. "Besides, the assault on Rauta Shèràa had reached its climax during the period this record was made. The Consulate had switched to emergency transmission only, to avoid sniffer bombs."

"How do you know? Don't tell me you were there?"

Big mouth. "Common sense." In truth, she'd found it out from John. He'd shown great interest in the circumstances surrounding the transport crash and had managed to uncover all sorts of details during her convalescence. "Why take chances?"

"Indeed?" Doyle watched Jani activate her scanpack. "What can I do to help?"

"I'll need a workstation. I assume yours is typed to you?"

Doyle pulled over the wheeled cart on which her sleek unit sat. "As you said, we're now working together on this, whether we like it or not."

Jani removed the code disc from its pouch and ran her 'pack over it to break the seal. She then handed the disc to Doyle. "Here. I'm sure you know what to do."

Doyle inserted the disc in one of the reader slots; Jani scanned the Consulate document to unlock the internal latches that would have prevented instrument reading. Her new chip functioned smoothly. She handed the unlocked document to Doyle, who set it facedown on a plate reader.

"I hope my station can handle an old code like this without locking down." Doyle's fingers moved over her touchboard. "I can't unlock my own damned machine—I'd have to call in someone from Justice. They'd use Betha's murder and the examiner's lien as excuses to shut me down, too." She tapped in a final series, then glanced at Jani. "Here goes." She muttered an initiation code, then held her breath as she watched her display.

Jani moved as close as she dared to the workstation and snatched peeks at the display's edge from the corner of her eye.

After a minute or so, Doyle's display flickered. "Here it comes," she whispered.

Jani watched the edge of the screen. "What does it say?"

"Just a list of names and dates so far." Doyle's eyes widened. "Wow, she *was* there then," she said, partly to herself. "Old school friend. Had a rep as a patho. Always told me she was on staff on Shèrá. Thought she was lying." She looked at Jani, then touched another area of the board. "Let me print you something solid. You look ready to jump out of your chair." Several sheets of paper emerged from a slot in the workstation's side, and Doyle handed them to Jani.

Jani took the papers in her left hand. The one that wasn't shaking. *Two women died because of what's on this paper.* She studied the column of names. Acton van Reuter's name was entered several times, as was Evan's.

Makes sense. Daddy messaging Sonny several times a day, demanding he get the hell out of the line of fire and come home like a good little van Reuter. Jani checked the date-time column. Most of the messages had been sent before the crash, while she had still been trapped at Knevçet Shèràa.

John said the transport had been sent from a Service fuel depot just outside the city. According to Lucien, that's where the bomb had been planted. The site had an odd code, an alphanumeric that corresponded to its location on a Service grid map of the area. *N-2-D—*

—1-4-3-7-L. Jani read the rest of the code, next to Evan's name. An outgoing call, made soon after the last in a series of communications with his father.

The buzzing in her head resumed. Intensified.

But he could have been talking to anyone there. The Service personnel stationed at the depot were the primary sources of information regarding Laumrau and Vynshà troop movements. Someone from the Consulate would have had to keep in touch with them regularly.

Don't make excuses for him anymore. Jani reread the entry. The right day. The right time. A short call. Only a few seconds. A call someone expected. A simple order. *Do it.*

"Is something wrong, Risa? You don't look well." Doyle leaned across her desk. "Is it important? What the hell do you see!"

More than two women died because of what's on this paper. Eight patients. Twenty-six Laumrau. Fifteen members of the Twelfth Rover Corps. Rikart Neumann.

And, in ways large and small, though not as important, Jani Kilian.

"Risa! Talk to me!"

You always took orders, didn't you, Evan? Jani heard a rustling to her left. Caught a whiff of burnt leather. She looked up to find Borgie standing beside her chair.

"Got your motive for Lady Lyssa's death now, don't you, Captain? She found out her husband gave the order to bomb your transport. Your old boyfriend. Saving his ass as usual. Keeping his eye on the ball. Not caring who got hurt." His fatigues stank of smoke and sweat. Dirt smeared his face. "I can't tell you anything you don't already know, Captain. Don't give me the wide-eyed look."

"I never would have guessed."

"Ah, bullshit, Captain. You remember what he was. You've been jumpy as a cat since you've been here. Glass in his hand all the time, just like back then. Making excuses, just like back then. Always somebody else's fault, just like back then." He looked at his T-40 and grimaced. "I think it crossed his mind more than once you might be on that transport. But his overbred ass was on the line. First things first—save the tears for later."

"I think you're right, Sergeant," Jani said. From far away, she heard Doyle calling her. No, not her. Someone else.

"Risa, who the hell are you talking to! Answer me, damn it!"

Jani stood up, almost stumbling as her back cramped. She shoved the papers and scanpack into her duffel and headed for the door.

"Tyi! Stop! Drop the bag! Put your hands where I can see them! Turn around slowly!"

Something in Doyle's tone made Jani stop. More than mere loudness. Panic. The kind that had drawn its weapon. The kind with blood in it.

Blood sings to me. I know the words. Jani let her bag slide to the floor, put her hands up, and turned. Doyle had indeed drawn her shooter—the bright red sight fix skittered across Jani's shirtfront like an insect. Better to stand still. Nervous hands made for messy shooting.

"*Roche!*" Doyle shouted. "Get the meds up here now!" She edged around her desk. "Don't move, Risa—I will shoot."

Blood sings. Strange songs. Jani heard the pound of footsteps in the hallway. Muffled shouts. *Blood talks, too. It asks, "Evan, how could you?"* Amid the voices, Jani heard Doyle call out, "She's in here." Then she felt a cool prickle between her shoulder blades. Then she heard nothing at all.

CHAPTER 30

"Of course you understand, nìRau, that much depends on your people's willingness to let bygones be bygones."

Tsecha looked Prime Minister Cao in the face as he tried to discern her meaning. The female raised her chin in acknowledgment of his attention and curved her lips without baring her teeth. On its own, Tsecha had learned over the past weeks, the expression meant nothing. Cao always smiled.

"I do not understand you, *nìa*," he said. "Please explain." The female's lips curved even more. *Yes, it is good to have called her nìa.* The only other humanish female he had called by the informal title in this damned cold city had been Hansen Wyle's daughter. *And she had not smiled.* She had shouted, in fact, and stamped her foot. Her voice had grown so loud, embassy Security had wanted to expel her from the grounds. How the young one had cried out. *I'm not my father!*

"Bygones, nìRau." Cao shifted in her high seat. Like Ulanova, her legs were not long enough to provide adequate counterbalance. She tottered and had to grab hold of the sides of her seat cushion to keep from falling. "We will ignore the fact the Elyasian Haárin are trying to monopolize transport refitting in most of the Outer Circle. In return, your colonial Council will cease its attempts to secure full and unrestricted access to Padishah GateWay."

Tsecha nodded, his eyes fixed on the Prime Minister's pale-knuckled grip on her chair. *If I moved quickly, she would tumble to the floor.* He had done such once before, to Ennegret Nawar, during the young male's Academy entrance interview. As Tsecha remembered, Nawar had not thought it very funny. *He bruised his hip, and split his trousers.* Nervous humanish, he had learned, needed to be treated carefully.

"NìRau? Are you listening to me?"

Tsecha studied Cao's round, golden face. Her eyebrows, thin as black pencil lines, had drawn down in puzzlement. "Yes, nìa," he replied. "You will allow my Sìah Haárin to continue to attempt to rebuild your most aged, unspaceworthy ships. In exchange, we the idomeni are to surrender in our efforts to gain more direct access to our Vren colonies, which suffer already from undersupply and dwindling populations. Thank you. Most generous. My Oligarch will be most pleased."

"NìRau—"

"Why do you not say what you mean? Why do humanish never say what they mean? As long as Padishah remains secure, you will have no worry that Haárin will try to settle on Nueva Madrid. Your Service hospital will remain safe from our observation. Your experiments will remain safe from our observation."

"NìRau!"

"We have known of the Ascertane work for some time, Your Excellency." Tsecha's use of Cao's humanish title upset the female, as he knew it would. Every trace of her constant smile disappeared. "We also know of the attempts John Shroud's colonial hospitals have made to recruit Haárin into other medical studies. So much have our outcasts been promised in return for their help. Access to business. Status. I wonder how Albino John is able to offer so much. I wonder who allows Albino John to offer so much."

The pleasing color drained from Cao's face, changing from Sìah-like gold to the bloodless sand of her tunic. Shards of pure color, formed by the lake reflection through idomeni window glass, danced over her face as though small flares burned beneath her skin. The lake itself, Tsecha could see, had calmed, the shore ice that had been shattered by the storm re-formed. A pleasing observation, a well-ordered reflection of the room itself: large, lake-facing, quiet, with chairs even a humanish would consider tolerable. With the exception of his own rooms, Tsecha favored this place most in all the embassy.

Cao breathed in deeply. "Since we're being so open and above-board with one another, nìRau—"

Ah, sarcasm.

"—perhaps you would be so good as to explain your actions of the past few days?"

"Actions?" Tsecha folded his arms into the full sleeves of his overrobe and shifted on his low stool. Had they found traces of his presence in the Exterior skimmer? Clothes? Hair? Skinprints? *But I took such care.* Would they be watching his hiding places tonight? *But I have so much to do!*

"The Exterior Minister has complained to me—"

Tsecha held his breath.

"—of your surprising attitude toward our requests for information concerning Haárin soil- and water-treatment systems in our Outer Circle. The reluctance of your Oligarch, of your Council and Temple, didn't surprise us, but we expected more of you, nìRau. Considering your history of kindliness toward us, even during difficult times, we find this sudden lack of cooperation on your part most unsettling—"

Tsecha watched the lake shimmer in the cold sunlight like metal foil. *My two favorites would have liked this room, I think.*

"—if not downright alarming." The Prime Minister paused to dab perspiration from her forehead with a wisp of white cloth she then tucked inside her tunic sleeve. Outside, the air could freeze one's blood, but the temperature inside the viewing room was most pleasant. "This place is set up to remind you of Rauta Shèràa, nìRau?" she asked as she made a small gesture toward the sand-painted walls and sun-stone-tiled floor.

"Yes, nìa."

"Even the temperature?"

"Do you not find it comforting?" Tsecha inhaled deeply of the hot, dry air. "I was told you would find it comforting." He had, of course, been told no such thing. The ease with which he lied about such an inconsequence was lessened by the fact that, for the first time since he had arrived in this frozen city, he felt truly warm.

Cao patted her forehead again. "I think you are pulling my leg, nìRau."

"Pulling your leg, nìa?" Tsecha looked at the female's cloth-covered limbs in alarm. He and the Prime Minister sat an arm's length apart—he had not touched her! "I only enjoy the warmth," he admitted, "and wish you to think I provided it for you." A humiliating admission, perhaps, but better that than to suffer such disorder!

Cao drew up straighter in her seat. "The strategy sounds familiar. Which of your Six taught you that particular lesson, nìRau?"

"My Tongue taught me most." Tsecha bared his teeth. "My Hansen."

"I should have guessed," Cao said, frowning. "I watched Hansen Wyle grow up. He schooled with my children. With all due respect, nìRau, learning humanish ways from that man was the equivalent of learning table manners from Vlad the Impaler."

"Vlad, nìa?"

"A long-dead dominant of ours. You would have considered him most disordered." A shadow of a smile revisited Cao. "Do you think much of Hansen these days, nìRau?"

Tsecha felt the female's stare, chilling where the sun had so recently warmed. "I think of Hansen every day, nìa."

"Do you think of any of the the others, as well?"

To lie successfully, Nema, you need to think of it as a game. His Hansen had sat in a room much like this one. Fallow time had come to the north-central regions; rain and wind had beaten against the window like souls screaming for mercy. *The best human liars think of it as a game. Don't think of the importance of what you're saying, or what you're trying to accomplish—if you do that, you'll lose. It's just a game Nema. Just a game.*

"No, nìa," Tsecha answered, "I think of no other." *I am as a young one, playing my game.*

"Exterior Minister Ulanova believes otherwise, nìRau."

A good liar knows how to use truth, Nema. He realizes its value better than anyone. "My Anais, nìa," Tsecha said, "has much of which to worry. Much which gives her trouble." He bit his lip to avoid baring his teeth as his Lucien's stiff posture at the theater sprang up from his memory. "The youngish lieutenant. Pascal."

"Yes." Cao's look held surprise. "Well, if *you* can figure out what's going on, someone had better have a talk with our Anais, and soon." She slid carefully off her seat. The click of her shoes on the bare tile echoed within the room. "I must go, nìRau. Time for my staff to begin the dance with your staff, I suppose. As usual, I have had an interesting time."

Tsecha followed Cao out of the room. In the hall, Sànalàn appeared from the shadowed interior of a side hall and took over the escort duties. Blessedly alone, Tsecha hurried back to his rooms. The time for midevening sacrament was fast approaching, and he had much for which to prepare.

He stripped off his clothing as soon as his doors slid closed and hurried to the sanitary room for a quick laving. Even as water dripped from his soaked head, Tsecha rummaged through his clothing cupboard for that which he needed for his evening's work: the silkweave cold-weather suit which would fit under his clothes like skin and the battered bronze-metal case containing other lessons learned from war.

Tsecha finished dressing. On its cupboard shelf, the metal case awaited his attention. He lifted it, its weight as nothing in his hands, and dumped its contents onto his bed. The two thin Vynshàrau blades he strapped over the sleeves of his coldsuit. The Pathen Haárin shooter he shoved into a pocket in the coldsuit's front. The weapon bulged from his chest as a second heart, but it would be most easy to reach if it proved needed. This he knew from experience.

With an ease he knew would have surprised his Lucien, Tsecha stowed supplemental shooter power packs and assorted scanning and blocking devices within other pockets in the suit. Shielded by the special polymer weave, his weapons would fail to activate embassy scanners. *I am most as Haárin.* He had felt such during the war, when he had allowed Hansen to persuade him to have the suit made. The materials were meant to be used in weapons-systems construction only—the fact a chief propitiator caused them to be used in ways not their own moved beyond disorder and into chaos.

I have always been as Haárin. Tsecha pulled on a fresh overrobe, then sat in his favored chair. *Because of such, I understand my Captain.* After a time, room illumins lulled by stillness darkened to thin half-light. Tsecha felt along his sleeves and touched each blade in turn. Through the altar-room door, he heard the soft sounds of his cook-priest and her suborn as they readied midevening sacrament.

I feel no fear. His hands were dry and steady. His heart did not thud beneath his ribs. *Soon I shall walk into the night, as my Captain did.* The thought should have sickened him, but it did not. He knew, as she had known before him, that a disordered way sometimes proved the only one possible.

CHAPTER 31

She lay on her back. She couldn't move. Efforts to flex her legs caused her right thigh to cramp. A tight strap pressed around her ribs just beneath her breasts, barely allowing her to breathe. A band like bony fingers encircled her right wrist and presumably her left, as well.

Jani opened her right eye and felt the depressingly familiar release of tension as her film split. She blinked. A slimy hydropolymer fragment slid off her eyeball and down her cheek, leaving a cold, damp snail track in its wake.

Well, let's see how much more damage we can do. She opened both eyes wide. Her left film remained intact, but her right continued to fissure. Her vision alternately blurred and sharpened as bits and pieces floated across her eye, then over the side, leaving her right cheek cool and sticky.

After a few determined blinks, Jani's vision cleared enough that she could look around. Up to a point. *Nice ceiling.* Dull white, from what she could tell, since the room's lighting left something to be desired. She lifted her head as high as she could. Darker walls, somewhere in the cheery blue family. In the far corner, near the door, two frame chairs squatted near a low, dispo-littered table. Someone had eaten their meal out of a box. More than one someone, judging from the number of containers.

They ate and watched me sleep? Jani tried to swallow and coughed as her dry throat prickled. Her mouth felt lined with absorbent, her lips, dry and rough. She summoned up what saliva she could and ran her tongue over her teeth. She pulled against her restraints again; her lower back tightened. She sagged back on the bed and tried to gather her scattering thoughts.

Not just any room. I'm in a hospital. Jani could tell from the smells in the air. Chemical. Antiseptic. Freshly cleaned bed linens and an underlying hint of metal. Especially metal. Instruments. Cold, sharp, and always too large.

This is for your own good, Captain.

Jani shivered at the memory of her examinations, embedded in flesh and bone and brought to life by her surroundings. John had gotten to the point where he flinched each time she did, which only made things worse. Val Parini, meanwhile, always examined her with the distracted air of one who had seen the worst, and rest assured, Jani, you aren't even close.

But that bastard DeVries had enjoyed hurting her. At first, she thought herself the unlucky recipient of his warped version of foreplay. But as time went on, she was compelled to conclude the man simply did not like her.

Hell, he hated my guts. He felt I distracted John from their greater purpose. She had heard the arguments. Raised voices in the hall outside her room.

"Open your little rat eyes, John! The A-G wants her, so hand her over. Hang on to her, she'll drag us and everything we've worked for right into the sewer with her. We've learned what we needed from her—give her up!"

Jani stroked the bedsheet. Warm, where her hand had rested. Smooth. Pure white. Like John. He never lost his temper during DeVries's tirades. He'd slip into her room afterward, pull a chair beside her bed, and watch her as she pretended to sleep. Always the same position, legs crossed at the knees, hands folded in his lap. The attitude of a man who owned the store and the street besides.

Hello, creation—my name is John Shroud, he'd said to her the first time she'd opened her eyes to find him there. *Unfortunate name for a physician, don't you think?* His milk white skin had seemed to glow in the harsh light, his voice rumbling from a source nowhere near his heart. Palest blue eyes had glittered like cut crystal. In the stupor following the reversal of her induced coma, Jani had thought him some sort of implacable, medically trained angel.

It was the color of his eyes that did it—turned out they were fake. John's eyes were pink, in reality. He'd been the one who taught her how to film. And how to walk, dress, and feed herself with the aid of numb, twitchy animandroid limbs. *Being a freak has its drawbacks*, he'd told her. *But it has its advantages, as well. Trust me, I know what I'm talking about.*

But he'd never shown her how to burst a restraint. Bad John. Jani pulled against the straps until the pain brought tears to her eyes. Then she raised her head and looked at herself. *I was wearing clothes, wasn't I?* If she had, they'd since been replaced by a plain-fronted white gown. In the crook of her right arm, a raised silver disc glittered in the dim light.

Oh hell—!

Too late. Cued by her increased movement and elevated blood pressure, the sedative pump activated. Jani felt the skin beneath the disc tingle. A heartbeat later, warmth rippled up her arm and across her chest. *I don't want to sleep anymore, damn it!* She yanked again at her restraints, but the straps held fast.

Sweat bloomed on her forehead, under her arms. Chills. Her stomach spasmed. Burning rose in her throat. *I'm going to vomit!* She tried to turn on her side, but the chest strap held her down. *I'll drown in it!* She forced herself still, breathed in slowly and deeply, willed the nausea to pass. Acid harshness percolated to the base of her tongue and stayed there. *For now.* If she continued moving, the pump would administer another dose after a buffer period had passed. Could be thirty minutes, or thirty seconds, depending on the drug.

Jani looked toward the door. Funny no one had checked on her. The sensors in the bed had to be monitoring her vitals. Didn't anyone notice the increased activity?

She worked her hands. The skin on her right wrist burned as she moved. *I'm hurting myself—these shouldn't hurt.* What kind of restraints were these? *Old.* And poorly applied. *I'm not in a place where they're used to strapping people down.* That seemed promising. Maybe they wouldn't know how to handle her if she broke loose.

She pulled against her left wrist restraint. Gently and firmly at first, then not so gently and much more firmly. All she felt was the compression. When her hand became stuck, she tugged harder still. A few muffled cracks sounded. It worked through the narrow opening more easily after that.

Jani held up the hand for inspection. The little finger twitched uselessly, corkscrew-twisted wrong side up. The thumb's movement was barely perceptible. The whole hand had numbed—she couldn't even detect pressure anymore. She loosened the strap beneath her breasts. *Thumbs come in handy when you're trying to work buckles*, she thought as she tried to unlatch the strap she couldn't see using fingers she couldn't feel.

"How's it goin' there, Captain?"

Jani glanced to the side. Borgie sat perched on her end table, cradling his T-40 like a bouquet of long-stemmed roses. "You could help," she replied.

Smoke puffed from the man's flak jacket as he shrugged. "Can't, ma'am. You know that." The fact seemed to desolate him—his hang-dog expression appeared even more gloomy than usual. "Yolan's here, too," he said, momentarily brightening. "She's found a new friend."

The chest strap fell away. Jani sat up and freed her right wrist and ankles. "Are they out in the hall, Sergeant? Does that mean you know where we are?" She looked again at Borgie, whose smile faded.

"Can't help you, ma'am," he repeated. "You know that." As Jani struggled out of bed, he stood up and shouldered the T-40. An odd odor wafted about him as he moved. Not scorched gloves, this time, but something familiar that Jani couldn't quite place. Scorched, yes, but not gloves . . .

"Oh, great!" She felt for the back of the knee-length gown and caught a handful of bare ass. "I had clothes, didn't I? Where the hell are they!" She caught Borgie's eye just as he was about to shrug another negative. His shoulders sagged.

"*—bullshit—!*" The sound pierced through the closed door. Jani backpedaled toward the bed, prepared to dive under the sheet if anyone entered, but no one came. Instead, the voices grew louder.

"—see you in hell before I call him in! Once you call in a facility chief, forget it!" A man's voice. Enraged. "—empty bedpans for the rest of my life—!" Jani tasted the panic, as well. Like bile. The taste reminded her of the pump. She worked her index finger beneath the thin disc—it left a raised, bloody welt in the crook of her arm. The itch had taken on a squirmy life of its own, as though worms crawled through her elbow and up her arm.

"You have no choice, *Doctor*!" Another man's voice. No panic, but you could fuel transports with the anger. "Look at the liver enzymes! When did you ever see values like those!"

The doctor countered, voice lower, shaky. "Are you sure you calibrated the blood analyzer properly?"

Silence. Which spoke volumes. "I ran the drug screen," the angry man finally replied. "She'd been dosed with Ascertane sometime in the past seventy-two hours. Her blood contains metabolite NCH-12. The last bulletin we got stated that if any patient turned up positive for that metabolite, we were to notify the nearest facility chief immediately. Now, Doctor, are you going to call Cal Montoya, or am I?"

The doctor spoke, his voice softer, words impossible to discern. Jani left Borgie standing by the door and walked back to her bed.

Near the headboard, a wheeled IV rack stood like a skeletal sentry. She hefted it, checked it for balance, swung it back and forth like a baseball bat.

"Heavy, Captain?" Borgie had started poking through the dispos on the low table, wrinkling his nose at what he found.

"Nope. Under control, Sergeant." Holding the rack in her right hand, Jani headed for the door. It swept open for her, revealing a larger room, an examination table, lab furniture, and assorted analyzers. The doctor and his angry colleague leaned over a desk, their backs to her, still arguing. The desktop was cluttered with readout cards, sheets of notes, and stacks of textbooks.

The angry man turned. Jani recognized him. Vaguely. *The duty nurse?* His eyes widened. He reached out to her just as she swung the rack around.

Both men wore medwhites. Jani stripped off the doctor's. Fewer bloodstains. She put them on, then scrounged through the glass-fronted cabinets, uncovering bottles of film former, a white medcoat, scuffed white work shoes. She washed away blood, dressed, refilmed her eyes. Light brown filming. Poor coverage. The greenness shown through—her eyes appeared phosphorescent in the office lighting.

"You look like a crazy wonko, Captain," Borgie said dryly as they left the infirmary. "Get the urge to drop 'em and bend over just looking at ya."

"Control yourself, Sergeant." Jani tried to smile, but one look at Borgie's face stopped her. It had changed in the past few minutes. Blackened in places. Blistered in others. One ear was gone. The peculiar odor that followed the man like a faithful hound had grown stronger. "Am I dying, Borgie?" she asked. "Or am I just cracking up?"

Her sergeant, her dead sergeant, stared at her through cloudy eyes. Cloudier eyes. His dark brown irises grew milkier as he spoke. "Captain, I can't help you. It's all you." His voice rasped with desperation. "*Your* questions! *Your* answers!"

They paused so Jani could get a drink of water from the hall cooler. After the fifth dispoful, Borgie began to fidget, so Jani reluctantly tossed the cup in the 'zap and fell in behind him. The people they passed in the halls looked at Jani's clothing, never at her. No one challenged them, or tried to stop them. *I mean, me. No one's tried to stop me.* Her sergeant had nothing to worry about. He possessed his own unique brand of camou.

Good ol' Borgie, Jani thought as she watched the man's smoking back. "*Sais-tu ou nous allons*, Sergent Burgoyne?" she asked him. *Do you know where we are going?*

"*Mais oui, ma Capitaine.*" Borgie looked back at her as he spoke. His other ear, along with most of his cheek, had burned away. White and yellow blisters glistened in the light.

The acid rose once more in Jani's throat. She recognized the smell now.

Borgie led her through an anteroom and into an office. Expensive paintings. View of a lake. Nighttime. Moon reflecting on rippling water. Jani expected to see a man sitting at the desk, but instead, she saw a woman. A friend. Dead, of course, like Borgie. Funny how that fact seemed to concern her less and less.

"Yolan." Jani approached the desk slowly. Her old corporal still wore her usual startled-deer expression. Her lazored blonde hair was as neatly combed as ever. Her steel blues appeared battered, though. But it was brick dust, not smoke, which puffed from the material as Yolan nodded weakly. The rubble had buried her fairly deep, after all. Oddly enough, her gamine face had remained untouched, but her body . . .

Bones in a bag. All that had been left. Borgie had waited for Jani to turn her back before he fell to his knees and gathered that limp body in his arms. Yes, his relationship with Yolan had crossed every line. Yes, Jani had known, and kept it to herself. The one time she got involved was when Borgie asked her to persuade Neumann not to leave Yolan behind at Rauta Shèràa Base. Neumann hadn't wanted to take her to Knevçet Shèràa. He trusted her even less than he had Jani. "I killed her, Captain," Borgie had cried. His weeping had seemed to sound from the walls themselves, following Jani as she left that section of the bombed wing, dogging her down every hall, echoing around every corner.

I helped, Sergeant.

"We had to come here," Yolan explained to Borgie, who loomed over her in his still-futile effort to appear domineering. "She got scared out in the open. Didn't want to risk seeing him again until she knew she could take it." Her delicate features set in stern lines, Yolan turned to Jani. "Captain or not, you say anything mean to her and I swear, I'll air you out. She's been through enough." The corporal leaned her head back. The chair rocked back as well. It dawned on Jani that Yolan had yet to move from the neck down.

"Fine, fine," Jani nodded. "Bossy-assed mainliner." A flash of movement captured her attention. She turned. "*You!*"

Betha Concannon stood in the middle of the office, her clothing rumpled, her hair tangled. She tried to speak, then winced and held a hand to her throat. Jani saw the steel blue scarf knotted around her neck and looked at Yolan, who regarded her levelly. "She wanted something to cover the bruises. She's sensitive about them."

"Well, bully for her," Jani replied. "She's left her best friend to be accused of her murder. She betrayed everyone she worked with and for. She's a liar and a cheat and an accomplice in Lyssa van Reuter's murder! And she's one of ours, damn it! She should have known better!"

"Being colony's no guarantee of goodness, Captain." Yolan spoke slowly, as though reprimanding a child. "You've lived out there long enough to know that. Besides, you knew what Betha was about, deep down. That's why you worried about her. But you cut her slack because she was colony. Because she was a dexxie. Maybe if you'd trusted her less, she'd still be alive."

"Not fair, Yolan," Borgie protested. His words came muffled and slurred, spoken as they were through lips now swollen and blistered. "Don't put that on her, too."

"But she wants it that way." Yolan's eyes never left Jani's face. "She wants to be nailed to the cross. She'll even pass out hammers and spikes to all comers, with instructions where to pound." The corporal's head lolled against the back of her chair. Borgie propped it upright with a gentle hand. "Doesn't help, does it, Cap? Won't help till the day you die, and after that, it won't matter." She looked at Betha. "No one deserves to die like she did. Do something about *that*. Take care of what you can."

Jani looked out the window, to the floor, the walls, everywhere but at the three people who stared at her silently. The three dead people. *How far gone are you, when the ghosts are more human than you?* Her right arm itched to the point of pain. Pinkish yellow seepage stained the medcoat sleeve. Her right shoulder felt hot. Breathing had become difficult, as though she wore a clogged respirator. She forced herself to look at Betha. "It was Ridgeway."

Betha nodded slowly, using her hand to stop the movement.

"You'd been working for him. All along."

Another labored nod.

"Ridgeway helped you bugger the docs Lyssa took to Nueva. He had an accomplice at the hospital, a doctor who purposely botched Lyssa's regularly scheduled take-down. Lyssa made it to Chira before hallucinating herself into the rocks, and Ridgeway thought the one person who knew Evan had transmitted the order to bomb my transport was dead." Jani paused to look at Borgie. What did she expect to find on his charring face, an expression of surprise?

"But you had friends at the PM's," she continued. "They told you what Cao and Ulanova suspected. You made friends with Lyssa before she left on that final trip, and she entrusted the proof she had compiled to you. At first, you planned to turn it all over to Ridgeway, in exchange for whatever. Then you got greedy. It never occurred to you he could kill you, too."

Betha's mouth moved in mute pleading. She managed a sharp squeak when sounds of activity reached them from the anteroom.

Jani slipped behind the shelter of a shoulder-high plant. Betha, Borgie, and Yolan remained where they were. Durian Ridgeway burst in, walking through his cowering victim on the way to the desk. He began a frenzied search, opening and slamming drawers until, with a bark of relief, he pulled a grey documents pouch from the bottom drawer and tossed it on his desktop. With Borgie and Yolan as fascinated bookends, he dumped out the contents and flipped through the pages, muttering under his breath.

Jani stepped out from behind the plant, ignoring Borgie's frantic gesturing for her to stay put. "It's not in there, Granny."

Ridgeway tensed. He looked up slowly. "Risa." His hands dropped below the level of the desktop. "I thought you were in the infirmary."

"I was." She took a step toward the desk in an attempt to circle around to Ridgeway's side, but he quickly countered, edging away in the opposite direction. "The Consulate comlog. The one that shows the call Evan made to the fuel depot. It's not there." Jani sidled closer to the desk, but stopped as Ridgeway backed away in the direction of the door. "It's in the hands of whoever Ginny Doyle is really working for. Judging from your behavior, that person isn't you."

"Captain Kilian. Jani. The call recorded on that log does not constitute proof. Our personnel at the depot were in constant communication with Consulate staff. Quite necessary, considering the circumstances. Surely you remember?"

"The way you're acting bitches that argument to hell, Durian. You raised the alarm that Betha was missing. Then you steered Doyle after Steve. When Steve disappeared, you shifted everyone's sights toward me. Anything to deflect attention from Evan. He told me you'll do what you think you have to. You're not stupid. If everything's green, why bother with it? Why clean it if it ain't dirty?" Jani watched Ridgeway's hands, still below desktop level.

He has a shooter. She glanced at Borgie, who now stood by a sofa on the other side of the room. Betha stood beside him, one hand at her throat, the other over her mouth. Yolan sat on the sofa, her legs propped on the low table in front of her, her arms limp, hands in her lap. "He's armed, Cap," she said.

"I know," Jani replied.

Ridgeway stiffened. "Still talking to yourself, Jani? Who answers? Riky Neumann?"

"Never. Why waste a good hallucination?" The burning itch in her arm had receded to a dull scratchiness. "I see Betha. She's over there, by the sofa." She raised her arm to point and Ridgeway flinched to one side as though anticipating a blow. He brought the shooter up and pointed it at her chest. Direct line of fire. One shot. Crack the sternum. Stop the heart. Not even augie could fight this one off.

This time, it would take.

Here's the hammer. Jani took another step toward him. *The spikes.* Another. *What are you waiting for?*

Betha's mouth opened in a soundless scream.

The shooter rasped. Jani stumbled to her left as the impact half spun her around. A fleeting pain, in her left shoulder, just above the joint. Then numbness. Her lungs cleared, her breathing eased. She looked down. Her arm jerked uselessly. What remained of it. The exit wound had obliterated the hand. Half the forearm. Rose pink carrier dripped through gaps in the heat-sealed stump, splattering over the synthetic flesh that now soiled the carpet. She looked at Ridgeway, who stared back in stunned silence. "You missed, you goddamn office boy. Point-blank range, and you fucking *missed*."

His eyes narrowed. "Is that your challenge, Jani?" She could smell the hate as he raised the shooter again.

So slow. He moves. So slow. Jani feinted to her right, then darted close. Right hand raised, fingers straight. Her sudden movement distracted Ridgeway. He discharged the shooter off target—the pulse packet brushed her left cheek just as she thrust at his neck just above the base of the throat. He collapsed to his knees, eyes goggled, grabbing at his throat as his breath wheezed and whistled like air being sucked through a cracked pipe.

"How does it feel, you son of a bitch?" she asked softly as she stepped behind him. The time for ritual had passed. The curve where his neck joined his shoulder whispered, *here*. This time, she listened. Felt augie's strength reinforce her own. Raised her right hand. Brought it down.

"Cap'n?" Borgie drew alongside her. They watched Ridgeway's body until it stopped twitching. Then Jani turned to her sergeant. His face was a crusted mass now. Eyes glazed white. He crackled when he moved. "Wuh be'er go."

Jani edged out into the hall and looked at herself in one of the safety-dome mirrors set in the ceiling. She had folded the empty documents pouch over her ruined forearm. The shooter graze had left a reddened brush burn on her cheek. *I look like a lab accident.* She smiled grimly. *I am a lab accident.*

"See anything, Cap?"

Jani checked the mirror, saw nothing behind her. Then she turned. Yolan smiled up at her, broken body bundled into a wheeled office chair. Betha pushed. Borgie brought up the rear, T-40 raised and ready. Tiny gouts of flame licked from beneath his flak jacket. His face was . . . unrecognizable.

Jani remembered where she was now. *Interior Doc Control.* She led the way, past the offices, toward the elevators. At every junction, she'd look up at a dome mirror and chart her solitary progress. *When I look up and don't see myself, I'll know I'm dead.*

Empty elevators. Deserted hallways. No one to challenge her, to stop her. *Like they're giving me room to maneuver.* Jani and her silent trio bypassed empty offices, entered a large anteroom, stopped before a door. *Like they want me to come here.*

"Once you go through that door, you're on your own, Cap," Yolan said. She'd become spokesman for the trio, seeing as she was the only one who could talk. "We can't help you."

"I know."

"Decision time, Cap."

"I know." Jani gripped the door handle and twisted. Sand shifted beneath her feet. Desert wind brushed her face and riffled her hair.

CHAPTER 32

Evan stood at the bar in his dimly lit office. "Excuse me," he said peevishly when he realized he had company. "I don't recall requesting a med—" He tensed as Jani stepped forward. "Jan." He offered a weak smile. "Glad to see you're up and about."

Jani let the doc pouch fall to the carpet. Tried to let it fall. The nappy material had stuck to the carrier that had crusted on the end of her stump; she wound up having to rip it away. Cloth parted company from synthetic flesh with a keening rasp. Evan moaned and gripped the edge of the bar with both hands. His eyes squinched shut.

"No one even tried to stop me, Evan. Did you ever get the feeling you were being set up?" She walked to the sitting area near his desk. "Have a seat. Bring your bottle. You may need it."

Evan remained in place for a time, breathing slowly, eyes still closed. When he opened them, he looked at Jani sidelong, sighing when he saw her settled into a chair.

"What did you think I was, Ev, a symptom?"

"No." He gathered up a glass and decanter. "That would have implied good luck. Mine ran out long ago." He sat in the chair across from her and deposited his glassware on a side table. "What's this about a setup?"

"I think certain people wanted me to come here. Tie up loose ends, save them the trouble."

"I hope you listened to the message I sent last night. It's true, you know. I do love you."

"You're a liar."

"You think so? You wouldn't say that if you'd heard the fights

Durian and I had over you. When we figured out you might be alive, he wanted to send someone to Whalen to kill you. I had to bribe him to leave you alone. I promised to wangle him a spot on the ballot in the next general election. Seems he has dreams of a deputy ministry. For starters." His hand shook. Ice rattled like chattering teeth. "I tried to convince him he operated better behind the scenes, but he insisted. I'm afraid exposure to the voting public is going to prove a shock for old Durian." He looked at Jani, taking care to avoid her mangled arm. "I'm hanging my janitor out to dry. That alone should convince you I'm sincere."

"You may have had a sincere moment or two in your life, Evan. I doubt they involved me." Without warning, Jani's left shoulder jerked. A sharp pain sang down her arm, flicked around her wrist, cramped her fingers. "I was just something to shake in your father's face." She looked down at her left thigh. Her left hand rested there. She could feel its weight, its trembling. She just couldn't see it.

"As I recall, you enjoyed upsetting your colony friends with me, as well."

"It doesn't matter." She watched the hand that wasn't there. Gradually, the shuddering eased to an occasional twitch. "It was a long time ago."

"I didn't think you'd trust me right away. I'm not an idiot, Jan." Evan emptied his glass. "I thought after you settled in, got used to things, realized how I felt, you'd see how good you could have it here." He cast a longing look toward the decanter. "Now, here it is, three days later. Plaster's flaking off the ceiling, and knickknacks are clattering on the shelves. The end is near." His eyes grew liquid as tears brimmed. "How much longer do I have?"

"Not long." Jani poked her left thigh with her invisible hand, felt the tiny impacts against her phantom fingertips. "Doyle's set the wheels in motion. She always suspected your complicity in Lyssa's death. She's working for someone else, by the way. Your Virginia. Service plant, maybe. Or else she's thrown in with one of the other Houses."

The comment fired some life back into Evan's face. His jaw firmed; his eyes sharpened. "Which one?"

"Your guess is worth more than mine. I'm surprised your janitor hadn't already flushed that out."

"Where is Durian, by the way? We were supposed to meet fifteen minutes ago." Evan waited for Jani to answer, fidgeted with his glass when she didn't. "I didn't kill Lyssa, Jan. She had evidence of my sins hidden all over the city. She told me if anything happened to her, she had someone in place to insure the evidence would be sent to the right people."

"That person was Betha Concannon." Jani etched figures in the air with her invisible fingers. "Bad choice on her part—Betha worked for Durian. Now Betha's dead." Her hand started to ache from the exercise. She stopped flexing.

"And Durian? He always notifies me when he'll be late. This isn't like him."

"I'm sure there's a reasonable explanation."

"If there is, I'd like to hear it, please."

Jani held both her hands out in front of her. The one she could see felt the same as the one she couldn't. "The alliance with Ulanova changed things with regard to Lyssa. With her aunt's backing, she became dangerous, instead of merely embarrassing." She straightened her left leg, shook the pins-and-needles feeling from her left foot. Funny that life should return to it now, when the rest of her felt so dead. "Do you remember that play they ran at the Consulate the night we met?"

"Jani." Evan watched her flex, then reached for the decanter. "*Becket*," he said as he poured. Liquor splashed against the ice and onto the table. "It was *Becket*."

"*Becket*." Sharp sounds. Jani had to concentrate in order to repeat them without softening them into Vynshàrau. *Mbeheth*. "I remember you liked it. I found it stupid. Man hires his friend to do a job, then gets pissed when said friend actually does it. And now look at us." Her chest felt tight. "Life imitates art." She touched her right arm. Even through the medcoat sleeve, it felt hot, swollen.

Evan leaned toward her. "Are you all right, Jan? Your lips are turning blue."

"I'm fine."

"Your eyes don't look right. There's a shooter graze on your cheek."

"I'm fine."

"Where's Durian?"

"I think I know what happened." Jani stared at Evan until he eased back. "You and Durian were talking. You'd just found out Lyssa had made the connection between your comlog entry and my transport crash. With Ulanova's help, she'd bring you down. After all, it was your big sin. No Acton to blame for this one—it was your call. You could have stopped it and you didn't."

"My father—"

"—was three weeks from Shèrá on the fastest ship he had. You could have handled it. Missed messages. Lost records. Lied. But no.

You wanted to be the hero. The one who pulled the van Reuter nuts out of the fire." Jani hesitated as her heart skipped a beat. In that instant, her breathing eased.

Hey, augie.

Hey, Cap.

"I didn't know you were on that transport." Evan reached out to her. "Riky told me he'd keep you out of it. He promised me—I made him promise when you left the city with him. Then I didn't hear from him anymore. No answer to the messages I sent him, and the ones from my father started coming in one an hour. Always the same. 'Do something, boy—we're depending on you. Act like a van Reuter for once.'" Evan's own breathing grew ragged. "Jani, I was alone. Scared. I'd acted as go-between for Rik and Dad—that made me culpable. Violating the Bilateral Accord was a treasonous offense. I faced prison. Maybe worse. I didn't know what else to do!"

Jani heard a familiar sound filter in from the anteroom. The sizzling crack of a shooter. "I didn't know what else to do, either." One report. Another. Another. *Twenty-six times. Before the dawn I will have fired twenty-six times.*

"They're all dead, Jan. We're still alive." Evan knelt before her, his hands closing over her visible one. "You said you wanted to remember what happened. You can do that here just as well as in prison. If you feel you have to suffer to make it count, trust me, you will. You'll have to bury yourself somewhere in Chicago. I'll have to resign. But I'll know you're here, and we'll be able to get together eventually. After the dust settles."

Jani eased out of Evan's grip. "You knew. All of it. About the patients. About Lyssa. Betha. When you left me that message ordering me to stop my investigation—Durian had just told you he'd killed her, hadn't he?"

"Jan, I didn't mean for any of it to happen."

She caressed the side of his face, ran her thumb over his unshaven cheek. He closed his eyes, rested his head on her knee, didn't even flinch as her hand slipped down around his neck. "I watched a man destroy his face with his bare hands. I helped pull what was left of my corporal from beneath tons of rubble. Evan," she said as he looked up, "there are some things you can't negotiate away."

"Jan—"

She pushed him away. "What was the name of Becket's friend? The king?"

Evan glanced toward the door. "Henry."

"Henry." Jani could feel the heat generated by too many people pressed into the Consulate auditorium, hear the rustle of evening gowns. "The one scene I remember. Henry's with his friends, his knights. His janitors, like Ridgeway was your janitor—"

"What do you mean, 'was'?"

"—and I'm sure you were drunk, like he was. Henry the king, losing his grip—"

"Jani?"

"—looking for someone to blame—"

"No."

"—knowing if she were dead, your problems would be over."

"Please!"

"Will no one rid me of this dam-ned priest." Jani's soft voice rang like a shout in her ears. "Lyssa and Betha. Make that dam-ned *priests*." Or maybe the reverberation was only in her head. "So Ridgeway maneuvered his mops and buckets and rid you of your priests. Ulanova didn't know about the comlog. You were home free." She coughed. Her arm ached again, but it no longer felt hot. Quite the opposite. She shivered.

"Jani?" Evan had slunk back to his chair. "Where is Durian now?"

"I left him in his office."

"Oh. Are you going to leave me in my office, too?"

"No." Jani watched Evan's gaze flick toward the door again. "They want me to kill you, I think. Whoever Ginny works for. Whichever of your colleagues is most fed up with you. But God, I really hate being maneuvered, and I'll be damned if I'll be the tool for another Family bastard." She smiled. "Besides, you knew. And you'll remember, too. That's the one thing we'll always have in common."

Evan swallowed. "We could have more," he said carefully. "We could have everything again—" He shot out of his chair, trying to dart past her to the door. But he moved too slowly, like Ridgeway had. Jani rose, kicked out, caught the side of his knee. The joint cracked with the wet snap of damp wood. He fell to the carpet and lay gasping, thumping the floor with his fist.

She waited until he looked at her with pain-glazed eyes. "I don't want to kill you. I want us both alive when they come. I want you around for a long time. Now I'll have someone to share my ghosts with."

Evan's shallow breathing gradually slowed, deepened. Jani couldn't say the same for her own. Her chest felt heavy. Her left leg cramped. Her right leg was the numb one now. She sat back down, and waited.

"Captain Kilian?"

The voice came from the other side of the door. A man's voice. She didn't recognize it.

"Captain Kilian, I'm going to open the door. I want you to come out here. Please advance slowly and keep your hands where I can see them. That's for your own good as well as mine."

Mine? Did that mean her visitor was alone? Augie tried to rattle Jani's bones in anticipation of a struggle, but she couldn't oblige with the customary battle chill. The only chill she felt left her clammy and numb. Dark patches flecked before her eyes.

"Captain?" The office door hushed open. "Please come out."

She struggled to her feet. With every incremental rise, the dark patches waxed, then waned. As she took her first steps, the room seemed to tilt. She grabbed the chair for support.

"Captain?"

A different voice now. Its source filled the doorway. Tall. Blond. Steel blue uniform wrapped around a steel blue spine. Red tabs on either side of his collar. Matching red wounds on his cheek.

"Lieutenant Pascal," she said.

Lucien fingered his shooter, still encased in the holster at his side. Then he drew to attention and snapped a salute, the sort that made stiff Service polywool crack like a wind-whipped flag on a pole.

Jani touched her forehead in return. "Save it for the A-G, Lieutenant. Allow me what's left of my sideline pride." The floor seemed to shift as though she walked across a deflating pontoon. She turned, found herself within striking distance of another man. Shorter. Stockier. Black hair. Beard trimmed to a sharp point. He offered a courtly bow.

"Dr. Calvin Montoya, Captain." He wore medwhites, carried a large pouch slung over one shoulder, held a large, featureless black cube in his hand. His dark eyes narrowed as he studied her face, then her mangled arm. "I've been charged with seeing you safe."

"Oh." Jani looked from Montoya to the cube, then back. "How is John?"

The point of Montoya's beard twitched. "He's as ever. I'll tell him you inquired. I'm sure he'll be—"

"Surprised?" She looked down at the cube again. "Time for the take-down? Well, Doctor, let's get it over with."

"Yes." Montoya's expression turned relieved. "I think we need to hurry." He held up the cube and fingered one side. Red lights glittered across the face Jani could see. "Watch the lights, Captain. Don't turn away. Concentrate on the sound of my voice and watch the lights." As Montoya continued to murmur directions, a tracery of red, like shooting stars, played across the cube face. Jani found herself tracking the flickering as a flower follows its sun. Her knees weakened.

"Watch the lights, Captain. Don't turn away. Watch—"

Patterns played, each more rapidly. Songs to her brain. Phantom pains shot through limbs destroyed long ago. Around her, flames flashed. Sounds. Yolan's scream as the wall collapsed. Smells. The nose-searing acridity of hyperacid. The stench of burning flesh.

"Come to the light, Captain," said the voice from the other side of the flashing red. "Don't fight it, or you'll feel—"

"Sicker. Yes, I know, Doctor." Jani took a slow step forward. The odor of berries enveloped her, overwhelming her taste and smell, overpowering the stinging smoke. Her vision tunneled, blocking out the flames, the tumble of falling debris.

Only her hearing remained true. The hardiest sense, John had told her. The last sense to die.

See you soon, Captain, Yolan said.

"Yes, Corporal," the Captain replied, as the last flicker of red winked out.

Patient S-1 remained hospitalized and under close observation for a period of four days. Because of extenuating circumstances and the fact the patient displayed her usual remarkable recuperative abilities, she was then released with the understanding that follow-up visits would take place regularly at a facility to be determined.

It is believed the patient can be expected to recover fully and to resume her normal range of activities, such as they are. However, it cannot be stated too strongly that the long-range effects of her condition are not known at this time.

—Internal Communication, Neoclona/Seattle,
Shroud, J., Parini, V., concerning Patient S-I

Aftermath

CHAPTER 33

Jani opened her eyes. The view was white and brightly lit. The air felt cool and carried the characteristic odor she had long ago dubbed hospital-metallic. She took a deep breath and stretched her arms. Both of them. One was phantom. The real one was encased from wrist to shoulder in a membrane bandage filled with clear allerjel. Jani shook it. The jelly sloshed.

When she tired of that, she sat up, wedged her pillow behind the small of her back for balance, and studied the watercolors hung on the wall opposite her bed. One was a seascape in greys and greens, the other, a gold-and-brown still life. Jani had spent most of the past few days picking out details in the paintings, little nuances she'd missed during previous examinations. If she concentrated hard enough on the exercise, she could almost forget certain things. Why she was in hospital, for example, and what had happened to put her there.

And more immediately, what lay beneath her covers. Or rather, what didn't.

Jani carefully ignored the telltale flatness of her bedspread. As long as she didn't look, she could pretend her left leg was still there. She could feel it, after all, like the missing arm. Funny how its absence bothered her more. *It's the vulnerability,* she thought, in a rare attempt at self-analysis. *You can still run with one arm.*

But run from whom? Calvin Montoya had been her only visitor thus far. He checked in on her five or six times a day, examining her with sure, gentle hands, a joke or a piece of gossip always at the ready.

The details of what had occurred at Interior Main, however, she'd had to pull from him with pliers.

The doctor and nurse from the Interior infirmary were still alive. Their encounter with Jani and the IV rack had netted them two concussions and one skull fracture. And three-month suspensions without pay for not notifying Montoya immediately of their singular patient. *They were arguing about me and looking things up in textbooks.* Her right film must have broken while she was unconscious; they'd probably seen her eye. One glimpse of that pale green orb would certainly be enough to drive any medico to the reference materials.

Her left calf itched. She tried to ignore it.

I did lots of damage that night. Evan's knee would never be the same. After suffering torn ligaments and a dislocated kneecap, his evening went rapidly downhill. The Justice Minister himself placed him under arrest. The warrant was served upon Evan in his well-guarded hospital suite, with Cao and Ulanova serving as the Greek chorus. All the major networks had been invited to record the unprecedented event.

Calvin had brought Jani a copy of the local CapNet broadcast. The wafer still lay atop her holoVee console, its seal unbroken.

She stared at the seascape. Contained by a pewter frame as shiny as summer, sunlight played on gentle waves. How often on Shèrá had Evan told her about his sailing adventures on the Earthbound lakes? His expression had always grown melancholy as he spoke; those were the only times she could recall him appearing at all homesick. *Are they letting you have a drink, Ev? Are they letting you have anything else?* Montoya had seemed worried. He had heard rumors of a suicide watch.

Jani twirled a corner of her blanket and switched her attention to the still life. A tasteful piece, nothing exceptional. Something Ulanova would hang in her dining room.

I can imagine the conversations ringing around that table. The gloating comments, the laughter. *Revenge is a dish best savored cold, to be served with the appetizers and the iced cocktails.* To those with the stomach for it.

Leaves me out—I don't have the stomach for much, anymore. Lucien had tried to visit her several times, but she refused to see him and rejected his bouquets of flowers. Ate without appetite when she ate at all. Ignored the holoVee and stacks of magazines and newssheets.

Montoya managed to hide his frustration beneath a cloak of humor and delicate prodding. *He threatened to toss me out into a snowdrift last night.* During this morning's examination, he assured her he'd push the skimchair himself if she'd just agree to a jaunt up and down the hall.

Jani's refusal had plunged him into watchful silence. His examination took a good deal longer than usual. He withheld his usual inquiries, but he also drew more blood and took more swab samples. The only time he spoke was when he announced what he was going to do, inviting her questions. Her response that he should just take it all and get it over with jolted him. As he left, Jani had heard the doorbolt slide into place.

So she'd slept for a few hours, studied the ceiling, slept some more, studied her paintings.

The door eased open, and a cautious Montoya poked his head into the room. "Ah, Jani. You're awake." He entered, pulling a wheeled trolley. A large black plastic bag rested on the trolley's top shelf. "If this doesn't get you out of that bed, I'm going to fill your membrane bandage with detonator gel and whack it with a hammer." He patted the plastic bag like a proud father. "Your new limbs are here."

Jani sat up straighter. "Already?"

"At Neoclona, we aim to please," Montoya said breezily, emboldened by her interest. "Get ready, milady," he said as he opened the door of an inset wall cabinet. "I intend to have you walking within the hour."

Jani kept her attention focused on the plastic bag. "I've only been here four days."

"Yes?"

"A standard arm takes a week to assemble. A leg takes at least two."

"Under normal conditions, that's certainly true." Montoya approached her bedside carrying a small metal tray on which instruments rattled. "But in your case, some preparations had already been made."

"How?" Jani swallowed as the doctor placed the tray on her end table. Several long, pointed probes glistened in the light. "Why?"

Montoya activated one of the probes, pulled down the left shoulder of Jani's medgown, and began prodding the smooth, shooter-burned membrane that served as the interface between her animandroid arm and the rest of her. "Once one reaches a certain level in Neoclona, your file becomes required reading." He worked around the outer rim of the junction, searching for dead spots. "The wise facility chief knows to be prepared."

Jani tried in vain to keep from flinching as needling tingles radiated throughout the hypersensitive junction. "What are you telling me?" she asked through gritted teeth. "That every Neo shop in the Commonwealth has a set of left-siders with my name on it sitting in a cold drawer?"

Montoya adjusted the shoulder of her gown and pulled up a corner of the hem. "I'm going to check the thigh junction now."

"You didn't answer my question." Jani grabbed a fistful of sheet and found a riveting light fixture on the wall opposite to focus on.

"The answer should be obvious, Jani," Montoya said as he probed, "to you more than anyone." After eliciting a couple of bearable twinges, he pronounced both junctions functional. Jani rearranged her gown as best she could while maintaining her shaky balance. Meanwhile, Montoya opened another of the room's recessed cabinets and rolled out a tall, silver monolith.

Jani watched him activate touchpads and enter codes. The limb sealer came to life with a characteristic hum. "Why replacements? Why not just fix the old ones?"

"Coming back to ourselves, are we?" The physician smiled absently, his attention focused on the instrument. "So many questions."

"And so few answers." Jani's stomach hadn't ached at all up to that point. She only noticed it in contrast. Now, it hurt like hell. "Why replace what you can fix?"

As Montoya pushed the limb sealer over to the bed, two disc covers on the instrument face slid open, revealing twin depressions. The upper one was small and green, the lower one large and dark blue. They looked like a pair of misshapen eyes.

"The reason for the new arm should be obvious. As for the leg—" Montoya hesitated. "I believe you'll find your back problems will be a distant memory once it's attached." He bumped the sealer up against the bed. The frame resonated in time to the sealer's vibration. Jani could feel the humming buzz in her teeth. "We'll do the arm first, I think. Then you'll have more leverage when we do the leg. Push your junction against the green."

Jani lowered the shoulder of her gown and pressed her stump into the shallow saucer. Tingling pressure radiated across her upper back as the disc membrane closed around the junction.

"You're implying the leg wasn't balanced. I had no problem with it for over seventeen years. My back just started acting up in the last six months."

Montoya disappeared behind the sealer. Jani heard his footsteps, followed by the whine of a zipper, a *pop*, and a rush of air as he removed the arm from its vacuum casing. "We change as we get older, Jani. Our bone density, muscle mass. Your animandroid limbs were older models in the first place—they stood no chance of keeping up the pace. In a more conventional environment, you'd have had them changed out three or four times by now." The sealer vibration ramped. "Press against the saucer," he said, peeking around the unit at Jani. "Hold your breath on three. Ready? One. Two. Three."

Jani pushed, inhaled. She felt a burning as the junction sintered, then split down the middle, exposing her shoulder joint. She felt as well as heard the soft click as new bone met old. Then came warmth as synthon lubricant flowed through the junction and into the joint, followed by the suction smack as tissue met bioadhesive.

"Looks good. Pull out, please."

Jani eased her new arm through the newly opened gap in the saucer. She rolled her shoulder, bent her elbow, counted off on her fingers to check—"*Hey*!"

Montoya poked his head around the sealer, which he appeared to be using as a shield. "Is something wrong?"

Jani winced as she pressed fingernails into fingertips. "I can feel with these."

"Of course."

"I couldn't before."

"An adjustment long overdue, don't you think?" The dark head again disappeared. "I'm going to call in someone to help with the leg." He left the room, returning soon with a burly nurse in tow.

This bout with the sealer proved clumsier, not to mention more painful. Tears blurred Jani's vision as she made a circuit of the room under Montoya's watchful eye. She muttered a prayer of thanks to whoever had had the presence of mind to slip a pair of underpants beneath the gaping medgown. "You're right, Doctor. My back does feel better." She hopped up and down a few times. "I didn't realize people could change so much at the ripe old age of forty-two."

The nurse glanced sidelong at Montoya, then excused himself with a curt nod. Once they were alone, Montoya pulled out a lazor and cut away the allerjel packing from Jani's right arm. As she washed away the gooey remains of the soothing jelly, he scrounged a set of medwhites and a pair of lab shoes.

"Hungry, Jani? Allow me to buy you a very late lunch." He handed her the clothes. "I'm getting you out of this damned room if it's the last thing I do." His dark eyes danced. "As reward, I'll tell you the exciting tale of how you got here in the first place."

"We escaped Interior Main a heartbeat ahead of Ulanova's people." Montoya forked through a tomato-sauced omelet, with occasional stabs at a green salad. "Your blond friend, that lieutenant, knew whom to look out for, which areas to avoid. He and the young red-haired man—"

Jani choked on her soup. "Steve! I told him to stay in Private."

"Well, he obviously didn't listen. He and Pascal bundled you onto a skimdolly he had purloined from the loading dock. Much bickering went on during this time. I gather Pascal found Steve wandering the Main halls in a furtive manner and set upon him. Steve had a black eye—"

"Why the hell did Lucien hit him!"

"—which went nicely with Pascal's air of 'last one standing.' They declared a truce when they realized your welfare was at stake, but it was shaky at best." Montoya dabbed a few beads of sweat from his brow. "I discovered during that time I wasn't cut out for excitement."

"I couldn't have been too exciting," Jani said. "All an augie does after a take-down is sleep and toss around a lot."

Montoya grimaced. "Your augment was the only thing keeping you alive. After I took you down, you began to slip into anaphylactic shock. Your blood pressure went into the basement—" He stabbed his fork at her like a fencing foil. "Those two morons knew that goddamn sedative patch was contraindicated in your case, and they used it anyway! Three-month suspensions—if they think it ends there, they're in for a grim surprise. Even *with* your augment, you could have died in that infirmary. The fact that you went on to do what you did . . ." He faltered and took it out on his salad, stabbing the vegetables into mashed submission.

Jani studied the view over Montoya's shoulder. The small dining hall was empty except for the two of them. Purple in all its shades dominated the color scheme, from tinged white walls to lilac grey floor and nearly black furniture. The funereal surroundings turned the mind to things best forgotten. "I killed Durian Ridgeway," she said quietly.

"Did you?" Montoya's chewing slowed. He set down his fork and pushed aside his half-eaten meal. "Pascal's skimmer was parked outside the docks. It was too small for the four of us. The situation became even more interesting when a hyperactive bundle of winter clothing bounded out to us yelling, 'Steve, Steve,' in a singularly feminine tone. Pascal pulled out his shooter, which caused Steve to spring for his throat like a cat. At that point, your blood pressure took another dive and the bundle started screaming that Exterior Security was hot on her trail." Montoya exhaled with a shudder. "Amazing how we suddenly all managed to fit into Pascal's vehicle. He took us as far as the boundary between Exterior and the Shèrá Embassy. I'm still trying to assimilate what happened next. *Tsecha* was waiting for us outside an Exterior guardpost. The idomeni ambassador."

Jani pushed her plate aside. The little she had eaten froze in her stomach. "Tsecha?"

Montoya nodded. "He drove us here. In an Exterior skimmer Pascal took great pleasure in telling us the ambassador had stolen. He wore eyefilms. Makeup. And an evening suit. Pascal treated this like it was the most normal thing in the world. Steve and his bundle, a young woman named Angevin, blinked perhaps twice, then piled you into the backseat of the ambassador's skimmer and shouted for me to, and I quote, 'hurry the fuck up.' " He sighed. "So I did."

He knows I'm alive. Did she ever really doubt he'd discover the fact? What had he told her on the Academy steps, when she handed him back his ring and told him she had every intention of remaining human until she died.

You will never die, nìa.

"Well," she said.

"Indeed." Montoya nodded absently. "Tsecha is a proponent of what he calls evading. He evaded us down side streets and alleys I never knew existed, and I've lived here all my life. We took corners at complete verticals. I yelled that if he didn't slow down, I was going to tear his head off. I couldn't keep you still enough to intubate you. Time was running out. Your throat was swelling shut. The shockpack alarm was blaring."

Jani eyed the entry. *He wouldn't come here, would he?* Risk his Temple's wrath and the Commonwealth's anger by calling upon a murderer. *Of course he would—he thinks killing is just something I do*. Part of the job description. Eyes and Ears . . . destroyer of diplomatic relations . . . toxin. . . .

Montoya rattled on, a captive in his own recollective jet stream. "He just smiled, if you can call what he does a smile, and told me, 'Ah, Doctor, you know my Captain will outlive us all.' I commented that that could be by a grand total of five seconds if we slammed into the side of a building. He then slowed down just long enough for me to reinsert and anchor the endotracheal tube." He bit his well-buffed fingernails one at a time. Just a nip here and there, an old broken habit undergoing spontaneous reassembly.

"So you were getting air. Thank God. We were being pursued, you know, until Tsecha started *evading*. The lieutenant had drawn his shooter, and the ambassador . . . he was armed, as well. A shooter in a chest holster. Knives up both sleeves."

Jani's throat felt dry and tight. "He would have used them, too." She stole a sip of water from Montoya's glass. "Idomeni martial order broke down after Knevçet Shèràa. Self-protection became the order of the day, even for those who had never had to think about it before. Nema always adapted quickly to change."

"Nema?" Montoya's eyebrows arched. "Oh, Tsecha's born name."

"He changed it after the war ended. Then he went into seclusion in his Temple enclave for five of our years." Jani's gaze kept veering toward the cafeteria entry. "And with all they knew about his beliefs, they still let him out of his cage."

Montoya nodded. "I've heard about those beliefs. That someday, the human and idomeni races will be as one." He played with his fork. "Did you feel the same way when you studied with him? Did you buy what he sold the way Hansen Wyle did?"

The sudden sharpening of Calvin Montoya's voice didn't surprise Jani. Anyone who had won John Shroud's confidence couldn't have been as ingenuous as he first appeared. "Hansen believed. But I think he enjoyed the thrill of it all, too. He liked flipping it off in people's faces."

"He died in an air raid a few hours before he was going to try to negotiate you away from my boss." Montoya smoothed away a ragged nail edge. "Seems to me our alien ambassador isn't the only one capable of making associates ignore their better judgment." He eyed her pointedly. "Let's get out of here," he said, gesturing toward a fluted paper cup nestled beside her soup bowl. "Take those. Chew and swallow them."

"Why?" Jani sniffed the dark brown tablets. They smelled like chocolate fudge made with sour cream. "What are they?"

"Enzyme tablets. They'll help you digest your food."

"What's wrong with my digestion?"

"It needs help."

"Why?"

"There's no time, Jani. Just trust that it's for your own good."

"I've heard that before." Jani chewed dutifully, chasing the bitter, gritty mass down with a swallow of water. "John's favorite line. Whatever happened next either hurt like hell or made me sick." The increased sensation in her left leg still jarred her, and she half walked, half hopped as she followed Montoya out of the dining hall.

It didn't surprise her that Lucien Pascal waited for them near the nurses' station, or that he carried her duffel as though he owned it. He looked tired; thin lines of scabs dotted one cheek. He offered her a cool nod, then turned to Montoya. "Think she's up to it?"

Montoya's nails again found their way to his mouth. "No. But it would be no next week as well. No right into next month, but we don't have the time, do we?" Muttering curses in Earthbound Spanish, Montoya ducked behind the nurses' station.

"You're not ready," he said as he emerged carrying a small polyfilm bag. "There's too much that needs to be talked about. Too much left up in the air. But I've been ordered to let you go anyway." He thrust the bag into Jani's hands. "The directions are in with the tablets. When you run out, stop at any facility. You have nothing to worry about, Jani. You're being seen to. If you don't trust anything I've told you, trust that." He squeezed her hand, glared at Lucien, then strode down the hall without a backward glance.

Jani turned to Lucien. "What's going on?"

He pantomimed an explosion. "All hell's broken loose." He gestured for her to follow and walked to a side door labeled, EMERGENCY EXIT ONLY. "We need to get you through as many GateWays as possible as soon as possible," he said as he ushered her though the door. "But before that, there's someone who wants to see you."

CHAPTER 34

"Where are you taking me?" Jani lagged behind Lucien as he led her through the garage. She swore under her breath as she searched for an escape route.

"My skim's charging. I'm just behind that," he said as he pointed to the silver-and-purple ambulance that jutted through a low arch like a metallic tongue. "I hope to hell I can pull around."

"*Where are you taking me!*" Jani's voice bounced off the cement walls. Her eyes teared freely, both junctions ached, the drying skin of her right arm tingled and itched, and Dr. Montoya's enzyme tablets had left a sickening metallic taste in her mouth. Oh, and there was the fear. Fear did wonders in countering take-down malaise. Jani planted in the middle of the garage, her hands curled into fists. "I'm not budging until you tell me where we're going."

Lucien turned back to her, his handsome face a study in angel innocence, his hand resting possessively on her duffel. "We're going over there," he said.

Jani squinted in the direction he pointed, trying to pick out details in the dark. A battered sedan nestled in a charge station, but the flow monitor atop the station's housing shone blue, indicating the vehicle's cell array was already fully charged.

Dark red. The vehicle's color was dark red. An old Exterior skimmer. Jani's stomach roiled as the driver's side gullwing popped up.

"I tried to talk him into stepping up to a better class of vehicle," Lucien said, "but he seems to have taken a shine to that old wreck, color and all."

Nema emerged from the vehicle like poured syrup and stepped

into the light. He had left his humanish evening suit behind, opting for the Vynshàrau clothing of an elder male of his skein and station. Full-sleeved, off-white shirt tucked into loose, light brown trousers. Dark brown knee-high boots. Wide bands of scarlet hemmed the edges of his cream over-robe. His thin, silver brown hair had been gathered into a single braid and looped like an oversize earring on the right side of his head.

"My Captain," he said in English, his High Vynshàrau accent softening the hard sounds. "I thought I would need Albino John's help to identify you, but to my joy I find you most as yourself. Glories of the day to you." He bared his teeth fully, an expression of highest regard. His bony face seemed to split, gold eyes opening wide. Grim Death with a Deal for You.

"NìRau ti nìRau." Jani stood up straight despite the stinging pain in her thigh junction and crossed her left arm over her chest, palm twisted outward. She tilted her head to the left. Nodded once. Thank God for the mechanics. If you could concentrate on the mechanics, you could block out everything else. She glanced to the side and saw Lucien watching her like an anthro student on his first field trip. "Push off," she said.

"I don't think so."

"Go, Lucien," Nema said. "I wish it as well."

"No, nìRau. I have my orders."

"Which were to guard. So guard out there." He gestured sharply toward the garage's entrance. "There is no need for guards here." He looked Jani in the eye and bared his teeth again. "My nìa and I are most safe with one another, and together, we win against all."

Lucien took a step in Nema's direction, ready to argue. But when Nema refused to look at him, he turned on his heel and strode out of the garage.

Jani waited until the echo of his footsteps died away. "You've hurt his feelings," she said in semiformal High Vynshàrau, etching fluid symbols in her air with her right hand. Her gestures accentuated the humiliation of a suborn cruelly mistreated by his dominant. "He is new to the ways of Vynshàrau, and he is not predictable. He might do something to hurt you in return."

"Perhaps," Nema replied, the angle of his head implying tentative agreement, "but then he will find I am not so predictable as well." He shook his head, humanish urgency leaching into his speech and gestures. "There is no time for him. Ulanova searches for you, nìa! She knows you are here in this damned cold city!"

"She wants to see me court-martialed that badly?" Jani glanced toward the garage entrance. She trusted Lucien. In this particular instance. Really. She just wished she'd had the presence of mind to ask him for her duffel.

Nema flicked his left hand in affirmation. "Eventually, I am most sure. My injured Lucien believes she first would force you to testify in Cabinet Court against van Reuter. The trial would be broadcast throughout the Commonwealth. Such a triumph for my Anais." His brow wrinkled in bafflement. "She hates van Reuter so. Lucien tried to explain it to me, but I could not understand. Things to do with business and your ways of marriage, among so many other stupid things. Such ridiculous disorder, inappropriate for dominants of their levels, and truly." He sighed. "So much I do not understand, and no one is to be left to me to explain." He looked Jani in the face and his posture grew somber. "Step closer to me, nìa, so I can see you."

Jani edged nearer, fighting down the urge to bolt back inside the hospital. When Nema grasped her chin and tilted it upward, her eyes stung and her throat ached.

"You have not changed, nìa."

"I look completely different to humanish."

"Humanish only look at the face. I see the gestures and hear the voice of one who is most as she was." Nema's amber eyes glittered like molten metal as he studied her. "I would have spoken with you in your hospital, after your damned transport explosion, but John would not let me. He hid you away, when I could have sheltered you better. He behaved in a most stupid manner."

"He had his reasons, nìRau."

"Yes, stupid humanish reasons. Did you choose him freely?"

"Yes. No." Jani pulled Nema's hand away from her chin. "I thought he'd turn me over to the military police if I didn't. By the time I realized he never would have done that, it was too late. The Haàrin had entered the city, the humanish were fleeing—"

"And he, your physician, did not see you safe!"

"I never gave him the chance, nìRau."

Nema took a step back from her, touching the side of his face in a way Jani couldn't interpret. For the first time she could recall, her teacher appeared at a loss for words. "You must go soon," he finally said in English, his speech stripped of gesture. "Lucien has found a ship which will take you as far as Felix. I do not know how he found it. He tried to explain it to me, but I could not understand! It is not as it was with you. My Eyes and Ears. When you saw and heard, it was as if I myself saw and heard."

"You had Hansen."

"Hansen was Hansen. He taught me games—he was not you. And now I have found you after so much time, and you must run again."

Jani took a deep breath. "I killed, nìRau."

"Yes." Nema tucked his hands into his sleeves. "You killed. In that way, as well, you are most as you were."

"I did what I did."

"Yes, nìa. We all do what we do."

She stared into her teacher's eyes, felt adrift in a sea of gold. "I'd do it again."

"Yes. Your own did not know you for what you are. The Laumrau believed your own, and see how they paid." Nema's attitude grew distant, as though he questioned her for an exam. "You have recovered from your injuries most rapidly, I understand?"

Jani nodded, addled by his presence and the abrupt change in subject. "Yes, nìRau?"

"Your Dr. Mon-toy-a, he is confused. Albino John is not so confused, I think."

"I wouldn't know, but—"

"And you, nìa, are not confused at all."

"We're not at Academy anymore, nìRau. We don't have time for philosophies."

Tsecha gestured sadly. "No, you are most right, nìa. The time for philosophies has passed us both." He fell silent, staring at her impassively. Then he pulled his hand from his sleeve. Held the closed fist out to her. Opened it. "Now is the time for realities."

Her Academy ring rested within. The jasperite glinted like the eye of a night creature.

"*Inshah,*" Jani said, addressing Nema with the informal High word for teacher, "you're wrong."

"Wrong?" Nema's brow wrinkled as he considered the concept.

"I'm not the one you want. Hansen would have been, maybe, but not me. I'm too disorderly."

Tsecha nodded, gesturing in strong affirmation. "You are toxin, Captain. You bring pain and change. Such is your way. You know no other." He reached for her right hand and placed the ring on her third finger. It was still too small—metal scraped over skin as he forced it into place. "Still some time yet, I think. But soon. Soon."

"I'm not your heir, nìRau. You've made a mistake." Jani sensed motion out of the corner of her eye and turned to find Lucien standing in the garage entry. He tapped his timepiece. "I have to go," she said.

Nema looked at Lucien and sighed. "Yes." He turned back to Jani and stood straighter. "But someday, when you have not killed for a time, you will come back to me. Then we can argue your suitability." His lips curved. It wasn't an idomeni expression of goodwill—he didn't bare his teeth a millimeter, or even cock his head. It was a humanish smile, the smile of someone who knew better. "*a lète onae vèste, Kièrshiarauta,*" he said as he gestured farewell to her, left hand extended, palm facing up. A farewell to an equal. Then he slipped back into his skimmer. The vehicle came to life with a smooth hum, then flitted away from its station and out of the garage like a bedraggled bat.

It took Jani a moment to realize she was shaking.

Lucien drew up beside her and handed her her duffel. "He drives like a maniac," he said, still smarting from his abrupt dismissal. "Not much for good-byes, either."

"No," Jani agreed, "none of the Vynshàrau are. They each live in their own little world. Nema figures if he likes you, you'll come to him again, and if he doesn't, why should he care?" She tried to fluff her pillow-mashed hair, then tugged at her medwhites in distaste. "Trade ya clothes," she said, eyeing Lucien's warm polywools with envy.

"I've got some for you in the skimmer." He headed toward his charge slot. "We better get going—your shuttle leaves in an hour."

Jani fell in quietly behind Lucien, noting with interest that he now drove a stolid blue sedan. "New skim?" she asked, as they drifted sedately into busy late-afternoon traffic.

"It does what it has to. It's also less conspicuous and loaded with antitracking." Lucien frowned at Jani as he maneuvered between lanes. "Yes, I had to give the other one back to Anais. Happy?" He reached behind her seat. "Here," he said, tossing a bundle of clothes in her lap.

"Who sideswiped your face?" Jani asked as she pulled a heavy shirt over the medwhite top. Service surplus winter-weight fatigues, baggy and dark blue. Her kind of clothes. "Anais or Claire?"

Lucien touched his injured cheek. "None of your business."

"Be that way. Are we going to O'Hare?"

"No. A private port." He unsnapped the top of his shooter holster as he eyed the traffic flowing around them.

Jani tugged on her heavy trousers. "How are Steve and Angevin?"

"Forell was locked up for a day and a half. Unfortunately, they found the code. Ange rousted some of her dad's old Academy chums. Your old chums as well, I suppose. They twisted arms. You could hear the sockets pop all down Cabinet Row."

"I would liked to have seen them before I left."

"Not an option. I'll tell them good-bye for you." Without warning, Lucien cut across five lanes of traffic and shot down an exit ramp. Jani took a few deep breaths to slow her heart, but kept her comments to herself. She knew the difference between reckless and evasive driving.

"Montoya told me you ignored the news," he said as he maneuvered down a side road. "No mention of Betha. Lyssa's death is still considered an accident." He paused. "Ridgeway's death has been ruled a suicide."

"I broke his neck," Jani said as she pulled off the med-shoes. "Wonder how the medical examiner explained that?"

Lucien shrugged. "It's Chicago. Precedent exists." He nodded toward the bag, which he'd tossed on the floor at Jani's feet. "Your boots are in your duffel." He stared at the side of her face until she gave in and looked at him. "I don't know why you should feel bad," he said. "He would have killed you."

"It's just post take-down." Jani stared out the window at the passing scenery. "Look, I do what I have to. It doesn't mean it doesn't affect me." She took a deep breath and opened her duffel. "Ah shit." She picked at the ragged-edged remains of her scanproof compartment.

"Sorry about that," Lucien said. "By the time I got my hands on it, Doyle had already torn it apart. I was able to sweep your room at Private before her people got there, though. Hope I got everything you need."

Jani thumbed through the bag's contents. Her boots. Two sets of coveralls. Underwear. Scanpack. Tools and parts. Her shooter, fully charged and polished. The tiny soldier saluted her from an inside pocket, where he stood guard over a static pouch containing an ID and cashcards.

She probed deeper. Her hand closed around the holocard. She studied it in the half-light of the cabin, tilted it back and forth. The racers swooped and glided, surfing the wind. She looked at Lucien out of the corner of her eye. Lucien the manipulator, who could always be counted on to keep his head. The frosty operator. The beautiful young man with the dead eyes. And a cheek that had been a scratched mess four days before, but was almost healed now. She touched her own shooter graze, mended to barest visibility. "You gave me this card for a reason. For a while, I thought it was your oblique way of telling me Lyssa was an augie. But that wasn't it, was it? You were letting me know. You're an augie, too." She waited until he answered with a scarcely perceptible nod. "When did you have it done?"

He touched the back of his neck, where bottom of skull met top of spine. "About ten years ago. It was my fifteenth birthday present from Anais."

"Is it like mine?"

"Not entirely. It's an improved version of the one Martin had. By then, they'd learned it was better to wait." He turned down a narrower road. In the distance, shuttleport lights blazed against the darkening sky. "I don't know if I'd be any different without it. Like they say, it only augments what's already there. Or in my case, what isn't." He bypassed the small charge lot, parking the skimmer at the edge of the tarmac next to a large baggage trolley. "Let's get a move on."

After a week of frigid cold, a comparative heat wave had settled over the city, making coldsuits and face shields unnecessary. Jani found the double layer of polycotton she wore adequate to keep her warm. She lagged behind Lucien, who broke into a trot as he neared a line of shuttles going through their preflight inspections. A serious-looking older woman in an olive green flight suit, pilot's headset dangling from her neck, walked out to meet him.

Jani circled the woman's ship. Late-model commercial shuttle. Sleek. Well maintained. Even the most suspicious Customs agent would think twice before searching it. It reeked of paid-up docking fees and clean inspection records. Therein lay the problem. *I can't afford to go anyplace you could take me*. Jani reached up to stroke the shuttle's smooth underside. *And anyplace I want to go, you'd stand out like a boil.*

She left Lucien and the pilot as they began the preflight walkaround and set off on her own inspection. She passed along the short line of shuttles, looking for signs of gold striping on the right side of the entry door. Customs' scarlet letter, a sign to all that dockscan had turned up something suspicious and you'd been boarded and searched. Most ships sported at least one such badge of infamy. Law of averages dictated you'd get nailed at least once if you flew long enough. Two or three meant bad luck or a lousy ship's clerk. More than that meant stupidity or bloody-mindedness.

No stripes, however, could mean one of two things. It could mean the ship was brand-new, too young to have a record with Customs. Case in point, Lucien's ship.

Or it could mean the ship had changed hands recently. New owner meant a clean bill of regulatory health for the vessel involved. New owner could mean someone anxious to keep it that way. Someone unfamiliar with the law of averages.

Jani stopped before the first vessel she came to that had no stripe.

A few reentry blisters marred the polycoat skin—other than that, it appeared in good shape. A serviceable shuttle. Older model. "Hello," she said to the pilot, who was in the midst of his own walkaround.

The man looked up from his recording board. A serviceable face. Older model. "What do you want?"

"Nothing." Jani smiled. "Just stretching my legs." She sidled up to him, peeking over his shoulder at the board display. Standard preflight checklist. She spotted three coding mistakes in the first four entries. Nothing that would interfere with the actual piloting of the vessel, of course. But Treasury Customs didn't give a rat's furry ass whether a pilot could hit his mark on an ocean float blindfolded. If that pilot could not fill out his forms properly, that pilot would live to regret the oversight.

The man tensed when he realized he was being watched. "Is there a problem, ma'am?"

Jani shrugged, backed off. Kept smiling. "Just checking out your coding."

The man's Adam's apple bobbled. "What's wrong with my coding?"

Jani pointed to the first entry. "You've entered takeoff data on a docking line. When the board tries to calculate your flight stats, you'll get an error message."

"So I'll just erase and reenter."

"If you don't code the deletion, it won't recognize your erasure." She took the board out of his hands. "You need to give it a reason, so that when you download the data to Luna dockscan, it will read 'entry error, deletion because of such and such, reentry.' Otherwise, it just sees an unexplained mistake. Being a Cabinet system, it thinks, sloppiness. Then it thinks, sloppy incompetent or sloppy on purpose? Then it calls a human." She activated the stylus and enacted the change. "A Customs docking inspection is a hell of a way to start the day."

"It's just a mistake." The pilot watched Jani make rapid multistep entries without a hitch. "You know this stuff, huh?" He rubbed his chin. "Have a look at the rest of it, if you don't mind."

It was so easy, Jani at first suspected a sting, a crackdown on non-Registry clerks. The manifest, however, proved to contain the sorts of convoluted, ingenious errors usually executed by someone who knew just enough to be dangerous. The look on her face must have alarmed the pilot. He started to say something as she handed the board back, but she cut him off with a headshake and an absent "G'night." She turned, started to walk away, counted. *One. Two. Three. Do you want—?*

"Do you want a job?"

Jani stopped, turned back, pretended not to understand.

"Only if you need one, of course. But if you don't, you know, I'd pay for your time. I can get you back here tomorrow. If you need to get back." He stuck out his hand. "My name's Zal." He approached gingerly, his face reddening. Obviously not the type to solicit strange women in shuttle-ports, but honest working-class fear had made him desperate. "Take you to Luna. Or farther. I'm starting a new transport business with my brother. He's handling the registration up there." He waved in the general direction of Earth's only natural moon. "We sure could use the help, though. Someone who knows how to fill out all these blasted forms."

The deal was cut quickly. Zal had been too relieved at the thought of handing off clerical duty to ask Jani her name, which was fine with her. It would give her time to think of one.

The stripped-down interior of this shuttle couldn't compare with the one in which she'd arrived a little over a week before. She strapped herself into her seat, stuffed her duffel into the grapple rack beneath, then started plowing through the manifest revisions. As the low powers rumbled to life and the shuttle taxied toward the runway, she twisted in her seat to look out the port. Lucien and his pilot had split up and were darting from vessel to vessel, accosting everyone they saw. Then the shuttle turned, and they disappeared from view. Within minutes, takeoff acceleration drove Jani into her seat.

"Sorry, Lucien. I just don't like being herded." She felt a pang of guilt that she hadn't said a proper good-bye after all he had done for her, but it soon passed. She liked him. Therefore, they would find one another again. She could adopt Nema's attitude, use it to keep her warm tonight.

Her old teacher's gift glinted in the cabin light as she wrote. Jani glanced out the port again as the shuttle banked over Chicago on the way to its exit corridor. It struck her how the ring's glittering red stone mimicked the lights of the city below. And foretold the lights of the cities to come. Wherever they were.

EPILOGUE

The stylus moved across the blank parchment. Beneath the moving tip of the writing instrument, the curves and whorls of High Vynshàrau appeared as though demon-written.

It is only science, Tsecha thought as he read his words, reconsidered, and made changes. Pro-dye impregnation. Ultraviolet light. Delocalization of electrons. So dull, such lucid explanation. He preferred to believe the words appeared on the paper's surface by magic, the work of demons.

His Temple and his Oligarch, if they could have read what he wrote, would no doubt have agreed.

> *. . . for humanish ways are not so different from ours. A piece of clothing. A color of eye. An intonation. Such are all that separate us.*

He frowned, stylus poised above the newly inscribed phrases. So obvious, the ideas. Did he really need to explain such?

"Steven is beyond this." He sat back in his favored chair, allowed it to stab him in the usual places, and meditated on the stark simplicity of his room. Yes, his Mr. Forell had come along quite quickly. But then, so eager had he been to learn. He had petitioned Tsecha personally for instruction in Vynshàrau document systems, saying he could not hope to further his Interior career without such specialized knowledge. Of course, Tsecha had not believed him. Not when he pulled Angevin into the meeting room after him like a reluctant youngish, and demanded Tsecha tell him the story of his Captain.

Yes, Steven had proved most seemly. So open to new thoughts. Almost as though Hansen had fathered *him*, and not Angevin. . . .

"I will not ask." Tsecha contemplated a carved bloom that rested in a wall niche opposite his desk. Humanish were sensitive to questions of parentage, and he did not wish to test his Steven's loyalty so soon. Not to mention his Angevin's temper. Best some things be left between the lines, for now.

This I know as fact, from experience. As always, I only write that which is already known, simply unacknowledged.

Instruction, at times, proved challenging. "Steven accepts as Hansen did, while Angevin fights . . ." Tsecha bared his teeth. "She fights as my Captain does." His Captain, who could read his writings as well as her born tongue, and who understood their meanings all too well. Where was she now? Lucien offered his guesses, of course. Such was his way, to never admit to not knowing. But he had misplaced her at the shuttleport, and his weeks of futile searching had left him morose and prone to sarcasm.

"My Captain is quite skilled at being misplaced, and truly." First by John Shroud, then by Anais Ulanova, and now by the odd lieutenant. How wondrous to be so unknown to so many. To be able to evade so well.

She can never be captured. She will live on, and lead on, into a time so different than this. This, too, is known but unacknowledged, for fear of the future prevents its recognition. This, of all manners, is the one of humanish adopted by idomeni. This is foolish, as I have written before. As I will write again. Until it, as my dead Hansen used to say, "sinks in."

Tsecha continued to trace stylus over parchment. In another room, much as this one, he had written such essays for two other humanish, instructing them how the universe would change. *So it began then*. So would it continue now. Until all would be revealed. One page at a time.

Rules of Conflict

In loving memory of Prince,
the best puppy in town

CHAPTER 1

"Name?"

Jani Kilian shifted her attention from her aching stomach to the admissions clerk who held her MedRec card by the corner like a dirty dispo. The woman tapped her stylus against the data-entry grid that rested on the desk in front of her, the staccato impact of plastic on polycoat sounding its *get on with it* song.

"Shane Averill," Jani replied, "just like it says in the card." She snatched a peek at her reflection in the highly polished counter. Chilly, too-dark eyes. Jaw tensed with discomfort. She forced a smile.

The clerk ignored the attempt at sociability. "Date and place of birth?"

Jani heard her voice quiver as she recited the information she'd memorized in preparation for this encounter. The Earthbound accents that echoed through the cavernous lobby made her nervous.

Coming to Felix had made sense after fleeing Chicago. The closest colony to Earth, it was an easy burrow to hunker down in. So obvious a stopping place was it that the Service agents who had no doubt pursued her would have bypassed it for someplace less likely. The Channel Worlds. Or Pearl Way.

But the burrow had proved to be made of quicksand. Expensive but necessary equipment purchases had devoured her finances, forcing her to remain until she could earn enough money to leave. Then her dodgy health had taken a serious downturn.

The stomachaches, I can handle. But not the nausea, the vomiting, the pounding heart. She knew she risked exposure by coming to Neoclona-Felix, but it was the only place on the planet that could treat her properly, and she had grown sick and tired of feeling sick and tired.

It was a matter of minutes now. One blood study or encephaloscan, and she'd be blown.

They promised I had nothing to fear. Cal Montoya, the doctor who had saved her life in Chicago, and those he spoke for. *Promises were made to be broken.* Her stomach clenched, and she leaned into the counter.

"Parents' names and worlds of origin?"

Jani looked around the Neoclona facility's glass and stone lobby as she gave voice to more of the fictitious Ms. Averill's invented history. Shades of purple—the company's signature hue—shone from every surface, even the tinted glass that softened the battering Felician sun. Bathed in shafts of grape-colored sunlight, she felt as though she stood at the bottom of a filled punch bowl.

"I don't suppose you can give me the first letter of your patient string?"

Jani took a steadying breath as the pain in her gut eased. "P-seven-eight-dot-one-two-dash-four-eight-zee—"

The tapping ceased abruptly. "You *know* your patient string *by heart*?"

Jani restrained the urge to turn on her heel, walk out of the lobby, and disappear into the Felix Majora crowds. "It's just a series of encodes. GateWay nearest my birth planet, followed by world code, followed by sector—"

The clerk ran the card through a scanner, then watched the disgorged data as it scrolled down the grid screen. "Shipping administrator for Felix Cruiseways, huh? Figures you can memorize forty-two-character strings." Her haggard features softened at this discovery of a kindred, data-crunching soul. She even cracked a smile. "Is Cruiseways a good place to work?"

Jani eyed the clerk's bright purple shirt. Silver caducei, every detail of snake, wing and staff visible in the holoetching, sparkled from collar and cuffs. The knowledge of what lay behind the symbols made her shiver. Or maybe it was the subarctic temperature of the lobby. "It's all right. I doubt it's any more exciting than what you do here. Besides, with the way Earth-colony relations are headed, the shipping and travel businesses are bound to take a hit. You're better off sticking with Neoclona."

The woman sighed and tugged at her dark blond bangs. Earthbound, judging by the odd twang of her Felician Spanish, and younger than she initially appeared. Mid-twenties, but her attitude aged her. "It just didn't turn out to be as exciting as I thought it would when I answered this posting. 'See the colonies! Meet new people!' " She fingered an entry into the grid. "Check in with the outpatient nurse on thirty-seven. She'll tell you where to go from there."

Jani reclaimed her record card and offered a commiserating grin of farewell. *Dear child, the last thing in the Commonwealth you want is an exciting life.* She waded deeper into the bowl, toward the lift bank. *Trust me.*

They asked her the same questions four more times as she scaled the floors to her doctor's office. Crude way to suss out potential healthcare fraud, but with the field of documents forgery as advanced as it was, the human element usually turned out to be the weakest link. Something about the increasing isolation and the proximity of sharp metal instruments and blinking analyzers tripped up less-determined con artists.

But we're the few, the sneaky, the hard-core liars, Jani thought as she followed the latest in the afternoon's series of white-coated backs down a hallway lined with examining rooms. She had reached the seventy-second floor, aerie of department chiefs and other demigods—her appointment had been made with a divinity named Tellinn. Deputy chief of endocrinology. Narrow, slumped shoulders. Shaggy black hair that needed trimming. Lapdog eyes deep-set in a drawn, pale face. Looked as though he could use a little of what he sold.

"This way, Ms. Averill," he said as he led her around yet another corner. "You're complaining of nausea?"

"Yes."

"And you're feeling jittery?"

"*Yes,*" Jani hissed. Two decades of experience compelled her to memorize the locations of the nearest exits, the security desk, the dead-end hallways. "At first, it just happened after I ate, but now it's constant."

"Could be one of the food allergies we've been encountering lately," Tellinn said glumly. "Are you from Elyas? Elyans have an awful time when they come here."

"No, I'm . . . not." Could they tell she was Acadian from her pattern of genetic mutations, or would her unique condition swamp out minor colony-to-colony differences? *What won't they find out about me, if they probe deeply enough?*

Jani sniffed the filtered air and shivered again. She hated hospitals. Not that this richly appointed corner of Neoclona's far-flung empire resembled in any way the jury-rigged basement in which, eighteen years before, the company got its start and she received a second chance at life. But old memories died hard, and every time she caught a biting whiff of antiseptic no filter could ever totally eliminate, three faces formed in her mind.

The three empire-builders. Eamon DeVries, who hated her guts. John Shroud, who . . . didn't. And Valentin Parini, who put out the fires that raged between the two polar opposites like the born fireman he was.

John and Val promised I would be looked after. Their representative had spoken in their names—she had nothing to worry about. She looked up and down the hallway as she trudged after Tellinn. *Exit to stairwell—unalarmed—second hallway to the left of the nurses' station.*

"Jesus Christ!" Tellinn slid to a halt so quickly Jani almost walked up his back.

"Not nearly so grand," said the man who had stepped out of the shadowed doorway. "Hello, Hugh."

"Val." Tellinn's voice shrank to a whisper.

"Sorry to drop in so abruptly." Valentin Parini riffled a hand through his ash brown hair. His hazel eyes were large and almond-shaped, his nose a finely molded arch, his cheekbones precipitous. Time's passage had left only thread-fine grooves near the corners of his mouth.

"What—are you—" Tellinn's complexion, moontan to begin with, had turned downright chalky.

The barest hint of recognition flickered in Val's green-brown gaze as it moved to Jani, then back to Tellinn. "I just punched through the GateWay two days ago. Forgive me for not messaging ahead, but being so near, I didn't see the point." Full lips curved in a cool smile. "Don't worry, this isn't a surprise inspection. John didn't send me to Felix with an agenda."

Tellinn drew the back of his hand across his mouth. "How did you get here? No one mentioned sending out the VIP shuttle."

Val shrugged lightly. "Felix Central Orbital Station to the city shuttleport. Chartered a heliskim. Landed on that new rooftop pad you installed last year. I must say, I do like the sensation of dropping onto my hospital from the clouds."

"Like God Almighty himself," Jani muttered. Val responded to the jab with a knowing smirk, but the glare Tellinn focused on her held murder. And something else. She looked again at Val, who winked.

"Actually, Hugh," he said, pointing to Jani, "I'd like to perform this physical, if you don't mind. I checked the appointment roster at the nurses' station. *Another* food allergy—my, my, they seem to be everywhere these days. They're a pet interest of mine—did you know that?" He waved off the other doctor's protest. "However, my role in all this is strictly *off-paper.* Keep your encode in her MedRec and draw up any scrips yourself. As far as we're all concerned, you're the physician of record." His all-business expression softened. "I'll explain it to you over dinner tonight." Jani swore his eyelashes fluttered. "But only if you can fit me in, of course."

Twin rounds of color bloomed in Tellinn's cheeks. "I—did have something, but I—can cancel." He blinked as though dazed, then handed Val the data-recorder board he had up to that point been holding in front of his chest like a shield. "I'll be in my office." He shot Val a last, stunned look, then walked slowly down the hall and disappeared around the corner.

Val watched Tellinn leave with the discerning eye a gourmet would direct toward the dessert display. Then he turned to Jani, and the look sharpened. "Oh Captain, my Captain." He pointed to the examining-room door. "In there. No sudden moves. Hands where I can see them."

Jani pushed the panel open; it whined under the force. "You haven't changed a bit, you shameless bastard. You sandbagged him." She held the door open while Val sauntered past. "You're more than he can handle, and you know it."

"But with me as a distraction, he won't give you a second thought, will he?"

"He's in love with you!"

"Yes, well. Believe it or not, after a few days with me, he'll be ready for six months without. I'm the white-chocolate cheesecake in his life—a little piece of me goes a hell of a long way." Val set the recorder on a table beside an analyzer. "But, first things first." To Jani's surprise, he held out his arms. "Just a quick hug, Jan. Because I've missed you. Because knowing I'd be seeing you again scared the hell out of me."

Jani hesitated. Then she walked, a little unsteadily, into Val's embrace. He enclosed her lightly, as though she might break. She squeezed back harder. He wore a crisp linen day-suit in light green; the stiff material crackled in her grasp like leaves.

"If you're trying to wring the years out of me, you're too late." He pulled back so he could look her in the face. His eyes glistened. "You look lovely. My one and only girl." He tugged at one of her short, black curls, then ran a fingertip down the bridge of her nose. "That's held up well, I must say."

Jani batted his hand away. "Social climber. You gave me a Family face. Damned bones you could sharpen blades on."

"Bullshit. I passed on the Parini countenance in the only way I cared to."

They grinned idiotically at one another. Then Jani sensed her instincts firing warning shots, and her smile faded. "How did you know I was here?"

Val sighed. "So much for sweet reminiscence." He frowned as Jani extricated herself from his arms. "Well, what can I say, except that there's nothing loyal employees and money can't accomplish. We have spies in every colonial city with a decent port—our Felician contact spotted you soon after you arrived. When you didn't depart immediately for a more out-of-the-way refuge, John started to worry. We decided I should come. John feared you'd bolt if you saw him."

"Did he?"

"Well, maybe I needed to convince him. Sit on him. Threaten him a little." Val crossed his arms and dropped his chin—his skeptical pose. "So?"

Jani shrugged. "I spent all my cash on gear. I needed to earn a berth." She wavered beneath his stare, weighty with paternal gruff. "And I haven't felt good for months."

"That's what John was afraid of." Val fingered the collar of her white trouser suit. "That's very pretty. *Très Felicienne.* You've got five seconds to peel out of it. We have work to do."

First came bloodwork, followed by a series of intrusive swabbings and scopings Jani could have done without, thank you. Then came an upper GI scan facilitated by her swallowing of a biodegradable, capsule-sized camera, and completed in spite of Val's insistence that she stand beside him at the display receiver and watch the full-color, three-dimensional workings of her digestive tract. Her equally adamant reply that he'd find himself *wearing* the camera if she did as he asked put a stop to his goading.

"Last part." Val rolled a stress screen the size of a full-length mirror into the center of the room. "Let's see how those new limbs of yours are doing. Off with the medgown. Get behind the screen. Stand up straight. Move only when I tell you to."

Jani stripped off the tissuelike gown and stepped behind the dull, milky screen. It brightened to translucent glass and emitted a barely perceptible hum.

She looked down at her left arm, then her left leg. No longer numb limbs driven by half-formed nervenets, but fully functional animandroid, the best Neoclona could produce. Replaced almost six months ago, during her first ever visit to Earth.

"Jani, atten-*hut*!"

She snapped to attention, chin up, shoulders back. The screen mirrored her image; she avoided looking at her face. Her light brown skin held up well under the room's chem-illumination. Her legs didn't look too bad.

But, as always, her eyes drew her in. They looked like two black holes staring back from the screen surface. She didn't like using that filming. It was the same brand holoVee actors used, formulated to show up well in the imaging, and less likely to fissure than commercial brands. But it was too dark for real life. People were starting to comment.

Bet they'd shut up if I let them see what was underneath.

"At ease, Captain. Your whole thorax has gone red. *Relax.*"

Jani took a deep breath and thought about white, puffy clouds. "Can I talk?"

"Yeah. Just don't gesture."

"How do I look?"

"All greens and blues—a veritable study in symmetry and stress distribution. The new limbs are fine, of course, but the old musculature has held up very well. We really did an exceptional job on you. I don't believe we've ever topped it."

"Well, you boys always worked best under pressure." Jani's hands clenched, and she thought about clouds again. "Trying to patch me together while holding off the Admiral-General's office and the Consulate—can't imagine much more pressure than that."

"Turn ninety degrees to your right, please." At first, it seemed Val would ignore further mention of their shared past. Then he cleared his throat. "The difficult part was justifying the supplies we ordered. Most of the Consulate staff had been evac'd out of Rauta Shèràa by then, and the ones that remained weren't sustaining the types of injuries to justify the materials we shipped in. It reached the point where I became a daily visitor to the Service Intelligence annex." He chuckled warmly. "Guess that's where I developed my legendary powers of persuasion. Turn your back to me, please."

Jani turned. "The Vynshà had taken the perimeter settlements by then. All they'd left to do was declare themselves 'rau' and send their Haárin advance troops into Rauta Shèràa to prepare the way. The Family members who'd supported the Laum were scrambling to realign themselves. Some pretty formidable names feared for their lives. You'd think Intelligence would have had their hands full getting them out of Rauta Shèràa alive."

Val sighed. "Yes, the Vynshà were exhibiting remarkably human vindictiveness, weren't they? I think Intelligence was concerned John, Eamon, and I were on the same short list. We were bad boys, remember? Turn ninety degrees, please."

Jani rotated slowly. The rough sensapad on which she stood made the soles of her feet itch. "Did you really think they'd have killed you?" She tried to shift her footing, but stopped when she heard Val grumble. "Nema considered the three of you esteemed enemies. A chief propitiator's regard should have been enough to save you."

Val huffed. "We had traveled pretty far into the land of forbidden knowledge by then. Besides, Nema was on his Temple's fecal roster. His regard and a vend token wouldn't have bought us a cup of coffee." A series of clicks sounded as he downloaded the screen data into the recorder. "All done. You can come out now."

Jani eased from behind the screen and reached to the floor for the crumpled medgown. The chill tile helped ease the burning on the bottoms of her feet, but before she could examine the damage, Val called to her.

"Let's have a look at those sweet baby jades of yours," he said as he wheeled the screen against the wall. "Strip off those eyefilms."

"My eyefilms?" Jani backed against the sinkstand. Her ankles prickled. She stifled a cough.

"What's the matter with you?" Val took a step closer. "What's wrong?"

Jani coughed again as her lungs filled with scancrete. "Can't breathe. My feet—" She slumped against the sink-stand. Black patches grew and faded before her eyes.

Val rushed to her. He knelt down, grasped her ankle, and snatched a glance at the bottom of her foot. Then he looked back at the sensapad. "Damn it! Damn it, damn it, *damn it*!" He hurried to the pad platform, tore the thin polymer film from its metal base, rolled it into a tight tube, and shoved it under his jacket and into the waistband of his trousers. Then he rushed to the door, pushing through the gap before it opened completely. "*I need a shockpack!*"

He returned, dragging an equipment-laden skimcart; white coats streamed in after him like a flood of milk. Two of them lifted Jani onto the scanbed while Tellinn clipped a monitor relay to her ear. "Hurry the hell up, Val," he snapped. "Her oxygen saturation's dropping like a rock."

Prodded with probes, raked over by scanners, Jani watched the frantic bustle with growing disinterest. Her world had become one of deadened emotion, blurring color, choppy sound and motion. Out of the corner of her eye, she saw Val work over her right arm, then felt the pinch of an injector. The heaviness in her chest eased, and she inhaled with a wheezy rattle.

"Blood pressure's up. A hundred over fifty-five." The source of the announcement, a silver-haired woman with CHIEF OF STAFF etched into her ID badge fixed Val with a glare. "What happened, Parini?"

Val's eyes locked with Jani's. *They know, Jan*, they said, as the once-glib mouth worked soundlessly. Sweat trickled down the face he'd copied for her, in a basement lab outside a war-torn alien city, when he and John and Eamon had learned enough about her to realize rebuilding her old one wasn't an option.

They know you're here.

CHAPTER 2

"Here, drink this." Val refilled the cup and pushed it over to Jani's side of the table. "Now, while it's hot."

Jani eyed the black, foamy brew with distaste. John's coffee had always tasted like a gift from the gods. Val's, on the other hand. . . . "Don't you think three cups are enough?" She belched quietly. "My stomach's going to go critical any second." She gazed longingly across the table at his iced lemonade. "I think we can ease up on the caffeine—my breathing's fine."

Val had returned to the bar, set in a sunken alcove in the middle of his spacious hotel room, and continued to rummage through coolers and cupboards. "Just keep drinking—you're not out of the woods yet. Damn it, I injected you with enough adrenosol to punch a resistant male one and a half times your weight through the ceiling, and it *just* brought your blood pressure up into low-normal. I couldn't risk giving you more, not with all those expert witnesses around." He slammed the cabinet door.

"I got enough of the fish-eye as it was. 'Wasn't that dose a tad *high*, Val? What were you *doing* to her, anyway?' They know the story of the patient we patched together on Shèrá, and not all of them approved of our methods. I swear they all think I was experimenting on you, and it backfired. You'd think that damned augmentation of yours could have helped you out."

"You know Service augies only work in threatening situations." Jani fingered the tiny round scar on the back of her neck where skull met spine. The large bore canula of a stereotaxic headset had punched a hole there over twenty years ago, then injected the self-assembling components of her little passenger. "Discharge a shooter across my bow, I can get as frosty and functional as you please." Only then would the tiny glands adjacent to her amygdala release their reservoirs of pseudocatecholamines. Sharpen her wits. Ease her panic. Dull her pain.

But if I'm not pissed off or scared senseless, I'm on my own. She pulled in a deep, wheezing breath, and choked down another sip of coffee. "So what happened?" Her stomach gurgled ominously.

Val returned to the table, the results of his explorations clutched in his hands. He piled all the stomach-settling food he could find, dispos of crackers and peppermint candies, by Jani's cup, then fell into the chair across from her. "I've got the head of Security running scan searches and background checks to see who the hell could have put the mat there. I'm not optimistic. It was either a Service or Cabinet plant, and they're probably off-world by now." He fumbled with a packet of crackers. "As for what was in it, I won't know for sure until I test it, and I can't test it properly until I get it home. Whatever it was, it had your number. You stood on it for no more than ten minutes, and the soles of your feet look like someone went after them with a strap."

Jani winced. Her heavily salved feet, encased in thick, truecotton booties, tingled with a maddening, itchy burn. The booties had been treated with anti-irritants and healing accelerants, but they couldn't work miracles. Walking promised to be a real treat for the next few days.

Wherever I happen to be. She checked her timepiece; six hours had elapsed since her episode. Most of that time had been spent in the office of Dr. Fanshul, the tart-tongued chief of staff, who had argued vehemently that it was in Jani's best interest to stay in the hospital overnight for observation. Val had put an end to the debate, and blown his cover in the process, by signing her out under his care. By the time all the signatures were in place, half the facility knew something strange had happened on the seventy-second floor involving one of the "Big Three" and a mysterious "woman in white."

"So?" Val laid claim to one of the peppermints. "Have I fucked up your situation here sufficiently, or should I try for full-page adverts in tomorrow morning's newssheets?" He smiled broadly, his teeth and lips coated bright blue by the candy.

Jani knew he wanted to coax a smile out of her. Under different circumstances, it might have worked. "I have to get off-planet. Within the hour."

Val slumped back in his chair and drummed his fingers on the table. "My ship's having some refit work done. It'll be ready in two days. Let me take you—"

"I can't wait two days."

"You better find a way. Face reality. You almost died. As things stand now, I can hear you breathe across the room—that situation isn't going to change for days. And if you try to do much walking on those feet of yours, you risk a nasty infection."

"Can't you give me something to see me through?"

Val's expression grew pained. "Jan, I'm not sure how the drugs I have on hand would affect you. As you learned to your detriment in Chicago, your response to some common medications has become idiosyncratic." He stared moodily into his lemonade. "For all I know, there's nothing wrong with that sensapad. You may have simply developed a sensitivity to that particular biopolymer, and damn it, if exposure to something like that is enough to knock you for a loop, what else out there could affect you?"

"That's not your problem."

"*Monkey's ass it's not my problem! You—*" Val fell silent. Jani could almost hear the click of a balance as he weighed his words. "Jan, your body is going through some changes right now. We know why, but the how, what, when, and where have us a little baffled." He looked at the ceiling, into the depths of his glass, everywhere but at her.

"Why can't you say it, Val?" Jani took another sip of coffee, and swallowed hard. "Eighteen years ago, you patched me together with tissue manufactured from human and idomeni genetic material. You thought you'd deactivated most of the idomeni genes, but you hadn't. You thought you'd made it so I'd live for two hundred years, but you didn't stop to think what I might live *as*."

Val blinked rapidly. "Jani," he said, his voice cracking, "you're wrong."

"I'm hybridizing. I'm not human anymore, but I'm not idomeni either. I can eat Haárin spices that would blister the inside of your mouth, but some of their herbs and nuts go through me like poison. I can't drink human tea anymore. I can barely choke down anything sweet, but I can peel a lemon and eat it like you would an orange." Jani heard the tremor in her voice. When she tallied up the small things—that was when it scared her. "Nema was right. He said this would happen, that no matter how you tried to stop it, I would continue to change."

"Jani, Nema is a religious fanatic with an agenda as long as my arm. Let's leave your medical care to experts, shall we?"

"And which experts would those be, Val? The ones who got me into this mess in the first place?"

Val flinched as though she'd slapped him. The room lighting accentuated the lines near his mouth, signs of age Jani couldn't find around her own no matter how hard she looked. "Jani, we did the best we could for you."

"That you did, Val, that you did. Thanks to you, I have eyes that look like two corroded copper discs and eating habits that make people stare. I york my guts a couple times a week, and between the nausea and the shivery shakes, my every day is a joy. And let's not forget that this condition of mine has reinforced Nema's grand theory that I'm his heir apparent, which gives him the right to take charge of the rest of my life if I ever let him get his hands on me, which I don't believe I will, thank you!" She glared at the stricken man. "I've had time to think these past few months. Way too much time. I hate being this way and I didn't have a choice. And now that the Service and the Commonwealth government know I'm alive, all they have to do is follow the trail. I'm a goddamn walking disaster siren!"

"Jani, we—" Val's voice cracked. "Do you hate us that much?"

"Do you really want me to answer that?"

"No." He sniffed. Cleared his throat. "You need more in-depth assessment than I can give you here. Come back with me to Seattle. You and I always got along, and Eamon isn't around much these days." He hesitated. "And whatever you think of John, he would like very much to see you."

Bits of memory flitted through Jani's mind. Some were more vivid than others. "Does he still play the violin?"

"Yes." Val's voice lifted hopefully. "You'd enjoy listening to him now—he's gotten rather good."

"Just the three of us basking in one another's company and listening to John fiddle. That sounds familiar." Jani looked out the tableside window. Fifty floors below, early-evening skimmer traffic crammed Felix Majora's main thoroughfare. Above the nearby mountains, barely visible through an artificial forest of scancrete and glass, the setting sun glowed like a weld spot. "You and John live in a dream world. Eamon would know better. He wouldn't be able to shove me out the door fast enough." A cramp shot through her abdomen. She tore open a packet of crackers and forced them down.

"Jan, we can keep you safe. No one will even suspect you're Earthside."

"Really? Is Neoclona a sovereign state? I read the news-sheets, Val. I watch the 'Vee. Funny the stories that keep cropping up. Rehashes about how human-idomeni relations took a dive after Knevçet Shèràa. Garbled rumor about the death of Rikart Neumann. Portraits of Evan as the emotionally battered son and lover. Can't you see what's happening? His attorneys are scrambling for a defense, and I'm it."

"Jani, he gave the order to have your transport blown out of the sky to cover up his involvement in Knevçet Shèràa. Nobody's that good a scrambler."

"Oh yeah? Has he been formally charged?"

"John knows he's guilty. He told me—"

"Has Evan been formally charged?" Jani nodded as the uncertainty flickered in Val's eyes. "The term is *plea bargain.* He's telling the Service all about me. I won't even need a trial—they'd just shoot me at O'Hare."

"We have influence."

"Val, I killed Neumann. My commanding officer. The first N in NUVA-SCAN. The Families are closing rank." She stood and headed for the door. "Your influence and a vend token." She took one step. Two. Before she could take a third, popping sensations worked across both soles, followed by stinging wetness, then raw agony as though she skated over metal blades.

Jani didn't feel herself fall; she only knew she was on the floor. As pain radiated up her legs and she gasped for breath, she felt a hand close over her shoulder.

"You're not running out on us, Jan," Val said gently. "Not this time. And when you finally do go somewhere, it's going to be with me."

In the end, they compromised.

"I don't like this one damn bit." Val snaked the Neoclona staff skimmer down one of Felix Majora's less-traveled side streets. The sleek, silver two-seater didn't meet Jani's standards as a getaway vehicle. It drew the eye like a stone skipping over water. Pedestrians stopped to stare as it passed.

At least it wasn't purple.

"You have to keep your date with Hugh," she said. "He can tell you what they're saying about us in the staff room."

Val checked a street sign, compared it to the name on his directional screen, and frowned. "He's not like that. No matter his feelings, he's always kept his own counsel."

"Oh, I'm sure you can work around his better judgment. Use your legendary powers of persuasion." Jani watched out her window as large commercial buildings gave way to the smaller residential structures of the city's mountain side. It took her some time to realize

Val hadn't spoken; she turned to find him eyeing her with ill-concealed discomfort.

"I don't like playing the tart while you're running loose doing God knows what."

"Staying put in my apartment. Packing."

"Packing. Right." Val pointed to the directional's touch-pad. "I like Hugh. The idea of working him repulses me."

"Considering your performance this afternoon, I find that difficult to believe."

"That was *fun*!" Val sighed. "Would've been fun. This is different. There's too much at stake, and I don't know what the hell I'm doing."

"Just find out what they're saying about us. If Hugh asks about me, bring up the massive clinical study you're planning. Tell him you want to base it in a colonial facility for a change. Mention it will need a director. Throw in that famous smile, and you'll be in like a greased weasel." Val shifted uneasily, and Jani forced a grin. "Look, if it's any consolation, I've done the tart thing once or twice. If *I* can do it, you're a lock."

Val stopped at an intersection and glanced at the directional. "You say left, it says right."

"Take a left."

He shrugged and turned left. "Sometimes, at the end of the day, when we've worked to the point of exhaustion and all our internal safeguards have burnt out, John and I will uncork a bottle of wine and talk. About you. Where you could be living, what you could be doing. John does most of the talking." He glanced at Jani sidelong. "I don't think I'll repeat this conversation to him anytime soon."

They turned another corner. The sudden brightness of the streetlights hit Jani full in the face. She closed her eyes against the battering glare; they watered anyway. "Fuck you," she said. "Stop here. I'm getting out."

"What!" Val jerked the wheel in surprise, sending the skimmer over the curb boundary and up onto the sidewalk. The vehicle's proximity alarms blatted as he tried to regain control from the autonav, which fought to turn the skimmer in the opposite direction. By the time he maneuvered into an idling slot near a small playground, residents from nearby buildings had gathered in windows and doorways to watch. Scattered applause sounded as the vehicle shuddered to a stop.

Jani watched a woman across the street point at the skimmer and laugh. "You have a future in this business, I can tell."

"Oh, bullshit!" Val glared at their surroundings. Much of the playground equipment had been dismantled, lighting was intermittent at best, and several less-polished-looking skimmers had already veered by for a look at the spiff new visitor. "I'll be damned if I'm letting you out here—this place is a dump!" He pointed to the directional touchpad. "I don't know why you told me to bring you here, anyway—the address code on Shane Averill's MedRec says—"

Jani popped open her door, but Val dragged her back inside the skimmer before she could flee. His grip on her animandroid upper arm made her gasp—he knew just where to grab and how hard to squeeze. "Shane Averill was a one-shot, wasn't it? Something you patched together to get through the visit to Neoclona? You don't work at Felix Cruiseways, and you don't live at the address in your file!" He struggled to pull the door closed with his free hand. "We're supposed to meet tomorrow morning at your apartment, Jani. Now how the hell are we supposed to do that when I don't know where you live!"

Jani tried to wedge her right leg through the shrinking gap between door and seal. "I'll meet you at your hotel."

"You said you didn't want to go back there anymore. You said it was too risky." Val swore as Jani wriggled halfway out of the skimmer. He tried to drag her back into the cabin without releasing his grip on the door pull, but before he could set himself, the gullwing flew upward, pulling him headlong across Jani's lap before finally wrenching free.

Hot, dry night spilled into the cabin.

"Hey, *lindo, que pa*?" A wiry Feliciano, bare to the waist and sporting a half-shaved head, stood in the gaping entry. He leaned forward while still holding on to the door pull; the stretched pose accentuated his thin waist and bony chest. "What's wrong, pretty man with the pretty skim, you don't get your money's worth?" He leered at Jani. "Hard girl like this don't earn her pay?" He rapped the door sharply, and shapes moved into the range of the skimmer headlights. Four of them. "Maybe we give you both your money's worth."

Jani eased her other knee from beneath Val's body. "When I bolt, you floor it and go."

"Oh shit, Jan, don't—"

Jani kicked out. Before she'd left Val's hotel room, she'd supplemented her booties with three pairs of his socks and a pair of his hiking boots. Her padded and armored feet connected perfectly with Shaved-head's solar plexus; he dropped to the ground. She scrambled out of the cabin and over his gasping form, pounding off in the direction opposite his cohorts before any of them could react. After a few strides, she heard the gratifying whine of an accelerating skimmer, followed by the much-less-welcome sound of pursuing footsteps. She tried to pick up her pace, but her feet burned as though she ran through flame. Her chest ached. Her legs turned to cement.

Behind her, the pounding grew louder.

Then, like a bracing wave breaking over her, an old friend dropped by to pay Jani his respects. Her feet numbed. Her lungs cleared. Muzzy perception crystallized. The ovenlike night air parted before her, then closed behind, buoying her along. She pelted down a side street and through an alley, aware as a cat of the fading noises behind her. The thought that she'd been sick a few hours before and should slow down flitted through the cold white that had become her mind, but she shook it off. Fatigue was for other people. She could surf this way for hours. And maybe she would, just for the sheer animal joy of it.

Hello augie—about damn time.

Through every cell in her body, Jani's augmentation whispered his regards.

But her Service-implanted bootstraps could only take her so far. As she slowed to a trot, Jani felt the first tendrils of panic push through her calm. The neurochemical rush that had eased her pain and opened her lungs slowed to a sputter. Augie worked best and longest for intact soldiers at the top of their game, not for half-animandroid never-weres just released from the hospital.

Jani eased to a walk, in part to conserve her flagging strength, but mainly because she'd entered a section of Felix Majora where a running woman would attract attention. Office towers and manufacturing facilities loomed on either side as she headed down a wide, well-kept alley. When she reached an entry next to a small loading dock, she knocked twice, then sagged against the doorframe and pressed her hot, wet face against cool, dry metal.

The door opened.

"I saw you coming on the scan." The woman looked Jani up and down and grimaced. Her name was Ileana, and she was Jani's boss. "What the hell happened?"

Jani ducked past her. Inside, the air felt cool and held a soft floral fragrance. "Almost got mugged."

"Where?"

"The Cuarto Montaña."

"What the hell were you doing there!" Ileana flipped her long black braid over her shoulder. "At night? Alone?"

"Fell asleep on the *hojea.*" The Felician Spanish slang for the automated public-transport system slipped off Jani's tongue as though she'd used it all her life. "Didn't hear the end-of-the-line alarm until it was too late. They just spooked me. I'm fine."

"Hmph." Ileana eyed Jani's rumpled white trouser suit. Then she looked down at Val's heavy brown boots and wrinkled her nose. "Tell me you didn't do that on purpose." She had matched her own flame orange wrapshirt and trousers with high-heeled sandals of the same color, and had wound a desert-print scarf around her neck. Her thick braid reached to her waist and gleamed with gold oil. Tall and lithe, with a long, angular face, she appeared the well-to-do Feliciana, a mature lady of business. Perfume dealer, in this case.

Appearances could be deceiving.

"It's a long story." Jani entered the main work area, where a man and woman watched over the array that packed the rolls of perfumed adhesive patchlets into cartons. "Maybe I'll tell you about him sometime."

"Ah, man trouble!" Ileana clapped her hands in glee. "Finally, my paper robot shows humanity!" She followed Jani into the tiny employee locker room. "Bring him to lunch tomorrow, Tasia. I must meet him."

Tasia. Jani sat down on the narrow bench in front of her locker. Oh yes, a "T" name; lately, she found it hard to keep track. "Sure. When and where?"

Ileana debated times and places out loud; Jani stifled a yawn as she willed her voice into the background. Post-augie fatigue had overtaken post-augie jitters more quickly than she remembered. But then, lately, lots of things were happening differently than she remembered.

The entry comport buzzed; Ileana, still nattering about restaurants, left to answer it. As soon as she was alone, Jani keyed into her locker and removed a small duffel. The Service surplus bag was made of stiff, dark blue polycanvas, and contained everything she owned. She had taken a risk leaving it there, but she hadn't dared take it into Neoclona, and she didn't trust the security of her flat.

Jani did a quick inventory of her duffel's contents. *My preflight check.* Two pairs of dark grey coveralls, rolled into tight tubes. A pair of battered black boots. Assorted underwear. Her keepsakes: a toy soldier, a holocard depiction of two sailracers, and a gold ring with a red stone.

She examined her boots wistfully. Val's hikers chafed her ankles despite the padding, but felt tight around her feet. That meant her feet had swelled. *If I take his boots off, I won't be able to get mine on.* She pushed her old faithfuls aside and dug farther into the bag.

The scanproof material that lined the false bottom of her duffel had cost Jani most of her cash reserve, but would have been worth it at twice the price. Within the slippery blue envelope rested her shooter, a bulky Service-issue over twenty years old, and assorted gadgetry hooked together by a braided length of red cloth. The devices allowed her to reset a touchlock or interfere with an eavesdropping device. Nothing to strike fear in the hearts of an antiterrorist squad, but they would draw the notice of Treasury Customs and Transport Ministry Security.

Jani stuffed the gadgets back in the envelope, then removed a cracked plastic case from a well-padded pocket. "Hello, you," she said as she unzipped the case and removed her scanpack.

The palm-sized oval's scratched black cover shimmered dully in the glare of the overhead lighting. Driven by Jani's farmed brain tissue, the device functioned as the repository of a quarter century's worth of documents knowledge. It would have won her envious stares from the other doc techs Jani had met at Felix Majora's Government Hall, and pointed questions from Ileana. Only Registry-listed documents examiners carried scanpacks, and only four others in the forty-nine-planet Commonwealth carried ones that looked like Jani's. And they all worked on Earth.

Pointed questions, followed by pointed sticks. Jani stuffed the device back in her duffel and sniffed the air again. *Isabellita.* The light floral scent had become popular in some rather far-flung regions of the Commonwealth, a reason sufficient to explain the small perfume house's 'round-the-clock operation. Every morning, boxload after boxload departed the small loading dock, bound for the rich colonies of the J-Loop as well as their not-so-rich brethren in the Channel and the Outer Circle.

Wonder if External Revenue's caught onto the fact there's a lot of sweet-smelling sewage out there lately. Jani grinned. The perfume was a water-soluble concoction that could be flushed out of the patch polymer; the polymer could then be reworked into some of the best scanshielding Jani had ever seen. Not on par with the military-grade material lining the bottom of her duffel, but good enough to allow the occasional cruiser filled with unregistered, untaxed cargo to flit through the GateWay chain under the noses of sundry Cabinet branches.

Jani unrolled one of the pairs of coveralls, then began the tricky task of pulling off her pants without removing Val's hikers. Ripping proved necessary, but that didn't bother her. The suit, fashionable and delicate, belonged to someone named Tasia, and Tasia had only minutes to live.

Laughter trickled in from the packing room. This was, without a doubt, the happiest smuggling ring she ever worked with. *Wonder how long it will last?* No operation like it ever floated for long without springing a few leaks. The fact that most of the revenue earned by the small network went to finance colonial secessionist groups didn't bode well for its life span, either.

That was the main reason for her delay, when every nerve in her body sang for her to *get out now.* She had to finish out the night, leave things tight. If it ever went to hell for these people, it wouldn't be because of anything she had done. Or failed to do. She might have worked at many jobs, under many names, on a score of worlds, but Jani Kilian had done them all very well. The habit had sunk its roots during her short but eventful Service career. *Whatever job you undertake, perform it to the best of your ability, and see it through to the end.* And so she had, now as then.

Well, no. There had been one particular *then* when she had not done her best. Oh, she had survived. No one else had, though, except in her memory.

Knevçet Shèràa, the one bad job that outweighed all the good.

"*Tasia!* What's taking you so long!"

Jani bundled the ruined trouser suit into her locker and limped out to the packing room to find Ileana waiting for her, holding a documents pouch.

"Guv Hall. Hurry. You have sixteen minutes to file these quarterlies or those bastards will come after me!" She thrust the pouch into Jani's hands, then grabbed her elbow and steered her toward the door.

"It's only half a block." Jani tried to ease out of the woman's grip. "I could stop for dinner and get there in time."

"Maybe, the way you eat." Ileana eyed Jani's coverall with distaste. "You eat like you dress. No thought. No one would ever mistake you for a true Feliciana." She pushed Jani out the door. "Now move!"

Jani hurried down the street in a lurching double time, her eyes focused on the brilliantly lit triple towers of Government Hall. Then she glanced back to see if Ileana watched her, and slowed down when she saw she didn't. Her chest ached again. Her thigh muscles trembled. She wondered what Val was doing. Worming secrets from his sometime love? Or tearing the city apart looking for her?

Good old Val. Her steps slowed as she recalled his embrace. It worried her that it took only a single kind gesture to knock her off-balance at a time when she couldn't afford the least wobble. Now more than ever, she could not drop her guard.

But I'm tired. Tired of feeling sick, of running, of trying to remember what her damned name was. Fed up with being alone.

Jani flashed her Tasia ID for the last time at the Guv Hall security desk—one of the few benefits of being non-Reg was that she didn't have to worry about hand or eye scanning. After she stuffed the pouch in a lobby drop box, she keyed in a request that the receipt be fiched to Ileana instead of to her.

That final loose end tied off, Jani crossed the wide avenue and headed for the *hojea* platform, dodging skimmers and jostling through groups of the well-dressed leaving their businesses for a night on the town. One, a day-suited man whose night out must have started that morning, bumped her roughly, then staggered on, muttering curses at the world in general. Not a Felician accent, Jani noted. Earthbound. No surprise there. Lots of Earthbounders worked on Felix.

She stepped onto the platform and surveyed the scene around her as she waited for the train. Across the street, she saw the man who had bumped her standing in the Guv Hall entryway, watching her. Then the street weaved and roiled like a banner in the wind. Just as she sagged to her knees, Jani heard footsteps close in from behind. Then it all went black—

CHAPTER 3

"So what do we do now, Quino?" Evan van Reuter flipped his stylus from one hand to another. "We've been waiting for one goddamn piece of paper for two hours."

Joaquin Loiaza shot a look uptable at the SIB chief investigator. But Colonel Veda was engaged in anxious discussion with the Judge Advocate's representative, and didn't appear aware of the mutterings at the far end of the conference table. "In truth, Evan, we've been waiting for two goddamn pieces of paper. The *Hilfington* roster would be nice, but we'll take the *Kensington* master if we have to."

"By my count, this makes the fourth time in a month they've misplaced documents."

"Yes, their track record does fail to impress. I must consider how to turn that to our advantage." Joaquin rubbed his chin thoughtfully. As always, the old-coin aspect of his close-cropped brown hair and regal nose was offset by the pinched look around his turtlelike eyes.

Caesar with a migraine. Evan tapped the stylus on the table and stole another glance at Colonel Veda. Since she sat, he could only see her from the waist up. Closely trimmed black hair. Creamy brown skin. A noble face, handsome rather than pretty. He'd yet to see her smile, but he guessed those dark brown eyes could sparkle given the right encouragement. He knew from other stolen glances that her Service summerweights hugged lovely curves.

Her first name's Chandra. A soft, lovely name. Yes, in another lifetime, he would have asked Durian Ridgeway to don his go-between hat and invite her to an assignation in one of the rented flats the Interior Ministry had scattered throughout Chicago. In that other lifetime, she would have accepted.

But in this lifetime, Durian is dead and Veda thinks I'm a worm. Evan struck the stylus against the table—tiny shards of poly sprayed across the surface as the writing tip shattered. "What difference do the ship records from the evac make?" He swept the plastic bits over the tableside and onto the carpeted floor. "They know I was there—that's why I'm in trouble now."

Joaquin sighed. "Pretend you're still a cabinet minister and use your brain. We want to build sympathy. Highlight the hardships you endured during the idomeni civil war and the evacuation, the hardships that still haunt your memory eighteen years later. The terror as the Haárin stalked Rauta Shèràa, slaughtering the fallen Laum, while their Vynshàrau puppetmasters watched from the surrounding hills."

"You make it sound like a 'Vee melodrama. All that's missing is the closing clinch with the girlfriend to the strains of the Commonwealth anthem." Evan smiled to mask his unease. He had many reasons to dread his memories—he didn't relish the thought of his own attorney dredging them up again.

Especially the memories he'd deny to the grave.

Joaquin's stylus scraped across the surface of his recording board. "Only you would see it that way. A more sober-minded individual would have lived in constant fear."

Evan's smile died. Fear? Of what? The bombs? The panic? The rumors of a massacre by a human of twenty-six Laumrau in a place called Knevçet Shèràa? That the Haárin might ignore their cultural conditioning and avenge the disorderly deaths of their enemies by slaughtering the remaining inhabitants of Rauta Shèràa's human enclave?

That his government would find out the things he'd done? That escaping execution in Rauta Shèràa only increased his chances of meeting that fate back on Earth?

"Fear?" Evan felt the sweat trickle under his shirt. His hands shook. His left knee ached. He needed a drink. "What do you know about fear?"

Joaquin ignored the question. "Most especially, we need to emphasize that there were times during the voyage home that you didn't think you'd make it back to Earth alive."

His stylus broken, Evan dissipated the urge to twitch by tugging on his security cuff. *My electronic leash.* Nice of his jailers to make the black-banded monitor look like a timepiece. He wondered if it fooled anyone. "Living through two months of crappy food and cramped quarters isn't going to win me any sympathy from this crowd. It's their way of life."

"Keep your voice down!" Joaquin glanced anxiously at Veda. "Remember your place. No one has to tolerate your pithy commentary anymore." He clucked his tongue, then returned to his note taking.

Evan felt the lump in his gut grow and twist. Not long ago, people stood in line to tolerate his pithy commentary and whatever else he cared to dish out. It had been six months since the life he'd always known had ended. Six months since the roof had caved in.

And we know who snapped the support beam, don't we? Evan could see her face as clearly as if she sat across the table from him. Hair as short and black as Veda's. Eyes as dark. Skin as smooth. Look, as cold.

Jani, who killed the Laumrau and, before that, his Uncle Rik. Whom he tracked down and pulled from the gutter eighteen years later, because he had needed her a lot and still loved her a little. Who repaid him first by killing his friend Durian, then by destroying his life.

Jani.

"Excuse me."

Evan looked up to find Veda standing before him. Up close, he could see the fine etching of lines that decorated the corners of her eyes. So, there were smiles bottled up in that well-conditioned body. He wondered for whom she saved them. He tried to inject some softness into his expression—imagining what lay hidden under that trimly tailored summerweight shirt made it easy. *Grey isn't her color;* he forced himself to focus on her face. No, it would have to be soft yellow or cream, something that would complement the undertones of her skin. . . .

Joaquin's puckered asshole of a voice shook Evan out of his sexual reverie. "Have the vanished rosters reappeared yet, Colonel?"

A muscle throbbed in Veda's cheek. "No, Mr. Loiaza, they have not. The ranking documents examiner has been contacted, however, and we hope to have them first thing tomorrow morning."

"Do you?" Joaquin managed to inject more cynical skepticism in those two words than less-skilled attorneys could in an entire summation. "I find it very distressing that documents that could play an important role in my client's defense have gone missing as easily as last week's newssheets."

Veda's chest rose and fell. Evan found the movement hypnotic.

"Not a very skillful diversion, Counselor." The Judge Advocate's representative, a geeky youngster whose name Evan kept forgetting, drew up to his full-yet-unprepossessing height. "Let's not lose sight of the essential facts. Your client is responsible for ordering the deaths of sixteen members of this Service. Add to that his collusion in the deaths of the Bandan research team at Knevçet Shèràa and his role in the illegal importation of idomeni augmentation technologies—"

"All alleged, Counselor. My client has not been charged." Joaquin's voice grew dangerously soft. "He's here to assist you in your investigation of Jani Kilian's murder of her commanding officer. Unless you're having difficulty uncovering documents pertinent to that case, as well."

The meeting ended with a terse assurance from Colonel Veda that the documents would be available by morning. Evan watched her stalk out of the conference room, his eyes greedily recording the sway of her walk in the long-deprived recesses of his memory. "Was that necessary?"

Joaquin tossed his recording board into his briefbag. "Evan, just because you have a hard-on for Veda doesn't mean I have to cease doing my job."

"Pithy, Quino."

"Let that be a lesson to you."

The SIB hallways mirrored the stripped-down aesthetic of the conference room. Evan fingered the austere beige sacking that cloaked the walls near the lift bank. *Roshi probably picked out the wall coverings himself.* Hiroshi Mako took pride in his functional, unadorned Service. He had battled to the dizzy heights of the Admiral-Generalcy with one goal in mind, to salvage his beloved Blue and Grey. They were a true military now, he claimed, instead of the Family police force they had been in the Bad Old Days.

Those Bad Old Days were pretty good to me. But then, Evan could admit his bias. Anything that improved a Family's place in the Commonwealth was right and commendable, and anyone in the NUVA-SCAN Family network who claimed to feel differently lied. Now, however, in these days of restless colonies clamoring for autonomy and argumentative idomeni demanding trade agreements that encroached more and more deeply into human territories, wise Family members kept such sentiments to themselves.

Family first. Even though, as far as the van Reuters were concerned, the Family had for years consisted of him and him alone.

"Rather fine qualifying match on the 'Vee this evening," Joaquin said. "Live from Geneva—Gruppo Helvetica vs. some poor colonial appetizer."

A scene flashed in Evan's mind. Tanned, coltish legs pumping—black ponytail flipping. *Daddy, watch me—!* His eyes stung. "Soccer's not my game, Quino."

"It *is* the Commonwealth Cup." Joaquin grew thoughtful. "Although God knows what the upsurge of colonial pride will wash out of the drains if one of those teams actually wins it this time."

"Serena used to play on her school team." Evan blinked until his vision cleared. "I haven't watched a match since she died."

Joaquin shifted his feet. "Evan, I—"

"Just drop it." He braced for a clumsy apology. When none proved forthcoming, he turned to find his attorney regarding him with impatient admiration.

"If the people of Chicago could see you at this moment, they'd storm Sheridan to free you." The man exhaled with a rumble. "You're my client. My responsibility is to you. Everyone's heard the rumors. Let me place one official story about the children—"

"No."

"Damn it, it's the prime example of how your late father manipulated everyone around him! He subjects Martin to an experimental personality augmentation at the age of three—eleven years later, Martin dies during the boating mishap he'd arranged to kill Serena and Jerrold."

"Thank you for mentioning it. I needed that."

"The deaths of your children destroyed any chance you and Lyssa had to rebuild your marriage."

"Our marriage was a joke from the start." Evan thumped the lift bank keypad with his fist. "We've discussed this before. I haven't changed my mind. Use anything but the children. Let them rest in peace. End of subject." The lift door finally opened. He limped in, left knee clicking with every stride.

"Since you brought up colonial pride, Quino, here's a question. I heard on CapNet that Acadia and the other Channel Worlds have lodged some kind of protest concerning the arrests of political prisoners despite insufficient evidence. One of those prisoners wouldn't happen to be Jani, would it?"

"As soon as Kilian is found, the SIB is required to notify us. If Veda lets us down in *that* regard, not even your esteem will prevent me from tearing her apart." Joaquin boarded the lift and punched the pad for the ground floor. "Apropos of nothing, how is the Crème Caramel doing?" The mention of roses erased the discomfort from his bony face.

"Fine, Quino." Evan bit his lip to keep from grimacing. At his flower-loving attorney's insistence, he had planted a small rose garden in the rear yard of his prison-home and tended the blooms faithfully every day. Joaquin claimed that the image of a disgraced ex–Cabinet Minister tending his garden as he once tended his constituents would excite sympathy from the public, but Evan nursed the conviction that the man just needed a place to stash the overflow from his own extensive cultivations.

"I hope you didn't fertilize it yet. You need to wait at least another two weeks."

"Yes, Quino."

"Then you must use the special mix I gave you for the Jewellers' Loop hybrids, not the standard mix I gave you for the others."

"Yes, Quino."

"And you must wait until late afternoon. Spread no more than two hundred grams around the base of the plant, then follow with a liberal watering."

God help me. "*Yes*, Quino."

By the time the lift reached the ground floor, Evan had mentally dismembered the Crème Caramel with an ax and was about to start on his attorney. The door swept aside; he stepped out of the car and almost collided with a man dressed in summerweights. Short. Stocky. A round, tawny face cut by a perpetual scowl. Black eyes hidden by sloping cheekbones and drooping lids.

"Hello, Roshi." Evan stepped around the supreme commander of the Commonwealth Service, then dodged sideways to avoid his aide. "Inspecting your fences, are you?"

"Evan." Admiral-General Hiroshi Mako pulled up short, then looked in apparent disinterest from him to Joaquin. Only if you looked hard could you detect the mild working of his broad jaw that betrayed his unease. But then, what could he say? *How are you? What brings you here?* "Hellish weather we're having." When in doubt, there was always the weather.

Evan racked his brain for a suitably neutral reply. "Plays hell with the roses."

Mako's eyes clouded as he watched the lift doors close. He stepped aside as his aide grabbed for the closing door and thumped the keypad—unfortunately for him, the man's efforts proved wasted. "You raise roses? Ah yes, I saw something about that on one of the news shows." Mako's guttural bass kicked upward a tone in grudging interest. "Tamiko raises them, too." His voice warmed as he spoke his wife's name. "The J-Loop varieties give her the hardest time, judging from her muttering. She refuses to accept mere climate as an excuse for failure to thrive."

"She should contact Dr. Banquo at the Botanical Gardens—the woman was born on Phillipa and knows everything about Jewellers'

Loop hybrids." Joaquin leaned forward in shared conspiracy. "The secret is in the fertilizer."

That's government in a nutshell. Evan caught the aide eyeing him and tugged at his somber, dark blue jacket. *Do I look that bad?* He had lost weight, and he hadn't been sleeping well, but what else would you expect—?

"*Damn.*"

He turned to find Joaquin standing with his hand pressed to his stomach and a look of stricken concentration on his face. "Watch my bag." He dropped his briefbag at Evan's feet and hurried toward a discreetly marked door near the lobby entry.

Evan answered Mako's questioning look. "New cook. She tends toward a heavy hand with some of the more pharmaceutically active colonial herbs."

Mako winced in sympathy, then turned to his aide. "See if you can find out which herbs she used, Colonel. The last thing we need at next month's off-site is an attack of the trots."

"Yes, sir." The man pulled a small handheld from the slipcase on his belt and muttered a notation.

Evan watched the man; whoever he was, he didn't look like the typical Base Command poop boy. Distinctive, in the close-clipped, wire-lean way that typified Roshi's New Service. The nasty scar that grooved his face from the edge of his nose to the corner of his mouth accentuated his sharp-featured homeliness, its dull white color a marked contrast to the sunburnt red-brown of his face.

But it was the way the man looked at Evan that drew his attention. Not the pointed monitoring of the bodyguard, but the more analytical assessment of one who searched through his mental ID file, matched, tagged, shrugged, and moved on.

I know a hatchet man when I see one. Evan had employed enough of his own. He snatched a glance at the man's name tag. "Colonel Pierce." He offered a nod, but didn't try to shake. One too many snubs when he had held out his hand had driven that lesson home.

"Sir." Pierce nodded back, but kept his hands at his sides.

"You're lucky to be lakeside in this weather." When in doubt . . . "At least you get some breeze."

Pierce made a point of not looking Evan in the face, instead concentrating on the floor indicator located above the lift doors. "Yes, sir. That we are, sir." His voice proved nasal and harsh. It could have been the lower-class version of Evan's own Michigan provincial, but odds were the muted remnants of a Victoria colony twang would prove the more accurate choice.

From Pearl Way, are we? Evan felt his long-dormant curiosity stretch out a paw. It was a hell of a long trip from that far-flung network of worlds to the Admiral-General's side. At one time or another, Pierce had proven himself extremely talented. Or extremely useful.

The lift returned to the first floor. "Good-bye, Evan." The relief in Mako's voice was gallingly evident as the door opened and he and Pierce stepped in. "Enjoy your roses."

Evan watched the door close. Mako took care to avoid his eye. But Pierce glanced at him just as the panels meshed, his scar twisting his disgusted curl of lip into a caricature of a sneer.

"I'm back. What's left of me." Joaquin drew alongside, then bent slowly to pick up his bag. His complexion was waxen, his eyes, narrowed to slits. "Let's go."

Evan followed him out the door. After the coolness of the SIB, the late-afternoon heat made him gasp. "How are you feeling?"

"Like I've been punched in the stomach." Joaquin gestured to his driver, parked in the nearby visitor's oval. "I can't decide if it was the cherryvale leaves in the salad or the folsom in the gravy."

"Probably a combination of both." Evan watched his lawyer's sedate black double-length slide to the curbside and felt the envy twinge. He'd had an entire fleet of black double-lengths at his beck and call, in that other lifetime. Triple-lengths. Sedans. One cherry red Sportster he missed particularly. He had planned to take Jani for a ride in it, as soon as the weather and her stiff-necked mien had permitted.

The best-laid plans, all blown to hell.

He eased into the passenger seat beside his rose-loving attorney and looked out at the bowl of poured concrete that some architect had inverted and dubbed the Service Investigative Bureau. Odd area of Sheridan for the supreme commander to be wandering, despite his reputation for digging into the daily workings of the base.

Whatever's going on, he needed his hatchet along to check it out. Evan remembered the feeling—he had dragged Durian Ridgeway along on so many cleanup projects, the man had earned the nickname *the janitor.*

Made one wonder what service Scarface had performed to merit the confidence.

"Did an officer named Pierce serve on either the *Hilfington* or the *Kensington*, Quino?" Evan must have done a good job keeping the curiosity out of his voice—Joaquin barely glanced up from his handheld.

"Crew rosters are included in the documents we've requested from Veda, Evan. I can't answer that question until I have them in hand."

Evan nodded. "It's just that he looks familiar." He tapped his thumb on his knee and watched Joaquin's face in the angled reflection of the driver's rearview mirror. "I could have seen him at the Consulate, I suppose."

"Those rosters we have, thanks to your father's meticulous recordkeeping. I'll have one of the clerks check when I get back to the office." He looked at Evan with an air of quiet interest. "Do you recall the circumstances under which you think you saw him?"

Evan shook his head. "No. Sorry. If anything comes to me, I'll let you know." With that, he dropped it. He had known Joaquin for over thirty years and had worked with him professionally for fifteen. The man sensed a possible lead; therefore, he would *check.* Whichever Service records he could access. Whatever other official sources he could tap. Then, just to make sure he hadn't missed anything, he would assign an agent or two to work the unofficial side of the street, to research Pierce's past from the cradle to what he had for breakfast that morning, and see where the reports overlapped.

Or didn't.

And then I'll know. It didn't have to be big—it just had to hurt. A failed marriage. An embarrassing relative. A rumor of cheating in school. Something to fling in Pierce's battered face the next time they met. *Pierce, Pierce, I'd heard of a Pierce who—oh, I'm sorry. Are you related?*

The skimmer passed beneath the base entryway. The shadow of the Shenandoah Gate darkened the vehicle interior; the illuminated names of the Greatest War dead inscribed on the stone's surface shone like stars. The sudden nightfall shook Evan out of his bitter daydream. *Why the hell am I bothering?* Did he crave a respite from his legal travails? Or did being rebuffed at by a colonial counter-jumper aggravate him that much?

Which colonial counter-jumper am I thinking about? He rubbed his aching knee and pushed thoughts of Jani from his mind.

CHAPTER 4

"I can't find it, Mr. Duong."

Sam looked up from the stack of files that he had balanced precariously on his lap. "Which is *it*, Tory? The *Hilfington* passenger roster or the *Kensington* master?"

The Clerk Four shifted from foot to foot. "Both. Neither." Her eyes filled. "Mr. Odergaard said that Mr. Loiaza threatened to notify the Prime Minister."

Sam closed the file he had been rooting through and hoisted the pile from his lap to the tabletop. "He can try," he said as he smoothed his rumpled civilian greys. "Prime Minister Cao does not jump to the beat of lawyers who make a show of stamping their well-shod feet."

"But Mr. Loiaza is *Mr. van Reuter's* lawyer."

"That's no great honor." Sam stood, shivering as conditioned air brushed across his sweat-damp back. He could visualize the light grey shirting darkened to charcoal, and wondered if he dared escape to the locker room for a shower and change of clothes. It wouldn't make the hell that the day had become go any more smoothly, but at least he would feel better. Comparatively speaking. He felt a battered wreck now.

"Mr. Odergaard says that if we can't track down the docs in the next half hour, you have to contact Lieutenant Yance." Tory's eyes widened. She was seventeen years old—the Clerk Four position was her first job since graduating prep school. Judging from the mounting panic on her round, fresh face, she would be starting her second position sometime next week. "Mr. Odergaard says—"

"As second shift Tech One, Mr. Odergaard is responsible for the live documents on his watch." Sam folded his arms. "I am the archivist. The dead belong to me."

Tory's agitation ceased, replaced by the so-still attitude Sam had encountered more and more frequently as the weeks passed. The weeks since ex–Interior Minister van Reuter and his lawyer had begun visiting Fort Sheridan. The weeks since they had begun asking for documents from the Service Investigative Bureau Archives. Documents describing murder. Mutiny. Conspiracy. Documents that could not be found.

And everyone blames me. Little Sam—you know him. Small, wiry chap. Hair like tar. Face like a daze.

He stepped from behind the table and beckoned for Tory to follow him back to the aisle after aisle of paper-crammed shelving that constituted the SIB stacks. *Because they think I'm . . . unwell.*

"Unwell or not, *K* still comes after *H.*" He waited at the stack entry for Tory, who lagged behind. He'd gotten used to that, too. The aversion people evinced at having to work with him, talk to him. The vague feeling that people just wished he'd go away.

We have that in common, van Reuter. The ex-minister's hawklike visage surfaced in Sam's memory. From the stairwell scuttlebutt he had heard, the man who had once been the *V* in the NUVA-SCAN technology conglomerate had become a pariah amongst his own. Isolated. Maligned. Blamed for every misstep taken by the Families in the last twenty years.

Sam felt a chill sense of kinship with van Reuter, in spite of the crimes the man was alleged to have committed. *It's all your fault, and no one wants to hear you explain.* He held the door open for Tory, and maintained his air of polite reserve as she dodged past him into the stacks. A great thing, to have so much in common with such a great man.

"I apologize for taking you away from your work, Sam. I understand you've been very busy."

"That's all right, Doctor."

"Look into the light."

"Yes, Doctor." Sam lifted his head and stared into the red glow, positioned a scant meter in front of his face. At first, it shone with a single, steady beat. Then it fluttered, skipped, skittered across its source surface like a bug in a bottle.

Another light joined it. Another. Finally, an entire series of red pulses stuttered and popped, filling his range of vision like a silent, monochrome-fireworks display.

After a few minutes, the reversal began. Fewer lights. Fewer. Mad perturbations slowed and steadied. A handful of lights. Five. Three. Two. One.

Stopped.

Sam blinked, worked his neck, yawned. Sitting in the dark had reminded him how tired he was. The *Hilfington* rosters had finally turned up. Tory had found them shoved in between two accounts-receivable folders, under the letter *P. One crisis averted.* But the *Kensington* rosters remained missing, as were so many other things. The day's single success did little to lessen the pressure Sam felt from Odergaard, who felt it from Yance, who felt it from the Head of Archives, who in turn had to deal with Veda's foot on her neck.

Normally, he despised his visits to Sheridan's Main Hospital. But today, the relief he felt at being able to leave the SIB basement made him want to cry.

The room lights blazed to life. Sam shut his eyes against the assault.

"Did that bother you at all?"

He opened one watering eye to see Dr. Pimentel standing near the examining-room entry, his hand still resting on the lighting pad. He shrugged. "I found it interesting, at first. Then it became irritating."

Pimentel hung his head. He seemed to grow older with each passing visit. The blond hair, more dull and lank. The eyes, more fatigued. He had to be at least twenty years younger than Sam, no more than thirty-five. What did he do that drained him so? "Irritating? How?"

Sam struggled to construct an explanation. It seemed such a trivial thing, hardly worth the effort. "It appeared so . . . tentative. I kept waiting for it to make up its mind."

Pimentel continued to watch him from his post by the door. Then he walked back to his seat next to Sam's examining table with the round-shouldered trudge of someone who bore the weight of the world. "Sam." He always took care to pronounce Sam's name in proper Bandan fashion—*Sahm* rhymes with *Mom*, not *Sam* rhymes with *damn.* "I subjected you to that test for a reason. If you were indeed augmented, as you claimed during your last visit, you would not have been able to look into that light for more than a few seconds without it affecting you."

Sam thought back to his previous visit. Tried to think back. It had been sunny . . . no, rainy . . . wait, they hadn't had any rain for over a month. Or had it been two? "Affecting me?"

The ergoworks in Pimentel's seat creaked as he leaned forward. "Blink patterns are designed to affect Service augments in very specific ways. You've been here often enough in the past few months to have heard the term *takedown.* That's when we use blink patterns to halt the progression of an unwanted overdrive state, a situation where the panic-dampening function of the augment asserts itself in a nonconflict situation. We do it both as a semiannual precautionary treatment, and, when necessary, to short-circuit an acute event."

"I told you I was augmented?" Sam reached into his shirt pocket and pulled out his Service-issued handheld. He kept all his appointments in it. And his little notations. Where the men's room was, for example. Well, the SIB was a large building—it was an easy thing to forget. *What did I tell Pimentel, and when?* He'd kept no record of that, unfortunately.

"Yes, Sam. You did." Pimentel glanced at the handheld, his tired eyes flaring with curiosity. "The aftereffects of a takedown aren't pleasant. The patient can feel fatigued and disoriented for as long as a week after treatment. Unfortunately, much milder versions of blink patterns can have a similar, though lesser, effect. For that reason, many augments develop an aversion to the color red, and become highly agitated when exposed to arrays of blinking lights. We take that into account here at Sheridan, where the augmented population stands at twenty-seven percent. Certain types of lighted displays and exhibits are expressly forbidden. Enforcement becomes difficult during the various holiday celebrations, of course." He grinned weakly. "But it's different in the world outside the Shenandoah Gate. No holds barred in Chicago, a city you visit three to four times a week." He grew serious. "Am I right?"

Sam nodded, resisting the urge to check his handheld again. "I visit the city, yes."

"You visit the various Service Archives to research the names for inclusion in the Gate. You travel at night, from what you told me. You find it easier to work when no one else is around. You take the Sheridan Local Line, which passes the Pier exhibits, the Bluffs Zoo, the Commonwealth Gardens. They each have thrill rides. All-night exhibits." Pimentel's weary gaze never left Sam's face. He seemed to be prompting him, reminding him of his life. As though—

As though he doesn't think I can remember on my own.

"I guarantee you, Sam," the doctor continued, "if you were augmented, you couldn't look at those exhibits, because *every* augment I examine mentions having a problem with at least one of them when they visit the city. Some wear special eyefilms to filter out the light.

Some wear hearing protection because they've developed related sensitivity to any sound resembling emergency sirens or explosions. But every one of them does *something*, because otherwise, they become very sick very quickly.

Sam's chest tightened as his anger grew. "You knew from my encephaloscan that I didn't have a Service-type augmentation?"

"Yes, Sam. You're the one who seemed to require convincing."

"My augmentation is different." Yes, that was it. Pimentel must have only asked him whether he was augmented, not what type of augmentation he had. He hammered Sam with vagueness, then called foul when Sam responded in kind. *Don't ask me what I remember, Doctor, ask me what I know.* "It's not a Service augmentation. It's something else."

"Define *something else,* Sam."

"It was supposed to make me hear things. See things. Feel things, deep in my body."

"That's an odd function for an augmentation. Why was it made that way?"

"Because they wanted to study my reactions. Because they wanted to see what I'd do."

"They?" Pimentel glanced down at his recording board, then back at Sam. "Who's they?"

"The ones—" Sam blinked away images that flashed in his eyes like the patterns. Faces. Gold. White. The gold ones spoke. He couldn't understand the words. "The ones who put it there."

Pimentel continued to write, the scratch of his stylus filling the small room. "Were you implanted against your will?"

"Yes."

"You felt paralyzed? Not in control?"

"Ye—" Sam could feel it again. The clench of anger that told him he was being maneuvered "Have I told you this before?"

Pimentel shook his head. "No, this is new. For the past few months, you've been insisting you're a xenogeologist. You showed me papers you'd written, books you'd had published." He pocketed his stylus and rocked back in his seat. "You had taken those papers and books from the SIB Archives, Sam. They weren't yours."

"No, I—"

"Sam, the e-scan didn't reveal a Service augmentation. It only confirmed what we've known for months. You have a tumor, in your thalamus, that's affecting your memory. It causes you to forget events that really happened, and to substitute fabrications to fill in the gaps."

"A tumor?" Sam poked the back of his head, then let his hand fall back into his lap. Silly. It wasn't as though he could feel the thing if he probed long enough.

Pimentel nodded. "It hasn't increased in size over time, but we need to remove it."

"I'll die."

"If we take the tumor *out*, why would you die?"

"They—they told me I'd die, if anyone took it out."

"No, you won't, Sam."

"Yes, I will!" *I know.* "This . . . tumor—it's not hurting me, it's not affecting my life, my work."

"Sam, it *is* starting to interfere with your ability to do your job." Pimentel stood and walked to his desk. "You've built a reputation over the years as a first-class archivist. But now you're losing papers, forgetting where you filed them, making up stories that they were stolen." He leaned against the desk as though he needed the support. "You need treatment."

Sam stared down at the floor. Dull grey lyno, flecked with white. He recalled seeing a stone that resembled it. Holding it in his hand. The where escaped him, however. The when.

"Sam, you don't state the names of any family or friends in the Emergency Notification block in your chart."

"There is no one."

"No one you can talk to? No one you feel you can trust?"

"No."

Pimentel returned to his seat. "Do you know what a ward of the Commonwealth is?"

The clench returned, stronger this time. "It means I'm supposed to trust a member of the government to take care of me."

"No, to help *you* take care of yourself. And it isn't just one person. It's a committee. In your case, it would consist of an impartial civilian official, a Service adjudicator, and a medical representative." Pimentel smiled. "Most likely me, as your attending physician."

"No." Sam slid off the examining table. His feet struck the lyno that reminded him of stone. "I've trusted members of the government to take care of me before. That proved a mistake."

"When, Sam?"

"I don't remember." *Don't ask me what I remember. Ask me what I know.*

He waited until after midnight to return to the SIB. Odergaard had left a note requesting Sam stop by to see him before start of shift later that day. That didn't bode well. If previous events repeated, that meant another document had turned up missing.

Sam sat at his desk, head in hands. Pimentel had made him promise to consider the wardship, and he had said he would. Anything to get out of that place.

No one cuts into my head. Ever. He left the cubicle maze of the doc tech bullpen and walked down the hall to the vend alcove. He bought a cup of tea, striking the beverage dispenser with a timed series of thumps the techs had discovered made it disgorge an extra mouthful into the cup. Since he was the alcove's only visitor, he had his pick of tables. He chose one in the corner, farthest from the entry.

He activated his handheld and pulled up the file he had unfortunately found many reasons to update over the past weeks. In one column, he had listed all the documents that had gone missing, in the other, the ones that had eventually turned up. He sorted, ran a discard, and examined the few items that still remained outstanding.

The roster. Shipping records. Death certificates. The roster and records belonged to the CSS *Kensington*, the flagship of the group that executed the evacuation of Rauta Shèràa Base.

And the death certificates? *Ebben. Unser. Fitzhugh. Caldor.* Three officers and a Spacer First Class, who died during the evacuation.

Sam stared at the small display and tried to divine a pattern from the list of documents. Like flecks in stone, they seemed anarchic, unconnected. But he sensed history, just as he would if he studied the stone. If he subjected the stone to elemental analysis and investigated the site at which he'd found it, he would know how it formed, and why. So, too, with these documents—they could be broken down, as well. Every entry had another piece of paper to back it up, and when he had uncovered those pieces, well, then he'd know, wouldn't he? He never liked to conclude ahead of his data. At the beginning, it was enough to know that sufficient reason existed for the data to be collected.

He sipped his tea, heavily creamed and sugared to obscure the bitterness. Not like at his old stomping grounds on Banda. *The university.* There, they knew how to make tea.

"And I knew how to drink it." He recalled overhearing a shopkeeper brag to another customer one day as he made his purchases. *No one in Halmahera knows tea like Simyam Baru—*

Sam paused, then checked the nameplate on his handheld. *Duong.* First name Sam, rhymes with Mom.

"My name is Sam Duong." But pictures formed in his imagination again. He saw himself encased in ice, then heard the hissing crackles as fissures formed in the block. Water dripped as the melting progressed, revealing who he truly was. Another man, who hated hospitals, too.

Again, not something he remembered. Something he knew.

CHAPTER 5

Evan stood before his shallow bank of roses and inventoried the status of each bush in turn. "The Crème Caramel's looking good." He dictated the observation into his handheld as he hefted a branch laden with butterscotch blooms. "Tell your Dr. Banquo she knows her fertilizer."

Banquo . . . Banquo. Evan paused, his finger pressed against the handheld touchpad, as the names cascaded in his head. *Banquo . . . Mako. Mako . . . Pierce.* "It's been over two weeks, Quino. I just wondered if you'd scrounged anything about Colonel Pierce. The more I think about that name, the more familiar it sounds." That was a lie, but he'd had lots of time to ponder the colonel's snub, and the more he thought about it, the more it bothered him. Information flitted throughout military bases at speed—he wondered if Pierce knew something, something that made him feel he didn't need to hide his dislike for his fallen minister. Perhaps the Service had reopened its investigation of Jani's transport explosion. Perhaps it had found a witness, someone who had stumbled past the comroom just as Evan had contacted the fuel depot where the transport was hangared. Saw him enter the comcode. Heard him say the words.

Do it.

He grunted in pain, and looked down to find he had gripped the Crème's branch too hard, driving the thorns into his hand. He hunted through his pockets for a clean dispo, dabbed at the welling beads of blood, and moved on to the next shrub. "I'm not sure about this Wolfshead Westminster. It's still washed-out rust instead of bright orange, but I don't know what you expect. It's a cold-weather hybrid that thrives by waterside, and we're only in the middle of the hottest, driest summer in thirty years." He flicked off the device and shoved it in his pocket. "Report's over for the day, Quino. You want to see how your goddamn roses are doing, drive up here and check them yourself."

His knee ached less than it had for weeks—a walk seemed in order. He strode to the end of the garden, then turned and paced alongside the two-meter-tall hedge that defined his boundary with the neighbor who he'd been told worked for Commerce Purchasing. Then he made a balance beam of the edge of his patio and finished the traverse by walking along the latticed polywood fence that formed the barrier between him and the neighbor who he'd been told slaved for the Commonwealth Mint. He knew better, of course. Prime Minister's Intelligence, both of them. He'd have bet his last bottle.

When he cut by the garden and stood again at the spot at which he had started, he checked his timepiece. "Elapsed time for inspection of the van Reuter fences—seventy-two seconds." And he had even walked slowly this time.

How do people live like this? Cheek by jowl. Sounds of their lives commingled into one vast blare. Everyone knowing their business and them knowing everyone else's, without one minute's privacy or peace. They all must have developed a zoo-animal mentality, he decided, living their lives as their instincts compelled them without caring who saw what.

"Sir!"

Evan turned. Halvor, his aide, stood on the patio, looking befuddled as usual. "*Yes?*"

The young man hesitated. "You have . . . a visitor, sir."

Evan trudged up the shallow incline toward the house he thought of as his Elba. "Quino isn't supposed to stop by until tomorrow."

Halvor's face, smooth and rounded as an overgrown baby's, flushed pink. "It's not Mr. Loiaza, sir."

"Well, who is it?"

Halvor told him.

Evan took care to follow his aide at a carefully calculated distance. Too close, and he'd seem anxious. Too far, and he'd seem apprehensive. *Stay calm . . . stay calm.*

After the glaring brightness of the outdoors, it took a few seconds for his eyes to adjust to the dimmer light of the sitting room. He didn't register the figure standing in front of the curtained window until it spoke.

"Hello, Evan." John Shroud stood with his back to him, his attention focused on the view of the rear yard. "You're due for a medical checkup. Compassionate visitation, the Jo'burg Convention calls it. Guess who drew the short straw?"

Evan motioned for the flustered Halvor to leave the room. He sank into his favorite lounge chair and waited for the hushed click that indicated the door had closed. "You expect me to believe you flew in from Seattle just to check my vitals?"

"You're an ex–Cabinet Minister, Evan. You rate Big Three attention."

"Bullshit."

Shroud turned slowly. "As you wish." He had employed his albinism like a fashion accessory, as usual. Today, he resembled a polished marble of a medieval monk. He'd brushed his stark white hair forward and had dressed in ivory from head to toe, the collar of his jacket draping like a cowl. His height, thinness, and long face reinforced the image, as did his blanched skin, drawn tight across cheekbone and brow. Disturbing, no matter how often you'd seen him. The ambassador from the Other Side.

I should have expected this. Evan wished he'd had the sense to prepare, but except for a quick swig prior to tending his roses, he'd had nothing to drink that morning. As ever, abstinence proved a mistake. He always felt more in control with a half liter of bourbon warming his insides. "What really brings you to Chicago, John?" As if he couldn't guess.

"It's been raining for two solid weeks back home." Shroud's bass voice rumbled like a knell. "I need sunshine, even if all I can do is look." He strolled to the sofa and sat down. "Besides, I don't often get the chance to visit the capital." He stretched out his long, thin legs and crossed them at the ankles, then looked around the room, sharp eyes taking in the cramped dimensions, the shabby furniture, before coming to rest on Evan. "Cozy," he said, with a ghost of a smile.

Evan responded in kind. "I think so."

"Quite a change from the old Family estate."

"Quite."

"Smaller."

"Yes."

"A woman's presence, of course, is what makes a home." Shroud's smile withered. "I never had the opportunity to offer my condolences. Lyssa's death came as a shock to us all."

Evan tensed at the sound of his dead wife's name. "Thank you."

"I spoke with Anais last evening, at one of Vandy's interminable dinner parties. Milla's staying with her for the summer. Lyssa's aunt and mother together again, after so many years. Sad how it takes such tragedy to reunite sisters." Shroud shook his head. "Anais had a great deal to say about Lyssa's death. I think she used it as a shield to avoid discussing that idiotic food-transport screwup she helped engineer that upset the idomeni so, but then Family gossip has always been more riveting than idomeni food philosophies."

"Transporting foodstuffs in sight of their embassy was incredibly stupid." Evan leapt at the chance to dismantle Anais's diplomatic blunder. He was starved for news from the capital. Besides, he didn't want to discuss Lyssa's death. "I understand the idomeni almost packed up and returned home?"

"Not as long as Nema draws breath." Shroud's air of mild interest never altered. "Tell me, was Lyssa's skimmer crash really an accident or did you arrange matters, as Anais claims?"

"I didn't—" Evan's fingers curved around a nonexistent glass. "Despite assurances to the contrary, I'm fairly certain the walls have ears." He pulled up his sleeve to expose his security cuff. "And I'm not altogether confident about the jewelry, either."

Shroud pressed a hand over his heart as though taking a pledge. "Jo'burg also allows us our privacy. And in case anyone's forgotten that, I'm well fitted out in the counter-monitoring department. Now, back to Anais—"

"I didn't realize you and she were so close."

"We're not." Shroud draped an arm along the sofa back. "But she does bend every ear she can these days." The smile again. "And you do have a history of engaging in that sort of thing."

Silence stretched. Just before it snapped, a muted tapping sounded. Evan offered up a silent thank-you. "Come in."

Markhart, his housekeeper, entered pushing a beverage trolley. She was elderly, short and compact—a white raisin of a woman in a shapeless tunic and trousers—but she possessed enough wit to compensate for Halvor's lack of same. Despite the smiling greetings, she detected the tension between the two men. She maneuvered the low-slung trolley between them like a barrier and, after waiting for a small nod from Evan, left them to serve themselves.

"As I was saying." Shroud leaned forward and poured himself coffee from the carafe. "An old habit is an easy fallback, and you've one that's hard to break. Killing people when they become dangerous, or inconvenient—"

"I've never killed anyone." Evan cracked the seal on a bottle of bourbon. "My attorney would be very interested to hear you've been telling people otherwise." He filled his tumbler, then added a splash of soda. His hands shook. His voice didn't.

Shroud's shoulder twitched. "You've never done the dirty yourself, no. Someone else interfered with Lyssa's augmentation so that she hallucinated herself into a fatal crash. Durian Ridgeway strangled that poor dexxie last winter." He stared into his cup, grimacing as though some ugly scene played itself out on the coffee's reflective surface. "Someone else placed the bomb on Jani's transport."

Evan took a large gulp of his drink. Liquid heat warmed him like an internal sun. "*Someone else.* Those are the two words that will have me sleeping in my ancestral bed by Christmas."

"You think so?" Shroud set his cup down on the sofaside table. He stood, reached inside his jacket, and removed a folded documents slipcase from his inner pocket. "I received this by special messenger two months ago, about the time the first of those pro-Evan stories appeared in the news." He unfolded the slipcase and removed a single sheet of parchment. "That is, I received the original, which is safely locked away. This is a copy."

Evan's heart skipped as his stomach went into free fall. It took all the willpower he could muster to keep from pulling away as Shroud held out the blue-trimmed white page for his perusal.

"It's an old Consulate comlog, a list of all the outgoing communications made by executive staff on the day Jani's transport exploded in midair." When Evan made no move to take the document, Shroud placed it across his knees. "You gave the order to have the bomb placed on board. The time, location, and comport code all identify you as the person who called the Service fuel depot outside Rauta Shèràa just before the transport that was assigned to pick up Jani and the other members of the Twelfth Rover Corps departed for Knevçet Shèràa."

Evan took a sip of his drink, more to moisten his dry mouth than for the alcohol. "That isn't enough evidence to convict."

"It's a start." Shroud returned to his seat. "It may even be enough to persuade Li Cao to turn you over to Commonwealth Intelligence for a dose of Sera."

"Truth drug?" Evan managed a harsh laugh. "Even if her Prime Ministry was at stake, Li would never set that precedent. Not if she thought there was the slightest chance it could come back to haunt the Families."

"If the colonies keep threatening to cancel Service base leases and limit port privileges for Commonwealth shipping, she'll set it." Shroud tasted his coffee and sighed contentedly. "If Nema keeps dangling access rights to idomeni GateWays in front of her nose like the weighty carrot it is, she'll inject you herself."

"Nema's a figurehead. The Oligarch will never allow him the authority to make deals like those."

"On the contrary, his influence grows every day. Cèel may despise him, but he knows the old bastard understands us better than any other Vynshàrau in his government. He needs him."

Evan took another swallow of bourbon. The colonies could be slapped down with a few good embargoes, but the unpredictable Nema added a new dimension to the term *wild card.* "I can't speak for the idomeni," he said in an effort to rally, "but I know for a fact the colonies have no authority to cancel those leases."

"Well, they're using the argument that if their signatures were necessary to validate the agreements, there must be some power behind them. Would you want to be the Prime Minister who tells them, no, we just let you sign off so you'd think you mattered?" Shroud plucked a cookie from the sweets tray. "You're in a nasty position, Evan. Li needs a head to stick on a pike to show the colonies she's acting in good faith, and yours is the most expendable. You're the last van Reuter. No desperate relatives to scurry about assembling a defense, no wide-eyed offspring to parade before the holocams—" He stalled in mid-chew, his face reddening.

Evan watched the man's growing embarrassment with grim satisfaction. "You were saying, John?"

"My apologies. Some things are off-limits, even during the final rounds."

"Go to hell, you bleached bastard."

Shroud dropped the remains of the cookie on his saucer. "You're alone. I'm offering you a chance to keep your head."

"At the risk of losing yours? Withholding evidence in a murder investigation is a capital crime."

"You're the murderer being investigated. I doubt you'll be filing a complaint." Shroud shook his snowy head. "No, what *is* in your best interest is to develop amnesia when Service Investigative asks you questions about Jani."

"I couldn't do that. They've already received preliminary reports from my attorney as to what I'll be saying. If I back down, they'll know something's wrong. And if they don't, Joaquin sure as hell will."

"You're a maintenance alcoholic who's gone without proper medical care for months." Shroud's look turned professional—it was obvious from his stern expression that he didn't like what he saw. "You've lost weight. You look like hell. I'm sure your nutritional indices would indicate several key deficiencies, some of which can lead to memory disturbance." He spread his long-fingered hands in an offering gesture, as though what he promised was worth a damn. "It's the cleanest way, and with me signing off on any diagnosis, there will be no questions."

"Selective amnesia?" Evan picked up the comlog with his thumb and index finger and tossed it atop the beverage trolley.

Shroud folded the document back in its slipcase and tucked it away. As was his habit, he'd filmed his eyes to complement his clothing—the pale gold-brown irises formed the only spots of warmth in his cold face. "I'll schedule you for a complete work-up at the downtown facility. We can discuss matters further then." He set his cup aside, then reached alongside the sofa and hefted a large carryall onto his lap. "Now, in case one of us ever has to testify as to what occurred here, if you wouldn't mind undressing . . ."

Shroud's preliminary examination proved mercifully quick. He drew blood deftly and completed swab samplings well before muscles tightened and gag reflexes kicked in.

"Do you just dislike eating," he asked as he watched Evan dress, "or are you consciously trying to starve yourself?"

Evan yanked on his shirt. So what if his ribs showed? They had for as long as he remembered. "I like good food."

"As a modest complement to plenty of good wine, I'm sure." Shroud rummaged through the carryall, removing a variety of bottles and cartons. "Get started on these. The bottles contain supplements. The cartons contain food additives and mixes. Drinks. Soups." He concentrated on arranging the containers atop the trolley. "I only ask because I'm required by law, not because I personally give a damn, but are you sure you want to continue with things as they are? A brain insert and a gene retrofit, and it could all be a distant memory."

Evan tucked in his shirt. "I'm a content drunk, John. Leave me be." He tightened his belt, using the last of the holes he'd punched only last month.

"As you wish. Your left knee requires a rebuild. The stabilizers you had inserted last winter were only temporary." Shroud hestitated. "I heard Jani had something to do with that."

"Ah, don't mince words, John. She cornered me in my office and cracked my knee to keep me from running off." Evan flexed the joint, which emitted its inevitable click. "Just before she crippled me, she killed Durian Ridgeway. The sheets called it suicide, but she broke his neck." He remembered it well, since he had been ordered to identify the body. In the interest of efficiency, he'd been told, but he had known better. He had stood in Durian's office, supported by Justice officials on either side, injured leg numbed to the hip. The crime-scene tech lifted the corner of the tarp and someone bit out, *Take a good, hard look.*

The images sneaked up on Evan now, sceneshots etched into his brain. Durian's goggled eyes. The unnatural twist of his neck.

He walked over to a wall-mounted mirror and concentrated on hand-combing his hair. "Durian. Rik Neumann. The Laum encampment at Knevçet Shèràa. Our Jani has a pretty lengthy history herself, and those are only the deaths we know about." He watched Shroud shift containers back and forth. "She's lived on the thin edge for almost twenty years—God only knows what else she's guilty of."

Shroud's head shot up. "I don't care." His eyes glittered, their fervor promising stakes and bonfires to anyone who crossed him. The monk gone mad. "I'll do whatever it takes to save her. If that means jumping down the hellhole and dragging the entire Commonwealth in after me, I'll do it."

Evan watched the color rise in Shroud's cheeks like fever. *You lovesick fool.* What did he expect in return for his risk-taking, gratitude? *You've picked the wrong girl, Johnny boy—trust me, I speak from experience.* He walked to the trolley, picked the largest cakelet he could find, and popped it into his mouth. "Jani had managed to get her hands on that log just prior to my arrest. After that, it disappeared. Any idea who sent it to you?"

Shroud eyed him warily, then shook his head. "None. All my efforts to retrace the delivery route petered out." His manner grew more distant as he calmed. "Whoever it was, they knew how to cover their trail. And they knew I had the background to understand what the information in that log implied. And the willingness to use it." He closed the carryall and hoisted it to his shoulder. "Good-bye, Evan. See you in a few days."

Evan charged Markhart with seeing Shroud to the door. He refilled his glass, this time without soda, and wandered out into the backyard.

He tried to consider his options, but thoughts skittered away like beads from a broken string. He studied his fingers, which had stiffened, the nail beds tinged with blue. He shivered. *I'm in shock.* He remembered the sensations from that day on the lakeshore, just as he remembered the other things. Lyssa's screams. The chill smoothness of Serena's small hand as he touched it for the last time.

"He doesn't like you."

Evan wheeled to find Markhart standing behind him. She stood only a stride away, so near that she had to tilt her head back to look at him. *She's so short.* He'd known it, of course. He just hadn't realized it. "I don't like him, either. You don't have to like the people you work with."

The woman pondered, her worn face grave. "My sister scolds me for working for you. She says you're a killer. But she works at Sheridan, and her husband's retired Service, so her viewpoint is skewed." Her voice, made ragged by nic-sticks, was shaded by a muted accent Evan couldn't place. "Others don't think that way."

Down the street, a dog barked. Evan stiffened. "And what way do those others think?"

"They think that whatever you did, or didn't do, you paid." Markhart's normally aloof demeanor softened. "Because of the children."

The barking increased. Another dog joined in, followed by the whining hum of older-model skimmers. Evan's heart thudded. "Is that what you think?"

Markhart sighed. "I think you're a very sad man." She frowned at the glass in his hand. "I think you drink too much." She smiled sadly, lined face crinkling. "Maybe you don't want me to think anymore." She squared her hunched shoulders. "Now I have a dinner to prepare. Another one that you won't eat."

"What are we having?"

"Tomato-dill soup from one of the boxes Dr. Shroud gave you. And kettle beef." She raised her chin in response to Evan's scowl. "They only allow me so much to run this house, sir, and I can't afford real animal on what they give." She nodded. "But there's fresh peas I need to shell, so if you'll excuse me."

"Wait a minute," Evan said, "I'll help." He started out walking alongside her, but as shouts and laughter sounded from the surrounding homes, he quickened his pace until his knee crunched with every stride. Shroud's visit had rattled him—he normally sequestered himself indoors long before this. He always avoided the outside in the afternoon, when school had let out for the day, and the children returned home.

CHAPTER 6

The skimchair stalled as it floated down the gangway leading from the shuttle gate into the O'Hare Service Terminal concourse. Jani gripped the sides of her floating seat as two members of her escort tried to wrestle it through the narrow arch. After one particularly hard push, the chair shuddered, bucked, then bounced to the floor and back up into the air. Her stomach turned. The acid rose in her throat.

"How many mainliners does it take to push a skimchair?" Jani *thought* she muttered under her breath. Every other person and device in the concourse chose that moment to fall silent, however—her commentary cut the air like inappropriate sounds usually did.

The mainline lieutenant who steered glanced over her head at the mainline lieutenant who ruddered, then at her. "Do you have any suggestions, Captain?"

"The signals from the doorscan and the skimchair lift array are confounding one another. Ask someone from Port Security to shut down the doorscan until you can push me through."

The looie grimaced. He was a man of action, who preferred pulling and grappling and nauseating his passenger to asking for help. He released the chair grudgingly and strode off in search of a Security guard, the red stripe on the side of his trousers flicking like an ambulatory exclamation point.

Jani crossed her arms over her queasy stomach. Then she looked through the arch at the third member of her escort, who had entered the concourse ahead of them and now sat perched on the arm of a nearby bench, regarding her with mock solemnity. He had worn the same sideline summer-weights since they'd departed MarsPort; days of wear had left the light grey short-sleeve and steel blue trousers rumpled, the sideline white trouser stripe puckered. His pale skin, black, curly hair, and stocky build would have marked him as Josephani Dutch even without his accent, which sounded like Hortensian German with the edges ground down.

Piers Friesian. Major. Defense command, out of Fort Constanza. Appointed by the staff Judge Advocate to see to her defense. A nice enough man. She wondered what he had done to deserve her.

He rocked back on his tenuous seat and locked his hands around his knee. "I heard the news walking by one of the kiosks. Acadia Central United won its final qualifying match. They defeated Jersey Conglomerate four to one."

Jani managed a smile. "That means they've drawn a first-round bye."

"The merry dance starts in two weeks. Guess who I'm rooting for?"

"Josephan Arsenal."

"You got it."

"Won't make it out of the quals." Behind her, the rearguard looie swallowed a chuckle.

"Says you." The light in Friesian's eyes dimmed. He glanced over the top of Jani's head at Rearguard, who stepped around the skimchair into the concourse and took a seat beyond hearing range. "How are you feeling?"

"Fine, sir."

Friesian ran a hand over his face. "Fine, sir. You said that at Fort Constanza, just before that stomachache dropped you like a rock. You also said it just as we broke through Felix GateWay. Right after that, you passed out, then awoke two days later speaking street Acadian and insisting you were fifteen years old. I don't think the medical officers will ever be the same. Neuro was *not* his specialty."

"I was fine by the time we reached MarsPort."

"Yes, you were. You did tell me that. I thought we might actually get some work done. Then you ate lunch and became royally sick." His impatience broke through his even speech like flecks of foam on smooth water. "Your 'fine, sirs' aren't worth much, are they?"

Jani tugged at her own baggy short-sleeve. From what little she could remember of the last three weeks, it had once fit her perfectly—otherwise, she wouldn't have been issued it. How much of a weight loss did that imply? Five kilos? Ten? "What do you want me to say, sir?"

"I want you to call me Piers, and I want you to level with me."

Jani examined her right arm, halfway between elbow and wrist, where a tiny, round wound had healed to form a darkened scar. Her new Service ID chip lay implanted beneath. They had her now. If Security activated the proper codes, they could pinpoint her exact location in a room and tell whether she sat, stood, or did push-ups.

She looked through the arch into the heart of the concourse. Functional furnishings, well maintained and spotless. Lots of steel blue and silver on the walls and floor, accented by splashes of mainline red in the chair cushions and fixtures. Through the wide windows opposite her, trim shuttles and sleek aircraft glinted in the summer sun.

Every object she looked at, every surface, every blue-and-grey uniform, told her where she was, and what waited for her. *My name is Jani Moragh Kilian, Captain, United Services. Eighteen years ago, at a place called Knevçet Shèràa, I killed Colonel Rikart Neumann, my commanding officer. Now I've been brought here to pay.* He had deserved to die, but that wasn't the point. The Service frowned on the individual Spacer making that judgment, and they had a time-honored method for showing their displeasure. The firing squad. "I'm scared, Piers."

Friesian eyed her in puzzlement. "I'm not saying you have nothing to worry about. But considering the state of your health, you're doing yourself no favors holding back from me." He stood as Lieutenant Forceful came into view, a Security guard in tow. "We'll talk after we get checked in at Sheridan. After you check in at the hospital."

Shutting down the doorscan worked as Jani said it would, much to Forceful's disappointment. Their journey to the lower-level parking garage was punctuated by his comments as to how he could have jazzed the mech if only he'd had the time.

He made up for the loss, however, by brute-forcing the side conversion panels of their skimmer so the passenger opening could accommodate the skimchair. His joy multiplied manyfold when Friesian asked him to expand the interior space by pulling out one of the seats. Rearguard and the driver, a corporal with a squint, struggled to keep from laughing as they fielded the components that came flying out the door.

Jani eyed the pearl grey, triple-length that had been provided for their transport. The enamel coating shone wetly, even in the dull light of the garage. "What's with the chariot?" she asked Friesian.

He pointed to her seat. "It was the only vehicle available that could hold a skimchair."

"What about a brig van?"

Another look of puzzled appraisal. "Jani, why would you expect a brig van?"

Jani fell silent. *They stuck me with an idiot,* she thought as Forceful and Rearguard loaded her into the skimmer. The Judge Advocate was required by charter to provide for her defense, but the charter said nothing about the quality of defense they had to provide her with. Friesian obviously had no idea what crime she'd committed or what the Service planned to do to her after they convicted her. He'd sit at the Officers' Club bar after her execution and wonder where the hell it all went wrong.

As they departed the garage, the sudden change from half-light to full glare of summer caught them all by surprise. Jani shut her eyes to stop them tearing, while Rearguard exploded with a sharp burst of sneezing. The Boul artery on which they rode seemed to glimmer in the heat. Chicago had been buried beneath mountains of snow the last time Jani had visited. Now, she could see the verdant patches of parkland and clusters of low houses, backed by the distant skyline.

Their driver took them on a route that skirted the city—within minutes, they left the crowding traffic behind. The four-lane skimway they rode cut along a line of homes obscured from view by large stands of trees.

"The South Bluffs." Forceful gazed out the window and sighed. "This is the low-rent section, and still all I can afford to do is look."

"Why would you want to live here, Don?" Rearguard sniffed as he took in the view.

"Because it's the *Bluffs*, Lou. Once a man can call this place home, he knows he's arrived."

Jani caught the look that passed between Friesian and Rearguard Lou, the chins-up camaraderie of those who had scaled the barriers of opinion since they decided to make the Service their career. That opinion originated in the homes they passed now. *All you with the wrong parents, wrong names, wrong accents, raise your hands.* Friesian looked down at his lap, while Lou concentrated on the view out his window.

The skimmer exited down a corkscrew ramp, then turned onto a two-lane road that ran along a massive fence built of arched whitestone and metal bridging. The five-meter-high barrier stretched ahead as far as Jani could see.

"Have you ever seen the Shenandoah Gate, Captain?" Rearguard Lou asked her. "It was erected to honor the tens of thousands who died at the Appalachian Front during the Greatest War." That those thus honored had died for the Earthbound side could be discerned from the gleam of resentment that lit his eyes.

"This year's the seventy-fifth anniversary of its completion."

Don seemed oblivious to the other man's displeasure. "The archivists are working night and day researching names for addition to the Placement Rolls." He shook his head in wonder. "It took the artisans eleven years to encode the grid-work and apply the coatings. Isn't it gorgeous?"

Jani caught the iridescent flickers of the names of the fallen as the sunlight played over the holoetching in the stone. "Lieutenant, in case you haven't noticed, you're talking to three colonials."

"It's a *Service* monument, ma'am." Don smoothed the front of his short-sleeve. "Besides, well, I hate to state the obvious, but the reason you're touchy is because your ancestors were asked to leave after the dust settled. Because they lost."

" 'Asked to leave'?" Jani smiled. "I like your choice of words, Lieutenant. Just for clarification, what words does your side use to refer to the internment camps and prison ships?"

Friesian tugged at his collar. "I read an editorial in *Blue and Grey* requesting a reevaluation of the Gate," he said hurriedly. "Over two-thirds of Service recruits come from the colonies. It does seem counterproductive to risk alienating them before they set foot on the base."

Don's eyes widened in surprise. "But sir—!"

"It's a matter of perspective, Lieutenant," Jani interrupted. "You're honoring yourselves because you won. You had the biggest governments and the richest companies behind you. You won control of the technologies and the freedoms and the privilege to dole them out. You won the right to send my ancestors to the colonies to work in your friends' factories and fields. You were quite happy with the outcome—you didn't need to examine it further. It was left to us as the losers to figure out the hows and whys, and after we did, we felt a little irked." She ignored Piers's warning look. "What do you know about the Battle of Waynesboro?"

Don frowned, as though she'd insulted his intelligence. "It was the turning point in the battle for eastern North America, ma'am. Major Alvin Cao came to his senses and brought his fifty thousand over to hook up with van Reuter's Fourteenth Armored out of Philly."

Jani nodded. "And if he hadn't come to his senses, as you say—we prefer the phrase *turned traitor*, the *C* in NUVA-SCAN was his price—Everhard would not have lost DC and the rest of the Eastern Seaboard wouldn't have dominoed in response. And there would have been no March to Albany."

"Yes, ma'am, but—"

"Seven thousand four-hundred eighteen losers died during that march. Their bodies were sprayed with dissolvant and tossed in ditches because your side judged *them* the traitors, undeserving of proper burial. A many-times-great-grandfather of mine was one of those losers. The only place his name is inscribed is in a Bible my father keeps in his workroom. Like I said, it's a matter of perspective."

Don nodded. He actually seemed to be listening, which was more than many Earthbounders did. "Can you say your side wouldn't have done the same thing if they'd won?"

Jani hesitated. She was colony, yes, and proud to be so. But life had left her few illusions about people, especially after the blood started flowing. "No, I can't. But that's not the point. The point is, all the dead merit remembrance. Even the ones who lost. Because first you forget who, and then you forget why. And then it happens all over again."

The skimmer turned onto the Fort Sheridan entry and passed beneath the Gate's main archway. The cabin darkened; the names inscribed inside the arch winked and faded. Then the view lightened; the sight of the numerous shade trees and multicolored shrubbery decorating Sheridan's rolling lawns dissipated the tension.

Borgie would have been in heaven, Jani thought as they passed teeming walkways that joined row after row of low-slung white-and-tan buildings. Her late sergeant hadn't been the most conventional of Spacers, but if you'd scratched him, he'd have bled blue and grey. He'd often told her that the only reason he'd ever visit Earth would be to walk the paths at Fort Sheridan. *I wish you were here.* She would have enjoyed listening to his blunt-edged take on her current predicament. She could have used the laugh.

"We'll be checking you into the Main Hospital first." Friesian leaned close to Jani so he could speak softly. "If you're through with the history lecture, that is." He sat back, eyes slitting as though a headache had placed a call.

In contrast to the glass-walled grandeur of every Neoclona facility Jani had ever seen, Fort Sheridan's Main Hospital showed squat and homely. Its white-cement surfaces were smooth and squared off, its windows short and narrow. Only ten floors, but what it lacked in height, it made up for in sprawl. Patients undergoing fitness therapy could get their day's exercise simply by trotting around its circumference.

Lou took it upon himself to maneuver Jani's chair to the hospital entry as Friesian supervised Don's refit of the skimmer. "*Bienvenu à Chicago, Capitaine,*" he whispered as he leaned forward to adjust the lift settings, touching his fingers to his forehead in a surreptitious salute.

"*Vous êtes un Manxman, Lieutenant*?" Jani didn't need to ask—the harsh tones of Man French branded him easily.

"*Oui, Capitaine.*" He backed away as Friesian approached. "*Vive la Manche,*" he mouthed, using the Channel Worlder's nickname for their network of planets.

A subversive Manxman. Jani touched her own forehead in return. *Quite a happy family the Service has here.* She sat back with a jolt as Friesian propelled her a shade faster than necessary into the cool depths of the hospital.

"Turn slowly, and walk back toward me."

As Jani tried to reverse her course, her right knee buckled. She grabbed the rails of her treadway just in time to keep from falling. "This thing is hard to walk on."

"There has been motor-nerve axon damage," a voice piped from behind the large analyzer that received signals from both the treadway and the numerous sensor buttons that studded Jani's arms, legs, trunk, and back. "I'm downloading the specific sites into her chart now."

The doctor who stood at the far end of the track offered Jani a quiet smile. Tall, thin, tired-looking—Hugh Tellinn's blond brother. "We'll be starting rebuild immediately. Along with digestive-enzyme adjustment and heme infusion." He held out his hand and helped her down the two short steps to the floor so the waiting nurse could pluck the buttons. "Are you feeling all right, Jani? You look dazed."

"I didn't expect to get herded into myotherapy so quickly." She glanced at the man's name tag. *R. Pimentel.* No rank designator visible on his medwhite shirt. Jani had yet to hear a title other than *Nurse* or *Doctor* over the past few hours, but she figured Pimentel for at least a major, judging from the way the other white coats deferred to him. Possibly even a colonel.

"We've been receiving your MedRecs via message central transmit for the past ten days, so we had a good idea what to expect. The *Reina*'s medical officer had a lot to send—let's just say this department's Misty account has topped out for the quarter." He continued to support her as they walked out of the therapy room and into an adjoining office. "Now, we need to ascertain your current status, judge whether it has improved or worsened, and commence the appropriate treatments as soon as possible." He helped Jani lower into a visitor's chair, then took a seat on the other side of the cluttered desk.

Jani looked around. Two filled bookcases, double-stacked with bound volumes and wafer folders. Holos of Admiral-General Hiroshi

Mako and Prime Minister Li Cao. A watercolor of a pleasant-looking woman holding a little girl. "So what happened to me, Colonel?"

"Colonel?" Pimentel's brows arched. "How did you arrive at that conclusion?"

Jani pointed behind him, to the narrow window. "You have a view."

"Well, I hate to break it to you, Captain, but this is Fort Sheridan, and we have windows to spare." Pimentel sat back. "But yes, I am a colonel."

"Full?"

"*Yes.* But I'm also a psychotherapeutic neurologist. Owing to the types of conditions I treat, I find it easier for both me and my patients if we leave the ranks in the lobby." Pimentel picked up a stylus from his desk and regarded the unlit tip. "We think the drug used to subdue you on Felix triggered this idiosyncratic reaction of yours. We may be dealing with a disease called porphyria, but thus far, we've been unable to identify the specific genetic mutation."

"A human genetic mutation?"

Pimentel hesitated. "For now. Until we have more data."

"Neoclona has a lot of data—why don't you request my file?"

Pimentel tapped the stylus on his knee. "Heme is manufactured in the bone marrow and the liver. Heme in the bone marrow is incorporated into hemoglobin; heme in the liver is incorporated into electron transport proteins, some of which metabolize drugs. The synthesis of the molecule is complicated; several intermediates and enzymes are involved. When a person possesses lower than normal activity of one of the enzymes, the precursors build up in either the bone marrow or the liver, depending on the enzyme involved."

When he's angry, he spouts techno. Jani decided to play good girl. He seemed to mean well—if she was nice to him, maybe he'd tell her why she was talking to him in his office with his family's picture on the wall instead of in a locked room in the brig infirmary. "I'm deficient in one of these enzymes?"

"Yes. Porphobilinogen deaminase, to be precise."

"Your wife married you because of your way with words, didn't she?"

Pimentel looked startled for a moment. Then he grinned bashfully. "PBG deaminase, for short. That makes your flavor acute intermittent porphyria. Its cardinal symptoms are the abdominal pain you developed at Fort Constanza, the psychotic episodes you experienced on the *Reina Adelaida*, and the neuropathy, or muscle weakness, you're showing now. It's extremely rare these days. Not life-threatening, usually—most people who have it don't even realize it. We normally only find it in the far-flung colonial outposts, where things tend to slip through the cracks."

"So people are usually born with it?"

"*Always* born with it. It's a genetic disorder, not something you acquire."

"That depends, doesn't it?"

Pimentel tossed the stylus back on his desk. "You know, whenever two or more doctors get together in the same room, the talk eventually turns to Neoclona's first patient. 'S-1.' Shèrá-1. The woman John Shroud wanted to make live forever." He seemed to stare past the painting of his wife and daughter, to someplace far away. "I've never met a legend." He looked at Jani. "Do I think something he did to you in Rauta Shèràa has come back to haunt you? I'm by no means Dr. Shroud's greatest fan, but I'd like to keep an open mind, for now. First, we need to stabilize your diet and repair the nerve and liver damage you've sustained." He reached for his comport pad. "You look exhausted. I'm going to have you taken to your room."

"My room?"

"I'm admitting you, Captain." The tired eyes grew steely. "I'll make it an order, if that's the only thing you'll accept."

They gave her a private room, owing to her rank. Dinner consisted of a fruit milk shake and dry toast; when she complained about the sweetness of the shake, they scrounged hot sauce to kill the flavor. She waited for Pimentel to burst in and order her out of his hospital for the murderer she was, but all he did was poke his head in and say good night. She waited for the guards to be posted outside her door, but they never came. She waited for Friesian to come and inform her of the charges against her, but the second-shift head nurse, a no-nonsense blonde named Morley, told her Pimentel had asked him to hold off until tomorrow.

They're not going to shoot me for Neumann's murder; they're going to shock me to death. Jani lay back against her soft Service-issue pillows, in her dove grey Service-issue pajamas, and worried herself to sleep.

CHAPTER 7

"Good morning, Jani."

Jani looked up from her magazine to find the morning nurse standing in the sunroom doorway.

"You have a visitor." He stepped aside. "You can go in now."

"It's about time." Lucien Pascal brushed past the man and strode into the room. When his eyes locked with Jani's he smiled broadly, at first glance the walking equivalent of a bright summer day.

"Hello." He dragged a chair over to the sunny corner Jani occupied, white-blond hair flashing in the diffuse sunlight. He'd acquired a tan since she'd last seen him—his grey short-sleeve looked silver against his skin, now almost as brown as hers.

"How did you get in to see me ahead of my lawyer?" Jani watched his shoulder muscles flex beneath the fitted shirt as he positioned his chair. The southerly view wasn't bad, either. "They're not going to let him in until this afternoon."

Lucien held up his arm to show her the thin silver band encircling his wrist. "Outpatient monitoring."

"They let you come here for your takedowns? An Intelligence officer?" Augmentation was one thing she and Lucien had in common, although his prototypical version had boosted the nonempathetic aspect of his personality in addition to adjusting his panic response. "I thought they'd put you in secure lockdown in case you started talking."

"No, I only come here for psych evals." Lucien's eyes, rich brown and normally as lifeless as spent embers, flared with disdain. "I had my last takedown at the Intelligence infirmary. Before that, they were supervised by Eamon DeVries—he's Anais's personal physician."

"Now that's a match made in hell." Jani shivered at the memory of DeVries' rough examinations. *Did that hurt, Kilian? Well, too damned bad.*

"But enough about me." Lucien fixed her with an angry stare, every trace of good humor extinguished. "You never even said good-bye."

"I'm sorry."

"I had your escape route all planned. I also had interested parties to answer to for your disappearance. What happened, didn't you trust me?"

Not completely. "You know I don't trust easily."

"I thought you understood me well enough to make an exception." He tugged at his outpatient band. "Hell of a lot of good your secrecy did you. They still caught you."

"If you came here to cheer me up, you're doing a good job."

"I came here to deliver a message." To Jani's surprise, Lucien slipped into Middle Vynshàrau, complete with posture and gestures. "*The chief propitiator of the Vynshàrau bids the glories of the day to his most excellent Eyes and Ears.*"

"You—" She stopped. Counted to ten. Twice. "You're working with Nema?"

"Attached to the idomeni embassy—security liaison," Lucien said in English. "I'm under arms at all times"—he lifted the flap of his belt holster, revealing an empty compartment—"except when I enter the loony bin and need to check my shooter at the front desk. Can't let the crazies get their hands on the weaponry, can we? They might take over, and then where would we be?"

"About where we are now. Who do you report to?"

"All embassy staff report to the Xeno branch of Justice. So, not only am I in constant contact with your most powerful ally, I also have an in at the ministry that's building the case against your old boyfriend." He grinned wolfishly. "Kind of makes you want to treat me nicer, doesn't it?"

"What else did Nema ask you to tell me?"

"Is that an apology?" Lucien held a hand to his ear. "I can't tell with all this interference."

"*Lucien.*" Jani tried to stare him into submission, but he glared back in sullen stubbornness. He could get testy when he felt unappreciated, but in this case he had justification. He had earned Exterior Minister Anais Ulanova's enmity when he forsook her patronage to throw in with Jani, and the animosity of a Cabinet Minister could destroy more than just a career. *Right, Evan?* "I'm sorry I bolted."

"Apology accepted." Lucien's smile bloomed anew.

"So what else did Nema say?"

"That you must watch and listen, as is your way. He also wanted me to ask you if the ring fits yet?" He ended with a teeth-baring grimace, an imitation of Nema's version of a smile.

The red-stone ring. Her Academy graduation gift from her esteemed teacher. Each of the six special students who had received their degrees in documents examination from the vaunted idomeni university had received one. Everyone else's had fit, but when Jani had tried hers on, she couldn't push it past her second knuckle. *Not anymore.* Several nervous sizing tests in Felix Majora confirmed the now-comfortable fit. "Tell him no."

"He told me that ring's a monitor. When it fits, you'll be hybridized enough to begin training to become his successor. Is that true?"

"Lucien, I'm human." *Officially. For now.* "That mitigates against me becoming the religious leader of a whole other race, don't you think?" *That and the fact the Service will have come to their senses and shot me by then.*

"But he said—"

"The hell with what he said. Just because he says things doesn't make them fact!"

"Keep your voice down!" Lucien looked toward the sunroom door, on the alert for eavesdroppers. "You know, he wanted me to rig myself so I could record you. He said he wanted to hear your voice. I don't think I'd want to be in the room with him after he heard *that.*"

"Oh, it wouldn't be bad. He'd disregard it as unimportant." She was only the Eyes and Ears, after all. A tool. Her thoughts and fears didn't matter. *And I have thoughts and fears, you bet I do.*

Lucien rose and walked across the room to the holoVee display. "Keep your mouth shut until I set up some interference." He activated the unit and flipped through the programs, stopped at an opera broadcast, and jacked up the audio until the swell of voices filled the room. "What's the matter with you?"

"Ask my doctor—he keeps the running tally." Jani watched Lucien stroll back to his chair. Part of her could have watched him forever. The part with the brain wished he'd go away. "What's happening with Evan? What sort of plea bargain has Justice offered him? What's he given them concerning me?"

"Slow down." Lucien sprawled unServicelike and picked at his nails in irritation. "His attorneys are worried—they don't like the publicity this case is drawing."

"They need publicity. They need to show what a great guy Evan was and what an evil influence I was."

"Well, that's not what they're getting. The Earth news services aren't carrying anything about you. The colony services are another story. On FelNet, Felix is complaining about the arrest of colonials with insufficient evidence. In the smoke-filled rooms, the Felician governor called your capture kidnapping and filed a formal complaint against the Service. She's threatening to cancel the landlease for Fort Constanza. She can't do that, legally, but that doesn't seem to concern her. Acadia and *toute La Manche* back her up. They're threatening to boycott the Commonwealth Cup—"

"*What!*"

"—but they've been sweeping the prelims, so they may decide defeating the Earthbound teams serves their cause better." Lucien chuckled. "Nema takes a different tack. He asks about you in meetings with the PM, usually after she inquires after rights to use the idomeni GateWays near the Outer Circle."

"That doesn't answer my question about Evan."

"If he attacks you, he has to admit the part he played in your transport explosion."

"That's the point of the plea bargain. He tells them how much I hated Neumann, and they let him off the hook for ordering the bomb to be planted on my transport."

"His pride won't allow him to admit what he did. That being the case, he'll sit in his little house forever."

It can't be that easy. "They haven't charged me with Neumann's murder yet." Jani rolled up the magazine and whacked herself on the thigh. "I shouldn't be here. I should be in a brig infirmary waiting to get scanned and strip-searched."

But instead, colonial governors were lodging protests on her behalf.

What the hell is going on?

Lucien looked at his timepiece. "Test time—I have to go. Then it's off to the city. I'm in charge of an advance team checking out Chicago Combined. Nema will be meeting with their botany professors. They're going to discuss the possibilities of idomeni-humanish hybridizations. For plants." He stared down at his shoes.

"Lucky you," Jani said, ignoring his allusion. "Has he been behaving himself?"

"No." Lucien looked up with a smile. "He left the embassy without his guard the day before yesterday. They corralled him in a park. Some kids were teaching him how to use the seesaw." He stood, then pulled her to her feet as well. Before she could react, he leaned down and kissed her on the cheek. His lips felt warm and soft; he smelled of soap and clean clothes.

Jani backed away. When he tried to pull her to him again, she placed her hands against his chest and pushed.

"That's OK, I thrive on rejection." He hunched his shoulders and kicked at the floor. "The least you can do is walk me to my appointment."

The halls were filled with people, including two colonels and a major, all mainline. The sight of all that red-striped brass compelled Lucien to behave. Somewhat.

"If you still feel strongly about that strip search after you get out of here, let me know." He walked down the hall toward the testing labs. "I'm an expert in that sort of thing." He paused to wink at her before disappearing around the corner.

Jani leaned against the wall for a few minutes and recovered her blond-addled wits. Then she wandered back to the sunroom. *The colonial guvs are making a stink.* And if the tension over the Shenandoah Gate was any indication, Service solidarity in a colonial crisis was not guaranteed. *And Nema's raising his own brand of hell.*

But in the end, what good would their interferences do? She traced the Pathen Haárin word for garbage on a wall with her finger. *Their protests and a vend token, Lucien.* Or a Vynshàrau ring.

Pimentel placed a drop of her blood on a cartridge tester. "The only reason John Shroud is still walking the streets rather than occupying a prison cell is because he's convinced certain people he's closing in on the secret to eternal life."

Jani sat on the edge of her bed. *I hope he won't be drawing any more blood.* The crook of her right arm already looked like a dartboard and stung to the touch. "What happened to your open mind? He saved my life." She waited for Pimental to reply, but he continued to manipulate testing materials and capillary tubes. "Cal Montoya from Neoclona Chicago treated me about five months ago," she said as she settled back against her pillow. "He prescribed enzyme supplements to help my digestion. He didn't say anything about porphyria."

Pimentel returned the testing equipment to his crammed carryall. "What else would you expect? Can you imagine the damage to Shroud's reputation if it got out that he had inflicted a genetic disorder on his legendary patient? That 'word from the mountaintop' aura is the main thing Neoclona has going for it. Service Medical has never bought into their mystique. Our physicians all receive their training in unaffiliated schools. And even Shroud will admit, if squeezed hard enough, that our people can hold their own against his by any measure you can think of."

Jani squirmed beneath her covers. She would be the first to admit her feelings for John had never made sense. In the months they'd been sequestered together, he'd treated her as either goddess or entitlement, depending on his mood. *Galatea to his Pygmalion one minute, oyster to his pearl knife the next.* For her part, she'd exploited his affection even as she ached for his touch; as the years passed, she'd come to resent him mightily for the things he had done to her. Every time her gut cramped or her muscles spasmed as though torn, she cursed him, yet when someone attacked him, she felt compelled to jump to his defense. "He thought he was helping me," she said, knowing how weak it sounded, to her ears as well as Pimentel's.

"He helped you, all right. I've spent the morning studying your tissue scans." He straightened her blanket with a sharp tug. "It amazes me you can speak kindly of him, considering what he did to you. He treated you like an experimental culture. Genius he may possess—unfortunately for you, he lacks the judgment and ethics to go with it. Every half-baked hypothesis that stewed in his brain concerning the benefits of human-idomeni tissue hybridization, he tried out on you. And now here you are, forced to cope with the consequences of his criminal negligence." Pimentel picked up the carryall and regarded her levelly. "You need sound medical care. You don't need John Shroud or one of his acolytes trying to fix you with the same useless tools with which he broke you in the first place."

Friesian breached the Morley-run defenses at midafternoon break. The enforced downtime had done him good. His fresh summerweights fit crisply, with not a pucker to be seen. He had gotten a haircut as well, and had shaved so closely his cheeks shone like a baby's.

"It felt good to sleep in a grounded rack." He led her into a vacant office located around the corner from her room. "All my friends live for ship duty, but I'll take a nice, solid planet any day." He closed the door, sat down at the desk, and pulled file folders and loose papers from a black-leather documents case.

Jani sat across from him and watched the desktop disappear beneath a layer of Service paper. "You've been working?"

"Oh, yes." He glanced at her in surprise, as though hitting the stacks directly after coming off a three-week-long haul was the most normal thing in the world. "Spent the better part of yesterday afternoon filing motions. Extensions, mostly, since you and I weren't able to work together to prepare your case. I also visited the Service Investigative Bureau Archives." The eager look in his eyes altered, becoming harder, more cold-blooded.

Jani caught a glimpse of Friesian-in-court and grudgingly admitted she liked what she saw. "What did you find there?"

"Better to ask what I didn't find." Finally, he removed a small watercooler and a couple of dispo cups from the case's side pocket, then dropped the case to the floor beside his chair. "Anything relating to your history after your transfer from First Documents and Documentation to the Twelfth Rovers. It's as though you disappeared."

Jani picked through a stack of papers. Most were formal requests to examine documents, formatted in the current style—lightest blue parchment with a stylized eagle watermark. Friesian had noted the places where she needed to sign. "That makes no sense. That's their case."

Friesian grinned. "Exactly."

"They're up to something." Jani crossed her arms, tucking her hands in her sleeves in an effort to warm them. *Why do they keep these rooms so damned cold?* She'd supplemented the long-sleeved winter-issue pajamas with a winterweight robe and two pairs of socks, yet she still felt cold. "They can't let me get away with this."

"Get away with what?" Friesian's voice grew measured. Another courtroom tic surfacing. "Jani, why do you believe you're here?"

Is this a trick question? She tried to cross her right leg over her left. The weak limb wouldn't budge, forcing her to grab a handful of pajama leg and hoist up and over. "Check the posting board in any colonial Government Hall."

"We aren't in a Government Hall now, and I want to hear it from you."

But I don't want to say it. Once she said the words, that would be it. No going back. No pretending the past eighteen years had never happened, that her Service career had continued uninterrupted, that she was simply in hospital for her annual physical. She stared over Friesian's head at a point on the blank wall and listened to her words as if they emerged from another mouth. "I'm wanted for murder. The murder of Colonel Rikart Neumann, my commanding officer."

"The correct wording is, *Wanted for questioning in connection with . . .* Hardly the same."

"Words."

"In my game, words count." Friesian freed a recording board from beneath one of the piles. "Jani, what you're actually charged with is Article Ninety-two of the Service Code. 'Missing movement.' " He unsnapped a stylus from its board niche, activated it, and began writing.

"Miss—" Jani tried to speak, but the words stalled in her throat. *They're saying I missed a ship.* Neumann dead. The patients dead. Twenty-six Laumrau and fifteen Rovers. *And they track me for eighteen years and arrest me for missing a ship.* "That—that's a joke."

"You think so?" Friesian continued writing. "As the highest-ranked documents examiner in the Twelfth Rover Corps, it was your sworn duty to ensure that the paper under your control made transfer during the evac of Rauta Shèràa Base. According to the charge, you failed to appear at your post the night the evacuation took place." Friesian picked a document off the top of one of the piles and studied it. Older Service paper—pale grey parchment. Paper from Jani's time. "The Night of the Blade. The night the Vynshàrau took over."

"The Twelfth Rovers—" Jani shivered. She felt even colder now. "The Twelfth Rovers never made it back to Rauta Shèràa Base."

"No, but you did, according to Colonel Veda. One of the documents that went missing recorded your transfer, via people-mover, from Knevçet Shèràa to Rauta Shèràa Base."

"That never happened!"

Friesian tapped his thumbs on the edges of his board. "What did happen?"

"From the beginning?" Jani pulled her robe more closely around her. "We were sent to Knevçet Shèràa to hook up with the group of Bandan xenogeologists who had been trapped by the fighting and escort them back to Rauta Shèràa."

"You were a documents examiner. Why bring you on a pickup?"

"Neumann said he needed me to confirm their papers. What he really needed me for was to validate and code their patient files for transport back to Earth, but I didn't realize that until too late." Jani blew on her hands—so cold. "The first patient died soon after. Her name was Eva Yatni. Then Simyam Baru mutilated himself, and I tracked down Neumann to find out what the hell was going on. We fought. That was when I killed him." She stared at her hands, skin paled from inner chill. "The Laumrau staff fled to the hills, warned their compatriots that word of their collusion with humans would get out if they didn't act. So they started bombing. Yolan Cray died during the first wave. She was my corporal. A wall collapsed on her. Then the bombing stopped."

She could hear the silence again, the silence that fell after the last shatterbox found its target. Silence too afraid to open its eyes. Silence with its heart torn out.

"A Night of Convergence." Friesian cleared his throat, then poured himself water from the cooler. "The idomeni government conducted an investigation that confirmed the action you took against the twenty-six Laumrau encamped outside Knevçet Shèràa."

"It wasn't an action—I killed them one by one as they took a sacramental meal in their tents."

"They also advised us that they have no interest in pursuing any type of case against you at this time." He paused to drink, then pressed the cup against his forehead. "That part of your story, at least, can be confirmed."

Jani recrossed her legs. She still needed to hoist her right. "What do you mean, confirmed?"

Friesian sighed. "Ever since I started working this case, all I've encountered is one rumor after the other." He pressed fingertips to forehead. "Rumor that the doctors who founded Neoclona salvaged you from the transport van Reuter allegedly arranged to have bombed. Rumor that they kidnapped you off the street and smuggled you offworld to experiment on you. I hear different stories every day concerning how Rikart Neumann died." He picked up the documents bag and rummaged through the flaps and pockets until he freed a small packet. He tore it open, shook a bright pink tablet into his hand, and tossed it into his mouth, washing it down with water.

Jani reached for one of the dispos—Friesian took that as a cue to pour her some water. She let him. Her hands had started to shake—if she tried to serve herself, who knew where the water would end up? "What other stories do you need? I'm admitting I killed Neumann."

Friesian handed her the cup. "On the *Reina*, when you were still holed up in the infirmary and giving the medical officer fits, you insisted you had sneaked out during a shift change and disabled the fire extinguishers. Your accounting of your movements was so accurate, the chief engineer ordered a ship-wide inspection. You hadn't touched a thing, of course. You'd never left the infirmary."

"You don't believe me."

"What *I* believe doesn't matter. What anyone else believes doesn't matter. Solid proof, *paper* proof, proof that can be researched and confirmed, is what the prosecution needs to support this or any charge and the only thing against which we need to mount a defense. And so far, they've shown me nothing to connect you with Neumann's death."

"You're—" Jani loosened the neck of her robe. She felt much

warmer now. Her heart pounded. "You're saying they won't charge me, that I spent all these years running for nothing. You're saying they have no case."

"That's exactly what I'm saying."

"Because the paper's gone missing."

"If it ever existed at all."

"I don't understand any of this."

Friesian leaned forward and selected papers from the various piles. "I had a long talk with Roger before coming to see you." He grinned at Jani's puzzled look. "Dr. Pimentel. He feels you're under a great deal of stress. Much of it, he adds, is self-imposed." He handed her one of the documents requests, along with a stylus. "I want to do what's best for you, Jani. I wish I felt you trusted me more."

Jani braced her hand on the arm of her chair. In spite of the support, her hand still shook so badly that her normally crisp signature showed blurred and crooked. "Do I have a choice?"

"That is not what I want to hear." Friesian took the document and handed her another. "Roger did tell me he feels you're improving. The muscle weakness may last for a few more weeks, but you're responding well to the diet they've put you on and the other therapies they're trying out. You could be released in the next few days."

"To do what?" Jani stared at the paper she held. *Extended Residence Agreement.* A Transient Officers' Quarters contract. "Work with you?"

"Such a luxury, the Service cannot afford. They have an Academy-trained documents examiner in their grasp, and they can't afford to let her go unutilized." Friesian pointed to the TOQ contract. "You're being returned to duty, Captain Kilian. With restricted movement, I should add. You'll be confined to base until we close the book on this." He reached into another pile and removed an official-sized steel blue envelope, its flap crosshatched with white security seals. He smiled cautiously and handed it to Jani.

She traded the TOQ contract for the envelope. The crisp parchment snapped like plastic between her fingers. "Do you know what's in here?"

"Um-hmm."

"Are you going to tell me?"

"No. You have to open it."

She held her breath as she broke the threadlike seals, removed the sheets of pale blue parchment, and unfolded them.

"What do you think?" Friesian's smile strengthened. "You've been assigned to your old outfit. First Documents and Documentation."

Reporting to Lt. Colonel Frances Hals. Foreign Transactions, third floor, Documents Control. Simple wording for simple actions. Three days from today, at 0830, she would present herself to Lieutenant Colonel Hals, dressed out, scanpack in hand. The Service's Oldest Living Sideline Captain reporting for duty.

Friesian gathered the documents and returned them to his case. "Roger feels it's in your best interest to work again. Use your skills. 'Chip off the rust,' he calls it. In the meantime, I'll work my end, and we'll meet regularly to discuss any developments."

Friesian insisted on playing the gallant, so Jani let him escort her back to her room. On the way, they passed a patient leaning against the wall, arms crossed in front of his chest, staring at nothing. He looked like he'd been through a war himself—bronze-haired and lean, with a long, weathered face cut from edge of nose to end of mouth by a deep, age-whitened scar. He looked at them as they passed—his eyes held confusion and bewilderment and mute question. *Takedown malaise.* Jani knew how he felt. The next time she looked in a mirror, she'd see the same eyes staring back.

CHAPTER 8

They discharged her two days later.

"You've shown marked improvement." Pimentel said. "But you're to check in every other day until further notice. The noise from the firing range occasionally entertains us—if it bothers your augie, come in and we'll fit you with hearing protection." He handed her a rectangular blue bag that looked like a Service toiletry kit. "Your scrips and instructions are in here. If you have any questions, anytime, call or stop in." He reached into the front pocket of his medcoat and pulled out a small, cartridge-tester-like device.

"This is your diet monitor. It's like a scanpack for food. Run it over every item you want to eat—it determines kcals as well as fat grams, protein, etc, and it keeps a running tally. If it squeals, you can't have what you just scanned." He held the small box out to her. "We'll be able to tell if you cheat and trust me, so will you."

Jani accepted the device with a grudging nod. "I know what it's going to tell me. More fruit milk shakes." The sweet sludge had remained a staple of every meal. She had run through the kitchen's entire supply of hot sauce in a day and a half, and had been forced to resort to plain black pepper to kill the taste.

Pimentel led Jani out to the lobby and was about to show her out the door when a woman standing near the entry desk raised her hand. He ran a hand over his rumpled medwhite V-neck. "Jani, I'd like to introduce you to someone."

The woman made no move to meet them, but remained by the desk. She was perhaps twenty years older than Jani, with steel grey hair trimmed in a blunt, chin-length style. Her eyes were dark, her skin, olive. She wore summerweights and a crisp white medcoat, and cradled a recording board.

"Ma'am, it's good to see you." Pimentel executed the straight-backed sharp nod that took place of a salute indoors. "Captain Kilian, I'd like to introduce Dr. Carvalla, our chief of staff."

Dr. Major General Carvalla, Jani amended, taking note of the twin silver stars adorning the sides of the woman's short-sleeve. "Ma'am."

"Captain." Carvalla's broad face broke into a genuine smile. "You have been giving my people a workout." She glanced at Pimentel, who looked starstruck. "It's not often I meet someone who served on Shèrá. We're contemporaries of a sort. I served as medical officer on a ship stationed in that area. The *Kensington*. You may not have heard of it, considering the circumstances at the time."

Jani's grin froze. "The flagship of the group that evac'd Rauta Shèràa Base—yes, ma'am, I had heard of it." After she escaped John's stifling care, she had spent several nerve-wracking days evading the crews that took over the human sector of the Rauta Shèràa shuttleport as she tried to wangle a billet on a civilian ship. Everywhere she had turned, she had seen someone sporting the names *Kensington, Hilfington*, or *Warburg* on a jacket or lid. "I'm sure the evacuees recall you fondly."

"*Perhaps*," Carvalla replied dryly. "Quarters were close, and supplies were scarce. I think the fondest memory the evacuees have of us was saying good-bye." She glanced at her timepiece. "Well, it's time for rounds. Take care of yourself, Captain. I'm sure I'll see you again." She nodded to Jani and Pimentel in turn, then walked to the rear of the lobby to join a doctor cluster waiting near the lift bank.

"She's wonderful. The best thing that ever happened to Service Medical. Fair. Forward-thinking." Pimentel's bounciness lasted until he walked out of the hospital and into the full blaze of summer. "God, it's hot! Are you sure you don't want someone to drive you to the TOQ?"

"No. I looked it up on the base map Morley gave me—it's not that far." Jani took a deep breath of hot, dry air, felt the chill leave her for the first time since her arrival, and waved good-bye to Pimentel.

She walked down the long drive leading from the Main Hospital, then turned down a series of shorter, tree-lined streets named after famous generals. Hillman Avenue. Dragan Row. Starcross Way. Earthbound generals. She could imagine Borgie's peeved Man French mutterings as to the inequity of the situation. She could sense him walk beside her, as he had a hundred times at Rauta Shèràa Base.

They'd both acquired reputations by then, Jani as the stiff-necked anti-Family doc jock who reacted to threats by making her own, Borgie as a quick mind ruined by a quicker temper and the penchant for the freelance deal. Jani had uncovered evidence of one such operation, an attempt to divert scanpack supplies to a Pearl Way broker. She had quietly shut it down, then had taken Borgie aside and explained why it was in his best interest to keep his damned hands out of her patch. Struck by the fact that she had figured out his plan so easily, *and* that she declined to turn him in to Base Security, he had decided to adopt her. Hers was a worthy mind, he had told her, for an officer. From then on, he took her on rounds of his own, and explained to her the things he felt a deskbound paper-pusher needed to know to survive in the Old Service. Much of the information had come in handy during her years underground. To say she owed Borgie her life didn't say enough. To say she'd let him down . . . well, that didn't say enough, either.

Jani took her time examining the Sheridan grounds. The rolling lawns. The locations of intersections and main drives. She walked easily, her discharge summerweights and relaxed manner marking her as a new release on her way home.

She and Borgie had talked about many things over the months. The fine art of breaking and entering. How to plan an escape. Primary routes. Back-up plans. Acquiring and secreting provisions and weapons. And other preparations.

They get us with that damned chip, Captain. They can track us anywhere with that thing. All they have to do is enter your code into systems and activate. How you deal with that depends on how desperate you are.

Jani checked her trouser pocket, the one that contained the scalpel she had swiped from a supply cart. In another, she'd stashed the half-used tube of incision sealant she'd found sitting atop the nurses' station counter, along with the topical anesthetic and a bandage pad. She'd operated on her scanpack often enough. She wasn't squeamish, and thanks to augie she had a high tolerance for pain.

The most important thing, Captain, is to choose your moment well. They won't give you a second chance.

"Frankly, Sergeant, I'm surprised they're giving me a first one." Jani slowed to a stop in the middle of the road and considered the strangeness of it all. *Piers thinks I'm lying about Neumann.* Because Veda needed paper to back up charges, and Jani's records were missing. *Where are they?* Who was responsible for their disappearance? Why were they involved? What did they expect to gain? Did they think to lull her into a false sense of ease, only to spring charges on her later? The unexpected attack was the hardest to fend off—she didn't want to be caught unawares. *I need to know who's been fiddling with my records.* And her records were stored at the SIB.

She started walking again, reaching a nameless cul-de-sac and trudging up a path leading to a five-story whitestone box set well back from the road, surrounded by low hedges. South Central Transient Officers' Quarters. Her home for the duration, however long that turned out to be.

The TOQ lobby proved just as plain as the exterior. The cheers and excited commentary that sounded from a side room indicated a well-attended Cup broadcast in progress.

Jani found her room on the mezzanine floor, a quick ten-step flight up from the lobby. Three small partitioned spaces: a sitting room cum office equipped with a desk and comport, a bedroom, and a bath. Spare furnishings of honey-colored polywood. Cream walls. A single narrow window in the sitting room, looking out over the cul-de-sac.

Her enthusiasm ramped when she laid eyes on her old duffel, resting small and lonely on the frame couch. "They really worked you over," she said as she dug through the depleted contents, removed her scanpack from its half-fastened pouch, then fingered the ragged edge of what had once been the scanproof compartment. They'd confiscated her shooter and gadgets. Someone, however, had taken the time to wrap her keepsakes in a tissue envelope.

She stashed her stolen medical supplies, the scalpel in the catch-all tray on her desk, the anesthetic, glue, and bandage, in her bathroom cabinet. *Hide in plain sight.* A nosy visitor would think she had a strange taste in letter openers and the tendency to cut herself with same, not that she planned to make a run for it as soon as circumstance allowed.

She opened her small closet to find the Clothing Elf had seen to her gear. She perused the six different styles of uniforms hanging within, then removed her unmarked hospital summerweights and donned a fresh set of her very own.

Jani found her ribbons and badges in a small box atop her dresser. She attached her bronze sideline captain's tabs to her collar, the silver scroll and quill of Documents Services to her shoulder tabs. They'd awarded one-year colonial service ribbons back in her day; she pinned the two green-and-gold-striped rectangles over her left pocket, where they glistened like pieces of spun-sugar candy.

They'd even allowed her the gold marksman badge she'd worked so hard to win when her mainline cohorts had told her she had no chance. Expert. Short shooter. *You'd think they'd have held that one back.* Might as well shout it to the worlds. *Hi, I'm Jani. Shot twenty-seven—killed them all. And you are . . . ?*

She applied makeup. Spritzed her hair with water and trimmed her more straggly curls with the nail cutters that came in her toiletry kit. *Captain Paragon girding for the File Wars.* She smiled despite her disquiet.

Her feelings toward the Service made about as much sense as her feelings for John Shroud. Pride in her Commonwealth had nothing to do with it—she'd been too much a colonial to feel patriotic and too much of a skeptic to see Acadia's rebel factions as any more than self-serving delusionaries. *I joined up for the same reasons that receptionist joined Neoclona.* To get away from a deadend homeworld. To meet different people. To learn. She'd never resented the routine, since working with the idomeni guaranteed things never remained routine for long. She'd even liked the uniforms; she'd never been an avid follower of fashion, and had been quite happy to turn the clothes part of her life over to someone else.

Give me a scanpack and a stack of paper, and I'm happy. If they'd assigned her anyplace but Rauta Shèràa Base, she might have even made the Service a career. *I like to fade into the background, and there's no place you can fade better than the Service.*

The one time she had broached that opinion to Borgie, however, he had laughed till he cried. *You're an action person, Captain,* he told her after he recovered sufficiently to speak. *You like digging into things you shouldn't. Turning over rocks. You don't toe the line—hell, you're a peacetime nightmare. You're one of those poor souls who needs a war.*

As it turned out, she was a nightmare even then.

She was in the middle of brushing her teeth when the door-scanner buzzed.

"Hello!" Lucien pushed past her into the sitting area, laden with packages. "I unpacked your gear this morning," he said as he tossed his brimmed lid on the couch and set a basket of cut flowers atop the end table. "I hope you appreciate it."

"So you're the Clothing Elf." Jani stood by the door, toothbrush in hand, and watched him unpack and store disposable cups and wipes, sundries and supplies for the desk. Instead of summerweights, he wore dress blue-greys. A black-leather crossover belt cut a diagonal swath across his steel blue tunic. His grey trousers were cut down the sides with the requisite mainline red slash, and the holster on his belt was fully packed. “Was today ‘take your idomeni ambassador to university’ day?”

“Yeah. His security picked the time at the last minute. Most propitious, they said, but I think they just wanted to shake the reporters. Nema was as excited as hell. He got into everything.” Lucien reached into one of the bags and removed a small glass-and-gold clock. “This has a *good* alarm,” he said as he set in on the desk. “The one on the comport isn’t loud enough, and you can’t set it to repeat.”

Jani ducked into the bathroom to finish her teeth. “I found soap, hairwash, and toothpaste in here. I’m surprised they couldn’t stick a clock somewhere.”

“They used to. Stopped last year. They said it was the officers’ responsibility to keep their own time.”

“Are you sure it wasn’t because the clocks were getting swiped by the occupants?”

Lucien poked his head around the bathroom entry. “We are talking about officers and gentlepeople, not *occupants*. And the word is *reappropriated*, not *swiped*.”

“They must have been good clocks. How many got reappropriated in a year, on average?”

“One hundred fifty-three. They could even survive direct shooter fire. When magnebolting them to the tables didn’t work, Housekeeping called it a wash. You really do have a suspicious mind, you know that?”

“Only because people keep living down to my expectations.” Jani rinsed her mouth, then fixed the damage the toothpaste and water had inflicted upon her makeup. “I doubt human nature gets checked at the Shenandoah Gate.”

“Don’t let a superior hear you say that, or you’ll get an earful. The New Service is a proud organization. It does not embrace the malcontent.”

“Then why does it have its hand down my trousers?”

Lucien laughed. “You’ve got me there.” Shoulders still shaking, he tossed a wrapper in the trashzap and disappeared around the divider.

Jani edged out of the bathroom, leaned against the divider, and watched Lucien set out an assortment of newssheets. When he still worked as a security officer on Anais Ulanova’s staff, he had been deftly inserted into the crew list of the CSS *Arapaho*, the ship Jani had traveled on during her first trip to Earth. His duty had been ostensibly to serve as her steward; his true function had been to uncover her real identity. Even after the ruse had fallen through, he had still insisted on performing his cabin-attending duties. She'd had fresh flowers every ship day, liqueur waiting after dinner, laundry done daily.

He even massaged my neck once. She had just spent hours combing over some of Evan van Reuter's files, and the conclusion that her ex-lover was guilty of bribery and conspiracy, among other nasty things, had resulted in a tension headache that left her photophobic and unable to move her neck.

But Lucien fixed. Did he ever. In the five weeks they spent together, that was the closest he came to getting her into bed. Letting him get those hands on her was one mistake she had no intention of repeating. But, if he wanted to spend part of his day replenishing her flowers and reading materials, she wouldn't turn him down. "Is that everything?" she asked as she watched him stuff more wrappings into the trashzap.

"No." He stepped into her bedroom, then turned to her and crooked his finger for her to follow. "One final surprise." He held up the last package, removed the silver-and-black wrappings with a flourish, and held it out for her inspection.

She found herself staring into two shining brown eyes framed by a fringe of fur. "A teddy bear?"

It was an old-style toy, designed to do nothing but sit. Light brown fur, the closest match Lucien could find to his own hair. A black-plastic nose capped a snubby muzzle and a winsome, sewn-on smile. The uniform of the day consisted of a dark blue field sweater and fatigue pants, complete with a little blue garrison cap clutched in one fuzzy paw.

"What do you think?" Lucien propped it against the pillow, then reached out to adjust its sweater.

"It's too cute for words." Jani eyed the creature in bemusement. "I haven't had a teddy bear since I was three."

"That explains a lot." Lucien ran a finger along the edge of the bed. "You know, I've been told I have teddy-bear-like qualities."

"Yeah, you're both glassy-eyed and stuffed." Jani tapped her timepiece. "I have things to do."

"The first thing you're doing is dinner with me, but you're not going anywhere looking like *that.*" Lucien pulled a comb from his trouser pocket. "This is Fort Sheridan. There are Appearance and Standards officers behind every bush." He recombed Jani's hair and made her retuck her shirt. Then he reached into his inside tunic pocket, removed a thin black rod, and tapped the side—a blue-green light flickered from one end.

"You carry a *micrometer*?" Jani watched him run the lighted end over her badges, check the readout, then pop the rod in his mouth like a nicstick as he adjusted the placement of one of her colonial service ribbons. "You can't tell me the A&S-holes are that picky."

"The wha—!" The micrometer wobbled as Lucien tried to suppress a laugh. "Depends whether they've met their quotas. They go on a binge about once a quarter; those demerit fines can really chew up your pay. You learn not to take chances." He touched Jani's shortshooter badge. "Expert. Really?"

"No, some officers steal clocks, I steal badges." She pointed to the micrometer. "That's bullshit."

"And you're all roses, my DI used to say, so suck it up." Lucien knelt carefully on the carpeted floor and measured Jani's trouser hems.

"You had a DI? I thought you emerged fully formed from a recruiting holo." She watched him run a dispo over one tietop. "And don't tell me that shoe's dirty because I just polished it."

Lucien looked up at her and shook his head in dismay. "You'll thank me for this later."

"This entire exercise is just an excuse to touch me."

"If I wanted an excuse, I could think of much more interesting ones than this." He yanked at her other fastener and retied it more neatly. "What are you going to name him?"

"Who?"

"The bear. He needs a name."

"Oh, it's a 'he,' is it?"

"Of course." Lucien straightened up and stood before her in all his mainline glory. His hair shone more brightly than his badges, which in turn gleamed enough to flash the room-light like stars. He'd pass any measurement test devised by man—oh yes, if you struck him, he'd ring. "What are you going to name him?"

Jani took a step backward. "Val," she replied quietly. "After my old friend, Val Parini."

Lucien looked heavenward and sighed. "I set out your gear, do your shopping, save you from A&S wrath, and what thanks do I get?" He pointed to the two badges decorating his own tunic pocket. "I have you beat. Expert, short *and* long shooter."

"You had a head start. You were born with half the equipment." Jani grabbed her scanpack from the desk, stuffed it into her belt pouch, dashed out the door, then waited for Lucien to catch her up.

After some bickering while he adjusted her garrison cap, they proceeded to dinner.

They ate at the South Central Officers' Club, and watched a freshly transmitted Cup qual match on the bar-mounted 'Vee. The German provincial team versus Elyas Amalgam in an Earthbound-colony tussle. Elyas was up five–zip at half-time—most of the faces at the bar appeared rather glum.

The temperature outside had reached record levels, according to the ServNet weather broadcast. Forty Celsius, with no cool-down expected for at least a week. The 'Vee viewers nursed their drinks and looked out the floor-to-ceiling windows to the bright, shimmering lawnscape beyond, delaying as long as possible the inevitable walk outside.

Jani stepped out onto the patio, sighing with pleasure as a Rauta Shèràa–quality blast of hell-spawned wind sucked the moisture from her eyefilms.

Lucien drew alongside. "Want to check out the beach?"

"We're not dressed for the beach."

"We can change." He handed her a dispo of water. "You don't even have to buy a swimsuit. You were issued one."

"Was I?"

"Yep. They're dark silver this year." His look grew pointed. "That color would look great against your skin."

"Would it?" Jani brushed off Lucien's subdued leer. "I want to go to the SIB." She chewed a mint leaf she'd plucked from her fruit cup—the fruit had been torture to choke down, even with pepper and hot mustard, but she found the gnawed mint leaves followed by a cold water chaser refreshing. "I need to talk to an archivist."

"You start working tomorrow, not tonight. Tonight, you're supposed to relax and have fun." Lucien flashed a smile, white teeth brilliant against tanned skin. "That's what I'm for."

Jani let his rich brown stare draw her in. A less-experienced soul could drown in those cool, dark pools. Luckily, she knew how to swim. "Can I ask you a question?"

Lucien leaned closer. "You know you can ask me anything."

"Are you using me to get close to Nema, or Nema to get close to me?"

His head snapped back. His smile vanished. He strode out onto the lawn. "A little of both. Does that matter?"

Jani remained silent. She knew he didn't like it when she tossed his affections, such as they were, back in his face, but she didn't relish him treating her like one of his suckers either.

He paced in front of her, with the occasional glance to see if she watched. "At least I tell you."

"Only because I already know."

He slowed to a stroll, then to a halt, and looked at her, his face a study in line and shadow devoid of emotion. Then the smile returned, grimmer and more knowing. "It's too hot for the beach. How about a walk along the South Marina docks? At least the walkways are covered."

"SIB."

"There's the indoor games room."

"SIB."

"We could see what's playing at the Veedrome."

"SIB."

"SIB." Lucien tugged at his tunic collar, then fanned his face. "Can I at least change into summerweights first?"

Jani studied him with what she liked to call her criminal eye. *If I were stealing documents, would I worry if I saw you show up in the middle of my shift?* She contemplated his trim, rangy frame, displayed to perfection in the formal uniform. His hard stare. Most particularly, she studied his packed shooter holster. "No. I like you just the way you are."

SIB Archives, like most repositories Jani had known, had been originally designed to be much smaller, then expanded over time to its divinely ordained size. The area, which took up half the basement, was comprised of an interwoven network of secured storage rooms and jury-rigged tech bullpens. She and Lucien walked through the hallways twice, drawing questioning looks from the techs who filed and performed preliminary doc checks in cubicles or at open tables.

Lucien eyed his surroundings with a complete lack of interest. "Forgive me for questioning your absolute authority, but what are you going to do?"

Jani stopped before a bulletin board and read some of the postings. The usual announcements of parties. Lost jewelry in the washroom. A memo from SIB Safety complained about the lousy clear time during the last evacuation drill, and promised repeat exercises until people "got it right." "I thought I'd play the registrar. Poke around. Ask a few questions."

"Oh. You mean overstep your jurisdiction and meddle in things that are none of your business."

"It's my ServRec that's missing—I have a right to look for it."

"Hmm. What do you want me to do?"

"Look like your day won't be complete until you arrest somebody."

"You know, I like being a lieutenant. Someday, I'd like to like being a captain."

"It's overrated." Jani entered the archives room with the most traffic and walked around the perimeter. She opened a file drawer, leafed through a report that lay open atop a desk, and smiled at everyone who looked her way.

"May I help you?"

Jani turned and found herself being subjected to the critical appraisal of a rotund man in civilian summerweights. "I'm Odergaard. Tech One on this shift." His face was flushed, his skin shiny, as though he'd just been taken from the oven and basted.

"Captain Jani Kilian, First D-Doc." She cocked her head toward Lucien. "This is Lieutenant Lucien Pascal, Intelligence."

Around them, the skritch of styli stopped. Whispers fell silent.

Odergaard's gaze widened as it flicked from Jani's name tag, to her scanpack, then to Lucien's sidearm. "Is there a problem?"

"I'm trying to obtain access to my Service record, but I've been informed by my attorney that portions of it have been mislaid."

What ruddiness remained in Odergaard's face after *Kilian* and *Intelligence* vanished upon mention of the word *attorney.* "We have been transferring files from the Judge Advocate's to new bins in this building for the past few months, and the inevitable cross-ups have, of course, occurred—"

"I'd like to speak to the shift archivist." Jani made a show of looking around the room.

Anger flared in Odergaard's eyes. "That would be Mr. Duong." He took a step, then hesitated, but another look at Lucien's sidearm decided him. "This way, please."

They walked to a more sheltered work space in the far corner of the room. A small, dark-haired man sat at a workstation, entering document tag numbers into a grid. Most of the numbers were blue, but the occasional red string could be seen. Red had meant "missing in action" when Jani interned in Consulate Archives. She doubted that had changed in the years since.

"You're running inventory." Her voice lowered in commiseration. "I always hated inventory."

The man turned with a start. Older, fifties probably. Earthbound Asian or Bandan—Jani wouldn't know until he opened his mouth. And suspicious. The look he shot at Odergaard held that special brand of distrust reserved for meddling managers.

Odergaard spoke first. "Sam—"

Sahm—he's Bandan. Jani smiled. This could wind up working quite well.

"—this is Captain Kilian from First Doc—"

"Apa kabar, señorìo." Greetings, sir. Jani's Bandan wasn't perfect, but it was formal, which came in handy when working with the pedantic precisionists that usually populated the archivist ranks. She held out her hand to the man. *"I'm looking for my life—can you help me find it?"*

He looked up at her. His eyes were old brown—dull, with yellowed sclera. His face held confusion, as though he remembered her face but couldn't recall her name. *"You speak Bandan?"* His handshake consisted of the barest touch. His voice emerged very small.

"I lived there for a time. Near the university."

"You know the university! I worked there for years—"

As Duong rattled on, Jani heard Odergaard grumble under his breath. Yes, they were being rude, but she needed Duong's help more than his boss's, and she couldn't help thinking that Odergaard deserved to get his tail twisted.

Duong rose from his chair. *"I'll show you my dead,"* he said as he gestured for Jani to follow him. *"Maybe in my dead, is your life."*

"Maybe." Jani wondered if Duong's Bandan expressions ever colored his English. Bandan was an interesting language, but it tended toward the poetic, and some of the literal translations struck the uninformed as odd.

Just as they were about to cut across the hallway into Duong's file bin of choice, a younger man in sideline summerweights blocked their path. His yellow collar tabs marked him as a lieutenant. His holstered scanpack marked him as the ranking examiner on the shift.

"Lieutenant Yance." Odergaard transformed into a round-shouldered hand-rubber. "This is Captain Jani Kilian. Her attorney, Major Friesian—"

"Captain." Yance nodded sharply. "I think the documents you're looking for may prove much more accessible than you've been led to believe." He brushed past her into the bullpen, all shined shoes and elbows.

Jani glanced at Lucien. "I don't want to talk to the ranking."

"They sure as hell don't want you talking to Duong." The first glimmers of attention showed on his face. "Odergaard almost jumped out of his skin when you started speaking Bandan."

"I did not put those there!"

Jani hurried back into the bullpen, Lucien at her heels. She recognized Duong's voice, and the mounting panic she heard in it.

The bullpen residents had swarmed around Duong's work space. Jani shouldered through them in time to see Yance pull a thick file from a desk drawer. Light grey parchment in a light grey folder. Old Service paper.

"What else has he got in there?" Yance craned to look around the bulky Odergaard, who was down on his knees, pulling more files out of drawers.

"I did not put those there!" Duong rocked from one foot to the other as though the floor scalded his soles.

One of the techs made a "slow down" motion with her hands. "Mr. Duong, please—"

"*I did not put those there!*"

Jani thumped Yance on the shoulder. "Lieutenant, what's going on?"

"Captain, please." He leaned close. "He's done this before, ma'am. He has a problem."

Odergaard twisted around. "I found some of the van Reuter stuff, too."

Jani glanced at the faces surrounding them. Some held surprise, others, disappointment. One or two sneered. "I don't like this," she said to Lucien.

He held up an open hand in an "oh well" gesture. "But it looks like you've got your records back, so what difference does it make?"

"You would think that, wouldn't you?" Jani stepped around Yance, who was busy talking into a handcom, and planted herself between him and the shaking Duong. "Mr. Duong?"

Duong looked up at her, eyes wide and glistening. "I did not put those there."

"You didn't lock my life away in your drawer?"

"*No!*"

Jani looked into Duong's stricken face. She had no reason to believe him—she had known him for all of five minutes. *He's an archivist.* Archivists had earned a well-deserved reputation for strangeness. Sometimes they grew jealous of the documents in their charge, resented others touching them, using them. Sam Duong could just be one of those disturbed few who had decided that if he couldn't have them, nobody could.

Do I believe that? She considered the trembling figure before her, and tried to get the sense of him. She had lived by her instincts for eighteen years—they'd served her well. It was only when she disregarded them that she found herself in trouble.

She touched Duong's arm. "I believe you."

It took a moment for her words to sink in. When they did, the tension drained from Duong as though someone had flipped a release, and he slumped forward.

Jani snaked her arm around him to keep him from falling. "Get this man to the infirmary!" She eased him into the arms of two techs, who helped him out of the room.

"You really shouldn't have said that, Captain. It only encourages him." Yance ran his scanpack over one of the papers, waited for the display to show green, then repeated the action with the next. Judging from the thickness of the piles, he had a long night of ID confirmation ahead of him.

Jani fingered a page from her Service record. *My transfer orders to the Twelfth Rovers.* She could almost feel Rikart Neumann's presence in the paper, like a layer of grime. "So he's done this before?"

"Nothing this blatant. Misfiles that he claimed someone else must have done."

"What made you suspect?"

"A tip."

"Anonymous?"

"*No*, ma'am. A very reliable source." Yance hesitated in midscan. "I don't like this either, ma'am. But if he's a threat to the paper, we have to shut him down."

Jani looked at Lucien, who responded with a shrug. "I'd like two copies of these docs. Send one set to Major Piers Friesian, Defense Command, this base. Send the other to me at the South Central TOQ."

"Yes, ma'am." Yance entered a notation in his handheld, then returned to his scanning.

Lucien left the bullpen with the light step of a newly released prisoner. "I didn't know you spoke Bandan." He slipped a finger between his tunic collar and his neck and cursed the uniform designer responsible.

"Enough to get by." Jani felt a twinge of self-reproach as she recalled the excitement on Duong's face as he conversed in his native tongue. It was pathetic how little it took to win a person over.

She strode ahead of Lucien up the stairs and through the lobby. As she burst through the lobby door, she barely missed colliding with a man trying to enter. The red trouser stripe combined with the hardware blared "mainline colonel." She was treated to a surprised glare as he brushed past her.

Jani stood in the entry and watched him snap across the lobby and down the stairs. Typical hard-ass brass, but he had a couple of distinctive features. Hair the color of bronze, and a long, weathered face cut from edge of nose to end of mouth by a deep, age-whitened scar.

CHAPTER 9

The incident with Sam Duong nibbled at Jani's tenuous calm as she readied for her first day as a reactivated Spacer. After a scanner-approved breakfast in her rooms, she strode the walkways to Documents Control, adjusting the tilt of her garrison cap until it mimicked everyone else's. She slung her black-leather briefbag over her left shoulder, again in imitation, and rested her arm across the top. *Everything the same as everybody else.* Just another way to disappear into the crowd.

The morning air held a metal tang, as though it had been on the fire too long. The hot wind desiccated everything it touched. She savored the heat as she followed the signs and markers, finally pulling up in front of a building that, but for the rimming of hedges, could have twinned the TOQ.

Jani trotted up the Doc Control steps as quickly as her weakened right leg would allow. She paused in front of the doorscanner, waited for it to read her retinas, then held her breath as the lock whirred and the door clicked open and she entered a close-controlled building as Jani Kilian for the first time in eighteen years. She listened to the echo of her tietops as she strode across the tiled lobby, and wondered at the firm tone of her oh-so-Service voice as she asked a passing lieutenant the location of the Foreign Transactions Department.

Before she entered the anteroom leading to Lieutenant Colonel Hals's office, Jani dug her orders out of her briefbag and checked the date and time against a wall clock. *Right day?* Check. *Right time?* Check. *So where is everybody?* All of the office areas she had passed on the way had been empty. She scanned the doorways and desktops for clues to explain the lack of human occupation, but no scrawled note informing all that the department meeting had been moved or that someone down the hall had brought in doughnuts surfaced to clarify the situation.

At the sound of the half hour, she stepped up to the adjutant's desk, positioned just outside the colonel's door. Lieutenant Ischi, who according to the nameplate should have been manning same, was nowhere to be seen.

Then Jani heard sounds emerge from the inner office. Sharp rises. Sudden falls. The cadences of argument. Either the voices were very loud, or the office soundshielding very poor. She'd have bet her 'pack the quality of the shielding was just fine.

She knocked on the door, and the voices cut off abruptly. One beat later, a woman called out, "Come in."

Jani touched the entry pad. The door swept aside to reveal two men and one woman standing around a large goldwood desk. The woman stood on the business side, hands braced on the edge. The men, one older, one younger, stood opposite her. The older man looked angry. The younger looked like he wished he were somewhere else.

"Colonel Hals?" Jani remained in the open doorway, looking from one worn face to another. "Captain Kilian reporting, ma'am." *What the hell have they been doing?* Their summerweights were sweat-stained and rumpled, their hair, matted, the older man's face alarmingly flushed.

"Do we look that bad, Captain?" Hals asked. Her voice held tired humor, along with the barest trace of New Indiesian singsong. She was shorter, heavier, and lighter-skinned than Jani, her curly, dark brown hair twisted in a tight bun. Pleasant-looking, if you ignored her heavy-lidded eyes and fatigue-drained complexion. "Please. Come in."

The younger man gestured toward the older. "This is Major Vespucci, ma'am," he said to Jani. "Our Procedural specialist."

Vespucci nodded. He was dark-haired and fleshy, his small eyes set in a permanent squint. It was Procedural's job to make sure a department had access to the latest form revisions—Vespucci had the humorless look of a man who liked controlling the codes.

"And I'm Lieutenant Ischi," the young man added with a smile. "Tech wrangler and department dogsbody." He was Eurasian, tall and trim, with big, bright eyes and good bones.

Jani removed her orders from her briefbag and walked across the office to hand them to Hals. "Ma'am."

Hals accepted the documents with a small smile. "We'll start you off by having Lieutenant Ischi show you to your office, Captain. I'd like to see you back here at oh-ten." She acknowledged Jani's "good morning, ma'am," with an absent nod, and resumed her conversation with Vespucci, this time at a lower volume.

Ischi bounded out of Hals's office, his relief at escaping evident in his wider grin and expansive gestures. "This way, ma'am." He led Jani down one short hall, then another, finally pulling up in front of an unmarked door. "I'm expecting your doorplate in this afternoon's delivery from Office Supply. They drop off three times a week—let me know what you need, and I'll add it to the next list."

Jani stepped past him into her office, close enough to catch a whiff of deodorant on the cusp of failure. *If an A&S-hole catches sight or scent of you, Lieutenant, you're a goner.* What had he and Hals and Vespucci been up to?

The office was long and narrow. No furniture except for a desk and couple of chairs. Inset bookcases, so at least she had shelves. A single-pane window centered the far wall. Through the portion not blocked by tree branches, she could see the edge of a charge lot. Pimentel was right—Sheridan did have windows to spare.

"Sorry about the view, ma'am."

"At least I'm not looking through bars."

"Ma'am?"

"Nothing." Jani wandered over to her desk. The workstation, comport, and parchment imprinter all looked like they'd just been removed from their cartons—the workstation touchboard still bore its protective plastic wrapping. "Has Systems initiated this yet?"

"This afternoon, ma'am." Ischi's grin tightened. "My apologies."

"Hmm." Having an uninitiated system meant she'd be spending the morning straightening her desk. She walked to the window, looked out at her tree, then turned back to Ischi. "Do you mind if I ask . . . ?" She gestured toward his unkempt uniform.

The light left Ischi's eyes. "We spent last night at the idomeni embassy, ma'am. They keep it pretty warm in there."

"The *whole* night?"

"Yes, ma'am."

"What time did you arrive?"

"Nineteen-up, ma'am."

Jani counted. "You spent over twelve hours there? Doing what?"

"Verifying and cataloging instruments of negotiation, ma'am. Concerning the Lake Michigan Strip."

"I've never heard of that."

"You will," Ischi replied flatly. He nodded sharply and turned to leave. "By your leave, ma'am. I'll nudge Systems about getting you up and running."

Jani watched the door close. Her door. In her old department. In a close-controlled building. On a Service base. *And everyone's fighting, they look hot and confused, and the idomeni have them back on their heels.* Almost two decades and six GateWays removed . . . and nothing had changed a bit.

"Come in, Captain. Have a seat."

Jani walked slowly across Hals's office to disguise her residual limp, and lowered into the visitor's chair.

Across the desk, Hals continued to page through her ServRec. She had showered and changed her uniform. The ends of her bound hair were tightly curled from damp, the creases of her short-sleeve sharp enough to cut parchment.

Jani tensed each time the woman's gaze was arrested, then raked her memory to recall which item could have claimed her attention. The SIB-decimated file held little useful information. Jani's Rauta Shèràa job history. Her specs. Her education and training. She knew it didn't contain what Hals no doubt most wanted to know.

So, Captain Colonel-Killer, what did I do to deserve you?

Hals closed the ServRec, then traced along its sides with her fingertips. "So—"

Jani squeezed the arms of her chair.

"—you're Two of Six. The Eyes and Ears." The woman offered a quick half smile.

"Yes, ma'am," Jani replied carefully.

"I'd just begun my sophomore year at Montserrat when the news arrived that six humans had been chosen to study documents sciences at the Rauta Shèràa Academy. That made my decision to major in paper rather than law easier for my parents to swallow." Hals tipped back her chair and tapped her fingertips together. Index to index, middle to middle. "How did that bit of doggerel go? One of Six for Tongue of Gold, Two for Eyes and Ears, Three and Four for . . . for—"

"Hands of Light." Jani felt the heat crawl up her neck. "Five and Six for Earthly Might."

Another fleeting smile. "The late Hansen Wyle was your mouthpiece. He was One of Six."

"Yes. Ma'am." Jani glanced around the lieutenant colonel's spare office. Of all the things she expected to be questioned about, this hadn't even made the top twenty. "Gina Senna was Three. Carson

Tsai was Four. They were musicians—musicians impressed the idomeni. That's what *Hands of Light* means." She waited for Hals to respond, but the woman only watched her silently. "Dolly Aryton was Five. Her mother was a Neumann. Ennegret Nawar was Six. He's the *N* in SCAN. Hence the Earthly Might." She wished she had the nerve to sit quietly, wait out Hals's silences. Memories of past calls-on-the-carpet returned *en force*. The dry mouth. The ragged thoughts. The gabbling to fill the relentless quiet. "We were eighteen when we wrote it. We thought it sounded very enigmatic."

"I'm not asking you to defend it, Captain." Hals paused and held a hand to her mouth. Her jaw flexed as she suppressed a yawn. "As you no doubt recall," she continued, eyes watering, "Foreign Transactions covers a rather broad range of dealings. These usually involve records and equipment transfers to the colonies. We do, however, occasionally monitor transactions with the idomeni. Unfortunately, as you also no doubt recall, that five percent of our duties can take up eighty percent of our time."

Jani nodded. "Food shipments into Rauta Shèràa Base used to result in some marathons. I remember the one time we tried to ship in beets. The idomeni have beetlike vegetables, but they're grown in the Sìah valleys in the central plains. They don't grow in the northern regions, so the Laumrau didn't want to let them in."

Hals leaned forward. "So what happened?" She spoke quickly. More than polite interest—she *wanted* to know.

"We gave up after three straight days with no breaks. Nobody liked beets that much." Jani could still remember the hot, stagnant air, the simultaneous collapse of everyone's deodorant, her CO at the time nodding off in a corner. "Sometimes, you have to give them what they want. It usually pays off. They gave in to us later when we wanted to bring in peanut butter. Of course, we were willing to fight for peanut butter. I think they knew that." She chuckled, until a glance at Hals's blank expression silenced her.

"You make it sound so homey, Captain." She fingered a corner of Jani's file. "Why are they so picky about their food?"

Ask me something easy, like the meaning of life. "They place great value in order—that significance cuts across sect lines. Order that nourishes the body also nourishes the soul. Eating certain types of food at certain times maintains that sense of order. Exposure to certain foods only during certain seasons of the year. A balanced diet taken to the extreme."

"Don't they ever eat anything just because it tastes good?"

"They're not a very sensual people when it comes to appetites, ma'am. One theory has it that their brains work similarly to those of humans who've been stressed to the point of burnout. They only feel extremes. Nuance escapes them."

"Do you believe that?"

"I'm not a xenoneurologist." Jani wavered under Hals's probing gaze. "No, ma'am, I don't believe that. They're alien. We just don't understand their nuance."

Hals's eyebrows arched. "Do you include yourself in that *we*, Captain?"

Jani hesitated, then shook her head. "No, ma'am. However, I also don't underestimate their capacity to surprise."

Hals nodded wearily, as though she'd had the idomeni capacity to surprise up to *there*. "Ask Lieutenant Ischi to provide you the background information concerning our involvement with the Lake Michigan Strip. I'll be interested to hear your take." She tapped absently at her comport pad. "By the way, during your time in Rauta Shèràa, did you ever know a female named Onì nìaRauta Hantìa?"

"Hantìa?" It had been years since Jani had heard that name. She recalled a smooth, arrogant voice, like barbed satin. "She was member of a scholarly skein, training to be a Council Historian. The equivalent of an archivist."

"She may have been an archivist then. She's the Vynshàrau's chief documents examiner now." Hals opened, then closed Jani's folder. "Did you know her?"

Yes. Jani watched Hals fidget. *But I think you knew that.* It looked as though her new CO possessed a capacity to surprise, as well. "We were at the Academy together."

Hals nodded. "I thought it might be likely, judging from your ages." She looked at Jani. Through the fatigue in her eyes, a hard light shone. "It will be nice to have someone with your experience in this department."

"Ma'am." Jani knew a dismissal when she heard it. She stood, rubbed her damp palms against her trousers, then came to attention. "Good morning, ma'am." She backed up one step, executed aboutface, and headed for the door.

"Captain."

Here it comes. Jani stopped. Turned slowly. What would it be? A question about Neumann? Evan?

Hals sat back, her brow furrowed. She wanted to ask Jani *something*—that was obvious. Maybe she was having trouble deciding where to start. How do you question mutiny, when you're on the business side of the table? "Never mind," she said. "Make sure you see Ischi about the background report."

"Yes, ma'am." Jani walked out of the office, left a note for the absent dogsbody requesting the report, then cut through the anteroom into the desk pool. Most of the chairs were filled; a few of the uniformed occupants paused in their work to cast her curious glances.

She entered her office to find someone from Systems bent over her workstation. She fled to the quiet of the women officers' lounge, locked herself in a toilet stall, and slumped against the cold metal partition. *Crazy.* Her heart pounded. Her stomach ached. *They want the wait to drive me crazy.*

By the time Jani felt settled enough to return to her office, the Systems tech had departed. The presence of a steel blue folder in the middle of her desktop told her that Ischi had delivered the background report.

She closed the door and sat at her desk. Paged through the file. Inserted the attached data wafers into the workstation slot. The mechanics of work calmed her. She slipped the report on like a favorite shirt, and read. Eventually, she sat back and propped her feet up on the desk. Laughed out loud a few times.

It was the funniest story she'd read in years.

"Ma'am?"

Jani glanced up to find a freshly fitted-out Ischi standing in the doorway, holding a steaming mug in one hand and a covered plate in the other.

"I thought you might want something to eat." He held up the plate with the hopeful air of a father trying to persuade his child to come out from under the bed. "You've been in here for over five hours."

"I have?" Jani checked her timepiece, and whistled. "I have." She lowered her feet to the floor. "Time flies when you're having fun."

"A couple of us did hear you laugh once or twice." Ischi walked in and let the door close behind him. "Three times, maybe." He set down the cup—the heavenly aroma of true-bean drifted across the desk. "We tried to figure out what was so funny." He removed the protective cover from the plate to reveal a sandwich and a piece of cake, and placed it before her.

Jani wrapped her hand around the mug, then motioned for Ischi to sit. "What the hell was Anais Ulanova thinking?" She sipped the coffee. Black. No sugar. Strong enough to warp enamel. She almost moaned in rapture. "She orders a lakeskimmer to transport mixed foodstuffs to the Commerce Ministry, even though the idomeni embassy sits smack between them and the verandas where all the idomeni take meditation facing the water."

"*Exposure to unknown food.*" Ischi perched on the edge of his chair, elbows on knees. "*Breaking the sacred plane.* Those phrases have been ringing in our ears since this began. Tsecha and the other priests spent three months decontaminating the embassy, and they're still not happy."

"And to keep it from happening again, all they want are land, sea, and air rights to a two-kilometer strip stretching from their embassy proper, across the lake, to the eastern side of the Michigan province."

"And scanning rights. And boarding rights. It's the scanning rights that we're worried about. They could monitor flyovers of experimental craft." Ischi's clear young brow furrowed in consternation. "I think they're overreacting, personally."

"You're lucky they're still in Chicago." Jani took a bite of the sandwich. Cold roast beef on buttered bread, with slices of pickled hot pepper on the side. "If the Oligarch had had his way, he'd have recalled the whole crew back to Shèrá. Morden nìRau Cèel has been looking for an excuse to cut diplomatic ties with us ever since they reopened." She bit a slice of pepper—Ischi cringed as he watched her chew. "It was a miracle that Nema talked him into only decamping to the Death Valley enclave. I wonder how he twisted his arm?"

"Nema?" Ischi chewed his lip in puzzlement. "Oh, the ambassador's other name." He eyed Jani intently. "Would you call him that to his face, ma'am?"

"No. To his face, I'd call him *nìRau*. Or *nìRau ti nìRau*, if I wanted to be really formal. Or *inshah*—that's informal High Vynshàrau for *teacher*. Not that he'd mind if I called him Nema, but I wouldn't feel right." Jani pondered her half-empty cup. "So, Lieutenant, what's the word. Did the Exterior Minister insult the idomeni on purpose?"

Ischi's guileless manner altered. His eyes narrowed. His voice deadened. "That's Diplomatic's call, ma'am. They don't discuss those matters with us."

"Why not? You're part of this enterprise. You can watch as well as they can."

"We're not qualified, ma'am. So we've been told. We've been told a lot of things, lately."

He wants to say more. That was obvious as hell. *He just needs a push.* And unlike with Hals, she could provide the helping hand. "Out with it, Lieutenant," she said coldly.

Ischi's words tumbled, laced with frustration and anger. "We've been getting questions from Diplo for weeks, ma'am. 'When's she coming? When's she going to be here?' "

"Their point?"

"Burkett, ma'am. Brigidier General Callum Burkett. Head of Diplo. He said you're halfway to being idomeni and you have no business being in a uniform, much less as a member of FT." Ischi swallowed. "I'm quoting, ma'am."

"I understand."

"FT doesn't hold with that opinion, ma'am."

"Glad to hear it."

"Inasmuch as we're allowed to express opinions. Ma'am."

Jani stood, stretched her stiff back, and walked to her window. "The first students the idomeni allowed into the Academy weren't diplomats, but documents examiners. To the idomeni, the order is in the paper, and order is all. They expect you to participate. They expect you to be able to make decisions and negotiate binding agreements because, I guarantee, their examiners sure as hell can."

"Hantìa," Ischi grumped. "She keeps trying to push Colonel Hals into saying things—"

"And Hals has been told to keep her mouth shut and scan the paper." Jani tugged at the window shade so hard she crooked it. "I went to school with Hantìa. If she senses weakness, she is merciless unless you hit her and hit her hard. She expects you to—that's the born-sect tradition of challenge and counterchallenge. She's making overtures, inviting Hals to begin the negotiation process. If Hals keeps ignoring her, first she'll become confused, then she'll feel insulted, and at that point, no amount of diplomacy is going to lessen the perceived offense."

"We're more important than Diplo thinks we are?" Ischi's voice bit, like he'd just had a long-nursed belief confirmed.

"Oh, yes."

"What can we do?"

"I don't know." Jani returned to her desk and picked up her cup. "Hals seems to realize she needs to do something. I kept getting the feeling that she wanted to ask me questions, but she couldn't work up the nerve."

"That's Vespucci. By the book—" Ischi swallowed his comment and stood up. "By your leave, ma'am—I have a tech meeting to prep."

"They were arguing about me, weren't they? About how involved I should get in this?"

"I think you'd better speak with Colonel Hals about that, ma'am." Ischi kept his eyes fixed on the floor. "I can set up an appointment for you first thing tomorrow morning."

"Please do, Lieutenant." Jani took another sip of coffee, then leaned against her desk and absently examined her cup—

"By your leave, ma'am." Ischi about-faced and made for the door.

—bright blue with a black griffin rampant on a gold shield. "Stop right where you are, Lieutenant!"

"Ma'am." Ischi snapped to attention a mere step from freedom.

"What is this?" Jani held the cup within centimeters of his nose.

"It's—a coffee cup, ma'am."

"And?"

"It's blue, ma'am."

"*And*?"

"It has a bird on it."

"No, Sergeant, this is not a bird. This, Corporal, is a griffin. Do you know what a griffin is, Spacer?"

"Ma'am."

"It's the emblem of something called a Gruppo Helvetica, a worthless assemblage of overpaid has-beens who are going to get their asses flayed as soon as they play a *real* team."

Ischi remained at attention as he looked at her sidelong. "Bet?"

"Name it."

"The officers have a pool."

"Put me down for Acadia Central United, all the way."

"You're on, ma'am." Ischi removed a handheld from his trouser pocket and coded an entry. "It's a fifty-Comdollar stake, payable before the first round begins. Ten percent off the top goes to the charity of your choice so we don't get gigged for gambling. Where do you want yours to go?"

"Colonial Outreach."

"Colonial Outreach, it is." Ischi tucked the device back in his pocket. "It'll be a pleasure to take your money, ma'am," he said as he departed, with a clipped coolness that would have given Lucien pause.

Jani stuck her tongue out at him as the door closed. Then she returned to her desk, and her report, and the balance of her meal.

It was dark by the time Jani departed Doc Control. Had been dark for hours—the only people out and about were third-shifters on their way to work. *Pimentel is going to have my ass.* She stopped by the South Central out of guilt and assembled dinner from the leavings of the salads and soups. Everything scanned edible. Good thing. She'd forgotten to scan the sandwich and the cake, and one of them had made her wheeze. Considering the only other things that made her wheeze were shellfish and biopolymers, unscanned foods were now officially expunged from her menu.

Her walk had slowed to a trudge by the time she entered the hostel lobby. But she detoured to the holoVee room anyway, just to decompress.

"In other news," the disembodied voice of the announcer continued, "reaction to the idomeni ambassador's visit to the Botany Department of Chicago Combined University, undertaken in an effort to promote scientific exchange between the Commonwealth and the Shèrá worldskein, remains mixed. Negotiations are currently under way to allow teams of human and idomeni botanists to conduct joint research in selected sites throughout both our domains. This would be the first time such exchanges would be allowed since the idomeni civil war, and agriculture officials fear these programs could draw attention and funding from the more traditional research that has been conducted in the colonies for decades."

As the announcer continued his narration, Arrèl nì Rau Nema came into view, flanked by white-coated human scientists. His golden skin seemed to shimmer in the bright sun. Gold coils flashed from his ears. His straight, pale brown hair had been braided into a series of thin loops that trimmed his head like fringe. He wore the usual clothing of a male of his skein and station: light brown trousers tucked into knee-high brown boots, open-necked shirt in the same dusky color, an off-white overrobe trimmed with crimson. A human wearing so many clothes in the extreme heat would have looked sweaty and wilted, but Nema looked sharp and energetic.

Jani stepped closer to the display. Several Service officers stood behind Nema, eyes fixed on the crowds. Lucien, she noted, wasn't among them.

"I have most enjoyed my visit to this place," Nema said. His light voice sounded clipped, flat, English falling easily from his thin lips. "So much have I learned, and truly."

One of the reporters shouted a question. The scientists frowned and tried to herd Nema away, but he planted his feet and rounded his shoulders. His stubborn posture made Jani smile.

"I am curious of all things in this city," he said. "*All* things." He paused, then looked straight at the holocam. "My eyes and ears are always open to that which I must know." Amber eyes tunneled.

Through the hours. The distance. Straight at her. "Knowledge is power, isn't that what all humanish believe? Then so must we labor together, to build our power."

He bared his teeth in a skeleton-like grimace. The expression was the idomeni equivalent of a smile, though it looked in no way benign. Jani had always referred to the expression as *Grim Death with a Deal for You.* The term seemed more appropriate now than it ever had.

Another reporter shouted another question, but before Nema could respond, the white coats maneuvered him into a nearby building.

Jani turned and walked slowly from the room. Up the stairs. Down the hall.

Nema's turning the screws to keep me out of jail because he wants me to look for something. She changed into pajamas, set out her late dinner, ate. *Something powerful.* She washed, burrowed into bed, nestled Val the Bear on the adjoining pillow. *But what?*

Did it matter? She esteemed Nema, and always would. And who could help liking him? *But he could teach John a thing or two about treating people like objects.* She had taken care to leave his ring in her bag. It was a keepsake, from a time long past. She didn't have the ability, or the will, to jump when he called anymore.

She punched her pillow, thought of the scalpel on her desk, and knew she should start planning her escape. *Not now.* Later, when she could think more clearly. When thoughts of victimized archivists and troubles with the idomeni didn't prey on her mind. When she'd seen everything through to the end. Left things tight.

She fell asleep slowly, fitfully. Her stomach had started to ache again.

CHAPTER 10

Sam sat on the scanbed and watched the morning sun stream though the examination-room windows. The light fractured into rainbows as it struck analyzer displays, flashed like flares as it reflected off metal stands. He found the brightness cheering. So different here than in the SIB basement.

In some respects.

"You understand my problem, don't you, Sam?" Pimentel activated one of the analyzers. "Why I'm reluctant to discharge you?"

Sam twisted the end of his bathrobe sash around his fingers. "I understand why you believe you have a problem, Doctor. I do not, however, understand why you feel it must become mine."

Pimentel dragged a lab stool next to the scanbed and sat down. He closed his eyes and pinched the bridge of his nose. "Sam, it's gone beyond simply taking on other people's pasts and calling them your own. You've been caught in a direct lie about your work. You'd never lied about your work before. Your condition is deteriorating."

"Your opinion."

"My *medical* opinion, Sam. It's worth a lot." He leaned forward, his hands splayed across his knees. Narrow hands, for a man. Thin fingers. "I've spoken with your immediate supervisor, as well as his supervisor. They told me what happened the other night. They told me about finding two drawers' full of missing documents in your desk."

"I did not put them there."

"You checked out those documents. Your name is on the sign-out."

"Be that as it may. I did not hide them."

"Sam, according to Lieutenant Yance, no one else has access to those particular papers." Pimentel stood. He wore summerweights, although as usual he had left his rank designators in his desk drawer. "You were put in charge of everything connected with Rauta Shèràa Base because you possessed a reputation beyond reproach and organizational abilities Yance called second to none." He paced in front of the bed, his hands inscribing strokes and circles in the air, a conductor without his baton. "You were able to surmise a series of events from just a few documents. You knew where the holes were, where people needed to look to fill them. You figured out paper protocols the idomeni hadn't used since the Laumrau fell from power. 'Almost as if he'd worked there himself,' was how Yance put it."

Sam nodded. "I understand research."

Pimentel stopped in front of him. "Yes, you spent years building your reputation. Refining your expertise." He braced one narrow-fingered hand on the edge of the bed. "Every day you delay the removal of the tumor increases the chances that you could suffer permanent brain damage, and with that, permanent damage to your expertise. Even with the knowledge base we have, some things can't be fixed." He leaned close. "Sam, please let me schedule you for surgery."

Sam edged away from Pimentel. His view of the door was blocked by the way the doctor had positioned himself. If he tried to slide off the bed, Pimentel only had to move a little to his right to stop him. He didn't like that. He hated the sensation of feeling trapped. He hated the sight of Pimentel's spindly hands. "No."

"Sam—!"

"No, Doctor! That's my decision, and unless you hold me prisoner here, there's nothing you can do about it!" He slid off the bed and darted around Pimentel until he stood in a direct line with the door. "I will be leaving this place as soon as I change my clothes."

"*Sam.*" Pimentel struck the scanbed with his fist. Once. Twice. "I assume you've given no thought to what we spoke of the other day."

"No."

"I can't stand by and watch a man destroy himself. If you persist on this course, I will initiate the paperwork necessary to have you declared a ward of the Commonwealth."

"You can try, Doctor." Sam bolted from the room, almost colliding with an orderly pushing a skimcart laden with equipment. He mumbled an apology and scurried down the hall, the ends of his sash bouncing off his knees like clappers in a silent bell.

No doctors inside my head, ever again. He'd die if he let them in. He knew it.

He weaved up and down halls, ignoring the signs, using doors and nurses' stations and inset lights as his guides. Things that couldn't be moved, couldn't be changed. *There's nothing wrong with my memory.* Not for the things that mattered. Escape. Freedom. Keeping the doctors out of his head.

Sam turned the corner onto the hallway that led to his room and collided with a uniformed man walking in the opposite direction. Dress blue-greys, unusual for that area of the base. Sam looked up into the man's face and stifled a cry. *Scar.* From his nose to his mouth. It drew the eye like any accident. Sam barely kept from blurting out that he was in the right place to get it fixed.

The man brought his hands up to chest level, palms toward Sam, as though to grab him. But in the same motion, he backed off a step. The hands dropped. "My apologies." He smiled—not the most pleasant sight. "I came by to pick up some test results, but I can't find the lab drop."

"Scan or wet analysis?"

"Scan."

"Two halls to the right. Middle door. Blue." Sam's gaze flicked over the man's badges and designators. Any more, and he'd have looked ridiculous; any fewer, and he'd have looked like everybody else. Then Sam looked at the name tag. "Colonel Pierce."

"Yes." The man looked over the top of Sam's head, toward the distant goal of the ScanLab.

"I've seen you before." Sam nodded in recognition. "On ServNet broadcasts. You accompany the Admiral-General to meetings." He rattled off the particulars as though the man's ServRec lay open on a desk in front of him. "Pierce. Niall. One I, two Ls. C-number M-five-six-dash-three-three-dash-one-one-one-S. You were a sergeant, assigned to the CSS *Kensington.* You led A Squad, Platoon Four-oh-nine-eight, during the evacuation of Rauta Shèràa Base, during the Night of the Blade."

Pierce lowered his gaze slowly, his scar smoothing as his smile died. As each detail found voice, he grew more and more still, until Sam thought he had turned to stone. "You have the advantage of me, sir," he said, so quietly not even his scar moved.

"Yes," Sam said, "I do." He sidestepped Pierce and broke into a trot, darting into his room and pushing the door closed. He pressed his ear to the panel, straining for any sound. He didn't trust doctors, no, but he trusted colonels even less. He couldn't remember why, although he knew there had to be a reason. Sufficient for now that he simply knew, that the instinct that helped him hack his trails through paper would see him clear to the door with regard to doctors who wanted to take away his freedom and colonels who wanted to know his name.

He tossed the robe in a corner, followed by the pajamas. Pulled his clothes from the tiny armoire and dressed as though the room were on fire.

Ward of the Commonwealth. Sam cracked the door open, eased his head out, checked the hallway for colonels and doctors. Then he dashed out of the room and down the hall in the direction opposite the way he had come, not stopping until he found a doc tech office.

"Excuse me." He stepped just inside the doorway and waited for one of the techs to attend him. "I can make changes to the personal data in my file here, can't I?"

"Yes, sir." A young woman approached him, smiling. Younger even than Tory, and no one was younger than Tory. "What changes do you need to make?"

"Next of kin."

The tech scanned his patient bracelet with her handheld, then waited for his file to open. "Name, please?" she asked, her stylus tip poised above the device input.

"Jani. Kilian. She is a captain, on this base."

"Could you define the relationship, please, sir?"

"Friend." His only friend—this he believed with all his heart. *She believed me.* She had looked him in the eye and told him so, when everyone else preferred to trust in the lies. *She'll take care of me.* He couldn't pinpoint why he felt so sure, but he did. He knew he could trust her. He just knew.

CHAPTER 11

Evan burrowed into the plush rear seat of the Neoclona double-length and watched with a mixture of excitement and dread as the Chicago skyline filled the windscreen. Months had passed since he'd last seen the city.

My arraignment. He had stood before the Ministers' Bench of Cabinet Court and watched men and women he'd grown up with look upon him as a stranger as they exiled him to his rose-infested Elba. *All except Anais.* Her scrawny face had been aglow with gloat. Evan treasured that memory, sick though it seemed. At least she'd considered him an enemy vanquished, rather than an embarrassment to hide away.

Since then, but for his sojourns to Sheridan, he'd remained rooted to his suburban patch. His jailers met his medical needs with biweekly visits from the local Neoclona annex, and had shunted aside his other needs as unworthy of their attention.

But what John wants, John gets. Joaquin suspected nothing. He'd even waxed enthusiastic about Shroud's sudden interest in Evan's health and dismissed his client's protests that the good doctor's real interest revolved around Jani Kilian. *John's a good Family man,* he'd said. *He didn't get where he is today by acting like an obsessed fool.*

"Quino, I'm afraid that's exactly how he got where he is today." Evan ignored the driver's questioning stare in the rearview, and soaked in the city views with the rapt attention of a condemned man watching from his tumbrel.

The driver maneuvered down traffic-jammed State Street. "We're early, sir," he said as he weaved around a triple-parked people-mover. "I can drive around the block, if you wish."

Evan held out his hands, palms facing down. No trembling. The half liter he'd downed for breakfast had seen to that. "Go on in. I'm ready."

Finding Val Parini waiting for him by the VIP-lift bank didn't surprise him. Shroud was the master, Parini the dog. *And I'm the stick of the day.*

"Hello, Ev." Parini looked ill—ashen skin, bleary eyes. His trousers and short-sleeved pullover were rumpled, as though he'd slept in them.

"Val." Evan congratulated himself that his own black trousers and black-and-blue-striped pullover looked much sharper. *The last thing I need is that bleached bastard thinking I don't give a damn.* He followed Parini into the lift, and swallowed hard as the car shot upward and he felt his feet press against the floor.

"How've you been?" Parini stuffed his hands in his pockets and leaned against the wall. "Considering."

"All right. Considering." Evan forced a smile. "Tired."

Parini stared up at the ceiling. "Yeah, I know the feeling. I just got in from Felix. Six-week round-trip, not counting the couple of days in between to catch my breath." He yawned. "I'm getting too old for that stuff."

Evan nodded politely. "Business?"

"Special patient. Someone you know."

"Our social circles overlapped, Val. Care to narrow it down?"

"Jani Kilian," Parini said, contemplating the light fixture. "You remember her. Tawny damsel. Had a little accident a few years back."

Evan flinched as the car decelerated. At least the lift mechanism's hissing whine drowned out the roaring in his head. "You saw her?"

"Yes. She slipped out from under, though, as she is wont to do. Unfortunately, she walked right into a Service trap. She's at Sheridan now." A corner of Parini's mouth curved. He knew surprise when he smelled it, the son of a bitch. "Didn't Quino tell you?" He tsked. "Bad Quino. She's been there almost a week." The lift slowed to a stop and the door opened.

Evan lagged behind Parini, eyes locked on the back of his neck. *Just one good shot*—Ridgeway's crumpled body flashed in his mind, and the urge evaporated. "There was nothing on the 'Vee or in the sheets."

"Yeah, I don't know how the hell they managed to keep it quiet." Parini led him down a wide corridor. One side was glass-walled—glimpses of the Commerce Ministry compound and the lake beyond could be seen between the high-rises. They stopped in front of an unmarked door enameled with a purple so dark Evan at first mistook it for black. Parini palmed it open.

Evan expected to enter an examining room—matte white surfaces, analyzers and viewscreens, a scanbed in the corner. Instead, he walked into an opulent sitting room—eggplant-colored walls, bloodwood bookcases and tables, Persian carpets.

A panel slid aside and Shroud stepped into the room. The feverish glisten in his eyes spoke of freshly applied filming. Violet, this time, a perfect match to his daysuit jacket. "You're early."

"Sorry, John," replied Parini, not sounding sorry at all. "Guess what? Loiaza didn't tell Evan that Jani's at Sheridan."

Evan glanced around nervously. A large holoVee display dominated one corner, a pillow-strewn daybed, another. *No way in hell I'm letting these two creeps examine me in here.* "I'm sure Quino had his reasons."

Shroud gestured for Evan to sit. "He must be realizing that taking you on as a client wasn't the wisest career move he ever made. I sense damage control in progress. You need allies." His rumbling voice grew measured. "*Quid pro quo*, as we discussed before."

Evan looked at Shroud, who regarded him with relaxed contempt, then at Parini, whose distaste held an edge. *Master told dog I'll help them.* He sank into a cushioned lounge chair and immediately reached for the bourbon decanter that rested on the nearby low table. "I've known Quino for over thirty years. He doesn't leave clients to twist in the wind." He poured a shot, tossed it back. Of course Joaquin had a reasonable explanation for not telling him about Jani. Which Evan would be damned interested in hearing as soon as he returned to Elba.

Parini flopped into a chair opposite Evan. "Jani's not in the news, either. ServNet's no surprise—they do what Roshi Mako tells them to do, and he doesn't think Service issues are the public's business. But I talked with Dory in Commonwealth Affairs, and she said CapNet must have agreed to self-censor. She said that they only do that when they get pressure from the PM."

Shroud joined them. The chair he chose was less padded and straight-backed. You could have used his spine to draw a plumb line. "Jani's news on ChanNet because she's from La Manche. She's news on FelNet because she was captured there under circumstances embarrassing to the Service and Felix is looking for an excuse to renegotiate the lease for Fort Constanza. No one's made a fuss over her in Chicago because she's not news in Chicago."

"You're wrong, John. There's a sizable Acadian population here in the French Quarter who would love to know what's going on." Parini ignored the beverage service and instead plucked at a bunch of grapes, popping them into his mouth with ballistic force. "I bet Nema has something to do with it. He's been twisting arms all over town. He'd start a shooting war on the Boul Mich if he thought it would free his Eyes and Ears."

"Nema doesn't exert any control over Earth-based broadcasting."

"Just because you hate him doesn't mean he has no influence, John!"

Evan listened to the two men bicker with the uneasiness of someone who found himself the captive audience to a marital spat. He looked from the animated Parini to the over-controlled Shroud, and the question that had been the subject of dinner-party debate for twenty years parked itself inside his head and refused to leave.

Do those two . . . fuck? Both sides offered cogent arguments, Parini's many boyfriends and Shroud's revolving-door women notwithstanding.

Evan refilled his glass as his well-calibrated people-filter chugged in the background. *No, not lovers.* He still felt his master and dog theory explained the relationship. *And sometimes dog refuses to stop barking and master has to go to the window to see what the fuss is about.*

Shroud picked up a nicstick dispenser from the table and turned the rectangular case end over end. His spindly fingers invited the image of spiders tumbling a victim in a web. "Why would Li and Roshi want to keep Jani's story quiet?"

"I can tell you the reason they gave," Evan offered. But first, he sipped. Shroud had him by the short hairs, true, but he also stocked the finest bourbon. "Commonwealth security. CapNet will sit on news if they're told releasing it could threaten internal stability." He'd exercised that option many times when Lyssa still lived, as her behavior grew more uncontrollable and her public displays more embarrassing.

Shroud snorted. "What could Jani do to threaten Commonwealth stability!"

The three of them looked at one another. For one brief moment, their thoughts coalesced. Only Parini felt it appropriate to smile.

Shroud coughed. "Let me rephrase that. What happened to her on Felix that could threaten Commonwealth stability?"

"John, she almost died!" Parini looked at Evan. "Those Service morons injected her with Tacit, an experimental sedative. It knocked her liver for a loop."

Shroud struck the nicstick case against his thigh. "Tacit is safe."

The rattle of the plastic sticks against metal punctuated every word. “Instances of hepatotoxicity have never been recorded.”

“For *humans*, John. It hasn’t been tested on idomeni—”

Evan shut out the men’s argument and considered his own uncomfortable thoughts. *I asked Joaquin about illegal arrests of colonials and he brushed me off.* The man had offices on Felix—the staff would have Misty’d him immediately if rumors of Jani had surfaced.

My own attorney’s holding out on me? Why?

“Evan?”

He looked up to find Shroud glaring at him.

“Let me repeat the question. In your opinion, is Jani’s case important enough to cause a furor?”

Evan nodded. “You said it yourself, John. The colonies are flexing their muscles, and the idomeni, especially Nema, are jumping feetfirst into the fray.” He should have worked it out himself, but living in exile, he couldn’t access the catalyzing snippets of information that had once fueled his life. “Li faces reelection next year. I’m betting that right now she wishes Jani had never been found.”

Shroud scowled. He had the moody, tightly wrapped look of a blanched El Greco. “What about Roshi?”

“He’s in a more difficult position. His proud New Service is over two-thirds colonial. If he prosecutes Jani, he risks a breach that may never heal at a time when a mixed-bag force may be called upon to quell colonial unrest. But on the other hand, it’s not in his best interest to seem soft on mutiny and murder.” Evan tried to put himself in Mako’s shoes—problem was, he didn’t know the man well enough. How far would he go to preserve what he had worked so hard to build? “He could be planning a quiet trial and execution.” That would explain Roshi’s presence at the SIB. The born field officer, checking personally on the progress of his investigative branch’s most sensitive case in decades.

Shroud’s voice droned funereal. “There’s no such thing as a quiet execution.” He reached for the beverage tray—to Evan’s surprise, he chose bourbon, too. “Well, Val, what do your sources tell you about the mood on Sheridan? Is Jani’s presence rallying the colonials?” He poured three fingers, added a single ice cube, and threw back a healthy swallow.

Evan checked his timepiece. Only midmorning. *Not a good sign, Johnny—don’t tell me I’ve found a drinking buddy.*

“I’ll admit, it’s pretty quiet.” Val slung his leg over the chair arm and flicked grapes into the empty vase in the center of the table. In between tosses, he shot anxious glances at the door. “Considering that Service Diplomatic has been pulled in to help settle that idomeni food fiasco, I wouldn't be surprised if they dragged Jani in as well." He shrugged at the surprised looks that greeted the statement. "That's what she used to do on Shèrá. She has more head-to-head experience with the idomeni than anyone else at Sheridan."

Shroud's jaw dropped. "They wouldn't."

"They would if they're desperate." Evan could hear the disbelief in his voice when he, of all people, should have known better. "I've sat across the negotiating table from idomeni. After a couple of hours, you've forgotten your name, much less what you're there for. If you meet them on their turf, you have to contend with the heat and the paralyzing sensation that every move you make is the wrong one. If they meet you on yours, you have to sanitize rooms, knock out walls, and relocate all the vend alcoves." And if the Service needed Jani now, they sure as hell didn't need him to give evidence against her. God, he must have been brain-dead—why didn't he think of it before?

The door opened, and a man entered. Mid-thirties. Tall, thin, and mopey. The type Lyssa would have dubbed *homeless puppy.*

"Sorry I'm late." He wore medwhites; his dark hair covered his ears and fell to his collar. He displayed the all-knees-and-elbows gangliness of a twelve-year-old as he lowered into the chair next to Evan.

Parini, Evan noticed, watched the man's every move with a look of eager expectancy. *This is his new toy*? Quite a change of pace from old Val's usual pretty boys.

Shroud looked aggravated. "So happy you could finally join us, Doctor." He refilled his glass, this time adding ice. "Evan, this is Hugh Tellinn. He's an old friend of Val's, from our Felix Majora facility."

To Evan's surprise, Tellinn held out his hand. If he knew his ex–Interior Minister's recent history, it didn't show in his face or his attitude. "Endocrinology," he said, as though that explained everything.

"That's Hugh's way of saying, 'hello'," Parini said with an uncertain smile.

Tellinn looked at the floor rather than his boyfriend. "I've been studying the results of the tests Val performed on Jani Kilian." He braced his feet on the edge of the table. "Has anyone bothered to bring you up to speed on the state of her health, Mr. van Reuter?"

Parini held up a hand. "Hugh—"

Tellinn ignored him. "I thought that's why we were here. I

thought that's why you're suborning perjury, because of your fears for Jani's health."

Shroud tilted his glass back and forth; the clink of ice echoed. "My fears for Jani's health consume my every waking moment, Doctor."

"She's very ill."

"Is she?"

"I believe she suffers from multiple metabolic and endocrine disorders, the most serious of which is a type of acute intermittent porphyria."

"Really, Doctor?"

"Really." Tellinn either didn't see Parini's increasingly frantic gesturing, or once more chose to disregard it. He looked at Evan. "Porphyrias are genetic diseases. Miscues at various points along the heme biosynthetic pathway. Jani wasn't born with the condition, according to the Service scans in her patient file. Therefore, she must have had it thrust upon her during a period when she was undergoing tissue rebuilding, rebuilding performed by someone who didn't know as much as he thought he did about the idomeni genome." He looked down the table at Shroud. "First, do no harm."

Parini's hand stopped in mid-slash.

Evan watched Tellinn. What had first seemed like clumsiness now revealed itself as an overwhelming effort to retain self-control. The man clenched his armrests. His whole body seemed to vibrate with deep-seated rage. *He wants to pound Shroud into the carpet.* Suddenly, he looked capable. The pup had wolf blood. "Well, well, John. Hugh's saying that when you reassembled Jani, you gave her a life-threatening disease."

Shroud ignored him. His stare never left Tellinn. "In your opinion, Doctor."

Tellinn's glower remained just as steady. "I believe the facts speak for themselves. Dickerson and Yevgeny have published a series of papers in *JCMA* describing an illness affecting members of a Haárin enclave on Philippa that is analogous to acute intermittent porphyria. The genetic mutations involved do not match those for the human AIP variant, and the idomeni ban on exchange of medical information has made it impossible for us to pinpoint them." His voice leveled as his eyes deadened. "Therefore, while Service Medical may have an idea what's wrong with Jani, they're unable to nail the diagnosis and therefore the definitive genetic retrofit. Which means they're falling back on heme infusions and dietary controls until they design methods to identify and fix her particular mutation."

Parini jumped in. "I'm also very concerned with the quality of the medical care Jani's receiving—"

Tellinn's blank look silenced him. "On the contrary, I have always found the Service Medical staff I dealt with at Fort Constanza to be very sound. What *I* fear is that Jani's ongoing hybridization has led to the development of so many anomalous metabolic disorders that the diet and drug therapies Service Medical has put her on could lead to serious adverse reactions."

Shroud started to speak, then stopped. His gaze flicked from one face to another, gauging mood without daring to look too deeply. Then he dug down and excavated a fragment of the old John. "In your opinion, Doctor," he said, his voice like a tomb.

Evan understood Shroud's reluctance. He'd felt it himself these past months. *Will you please tell the court what you knew and when you knew it?* And Shroud knew, damned right he did. He knew that Jani's hybridization had led to problems, and that Service Medical wouldn't know how to treat her. *And you've alienated them to the point that they won't ask for your help or let you anywhere near her.* Enter Evan, stage right.

Tellinn graced his agitated lover with a bare glance. "That's why Val persuaded me to accompany him to Chicago, because my opinion counted."

"I wouldn't overestimate your value to this enterprise," Shroud replied. "It wouldn't be the first time Val thought with his prick."

Parini's face flared red. "You should bloody talk!"

Tellinn showed no reaction to either Shroud's insult or the breaking storm. He stood up and turned to Evan. "When is your next visit to Sheridan scheduled, Mr. van Reuter?"

Evan could feel Shroud's glare brand the side of his face. "Early next week."

"Well, perjure yourself as you never did before. Jani won't live out the month if you don't." Tellinn nodded to him, then shambled out of the room.

Parini struggled to his feet. "Damn it, John!" He tripped over the edge of a rug but bulled onward, rubbing his knee and cursing as he stumbled out the door. *"Hugh! Wait!"*

Shroud watched the hot pursuit with a disgusted grimace. "Poor Val. He certainly can pick them."

Evan listened as Val's shout rang down the hall. "Jani's survival instinct is knife-edged—she knew the Service was looking for her. She knew her medical problems were so distinctive, she'd attract immediate attention. Yet she still braved a visit to Neoclona-Felix." He remembered the last time he saw her, just before Justice arrived to arrest him—her lips tinged blue from lack of oxygen, her breathing a rattle he could hear through his haze of pain. "She must have felt like hell."

"I'd worry about myself, if I were you." Shroud stared into the dregs of his glass. "Now repeat after me, I do not remember . . . I do not recall . . ."

After a final warning from Shroud on the benefits of acquiring alcoholism-induced amnesia, an actual condition with the name of Korsakoff's syndrome, Evan was passed off to a series of staff physicians. They lectured him on diet, scanned his brain, and scoped his knee. No one gave any indication that they cared who he was or who he had been. Oh, how the mighty had fallen.

His rage mounted as he descended to the parking garage, entered Shroud's loaned skimmer, fast-floated through the Chicago streets. By the time the driver deposited him in the front yard of Elba and reset his security bracelet, his hands shook and his head pounded. Markhart showed her good sense by remaining silent when she met him at the door. Halvor showed even greater sense by staying out of sight entirely.

Joaquin's secretary put him on standby. By the time the attorney's sere image formed on the comport display, Evan had to grip the edge of his desk to keep from punching his fists through it. "*Why the hell didn't you tell me Jani was at Sheridan!*"

Joaquin blinked slowly. "You heard that from Parini, I'm sure. The man's a shameless gossip. Why Shroud tolerates him, I'll never know." He pressed a hand to his forehead. "Evan, I only learned myself the day before yesterday."

"So why didn't you *tell* me the day before—"

"Because I knew you'd do just what you're doing now—work yourself into needless panic." He paused to sip from a cup. Tea, most likely. Earl Grey, flavored with plenty of personality-enhancing lemon. "She was seen being pushed through the O'Hare Service concourse in a skimchair. Immediately upon arrival at Sheridan, she was admitted to the Psychotherapeutics Ward. I understand she has since been released, but is under constant medical monitoring."

Evan's fingers cramped. He eased his grip on the desk and sat down. "They've got her working with the idomeni, don't they?"

"She is on restricted duty, yes." Joaquin riffled through a folder. "In the Foreign Transactions department."

"Her old department at Rauta Shèràa Base." Evan opened the bottom desk drawer and pulled out a half-empty bottle. "Shit."

"Evan, calm down. She hasn't been deposed yet, but she will be. We can't control what she'll say, but we will be able to counter. Is that clear?"

That's what you think. "Yes, Quino." He cracked the bottle seal and took a healthy swig.

"Good." Joaquin closed the folder and pushed it aside. "So, how did your examination go?"

Shroud grabbed me by the balls and squeezed. "Fine."

"Good, good." Joaquin stilled, then reached for another file. "By the way, why did you ask me to check into Niall Pierce's background?"

Pierce? The visit to Neoclona had rattled Evan so much, everything else had slipped his mind. *Oh, Scarface.* He shrugged. "I don't know." Finding the man's Achilles' heel didn't seem important anymore.

"Well, you always did have a nose for the nasty." Joaquin sniffed. "He's a Victorian. Orphaned at age four. Ward of the Commonwealth. Entered the Service twenty-three years ago under the Social Reclamation Act, a nice way of saying join up or go to prison. Numerous disciplinary actions against him—a wonder he wasn't booted out." His eyebrows arched. "As a last resort, he was transferred to the Fourth Expeditionary Battalion. After that, he seems to have grown up, and the nasty ends."

"Fourth Expeditionary?" Evan perked up. "They're the ones who got us out of Rauta Shèràa."

"Yes, the Fourth was Roshi's old crew, wasn't it?" Joaquin continued reading. "Roshi's good with the hard cases. Pierce thrived. Promotion through the enlisted ranks followed. To top it off, his actions during the Rauta Shèràa evac earned him a battlefield commission." He glanced up over the top of the file. "Was it that bad?"

Evan took another swallow before answering. "Yes."

"We should make more use of it." Joaquin read on, his brow wrinkling. "Pierce has actually become something of a scholar in his spare time. Master of Literature from Chicago Combined. Published a well-regarded essay on *Macbeth*—who would have thought? For the past few months, he's been a regular visitor to the PT Ward. He's augmented, of course—most combat Spacers were back then. Some of them go on to develop augment depression—he's apparently one of the unlucky."

Past few months—define few! Evan had always hated it when aides became vague about time—it always meant they hadn't done their homework. "Can you be more specific as to the date?"

Joaquin looked up with a start. "Early this year. Right after your arrest, as a matter of fact." He pulled a disc out of the file. "Here, why don't I just transfer this to you. I'll code it as legal communication so no one can monitor it. If you think you recall meeting him during the evac, let me know." He inserted the disc into his comport. "Now, if you're sufficiently becalmed, perhaps you'll let me get back to work." It wasn't like Joaquin to request permission, and this time proved no exception. His image sharded, leaving Evan to stare at the blue standby screen.

He waited for the data transfer to complete, then called up Pierce's file on his comport display. Joaquin had covered the high points, but the details revealed the more complex picture of a self-destructive young man undergoing a complete transformation under the firm guidance of the only father figure he had ever known. "Boy, Niall, you'd fall on a sword for Roshi, wouldn't you?" If every great man had his dog, Mako had bred an attack animal in Pierce.

Evan rested his head against the chairback and let his mind wander. *I get arrested.* Directly afterward, the son the A-G never had starts cracking up. "But Roshi doesn't let him down. He keeps him by his side to play escort and take notes on diarrhea-inducing herbs." However much Pierce esteemed Mako, the feeling seemed mutual.

"What else happened after my arrest?" Well, relations with the idomeni became more interesting. Nema started talking GateWay rights and trade routes as soon as the fact that Jani Kilian lived became widely known.

"Jani's alive—Pierce goes downhill." Evan pondered, then shook his head. "Coincidence." He stared into space for a time. Then he scrabbled through his desk for a recording board and stylus and reread Pierce's file, making notes along the way.

CHAPTER 12

It might have been a dream. Could have been a dream.

Jani rode a waveglider. But she had no arms to steer the board, and skimmed out farther and farther on the lake. The shoreline disappeared from view. Skies darkened. Wind howled. The waves grew higher and higher, breaking over her again and again before finally flipping the glider like a vend token. She tumbled through the air. Into the water. The cold wet closed over her, pulled her down. She could see nothing in the frigid blackness, but she could hear.

Voices.

No.

One voice.

Neumann's.

Welcome to my home base, Kilian.

Deeper. Darker. Colder.

I've been waiting for you.

Pain. In her stomach. She pressed the side of her body against the floor, and tried to drive it out with cold.

"Jani!"

She curled in a ball.

"Somebody call an ambulance!"

Tighter. Tighter. If she made herself small enough, she could sink between the tiles, disappear into the floor, and leave the pain behind. It wouldn't fit. It was too big.

"Hurry up! She's in here!"

* * *

Pimentel glowered at the cartridge tester. "You're the gatekeeper, Jani. You're the one who controls what you eat. Your scanner doesn't come equipped with little hands to clamp over your mouth." He looked at her over the top of his magnispecs. He wore summerweights rather than his usual med-whites; his shirt was rumpled, and his hair needed a trim. Some A&S-hole would make his or her quota and then some the next time he stepped outside.

Jani sniffed the air, then continued to breathe through her mouth. According to Pimentel, Lucien had stopped by her room to take her to breakfast. When she didn't answer the buzzer, he had broken in and found her semiconscious on her bathroom floor. She had come to in Triage. Taken a deep breath. Passed out again when the smell from the next alcove hit her. There, a burn team attended to a firing-range accident. The young woman's shooter had backflashed; the half-formed pulse packet had burnt through her summerweights and seared her right side from shoulder to knee.

"Please don't admit me," Jani whispered. Even though she now sat in an examining room on the opposite end of the building, she swore she could detect the odor of burnt flesh in the air. Burnt, like Borgie and the others. Burnt as she had been, too, but she had survived. "I don't want to stay here."

Pimentel removed the magnispecs. "Jani, you are in no condition to leave. Acute intermittent porphyria can affect the autonomic nervous system. Part of that system controls the adrenal glands, which, along with your thyroid, are the sites of your secondary augmentation. While you were in Triage, you started talking to someone who wasn't there. I'm concerned that stimulation of your adrenals is aggravating your primary insert, and you don't need the threat of augie psychosis on top of everything else." He held out the recording board and stared at it. "I'm going to schedule you for an augmentation imaging. Today. And you're staying here until that's done."

Jani sat on a skimchair in the imaging lounge and spooned another mouthful of fruit sludge from the overlarge container. Strawberry, supposedly. Judging from the texture, "straw" was a given, but she'd fight to the death the "berry" part.

The clip of footsteps in the hallway gave her an excuse to drop the spoon in the remains of the semifrozen glop. The door swept aside and Friesian bustled in; he slid to a stop when he spotted her.

"Pimentel called," he said as he took in the skimchair, her hospital-issue robe and pajamas. "Said—they found you—in your room." His voice was choppy, his face flushed. It was a healthy run from Defense Command. "What happened?"

"Didn't eat right. Got sick."

"*Jani.*" Sweat beaded his forehead and soaked his short-sleeve. He pulled a dispo from his trouser pocket and mopped his brow. "How do you feel now?"

"Fine."

" 'Fine,' she says." He sat down on the sofa next to her chair. "And we know what that's worth, don't we?"

Jani remained quiet and stirred the remains of the sludge.

Friesian shook his head. "Pimentel thinks one of the reasons you suffered this episode is because you're under a great deal of stress. I told him I had a piece of news I thought might reduce that stress substantially. When he heard what it was, he suggested I share it with you." He sat back, arms at his sides. He looked as exhausted as Jani felt. "I received a call early this morning from a Colonel Bryant, a member of the prosecution. We had a very interesting talk. I'm expecting an offer to work out a deal anytime now."

Jani kept poking at the sludge. "No trial?"

"Just a hearing."

"How do you know they're not just pulling your leg?" She set the container on her chairside table and wiped her condensation-wetted fingers on her robe.

Friesian tugged at his damp short-sleeve. "I've been at this game a while. I know when someone's playing with me and I know when they're scrambling. This is a scramble like nothing I've ever seen. They want you settled and out of here."

Jani sat back. As she shifted, the skimchair rocked. The motion sickened her—she had to swallow hard before speaking. "Makes you wonder what's the rush, doesn't it?"

Friesian flexed his neck forward, back, then side to side. His cervical vertebrae cracked like knuckles. "*No*, it doesn't. My job is not to run after the prosecution and ask them why they're not going after you harder. My job is to get you out from under with as little penalty as possible. *And* to keep you from shooting yourself in the foot, which from the notations in your record appears to have bordered on a second calling!"

After a flare of anger that set her stomach to clenching, Jani decided not to argue. She felt too sick. Besides, truth was truth. "So what would I be looking at?" She leaned forward. Her lower back balked, and she braced her elbows on her knees for support. "A plea bargain?"

Friesian glanced at her, then looked away. "Not quite. More an arrangement that would see justice served, while taking your condition into account."

"My condition?"

"Your emotional and physical health, both now and at the time of the infraction."

Infraction? That made it sound so . . . A&S. Jani sat up carefully. "Go on."

Friesian hesitated at the tone in her voice. "This arrangement would be worked out by a panel of experts. In your case, the panel would consist of an adjudicating committee, your attending and consulting physicians, a prosecutor from the JA, and me."

"Who sits on the adjudicating committee?"

"A judge and two members of Service Medical unaffiliated with your case."

"No trial?"

"What would be the point? We would admit you did what you were charged with. Your physicians would explain why you did what you did. The prosecution would delineate the consequences of your actions. Then, it's up to the committee to decide a fair punishment, while at the same time protecting you."

Why do I have a feeling what I need protecting from is the committee? "And you expect what?"

"A general medical discharge. A verdict that while you may have been somewhat aware of what you were doing when you missed being evac'd from Rauta Shèràa, your physical and emotional states contributed to your disregard of the consequences."

"How can you define my physical and emotional states when no one will believe me when I tell them what happened?"

"Jani, we need to make a determination according to what we *know* happened. What we have paper on. The effects of the experimental treatments you received from John Shroud. Your guilt over the deaths of your comrades in the transport crash. Your inability to prevent the deaths of the patients at Knevçet Shèràa."

Jani rested her hands on her stomach. The nausea had eased, but the fruit sludge settled like a weight, heavy enough to push her through the chair. "What does a general medical entail these days?"

Friesian's shoulders slumped. It was as if he'd braced for a fight, then realized there wouldn't be one. "It entitles you to a partial pension. You'd give up the right to sign yourself as *Captain, Retired.* No access to ship-stores discounts or emergency travel on Service vessels. But you'd still retain rights to medical care, which in your case, I believe, is the most important consideration."

"Jail?"

"Sentence would be limited to time served."

"Which was?"

"Your incarceration at Fort Constanza."

"One week in the brig infirmary?" She searched Friesian's face for some sign of wonderment or confusion, any indication that he felt mystified. She certainly did. "You really believe they will offer me this deal?"

"Bryant indicated it could be finalized within a week."

"And that I should take it?"

"I would recommend you do, without hesitation."

"Just walk away?" She watched Friesian nod.

The realization settled over her gradually, like the slow-motion buckling and flattening of a sailchute after a landing. *They're letting me off the hook.* She licked her dry lips, swallowed. *I killed Rikart Neumann, and they don't care.*

I wonder why?

Jani felt a slight tingle, the mild frisson of the shock not completely unexpected. She used to feel it back at Rauta Shèràa Base, when she'd show up for an audit. The catch in a voice. The sidelong glance. The sense that things were going on that other people didn't want her to know about.

I'm being diddled. She sat back and clasped her hands over her still-sore stomach. It didn't do to get excited—a person could miss things if she let herself get carried away.

Eyes and Ears open—that was always the key.

Friesian rose, walked to the wall opposite, and thumbed through the tacked-up notices on a message board. "By the way, I received a packet in the interdepartmental mails from a Lieutenant Yance in SIB Archives. It contained missing portions of your ServRec. He noted in his cover memo that he had sent copies to you, as well. At your request." He walked back and stood in front of her. "What were you doing at the SIB?"

Jani grew conscious of a disquieting sensation. A flash-back to her teen years, and her papa standing before her. Same stance as Friesian. Same probing glare. "Just looking around," she replied softly. A voice caught out past curfew.

"Just looking around?" Friesian rubbed his face. He suffered the curse of the dark-haired and pale—only midmorning, and he already looked like he needed a shave. "The next time you feel an overwhelming urge to stick your nose where it doesn't belong, call me."

"I have the right to find out what happened to my ServRec."

"No. You have the right to come to me, and say, 'I wonder what happened to my ServRec.' To which I would reply, 'Why do you believe it's applicable to your case?' And if I liked your answer, I would contract with a registered legal investigator and have them look into it, so that if something did turn up, it would have been uncovered properly and we will have had a chance to deal with it. Your case is still open, Jani, and that means the rules of discovery are in force. Everything we find, the prosecution gets to see and vice versa. That being the situation, it really isn't advisable to turn over every rock you find just to see what crawls out!" He covered his face with his hands. "Damn it! You're a documents examiner. You of all people should know better."

Jani folded her arms. The chair rocked some more, but it didn't upset her stomach as much. She felt stronger. "If it's the truth, why bury it?"

"So that we don't wind up uncovering a mess we can't deal with!"

"You mean you don't want to know what you don't know." Jani cocked her head to look him in the eye. "All those things you've heard about me. It's starting to occur to you that they might be true, isn't it?"

"Not related to this case. Therefore, not my concern." Friesian flexed his neck again and returned to his seat. "I don't think Pimentel would be very happy with me right now. That's the end of legal talk until you get out of here."

Jani picked up her fruit sludge and stirred the melted remains, just to have something to do with her hands. The repetitive motion helped her think. "Sometimes you walk around a big place like Sheridan, you keep seeing the same faces. Makes the place seem smaller somehow."

Friesian rocked his head back and forth in a "so-so" nod. "They probably live or work in this area of the base. Makes sense they'd crop up regularly."

"Hmm." Jani gave the spoon another turn. "There's this one guy who's popped up a few times. Full colonel. Nasty facial scar."

"Oh, him." Friesian frowned. "Niall Pierce. Special Services."

"What, is he famous or something?"

"No. He's just the A-G's right hand." The frown turned to a grimace of concern. "You haven't made yourself known to him in any way that I should know about, have you?"

"I don't know what you mean."

"No, of course you don't." Friesian clasped his hands and slowly twiddled his thumbs. "You remember what Spec Service is?"

"They're the hatchet team."

"No, they provide special assistance and advice to the commander on technical matters and other O-three situations."

"Out of the ordinary?"

"You remember that? That is reassuring."

"I remember lots of things." Jani grabbed a handful of pajama trouser and hoisted, right leg over left. "That's a pretty wide gulf between the A-G and a colonel in Spec Service. What's the deal with Mako and Pierce, they marry sisters or something?"

"Better than that." Friesian eyed her thoughtfully. "They served together on the CSS *Kensington.*"

"Really? The *Kensington* flagshipped the evac of Rauta Shèràa's human enclave."

"Yes, it did. Mako was her captain. Sergeant Pierce played an integral role in the ground assault."

"*Sergeant* Pierce?"

Friesian nodded. "Yeah, that man earned himself a field commission. For that matter, all the members of the *Kensington* crew have done well over the years. Dr. General Carvalla was Medical Officer. General Gleick, the Sheridan base commander, was Mako's exec. Aliens, anarchy, hostile fire, a threat to the Commonwealth—that evac had it all. Even the hot water they got into after they returned to Earth added to the aura."

Jani uncrossed and recrossed her legs, worked her neck, did her best to seem only mildly interested. "Did they botch the evac?"

"No, nothing that serious. They mishandled some remains. Problem was that the remains belonged to Family members. Mako had to testify at a Board of Inquiry about what happened. He knew a witch-hunt when he saw one, and went on the offensive. Named names with regard to some of the garbage that went on at Rauta Shèràa. Rumor has it that those records will remain sealed for two hundred years." He looked at Jani, and stood.

"That's it. You look beat, and I don't want Pimentel coming after me with a bone cutter." He looked at her with kinder eyes, and smiled. "This is going to work out for you. You just need to get your strength back, listen to your doctor, and stay away from the SIB." The courtroom light flared. "Promise?"

Jani nodded. "Whose remains?"

Friesian sighed. "Oh, no one important. Just the members of

Rauta Shèràa Base Command who died during the evac. You probably knew them—Ebben, Unser, and Fitzhugh."

What do you know—those three bastards didn't make it offworld alive. "Think they died accidentally or on purpose?"

"Not your problem. Do you promise?"

Jani nodded in the here and now as, meanwhile, a part of her returned home to Ville Acadie. Her father had meted out her punishment, and explained to her that it was for her own good. And that part of her sat on the couch, head hung low, and murmured agreement as she planned her next escapade. *Mais oui, Papa.* "Promise."

Pimentel fingered his workstation touchpad once. Twice. "The augmentation scan does show some low-level stimulation in the regions around your primary insert." He spun the desk display so Jani could see it. "See." He pointed at a multicolored blob that pulsed in the lower middle area of the translucent overlay of her brain. "We're seeing moderate hyperactivity in your thalamus and in the area of the insert nearest to your amygdala. Now, your tendency toward vivid dreaming is indicated by your elevated Dobriej values"—he tapped a row of numbers that scrolled along the top of the display—"and combining that with the excitation in your limbic system and diencephalon—"

"*Roger!*"

"Fight or flight and sensory areas," he said, switching to layspeak without missing a beat. "Memory." He snatched a dispo out of a box on his desk and wiped a smudge from the surface of the display. "I don't think I'm telling you things you don't already know. You're one of those augments who tends to hallucinate under stress. The porphyria may be aggravating this tendency. The usual monitoring we perform may need to be stepped up in your case." He shredded a corner of the dispo.

Jani thought back to Pierce's post-takedown expression. The bewilderment. The desolation. *Is that what you're offering me, Roger?* "What do you recommend?"

Pimentel shrugged. "Well, my first suggestion is always to remove the augmentation. Your records show you were a borderline case. We have ample justification." He rested his elbow on his desk and tapped a finger along his jaw. "Of course, even the most challenged augment is reluctant to give up the benefits. I don't believe I need to explain those to you."

"No." Augie had saved Jani's life too many times for her to give him up now. *Like most men, you're trouble, but I still think I'll keep you.* "Next option."

"Hmm." Pimentel's jaw-tapping slowed. "We'd be entering to experimental areas."

"Roger, my entire adult medical history has been an experimental area."

Pimentel gave a snort of laughter. "Quite." The tapping stopped. "I'd like to try to take you back."

"Take me back where?"

"To what you were before Shroud got his hands on you. I've been consulting with some researchers in our Gene Therapeutics lab. To say they're itching to get their hands on you doesn't do their enthusiasm justice." He smiled like he had a present for her hidden in his pocket. "I'd like to try to make you human again. One hundred percent."

Jani pulled her robe closer around her and looked past Pimentel to the sunlit scene outside his window. She longed to sit in the dry heat and let it bake her to the bone. *Always cold . . . always sick.* And what if she developed a bacterial infection and the bug did things to her that it wouldn't do to someone normal? Someone human?

I'm one of a kind. And a damned lonely one, at that.

Nema will be devastated. But then, he wasn't the one passing out on the bathroom floor, was he?

She wouldn't have even considered the option if Friesian hadn't told her about the deal. Odd feeling, having a future to worry about again.

What do you want to be when you grow up, Jani Moragh? To be left alone. And the best way to guarantee that was to be like everyone else. "I think I'd like to give it a try." She shoved her hands into her sleeves to try to warm them.

"It won't be pleasant."

"I'm used to that."

"I know." Pimentel tapped an entry into his workstation. "Like I said, I'd be turning you over to the Gene Therapeutics group. I wouldn't even think of treating you myself. I know my limitations, unlike some." He eyed her sharply. "I'd like to wait until you get this legal mess behind you. Piers feels it may be wrapped up in a week or two. I'll set up the first appointment for you for month's end."

"Fine." Jani tried to scoot out of the visitor's chair, a task made more difficult since she didn't want to remove her chilled hands from her sleeves. "Can I leave?"

"Hang around for another hour and make an appointment to come in tomorrow for a follow-up. Then you can go." Pimentel raised his hand. "There is one more very small thing. Sam Duong."

Jani sat back. "That man from the SIB. The archivist."

"Yes." Pimentel's shoulders sagged as his bright mood evaporated. "How well do you know him?"

"I don't, really. I'd never met him before two days ago."

"Never met him before." Pimentel picked up his recording board and entered a notation. "The reason I ask is, he has no relatives. Up until this morning, he had no friends, either. None he'd admit to, anyway." He massaged the back of his neck. Talking about Sam Duong seemed to tighten him up. "He authorized a change to his MedRec a few short hours ago. He named you as his next of kin."

"*What?*" Jani slumped in her chair—the ergoworks whined in their effort to keep up. "Did he say why?"

"I was hoping you could tell me."

"I was there when he fainted. His supervisors were pulling missing documents out of his desk and he was yelling that he hadn't put them there. . . ." *Oh.* "And I told him I believed him."

Pimentel knocked the back of his head against the headrest of his chair. "Jani, why did you tell him that?"

"Because I didn't like what was happening. His supervisors were taking him apart in front of his coworkers, which you do *not* do, I'm sorry, and he was in a state. I tried to calm him down." Pierce's face appeared in her mind again. Mako's right hand. "Thinking back, I don't consider it outside the realm of possibility that Sam Duong was framed."

"Framed?" Pimentel's massaging action moved to his forehead. "Jani, if you knew his medical condition, I think you'd change your mind."

"So tell me." Jani crossed her left leg over her right—the left felt stronger and she didn't need to hoist. "If I'm his official next of kin, I have the right to know."

Pimentel rapped his work station touchboard; the image of her brain splintered into oblivion. "Sam Duong first visited me about six months ago. It was at about that time that papers in his charge began disappearing, and his supervisor was concerned that perhaps Sam was having some problem he didn't want to talk to an on-site counselor about. Encephaloscan revealed the presence of a tumor in the paramedian posterior region of Sam's thalamus—"

"*Roger.*"

"—and you need to know where it is, because the location

defines the clinical symptoms. He suffers memory defects, amnesia. Immediate memory is especially affected."

Oh. "So if he did something this morning, he'd forget it by this afternoon." *Like putting papers in his desk.*

"Yes." Pimentel reached into the front pocket of his short-sleeve and removed a small packet. "He will also work to fill in those missing memories. In addition to distortions of fact and outright lies he has shown the tendency to adopt the lives of those in his archives as his own." He stood up and walked to his bookcase, atop which a watercooler rested. "Two months ago, he brought me a book. I don't recall the title, but the subject was geology. Not popular geology, either. This was a university-level textbook." He tore open the packet, dumped the contents into a glass, and added water. "He said he wrote it." Pimentel stirred the resulting pale yellow liquid with his finger, then tossed it back.

"Maybe he did."

Pimentel set down the empty glass. "The book had been written by a man named Simyam Baru."

Jani's mind blanked. She had to consciously make the effort to not cry out. To breathe. "Did—" She stopped, and tried again. "Did he say he was Simyam Baru?"

Pimentel shook his head. "Not outright. But he insisted he'd written the Baru book, as well as another written with a woman, a fellow professor—"

"Eva Yatni."

"Yes." Pimentel walked back to his desk and sat on the edge near Jani's chair. "To complicate matters even further, he consistently refuses treatment because he claims removal of the tumor will kill him. Then along you come, telling him you believe him when he says he didn't take your files. He probably figured you'd believe the rest of his story, too." He touched her shoulder. "You don't know how much it pains me to tell you this."

Jani stared past him out the window. "I visited Banda about fifteen years ago." She'd arrived during the summer. Just as hot as Chicago, but more humid. She'd spent the first three months of her visit indoors—she didn't possess the heat tolerance that she did now. "I wanted to know them. What they had done, how they had lived. I studied their work, what I could understand of it. Talked to their friends." The view blurred—she blinked it clear. "The tumor's in his thalamus?"

"Yes."

"I had been able to get hold of the Knevçet Shèrâa patient files, but I didn't understand most of what I read. I knew the Laum researchers were experimenting with altering perceptions. Sensation. And I remember Service Medical tested my thalamus repeatedly before they augmented me. So the thalamus is involved in those functions."

Pimentel nodded. "Very much so."

"Then the Laum would have implanted there."

"Oh, Jani . . . There is no reason for you to have to go through this. I can have someone from MedRec bring up a waiver of rights. You sign it, and your name will be removed—"

"No." She stood up slowly. Her left leg felt strong, but her right was still wobbly. "Not until I talk to him."

Pimentel held out his hands in exasperated plea. "He has an explanation for everything. He will tie you in knots."

"Then I'll bring an all-purpose knife." She shuffled to the door. "I'll explain to him why I can't act as his next of kin, then I'll come back and sign your waiver." She waved good-bye without turning around. "Promise."

Jani returned to her room to find Morley bustling in an unusually bubbly fashion. Lucien had stopped by to see his favorite captain, she said, and he had brought her some clothes, wasn't that nice of him?

"He's a peach." Jani waited for the nurse to leave, then picked through the small duffel Lucien had packed for her. *Wonder how he got in my room in the first place?* Had he broken through a panel? Jazzed the lock? Charmed the building manager into giving him the code?

She pulled her panties out of the bag. As she shook them out, a small piece of paper fluttered to the floor. Handwriting of calligraphic neatness, written by someone who placed a grid sheet beneath his notepaper to keep the lines straight.

Call me at I-Com Four West-7. L

"Signing our name with an initial now, are we?" Jani tucked Lucien's note into the pocket of her summerweight trousers. "Intelligence, Communications branch." Hell, if he'd wanted her room code, he probably just brute-forced it out of systems.

She finished dressing. Styled her hair. Put on makeup. Tried to avoid consciously thinking the thought that skirted the edges of her mind.

What if someone else got out? What if I'm not the only one anymore?

"No." She checked her badges, packed her gear. "I'll talk to him.

That's all. I'll explain to him why I can't do what he wants me to do." And if she slipped in a few questions about life on Banda, or the university, or the best place to buy kimchee, or the Great Boiled Shrimp Debate, well, that was fair. Her questions deserved answers, same as anyone else's. And she'd get them. Not wanting to know what she didn't know was a philosophy she wasn't familiar with.

CHAPTER 13

Jani walked into her TOQ suite, tossed her cap and duffel on the chair, and walked from room to room looking for signs of Lucien. He had replaced her old newssheets. Not with the *Tribune-Times* or the *Commonwealth Herald,* however, but with colonial sheets. Weeks-old issues of the *Ville Acadie Partisan* and the *Felix Majora Vox Nacional*, transmitted to Service Intelligence via Misty and printed out on fiche.

The *Vox* was littered with editorials demanding the shuttering of Fort Constanza, interspersed with the usual calls to secede. The *Partisan* reported the presence of the Acadian governor in Chicago to discuss matters related to "colonial rights." The article mentioned "an incident involving an Acadian colonial in Felix Majora that remains shrouded in mystery."

"Nothing mysterious about it. I was shanghaied." For the express purpose of being coddled and petted while the Judge Advocate tore apart the Service Code looking for an excuse to let her go. "After that, they're going to make me human again." Then what? A civilian consultancy? An extravagant flat in the city? The social whirl, capped off by her favorite lieutenant sunny-side up whenever his schedule allowed?

"Pull the other one—it sings 'Oh, Acadia.'" Jani tossed the newssheets aside and continued her inspection. She found fresh flowers in both the sitting room and bedroom. Val the Bear sat perched against the bedroom vase, a banner pinned to his chest.

"You're out of uniform," she told him as she detached the note. *I found the scalpel on your desk—don't even think about it.* This time, Lucien hadn't even bothered with an initial. Jani crumpled it and tossed it in the trashzap, following with the missive she'd found tucked in her underwear.

She had made another circuit of the bedroom before she spotted the thick, pale blue envelope lying on her bed. Another slip of white paper had been attached to the closure flap.

My, aren't we the colorful personality?

Jani shredded that note before consigning it to the flash-flame. Messages in underwear were cute, and knowing Lucien had been rummaging through her bedroom had its seductive aspects. "But there's a line, Mister, and you just crossed it."

She hefted her ServRec and adjourned to her sitting room, plucking Val the Bear from his floral roost on the way. "Simyam Baru escaped from his room," she told him. "I thought I'd locked him down well enough, but he wasn't as far gone as the other patients, and he figured out how to crack the Laumrau code locks." She sat on the couch and propped Val against a pillow in the opposite corner. "Only two other patients still lived at this point—he released them from their rooms. Orton was blind—they'd severed her optic nerves so they could input directly into her visual cortex. Fessig could still see. On him, they'd performed a tactile-aural synesthetic reroute." Jani looked into the bear's shiny eyes. "He felt everything he heard. Whispering and instrument hum felt like ants crawling over him. Normal speaking voices felt like slaps and punches, depending on their pitch."

The three of them jumped Felicio and Stanleigh, who had run down to the garage to secure the exits as soon as they realized patients had escaped. "They had to secure the exits manually because we couldn't control ingress and egress from central systems. You see, the bombing started right after the Laumrau hospital staff cleared the building and fled to their sect-sharers in the hills."

Shatterboxes first, to disable systems and blow infrastructure. "That was when Yolan died, when one of the operating theater walls collapsed on her."

Then came pink, the brilliantly hued microbial mist that took up where the explosives left off. "We tried to wash it out of the air with water—within the first half minute after release, it's still concentrated enough that you can do that—but the shatterboxes had damaged the pumping system, and we couldn't maintain pressure in the hoses. The pink diffused and got into everything."

Instrument cards liquefied. Boards turned to jelly.

"So we couldn't control the doors—we had to shut them manually. That was the first mistake I made—I should have guessed the Laumrau would try to pink us. I should have locked down the doors and vents as soon as they'd fled."

Val regarded her patiently.

"I know. I'm digressing." Jani prodded him with her toe. "So Fel and Stan ran to the garage to check the doors, and Baru, Orton, and Fessig jumped them and stole the control card for the people-mover." But the vehicle had been damaged by the shatterboxes. "I think the pink got to it, too. I watched it from the roof—it barely made it over the first rise."

Then she saw the Laumrau pursuit craft, a sleek, bullet-shaped demiskimmer with bank-and-dive capability. "It flitted over the rise after the 'mover." She picked up one of the throw pillows and hugged it to her chest. "I heard the explosion. Saw it. A blown battery array emits a very distinctive green-white flash. John confirmed it later." Granted, over two months passed before he could examine the site, but he'd had a lot of experience in crash investigation by then, and he knew what to look for. "He said from the condition of the wreckage and the human remains he found, no one could have survived."

Val the Bear cocked an eyebrow. Well, not really, but it was easy to imagine.

Jani nodded. "Yes, I know. You could have said the same thing about what happened to me." She cracked open the envelope and removed her file, shaking and riffling both in case any more *communiqués petits* awaited discovery. Then she lay back, rested her head against the bolster, and paged through her Service record. Most of the material that covered her time under Neumann was still missing, but what remained still told quite a story.

The excerpts she read could be considered hilarious or depressing, depending on the judgment of the reader. She could understand Lucien's dismay. The role she played in the midnight requisition from Central Supply of several sorely needed parchment imprinters and systems cards had earned her the undying enmity of the Rauta Shèràa Base Supply officer, the threat of a court-martial, and a personal invitation from Colonel Matilda Fitzhugh to eat a shooter.

"No mention is made, of course, that the reason they kept Documents and Documentation undersupplied was because they'd been shunting equipment into the J-Loop black market for a year and a half." Jani glanced over the top of the report at Val the Bear. "Instead they dropped the charge against me because of 'insufficient evidence' and spread the rumor that Evan used the Family *du piston* to get me off the hook. Forget the fact we hadn't spoken in six months." She straightened the pages and moved on to the next episode.

"Oh yes. My first run-in with good old Rikart." Jani could visualize Neumann in his dress blue-greys, the narrower black belt of the older-style uniform squeezing his thick middle like a tourniquet. Broad-beamed. Wide, jovial face cut with a narrow mustache. Father Christmas in middle age. "A personal buddy of Phil Unser, which told one everything one needed to know right there. He started out second-in-command of Base Operations. When he tried to kneecap Documents and Documentation by incorporating us into Ops, I wrote a report." She leafed through the fiched copy, forty-eight pages of carefully delineated argument as to why a nonindependent documents section would be detrimental to the Service as a whole and Rauta Shèràa Base in particular. Her "fictional examples" had contained everything but the names and dates.

"There were twenty-three transfers after I submitted it for General Review." Her commanding officer had reamed her for not clearing the report with him before submission, and yet another notation of "insubordination" was added to her record. "I couldn't figure out why they didn't just boot me out."

The answer came in a message, which she had found tucked in the outer pocket of her scanpack pouch during an idomeni-Service conclave a few weeks later. The pouch hadn't left her belt—she'd never been able to figure out who passed the message to her and when.

Think if this had been a knife, the first line had read. It got better after that, but not much.

> *Nice report, Kilian. You think like a crook, but you need seasoning. When you get sick of protecting the litter-runts of the Commonwealth, I'll be waiting. Rikart.*

"And do you believe he signed that note?" A few weeks later, he had her seconded to the Twelfth Rovers to help her make up her mind.

Jani reassembled her file and tucked it back into the envelope. Val the Bear had toppled over and lay flat on his face. *I know the feeling.* She sat back, cradled her head in the crook of her arm, and let her gaze drift. "Piers didn't answer my question about how Ebben, Unser, and Fitzhugh died. I'd bet 'on purpose' myself." Her eyelids felt heavy. Her stomach growled.

She stared at her comport message light for a full minute before she realized it blinked. "Lucien, go away." She struggled to her feet and shuffled to her desk. "I'm mad at you." She hit the playpad so she wouldn't have to look at the flickering light anymore—she meant to delete the message immediately, but the face flashed before her fatigue-blunted reflexes could kick in.

Lieutenant Ischi's pensive aspect filled the display. "Captain? Ma'am, I know you're not feeling well. But if there's any way at all you can manage to stop by the office today, it would be greatly appreciated."

Jani checked the time-date stamp on the message. *Only an hour ago.* Odds were good the bodies hadn't cooled yet, although Ischi's expression aside, she had no reason to assume Hals and Vespucci had gotten into another fight about her. *And if you pull this one again, it sings "The Hymn of the Commonwealth."*

"All eight bloody verses." She recovered her garrison cap from its resting place and tottered out the door.

Jani entered the Foreign Transactions desk pool to find Ischi and several techs clustered by the coffee brewer. Ischi stood fists on hips and head thrust forward—the traditional lecture posture of a frustrated tech wrangler trying to cut the stampede off at the pass.

"Colonel Hals is a helluva lot more aware than you are of the problems we're facing, Mister!" he barked, his nose a finger's breadth away from that of a pasty-faced SFC. "And the sooner you stop bleating your unique blend of garbled fact and outright fiction, the better off we will *all* be!" He was about to launch into round two when another tech's eyes rounded, and he turned to follow her stare.

"Captain Kilian, ma'am!" His turnabout-and-present was so quick, the object of his ire barely ducked an elbow in the nose. "The colonel will see you shortly. Please follow me."

Jani fell in behind Ischi in the best Officer's Guide manner, waiting to draw alongside until they had passed into the anteroom. "Having a bad day, Corporal Coffee Cup?" That got a smile out of him. "Ah, the joys of personnel."

"Doylen's an idiot. He listens at doors, catches half the words, and rearranges them in the worst order possible." Ischi stopped at his desk and paged through the assorted stacks. "The problem is, it's hit the fan, everyone knows it, and they're diving for cover."

"So what's the latest?"

"Hals is being relieved and FT split up. Some of us will be shipped to colonial postings and the rest shoved back in the main pool."

"*What?* What brought that on?"

"A complaint by Hantìa. She claimed Colonel Hals is incompetent and that her mistakes have hampered negotiations." Ischi kept his eyes fixed on his paper rearranging. "All the errors are Hantìa's fault. She held back vital data, waiting for the colonel to ask for it. But she wasn't allowed."

Sounds like the Hantìa I knew and hated. Jani jerked her head toward Hals's door. "Who's in there now?"

"The colonel, Major Vespucci, and Colonel Derringer from Diplo." Ischi exhaled with a rumble. "Come over to *explain* the situation."

"Right." Jani circled around the distracted lieutenant and punched Hals's doorpad. She ducked into the office and forced the panel closed on Ischi's wailing "Ma'am, not yet—"

Hals sat at her desk, face drawn. Vespucci sat across from her, the look he directed at Jani suffused with outrage.

Derringer sat on the short side of the desk between the two, his mainline stripe drawing the eye like a warning flare. He stiffened when he saw Jani—the leg that had been crossed ankle over knee slowly lowered until foot hit floor. His was the rangy build and sun-battered face that came from a bin labeled "middle-aged officer-standard issue." He looked like he knew the answers. Jani would have bet her 'pack he didn't understand half the questions.

"Ma'am." She snapped to attention as well as her weakened right leg would allow. "Captain Kilian reporting as ordered."

Vespucci's voice emerged level and hard. "You don't have an appointment scheduled, Cap—" He had twisted so his back faced Hals, but they must have worked together for so long, they'd developed psychic communication. Hals's stare bored through the back of his head—he turned to face her slowly, as though in a trance, and fell silent.

"Captain, it's obvious some mistake has been made," Derringer said sharply. "Please leave us."

Jani clasped her hands behind her back. Lifted her chin. Dug her heels into the carpet. Just like old times—ready, steady, into the deep end. "I know what this meeting is about, sir. I find it alarming that Diplo has taken it upon themselves to decide a course of action without consulting the one officer in Foreign Transactions who is a known authority on idomeni affairs."

Derringer stared past Jani at the door, as though waiting for Ischi to make an appearance. "And who would that be, Captain?"

"That would be me, sir."

His gaze shifted to her. Even Vespucci's had held more warmth. "Captain, I realize sideline conducts itself more loosely than mainline, and I also realize documents examiners as a whole pride themselves on their unmilitary behavior. But you are out of line here, and I am ordering you to leave this room."

"Captain Kilian is *my* direct report, Colonel, and we are in my physical jurisdiction." Hals's soft Indiesian accent contrasted sharply with Derringer's twangy Michigan provincial. "If we are indeed so concerned about proper military behavior, I believe those two points give me the deciding vote as to whether she stays or leaves." The look she directed at Jani said, OK expert, this better work." "Carry on, Captain."

Jani heard voices outside. She reached behind her and pressed down on the doorpad—the doormech scraped as Ischi tried to open it from the other side.

"Sir." The scuffling outside the door grew louder, and she leaned harder on the pad. "It is my informed opinion, as a Service officer experienced in dealing with the idomeni, that removing Colonel Hals from any further contact with this matter is not a sound decision. It will prove detrimental not only to immediate Service dealings with the idomeni, but to future Service and Commonwealth dealings with them as well."

Derringer looked from Hals to Vespucci, then back at Jani. He hadn't expected this. He had no fallback position, no support, and no idea what to do next. "It has not been officially determined that you outstrip everyone in the Diplomatic Corps with respect to idomeni experience, Captain."

"Fair enough, sir—in that case, I have two questions for you. One, how many years did the senior Service negotiator attached to this matter live on Shèrá and two, how many idomeni languages do they speak and is High Vynshàrau one of them?"

"That's three questions." Hals's expression was bland, but tiny embers of rebellion glowed in her eyes.

"My mistake, ma'am," Jani replied with equal flatness. "I do apologize." She looked at Derringer. "Sir?"

Derringer shifted in his chair. He wanted to refuse to answer, but three pairs of sideline eyes let him know that wasn't an option. "General Burkett spent one year at Language School and a six-month stint at our embassy in Rauta Shèràa."

"Is he a colonial? Some colonials have had a great deal of day-to-day experience dealing with the Haárin."

"No, he is Earthbound by birth. However, he did do a ten-year stint in the J-Loop, where large populations of Haárin do reside. He tells stories." The corner of Derringer's mouth twitched as the gauntlet hit the floor.

Jani nodded. "I began my course of study in documents examination at the Rauta Shèràa Academy at the age of seventeen. Four and a half years to degree, with my final year spent under direct tutelage of the being who currently serves as idomeni ambassador. After that, two and a half years at Rauta Shèràa Base, the majority of that time spent as a Food Services Liaison and an Import-Export Registrar. After that, eighteen years—"

Derringer held up his hands. "Captain, no one is denying your expertise—"

"Only my loyalty?" She stared at him until he looked away. "I am fully aware of the low opinion any member of the traditional Service would hold of me. But your opinion of me is not the primary consideration here. The primary consideration here is the continued lack of regard being shown the documents examiners assigned to this matter and the confusion this engenders in the idomeni, who consider examiners as qualified to negotiate and determine policy as any diplomat."

Derringer sucked his teeth. "Captain, we have discussed this with the ambassador at length, and while he questions our reasoning at times, he has shown himself willing to see the human side of things."

"Sir, FT isn't dealing directly with the ambassador, who is an exception to almost every rule regarding traditional Vynshàrau behavior. FT is dealing with the documents examiners, who have been reared from birth to operate in the diplomatic sphere." *Except for Hantìa, but I'll worry about that inconsistency later.*

Derringer glanced at his timepiece. "Captain Kilian, negotiations for the Lake Michigan Strip have grown more and more heated over the past several days. The Prime Minister and members of her Cabinet are currently attending at the embassy, and we have been called in as well. There is no time to waste." He stood. "The decision on how to proceed has been made."

Jani leaned against the doorpad. The voices and scrabblings had stopped long ago. All she could hear was the voice in her head that whispered *gotcha.* "NìaRauta Hantìa issued the complaint against Colonel Hals and the Vynshàrau demanded FT presence *all* this afternoon?"

Derringer hesitated. He'd grown sick of answering her questions—that was obvious—but he knew alarm when he heard it. "Yes."

Hantìa, you witch, you set me up. "Sir, they know I'm here. They want me to attend. They've issued the sort of challenge they know will flush me out." *They know me.*

Vespucci screwed up the nerve to open his mouth again. "Aren't you taking a lot on yourself, Captain? You'd think the outcome of these negotiations hinged on you."

Jani worked her neck. Her back hurt. Pimentel would strangle her if he knew where she was and what she did. *I wish I had never checked that comport light.* "Sir, I'm sure I sound arrogant, but I know them. They've always acknowledged the actions I took at Knevçet Shèràa. This is their way of formally recognizing me. Everyone here wishes I'd dry up and blow away, but ignoring the unpleasant in the hope it will disappear is not their way. I'm anathema to them, but I'm the devil they've always known. In a culture that values open disputation and the concept of the esteemed enemy, the thought that you could be hiding me is as repugnant to them as a food hoarder during time of famine is to us. They want to see me. Let's get it over with."

CHAPTER 14

Brigadier General Callum Burkett proved the taller, greyer edition of Colonel Derringer. And more frazzled. Seeing Derringer arrive at the embarkation zone with Hals and Jani in tow did nothing to calm him down.

"*Goddamn it!*" He slid into his seat in the rear of the Diplomatic steel blue triple-length and glared across the compartment at the three of them before settling on Derringer. "Intelligence is stepping on our necks for even talking to the idomeni about the Strip, the PM is mixing up Family politics and defense policy *again*, and now you take it upon yourself to jettison the only firm decision we've been able to make in three months!"

"Who drove the decision?" Jani looked from Derringer to Burkett. "It was a bad decision. Who drove it? Ulanova?" She flinched as the skimmer passed beneath the Shenandoah Gate. It wasn't political opinion, but a shocklike tingle that radiated up her right arm. "It's in her interest to destabilize colony-idomeni relations. One way to do that is to blow systems here, and let the backflash take out a few of the Haárin-colony arrangements that have formed over the years." She flexed her arm, then rested it in her lap instead of on the armrest.

"The origin of the decision isn't your concern, Captain." Burkett didn't bother to look at her, or even turn her way.

"Captain Kilian raised some valid points, sir." Derringer sat with the tense nerviness of a man who wanted with all his heart to punch out the canopy and go out over the shooters but had been ordered to go down with the demi instead. "Major Hanratty's been pushing for months to allow dexxies into the negotiations."

"Hanratty's a *xenolinguist*, Colonel." Burkett's sarcastic tone bit almost as much as the pain in Jani's arm. "Are you suggesting we let someone who watches sceneshots of conversations for a living decide Commonwealth defense policy?"

"Can't do any worse than you're doing now." Jani's right arm throbbed now—she tried massaging it and barely suppressed a cry. "Hantìa and her skein-sharers are attempting to treat Colonel Hals and her skein-sharers as equals. She assumes Colonel Hals is playing coy, and she wants to shake her up by challenging us all. She doesn't expect you to drop the colonel like a hot rock; she expects you to stand behind her. If you show her that isn't the case, you've only reinforced the Vynshàrau opinion that humanish are disordered and unseemly, and you've done it by insulting a documents examiner, which just triples the injury. Is battling for a strip of airspace so important that you're willing to risk an irreparable fracture between the Commonwealth and the Shèrá worldskein?"

"You're suggesting we allow an alien race with whom relations are tenuous at best the unfettered ability to scan any flyover that cuts through that slice of sky?" Burkett's voice twinned Evan's—level, deep, and sharp. Reason enough to dislike him. "It's—"

"A primary corridor into and out of O'Hare, yes, I know." Jani struggled to keep from yelling, to keep from responding to Burkett's voice. "Are you naïve enough to believe they aren't already doing just that?"

Derringer shot her a "please shut up" glare. "Publicly admitting the fact could set a nasty precedent."

"With whom? The colonies? Are we so independent that you need to worry about negotiating treaties with us?" She tried to work her fingers, and her thumb cramped. *Augie, cut me some slack.* "You want some advice from someone who's negotiated with the idomeni for years? Give them the Strip. Show them that you acknowledge that Exterior Minister Ulanova's actions were insulting and that you want to repair the damage." Their skimmer floated down a wooded lane—the trees met over the top to form a leafed canopy. *I'm sure this is lovely.* She wished she could appreciate it.

Burkett glowered across the compartment at Derringer, who tried to sink into his seat. They'd reached the first low-rise complexes that marked the northern outskirts of Chicago. The driver exited the thoroughfare and ramped onto the Boul artery. It wouldn't be long now.

Hals tapped her window softly with one knuckle. "Maybe we can talk to the ambassador about Hantìa, and he can order her to back down. The consensus, as I understand it, is that if we can convince him of something, he'll drive the point home to the Oligarch."

"No, ma'am—we definitely do not want to do that." Jani tried to filter the impatience out of her voice. Trying to find the words to explain the obvious aggravated her anyway, and her aching arm didn't help. "You have been challenged, and you must meet that challenge openly."

"But the ambassador understands us."

"Nema *is* different than the rest of his sect-sharers, ma'am, yes. He likes us. He finds us fascinating." *He has plans for us, too, but if Gene Therapeutics has its way, that won't be my problem anymore.* "He understands our concerns to some extent, but only on an abstract level. Just because he looks you in the face when he talks to you doesn't make him an honorary humanish. He's not your addled Uncle Arthur, he's the chief priest of his sect. I've watched him accept and offer *à lérine.* I've watched him fight and I've seen him bleed."

"I've seen the scars on his forearms. They look like he's wearing lace sleeves under his robe." Derringer winced. "But *à lérine* are only ceremonial fights. Acknowledgments of your enemies. They're not real battles—no one dies."

"Not usually." Jani rested her head against the seat back. The pain had stabilized to a steady pulsation. "Nema fought many of those battles for the right to come here as ambassador. His religious skein-sharers followed him here because he's their dominant and his way is their way. Same for the diplomatic seculars who owe primary allegiance to Morden nìRau Cèel, the Oligarch. They came here because it was their leader's wish. But we're the disordered humanish who do not know our food, and they believe that in living with us, they've sacrificed their souls. Your refusal to concede them the strip tells them you do not consider that sacrifice important. Give them the Strip. They will give it back. That's not what they want—what they want is an acknowledgment of what they've lost." Even though she answered Derringer, she looked at Burkett. "You're thinking like a humanish soldier, and in doing so, you're making a mistake."

Their skimmer ramped off the Boul and down a two-lane access road lined by thick hybrid shrubbery that served the dual purpose of absorbing sound and obscuring idomeni property from prying humanish eyes. As they wended down the road, they passed the first of the manned checkpoints. A tall, ropy Vynshàrau stood in the guardhouse, a long-range shooter hanging by a cross-strap across her back.

"Is that the sort of being you want to allow access to our nav paths, Captain?" Burkett snorted softly. "It's obvious you aren't much of a soldier."

Jani looked him in the eye. He lifted one brow in surprise—he must have thought he'd insulted her. "No, sir, I am not. I will be the first to admit it and the last to deny it."

"You have no business participating in this matter."

"They just need to see me, sir." *After that, I can go back to being your private shame.*

After the gate guards checked the skimmer through, it pulled inside the embassy courtyard, an austere, sunstone-tiled space lined with shoulder-high silverleaf shrubs. The small triangles of sunstone, colored in shades of creamy gold, had been laid in whorled patterns. The courtyard surface looked as though huge fingers had pressed down from above, leaving their prints behind.

As junior officer in the happy convoy, Jani disembarked first. Her arm still ached, and her stomach had joined the chorus, yet she took the opportunity to stroll around. The late-afternoon sun warmed her; the glare of its reflection off the light-colored stone hurt her eyes.

This brings back memories. The bare façade of the embassy was featureless but for a set of banded bronze doors. The poured scancrete fence that barred their view of the sweeping grounds and the city beyond was three meters high and topped with crosshatches of ornamental blades.

At least, they're supposed to be ornamental. Jani wouldn't have wanted to be the one to determine whether the edges had actually been dulled. Idomeni steel cut deep, and the hair-thin wireweave that ran down both sides of the edge ripped flesh and left nasty scars.

A few minutes later, the people-movers bearing the rest of Foreign Transactions and Diplo lumbered into the courtyard. Disembarkation began immediately, but it still took time. Jani had plenty of opportunity to bask in Major Vespucci's scowling regard as he watched her through the FT mover's rear window.

As soon as the vehicles had emptied, the embassy doors swung open and a brown-robed Vynshàrau diplomatic suborn beckoned to them. The Service personnel lined up single file, lowest-ranking first, with the civilian techs inserting themselves at predetermined points according to their number of years in the department. Jani looked at Hals, who stood off to one side. The woman walked over to her, her face grooved with tension.

"Burkett told me I'm to remain out here." Her eyes glistened with barely contained tears. "Sit in the FT mover and wait for you." She blinked rapidly, then turned away.

"And your response is what, ma'am?" Jani edged away from the gathering of closed mouths and open ears. "I will back you to the wall, for what it's worth."

Hals looked across the courtyard, where Burkett stood in huddled conversation with Derringer and another mainline officer. They'd changed their trousers in the interim, switching out their crimson stripes for slashes of dark green. Nema would be the only being in the embassy allowed to wear red in his clothing. The idomeni considered it a holy color.

"He'll change his pants for them, but not his mind." Hals shook her head. "If I buck him on this, he'll level me."

Jani dragged her toe along a whorl of stone. "One Service dictum I remember—and I don't remember many—states that if you value your career more than you value your job, you're the wrong person for both. Now if you stay out here like a good little sideliner, you'll still have a career. You may pass some of it in a shelter waiting for the idomeni shatterboxes to stop falling, but you'll still have your scanpack if the pink doesn't eat it and you'll have a pension if we've reestablished a viable monetary system by the time you retire. Assuming you're still alive."

A flare of temper erased some of the strain from Hals's face. "Kilian, has anybody ever told you you're a judgmental pain in the ass?"

"Good, ma'am, I hope that made you feel better." Jani reclaimed her place in line, one step ahead of the stone-faced Vespucci. "Doesn't do a damned thing to answer the essential question, but one should take every opportunity to vent one's frustrations, I've always believed."

Hals adjusted the set of her garrison cap. "You honestly feel my not participating in these negotiations could alter the tone of idomeni-human relations for the worse?"

"Yes, I do."

"I will have to deal with the consequences of this much longer than you will."

"It will affect your *career*, yes. It may even end it. But I can give you the names of four people who would be more than happy to take on a dexxie who knows how to do her job."

Hals hesitated. "Senna, Tsai—"

"Aryton and Nawar. Yes, ma'am."

A small grin brightened Hals's features. "Not you?"

Jani shook her head. "You don't want to work for me—I'm a judgmental pain in the ass."

The grin flashed. Then Hals reset her cap once again and slipped into line behind a stricken Vespucci.

"She could be court-martialed for this," he rasped in Jani's ear.

"Thanks for the support, Major," Jani tossed over her shoulder as the line started to move.

The first thing that struck her was the heat, followed by the stark, ascetic look of the unadorned hallways and rugless, tiled floors. The Vynshàrau favored the colors of the desert in their interior decoration—cream, white, and tan predominated. But in deference to their allied sects, they allowed some splashes of variety, such as the leaf green and sky-blue curlicues inset in all the lake-facing windows. *Pathen,* Jani recalled. The silver-and-copper wireweave chandeliers, however, that resembled the blades lining the top of the fence, were of Sìah design, since the Sìah were renowned for their metalwork.

So stark, yet so beautiful. Jani struggled to remain in formation as exhilaration washed over her. She felt drunk. Ecstatic. She wanted to skip down the hallway and pound on all the doors. *That would go over big.*

"Colonel!"

Jani heard Hals groan. She turned in time to see Burkett storm up the hall.

"You will return to Sheridan immediately." He drew alongside Hals and beckoned for her to accompany him.

Jani sidestepped out of line to stand beside Burkett. "You're making a mistake, sir."

He turned on her, his voice deadening. "You are expected to defer to the trained diplomats on this team, Captain. After you make your token appearance, you're out of here right behind her."

Jani nodded. "Yes, sir. I'll go," she said in a voice loud enough to echo down the cavernous hall. She pointed to Hals. "She. Stays."

The faint buzz of humanish and Vynshàrau voices reached them as Cabinet and Council officials filled the open doorways. Burkett's sweat-slicked face showed his extreme displeasure at putting on a show. "This discussion is finished, Captain. You have your orders." He gestured to one of his staffers, who had drifted uneasily into the hallway. The woman immediately beckoned to a larger, less timorous-looking Service Security officer, who started toward them.

"Glories of the day to you, my dear-rest friends!"

The familiar singsong stopped the Security officer in his tracks. Hals gasped. Burkett closed his eyes. The other members of FT and Diplo buzzed and whispered.

Jani smiled.

Nema stalked toward them, his off-white overrobe billowing

behind him like a churning wake. "Such argument. I left Cabinet Ministers in order to hear more." In person, his skin appeared darker than Jani remembered from the winter, gold-brown rather than ocher, the result of frequent trips to the Death Valley enclave.

Burkett stood at attention. "NìRau, permit me to apologize—"

"For what, General? Open disputation is most seemly. Most as idomeni. Otherwise, humanish are so as walls, we do not think you alive." Nema looked each of them in the face, a born-sect taboo he seemed determined to topple single-handed. His eyes widened as he bared his teeth, resulting in a startling, and to some, unpleasant expression.

They don't see what I see. To Jani, Nema's rictus sardonicus was the welcoming grin of an old friend. An *aggravating* old friend. Presumptuous. But nevertheless . . .

Nema stepped between Jani and the rattled general and gripped her chin between his thumb and forefinger. "You have brought me my Eyes and Ears." He tilted her face back and forth. "*a lète onae vèste, Kièrshiarauta,*" he said to her, voice pitched higher than normal as a show of regard. *Glories of the day to you, toxin.*

"*a lète ona vèste, Nemarau.*" Jani pitched her voice high as well, and added a greeting gesture, crossing her left arm over her chest, palm twisted outward. She tried to tilt her head to the left and offer the traditional single nod, but Nema's firm grip prevented her. "NìRau, I can't move my head."

"Apologies, nìa." His hand dropped away, and he stepped back. "So, you have come to assist me with this stupid food business. Such ignorance. You are most well?" His voice held a touch of skepticism, but he restrained the gestures that would have clarified his feeling. Whatever Lucien had been telling him, he either didn't believe, or didn't like it.

"NìRau Tsecha." Burkett's eyes held that wild look most humans acquired after they'd been around Nema for more than five seconds. "We didn't expect to see you this afternoon."

"I know that, General." The glint in Nema's amber-on-amber eyes indicating that dashing the expectations of humanish Burketts was all part of the fun. "But when I heard my Eyes and Ears was to be here—" His gaze fell on Hals, and he bared his teeth again. "Ah, Colonel Hals, you have met challenge! Onì nìaRauta Hantìa will be most pleased—she thought you dead." He took her by the arm and towed her down the hall and into the documents examiners' meeting room.

Burkett bent close enough to make Jani flinch. "This does not end here, Captain." He turned and whispered something to the Security officer before disappearing into the Diplomatic meeting room.

Jani followed the still-stunned stragglers down the hall to the examiners' room, realizing after a few steps that the Security officer shadowed her. She probed her arm again. The ache had intensified in the last few minutes—the muscles in her lower arm had started to twitch. *What the hell is this?* Delayed reaction to Pimentel's prodding and poking?

"My, my, my."

Jani turned. Exterior Minister Anais Ulanova stood in the nearest doorway, regarding her with the cool arrogance Jani recalled from her first visit to Chicago. In deference to idomeni religious sensibility, she wore a wrapshirt and trousers in dark brown rather than the usual Exterior burgundy. A younger woman stood next to her. Ivory skin and hair. Pale blue eyes glittery with nerves. She wore black and grey, the official Interior colors. McEnnis, Jani recalled from news reports. Evan's interim replacement.

"Captain Kilian." Ulanova nodded. "Although I recall you went by the name 'Risa Tyi' when you visited us last." She leaned toward McEnnis and whispered something in her ear. The woman's eyes widened.

Jani smiled at McEnnis, who took a step backward. "I can imagine what she's told you about me. Some of it might even be true. I hope for your sake you can figure out which is which—you need that skill dealing with her." She waved farewell and started down the hall. "I'll give Lucien your regards, ma'am, the next time we come up for air." The look of outrage that Jani saw on Ulanova's face just before she slipped into the examiners' room was worth the little fib.

The windowless meeting room proved hotter than the hallway by several crucial degrees. Judging from the mutterings Jani heard, summerweights felt itchy and clingy; dress blue-greys would have been downright dangerous.

She only felt mildly warm herself, but if another twelve-hour marathon stretched before them, who knew how she'd hold up? *But that's a big if.* She glanced behind her and saw the Security officer standing in the doorway, watching her. A lieutenant, his mainline red bars switched out for religiously insignificant dark green. Unarmed, since he technically stood on idomeni soil, but far from helpless, judging from his muscular arms and chest.

If I tried to bolt, he'd just pick me up and toss me over his shoulder. Or break her in half, depending on how much of a fuss she made. She approached him slowly, arms at her sides, hands open and visible. "Lieutenant."

He nodded. "Ma'am."

"May I ask why you're following me?"

"After you meet with nìaRauta Hantìa, I'm to escort you back to Sheridan, ma'am."

"Odds are I'll be needed here."

"General Burkett's orders, ma'am."

Right. Jani walked to the central U-shaped table, where Nema stood surrounded by the members of Foreign Transactions. Most faces held shock or surprise. Ischi's shoulders shook. Hals had covered her mouth with her hand. Even Vespucci grinned.

"And only the player standing in the net can use hands?" Nema toed weakly at the floor. "All the others have to *kick*?"

"Like this, nìRau." Ischi mimed a short, hard pass to Vespucci, who in turn pretended to block the nonexistent soccer ball into the floor with his formidable stomach.

"Really? Such I do not understand." Nema looked at Jani, his posture crooked with dismay. "Why did you never tell me of this, nìa!" He clasped Ischi by the arm and pulled him to one side, gesturing for Vespucci to follow. The sounds of crumpling parchment soon emerged from the huddle. The two men then broke away and kicked a paper ball back and forth as Nema stood on the side and scrutinized every move.

Jani watched the exhibition until she grew conscious of a stare boring through the side of her face. "Colonel."

Hals sauntered to her side. "Captain." She peeked around Jani and nodded toward the strapping lieutenant. "Is he here for you, me, or us?"

"Me. As soon as Hantìa and I meet, Burkett wants me out."

"Then we must meet now," entoned a voice from behind. Feminine, but grating, like nails down a slate. "So that I can laugh as you leave."

Jani turned slowly. She kept her eyes straight ahead, so she would look the idomeni in the upper chest, not the face. Tan robes. The lower curves of shoulder-grazing gold oval earrings. Light brown hair twisted into short helices and wrapped with silver cord. Same regal posture she remembered from Academy. Same damned voice. "Hantìa."

"Kièrshia." The Vynshàrau stepped back and studied her. Side-to-side examination, followed by top to toe, looking everywhere but in her eyes. "You are not what you were." She tilted her head slightly to Jani's right, a posture of moderate respect acknowledging their shared past.

Jani tilted her head to the left, mimicking Hantìa's regard, as she allowed herself oblique glances at the jutting cheekbones and squarish jaw. "Only physically." She lapsed readily into High Vynshàrau; it seemed more appropriate, somehow. "In my soul, I am as ever."

"You left your soul at Knevçet Shèràa. So you are as nothing. That, I always knew."

Jani twitched the fingers of her left hand, a gesture of disregard. She heard no other voices, and knew all eyes were on the two of them. "You are not an archivist, as was planned."

"No." A bow of head as right hand reached up and gripped left shoulder. A posture of sadness. "NìRau ti nìRau Cèel had need of me here." The hand dropped. Hantìa straightened. "A great need, and truly." She turned to Hals, and switched back to English. "Colonel."

Hals nodded stiffly. "Hantìa."

"We must work now. Soon, there will be too many damned papers to count." Hantìa stalked toward the other Vynshàrau examiners, who had gathered on the opposite side of the room.

Hals cocked her head. "Did she just say what I thought she said?"

"She's been taking English lessons from Nema." Jani smiled, but her good humor faded as she watched the lieutenant cross the room toward her.

"Ma'am." He stopped in front of her and gestured in the direction of the door. "This way, please."

Jani looked at Hals, who watched her warily. *I could stand my ground, and fight to stay.* Nema would rush to her aid—he'd probably even offer her asylum. *Wouldn't that do wonders for diplomatic relations?* Ulanova might even persuade Cao to send in armed troops to take her back. Not that they'd succeed, but the invasion itself would constitute a declaration of war.

What do I care—I'd be free.

But at what cost? She looked at Ischi, who bounced the paper ball from knee to knee. At the other members of FT, who grinned and watched. She didn't even know their names.

Better I don't—the list is long enough. No more, if she could help it. No more.

"All right, Lieutenant." She took one last look at the unadorned, sand-colored space, then fell in behind.

"*Nìa?*" Nema broke away from Ischi and Vespucci and beelined toward them. "Where are you going?"

"Back to the base, nìRau. General Burkett's orders."

"*Orders?*" The pitch of his voice lowered so he sounded hoarse. His shoulders rounded. "Is it not true that to stand here is to stand in Rauta Shèràa? Is it not true that in this room, my word is as orders?"

The lieutenant's eyes widened as the tall, *angry* ambassador closed in. "Sir."

"So do I order you to leave this room, Lieutenant."

"Sir—nìRau—General Burkett—"

Jani stepped between the lieutenant and the oncoming Nema. "NìRau! Please!"

"Go to your paper, nìa! Obey me!" Nema's guttural voice sounded a distinctly idomeni warning. He waited for Jani to back away before closing in on the hapless Security guard. "I will speak of this to General Burkett, who gives orders within my walls!" He grabbed the young man by the arm. The lieutenant tried to pull away—his eyes widened when he realized he couldn't break the Vynshàrau's grip.

"So." Nema pushed him out the door and directly in the path of a young diplomatic suborn, who sidestepped neatly.

"NìRau ti nìRau? You are needed." She spoke English with a heavy Vynshàrau accent, swallowed *t*'s and back-of-the-throat *r*'s.

"Not now, nìaRauta Vìa."

"*Now*, nìRau ti nìRau." Vìa rounded her shoulders in a posture of aggravation. Not as hunched as Nema, but the twist and twirl of her right hand indicated that it was only a matter of time. "Exterior Minister Ulanova and Suborn Oligarch nìRau Lish are discussing taxation of Elyan Haárin settlements."

"*Discussing*, nìa?"

Vìa hesitated, then raised her right hand, palm facing up, in silent plea.

Nema's voice dropped to a John Shroud-like resonance. "My Anais makes trouble, as always. I would challenge her myself, but she is too short to fight." He looked at Jani, and his posture saddened. "I see my nìa Kièrshia for so short a time, and now I must leave!" He walked back to Ischi and took the wad of paper from his hand. "I must play goalie." He tossed the parchment ball from hand to hand as he strode out of the room.

Jani turned back to the table, which held surveys and maps and other documents applicable to the Strip negotiations. She couldn't recall the last time she'd seen Nema that angry. *And all because of me.* "How much longer do you think I have to live, ma'am?"

Hals sighed. "At least until you get back to Sheridan." She unholstered her scanpack. "Burkett wouldn't want civilians to find the body."

The verification session lasted six hours, not including the forty-five-minute interruption for the Vynshàrau's late-evening sacramental meal. By the time they adjourned, Jani's stomach ached from hunger and her right arm had numbed and stiffened from pain. The meeting room smelled like old socks. She hadn't broken a sweat to speak of, but everyone else in FT looked like they'd been caught in a shower. The only consolation was that she felt so exhausted, Burkett's welcoming scowl as he met her in the hallway didn't make her feel worse.

"If you think the ambassador's influence is going to get you off the hook, Kilian, you're sadly mistaken." He hustled her and Hals past the rest of FT and Diplo, through the entry and out into the courtyard, where the lieutenant from Security waited by the triple-length.

"*General Burkett!*"

Everyone stopped, turned, stilled.

Nema stood in the embassy entry, surrounded by a half dozen of his brown-clothed guards. The shortest equaled him in height. The tallest outstripped him by a head, which made her at least two-one. All were armed. Twin shooters. Knives.

"You are taking my Eyes and Ears away from me!" His sibilant wail echoed off the blade-topped walls. He tucked his hands into his sleeves while six gold faces watched every humanish move. "But you will not take her for long?"

One word from him. Jani watched six pairs of gold hands hover near weapons while around her, grim-faced mainline Security patted their empty holsters. *All they're waiting for is one word from him.*

Burkett gaped. Swallowed. Found his voice. "Bloody hell." Service decorum went out the window as he pushed Jani into the skimmer, then bulleted in behind her as Hals and Derringer piled in through the other side. The driver shot out of the courtyard and sped past the checkpoints without slowing. No one spoke until they cleared idomeni property.

CHAPTER 15

Jani barely managed to undress and set her alarm before tumbling into bed, visions of the glowering Burkett dancing in her pounding head. She had overheard him in heated discussion with Derringer as they had departed the embarkation zone—the phrases *Office Hours* and *nail down our options* had cropped up with depressing frequency.

Well, if Hals had a shot at nonjudicial punishment, she might not wind up too badly off. Besides, wasn't there an old Service saying that a Spacer without at least one Article 13 on his or her record was unworthy of the name?

Makes me a Spacer for the ages. Jani had stopped counting after number five. She buried her face in her pillow and fell into troubled sleep.

"—anytime now."

Jani jerked awake at the sound of the intruding voice. Reached out. Grabbed a handful of—

What the—? She opened her eyes and saw herself reflected in a glassy brown stare. She released her grip on Val the Bear's throat and lifted her muzzy head.

"I said, feel free to wake up anytime now." Lucien had dragged her desk chair into the bedroom. He appeared much too comfortable, feet propped on the mattress's edge, chair tipped back precariously.

"How 'n hell d'you get in here?" Jani worked her jaw, yawned, stretched her stiff legs.

"Facilities should invest in better locks," he said by way of explanation. "If you get up now, you'll have forty minutes to shower and dress before you have to hightail it to FT."

"I need to eat—"

"So you shall. I have breakfast set out in the sitting room."

"It has to be scanned—"

"I came and got the scanner before I got the food. It's all clear."

"Aren't you the efficient one?"

Lucien tugged at his short-sleeve. "Why's it so warm in here?"

"Because I like it." Jani's voice rang clearer that time. "How long have you been sitting there?"

"Half hour." He offered her the knowing sort of smile that made her teeth clench. "Did you know you talk in your sleep?"

"Do tell." Jani twisted around and sat up, catching her bedcover just in time. She still wore panties, but her bandbra rested amid the muddle of clothing heaped on the bedroom floor. *Make that, "had been heaped."* Le steward extraordinaire had taken care of her dirty laundry along with everything else.

"You're going to have to tell me about Piers sometime." Lucien's gaze drifted from her face to points south, lingering on her bare shoulders. "I see you don't believe in pajamas."

Jani yanked the sheet up to her neck. "Out."

"I don't either."

"Get *out*!" She tried the melodramatic "pointed finger thrust toward the door" move and almost dropped her coverage.

"I love it when a woman loses her . . . temper." Lucien did a side roll out of the chair and darted to the door. He ducked through the opening just as Val the Bear impacted the panel at a height even with the back of his head.

"So, tell me about your trip to the embassy." Lucien poured coffee for both of them, then settled back, mug in hand.

Jani crunched toast as she checked out her scanpack. "How much have you heard?"

"Only the disobeying a direct order part."

"How did you hear about that so soon?"

"Diplo contacted I-Com to ask if they could borrow some recording equipment. Night Desk contacted me because I'm in charge of the storage bins." Lucien reached across the desk to Jani's plate and snatched an apple slice from her overladen fruit cup. "Woke me out of a sound sleep at oh-three up. Burkett must have started amassing his weapons as soon as you returned to Sheridan."

Jani dropped her half-eaten toast on her plate. "And those weapons would be?"

"You'd better contact your lawyer first thing you get to your office." Lucien brushed a nonexistent spot from his immaculate shirtfront. "His name wouldn't happen to be Piers, would it?"

"I'm surprised you have to ask." Jani stabbed halfheartedly at her fruit. "Did you hear any fallout concerning Sam Duong?"

"Why would I?" Lucien finished his coffee and started piling dirty dishes onto the take-out tray. "That sorry situation is none of my business."

"Since when did that ever stop you?"

"It's none of yours, either."

"He made it my business." Jani set down her fork. The memory of the man's desperation ruined what remained of her appetite. "He put me down as next of kin in his MedRec."

"Because you said you believed him?" Lucien made a point of setting Jani's fruit cup on the desk before picking up the tray. "I knew you'd regret saying that."

"I don't regret a thing. I think he may have been set up."

"And why would anyone bother to do that?" Lucien walked about the room gathering newssheets and plucking wilted flowers from the bouquet. "He's a clerk."

"He's a clerk who's been overseeing the compilation of Rauta Shèràa Base and Knevçet Shèràa documents for years." Jani felt a twinge of satisfaction as Lucien hesitated in mid-pluck. "I think he uncovered something, and that something's buried in the missing documents. I think somebody stole the paper, then hung Duong with a *crazy* tag so that he'd get blamed for the docs being missing."

"That's a lot of thinking."

"Admit it—did you ever observe a scene better calculated to destroy a man's reputation?"

"So he works for an asshole." Lucien took his time folding an old newssheet into a loose cylinder. "Make that two assholes." He shoved the paper tube into the 'zap. "What do you think he knows? Or doesn't know he knows?"

Jani didn't answer. Instead, she picked another mental spare fitting out of the bin and checked it for size. "Did you ever hear of Niall Pierce? He's a colonel in Special Services."

Lucien frowned. "The guy who almost ran into you in the SIB lobby."

"Does everybody know him?"

"Just by reputation." Lucien glanced at the clock. "We better get going."

They spent valuable minutes arguing about the breakfast she hadn't eaten. By the time they departed TOQ, the walkways had cleared of first-shifters, which meant that if Jani didn't get a move on, she'd be late. *Not at a time like this.* Her back issued a string of complaints as she broke into a double-time trot.

"I saw Pierce at the hospital, too. He was standing outside the office where I met with Friesian." She pressed a hand to her right side as a stitch took up residence.

Lucien loped beside her with disgusting ease. "Think he was listening?"

"He wasn't that functional. Takedown malaise had him by the throat."

"So he had a good reason to be there. Your running into him was a coincidence."

"We've got quite a few coincidences jostling for space here, don't we?" Jani eased to a slow jog as the Documents Control white box came into view. "You said he had a reputation."

Lucien hesitated. "I've heard things about him."

Jani detected an edge in his voice. That meant he didn't want to discuss Pierce. *That* meant it was time to push. "I know he was at Rauta Shèràa. I know he nailed a field commission after the evac, and that he's Mako's man."

Lucien shot her a "how did you know that?" look. "He and Mako are an odd couple. Mako comes from a cultured background—he doesn't like to admit it, but he's descended from a long line of Family affiliates. Pierce joined the Service to stay out of prison."

Jani gasped in relief as they eased to a walk—her side-stitch had evolved into an entire wardrobe. "What was he up for?"

"Weapons-running." Lucien tapped her on the arm to get her attention—together they saluted a pair of sideline majors walking toward them. "Even after he joined up, he still got into trouble. Fights. Smuggling. Disobeying orders. All that changed after he was transferred to the Fourth Expeditionary. Mako straightened him out. When they returned to Earth, Pierce even went back to school, got a degree at Chicago Combined. Literature, of all things. He doesn't look the type."

Jani pulled in a deep breath. Another. "So? What are you—not telling me?"

Lucien blinked. "What makes you think—?"

"Save the coy-boy routine for someone who buys it and—spit it out!"

Coy Boy eyed her in disapproval. "If you got out of bed at a reasonable hour, you wouldn't have to push yourself."

"*Lucien.*"

"I found the anesthetic, glue, and bandage in your bathroom. I trashed them and hid the scalpel."

"I'll get more."

"You don't want to escape now. You're having too much fun sticking your nose where it doesn't belong."

"Answer the damned question!"

"Mako saved the Service."

"That's old news." Jani kept an eye out for Hals as they pulled up in front of the Documents Center. "Tell me something I don't know." She walked a figure eight. Her pounding heart slowed.

Lucien strolled to the walkway's edge and kicked at the stone border. "At first, it didn't want to be saved. The Old Guard needed to retire. Some of them didn't want to go."

"But Mako, with the help of loyal underlings like Pierce, helped them make up their minds."

"He was promoted to J-Loop Regional Command after Rauta Shèràa. The promotion was designed to reward him officially and at the same time get him out of the way. It didn't work." Lucien stepped over to Jani and leaned close to her ear. "That's where he started cleaning house. Not everything he did was by the book. That's not common knowledge."

"It was well before your time, too. How did you find out?"

"I *am* in Intelligence."

"And you've sneaked peeks at files. And Anais probably told you things." Jani sniffed. Lucien had used scented soap that morning. A light, musky odor, barely detectable. "And you have this way about you that makes people spill their guts."

"You think so?" He moved closer and brushed against her arm. "Care to tell me what way that is?"

"Oh, I think you know." She stepped away and started up the Doc Control steps, then turned back. "I wonder if Pierce had anything to do with what happened to Sam Duong?"

Lucien shook his head. "Why would he want to bury Rauta Shèràa documents? If anything, he'd want to get those out in the open."

"You'd think that, except Mako was called before a Board of Inquiry after the evac team returned to Earth. He bulled his way through it, and emerged victorious."

"So?"

"So maybe something in the Rauta Shèràa documents would sully that victory."

Lucien sighed in annoyance. "I suppose anything's possible."

"Think you could find out more about ex-weapons runner Pierce?"

"That's what I like about you—you never ask for much."

"You owe me." Jani stared at Lucien—he dropped his gaze eventually. "You had no right to pick through my stuff, no right to take that scalpel, and no right to read my ServRec."

"It made for an enlightening afternoon." He looked up at her, cheeks flushed from exercise, stony eyes alight with cool appraisal. "You really could have gone places if you'd behaved, you know that?"

"If I'd shut up and played along, you mean?"

The light dimmed. "There are plenty of ways to make your point without impaling yourself in the process." Lucien snapped a salute and clipped down the walkway to wherever he went, sweat-darkened hair gleaming in the sun like a tarnished halo.

"Your mail, ma'am."

Jani looked up from her equipment transfer report. Ischi stood in her doorway, holding a thin packet of paper mail. If past behavior held, he was using mail delivery as an excuse to talk to her. That was fine—she had a few questions for him, too. "Come on in, Lieutenant. Have a seat."

He slipped inside and settled into the visitor's chair. "I hope you're well after last night, ma'am." Residual excitement animated his haggard features. "I taught the idomeni ambassador how to play soccer!"

Jani smiled. "Yes, you did."

"He sure got upset when Burkett tried to get you bounced." Ischi placed her mail on the desk, one piece at a time. "Think he could put in a word for the colonel?"

"Where is she?" Jani had gone directly to Hals's office as soon as she'd arrived, only to find it dark. She had reconnoitered intermittently ever since, but it was after lunch and there was still no sign.

"Emergency meeting scheduled with Major General Eiswein, head of First D-Doc."

"In this building?"

"No, ma'am. Eiswein sits up at Base Command. North Lakeside sector."

"I should go." Jani closed her report folder and stood up, but the look of alarm that flared across Ischi's face compelled her to sink back down in her chair.

"We've been told to stafo, ma'am."

Sit tight and await further orders. "By whom?"

"Eiswein, ma'am. Her exec transmitted the order when he came to escort Hals to North Lakeside."

Shit. Jani sat back down and thumped her fist on the arm of her chair. "She did the right thing. The Vynshàrau would not have understood her absence, and that would have crippled negotiations."

"Yes, ma'am." Ischi poked moodily at her mail, then slipped an ivory envelope out from the pile. "Your raffle number came."

"My what?"

"Your raffle number." He slid it across the desk to her. "Every month, the A-G hosts a garden party at his house at Far North Lakeside. Invitation's by raffle—everybody gets a number issued them once they get entered into Base systems." He offered a perfunctory grin. "Hottest ticket in town."

"Is it that great?"

"My number came up last spring." He wrinkled his nose. "It was still cold, and it rained. The tent was heated, though, and the food was great." His smile brightened. "Mrs. Mako's beautiful. She took folks on a tour of her greenhouse. Lot of the guys went just to check her out."

Jani opened her desk drawer and swept the envelope inside. "Well, neither flowers nor beautiful women interest me, Lieutenant, but thanks for the heads-up."

Ischi's face darkened. "Sorry, ma'am." He stood. "Do you think the ambassador could do anything to help, ma'am?"

"I'll see what I can do." Jani punched out the one base code she knew. "What's Major Vespucci's take on this?"

"Um." Ischi rose and backed his way to the door. "No one's talked to him, ma'am. At least I haven't." He departed, leaving Jani alone with the blooming face on her comport display.

"Hello." Even a transmission of Lucien's smile lit up the room. "Called to ask me out to dinner? The answer's yes."

"Actually, I called to ask you for Nema's private code."

The happy expression snapped off. "I can't give you that."

"Can you tell me if FT's comports are being monitored for outgoing."

"No."

"No as in 'no, they're not,' or no as in 'go to hell'?"

"*Will you*—" Lucien's face blanked as his eyes followed something over top his display. A walk-through, most likely, which meant he resided in a desk pool.

"Don't you have an office?" Jani asked, just to rub it in.

"In a sane world, the lieutenants would have the offices and the captains would be out on the street, but that day is not yet come."

"You've become a philosopher."

"And you're still a pain in the ass."

"Hals has been at North Lakeside all day."

"And they told you to stafo?"

"Yes."

"Then do it!" The display sharded as Lucien signed off.

Jani rested her head on her desk, every once in a while pressing her fingertips to her tightening scalp. By the time she lifted her head, her incoming call alarm rang.

"Jani." Friesian's expression would have darkened the bottom of a mineshaft. "Why didn't you call me immediately?"

"I—"

"Things like this aren't just supposed to drop down on me from the sky. Things like this are supposed to be told me by my cooperative client."

"But—"

"Are you busy at fifteen up? Good. See you here. Defense Command Three South, Room Three-oh-four."

"I don't need legal counsel for Office Hours."

"You need legal counsel to get up in the morning." The display fractured once more.

Jani stared at the message light, which still blinked. Someone had called her while she talked, or rather, listened to Friesian. All of a sudden, she had become very popular.

"Good afternoon, Captain Kilian, this is Captain Brighton from Diplomatic," said the professionally dour woman. "I am calling to inform you of your Office Hours appointment with Brigadier General Callum Burkett for the day after tomorrow. The exact time and date have been applied to your calendar. Details have also been provided to your attorney, Major Piers Friesian, Defense Command. Good day."

Jani fled her office just as the incoming message alarm rang yet again. She hurried into the desk pool and over to one of the techs, who was busy stuffing paper mail into mailboxes. "Do you have anything that needs to be walked anywhere?"

"Ma'am?" The young woman dug into one of the OUT bins. "This needs to go to the SIB, but I can—"

"Perfect." Jani grabbed the envelope and darted out the door. *Always have a reason to go where you're going.* Especially if it gave you a reason to get the hell out of where you were.

The afternoon proved a copy of every one previous—deliciously hot and dry. On her way to the SIB, Jani stopped off at a ship's stores kiosk and shopped. She bought a creamy white coffee mug decorated with a brushlike crimson flower. *La fleur feu*—the fireflower, the emblem of Acadian Central United. Just enough of the old red to make a statement, but not enough to drive her augie up the wall. *Take that, Corporal Coffee Cup.* She'd savor the look on Ischi's face the next time she visited the brewer.

If we're all still working together, that is.

She also bought a canister of Bandan loose tea. Halmahera Black, an expensive blend of hothouse hybrids. She asked the items be packed in separate carriers, and headed to the SIB.

She dropped the envelope in the appropriate mail slot, then descended the stairs to the basement. *He may not be in yet.* Second shift didn't start until fifteen up. But Jani knew Sam Duong would be at his desk. She doubted he had anywhere else to go.

CHAPTER 16

Sam leafed through one of the few files that remained on his desk. Names to check for inclusion in the Gate—at least they still allowed him that much. It meant more trips into Chicago, since Yance had revoked his SIB archive access. But, truth be told, he needed the time away from the basement. Not that people said anything to his face, but he knew they talked. He could tell by the way that they looked at him. Pity could come in many flavors—angry, disgusted, disappointed. But it was still *pity.* He'd have preferred it if they'd hated him. At least hatred stood on its own two feet.

He heard the voices in the cubicles around him waver, and assumed yet another visit from Odergaard. He braced for the sight of that red face rising over his cubicle partition like a florid sunrise.

"Mr. Duong?"

Sam stilled at the sound of the voice. He looked up slowly.

"Hello." Jani Kilian smiled down at him. "I wanted to talk to you about . . . well, I think you know what I want to talk to you about." She held out one of the two silvery plastic bags she carried. "I've even brought a facilitator."

Sam smiled weakly. "In Chicago, we just call them bribes."

"How indelicate." She beckoned for him to follow with the hurried backward hand wave of a child. "Let's go."

Sam stood, paused, then stepped out of his cubicle. All eyes fixed on him, from the split-shifters readying to leave for the day to the second-shifters straggling in like the first wet splotches of a rainstorm. He followed Kilian into the hall—the pressure of stares lifted like the removal of a weight.

"Is there a breakroom around here?" She looked one way, then the other. "I have a meeting at fifteen up. That doesn't leave us much time."

"This way." Sam led her down the hall to the vend alcove. Three split-shifters sat at one of the tables by the entry, reading newssheets and smoking nicsticks. He led Kilian to his favored table in the back of the room. She fell into one of the chairs and handed him the bag.

He opened it. "Shrimp tea! I used to drink it all the time." He removed the dark green canister and turned it over and over in his hands. "I can't afford it anymore since the tariff increase." He hurried across the alcove to the beverage dispenser and drew a dispo of hot water. "I should have properly boiled water in a pot," he said as he slid back into his seat, "but I will make do." He cracked the canister seal, removed the slotted scoop from the inside of the top lid, filled it with the loose leaves, and snapped the lid closed. "I need orange rind for proper brewing, but oh well." He dipped the scoop into the hot water and watched the ebon essence leach from the black leaves. It dawned on him that Kilian hadn't spoken for a while. He glanced over at her to find her staring at him.

"You know it's called shrimp tea?" Her voice sounded weak. "It says Halmahera Black on the label."

Sam shrugged. "It's shrimp tea. Some people think if you filter it through boiled shrimp shells, it's supposed to unlock hidden flavors."

"Does it?"

"No. Makes it taste like crap." He removed the scoop, tapped it gently against the rim of the dispo to remove the excess liquid, then set it aside. "Some people can convince themselves to like anything, I suppose, if it's outrageous enough. Big fight about it at the university, sometime back."

"The Great Boiled Shrimp Debate." Kilian sat back and folded her arms across her chest. She looked as though she shivered, but how could anyone feel cold in this heat? "Mr. Duong, when did you work at the university?"

Sam thought. Thought some more. He knew the wheres, most times. As always, the whens gave him problems. "Twenty years ago, I think. Could be more. Could be less." He tapped his temple. "It's my head. I have a problem with my memory that bothers Dr. Pimentel."

"He told me about your condition. I had the right to know, since you'd knocked me."

"Knocked . . . ?"

Kilian cocked her head to one side, then the other. "N.O.K. Nok. It's dexxie slang for naming someone your next of kin." She exhaled sharply, like a breathy laugh. "Like I said, Pimentel told me about your condition. I'm going to test your allegedly poor memory by asking you some questions, OK?"

Sam set his cup down. Oh well, it was fun while it lasted. "I didn't hide your papers in my desk."

Kilian waved her hand dismissively, her face grave. "I'm not asking you about that. I want to know about the other papers."

Grave is the right word for her. Like the grave light that shone in her too-dark eyes, black as the tea in his cup. "*Kensington* records." He took a sip of the grave. "The death certificates showed up this morning."

"In your desk?"

"In my locker."

"Really?"

"I did not put them there."

"I believe you." Her voice held a quiet strength. "What kinds of *Kensington* records?"

"*Kensington* records from the *Kensington.*" Sam grinned at his bad joke. That made one of them. "Rosters. Shipping records."

"And the death certificates?"

"Four certificates. Ebben, Unser, Fitzhugh, and Caldor."

"Major General Talitha Ebben. Base commander, Rauta Shèràa Base." Kilian grimaced, as though it hurt to say the name. "Colonel Phil Unser was her exec. Colonel Matilda Fitzhugh ran the Special Services branch, and reported directly to Ebben."

"Wasn't that unusual?"

"No. Spec Service always reports to the base commander." Kilian struggled to her feet and walked unsteadily to the beverage dispenser. "When did those particular documents go missing?" She chose black coffee, and held the dispo with both hands as she trod back to her chair.

"I don't—" Sam paused to drink, and wished he could enjoy the tea without the questions. "I don't remember."

"Do you recall the causes of death?"

He shrugged. "There were rumors the Haárin killed them."

Kilian's eyes clouded. Cold tea. She looked down at the steaming dispo, which she still held in both hands. She didn't seem interested in drinking the coffee, only in absorbing its heat. "That would mean they died from stab wounds, since they died during the Night of the Blade."

Sam nodded. "The Haárin only used swords and knives that night, to kill the Laum. To cleanse the city."

Kilian set down the cup then pressed her palms to her cheeks. "You mentioned a Caldor, too. I don't remember a Caldor in the command staff."

"Spacer First Class. Died during the final round of bombing. A barracks wall collapsed on her." Kilian's look grew pained—Sam wondered why.

"I heard Mako mishandled the remains." She drew her hands away from her face; their coffee-warmth left redness behind. "He had to answer questions when he returned to Earth, but those records are sealed."

Sam shrugged. "So we'll never know. They all died during panic, so there was no follow-up investigation. No images of the scenes of death appended to their certs."

"No proof," Kilian said.

"Proof." Sam drank down the balance of his tea, before it looked like Kilian's eyes. "I think of so many deaths. They left behind no images, either. No proof." He crumpled the dispo between his hands. "All I have are flashes of thought, things I know."

Kilian leaned forward, eyes downcast. She looked like someone trying to see over the edge of a cliff without drawing too close. "Like what?"

"Like . . ." Sam ground the crumpled cup against the tabletop, and blurted out all the things he knew. "Like I never walk on the beaches here because of the sand. I hate sand. And heat. And hospitals and doctors and the way Pimentel looks at me when he tells me he wants to cut into my head for my own good." He worked his hand back and forth, grinding the cup into the marble-patterned poly. "There is no good in that, not for me. And he promises I'll be fine and he says they'll take care of me but even though he speaks I hear the words come from somewhere else and I don't remember where. I just know it isn't here." He picked up the flattened cup. "And I can't remember why I hate any of it. I just know I do."

Kilian sat back slowly. She looked older now, years of age added in minutes. "You don't want the surgery?"

"No. No cutting in my head. I know I'll die if they cut into my head." He reached across the table and touched her hand. Still so cold, as though no amount of heat could warm her. "And I knew, I *knew* when you said you believed me that . . ." He pulled back. "That if Pimentel tried to force me, you'd stop him."

Kilian tucked her hands beneath her arms. "How do you know?"

"Because I just know. Like I've been telling you." Sam stood, picked up his smashed cup, and tossed it in the sink so it could dissolve. Water-soluble cellulosic. No trashzaps in the SIB archives. Too great a risk of fire, and fire here would destroy so much. "Do you know what it's like, to know something in your bones?"

Kilian hesitated. Her eyes looked strange, glistening, as though she suffered from fever. "Yes."

Sam bent close. "Well, that is how I know I can trust you." He stood back, and pointed to the wall clock. "Five minutes to fifteen up. You'd better go."

Kilian followed him down the hall, into the stairwell, up the stairs, not drawing even with him until they had crossed the lobby. "You can trust me this time. I won't let you down." She left without smiling, or nodding, or offering him her hand to shake.

Sam stepped up to the lobby window. He watched Kilian leave the building, set her garrison cap on her head, and walk out into the brutal sun, and wondered why she said, "this time." He watched her cross the lawn to a stone bench set beneath a stand of oaks, and wondered why she took the time to stop and sit if she needed to make her fifteen up meeting. He watched her set her bag on the ground, then lean forward and cover her face with her hands. He thought back to her tired eyes and drawn face, and wondered if she suffered a headache and whether he should run out to her and offer her some painkiller.

Then he watched her shoulders shake, and wondered why she wept.

CHAPTER 17

"*Sir!*"

Evan cringed as Halvor's voice cut through the humid afternoon air. His hand jerked. The motion activated the trimmer he held; the edge brushed across a branch of the rose he'd been pruning. He swore as a fist-sized Crème Caramel lolled on the end of its damaged stem like a broken-necked doll's head. Reactivating the trimmer, he made one more slash and put the fragrant bloom out of his misery.

"Sir!"

"*What is it!*" Evan wheeled to face his bleating aide.

Halvor stopped short. He looked from Evan's face to the flower in his hands. "S-sorry, sir, but Mr. Loiaza's here."

Evan entered the sitting room to find Joaquin sitting on the sofa leafing through the contents of his documents case.

"Sorry for the surprise visit, Evan." He removed a recording board and several folders, placed them at his side, then dropped the case to the floor. "I received some rather alarming news this morning, however, that necessitates a reevaluation of our strategy."

"Let me guess." Evan lowered into a lounge chair opposite the sofa. It wasn't until he tried to grip the armrests that he realized he still held the trimmer and the rose. He tossed them one after the other atop a chairside table as though he had meant to carry them inside, as though this unexpected visit from his attorney hadn't rattled him in the least. "Something to do with Jani."

Joaquin nodded. "I received a call from your dusky Colonel Veda this morning. She informed me that the SIB can find no evidence linking Jani Kilian to the mutinous murder of Rikart Neumann."

Evan picked up the slaughtered rose and examined it. The petals looked edible—warm butterscotch tipped with peach, like blush on smooth skin. He gripped one velvet edge and yanked. "Did she tell you what they *did* plan to do with her?"

"You aren't going to like it."

Evan laid the petal on his knee, then tugged at another. "I don't like it already." He'd expected news like this since his visit to Neoclona, but he'd hoped he was wrong. He should have known better. Politics, not to mention life, had taught him that what you dreaded most usually came to pass.

Joaquin tapped the writing plane of his recording board with his stylus. "She's to be tried by an adjudicating committee. All indications at this time point to a medical discharge."

"Prison time, at least?"

"No."

"You're kidding!"

"Her health, by all accounts, is not good. Add that to the lack of evidence against her."

Evan tore the petal he held in half. "Oh for chrissake, everyone at the Consulate knew how much she hated Neumann!"

Joaquin smiled grimly. "A funny thing happens to people after they swear an oath. Suddenly, their words become gold and they become misers."

"I'm a free-spender. Why doesn't Veda ask me?"

"Again, it's a question of corroboration." Joaquin unclasped the fasteners of his jacket and sat back more easily. "Everyone knows what you have to say. But without anyone to back up your story, and without the paper to back them up, it's your word against Jani's, and, like it or not, she does have her sympathizers. Some of them are very vocal, and one in particular is riveting."

Evan added the bisected petal to the row forming on his knee. "Nema?"

"He does cut an intimidating figure when he isn't invading playgrounds and wowing them at Chicago Combined." Joaquin frowned in disapproval—in his dignified universe, responsible diplomats did *not* engage in invasions and wowings. "And as much as Cèel despises him, he'll support him when it comes to harassing us."

"Imposing trade sanctions." Another petal. "Looking the other way when colonial smugglers take refuge in their ports."

"Exactly."

As Evan annihilated his flower, Markhart entered bearing a tray. She glanced at him out of the corner of her eye—whatever she saw made her quicken her pace. She set the tray down on a side table and, since Joaquin preferred to be waited on, did the honors as server. She poured his tea and Evan's bourbon in efficient silence.

"She's a prize, Evan," Joaquin said after she had departed, sipping his tea appreciatively as he paged through a file. "Now, where were we?"

"Discussing our contingency plan." Evan swept up the petals and tossed them, along with the rose remains, back on the table. Then he dug into his trouser pocket and removed the recording-board wafer that contained his work-up of Niall Pierce. He carried it on his person as a precaution. He hadn't wanted to risk Halvor or Markhart accidentally erasing it or throwing it away. Or reading it. "Here. Have a look at this."

Joaquin accepted the wafer hesitantly. "What is it?"

"You said we should use more of my Rauta Shèràa experience. Now's our opportunity."

Joaquin pursed his lips. Aggravated turtle. Then he slipped the wafer into his board's reader slot, sat back with cup in hand, and did as Evan asked.

His brow furrowed every so often. He laughed once. That angered Evan, since he hadn't written anything funny.

When he finished, he set the board beside him on the sofa and contemplated his tea.

Evan ignored his bourbon, picking up the mangled rose instead. "Well?" He stripped another petal.

Joaquin didn't look at him. "Have you ever considered writing thrillers?"

"What the hell's that supposed to mean?"

"I mean that this tale of yours is the most convoluted, seat-of-the-pants thing I've read since Vladislav's *The Hijack of the Sainte Marie.*"

Evan sent rose parts scattering as he bounded to his feet. "Oh come on, Quino!" He paced the room. "Name the Family that doesn't have something like that in their history!"

"Evan, there's a difference between the information bandied at parties and that used to defend oneself in court. What you have here"—Joaquin pointed to his recording board—"is speculation, and defamatory speculation at that."

Evan parked himself in the window seat behind Joaquin. "I thought if you wrote it down, it's libel."

"It needs to be published in a public venue to qualify as libel, and no one will publish this if I have to smash the wafer to bits myself."

Joaquin twisted around so he could look him in the face. "You honestly believe it?"

"Yes."

"That Niall Pierce was involved in felonious activities at Rauta Shèràa Base and that Roshi Mako has squelched the Kilian investigation to prevent those goings-on from being discovered?"

"*Goings-on?* Christ, Quino, you make it sound so polite." Evan swung the rose by the stem, whacking the remains of the bloom against his thigh like a riding crop. "*Yes.*"

"You give me nothing to work with. You say ships from the Fourth Expeditionary often docked at the Rauta Shèràa transfer point, but you offer no proof that Pierce crewed on any of them. You don't even give me the names of the ships so I can check."

"He must have been on one of them. It's the right time frame." Evan pointed the vanquished rose at Joaquin. "All you have to do is get hold of the Fourth Expeditionary vessel records and comb the docking data and the crew lists."

"Track every move made by a half dozen GateWay-class vessels over a period of at least three years. Is that all?" Joaquin pinched the bridge of his nose. "And if we found Pierce had indeed visited Rauta Shèràa, even that he had visited the city multiple times, what good would that do? The same people who can't remember Jani Kilian's actions aren't going to recall the occasional pass-throughs of a nonresident enlisted man."

"You left out the clincher." Evan stood and paced some more. It made sense, damn it—why couldn't Joaquin open his mind! "Pierce's emotional health went into a tailspin after it became known that Jani was alive. Jani knew everything about what went on there—she'd know what Pierce did and when he did it. He sees his career diving into the 'zap—he's scared to death she'll rat him out."

"Evan." Joaquin pressed his fingertips to his forehead. "That's too much coincidence, even for Vladislav."

"You said yourself that Pierce had a criminal past, and that he didn't change his ways after he joined the Service."

"He did change his ways in the Fourth."

"Are you sure! How do you know he just hadn't learned to hide his crimes better?"

Joaquin blinked. He had the dazed look of a man who'd taken one too many punches. "Evan, my sources are very sound, and they tell me—"

"*Just get off your bony ass and check, you son of a bitch—that's what I'm paying you for!*"

Silence fingered through the room like ice crystals spreading through freezing liquid. Joaquin blinked with reptile slowness, as though unable to believe that he'd heard what he'd heard.

Then the comprehension dawned, and his face reddened. "We'll blame that outburst on the tension you're under and move on." He fingered the lapel of his staid dark blue jacket. "So, you claim Pierce was involved with the criminal networks working out of Rauta Shèràa Base, that an investigation of Jani's relationship with Rik Neumann would have revealed his guilt, and that Roshi arranged to scuttle said investigation, not to mention jeopardize a thirty-plus-year career, in order to protect him." He picked up his recording board and readied his stylus. "Explain the field commission."

"I touched on that at the end." Evan stalked the room, picking up petals as he went. "I think Roshi threw the lieutenancy at Pierce as a bribe, to make him behave." He shrugged. "The other possibility is that Pierce really earned the promotion. Being a criminal wouldn't necessarily prevent him from acting bravely."

"You're leveling serious charges against a man who is widely acknowledged as the savior of the Service."

"His decision to save the Service could have started with Pierce. He salvaged one lost boy, decided he'd found his calling, and went on to rescue the whole damned system."

"You honestly believe this?"

"*Yes.* How many times are you going to ask me that?"

Joaquin deactivated his stylus and powered down his recording board. "John Shroud called me yesterday. He needed to speak to me about your medical condition."

Oh shit. "I can imagine what he said."

"No, I don't think you can." Joaquin stashed the equipment in his documents case, then gathered the files. "I was going to delay telling you. I thought the news about Kilian enough of a blow for one day." He motioned for Evan to sit.

Evan returned to his chair. The glass of bourbon at his elbow whispered *remember me.* "Shroud would say anything to save Jani's skin, Quino. Keep that in mind." He took a golden swallow and waited for the next volley.

Joaquin leafed through a folder, then closed it and stuffed it in his bag. "You've been classified as a maintenance alcoholic since your mid-teens. During most of that time, you received the quality of medical care necessary to guarantee your good health while allowing you to indulge your dependency." He shot Evan an irritated look.

"But there were times, John said, when you didn't care for yourself as you should have. Your tour of duty on Shèrá was one of those times."

"He's a liar! I—"

"According to medical-annex records, you failed to follow your mandated treatment regimen. You worked too hard. Played too hard as well. With that Kilian woman, and other wild companions."

Evan drained his glass and reached for the bottle. "You make it sound like the second rise of Sodom and Gomorrah. We threw a few parties."

"Quite." Another moue of distaste. "The point is that John's opinion of your past health casts doubt on whatever testimony you have to offer, while his diagnosis of your present condition has effectively scuttled your ability to act in your own defense."

Shroud, you bastard. "I'll have a talk with him."

"I would advise against your contacting him personally, Evan. Going through proper channels at a time like this can only work in your favor."

Evan knew how to decode that remark. "You've already discussed his findings with Veda."

"I was compelled to by law. To allow things to continue with your competency in doubt would have constituted the worst sort of malpractice."

"My. *Competency?*" Evan sagged into the seat. "Any test that old Snowy wants to throw at me, I'll take. Just set the date."

Joaquin avoided his eye. "I don't want it to come to that, Evan. Really I don't."

"He's got you believing it, hasn't he? That my mind is gone."

Joaquin clasped the fasteners of his documents bag. "I need to reopen some doors I felt we could close, start exploring the Haárin connection to the goings-on at Rauta Shèràa Base."

Evan felt his reflexes slow, his mind numb, as though he'd already downed the second liter of the day. "I don't recall that ever being more than rumor."

"It is now. Do admit, it's not completely outside the realm of probability. Hansen Wyle did die in one of their bombing raids, and the images of the slaughter of the Laum during the Night of the Blade are very potent. You feared for your life, Evan. You were ill. You became involved in things you shouldn't have, something we will admit. You thought it possible the Haárin could come after you the same way they went after Kilian after Knevçet Shèràa."

"You're going to blame the transport bombing on the Haárin?"

"Based on the tone of the time, it's possible." Joaquin stood and refastened his jacket. "Reasonable doubt, Evan. Let that be your mantra for the next few months." He picked up a rose petal that had drifted onto the sofa cushion and flicked it absently onto the serving tray.

Evan watched him. Funny, the Joaquin Loiaza he had known for years had never ignored an injury to a rose—odd that he hadn't yet commented on Evan's prolonged torture of the Crème Caramel. Very odd. "Quino, give me the wafer back."

Joaquin gave him a blank look. The turtle befuddled.

"The *wafer.* You accidentally left it in your recording board. I'd like it back, please."

"All right." Joaquin unfastened his bag, removed the board, and popped out the wafer, all with the thin-lipped haste that implied he had more important things to do. "Here."

Evan took the disc and slipped it in his pocket. "What are you up to?"

Quino released a rattling sigh. "I'm up to getting you out of this house. What else would I be up to?"

Following his solitary dinner, Evan sat at his workstation and perused the public data banks open to someone with his restricted access. He looked up Korsakoff's syndrome, and studied the descriptions of the associated memory defects. They were rare thanks to the advances in addiction maintenance, but they did occasionally occur in alcoholics who received inadequate medical care.

"Bullshit." Evan activated his recording board and spent some time writing descriptions and events from his past, beginning with his mid-teens. Then he checked the facts against the holos and sceneshots archived in desk drawers and cabinets.

The neckpiece his father wore to his graduation from Sarstedt. Black-and-gold diagonal striping. *Check.*

The color of the bunk blankets on the *Excelsior*, the cruiser that transported him to Shèrá and his first diplomatic posting. Maroon. *Check.*

The flowers Lyssa wore in her hair on their wedding day. White Mauna Kea orchids. *Check.*

The weather on the day he was sworn in as Interior Minister of the Commonwealth of Planets. Blue sky sunny and cold as a witch's tit. *Check!*

He left the room only once, to confirm with a befuddled Markhart what he'd had for lunch the previous day. Vegetable soup.

Cheddar bread. Pear tart. *Got it.* Combed the newssheets to assure himself he had indeed watched the holoVee drama he remembered from the night before.

He slumped in his chair, the desktop and the surrounding floor scattered with confirmatory remnants. *There's nothing wrong with my memory.*

And if he didn't act quickly, that fact could keep him marooned on Elba for the rest of his life.

He adjourned to bed, exhausted. Slept. Dreamed. Of Jani.

She looked as she had before the crash. Rounder, cuter face. More compact, curvier body.

She wore the nightgown he'd bought her for their first anniversary. A gift both for her and his twenty-four-year-old hormones, a murderously expensive confection imported from Phillipa. Transparent film from neckline to floor, cut with an opaque swirl that covered just enough and no more.

She straddled him, the gown's skirt hiked up to reveal her satiny thighs. She said something that made them both laugh. Then she leaned forward, shoulder-length black hair veiling her face, and kissed him.

The scene shifted. No more nightgown. Just her flawless skin, lit by unseen illumination to the shade of the Crème Caramel. Perfect breasts. Narrow waist. Swell of hip. Head thrown back as she moved above him, called his name, cried out—

He snapped awake, mouth dry, heart pounding. *Damn it—anybody but her—!* He groaned as the ache of an erection overtook him; he dispatched it in the usual manner.

He got out of bed, showered, switched into fresh pajamas. Then he collected a bottle and padded downstairs and outside to his sheltered patio.

The night air was weighty with heat and the unfulfilled longing for storm. Evan sat, propped his bare feet on a table, and drank. Then he laid back his head and counted the stars.

I visited some of you. Committed crimes. Then returned home to the life that had been made for him, a glossy thing with a hollow center built on a foundation of sand.

"Didn't turn out the way you planned, did it, Dad?" He kept his eyes focused on the night sky as he spoke to his dead father. Then he decided that was being optimistic, and looked down at the flagstone instead. "I started out so full of promise." But the posting to the Rauta Shèràa Consulate, meant to be the first step in a great career, devolved into disaster, followed by full-blown, tail-between-the-legs retreat.

The journey from hell. A detour to Phillipa to take on supplies added two weeks to an already-interminable journey. By the time Evan touched down at O'Hare, he had lost fifteen kilos and, despite the efforts of the *Hilfington* medical officer, much of his hair. Stress, he'd told his mother, who had broken down at the sight of him. To Dad, he'd said nothing. *You did the right thing,* his father told him as they walked down the VIP Concourse. *You did it for Rik.*

He'd come home to the hard looks the bereaved sometimes bestowed on the survivors. *And to the funerals.* Rikart Neumann's memorial service, sans body, followed by Ebben's, Unser's, and Fitzhugh's, that might as well have been. Closed caskets all, because of the condition of the bodies. Severe decomposition caused by improper storage, his father had said. Criminal negligence, the mourning Families maintained.

Sloppy of Mako. The forceful performance he'd given before the Board of Inquiry assured that the furor didn't damage his career, but still. . . . *All he had to do was put the bodies in the damned freezer.* What the hell had he done, stuffed them in body bags and shoved them in the hold?

Evan sat and watched the moon, his mind emptying with the bottle. No more thoughts of death. Jani. Lyssa. His children. By the time he returned to bed, he felt numbed. *Nothing wrong with my memory.* But then, that was the problem, wasn't it?

CHAPTER 18

Jani sat at her desk, her hands moving over her workstation touchboard at their own pace, in their own world. She was sufficiently adept at report assembly that she didn't need to concentrate on what she did in order to do it. Lucky for her.

With the help of some cold water and borrowed makeup, she had pulled herself together by the time she met with Friesian, at least on the outside. Their discussion began contentious, with a gradual shift to tense treaty by the end. Yes, he would sit at her side during her Office Hours with Burkett and yes, this did complicate any possible deal with the Judge Advocate. Her special knowledge of idomeni customs would weigh in her favor. Any pressure applied on her behalf by the idomeni ambassador would not. Nema had been told exactly that after he called Burkett in person to protest her treatment, and seemed to understand when told that his interference would only complicate an already-messy situation. At least, he had nodded his head in a positive manner. When Jani had commented on the many ways such a head-nodding could be interpreted, Friesian had once again broken out the bright pink headache tablets.

That meeting finished, she had returned to FT to find no one had heard from Hals. The desk-pool techs watched her with coiled-spring wariness when she emerged from her office to get coffee, which she drank from a dispo. Her Acadia Central United mug joined the Gruppo Helvetica in the bottom drawer of her desk. Ischi hadn't been in the mood to take a joke, and she certainly hadn't been in the mood to make one.

Jani entered the last of the data-transfer parameters into the report grid, applied the macro, and sat back to watch the report assemble itself, section by section. Part of her monitored the formatting and data retrieval with an eye that could detect a problem without consciously thinking about it. The rest of her decamped to the dark corner of her soul and pondered whether Sam Duong could actually be Simyam Baru.

He looks so different. She caught a glimpse of her skewed reflection in the display surface. *Join the crowd.*

She wondered if she could dare broach the subject. She wondered where she would start. *Hello, Mr. Baru. Do you remember me? I'm the one who let it happen, the one who didn't act quickly enough, the one who let you die.*

Do you remember me?

I've never forgotten you.

"So this is how the other half lives."

Jani looked up to find Lucien leaning against the doorjamb, arms folded, examining her office with a doubtful eye.

"I thought there'd at least be furniture." He sauntered in and paced a circle in the large empty space between her desk and her window. "Great view," he sniffed as he walked past the pane. He flopped into her visitor's chair and put his feet up on her desk. "Do you know what time it is?"

Jani checked her timepiece. "Twenty-one seventeen."

"Have you had dinner?"

"No."

"When's your next appointment with Pimentel?"

"Tomorrow."

"He's going to be perturbed."

"Probably."

"Well, that makes three one-word answers in a row." Lucien tugged at his trouser crease. He looked extremely crisp, as though he'd changed into a fresh uniform just prior to dropping by. "Are you angry with me for not giving you Nema's code?"

"No." *Not much.*

"Good, because I spent the whole day busting tail for you."

"Really?"

"That's *five* one-word answers in a row. What's wrong?"

Jani watched page after page of her export-license agreement pull itself together from portions of other people's reports. *That's how Roger thinks Sam's mind works.* Every day, every hour. *And I have no good reason to think otherwise.* "I talked with Sam Duong today."

"And?"

"He's sick."

"I could have told you that."

"I think he might—" No, she couldn't give the possibility voice. Not yet. "I think he might have a very good reason for being the way he is."

"That's not what you were going to say." Lucien plucked her stylus holder from her desktop and toyed with the charger. "Doing anything tomorrow afternoon?"

"Burning a candle for my Office Hours appointment. Otherwise, no." Her workstation signaled the report complete, and she forwarded it to Hals's system for sign-off. "Why?"

"Interdepartmental soccer match. I'm captain of the Fourth Floor Wonderboys. Star halfback, and a joy to watch."

"Modesty becomes you."

"We're playing a team from North Lakeside." Lucien rattled off a tinny drumroll with two styli. "The Specials."

Jani smiled for the first time since her SIB visit. "Spec Service?"

He grinned. "I thought that would get your attention."

"Pierce play?"

"No, but he attends all the games." One stylus became an orchestra-leading baton. "I juggled our schedule and brought the match forward six weeks. The Sports and Activities department is not my friend anymore, if you know what I mean. That's what I spent all day doing, when I should have been reading security investigation reports about the next place Nema's visiting." Lucien pointed the other stylus at Jani like an overlong accusing finger. "If anything happens to him at the Commodities Exchange next month, it's all your fault."

"I'd worry about the Exchange, if I were you." Jani brushed off his aggravated stare. "I need to think of how to approach Pierce."

"You need to think why you're putting your ass on the line for a sick old man you don't even know." Lucien hunched his shoulders and sank down in his seat. "I bet you wouldn't do it for me."

Jani considered the not-so-veiled cry for sympathy. "You know what I think about sometimes?" She deactivated her workstation and dimmed the desk lamp. "What you told me in the sunroom, the first time you visited me."

Lucien shifted uncertainly. He had expected her to protest or reassure him—he wasn't sure how to respond. "I told you I was working with Nema."

"You also said you reported to Justice. Now that makes me wonder—after Nema gets his and they get theirs, what's left for me?"

Lucien pouted. "What do you want?"

"Your mind." Jani finger-locked her desk drawers. "According to Sam, all the missing documents have shown up except for some records for the CSS *Kensington.* Death certs bubbled to the surface today. One, an SFC named Caldor, was directly attributable to the Haárin bombing. But the other three, Ebben, Unser, and Fitzhugh—mishandling their remains was the main reason Mako was called before the Board."

"Ebben—Anais used to talk about her." Lucien kept his gaze locked on his shoes. "They were best friends."

"They deserved each other. Talitha Ebben CO'd Rauta Shèràa Base. Phil Unser was her exec, and Matilda Fitzhugh headed Spec Service."

"Anais always felt the Haárin killed Ebben in revenge for Knevçet Shèràa." Lucien glanced at Jani and shrugged apology. "That's a big reason why she likes to stick it to the idomeni whenever possible. She knows it's bad policy, but she can't help herself. She hates them. She thinks they used the Night of the Blade as a cover to settle scores."

Jani shook her head. "The idomeni don't operate undercover like that—that was why the Laumrau's conspiracy with Neumann upset them so."

"Maybe if they felt angry enough, they'd make the exception."

"No." Jani twisted in her chair to stretch her stiff back. "They'd feel no compunction about admitting to killings they felt were justified.

Lucien removed his feet from her desk and leaned forward. "So how did they die?"

"The obvious answer is that they were murdered by humans. Problem is, the list of suspects is endless. They were involved with every smuggler, fence, and racketeer in the J-Loop and Pearl Way. It could have been that as the war entered the final stages, they defaulted on agreements with people who wouldn't take 'sorry, there's a war on,' for an answer."

"But you'd know if someone like that had killed them, wouldn't you?" Lucien asked. "What's the point of making an example if it's just going to get swamped out by background noise?"

"Maybe the signs were there, but Mako's botching erased them." Jani contemplated her comport, then glanced across the desk to find Lucien eyeing her in a much-less-attractive manner.

"And where were you during the night in question?"

"Very funny."

"You were in the city that night, weren't you?"

"I had just fled the hospital. I was trying to get to the shuttleport, wangle a berth out of there."

"Any witnesses?"

"*Thanks.*" Jani tapped out a search on her comport, then rang through the code that appeared on the display. "Good evening, Mr. Duong," she said to the sad face that appeared.

"Captain!" Sam Duong's expression lightened. Then his brow furrowed in concern. "Are you feeling better? You didn't look well when you left."

"I'm fine," Jani replied, avoiding Lucien's questioning look. "Mr. Duong, who signed the death certs for Ebben and the rest?"

"Oh. They're locked away now, and I can't—" His eyes widened. "Car—*Carnival!*"

Jani shot a dirty look at Lucien, who had clapped his hand over his mouth to muffle his laughter. "Don't you mean Carvalla?"

Duong blinked uncertainly. "Maybe." He jumped as an alarm bleat sounded at his end. "Disaster drill—I must go!" His face froze, then fractured, leaving Jani to stare at the darkened display.

Lucien stood up with a growl. "Work day over—let's go. We can go to the South Central Club and watch soccer and argue."

The darkness felt comforting, like a warm blanket. Jani felt her mood lift at the sight of people dressed in base casuals—light grey T-shirts with steel blue shorts or pull-on pants—and at the squeak of trainers on scancrete that cut the still air.

But she needed to talk to someone, and Lucien wouldn't do. Not for this. He had no use for sympathy. She doubted he had much use for hope either.

She tapped his arm. "Is there a Misty Center nearby?"

"Why?" He pointed down the walkway, toward the brightly lit entrance of the South Central Officers' Club. "At twenty-two up, drinks are two for one."

"I don't think Pimentel wants me to drink."

"So I'll drink yours, too."

"*Lucien.*"

"Why now?"

"Because I need to talk to someone." Two someones, really, whom she should have tried to talk to long before this.

"Code?"

"Acadia one-two. Ville Acadie TG-one-seven-X-one."

"Name of contact?"

"Declan and or Jamira Kilian. Ninth Arrondissment, Seven Rue D'Aubergine."

The civilian clerk continued to read items off a checklist attached to a recording board. "You realize sending family messages via Misty is considered nonessential use of an essential service?" She sniffed quietly.

Jani leaned against the wall of the transmission booth and folded her arms. "I seem to recall that the real reason message central transmit was invented was to relay Cup match results more quickly between bases." She sniffed louder. "Apocrypha, I'm sure."

"If you brought a Form Eight-twelve from your CO defining this as an emergency communication, I could waive the fee." The clerk's high-pitched voice kicked up an additional third. "This is going to chew up half your monthly. Are you sure you don't want to go ServNet?"

Jani nodded. "I'm sure." In a way, she was punishing herself for taking so long to get around to this. She should have done it sooner, but when she thought they were going to kill her, she didn't see the point.

She handed her ID card to the clerk for scanning, then pressed her thumb against the input pad to authorize the deduction from her salary account.

"The instructions are—"

"I've Misty'd before." Jani slid into the chair behind the console. "Thank you."

The clerk executed a jerky about-face and closed the door after her. The last thing Jani saw was Lucien's face disappearing behind the sliding barrier, lips thinned in exasperation.

She straightened her shirt, fluffed her hair, then fiddled with the adjust angle on the relay screen until the slider base squealed in protest. She sat quietly, took a couple of steadying breaths, then punched the timer countdown on the side of the screen.

The changing colors marked the seconds. Red. Orange. Yellow. Green.

Green.

"*Âllo, Maman. Papa. C'est Jani.*" She fought the compulsion to stare down at her hands, forcing herself to hold her head up so the relay could light her properly. "I know I look different. I was assured my voice hasn't changed, though. I hope you can recognize it." She spoke slowly, pronouncing words in her head before saying them, but they still sounded strange when she said them aloud. That's what she got for working so hard to lose her Acadian accent.

"You probably know what's going on here." Memories of

ChanNet's scandalmongering reputation dampened her enthusiasm. "It's not all true, what they're saying. I hope I can explain it all to you soon." She struggled to think of a neutral topic, something as far removed from Knevçet Shèràa and Evan van Reuter as possible.

"*Vive Le Rouge!*" Well, the supposed nonpolitical status of the Commonwealth Cup was a joke, but she had to say something. "They drew a first-round bye. I wish they didn't have to depend so much on Desjarlais, though. One-man teams don't win the Cup. I wish Gilles would get off the disabled list. If they knew his leg wouldn't heal in time for the prelims, they should have signed Stewart. He was worth the money. Good halfbacks are always worth the money." OK, that did it for sports. What was next . . . ?

"It's very hot here." She saw half her paychit disappearing under a sea of banality, and berated herself for not planning the call better. "I don't mind it, though." She watched the timer blink, studied the controls rimming the display. She had trouble looking at the display directly. Too much like looking someone in the eye.

"There's a tag line that runs along the bottom of the message—you need to use same systems to reply. So you can't go to Vickard's—he used out-of-date equipment when I still lived home, and I doubt he's changed. Go to Samselle, or Fredericka." It struck her that it had been over twenty years since she'd walked down a Ville Acadie street. "If they're still in business, that is.

"I couldn't—" Her throat ached, thinning her voice until it sounded like the clerk's. "I couldn't contact you before now. I wanted to. I even tried a few times, but—" She looked into the grey depth of the display. "I'll explain, someday soon." She dropped her gaze. "If you want to listen.

"Say hello to Mirelle. And Yves. And tell Labat that if he's making book on my sentence, whatever he guessed, he guessed high." She doubted that line would get past the censors, but no harm in trying, especially if the thought of a light sentence might give her parents some peace of mind.

The timer light pulsed faster. An alarm chirped. "I have to go." She forced a smile. "I'm going to watch a friend's match tomorrow. Everyone plays soccer when the Cup rounds are on. But I understand he's quite good. He told me so himself, so it must be true." She watched the timer count down, concentrating on the colors as she struggled to keep her voice steady.

Yellow. *There's this man, Maman.*

Orange. *I thought he died because of my mistakes, but now I think he's alive, and I don't know what to do.*

"I love you." She waved weakly. "*Au revoir.*" She watched the timer flutter red and wink out.

She sat in the dark and tried to collect her thoughts. Her heart skipped as a pounding knock fractured the silence.

Lucien dogged her elbow as soon as she stepped into the hall. "He told me so himself, so it must be true. I agree with your remark about halfbacks, though—small thanks for little favors. Who the hell is Yves?"

"What did you do, flash your Intelligence ID at the control room door and muscle in?"

"Better me than standard censors." He leaned close. "I let through the line about the short sentence. Feel free to thank me again." He eyed her expectantly. "Yves?"

Jani brushed past the Communication annex's single lift and pushed open the door to the stairwell. "I went to school with him. Just a friend."

"He must have been some friend if you're saying hello after twenty years." Lucien's voice bounced off the painted walls, drowning out the clatter of their hard soles on the stairs.

"Mirelle's an old school friend, too."

"Hmm." Mirelle didn't interest him.

"Labat runs the local off-track." Jani led the way through the building's clunky double doors. "When I joined the Service, he laid four to one I wouldn't make it through OCS."

"Did he ever give you a reason why?"

"He said I never met an argument I didn't like." Jani ignored Lucien's not-so-muffled guffaw.

Noise and officers packed the South Central from wall to wall. Casuals and summerweights stood three deep at the bar—Lucien executed cuts and weaves that offered an enlightening preview of the next day's match. Jani, meanwhile, staked out the sole empty table, a wobbly two-seater with a commanding view of the men's room door.

"Place is a madhouse." Lucien set down the drinks, followed by a basket of popcorn. "You should have told your parents hello from me. Let them *think* you're having fun."

Jani stared glumly at her fruit soda, interspersed with a few envious peeks at Lucien's beer. *I wish I could get drunk.* Hoot and holler and roll up the rugs. Find a warm, hard body who'd be as happy to vanish with the dawn as she would be to let him.

"Heard anything about Hals?" Lucien shifted his chair so he could watch the door, the 'Vee match, and the room panorama all at the same time.

"No." Jani picked at the popcorn. "I wish Eiswein would tell us something—the pressure's building, and people are starting to snap."

"Who's next in line?"

"Guy named Vespucci. Major. Doesn't like me a bit."

"What did he have to say?"

"Nothing. I don't think he left his office all day." Jani had been relieved that she didn't have to put up with Vespucci's accusing glares, but it did bother her that he didn't try to rally the troops behind their absent leader.

"Think he's a pouter?" Lucien clucked in disgust. "It's always fun to have a pouter in the department. They want people to come to them, and when no one does, they crawl in a hole and seal the entrance." He took a swallow of beer. "Funny he didn't send Hals's adjutant around with the 'I'm in charge' announcement. That kind usually does."

Jani squinted in the direction of the 'Vee screen to try to see who played. But the haze from multiple flavors of nicsticks hung in the air and seeped into her films, stinging her eyes and blurring her vision. "Ischi came to see me, but he said he hadn't checked with Vespucci about anything."

"He came to *you*?" Lucien's arm stopped in mid-swig. "Really?" He set the bottle down slowly. "Hals talk to you a lot?"

"Not too much."

"She took your advice about bucking Burkett, though, didn't she?" He nodded knowingly. "And your advice ran opposite Vespucci's, I bet."

"Yeah, but—"

"He thinks you've end-arounded him. He's jealous."

"Oh, come on!"

"I've seen it before." Lucien waved a sage finger. "You have to nip this in the bud. If Hals doesn't show up tomorrow morning, you need to go to Vespucci and ask his advice."

"He won't give me the time of day."

"Nah, he sounds like the gloating type. You'll want to punch him in the mouth by the time you're through, but at least people will know order's been restored." He shrugged at the look of profound dismay on Jani's face. "Sorry, that's the way it is."

Oh goody—something to look forward to. Jani sipped her fruit juice. Carbonated, which did nasty things to her still-achy stomach, and much too sweet. She stood up and surveyed the surrounding tables in search of a spice dispenser, her eye scanning for shape without transmitting details to her brain. When she finally realized who sat across the room at the far end of the bar, she barely ducked in her seat in time to avoid being seen.

Niall Pierce was alone. People crowded him from every side, but that didn't make a difference. You could always tell. The eyes focused straight ahead. The hunched shoulders. The only communication between him and what filled his glass.

You look the way I feel. It crossed Jani's mind that he might have waited outside Documents Control for her to emerge and then followed her to the Misty Center, then here. The thought didn't bother her as much as it should have. She watched him sit still and silent, then tipped her soda imperceptibly in his direction, a toast to their shared misery.

CHAPTER 19

Jani left Lucien on her doorstep, pleading fatigue and the need to prepare herself to play supplicant to Vespucci. He looked dubious but departed quietly, leaving her with the promise to stop by at 0730 to take her to breakfast.

She talked to Val the Bear about Sam Duong. Wondered what Borgie's take on Lucien would have been. Slept fitfully. Dreamed of drowning again, Neumann's jolly chuckle providing background music.

Oh-five up found her suffering the wide-awake lassitude of the truly exhausted—too numb to sleep, too enervated to rise. She got up anyway, showered and dressed in a plodding daze, and departed the TOQ just as the sun began its creep above the lake horizon.

She bought breakfast at a kiosk, then dumped it in the trash untouched. Watched a frazzled lieutenant endure an impromptu inspection by two A&S-holes with recording boards. Kept a weary eye open for Pierce as she trudged to Documents Control, arriving just in time to meet Vespucci coming from the opposite direction. She saluted. "Good morning, Major."

"Captain." Vespucci returned the salute grudgingly, then hurriedly mounted the steps.

Oh no, you don't! Energized by a jolt of anger, Jani chased him up the steps and through the entry, finally catching up to him by the lift bank. "I wondered if you'd heard anything from Colonel Hals, sir."

Vespucci's face brightened in surprise. "You mean she hasn't been in touch with you?" He drew up straighter, the first glimmerings of smugness imbuing his fleshy features. "She called me first thing yesterday morning. Meetings with General Eiswein all day yesterday. Hammering out proposals for a revamping of Foreign Transactions."

Jani stepped aboard the lift, her benumbed brain struggling to wedge that tidbit amid all the others. *You were in contact with her yesterday and you didn't tell anyone!* Lucien had overestimated her tolerance. They hadn't even entered the office, and she already felt like punching Vespucci.

Instead, she stepped to the front of the car and concentrated on the control-panel lights. Red, of course. Not the smartest decision to stare at them, considering her current state. *Screw it,* she thought, as the indicators flickered. The fatigue faded from her limbs as she rode the glow. "What else did she have to say, sir?"

"That's confidential, Captain."

"Can you at least say if she's—" *—under arrest?* "—if she's well, sir?"

"As well as can be expected, considering the trouble you stage-managed her into." The lift stopped—Vespucci crowded out the door as soon as it opened wide enough and bustled down the hall. "You may think that Academy mystique of yours fools people, but some of us know a destructive malcontent when we see one."

Jani's tietops slid on the slick flooring as she wheeled around the corner. "Whatever you think of me, sir, the rest of FT deserves to hear something. Is the department breakup on hold? Are folks going to be shipped out to colonial postings tomorrow?"

"We were ordered to sit tight and continue at our jobs, Captain. That's all anyone needs to know right now." Vespucci strode through the desk pool, ignoring the hopeful "good morning, sirs" that greeted his appearance.

Jani glanced around the desk-pool area. Already, the paper mail had piled up in the collection boxes, and dirty dispo cups and plates littered desktops and tables. The coffee odor permeating the air had that sharp, stale tang. The high gloss had dulled already, and Hals had only been gone a little over a day. *Ah, shit.* Vespucci showed his worth by allowing it to happen, but he was all they had to work with right now, and it was apparently up to her to nudge him into his designated mooring. *I've become a diplomat.* And she had about two seconds to figure out the drill.

I hate this. She pulled up beside Vespucci as he palmed his doorlock. "Sir, if I could be allowed to make a suggestion?" She waited, her teeth grinding as Vespucci hesitated in his open doorway. She could see the mechanisms turning, his eyes flicking back and forth as he weighed his options. *You self-serving son of a bitch.* "I don't possess the authority to speak to them, sir. They're waiting to hear something from you."

"Ischi spoke with you yesterday." His voice held the barest tinge of verbal pout. "I saw him go into your office."

"Lieutenant Ischi brought me my mail, sir, as I'm sure he did yours."

"I didn't—" Vespucci stopped.

You didn't let him in the door because you're mad at him for liking me. "Sir, this is your department until Colonel Hals returns. I understand completely that I am in no position to presume any sort of authority. I am, of course, available to provide any advice you might wish—" the words ran together as he stiffened "—but I know where I stand." Her head pounded. "*Please*, sir."

That was the magic word. Vespucci shot her a superior smile. "A little different, dealing with a real department instead of that fly-by-night collection of losers you worked with, isn't it, Kilian?" He sauntered into his office and tossed his briefbag on his desk. "Give me a few minutes. Have everyone gather in the anteroom."

Jani flexed her left hand, the one hidden from Vespucci's sight. Formed a fist. Forced it open. "Yes, sir. Thank you, sir."

"—and the colonel requests I let you know that as soon as these rather intense meetings are over, she will be back in her office, just in time for our annual performance evaluations." Vespucci grinned at the chorus of mock moans and groans that greeted that portion of his announcement. His pleasure seemed genuine. He liked being the center of attention and the fountain of all Service wisdom, and his delight filled the room.

The group dissolved into happy gabble. Three of the techs jostled to sort the mail, while two others disassembled the brewer. *And peace reigned again in the valley.* All Jani had to do was roll over on her back, expose her throat, and point out the targets.

Ischi wandered up to her, his face lightened by a subdued grin. "Thank you, ma'am."

"Major Vespucci is second-in-command here, Lieutenant."

"Yes, ma'am." His eyes shone with wisdom beyond his tender years as he jerked a thumb toward the gurgling brewer. "Coffee?"

Jani bit her lip to keep from smiling. "Why, thank you, Lieutenant. Just let me get my cup."

* * *

Jani sipped from her Central United mug, and grumbled foul words in Acadian as she scanned the report she had transmitted to Hals's system the night before. Vespucci, now sufficiently persuaded as to his worth to do his job, had taken it upon himself to make changes that would have resulted in the document being bounced back from Legal within the time it took an outraged paralegal to smash his fist into his touch-board. She deleted one of his "corrections," ignoring her bleating comport until the fifth squawk.

Lucien's face in no way resembled the sunny visage she had come to know. More overcast, with a threat of storm. "Where were you this morning?"

"I peeled out early." She tapped her board again, deleting a phrase that would have resulted in twelve crates of cabinets being classified as small arms. "I was nervous."

"*You*?" He wadded a sheet of paper and bounced it off his display. "How did it go?"

"Hals had spoken to Vespucci yesterday morning. He sat on it the whole damned day."

"A pouter. I knew it." He smiled proudly, a professor watching his valedictorian strut across the stage. "But you charmed it out of him."

"I feel like I need a shower."

"Want some company?"

"Good-bye." Jani thumped the disconnect with a fast chop of her open hand, then returned to debugging her report.

Her comport squawked again. This time, she caught it on the first alarm. "Damn it, Lucien, leave—!" She choked back the balance as she found herself staring at Frances Hals's puzzled countenance.

"Good morning, Captain."

"Ma'am!"

"I'm still alive."

"We were beginning to have our doubts."

Hals offered a tired grin. "So was I." She massaged the back of her neck. "Things started out badly. But once Eiswein realized you were right and Foreign Transactions had legitimate cause to complain about how Diplo treated us in this matter, it was all over but the drafting of the formal report." She stared out of the display. "You look surprised, Captain."

The only thing worse than taking the shot is finding out you took it for nothing. "I only heard about a meeting with Eiswein and a revamp of FT, ma'am."

Hals ran a hand across her eyes. "*When?*"

"This morning, ma'am. I spoke with Major Vespucci and requested he address the department. People were starting to get edgy, if you know what I mean."

"I told him to use his discretion. Unfortunately, he takes that as permission to keep his mouth shut." Hals's look of tired disgust didn't bode well for Vespucci's future in FT. "Things are in the draft stage, so I can't be too specific about details. Suffice it to say, General Eiswein was extremely interested to hear all the things I had to say about how the idomeni regard documents examiners. I haven't spent the past day and a half getting my ass chewed on. I've spent it helping to assemble a proposal that should, if it gets past the Administrative flag, result in FT being reclassified as a Diplomatic adjunct."

Jani laughed. "Burkett will flip."

"Serves him right. The day the first of my people start Dip School is going to be one happy day for me." She stared off to the side, her expression pensive. "Do you understand any German, Kilian?"

"Very little, ma'am. Enough Hortensian to get by."

"Does *Scheißkopf* mean what I think it means?"

Shithead! Luckily, coffee beaded nicely on summerweight polywool. "Yes, ma'am, I believe it does," Jani said as she dabbed at her trousers with a dispo.

Hals nodded. "Eiswein muttered that a lot when I told her how Burkett tried to lock us down." She yawned again. She looked like she'd been wrung out and tossed in a corner to dry. "I'm exhausted. I need a shower and a hot meal and about ten hours' sleep."

"Would you like me to do a room sweep and bring you some gear?"

"No, thank you. My husband brought me a kit. He's a civilian, but he's learned to pack in a rush with the best of them."

Jani started. "I didn't know you were married, ma'am."

"Nineteen years." Hals's face closed. "The past few weeks have made for an interesting time."

"Children?"

"Three. All in prep school." The dulling in her eyes hinted at the pressure the situation had brought to bear on her life outside Sheridan. "We're on our way to getting this straightened out. Can't come soon enough. I hope to be back in the office in a few days."

"My Office Hours with Burkett is scheduled for tomorrow." Jani knew she couldn't discuss the matter with Hals *per se*, but a hint that she could anticipate a cancellation of the little get-together would have done wonders for her mood.

"Yes." Hals's dour countenance gave away nothing. "He may try to get his last licks in. I understand he's working up a head of steam over rumors he has heard that aren't really rumors a'tall." Her thin smile allowed a glimpse of an agreeably vile sense of humor, but the curtain soon fell. "We didn't do our careers any favors, but we did our jobs, and the entire department is going to benefit from it. It's a good feeling." She nodded. "Captain."

"Ma'am." Jani waited for the display to blank before turning back to her workstation. She dumped a few more of Vespucci's edits, then set the unit to standby. She had picked up her cup and was just about to leave in search of fresh coffee when her comport alarm bleeped again.

"Jani." Friesian's face held the contented fatigue of a workman who had taken a step back to admire his handiwork. "Could you be at my office within the hour? I have some news for you."

"If this goes as planned, with no paper snafus or further visits to the idomeni embassy, your hearing should take place late next week, and your discharge early the following." Friesian tapped a happy drumbeat on the tabletop. "A week and a half from now, you'll be a civilian again."

Who are you kidding, Jani thought. *I'm a civilian now.* They sat in the breakroom down the hall from Friesian's office. The room faced the lake. Brightly colored sails of assorted watercraft shimmered like pearly scales on the water's calm surface, while lakeskimmers whizzed in all directions like skipping stones.

"Try to restrain your excitement." Friesian pushed back in his chair. The flexframe hummed as his weight shifted.

"I'm sorry." Jani felt genuinely contrite. He had looked so proud as he described the terms of her discharge. "I just have a difficult time accepting that I'm being let off the hook."

"Off the hook for *what*?" Friesian took a swallow of his black coffee. "The missing-movement charge is a harsh one. You're losing half your pension, many of your benefits, and if not for the medical aspects, you'd be facing a dishonorable discharge. Hell, they're even letting you go out a captain—they had every right to bust you to lieutenant!" Dark circles rimmed his eyes, and his skin had greyed. He looked as drained as Hals.

It's the pressure of their jobs. Had to be. It couldn't have anything to do with the fact they worked with her. Could it? She looked at her hands. They had grown so cold that the nail beds looked blue.

"It's not that I'm not grateful. But compared to some of the things I've gone through in the past few years, this didn't make the top one hundred. I expected . . . much worse."

"Well." Friesian got up and walked across the room to the vend coolers. "The only thing you have on your plate now besides the hearing is to provide some info to Colonel Chandra Veda. She's the SIB investigator assigned to your case." He patted his pockets in search of a vend token. "I pledged your cooperation in some other investigations she's closing out. She just wants some information about Rauta Shèràa Base. She also mentioned some questions about Emil Burgoyne."

"Borgie." Jani looked toward the window. The reflection of the bright sun on the lake made her films draw and her eyes water, forcing her to squint. "We called him Borgie."

"Borgie had problems with Neumann, from what I could glean from your ServRec. Some were rather serious."

"Neumann pushed him. He enjoyed tormenting him."

"He pushed him into at least one assault on a superior officer."

"Trumped-up charge." Well, not really. Jani had helped Borgie wash Neumann's blood out of his short-sleeve herself.

"Borgie admitted to having an affair with his corporal. Nothing trumped-up there."

"Yolan Cray." Jani could see them now, the short, dark-haired Borgie and the willowy blond Yolan. "At Rauta Shèràa Base, a good-looking body belonged to whichever member of base command laid claim to it. Yolan was attractive. She went to Borgie for protection, and things took off from there."

Friesian's lip curled. "He worked the situation to his advantage, you mean?"

Jani recalled the light in Yolan's eyes the day she showed Jani a ring Borgie had given her. It hadn't been expensive—Borgie had his pay docked so many times, he barely cleared enough to cover his incidentals. A plain silver band—you'd think he'd given her the Commonwealth Mint. "They loved one another. Maybe to you, it was a threat to order and discipline. You have a different measuring stick against which to judge it. To me, it came as a relief. At least it was clean."

Friesian plugged his token into a cooler slot and removed a sandwich. "You can say things like that to me. It won't go beyond these walls. But keep your opinions to yourself when you talk to Veda—she tends to be a little straight-laced."

"I'm glad she can afford to be." Jani wedged her hands beneath her thighs to warm them. "I assume you're going to sit next to me when I talk to her, too."

Friesian tore the wrapping off his sandwich and tossed it into the trashzap. "You're damned right," he said, as the polycoat paper flashed, then flamed to powder.

CHAPTER 20

Jani checked in at FT after her meeting with Friesian, and found the desk pool scrubbed and straightened to its former glory. She finished editing her report back to its earlier pristine state, and forwarded it to Hals's system on a delay that would guarantee it wouldn't be opened until the colonel herself was at her desk to read it. She checked out for the day to sounds of Vespucci singing along with an opera recording someone had inserted into systems. He proved a remarkably sound tenor. Jani considered sticking her head in his office and recommending he transfer to the Entertainment Corps, but after some thought, she decided against it. Unaccustomed restraint on her part. She felt extremely pleased with herself, as though she'd passed a grueling test.

She returned to her rooms to find her comport message light fibrillating. A clerk from the Misty Center confirmed that they'd transmitted her communication to her parents, and that her salary account had been billed accordingly. Since she had yet to receive any salary, she owed them money. They had therefore applied to garnish her account, but she was not to worry since this was standard practice and would not reflect negatively on her credit rating.

"I didn't know I had a credit rating." Jani erased that message and went on to the next one.

"Hello, Captain!" Sam Duong appeared much happier than he had earlier, which probably meant his supervisor was somewhere else. "Can we meet tomorrow? I have news that may interest you." He fiddled with an object below display level. "I have entered the time into my handheld. I hope twelve up is fine. We can meet in front of the SIB. Please reply if not possible; otherwise, I will assume you will be there."

"Damn." Jani held her finger on the response pad, and debated sacrificing Lucien's soccer game. She would have liked to barge in on Duong and see what he information he had. And to see how he was doing. Whether he enjoyed his shrimp tea. If he remembered anything now, rather than just knew.

"Lucien would kill me." He had, after all, sacrificed his relationship with Sports and Activities in order to bring her Niall Pierce. Pierce, who kept turning up. Who followed her. Who stared into his beer like a man with a rip in his soul. Yes, she needed to meet Pierce.

She hit the pad for the last message.

"Hello, Jani." Pimentel glowered at her. "You missed your appointment today—"

Damn again.

"—so I've rescheduled you for tomorrow at sixteen up. Please be sure to stop by, or else I will track you down using every tool at my disposal." The display blanked, leaving Jani to stare at the slow fade to standby blue until a glance at her clock told her she needed to get moving.

She showered, then donned her base casuals for the first time. The trainers were dull white, with removable sock liners. The T-shirt fitted more snugly than she'd have liked, and the shorts, while attractive and comfortable, were above all, *short.* She couldn't recall the last time she'd shown her legs in public. Baggy clothing and no makeup had been her uniform of the day for almost two decades. Unattached women attracted unwanted attention in the places in which she'd been forced to earn her keep. She'd learned to avoid trouble.

But that isn't an issue anymore. That sort of trouble had become something to welcome, to embrace with open arms. *Somebody nice and safe, I think, like a test pilot.* Much more dependable than any I-Com lieutenant of her acquaintance.

Just before she left, she buzzed the Misty Center and asked if any messages had arrived for her. It was ridiculous to expect a reply so soon. If nothing else, the laws of physics dictated against it. But it didn't hurt to make sure she had given them the right code. Just as it didn't hurt to turn her comport on its base so that she could see whether the message light blinked as soon as she opened the door.

Jani found a seat on the end of the half-filled bank of bleachers, away from the bulk of the crowd. Both teams still warmed up. She could see Lucien's towhead flash in the sun as he trotted downfield and lifted a soft pass to one of his teammates. He spotted her as soon as he turned upfield, and froze just long enough to catch a return off the side of his head. Amid rude laughter, he ran to the sideline.

"Where were you?" His face was flushed, his blue-and-gold striped jersey already sweat-soaked. "I waited by the field house for over an hour."

"I had things to do."

"Like what?" Before she could answer, he jerked his head toward the opposite sideline. "He's over there."

Jani looked across the field. Pierce stood near the cooler bank. He wore base casuals—his arms and legs were as tanned and hardened as his face. Sunshades shielded his eyes—Jani couldn't tell whether he watched them or not.

Lucien glared at her. "He was standing there when I arrived. He took off his shades to watch me stretch. He hasn't budged. I don't know whether to water him or ask him out."

Jani wrinkled her nose. "He's not your type."

"Ha-ha. Laugh, I thought I'd die." He wiped his face with the hem of his jersey, flashing an attractive expanse of flat, tanned stomach in the process. "I should have fitted you with audio pickup. He's the wound-up type that blurts incriminating details, I know it."

"I'll be fine."

"You will? *Good.* I'll tell Nema you said that. Maybe it'll buy me a ten-minute head start."

Jani watched Lucien fidget with his sleeves. It would have been a stretch to call him jumpy. Concerned, more like. Definitely concerned. "What are you so worried about?"

Lucien bent close to her ear. "Because before I thought he was just a hard-ass, but now I know he's strange, and you can't predict what strange will do." One of his teammates called to him. "Don't let your guard down." He loped back to the middle of the field to join the referee and the Specials' captain.

The Specials, clad in plain green, won the token flip and elected to receive. Both teams huddled, broke, then spread out in formation. The starting whistle blew. The crowd whooped as the ball sailed.

Jani followed the arc of the ball's flight. As she did, she caught a flicker of motion out of the corner of her eye.

"Excuse me." Pierce brushed by her, stepping over her bench seat to the one behind. His voice fit him—rough, middle-pitch, nasal. Victorian accent. He wasn't much taller than she was. Solid muscle, though—the bench creaked when he sat.

Jani waited.

"He's not your type."

Jani turned and looked up at him. Against the ruddy, worn skin of his face, his scar glinted like something polished and new. "Are you talking to me?"

"Pretty boy." Pierce's sunshades obscured his eyes—even up close, Jani couldn't tell whether he looked at the field or at her. "He knows it, too."

"So do you, apparently."

"What makes you say that, Jani?"

"He told me you've been watching him."

"Bugs him, does it?" Pierce grinned. Nobody would ever call him pretty. "Good to know."

"You did it on purpose?"

"Pretty Boy's been asking questions about me. I traced back his comport calls."

"You have a search lock on your name?" One that could override any protections Lucien with all his I-Com knowledge had most assuredly put in place. "Isn't that excessive?"

"I have a right to know if people are talking about me."

"Sounds like you're concerned with what they're saying." Jani searched Pierce's face for a twitch of muscle, any movement that would betray fear or nerves. "Now why would that be?"

Pierce hesitated. "Because they'd miss the point." His grating voice dropped to a whisper. "They wouldn't understand." He removed his shields to rub his eyes, then quickly shoved them back on. "Take your Service record," he said, speaking normally. "Anyone reading it would assume you to be a willful, arrogant, insubordinate screwup. Would they be right?"

Jani glanced toward the field in time to see Lucien look in her direction. He almost missed a pass in the process—one of his teammates yelled at him to wake up. "To an extent." She tried to think of something to say that would drag the conversation back on course without spooking Pierce. "Sounds like you've been asking questions, too."

Pierce crawled down from his seat to the open space next to her. "Actually, I have a few that only you can answer." His voice turned lighter, sharper. "You've been in and out of the PT ward as much as I have lately." His bare knee brushed hers as he leaned toward her, the reddish hair glinting like finest wire. "What's the verdict?"

Jani edged down the board away from him, rubbing the place where their skin had touched. "You read my ServRec. You tell me."

"Well, there are your physical difficulties, caused by your hybridization. The rumored bioemotional problems—same cause."

Pierce's Victorian twang had softened. Now he sounded thoughtful. Scholarly. "Do you remember the transport explosion?"

"According to my ServRec, I wasn't on the transport."

"I've heard that rumor—I don't believe it. I don't think Shroud could have gotten his hands on you any other way." Pierce tilted his head. Jani still couldn't tell what he looked at. " 'Hurled headlong flaming from th' ethereal sky, with hideous ruin and combustion.' "

What? Jani felt a gnaw of curiosity. Coupled with her wariness, it made for an interesting combination, like admiring the snake while waiting for it to strike. "I don't think you got *that* from my ServRec."

Pierce cracked a smile. His scar contorted his curved upper lip, exposing the jagged point of his eyetooth. "Milton. *Paradise Lost.* Book One—the expulsion of Lucifer from Heaven." One shoulder jerked. "I wasn't drawing any comparison. The imagery just seemed particularly apt." His head dropped. No problem determining where he looked now. "Your arms and legs don't look different. They're the same color. Same shape."

I should have worn the damned pants. And a long-sleeved shirt. "The leg had to be switched out earlier this year," Jani snapped as she crossed her arms in front of her chest. "The arm's new, too."

Pierce detected her annoyance, and pulled away from her. "I didn't mean to be forward. Just making an observation." He nodded toward the field just as the crowd noise ramped. "Pretty Boy just made goal."

Jani watched Lucien run across the field, arm pumping. She took her cue from his display—times like this didn't call for subtlety. "You're framing an innocent man for documents theft. Why?"

Pierce drew close again. "If you ever got to know me, you'd see we have a lot in common." He held one hand in front of him. " 'Full of doubt I stand, whether I should repent me now of sin by me done and occasioned, or rejoice much more that much more good thereof will spring.' " The open hand closed to a fist and lowered to his knee. "Book Twelve. The archangel Michael shows Adam the future of the human race just before he's cast out of the Garden, the eventual triumph of good over evil. Adam is comforted. He realizes his suffering has a purpose." His voice grew harsher, scolding. "You should read more, Kilian. It soothes the soul."

He just admitted he set up Sam Duong. It wasn't the sort of admission that was worth a damn legally—for one thing, she didn't think Pierce was emotionally stable enough to testify. But it was enough for her. "Do you really believe that it's worth destroying a man's reputation to save yours and Mako's?"

"What's one man's reputation? We have a way of life to protect."

"You broke the law at J-Loop RC when you forced out the Family hacks. Fine—nothing wrong with that. But now you're attacking an innocent. You call that honorable?"

"For the good that thereof will spring." Pierce thumped his fist against his knee. "Yes, I do." He flinched, muttered a curse, and reached into the pocket of his shorts, pulling out a handcom. "I have to go." He muttered a few words into the device, then stuffed it back in his pocket. "I can send you a reading list, if you'd like. To your office or your TOQ suite, whichever you prefer." He stood and nodded to her. "Let me know." He looked as though he practiced for the parade ground as he strode away, back straight and arms swinging, around the end zone and down the steep incline that sloped from the Yards toward the base proper.

The game continued past sunset, the usual combination of blown calls, sloppy play, and outright confusion. The Wonderboys, unfortunately, weren't. Final score: five to four in favor of the Specials.

Jani joined the crowd of players and spectators that milled around the coolers. She found Lucien standing by the ice dispenser, scooping melt out of the drain with a dispo and pouring it over his head. "You had a good game. Scored twice."

"Three times. Glad to see you paid attention." He slipped into soft-spoken French. "I saw him take off. What happened?"

"Nothing. He got a call."

"Did he say anything interesting?"

"He thinks we have a lot in common." Jani filled a dispo with ice chips and popped one into her mouth. "He thinks I should read more."

"Strange—I knew it. Anything about Duong?"

"He admitted he framed him." He seemed to have admitted other things, too—Jani just couldn't figure out what they were.

Lucien pulled his sodden jersey over his head and snapped it like a wet towel. "I knew I should have fitted you with a pickup." He walked toward the field house. "Shower," he called out in English as he vanished through the door. "Out in ten."

Jani passed the time tossing ice chips into the trashzap and watching them crack and steam. "'Hurled headlong flaming.'" Though in this case, sputtering described it better.

She pondered Pierce's odd explanation. "He's been following me because he wanted to talk to me. He wanted to make me understand." Understand what? That Sam Duong's reputation was a fair price to pay to cover up his and Mako's character assassinations? "That's what you think, Niall."

"You're talking to yourself again."

Jani turned to find Lucien grinning at her. He'd changed into clean casuals—his hair was towel-damp, his cheeks shiny from lazoring. He looked so fresh and normal—a balm to the senses after the bizarre Pierce. She found herself grinning back. "And you're eavesdropping again."

"It's the only way I can find out what you're thinking." His gaze drifted down, settling on her legs. "Maybe during our next match, you could stroll around the end zone and distract the opposing goalie. I'll run it by the guys, take a vote."

"Stop it."

"But it's for the team." He yawned loudly. "So, back to the Club for dinner? It's a cookout tonight."

On cue, the odor of grilling meat drifted across the Yard, borne by the breeze. Jani's roiling stomach tightened in rebellion. "I'm not hungry."

"You have to eat."

"I need to do some things first." See if her parents called. Check on Sam Duong. Figure out what Niall wanted her to understand. "Let's go back to my room."

Lucien pursed his lips and shouldered his duffel. "Whatever you say."

The TOQ lobby was empty. The sounds of the 'Vee filtered in from the game room. Jani took the stairs slowly, keyed into her suite, checked the comport message light. Nothing. She patted the top of the display and wondered if Mako had ordered her room bugged. "I wonder if Pierce is covering up more than chicanery at J-Loop Regional?"

"I guess I can't leave your side now that he knows you suspect him." Lucien slipped his duffel off his shoulder and let it drop to the floor. Jani tried to back away as he closed in, but the divider that separated the bathroom from the sitting area stopped her. He leaned into her and let his lips brush hers. So light. The barest touch. His breath smelled of mint, like her favorite lunchtime leaves.

Jani tried to turn her head away. "There's a time and a place."

"Right here." Another kiss. "Right now."

"You call this protection?"

"Of course." He placed his hands on the wall on either side of her head. "After Nema gets his—" He kissed her cheeks, her eyes, along the lines of her jaw, her neck. "—and Justice gets theirs—" He lingered over her pulse points, raking them lightly with his teeth. "—this is what's left for you."

Jani leaned harder against the wall as her knees threatened to buckle. *I can't do this now.* Her heart pounded. Her clothes grew tight. *Maybe I can.* She wrapped her arms around him, pulled him close, felt his hard muscles beneath her hands. He buried his head in her neck and murmured things in French that made her gasp.

As they pulled at one another's clothes, Jani heard a cough. She looked over Lucien's shoulder.

Rikart Neumann sat in an armchair at the far end of the room, near the window. He wore desertweights—the tan shirt and trousers faded as she watched. "Tsk, tsk." He shook his finger at her—Jani could see the curtain through the translucent skin and bone. "You always were one for the boys, weren't you, Kilian?" he said as he vanished.

Jani pulled her hands from Lucien's back, bunched them into fists, brought them down past his arms and up through, breaking his hold and pushing him backward.

"What the hell!" He stumbled and sprawled across a low table. "What's the matter with you!"

"Get out."

"What!" His unfocused gaze sharpened. "Why?"

"Because I said so."

Lucien stared at her. His breathing slowed. "You know, I see the way you look at me." He'd reverted to English. Crisp. Sharp. Cold. "The feeling's mutual." He pushed himself into a sitting position. "Look, you're sideline—I'm mainline. We don't work together. No lines crossed. Is that what you're worried about?"

Jani shivered and hugged herself as a fat chuckle sounded from the far corner of the room. "No."

"Then *what*?" He boosted to his feet. "Pierce thinks you and he have things in common. Well, you and I have things in common, too. We know how to work people. We keep it simple and travel light, take what we want and leave the rest. We're a matched set—why waste it?"

Just as Jani opened her mouth to speak, Neumann reappeared at the bedroom entry. He held a finger to his lips. Then he formed an O with his index finger and thumb and poked his other index finger through the circle. In. Out. In. Out. "You do it because you like to," she said hurriedly. "I do it because I have to."

"Oh, really?" Lucien picked up his duffel. "I don't understand you completely, and, frankly, I think you're wrongheaded about a lot of things. But I never figured you for a tease, and I sure as hell never figured you for a hypocrite!" He hit the doorpad and left without looking back.

A greasy snicker sounded. "Looks like your little rent boy took off, Kilian." Neumann's form had disappeared, but his voice remained. "I don't think you can support him on a captain's pay. He's Cabinet class all the way. You don't earn enough to cover his mint-flavored oral rinse."

Jani pressed her hands to her ears and stumbled to her bed.

"Think you're off the hook because Mako says he'll cut you loose?" Neumann's voice sounded from one dark corner, then another. "Well, think again."

"You're *dead*!" Jani fell back against her pillows, pulled her damp shirt from her sweaty skin, and breathed deeply and slowly.

When the fluttering in her chest subsided, she eased to her side and struggled to her feet. Bedrooms felt too much like hospital rooms—she stumbled into the sitting area and lay on the sofa. It was too short to sleep on—one bolster caught her in the back of her neck, the other, just below the backs of her knees—so she curled her legs and hunched her shoulders and resigned herself to discomfort.

The inactive comport display reflected the dim light that seeped around the window seals. Jani watched it until Neumann's mumbles lowered to nothing and the sweating stopped and she was able to fall into something resembling sleep.

CHAPTER 21

Sam disembarked the tramline that shuttled from the civilian apartment blocks to the base. Even at that early-morning hour, the heat enveloped; by the time he descended the stairs from the elevated passenger drop-off to ground level, he could feel sweat trickle beneath his shirt.

He stopped to study the building signs, and earned a muttered "watch where you're going" from the civvie who banged into his shoulder. *I hate this place in the morning!* Uniforms and civvies bustled in his path. Delivery skimvans laden with supplies blocked entries and walkways. Muffled rumbles emanated from the weapons ranges, echoing off buildings like thunder.

Sam cringed as a sharp report sounded—he stepped off the walkway and ducked beneath the sheltering shade of a black maple until his pounding heart slowed. Of all the things he hated, the booming roll and reverb that issued from the ranges topped the list.

But it was louder this morning—like bombs. *They've broken out the Y-40s today.* The latest-model long-range shooters made a great deal more noise than had their predecessors, the V- and T-series, but design improvements had supposedly made them safer and easier to control.

"Yes, this one will only blow your target to bits if you want it to." He tucked his briefbag under his arm and dashed out into the open. The faster he found a quiet indoor haven, the better he would feel.

He hustled into the safety of the South Central Facilities lobby and removed his handheld from the outer pocket of his bag. *Where am I going?* Who could find their way when surrounded by all these bloody identical buildings!

He flipped through his list of "Reminders." *Odergaard is my Tech One . . . my name is Sam Duong . . . I live in Flat 4A-Forrestal Block.* He paged to the next screen. *South Library!* That's where he wanted to go. A good place to do Gate research, or rent a few hours on a workstation, or catch a nap before the start of a second-shift day.

"Are you all right, sir?"

Sam looked across the lobby at the desk corporal, who eyed him with concern. He forced a smile. "Just taking a break from the heat." He waited a few more minutes, then rose and walked back outside. *I am going to the South Library.* He followed the signs and markers until he reached the five-story white scancrete box.

He crossed the lobby, then wandered aimlessly through the stacks. Departed through one of the side doors. Hurried down the connecting walkway to one of the many satellite office buildings that dotted the base, which was where he meant to go all along. Darted down the hallway and disappeared into the first vacant office he found. It made sense for an archivist to go to a library. Therefore, a library was the last place he wished to be. He suffered from a brain tumor, not stupidity.

Sam didn't know for sure whether someone followed him. The movements he'd glimpsed in entryways and beneath trees the previous night as he walked across the Yard to the tramline platform could have been tricks of moonlight and shadow. The display flutter when he tried to use the comport in his flat could have been random interference from base systems. The trip of his heart each time he locked eyes with a stranger or heard an unfamiliar sound could be due to his medical condition, not the ancient portions of his brain telling him to beware.

No one knows what I found. He and Tory had journeyed to Chicago, to the Active Vessel Archives building. He'd been helping her search for an old equipment record when he'd uncovered the Station Ville Louis-Phillipe cargo transfer. Technically, it did belong in the unsecured bin in which he'd found it, since it contained no obvious Service markers. Only the date, time, and dock entries linked it to the CSS *Kensington*, and that would only set off alarms if you knew what date, time, and dock entries to look for. Which Sam did. Some details managed to stick in his mind, despite Dr. Pimentel's fears and his own disintegrating self-confidence.

He reached into his briefbag's inner compartment and once again reassured himself of the transfer's presence. Encased within its flexible plastic slipcase, the document crackled, the aged parchment dried, almost brittle to the touch. Cheap colony paper, a simple record of what was loaded onto a certain ship at a certain time. Not meant to be saved.

Food. Nothing unusual there—it made sense that the *Kensington* would load more supplies to feed its extra passengers. But synthetics and high-density nutritionals would be the consumables of choice. *Not real meat.* And certainly not real meat packed in agers. Sam had archived active vessel records for many years, and the only ships he recalled taking on agers were command vessels with high-level guests to impress, not combat vessels in emergency status. The containers took up too much room; they required specially trained technicians to maintain calibration or the contents would spoil. If Mako had wanted to feed his evacuees high-quality protein so badly, that's what the kettles were for.

Sam nestled into a chair, maneuvering it so it faced the door. Captain Kilian would approve of his actions, of that he felt sure. She seemed a cautious soul. He hugged that thought close as he did his briefbag, and waited for the hours to pass before their meeting.

He arrived at the SIB a few minutes before twelve up and sat on one of the tree-shaded benches in the building's front yard. He wiped his sweaty face with a pre-dampened dispo, and checked the transfer record again. Then he looked up—his heart lifted as he watched Kilian cross the lawn from the direction of the South Central Base complex.

She wore summerweight trousers, but with the dressier white shirt Sam had seen Yance wear when he had to give a presentation. Unlike most Service clothing, it flattered a woman's figure. The wrap styling accentuated Kilian's waist and bust while the crossover collar framed her dark face.

She terrified him physically—so tall and straight, a woman of line, not of curve. Still, he found himself appreciating her with a bolder eye than he normally would have dared; he felt a surge of pride as he watched other men's gazes follow her. *My Captain of Dark Ice.* He stood as she approached the bench.

"Mr. Duong. I hope you're well." She smiled. "We don't have a lot of time. I'm scheduled for an important meeting at thirteen up. I didn't arrange it, so I couldn't move it. Sorry."

"You have so many meetings." Sam remained standing, finally gesturing for her to sit down first. "This one must be very important. You look very nice."

"Thank you." Kilian dropped her briefbag to the ground. She lowered to the edge of the bench, then moved down with a start as though something surprised her. "It's Office Hours. With a mainline general. I might live." She tensed, hunching her shoulders like Sam did when people pressed around him in the lift.

He leaned toward her. "Are you feeling all right, Captain? You don't look well."

"I'm fine." She had lost her smile. "Would you mind if we went somewhere else?"

"Where?"

"Not indoors." A loud blast sounded from the ranges, and she flinched. "The covered walkways, maybe? I know you don't like the beach."

"I will walk on the beach." Sam injected his voice with a confidence he didn't feel and hoisted his briefbag to his shoulder. "If you're with me." He looked down at her—was it his imagination, or did she shiver? "It's the noise from the weapons ranges, isn't it?"

She stiffened, then nodded. "That's not helping."

"We could go in—"

"*Not inside.*" She offered a sheepish curve of lip that was more grimace than grin. "I'm feeling a little crowded today."

They walked silently across the East Yard, then down the flights of steps that descended to the beach. Sam held his breath as he stepped onto the sand and sank in up to his shoe tops. He stopped. Took another step. Stopped again.

Kilian reached out to him. "Give me your hand, Sam."

Sam held out his hand, sighing as Kilian closed her fingers around his. They felt cool. Dry. She had a strong grip for a woman. He felt her strength course up his arm, through his body.

He looked up the shore and saw the red, blue, and green splashes of sun umbrellas, running children, a group in base casuals struggling to right a volleyball net. *There's nothing to be afraid of here.* Not on this sand. Not now.

Kilian led him to a round wireframe table that was sheltered from the relentless sun by a red-and-white-striped awning. "You said you had some news that would interest me?" She released him, dragged a chair into the center of a wide strip of ruby light, and sat heavily.

Sam looked at the place where she'd touched him—he imagined the imprint of her fingers, like a signet. He slid into the chair opposite her and reached into his bag. "I found this in the city." He tucked the transfer into the fold of that morning's issue of *Blue and Grey*, and pushed it across the table toward her. "Early morning is the best time to search through Active Vessel Archives. The security is not all it should be."

Kilian opened the newssheet—her eyes widened as she studied the document nestled within. "Cargo transfer."

Sam nodded. "Check the date/time stamp."

Kilian did. "Well, well." Her voice emerged stronger, surer. She didn't look cold anymore. "You wanted to see how my idomeni-made scanpack worked—that's the story if anyone asks, OK? I scanned the newssheet." She waited for Sam to nod before she reached to her belt and removed the device from its pouch. "Where did you find this?"

"In an unsecured bin, while I searched for something else." Sam glanced up and down the beach, on the lookout for spectators. "There's nothing on the document that identifies it as Service paper. That's why they let it go."

"All they had to do was check the date." Kilian activated her scanpack; the palm-sized unit's display shimmered bright green. "That tells me that whoever took the other records had little or no experience with documents. Covering the main doc trail is a snap, it's the peripherals that'll trip you up every time." She brushed the 'pack's bottom surface over the document in a regular left-to-right, top-to-bottom pattern. When her scanpack display flashed green, she deactivated it and returned it to its pouch. "It's the real thing," she said as she fingered a browned corner. "Not high-quality paper. I'm amazed it held up for eighteen years."

Sam nodded. "I don't think that bin was opened much. We got lucky."

Kilian studied the transfer. "Agers. Two of them." She looked across the table. "Feeding those evacuees well, weren't they?" The act of examining the paper had energized her—her dark eyes glittered.

Sam swallowed. When Yance looked at him the way Kilian did now, it never boded well for some poor would-be paper fiddler. "The evacuees were Family. I suppose they were entitled." He scraped the soles of his shoes against the scancrete. "I think I wasted your time—that document means nothing."

Kilian stared out toward the lake, where a couple of wave-gliders banked and weaved across the still surface. One glider cut a turn too sharply—his iridescent board shot out from under him and tumbled through the air. "Mako faced a court of inquiry when he returned to Earth." She waited for the board to strike the lake surface before turning away. "He mishandled remains. Ebben's, Unser's, and Fitzhugh's."

"Caldor's." Sam squirmed under Kilian's startled stare. "Her death cert had gone missing, too."

"So it did." Kilian crossed her legs and locked her hands around her knee. The red light that filtered through the awning rouged her complexion, making her look sunburnt. "How many died during the evac, total?"

"Sixteen."

"That's a lot of bodies to store in three cramped ships."

"The morgue coolers—"

"Three per sick bay. That's nine bodies—what did they do with the other seven?"

Sam rubbed his stomach. The conversation made it ache. "Body bags in the hold?"

"Want to know what I think?" Kilian smiled, a frosty twist of lip that reminded Sam uneasily of Pierce. "I think they ran out of body bags. And someone thought, oh aren't these convenient, and emptied out the meat and shoved the bodies in the agers. They probably thought they were reefer units." She chuckled. "I'd have hated to be the poor bastard who cracked those seals after two months." Her happy expression vanished when she looked at Sam. "Sorry. My sense of humor." She sat forward and spread her hands out on the tabletop, spacing them so that they both were bathed in red-tinged light.

Sam imagined the shadowing as the thinnest film of blood. "Captain, are you an augment?"

"Yes."

"Dr. Pimentel told me things, too. About agitation and feeling sick."

She smiled brilliantly. "You remembered that!"

"Yes." Sam tried again. "Should you be sitting in the red like this?"

The smile turned strange. "I find it energizing." She grew serious. "Has a mainline colonel with a nasty facial scar been turning up at the SIB over the past few weeks?"

"You mean Niall Pierce?"

"*You* know him, too?"

Sam shook his head. "I know of him, from the Rauta Shèràa Base files."

"He was part of the evac."

"Yes. And I saw him at the hospital once. He was there to pick up scan results. I haven't seen him at the SIB."

"I have." Kilian stood up and walked out into the blazing sun. In the distance, the booms of the Y-40s shook the air, but she didn't seem to hear them anymore. Her timorousness had disappeared—energy seemed to ripple from her now, like heat from a roadbed. "Do you think you're being watched?"

"Yes." Sam's hands shook—he braced them against the table.

"Do you own a weapon?"

"No. You think I'll need one?"

"If you don't know how to use it, it may do you more harm than good."

"I'm very good at running and hiding."

"Not bad skills to have." The grim smile again. Then Kilian glanced at her timepiece. "I have to get going." She walked back to the table and hoisted her bag, then gestured to Sam with that child-like backward wave. "Let's go."

"No." Sam shook his head. "I want to sit here a while." He looked out over the water, at the lakeskimmers and sailboards. "Maybe I'll even walk in the sand."

"You're sure?"

"Yes."

The dark in Kilian's eyes softened. The goddess touched. "You're a very brave man."

"As long as I know you're here." Sam smiled up at her. "I couldn't do it alone. I could never do it alone."

Kilian started to speak, blinked, turned away. She strode across the sand, her step hurried. As though there were someplace she needed to go. Or someplace she needed to leave behind.

CHAPTER 22

Evan slept fitfully and awoke feeling restless. As pink-orange wisps of cloud drifted through the sunrise sky, he tended his roses, following the checklist Joaquin had given him to the letter. Hours passed as he applied nutrients and fungicides, cut back straggly branches, slaughtered the weeds that had dared poke through the raked and treated soil.

For the first time, he found himself enjoying the work. Sweat and repetition helped him think.

"So, Quino would rather think me brain-impaired than believe Mako killed the charges against Jani to save Pierce." Evan yanked at a stubborn pig's ear, breaking the plant at ground level. "He controls my access to secured information, which means I can't investigate further without his buy-in." He knelt and dug into the ground with his hands. After a few strong tugs, he wrenched the root free, spraying clods of dirt in all directions. "Shroud was right. Quino wants to cut me loose—he's tossing up that Haárin option as a smoke screen." Well, he had learned a lot about the esteemed Mr. Loiaza in the thirty years of their acquaintance. "You snake me, I may just make some notes about you, too." He wiped smeared earth from his face and hands and continued weeding.

"So who got to him, Anais or Roshi?" Evan paused in front of a creeping Charlie that had taken over a shady corner near the Wolfshead Westminster. "I'd bet Anais. Quino doesn't give a damn about the Service, but he sure as hell cares about Cabinet Court retainer fees."

He tore out the creeping Charlie with a hand rake, then collected the round-leafed tendrils and stuffed them into a decomp bag. In a few days, he'd remove the rotted plant matter and fold it back into the soil to nourish the roses, the vanquished enemy reworked for his purpose. Government in a nutshell, part two.

He collected his implements and concoctions, trudged to the small shed adjoining the house, and returned them to the appropriate hooks, racks, and shelves. Pulled the flask from his trouser pocket and took a draw.

The *breep* of the front-entry buzzer greeted Evan as he entered the house. Halvor had already departed to run errands, and Markhart worked upstairs before lunch, which left him with the unusual task of answering his own door.

He didn't check the security display to see who waited outside. If the door system announced a visitor, then his jailers must have already cleared them. So he released the panel, swept it aside, and found himself nose to nose with an agitated Hugh Tellinn.

"Mr. van Reuter." Tellinn looked over his shoulder, then back at him, his movements as stiff and awkward as they had been in Shroud's parlor.

Who does he want to pound into the carpet now? "Dr. Tellinn." Evan looked past the man to see if either of his neighbors had wandered to their front yards to check out the action in person. Both areas looked clear, which meant they had stayed inside and used scanners instead. "Come in."

The physician stepped inside. "Thank you for seeing me," he said softly. "I understand this isn't the best time for you."

"Not your problem, Doctor. Don't give it a second thought." Evan regarded Tellinn with a critical eye. *So, Val, you forsake young and dumb for old and smart and look what happens.* He gets jittery and seeks out the enemy. "Is this a medical visit?" he asked for form's sake.

"Only officially. So I could get permission to come here." Tellinn took a tentative step toward the sitting room. "I—I need—I need your help."

"I'm not in the position to help myself, much less you."

"Just hear me out. I think after you do, you'll change your mind." Tellinn walked around Evan into the sitting room, then glanced back at him in nervous expectation. "I'm here about Jani Kilian."

Oh no. Evan fell in behind him and sat in his usual lounge chair. "Val didn't send you here in an effort to bypass John, did he?"

Tellinn perched on the edge of the sofa. "No. If Val knew I'd come here, he'd kill me." He started to rock, a slight forward-and-back motion, like a continuous nod of the head. "I need you to contact

Jani the next time you go to Sheridan. I need you to give her something."

Evan studied Tellinn's face for some sign he joked, but saw only dour sincerity laced with panic. "I won't be returning to Sheridan for some time." *If ever.* "The most serious charges against Jani are to be dropped, and she's to be given a medical discharge. Since that's the case, the SIB no longer needs what information I have to offer."

"But surely you can think up some excuse, tell your attorney that you've remembered something important." Tellinn stilled his rocking long enough to reach into his inner shirt pocket and pull out what looked like a cigar case. When he snapped it open, however, steam puffed—he removed a frosted cylinder the size of Evan's index finger. "She needs to have the contents of this syringe injected as soon as possible." He slowly inverted the cylinder, displaying the straw yellow liquid contained within.

Evan eyed the cylinder with dismay. For years, his own physicians had threatened him with similar devices. "That's a gene-therapy cocktail."

"Yes." Mild surprise dulled Tellinn's edginess. "If you know what it is, you must realize the condition she's in."

"I remember what you said in John's parlor. John didn't think you knew what you were talking about."

"Dr. Shroud had allowed his ego to come before the needs of his patient." Tellinn rendered his own diagnosis of the situation quickly and coolly. "I had to bribe one of his hybridization specialists to help me manufacture this. It's primarily designed to repair the defect in Jani's heme pathway, but it also contains components to fix the worst of her metabolic abnormalities as well." He resumed his rocking. "They're packing her with engineered carbohydrates because that's the diet prescribed for patients with AIP, but she's synthesizing idomeni digestive enzymes that are cleaving the molecules in different places, which is leading to the buildup of toxic metabolites in her tissues—"

Evan jumped in before the torrent of words turned to flood. "Dr. Tellinn! I can't help you!"

"But . . ." Tellinn stilled, and blinked in bewilderment. "Val said you agreed to help us. You felt guilty because of the way you treated Jani years ago and you wanted to make it up to her."

Vladislav's got nothing on you for dramatic nonsense. Evan squeezed the arm of his chair. His hand closed over a Crème Caramel petal left over from yesterday's encounter with Joaquin, and he rolled it between his fingers. "Dr.—"

"Call me Hugh," Tellinn interrupted hopefully.

Evan glanced at the wisp of flower in his hand. "It sounds as though you don't know the entire story where Jani and I are concerned."

"I confess, I don't keep up with events as well as I should." Tellinn's face lightened with an apologetic smile. "But Val said you almost married—"

"John Shroud has circumstantial evidence linking me to Jani's transport explosion. I had nothing to do with it, of course"—Evan's fingers worked harder, grinding the petal to fragments—"but it looks very bad, and I'm in no position to fight it. In other words, he held a shooter to my head. That's the only reason I agreed to perjure myself. I don't care what happens to Jani." He brushed the bits of rose to the floor. "But now that she's to be discharged, it's all academic."

Tellinn's eagerness evaporated. "No, Mr. van Reuter, not *all* of it." He glared at the cocktail cylinder, then shoved it back into its case. "You won't help?"

"I can't."

"Her organs will fail, one by one. Her brain will be irreversibly damaged. She will die."

"Even if I could talk myself onto the base and somehow arrange to meet Jani, I could never convince her to take anything from me." Evan felt his pocket for the flask, then pulled his hand away. *Not in front of the children.* "I assume you've tried to contact her Service doctors yourself."

"Just last night. Begged my way as far as a Roger Pimentel. Received a very cold, 'thank you, Doctor, but we have things under control' in response." Tellinn's face had paled to a Shroud-like pallor. He sat forward, elbows on knees, hands clasped across his forehead.

Evan looked over the top of Tellinn's head to the window and the outdoors beyond. He wished he'd remained outside, never heard the buzzer. "John loves her. If he has to resort to brute force or invoke compassionate intervention to get into Sheridan, he will."

"I don't think you understand the extreme animosity that exists between Service Medical and Neoclona."

"I know all about that. If John hadn't accused the Service Surgeon-General of promoting butchery last year when she refused to allow Neoclona to assist in the training of Service physicians, he wouldn't find him on the outside looking in now."

"There's more involved than that." Tellinn's face had the nauseated cast of a man who had bitten into an apple and found half a worm. "I think the Service higher-ups who remember the idomeni civil war hold John responsible for the destruction of Rauta Shèràa Base. They feel that if he hadn't angered the idomeni by getting involved in illegal research, there would have been much less outrage directed at the remaining humans as the war wound down."

"Knevçet Shèràa led to what happened at Rauta Shèràa Base, and John Shroud had nothing to do with that." Evan massaged the rough upholstery until his fingers stung. "How many times do I have to tell you, Doctor? I can't help you."

"She's been through so much."

"I hate to sound cold, but she brought a lot of it upon herself."

Tellinn stared at him, tired eyes searching in vain for something. Then he stood slowly and walked, back bowed, step heavy. He paused in the room entry and turned back to Evan. "Val tells me stories about Rauta Shèràa Base. He leaves a lot out—I can tell from the way he jokes to fill the holes." He hesitated, dark eyes reflecting the horror described. "He talks about the last night. The Night of the Blade. The dead quiet when the bombing finally stopped, and the Laum streamed out of their homes and lined up to be slaughtered." He looked at Evan. "Humans don't line up to be killed."

"Not unless they're forced, no."

"So the humans who died there probably weren't killed by Haárin, because the Haárin weren't carrying the sorts of weapons that could compel them to stop. Val thinks they were executed by criminals for failing to come through on contracts, or just to keep them from talking."

"That's certainly possible."

"Jani wasn't a criminal. She got into trouble for fighting the criminals." Tellinn's hands twitched. He kicked at the carpet—the tread of his shoe caught so that he almost lost his balance. Gone clumsy again. "So how can you say Rauta Shèràa Base was her fault? Seems to me quite a few *humans* went over the edge there. Panicked. Rode the madness of the moment. They're the ones to blame, not her."

Evan reached for his flask again. Stopped himself again. "Jani won't die. Remember that she has Nema on her side, and Prime Minister Cao knows she dare not anger him." He stood, hoping that Tellinn would take the hint. "Something will shake loose."

"I hope you're right." Tellinn accepted the invitation to get lost. "Thank you for nothing, Mr. van Reuter." He headed for the door—it swept aside, and he almost collided with a grocery-carton-laden Halvor.

"I'll be outside," Evan informed the confused aide. He had the flask out of his pocket before he stepped out of the house.

It would have been nice to officially blame the Haárin or some criminal syndicate for the deaths of Ebben, Unser, and Fitzhugh. That would have provided answers enough to cut off the questions and the rumors that sprang from the events of that night. And the magic Joaquin could have worked with a few holos of the blade-cut dead or signs of ritual execution would have dispelled once and for all the cloud of suspicion hanging over Evan. *Nothing works like firm, hard paper.* From there, it would have been an easy leap to suppose Jani's transport crash the product of Haárin vengeance or criminal bungling. *And I'd have been out of this house by autumn.* He ducked into the shed, leaned against the sheet-metal wall, and emptied the flask down his throat. *If not for Roshi's screwup.*

He kicked at the decomp bag, distended by weed bulk and digestion gasses, and gagged as a warm belch of half-rotted vegetation stench puffed through gaps in the opening. He grasped the handle of the bag and dragged it across the floor to rest near the solvent storage ventilator. The digestion mechanisms built into the sack worked quickly—in a few days, there would be no sign of what the muck had been or where it had come from—

Something flitted in Evan's head, like a whisper. He picked through his myriad thoughts trying to recover it, but it wriggled away like a fish.

The madness of the moment. . . .

He stood in the doorway of the shed, Tellinn's words echoing in his head, and stared at the decomp bag until Markhart called him in to lunch.

CHAPTER 23

Jani set aside the issue of *Blue and Grey* that she'd been paging through, and stifled a yawn as post-augie languor settled over her. Sitting in a stream of red light wasn't the medically approved way to deal with Neumann's hallucination, but she'd grown desperate since she'd awakened that morning to hear his off-key bass emerge from her bathroom. *I always dreamed of this, Kilian,* he said when he stuck his shower-damp head out the door. *All you'd have to do is strip and join me to make this moment complete.*

A few minutes later had found her trudging barefoot across the South Yard, wearing the same base casuals she'd slept in, duffel on her shoulder. It had still been dark, thankfully. No A&S-holes out and about to find her in sweat-stained dishabille.

Working on sleep-deprived autopilot, she had showered in the women's locker room of the South Central Gymnasium. Dressed. Applied makeup with a trembling hand. And walked out into the blaze of day to find Neumann leaning in the gymnasium doorway, waiting for her. He'd stood close enough for her to smell his breath drops, the cinnamon candies he had sucked incessantly.

I watched you through the gap in the shower curtain, and you didn't see me.

"Nervous, Jani?" Friesian shuffled through a file and made a notation into his handheld. He had gone the "B" shirt route, as well. And had his hair trimmed.

"No more than usual, considering the circumstances."

"They will probably holocam this, even though it's a non-judicial. Just forget it's there and act natural."

Act natural, he says. She'd have a hard enough time staying awake. She had tried to give Neumann the boot by breakfasting decently, then making sure her morning in Foreign Transactions remained uneventful by locking herself in her office and letting her comport screen her calls. He hadn't shown up—she thought she'd beaten him.

Then he had reappeared during her meeting with Sam Duong, dogging her shoulder and offering advice on how to get Burkett off her back. Foul comments all, and some physically impossible besides.

So she drove augie to the edge, felt the white light in her head and the hurricane gales at her feet, and pitched Neumann over the side, at least for a while. *Roger would kill me if he knew.* But augie's neurochemical magic had worked wonders—she felt better than she had for a week. *Just a little wobbly . . .*

A gentle throat-clearing sounded from the opposite side of the anteroom. General Burkett's adjutant spoke a few words into her comport, then glanced at Jani and Friesian. "You may go in, Major. Captain."

Jani stood slowly, gripping the arms of her chair for support. She sniffed, smelled only filtered office air, and offered silent thanks. She followed Friesian to the door, let him palm it open, and preceded him inside. As expected, she saw Burkett sitting at his glossy bloodwood desk, glare at the ready.

She didn't, however, expect to see Frances Hals sitting across from him, nor another older, blond-haired woman who, judging from the stars on her collar and the scanpack on her hip, could only be Major General Hannah Eiswein, commander of the First Documents and Documentation Division.

I'm gonna die. "Captain Kilian reporting as ordered, sir."

"Come in, Captain." Burkett's gaze shifted to Friesian, and his frown deepened. "Major?"

"Major Piers Friesian, General. Defense Command." His voice sounded tentative as he looked at Hals and Eiswein. "I'm Captain Kilian's legal counsel."

"There's no need for that, Major." Eiswein smiled. She appeared companionable, with the sort of relaxed, unlined face that *implied* an even temper. "This isn't a disciplinary action."

Friesian shot Jani a befuddled look. His thick, black eyebrows knit. "Ma'am, my client was given to understand—"

"Circumstances have changed, Major." Eiswein smiled again, more coolly. "Captain Kilian's role here will be more in a consulting capacity. If you feel at all uncomfortable about this, of course you may stay. But you'll be wasting your time."

Friesian settled back on his heels, chin raised, eyes narrowing. Jani could read the questions in his expression. The concern. The stars.

"If it's all the same to you, ma'am, I'd prefer to sit in on this." He gave Jani a "be careful" nod as he walked to a small conference table that basked in the light of the office's window-wall. "I do possess top-level security clearance, if consultations reach that point."

"They shouldn't," Eiswein said softly as she withdrew a recording board from the briefbag by her chair. Pink-skinned and cushy, she looked the polar opposite of the tanned, narrow-faced Burkett. "Captain Kilian. The famous Eyes and Ears." She gestured toward the empty chair between her and Hals. "I've been looking forward to meeting you."

Hals offered the barest smile as Jani approached; the expression altered to one of concern as she took her seat. "Are you feeling all right, Captain?"

"Yes, ma'am." Jani caught herself on the chair arms just in time to keep from collapsing into it. "Trouble sleeping." She noted that Hals wore the less formal light grey "A" short-sleeve, as did Burkett and Eiswein.

We're overdressed, Piers. Jani looked around Burkett's office, a showcase of wine-red cabinetry and satin-finish steel, on the alert for hidden lieutenants with holocams. She faced front to find Burkett glowering at her.

"Looking for something, Captain?"

"Just admiring your office, sir." It took true force of will for her to smile at him. He made no effort to hide his feelings—the animosity rolled across his desk and buffeted her like a wave.

"Well, General, why don't we get started." Eiswein's voice, flavored by her German provincial accent, sounded at the same time soft and clipped. The rules of the game being what they were, if her sideline double stars had been able to stand up to Burkett's mainline single and quash any disciplinary actions against Jani and Hals, that meant someone in Supreme Command had thrown their vote her way.

Jani could imagine the scene. Perhaps it had even been Mako himself who had said, *you gave the wrong orders, Cal, and I'm ordering you to back off.*

Eiswein proved gracious in victory, at least for the time being. She ignored Burkett's choppy mood, and had only smiles for her two rebellious dexxie underlings. "Colonel, please bring Captain Kilian up to speed."

"Yes, ma'am." Hals activated her board; an open file bloomed on the display. "Captain Kilian is, of course, an old hand in dealing with the idomeni. She already understands our major issues."

"Such as figuring out the difference between what's important to us and what's important to them, ma'am?" Jani looked around innocently. Burkett met her eyes, his face like stone.

"But surprises still occur," Hals added hastily. "Scanpack health, for example, has suddenly become a pressing concern." Her voice lowered in genuine distress. "Lieutenant Domenici's 'pack suffered a stroke soon after we returned from the embassy. It can't recognize certain symbols anymore, and can't decode the right sides of chips. Scantech blamed the elevated temperature in the embassy. They said nutrient degraded, formed a clot, and blew out her fourth octant region."

Jani thought back to the embassy visit. Everyone had complained of the heat except her. "If 'packs are experiencing heat distress, the embassy interior must have been at least forty-five degrees. You need to switch out spent nutrient more often. Make sure you're using a warm-weather brand, and that fluid levels are topped off. Has that been the only stroke?"

Hals nodded. "Yes, although we have had some scares during previous visits. Transient ischemic attacks—the 'packs malfunction for a few hours, then snap back. Tech Service is starting to write papers about our problems, and that is a worry."

"Lieutenant Domenici will, in fact, need to have her 'pack replaced," Eiswein interjected. "I approved the requisition an hour ago. The damage proved so extensive that it's cheaper to grow her a new one than try to fix the old." She patted her own 'pack pouch absently. "They'll farm her cells tomorrow. It will be six weeks before she'll have something she can begin to teach." Her eyes bored into Jani's. They shone palest blue, like Burkett's steel. "So not only are we dealing with the replacement of an extremely expensive piece of equipment, but I'm also out one experienced dexxie in an already-stretched department for the time it takes her to retrain her 'pack. How long does that take on average, Colonel?"

Hals called up another screen on her board. "Four months, ma'am. On average."

"And that's assuming she returns to FT, of which there's no guarantee." The color rose in Eiswein's face as she hit her stride. "Dexxies get edgy when their equipment's threatened, and the knowledge that merely doing their *routine*, *uncomplicated* jobs could result in irreversible damage to the devices on which their livelihoods depend is enough to make them pretty damned edgy!" Her anger held a particularly distressing aspect, like being chewed out by your favorite aunt.

Burkett remained silent throughout, although he did twitch about in his leather-upholstered chair as though he needed to adjust his underwear. Especially after Eiswein spat out the words *routine* and *uncomplicated.* Direct quotes, no doubt. Jani almost felt sorry for him. If Eiswein hammered him like this in front of subordinates, what had she said to him one-on-one?

Scheißkopf? She struggled to keep a straight face. "So, along with the measurable loss in equipment and efficiency, FT may also find itself dealing with a serious morale problem."

Hals sighed. "There are so many minefields where the idomeni are concerned, things we think nothing of. We know we can't wear red. That we can't carry in food, not even so much as a pack of gum. My concern is that one or more of our rebellious souls might resort to sabotage. Considering how important the idomeni think we are, the magnitude of the perceived insult would be great indeed."

Burkett finally opened his mouth. "And you've made no effort to supply me with the names of those souls, Colonel, despite my repeated requests."

"Give those souls the tools to maintain their equipment and you'll stop the revolution in its tracks." Jani pulled her scanpack out of its pouch and studied the underside. "My 'pack was manufactured on Shèrá as part of a joint humanish-idomeni project. Lots of effort went into synthesizing the heat-dissipation system. It's functioned flawlessly for over twenty years. I don't even consider it exceptional anymore." She looked at Eiswein. "Did anyone talk to Three through Six about this? They have the same type unit I do—they could have advised you on what to expect."

"Three through six?" Burkett muttered crankily. "What does that mean?"

"The Captain is referring to her fellow Academy graduates." Eiswein made a notation into her board. "The funny thing is, Captain, that whenever we dexxies talk about the fabled Academy days, we talk about you, and we talk about the late Hansen Wyle. The others don't make the cut." She regarded Jani intently. "Shortsighted of us, was it not?"

"Ma'am," Jani replied. Eiswein's examination possessed a distinctly maternal quality, if one's mother had the talent for seeing through to the back of one's head. "If you're going to keep working with the idomeni, you need to act. Right now, FT is taking all the hits. You need to start dishing out."

"That's Diplo's job," Burkett growled.

"From what I gather," Eiswein countered, "any negotiation with the idomeni must take place on many different levels. They believe existence is a series of incremental steps, like multiple stairways approaching from all different directions, and every undertaking is approached the same way. Any resolution of this Lake Michigan Strip matter will be reached in the records room as well as the negotiating room."

"My thoughts on that, I believe, have been added to the record, General."

"Yes, General, but be that as it may, we have our mandate from Supreme Command—"

Jani glanced sideways at Hals at the same time Hals glanced sideways at her. Then Hals activated her stylus and executed a quick sketch. With a few rapid strokes, she outlined a pudgy matador, cape in one hand, scanpack in the other, advancing upon a snorting bull that had been branded on his backside with a single large star—

Jani faced front and focused on a point on the wall above Burkett's head.

"—and participate in this process, we will." Eiswein smoothed an errant lock of hair behind her ear and eased back in her chair.

Burkett drummed his fingers on his desktop. Once. Twice. Thrice. "Could we just ask the idomeni to turn the heat down?"

"You could, sir," Jani answered carefully. "But it would be better if you made a bigger splash. They know you're miserable—all they have to do is look at you. They're enjoying watching you sweat, both literally and figuratively."

She paused before continuing. "A visual display of your adjustment to their conditions would act as an issued challenge, and win you a little of your own back. It needs to be something obvious, something the idomeni can appreciate. They find us so difficult to read that an explicit action by us would both please them and take them by surprise." A spot of personal whimsy popped into her head, and she tossed it out to the house. "Wear base casuals the next time you're called in."

Hals sighed. "God, that would be *so* comfortable!" She starting making notes. "Do you think we could bring little cooler units, too? The ones you can set up on your desk—"

"*Colonel!*" Burkett's bronzed skin flared maroon. "That's outrageous!" He thumped his fist on his desk. "I'll be damned if I ever represent my Service in a T-shirt and trainers."

"Don't forget the shorts, sir." Jani heard a tiny, strangled sound emerge from Hals's throat. Burkett twisted around in his chair to face her, but before he could erupt, Eiswein cut him off.

"Calm down, General." She beamed like Mère Christmas. "I like it."

Burkett's jaw dropped. "General—!"

"Well, why not! I'm always hearing about the idomeni's playful side, their need to make and accept challenge, the constant one-upmanship they seem to thrive on. And here we are, with a golden opportunity to stick it in their ear, and you want us to back off in the name of *propriety*?" Eiswein gave the word a gamy twist, making it sound like something nice people didn't talk about.

Burkett looked stricken. "Aren't there any alternatives?" The hard look he directed at Jani held a hint of pleading. "What did you wear, Captain, when you were stationed at Rauta Shèràa Base?"

"We were issued desertweights, sir."

Burkett nodded in relief. "We can ship some of those in from Bonneville or Aqaba. We'll have them in a couple of hours."

Hals shook her head. "Base casuals are an official part of the Sheridan-issue uniform set, sir. If you name it Uniform of the Day for our trip to the embassy, no matter how strange it may seem to some, we are technically in A&S compliance. But desertweights are *not* an official part of the Sheridan-issue uniform set; therefore, we would need sign-off from A&S before we could even place the order."

"We're in a crisis situation, Colonel."

"Yes, sir. The problem is, sir, that if you go to A&S with this type of request . . ." Hals faltered. "It's the Joint Perception Committee, sir. The Cabinet-Service group that monitors how the civilian public perceives the Service. They'll get wind of it, and once they do they're going to stick their—get involved."

One little vein stood out in Burkett's temple. "Which Cabinet Ministers sit on that committee?"

"Exterior Minister Ulanova, for one—"

"Scratch that," Eiswein entoned glumly. "Ulanova would kick our sand castle over just to watch us cry." She pondered. "We place the nice, aboveboard order for the desertweights, via A&S, and amass our weapons for the fight. For this next visit, which is scheduled for early tomorrow morning, we go casual."

"You need my buy-in for any off-the-beaten-path scheme." Burkett's voice had thinned. The stressed metal had been drawn very fine, and seemed about to snap. "I want it on the record that I disagree strongly with our constantly and consistently putting idomeni sensibilities before those of our own people." He didn't look at Jani as he spoke; he didn't have to. "Why are we always giving in to them?"

"They gave in to us just by the act of coming here," Jani said to the side of his face. "Just by the act of living here. We've discussed this before, sir. Your refusing to see the point doesn't make it any less valid or any less important."

"In other words, what's a little dignity if it saves us the Lake Michigan Strip?" Eiswein deactivated her board and stuffed it back in her briefbag. "Your buy-in, as you call it, would certainly make the row easier to hoe, but if it doesn't prove forthcoming, I suppose we'll have to carry on without it."

Before Burkett could counter, a voice piped from the far corner of the room.

"Ma'am? Sir?" Friesian spoke quickly, as though he'd been trying to fit a word in edgewise for some time. "If Captain Kilian is to leave the base so soon, we need to clear her through the JA immediately." He looked at Hals. "Colonel, with whom did you talk to arrange clearance for the captain's previous trip off base? I did not receive a restricted-movement repeal related to that trip, and with her status, it's vital I have those on file."

Burkett stared at Jani. "You're restricted to base?"

"Yes, sir." She cast a wary eye at the four confused faces watching her. "I assumed everyone knew."

"I did, but . . ." Hals fell silent.

Burkett seemed to be having trouble wrapping his mind around Jani's status, too. "You were under *official* restriction when you traveled off base to the embassy?"

"Yes, sir," Jani answered, more harshly than was prudent. "Is there a problem?"

"I don't understand this at all." Pimentel stood in front of the imaging display and flipped through the multiple deeptissue scans of Jani's right arm. "Where did the calcification come from?"

One of the many new medical faces that had surrounded Jani for the past two hours spoke up. "My best guess is that when they implanted the chip at Constanza, they used standard nerve solder, which is, of course, human-compatible." She nodded toward Jani. "Captain Kilian rejected the solder as foreign material and sealed it off from the rest of her tissue. In sealing off the solder, she sealed off the rest of the chip as well, causing the security function to fail."

"Not all the way." Jani massaged the crook of her right arm, from where William Tell Pimentel had withdrawn about half her blood. "My arm hurt like hell as soon as I passed through the Gate. By the time we returned from the idomeni embassy, it had gone numb."

The internist waved a hand. "Captain, trust me, 'hurt like hell' doesn't begin to describe the pain restrictees feel when they try to leave their allowed area. Prisoners pass out. We've even had a few try to cut the chips out themselves—luckily, we got to them first." She wandered up to the imaging display. "Has anyone notified the Judge Advocate?"

Jani had been thinking longingly of sleep, but mention of the JA jarred her alert. "Why do you need to call them?"

"Your chip's security function needs to be reset. Only someone from the JA can do that." Pimental studied the image again, and shook his head. "Judging from the looks of this thing, they'll need to insert a new chip. We're going to have to keep you here until we can perform the surgery." He walked to the door, the rest of the medicos falling in behind him. "Major Friesian is holed up in the sunroom. I'll speak with him. Under the circumstances, I think he should notify the JA."

The removal of Jani's calcified ID chip and the implantation of her new one were performed in a cramped operating theater, under the official eye of a blasé sergeant major who observed the magnified interior of Jani's lower arm without a blink of discomfort.

They anchored the chip with surgical glue rather than nerve solder. They couldn't risk using anesthetic, the neurosurgeon told Jani, because of her history of idiosyncratic reactions to common medications. Instead, after they clamped her arm into the surgical sleeve, they applied pin blocks that supposedly disrupted nerve transmissions just as well. They didn't. Not without the magnetic-pulse adjuncts, which they couldn't use because a magburst could blitz the new chip. Pimentel stood behind her and massaged the knots out of her shoulders, and they gave her a dental appliance to bite down on so she wouldn't damage her teeth when she clenched her jaw.

After the neurosurgeon finished, she recommended cold packs for the pain. Jani's street Acadian reply drew blank stares from both her and Pimentel. The sergeant major, however, betrayed her origins by chewing her lower lip and staring at the display until her eyes watered.

As soon as Jani had been settled with a cold pack and instructions for caring for the incision, everyone left. Except Pimentel.

"I'm sorry about that, Jani." He dragged a stool near her surgical chair and sat. "I've scheduled you for an appointment with someone from Gene Therapeutics tomorrow."

Jani repositioned the cold pack. "I thought you wanted to wait."

"I don't think we can." Pimentel stared at his hands. For the first time, his voice sounded tentative. "I ran a routine liver-enzyme scan while we were waiting for your imaging analysis. I'm seeing values I've never seen before, and I'm not seeing things I should see." He looked at Jani, eyes pitted by circles, skin grey. The self-confident physician of only a few days ago seemed never to have existed. "Internal Medicine has a team of med techs working to develop assays that can identify and quantify your enzymatic activity. Hepatology has advised we farm your liver immediately so we can start growing a replacement, and so we can assemble an adjunct in case you go into failure."

"I feel *fine*." Jani forced her voice to be strong. "Not great, but not that sick. My department is required at the idomeni embassy tomorrow morning. I *have* to go."

"Not if I feel you're in danger," Pimentel replied, in a voice that sounded surer than it had all afternoon.

Jani spent over three hours in Gene Therapeutics being sampled, scoped, and scanned. More pin blocks, this time augmented by the magnetic pulse. Together, they deadened the pain, though not the eerie sensation of *things* being removed from her abdomen.

The med techs' cobbled assays told the hepatologist some of what he needed to know about the state of her internal organs. That allayed Pimentel's fears sufficiently that he agreed not to admit her. He did, however, make her spend a few postop hours in the sunroom. Just to be on the safe side, he said, which didn't make Jani feel safe at all. She cheered up a little, though, when Ischi stopped by on his way home to the BOQ to drop off her paper mail.

"You didn't have to do this, Lieutenant," Jani said as she laid out the few thin envelopes before her on the table. One contained an offer to join the South Central Players, while another held an invitation to the All-Base Volleyball Tournament.

"Oh, yes I did, ma'am." Ischi leaned down and with one finger, tapped a crimson-edged white envelope out of the stack like a trickster picking his card. "Read the front."

"One North Lakeside." Jani felt her tender stomach clench as she peeled the envelope seal and removed the stiff, gold-edged card. "Admiral-General and Mrs. Hiroshi Mako cordially invite you and a guest to attend an Open House . . ." Her voice faded.

"How about that!" Ischi bubbled. "Some people wait for *years* to get their invitation. But you've only had your number a couple of days."

Oh, I think someone's had my number for longer than that. "Yeah," Jani replied. "How about it."

CHAPTER 24

The next morning dawned, as had all the previous ones, clear and hot. Jani stood by the people-mover, dispo of fruit drink in hand, and watched the rest of Foreign Transactions gather. She'd had an early night—Pimentel's dour pronouncements concerning the state of her health, combined with the lack of news from the Misty Center, had made her too grumpy to socialize. She'd remained in her rooms. Read newssheets. Debated calling Lucien and decided against. Discussed Niall Pierce's odd behavior with Val the Bear.

She had also waited for Neumann to reappear. He hadn't. At least something had gone right.

The sound of laughter brought her back to the present; she watched the rising sun illuminate her coworkers' sleepy eyes and sheepish grins. Dressed in T-shirts, shorts, and trainers, scanpacks hanging from belts and shoulder slings, they looked like Sheridan's first team in the all-dexxie Olympics.

"What do you think, Captain?" Colonel Hals gestured toward the milling group. Ischi, athletic-looking enough to appear at home in the abbreviated uniform of the day, busied himself checking off names on a recording board. Meanwhile, the less toned Vespucci, red-faced and fidgety, assisted a couple of underlings with last-minute 'pack assessments.

Jani eyed assorted flaccid limbs. "I think there's going to be a stampede on the gym when we get back." She looked at Hals, who regarded her impatiently. "When word of this leaks out, the self-appointed arbiters will have plenty to say."

"That's a given." Hals sipped her steaming coffee. "What about the Vynshàrau?"

Jani bit into a slice of carefully scanned breakfast cake. The smell of the coffee hadn't agreed with her stomach, but otherwise, she felt good. Not one bit sleepy. Hyper, actually. Floaty, as though she'd drunk a glass of wine. "Officially, I think they'll be relieved. I can't predict individual reactions."

"But you went to school with them?"

"Yes, but we didn't mix."

"Except for Hantìa?"

"Only because she approached us."

"Wasn't that unusual? I would have thought they'd have waited for you to come to them. I thought that except for Tsecha, all the idomeni felt themselves superior to you." Hals coughed out Nema's official name. A good job, as though she'd practiced.

Jani shrugged. "The Vynshà hadn't yet ascended to rau, so they still had room to maneuver. It was up to the Laumrau to hold the snobbery standard." She flashed a smile she didn't feel. "Hantìa was disputatious, even by Vynshà standards. She liked sticking her fingers between the bars."

"Did any of you ever bite?" Hals grew restive as the silence lengthened. "I'd like an answer, Captain."

Oh hell. It never failed. Why did the events from your past that you hoped remained buried forever always disinter themselves at the worst possible time? "I . . . hit her, once."

"You *hit* her!" Hals lowered her voice as people turned to look. "Define *hit*."

Jani mimed a right uppercut. "It was our first term at Academy—"

"I don't need a history lesson."

"Yes, ma'am, you do. She found out that Hansen Wyle and I had been sneaking food into our study carrels. We stayed in the equivalent of a dormitory, but we couldn't eat or even store any food there. If we wanted to eat, we had to travel to the human enclave, two kilometers outside Rauta Shèràa's perimeter. It took an hour or more to skim there on an average traffic day. Three or more hours to make the round-trip. We already traveled there twice a day for regular meals. We had so much work to do, we couldn't spare the extra time." Jani felt a sick chill. "And we just got tired of being hungry." Even decades later, the episode bought back feelings of guilt. Fear. Anger. "We tried our best to follow their dictates, and only bring in the kinds of foods that were sold on the futures markets on a given day."

"She threatened to fink?"

"She would have gotten us expelled. Not even Nema could have saved us from that one." Jani clenched her hand. "She came to my room and told me what she was going to do. She has a very aggravating laugh, even for an idomeni." She heard it in her head now, that monotonic staccato. "I was scared. Upset. I thought I'd blown it for everybody. Before I knew it, I had knocked her to the floor."

"What did she do?" Hals's voice was flat.

"Blinked. Stared right at me, which surprised me. Picked herself up off the ground and left."

"That was it?"

"Yes, ma'am." Jani worked her fingers. She could still remember her aching knuckles, Hansen trying to console her as he packed her hand in ice.

Hals shook her head. "And you think that in spite of that run-in, she accepts you now?"

"She knows I killed twenty-six Laumrau at Knevçet Shèràa. They all do. They accept it. Like I've said before, they'd be insulted if you tried to hide me or pretend I didn't exist. It would be an affront to their intelligence." Jani sighed at Hals's confused look. "It's difficult to explain. Honoring the unpleasant isn't a sensibility most humans are familiar with."

Before Hals could respond, a stiff-looking young woman approached them. She wore dress blue-greys cut with a mainline stripe, and eyed the bare limbs around her with distaste bordering on horror. "Lieutenant Guid, ma'am." She saluted Hals. "Judge Advocate's office." She offered Jani only a vague nod, in acknowledgment of the fact that she represented the prosecution while Jani embodied the prosecuted.

Hals gestured for them both to follow her to the other side of the people-mover, away from prying eyes. "Lieutenant Guid is here to see about your chip, Captain."

"I was starting to wonder about that." Jani held out her still-sore right arm to the pinched young woman, who removed a tiny blip scanner from her trouser pocket.

"This release is on a timer." She ran the scanner along the inside of Jani's arm. As soon as it beeped, she tapped it against the bandaged area, leaving a red dot behind. Then she removed a stylus from her shirt pocket, activated it, and placed the glowing orange tip against the dot.

Jani felt a warm tingle at the site, followed by a painful jolt as feedback from the chip radiated through incised tissue and nerve. Her arm jerked.

Guid struggled to hold the stylus in place. "You must return to

Sheridan within four hours, Captain." The stylus emitted a sharp squeak, and she released her grip as though Jani burned.

"I asked for six, Lieutenant." Hals had paled when Jani's arm started twitching. She stood a long pace back and declined to draw closer. "I distinctly remember petitioning Incarceration for six."

"Four hours, ma'am. That's standard."

"This is a decidedly nonstandard situation."

"Then you need to take it up with Incarceration, ma'am." Guid repocketed her devices. "Someone will be available at oh-nine."

"You—" Hals struck her bare thigh with the flat of her hand—the impact sounded like a slap. "Thank you, Lieutenant. That will be all." She grudgingly acknowledged the young woman's salute. "Damn it," she said as the representative of justice disappeared over the rise, "that's cutting it close."

Jani flexed her arm. Liberated felt no different than trapped. *Not yet, anyway.* "If what I felt before was any indication, when it kicks in, it kicks in full-force. It won't increase gradually."

"Should we have a medic standing by?"

"Do you believe we're going to be there more than four hours?"

Hals paced in a tight circle. The casuals accentuated her plump roundness—she looked like she should have been carrying a trowel and a flat of seedlings rather than a scanpack and the weight of an entire department. "Burkett's been good about making sure our time isn't wasted. According to what I've been told, we're just supposed to validate the provenance of some survey grids and maps being used in the talks."

Jani ran the toe of her shoe along a hairline fissure in the walkway. "Hold off for now. If it looks like our visit will run over, we can call. It shouldn't take them long to get there. All they have to do is blow the chip out with a magburst." She peeked around the mover just in time to see the amused sergeant who would serve as their driver amble down the walkway.

Two orderly lines formed in front of the vehicle's fore and aft doors. Hals hung back, gesturing for Jani to remain with her. Ischi bustled past them, recording board tucked under his arm, eyes shining at the prospect of diplomatic derring-do. "We're going to Camp Ido!" he sang as he leapt aboard the mover. "We're going to Camp Ido!"

Vespucci approached them, white knees flashing in the sun. "Everything's airtight, ma'am." He remained with Hals, waiting pointedly until Jani broke away and headed for the mover.

Jerk. Jani took a seat near the rear, one row up from where Hals and Vespucci would sit. As they pulled out of the charge lot, she glanced out her window. Lucien sat alone on a bench beneath a stand of trees, a place hidden from view from the charge lot, but visible now. He looked up just as the mover passed by, a morose expression on his fallen-angel face. He wore summerweights. And a packed holster. Jani watched him track the vehicle until they floated around the corner of an Admin building and out of sight.

Everyone seemed relaxed as the trip began. Ischi even tried to organize a sing-along, but as soon as the mover passed beneath the Shenandoah Gate, the first verse of "All Around the Campfire" dwindled to a few halfhearted warbles. Then one of the civilian techs said, "Shut up," very softly. Ischi shot her a hard look, but kept his protests to himself. Jani looked over her shoulder at Hals, who stared back, face set.

The nervous backward glances started as soon as the mover ramped onto the Boul. Jani felt them like gnat bites, and did her best to ignore them. But the growing tension managed to wend around her calm—she started when Vespucci touched her shoulder.

"I hope you know what you're doing, Kilian." He tugged at the neck of his T-shirt as though it choked him.

"This was *Eiswein's* call, Major." Hals's voice was tight. "Kilian may have suggested, but it was Eiswein's call all the way.

Vespucci's mouth opened, but one glance at Hals and it snapped shut.

Jani turned around to face the front. Everyone else did, too.

The mover traversed the same route as had Burkett's skimmer. Through the Bluffs, then onto the Boul artery that ran within view of the lakeshore. Soon, the Chicago skyline filled the windscreen; some of the older, reflective-glass towers flashed the light of the rising sun.

Temporarily blinded, Jani didn't spot the demiskimmers at first. But as the mover veered toward the lake and her viewing angle changed, she saw them glide over the water toward the city, metal skins gleaming. They banked in groups of three, first rising, then swoop-landing out of sight amid the buildings lining the shore.

"I'll bet my 'pack they're coming from HollandPort," Vespucci said. "That's the shuttleport on the eastern shore that's set aside for idomeni use."

Idomeni, coming to their embassy. Jani counted the demiskimmers, and lost count after thirty. *Lots and lots of idomeni.* Important idomeni, to command demis. Along with the rest of FT, Jani watched the graceful craft bank and glide.

Whatever it was, it looked big, and she hoped like hell that it had nothing to do with her.

* * *

The fingerprinted courtyard felt almost cool, sheltered as it was from the morning sun. Quiet, too, like the vestibule of a church.

"By the way," Hals said to Jani as she stepped down from the mover, "keep your fists to yourself in there."

Jani nodded. "Yes, ma'am."

They fell into their rank-line and walked up the short flight of steps and through the door. Six Vynshàrau diplomatic suborns bookended the entry this time instead of the single female who had stood for them before. Three males on one side, three females on the other.

Oh . . . shit. Jani looked past them down the hall, where even more suborns lined the way. Five on each side, lined up by sex. A total of eight paired escorts, one for each major god. Her mind stumbled over itself as she tried to determine the reason for the formality. So intent was she, she didn't feel Vespucci nudge her until he prodded her aching arm.

"Do you have any idea what's going on?"

Jani nodded, her stomach roiling. "Someone plans to offer challenge."

"*À lérine*?" He surprised her by pronouncing the term properly. Ah lay-reen, with a trilled r.

"Yes, sir."

"Who?"

"I don't know, sir." Someone who had arrived in one of the demis, perhaps. *But whom would they fight?*

They passed through the silent gauntlet to find Burkett waiting for them by the documents-room entry. Even dressed in casuals, no one could mistake him for anything other than highly polished brass. "Morden nìRau Cèel is here."

The Oligarch? A vague image of lanky height and dark hair formed in Jani's mind. She had never seen him in person, even though he had studied at the Academy at the same time she had. He didn't like humanish then. He still didn't.

"Just flew in from the Death Valley Enclave." Burkett's eyes were on Jani. "The PM is here with half the Cabinet. They're playing catch-up because no one can figure out what Cèel's doing here. He and Tsecha holed up in the main altar room as soon as he walked through the lakeside door—no one's heard a word from them since." He turned to her, his dislike swamped out by his need to know. "It's a challenge, isn't it, Kilian? A big one."

"Yes, sir," Jani replied tiredly. It figured that the knives and fighting part of the idomeni philosophy would be the part Burkett would get right.

"Think Cèel challenged Tsecha?"

"I hope not, sir."

"That would explain the number of demis, though—a formal bout between the Vynshàrau's secular and religious dominants would definitely draw a crowd." Burkett stood tall, hands clasped behind his back. "Not to mention precipitate an intrasect rift that would cripple the Vynshàrau's power and influence over their affiliated sects." His nostrils flared, giving his narrow face a snorting-stallion cast. Confusion to the Vynshàrau held definite appeal for him.

"You may think you want that, sir, but you don't." Jani caught a glimpse of Hals, who stood behind Burkett, mouthing an emphatic "shut up." "Nema has fervor on his side, but Cèel has forty years. Their mutual enmity's ground in the bone. À lérine may technically be ritual fighting, but knives have been known to slip. The Vynshàrau are the most pro-humanish born-sect, thanks to Nema's influence. You don't want anything happening to him."

Burkett looked down his nose at her. "Don't presume to know my mind, Kilian."

"I was in Rauta Shèràa the night it fell to the Vynshàrau. I repeat, you do not want anything to happen to Nema!"

"*I hear my name!*"

They turned as one toward the voice.

The overrobe churned less vigorously, befitting the formality of the occasion. "I find my nìa arguing with you again, General." Nema's face split in a ghoulish grin. "Such habitual disputation—you should declare yourselves. We have blades you may borrow for the task."

Burkett's face reddened. "We don't handle disagreements that way in the Service, nìRau."

"Ah." Nema cocked his head to the left as he cupped his right hand and raised it chest-high, his tone and posture indicating question of yet another aspect of humanish behavior. His eyes met Jani's, and he bared his teeth. "Nìa," he said, touching a fingertip to her chin. Then he looked at each of them in turn, examining them from head to toe one after the other. He reached into his overrobe as he did so, and removed a battered black ovaloid that twinned Jani's scanpack. His handheld, however, functioned as a Vynshàrau-humanish dictionary. It held French, English, and Mandarin, formal and foul, idiomatic and slang. The occasional amusing muck-up occurred, but Nema's research and extensive cross-referencing would have impressed any linguist.

He tapped at the worn unit's touchpad. "We have been *cooking you in your skins.*" He shut down the handheld and bared his teeth again. "And you have accepted challenge. A glorious thing. My compliments, General, for finally waking up." He thrust his hand toward Burkett and nodded vigorously as the man gingerly shook it. "Now, let us work, for we have much to do." He swept down the hall, the members of Foreign Transactions playing butter to his Sìah blade. "Come! Come! Much to do!" he cried as he vanished around the corner.

Burkett watched him, mouth agape. "He's a goddamned Pied Piper."

"And he's the only idomeni who can pipe a tune you can dance to," Jani said. "Remember that the next time you wish a knife in his ribs." She waited for Burkett's face to flare anew before she turned her back on him and walked slowly into the documents examiners' meeting room.

Jani braced her hands on the U-shaped table for balance and leaned back in her three-legged easel seat.

So where are Hantìa and company? Foreign Transactions had been validating documents for almost forty minutes, and the Vynshàrau had yet to make an appearance. *Only a couple of hours left.* Jani felt the muscles in her right forearm twitch. They knew what would happen if the princess didn't leave the party on time.

She looked at the others. Vespucci turned away as soon as she glanced uptable at him. She had caught him eyeing her several times, beetle brow knit in consternation. And dripping sweat.

She breathed through her mouth as Ischi leaned close to spread a set of nautical survey maps before her. His deodorant still worked. Barely. *Wish I could remember what we used in Rauta Shèràa.* A colonial brand, formulated for above-average temps. Limited distribution. Odds were it wasn't even manufactured anymore.

Wonder who could find out?

Well, there are my parents.

She imagined the dead comport light, and busied herself scanning the maps.

"How are you holding up, Captain?" Hals, seated next to her, asked for the umpteenth time. "There's ice water and electrolyte replenishers in a supply vehicle just outside the embassy perimeter." The easel seats, like all Vynshàrau daytime furniture, weren't designed for comfort. They also weren't designed for the average human—the one-four Hals was having a hell of a time keeping stable in a seat designed for a one-nine Vynshàrau. "We can break at any time—our mover can get us there in five."

"I'm fine, ma'am." Jani met Hals's examination head-on. "Really."

"You're not even sweating." Hals wiped the tip of her nose with the edge of her T-shirt sleeve just before she dripped on her aerial survey grid. "I don't know if that's good or bad."

"Could be heat stroke," Ischi chimed helpfully.

"I'm not moving around as much as you are," Jani said. "And I picked the seat by the vent."

"Moving hot air is still hot air." Ischi tugged his blotched T-shirt away from his skin. "I think we should invite the Vynshàrau to the base and stick them in the arctic test facility. Crank it *all* the way down."

"Thank you, Lieutenant," Hals said.

"Chip 'em out with chisels."

"That will be all, Lieutenant." Hals waited until Ischi found another ear downtable to complain into. "Was it like this in Rauta Shèràa?"

"Worse." Jani felt her forehead. Slightly damp. A little warmer than normal. "The only air-conditioning was in the human enclave. Once you entered the city, you were at the mercy of nature and idomeni utilities." *I know the symptoms of heat stroke.* She'd seen it enough in Rauta Shèràa. *I'm still lucid.* She felt fine.

The general buzz of conversation died as work claimed everyone's attention. So intent were they, no one looked up when the door opened.

"Ladies and gentlemen."

Heads shot up. Hals had a better view of the door than Jani. Her breath caught. "It's Burkett. He looks sick. Or mad as hell. I can never tell the difference."

Jani twisted in her easel seat too quickly and grabbed the edge of the table to keep from tipping over. "Anyone else?"

"The PM and some Ministers—Ulanova, damn it—Tsecha and all the Vynshàrau dexxies and a whole bunch I don't recognize and—oh damn! Cèel's there, too!"

Jani balanced on the seat rungs to peek over Hals's head, and caught a glimpse of the Oligarch. He was half Nema's age, lighter-skinned and darker-haired. They were arguing—you didn't need to be a trained Vynshà-watcher to interpret the choppy hand movements and twisted facial expressions. Hantìa stood with them. Her hairloops had been gathered and clasped. Instead of the tan-and-grey clothing of a documents suborn, she wore white lightweave trousers and a sleeveless overshirt. "The better to show the blood." Jani pressed a hand to her churning stomach.

"What?" Hals glanced back at her, frowning.

"Remember when I promised not to use my fists, ma'am?"

"Yes?"

"I'm going to have to take it back."

"Kilian, what are you talking about?"

"You know that challenge that's going to be made?"

"The guessing games stop *now*, Captain."

"Yes, ma'am, I believe they will." Jani watched Burkett break away from the group and walk along the table toward her, followed by Nema.

Hals leaned close. "What are you talking about!"

Jani slid off her seat. "Twenty-five years later, it's finally Hantìa's turn."

Before Hals could ask any more questions, Burkett stopped in front of Jani. "Captain."

Jani nodded. "Sir."

"I imagine you don't need to be told what's going on."

"No, sir. Hantìa's requested permission of nìRau Tsecha to make challenge. He gave her leave. Then he made the request to you, as my most high dominant. I'm assuming you're reluctant."

"Yes." With Burkett, uncertainty came clothed as stiffness and an inability to look one in the eye. "I understand refusal is an insult." He stared at a point somewhere over Jani's shoulder.

"Without cause, yes. Simply not wanting to fight isn't enough. Health reasons can serve, but I'm here working, so it's difficult to argue that I'm unfit." Jani flexed her hands. It was safe to say she was already warmed up. "It's ceremonial fighting. Doesn't last long. Injury occurs to the arms, mostly. The shoulders. Superficial wounds. They leave ugly scars, because of the types of knives used, but they're not in themselves dangerous."

"Nonetheless, I've messaged Doctor Colonel Pimentel. Nothing proceeds unless he's standing by. I asked him to bring a trauma surgeon, as well. Something someone said about knives having been known to slip." Burkett lowered his voice. "I am deferring to your judgment, Captain. I've never acted as someone's second before."

"Sir, Captain Kilian has been at Sheridan less than two weeks." Hals's voice was strained. "She's spent more than half that time in hospital, and remains under close medical supervision. She is in no condition to fight anyone. I don't care how ceremonial it is."

Jani looked uproom at the assembled Vynshàrau. She recognized several of them from her Academy days. *Hey, a class reunion.* "It's not a fight to the death. I don't need to be in top form. It's simply a declaration. Hantìa and I are acknowledging to the world that we hate each other's guts." She stared at the female, who turned to look in her direction. Jani nodded; Hantìa bared her teeth. "That shouldn't take long."

Nema, who had remained uncharacteristically silent to that point, stepped forward. "I have accepted challenge sixty-seven times, and offered challenge twenty-two times." He extended his arms and pushed up the sleeves of his overrobe to his elbows. The silvered remains of old scars, accented by the occasional red slash of a fresher wound, crosshatched the bronze skin of his forearms and wrists. "It is an honor to be challenged by one such as Onì nìaRauta Hantìa. She shares skein with Cèel, through their body mothers." He tilted his arms back and forth. The scars, jagged and raised, seemed to shimmer in the roomlight. "Such an esteemed enemy is greatly to be wished."

Hals and Burkett both stared at the wounds. "Hantìa and Cèel are *cousins*?" Burkett asked. He sounded choked.

Jani looked at Nema, who patted his pockets for his handheld. "In a way. Vynshàrau family organizations are difficult to explain." She shut down her scanpack and stuffed it into its pouch. "Right now, I need to get ready, and since the opening ceremonies can get a little protracted, I can't afford to waste any time."

Burkett glared at Hals. "I thought you took care of that, Colonel."

Hals glowered back. "They gave me *four* hours, sir."

"I specifically asked for six."

"Well, askin' ain't gettin' around here, is it!" Hals closed her eyes. "Sir, I apologize—"

Burkett ignored her. "Captain—"

Jani held up her hands. "I realize you're both upset because you're confused and hot and completely out of your element, but I know what I'm doing, so there's no need to worry." She handed her packpouch to Hals for safekeeping and ducked under the table. "Let's try to maintain a united front, all right, Spacers?" she called out as she emerged on the other side. Nema bared his teeth and beckoned to her, and she followed him out of the room.

CHAPTER 25

"To which god do you pray, nìa?" Nema pointed to the cluster of statues and symbols arranged atop the altar. The beads, medals, and smaller figurines had been obtained from the pockets of members of Diplo and Foreign Transactions, while the larger pieces had been hastily acquired from nearby shops by an Ischi-headed strike force. "You have more than we. Such confusion." He backed away, so that Jani could step up and choose. They were the only two in the embassy's secondary altar room. Normally, both foes would have offered prefight sacrifice in the same place, but since such a profound difference in religion existed, the home team had been granted use of the primary room, a windowed veranda that contained shrines to all the Vynshàrau's eight dominant gods.

I, meanwhile, get the closet. But it was a nice closet, quiet and cooler than the rest of the embassy. Nema had chosen to accompany her, a fact that had visibly irked Hantìa and resulted in even more heated discussion between Nema and Cèel. *He's declared himself my supporter.* In the face of his ruler. In spite of Knevçet Shèràa. *I have to fight well.* Her stomach ached from tension.

She picked up a small stone elephant. "Ganesha, the god of wisdom. I prayed to him when I was little."

"Ah." Nema took the tiny figure from her and examined it thoughtfully. "Why did you stop?"

"I don't know." She picked up the teakwood seat on which the elephant had rested and studied its minute carvings. "Maybe I didn't think it helped." She set the seat back down on the altar. "Sometimes, he's called Vinayak, when he's worshipped as the god of knowledge, and other times, he's called Vighneshwer, when he's honored as the remover of obstacles."

"Ah." Nema handed the figurine back to her. "Do you worship any gods that are less complicated?"

Jani smiled. "My mother is Brh Hindi. My father grew up Freehold Catholic, and converted to the Hortensian Presbyter just before I left for the Academy." A memory of the baptism ceremony flashed in her mind's eye, and she almost burst out laughing. *They held it outside. It was cold and the pool leaked and the minister wrenched his back dipping Mrs. Louli.* "I guess the answer is no."

"Then I believe the remover of obstacles would be a good god for now." Nema looked around the room. "What does he demand as sacrifice?"

Jani set the elephant back on its seat. Then she stripped some petals from the blanket of bright orange cymbela that had been draped across the altar, and sprinkled them before it. "Help me, Lord," she said, just as she had when she was eight and asked for the wisdom necessary to pass maths.

She knew her father would be disappointed if he somehow discovered she hadn't given his God a chance, so she picked a plain gold cross from the collection and whispered a quick Act of Contrition. The one formal prayer she remembered. She knew many informal ones, spoken from the heart, usually a variation of "please, God, get me through this." Any God. Whichever one cared enough to listen. And up to now, she'd managed to survive it all and didn't despise herself any more than she ever had, so someone must have thought her worth the bother.

"We must go, nìa," Nema said. He watched Jani as she set the cross back down on the altar. "You feel strong?"

"Yes, nìRau."

"Hantìa will try to draw much blood. That is her way."

"I understand."

"If she fights too vigorously, you must knock her down, as you did before."

Jani stared at Nema. His expression was bland, for him. Grim Death in Repose. "You knew about that?"

"Yes, nìa." He rearranged the draping of his red-rimmed cuffs. "I know all."

"You could have told me."

"No, nìa." He walked ahead of her, which since he was her dominant was a serious breach of protocol. "You prefer your secrets, even if they are secret only to you."

"You've come to know humanish so well?"

"Humanish have no place in this." His auric eyes seemed to glow. "I know Rauta Haárin. I know you."

The room was oval, windowless, with smooth, dun-colored walls and floor. A high ceiling, the light provided by simple sunglobes suspended from helical chains.

The audience had already assembled. Humans filled the banked seating on one side, idomeni, the other, each following the idomeni convention of lower ranks to the rear. That allowed Prime Minister Li Cao a seat of honor on the floor, very close to the action. Closer than she would have liked, judging from the way she jerked back as Jani walked near the edge of the fighting circle.

Anais Ulanova sat at Cao's side, the slight elevation of her seat denoting her lesser status. "An interesting way to start the day, is it not, Captain?" No false bravado was detectable in her voice or manner. In fact, she seemed rather bored. Somewhere in her ancestry lurked women who yawned during executions.

"Yes, ma'am." Jani shot an encouraging look toward the back rows. Hals stared back, grim and tight-lipped. Ischi sat behind her, edgily tapping his feet. Vespucci chewed a thumbnail. Burkett sat arms folded, eyes on the floor.

The Vynshàrau side looked even cheerier. As ranking secular dominant, Cèel sat in a very low seat, mere centimeters from the floor. The best seat in the house, idomenically speaking, belonged to Nema as ranking religious dominant and, as such, Cèel's propitiator. Like Cao he rated the floor itself. Jani watched him lower slowly, his back straight, his face unreadable. *He won't root for me.* Not openly, anyway.

As the challenged, the choice of blades fell to Jani. She considered the assortment laid out before her. Long and short, curved and straight, all bearing the stark elegance and implied efficiency that marked classic Sìah workmanship.

Her earlier self-assurance ebbed as she hefted a couple of the longer blades. The incision in her arm pulled every time she squeezed. *When was the last time I fought with a knife?* Not stabbed someone, but *fought.* Like any other martial art, it required training. It also took skill to fight without seriously hurting your opponent. Hantìa had trained for ceremonial bouts like these since she was old enough to walk—her experience showed in her heavily scarred arms. *I only know how to cut and run.*

Jani settled for a short, straight sword that resembled a really nasty carving knife. Hantìa bared her teeth when she saw her choice of weapon. She picked up the matching blade and made several skillful cuts through the air.

Show-off. Jani tilted her blade back and forth. The anodized wireweave, fine as spider silk, shone beneath the lamps like multicolored threads. The razorlike wires would shred as they cut. The wounds she'd receive would sear as though rubbed with salt, while the edges would heal raised and ragged.

Pain. The prospect worried her. As much as she disliked Hantìa, she didn't want to fight this fight. Not because she didn't know what she was doing, and not because she feared the pain. But the aches and twinges she'd tolerated for years were different from the agony experienced when someone cut you with a knife. And kept coming. And kept coming.

Augie likes that kind of pain. She could sense him in the back of her mind, telling her exactly where she needed to strike. He didn't fight for the beauty of the process. He didn't fight to make declaration, or honor any god. He fought to hurt. He fought to kill.

The status of humanish-idomeni relations again depended on what she feared, and how she felt, and where she aimed.

Please God, don't let me kill her. Any God. Whichever one cared enough to listen.

As if on cue, hushed conversations silenced. All eyes shifted to the two females standing in the middle of the room.

"*We will begin now,*" Hantìa said in informal High Vynshàrau, her voice level and without gesture. She circled Jani, arms opened wide, slightly bent at the waist. *Hain.* The Stance of Welcome. A great position if you wanted to be gutted.

Get it over with. That was augie talking. Jani blocked him out. "*Yes,*" she answered, forcing herself into the same stance as Hantìa. "*We will begin now.*" The soles of her trainers squeaked against the bare floor as she maneuvered. That and the pound of the blood in her ears were the only sounds she heard.

She played it safe at first, blocking Hantìa's tentative initial thrusts, restraining the urge to come in behind the blocks and do damage of her own. She knew Hantìa, a skilled fighter, would try to draw her in. *She wants a quick shot.* A chance to cut near an elbow or a wrist, to nick a tendon and impede Jani's ability to wield her weapon.

Hantìa struck repeatedly. Jani parried attack after attack, each more confident than the last. Her incised arm ached. The impacts Hantìa threw behind the blows forced her back, left her off-balance. Open.

I am not weak. Yes, she was. *I'm—not tired.* Yes, she was.

Sweat flowed. Her knees trembled.

Her hands dropped.

Hantìa struck. Blade in. Blade out.

The gash tore Jani's left arm from elbow to wrist. The wireweave worked its magic, making vessel-grown nerves sing as though real. One note. High and long. Rose-pink carrier welled and dripped, squelching beneath her shoes as she dodged Hantìa's follow-up.

"*Bring your hands up! Cover—!*" Ischi's shout, silenced mid-warning.

No coaching allowed. Jani raised her hands just in time to avert another blow. Carrier flowed down her arm and coated her hand. It didn't clot as quickly as blood. It would remain liquid for the balance of the fight. She'd drop her knife if she tried to switch hands.

Her heart pounded. Skipped a beat. A side stitch stabbed like an internal knife. Hantìa's face wavered. The room darkened.

Jani's heart skipped again, then slowed. Like new life, the pain ebbed. She knew why.

Hantìa again closed in, arms spread wide, torso exposed.

You owe me! augie shouted. *Hit her now!*

Jani ignored the fatal opening. She blocked another thrust with her injured left arm. Found her chance. Slipped her blade through.

Hantìa jumped back, blood streaming from the hack across her right bicep. Her dominant arm. Jani saw her wince as she tried to grip her blade. Heard the mutters from the Vynshàrau side of the room, the muffled "yes" from hers. She could hear the rasp of Hantìa's pained-tinged breathing. See every bead of sweat on her face. Smell the syrup sweetness of the carrier mingled with the metal tang of blood.

Time slowed. Motion. Jani saw Hantìa's answering blow coming as if she'd announced it. She swept aside the blade edge with her right arm, driving the Vynshàrau back toward the wall, taking the cut as she knocked the knife from her hand. *Follow it in.* She did. *Grab her around the neck.* She did, the slickness of her left hand forcing her to grip Hantìa's throat so tightly she could feel the pulse.

Either side of the neck. Just under the jaw. Do it. Do it!

Jani pressed Hantìa against the wall. Pushed tip of blade against hollow of throat. Saw, for one fleeting moment, the alarm in the Vynshàrau's cracked marble eyes.

Then she stepped back. "*Declaration is made.*" She switched the blade to her left hand. No matter if it slipped now. Edge to right forearm, taking care to avoid the bandage. Back. Forth.

Somebody screamed. It wasn't her.

"Finished!" Nema bounded to his feet. "A marvelous fight, and truly. Full of hate—a glorious thing!" He swept toward them, eyes alight. "My Eyes and Ears' first declaration. When she turns my age, her arms will look as mine, I predict!"

"I'd be dead by then." Jani opened her left hand and let the blade fall. Metal clacked softly against coated flooring.

"No, no, no. You will be most gloriously alive." Nema picked up the blade, turned to his side of the room, and lifted it above his head. His eyes focused in Cèel's direction, he lowered it slowly and wiped the edges on his sleeves, leaving behind ragged smears to complement the neat red trim.

Hantìa approached her. "You are cut more than me." She sounded disappointed. "I should demand rematch." She grasped Jani's left wrist and turned it, examining the wounded animandroid flesh. "Does that hurt?"

"Yes."

"Good." Hantìa nodded, her tone as clinical as John's at his most detached. "Mine, also." She studied the cuts on Jani's other arm, touching the self-inflicted one that signaled the end of the bout. "The wound you gave yourself is worse than the one I gave you."

"No surprise there."

Jani turned, catching herself just before it devolved to a wobble. "Good morning, Doctor."

Pimentel scowled. "Good morning, Captain. It's been hours." He wore medwhites instead of summerweights. A woman stood behind him. She wore medwhites, too, and a stunned expression. She also toted a sling bag. Without being asked, she reached into the bag, pulled out a stylus, and handed it to Pimentel.

"Let's see how far gone you are." He frowned as he stepped around the carrier drying on the floor. Then he activated the stylus and flicked the light in Jani's eyes.

Red light. Pulsing. This time, she wobbled.

"We have to get you out of here now." Pimentel pocketed the stylus and gripped Jani by the elbow.

"No!" Nema's hand locked around Pimentel's wrist. "She cannot go. There are ceremonies. There are—"

"NìRau ti nìRau." Jani slipped her fingers around Pimentel's wrist and pried Nema's fingers away. "I'm wearing a security chip on a time release. I have to go back."

"But your first *à lérine!*"

"NìRau." Pimentel massaged his abused wrist. "She should never have left the base in the first place." His voice shook. "She is sick, weak, in the first stages of augie overdrive, and if I don't get her back to Sheridan within thirty minutes, there isn't a pin block in existence that will stop her from going into shock."

"*À lérine* must be properly closed." Cèel swept through the Vynshàrau gathering. On closer examination, his face looked familiar. If Val Parini could be jaundiced and stretched, he could pass for the Oligarch's twin. "You forced this, Tsecha. Now we are to be cheated of what small order we could have salvaged." His English held only the barest born-sect throatiness. His clipped disapproval was more easily detected.

Nema rounded his shoulders. "My nìa won."

"No finesse. No beauty. She beat back nìaRauta Hantìa like Haárin. Like humanish. The fight ended before it began." Cèel's chin jutted. Since he had typical Vynshàrau bones, he had a lot to jut. "I could declare it no fight at all."

In other words, your girl lost, so you're kicking the gameboard over. Jani fingered the bout-ending wound on her right arm. "If that was no fight, why am I bleeding?" She held up her arm in front of Cèel's face. He didn't look at her, of course, but he knew she was there. "*I found opening. I disarmed. I won.*" She slipped easily into the stylized posture of High Vynshàrau, despite the growing agitation caused by augie's dressing up and finding nowhere to go. "*I should challenge you for questioning me.*" She raised her left hand, palm facing down, and turned her head to the right in injured pride. "*I do challenge you for questioning me.*"

Vynshàrau and humanish fell silent.

Cèel looked at her in his periphery. His eyes were unusual for a Vynshàrau, neither brown nor gold but a pale sea green that contrasted sharply with the tarnished gilt of his skin. "You have no right or cause to challenge me," he said in English. "You do not understand hierarchy."

"But lousy sportsmanship, nìRau, I understand perfectly." She turned her back on Cèel's puzzled glower. "Ask my teacher to explain it to you. He has the handheld." She headed for the exit. Pimentel hurried after her, followed by his colleague.

Nema cut past, around, and through to catch Jani up. Desjarlais at his best never moved better. "Your first declaration." He sounded giddy.

"Hantìa had been training as a Temple archivist." Jani touched the wall every so often just to make sure it was there. "Instead, she's here as an examiner. You forced her to change her life's work. Then you brought her here, because you knew she would challenge me. You knew if she did, it would force Cèel to acknowledge me because they share skein. Gotten devious in our old age, haven't we, nìRau?"

“You are angry, nìa?” Nema’s voice wavered in disbelief.

“You set me up.”

“You must assert yourself as my heir, nìa. You must fight for your acceptance.”

“I am not your heir! I will never be your heir!” She darted out the doors and toward the first vehicle she saw, a Service grey triple-length with a caduceus and two silver stars etched on the rear door. She turned to Pimentel. “Carvalla’s staff car?”

“It’s fast.” Pimentel closed in behind her. “Hals told me what happened. Somebody at the JA is going to get their ass handed to them on a plate.” He yanked up the door and pushed Jani inside. The other doctor followed close at his heels; Burkett, to her surprise, brought up the rear. He yanked the gullwing closed. The vehicle shuddered.

“Let’s go!” Burkett thumped the privacy shield with his fist. The skimmer lumbered out of the courtyard, then picked up speed as it hit the skimway.

CHAPTER 26

"How are you feeling?" Pimentel again flicked the stylus in Jani's eyes. Muttering darkly at whatever he saw, he dug into the sling bag and pulled out a larger scanner with an attached sphygmomanometer cuff.

"Flicking red lights in a challenge room—you're lucky Cèel didn't ask you to choose your weapon." Jani rested her head against the seat back. The smooth leather felt odd. Damp.

"So is he." Pimentel wrapped the cuff around Jani's right arm, but as soon as he hit the contraction pad, the pressure caused blood to well in the gashes. "I need to close those wounds."

Jani sniffed. The upholstery smelled, too, like wet rodents. "You can't close them. They have to heal naturally."

Pimentel punched at the scanner pad. The device squeaked in protest. "It looks like someone went after your arms with a piece of sheet metal." He took the blood pressure reading, then stripped off the cuff. "Even with your augie, they're going to scar."

"They're supposed to." The smell intensified. Her stomach churned. "The uglier the better. It means your hatred has been well and truly declared."

A ripple of dismay crossed Burkett's face as he watched Pimentel scrabble with his equipment. "What did Tsecha mean when he called you his 'heir'?"

Jani found Burkett's queasiness amusing, which told her how badly off she was. "You're aware of my medical history?"

A sharp nod, followed by hesitation. "You're turning into one of them."

"No, not completely. I'm hybridizing. The ambassador thinks

after I hybridize completely into a half-human, half-idomeni, I can begin training as his religious replacement."

"Chief propitiator of the Vynshàrau!"

"Yes, sir."

"You won't have to worry about that once Gene Therapeutics gets started on you," Pimentel muttered as he and the trauma surgeon took turns attaching pin blocks leads.

"My God." Burkett rested his head against the seat back. "I hope I did the right thing letting you fight Hantìa."

"You would have insulted the Oligarch if you hadn't." Jani paused. The damp rat smell had ramped to an appalling stench, and she tried to breathe through her mouth and talk at the same time. "Then who knows, he might have challenged you." She smiled. Cruelty could be fun, with the right target. "I'd brush up on my bladework if I were, sir. You may need it."

Burkett looked at her. Outside, the workday was just beginning for most inhabitants of Chicago, but his long face already showed the effects of a head-on collision between a rough morning and an afternoon that promised more of the same. "You held your augie in check during that fight. I could tell."

Jani's smile faded. "Yes, sir."

"That takes . . . an extreme amount of willpower."

"I've learned how to control him. All it takes is practice." A wave of shivering overtook her. She could hear her teeth chatter.

Burkett swallowed hard, then twisted in his seat and thumped his fist once more against the privacy shield. "Damn it, hurry up!"

"Yes, sir!" The young man's voice sounded tight. "We're almost topped out, though." The skimmer's insect hum increased in pitch. They had left the last of the city buildings behind. Forests and parks now whipped past in a series of green blurs.

"The Bluffs." Jani grinned. "I know people who live here, but I don't think they'd admit to the acquaintance." She sniffed. Amid the wet rat, she detected the unforgettable rank of corpse. "Roger?"

Pimentel looked up from the recorder display. "Yes?"

"Does this cabin smell funny to you?"

"Do you recall that smell, Jani?"

Jani nodded carefully. "A cellar. On Guernsey. Spring floods—we found all these dead rats in the cellar. Drowned. And a body—"

The trauma surgeon thrust the recorder at Pimentel and dived into the bag. "She's accessing sense memory. We need to take her down now. If she flies off, we may not be able to control her."

"No!" Pimentel grabbed her wrist. "We only have a few minutes to set up the pin blocks. We take care of the pain first, then we worry about her augie!"

A sharp tingle, like an electric shock, radiated through Jani's right arm. "How much time do we have left?"

Pimentel checked his timepiece. "We're still supposed to have fifteen minutes!" He turned and pounded on the panel. "Speed up!"

"I'm going as fast as I can, sir!" The driver's knuckles showed white as he clamped down on the wheel. "I'm losing her on the curves as it is!"

"You should have called for air transport, Colonel," Burkett snapped.

"I tried, sir." Pimentel's hands flew as he clamped the pin block array around Jani's forearm. "I couldn't get approval for an in-city trip."

"Then you should have lied!"

"I'll file that recommendation away for future use, sir, thank you!"

Jani stiffened as the second wave broke like a studded club across shattered bone. She reached out her carrier-encrusted left hand. Pimentel grabbed it and squeezed. "I didn't think it would give any warning." She winked at him. "Write it up. Maybe you can get a journal communication out of it."

Pimentel thumped the block touchpad with his free hand. "I've just activated the blocks, Jani. Hang on for a few more seconds."

"That's easy for you to s—!" Her back arched as the third wave hit. No mercy this time. No quarter. And, after a split second of white-hot pain that exploded from within like a swallowed shatterbox, no consciousness.

She inhaled.

No rats, this time.

Metal.

Antiseptic.

Hospital.

Jani eased open her eyes just as Morley's familiar face poked into view.

"Don't move too much. Your arm is going to be pretty sore for a couple of days."

Jani looked around as well as she could. It wasn't worth the effort. This room mirrored her last room, which in turn mirrored the one before that. "Are you still on afternoons?"

Morley checked the readouts on the monitors surrounding Jani's bed. "In answer to your unspoken question, you've only been out four hours. It's about what we expected. There are only two sedatives we could risk using on you, and neither is worth much. They pumped you full as soon as they skimmed you into Triage, but your augie fought off most of it."

"Oh." Jani stifled a yawn, then ran a tongue over her dry teeth. Her head throbbed. She swallowed again, and detected the tell-tale odor of berries. "They took me down, didn't they?"

"They had no choice." Morley held a straw to Jani's lips and supported her head as she drew down a wonderful swallow of cold water. "You came to a few minutes after the chip stopped emitting, and you came up swinging. You wouldn't let anybody touch your arm." She pulled the straw away.

Jani gazed longingly after the water. "What else happened?"

Morley grinned. "First Pimentel stormed over to the JA's and went critical all over Incarceration. Turns out their four-hour grace period really equaled three hours and forty-five minutes. The traditional warning shot, they said. Endangering the life of my patient, Pimentel said. I think it was the attempted murder threat that really made their day. Some of them are augmented, but they're going to be reluctant to come here for their precautionaries for quite a while." She dragged a chair between the monitors and sat down.

"Watching what you went through with that chip shook the hell out of Burkett—he was green-faced when he shot out of your skimmer. Tore off to the JA Executive Offices right behind Pimentel, sweaty casuals and all, and threatened everyone within shouting distance with a charge of treason, saying that what happened to you endangered sensitive negotiations, thus imperiling Commonwealth security. *Then*, last but far from least, the idomeni ambassador called the A-G. Something about the Oligarch's extreme displeasure and the disruption of sacred rituals. He also mentioned Lord Ganesha?"

"He's a Hindu god."

Morley chuckled dryly. "Talk about threats to body and soul. Everyone at North Lakeside must be afraid to walk outside for fear of lightning strikes." She thumped the arms of the chair and rose slowly. "Well, I'm going to let you get some rest. Pimentel will be around soon, if he hasn't staged an assault on Base Command." She straightened Jani's sheet. "Hit the rail pad if you need anything."

Jani licked more cotton coating from her teeth. "I'm really thirsty now."

"Thank the sedative for that," Morley said. "We need to hold off. Your fluid levels are satisfactory, but post-takedown vomiting is still a threat, and the usual antinausea meds we give might do you more harm than good."

Jani stuck out her tongue at the closing door. "I have such glamorous illnesses." She stared at the ceiling, hunting for any interesting blemishes that would set it apart from the other hospital ceilings she had known.

"Hello, Kilian."

Jani raised her head too quickly. The room spun.

Neumann sat in Morley's recently vacated chair. He wore desertweights. A rancid smile. "Didn't think you'd see me anymore, did you?"

Jani stared at the years-dead man. "Guess the takedown didn't."

"Yeah. Can't trust technology. Pin blocks. Shooters. Pulse bombs." He straightened so he could look over at Jani's bandaged arm. "So, your marble-eyed buddy set you up. With friends like him, who needs a death sentence?"

"I was never in any danger."

Neumann snorted. "Shows what you know. Hell, you said it yourself. Knives have slipped during those little bouts before, and Cèel's a hard-liner who'd like nothing better than to offer a prayer of thanks over your corpse."

"But instead, Nema forced him to accept me." Jani tried to sit up, and made the mistake of using her right arm for support. Stars exploded. She slumped back against her pillow, breathing in quick gasps to keep those precious sips of water where they belonged. "He's ten steps ahead of all of you. Always was. Always will be."

"You better hope so. Your continued existence depends on it." Neumann stood and walked to the window side of the room. The wash of daylight highlighted odd shadows in his pale tan uniform, darkenings across his torso, his right trouser leg and sleeve. "Yeah, he's got them all running scared."

"Cao can't afford to lose whatever idomeni support she has." Jani sat up, this time more carefully. "Colony-Haárin trade increases every month. Financial stakes are huge. The colonies will vote her out of office the second her policies affect their pocketbooks."

"Since when did you become a political analyst?" Neumann sneered. "Well, you were always good at flummoxing those too ignorant to know better." The taunting expression turned self-satisfied. "But you never fooled Acton van Reuter. And you sure as hell never fooled me."

"I *killed* you."

Neumann shrugged. "My shooter caught in my holster." The front of his shirt had darkened further. Looked shiny. Wet. Red. "You'd have never outdrawn me in a fair fight." He turned from the window to face her. The blood from the shooter entry wound in his abdomen had soaked from the V of his collar to below his beltline. "But you don't know a goddamned thing about fair fights, do you, Kilian? All you know is fucking your way to the top and interfering with your betters."

Jani watched the bloodstains bloom. The killshot. The exit wound that blew out his right leg. The wound in his right arm, that seeped instead of bled. That was where the shelving had fallen on his corpse during the first round of Laumrau shelling, severing the dead arm. *He's a hallucination.* Yet he seemed more real than any person Jani had seen that day. *Big as life and so damned ugly.* "One of the last times I spoke with Evan, he sounded as though he missed you. Why?"

Neumann leaned against the window. The blood from his damaged arm streamed down the glass. "Evan was a good kid. Normal blowouts growing up. The drinking—that started way too early, but Acton wouldn't listen to me." He smeared a line of blood with his finger. "Evan understands tradition. He respects it."

"What he respects are the privileges of being the *V* in NUVA-SCAN."

"Ours by right of conquest, Kilian, paid for with those names on the Gate. Top dog gets the best cut of meat—first law of life in the Commonwealth."

Jani watched Neumann draw on the glass in his blood. One line. Another. Then crosshatches, like a small grid. *He's here for a reason.* Her ghosts always appeared for a reason. It was her job to figure out what the reason was. "Speaking of dogs, ever run into Ebben, Unser, or Fitzhugh?"

Neumann drew an *X* in one box. "Once in a while."

"Did they ever tell you who killed them?"

"Oh, now she wants information." He filled another box with an *O*. "Even though she knows I can't tell her anything she doesn't already know or have the ability to figure out." When the blood on the window became too thinly spread to work with, he refilled by dipping a finger in his oozing arm. "No, Kilian, you have to work for your supper like everyone else. No more easy rides. No more getting by on your Two of Six mystique."

"That mystique was the reason you forced my transfer to the Twelfth Rovers." She watched him puzzle over the half-filled grid. "You need a naught in the upper-right corner."

"Oh, thank you." He drew it in, then cut a diagonal slash through his line of *O*'s. "Being dead plays hell with the ol' cognition." He took a white-linen handkerchief from the pocket of his short-sleeve and wiped the window clean. "You think Pierce had something to do with their deaths." He tucked the bloody cloth away, then crossed his arms and leaned against the pane. His right arm shifted as he applied pressure—the elbow slipped down.

Jani tried to sit forward. Every time she moved, her right arm throbbed. "I know he did. It's just a question of what."

"He already told you. At the soccer match."

"He said we had a lot in common."

"Nah. He did you two better." Before Neumann could explain what he meant, the door swept aside. Lucien stood in the open entry and peered cautiously into the room. "Who are you talking to?"

Jani eased back against her pillow. "Just myself."

"Just myself," Neumann mimicked. "What a choice you have. Keep your mouth shut and piss him off, or tell him the truth and have him think you're crazy." He minced to Lucien's side and blew him a kiss. Then he pulled at his own belt. "Tell you what, Kilian. I bet he shows you his any second now. Then I'll show you mine, and you can tell us which is bigger."

Jani shot back in disgust, "I didn't know you had one, you son of a bitch."

Lucien stiffened. "What did you say?"

"Nothing."

"I'm only here because Nema ordered me to come. If you want me to leave, just say so."

"No." Jani waved toward the bedside chair. "I'm just tired. My arm hurts." She watched Neumann wander to the far corner of the room and turn his back. He stood hunched, right shoulder jerking up and down. Jani shifted so the seated Lucien blocked the view.

"You're not supposed to have visitors, but Nema wants an eye-witness account of your condition." Lucien's heavy-lidded stare moved over her as Neumann's grunting sounded from the corner. "So, how do you feel?"

"I just had my arm yanked out of its socket from the inside. How do you think I feel?"

"Nema said you fought most as idomeni. He crowed to me for over fifteen minutes. If he's doing the same thing at the embassy, Cèel's ready to kill him."

Neumann spun around. "Hey, Kilian, look what I can do!" He tugged at his right arm, gasping in fake surprise as it came away in his hand. "Wave bye-bye to Aunt Jani." He held it by the wrist the way a father would his son's arm, and worked it up and down. The limp hand flopped like a dying fish.

"Are you all right?" Lucien glanced at the monitors. "I don't want to be the one to tell Nema you look really sick."

"I'm fine."

"I heard you're going to a party tomorrow night."

"From whom?"

"Ischi. I stopped by FT to hear what happened. He wouldn't shut up about you, either." Lucien's peeved look altered to angel innocence. "You know, that invitation says you can bring a guest."

"Boy, that's a friend." Neumann had given up waving bye-bye, and now played one-sided patty-cake. "You're lying there half-dead, and all he can think about is trolling for new victims at Mako's shindig."

Jani watched Neumann toy with his limb. "Stop by during morning vis and I'll let you know."

Lucien eyed her sourly. "Is that a hint?" Something banged against the door, and he hunkered down as if to dive under her bed. "I better get going. After what I heard about Pimentel, I don't want him to be the one to find me." After an obvious pause, he leaned down and gave her a brotherly kiss on the cheek before slipping out of the room.

"Isn't that sweet?" Neumann tossed his arm onto the top of a metal-frame table, and struggled to adjust his leg. Judging from the balletlike turn-out of his foot, it must have slipped from its tenuous mooring. "Well, Kilian, it's been lousy as ever. I'll leave you alone. Let you *digest* it all." He limped to the door, empty right sleeve soaked and dripping. Then he slapped his forehead, returned to the chair, and picked up the limb. "Forget my head next." He waved good-bye with the detached arm. " 'Course, I'd have to give you a chance to blow it off first." He exited through the door, literally, the blood from his blown leg squelching in his shoe.

Pimentel visited toward nightfall. He wore summerweights. Dress "B" shirt. Creases sharp enough to shave with. Eminently suitable for reaming North Lakeside ass.

We'll see, he said, when Jani asked him about Mako's party. He transferred data from the monitors to the recording board containing Jani's chart and gingerly examined her right arm. He seemed distracted. He asked her questions about Cal Montoya's diagnosis, and about John, and left without saying good night.

Morley brought her a snack. Not fruit sludge, but nutritional broth. Chicken-flavored. Spicy. With crackers, even. Jani savored it like a meal from Gaetan's.

Wonder if Neumann will come back. The prospect angered rather than scared her. *He's part of me.* Like Cray, and Borgie. She'd seen them the last time she visited Chicago. *They helped me solve a murder, too.*

Her door had opened wide before she realized it had opened at all.

"Captain?" Sam Duong slipped in, then skirted to one side so no one in the hall could spot him before the door closed. "Shh. I don't want Pimentel to see me."

Jani looked him over. He wore civvie summerweights. No sign of an outpatient bracelet. "Are you all right?"

"Yes." He eyed her in bafflement. "I'm on dinner break. I just stopped by to visit. See if you needed anything."

"A working brain."

"What?"

"Sit down, Sam." Jani watched him as he walked to Lucien's recently vacated seat. He looked a little wobbly himself—he gripped the chair arms the way she did, as though he'd fall off if he didn't hang on tight. "I've been thinking about Pierce."

Sam shot her the same aggravated look Friesian and Pimentel had been bestowing on her since her arrival. "You shouldn't be thinking about him. You should rest. Get better." He looked at her arms. "You fought. Now you should recover."

"Pierce and I have a lot in common. He told me so himself."

Sam chuffed. "You have nothing in common with him! You're lovely and he's—" His face darkened with embarrassment. "He's not."

"You shepherded the paper, Sam. Do you remember why I'm here?"

"Stupid reasons. No proof."

"I was wanted in connection with the death of my commanding officer." Jani knew Sam admired her, and it pained her to destroy it. But better he should know her for what she was. Better she should tell him things he couldn't remember. "I killed him."

"No—!"

And Pierce—She gasped as Neumann's words hit her like a punch. "And Pierce did me two better." She slumped forward and pounded the mattress with her fists. "Two better. Two better. Two better!"

"Captain?" Sam leaned forward, bracing his hands on the edge of the bed for support. "You look like you did under the awning. I don't think you should look like that now."

Jani thumped the bed, her right arm singing in time. "Pierce killed them, Sam."

"Keep your voice down!"

"For the good that thereof would spring. Then he stole the documents connected with my case because they could lead back to him.

And he stole other documents and put them back and set you up to take the blame."

Sam stared. Then he clapped his hand over his mouth to muffle his cry. "I did not put them there!"

"No." Jani massaged her aching arms. "Pierce was sent to do a very important job. Doing that job would have been the first step in saving the Service, the Service he'd come to love, thanks to Mako. The Service he'd come to see as his life." She held out her hand, as Pierce had. "It was night. The air reeked of panic and the stench of burning bodies. The Haárin had constructed the Ring of Souls around Rauta Shèràa—he was one of the happy few who witnessed the Laum line up to be slaughtered and tossed on the burning piles."

Sam closed his eyes.

"The base was a shambles, I'll bet. Partly from the Haárin bombing, partly from the efforts of Ebben, Unser, Fitzhugh and the rest trying to cover their tracks. But that was all right. Pierce was a weapons runner in the life he's left behind. He was used to thinking on his feet. Improvising." Her voice dropped. "Up to a point. I'll bet he was just supposed to arrest them. But they ran. Toward the city. The shuttleport. He'd never find them then." She looked at the stricken Sam, who still held his hand over his mouth. "What do you do? They're human and you're human and it's all going to hell and they're running. What do you do?"

Sam spoke through his fingers. "I yell for them to stop. The MPs always yell—"

"They *don't* stop, Sam! They keep running. A few more seconds, and they'll be gone. What do you do?"

Sam had raised his hand to object, but the protest caught in his throat. Instead, he raised his arm higher, straightened it, squeezed off. "I . . . shoot them."

"You shoot them." Kilian nodded. "And you know that no one can die by shooter on the Night of the Blade. So you shove the bodies in agers to rot them and hide the cause of death. Call it an awful mistake if anyone complains. Then you spend the next two decades building a career and trying to forget that one night when it all went to hell, when you became the thing you'd been sent to destroy."

"But Caldor—?"

"Not involved. She was only put into one of the agers to make it look like an accident." Jani thought back to Pierce on the day of the match, wound to snapping with anxiety, bursting with all the things he wanted to tell her because they had so much in common. "Could you stop by the hospital library and get me a copy of *Paradise Lost*?"

Sam eyed her strangely. "I suppose so." He took his handheld from his shirt pocket and entered a notation. "I'll go right now."

"Wait. Is there someplace you can spend the night?"

"Well." Sam frowned. "Tory invited me to her eighteenth birthday party. She feels *sorry* for me." He moaned in pain. "The music alone will kill me."

"You should go. You should pretend to get very drunk. Make someone put you up for the night. It should all be over after tomorrow."

"What's tomorrow?"

Jani forced a smile. "You're not the only social butterfly around here. I've been invited to a party, too."

CHAPTER 27

It took Evan several days to work out what must have happened. He ransacked the Family records that he'd been allowed to keep, searching for any references to Rauta Shèràa Base from the early days of the civil war through the evacuation and the long journey home.

Bless you, Mother. Since Carolina van Reuter was an Abascal by birth, she had persuaded her brother—the then–Exterior Minister—to copy her on the Mistys he received from both Rauta Shèràa and Ville Louis-Phillipe, the colonial port nearest Shèrá. The fraternal generosity should have ceased for security reasons as soon as conditions in Rauta Shèràa became dangerous, but owing to the pressure applied by the frantic Carolina, they never had.

Evan had found the messages, encased in parchment slipcases and bound with dark blue cord, in a set of silver brocade boxes stashed in the closet-sized spare bedroom. Well, that explained why Joaquin hadn't claimed them. He must have taken one look at the containers, assumed Carolina's personal missives, and allowed his sense of gallantry to overwhelm his lawyerly reason.

Good old Quino. Evan arranged the most important messages in a neat row atop his desk and reread them. In a court of law, they'd be considered insufficient evidence. Too many gaps that needed to be filled in by Evan's memory and his gut instinct.

"That's where the court of public opinion comes in." Or rather, the court of public opinion that mattered.

The first marker on the trail was a communication from J-Loop Regional Command to the Consul-General, who had relocated his offices to Rauta Shèràa Base after the Haárin started shelling the city. A timetable, informing him that three cruisers, the CSS

Hilfington, the CSS *Warburg*, and their flagship, the CSS *Kensington*, were being sent from Station Ville Louis-Phillipe to evacuate the human enclave.

The ships would take on additional supplies in preparation for the evacuees. They would also take on additional weapons. T-40 shooters, both short and long-range. Screech bombs. Smoke screens. No blades of any sort, however. Regional Command didn't want the Haárin to think humans wanted to challenge them with their ritual weapons of choice.

Evan underlined the sentence about the blades, and continued reading.

Since the ships would be fully outfitted prior to their arrival, no stops would be made on the way back to Earth. Most of the evacuees were Family members and affiliates, highly placed officials with heads crammed with sensitive information. They needed to be returned to the mother world as soon as possible for debriefing.

Evan underlined that sentence twice. "So why the detour back to Station Ville Louis-Phillipe, Roshi?" That could be discerned from the next two documents.

The defense Mako assembled to justify the return trip had been carefully assembled, with enough basis in fact to withstand examination. His argument, combined with his proof of Family criminal wrongdoing and his threat to make it all public, had allowed him to keep his career.

Facilities and Environmental were taxed to the limit, Mako had written. *Space was at a premium.* Therefore, there was no room to house "exceptional cases," those who could batter already-tenuous morale and endanger other passengers and crew. One evacuee who suffered from claustrophobia was put ashore at the Station, as was an odd case who had taken to lurking in the women's showers.

It surprised Evan to see that he had been one of the examples cited in Mako's defense of his sidetrip.

> *Mister van Reuter refuses to eat. He sleeps fitfully, and has been found wandering in restricted areas of the ship. If his condition does not improve soon, it's the recommendation of my medical officer that we put him ashore at Station Ville Louis-Phillipe, since it is her belief that he poses a danger both to himself and the other passengers and crew of the Hilfington.*

The name of the *Kensington* medical officer turned out to be Sophia Carvalla. *So she was in on it, too.* Evan didn't meet her during the journey, although he did recall meeting her at a party several years back. Seemed a sound woman. Just the sort her frazzled colleague from the *Hilfington* would consult with concerning his high-born problem patient.

And Mother got to read this fresh from the receiver. No wonder she had fallen apart at the sight of him. "I wasn't that much of a problem." True, he refused to eat. And he had trouble sleeping. But his appetite had never been the sturdiest, he had always suffered from insomnia, and the lack of liquor had made both situations worse.

Yes, I infiltrated a restricted area. Suicide had crossed his mind, and he wanted to see what the weapons lockers had to help him along. But that only happened once. At the start of the trip. When the memories were still fresh.

He opened the bottom drawer of his desk and unearthed a bottle.

"So they put two people offship, and topped off supplies." Took on prepack rations. Medical goods. And two meat-filled objects referred to only as *TD4J1* and *TD4J2*. Evan's intuitive leap with the decomp bags had led him to ask Halvor to make a special trip to question their grocer. Yes, the model numbers were old, but she recognized them. Agers. Meat-curing chambers.

Or meat-rotting chambers, if a person wasn't careful about the settings.

Which led to the fourth document, a handwritten communiqué from the unlucky clerk who had been the first to crack the *Kensington* hold seals at Luna Station.

> *. . . hosed them out. Shoved them into hold, Gleick said. Too many evacuees, not enough room. No time to care for the dead—they had the living to worry about.*

Mako, of course, took full responsibility for the error. "But it was no accident—he rotted those bodies for a reason." This was where the leap in logic came. Gut instinct.

Evan stood, stretched, walked around his tiny office. Adjusted the window controls and let the first light of day into the room. It had been years since he'd pulled an all-nighter. Good to know he still had it in him when he needed it.

"The way Ebben, Unser, and Fitzhugh died points to Pierce. Pierce killed them. Maybe he planned it himself. Maybe his criminal cronies sent him. Whatever happened, he shot them. Then he realized that if it was discovered they died by shooting, he couldn't blame the Haárin. So he ran squealing back to Daddy Mako."

And Daddy Mako fixed. By disobeying orders and detouring to Station Ville Louis-Phillipe to take on the agers, then shoving the incriminating shooter-burnt corpses in the meat boxes and cranking the settings to maximum. "The putting-ashore of the two nutcases was a decoy." As was the addition of the SFC to the mess. "Make it look like an accident by throwing in a nobody."

It must have been a difficult decision for Mako to desecrate an innocent like that. Or was it? Survival instincts had kicked into overdrive by that point. A man could find himself capable of anything when faced with the loss of everything he valued.

"Yes." Evan leaned against the window and took another swallow from the bottle. "I can't have been the only one to figure this out." He knew he possessed a sound native wit, and he could reason in the policy stratosphere when he needed to. *But it's all here.* All someone needed to do was comb and piece, and Families paid people lots of money to do just that. *He wrote a paper on Macbeth, for crying out loud. A story of a murderer driven mad by guilt. Jesus, Roshi, how could you let him walk around loose?*

"So here I have it." His great defense—one-third bluff, one-third bullshit, and one-third hard fact. "Government in a nutshell, part three." He hoisted the bottle in the air and toasted himself for a job well-done.

Before he could seal the self-congratulation with more bourbon, his door buzzer sounded.

"You're up early, sir." Halvor blinked blearily at him, then at the documents covering the desktop. "Is something wrong?"

"No. Not at all." Evan felt so pleased with himself, he even smiled at the young idiot. "What's up?"

Halvor yawned. "It's Mr. Loiaza, sir. He's here. He says he needs to speak with you."

"That was last night. As of this morning, she's still in hospital." Joaquin dabbed at the corner of his mouth with his napkin. "The idomeni are in quite the happy uproar. Tsecha actually told the Exterior Affairs correspondent for the *Tribune-Times* that the embassy had finally been properly blooded. I suppose that means that was the first bout that had been fought there. One doesn't know whether to be relieved or appalled." He wadded the linen square into a ball and tossed it onto his plate. "What utter savagery."

Evan picked at his omelet and snatched glances at Joaquin's face. The lawyer's expression remained placid. He seemed to have enjoyed the hastily assembled fare Markhart had prepared. They had elected to eat outside, and the man had joked amiably about the fact that the two-seat table filled the miniscule patio.

Evan took a sip of coffee. Too damned bland—he hadn't thought to lace it until they'd sat down to eat. He set down his cup. Tapped the rim of his plate with his fork. Waited. "What does it mean, Quino?" As if he didn't know.

"It means Kilian had been officially acknowledged by the Oligarch. It means she's proven her usefulness to the Commonwealth in a way we wouldn't have thought possible months ago." Joaquin stared out toward the cramped rear yard, the truncated banks of roses. "It means we need to talk, Evan."

"Yes, I—" Evan looked into Joaquin's turtle-eye stare, and his tale died in his throat. Better to hold his fire until he could see down the enemy's gullet. "You first."

"Thank you." Joaquin shot the cuffs of his charcoal day-suit. Even in the morning heat, he kept his neckpiece snug and his collar fastened. "You were never a man for weasel words. Well, outside my chosen profession, neither am I. I've been forced to admit a couple of things to myself these past few days. One is that taking you on as a client was the greatest miscalculation of my career."

Evan tried to probe Joaquin's expression. No use looking for signs of joking—at their level, one didn't kid a fellow about tossing him over the side. He forced a laugh through clenched teeth. "If you cut me loose now, I'll have a hell of a time bringing a new attorney up to speed for my trial."

Joaquin smiled coolly. "There will be no trial, Evan. Anyone as politically shrewd as you must have figured that out by now. The Service's refusal to charge Kilian with Neumann's murder negated your usefulness to them. It also gutted her usefulness to you. You needed her, Evan. You needed a foe with as many strikes against her as you could uncover in order to draw attention away from your own missteps."

He's saying you *now.* Not *us.* Not *we.* "The charges against me are independent of the ones against Jani. There's no reason for them not to proceed."

"If they did, you'd have a greater problem." Joaquin *tsked* in disgust. "I should have seen it coming. Mako had his own agenda all along. He stuck Kilian in the Psychotherapeutics ward as soon as she arrived at Sheridan—she's been in and out like a fiddler's elbow ever since. It's on paper that she's not entirely well between the ears. Attacking a sane alleged murderer is one thing. Engaging in the character assassination of a woman diagnosed as mentally incapable of defending herself would not have been the way to rebuild a political career. Thus does the Service guard its own." He took a linen square from his jacket pocket, dipped a corner in his glass of ice water, and patted it over his forehead. "Let's walk. It's stifling to sit in this heat."

"It's stifling to sit, period." Evan rose shakily, leaning on the table for support. "They can't just shunt me aside."

Joaquin locked his hands behind his back. He walked easily. No shakes. No nerves. Just another morning spent setting someone adrift on the stormy Family seas. "The evidence against you seems to have disappeared. No surprise there—Lady Commonwealth has a long reach. It doesn't do to reopen old wounds with the idomeni, who in their distinctly odd way have accepted the fact that Kilian is alive and in the public eye. It doesn't do to appear fragmented before the colonies."

Evan shook his head. He still found it hard to comprehend. His screwed-up Jani, the fulcrum on which two civilizations balanced. "She means that much to them?"

"On the day she's discharged from the Service, Felix has pledged to withdraw its lien against Fort Constanza. In addition, the Channel Worlds will sign a pact promising full cooperation with Exterior's efforts to rein in the runaway smuggling operations based in their sector." Joaquin leaned over to sniff a fully opened Nathan Red. "And let us not forget nìRau Tsecha, who just last night put forth an offer of GateWay rights to the Samvasta Outlet, the granting of which will shave one week off Outer Circle long-hauls." He plucked a partially opened bud and inserted it in his collar notch. "I don't relish telling you this, but we're both realists. It's moved beyond you, Evan. You're yesterday's news."

Evan kicked at a clot of soil. It exploded into powder against a stand of rocks. "What do you get out of this? A Cabinet Court retainer fee? NUVA-SCAN contracts?"

"I had those before. When I took you on, I lost them, one by one. Now, I'm getting them back."

"So you're working for them now. You didn't come here as my attorney. The Families sent you here to make me an offer."

"Offer? No. They sent me here to tell you the way it's going to be." Joaquin kept his turtle gaze fixed on the roses. "Arrest will be rescinded. Gradually. You'll have this house, and a stipend with which to run it. Your personal assets will be held in trust for a period of five years, during which time your conduct will be monitored. Behave, and when the term ends, you get the money. Step out of line even once, every bit reverts to the Treasury."

"The personal assets are nothing compared to the NUVA holdings!"

"Which reverted to the company on the day of your arrest." Joaquin shot a quick look at Evan's shoes, as if assuring himself of the distance between them. "After a year or so, a board meeting or two is a possibility, but only as a courtesy. You will have no voting rights."

"You can't confiscate my family's property!"

"Consider it reparations." Joaquin hesitated. "Some of us were very fond of Lyssa."

That was easy when you didn't have to live with her. "You said no proof existed."

"There's trial-quality proof, and there's the opinion of people who watched you grow up." Joaquin plucked a dead leaf from the stem of a Tsing Tao Pink. "If several members of the Cabinet had their way, you'd spend the balance of your life on a Lunar construction site welding transport frames. As it is, you'll have your native sky above your head and native soil beneath your feet. And you'll be cared for." His mouth twisted. "All the *medical* treatment your heart desires."

Evan followed Joaquin's gaze, still fixed on the flowers. Why did people love roses? All he saw were twists and thorns; their pungent perfumes, released by the first wash of sun, sickened him. "I'm too young to be shut away like this—I'll go mad."

"You don't have a choice."

"I'll demand a trial. I'll name names." Evan nodded firmly. "The van Reuters weren't the only ones who made money off Knevçet Shèràa technology, and they weren't the only ones with something to hide. I could tell you—"

"Who will listen to the ravings of a mentally impaired maintenance alcoholic? I received a copy of John Shroud's medical findings last night. Suffice it to say that if a person asked you if it were night or day, they'd be well advised to look outside first." Joaquin turned to him, stiff and formal, thirty years' acquaintance gone by the boards. "The sad end to a promising career, perhaps, but you did it to yourself. I'm only glad your parents aren't alive to witness the fall." He nodded. "If it's any consolation, you went farther than most of us thought possible. Good-bye, Evan."

Evan watched Joaquin walk up the shallow incline, the leather soles of his shoes sliding on the grass. He grappled with the urge to grab a spade from the shed, to run the man down and split his skull.

He slipped and hit his head. Honest, Officer. It was Chicago, after all. The Bluffs. The ComPol dealt with accidents like that all the time.

Instead, he shoved his hands in his pockets. When Joaquin disappeared through the doors, he made his own slow way up the slope. His feet dragged. His perception played tricks. The house seemed to draw farther away the closer he came—he knew if he turned around, he'd see himself standing at the bottom of the yard, staring back.

He closed his eyes. When he opened them, he saw Elba in all its poky homeliness sitting where it always had. He reentered the cool quiet of his tomb, closed himself in his office, and entered a code into his comport. It wasn't a personal code—he had to threaten several peons before he was sent through.

The pasty face formed on the display. "Evan." Shroud scowled. "What do you want?"

"Your head on a plate, you son of a bitch!" Evan sank into his chair. "You gutted me."

"Well, in the end, it did seem the best way to ensure Jani's safety." Shroud's voice rose and fell, a singsong of mock condolence. "What are you upset about? You won't face trial. You won't die."

"I'll go public—"

The voice flattened. "The comlog ensures that you will do no such thing." Shroud sat back. He wore medwhites. Greyed circles beneath his blue-filmed eyes combined with his chalky aspect to make him look like a nervous patient's worst nightmare. "Don't contact me again, or I may recommend hospitalization. Trust me, that's the last thing you want."

Evan opened a drawer, drew out a bottle, then put it back. "Tellinn was here."

"That doesn't surprise me."

"He says Jani's dying."

Shroud gave the smallest start. For an instant, he looked ready to crumble. But just for an instant "Good-bye."

Evan stared at the blank display. He didn't move until a shadow cut across his view. He glanced up to find Markhart standing deskside, regarding him thoughtfully.

"Mr. Loiaza seemed confident this morning, sir. I hope that means things are going well?"

"Things are great."

"How many for lunch?"

"One." He tasted the sound of the way it was. "Markhart, you said your sister worked at Fort Sheridan, didn't you?"

Markhart nodded. "Half shift in one of the snack bars. But only two days a week."

"Is today one of those days?"

"No, sir. Tomorrow is, though."

Tomorrow. Evan swallowed down a growl of frustration. *Take advantage of it.* That would give him plenty of time. To word things properly. To decorate the few facts he had with just enough bluff and bullshit. "Ask her if she'd do me a favor."

Markhart stared at him. "Sir—"

"Nothing illegal." Evan grinned reassuringly. "I'd just like her to deliver a note. To a friend."

CHAPTER 28

Pimentel balked when Jani mentioned attending the A-G's garden party. She wore him down over breakfast and had him convinced by lunch. But late that afternoon, when Lucien arrived with her gear, he wavered once more.

"I don't like this one bit." He watched Lucien lay out Jani's dress blue-greys on her bed. "You're in no condition to be discharged, much less attend a party."

"It's not like I'm going to dance the night away." Jani nestled in her visitor's chair and tucked her bare feet beneath her. "It's just a sedate little gathering. I'll make small talk, avoid the buffet, drink water, and lean on the lieutenant for support when necessary."

The supportive lieutenant continued his silent organizing, setting out her mirror-polished black tietops and running a cloth over her dress lid's black brim. Then he reached into his duffel and pulled out hairwash, makeup, and underwear.

When he removed the bouquet of miniature roses, however, Pimentel's eyes goggled. "What the hell?"

Lucien turned to him and smiled. It was an odd expression, one Jani hadn't seen before. It wasn't a broad smile, or a boyish grin, but a half-mast bend of lip accompanied by hard-eyed evaluation. It said that he liked doing things like this, and would do them for the colonel if the colonel wished. It added that he would do a lot of other things for the colonel, too, if the colonel were at all interested.

Pimentel shifted uneasily. "I have to go." He nodded brusquely to Jani and darted out the door.

Lucien looked at Jani, shrugged, and arranged the flowers in a handy water glass. He had already donned his blue-greys; his glossy hair had the look of a fresh trimming.

Jani watched him bend and turn—it was a pleasure, as always. "He's a happily married man."

"Most of them are." He glanced at her slyly. "Jealous?"

"Only if I thought you gave a damn."

"You mean there's hope?" He dawdled over the bottles, rearranging them according to size. "Guess I'm going to have to learn to give a damn."

"You'd need a different implant in your head."

"Oh well, so much for that." He rummaged through the bag, then turned it upside down and shook it. "That's it. I don't believe I forgot anything."

Jani counted the containers vying for space atop the small dresser. "No, I don't think you did, either." She untangled her legs and stretched her stiff muscles. She still couldn't support any significant weight with her right arm; getting up meant sliding to the edge of the chair and boosting upright with only her left arm for stability. Since the animandroid flesh was still sore, her legs felt rubbery, and her back ached, it resulted in a significant portside lean.

Lucien took a step toward her. "Do you need help?"

"I'm fine."

"You're bent into a letter C."

"I'm fine."

"Let me be supportive."

"Maybe later." She straightened, flexed her right arm, mouthed an "ouch," and walked to the bathroom.

Lucien drew alongside and paced her, step for shaky step. "I can wash your back."

"Go harass a nurse." Jani leaned against the bathroom entry. "Track down Morley—she's ripe for conquest."

"No, she's not." Lucien kicked at the floor. "I know her."

"Is that a fact?"

"She's a lot like you."

"I knew there was something about her I liked."

"You're up to something." Lucien helped Jani ease into the passenger side of a wheeled scoot. "You are being too damned . . . *military.*"

Jani unbuttoned her jacket and flared the bottom outward to avoid rumpling it. "I thought that's what you wanted."

"If it crossed my mind for one second that you were doing it for me, I'd check myself in for a takedown." He squeezed behind the steerbar. "You saluted Pimentel, fer chrissakes."

"He's a superior officer."

"He almost readmitted you on the spot." He pressed the vehicle charge-through. The motor hummed to life, and they trundled up the track designated for wheelworks. Progress proved slow; brisk walkers on the adjacent path passed them easily, and one wag shouted that the playground was in the other direction. "You aren't going to tell me a thing, are you?"

The landscaping kicked up a few grades as they crossed the Memorial Quad that separated South Base from North. Colonial shrubs outnumbered native; the flowers possessed the glassine petals and jewel colors that were the current fads among plant designers. "What do you want to know?"

"I want to know if I'm going to be court-martialed!" Lucien tapped an agitated song on the steerbar. "I know it's a minor consideration for you, but we don't all have your complete disregard for the things normal people care about!"

"You're normal compared to me, huh?"

"What the hell is that supposed to mean?"

"Nothing." She waited until his fidgeting eased. "I know why they're discharging me."

"Nema and the colonies will raise holy hell if they don't, that's why." Lucien glanced at her. "You don't think so?" He looked away, his hands tightening on the bar. "Anybody ever tell you that you think too much?"

"Only anybodys trying to hide things from me." As if to illustrate her point, the Base Command complex came into view. "It's bigger than I thought," she said, as they passed building after building. "How many people work there?"

"At any given time, about half." Lucien didn't even bother to grace his own joke with a smile. "*Well?*"

She told him. When she mentioned Sam Duong's framing, he threatened to toss her out of the scoot. By the time she explained about the agers, Pierce's ghosting, and the timing of Mako's invitation, his protests dwindled to the occasional sharp question.

The working portion of Sheridan gave way to the leisure regions. After passing the Officers' Marina, they puttered through a sprawling park. Another turn of corner and the A-G's whitestone residence loomed into view, a boxy, four-story edifice that resembled a well-landscaped office building more than a home. Uniforms and dressy civvies streamed in from all directions, guided by the faint glow of half-lit patio lights.

"The tent's on the north side," Lucien said halfheartedly, as he wheeled the scoot into a remote charge lot. Then he muttered something dark and Gallic, and smacked the steerbar with his open palm. "What do you need me to do?"

"Just stay within shouting distance." Jani patted her trouser pocket, checking for the slip of paper she'd tucked there. Sam had made good on his errand—she had spent most of the previous night reading snatches of *Paradise Lost* beneath the covers. Memorizing. Making notes.

She slumped into her hard seat, tried to figure a way she could get through this without depending on Lucien for help, and realized she couldn't. She still didn't know where he and duty parted company, didn't know the point at which his fear of Nema outweighed his loyalty to the Service or whoever else had laid claim to his attentions.

Lucien sighed loudly. "Shall we go?"

"I guess." Jani tried to slide out of the scoot by herself, but her right knee gave out, forcing her to wait for assistance. She leaned against Lucien so heavily he murmured in pleased surprise, and they joined the rest of the crowds streaming toward the Residence like ants toward the world's largest honey trap.

The years spent as Anais Ulanova's protégé had trained Lucien to deal with situations most people found daunting. He negotiated the social reefs and shoals of the tent like the seasoned sailor he was, dropping bon mots and names, eliciting greetings, laughter, and the occasional lustful stare.

Jani just nodded, mumbled "good evening," and watched the master. "You're good," she said, when they finally took a break and laid claim to a table near one of the numerous buffets.

"Ani gave a lot of parties." Lucien had collected ice water for her and a piled plate of hors d'oeuvres for himself. "It was either learn to play the room or check coats and work in the kitchen."

"She made you work?"

"One less temporary staffer she had to hire. One way or the other, she always got her money's worth."

Jani surveyed the scene around her. The tent was immense, and already filled from end to end. The buffet tables and bars that lined the walls were crowded, and the soundshielding fought a losing battle with the noise level. "Didn't you care for her at all?" She knew as soon as she'd asked that it was a stupid question. Partly inborn and partly inserted, Lucien's ability to care stopped at the end of his nose.

He shook his head, dark eyes blank. "She gave me what I wanted. Nice room. Nice skimmer. Clothes. Money." He had chosen the most select offerings from the buffet, exotic seafood, cheeses, mushrooms, and breads. "When I graduated prep school, she wangled me an appointment to East Point. I ranked fourth in a class of fifteen hundred and seven. That qualifies as good return on investment, by any measure."

"Why the Service?"

"I . . . like rules." He had the sense to smile. "Most times. I like knowing what I'll be doing the next day."

"Then why me?"

"You're for the rest of the time." The smile turned saucy. "When I'm in the mood to be totally confused." He glanced out at the milling crowd. "Speaking of which, do you expect something to happen, or are we supposed to force their hand?"

"I think it's happening now," Jani said, as an unfortunately familiar face came into view.

The dress blue-greys looked hand-tailored rather than line-cut, and the number of ribbons and badges arraying his chest was formidable. Despite that, Niall Pierce should have given up long ago. His damaged face and sinister air would forever mar any attempt at North Lakeside polish. Jani took a swallow of water and held it in her suddenly dry mouth. *Wonder why he never got his face fixed?* Maybe the ragged scar served as his equivalent of the healing gashes on her arms. *Wonder if whoever gave it to him is still alive?*

"Good evening, Captain Kilian." He waved for her to remain seated, his quick smile appearing snarl-like in the tent's subdued lighting. "Heard about your match. Congratulations are in order, I understand."

Jani swallowed the water with an audible gulp. "Thank you, sir."

Pierce looked at Lucien, who had stood up like a good looie, and his manner frosted. "Lieutenant. Tough loss the other day."

"Yes, sir."

"Your sweeper stinks."

Despite his social training, Lucien's grin visibly tightened. "We're working on replacing him, sir."

"The sooner, the better." Pierce then caught Jani by surprise by offering her his arm. "I wondered if you'd accompany me on a tour of the house, Captain."

"Sir." As Jani rose, she shot a sharp look at Lucien, whose return glare could only be interpreted to read "he outranks me." She held Pierce's arm as lightly as she could, and allowed him to lead her from the tent.

"You should watch him." Pierce's 'across the Yard' voice lifted easily above the party din. "I've been asking a few questions of my own. He meets with Justice Ministry officials every day."

"I know." Jani brushed off his look of surprise. "If he's so dangerous, why do you go out of your way to twist his tail?"

Pierce shrugged. "I've no use for his sort. Self-serving. No loyalty to anyone or anything save themselves."

"When did you acquire your experience with his sort—during your weapons-running days?"

"My crimes are no secret."

Aren't they? Jani tried to pull away from him, but he tightened his hold on her arm. Not hard enough to hurt her, but hard enough.

"I waited to hear from you concerning the reading list," Pierce said. "I've prepared one especially."

"I've been very busy."

"You're never too busy to learn."

"I'm sure you're right." Jani glanced back over her shoulder and down the fabric tunnel that connected the tent to the house. *So much for shouting distance*, she thought as she watched Lucien's silvery thatch disappear amid the crowd.

The tour began and ended in the same place, a sitting room on the second floor. It no doubt resembled every other sitting room where such discussions had ever occurred. The chairs were large and well padded, the windows darkened against any threat of accidental observation. A sideboard held a narrow selection of hard liquor. The basics—whiskey, gin, vodka. A bucket of ice.

She recognized Admiral-General Mako. General Carvalla. The three-star had to be Gleick, the base commander. There was also a two-star she didn't recognize, but no one seemed inclined to make introductions.

"So." She stepped inside. "Let's get the story straight now, in case it ever comes up. Where were we during the time this meeting never took place?"

Carvalla fidgeted. Gleick scowled. The two-star swirled his whiskey.

Mako smiled. "You were touring the house with Colonel Pierce. You stuck your heads in this room, and spoke with General Carvalla, who had a yen to sample my excellent vodka in private. A display of

Channel World curios in my library held your interest for quite some time. Then you and the colonel returned to the party."

"Shouldn't I be able to describe these fascinating curios?"

"Colonel Pierce will take you to see them after our meeting."

"And what about you and General Gleick and General . . . ?" She thought her prompting obvious, but no introduction to the silent stranger followed.

"We will see to ourselves, Captain." Mako's smile dimmed. "Thank you for your concern." He gestured toward a vacant chair near the center of their grouping. "How are you feeling?"

As Jani sat, she sensed Pierce move behind her chair. "I'm fine, sir."

Mako turned to Carvalla. "Is that true, Sophia?"

"Her test results are as screwy as ever." Carvalla sipped from a small, frosty cylinder with a silver handle. "Roger's worried that the readings we're getting aren't telling us what we need to know. He's desperate enough to contact Shroud."

Jani recalled Pimentel's edginess. "He's changed my diet. He's manufacturing a new liver for me. Is there something else going on I should know about?"

"Not one for the military courtesies, are you, *Captain*?" That was Gleick. Grey-haired. Bullet-headed. Face like a fist.

"No, I'm not." She withheld the "sir" deliberately, and watched him squirm. "But I didn't think you'd mind, seeing as we all have so much in common." She did a slow three-count. "Officer-killers, all."

CHAPTER 29

Everyone stared at her. Jani sensed Pierce, still behind her, like you'd sense eyes in the forest.

Finally, Mako broke the tension with a small snort of humorless laughter. "Not much for preliminaries either, are you, Jani?" He wiped a hand over his face, regarded his empty tumbler. "That's fine. Neither am I." The angle of his chairside lamp highlighted his fatigue-grooved jowls. "I gather you arrived at this conclusion during your explorations with the odd Mr. Duong?"

"He's not odd—you just made sure everyone thought so!" Jani sat back as tiny flecks of darkness bloomed and faded before her eyes. "My attorney had difficulty locating Rauta Shèràa Base documents I told him should have existed. Documents I'm charged with having neglected."

"Indeed," Gleick growled.

Jani looked at the man. He sat rigidly straight—she would have bet her 'pack the clear liquid in his glass was water. Physically, he looked nothing like Durian Ridgeway, but she could see the similarities just the same. The cutting voice. The air of judgmental superiority. *Behind every great man stands a creep with a shovel.* "You know, General, I bet you made one hell of a poop boy."

"*How dare you, you—*" Gleick had half risen out of his chair, but settled back in shocked surprise when Mako held out his hand.

"Sit down, Gunter." The look he gave Jani was stern, but not unkind. "I've known Spacers like you before. When their expertise is needed, none are better. As you proved yesterday, at the idomeni embassy." He nodded slowly. "But your times are few and far between, and those betweens are the career-killers, aren't they, Jani?"

Throwing a fistful of stars at me didn't work, so now you're trying understanding. "I had the sort of career that killed itself. I conducted audits on Rauta Shèràa Base—that was no way to win friends." *Stay on course—don't let him distract you.* "One thing I learned is that the reason documents disappear is because they lead to bigger and better things."

"Paper disappears because nobody cares about it," Gleick grumbled. "It disappears because it doesn't matter."

Jani ignored him. "The *Kensington* shipping records, for example, that described the loading of two agers."

Mako waved a dismissive hand. "I admitted in closed-door sessions long ago that in our haste to free up space for evacuees and supplies, we accidentally packed bodies in unsuitable containers."

Jani nodded. "Yes, and it's a shame that that story doesn't hold up, because it's nice and simple. Short of space, let's get these bodies out of the way—whoops, we loaded them in the wrong sort of box, but we were in a hurry, you see. SFC Caldor was a sound move. Good randomization. If a little nothing colonial got stuck in an ager, well, it couldn't have been planned. Had to be an accident."

A cloud passed over Mako's face. "I did not consider Caldor a 'little nothing colonial,' Jani."

"Then I stand corrected." Jani touched her face—the skin felt hot and dry. Her heart pounded.

"Are you all right?" Carvalla set her drink on her chairside table, and sat forward. "Get her some water, please, Niall."

Mako looked at Jani, then at Carvalla. "Sophia?"

"I don't like how she looks at all."

"*I'm all right.*" Jani sat back, inhaled deeply, tried to relax. But when she attempted to cross her legs, the right one wouldn't work. She couldn't even lift it off the ground. "The question is, why go through the trouble to rot the bodies? What was it about them that you couldn't afford to let others see?"

She looked up just as Pierce leaned over to place the water glass on her table. His eyes proved his only handsome feature, rich gold-brown, like honey.

"They deserved it." His voice held an eager rasp, as though he felt he had to convince her.

Jani nodded encouragement. "They ran, and you had to stop them because they were headed into Rauta Shèràa, and once they disappeared into the city, you'd have lost them for good."

"They deserved it. Do you know some of the things they did?"

"I lived some of the things they did." Her dull tone made Pierce cringe. "You were just supposed to arrest them, weren't you? Those were your orders. But they ran. And you're another of Mako's Spacers—it was between-time for you. He gave you your big chance, and you let him down." They'd begun to breathe as one. Short. Sharp. Inhale. Exhale. " 'Which way I fly is Hell; myself am Hell.' "

"Book Four, Satan's entry into Paradise. Out of context. You need to study before you can toss lines at me. I lived it!"

"What did you do, Niall, blow them apart with a long-range?"

"They deserved it!" His beautiful eyes described the ugly details. He held out the glass to Jani with a tentative hand. As if whether or not she took it from him would forever define something between them.

Jani took it. "I can't argue with that." She sipped the metallic-tasting water and set it down. "I can't argue with that at all. But the problem isn't whether I agree or disagree, the problem is that I *know.*" She looked at Mako, Carvalla, and Gleick in turn. "So, that's my side. I'm assuming you asked me here to give me yours."

Gleick's lip curled. "We don't owe *you* any explanations."

Mako closed his eyes. "*Gunter.*"

"Damn it, Roshi, stop coddling her! She didn't do it for the good of the Service, like—"

"Like we did?" The eyes that opened held the dimming light of a suddenly older man. "No, Spacer Kilian didn't kill for the good of the Service. She killed because people were dying horribly, and she wanted to make it stop." Mako tipped his glass back and forth. It had been empty since Jani entered the room. Looked, in fact, as though it had never been filled. "Isn't that true?"

Jani listened to the sound of ragged breathing behind her. Pierce, reliving Hell. "Does it matter?"

Mako held out a hand, palm facing up. "Perhaps not." But something in the way he looked at her indicated that it did. When he donned his uniform and appraised himself in his mirror, he no longer felt the way he wanted to. And he blamed her for it.

Jani read his single thought easily, followed its flarelike track. "You'd have me executed, if you could. But I've become a symbol. The Channel Worlds would make trouble, and that could increase the dissension between the colonials and Earthbounders in the ranks. And you know a fragmented Service would lose against the idomeni. Nema's hinted at that, hasn't he? War. I think you blinked where that was concerned. He couldn't have convinced Cèel to go to war over me. But you had seen the Haárin fight in Rauta Shèràa. You didn't want to chance battling them with divided troops."

"You credit yourself with formidable influence, Kilian." Gleick still couldn't let go the old standard. "You're nothing."

Jani breathed, but couldn't sense her chest rise or fall. Her legs felt numb. She wondered if Pierce had poisoned the water. "If I'm nothing, then have Pierce escort me to the brig. Process me. Treat me the way I should have been since you nailed me on Felix. Prosecute me—for Neumann's death." She stopped to catch her breath. "Stop throwing roadblocks in the way of Colonel Veda's investigation. Then watch her reach the same conclusion I did, because any investigation of Knevçet Shèràa will lead her right back to Rauta Shèràa Base on the Night of the Blade."

Gleick's mouth moved, but no sound emerged. Carvalla tossed back the balance of her vodka. The silent two-star, whom Jani had forgotten about, watched her unmoving, like a snake on a rock.

Mako finally spoke. "What do you want?"

"What do I *want*?" Jani tried to shrug. "Nothing." Her limbs felt leaded. "To be left alone."

"A job befitting your training?"

"Anyone with a scanpack can earn a living."

"But people will still think you a killer. They'll think you got away with it."

"I don't care what people think of me."

"Don't you?" Mako cocked an eyebrow. "This isn't some Outer Circle backwater, Jani, this is Chicago. The Commonwealth capital. Home base for all us Earthbounders of whom you think so little. You're the Eyes and Ears, a famous woman. Nema has formally declared you. Your days of hiding are over. What some people in this city think of you will shape your life." He touched fingers to forehead in a mock salute. "The Prime Minister and the Exterior Minister, for example. Let me commend you. You've managed to acquire some very powerful enemies in a very short time."

"I'll leave Earth."

"Your medical condition prevents that. The only facilities that can treat you properly are located here. From what Sophia tells me, if you left Earth now, you could be dead in a month."

"That's ridiculous." Jani paused to breathe. "I feel fine."

"Why are you so determined to make it hard for yourself?" Mako gestured to the silent two-star, who set down his glass and reached into his inner tunic pocket. "Li Cao is agreeable to releasing you, but to appease some of her more vocal critics, she needs a victim. It's a matter of record that the late Sergeant Emil Burgoyne threatened the late Colonel Rikart Neumann on several occasions. The Judge

Advocate is prepared to make a ruling that all evidence points to him as Neumann's killer."

Jani looked at the eerily silent man, who had taken a piece of paper from his pocket and now noiselessly unfolded it. "You're the Judge Advocate General?" He nodded. "You want me to hand my sergeant over to save myself?"

"*Your* sergeant?" Mako smiled coolly. "He's dead, Jani. I hardly think he'll mind."

"He didn't do it!"

The JA held up his piece of paper. "Even the most cursory glance at the late Sergeant Burgoyne's record would give one pause, Captain." He again reached inside his tunic and removed a stylus. "All we need to close the case is a signed statement from you that you witnessed such threats, but failed to report for fear Sergeant Burgoyne would turn on you as well."

Jani looked from Mako to the JA. "Are you familiar with the concept of untoward influence?"

The snake didn't blink. "We have a Service to protect."

"I trusted Borgie at my back."

Gleick snorted. "You consider that a recommendation?"

"I wouldn't trust *you* out of my sight!" She felt her eyes grow heavy. "He was worth twelve of any one of you." Her shoulders slumped. "He was worth twelve of every one of you."

Pierce touched her shoulder. "Kilian, take the deal."

Jani shook him off. " 'Ease would recant vows made in pain,' Niall. Book Four, again. That's another way of saying I don't want to wind up like you." She sat forward. The room darkened. "I stood here. Neumann stood"—she stretched her aching arm, and sighted down—"four paces in front of me."

"Five." Neumann sat on the arm of Carvalla's chair, detached leg swinging sideways from his hip, back and forth like a pendulum. "And I was a little off to the right, but keep going, keep going. I'll dance at your execution yet."

"Not with one leg, you won't."

"Captain?" Carvalla glanced at the chair arm in alarm. "Are you all right?"

"*Five* paces." Jani pointed her finger at Neumann. "He told me about the patients." She squeezed the imaginary charge-through. "He made me an offer, too." Neumann blew her a kiss.

Mako and Carvalla looked at one another. Mako's eyes widened, and Carvalla sat back.

"I understand guilt," Mako said.

"No, if you did, you'd have locked down Niall long ago. He kept turning up, and I had to ask myself why?" Jani kept her finger pointed at Neumann—it felt as weighty as a long-range. "I shot Neumann. I didn't know whether he had drawn his weapon, and I didn't care. I'd have killed him if he'd been unarmed. If he'd been sitting at his desk. If he'd been asleep."

"Brava." Neumann stood, bowed to her and clapped his hands. "Do you want me to kick my leg across the room for emphasis?"

"I killed him. Then Yolan died. Then the patients. Because of me. Then I killed the Laum. Then Borgie and the rest of the Twelfth died. Because of me." She stopped to breathe. "I almost died, but John stuck his nose in. I wish he hadn't."

Pierce whispered, "Jani—"

"I admit to murder, yet you'll hand me the lie to save myself. Why?"

Mako had the gall to look humble. "Because you are a good Spacer who deserves a second chance."

"And you're the honorable man who'll give it to me." She watched him watch her. "I'm not honorable. I've known that for years. It's difficult, at first, admitting that you're no better than what you are, that you'll do whatever it takes to survive. Deal with whatever devil rears his head. But it gets easier as time goes on. Doesn't it, Roshi?"

"I'm offering you a new life."

"And all I have to do is abet the libel of a dead man." Jani held up her left hand so she could shake her finger. Since the arm felt numb to the shoulder, she had to watch to make sure she did it. "No, I'm wrong. You can't libel the dead. Supposedly." She let the arm drop. "I killed Neumann."

"The evidence doesn't exist."

"I admit it freely."

"The court will not accept your word as anything but the guilt-ridden ramblings of a traumatized woman," Mako said. "The world outside court is, of course, a different story."

"You have paper proof concerning Borgie?"

"Of sufficient scope that guilt can be assumed, yes."

"Where is it?"

The snake glanced up from his paper. "Hidden, Captain."

Jani nodded. Across the room, Neumann clucked his tongue, then stuck it out at her. She stood up slowly. "Good evening."

Carvalla tried to rise as well, but Mako held up his hand, and she sat back. "Good evening, Jani. You know where we are if you should change your mind."

Pierce caught up to her just outside the door. "They're giving you a chance." He grabbed her sore arm and spun her around. "Take it and run!" Jani stifled a scream, and he released her like hot metal and backed away.

She waited for the haze in front of her eyes to clear. "I said I couldn't argue with you about killing them. I meant that. But there are limits—you know that better than I do." She pulled the slip of paper from her pocket. "I had to write this down. No time to memorize everything. We're still in Book Four. It seemed to describe you so well." She blinked at the paper until the words came into focus.

" 'Horror and doubt distract his troubled thoughts, and from the bottom stir the Hell within him.' " She heard Pierce speak the words as she read them, and slowed her voice to pace his. He knew it better than she did, after all. " 'For within him Hell he brings, and round about him, nor from Hell one step, no more than from himself, can fly by change of place.' " She paused to breathe, and heard Pierce pause beside her. " 'Now conscience wakes despair that slumbered; wakes the bitter memory of what he was, what is, and what must be worse; of worse deeds worse suffering must ensue.' " She folded the paper and slipped it back into her pocket. "I think that means it's only going to get worse from here. I think it means Sam Duong and Borgie are only the beginning." She looked past Pierce's sliced face, and spoke to the unscarred man. "Smearing Borgie bothers you the most, doesn't it? It should. Shame on you, Sergeant. He was one of yours." She turned her back on him and walked slowly down the hallway.

"So, what do we do now?" Neumann crab-walked beside her, cartwheeling his arms, pushing the right one back up his sleeve every time it slipped.

"SIB."

"Oh, Christ, I hate that place." As they walked through the foyer, he looked toward the door leading to the party tent. "Where'd your rent boy run off to?"

"I don't know."

"Guess it's just you and me, Kilian. At each other's throats, just like old times."

"Just like old times."

CHAPTER 30

The other techs had gone on break. Sam sat at his desk and picked through his perfunctory task. *Alphabetize these lists, Sam*, Odergaard had told him, while strangers guarded his dead.

"Mr. Duong?"

Sam looked up. Kilian leaned against the wall of one of the other cubicles. Hanford's, the gum-chewer. He wanted to warn her that if she wasn't careful, she would stick to the partition, but something about the expression on her face told him she wouldn't appreciate the joke.

"Captain." He stood slowly, one eye on the entry, on the lookout for breaktime returnees. "How was your party?"

"Can you get into secured records?" Kilian's light brown face was purpled, as though she'd been running. Yet she didn't sweat—her skin looked papery, as though it would tear if Sam touched it. She stepped forward, dragging her right leg. She had undone the collar of her dress tunic—a crescent of white shirt showed in the V. "I need—Sergeant Burgoyne's record." She stopped to breathe. Her eyes glimmered with fever. "Can you get it?"

"I—don't have the codes."

"Can you find them?"

"I need to break into Odergaard's desk."

"What kind of lock is it?"

"A single-finger."

"Those are easy."

They both smiled, in spite of the odd tension, and her strange behavior.

"They're going to smear him." Kilian's smile faded. "Borgie.

They're going to say"—again, she stopped to take a breath—"he killed Neumann. But he didn't—I did."

"Because of us?"

"Yes." Kilian stared at him, her eyes filling. It was a terrifying sight, that abject vulnerability in one so contained, like watching the ground fissure at your feet. "You're Simyam Baru, aren't you?"

"Yes." Sam sagged against the desk. He felt so weak, but just on one side. He touched the right side of his face, tracing the jagged outline where the skin had peeled. Up to his temple, then alongside his ear, the line of his jaw, to his chin. "I wondered when you'd recognize me."

"You don't look the same."

"Neither do you, Captain." He felt a rush of compassion for her, this woman who lived only to dash herself against rocks. "But people are more than their faces, are they not?"

Kilian slumped against the partition, then edged along it and around the corner, finally scrabbling for purchase on the brink of a vacant desk. "How did you get away?" She squinted at him and blinked repeatedly, as though she had trouble focusing.

Her vision is going. He felt for his comport pad. "I should call the hospital—"

"Answer the question."

He pulled his hand back. "Orton had been our driver during our previous expeditions. She had never handled a people-mover of that size before, but—"

"Orton couldn't see. They'd severed her optic nerves so they could input directly into her visual cortex."

"The best pilots handle a craft by feel."

"Not to that extent."

"I was her eyes. I told her where to steer."

"Right over a blind jump and into the path of a Laumrau scout." Service disgust for all reasoning civilians dulled Kilian's overbright eyes. "I saw the flash from the roof of the hospital."

"I was never a soldier, Captain." Civilian disgust for all things Service darkened Sam's voice. "I did not understand the concept of ambush until too late." He touched his face again. "Orton died. Fessig. I was the only one to survive the crash."

"Any injuries?"

"My left arm." He flexed it. "Broken."

"How did you get—to Rauta Shèràa?"

"I walked for hours. The sun at my back. Toward the city. Just when I thought I could walk no farther, I was rescued by a group of xenoanthropologists. They had been conducting research in the central plains, and had received the evac order from their inpost in the city." Sam watched as Kilian's shoulders rounded, slumped. *She's too weak to sit up.* "How did you get here from the party?"

"I swiped a scoot and don't change the subject!" Again the pause to breathe. "Who were the xenos affiliated with? A university? A collective?"

"I was in no condition to inquire."

"Can you recall any of their names?"

"No." He had tried to remember. He recalled snatches of faces—dark eyes, kind smiles—but he could never remember more. "They bandaged my face and arm as best they could and took me to the shuttleport in Rauta Shèràa. From there, I begged passage from a merchant transport bound for Phillipa."

"How did you pay? Did your rescuers pass the hat?"

"No." Details had always been fuzzy there, too, but considering the circumstances . . . "I begged. They let me on."

"No one would have given a billet to a broke and injured incoherent."

"Compassionate people exist, Captain, even in shuttle-ports."

"Name one." Kilian squinched her eyes shut. Opened them. Shook her head. Then she paused, tensed, as though she heard a far-off sound and was trying to place it.

"Do you hear something?" Sam watched the doorway, on the lookout for returnees.

"No one important." She muttered under her breath, as though she argued with someone close by. When she finally looked at him, rage glittered in her fevered eyes.

"Everyone says—you're sick." Her voice shook. "You have a tumor in your thalamic region that induces—a type of amnesia. You can't recall your own past, so you substitute other people's. For some reason, you've fixated on Knevçet Shèràa—and Simyam Baru. It makes sense. You're both Bandan. Similar, physically. But he's dead, and you are, and have always been, Sam Duong." She wiped her hand across her cheek, and looked down at the floor. "Too much coincidence, otherwise. Why, after all these years—would you wind up here?"

Why, indeed? That area of Sam's life had always been fuzziest of all. *Why am I here?* "So I could thank you." Yes, the relief that flooded him as he spoke told him those were the right words. "For trying . . . for trying to save us. I knew, if I waited here along enough"—his voice quickened as his assurance grew—"if I waited here long enough, you'd show up. Eventually."

Kilian stared. "Thank me—?" Her voice cracked, and she pressed a hand over her eyes.

Sam fixed his attention on the door to allow her some privacy. And to watch for his officemates, who would be filing in any moment now.

Kilian wiped her eyes with her tunic sleeve, and looked across the gulf of years at him. "Could we try to get hold of Borgie's—"

The alarm klaxon blatted. It pounded eardrums with physical force, pressing around them with walls of sound.

"It's a fire drill." Sam swept the work orders into a drawer, and locked it. "Only a fire drill, Captain." He looked over at her. "Follow me—"

Kilian sat rigid on the edge of the desk. Her eyes had gone black glass, her skin, dun clay.

"Captain." He stepped up to her, nudged her arm, then grabbed her shoulder and shook. "It's just a drill!"

"You have to get out." Her breath smelled like sweet vinegar. "They're coming—"

"*Duong!* Move your ass!" Odergaard stuck his ever-red face in the door. "It took us three minutes to clear the floor last time. You know we need to break two!" His voice rang down the hallway. *"Move! Move! Move!"*

Kilian had hidden behind the partition during Odergaard's short tirade. Now, she jerked. Gasped. "*Run.*"

"Captain—"

"*Run.*" She looked him in the face, but whatever her eyes saw, he knew it had nothing to do with him, or anything else in the here and now. "Get out while you still have a chance. Neumann's made a deal with the Laumrau. They're going to perform tests on you. You'll die. You have to go *now!*"

"But they check for stragglers after everyone is outside—"

"Let them." She grabbed him by the elbow, dragged him out of the office, and pushed him down the hall toward the exit. Then she took off in the opposite direction and disappeared around the corner, her stride an odd skip-walk because of her stiff right leg.

He stood in one spot, the siren blare squeezing him until he thought he'd scream. *Run! Neumann's coming!* He pelted down the halls, his weak leg causing him to stumble, up the stairs, through the building entry, out the door, and collided with—

He looked up into the face that stared down at him, saw white and death and eyes like ice. This time, he did scream.

"Oh bravo, John." Another man slipped an arm between Sam and certain doom and pushed them apart. His hair was light brown, his skin pale, but he looked like night next to the grey-suited thing beside him. “My name is Val Parini. This is John Shroud.” His voice held that clipped, professional calm that reminded Sam of flavored ice—sweet, cold, nothing. “We’re looking for Jani Kilian—do you know who she is?”

“That lieutenant said she fled here from the party.” Shroud stalked to the SIB entry, his white skin glowing beneath the chemical discharge of the security lighting. “We need to get her out now. If what Pimentel says is true—”

“What do you mean, *if!*” Pimentel of the surgery threats broke away from a nearby huddle and strode toward Shroud, his finger raised like a shooter, medwhites fluttering in the night breeze. “Are you doubting my veracity *again*, Doctor?”

Parini stepped between Shroud and Pimentel. “If you two don’t shut the fuck up—!”

A Spacer in black night fatigues ran past them. “The doors are all locked,” she said to a similarly garbed figure who’d been talking to Pimentel. Behind her came outlines. Many outlines.

As Pimentel’s black garb drew closer, shadows resolved into a pushed-up hoodmask. Hair like corn-silk. “Did you try the emergency exits?” the young man asked as he pocketed a handcom.

“They’re locked from the inside.”

“Shit.” The handcom beeped, and he slapped it silent. “Is anyone left in there with her?”

“Not according to the Fire Drill Teams. Everyone present and accounted for.” The young woman hesitated. “Sir, I think she’s gotten into central systems. That means she’s controlling all access and environmental.”

“Override from South Central Facilities.”

“I tried them. They can’t. She’s blocked them.”

“How!”

“She said one-finger locks were easy.” Sam floundered when he realized everyone had stilled to listen to him. “That—that’s what she said.”

“Does she know that much about structures?” one of the fatigues piped.

“She was a registrar and a smuggler,” another said. “She knows where to look and where to hide.”

Glum silence fell. They turned as one to look at the building, as if to assure themselves it was still there.

“Her ID chip’s rigged with a security lock,” someone mumbled. “Just blast her one and get it over with.”

"*Who said that!*" Shroud's voice boomed over their heads. "Captain Kilian is gravely ill. She requires immediate hospitalization. She is unarmed and a danger to no one but herself. If you spot her, mark her position and notify a med immediately." He turned to the cornsilk blond, and his voice dropped. "She is unarmed, isn't she?"

"Yes," Cornsilk said. Both men sagged in relief.

Shroud's ice stare sought out Sam. "Is she hallucinating?"

Sam nodded.

"Do you know who she sees?"

"I think that's rather obvious, John," Parini said. "Considering the circumstances."

"You need to get in there." A thin, dark-haired man broke away from another huddle that had gathered by an ambulance. "Carvalla said she was showing signs of respiratory distress."

"Her breathing isn't right," Sam said. Again, he hesitated as everyone quieted to listen to him. "She's dragging her right leg."

"Did she seek you out?" Shroud asked, broad brow furrowing.

"That's Mr. Sam Duong," Pimentel said. "I told you about him."

"Oh." Shroud's gimlet eyes narrowed.

"Can we get back to the matter at hand?" Parini snapped. "We know her neuropathy's progressing. Is paralysis ever complete?"

"Rarely," the dark-haired man said. "It's not unheard of, however—"

"Answer the goddamn question, Hugh!"

"Could she stop breathing! Yes!"

Shroud paced the sidewalk. "We need to get in there."

"We're rousting someone from the JA with a spotter so we can pinpoint her location using her chip." Cornsilk's handcom squealed once more. This time he answered. Barked one-word questions. Signed off. "The cracker team is on their way with ramming equipment. They'll be here in two minutes."

"We may not have two minutes," dark-haired Hugh muttered. A ragged look passed between him and Parini.

"What the hell?" A single voice lilted in wonder. "What is she doing?"

Everyone turned, and watched as section by section, floor by floor, the lights went out all over the SIB.

CHAPTER 31

Jani flashed the stylus, flicking closed the last UV switch, shutting down the hospital's interior lights as she had the entrance-exit controls and the ventilation. It would be difficult to see her way out of the central-utilities chase with only the sulfur glow of emergency illumins to light the narrow walkway, but it was safer that way. The Laumrau monitored the building systems using remotescan, and aimed shatterboxes at any area that showed signs of electrical life.

"I should have thought of this before the first wave." The barrage that followed her killing of Neumann and the subsequent fleeing of the Laumrau staff to the safety of the hill camps. The barrage in which Yolan died.

"If fucking were thinking, you'd be a genius, Kilian." Neumann's voice sounded from a pitch-dark corner of the chase. "Otherwise, you're boxed rocks." He had followed her into the guts of the building as he had through the halls and offices, offering sarcasm and useless advice as she broke into desks and cabinets in her hunt for weapons and handy objects like the stylus.

"You only started calling me stupid after I turned you down." Jani closed the switch box and turned to walk to the door. Tried to walk to the door. Her right leg hung her up again. "I think your bias is showing." She leaned against the wall and tried to shake the feeling back into the numb limb.

"Still time to make up for any regrettable lapses in judgment." Neumann stepped between her and the door and waggled his bushy eyebrows. She would have maneuvered out of his reach if she could have seen him approach, but he seemed to follow quantum rules when it came to movement. First he'd be one place, then another, with no transition she could see.

"I'd rather be found dead in this basement," she said as she brushed past him, close enough to smell his cinnamon breath. His thick, grasping fingers closed around her arm, and she struck out. His cry of pain and rage as her fist connected with the point of his chin was worth the agonizing shock that rang from her knuckles to her shoulder.

"You're gonna get your wish, Kilian!" he called after her as she exited the chase. His voice sounded muffled, as though his mouth bled.

The thought made her smile.

"*Borgie!*" She sagged against a wall and struggled for breath, then grabbed for a door handle for support as her legs crumpled beneath her.

"He ran." Neumann leaned against the wall opposite and folded his arms. "Left you high and dry." The right arm slipped, and he shoved it back into place with a muttered curse.

"He'd never do that."

"Could, would, and did, Kilian." Neumann fussed with his bloody sleeve. "You always put your faith in the wrong people."

In the distance, a dull thud echoed. Jani pushed away from the wall, and looked down the hall in the direction of the sound. "What was that?"

"How the hell should I know?" Neumann ratcheted his leg, which had twisted out of position. "Maybe it's company."

"Second wave?" Jani limped down the hall. The thud sounded again, this time with a higher pitch.

"Shatterboxes don't thump, you dumb bitch, they sing." Neumann shambled toward her. "Sounds like a door ram to me."

"I set all the main doors to close before I deactivated the access controller."

"So whoever's out there is going to have to ram through a whole lot of doors before they get to us. Great. That should make them good and pissed by the time they get down here." He squinted. "What's that stuff yorking out from the stairwell?"

Jani looked to the end of the hall, where a thick stream of gaseous muck billowed under the sealed door. Gaseous, fuchsia-colored muck. "They're lobbing pink." Jani's throat closed at the memory of the thick, cotton-candy smell. "Pink's *heavy*—it drifts down."

"And we're in the basement." Neumann laughed. "Good job, Kilian. You've set yourself up to suffocate to death."

"Pink's *heavy*—the cloud will settle around my knees."

"And what knees those are." Neumann's leer stripped her trousers away like paper. "Well, the real one, anyway. The fake one, however, could be in for a bit of malfunction. In fact, those animandroid limbs of yours might be just what those little beasties need to whet their appetites for the comports and workstations."

Jani tapped the fire-alarm touchbox inset in the wall by her head. "It washes out if you catch it fast. You can hose bright red air clean in seconds." She removed the purloined UV stylus from her pocket, activated it, and pressed it to each corner of the alarm pad in turn. As she touched the last corner, the plastic shield disconnected and fell to the floor, revealing a host of fire safety contacts, all clearly marked. Elevators. Alarms. Extinguishers.

Jani touched the stylus to the Extinguishers slot. With a series of hisses, reservoirs in the walls and ceiling opened. Liter after liter of fire-retardant foam spewed from inset sprayers, coating all surfaces in heavy white cream.

"*You idiot!*" Neumann covered his face with his hands and dashed into the nearest clear space.

Jani followed. Stopped in the entry. Looked around. *What's a vending alcove doing in an idomeni hospital?* That disquiet made way for greater concerns when she saw that no foam streamed from any orifices in the alcove walls or ceiling. Any pink that wended down the hall would find refuge here, seeping into the air-handling system through the floor-level vents.

"I don't believe you did that!" Neumann spat foam, coughed foam, blew it from his nose and scooped it from his eyes and ears.

"Anything that can push the pink out of the air and down will work long enough for me to think of what to do next." Jani slapped foam from her arms and face as she opened the coolers, the cabinets, and dispensers, looking for anything she could use as a hammer. As Neumann muttered and sputtered, she yanked opened the last door.

What the—! She reached out, picked up what her eyes saw and what her mind called impossible. The long handle, that seemed molded to fit her hands. The sensuous curve of blade. What a Sìah fighting ax was doing in a vending alcove janitor's closet, she had no idea, but she wasn't going to argue with providence. She swung it at the plastic cooler and dispenser connections—water geysered to the ceiling and rained to floor.

"They're coming, Kilian." Neumann sloshed to the door and stuck his head as far as he dared into the jetting whiteness beyond. "Those bashes are sounding closer and closer."

Jani swung the ax through the private rainstorm, and heard another sound, a sound she knew Neumann couldn't hear. A sound of her very own.

Do that again, augie whispered as metal cut the air. *I like it.*

"Hey, Kilian, stop making like the Ride of the Valkyries. We need to find the way to the subbasements. I thing they're in the stairwell."

"I'm not going anywhere." Jani stilled the blade, held it up to her face, and caught sight of her bright eyes in the mirror metal.

You owe me, you know. Augie whispered sternly in her ear.

Jani nodded in agreement. She was never meant to escape. Never meant to be free. She was meant for steel and rainbow edges glistening in the light. "Didn't you say something recently, sir, about me waiting for the chance to blow your head off?"

"What?" Neumann turned to her, his eyes widening in gratifying horror as he watched her cut patterns in the air. "That was a joke, Kilian."

"Strange. I didn't think it funny."

"We have to get out of here!"

"Why do you care?" Jani contemplated the blade's wispy Sìah tracework. "You're dead."

"I'm not armed, Kilian." Neumann pulled his right arm out of its sleeve and waved it at her. "I mean, I'm really not."

"Haven't you figured out that among all my other sterling qualities, I'm also a dirty fighter when need be?" Jani slashed the ax through the rain—the very molecules screamed in agony.

"Kilian!" Neumann backed too quickly, and slipped on the carpet of water. "We can work this out!" He fell backward with a loud splash, then scuttled cripple-crablike behind the shelter of a table.

"No. No." Jani's voice reverbed inside her head. "I've had just about all I'm going to take from you."

Neumann shot upright from behind the table like a pop-up toy. "I'm ordering you to desist!" He tried to skirt to one side as Jani closed in from the other. His detached leg shot out from beneath, sending him sprawling across the tabletop. For a perfect moment, he lay on his stomach, arm spread out to the side, neck exposed.

Jani sidestepped into position. Swung the ax up. "*Declaration is made*," she said as she brought it down.

Neumann's head bounced off the table and across the alcove floor like a deflated soccer ball across a soggy field, leaving a red stream in its wake, finally rolling to rest against the bottom hatch of the beverage cooler. Jani limped over to it, nudging it with her foot until she could look into the staring eyes.

"You're gone. You're dead. You lose. I got them all out." She hesitated. "Except for Yolan." But then, she hadn't seen Yolan's body, so maybe she got out, too. She grinned in long-delayed satisfaction. "They're out of your reach forever. Yours and Acton's and Evan's." She let the ax slip from her grasp and fall to the floor. From down the hall, voices, confused and angered, deadened by foam, resonated flatly. They didn't sound like Laumrau, from what she could discern amid the slosh and shower of falling water. *Sounds like English.* How silly. She turned slowly and walked to a chair to sit, and wait.

"The patients are gone. Borgie and crew are gone. You stay behind. Think that's an even trade, Kilian?"

Jani wheeled. Her tietops shot out from beneath her, sending her careening into the wall. She cracked the back of her head against uncoated brick. Lights spangled before her eyes as she sagged to the floor.

Neumann's head rolled away from the wall. It spun to a stop in the middle of the floor and righted itself with a couple of wobbly loops.

He blinked the water out of his eyes. "You can't murder the already-murdered, Kilian." A gurgle bubbled up from the throat he no longer had. "I'm going to stay with you forever and ever and ever. Till the day you die. Which from the looks of you just might be today."

Jani slumped farther down the wall as augie leached away. Her legs had numbed. The room had greyed. Breathing seemed too much trouble.

"See you in hell, Kilian." Neumann winked at her, and smiled.

She fell to one side. Gradually became aware. Of the water. Soaking her hair. Running down the walls. Like tears. Puddling around her. Immersing her. Drowning her. Like in her dream. Drowning.

Sinking. Deeper.

Deeper.

Deep—

CHAPTER 32

Sam huddled in the passenger seat of an abandoned scoot and watched the turmoil unfold around him.

The fireskims arrived first, great scarlet brutes that spat out HazMat teams and equipment with startling efficiency. The teams entered the SIB through the ram-blown doors, fighting against the relentless stream of bodies in foam-covered night fatigues who struggled to get *out* through the same narrow openings. Startling descriptives in several languages cut through the still night, following the inevitable soggy collisions.

Sam hid in his seat as the members of a spent HazMat team clustered beneath a nearby tree.

"Foam." An older woman's voice, exhausted and disbelieving. "All four fuckin' upper floors. And the basement. And the subs."

"First floor's the worst," said a younger man. "Those jas-sacks with the ram punched through a support wall into the relay station behind and ruptured an air-filter array. Microbial sieve everywhere!" He cracked the tip of a nicstick and passed it to the woman. "The conference-center auditorium looks like the world's largest strawberry sundae."

"There were no fires," another team member said with a yawn. "Who the hell set off the foam?"

"Some nutty captain. Her augie went south—guy from Security said she broke into desks and cabinets, found a UV stylus someone had rigged to building frequency."

"No one outside Facilities is allowed to have a stylus!" The older woman groaned. "You can reset a whole building with one of those things."

"Apparently, some people keep them around as personal environmental adjusters." The younger man activated a nicstick for himself and turned to look at the SIB, now ablaze with lights and teeming with activity. "When was the last execution we had around here?"

"Thirty, thirty-five years ago."

"Well, there's going to be one toot sweet when they find whoever the hell that stylus belonged to." He pulled off his hood and pushed a hand through his matted hair. "Never saw a mess like this in all my life."

Sam watched the group smoke in tired silence, then turned his attention back to the still figure standing alone atop a low rise. John Shroud hadn't moved from his station since the ambulance arrived, a heartbeat behind the fireskims. He'd made no attempt to approach the lone skimgurney that had been pulled from the building, its burden obscured by attached monitors and emergency techs. The sole movement he made had been a clenching of one fist when a monitor alarm blared, causing the level of commotion around the ambulance to escalate accordingly.

Val Parini, his shirt pulled from his trousers and his jacket long since discarded, broke away from the anthill activity and trudged up the small elevation.

"How can you just stand up here like a goddamned tree?" He planted himself in Shroud's path and folded his arms.

"Because I can't do any good down there." Shroud's voice was level, matter-of-fact. "My years as a trauma man are long behind me. All I'd do is get in their way."

Parini hung his head, then dropped his arms and plodded a circle around the other man, finally coming to rest at his side. "A foam-encased mound by the name of Pascal informed me that if Jani dies, Nema is going to pick us off one by one like free range targets."

"Let me worry about Nema," Shroud replied quietly.

Parini shrugged. Coughed. Sniffed. "John, what the hell did we do?"

"The best we could at the time."

"Did we?" His breathing grew more and more shaky. Then he leaned against Shroud and pressed his face against his chest.

Shroud placed an arm around his shoulders. He remained quiet, his face like carved stone, and let Parini cry. Then he jostled him gently, the way a father would his son. "Val? Val, pull yourself together."

"Yes, John." Parini pushed back. Ran a hand over his face. Coughed again.

"Val?"

"Yes, John."

"I've spoken with Pimentel. If it looks as though—" Shroud stopped. Closed his eyes. Exhaled with a loud huff. "We stay with her until the end, and *we* pronounce her. We owe her that much."

"Yes, John." Parini's eyes squinched like a squawling babe's. Then he lifted his chin and swallowed hard, his face as masklike as his friend's.

All during that time, dark-haired Hugh stood at the base of the rise, watching. Parini beckoned to him as soon as he realized he was there, and the younger man strode briskly up to them.

"She's seizing. Your specialist thinks they should perform a De-Vries shunt. Her Hybrid Indicator Indices are skied—he's worried about excitotoxic brain damage." He tugged at his sweat-soaked shirt. "They need to get her to Cryo."

"Those shunts have an astoundingly low success rate—he is aware of that?" Shroud's voice sounded dull, as if he knew the answer. "Is that the only problem?"

Hugh hesitated, then shook his head. "Hepatic failure's imminent. I'm worried whether the adjunct has the capacity to clean her up. Pimentel says they haven't been able to harvest a viable transplant. Cal Montoya's searching all Earth facility banks for possibilities, but—" He had already backed halfway down the hill. "I think we better go."

"Hugh!" Parini trotted after the man, who didn't slow or even give any sign that he heard him.

Shroud remained in place. He watched the crowd disperse and distribute themselves amongst other vehicles as the crew loaded Kilian's stretcher and closed up the ambulance. His eyes followed it as it fast-floated away, sirens blaring, lights flashing.

Sam struggled out of the tiny scoot and ran to his side. "What does that mean! What you said?"

Shroud glanced down at him, a cocked eyebrow the only sign of surprise on his long, monkish face. "Mr. Duong, isn't it?"

"What's the matter with Captain Kilian!"

"It's difficult to explain to a layman."

Sam dug deep, and came up with his "oral defense committee" voice. "Do. Your. Best."

Shroud stared. "My specialist wants to insert devices into Jani's neck and brain that will bypass her circulatory system and perfuse the brain with a solution that can both nourish it and prevent and repair damage from the seizures she's having." He broke eye contact, and focused on the grass at his feet. "But that's not her only problem.

Some foods she's eaten and drugs she's taken in the past few weeks have poisoned her, and her liver is failing as a result. The toxic metabolites that have damaged that organ could affect others, as well. We don't know whether an artificial liver can do the job, and we can't locate a tissue replacement."

"She will die?"

Shroud stiffened. Then he picked his nails. The steady *click click* cut the still night like cricket chirps.

"Why did you do it?"

"Is that any of your business?" Shroud glanced at Sam, and offered a sad smile. The expression erased years, but as with Kilian's tears, the hint of exposed psyche rattled. "If you must know, I truly believed I was helping her. I was . . . very fond of her, and I wanted her to live forever." He turned away. Took one unsteady step, then another. Finally, he thumped his thigh with a cage-wire fist and quickened his stride, reaching the last remaining skimmer just as it was about to depart.

Sam remained atop the little hill and watched the vehicle float away. "No one lives forever, Dr. Shroud." He walked down the hill toward the SIB. The lawn in front of the building looked like a depot, the fireskims having been joined by a small fleet of empty tankers that had been bought over to "hold the foam." Activity, while still bustling, had slowed from "what the hell!" to "steady as she goes" as the discovery phase of the cleanup operation gave way to the actual cleaning-up.

The HazMat crews had disabled the building alarms to allow for the rapid deployment of hoses, suction pumps, and portable ventilators. Sam walked up to the staging area with the sure step of someone who had every reason to be there. He slipped a ventilator helmet over his head, freed a pair of boots and a coverall from the pile of discarded safety equipment and dressed. He had to fold over the coverall sleeves twice, and the amount of material he had to stuff inside the boots impeded his ability to walk. But even the best-fitting safety gear made people look like they'd dropped a load in their pants, so Sam decided he looked just fine.

Most of the cleanup centered around the first-floor conference facility. Someone had already tacked up a banner over the doorway leading into the space. Operation Soda Fountain had been crossed out in favor of Operation Scoop, which had in turn been countered by the less poetic, but more apt, Operation Suck. Rows of vacuum pumps already filled the huge rooms with their characteristic spluttery sounds. Sam walked past chest-high dollops of bright pink foam, and felt for one crazy moment like an explorer in a children's adventure story.

The stairwell leading into the basement proved gratifyingly empty. He limped down, unable to avoid the sticky, whipped-cream mounds that swallowed his boots to the knee. The hallway itself had avoided a major influx of microbial sieve, although he could easily trace the pink-outlined trails of those who had preceded him.

The tech bullpen . . . well, shambles seemed appropriate. Sam pushed a mountain of white foam from atop his desk—it *flooped* to the floor and continued to advance across the lyno like pyroclastic flow. He removed one coated glove, touched open his drawer, and removed the box of shrimp tea Kilian had given him.

He unfastened the front of the coverall, stuffed the canister inside, closed himself back up. If he stumbled into anyone now, he'd say that he'd come down to recover his mess card, and gladly accept the three-day suspension he'd draw for crossing the hazard line.

Sam slooshed into the hall. The foam damped out sound—the vacuum noises that had filled his ears in the stairwell proved barely detectable here. *So quiet.* Like a hospital. He looked in the direction Kilian had disappeared, then slipped through the hip-high layer of fluff.

On his way down the hall, an opened fire-alarm station caught his attention. Someone had painted a large yellow X over the gaping hole, through which assorted connections could be easily seen. He smiled, thinking of Kilian popping the cover and inserting the stylus. He relished the thought of her creating mayhem. He prayed she would remain alive to make more.

The vending alcove, the source of so much lousy tea, looked appropriately tatty. The floor was covered with a runny, white-streaked liquid, a blend of foam and . . . what? Sam saw the broken water connections, the spray still covering the furniture and counters, and shook his head.

"What was she trying to do?" What had happened at Knevçet Shèràa that she thought smashing water valves an appropriate response? Did she try to drown Neumann? The Laumrau? Did she even know what she did?

He kicked something as he crossed the floor, and bent to retrieve it. *A turnstick.* The long one Janitorial used when ceiling lights needed switching out. One of the polywood ends was cracked and dented. *She used this to smash the valves.* His mind plundered the thought. *What was she trying to do?* He had a right to know. They were in this together, after all.

Together.

Sam's eyes stung. He coughed, as Parini had coughed, to loosen his clenching throat. He leaned on the turnstick like a cane as he walked to the janitor's closet to return it to its rack.

Together.

All these years, he had known, in his bones, that despite all evidence to the contrary, Jani Kilian lived. As proofs of her death cropped up all over the Commonwealth like mushrooms, he treated them as conjecture only. Anecdotal evidence, not even worthy to be dubbed hypothesis. He knew her to be out there, somewhere. He knew that someone else had survived the hell he had lived through. He knew he wasn't alone.

He opened the closet door and inserted the turnstick back into its niche. He touched the places where Kilian's hands might have gripped, and a cry caught in his throat as the first hot tears spilled. He stepped into the closet, inverted the bucket used to catch leaks from the coffee brewer, sat down, and wept.

He wept for Eva, and for Orton, and the others. But mostly, as much as it shamed him, he wept for himself. This was what it meant, to choose Simyam over Sam. *If she dies, I'll be the only one.* The only one left to remember. The only one left to bear the weight.

She felt like this for years. The thought caught him like a sharp blow. His breath stopped, starting only when he consciously forced himself to pull in the air. *She felt like this . . . so alone.* The sole survivor.

He stripped the helmet from his head, let it fall to the floor.

"I don't want to be the only one! I don't want to be the only one!"

Then he thought of the dying other, and finally wept for Jani Kilian. Wept as Parini and Shroud refused to. Wept as people in HazMat suits splashed into the alcove and stared at him. Wept until Odergaard, much less red of face than he had ever seen him, escorted the two white-garbed men into the storage room and led him away.

CHAPTER 33

Quiet, cool, whiteness. It stretched around Jani for as far as she could see. She slept in it—it nestled her like velvet, soft as the wings of angels. She couldn't walk in it—when she tried, she sank in to her hips and fell over. But that was all right. She didn't want to walk anyway.

Neumann only bothered her once. He sprayed pink foam in all directions as he slopped toward her, his head nestled beneath his good arm. His mouth still worked, unfortunately. She told him to go to hell and he stalked off, muttering about colonial lack of respect for their betters.

At times, she'd see one in an assortment of faces. Male. Female. Dark. Light. Flashes only, barest traces of variety in an endless sea of white.

Sound. Her consciousness revolved around sound. It ebbed and flowed like the tide, fingering the white space with swirls of imagined color.

"—and after Gruppo Helvetica wins the Cup and I take your money, I'm going to—"

"—and the Lake Michigan Strip talks are still ongoing, but it looks better from our end. The Vynshàrau have backed off, just like you said. They've even turned the temperature down! And I spoke with Tsecha last week. Hantìa was with him, and he said, " 'Colonel Frances, you must tell—' "

"—foam everywhere, and guess who has to work cleanup detail for three fuckin' weeks because everybody said I should have been watching you—"

"—so Piers and I are having a little informal contest, to see which one of us has a heart attack first—"

"—I never stopped loving you, Please come back—"

"—I'm not mad at you anymore for ditching me in Felix Majora, but you owe me dinner for putting me through hell—"

Blues. She heard happiness in most of the voices, and happiness touched her as blue. Even the complainer, who muttered about lost gloves and crap in his hair. Granted, at times his voice radiated into violet, with the occasional flash of scarlet. Self-pity, she sensed. Worry, about himself.

But blues, mostly. All the emotion that touched her came to her in blue.

Except love. Love was white, like the velvet that enveloped her. She recognized the color of the voice.

A brick crushed her forehead. Every time she tried to open her eyes, it pressed down more and kept them closed. She raised her arm and tried to push it away, but something wrapped around her wrist and stopped her.

"L'go." She tried to pull away, and the grip tightened.

"Get Shroud."

"Roger will have a fit if we don't call him."

"Then get 'em all!"

Running. Swoosh of a door.

"Le' go!"

"Please don't struggle, Jani, you'll pull out your IVs."

"*Lemme go!*"

The brick smashed down.

"M'head."

"That's swelling from the shunt, Jani. Your head will ache every time you move it for a few more days."

Jani concentrated all her strength and will on forcing apart four parchment-thin flaps of skin. Slits of light. Stabs of pain. She closed them, then tried again.

Shapes. Surrounding her. Watching her.

A flash of white. Bending close.

"Hello." John's thin face filled her view. A smile. Light green eyes, the milk skin beneath cobwebby with fine lines.

"I remember you." Jani's words came slow, slurred. Poured, rather than spoken.

"And well you should." A last, wider smile. Then nothing.

"Me next." Val's head replaced John's. New haircut since Felix. Shorter, more Service-like.

"Cousin Finbar—is it really you?"

His smile broke like sunrise. It was one of their Rauta Shèràa jokes. He'd probably hurry to the nurses' station after he left her to jot happy notes about her long-term memory.

"Me last." Scraggly blond hair and bloodshot eyes.

"Hi, Rog. Consorting with the enemy?"

Pimentel grinned sadly. "I had no choice. Patient before pride." Val made soothing noises, but he ignored them.

"Hmm." Jani smiled. "Had your heart attack yet?"

His eyes widened. Twin rounds of pink bloomed in his sunken cheeks. "Not yet. Any minute now, though." He exhaled with a *whoosh.* "You remember that?"

"I remember lots of things." She turned her head as much as she dared and looked at John, but he pretended to fuss with the IV leads and refused to meet her eye.

A DeVries shunt, a procedure developed by and named after her least favorite *living* person in the Commonwealth, had been performed. The exit and entry scars, located at her hairline on either side of the base of her skull, pulled and tingled every time she moved her neck. She had a new liver. It was undersized since they'd been forced to insert it when it was still in its early growth stages, but it would reach full form and function within months. To fill the gap, they'd implanted a partial adjunct to help it along.

Beyond that, no one would tell her what had happened or what had been wrong with her. Her nurses fobbed her questions off on her doctors, who in turn fobbed her questions off on each other. Pimentel chewed his lip to blood. Val oozed charm and changed the subject. John, she saw not at all. That worried her more than anything else.

They wouldn't give her a mirror. She discovered the first time she touched her scalp that they'd shaved her head in order to jack in the shunt main and attach the moniter buttons. She estimated length as best she could with her thumb, and guessed that her new growth consisted of a centimeter of wave. Unaided hair growth averaged fifteen centimeters a year. Hers had been on the slow side since her rebuild. *I've been out over a month?* She checked the color in the curved reflection of her IV stand. Still black. No bald patches requiring implants.

They'd left her *à lérine* wounds alone. The gashes had healed to ragged red lines on her right arm, thinner, paler threads on her left.

They had removed her eyefilms. Threat of infection, Morley said. Green-on-green orbs goggled at her, warped to skewed ovals by the tubing surface. She turned away from them repeatedly, only to have morbid fascination draw her back. Judging from the blasé reaction of the nurses, however, her eyes' appearance bothered her more than it did any of them. A day and a half passed before someone honored her request for filmformer—the male nurse who finally brought it expressed disappointment that she'd decided to cover them. Several of the guys had commented that they liked the way they made her look.

Big pussycat, indeed!

By day two, the headaches eased enough that she could sit up. On day three, they removed the IVs and fed her soup. She shocked everyone on day six by walking the halls. Especially Pimentel.

"Your progress is mind-boggling. I'd ascribe it to the recuperative abilities of youth," he said as he squired her back to her room. "But you're older than I am."

"Watch it, Roger." Jani kicked off her slippers and perched on the edge of her bed. "So what do you think it is?"

He looked at her with the same hangdog expression he'd worn since she awoke, and left before she could demand he answer the damned question.

"Why did I release the retardant foam?"

"*That's* the million-Com question, isn't it?" Lucien propped his feet up on her bed and tipped back in his chair. "And not just the stuff in the ready tanks, but the stuff in the reserves and in the lines. You activated the synthesizers, too. Overrode the metering sensors. Yup, you shoved a UV finger down its throat and the whole damned system just went *blech.*"

Jani grinned. "I'm sorry about the cleanup detail."

Lucien had the decency to look uncomfortable. "Pimentel organized the tag-team talkers. He said you might recall what we said while you were in coma, so we had to be careful."

"Thanks for not taking the advice to heart."

"*You* hand-polish brass fixtures for three weeks and try to restrain your enthusiasm!" He eyed her with an expression of patience sorely tried. "Oh well. Nema says hello."

"Next time you see him, tell him hello back."

"He's inevitable, you know. Inexorable. All those *in* words." Lucien hunched deeper into the chair. "Besides, if you came around, you could keep him off my back. 'Lucien, you must tell my nìa—! Lucien, you must—you must—!' "

Jani studied him for some sign he might be joking, and couldn't find one. "If it's so bad, request a transfer."

"No." Lucien studied his nails. "It's still interesting."

"Haven't figured out how to work him yet, have you?"

"I'm going to ignore that. What he really wants is to see you. He has to hold off, though. Ceèl is still ticked about being forced to acknowledge you. Nema said he has to throw him a bone or two before he can mention the possibility."

"Did he really say 'throw him a bone'?"

"Yeah. That handheld of his has been getting a workout."

Before Jani could learn more, the door opened and Val sauntered in. He was sharply attired as always—dark green trousers and a patterned shirt in greens and browns. Late summer afoot. "Hello, I was on my way to a meeting and—" His eyes drank in Lucien, and his face lit. "I'm sorry, Jani, I didn't realize you had visitors. Lieutenant Pascal, isn't it? We spoke once during the night in question, but we've never been formally introduced—I'm Val Parini."

Lucien cast him a bored glance, then ignored him. "I have to get back to work." He rose and bent close to Jani. "I'll stop by this evening."

Jani tilted her head to receive his now-customary peck on the cheek. She wasn't paying attention, so she couldn't slip from his grasp when he wrapped his arms around her and pressed his lips to hers. He kissed her so hard she either had to open her mouth or risk a serious bruising. He tightened his grip when she tried to pull away, and nipped her lower lip when she pinched his thigh.

"Speaking of ten-minute head starts," Jani said in brisk Acadian when they finally broke apart. Lucien answered with a smirk, then brushed past Val as though he wasn't there.

Val waited for the door to close before speaking. "I don't think osculation *français* is on your list of prescribed meds."

Jani struggled to find a less distracting sitting position—stimulation of one highly sensitive region tended to travel. "You're just jealous."

"Nonsense. Merely concerned for your welfare." His expression grew thoughtful as he strolled around the end of the bed and flopped into Lucien's chair. "I've read his psych evals. Nasty augment he has. You deserve better."

"I've seen him without his shirt—he's just what the doctor ordered."

"Not this doctor." Val adopted a look of serious concentration. "Selfish. Narcissistic. Incapable of sympathy, much less empathy."

"No sloppy emotions to complicate matters—just the way I like it."

"You're not—" Val faltered. "You're not his only *interest.* Or his only loyalty, if I can even use that word in connection with him. He can't be trusted."

"You have been digging, haven't you?" Jani met his gaze—he dropped his first. "I have him figured out."

"Think of the opportunities you're letting slip away."

"Keep John out of this."

"Did I mention a name? I was speaking of life in general—did I once mention my best friend, my business partner, one of the wealthiest men in the Commonwealth?"

"It didn't work the first time. What makes you think now would be any different?"

"The best amongst us acquire certain traits as they age. Maturity. Patience. The ability to give and take."

"We're talking about the same John Shroud, aren't we?" Jani racked her brain for a suitable change of subject, and pounced on the first thing she thought of. "How's Hugh? Morley said he was here the night I was admitted, but I haven't seen him."

Val's rakish air vanished. He looked away, hands clenching. "He wants to visit you, but only if he knows he won't run into me. I'm meeting with Cal Montoya in the city tomorrow, so he'll stop by then."

"Emergency ditching in the lovelorn sea?" That had been another one of their Rauta Shèràa jokes. Jani suddenly felt the need to make him smile.

He did. A little. "White chocolate cheesecake—what did I tell you?" He picked at his trouser leg. "And he got upset. About you. Reading the files was one thing, he said, but seeing in the flesh what John and Eamon and I had done . . ." His hand stilled. "He's submitted his resignation. He's leaving Neoclona."

"I'm sorry."

"Yeah." He looked at her, eyes darkened with concern. Fear. "I asked you on Felix, and you didn't answer. I'm asking you again." He tapped his fingers against his thigh, faster and faster, as though building up momentum. Or courage. "Do you hate us?"

"You saved my life," Jani said, jumping at the pat answer. But Val's desolate look informed her that she wouldn't slip out from under that easily. *How do I feel about you?* Master go-between. John's apologist extraordinaire. She shrugged, catching herself as the scars from the shunt pulled. "Val, if we'd met under normal circumstances, I think we'd have been great friends."

"Jani?" Val's eyes dulled in question. "We're friends *now*."

"In a way." Jani studied her hands. Had the real skin grown darker than the animandroid? More bronze? If she compared herself to Nema, would she see a difference? "But you're a scientist, and by all accounts a good one, if a little shifty on the follow-through. I think you're anxious to see how the experiment turns out."

"Don't be so sure," Val said, too softly. "You haven't been on the other side of that door for the past five weeks."

"No, I've been on the business side." Jani's voice thinned as her throat tightened. "Every time I ask somebody a question, they dodge or clam up. What did you do to me?"

"You're not in any condition yet—"

"Val."

"John ordered us not to tell you until he deemed you ready, and he hasn't deemed you yet!"

"Hasn't he? Well, the next time you see him, tell him to get off his ass and deem away!" Jani kicked off her covers. "I'm going for a walk."

Val scrambled to his feet and hurried around the bed to her side. "Are you sure you're up to it?"

Jani eased her legs over the bedside and probed with her toes for her slippers. "Yes. I may even venture outside this time—it's a beautiful day."

She found herself the focus of all eyes as she shuffled down the hall on Val's arm. White coats smiled. Waved. Offered the occasional "Howya doin', Captain?"

"It's hotter than hell out there," Val said as he escorted her to the front entrance. "One circuit around the flower beds and I'm bringing you back in."

"I thought you had a meeting."

"Shit." He glared at his timepiece. "Stay put. I'm going to find someone to go with you."

As soon as Val disappeared from view, Jani took off in the opposite direction, weakened muscles distorting her walk into a limping skip. She had gotten the lay of the land during her previous visits—she knew exactly where she needed to go. She cut through as empty conference room. Up another hall and down a utilities chase.

The Basic Research Group dominated the east wing of the ground floor. Jani pressed the buzzer of the door leading into the largest, best-equipped lab. It swept open.

John sat at a large desk in the middle of the room, hunched over a recording board. Atop the surrounding benches, analyzers clicked and data-transfer stations chirped. In the background, a hint of music from a hidden system. Elgin. Or was it Mozart?

"Put the sequencer on the bench nearest the window," he rumbled. "Leave the samples on the cart."

"Where do you want me to put the violin?" Jani asked as she dragged a visitor's chair over to the desk.

John's head shot up. As soon as he saw her, his face colored candy pink. The cruel blush clashed with his jacket, a crossover cowlneck in palest pearl grey.

"Val told me you still play." Jani sat and swung her feet up onto the desk. The left leg worked fine, but the right still needed hoisting.

"Play?" John blinked in confusion. He'd filmed his eyes to match the jacket—the argent irises glittered like fish scales. He'd have cut a sinister figure if not for his face's boiled-lobster glow. He sat back and tossed his stylus on the desk. "Oh. Yes. Once in a while. I'm out of practice, though." He raised his left hand and ran his fingers along an imaginary violin neck. "I'm losing my calluses."

"Shouldn't let that happen—it'll take months to grow them back." Jani glanced around the lab for something else to comment upon. The featureless white walls? The blaze of summer, visible through narrow windows? Finally, she caught sight of a familiar device atop one of the benches, and shook her head. "Coffee brewer in the lab? For shame. Where's a safety officer when you need one?"

John's expression lightened. "I was about to make fresh." He rose and crossed the floor with the loose-limbed, liquid walk that age hadn't changed. "Do you want some?"

"Sure." Jani settled back and watched him brew the coffee. The surroundings were more posh and the circumstances less perilous than they'd been eighteen years ago, but in a way, it was as though nothing had changed. As though they sat in the same basement office and listened to the same recordings. As if nothing existed outside the walls that enclosed them.

She studied him, something she hadn't yet been able to do. He stood one-nine, but as always, his thin build and penchant for monochrome clothing made him look even taller. His hair shone in the diffuse room light, so white and crisply trimmed it looked like a plastic cap. Jani could still recall its feel between her fingers, like shredded silk.

She pushed the memories aside and concentrated on the man who stood before her now. Time's passage had done him a favor. *Homely* had become *striking.* Strangeness had become style. *Congratulations, Johnny—you won. Just like you told me you would.*

The brewer gurgled and hissed. Dark aromas filled the room,

heavy enough to cut with a Sìah blade. John poured and stirred, then ambled back to the desk and handed Jani her cup. Unadorned ivory ceramic—weighty and solid. "Black?"

"You remembered." Jani held it to her nose and inhaled the almost solid essence. "I drink this, I won't sleep for a week."

John frowned. "Val claims it etches tooth enamel." One nearly invisible eyebrow arched. "He told me *he* made you coffee on Felix, and you liked it."

"I *drank* it—it was either that or die." Jani sipped, then tried to think of the words to compare Val's bellywash with the nectar she tasted. "Trust me, you have nothing to worry about."

John smiled. "That's what I thought." The expression flavored his voice warm brown, like the coffee. He stared into his cup, then sighed. "I'd like to think this is a social call, but I'm guessing you came here for a reason." He returned to his side of the desk.

Jani nodded. "I waited for you to visit. When you didn't, I decided it was time for the mountain to come to Muhammad."

"You needed your rest." John gripped his recording board by the corner and pushed it back and forth. "Your recovery has progressed splendidly." He looked at her, and his metal eyes softened. "You look . . . wonderful."

Jani tugged first at the lapel of her mud blue robe, then at her pillow-mashed curls. She felt the heat flood her face—at least her skin contained enough melanin to obscure matters. "Pimentel thinks I'm healing like a kid. He's never seen anything like it." She labored to maintain a casual tone. "What happened?"

John set down his cup and tented his hands. "Your condition, when we pulled you out of the SIB, was extremely grave. Your liver was failing, and your metabolism was deranged. You began seizing—those seizures were of sufficient scope and severity we feared permanent brain damage. The DeVries shunt—"

"—cut my brain off from the rest of my body until the hepatic adjunct cleared toxic metabolites out of my system so I'd stop seizing. That much I extracted from a nurse named Stan, who is quite taken with my pussycat eyes." Jani flexed her right hand and compared it again to her left. The light was brighter here—did they still look different? "What else?"

John ran a hand along his jacket crossover. "If you're upset, we can discuss this later—"

"*No.*" Jani lowered her feet to the floor—the right one hit with a *thump.* "We discuss it now."

"You have a new liver."

"*I know that.*" She leaned forward and set her cup on the desk hard enough that coffee splashed over the side. "Pimentel was treating me for acute intermittent porphyria, a disease he thought you gave me when you rebuilt me. Is that true?"

"Don't say 'rebuilt.' You make yourself sound like a machine." John drummed his fingers on the desktop. "Yes, you suffered from a porphyria-like disorder that affects a scant percentage of the idomeni population."

"An *idomeni* genetic disorder?"

"Yes." The drumming altered to a slower turn of finger, as though he pressed a string. "The idomeni tissue we used when we grew the new organ was taken from an unbred born-sect. The born-sects don't bother to repair manageable genetic miscues until the member is ready to breed. Sometimes, not even then. I didn't learn that until after you . . . left." He glared at her. "Ridiculous, but there it is." Whether he referred to the idomeni practice or her running away, he didn't make clear.

Jani's skin prickled in alarm. "Which sect?"

Another curl of finger. "The disease is most common in Vynshàrau. It affects point two percent of their population."

"Did you use . . . Nema's tissue?"

"*No!*" John's face flushed anew. "Use your head, Jan! I despise him—do you think I'd give you his tissue?"

"Right." So she wasn't related to Nema in any bizarre ways. Make that any *more* bizarre ways. "You repaired this disorder?"

"Of course. Then . . . things snowballed."

"Snowballed?"

John nodded. "You suffered from one or two arcane connective-tissue disorders, and a defect in glycosaminoglycan metabolism. And a glycogen-degradation defect that I believe accounted for more of your symptoms than the porphyria."

Jani pressed her hands together. Were the fingers of her right longer than her left? "Human defects or idomeni defects, John?"

John's hand stilled. "Defects."

"Human or idomeni?"

"Jani—"

"Answer me! On a percent scale, how human was I when I came in here and how much has that number decreased in the last five weeks?"

John leaned forward. "Jani, your transplant incision is almost completely healed, and you were operated on only two weeks ago. Every patient we've seen who was ever treated using a DeVries shunt remained bedridden for at least six months and required extensive rehab. Rehab that, I may add, was seldom entirely successful. Only twelve percent of those patients recovered sufficiently to live unaided." He nodded firmly, as though that proved his point beyond doubt. "You're walking around on your own and engaging in complex social interactions after five weeks. And your distinctive personality"—he eyed her in injury—"doesn't seem changed in the least." He touched the fingertips of his left hand to the desktop, raising and lowering each in turn, like slow scales. "The advantages of hybridization are becoming more and more obvious, and we've learned better how to take what we need and leave the rest behind. You won't change physically—well, not much more, anyway—and the health benefits—"

"You pushed me farther down the road. Hybridized me at a much faster rate than would have occurred naturally."

"We had no choice! The disorders you could have developed if we hadn't—"

Jani held up her right hand. Maybe the skin hadn't yellowed—maybe it was the light. "If I went to Cal Montoya or one of your other facility chiefs and asked them to make me one hundred percent human again, would they be able to?"

John shook his head. "You've altered too much. They wouldn't know where to start. You could develop more life-threatening disorders, the treatment of which could lead to more problems."

"So you did this for my own good."

He looked at her. His long, sad face was the first thing Jani had seen when she opened her eyes after the explosion. For a time, it had been the last thing she had seen when she closed them at night. "That has always been our foremost consideration."

Jani crossed her wrists and compared the skin color. Maybe the animandroid skin didn't tan like the real thing. Maybe the muddy hue of her pajamas made her look more sallow than normal. Maybe. "Val worries that I hate you both, but I don't blame you for what you did in Rauta Shèràa. You were young and thought you knew everything, and you were honestly trying to help me."

"Of course—you know we were—"

"But that was then and this is now. Could you have modified your all-or-nothing approach? Made do with the shunt and the adjunct until I was conscious and could make an informed decision?" She looked at the man who had saved her life in the way he thought best because he loved her. The man she'd fled when she realized what his love meant. "Angel—"

John's breathing quickened. "Jani—"

"—could you have *asked*?"

He buried his head in his hands. "It was the only way to ensure your complete recovery!" He looked at her over the tops of his fingers. "You can trust me," he said, his voice gone velvet Soft, enveloping, suffocating velvet. "I know more now than I did then."

"You may know more about the science, John." Jani reached for her cup—more coffee sloshed over the rim as she pushed it farther away. "But you don't know a damned thing more about me." Her knee gave out when she stood, and she almost lost her balance. John reached out to help her, but when he looked her in the face, he sagged back in his chair and let her go without a word.

CHAPTER 34

The next morning, Jani entered the sunroom to find Hugh Tellinn sitting on a lounge, leafing through a holozine. Almost three months had passed since she'd first met him at Neoclona-Felix. In the interim, his hair had been inexpertly trimmed into a flip-ended mop, and his state of sartorial disarray had further deteriorated. He turned pages with a rapid, slap-hand motion, as though sitting in the sunroom set his teeth on edge.

Then he looked up. "Jani!" It was the first time she had ever seen him smile. The expression split his face from ear to ear. Instead of a thirty-five-year-old man with a bad haircut and grab-bag taste in clothes, he looked like a boy who had opened his birthday box and found the puppy. She could imagine Val performing handsprings for a chance to savor that open-faced happiness.

"Hugh." She walked slowly to a straight-backed chair opposite his lounge. She could sense his examining gaze, knew he watched her posture and coordination, whether she walked easily or had to concentrate on how to place her feet. "Do I pass, Dr. Tellinn?" she asked as she sat.

"You look good." He tossed the 'zine aside and sat forward, his hands clasped. "I'm glad." The brilliant smile wavered. "I assume Val told you what happened."

"The barest bones." Jani sat back, grateful for the support the stiff framing offered her muscles, which still tired quickly. "The less he discusses a breakup, the more it bothers him. He spent all of fifteen seconds summing you up."

Hugh blinked. "Really?" He tugged at a stretched-out cuff of his dull brown pullover. "I was very fond of him, too. But sometimes that isn't enough."

"He said you resigned from Neo."

"Yes."

"That was a drastic step."

"It was the only way. I knew it from the start. Every time I tried to talk about you, Val would nod and pat me on the back. Told me he understood my concern. Five minutes later, John's rattling off a list of all the things they'd try the second they got their hands on you." Hugh rubbed his cheek. His face looked drawn. Thinner. "I lived with them for over three months. Longest ten years of my life."

"Three months seems the turning point. That's how long I lasted, too." Jani felt a warm rise of concern for her fellow veteran. "What are you going to do?"

Hugh's shoulder twitched. "I have family in Helsinki. I thought I'd visit them for a time. After that?" He rocked his head back and forth. "Bullet train through the China provinces. Ski in the Andes. I've never been to Earth and I have enough savings to see me for a year or two. Who knows what I'll do?"

Jani covered her mouth with her hand to hide her grin. Was there anything funnier than listening to a workaholic discuss vacation plans? "You'll hook up with a hospital within a month," she said through her fingers. "You won't be happy until you're up to your elbows in glands."

That smile again. "You're probably right. What about you?"

"I'm stuck here until I'm stabilized to the world's satisfaction." She crossed her legs. Right over left, no hoisting required. "My lawyer told me yesterday that my adjudicating committee met two weeks ago and tried me *in absentia.* Sentence, ninety days, commuted to time served. Alice loses some privileges, but she keeps her head. I'll be discharged from the Service two minutes after I'm discharged from here." *Don't be surprised if they process you in the lobby,* Friesian had added dryly. "I'll need to find a place to live. A job."

Hugh cocked an eyebrow. "Val had mentioned hiring you into the Neoclona Documents Group."

"*Not bloody likely.*" Jani looked at Hugh to find him regarding her with sad amusement. "I didn't mean that the way it sounded."

"I understand. Believe me." He pressed his knuckles to his lips. "Well, I just wanted to stop by and say so long." He stood awkwardly, his too-large trousers rumpled and bagged at the knees.

Jani started to speak. Hesitated. Tried once more. "Could you do me a favor? I want you to read a MedRec." She handed him a slip of paper on which she'd written a name. "Then I want you to come back here, so we can talk about it."

* * *

One hour passed. *This is taking longer than I thought.* She knew that Hugh suffered a disadvantage not being a neurologist, but she felt sure he'd grasp the essentials. He'd read her Rauta Shèràa file. He'd make the connection.

Several patients had wandered into the sunroom for their post-breakfast/prelunch newssheet reading by the time Hugh returned. He paused in the entry, searching faces. When he finally saw her, the life drained from his eyes. He shoved his hands in his pockets and slouched across the room.

"I spoke with Roger." He reached out to her. "We're going to meet with him." He maintained his gentle grip on her hand as they departed the sunroom and negotiated the halls.

Pimentel sat at his desk waiting for them. Jani memorized the details of his office, the bookshelves, the watercolor, the view, in the sincere hope she'd never see them again.

"Jani." He glanced at Hugh. A look of back-and-forth argument passed between them. *You start. No, you start.*

Jani sat down in her usual chair and rubbed her damp palms over her pajama-clad thighs. "Well?"

Hugh walked behind Pimentel's desk and perched on the windowsill. His choice of seating gave the scene an "us versus them" flavor. "Roger told me that Sam Duong had named you his next of kin." He turned to look out the window. "He was admitted the same night you were. Discharged two weeks ago." He toyed with the light-transmission touchpad, the taps sounding harder as he continued talking. "During his stay, he revoked your NOK designation. Legally, therefore, you have no right to know anything about his condition."

Pimentel occupied his own nervous hands by paging through a file. "However, he did mention to me things that he wished he'd told you. I'm taking that as permission to discuss him with you. Besides, the faster we clear this up once and for all, the better for both of you." He pushed a hank of hair out of his eyes. "He spoke about you quite a bit. He even volunteered to help talk you through your coma, but I refused to allow it. He was too weak to be subjected to that sort of stress. We operated on him the night he was admitted."

Jani tried to read Pimentel's closed expression, his careful wording. "You removed the implant?"

Hugh sighed. "No." He finally turned from the window. "Sam Duong suffered from a benign neoplasm affecting the paramedian posterior region of his thalamus—"

Jani tapped her temple. "A mass in the middle of his head. Thank you. Roger told me all about it."

"Jani and I have discussed the particulars of Sam's condition. She believes some of the experiments the Laum conducted involved augmentation of the thalamus." Pimentel removed sheets of coated parchment from the file and laid them on the desk in front of him. "I have to admit, some of the things you said jolted me. So I contacted Bandan Combined University and requested they send me whatever ID they had for Simyam Baru." He slid three pages of parchment across the desk toward Jani. "I also requested that they search their records for a Sam Duong. Three men with that name turned up. Two still work there. The third left about five years ago, to take a job as a civilian archivist with the Commonwealth Service at Fort Sheridan."

Hugh turned back to the window.

"I took a sample from Sam. It matches that of the Sam Duong who came here from Banda. It doesn't match Simyam Baru's." Pimentel sat back slowly, gaze locked on her face. "Simyam Baru and Sam Duong are not the same man."

Jani looked from one scan to the other, her heart tripping, her hands damp. "Yes, but scans can change. The Laum may have conducted unrecorded experiments with tissue hybridization for all I know. I mean, look at me. My current scan doesn't match my Service scan." She kept reading. Line after line of comparator code. All different.

All different.

"Service ID scans are trace scans, Jani. Suitable for quick and dirty ID, in most instances. However, your ServRec also contained a full genomic scan, which was used to confirm your ID on Felix when the trace IDs didn't match up." Pimentel's voice remained low and steady. Calm. "The Bandans are similarly thorough. The scans they sent are full genomics. No chance of error or mix-up. No chance of confusion."

Hugh left his window seat. "Through a skillful melding of coincidence and storytelling, Sam Duong built himself a past to replace the one he'd forgotten." He rounded the front of Pimentel's desk and sat on the edge, close to Jani.

Pimentel picked up the story line. "He worked at the university at the same time Simyam Baru did. He may have even met him, but he can't remember and we'll probably never know." He cleared his throat. "Nothing would give me greater pleasure than to tell you, yes, it's possible someone else survived Knevçet Shèràa. But I will not lie to you. As a physician, I cannot, and as a friend, I will not." He reached across the desk and touched her hand. "I'm sorry."

Jani put a hand to her throat. The ache in her chest made it hard to breathe. "There's no chance?"

"Simyam Baru and Sam Duong are two separate people, Jani. No, there's no chance whatsoever." Pimentel paused. "Sam wanted me to tell you he's sorry. He said the thought of being the only one left with those memories terrified him into seeking help. He didn't want to be alone." He forced a smile. "He called you his 'Dark Ice Captain.' He said you were stronger than he was, and that he hoped you'd understand."

Hugh moved in behind her and placed his hands on her shoulders. "I wish the answer could be different. I wish something could be returned to you, for all you've lost." His touch melted the tightness. Jani leaned forward and rested her head on the desk; Hugh didn't let her go until she stopped crying.

Pimentel walked her back to her room. He sat in the visitor's chair instead of on his usual perch at her footboard, as if he thought she might not want him too close.

"Jani." He eyed her uncomfortably. "Are you all right?"

"Yeah." Jani circled to the far side of her room, and leaned against the window.

"You're sure?"

"I'd bet my license."

Jani traced a finger over the glass in the same place Neumann had sketched tic-tac-toe with his blood. "Did he tell you anything about that night? I don't remember what happened from the time I arrived at the A-G's party."

Pimentel shook his head. "He knew you hallucinated. He hinted you spoke with Neumann, but when pressed, he became highly agitated." He smoothed a hand over the freshly made bed. "At that point, it was enough for me that he didn't want to be Simyam Baru anymore. That he realized there was a Sam Duong out there that he needed to recover. Rebuild." He thumped the bedspread, which was so tightly tucked it *whumped* like a trampoline. "Speaking of rebuilding . . ."

"Are you going to say something about the SIB?"

"No." He chuckled. "I wondered if you were up to . . . taking a call?"

Jani saw the controlled eagerness in his face, and felt her heart skip. "From whom?"

"Someone real, who's been worried sick about you for the past five weeks." He hesitated. "And, I'm guessing, for a hell of a lot longer than that."

"You'll be all right by yourself?" Pimentel pushed Jani's chair close to the display. "After what you just went through—"

"I'm fine." She pushed the chair back to a more comfortable viewing distance.

"I'll be down the hall." He glanced back at her over his shoulder. "If you need anything."

"Thank you, Roger." Jani fingered the Misty replay activator pad, and hoped he couldn't see how her hand shook. "I mean that."

"Sure." Pimentel eyed her somberly, then slipped out.

She tapped the activator once. Twice. Third time proved the charm. The display blued. Lightened. The face formed.

"Janila?" Her mother squinted, as though she could just see Jani at the other end of a very long tunnel. At the age of sixty-seven common, Jamira Shah Kilian looked so much as she had nineteen years ago, it took Jani's breath away. Only the faintest wisps of grey lightened her black hair, gathered in a knot at the nape of her neck. Her brow and cheekbones were broad, her nose an arched curve almost Family in its sharpness. Her skin, a shade darker than Jani's, bore a few fine lines at the corners of her brown eyes, which still shone large and bright. As always, she wore a brightly colored short-sleeved tee—Jani knew her loose, belted trousers would contain a multitude of colors to complement the current turquoise hue. She had drawn two horizontal downcurves of henna in the middle of her forehead, which meant she had visited the Brh shrine that day. She kept a smaller shrine at home, and only visited the neighborhood sanctum when she wished to pray for something special.

Jani looked away from the display toward the wall opposite until her eyes stopped swimming.

"It's very vexing not being able to see you to speak to you," her mother continued. "I was quite shocked when I saw your new face. So much like my grandmother Jamuna, my father's mother whom you did not know. I had grown so used to you looking like your father, to see my family in you now—" She held a hand to her mouth as the seconds passed. Ten. Twenty.

The hand dropped. "I have received so many messages these past weeks. Some of them have been quite . . . startling. So many doctors, reassuring me you are all right. That told me how sick you were. You can imagine my thoughts."

Jani rubbed her forehead and imagined her hands around Val's throat. It would have been his idea, of course, to reassure her parents that she was just fine, then to nudge John into doing the same. And Roger. And God knows who else.

Her mother reached out and touched the display, her eyes soft with apology. "Your father is not here. He is helping Oncle Shamus install systems at Faeroe Outpost. He has been there two months common already, and the delays still multiply like *lapin*. He is furious, but if they do not install the relays now, they will miss the peak of the tourist season and have to wait until next quarter to renew the permits and you know how anxious Shamus becomes. Already, he jumps at loud noises. Of course, most of those loud noises are your father. But it is for the best. He would only want to go to Earth immediately to see you, and Dr. Pimentel warned us you need time to recover. Without undue strain, he said. He seems very worried about that. I quite like him. He seems . . . normal." Her unexpressed opinion of John and Val rang loud and clear.

"Your Colonel Hals also messaged. I quite liked her. Solid woman. Lots of common sense, if she is your friend, you are lucky. I feel I have less to worry."

She inhaled shakily. "It was very silly—" Her hand went to her mouth again. "Silly of you to think we would not want to see you. You're our daughter, our only child—" She once more touched the display. "I can't talk to a blinking screen. I want to talk to you in the same room. I want to hold my Jani-girl—" With that, all semblance of reserve shattered. She sagged forward, her face buried in her hands, shoulders shaking. "I don't want to cry in this booth by myself. I want to cry with you. Tears should be shared." She sat up and wiped her eyes with a tattered dispo.

"I will send another message in a few days, when I can talk without crying. Dr. Shroud told me I should send as many as I wish, that Neoclona will pay. That is very generous of him, but I do not like to take advantage." Her eyes narrowed, lit with a sharp light Declan Kilian always referred to as "roasted almond." "But maybe I will. I most look forward to meeting him, Janila, when we come to Earth." Again, the melting. "*Beaux rêves, ma petite fille. Au revoir.*" The display blanked.

Jani wiped her face. Then she touched the reply pad. She talked for almost an hour, telling her mother about life on the base. Acadia Central United's continuing quest for the Cup. The weather. Her upcoming life in Chicago, that she had not even planned. Three months' nonexistent income shot out into space when she pressed the touchpad, but if Neoclona could pay for her mother's messages, they could pay for hers, too. John owed her that and more.

Discharge came one week later. John and Val, who had made themselves scarce since Jani's blowup with John, were nowhere to be seen. Morley helped her pack, while Roger lectured her on diet and the need to take it easy. In order to stave off the heart attack he'd threatened her with for weeks, she relented and accepted his offer to carry her full-kit duffel. When he staggered under its weight, she took it back and told him to stop being silly.

Friesian waited for her in the lobby. To Jani's surprise, Hals stood next to him. They both wore dress blue-greys; Friesian held a bouquet of mixed colonial blooms that looked suspiciously like those growing around the buildings in North Lakeside.

"Remember what I said about a table in the lobby?" He handed her the flowers, then pulled a sheaf of papers from the documents case that rested on the floor at his feet. "I was being optimistic." He handed her the papers along with a stylus, then turned around. "Sign the bottom of pages one, four, and twelve, then touch the fingertips of your right hand to the sensor square at the bottom of page twenty."

Jani handed the flowers to Hals and dropped her bag to the floor. Using Friesian's back as the table, she wrote the coda to her Service career. "Any surprises?" She tapped him on the shoulder to indicate she had finished and handed the documents back to him.

"Nope. It's just like I told you." He slid the papers into a Service courier envelope, returned them to the case, then handed the case to a mainline lieutenant who had appeared out of nowhere. "Your first pension payment will be deposited into a general account at the Service Bank by month's end," he said as the lieutenant departed. "Go to any branch in the city to arrange transfer to your own account."

"Take your shooter badge," Hals added with a grin. "They'll give you two tickets to a Cubs game."

As Jani shouldered her duffel, she caught sight of another full kit resting beside the lobby sofa. "Whose is that?"

Friesian held a hand to his heart. "I'm shipping out. In two hours, I catch the shuttle to Luna, then the *Reina Amalia* back to Constanza. There's already a new brief waiting for me on board."

"Here's your hat, what's your hurry," Hals said softly. "The lawyer shortage at colonial bases is a well-known fact."

The three of them stared over one another's heads and struggled to keep the smiles off their faces.

Friesian broke away to the sofa and gathered his gear. Then they walked out into the burning afternoon. A steel blue four-seater hovered in the Ten Minute oval in front of the hospital. Friesian raised a hand; the officer behind the wheel waved in response.

"My ride is here already. Imagine that." He offered Hals a sharp salute. "Colonel. It was a pleasure meeting you."

"Likewise, Major." Hals saluted in return. "Safe trip."

Friesian turned to Jani, and held out his hand. "It's been . . ."

"Yeah." Jani laughed. "Sorry for all the excitement."

"Maybe in a few years, when the dust has settled, we can hook up. Have a good, long talk."

"Sure." Jani agreed easily to a meeting she knew would never take place. Time would interfere. Distance. Or most likely, sweet reason. Friesian would realize that he didn't want to know what he didn't know.

She waved to him one last time as his vehicle skimmed out of the oval. "I wonder what's waiting for him on Luna?"

"A nice attempted murder, he said." Hals frowned. "He may have been joking." She adjusted her brimmed lid and led Jani to a rent-a-scoot stand.

Jani glanced back toward the hospital. Through the tinted scanglass, she could see Niall Pierce standing in the lobby window, dressed in pajamas, his bathrobe wrapped tightly around him. She hesitated, then raised her hand in farewell. He kept his hands buried in his robe pockets; she could feel his eyes follow her as she boarded the scoot, and it pulled away.

"I'm sorry none of us made it in to see you the past few weeks," Hals said as she steered along the path.

Jani broke the code of that remark. "How is Burkett?"

Hals grinned. She seemed more relaxed now. Her shoulders had unclenched, and her hand rested easily on the steer-bar. "He's been surprisingly helpful. He arranged for everybody in FT to attend the weekly Diplo update meetings. And we'll all attend Diplomacy School, which means we all wind up with Foreign Service entries in our records. Nice little notation, come promotion time." She glanced at Jani. "He sends his regards, by the way. Trusts you'll make yourself available for consultation once you're settled."

"Tell him to get out his expense book. Advice from the Eyes and Ears will not come cheap."

"I think he knows that." For the first time, the contentment left Hals's face. "I could have used you here. Our interactions with the idomeni are going to get more and more complicated, and no one else here has your experience."

Jani glanced in the side mirror and watched the South Central Base recede from view. "You can handle the idomeni. As for me, well, I seem to encourage your unconventional side."

Hals nodded grudging agreement. "There is that." She steered into the drop-off oval adjacent to the station. "What time is your train?"

"Seventeen up." Jani checked her timepiece. "Just enough time for me to buy a newssheet and something to eat."

Hals helped Jani with her gear, then ambled around the oval. "Speaking of which, if you could suggest any news-sheets or periodicals we should subscribe to, I'd appreciate it." She glanced down the stairs that led from the train platform down to the charge lot, and stopped. "Oh. My. God."

Jani hurried to the railing to find Lucien looking up at them from the middle of the half-empty lot. His hair glimmered in contrast to his black T-shirt. His beige trousers were tasteful, but *fitted.* Black sunshades covered his eyes. The skimmer he leaned against looked like an oil droplet in a stiff headwind, and cost more than the entire population of Base Command made in a month.

Hals exhaled with a whistle. "Don't tell me—that's your nurse." She shook her head in wide-eyed wonder. "Next time I have a day off, maybe we can meet for lunch. You can tell me Tsecha stories." She sneaked another glance at Lucien. "And anything else you think needs an airing."

"Sure." Jani smiled. "Thanks for calling my folks, Frances."

"No problem, Jani." Hals gripped her shoulders in a quick hug. "Be seeing you."

Flowers in hand, feeling like an underdressed bride in her base casual tee and trousers, Jani descended toward the vision that awaited her.

"Hello." Lucien met her at the foot of the stairs. "I had the afternoon off. Thought you might need a ride into the city."

"That was nice of you."

"I have my moments." He tossed her duffel into the boot as though it weighed grams and not kilos, then helped her into the skimmer as though nursing actually was on the agenda.

Jani snuggled against plush black leather and ran her hand over the polished ebony dash. "Mind if I ask?"

Lucien maneuvered out of the lot and ramped immediately onto a Boul artery. "One of the Caos, in a small way. Husband's spending the summer touring the colonial holdings. She's spending the day sucking up to the in-laws."

"Does she know you're spending the day with her skimmer?"

"That's not nice."

"Sorry."

The Plan involved finding Jani a reasonably priced hotel, followed by a recon mission to get the lay of the land and possibly dinner. However, she had certain criteria that needed to be met regarding the hotel. By the time they found an establishment with easy access to train stations and major thoroughfares, a secure entry, and a room from which she could view the comings and goings on the street outside *and* rapidly access stairwells, emergency exits, and alleys, the clock had struck midnight and then some and her self-appointed guardian angel was muttering mutiny.

"Guess the lay of the land will have to wait until tomorrow." Jani stood by one of the room's narrow windows and checked her timepiece. "Make that later today."

"That was ridiculous." Lucien lowered to the small couch, testing the cushions with skeptical probes of his fingers. "Everyone who was looking for you found you and threw you back—you're off the hook."

"Humor me."

"I've been doing that since the day we met. I'm getting tired of it."

Whoops. Jani perched on one of the built-in window seats. Outside, the city lights shone. Ten floors below, skimmers coursed, bearing people who never had to worry whether their backs were covered. *I wonder what that's like?* Looks like she'd get the opportunity to find out. "Most folks have some kind of celebration on Discharge Day." She looked at Lucien, who looked perplexed.

"Who else do you know in Chicago?"

Jani pretended to ponder. "Only you."

His expression changed to one of profound concentration. "I'm signed out until oh-eight-thirty." He picked his words like delicacies from a tray. "If that will help you make up your mind."

Jani took in the cityscape one last time. Then she fiddled with the window adjustments until she found the privacy setting. The cast of the scanglass altered subtly, blocking the view from prying eyes.

"If you're toying with me again," Lucien said as she walked toward him, "I'm going to be really, really upset."

"You're so suspicious." Jani straddled him, eased down onto his lap, and wrapped her arms around his neck. "Looks like I have a lot of fence-mending to do." She planted butterfly kisses on his forehead, his lips and cheeks, at the same time brushing her fingertips along the back of his neck until he shivered.

"I should say so." Lucien didn't waste much time on preliminaries—he had gotten the lay of her land long age. He pulled her shirt up over her head. The bandbra followed. He eased her onto her back and finished undressing her; his clothes soon joined hers on the floor. He looked like a young god in the half-light, down from the mountain to help her celebrate her freedom. He didn't tell her he loved her—she wouldn't have believed him if he had. Love was something he did and was good at; right then it was what she needed. First, he said things to her that made her laugh. Then he did things to her that made her cry out.

Then it was his turn, and the first press of his naked body atop hers was a shock she didn't want to recover from for a very long time.

CHAPTER 35

Evan sat on the patio, his chair in the shadows, glass in left hand, right hand dangling over the side. The second bottle of the day, half-empty, rested on the table at his left elbow. He had decided to wait for as long as it took, but it had been a hell of a day. First, news of Jani's discharge had filtered in via Markhart. Then his attempts to reach several old friends had been bounced back, along with the notice that their services would not accept calls from his code.

One up. He'd give the son of a bitch until one up. Then he'd retire to the cool quiet of his office and compose a second letter to a wider audience.

He flexed his aching knee, then tensed as a rustle of leaves sounded from the rear of the yard. Something rattled closer, careless in its approach, like one of the neighbor dogs on a gallivant.

A few meters beyond the edge of the reflected streetlight, the sound stopped. Then, silently as the predator he was named for, Mako glided into view. He wore dark clothes—long-sleeved shirt and trousers. His hands hung at his sides, empty.

Evan tossed back the balance of his drink. "You took your god-damned time."

Mako grunted as he stepped onto the patio. His dark shoes made no noise on the flagstone. "I don't know if you heard, but we've been dealing with an incident. Neoclona has turned my medical services upside down and Cao and Tsecha are watching my every move." He sank into the only other chair, which Evan had taken care to position in the light. "Now, I'm here."

"How much interference are you throwing out?"

"Enough. I've been properly fitted against every sort of electronic surveillance." The soft patter of ergonomic clicks sounded as Mako shifted in his seat. "You'd be more comfortable, I'm sure, if you put that knife away."

Evan's right hand clenched. The knife, a serrated bread slicer taken from the kitchen, comforted him with its cool heft. "If you don't mind, I think I'll keep it."

"Put it away, van Reuter. If I'd wanted to kill you, I'd have done it a half hour ago, when you stepped into the bushes to piss."

"You were out there?"

"I've been here for over an hour, standing out by your lovely roses, watching you drink." Black eyes, scarcely visible through skinfolds and cheekbone, closed in pain as Mako worked his neck. "Killing you would provide me some repayment for the hell of these past weeks, but not enough." He opened his eyes, and gazed at Evan in quiet disgust. "What do you want?"

Evan flexed his right arm, gone numb from the position and the tension. "Just a foot in the door. Idomeni consultant. Seat on a Service-civilian commission. A chance to get in the 'sheets once in a while, keep me from gathering dust." The final words hung up in his throat. "I'll take anything."

"Bah-hah." Mako's rough laugh bubbled like a stuck drain. "You'll take anything *now.* I know you, van Reuter. Once you get that foot in the door, you'll force your way in and start stuffing your pockets."

"It's the Family way." Evan smiled. "I'm getting a renewed taste of the Family way. I catch the lucky break, comparatively speaking. I'm one of theirs, and they don't want to risk setting any unfortunate precedents with the tang of revolution in the air. That makes the verdict death by shunning." He refilled his glass. "But you're an outsider, Roshi. You're pro-colonial, in spite of your protests that you're apolitical, and what you pulled at Rauta Shèràa Base sure as hell proved that you're anti-Family. They'd chew you up and play flipstick with the bones."

Mako sat back, his spine straight and stiff as a flagpole. "If what you say about your predicament is true, who would believe you?"

Evan had prepared his bluff for that one. "The Unsers, for starters. Jerzy Unser's married to Shella Nawar, who just happens to be the Justice Minister's daughter. What's more, they all get along. I predict a domino effect."

Mako exhaled shakily. A long silence followed. Finally, a rumbling sigh. "These idomeni. They are a trial."

Evan's heart leapt. "Aren't they, though."

"I daresay we could use some advice, from time to time."

"Thank you, Roshi."

"Have you got another glass?"

Evan, as it happened, did. He filled it, then took care to maintain his distance as he handed it to Mako. Cornered animals could still strike, even when they seemed subdued. His fingers ached from gripping the knife handle.

But Mako remained seated. He even said, "thank you." Neither offered a formal toast, but they did sip at the same time. A deal sealer, of sorts, although Mako would never admit it and Evan would never think to push.

"You bollixed some of the details."

"But the essential argument is correct?"

Mako grunted an affirmative, his eyes fixed on nothing.

Somewhere down the street, voices carried in loud farewell, followed by the dull *thunks* of skimmer gullwings, an insect chorus of activation whines.

"Where'd you park?" Evan asked.

Mako swirled his drink. "Three blocks over. House party. Skims everywhere." He looked deflated. Exhausted. "I offered her a way out."

"She didn't take it, did she?"

"She had no choice."

"But she didn't say 'yes.' And she didn't say 'thank you.' And she made you feel like the scum of the earth for offering. Welcome to the club, Roshi." Evan stared at the stained flagstone at his feet. "Need a refill?"

But when he looked over at Mako, he saw only an empty chair, a half-filled glass balanced on the arm.

CHAPTER 36

Jani slipped out of bed, then showered and dressed. She took care not to trigger the lights—she needed to get where she was going by a certain time and she didn't want to risk waking Lucien. Odds were if he did wake, he'd simply want to make love to her again. But he was a curious soul, and would definitely question why she felt the need to stumble about in the dark at 0400 when she could be playing with him or for that matter, just *sleeping*.

She considered leaving him a farewell comport entry or a handwritten scribble on a piece of hotel stationery. Something to leave him mumbling imprecations as he drove back to Sheridan in his Family paramour's husband's skimmer. Instead, she blew a kiss to the tangle of arms, legs, and sheet sprawled across the bed and left.

The air was thick with pavement heat, the night sky faded to grey velvet by building lights. Chicago never truly slept, but it did take the occasional breather and early morning midweek appeared to be one of those downtimes. Few skimmers, delivery vans mostly. Fewer pedestrians. Jani bought coffee from an automated kiosk, then hurried down the main streets and byways she had mapped in her mind the night before. She didn't need to ask directions. She had done more during the previous night's hotel search than search for hotels.

Service Archives loomed like a holoVee castle on a corner across from one of her rejected hotels. She walked in the front door and directly up to the desk lieutenant, and handed her one of the IDs she had cobbled together during her short stint in Foreign Transactions, when she still thought she needed to plan her escape.

She waited for *Kisa Van, Major* to ring up clean and green, then she wandered from stacks to stacks, and eventually found Sam Duong huddled on the floor, picking through slipcases.

"Good morning, Mr. Duong."

His breath caught, but when he looked up and saw her, he grinned in relief. "Captain." He shook his head. "No, not Captain. Not anymore." He brushed nonexistent dust from his hands and stood. "How did you know—?"

"You said morning was best to do Gate searches. Not the best security. I guessed."

"I'm surprised you remembered." Sam struggled to his feet, gripping the shelving for support.

"I understand you were in hospital the same time I was?"

"Yes. I wanted to visit, but Pimentel didn't think it a good idea."

"He's a worrier. How are you?"

"Fine. You?"

"Fine. You had surgery?"

"Yes. Pimentel says it went very easy. Drill, freeze, cut, cut." Sam flicked two fingers in imitation of a pair of snips. "I don't mean to sound rude, but how did you get in here?"

"You don't want to know."

"Hah!" Sam grinned. "Want do you want?"

She told him.

"I don't often make the entries themselves." Sam activated the workstation, nestled in a closetlike office down the hall from the stacks. "It's possible my passwords have expired." He uttered a few Bandan phrases, then sat forward so the display could get a good scan of his eyes. It took several minutes—the workstation was old and required coaxing—but eventually the correct screens burbled up from the system depths. "Go ahead."

Jani hesitated until he turned to her, brows arched in question. "Cray," she finally said. "Yolan. Corporal. C-number M-four-seven-dash-five-six-dash-two-eight-six-R."

Sam uttered codes, touched pads, waited. "Next."

"Burgoyne. Emil. Sergeant. C-number M-three-nine-dash-one-four-dash-seven-seven-I." Jani studied the scuffed brown lyno, the ancient paper notice tacked on the wall notifying users to clean up their trash. "Can you place the names where you want, or do they have to fall in alphabetically?"

"I can force-fit."

"Then put Borgie's name right at the top of the entry arch. I want Mako to drive beneath it every time he enters and leaves the base."

Sam uttered another password. "Next."

Fifteen names, by the time they finished. Fifteen C-numbers. Then Sam punched the touchpad one last time, and spoke the final password, and fifteen new names etched themselves in the Shenandoah Gate.

"I give it a week." He shut down the workstation and tipped back his chair. "Two, tops. I'm not the only checker they send out, and the names are monitored regularly."

"Can't let colony names get on that Gate."

"Almost as bad as inmates taking over the asylum."

They both smiled.

"I need to get going." Jani stood and held her hand out to Sam. "Take care of yourself."

"You, as well." He took it gently. "Jani."

Who do you think you are now? Jani couldn't make herself ask him that, either. Instead, she settled for wishing him good-bye, and hurried from the room before she thought of any more questions he could never answer.

The desk smiled. "Did you find what you were looking for, Major?"

"Yes, I did." Jani nodded briskly to the young woman and walked out of the archives building into the new light of day. The walkways had filled in the scant time since she'd entered. The skimways had clogged. She darted between the stalled movers and taxis and down a side street, flicked the Kisa Van ID into a trashzap, then stopped at the first decent-looking café she found. Time for a leisurely breakfast, before the Documents Examiners Registry opened at 0700. The day was young, and Jani Kilian had a lot to do.

Law of Survival

Acknowledgments

To my newsgroup regulars, for keeping me motivated and making me laugh when I needed it.

To Julia Blackshear Kosatka, Dave Klecha, and Secret Dave, for First Readership above and beyond the call.

As always, to my parents, for their understanding and support.

And finally, a postscript . . .

I've been asked how to pronounce my idomeni names and places often enough that I felt I needed to do something about it. I've therefore added a Pronunciation Gazetteer to my webpage, which is located at *www.sff.net/people/ksmith*. There, you'll find some how-to's, along with a few whys and wherefores.

CHAPTER 1

"Come look at these."

Jani Kilian maneuvered through the morning workday crowd and joined Lucien Pascal at the shop window. The display proved typical for an establishment bordering Cabinet Row, quiet and opulent at the same time. The store specialized in fine tableware—the cutlery and metal plate that filled the velvet-draped display niches seemed to glow in the Chicago morning sun.

"This is a very good thank-you gift for your better clients." Lucien pointed to a small silver bowl that had been shaped into a half-shell, then satin-polished until it appeared lit from within. "Not too expensive, but not cheap either. It implies that the document business is good, but you're too astute to throw money about without good reason. It just so happens that you consider the recipient to be a good reason." He bent closer to the window to get a better look, his white-blond hair capturing the light like the silver. "Hand out a few of those, then sit back and watch the commissions pour in."

Jani examined the bowl. Lucien had acquired his eye under the tutelage of Exterior Minister Anais Ulanova—his taste, as always, proved sound but expensive. "I already have more commissions than I can handle." She turned away from the window and continued down the walkway. "I should be home working on a few of them now instead of walking you to the train." She slipped her hand inside her trouser pocket, working her fingers through the assorted vend tokens and keycards until they closed around a slip of paper. The crisp, Cabinet-grade parchment crackled—she jerked out her hand, then folded her arms and turned back to Lucien.

He stood in front of the window, watching her. He looked like a fairy tale soldier in his dress blue-greys, the steel-blue tunic cut on the diagonal with a black leather crossover belt, the grey trousers slashed along the sides with mainline red stripes. He'd set his brimmed lid with geometric precision. Even his red lieutenant's bars and expert marksman badges glittered like costume decoration.

Only the fully packed holster on his waistbelt belied the romantic image. That, and the light in his brown eyes, as cold as the metal on the other side of the glass. "Why are you so edgy?"

Jani forced a smile. "What makes you think I'm edgy?"

"Because you're answering my question with a question, for one thing."

"I do that all the time. You're not the only one who complains about it."

"But I'm the only one who knows what it means in this particular instance." Lucien strolled to her side. "At oh-six, you get a call from the lobby. It's your building manager, with an early morning documents delivery from Cabinet Archives. Nothing unusual in that—you've gotten those before. You tumble out of bed, throw on some clothes, and go downstairs to retrieve them." He leaned close to her, bringing with him scents of soap and freshly washed hair. "Except you don't return right away, and when you finally do show up, you're snappish and distracted. You refuse to eat breakfast, and you hustle me out the door before I've even swallowed a cup of coffee." He drew even nearer, until he brushed against her arm. "John would be upset if he knew you didn't eat. You know that you can't afford to mistreat yourself, considering your condition."

Jani backed off a step so that she could look Lucien in the face. And what a face, the full mouth and strong bones still softened enough by youth to imply innocence. An angel, perched on the brink of damnation. *Stay focused.* She knew he could distract her, then trap her with a question or an offhand comment. "I'm fine. It just hit me how much work I have to do. I've got that meeting at the idomeni embassy today, and if form holds true, it will run longer than expected. I've got three Treasury summaries due next week, and I haven't even looked at the data."

"So as you said, why waste the time playing escort now?" Lucien stood easily, arms at his sides, head cocked in artless curiosity. "Where are you going after you leave me at Union?"

"The only place I'm going after I leave you at Union is home." Jani turned her back on him and started to walk. Her weak right knee sagged with every step, the persistent reminder of an eventful summer. "I've found that the occasional break clears my head. Maybe I'll take another one later today, come back here and buy something for my best clients." She took a deep, steadying breath. The crisp fall air held a city melange of restaurant aromas, overheated skimmer batteries, and a whiff of pungent cologne from a passing pedestrian. "What time's your train?"

"Oh-seven and a half. Same as when you asked five minutes ago." Lucien moved up beside her, matching her stride for stride. "What's wrong?"

"Nothing."

"How can I help you if you never tell me anything?"

"I don't need your help."

"Who are you meeting?"

"I'm not meeting anybody."

As they continued up the walkway, Jani noted that people stepped aside for them. They glanced first at Lucien, then at her, their eyes questioning. *Who are you, lady?* A Family member on an early morning shopping spree with her officer boyfriend? A colonial diplomat out for a stroll with her bodyguard? She knew she cut an imposing figure in her black trousers and crimson shirt-jacket. She matched Lucien in ranginess and almost matched him in height, her short black hair and brown skin serving as dark contrast to his brilliant blondness and paling summer tan. *That's who I am—the soldier's shadow. Not the real thing—please don't make that mistake.* It was an error she'd made herself once, thinking herself a soldier. As was usual with those sorts of lapses, others had paid a steeper price for it than she.

They turned the corner, and Union Station loomed into view. Commuters streamed out, on the way to posts in the Cabinet Ministries, NUVA-SCAN, or Neoclona, and in, travelling to Fort Sheridan or other more distant points in the Michigan province. They entered the station, a train cathedral of stained glass and vaulted ceilings; the pound of footsteps and the keen of voices ricocheted off the walls and seemed to increase in volume with each successive bounce. Jani's pulse quickened as she elbowed through the crowd. She had hurried through many train stations over the years.

They reached the embarkation platform and scanned the Outbound display, then hurried along the line of trains and down the track just as the first call for the Sheridan Express sounded. Lucien stopped before an open car, then turned. "I'll see you at the embassy?"

Jani hesitated, then nodded. "You're going to be there?"

"I'd never miss a chance to watch you and Nema cause trouble."

He pulled her close and kissed her, his lips warm and bruising. "Enjoy your *break*," he whispered as he pulled away. He boarded the train, remaining in the entry as the door slid closed and the sleek bullet pulled away. They didn't wave good-bye, just as they never held hands, or hugged—it wasn't their style. They just stared at one another until the angle grew too sharp and Lucien disappeared from view.

Jani stood on the platform until the train vanished around the bend, then reached into her pocket once more. This time, she removed the piece of paper, her actions of earlier that morning replaying in her mind.

I met Hodge at the front desk. No one else was in the lobby. The only person outside was the doorman. I opened the documents case in Hodge's presence, like I always do. If the seals appeared tampered-with, or if anything looked strange, better to uncover it before a reliable witness. *I found nothing amiss. Seals appeared intact. The papers had been filed in an orderly manner.*

Then she had caught sight of the slip of pale green parchment sticking out of the corner of one of the slipcases like a marker tag. She had gone ahead and closed the case, waiting until she boarded the lift before opening it again and removing the scrap with a hesitant hand.

You possess hidden talents, Niall—it takes skill to crack a Cabinet-grade seal. She unfolded the note and studied it as she had earlier. A short sentence, written in the neat script she'd grown accustomed to over the past months.

Meet me at oh-eight. You'll know where.

"I will?" Jani turned over the scrap and examined the back for any clues she had missed during previous examinations. "Why the mystery, Colonel? And why the rush? We're meeting for lunch tomorrow—can't this wait?" She folded down one of the corners, then unfolded it—the weighty paper still rustled like new. "Pale green—that's the color Commerce is using for their official documents this year—" She stilled. "The Commerce Ministry."

Now she knew where she had to go. All that remained was to find out why.

Jani crossed the pedestrian overpass that spanned the twelve-lane Boul Mich, Chicago's main thoroughfare, and entered the lakeside sprawl of government buildings, parkland, and open land known as Cabinet Row. She reached a vehicle dispatch platform, and boarded a Commerce Ministry people-mover amid a group of green-clad employees. After everyone sat, the lumbering conveyance began its slow float down the wide walkway toward the kilometer-long Ministry main building. As it approached a subsidiary gate that led to a small employee park, Jani stood. The vehicle stopped, and she disembarked.

Jani watched the roofless vehicle resume its glide toward the Ministry proper. Then she pressed her hand to the gatekeeper square; the device scanned her palm, and the gate swung open.

Colonel Niall Pierce stood near the entry, talking to a younger man in lieutenant's gear as he pointed to a late-blooming hybrid rose. Like Lucien, he wore mainline dress blue-greys, but no fairy tale Jani could think of would have claimed him as its hero. In contrast to the prince's clean, broad brow and high cheekbones, this weathered pretender possessed a narrow visage, sun-battered and lined, the appearance of length accentuated by the scar that cut the left side of his face from the edge of his nose to the corner of his mouth. Young blond was replaced by old bronze; springy fitness gave way to wary tension.

Only his eyes spoke to the humor in the man. The warm gold-brown of the richest honey, they hinted at depths of emotion that Lucien had never experienced.

Niall straightened when he heard the gate slam shut. "Captain." He touched his fingers to his forehead in a modest salute. "That'll be all, Pull," he said to the lieutenant. "Meet you back at the skimmer."

"Sir." Pull snapped a salute, then turned to Jani. "Ma'am."

Jani nodded. "You're new."

"Lieutenant Randal Pullman, ma'am." The young man blushed. Since he was a pink-skinned redhead, the rouging made it appear as though he'd just popped out of a boiler. "Good morning." He backed away, his smile wide and fixed, then turned and clipped down the walkway that led into the Ministry.

"I've been telling him about you." Niall's voice twanged, middle-pitch and sharp, lower-class Victorian blunted by years spent on other worlds. "Suffice it to say that you have a new admirer." He moved from the rose to an autumn hydrangea, lifting one of the bloom-heavy branches to his nose.

"I wish you wouldn't do that." Jani wandered a wide semicircle until she stood beside him. He pushed the branch toward her and she bent to sniff the blooms, which were brilliant purple with a heavy, spicy-sweet scent. As she did, Niall released the branch and stepped away. Jani had flinched once when he accidentally touched her. Since then, he took care not to remain close to her for too long.

"Why not?" He drew up straight and locked his hands behind his back. "The work you did at Rauta Shèràa Base was admirable; even twenty years later, it manages to impress. And that flaw you found in

Transport Ministry docking protocols was a marvel of critical analysis."

"Niall, I was forging manifests for a smuggling operation when I uncovered that flaw." Jani paused, then looked up from the flower. "I don't think I ever told you about that, did I?"

Niall hesitated. Then he jerked his chin toward the garden entry, and sniffed. "Pretty Boy waiting for you?"

"No, he's on his way back to Sheridan." Jani picked a shriveled petal from one of the blooms. "I didn't tell him I was meeting you, but he knows something's up. Don't be surprised if you get back to Sheridan to find someone had checked into your whereabouts this morning."

"Isn't he the crafty one?" Niall sneered, his damaged lip accentuating his disgust. "Is he still . . . *dating* that father of four who runs the Justice Ministry Appeals Division?"

"Yes, and a few others as well. I've explained to you before—I don't mind. That way, he doesn't get bored, and I get a few nights a week to myself."

"You call that love?"

"You know I don't. I never did. Between Lucien's essential nature and prototype augmentation, he can't love anyone. My . . . experiences have taught me the value of his sort of outlook. He doesn't know how to ask for what I'm no longer prepared to give. We have just the relationship we want."

"I think you're doing yourself a disservice."

"Can we please cut to the chase?" Jani backed away from the shrubbery until she stood in Niall's path. "What's going on? You didn't go through the trouble to break into a sealed Treasury Ministry documents case in order to lecture me about my personal life, did you?"

Niall reached beneath his brimmed lid to scratch the top of his head. Then he readjusted the braid-trimmed hat to its former dead-on level, and brushed a speck of nonexistent dirt from the front of his tunic. "Ever been to Tsing Tao Station?" He tugged at his own expert marksman's badge. "Biggest shuttle transfer station in the Pearl Way, last stop before you hit the GateWay and enter La Manche, the Channel Worlds—"

"I know what it is." Jani watched him take great care to look everywhere but at her. "A few years ago."

"Four and a half?"

"Yes. Four and a half."

"Just passing through, or did you work there for a time?"

"I did a few odd jobs to earn billet money. Same as I did at every other station I ever passed through. I think I stopped over there for a total of six months."

"Five." Niall yanked a brown leaf from the branch of a late-blooming rose. "Kill anybody while you were there?"

Jani studied him for any sign he joked. She'd learned to spot the hints over the months of their acquaintance—the narrowing of his eyes, the working of his jaw as he bit the inside of his cheek to keep from laughing. But she couldn't find them this time. Unfortunately. "No, I didn't."

CHAPTER 2

"Let's walk out to the lake, where we can talk in private." Niall led Jani through the garden, past a triplet of clerks who had intruded in a flurry of giggles and whispers. They exited through the rear gate, which opened out onto the beach.

Jani shivered as the lake breeze brushed her. It was because of what Lucien referred to as her *condition,* she told herself. It had advanced to the point that she only felt comfortable in heat most people found oppressive. Her discomfort had nothing to do with Niall's questions. Nothing.

She trudged after him across the combed sand to a bench set at the edge of the breakwater. As always, he waited for her to sit first before lowering beside her, an unthreatening arm's length away.

They sat in silence. Overhead, seagulls swooped and screamed. On the water, Commerce lakeskimmers glided in silent patrol. Niall reached into the inner pocket of his tunic and pulled out a flat silver metal case. He shook out a nicstick through the slotted opening and bit the bulbed end—the ignition tip flared orange as it contacted the air.

Jani watched him smoke. He didn't do it often, she had noted, but he did it at very specific times. When he felt particularly agitated or troubled, or as he tried to screw up the courage to talk about what he called their "shared experiences."

"When to the sessions of sweet, silent thought I summon up remembrance of things past." Niall leaned forward, elbows on knees, and studied the 'stick's glowing tip. "Shakespeare's Sonnet 30." He looked out over the water, his voice so soft that the gulls threatened to drown him out. "I keep meaning to lend you the sonnets."

Jani folded her arms and tucked her hands up her sleeves. Her fingers felt like ice chips. "Tsing Tao Station, four and a half years ago. After a run of janitorial gigs, I managed to scrounge a non-Registry clerk's job for one of those seat-of-the-pants shipping companies. I don't even remember the name."

Niall exhaled smoke. "Mercury Shipping."

Jani watched the side of his face and waited for him to explain how he knew that. When he remained silent, she continued. "A brother-sister outfit. One rebuilt shuttle and a time-share lease on a thirty-year-old transport. Constant repair bills, high turnover, and the low-pay, bottom-feeder jobs that the bigger firms never touch."

"Sounds like the sort of outfit that might turn to a bit of smuggling to meet the payroll." Niall had wandered the wild side of the Commonwealth before deciding on the Service straight-and-narrow; his voice held the quiet sureness of someone with experience in the subject.

"Most of the time, smuggling was the payroll." Jani flinched when a gull screamed. "One thing led to another, and we got on the wrong side of a Treasury Customs agent. Not an official investigation—he'd just turn up unexpectedly and ask to see our records. Did that a few times. I figured he was trolling for a payoff, but he never got around to asking."

"He never got the chance. About the time he started digging into the inner workings of Mercury Shipping, he noted in his personal log that he began receiving threatening messages. He saved the paper ones." Niall took a deep pull on his 'stick—the dose ring moved halfway up the shaft. "Two station-days after the date on the last message, his body was found in his flat. Throat had been cut. One station-day after that, you upped and disappeared."

"I had my reasons, in case you've forgotten." Jani shivered as a bout of chills took hold. "Niall, what's going on?"

Niall again reached into his tunic, but instead of his silver box, he removed a folded-over documents slipcase. "I found this waiting for me in my mailbox this morning. After I read it, I figured I'd better pass it along." He handed her the slipcase, then reached into his tunic and once more pulled out his 'sticks.

Jani slid aside the closure and removed several pages of weighty, brilliant white Cabinet-grade parchment. "A joint ministry effort," she said as she searched the gold-bordered documents for a ministry ID code and didn't find it. She flipped back to the face page and read the summary header. "Commonwealth White Paper. Security Risk Evaluation—Jani Moragh Kil—" She fell silent as she found herself looking at a list of dates and page numbers arranged like a table of contents. Next to each date was the name of a city, or a settlement, or a station. The first page contained years one through five of her eighteen years on the run; the second page, years six through twelve; the third, years thirteen to the present.

"There's a data wafer tucked into a pocket inside the slipcase," Niall said. "It contains the full report. Names of companies you worked for, in what capacity, what sorts of . . . business you engaged in. Interviews with coworkers, acquaintances. Ex-lovers."

"I—" Jani swallowed a curse as her stomach cramped. She'd been doing so well on her new enzyme therapy—it hadn't ached for weeks. "I guess I should have expected this. I just didn't think it would turn up so soon." She tucked the papers back in the slipcase. "When do you need it back?"

Niall shook his head. "Keep it. There's plenty more where that came from."

Jani tucked the slipcase in the pocket of her jacket. "It's in general circulation?"

"In the various upper reaches, from what I could gather. PM got a copy. All the Ministers and their deputies. Security chiefs. It's been out for a week or so. Took a while to filter down to me, seeing as I'm on the second team."

"So the Admiral-General's office got one?"

"Oh, yeah."

"Mako have anything to say?"

"About what you'd expect."

Jani watched the dapple of sun on water. It calmed her enough to make her feel that things weren't as bad as they seemed. Almost. "I ran because I couldn't afford to be interviewed, not by trained criminal investigators. You know the drill. First would have come the encephaloscan, which would have revealed my Service augmentation. That would have given them just cause to call in a physician to perform a phys exam. After they'd found my animandroid arm and leg and all my other unique identifiers, they'd have assumed 'deserter' and moved on from there. Before I could whistle the first verse of The Commonwealth Anthem, they would have uncovered the Service warrant for my arrest."

"You could have stalled them."

"You think so? I don't know if you recall the last time we both met with Mako, but I don't interview particularly well."

"Really?" Despite the mood, Niall grinned. "Bit of a smart aleck, are you?" The expression wavered when Jani didn't respond. "Well, like you said, you expected it. How do you plan to counter?"

"Depends how bad it gets, and it could get pretty bad. I falsified shipping and receiving records. Stole scanpack parts. Reset credit chits. An entire host of Level A Registry offenses, any one of which could get me deregistered. Then there's my bioemotional restriction. If some psychotherapeutician decides my past behavior is an indication of future problems, they'll try to stick me in some type of permanent wardship. At the very least, they'll maintain the operational restriction—I won't be able to carry a shooter or drive a skimmer for the rest of my life." Jani stood and stepped to the edge of the breakwater. It was a short drop into the cold churn, only a couple of meters. The drops were always shorter than you thought.

"Maybe it's not as gruesome as you think." Niall's voice sounded rough comfort. "Read it first, then figure out what you need to do." Service tietops scraped on scancrete as he joined her at the edge. "I'll help in any way I can."

"Yeah." Jani gasped as her right calf cramped—her muscles tightened when she sat for too long. "I need to walk."

They strode along the breakwater until it ended, then followed the slope of sand down to the manicured shore. Gulls scuttered ahead of them, waiting until the last moment before taking to the air. In the distance, Commerce employees on break played a game of three-cornered catch.

Jani relaxed. She always felt better when she moved. Her limbs, both the real right and the animandroid left, adjusted readily to the shift and slide of the sand. "I wonder who drove it. The investigation."

"I hate to say it, but I'm betting it was someone on my team." Niall passed her and walked a little farther up the beach. "They probably started out gathering the evidence for your court-martial. When we medical'd you out instead, they wrote the report anyway. One thing Intelligence spooks hate is to let good garbage go unused." He kicked at a pile of pebbles, then picked one up and flung it into the water. "You've got your enemies at Sheridan, you know. They thought you should have been tried for Neumann's death, no matter what led up to it."

"I did shoot him, Niall."

"You had your reasons."

They headed back up the beach toward the Ministry. Jani slowed to give Niall a chance to catch her up. "Mako giving you a hard time about being seen with me?"

"A couple of closed-door talks. Reminders of 'the current conservative climate.' " Niall shrugged. "I remind him that you've got more experience dealing with the idomeni than anyone in Diplo, and that some of your recommendations over the past few months have saved us from some godawful blunders. He understands." His voice held quiet conviction, but he had followed where Admiral-General Hiroshi Mako led for over twenty years, and felt that the sun rose and set by order of the great man.

Jani didn't. "Niall, I'd bet my scanpack that Mako helped set this up."

"No, he didn't." Niall's voice lowered to a warning growl. "It's the Base Command desk jockeys that are causing the trouble. The same ones that want to nail you for Neumann."

"Have they been reminding you of the current conservative climate, too?"

"Yeah. I hand them a little Milton, a little Shakespeare, tell them in my Master of Literature way to butt out. I don't interview particularly well, either."

Jani slowed more as Niall labored to keep his footing on the loose sand. "Don't screw yourself over on my account."

"You'd do the same for me if I got into trouble. I've seen you in action, remember?" He pulled up, removed one of his shoes, and tapped out sand that had leaked in. "I'm going to dig into this when I get back to Sheridan. See if I can find out who signed off on the expense reports." He brushed an invisible smudge from the black tietop's glassy finish, then slipped it back on. "You've got enough going on right now without dealing with this."

They walked in silence. Jani grew conscious of Niall's examination—he tried to hide it, but he never succeeded for long. "If you want to say something, I wish you'd go ahead and say it."

Niall drew closer until they walked shoulder to shoulder. "Earlier this summer, I was a shade taller than you. You're taller than me now. When are you going to stop?"

"No one knows. The average Vynshàrau grows one-nine to two-oh. I'm one-eight-two." Jani held her hand a handspan above her head to indicate how much she could still grow. "John says I might not get as tall as that, being a mixed breed. But even he's ready to give up on the predictions." She heard her voice grow tight. The anger built on its own now, no matter how she tried to suppress it.

"Your eyes look different." Niall leaned in for a closer look. "You've filmed them green! They were always so dark before."

"Neoclona's developed a new color-dispersive film just for me. What's underneath has darkened to green marble. I have nightmares about a film fissuring when I'm out in public."

"They look nice now, though. Stuff seems to work." Niall hurried ahead of Jani as they mounted the breakwater and cut through the rear yard of the Ministry. "I thought they were looking into the possibility of making you all-human again?" He held open the back gate leading into the garden and waved Jani through ahead of him.

"John did call in Eamon DeVries last month." Jani fielded Niall's look of confusion. "Eamon's the third member of the Neoclona Big Three. He's distanced himself from the company in recent years. You don't hear much about him."

Niall's brow arched—he'd detected the sharpness in her voice. "You don't seem sorry."

Jani shrugged. "I despise him. He despises me. He did his best to persuade John to declare me dead at the site of the transport crash. He'd heard that the Service had begun investigating Neumann's murder, and he knew they'd be looking for me. Because of the hybridization research he and John and Val had gotten up to in the basement of the Rauta Shèràa enclave clinic, he knew they couldn't afford to attract attention." And she had attracted attention. Many were the hours she had spent huddled in utilities chases while Val persuaded the Service investigators that Jani Kilian no longer existed. "Almost twenty years had passed since Eamon had seen me." Jani paced a circuit of the small garden. "First thing he says as he walks into the examining room is, 'Why aren't you dead yet?' "

Niall braced against a tree, removed his shoes one at a time, and tapped out more sand. "Bet he didn't say it in front of Shroud—ol' John would've killed him."

Jani smiled. "I never figured you for a John Shroud fan."

"I'm not." Niall brushed off his socks and slipped on his shoes. "Val Parini's all right. The doctor you see most of the time—Montoya—he seems sound. I know Roger Pimentel likes him."

"How is Roger?"

"Fine. Still Chief of Neuro, but the workload is wearing him down. He made vague noises about retirement when I saw him last week. Asked how you were." Niall shook his head. "We could spend all day talking about our doctors, couldn't we?" He watched Jani walk with the sharp eye of the experienced medical amateur. "So?"

"So, after Eamon examined me, he hunkered down with John and Val. They concluded that any attempt at retooling would most likely kill me." Jani stopped in front of a bird feeder and unplugged a stopped dispenser with her finger, sending a thin stream of birdseed spilling to the ground. "Sometimes that doesn't sound like such a bad risk."

"You can say things like that to me—I understand. But remarks like that tend to make psychotherapeuticians nervous." Niall gathered up a handful of the spilled seed and tossed it to some squirrels that foraged in the grass. "Trust me—I know what I'm talking about."

Jani gripped the feeder post and swung around to face him. "How did your last check-up go?"

"About as you'd expect." Niall flung more seed with such force that the squirrels scattered. "Get your augmentation removed—the risks of depression and psychosis outweigh the benefits. Yes, we know it could save your life in case of severe injury, but if the injury resulted from the fact that you just slashed your wrists, define the benefit please, Colonel. Cut back on the workload, take a vacation, transfer to another area. At least no one suggested retirement this time." He brushed off his hands and cut across the garden to the front gate. "Need a ride home?"

Jani tagged after him. "No, I'll take public. I've got to go to the embassy later. Sitting in a people-mover and watching the city float by helps me think."

"More fun with diplomacy?"

"Yeah."

"If I don't hear from you in a week, I'll send in an assault team." Niall once more cut ahead of her as they came to the gate so he could hold it open for her. "The Cup semifinals are set for next week. Acadia Central United's playing Gruppo in the first match."

"United got Desjarlais back just in time." Jani shivered as her body once more decided it was cold, and closed her jacket fasteners up to her neck. "The government will go nuts if a colonial team wins the Cup. They're afraid that's all it would take for some of the more rebellious colonies to attempt to secede from the Commonwealth."

"That's ridiculous."

"You're a colony boy, Niall. You know better than that. It's all about politics, even when it's not."

Niall sensed that she didn't feel like talking football. "Heard from your folks?"

"Yeah." The 'mover that would take Jani back to the walkway drifted up to the stand. "They've gone to stay with Oncle Shamus at his lodge near Faeroe Outpost. I guess he needs help with his systems again."

"You guess?"

"They're not being real forthcoming. I'm wondering if times are bad in Ville Acadie, and they needed to sell the business."

"Times are never bad for systems installers."

"Well, something's wrong." Jani stepped aboard the open-topped 'mover and took a seat near the rear. "I don't think they're comfortable talking to me. Maybe they don't think it's any of my business."

Niall shot her a "let's have none of that" look. "Or maybe Shamus did need help. Sometimes the answers really are as simple as they seem." He stepped back as the 'mover pulled away. "I'll look into that report."

"Thanks."

"Take it easy." Niall smiled his crooked smile and again touched his forehead. "Captain."

"Colonel." As Jani returned the salute, she felt the slipcase jostle in her jacket pocket, and tried to forget it was there.

Jani changed people-movers three times on her way home. As she had told Niall, sitting and watching Chicago drift past her window helped her think. Unfortunately, she couldn't control what she thought about.

They got me. She felt the slipcase every time she moved, saw the gleam of the white parchment sheets, heard their crackle as she had unfolded them under Niall's concerned eye. *I wonder how long it took them to uncover it all? When did they start? Last winter, when they realized that I lived? Or did they wait until the summer, when they had me in hand?*

The six-lane tumult of the Boul Mich Sidebar gradually veered lakeward, narrowing and quieting into the tree-lined elegance of Chestnut Street. Jani looked through the branches to the establishments beyond . . . the glass-walled terrace of the restaurant where she and Lucien had dined the night before . . . the shops in which they'd debated other presents for her clients. Jani hadn't realized that she needed to worry about presents for her clients until Lucien had broached the subject. Her comment that considering the way they ran her ragged, the presents should all flow in *her* direction had fallen on unsympathetic ears. *You're in the big city now,* Lucien had said. *We do things differently here.*

"Do you?" Jani stood as the 'mover slowed to a stop. "Could've fooled me." The only difference she had been able to discern thus far between the wilder colonies and the Commonwealth capital was that life in Chicago required more paperwork. And, at times, even more caution.

She disembarked and headed north, crossing Chestnut and turning onto the even more rarified gentility of Armour Place. Her goal rested in matronly repose in the middle of the block, a twelve-story sanctum of safety and security. Eighty-seven fifty-six—a sedate, marble-faced building with a live doorman and, according to Lucien, a century's worth of Family secrets buried within the walls.

Secrets . . .

I have secrets. Jani's step slowed. *The funny thing is, some of them are common knowledge. But still they're ignored, denied, not talked about, in the hope that they'll disappear. A peculiarly humanish habit, one the idomeni mock.*

My name is Jani Moragh Kilian, late of the Commonwealth Service. One of the conditions of my discharge disallows me from using the title Captain, Retired, but that's what I am.

Just as John Shroud resurrected me and rebuilt me as he saw fit, so my past has been gutted and reconstructed for the benefit of the few. What remains speaks to the facts, but the truth lies elsewhere. I tried to speak the truth, and they called me crazy. Now I stick to the facts, and bide my time.

Jani shook herself out of her grim reverie as she approached her apartment house, eyeing the entries of the buildings directly across the street. She did so mostly out of habit, but partly from unease. The small multilevel chargelot seemed quiet as usual. The commotion echoing from the building next door to it, however, scuttled the gracious ambience the avenue usually projected. Bangs and clangs, interspersed with the occasional muffled boom of a pinpoint charge and the whine of heavy-duty construction machinery. The gutted former residence would soon twin its neighbor across the way—twelve stories of marble enclosing thirty of the finest flats money could rent. In the meantime, the carefully preserved white façades sheltered scaffolding, equipment, workers, and building materials sufficient to convert the shell into a hive.

Jani ducked beneath the low-hanging awning that sheltered her building entry and nodded to the morning doorman, who keyed open the triple-width door. The thick, ram-resistant scanglass swept aside and she stepped into the lobby, a low-ceilinged space filled with expensive furnishings, paintings, and sculpture. The sudden hush as the door shut behind her made her feel, as always, as though she'd been locked inside a vault.

She walked to the front desk, her shoes sinking to the ankle in the sound-deadening carpet; fellow residents passed her, their greetings muted, as though they spoke in church.

"You're back, Mistress Kilian." Hodge the manager smiled a subdued greeting. "Confound the racket across the way."

Jani sighed as she accepted the pile of paper mail he produced from beneath the desk. "Confound it, indeed."

“Not much longer.” Hodge’s voice held a hope-filled lilt—he’d mistaken her dismay at the amount of mail for weariness with the noise. “The rededication is scheduled for Thanksgiving weekend.” He grew subdued. “Armour Eight Seven Five Five. Seems a rather dull name.” He was a slight, older man with a schoolmaster’s air. He’d worked in the neighborhood all his life and felt the changes like a father watching his children grow.

“Well, at least they’re preserving the façade.” Jani tucked the mail under her arm and looked out at the bustle across the street. “But for the noise, they’re remarkably self-contained. You never see the workers.”

“There are restrictions regarding these matters, to minimize the impact on the neighborhood.” Hodge frowned. “But I have seen things. The workers are supposed to use a contractor lot three blocks west, near the University Annex. But I believe they sneak vehicles into our garage to avoid the walk.”

“Imagine that.” Jani bit back the comment that if she’d been in their place, she’d do the same thing. But that was a colonial sentiment, and she lived in the Commonwealth capital now. As Lucien said, they did things differently here.

CHAPTER 3

The lift deposited Jani on the sixth floor. She walked to the last door at the end of the carpeted hall and keyed into her flat. The door slid open to reveal the large sitting room, an expanse of bare bleached wood flooring, unadorned off-white walls, and uncurtained windows.

Jani walked to her desk, the sole piece of furniture in the space, and pushed aside a stack of files so she could deposit her mail. Compared to the rest of the room, the desktop looked as though it belonged to another person. Masses of documents in multicolored folders and slipcases covered the surface from end to end, abutting her workstation on three sides and all but burying her comport. *I've got too much work.* But the commissions kept coming. The requests. The contracts. Niall had spoken the truth. Jani Kilian had more experience with the idomeni than anyone in Chicago, and Chicago seemed determined to take advantage in every way possible.

"Who has time to buy furniture?" Jani muttered as she cleared a space around her comport. *Give me a credit line,* Lucien asked repeatedly, *I'll get you whatever you need.* But she had turned him down because she didn't want him to become too well acquainted with her finances.

There are companies that handle this, Niall had commented, his assumption being that after years of living in the Commonwealth's outer reaches, she didn't trust her taste.

But it was her friend Frances Hals who had nailed the perplexity as well as anyone could have. *The two sides of Jani Kilian—paper and nothing,* she had said when she visited earlier that week to find the floors still bare. *When are you going to start filling in, and with what?* She had served as Jani's CO for only a few weeks that summer, but years spent managing recalcitrant documents examiners had further honed an already keen insight. She didn't want to hear that Jani had no interest in life outside the documents realm, that the workload was too heavy, the responsibilities too great. *You're still running. You need to decide whether it's force of habit or fear of what you'll find if you stand still.*

"Always a pleasure, Frances." The comport's incoming message light fluttered in mad blue abandon—Jani flicked the activator pad and watched a harried male face form on the display.

"Hey, Jan." Kern Standish, the Deputy Treasury Minister, stifled a yawn. He'd already loosened his neckpiece, and sat with both hands wrapped around a cup of coffee. "We're having a meeting about you this morning, which will be a continuation of the meeting we had about you last night. I'm guessing that you know what I'm talking about."

Jani patted her pocket, and felt the outline of the documents slipcase. "Yes, Kern," she said to the recorded image. "I know."

"Anyway . . ." Standish tilted his wrist to glance at his timepiece, and sighed. "Gotta go. Just wanted to give you a heads-up. I'd appreciate if you'd erase this after you listen to it." His brown skin looked greyed in the harsh office lighting. "Most folks here think it's water under the bridge, but you know Jorge. He's worried about Anais, and how miserable she can make his political life if she finds out he's on your side." He smiled weakly. "I'll let you know what happens." The screen blanked. Jani duly erased the message, then tapped the pad to open the next one.

"Ja-ni." The man offered a mouth-only smile. Devinham from NUVA-SCAN Colonial Projects Division—one of her errors in professional judgment. He kept moving the targets and still expected her to hit every one with a single shot. "The presentation I'm giving has been moved up to next Monday, and I need the Phillipan dock data a little earlier than I'd anticipated—"

"That's news, Frank." She tapped the pad again.

"—please help—"

Again.

"—if you have the time—"

Jani checked the counter. *Twenty-one messages*. Judging from the number of pleas she'd heard so far, the white paper hadn't yet scared off any clients. *Too bad—I could use the break.* She settled for taking refuge in her bedroom.

Unlike the rest of the flat, Jani had furnished her bedroom.

Lucien had insisted. After all, he needed an armoire to store his clothes, a nightstand so he could reach a comport immediately in case of an emergency call from Sheridan, and lamps so he didn't kill himself when he arrived late at night to find her already asleep.

But most especially, Jani felt, he wanted a place to display his gifts to her. Last winter's tin soldier stood sentry atop the armoire. This summer's fatigue-clad teddy bear guarded the bed. They had since been joined by a set of nested matryoshka dolls and a watercolor of a costumed couple eyeing one another across a crowded room. The painting, which hung alongside the dresser, was exquisitely detailed and framed in tasteful gilt. The doll set, which had joined the soldier atop the armoire, had been hand-carved from wood and painted bright red and blue. Both objects contained flaws of use—the picture frame had been nicked in several places, and the fact that the tiniest doll in the matryoshka set could be opened implied that the littlest one had gone missing. In Jani's experience, only one type of person treated works of art like everyday objects, to be used as intended regardless of their value.

"Which of his Family lovers did Lucien steal you from?" she asked the largest matryoshka doll as she took her down from her resting place. "And why?" They certainly weren't the sort of gifts one usually bestowed on the object of one's rapture. Lucien took particular delight in showing Jani the clothes and jewelry that he received for services rendered—he ranked every present by its monetary value, and negligent admirers weathered the brunt of his indifference until they dug into their pockets and rectified the situation.

Jani returned the doll to its place. "Frances thinks that at heart, all men are children and that they show their truest feelings with childlike gifts." But then, Frances liked Lucien, and thought he had feelings to show. Jani liked him too, even though she knew that he didn't.

She walked to the window and deactivated the privacy shield. The milky scanglass lightened to transparency, revealing clear views of both the garden alley that ran along the rear of the building and Oak Street, a shopping lane that paralleled Chestnut and also merged with the Boul Sidebar. An escape route, one of many she'd worked out over the months. Not that she'd ever need them. She was yesterday's news, useful only as a subject of gossip and the occasional damning security evaluation.

Jani sat down on the bed, and girded herself for another go-round with her comport. And so they went in spite of the white paper. Requests for research updates. Meeting reschedules. Hat-in-hand queries into her availability. Jani demurred, assented, and rejected—if she applied herself, she could meet the most pressing of her deadlines and accommodate a few of the more challenging, and therefore more expensive, requests.

In theory. She'd been pushing herself the past few months, and only yesterday had caught several slips that would have proved embarrassing if they'd gotten into a final report. Niall had taken to calling her "the Red Queen"—her request for an explanation won her a lecture about the storied Alice.

Running faster and faster to stay in one place. She knew she spent too much time performing routine research. But she didn't trust the contractor firms, and her searches for help had left her muttering dark damnations about the current state of the documents profession.

When she had whittled the queue to the final message, she took a breather, sitting forward and letting her head drop between her knees to stretch her tightening back. Her stomach ached again. Hungry or not, she'd have to choke down breakfast. Her life had come to revolve around the care and feeding of her mutating body and her physician, Calvin Montoya, possessed a sorcerous knack for diagnosing patient noncompliance with a single look.

She hit the message pad, and stared open-mouthed at the face that formed.

"Hullo, Jan." Steven Forell grinned and pushed a shaggy auburn lock out of his eyes. "Bet yer surprised to see me." His lapsed altar boy face looked despairingly youthful.

"You might say that, yes," Jani said with a laugh. She'd last seen him that past winter, when she left him hiding in her Interior Ministry suite while she hunted down whoever had framed him for murder. She had uncovered the true culprit and much more besides, and almost died during the subsequent shakeout that wound up costing Evan van Reuter his Ministry.

"We're back—Ange and me—froom Helier." Steve's Channel-Guernsey accent ground his words together into a single lumpy mass. "Bit of a bang job. In and out—word from the nobbies—here we are and back again."

You and Angevin received a short-term special assignment from some higher-ups in Interior Colonial Affairs . . . got it.

"We'd heard about yer to-do, o'course . . ." Steve's brow drew down as his look sombered. "Rum go you had, gel. Ange thinks it were all a setup from on-high. She tried to tap some of her late dad's friends fer info. You'd think she'd asked them to give a few years off their lives." His words stalled as he searched his pockets. He uncovered a nicstick, ignited it, and was soon enveloped by the cloud of smoke Jani recalled so well. "So we're here. Still a few days till our return to the grind—Ange thought you might like a dinner. Tomorrow night? Gaetan's? Our treat, since we never got to thank you proper." He coughed and looked away. The seconds ticked. "Sevenish, then? Meet ya there." He turned back to the display. His grin froze and faded as the message ended.

Jani stared at the blank screen. *Ya see, there's this bang job,* she thought in Steve-speak. *I don't have the time,* she continued in her own. She reached out, her finger hovering above the reply pad. *I don't have the time.* A very simple sentence. By now, she could say it in her sleep.

Instead, she undressed. Showered. Chose a suit in dark green from the conservative array in her closet and dressed with absent care, her mind carefully focused on nothing. Styled her hair. Applied makeup. Avoided the mirror.

Finally, boots in hand, she removed Niall's slipcase from the pocket of her discarded jacket, padded out to the sitting room, and inserted the data wafer in her workstation's reader slot. She sat down and pulled on her boots, concentrating on adjusting the fasteners to the proper tension before looking at the display.

It scrolled before her, cross-referenced and footnoted. The officially researched life of Jani Moragh Kilian, written in bland government style. The anonymous authors didn't spend much time on her first seventeen years—a single paragraph defined her parents and her early schooling in the Acadian capital of Ville Acadie. Only when they discussed her performance on a formidable array of Commonwealth-wide qualifying exams and her subsequent acceptance into the idomeni Academy in Rauta Shèràa did they become more verbose.

" 'After her arrival in Rauta Shèràa, Kilian's lack of Family connections and singular personality caused her to seek support and companionship in unlikely quarters. Kilian's ready adoption of idomeni languages and customs alienated her from peers even as it increased her value in the diplomatic sphere. While her singling-out as a favorite by the Chief Propitiator of the Vynshà, Avrèl nìRau Nema, alarmed Consulate officials, the general feeling was that even this could be worked to Commonwealth advantage. Her subsequent commissioning into the Commonwealth Service, while a sound decision on the face of it, only served to highlight her flagrant disrespect for traditional seats of human authority and intensify her estrangement from those who could have assisted her in her reassimilation.' "

Jani smacked the side of the workstation display with the flat of her hand. "This is a reference to Evan, is it? The only reassimilating he wanted from me was the illegal transfer of idomeni brain research data into his late father's hands!" She didn't find that out until years later, however. *Just last winter, in fact. The uncovering of that information led to Evan's downfall.* She stood and paced a circuit of her barren sitting room before returning to her desk.

Knevçet Shèràa, the authors touched on only briefly. The deaths of humans as the result of mind control experimentation performed on them by Laumrau physician-priests, well, they had to discuss that since it was a matter of record to which the idomeni admitted freely. The role that Colonel Rikart Neumann played in planning and gathering the research was glossed over as unsubstantiated rumor; his murder was blamed on his sergeant, Emil Burgoyne, who supposedly sought revenge for a recent demotion. "Except Borgie didn't do it. Mako made him the scapegoat so that Prime Minister Cao would accept the idea of my medical discharge." Jani felt her throat tighten. "Mako couldn't afford to let me face court-martial. He has his own bodies to keep buried." She blinked until her eyes cleared, then continued to read.

" 'As the Vynshà worked to weaken Laumrau defenses around the dominant city of Rauta Shèràa, the Laumrau sought to maintain strategic positions in the mountainous desert regions that surrounded the city. Knevçet Shèràa, which they considered a holy place, was one of those positions. The presence of human beings in the area was, they felt, a mistake that they needed to rectify in order to regain the favor of Shiou, their goddess of order. For that reason, as was admitted later in a closed-door session cited below footnote addendum et cetera et cetera, they planned to retake the hospital-shrine from the remaining members of the Twelfth Rover Corps. The battle would follow a night of prayer and sacramental meal-taking that they referred to as a Night of Convergence.' "

Jani's voice slowed as her sense memory of that night returned. The sear of pain as she hacked her left arm with a mess knife. The warm flow of her blood, captured with strips torn from a red machinist's rag, the closest facsimile she could find to a Vynshà soul cloth. The growing numbness in her slashed arm, the rough dampness of the rag between her fingers as she braided the strips into a skein that would house her soul, and shelter it from the actions of her body. The slip of the sand under her boots as she walked down the hill toward the Laumrau encampment. " 'As the twenty-six Laumrau based at the encampment took sacrament in their tents, Kilian crept in under cover of night and shot them one by one.' " That much, the fact-finders nailed perfectly. But then, they'd found it out from the idomeni. Unlike humans, the idomeni always admitted truth freely, no matter how damning the result.

After that, details muddied quickly. While unofficially, everyone knew that Evan van Reuter had arranged that a bomb be planted on the transport that had been sent to return Jani and the rest of the Twelfth Rovers to Rauta Shèràa, he had never been officially charged with murder. Even though everyone knew that John Shroud had salvaged Jani's shattered body from the wreckage and rebuilt her with illegally acquired idomeni genetic material, no one wanted to put the details to paper. John could have faced charges of kidnapping and illegal utilization of technology, and John was a powerful man. Evan, meanwhile, though no longer a powerful man, still had his memory and his mouth.

"You'd spill it all if they tried you for murder, wouldn't you, Ev? You'd drag all the Family members who conspired with Neumann and your father into the hellhole with you." Which explained why Evan remained free to nibble on the edges of the idomeni diplomatic pie, a peripheral presence at some of the meetings Jani attended. They took assiduous pains to avoid one another, much to the disappointment of those who hoped for an altercation. "As if it would make a difference." Maybe someday they would be forced to face their shared past. With any luck, *someday* would never come.

Jani broke off her meditation to look once more at the workstation display, and read of her escape from Rauta Shèràa during that final Night of the Blade, when the Vynshàrau asserted their claim to the city. Then came the details of her life on the run. The names she had used. Men she had known. Dirt she had done.

So they found out about the faked bank transfers in Ville Louis-Phillipe. The altered manifests and receiving documents she had constructed on a score of worlds. And the shipping clerk in New St. Lô must not have been at happy with her cut of the proceeds as she had seemed at the time—she had revealed everything about the scan-pack parts skimming operation in which Jani had been involved. *No, not involved—it was mine from start to finish.* But her scanpack had needed refurbishing, and she had been desperate. *I just took a part here, a part there. I never got greedy.* Unfortunately, that qualifier hadn't made it into the report.

She paged to the top and read through once more. She searched for conclusions. A recommendation for censure or expulsion from Registry. A proposal to convene a grand jury to explore possible criminal charges. She didn't find them, though, just as she didn't find mention of certain other salient events. A small gap. One missed stop in her round-the-Commonwealth journey, but it dwarfed the other matters delineated in the security report.

They're probably saving that for the next white paper. She pushed the idea to the back of her mind and waited for her nerves to settle enough that she could consider eating.

Jani adjourned to the kitchen. She dug through the cupboards for a Neoclona prepack meal and tossed it label-unread into the oven, then poured herself coffee from the morning's dregs. By the time she flushed out the brewer, her breakfast was ready. She popped the lid on the container and stared at reactor-kettle meatloaf and a shredded purple vegetable that the container claimed was beets but that smelled like no vegetable she'd ever encountered. She excavated a fork from her muddled utensil drawer and boosted herself up on the counter. She ate and mulled until the buzz of her comport called her out to the sitting room.

"Jani." Colonel Eugene Derringer, adjutant to General Callum Burkett, the head of Service Diplomatic, regarded her with his usual air of impatience. He looked a study in tan—skin, hair, desertweight uniform. Burkett the Younger, with his clipped demeanor and horse face; it was a running argument among the rest of Diplo whether the similarities were happenstance or if Derringer worked at them. "I'm calling from my skimmer. I've just left the base. Why don't I zip by your building and give you a lift to the embassy?"

"It's a little out of your way, Eugene. And it's almost two hours early."

"We can use the extra time. There's something you and I need to discuss."

"What?"

Derringer smiled coolly. "See you in a few." His face fractured and faded.

Jani poked her fork into the remains of her meal. She suspected a bout of on-the-road reeducation in the offing. Derringer felt her behavior toward the idomeni too familiar, her relationship to the ambassador too close—

The comport buzzed again. She hit the receive pad harder than she should have, and the unit screeched.

"I heard that." Niall sat at his desk in his Base Command office. He paused to partake of his soldier's breakfast—a swig of coffee, a pull on a nicstick. "Things not going well?" He made no reference to which things he talked about. Neither of them trusted comports, even ones like his and Jani's that were supposed to be secured.

"Eugene just called." Jani rolled her eyes. "He's picking me up in person to take me to the embassy."

"Well, well. Fixing to pop the question, is he?"

Jani forced a laugh. "Yeah, I think he has the ring and the date all picked out. Right after I say yes, he's going to ask Nema to be best man."

Smoke puffed from Niall's nose and mouth as he laughed. "Has the esteemed representative of the Shèrá worldskein pulled anything since the Pokegrass Episode? Any more vegetation-stuffed chair cushions for our dear Eugene to sit on?"

"No." Jani smiled more easily, the memory of Derringer twitching about in his booby-trapped seat over the course of one memorable four-hour conclave replaying in her mind. "Nema's moved on to other torments. I keep telling him, 'You're humiliating a Service diplomat—stop it.' But he won't listen."

"He's idomeni. He knows Derringer doesn't like him, and he enjoys tweaking him." Niall sat back, nicstick clenched between his teeth at a jaunty angle. "So what's happened lately?"

Jani pressed a hand to her forehead. "They met in Nema's rooms last week—I forget what about. Somehow, Nema arranged to have an audio track of the Commonwealth anthem piped in, at a very, very low volume. So they're talking, and Eugene's just barely hearing this music—"

"And wondering if he should stand at attention or check into the Neuro ward."

"Nema said the look on his face was 'a sight to behold, and truly.' I keep waiting for Eugene to retaliate. Somehow, I don't think that will prove nearly as humorous." Jani sighed heavily and sat up. "That being so, I shouldn't aggravate him by making him wait. I better get ready."

Niall's eyes narrowed. "You OK?"

"Yeah." She nodded once, then again.

"You don't seem too sure."

"Just a feeling. Just—" She braced her hands on her chair arms and boosted to her feet. "We'll talk later."

"All right." Niall frowned. "Later."

Jani waited for the display to blank. Then she carted the remains of her meal to the kitchen for disposal. Washed her fork and coffee cup and stored them away. Wiped down the counter. Thought.

Here's my feeling, Niall—the white paper contains one important gap. Two serial events in the same botched scenario, the discovery of either one of which could result in her imprisonment for life.

Jani returned to her desk and stuffed her scanpack and a few pertinent files into her battered Service surplus duffel. *How could they uncover my one-week stint as a deckhand on a Phillipan cruise shuttle, and miss those two things?* She put the duffel aside and sat down, burying her face in her hands as the past returned, an unwelcome shadow in the doorway that said, *Hello, remember me?*

Document forgery as a whole was a crime, of course, but under the general heading came three classifications with steadily increasing penalty in proportion to the adjudged severity. Simple forgery, the construction of a unique document that had no legal right to exist, was the least grave—such objects were bastard children, embarrassing to the putative relatives but easily dealt with. Wipe them out, lock them up, take steps to make sure that particular avenue of deceit was closed and remained so. Second came alteration of existing paper. That misdeed carried heftier fines and sentences because something once pure had been sullied, something once reliable had been rendered untrustworthy.

But copying a document, divesting it of its unique identity by sending a twin out into the world as if it were the original, was considered the worst of the three. Simple forgeries were more sporting—a contest between the forger's skill and the investigator's ability to detect. But executing a copy of an existing document, down to the weave of the paper and the position of the insets, took that competition and warped it. Worse than a bastard, such an object was a changeling that subverted the rightful document's place in the paper world, and robbed it of its inheritance. It shook the stability of the paper system, a construct in which every document played a role, had a history, promoted order.

Jani lifted her head and rested her chin on her arm.

"I made a copy once." Five years before, in Hamish City, a dreary town as off the beaten path as a colonial capital could be. *The capital of Jersey, the hind end of the Channel Worlds.* She tried not to think of Jersey too much.

Jani could see out her sitting room windows to the bright sunny morning on the other side. Bright sun didn't evoke memories of Hamish City. For those one needed grey skies, grimy streets, the stinging odor of battery hyperacid mixing with the rank of desperation.

"Sasha needed my help." But then, Sasha had always needed somebody's help. Short and spindly, a shaggy brune with bitten fingernails and a nervous smile, he was a member of the loose-knit group of techs and clerks to which Jani belonged during her Jersey stay. Another member of the group had labeled Sasha clumsy, which was a shorthand way of saying that he missed warning signs and never listened.

"He decided one day that he wanted to pull out of Hamish." Jani rose, twisted back and forth to stretch her back, then walked to the window. "But he needed money." And someone offered him some, Sasha had told Jani, the excitement pitching his voice high like a young boy's. All he had to do was figure out a way to obstruct an investigation into the true ownership of a parcel of land on which someone wanted to build a fuel depot. "I should have known as soon as he told me about it that a Family was involved. The Families had a vise grip on fuel services in the Channel." But she was working as an inventory hack and going mad from the boredom, and the idea of throwing a wrench in somebody else's works appealed.

So when Sasha brought Jani the original deed of ownership and asked what she could do, she pulled out her scanpack and the best documents training extant and went to work. It had taken her a week to diagram the original, then two more to steal the necessary components and assemble the backdated copy. It was a sound piece of work, she knew, the best that could be done without a Registry copying device. It even got past her scanpack analysis, if she ignored some of the dodgier variances.

"But I warned Sasha that it wouldn't get past a Family examiner." Jani watched the well-dressed midmorning bustle on the sunny street below and envisioned a gloomier scene: the pedestrians bundled in weatheralls and field coats, late fall wind driving the cold mist like smoke. "I told him to arrange for a fifty-fifty drop." The buyer would leave half the money at a prearranged site; Sasha would take the money and leave the copied deed. "The next step would be for the buyer to pick up the copy and leave the rest of the money. A sucker bet, yes, but it didn't matter because I had told Sasha not to wait. The half payment was enough to get him off Jersey. I told him to take it and go. He took too great a risk if he hung around."

She still didn't know why she followed him the day he made the drop. Guilt, maybe, that she'd helped him get in well over his head. Shooter in hand, she tailed him to an alley behind some warehouses, watched him pluck the documents slipcase containing the first half of the payment from a space behind some empty crates, then insert the copy into the same niche. "I rousted him then, made him come with me, told him to get offworld *now*." She should have escorted him to the shuttleport herself and seen him aboard the next merchant vessel out, but he had promised her he'd leave, and she'd believed him for the ten minutes it took him to disappear from her sight.

By then, the realization hit. That Jani had asked Sasha to leave a great deal of money behind, and that Sasha never listened. By the time she reached the drop site, she found him felled like a tree. A man stood over him, shooter in hand. A man like Niall. A coiled spring. A professional. But even professionals could be surprised—he spotted her an instant after she saw him. An instant too late. She had earned an Expert marksmanship badge in the Service and never lost the eye.

Jani knew she'd killed him—she could tell by the way he lay, like a rag crumpled and tossed to the ground. She left him and saw to Sasha, dragging him into the open as carefully as she could, then watching from a safe distance as the first passerby found him and called for help. Then she fled, the need to reach the shuttleport and nab a billet on the next ship out overwhelming the desire to remain behind and discover whether Sasha survived. Clumsy Sasha, who had needed a mentor but had been given a changeling instead.

"Copying. Murder." Of a Family agent, most likely. "How did they miss it?" Jani stood at the window, watching but not seeing. Then thoughts of Derringer intruded, and she trudged to her bathroom to brush her teeth. She did so twice, in deference to Vynshàrau sensibilities. All idomeni considered the act of eating a private communion between the worshipper and their gods, food and drink the links that forged that sacred bond, but the Vynshàrau were the most rigid in their beliefs. Even Nema, as audacious as he was, adhered to his sect's dietary laws, and Jani didn't want a whiff of coffee breath to further aggravate already tense relations.

By the time Hodge called her from the lobby to tell her that the colonel's skimmer had arrived, she felt prepared to face whatever Derringer had to throw at her. Before she left her flat, she removed Niall's wafer from the workstation reader, returned it to the slipcase, and tucked it into the safety of her inner tunic pocket.

CHAPTER 4

Derringer's steel-blue double-length hugged the curb in front of the apartment house. As soon as Jani hit the sidewalk, the doorman and Derringer's driver engaged in a footrace to see who would play the gentleman. The point was declared moot when Derringer popped the door open himself and stepped out of the vehicle.

"Jani." Even though the red stripe had been removed from his desertweight trousers in deference to the Vynshàrau's color protocols, no one would ever mistake him for anything but highly polished mainline brass.

"Eugene." Jani brushed past him and bent low to climb into the jump seat across from him. "What did you need to see me—" She fell silent when she saw a young man already sitting where she wanted to sit. "Who are you?" She could hear the sharpness in her voice, but she didn't savor being forced to sit next to Derringer. She scooted down the bench seat, as far away from the colonel as possible.

Derringer doffed his garrison cap and eased in beside her. "This is Peter Lescaux." He nodded to the intruder, who smoothed the neckpiece of his somber brown daysuit. "Exterior Minister Ulanova's new Chief of Staff."

"The storied Jani Kilian." Lescaux smiled shyly and extended his hand. "I'm thrilled to meet you at last."

Jani took in the brilliant blondness offset by brown eyes. The sharp bones, slim fitness, vague, indefinable accent. *So you're Anais's new Lucien.* His skin felt cool and smooth; he'd buffed his nails until they shone like glass. She likened him to a snake that had just shed its skin, then pushed the thought from her mind before it showed in her face.

"I thought we'd stop at a place I know nearby, grab some lunch." Derringer nodded to his driver; the skimmer pulled away from the curb. "Lord knows how long we'll be holed up at the embassy—we better stoke up while we can."

"*Excellent* thought, Colonel," Lescaux nodded as though someone had spring-loaded his neck.

Oh brother! Jani knocked the back of her head against the seat bolster.

"Fancy setup you've got." Derringer cast a sideways glance in her general direction. "I'd heard you'd taken a flat near the Parkway, but Armour Place? Now I know what happens to all those consultant fees we pay you."

Jani counted to three before answering. "The Registry employment adviser advised my renting at the best address I could afford. It instills confidence in the client." She wanted to add that since her flat overlooked the alley and commanded views of neither the Chicago skyline or the lake, she paid half the rent of her more scenically gifted neighbors, but she'd be damned if she'd justify her living arrangements to Derringer.

"It is a good address," Lescaux said, nodding knowingly. "All the Families have residences nearby."

Jani watched the passing city views, and waited. And waited some more. "Are you two going to tell me what's going on"—she swung around and glared at Derringer—"or are you going to make me guess?"

Derringer nodded again to his driver, who raised the privacy shield between his seat and the passenger cabin. "How much do you know about problems on Elyas?"

Jani flash-filtered all the scuttlebutt she had heard over the past weeks. "The problems I've heard about are confined to Karistos. It's a typical colonial capital, grown too big too quickly. The infrastructure hasn't kept pace. Skimways can't handle the traffic. Water treatment facilities are overtaxed. Last month, a majority of the population got dosed with a microbial contaminant that had infested the treatment system of the primary facility. Several people died."

"Twenty-two," Lescaux piped. Jani acknowledged the information with a nod, Derringer not at all.

"The plant needs an upgrade—that's a given. A new plant is the best solution, but you're talking two to three years down the road before that's completed." He thumped his thigh with a closed fist. "Take a wild guess who's volunteered to help the Elyans with their micro problems in the meantime. Just guess."

Jani blinked innocently. "The regular crop of Family-connected suppliers, the ones who designed the inadequate plant in the first place."

Derringer glared from Jani to Lescaux. "Tell her."

For an instant, Lucien's sharpness flashed in Lescaux's eyes. Then he looked at Jani, and the boyish aspect returned. "The Elyan Haárin surprised us all. They struck a deal with the Karistos city government for a microbial filter assembly with sufficient capacity to tide over the Karistosians until the new plant is built."

"The Haárin sold us a component that they use in their own water treatment?" Jani looked at Derringer. "The Rauta Shèràa Council will consider that a violation of their dietary protocols. The Oligarch won't allow it."

"You'd think that, wouldn't you?" Derringer deigned to glance at Lescaux once more. "Show her the big surprise."

Lescaux rummaged through the briefbag on the seat beside him. "It took several passes through the stacks of contract documentation before we realized what we had." The shy smile shone once more. "I'm sure I don't need to tell you how easy it is to overlook that one vital piece of paper." He fumbled through his files once, then again. His searching grew more agitated as the soft *patpatpat* of Derringer's fingers drumming on the leather upholstery filled the cabin. *"Ah!"* He yanked a document out of its slipcase—the high-pitched tearing noise of smooth parchment sliding over pebbled plastic made Jani cringe.

"Thank you." She took the document from him as though it was wet tissue, her thumbs and index fingers gripping the top corners. "Ease it out of the slipcase from now on—abrasion can play hell with the inset chips."

"Sorry." Lescaux wavered between sheepish apology and expectant anxiety as he watched Jani examine the document. "You see what that is, don't you?"

Jani draped the paper across her knees. "It's an analysis of the Karistos city council decision to contract with the Elyan Haárin." She ran her fingers along the edges once, then again. The paper possessed the substantial, almost fleshy feel of highest quality parchment. "Best grade of paper. Premium inks and foils." She reached for her duffel. "If you want me to scan—"

"Just read the bottom paragraph," Derringer growled.

"I'll read the entire thing." Jani activated her scanpack and set it beside her on the seat. "Neat little precis describing how the Karistos city government has come to depend on the Elyan Haárin for many things—shipping and receiving of goods and documents, design and maintenance of everything from devices and instruments to buildings." She shrugged. "It's the way of the colonies—human and Haárin doing business together. Some Haárin enclaves have been in existence since before the Laum-Vynshàrau civil war. They remained in place even during the postwar cessation of human-idomeni diplomatic relations. Over the course, the Haárin have sold us things that violated their dietary protocols. But they never wrote it down, and they sure as hell never drew up a formal agreement that required a buy-in from Shèrá."

"Keep reading." Derringer kept his gaze fixed on the view outside. They'd entered the far north region of the city, a place of narrower streets and smaller buildings separated by stretches of parkland, and he seemed to be savoring the early fall scenery.

You're not the sight-seeing type, Eugene. Jani turned back to the document. "The writer concludes the piece by stating that"—her voice faltered—"that the Haárin have set out purposely to win the trust and confidence of the human population of Karistos with a mind toward undermining colonial security. Acquiring control over utilities and infrastructure by supplying vital services and equipment will serve as the first step in this infiltration." She flicked at the document with her thumb and forefinger—the sharp crack filled the cabin. "That's bull."

Lescaux's chin jutted defensively. "Exterior takes these opinions very seriously."

"The reason the Haárin want to provide us with vital services and equipment is because there's money to be made." Jani thought back to some of the Haárin she had known. "They like money. They like the reputation they've garnered for sound business practices. Those things give them a freedom they don't have within the Shèrá worldskein—they're not going to do anything to screw that up."

Lescaux cleared his throat. "Exterior believes the Elyan Haárin were specifically ordered by the Oligarch to infiltrate Karistos. Exterior believes Karistos is a preliminary step in Morden nìRau Cèel's plan to weaken Commonwealth defenses from the outside in."

"By Exterior, you mean Anais Ulanova." Jani waited for Lescaux's nod. "Anais is prejudiced where the Haárin are concerned. She believes them responsible for the death of her good friend during the idomeni civil war. She also derives a substantial portion of her fortune from her ownership of companies with which the Haárin are competing. It's in her interest to stop their expansion."

Lescaux licked his lips and tried again. "Her sole interest is in protecting the Elyan citizens."

"Her sole interest is in maintaining an income stream," Jani countered. "Family companies have worked for years to stifle competition in the colonies. That water treatment plant was built to fail so that someone could rake in exorbitant repair fees. And if fond recollection serves, any deals that the Karistos city government tried to work with unaffiliated colonial businesses were countered with veiled threats of sabotage and sudden unavailability of vital parts. The Elyan Haárin were their last resort." She glanced at Derringer, who still looked out the window. His silence was uncharacteristic. He should have questioned her loyalty to the Commonwealth at least once by now.

"Anais's prejudice, as you call it, against the Haárin isn't unfounded," Lescaux said. "She showed me evidence linking them to the death of Talitha Ebben. That was her friend's name."

I know all about General Ebben. A sergeant named Niall Pierce killed her and two other officers during the human evac from Rauta Shèràa, and a colonel named Hiroshi Mako covered it up. Those are the bodies Mako needs to keep buried. Any investigation into Knevçet Shèràa would have uncovered them—that's why Mako arranged to medical me out of the Service rather than risk an open trial. Niall talks to me about Ebben . . . a lot. That's our shared experience, that we both killed officers. Only I paid my own bill, but Borgie paid Niall's and the guilt eats him alive, so let's not talk about Ebben, all right? "Let's get back to this precis," Jani said. "I assume it was written by an Exterior agent working in Karistos?"

"Well, we're here." Derringer rubbed his hands together as the skimmer docked in a secluded chargelot. "I can't bear to keep you in suspense, Kilian, so let me cut your legs out from under you while you're still sitting down. Your old teacher wrote that precis. His Excellency Égri nìRau Tsecha, the ambassador of the Shèrá worldskein. Only you still call him Nema because you two are such good friends." He shot her a cruel grin. "Now, shall we go to lunch?"

Derringer's restaurant of choice was located at the end of a tree-lined shopping street. He chose a table in the outdoor dining area; as soon as they sat down, waitstaff appeared, watered, appetizered, and vanished.

"You're awfully quiet, Jani." Derringer's voice, muffled by poppy seed bread and stuffed egg, sounded smug.

"Just massing my artillery." Jani picked through the assorted baskets and plates as John's ever-growing list of forbidden foods looped through her mind, searching for something to quell her roiling gut.

She settled for a piece of flatbread; the taste lived up to the name. "If you're looking for an initial volley, I think you're both full of shit."

Derringer responded with a cocked eyebrow and a nod in Lescaux's direction. "Careful. You'll shock young Peter."

Jani looked at Young Peter, who stared fixedly at his water glass. "Do you have any idea the magnitude of the accusation you're leveling?" Lescaux's eyes, awash in full defensive smolder, came up to meet hers, but before he could answer, Derringer intercepted the conversational pass.

"It makes sense. Tsecha's the most pro-human idomeni alive. He thinks you're his heir, that we're all destined to become human-idomeni hybrids, and that our futures are as one." He broke bread, scattered crumbs. "Oligarch Cèel has had Tsecha's delusions up to *here* and has started blocking him at every turn. Tsecha's old and getting older, afraid he'll die before his dream is realized. That fear has made him desperate enough to give us a leg up."

The anger in Lescaux's eyes transmuted to shocked realization. "That's right! Anais told me that Tsecha started grooming you at the Academy. He thinks you're to succeed him as the next chief propitiator of the Vynshàrau!"

The silence that fell held a tense, after-the-thunderclap quality. Jani studied the diners at the other tables, the flagstones at her feet, the flowering shrubs surrounding the patio. Anything to avoid the two faces that regarded her, one with distaste, the other with rapt curiosity.

Waitstaff arrived to refill and take orders. That broke the tension somewhat, even though Lescaux looked uncomfortable when Jani declined to order any food. Derringer, however, let it pass. He knew about her dietary difficulties. Their relationship being what it was, he had taken special care to bring her to a restaurant that specialized in the dairy-drenched food she could no longer stomach.

While Derringer and Lescaux devoured the creamy, cheese-laced appetizers, Jani scanned what she had already christened The Nema Letter. She placed her palm-sized scanpack over the upper left-hand corner of the document and began the slow back and forth initial analysis. She had only gone a few centimeters when her 'pack display flared red and the unit squealed so loudly that a woman sitting at the next table dropped her spoon in her soup.

"That's what made Exterior Doc Control suspicious about the document's origins." Lescaux's face reddened as the soup-spattered woman graced them with a highbred scowl. "That letter was subjected to five full-bore scans and each time, seventeen separate incompatibilities registered."

Jani lowered the volume on her 'pack output and rescanned the same spot; this time, the device emitted a barely detectable chirp. She read the error coordinates on the display, and frowned. "Did all the inconsistencies show up in the same places each time?"

"Yes." Lescaux fell silent as the waiter arrived with their main courses.

"Do you have a copy of your chief dexxie's report delineating the locations and types of errors?"

"Y-yes." Lescaux fidgeted as the waiter hovered.

"Better give it to her now, boyo. She's going to keep asking questions until you do." Derringer tore his attention away from his sauce-drenched steak just long enough to shoot Jani a self-satisfied smirk.

"Just doing my job, Eugene."

"I know, Jani. And nothing kicks your overofficious ass into high gear like a professional anxiety attack." He hacked the meat with a heavy hand, bloody juice spilling across his plate. "That's the initiator chip that's set your 'pack to bleating. All it does is tell your scanpack that it's about to scan a document. It's basic, a throwaway, a nonissue, and your 'pack can't read it." He shrugged off Jani's unspoken question. "I've been taking a crash course in chip placement, courtesy of your good friend, Frances Hals. It's been a pretty goddamn interesting last couple of days."

Lescaux removed a slim packet of files from his briefbag and handed it to Jani. "Here's our doc chief's report, along with her affidavit that she stands by her conclusions. She's worked for Exterior since her graduation from Chicago Combined. She has extensive colonial experience and she acted very carefully once she realized what she had." His chin came up again. "Yes, I guess you could say we all understand the accusation we're leveling."

Jani unbound the packet and riffled through the documents until she found the chief's report. *So, Roni McGaw, you think you know from idomeni paper.* She read the first few lines. "McGaw's basing her conclusion that this document is of idomeni origin on the fact that she and her staff can't read a few chips." She read further. "There's no discussion here of prescan testing of any of the 'packs, no record of paper analysis stating whether it's of human or idomeni origin, no mention of the conditions under which the documents were stored and transported or whether they were stressed by temperature or humidity extremes—"

"You're grasping at straws, Kilian," Derringer snapped.

"You realize that this level of subterfuge is alien to the idomeni mind-set?" Jani directed her attention at Lescaux, knowing Derringer a lost cause. "They despise lies and secrecy more than the crimes they're meant to cover up. That's why they accept me despite the fact that I was the first human to ever kill any of them in one of their wars, because no one ever tried to hide the fact that I had done it. That's why they refuse to acknowledge Gisela Detmers-Neumann and the other descendants of the instigators of Knevçet Shèràa, because they've denied to this day that Rikart Neumann and his co-conspirators did anything wrong."

"Human experimentation." Lescaux looked down at his own rare steak, and nudged the plate aside.

"Rikart and crew couldn't have arranged any experimentation without Laumrau participation." Derringer took a sip from his water glass and grimaced as though he longed for wine. "Seems to me they took to secrecy and subterfuge rather well."

"And they paid for it during the Night of the Blade. What was the last estimate you heard of the number of Laumrau who were executed that night? Twenty-five thousand? Fifty thousand? An entire sect, wiped out within hours." Jani pushed her chair away from the table and the stench of charred meat, the sight of blood, the memories of that final terrifying dash through the city. "That's how the born-sect idomeni punish secrecy and lies among their own. Does this give you some idea of how they would punish Nema if they discovered he had perpetrated such a deception, and do you believe for even a fraction of a second that Nema doesn't realize that?"

Derringer pointed his steak knife at her. "Spies have always risked death. It's part of the job description."

"You're basing your conclusions on human behavior. You've made that mistake before and damn it, you just won't learn!" Jani returned the chief's report to its slipcase. "The Elyan Haárin are outcast of Sìah and hard-headed as they come. They never had a great deal of patience with either Nema's plan for the universe or Cèel's distrust of us. They do, however, possess a deep and abiding respect for a signed contract. Karistos needs Haárin technology, and the Family-affiliated businesses are worried enough to try to upset the deal by defaming Nema. It all boils down to money, gentlemen, and it's going to take a hell of a lot more than one jazzed precis to convince me otherwise."

"Jazzed?" Lescaux's face flushed. "You mean *faked,* don't you? If you're saying that Her Excellency—"

Jani held up her hands in mock surrender. "I'm not saying who, Peter. I'm just saying what." She picked up The Nema Letter. "This arrived, I assume, with the rest of the contract documents in the regular diplomatic pouch from Karistos?"

Derringer bit down on a breadstick—it crunched like brittle bone. *"Yes."*

"Did any of the other docs in the pouch show the same faults? McGaw's report doesn't mention supplementary testing."

Lescaux hesitated just an instant too long. "No."

Jani nodded as though she believed him. *You didn't check. You found one anomaly and ran barking to Derringer, who got so jacked about the prospect of placing a mole in the idomeni embassy that he didn't run any confirmation either.* "To prove definitively that this document is what you claim, you'd need an idomeni to scan it with their scanpack and prove the chips aren't simply damaged or faulty."

Derringer shook his head. "We don't want any of them to even know this exists. Couldn't you just load an idomeni chip in your unit?"

It was Jani's turn to respond in the negative. "Chips are designed to operate in unison with the thought processes of the brain matter that drives the 'pack. Idomeni brains and human brains function differently in several key areas. An idomeni chip wouldn't work in a human scanpack."

"Not even yours?" Derringer didn't quite manage to keep the slyness out of his voice.

This time, Jani counted all the way to ten. "The brain between my ears may change over time. The brain in *this*"—she held her 'pack up to his face—"is a self-contained unit—it won't change unless I do a refarm-rebuild."

"I suppose I could have our labs analyze the chips." Lescaux's voice sounded tight—the accusation that he peddled a fake document still rankled.

Jani waved him off. "This is a diplomatic-grade document. Therefore, if you attempt to remove the chips from the paper or try to analyze them with anything other than a scanpack, they will self-destruct. The only way you will ever know for sure if an idomeni assembled this document would be to get one of the embassy examiners to scan it."

"I thought you could just ask he who wrote it." Derringer plucked another breadstick out of the basket and snapped it in two. "During our embassy visit today, just before you ask him whether there are any other useful tidbits of information he thinks we should know."

Jani looked at Lescaux, who looked away. "What?"

"You heard me." Derringer pressed the two breadstick halves together lengthwise, and broke them again.

The noise around Jani faded. The babble of conversations. The clatter of plates and cutlery. The rustle of the breeze through the trees. "You want me to spy—"

"No. Tsecha's doing the spying. You just need to ferry the information from him to us. He wants to help us. We only have to provide him the opportunity." Derringer grinned. "You were the first person I thought of when this fortuity presented itself."

Lescaux tossed his napkin on his plate and rose from the table. "I need to clean my teeth." He held out his hand to Jani. "The precis, please." A look passed between them—on his part, it held fear, and dislike, but also a shade of uncertainty. "You can keep McGaw's report overnight, but I need it back tomorrow first thing." Jani handed him the letter—he slid it back into its slipcase and tucked it into his bag. "I'll meet you both back at the skimmer." His shoes clicked on the flagstones. He looked like a well-dressed prep schooler on his way to address student-teacher assembly.

Derringer watched him. "Think it's true what they say about him and his boss? He only did time in a couple of dinky colonial posts before he nailed the Chief of Staff job—I mean, he must have nailed her first, right?" He glanced at Jani. "Cheer up, Kilian. Tsecha bubbles like a fountain around you—once you get him started, you won't be able to shut him up."

"Don't you remember what I said would happen if Cèel suspected him of this level of duplicity?"

Derringer shrugged. "We disavow immediately. Standard cut and run."

"No, not what happens to your operation. What happens to *him*!"

"I could not care less."

"You bastard."

Derringer leaned toward her. "No. Not a bastard. A human being. Which is what you still are too, at least officially. I'm just offering you a chance to prove it." He pointed his fork at McGaw's report. "You take that home to your posh flat on posh Armour Place, and you study it as much as you want. Then you take a good, hard look at your posh walls and your rapidly growing credit account and your flash lieutenant boyfriend, and then you do what you are told."

Jani took a deep breath. She felt agitated enough for her augmentation to weigh in, and an aborted augie overdrive was the last thing she needed right now. "You are threatening a Registered documents examiner. You are trying to intimidate said examiner into making grave and important—I quote these words from the Registry Code of Ethics—*grave* and *important* decisions based on the conclusions drawn from a document that she does not trust. That's a Commonwealth felony, Eugene. I may lose my posh flat when all this settles, but you'll lose a lot more."

"You're crazy, Kilian. It's public record. No one will believe you."

"If that's the case, why would anyone believe anything I say I heard from Nema? That little blade cuts both ways."

"That little blade is supposed to get lifted from your slender throat by year's end. Employee assessments are going to have some bearing on whether that in fact occurs." Derringer sat back and hooked his thumbs in his trouser pockets, like a gambler who knew he held the winning card. "Do not cross me on this. Burkett's not exactly wild about you—if I push a recommendation that they yank your 'pack, he'll listen." He glanced at his timepiece and looked around. "Do it. You have no choice."

"Eugene, the last time someone thought they'd left me without a choice, I wrote a chapter in idomeni mythology."

"You wrote a few other chapters, didn't you? I read that white paper, Kilian—my, my, what a bad girl you were. Combine that with your present emotional state, I see someone who can't afford to say no." Derringer stood, removed his garrison cap from his belt, and set it on his head. "I'm willing to let you start slow. Grab a few minutes with Tsecha during a break in today's meeting, feel him out. He loves to talk to you—you're his pet. It shouldn't take much effort to get this rolling." He started walking in the direction Lescaux had gone. "Now let's go. We're keeping Young Peter waiting."

Jani watched Derringer stride away. In her ear, she heard her augmentation whisper about pressure points and methods of dismemberment and the best ways to dispose of body parts, but augie tended toward the direct approach when it sensed she was in danger and that wasn't what was needed right now. She wasn't sure what was, but she'd think of something. For Nema's sake, she had to.

CHAPTER 5

"And with this bite of ground, of soil, I—" Tsecha fell silent and stared at the slice of *faria* impaled on the end of his fork. *"Bite of ground . . ."*

The piece of purple-skinned tuber offered him no clue as to the words he needed to say to complete the prayer. No prompting scrolled across its glistening white surface, as it did across the broadcasters' eyepieces at the holoVee studio he had visited earlier that humanish week. Instead, it stared in death glaze, as white and blank as a humanish eye, leaving him to suffer the humiliation of a chief priest who had forgotten how to petition his gods.

"I have prayed such for years," Tsecha murmured in English. He often talked to himself in English. He found the language's hard sounds complemented his mood. "I prayed such only yesterday." But yesterday seemed an age ago.

"Now yesterday is today and all is hell." He shoved the slice of *faria* into his mouth and chewed without the benefit of prayer. The bitterness of the vegetable stung his throat—he coughed into his sleeve so his cook-priest wouldn't hear. He knew she waited near the outer door of his private altar-room, pacing the hall like a nervous beast as she prayed for his soul. She esteemed him—he knew that. She possessed the proper skein and standing. He sensed she might ask him to breed her, and if she did so, he could not refuse.

Then she would leave me to make her birth-house, and I would need to find a new cook-priest. One who didn't worry so much. Yes, that would be most pleasant. It weighed upon Tsecha, the way others worried after his soul.

He removed his handheld from his overrobe's inner pocket and entered the English word "weight." The aged device took some time to search and collate. It had been built for him many seasons before, prior even to the War of Vynshàrau Ascension, when humanish had first begun to visit his Shèrá homeworld. It contained his favorite humanish languages: French, English, and Mandarin, along with the many odd terms and definitions he had compiled during the glorious Academy days more than twenty humanish years before, when Jani Kilian and Hansen Wyle taught him so much.

Such days. He studied his handheld's scratched display. *Weight.* He shook the device gently as words appeared, then faded. *Ballast. Tonnage. Anchor. . . .*

Anchor. Yes, that was the word. The fears of others weighted him as an anchor. They immobilized him, kept him motionless, static, changeless, at a time when change meant life and stasis meant something quite different.

Tsecha sipped his water, warmed and sweetened with *veir* blossom. It soothed his throat, and quelled the burning on his tongue.

"Pain focuses the mind." He spoke softly, so his cook-priest would not hear his ungodly English. "With the pain I have experienced this day, mine should be the most focused mind in the universe." First, he awoke to the ache of age in his knees and back. Then he recalled his upcoming meeting, which like most such gatherings promised hellish depths of boredom and confusion. They were to discuss the Karistos contract today—such a ridiculous thing, and truly. Haárin and colonial humanish had entered into such agreements since before the last war, so many that one lost count. Why Anais and her allies objected so to this particular agreement, he could not understand.

He set down his cup, and picked with ungodly indifference at his food.

"They are assembling, nìRau."

Tsecha looked up from his reading. Sànalàn, his suborn, stood in the doorway of his front room. She had already donned her own formal overrobe, and carried his draped over her arm. "Is it time already?" He folded the Council reports with heavy hands and inserted them back into their sheaths.

"The Exterior Minister arrived most early." Sànalàn lapsed into the curt cadences and minimal gestures of Low Vynshàrau as she fussed with the overrobe's folds. "She asked one of the Haárin to show her the allowed areas of the embassy, and he did."

Tsecha rose slowly from his favored chair. The frame had stabbed him in all the usual places, but even that discomfort had failed to sharpen his mind. "It is allowed that our Anais tour the allowed areas of the embassy, nìa." He let Sànalàn help him don his robe, since such was her temper that he did not think it wise to reject her assistance. "That is what the word means."

"It is unseemly." Sànalàn prodded and yanked as though she dressed a squirming youngish and not her aged dominant. "You must reprimand him. He should have directed her to me or to nìaRauta Inèa instead of taking charge of her himself."

"I must take care how I admonish any embassy Haárin, and truly." Tsecha adjusted his twisted, red-trimmed sleeves as unobtrusively as he could. "They maintain our utilities. Our air and our water, our fire and our foundation. I berate this one you speak of too strongly, and we may all freeze in our beds."

"Not this one. He is the tilemaster."

"Ah. You have complained of him before."

"And still you have done nothing."

Tsecha offered a hand wave of acquiescence. "I will speak to him. I will threaten him with the anger of the gods." He waited for Sànalàn to precede him to the door, then fell in behind her. "What is his name?"

"Dathim Naré." Sànalàn gestured abruptly. "He is unseemly."

"So you said, nìa. So you said." Tsecha tried to recall the last time he had witnessed such agitation in his suborn as he continued to wrestle with his sleeves. "Jani is here?"

"Your Kièrshia has just now arrived, along with Colonel Derringer and Lescaux, Ulanova's suborn."

"The one who looks as my Lucien? He did not arrive with Anais?"

"*No, nìRau.* With Derringer and Kièrshia, as I said."

"Ah." Tsecha slackened off his pace so that he fell a stride farther behind the aggravated Sànalàn.

He entered the windowless meeting room to find it as Sànalàn described. Humanish filled one side of the banked spectator seats, Vynshàrau the other, the murmurs of conversation stilling as all faces turned to him.

How different we look. The contrasts struck him particularly in these meetings. The humanish appeared stunted, truncated in every way. So short they were—even the tallest only reached Tsecha's nose, while the shortest . . . well, one had to watch where one stepped. Males and females both wore their hair in clipped styles that showed their ears and the shapes of their heads, and dressed in fitted clothing in dark, forest colors of leaf and wood and pool. Even his Jani, who sat in one of the banked rows of seats behind the tan-garbed Colonel Derringer, wore a green as dark as the depths of a well.

Against the multihued gloom of their clothing, their skins shone every color from worm-white to wood-brown, their pale-trimmed eyes glittering with feverish death glaze. Not an aesthetically pleasing people, humanish—Tsecha could admit this despite his affection for them. As ever, they seemed to war with their surroundings, rather than blend with them.

So different are my Vynshàrau. Gold-skinned and gold-eyed, garbed in flowing robes of sand and stone that complemented the muted hues of the walls and floor, long of limb and fluid of line and motion. Like him, most wore their hair in the braided fringe of the breeder; the few unbred, like his Sànalàn, wore theirs in tight nape-knots. All wore shoulder-grazing hoops or helices in their ears. *We are the Gold People of the High Sands. A dène vynshàne Rauta Shèràa.* He never felt the surety of this more than in the contrast with humanish. Never more than now, the differences daunted him. So vast. So overwhelming.

He took his seat at the point of the arrowhead-shaped table, in a chair so low that his knees complained as he lowered into it. On one side of the arrowhead sat the secular dominants who acted in Cèel's stead, Suborn Oligarch Shai and next to her, Speaker to Colonies Daès, their chairs pitched slightly higher than Tsecha's in deference to his status as their religious dominant. Tsecha stretched out one leg beneath the table as surreptitiously as he could, and wished that they had deferred to the status of his old joints instead.

He looked to his Jani again. She looked back, her eyes half-closed as though her head pained her, her face as a wall. He nodded, and she responded with a flick and waver of the fingers of her left hand, a Low Vynshàrau gesture of agitation and the need for explanation. Then Derringer turned around to speak to her, and she let her hand drop.

Derringer. Tsecha watched the man point his finger in Jani's face, his expression stern. He scolded her constantly, for reasons Tsecha could never comprehend and Jani refused to discuss. *But only when his dominant is absent.* When General Callum Burkett attended meetings, he and Jani talked as Derringer sat most quietly. Which was not to say that Burkett never scolded Jani, or that Jani never scolded him in return. In the end, Burkett listened. Derringer never did.

I have used up all my dried pokegrass, Eugene. But the Haárin who managed the ornamental gardens did grow leafbarb to discourage the feral animals that evaded embassy security barriers. A wondrous plant, leafbarb, and truly. Not only did the blade-sharp yellow leaves poke through clothing admirably, but their clear juice contained a chemical that caused humanish skin to erupt in a seeping rash. . . .

"Minister Ulanova." Suborn Oligarch Shai gestured toward the chair at her side. "Join us at table, so we may begin."

A miniature figure rose from her front row seat beside Lescaux and walked to the table. Her hair and clothes were as wood-brown, her face as sharpened stone, her steps as minced as a youngish. "My gratitude is yours, and truly, nìaRauta," Anais Ulanova replied in stilted High Vynshàrau as she mounted the chair across from Shai. Her knuckles whitened as she clenched the rim of the seat to keep her balance, her tiny feet dangling half an arm's length above the floor.

Tsecha glanced at Jani, who bit her lip and looked away.

"In deference to Vynshàrau directness and openness, I will simply begin." Anais had returned to English, which sounded as forced as her Vynshàrau. Many of the assembled attached translator headpieces as she spoke, while others paged through their copies of the official Exterior report that had been provided them. "I wish to state for the record how much the Commonwealth esteems the Oligarch's candor in dealing with this unfortunate chain of events. I would also like to state that this idomeni custom of facing difficult matters in such a straightforward manner is one that humanish also esteem and appreciate, and one that we will seek to maintain as our diplomatic relations strengthen."

How glorious, Anais! Tsecha had to clench his hands to keep from erupting into humanish applause. *Somewhere in that speech was a point, I believe, although it would take a crew of deep-pit miners many seasons to uncover it.*

Anais continued. "The situation I speak of is, of course, this regrettable circumstance in Karistos, which is the capital of Elyas, one of our Outer Circle colonies. It is indeed unfortunate that Karistos city officials failed to explore all avenues of recourse available within the Commonwealth before taking it upon themselves to set precedent."

Out of the corner of his eye, Tsecha watched Shai tap her headpiece and gesture to Daès, who curved his right hand in supplication. "You should clarify your thoughts for we the direct and open, nìaRauta." Daès glanced at Anais's report on the table in front of him, which even now the Vynshàrau xenolinguists studied for the hidden meaning that existed in all humanish documents, the words between the lines. "You are angered that the Karistos dominants acted without consulting you. Except that they have consulted with you for many months, and pleaded for assistance in solving their water problems. Elyan humanish died, yet you told them to wait. Elyan humanish died, yet you told them to draw up plans and obtain estimates."

Anais raised a hand, palm facing up. A subtle variation of a plea, Tsecha had learned, a request for the speaker to rethink their words. Not her usual reaction to Daès's questions—she usually fluttered her hands and turned most red. "A great tragedy, which occurred because the water treatment facility in question was built too hastily, from a design that had not been adequately thought out. We must take the time to think now, nìRau. We are most concerned that to act in haste again could result in even greater tragedy."

Tsecha closed the report before him with one finger, then pushed it away with such force that it slid to the middle of the table. "You are most concerned, you say. Most concerned. Yet when the Elyan Haárin offer a way to stop the dying *now,* you protest. Because your colonial business interests lose money, you assemble reports with graphs and charts and financial analyses, reports that could not be assembled when it was only your *people* whom you lost."

Anais's face reddened in a most gratifying manner as in the banked rows, whispered conversation rose. "Are you accusing me of allowing my people to die in the interest of financial gain, nìRau?"

Tsecha folded his hands before him. "Is there any question—"

"Tsecha."

The droning humanish conversation silenced. Jani sat up most straight, her gaze fixed on Suborn Oligarch Shai, whose shoulders had rounded in anger.

Shai gestured to her suborn, who reached to the table's center and removed Tsecha's copy of the report. "Allow nìaRauta Ulanova to finish," she said as she opened her own copy.

Tsecha barely restrained his laughter as he watched Shai study a triaxial graph as though she understood what it meant. "Shai—"

"Allow nìaRauta Ulanova to finish." Shai spoke to him without any clarifying gesture, which was most unlike her. "We are all most aware of your thought in this."

Anais inclined her head toward Shai. "Many thanks, nìaRauta." She bent her head over her own report, and read words that all in the room realized she knew, as humanish said, by heart.

As Anais yammered about cost estimates and medical

ramifications, Tsecha caught a flash of palest platinum hair move into his periphery. His Lucien raised his hand in a subtle greeting as he stepped among the seated crowd. Unlike his fellow humanish, he did not seem stunted at all. His smooth movement and quiet arrogance reminded Tsecha of the cats he sometimes saw stalking across the embassy grounds, their contempt for the gardeners' leafbarb evident in their every motion.

"When it became clear—" Anais's voice faltered as she caught sight of Lucien. Her pale skin once more colored. "When it became clear," she repeated, her tone sharpening so that humanish eyes widened, "that the drafters of the contract failed to properly consider the many issues involved in this situation, we in Exterior felt it our duty to step in and take charge of the proceedings. We took this step despite the risk of angering the Elyan Haárin, who set great store in signed agreements, as do we all. We now formally request that the Shèrá worldskein accept our humblest apologies for this misunderstanding, as well as financial reparations well in excess of those lost by the Elyan Haárin in the cancellation of this contract."

As Anais ended her speech with wishes of good fortune for all, Lucien positioned himself against the wall directly opposite her. Their gazes locked. Her voice faltered once more.

Tsecha looked at Jani, whose face appeared as the wall against which Lucien rested. Then he looked at Lescaux, the youngish that seemed so poor a replacement for such a startling animal, and pondered the flush he saw on his face. Was it anger? Jealousy? Both? He could not tell.

Tsecha glanced around the room at the uncomfortable humanish, the confused Vynshàrau, and inhaled deeply of the suddenly charged air. Such a marvel, his Lucien, like a humanish shatterbox.

"The Elyan Haárin are indeed most dismayed at this action by the Exterior Ministry." Speaker to Colonies Daès entoned in High Vynshàrau, oblivious to the emotional maelstrom that surrounded him. "The assemblage had committed to a shuttle purchase on the strength of the contract affirmation. This pledge now needs to be cancelled, as well as the pledges made by the shuttle dealer for her own purchases. Broken agreement after broken agreement will proceed from this, a simple contract no different from many that colonial humanish and Haárin have entered into over many seasons."

Anais waited until the full translation of Daès's speech filtered through her headpiece. Then she bared her teeth—the expression barely widened her narrow face. "As I have stated, nìRau Daès, we are prepared to make generous reparations to all concerned—"

Tsecha flicked his left hand in curt dismissal. "Reparations." He knew his English to be most sound and easily understood, thus he ignored Derringer's aggravated tapping on his headpiece as though the translators erred. "Do you believe, Anais, and truly, that *reparations* are sufficient—"

"Tsecha!" Shai brought the flat of her hand down on the table. "Allow nìaRauta Ulanova to finish or leave until she does so!"

Humanish spoke of "shattered silence," as though an absence of sound could be as a solid thing, tangible and breakable. Tsecha often had trouble comprehending these strange meanings, but sometimes they revealed themselves to him with almost godly insight. *Shattered silence.* Yes, the quiet that filled the room now felt as corporeal, as stone and metal, waiting only to be smashed by more of Shai's words, by her strange behavior. *She silenced me?* Even though Tsecha knew this to indeed be the case, he felt difficulty accepting it. *She silenced me.*

How the humanish stared at Shai, even Anais. Only Derringer and Jani looked at Tsecha. Derringer glowered, his long face dark with the dislike Tsecha knew he felt, but until now had managed to hide.

But it was his Jani who alarmed him the most. Confusion, yes, in her furrowed brow and narrowed eyes, but anger, too.

Then he watched her gaze drift to Derringer, and the anger sharpen. *If looks could kill,* as his Hansen used to say. Tsecha felt the grip of wonder as the meaning of even more humanish imagery bore down on him. If his Jani's eyes had been knives, oh, the blood that would spill.

"I am finished speaking, nìaRauta." Anais once more inclined her head. "My concerns are more completely expressed within this report, copies of which were submitted to your xenolinguists ten days ago to allow them time to interpret the material contained therein."

"Ten days?" Tsecha looked out at his Jani, who stared back at him, the knives in her eyes gone dull. "I did not see—"

"I have conferred with nìRau ti nìRau Cèel on this matter." Shai addressed the assembled, seemingly oblivious to the fact that she had once more interrupted her ambassador and priest. "He agrees with nìaRauta Ulanova. There are issues of seemliness involved here. Our dietary protocols are most strict on the subjects of exchange of food and water and the possibilities of cross-contamination. The Elyan Haárin are expected to arrive here in a matter of Earth days. During their stay, they will be retrained in these protocols. They will also be awarded reparations for the broken contract." She gestured agreement to Daès, who tilted his head in the affirmative. "Cèel will be pleased that it has been handled so cleanly."

Tsecha flicked his thumb over his ear in disdain. "Cèel would be pleased if Haárin and colonial never bought any equipment from one another ever again. He would be happier still if the Elyan Haárin decamped from Elyas and returned to the worldskein. He would declaim in rapture if every Haárin enclave ceased to exist and every humanish returned to their Commonwealth. His opinion is not the most balanced on the matter, and I do not feel it can be applied here!"

Shai's back bowed in profound anger, a posture understood by even the most ignorant humanish. "Tsecha, you are Cèel's representative—"

"I am the ambassador of the Shèrá worldskein. Thus do I speak on behalf of all idomeni, not just Cèel. I am also chief propitiator. Thus do I speak the will of the gods when I say that you err gravely here."

"Tsecha." Shai pitched her voice higher than normal in respect, and directed her gaze above his head to indicate same. Her words, however, held a Haárin's intransigence. "The decision is made. The discussion is ended. The meeting is adjourned."

"With all due respect, nìaRauta ti nìaRauta?"

At the sound of the voice, Lucien started. Anais clenched her hands. Derringer scowled. The humanish rustled and the Vynshàrau stilled.

Tsecha bared his teeth as his Jani stood. She spoke English, but gestured as Vynshàrau, so that the tone of her thoughts would be clear to the Vynshàrau along with the translation of her words.

"I know of the Elyan Haárin, and have dealt with them on many occasions in the past." Like Lucien, she did not seem in any way short in height. She gestured as smoothly as any idomeni, even as the Oà, who spoke the most beautifully of any of the born sects. "They are outcast of Sìah"—she gestured toward the half-Sìah Sànalàn—"and the Sìah were the first to codify idomeni secular law and develop the documents protocols we all adhere to. They carry the highest regard for all that is written, and for all that is composed within the boundaries of law. They will most assuredly *not* understand the cancellation of this contract, and they possess ways of making their displeasure felt."

Anais waved a dismissive hand. "We are discussing a single contract—"

"I believe, Your Excellency, that if you examine various shuttle dock and infrastructure maintenance contracts signed by the Elyan colonial government in recent years, you will find you have more cause for concern as to the feelings of the Elyan Haárin than you might wish for. In addition, the immediate needs of the Karistosians must be met. The safety of their water supply is of paramount importance—"

"The contract will be put aside—"

"The cancellation needs to be examined—"

"It will be put aside," Anais snapped. "Thank you for your input, Ms. Kilian, but the matter is settled."

"Is it? How? By your words, which cannot even convince the only one here who knows the Elyan Haárin well!" Tsecha stood and pointed to Jani. "She knows the ways of the enclave and the assemblage as she knows the ways of these ridiculous meetings, and she knows that the Elyan Haárin will not understand. She is of us and of you. She is the hybrid who knows us all. She will wear my ring and robe after I die. If you have not convinced her of your argument, then it is as worthless!"

The translation filtered through. Shai resorted to banging her fist on the table to restore order so she could formally adjourn. The meeting dissolved into whispers and gesturing and huddled groups. Tsecha tried to push through the clusters to reach his Jani, but Derringer had grabbed her by the arm and herded her out the door before he could do so.

CHAPTER 6

Tsecha stalked the halls, alert for the sounds of argument that would signal the location of Jani and Derringer. He passed humanish along the way, dressed in gloomy Cabinet colors or the tan uniforms as the one Derringer wore, now sanctioned by the Service for their personnel to wear when they visited the embassy. It did not surprise him unduly that he could not recognize the postures and faces he passed—meetings frequently took place at the embassy of which he knew nothing, and for that, he offered the gods thanks.

After a time, he grew conscious of a presence at his back. He thought once more of cats, and put a name to the sensation. "Lucien. It is unseemly of you to follow me."

"I didn't want to alarm you, nìRau. You seemed so deep in thought." Lucien drew ahead of him in a few strides, even though he did not appear to quicken his pace. "You let Jani walk behind you sometimes. I've seen it."

"That is my Jani. You are not she."

"True." As usual, Lucien accepted the rebuke without a quarrel. Such behavior always caused Jani to remark that he was "conserving his ammo," whatever that meant. "You certainly know how to break up a meeting."

"If your people or mine cannot accept the truth, it is not reason for me to refrain from speaking it." Tsecha stopped before a meeting room door and listened, but the voices he thought he heard proved to be the whine of drills and the clatter of building materials that managed to seep through the soundshielding. "So much renovating. It is a wonder this embassy does not collapse from the pounding and banging. . . ." He herded Lucien ahead of him and continued down the hall.

"I saw her arrive with Derringer and Lescaux." Lucien tugged at his tan uniform shirt, spotted with the first dark dots of sweat. Many humanish still found the temperature of the embassy uncomfortable even though the Vynshàrau had lowered it earlier that summer, thus guaranteeing misery for all.

Tsecha opened another door and stared into the quiet dark. "Well, she has not left with them. I asked my Security suborn, and she told me that no one detected them leaving."

"NìRau." Lucien stopped in front of a narrow window that looked over a seldom-used veranda. "Over here."

Tsecha walked to Lucien's side. His ears heard before his eyes saw; he bared his teeth wide at the sound.

"He doesn't know anything about it—"

"—think you know every fucking thing—"

"—you've made a mistake—"

"—when I tell you to do something, you do it!"

"One day I will offer them the blades, and they will take them. *À lérine* they will fight, for such is the only way." Tsecha nodded to Lucien. "Such hatred must be declared openly, or it festers like a sick wound." He swept aside the portal and stepped out into the weak sunlight. "Colonel Derringer, you are needed in the meeting room. Anais Ulanova wishes to speak with you."

Derringer wheeled, his face reddened from embassy heat and undeclared anger. "Her Excellency? In the meeting room?" He looked from Tsecha to Lucien. "Is this true, Lieutenant?"

"Her Excellency wishes this matter resolved as soon as possible, sir." Lucien stood most straight and tall, his eyes focused on a point somewhere above Derringer's head.

Derringer looked back at Jani, who stood obscured in the shadow of a wall. Then he nodded brusquely to Tsecha in the humanish manner. "NìRau."

"Colonel." Tsecha stepped aside to allow the man free passage to the door. "I should challenge him for asking you if my words held truth, Lucien," he said when he heard the door seal catch. "I have never before been called a liar so openly."

"You're both going to get your heads handed to you when he figures out you sent him on a fool's errand." Jani stepped into the light. Anger stiffened her stride and made her face as painted sculpture. "But then, I don't know what other kind you'd send him on."

Lucien shrugged. "Ani will come up with something for him to do. That's what she thinks colonels are for." He took a step toward her. "We caught some of the shrapnel out in the hall."

"I caught the rest in the neck." Jani stood still as Lucien approached, but she did not bare her teeth or reach for him as some humanish females did when their males drew near.

They have an arrangement. Tsecha watched Lucien question, Jani twitch a shoulder in response. The breeding protocols of humanish confused him in the extreme, but he thought them a most seemly pairing. Except. . . .

The way they watch each other. . . . Was such the way with all humanish pairings? Tsecha did not have enough experience to know for sure. But whether or not such was indeed so, he needed to set his curiosity aside for now. "Nìa, we must speak."

"Yes, I think that we had better." Jani stepped away from Lucien without gesturing or speaking farewell, walking past Tsecha and through the door into the hall.

"She is very angry," Tsecha said, because he felt one of them should acknowledge what had happened and he knew from experience that neither Jani nor Lucien would. He raised his hand in salutation to Lucien, who regarded him in his particularly empty way that made even Jani seem expressive.

They walked the embassy grounds, as they often did. They both dreaded the coming cold, and savored the last warm rays of the sun.

Jani did not speak until they had walked one complete circuit around a Pathen-style water garden. She stopped before one of the stone arrangements, an upright hollow-center circlet through which one diversion of the stream flowed. "You think the Karistos contract is a good thing?"

Tsecha raised his right hand palm facing up, his equivalent of a humanish shrug. "Of course, nìa. Any such interaction between idomeni and humanish is greatly to be wished."

"You don't . . . consider it a threat to your dietary laws, or to anyone or anything here on Earth?"

"Nìa?" Tsecha bent nearer to study Jani's face, to no avail. He would have learned more from studying the stone circlet. "You have a reason for these strange questions?"

"Just confirming the blindingly obvious, nìRau." She twisted first to the left, then to the right—the bones of her spine made a crunching noise. "Shai interrupted you several times. That's not good."

"I have always angered her, nìa."

"You're her priest. You outrank her. She should let you finish speaking, then take your head off." Jani bent over and swept her fingers through the water. "She and Ulanova discussed this contract days ago. Shai shut you out of the final decision."

Tsecha watched her spray droplets at some insects that had clustered at the rim of the pool, sending them flying. He brushed away one of the fleeing creatures, which buzzed and hovered near his head. "She cannot do so, nìa—I am ambassador."

"NìRau, she just did." Jani straightened and dried her fingers on the hem of her jacket. "When is she returning to Shèrá? She came here months ago, right after Cèel packed up and pulled out. The Suborn Oligarch's role is to act as Council dominant, lead conclaves, monitor voting and debate. She can't do that from here."

"She . . . likes Chicago, nìa." Tsecha felt as though he stood under the questioning attitude of the Council tribunal, as he had so often in the past. But he had always been able to conjure answers for the tribunal, when the wrong ones would have meant his life. Why did he feel so confused now, when all he risked was a sharp rebuke?

Jani turned and looked at him, her green eyes shining as the water. "She isn't going back, is she? Cèel sent her here to replace you as ambassador." She bent and splashed water at the insects again, this time more vigorously. A few managed to fly away, but two failed to take to the air in time. They lay swamped in the puddle, their legs waving feebly.

Tsecha watched one of the black and yellow creatures shudder, then lay still. "You are killing them, nìa."

Jani threw more water, washing the stunned insect into the rivulet. "They're wasps, nìRau. I don't know anymore how I'd react if one stung me. I'd rather not chance finding out."

"If you left them alone, perhaps they would not bother you."

"If I get rid of them now, I don't have to worry about 'perhaps.'" Jani frowned as more wasps alit on the edge of the puddle. She backed away from the water garden and onto the lawn, working her shoulders as she walked. "Humanish diplomats attend classes on Vynshàrau behavior. We know that Vynshàrau study humanish, as well. Everyone knows you and Cèel don't get along. We humanish interpret that as disunity in the ranks, a sign of weakness. In cases like that, the leadership needs to act decisively to close the perceived schism, or they are seen as weaker still." She stretched out her arms toward the sun and swept them in wide circles. Then she let them fall to her sides, and tilted her head from side to side. "You do not work with Shai to present a united front. Every time you open your mouth in one of these meetings, you outrage everyone. You tell humanish and Vynshàrau that I'm your heir when you know that my condition scares them and that the idea of hybridization terrifies them." She turned to him, her posture as tense and troubled as it had been during the war, when she had worried for his life. "Every day, in every way, you make it more difficult for Cèel to allow you to remain here and more difficult for me to do my job."

Tsecha crossed his arms and shoved his hands into the sleeves of his overrobe. "And what is your job, nìa?"

"To keep you from wrapping yourself around a tree." Jani swatted at another insect that buzzed past her head. "To keep the wasps away."

"To keep the wasps away." Tsecha pronounced each word most distinctly. "You are my protector, in the way a suborn sometimes is?" He watched Jani's motions still, and knew they shared the same thought. He slipped close to her, grasping her right hand in his before she could move away. "Then where is your ring, nìa? My suborn should wear my ring." He straightened her fingers, so long and thin and brown, then held out his beside them. His ring of station glittered, cagework gold surrounding an oval of crimson jasperite. "It looks much as this one, I believe. You have not lost it, have you?"

Jani refused to look him in the eye, as she always did when he inquired about her ring. "No." She pulled her hand away, slowly but firmly. "It's in a bag, on the shelf of my closet."

"In a bag. On a shelf in your closet. Perhaps I should ask you to keep your concern there, as well."

"NìRau—!"

"Our Hansen died wearing his."

"His ring fit him out of the box. You didn't have his ring made too small so he'd have to shrink into it. The fact that he wore his didn't signify that he had become point man for a new race!"

"Point man . . . out of the box . . ." Tsecha patted his pockets and wished for his handheld. "You confuse me with your words as no other."

Jani strode away from him, flexing her arms as a youngish bird. "If you're so easily confused, maybe you shouldn't talk so much."

"I did not risk my life and soul to come to this damned cold place so that I could remain silent!" Tsecha rounded his shoulders in irritation. Jani's constant twisting made his own muscles ache. He closed in on her, his back hunched in anger. "All I hear from you is censure! Lecture as to how I should act. Why? There are no wasps. They cannot threaten to kill me anymore."

Jani slouched in response, so quickly and smoothly that Tsecha straightened in surprise. "Don't be so sure." She slipped into Low

Vynshàrau, her muted gestures hard and swift. "If I told you it was as Rauta Shèràa, I would not be far from wrong."

Tsecha looked up at the sky, its clear blue broken only by the swoop of seabirds. "As Rauta Shèràa, is it? Then where are the demiskimmers, nìa? Where are the bombs?"

"Explosives aren't the only things that can blow up in your face." Jani must have sensed his abating temper, since she drew up straighter as well. "Will you behave until I tell you it is safe?"

Tsecha twitched his shoulder as he had seen her do so many times, when she wanted to seem to answer without actually telling him anything. He had gotten quite good at it, in his opinion. "No more disputation with Anais?"

Jani smiled. "On the veranda, or in your rooms, fine. But not during public meetings."

"No more musical gatherings with Colonel Derringer?"

"Good God, no."

"You worry after me."

"Constantly."

They regarded one another. Tsecha sensed fondness in Jani's relaxing posture, which he always knew to be there. He sensed exasperation, as well, which he had grown to accept. He turned to walk back to the embassy, beckoning her to walk ahead of him, as was seemly. If he needed to behave, now would be a good time to start. "You are well, nìa? I notice that you seem pained."

Jani looked him in the eye. The afternoon sun struck her full-face, lightening her green irises to the color of new leaves. But the bright light overwhelmed the diffusing ability of the filming—her pale green sclera showed beneath the hydropolymer the way a dark shirt showed beneath a pale overrobe. "I'm all right. Just a little achy." Then the shadow of a tree branch played across her face, sharpening bone and darkening skin to gold-brown. She lifted and cupped her right hand in a gesture of resignation, the movements as smooth as though performed beneath water.

Tsecha watched her move as no human could, and felt the clench in his soul. *You are as Rauta Haárin now, and truly.* She had become as he always knew she would, as he always wished she would. Why then did he feel sadness? Why then did he feel fear? "Winter comes," he said, because he could think of nothing else to say.

"Yes, nìRau. I can feel it in my bones." Jani's voice sounded as dead. As she turned her back to him, a wasp swooped near her face. She reached out and caught it in her animandroid left hand, then with a single swift movement opened her hand and smashed her palm against the grid of the pestzap installed alongside the entry. The wasp shot through the grid opening and vaporized in a flash of blue. Jani brushed her hand against her jacket and disappeared into the darkness of the embassy.

They heard the commotion well before they saw the cause: the babble of voices from around the next corner, Anais Ulanova's piping above them all.

"I told you, Colonel. Isn't it lovely!"

Jani looked back over her shoulder at Tsecha, then quickened her pace. Tsecha hurried, too. He recalled only too well the rooms located down that hallway, the clatter of renovation that perpetually sounded from them. The buzz of drills. The hum of sealers.

The shatter of old tile.

"I haven't seen work of this quality since I toured the Pathen Mosaica on Nèae. Flowers so well detailed, they looked real. The shadings! The hues!"

Tsecha broke into an unseemly trot, catching up with Jani just as she rounded the corner.

The crowd stood packed around the doorway of one of the rooms undergoing refurbishing. A secondary altar room, Tsecha recalled, the same one in which he had prayed with his Jani prior to her very first *à lérine*. The embassy workers had installed a small laving area for the washing of blessed vessels and cloths, but the final decorations had yet to be applied.

Jani pushed through the crowd. Tsecha shoved after her, his eyes locking on the anger-bowed back of Suborn Oligarch Shai, who stood just inside the doorway next to Anais Ulanova.

"It would not be seemly, nìaRauta." Shai gestured stiffly, her hands clenching when they should not have, her voice catching when it should have flowed.

"But it could serve as a gesture of good faith during a tense time." Anais nodded to Lescaux, who nudged to her side. "We would be most happy to arrange some sort of exchange. One of our finest craftsman could design something suitable for your embassy." She said something to Lescaux, who shook his head. "We must admit, though, that we will be hard-pressed to compete with this." She crossed her hands over her chest, glittery-eyed rapture softening the harsh planes of her face.

Tsecha looked past her into the altar room, where an Haárin male dressed in dull blue work garments wiped the surface of the freshly tiled wall that served as the backsplash for the altar sink. He wore a leaf-patterned wrap around his head to keep the grime out of his hair. He also kept his back turned toward the crowd so none could see his face or his attitude.

Tsecha looked at the wall on which the Haárin worked. The cava shell was only half-completed—the head and the horn-like flare of the opening had yet to be tiled, and shown in lead-sketched simplicity beside the finished portion. Nature scenes were common décor in Vynshàrau rooms—at first, the shell did not appear at all remarkable.

Then Tsecha studied the work more carefully. The lower half—the sand-colored body striped with darker brown, the pink-tinged curve where the shell opening began—at first seemed painted. Upon closer examination, the shell would devolve into precisely cut triangles and curved slivers of carefully colored ceramic. But for now, graced by distance, the fragments seemed to form a glorious whole, an emerging perfection, as though the shell itself had been buried within the wall and was now being slowly uncovered. A wondrous work, assembled by an artist of godly skill.

The Haárin continued his polishing, oblivious to the commotion behind his back.

Tsecha flinched as an elbow jostled him in the side. *"Dathim Naré,"* Sànalàn hissed in his ear, her Low Vynshàrau roughened by anger so that it sounded harsh as Haárin dialect. "I told you of him. I told you to speak to him! Now look what he has done!"

Tsecha glanced over the heads of the crowd, and sighted his Jani on the opposite side of the gathering. She stood between Lucien and Treasury Suborn Kern Standish, her arms folded, watching the Haárin.

"I do not know what your craftspeople can bring to us," Shai said. She, too, watched Dathim. Her back had unbent, but her voice still held the guttural sharpness of anger.

Anais waved a small, bony hand. "Precedent exists in the colonies. I know of several instances in which humanish craftspeople worked in idomeni buildings, and your tilemaster mentioned several more when he escorted me through the public portions of the embassy."

Dathim the tilemaster, having now lost his ability to mention, tossed his polishing cloth aside and resumed insetting bits of tile.

Tsecha pushed past Derringer and Lescaux so that he stood at Anais's shoulder. "How easily you accept our Haárin's presence when they have something you want, Ana—"

"We will discuss this in private, Minister Ulanova," Shai interrupted. She backed out of the altar room, pushing the crowd behind her as if they formed one body. "In my rooms." She beckoned in a humanish manner for Anais to walk with her. Tsecha watched in befuddlement as they proceeded down the hall, humanish and Vynshàrau alike trailing after, until only he and his Lucien and his Jani remained.

"What did I tell you? They've shut you out. You need to take care, nìRau." Jani did not look at Tsecha as she spoke. Instead, she watched Dathim Naré tap and arrange.

Only once did Dathim look at her. Their eyes met for only the briefest time; he then returned to his work, taking care to position himself so that she could not watch his hands, or see over his shoulder.

CHAPTER 7

Jani trudged up the access road that ran along the idomeni embassy property. The blue-green groundcover that the Vynshàrau had imported from Shèrá gave way to terrestrial grasses and shrubs as she entered the "demilitarized zone" that served as boundary between the embassy and the Exterior Ministry. Her back ached. Her stomach growled. The L station lay a few hundred meters ahead, elevated tracks and silver bullet cars glinting in the afternoon sun.

The Exterior Minister's disruption of the afternoon's agenda had released Jani from an afternoon's diplomatic servitude and prevented another confrontation with Derringer. With luck, Anais's determination to have the Haárin tilemaster redecorate her annex would keep the colonel occupied for several days. That probably wouldn't give Jani enough time to figure out why someone tried to set up Nema as a traitor to his people, but it would let her do some initial fact-finding.

Shai's had it with him. Jani didn't believe Shai had arranged the faked precis—that would have scaled heights of Byzantine treachery beyond the reach of most humans. *But if she suspected that he had betrayed the idomeni, she would send him back to Shèrá in restraints.* And there Cèel would be waiting, eager to mete out the justice that had been denied him so many years before, and repay Nema for bringing humanish into their lives. Nema had talked his way out of execution once. He wouldn't be allowed to do so again.

Jani stepped onto the grassy berm when she heard the hum of a skimmer approaching from behind, and turned as it slowed to a stop beside her. A deep gold sedan, lightened to gilt by the sun.

The passenger-side window lowered. "Jan!" Kern Standish called through the gap. "You need a ride?" He jerked his head toward the woman sitting beside him in the passenger seat. "I'm dropping off Dena at Commerce—I can swing by Armour no problem."

"We tried to catch you after the meeting, but Gene tackled you first." Dena Hausmann, the Commerce Finance chief, raised her hand to shield her eyes from the sun. She was a straw blonde with skin almost as pale as John Shroud's—even the weaker autumn light overwhelmed her. "He didn't look happy. Did you have a falling-out?"

"Eugene thinks I should be seen and not heard." Jani strolled up to the skimmer, mindful of the two pair of politically astute eyes watching her. *This road heads north—they'd normally use the south exit to return to the city. They tracked me on purpose.*

Kern snorted. "Ivy said she heard you two barking at one another all the way down the hall." Ivy was his Admin-slash-spy. "So what do you think about what happened?"

Jani didn't need to ask which *what* he referred to. "I think the idomeni study us as much as we study them. They've figured out that Nema contradicting everyone in public makes them appear disorganized. Shai may be trying to reel him in."

Dena squinted up at her. "Rumor has it that Shai's been sent here to replace him—think there's anything to it?"

Rumor's been getting up to no good, hasn't he? Jani hesitated. Kern and Dena were two of her supporters in the Cabinet purview—she owed them some sort of answer. "Nema will remain an influence, no matter in which capacity he serves."

"But he's the most pro-human of all the idomeni. If he loses any influence, we're in trouble." Kern waited for Jani to speak—when she didn't, the pretense of good humor fell away. His voice sharpened. "Jan, we should be working hand-in-glove with Anais on this, but whatever she knows, she refuses to share. Our Outer Circle Annex is on my back because of this Elyan thing. I've got Commonwealth–Shèrá trade and GateWay licensing agreements to examine. I've asked Anais for help, I'm not getting it, and frankly, my idomeni expertise could be inscribed on the head of a pin."

Then what the hell are you doing in this job? Jani thought of the piles of paper on her desk, and sighed. "Shoot 'em over—I'll see what I can see." She returned Kern's smile, as much as she could. "Any word on what she had to say about the white paper?"

"About what you'd expect." Dena grinned. "You're the Antichrist whose appearance signals the end of the Commonwealth, didn't you know that?" She glanced at her timepiece, and gasped. "Staff meeting in an hour—"

"Gotta run." Kern nudged the skimmer out of standby. "Jan, I owe you. I'm going to ask Jorge to kick you up to permanent retainer status."

"He won't do it."

"Bet you lunch. You'll keep us updated on Tsecha?"

"If I find out anything worth a damn, I'll let you know." Jani waved after the skimmer as it pulled away. "If I live that long." She kicked at a tuft of grass, then resumed her trudge to the L. "No. N-O. It's a very simple word—why the hell can't I learn to use it?"

She veered onto the berm again as another skimmer approached. A dark blue four-door this time, the mainstay of the Fort Sheridan vehicle pool. The driver's-side gullwing popped up, and Lucien poked his head through the opening. "Get in. Nema ordered me to drive you home." He disembarked and walked around to the passenger side. "He thinks you're not feeling well."

"I'm fine." Jani hitched her bag and bent low to enter the skimmer. "I—" She fell silent when she spotted Lescaux sitting in the backseat.

Lescaux held his briefbag up to his chest as though he expected her to grab him by the lapels and drag him out. "Lucien's giving me a lift into the city."

"How nice of Lucien." Jani glared up at the nice Lucien, who regarded her blankly as he pushed the door closed.

They rode in silence. Jani sensed Lucien's sidelong examination. He knew he'd dropped a small bomb, however unwittingly; she knew he relished the resulting tension.

As they swept up the ramp onto the Boul artery, a throat-clearing sounded from behind. "I guess we're going to have an Haárin laying tile at the annex sometime soon. That should prove a joy to organize."

"I'll be surprised if Shai allows it." Lucien spoke with the cool assurance of one who had taken a class on the subject. "If what I've seen in the colonies is any indication, that Haárin was advertising his services. He wants to do more than tile one wall in the Exterior Annex—he wants to start a business. Once Ani realizes what happened, she'll retract. She can't block the colonies doing business with Haárin, then turn around and do so herself. That would be ballsy, even for her."

"Nothing she does would surprise me anymore." Lescaux paused to ponder. "Does the shell have any significance? I saw it on a lot of Haárin walls during my colony years."

"The Vynshàrau like representations from nature," Lucien replied when he realized Jani wouldn't. "Shells, flowers, scenery. The Laum preferred symbols—geometric tracery and scrollwork. I don't think any of the born-sects go in for faces or figures, do they?" He looked at Jani and arched his brow in question.

"The Oà like portraiture," Jani mumbled.

That was all the opening Lescaux needed. "You made quite an impact at the meeting."

"Not enough," Jani replied eventually.

Lescaux grasped her words like a rope, pulling himself forward until his head poked between the front seats. "But do you really feel that a colonial government should contract with Haárin at the expense of their own people? Wouldn't it be better if we streamlined a way that the Karistosians could obtain materials and services from businesses on Elyas or elsewhere in the Outer Circle?"

"Yes, but what do they do for water while they wait for a half-dozen merchants' associations to argue whether the intercity dock tax should stand at a quarter or a third percent of sales price?" Jani exhaled with a grumble. She had sat in on those sorts of meetings over the summer, and had barely restrained the urge to throw her chair through a window. "If the Elyan Haárin have a filter system that works, Cèel should allow them to sell it to the Karistosians, and they should be allowed to install it. If a new plant comes two or three years down the road, let it come. But let's take care of *now* what needs taking care of now."

"But we have systems in place to handle these situations." Lescaux shook his head between the seats like a colt worrying in his stall. "You can't just ride roughshod over the process."

"Why not?" Jani ignored Lucien's frown. "The system is supposed to serve the people, Mr. Lescaux, not the other way around. If the system stops working, you change it. If the Karistosians can't obtain the equipment necessary to refit their water filtration system from their own people, they should be able to get it from the Haárin. And I'm not saying this because I'm pro-Haárin or anti-Commonwealth or a troublemaker or unrealistic. I'm saying it because the people at the sharp end of the stick come first and that's one thing that always gets lost in any trade discussion that I hear."

"But that's what I'm saying—"

"No, you're not. What you're arguing for is yet another variation of the same old song we've heard in the colonies for years. NUVA-SCAN affiliates. Sanctioned businesses. Preferred vendors. It's just one more way of forcing us to keep it in the Family. That's Family with a capital F, in case you missed it." Jani pounded her fist against the door. "Paid-for shipments that never arrived because they were diverted to somewhere with a bigger line of credit. Manufactured shortages. Buildings and skimways and equipment that were built to fall apart so that the vendors that sold them in the first place could collect premium prices for repairs and replacements. That's what this colony kid remembers growing up. From what she hears, it's getting worse. Well, not in one little corner of the Commonwealth. Not if she can help it. Sorry."

Lescaux released the conversational line and eased back in his seat. When they drifted to a stop at an intersection near Armour Place, he muttered "Merci" to Lucien and slipped out.

Jani watched Lescaux circle in front of the vehicle and merge with the lunchtime bustle on the tree-lined sidewalk, then turned to Lucien to find him regarding her beneath his lashes. "What?"

"You *are* pro-Haárin and anti-Commonwealth. And a trouble-maker." He re-merged with the midday traffic. "Not to mention flagrantly disrespectful. Estranged and unassimilated—"

"You read the white paper."

"Only a summary. I'm not high enough up the ladder to read the actual report." Lucien sighed his regrets. "But knowing you as I do, I can imagine the details. That being the case, do you really think ticking off the Exterior Minister's Chief of Staff is a good idea? Peter loves brushes with greatness—a few nice words from you and he'd sprain his arm throwing Exterior business your way." He tapped the steering wheel as the seconds passed. "So why don't you like him?"

Jani made it a point to sigh just as loudly as he had. "I never said that I didn't like him."

"I thought you were going to toss him out of the skimmer."

"I was just surprised to see him. I would have assumed you to be the one who wouldn't like him."

"Why? Because of Anais? I was well out of there before he came to take my place."

"You upset him at the meeting. He's jealous."

"Perhaps." Lucien shrugged as though he heard that every day. "But I'm a veteran of the war he's fighting. When he asks for advice, I give it. When he wants to talk, I listen."

"How understanding of you."

"I also find out some of the most interesting news that way." He turned the corner onto Armour Place. "You arrived with him and Derringer today. Change of pace for you—you always come alone."

Jani toyed with her duffel, taking care not to look Lucien in the face. "Lescaux had provided Derringer with some information about Elyas. Derringer thought I should have a look at it before the meeting."

"That was uncharacteristically nice of him." Lucien steered the skimmer into the garage—the interior darkened to night as they drifted inside. "What sort of information?"

"Trade propaganda—the kind of thing Peter talked about here." Jani popped her gullwing as Lucien drew alongside a charge station. "He tried to lobby me. It didn't work."

"You're lying." Lucien slammed down his gullwing, then yanked the connect cable from the station and jacked it into the skimmer battery access. "I've watched Cabinet staffers lobby you all summer—you brush them off like mosquitoes. You don't get angry, and you're angry with Peter." He pulled his garrison cap out of his belt and put it on. "I called you an hour before the meeting. You didn't answer."

Jani headed for the exit ramp that led out to the street. "I'd already left." She limped up the incline, her knee griping with every stride.

"It only takes a half-hour to get to the embassy. Did they pick you up early, or did you take another *break*?"

"Are you keeping tabs on me?" Jani pushed open the access door, but before she could step outside, Lucien reached over her shoulder and grabbed the door pull, blocking her passage.

"I just wanted to talk to you. Is that a crime?" He stepped out onto the sidewalk in front of her, then held open the door, the sunlight sparking off his hair.

Jani watched a pair of women turn to gape. "It was certainly uncharacteristically nice of you." She tugged at the front of his sweat-splotched desertweight shirt. "You look wilted—are you going to change?"

"Change. Shower. Crawl in your cooler." Lucien sucked in a lungful of crisp fall air. "The heat at the embassy really doesn't bother you?"

"Nope."

"It's not fair."

"Want me to talk to John? He can have you throwing up inside a week."

"You make it sound so inviting."

They crossed the street, their steps punctuated by a series of sharp reports as pinpoint charges detonated within the renovation. Lucien patted his holster as the shooter-like noises continued to sound. "Doesn't that noise get to your augie?"

Jani hurried past the doorman into the quiet of the lobby. "If I avoided everything that got to augie, I'd spend the rest of my life in a soundshielded cell, no blinking red lights allowed."

"I thought you couldn't handle red at all."

"John brought that under control this summer." Jani nodded to Hodge as she crossed to the lift bank. "Much to my relief. You wouldn't believe how many people I know think red is a good color for a wall." She didn't notice that Lucien lagged behind her until she had entered the lift.

"Oh, damn." He had pulled up, gaze fixed in the direction of the lobby sitting area.

A young woman stood in the middle of the space, poised as though unsure whether to retreat or step forward. Her face was small-featured, a series of wispy upturns, the delicate effect complemented by clipped light brown waves. Slim and of medium height, she wore a wrap shirt and trousers in darkest burgundy.

"Roni." Lucien doffed his cap and tucked it in his belt. "It's been a while."

"Yeah," the young woman replied, in a tone that hinted that the while hadn't been long enough.

Roni? Jani stepped out of the lift. "Roni McGaw? The Exterior Documents Chief?"

Wide-set, slanted eyes narrowed further as they fixed on Jani. "Jani Kilian." McGaw's was the accent of privilege, twangy Michigan provincial. "I wanted . . . to talk to you." She looked again at Lucien, and her voice deadened. "If you're busy, we can meet another time."

"We are, as a matter of fact." Lucien tried to herd Jani back into the lift. "Sorry, but—"

"Wait." Jani stepped around Lucien and beckoned to McGaw. "I can spare a few minutes, if you don't mind a ride upstairs."

"I'm in a hurry myself. Late for a meeting." McGaw boarded the lift, taking care to stand as far away from Lucien as possible. "Forgive the informality, but I wanted to ask your advice and such requests are better made in person."

In other words, you didn't want to risk anyone from Exterior intercepting the message. Jani studied Roni more closely. The muted light of the cabin combined with the too-dark Exterior uniform to accentuate shadows beneath eyes and cheekbones and tinge ivory skin with blue. It was a picture Jani recalled well. *She's like Yolan—worry deadens her face.* It surprised her to think of her late corporal at a time like this, in the quiet of the vault. She usually only thought of Yolan Cray during the day, when she walked outside, and heard the *boom* of the charges.

McGaw's eyes widened when she entered Jani's flat, but she kept her interior decoration commentary to herself. "Nice place," she said as she walked to the window. "Nice view, too."

Jani joined her. "Yes, it is. You can see the intersection, and Armour Place all the way to where it veers onto the Boul Sidebar." She lowered her voice. "Do you think you were followed?"

"No." McGaw made as if to say more, but the sound of Lucien's footsteps silenced her.

"How's Miryam, Roni?" He wedged between them, his voice laced with petulant bite. "I heard she moved back to Lyon."

"She's fine. She . . . did leave, last month, yes, she started a consulting business with some friends." The blush crawled up McGaw's neck, then fingered along her jaw. Yolan had reacted the same whenever Neumann goaded her, her pale skin broadcasting her every emotion.

Jani interrupted Lucien's baiting, just as she had Neumann's years before. "Would you like a drink?" She headed for the kitchen, gesturing for McGaw to follow.

"Please." McGaw hurried to catch her up.

Jani swept through the door and yanked open the cooler. "Is this about The Nema Letter?" She removed a dispo of fruit drink and handed it to McGaw.

"Nema?" McGaw stared at the dispo, her expression clouding. Then her head came up. *"Yes,* I—"

The kitchen door slid aside once more. "Are you ladies avoiding me?" Lucien asked as he sauntered in. "Ron, is that any way to treat an old friend?" He joined Jani in front of the cooler and put his arm across her shoulders, pulling her close.

Since when? Lucien never put his arm around her—he wasn't the drapery type. Jani looked at McGaw to find her staring at Lucien, eyes hard and shining.

"All this increased business with the idomeni is highlighting the deficiencies in my staff's training. We could use input from someone with your experience." McGaw cracked the dispo seal and took a sip. "If you'd agree to conduct a seminar, I can guarantee a room packed to the roof."

"Ron, where have you been?" Lucien gave Jani a squeeze. "Ani will never allow Jan to set foot on Exterior grounds."

"Anais and I have a deal. She doesn't interfere with documents, and I keep my nose out of politics." McGaw took another swallow from the dispo, wincing as she did so. "Please think about it and get back to me, won't you?"

"Sure." Jani slipped from under Lucien's arm and followed McGaw out of the kitchen. "Lescaux doesn't know you're here."

"God, no." McGaw handed Jani the juice dispo. "It's so sour."

"Sorry."

"Anais will be in the city all day tomorrow. Stop by the Annex."

"Shouldn't we meet somewhere else?"

"I've mentioned you to my staff. They'll expect to see you. It's all right." Disgust rippled across McGaw's face as Lucien approached, intensifying when he once more slipped his arm around Jani. "I'll see what I can arrange," she said more loudly. "I will certainly appreciate your help." She stuck out her hand. "Call me when you have the time."

"Sure." Jani took McGaw's hand, shook it lightly, dropped it. It felt warm, not cold. Alive, not dead. So why couldn't she bear to touch it . . . ?

McGaw looked at her hand, then at Jani. "Is something wrong?"

Jani looked into her eyes. At least they were hazel, not pale grey like Yolan's. That would have been too much. "You . . . just remind me of someone I used to know."

"Oh? I can't tell from your face whether that's good or bad." McGaw backed out the door. "Until later." She ignored Lucien's weak wave and hurried down the hall toward the lift.

"Well, that brought back memories." Lucien's arm fell away as soon as the door closed. "She's trouble. Always sticking her nose where it doesn't belong. I lost track of the number of times I asked Ani to fire her."

Jani stepped around him to her desk, taking a drink from the nearly full dispo along the way. "Why didn't Ani listen?" She swallowed, then glanced at the dispo label. *It's just lemon tonic.* She'd always found it sweet.

"Roni's mother is Ani's cousin. Ani lets family get in the way. That's family with a small 'f,' in case you missed it." Lucien tossed his garrison cap atop the desk, then pulled his rumpled shirt out of his trousers and undid the fasteners. "I'm going to shower."

Jani sat and pulled a file off the top of a stack. "Have fun."

"I could use someone to wash my back."

"First rule of the Service—never volunteer."

"And a soldier's life is a lonely one." Lucien pulled off his shirt as he walked down the hall toward Jani's bedroom, allowing her an unimpeded view of his back before the door closed.

Such an admirable view. Thoughts of it warred with the upset that McGaw's surprise appearance had caused, but before either thought could claim precedence, the buzz of Jani's comport spooked them all back to their burrows.

"Documents, Mistress," Hodge imparted in hushed tones. "Treasury courier."

Boy, Kern—you didn't waste any time. "Send them up." Jani counted to twenty, then pushed away from the desk. By the time she reached the door, the entry bell sounded. Hodge passed the gold carrier across the threshold with solemn ceremony; Jani cracked the seals, sighing inwardly when she saw the amount of paper contained therein. *Retainer? Try a damned deputy ministry.* After Hodge departed, she hefted the case back to the desk, pulled the top file out of the portable bin and tried to concentrate on the tables and charts.

Only a few minutes had passed when she heard the bedroom door open, but Lucien seldom dawdled when he showered and dressed alone. She glanced up. "Are you going straight back to Sher—?"

"Straight back to Sheridan? I don't know." He smiled as he padded toward the desk. He had showered, judging from his damp hair and the stray drops of water glistening on his shoulders. He just hadn't bothered to dress.

Long thighs. Flat stomach. Just enough muscle—breadth without bulk. *Blond all over—well, we knew that, didn't we?* Jani struggled with an "animal in the skimmer headlamps" feeling. Hypnotic view—inevitable outcome. "Forget something?"

"My cap." Lucien reached across the desk and picked it up, allowing her to catch the scent of musky soap arising from his bare arm. He studied the cap absently, then planted his elbows on the desk and jerked his chin at the Treasury carrier. "Those are new."

"Yeah." Jani dragged her attention back to the documents. "Kern asked me to have a look at them. Idomeni issues. Anais is supposed to be helping him, but she's ignoring his pleas."

"That means his boss ticked her off. It's Kern's job to heal the breach, not pass off the mess to you."

"I said I'd help."

"You're always helping. The more you help, the more they ask. What's Kern offering in return this time?"

"Permanent retainer."

"Did you get it in writing?" Lucien leaned closer. "Roni. Kern. Yesterday, it was someone else. Tomorrow, it'll be someone else again. They all want your help, but what do *you* get in exchange?" His eyes darkened in frank invitation. "With all you've been through, you still haven't learned the difference between people who earn their keep and people who don't."

Jani inhaled. The musky scent seemed to envelop her now, but McGaw's visit had unsettled her too much to consider the inevitable outcome. She nodded toward the clear windows, through which the afternoon sunlight streamed. "The privacy shields aren't up. Someone's getting an eyeful."

Lucien looked toward the unimpeded view of the nearby buildings. "Perhaps that someone will show an interest. I'm certainly not getting any in here." He straightened, then opened up the cap and set it at a jaunty angle atop his head. "My desertweights were rancid. I stuck them in your cleaner and set it for an hour."

"I'll take them out when they're done." Jani watched his perfect form recede down the hall, taut muscles working under tanned skin. Many thoughts occurred, none of which would have given Lucien any pleasure.

He's trying to distract me. But from what? Not work—he never interfered with her job except to opine that she didn't charge enough for her services. *Peter?* Possibly. It did strike her as odd that they got on well enough to confer about the care and feeding of Anais Ulanova, especially considering Peter's reaction when Lucien interrupted Anais at the meeting. *They're rivals, oh yes they are.* But allies of a sort too, apparently, inasmuch as circumstances and Lucien's misshapen personality allowed them to be.

What about Roni McGaw? His former coworker. *They despise one another.* Were they ex-lovers? No. *He'd flaunt that, not hide it.* Besides, Jani had sensed no heat between them, only the acrid odor of profound dislike.

He kept interrupting us. Why?

Lucien reemerged from the bedroom, this time fully clothed in a fresh set of dress blue-greys. "I'm off." His black tietops clipped on the bare wood. "I'm not sure if I'll be by again this week—my schedule's a little choppy."

"Whenever you can spare a few moments." Jani reached for the Treasury carrier to pull out another file, but before she could, Lucien flipped the lid closed.

"If I never came back, would you care?" His voice held the deadness he reserved for people he had no use for, which meant he wasn't real happy with her at the moment.

"I don't know." The words slipped out before Jani could stop them, driven by Lucien's odd behavior, the memory of Roni McGaw's agitation, and her own rising sense of disquiet.

"You. Don't. Know." Lucien slipped his hand behind her head and pulled her to him, kissing her hard enough to hurt. He'd rinsed his mouth with a peppermint concoction—the sharp taste filled Jani's sinuses and made her eyes water.

"Tell Kern he better come through with that retainer," he whispered as he broke away. The door had closed after him before Jani thought to breathe.

She spent the balance of the afternoon alternating between Kern's files, Devinham's dock data, and the other Treasury reports. As the sky darkened, she prepped a strange supper of Neoclona Chicken Surprise washed down with lemon tonic. The chicken did indeed surprise her by tasting good. She buried thoughts of how a fully human mouth would perceive the tangy wine-herb flavor she enjoyed, and sopped up the sauce with bits of bread.

Late evening found her restless, brain churning with Nema's troubles, Lucien's actions, Roni McGaw's trepidation, and her own white paper-lined collision with her past. She tried to decompress by flipping through a holo album her parents had sent her the month before. First came sceneshots of north Acadian wilds near Oncle Shamus's tourist compound, the moors and the rolling hills. Then came the more personal images. Her mother, Jamira, grey-edged black hair twisted into a loose knot, holding up a rainbow-hued sari she bought for Jani to wear during her expected visit home. Her father, Declan, sleeves rolled up to expose sinewy arms, displaying with self-conscious pride the oaken salmon he had machined to hang over the mantel of Shamus's lodge fireplace.

Jani stilled the rolling image and studied her father's face—the turned-up nose, snub chin, straight black hair—and saw the face she had worn before Evan van Reuter's bomb blew her out of the Shèrá sky. Her chest tightened. She slammed the album closed and shoved it back in her desk drawer, then pulled a Service-surplus field coat from her front closet.

The urge to bolt, which never lurked too deep beneath her surface, broke through several times as she walked to the lift. She could pack in minutes, catch any of a dozen trains or 'movers to O'Hare, lift off for Luna within the hour, be halfway to Mars before anyone realized that she had left Chicago.

No, I don't do that anymore. I've signed a rental contract. I have clients, obligations. I'm a free and functioning member of society.

Then why did she feel more trapped now then she ever had as a fugitive?

The air held a hard, brittle quality, as though it would sing like glass if Jani brushed her fingers through it. She pulled up her collar and stuffed her hands in her pockets, her internal thermostat having decided now was the time to freeze her to death. She trudged down the empty sidewalk and across the deserted street, past the tarpaulined silence of the renovation and down a side lane, until she came upon a small park nestled between two Family townhouses. She wiped an unseasonable dusting of frost from a slatwood bench, and sat.

Despite the cold, she savored the night silence. She hadn't been entirely truthful with Lucien—the blasts and clatters of construction did bother her. Not her augmentation, no. What they did was uncover memories. Of the bombs. The stench of smoke and char. The rubble, and what lay beneath.

Yolan Cray died during the first round of shelling at Knevçet Shèràa, when the Laumrau shatterboxes wrought their first wave of destruction. Windows had sharded. Safety doors had blown. Walls collapsed, and killed. Buried. Entombed.

Jani closed her eyes as once more, Borgie's sobs filled her ears. She could see him, clear as relentless remembrance could be, as he lifted Yolan's broken body and buried his face in her wispy blonde hair.

Silence. Silence felt like heaven. Jani tensed as the distant scree of a ComPol siren broke through. She thought of a seat on an outbound shuttle, and clenched her hands into fists. She forced herself to sit still as silence, and watched the shaded windows until the last light faded.

CHAPTER 8

Jani awoke with a start to find she had worked her way over to Lucien's side of the bed. She buried her face in his pillow, filling her nose with his scent as fragments of a rather pleasant dream drilled heat-tracks through her brain and down her spine.

I'm not in love. She struggled into a sitting position. *I know what love is, and this ain't it. This* was lust, the enthusiastic appreciation of a beautiful body and all the wonders it could perform. It worked beneath her skin like a constant prickling, as though nerves that had never felt before had suddenly come alive. It was ridiculous. It made no sense.

It was profoundly human and she would cherish its every ache and throe for all the human time she had left.

Love had nothing to do with her feelings for Lucien. Nor trust. She didn't trust him to give her the right time, but she had never felt that was part of the deal. She allowed him access to Nema, and a chance to build his career; he took her out of herself for a little while, and accepted her at face value. In the series of deals and trade-offs that had comprised her life for over twenty years, this one worked better than most.

Love, on the other hand, felt like a calm refuge in the midst of a raging storm. Nasty thing about love—it let you get comfortable, then threw you a curve. She'd loved Evan van Reuter once, with the handed-down-from-heaven certainty of a twenty-one-year-old who thought it all started with her. That ended when she realized what giving herself over to a Family member really meant. When she learned that the public Evan and the private Evan were two distinctly different men, and that while he didn't think that mattered, she did.

She tottered to the bathroom, collecting clothes along the way. *And then there's John Shroud.* A few weeks before, she had made the mistake of spending a day in the Neoclona documents archives to research a last-minute project. Funny how John needed to look up some data that very day. They'd spent hours discussing, bickering, and laughing over everything from the results of the latest Cup match to *exactly what color are Val Parini's eyes, anyway?* And when they didn't talk, they worked at their respective tasks, or read, or daydreamed, content simply to be in each other's company.

Jani didn't realize until she'd returned to her flat that she had once again *given herself over*. That she'd let John choose the chair in which she sat, the food she ate, the color of the folder she used to bind her report, and that she'd set her conscious will aside and allowed it to happen. She didn't blame him. Not entirely. They were inextricably bound, as only creator and created could be. He had saved her life, rebuilt her to the best of his ability, sheltered her from Service justice until she dug deep and found the will to shake him off.

He was the first thing I saw when I opened my eyes. Her mutant eyes, as green as the edge of a pane of glass. The harbinger of what was to come, the point man for the changes her body was going through.

Jani arranged her clothes and showering gear in the over-mirrored bathroom, all the while avoiding her myriad reflections. She bent over the sink to brush her teeth—the strong mint odor of her tooth cleaner irritated the inside of her nose. She sneezed, then groaned as she felt the telltale loosening over her right eye as the film fissured. She peeled away the ruptured hydropolymer and rummaged through the drawers for her filmformer. Bottle in hand, she made ready to *apply and let dry,* then stopped herself. "I need to look in the mirror to make sure it spreads evenly." Her filmed eye could wind up looking like a fried egg if the polymer didn't coat properly. *One . . . two . . .* She took a deep breath, and looked at her naked eye.

The iris had increased in size and darkened profoundly over the summer, thanks to her accelerated hybridization. Half again as large as a human iris, a forest green shattered marble accentuated by the lighter hue of her visible sclera. She pulled down her lid, exposing the edging of slight darkening that inscribed the border between green and white. *Sweet baby jades*, Val had dubbed them, as though giving them a nickname would help Jani accept their inevitable change.

John did this because he loved me. Because he didn't know how else to save me. Because he had convinced himself that he possessed the know-how to construct a human-idomeni hybrid that combined the best of both species but left the unwanted effects behind. Because he felt that since he did what he did with the best of intentions, for love and for science, that the law of unintended consequences didn't apply.

"That's love for you." Jani shook the drops of filmformer onto her eye and counted off the setting time.

She adjusted the shower to a pounding spray that massaged the constant stiffness from her muscles. She dressed for comfort, in a white Service surplus pullover and dark blue fatigue pants, since she had no appointments until her dinner with Steve and Angevin that evening. *Not unless Derringer drops by.* She didn't look forward to that. He'd pick up their argument where it left off at the embassy, and she'd have to employ every duck and dodge she knew to keep him from breaking out his particular set of thumbscrews.

She was in the midst of toweling her hair when the bedroom comport squawked.

"Good morning, Mistress Kilian," Hodge entoned formally. "Colonel Pierce is here."

"Good morning, Hodge. Send him up."

Hodge glanced off to the side, and nodded. "If you would, Mistress, attend here please. Colonel Pierce would prefer to discuss the matter in another venue."

In other words, Niall wanted to talk outside. "Tell him I'll be right down."

By the time Jani entered the lobby, she found Niall had already adjourned to the sidewalk in front of the apartment house. He wore fallweights—dark blue trousers cut by a mainline red stripe, paired with a long-sleeved grey shirt. He set his dark blue garrison cap on his head, then dug into his shirt pocket. When Jani saw him remove the nicstick case and shake out a 'stick, her stomach roiled.

"Pretty Boy up there?" He spoke without turning around, his eyes fixed on the street activity.

"No." Jani pulled up beside him, and caught a whiff of the astringent smoke. Her nose tickled ominously—she circled around Niall in search of clean air and started up the walk.

Niall fell in beside her. Luckily, the light breeze blew his smoke in the opposite direction. "Plan to see him today?"

"No. He does occasionally show up out of the blue, though. He's keyed into the flat, and he keeps things there." Jani stopped at a kiosk and purchased a packet of crackers. Her stomach was letting her know that skipping breakfast had been a dumb idea, and tasteless with a little salt had proved safe in the past. "Is there a point to these questions?"

"Yes." Niall glanced around uncertainly, then reached into his shirt pocket again.

Jani watched him shake out and ignite another 'stick. "OK, Niall, what don't you know how to tell me?"

They had come upon a small playground. Niall leaned against a low fence and watched two small boys launch a tiny pondskimmer in the shallow pool of a fountain. "It's your parents." His eyes widened. "I began that badly. I'm sorry. They're fine. They're—they're on their way here. They hit MarsPort tonight. They touch down at O'Hare the day after tomorrow."

Jani ran the words over in her mind once, then again. She knew what she'd heard, but it made no sense to hear it from Niall. "Repeat what you just said."

"Jani, you heard me."

"Why didn't they let me know?"

"I don't know. I have a few guess—"

"What happened?"

"I don't know. I got a bare bones Misty earlier this morning from a buddy in Guernsey. Ares Station called to confirm that they're on their way."

The boys argued over which of them should control the skimmer. As their high-pitched quibbling intensified, they lost track of the craft. Jani watched it veer off-course, bounce off the side of the fountain, and spin in tight circles. "Does this have anything to do with the white paper?"

"I don't know." Niall leaned out over the fence as the toy popped out of the pool, catching it before it clattered to the cement. "We're going to debrief them during the trip from Mars to Luna." He held up a hand to silence her protests. "They're coming here under very strange circumstances. We have to find out what compelled them. Were they told something about you that made them fear for your safety? What? From whom?"

"From whom?" Jani waited. "Spit it out, Niall."

Niall ran a finger along the pondskimmer's bow, and scraped a thumbnail over a colored decal. "Ever hear of a group called *L'araignée*?"

"Spider?" Jani shook her head. "Sounds like one of those trumped-up gangs that takes over a loading dock and calls itself a syndicate."

"This is a little more than a trumped-up gang." Niall flicked the skimmer's safety switch, then tossed it back in the water. "It's a well-organized alliance of colonial businesses. Their stated goal is to 'maintain standards and markets throughout the Commonwealth,' whatever the hell that means. The problem, according to my Guernsey friend, is that the membership wasn't very well vetted. They range in legitimacy from rock-solid to ones like you mentioned, gangs taking over loading docks. Unfortunately, the gangs seem to be taking over *L'araignée,* as well. My buddy says that in the months since its inception, *L'araignée*'s been responsible for all sorts of interesting incidents. Money laundering. Diversion of goods. The odd hijacked transport." He watched the bickering boys, still oblivious to their dead-in-the-water ship. "They're based in the Channel. That's why I wondered if you'd heard of them, if your folks had ever mentioned them."

"No." Jani backed away from the fountain, her hands pressed to her ears—the boys' screeching made her head pound. She envisioned her parents disembarking at MarsPort, surrounded by uniforms. Did Spec Service receive training in making smalltalk with parents? Could Niall snag her a seat on a shuttle so that she could meet them at Luna? Were they afraid? "Does Mako know they're coming?"

"Of course Mako knows they're coming." Niall herded her up the street. "He assigned me to head up the welcoming committee." His weathered face set in grim lines. "They've become his new special project. He knows you'd ring the curtain down on him if anything happened to them."

"I'd never do anything that could take you out."

"You say that now. I've watched you look through holo albums for the past four months."

"Niall."

"Yeah." Niall pulled out another 'stick. "I told you I would check on who had been involved in compiling the information in that white paper, right? Well, matters got interesting in one hell of a hurry." He snorted smoke like a Tsing Tao dragon. "Guess who spent the first six months of this year zipping to most of the same cities covered in your report? Guess who met with agents based in the locations that he didn't manage to visit in person? Go on, guess."

"The Service was looking for me at the time, Niall." Even as she spoke, Jani felt a chill flood her limbs that had nothing to do with her wonky internal thermostat. It was augie, she knew, clamping down on the blood flow to her extremities, prepping her for the dash to safety that she couldn't afford to make. "It made sense to send Lucien after me. He did know me and he is in Intelligence."

"Intelligence." Niall gave the word a gamy twist. "Speaking of

trumped-up gangs." They pulled up in front of Jani's building. "I'm going to be a little hard to get hold of until your folks arrive. I'll keep you posted, and I'll notify you as soon as we have them."

"I want to be there."

"Not a good idea. Save the reunion for the safe house. I want them in plain sight as little as possible, and I don't want the three of you together in public." He touched her arm, a brush of the fingers only. "I've got them. They'll be fine. You have my word. We have them sighted. We know when they'll arrive at MarsPort. We have people there to take charge of them. They'll be under close guard until they get here. I will meet them at O'Hare personally and place them in protective custody immediately."

Niall escorted Jani back to her flat. She tried once more to talk him into letting her come along to O'Hare, and he again stated reasonably and firmly why he felt that wasn't a good idea. He then took his leave, his the light step of someone who had an order of mission and a timetable and all those other things that kept the hours from hanging over your head like a sword suspended by a steadily unraveling thread.

"We also serve who only sit and go mad." Jani walked to her desk and fell into her chair. Her comport incoming message light showed dark for the first time in weeks, and she had her for-hire projects under control for the moment. She dug McGaw's affidavit out of her duffel and tried to examine it, but couldn't muster the concentration she needed. The image of two figures huddled in a ship's cabin had formed in her mind and refused to yield the floor.

Her stomach grumbled, and she went into the kitchen to shut it up. Her throat clenched with every swallow of the Neoclona premade, and she expected at any point to expel into the sink everything she had just swallowed. But augie ran her now, and his orders were always simple and to the point. Eat first. Sleep. Study. Evaluate the facts. Then act.

She lay down on her side of the bed. Lucien's scent didn't interest her now. The problem with Niall's quick and dirty assessment of the source of the white paper was that she could indeed imagine Lucien compiling it. "I can't see him leaving anything out, though." He enjoyed creating anxiety. Jani could imagine him dropping details of her deed-copying for months, then savoring her every start and display of unease.

She struggled to forget about Lucien by performing thought exercises that she'd developed during her years on the run, when augie threatened to blow out the top of her head unless she acted and she knew action was the last thing she should do. She inhaled slowly. Exhaled. Visualized her limbs sinking into the mattress. Concentrated on a mental image of Baabette, a storybook character from her youth. In her conception, the white sheep with the black face sat at a workstation and assembled a hologram landscape, an absurdity that for some odd reason Jani found calming. She had just reached the point where sleep seemed possible when her comport screeched.

"Mistress? I couldn't stop him." Hodge blinked rapidly, his equivalent of an emotional breakdown. "Colonel Derringer, Mistress. He's on his way up."

"It's all right, Hodge. I've been expecting him." Jani swung her legs over the side of the bed. Stood. Counted. By the time she reached her front door, the entry bell rang.

"Anais Ulanova should be shot," Derringer muttered as he stormed in. He wore dress blue-greys and clutched his brimmed lid in his hand like a weapon at the ready. "Fifteen hours I spent at the embassy discussing tile specifications! Delivery dates! I felt like a goddamn building contractor." He stopped in the middle of the floor and looked around. "What the hell?" He turned back to glare at Jani. "Where's your furniture?"

"Don't believe in it. Makes visitors think they're welcome." She folded her arms and leaned against the wall.

Derringer's scowl altered to a frown. "Are you feeling all right, Kilian?"

"No, sir."

Derringer flinched at the "sir." He knew she didn't mean it. "One of your many ailments, I assume." He backed farther into the room. "You slipped out from under yesterday. We never had a chance to *talk.*" He offered a superior half-smile. "Tsecha. Information." He walked to the window and sat on the sill. "Report."

Jani fought the urge to stand at attention. "He knows nothing about that letter. He reaffirmed his belief that any and all interactions between humanish and idomeni are desirable."

Derringer's hand tightened around his hat brim. "And you accepted this at face value? You didn't try to dig deeper?"

"All there is with Nema is face value. There is no deep to dig into." Jani let her arms drop and stepped away from the wall. "He's being set up by someone with an interest in getting him out of the way. I have reason to believe that his position at the embassy is tenuous and that even the appearance that he is involved in subterfuge of this nature will result in his recall and possibly his execution."

"You said that at lunch yesterday. I don't buy it." Derringer sounded bored. Callum Burkett, his CO, had spent ten years working with the colonial Haárin. Derringer had heard all his stories and felt that he now knew all there was to know about the idomeni. "Tsecha's still invited to the meetings. I've received no official notification that from such-and-such date on, he no longer speaks and acts for the Shèrá worldskein."

"Didn't you see Shai's posture at yesterday's meeting? How she interrupted Nema when he tried to reprimand Ulanova about the tile?"

Derringer brightened. "Wish he'd succeeded. Would have saved me a lot of trouble."

"Shai *cut* Nema *out.*" Jani's voice rasped as her throat tightened—she waited until the worst of the clench abated. This was her best shot at convincing Derringer to leave Nema alone. If she lost her temper now, he'd never give her another chance. "Shai"—she paused—"Shai took over the discussions with Ulanova herself. She's acting in Nema's stead, preventing him from acting as the worldskein's voice."

Derringer's gaze moved from Jani's face to some point above her head. "Why is she doing this? She's always deferred to him before. Why the sudden change?"

Jani spoke slowly, pacing her argument. "I think the Vynshàrau are studying us the way we study them, and they've realized that their habit of open disputation doesn't play well with us. We see it as a sign of weakness, a crack in the united front. Shai knows Nema will never change his ways, no matter how it looks to us, so she's trying to shut him out. If she does this, he's little use as ambassador. Cèel has been looking for an excuse to shut down Nema for years. The least misstep on his part could mean recall, and if there's a suspicion that he's betrayed his people, the penalty will be much greater. We can't afford to lose him. He's our best friend. He's the one who badgers Cèel to open up idomeni GateWays to our shipping, to permit technology exchanges. He's the doorway—we don't want that door to close. You've visited idomeni factories and military bases. You've seen their technologies. Do you really want them to shut themselves away, to develop and expand where you can't see them? You don't trust them? You think they're the enemy? Well, what's that old saying—keep your friends close—"

"—and your enemies closer." Derringer's gaze dropped. He fussed with his lid, brushing invisible specks from the crown and running the cuff of his tunic over the brim.

Jani watched him ponder, and offered up a prayer to Ganesha, the favored god of her youth. The Remover of Obstacles. *Please, Lord, make this idiot see sense.* She thought of the shrine she had meant to construct for months. *Tomorrow—I'll build it tomorrow.* No. If the Temple store on Devon Avenue was still open, she'd build it today.

Then, slowly, like a clouded sunrise, Derringer's head came up. "Sorry, Kilian, I don't buy it. If the Vynshàrau are so averse to subterfuge, they wouldn't have let Tsecha come here in the first place. He pulled a few tricks of his own during that last war of theirs. Hell, I heard he helped plan your evac from Interior the night van Reuter was arrested." He shook his head. "He's their boy, like it or not. The gods chose him, so the idomeni are stuck with him. He's chosen us, and I have no intention of letting the opportunity go to waste." He stood up, tucked his lid under his arm, shot the cuffs of his tunic. "Since your meeting with him got cut short, I've arranged another visit for tomorrow. Some documents transfers that just won't wait."

Jani stepped out to the middle of the floor. The chill had flooded her limbs again—standing too near the wall made her feel trapped. "I will not go."

"You have no choice."

"I will not endanger Nema's life."

"You will do as you are told." Derringer started toward the door. "I'll send a skimmer for you. Save you having to hike to the L. End of story."

Jani remained silent. Her throat ached too much to try to talk. She stepped to one side as Derringer brushed past her, her hands clenched, nails gouging her palms. She fought to ignore augie as he urged her to strike, and stood frozen until she heard the door close.

CHAPTER 9

Jani remained standing in the center of the room for some time after Derringer left. She performed her breathing exercises, then tried to concentrate on Baabette and her landscape design. Derringer's face, however, kept superimposing itself over that of the sheep's. The image of him coated in white wool quieted Jani's wire-drawn nerves, much as envisioning a naked audience calmed an edgy speaker.

The ploy didn't work for long, though. Her throat soon ached again. Her stomach hitched along for the ride. She dragged her feet loose from their invisible moorings and paced the perimeter, her mind veering from thoughts of dockings at MarsPort to how she could pry Derringer off Nema's back to—.

I have an appointment with Roni McGaw. Lucky thing. The walking, riding, working out of her route would give her racing mind a track to ride on.

She lowered to the floor beside her desk and checked the contents of her duffel. Her scanpack and other devices she had inserted into the scanproof compartment she had rebuilt into the duffel's bottom. She fingered two torn edges where she had attached compartments that had been hacked out by over-officious investigators. *My history in the bottom of a bag.* One torn edge marked her detainment just prior to Evan's arrest; the other served as reminder of her capture by the Service that summer. *Bad things come in threes,* Jani thought as she tugged at one of the polyfilm fragments. She struggled to her feet, hoisted the duffel, and grabbed a Service surplus jacket from the entryway closet on the way out the door.

* * *

Jani disembarked the L at the station located just outside the entrance to the Exterior Ministry, and took some time to examine her target from the elevated platform.

The Outer Circle world of Amsun served as the true home of the Cabinet office to which fell the job of administering the Commonwealth's forty-six extrasolar colonies; to that placement belonged the sprawl one normally associated with a Ministry HQ. Therefore, since it was considered an annex only, the Chicago compound paled when compared to the other Cabinet installations that stretched from just north of Chicago to the lower tip of Lake Michigan. Unlike the neighbor Interior Ministry, which was comprised of an immense Main building, a score of subsidiary structures, and a private estate for the minister, Exterior consisted only of a smallish office tower and a few security and utility outbuildings. Instead of grounds measured by the square kilometer, it possessed a yard of mortal scope, easily traversed by skimmer in a couple of minutes. And as for the estate, Anais Ulanova solved that problem by residing in the Family home that was located a block or so east of Jani's own flat.

Jani shaded her eyes and looked to the south, where the sudden shift from the grey-green of native scrub grass to the bluish tint of the Shèrá hybrid species marked the boundary with the idomeni embassy. Only that southern boundary possessed any significant security presence—Jani could just detect the top of one of the boxy concrete booths that dotted the border from the western line of the Ministry access road east to the lakeshore.

That's not my problem. If Jani ever needed to infiltrate Exterior grounds from that direction, she need only ask Nema how he did it. He had, after all, penetrated the boundary regularly that previous winter, hiding clothing and makeup in one of the booths and using it as a jumping-off point for disguised forays into the city.

He blended right in. Well, truth be told, he must have looked rather strange. *So tall and stick-thin.* Cracked amber eyes obscured by filming. *But excellent clothes, and lightly accented English.* People must have taken him for one of Chicago Combined University's more eccentric professors.

The more Jani thought about it, the more she realized how well that particular shoe fit. *He does understand subterfuge, you know.* And plotting. And planning. *He's not the naïf you think he is.* So why did she feel so bound to protect him? What made her think he couldn't talk himself out of this jam as he had out of so many others?

Because at times, he is as blind and deaf here. At such times, I become his Eyes and Ears. I watch his back. I kill the wasps. A duty long-evaded, reclaimed. *My job.*

She switched her attention to the Exterior Ministry entrance. The long, curved drive was filled with double- and triple-length skimmers. Chauffeurs stood in groups, chatting and smoking, while security guards walked among the vehicles, scanning Registrations and making notes in recording boards. Of course, the skimmers had already been identified, cross-matched, and effectively searched when they turned onto the drive and passed through the sensor fence, but that was invisible and therefore had little effect on the nerves. Better for potential infiltrators to see the burgundy-clad guards, holstered shooters hanging on their belts, walking from vehicle to vehicle, opening boots and huddling in low-pitched discussion.

Jani brushed a hand over her jacket front and started down the stairs.

"Name?"

"Jani Kilian." Jani handed the lobby desk her ID, then waited as the young woman scanned her eyes. A distinct change of pace, announcing herself to a guard using her real name.

The guard checked her workstation display. "Ms. McGaw will be right out, ma'am. Please have a seat." She handed Jani back her ID, professional seriousness framed by a Service short-back-and-sides and the brilliant white collar of a fallweight "A" shirt.

"I'll stand, thanks." Jani strolled across the marble tile floor and pretended a pointed examination of the lakescapes on the walls. *I wonder if the Haárin tilemaster will be retiling this particular floor?* If Lucien's assessment proved accurate, and Jani felt it would, such a public display of his singular artistry would lead to more requests. *And after the tilemaster will come a painter, or a woodworker, or a skimmer designer. Anais, you do realize that you opened the door you wanted to keep shut?* Unfortunately, months or years would pass before open trade sank its roots in Chicago, and that would be much too late to do the Karistosians any good.

Jani turned as she heard the brush of a door mech and the high-pitched clip of thin-soled shoes.

"I wondered when you'd show." McGaw tugged at the pockets of her wine-red trouser suit. She looked even more drained and restive today than she had at Jani's flat. "My office."

McGaw closed the door, then touched an inset pad that Jani hoped activated an anti-surveillance array. "It's funny. Anais has been taking your name in vain on a regular basis ever since you started working closely with Tsecha. All I could think of was, 'Wow—Jani Kilian. She studied at the Academy. She walked the streets of Rauta Shèrâa.' "

Jani sat in the visitor's chair on the opposite side of the desk. "Except for the night the Vynshà ascended to rau and their Haárin overran the place. Then we ran."

"You know what I mean." McGaw eyed her peevishly as she sat behind her large desk, which was covered from side to side with stacks of documents. "Must be something to turn to the face page of the Registry and find your name there."

"I don't really think about it anymore."

"You aren't going to give me a break, are you?"

"What break? You've romanticized it. I lived it. It loses a lot in translation, believe me." Jani's thigh muscles twitched as her news-from-home nerves finally abated and post-augie tremors settled in. Afterward would come post-augie languor, a muddle-headed state that would spell the end to her fieldwork for . . . how long? *Minutes? Hours? Days?* Her physical condition, once so reliable, had become more and more unpredictable. She could no longer time her augie stages as she used to—her increased hybridization had altered the old, familiar progression to a stop-and-start dissonance.

"Hansen Wyle and Jani Kilian, the senses, the infiltrators," McGaw continued, determined to shoulder on regardless. "Gina Senna and Carson Tsai, the musicians. The pacifiers. Dorothea Aryton and Ennegret Nawar, the Family members. The muscle." The recitation did some good—her calm seemed to reassert itself as she discussed Jani's history. "One of Six for Tongue of Gold, Two for Eyes and Ears, Three and Four for Hands of Light, Five and Six for Earthly Might."

Lives there a dexxie anywhere that doesn't know that damned verse? Who would have thought that the rhyme the six of them had concocted during a late-night study burnout would dog them for life? "Ms. McGaw, I thought you were in a hurry."

"I admire you. You helped mold my profession."

"You're confusing a set of circumstances with the person who lived through them. That's a common mistake, a dangerous one, one that a woman in your position can't afford to make."

"I—" McGaw sat back, the blear in her eyes slowly sharpening. "Angie Wyle's a friend of mine. We had a long talk about you last winter, before she headed off to Guernsey. She said you were different from the others." She shifted uncertainly. "Please call me Roni." It sounded more a plea than a request. She sat forward, elbows on desk, and covered her face with her hands. "Hurry. Yes. Where does one start? Audits brought me the letter a week ago and asked me to scan it. The first time my 'pack balked, I figured the mirrors needed cleaning, so I cleaned them. The second time it balked, I switched out filters and lenses. The third time, I thought the brain had suffered some sort of tissue damage, so I called in a friend from Commerce to check it out. My 'pack was fine, of course, so I asked him to scan the letter. That's when all hell broke loose."

"Why?" Jani spread her hands in question. "You should have let Labs check it out. A chip can hang up for many reasons. Oxidation. Degree of protein crosslinking. You always have some, but sometimes you can exceed the critical limit, and you're left with a worthless chip that scans like garbage."

Roni's head came up. "That's what I wanted to do, but Peter Lescaux wandered in. He had heard I had called in someone from Commerce on a consult, and he thought I was giving away the Family jewels. He hates to share." She snorted. "I told him not to fly off to Derringer until I had time to go over the letter with Forensics, but he saw a chance to make points with Service Diplo. God knows why." She lowered her hands, then let them drop to her desk. "He's always jumping the starter, always trying to come off like the big shot Exterior mover-and-groover. Little bastard sows chaos wherever he goes."

Jani thought of Lescaux's wide-open face. The earnest questions. *Save us, Lord, from simple, uncomplicated ambition.*

"I don't believe he let you scan it. He made us all look like *fools.*" Roni fell back in her chair; the ergoworks hummed and squeaked. "I'm still waiting for the quality records for that batch of initiators. If they were manufactured near the upper cross-link limit, and the document resided in an uncontrolled environment for too long, that could be the answer."

"There's another possibility." Jani paused to look around the large office. Expensive hardwood furnishings, befitting a department chief. The requisite potted plants inhabiting the corners. Windows facing the lake. Holos adorning the walls. Roni's diploma from Chicago Combined. Nice, normal surroundings, inappropriate to the discussion. *We should have met someplace else—I should have insisted.* She hated the walls, and what could be hidden within. "What if the errors weren't accidents? What if they were purposely put in place to toss a stinkbomb in the midst of human-idomeni relations?" She took a deep breath, and opened a door she would have preferred to keep closed. "Why didn't you want to talk in front of Lucien? He's been out of Exterior for months, and he left under a cloud. You've nothing to fear from him."

"He works for the competition. He probably knows about this letter."

Yes, well he might. The fact that he didn't mention the fact to Jani . . . well, Lucien adhered to his own pattern of consistency. "Peter apparently consults him on a regular basis."

Roni rolled her eyes. "That's a pair—the ventriloquist and his dummy. Peter opens his mouth, and Lucien's words pop out."

Jani examined Roni's face for some sign she joked, but saw only tight-lipped disgust. "I didn't realize they had known one another that well."

"Lucien met Peter during some colonial assignment a little over a year ago. He's the one who introduced him to Anais. Groomed him to succeed, as it were." Roni's gaze moved to her windowed view. "Lucien may have departed Exterior officially last winter, but in too many ways, it's as though he never left. If you told me that he had something to do with this letter, I wouldn't be at all surprised."

Jani pulled her duffel onto her lap and fiddled with the straps to give her hands something to do. "One thing I know beyond doubt is that Lucien finds the idomeni fascinating, and anything he finds fascinating he lets live." She spoke as much to convince herself as Roni. "I don't believe he'd do anything to damage our relations with the Shèrá worldskein."

"I think he'd break anything just to see what would happen." A touchlock clicked as Roni opened one of her desk drawers. "I tried to research his life once. He had . . . come between me and someone I was very fond of, and I wanted to do something, *anything,* to sabotage his relations with Anais."

Jani nodded. She had done a little research into Lucien's background herself. Her reasons were less personal, nothing more than the fact that turning over rocks had become her habit long ago. "He was born in Reims, in the northern French province." Given the nature of the documents she had uncovered, she had gotten to the heart of the matter rather quickly. "His bioemotional deficiencies began causing real problems as he entered his teens. Luckily for him, that's when Anais came along and persuaded his parents to consign him to her care."

Roni's jaw dropped. "You found out a hell of a lot more than I did!"

"Friends in high places." Jani paused, recalling Val Parini's shouted description of the penalties for cracking sealed juvenile court records.

"I came up against brick wall after brick wall. Anais finally called me into her office one day and ordered me to cease and desist. Even she acted nervous." Roni hesitated. "What I'm trying to say is . . . he has a past worth hiding, and that begs the question of what he's gotten up to in the present." She held up a documents slipcase. "And, unfortunately, all I have to go on is this letter, purportedly from the idomeni ambassador, and I don't know how to make it tell me what I need to know."

Jani eyed the slipcase, which had a smooth finish rather than pebbled. "That's The Nema Letter."

Roni nodded. "Peter commented that you took exception to the rough finish of the slipcase you saw yesterday. You were correct, of course. We've been using them for, oh, two months now, and our Doc Repair hours have tripled. You can't stack the damned things—the pebbles push into and damage any insert they touch. I memoed Purchasing about them myself, but we buy them from one of Her Excellency's companies. I may as well spit into a hurricane." She pushed aside a pile, then extracted the letter and placed it in the cleared space. "I've taken to switching them out myself on the sly."

"I didn't get the chance to scan farther than the initiator chip." Jani removed her scanpack from her bag and activated it, then set the bag and the scanpack on the desk as she dragged her chair closer. "I want to—"

The office door opened, helped along by several Security guards. Two entered, splitting off like demiskimmers in formation and circling to either side of the desk. Two remained outside, bracketing the door like statuary.

Then Lescaux strode in, hands locked behind his back.

"Peter!" Roni shot to her feet. "How bloody dare you!"

Lescaux walked up to the desk and rooted through Jani's duffel. "How bloody dare you let this woman on the premises without clearing it with me." He picked up the top file, read the title tab, then shoved it back inside.

"You have no jurisdiction here!"

"I have every jurisdiction when I feel the security of the Commonwealth is at risk."

"Anais is going to hear about this."

"Anais is behind me one hundred percent."

As the argument waged around her, Jani eyed the letter, sitting like a holiday plum in the middle of Roni's desk. She then glanced at the guards, who deserved note mostly for their height and musculature. *If I made a grab for the letter, it would be a race to see which one broke my arm first.* Odds were square that they'd break her left arm, and she'd be inconvenienced only for the time it took John to switch out a new limb. Even a right break would put her out of commission for no more than a few hours. *Wouldn't solve the essential problem, though.* Namely, how to get the letter off Roni's desk and into her duffel.

"—trumped-up little bastard!" Roni's breathing had gone ragged from rage. "Aryton at Registry will hear about this, you can be damned sure!"

Dolly? Yes, Five of Six did work at Registry, didn't she? Registry Inspector General, so her title went. Pretty much ran the place. Jani hadn't tried to contact her since she'd settled in the city. They had gotten along well enough at Academy, but between work and health, there just hadn't been time.

"Dorothea Aryton is a good Family woman. She will not involve herself in matters of state"—Lescaux shot a disgusted look at Jani—"unlike some documents examiners I could name."

Roni braced her hands on the edge of her desk and leaned forward. "Listen, Beddy Boy—"

"It's all right, Ms. McGaw." Jani stowed her scanpack and rearranged the files Lescaux had muddled. "Just return me my sample docs, and I'll be on my way."

Roni proved at that moment that she could have guarded the third baseline for any professional baseball team in the Commonwealth. Her eyes lit with anger-fueled glee. "Of course, Ms. Kilian. I appreciate your . . . understanding." She plucked a few random documents off the top of one of her piles, then stacked them together with The Nema Letter and tucked them into the substitute slipcase that Jani hoped and prayed Lescaux hadn't seen before. "I appreciate you taking the time to consult with me on this matter." With steady hand and steely countenance, she held out the case to Jani.

Jani took her time tucking the slipcase into her duffel. She made sure the guards could see everything she did, and didn't move too quickly or stealthily. She shut the bag and shouldered it. Her heart beat slowly. Her hands felt dry. The twitchiness in her limbs vanished as augie took the controls.

She turned, and walked to the door.

"Hold it!"

Jani pulled up. *Oh well.* Roni had shown unexpected nerve, which probably signaled the end of her career at Exterior. But she'd find another job—Jani would help—

Lescaux stepped between her and the door. Anger firmed the line of his jaw and chilled his eyes, strengthening his resemblance to Lucien. "The affidavit, if you please."

Jani looked down quickly. "Of course, Mr. Lescaux." She undid the clasps of her duffel and picked through the files until she came upon the familiar pebbled slipcase. She removed it from the stack, handed it to Lescaux, and closed her bag.

"I should have expected this from you, considering our last conversation." He tucked the file under his arm and stepped to the side. "This was not the time for cheap dirty tricks."

Jani departed the office. Two of the guards preceded her. Two brought up the rear. She waited for the pound of footsteps from behind, the shout for her to once more *"Hold it!"* But the only steps she heard were those of the guards, and her own easy stride.

She walked through the lobby. Out the door and down the drive. Her heart tripped as she approached the sensor fence and it struck her that Exterior might lock-chip its documents and that third baseman McGaw hadn't had the chance to perform an unlock. But she passed through the sensors with nary a blip or beep.

The rear guard peeled off as Jani mounted the steps to the L platform. The lead pair stayed, bookending her silently as she waited, and remained on the platform until she boarded and the train pulled away.

Jani sat, still and silent, duffel cradled in her lap. She studied the other passengers, on the alert for someone who sat too close or looked at her for a little too long. After a time, she lowered her bag to the floor and opened it. Using the blip scanner she had secreted in the scanproof compartment, she checked the letter and slipcase for any tags, collars, or leashes. The testing proved negative, to her relief. She would have hated to ditch the valuable document beneath the seat if she had found an attached sensor, but she also had no intention of allowing Exterior to track her every waking move.

She then checked the soles of her shoes. Roni's office had been carpeted, and carpets could transfer all kinds of nasty things. Most people knew enough to search their pockets, the cuffs of the trousers, their hair. But they seldom checked their shoes.

After assuring herself of bug-free status, Jani disembarked at the next stop. She then waited for three trains to depart before boarding the fourth, a local that stopped at every lamppost. She rode it past her Armour Place stop, into the heart of the shopping district, getting off with the bulk of the passengers at the station across from a large mall.

She used the main entrance, taking care to stay with the crowd. Boarded the lift, hit the pad for the fourth floor, and got off on the third. Hurried to the nearest bathroom and shut herself in a stall. Only then did she sag against the wall, and pound her fist into her open hand.

CHAPTER 10

Jani wandered the mall to kill time, and surprised herself by actually committing *purchase*. She visited a religious shop, and pored over the shelves of figurines until she found her Lord Ganesha. The statuette she chose stood about ten centimeters high. The four-armed elephant sat upon a lotus throne, a mouse at his feet. He held a lasso in one hand, and wore a gold-weave snake around his waist.

Remove the obstacles that impede my mission, Lord, I pray. Jani cradled the Ganesha in her arms as she roamed the store. She picked a brass bowl to hold offerings, and a teakwood pedestal to serve as an altar. The size and weight of the pedestal precluded her carrying it with her, so she arranged to have everything delivered unto Hodge's sterling care.

She bewildered herself even more with the next items she bought. She didn't like shopping for clothes. Her business attire copied the uniform style she'd grown used to in the Service—conservative in color, severe in cut. Casual clothes were anything she could talk Lucien into scrounging for her from Service stores.

And then there were *nice* clothes, the evening dresses that John Shroud sent her in the unfulfilled hope that she would wear them in his company. Murderously expensive confections all, perfectly fitted and exquisitely shaded. She had yet to wear any of them, despite Lucien's assurances that he was more than willing to act as dresser.

I don't like to dress up. Even so, she couldn't tear away from the display of saris. The one that claimed her attention shone blue-green as sunlit seas, bordered in a chainlink pattern of gold and silver threads. She finally entered the shop to inquire as to the sari's price, gasped, and bought it anyway, escalating the damage by adding the platinum-dyed short-sleeve top, wrap trousers, and slippers that completed the outfit.

I need something to wear for the folks. Her mother, Jamira, always dressed in bright colors—she said they cheered her in the Acadian cold. *This will make her happy,* Jani thought as she fingered the turquoise silk. She then followed her newly acquired habit and had everything sent to Hodge.

Just remember to scan it before you bring it inside the flat. Jani made that note to herself as she settled into a comport booth in one of the public stands that dotted the mall. She'd determined by her many passes through the area that no one had followed her from Exterior. Now she dug an untraceable credit chit—the sort one could buy from a vend machine—from her pocket, ran it through the comport pay slot, and punched in a code.

A prim young face appeared on the display. "Registry?"

"Aryton, please."

The young woman stared. "You're—"

"Yes." Jani forced a smile.

"I'll . . . tell . . ." The desk emitted a tight little sigh as the display blanked.

Jani picked through the files in needless confirmation of the presence of The Nema Letter. "Bet she knows the words to that damned poem, too."

The display came up again, more quickly than she'd hoped.

"Jan?" Dorothea Aryton looked out at her with the solemn quizzicality that Hansen Wyle had christened "Juno rising." "My God." She still wore her thick black hair bound in a head-wrapping braid. Sharp Family bones, broadened more than usual across the cheekbone and brow, served as frame for clear blue eyes. Her skin had tanned red-brown from a summer of outdoor activity. Sailracing, if Jani remembered correctly. A risky sport for the seasonal amateur, but Dolly had always been willing to skirt the edges when they lived on Shèrá. Apparently, that still held true.

Apparently.

"You look . . . a different sort of person." Dolly squinted, grooving the skin around her eyes. Her voice still emerged in its own good time, drawled Virginia Provincial. "Impish, before. Now . . ." She sat back and folded her arms. "Solemn." She touched a hand to her chin. "I don't believe it."

"That it's me?"

"That you've grown solemn to match your face." Dolly pushed papers about her desk. "We've waited for you to call. Carson and I.

He heads NUVA-SCAN Fraud, you know. Right down the street from Registry. We're the only others in town. Ennegret manages the Family money in London, and Gina consults out of Jo'burg." Her hand stilled. "You're calling from a public place."

Jani exhaled with a rumble. She'd forgotten Dolly's charming habit of approaching from all sides at once. "Yes."

"You always did." Dolly smiled, a minute shallowing along the corner of her mouth. "And I'm doing all the talking, as ever and always."

"I received a notice that there's a problem with one of my position filings." Jani tilted her head to the left as she held out her right hand, palm open and facing down. A Laum gesture, signifying grave worry. "If you have the time, I'd like to discuss it with you."

Dolly's eyes narrowed. The pleading inherent in the gesture didn't match the sort of routine document dispute Jani described. "I have some time now, as it happens."

"Allow me fifteen minutes." Jani gathered her gear, then paused and looked back at the display. "How's Cairn?"

"She's well, thank you." Dolly smiled again, winter-cool. "Social niceties discharged, Jani Kilian. You can come out now." The display blanked, leaving Jani to stare at the fading blue-to-grey.

Afternoon commuters filled the train—Jani switched her duffel from one shoulder to the other so she could change her grip on the overhead strap. Her back bothered her enough that she would have preferred sitting, but the standing view served her better. She stood near the rear of the car and monitored every embark and debark, watched every head and action. She imagined Nema's letter growing heavier in her bag with each passing minute, and wondered how well Roni could lie when pressed. If Lescaux possessed any wit at all, he would have wanted to reassure himself of the letter's presence immediately after ordering Jani off Exterior property. That meant Roni would have had to stall. *Straddle that third base line, McGaw*. What Jani planned to do, she could complete in a few hours. After that, let Lescaux track her down.

The train slowed. Stopped. Jani pushed along with the crush, shifting her duffel so she could guard it by holding it against her chest, grabbing at the handrails to keep from falling as her right knee grew wobbly.

The Registry resided on LaSalle Street, in a silvery glass tower that possessed the smooth, featureless surfaces of refrozen ice. Jani pushed through the nonscan front entry into the skylit lobby, then immediately veered to the right and palmed through another set of doors that funneled down a narrow hallway. As the doors swept aside, she saw Dolly Aryton standing at the hall's far end, distant smile still in place.

"Prompt, as always. Hansen always said he trusted you more than any timepiece." The reserve cracked as she watched Jani walk toward her. She folded her arms and touched a fist to her chin—the contact turned to tapping that became faster and faster as the distance between them shortened. "My God."

"You already said that, Doll."

"Then I'll say it again. My God." Dolly looked Jani up and down, ticking off the differences between the woman with whom she'd schooled and the one that stood before her now. "It suits you, though. It hides. Gives the impression that you are what you're not." She took a step back—she wore trousers and wrap shirt in an autumnal shade of melon, and the flowing material swept around her wrists and ankles. "Collected. Contained."

Jani suppressed a sharp comment. Her back griped from the walk, and she was in no mood for Dolly's pronouncements. "I *am* collected and contained."

"If you insist." Dolly took a step closer, her gaze fixed on the top of Jani's head. "You're taller than I am now."

"Yes." Jani stared until Dolly arched her brow and backed away.

"As I said, Carson and I have been waiting for you to call." Dolly turned and walked up the hall toward the lift-bank, gesturing for Jani to follow. "Now you have. Since we both know you're not the sentimental sort, to what do I owe this reunion?"

Jani realized protest would be futile. Dolly had pegged her during their comport conversation—it was one of her more disconcerting talents. *Business. I'm here for business. That's all I ever had in common with you and Carson, and Gina, and Ennie.* Only the long-dead Hansen had been a friend. *You others are just people I used to know.* She followed Dolly into the lift car and waited for the doors to close. "It's Nema."

Dolly frowned. "I understand he's having a hard time working with Shai."

"It's gone beyond that. I believe Shai and Cèel are trying to force him from office."

"That's *our* style. The idomeni don't operate that way."

"I think they're starting to learn."

Dolly appeared to stare at the floor indicator, but Jani could detect the far-off look in her eyes, the telltale sign of a wicked turn of thought. "You think Nema's in danger."

"Yes, I do—" The lift decelerated, and Jani grabbed the railing as her head rocked and a wave of chills shook her. *What the hell's wrong now!* Maybe she should have eaten at the mall. Maybe her second dance with augie neared its finale, signaling the end to her ability to concentrate. Or maybe yet another new wrinkle had developed in her ever-changing physical state.

"Are you all right?" Dolly moved toward her, voice mellow with concern.

Jani hurried out of the lift as soon as the door opened and ducked into a furnished alcove. "Dolly, I may not have much time." She lowered into a chair and dropped her bag over the side. "I need a vacuumbox, a full set of tools, and access to paper and chips. I need . . . a copier."

Dolly crouched in front of her. She pressed a hand to Jani's forehead, then to her cheek. "You're *freezing*. You need a doctor."

"I'm used to it—it will pass!" Jani grabbed Dolly's wrist and yanked her hand away from her face. She didn't think she squeezed that hard—why did Dolly wince? "I have a lot to do and not much time in which to do it. Someone is depending on me—I need to get started now."

Dolly straightened smoothly, like the athlete she was. "You want to copy a document, then alter the copy." Her dulcet voice hardened. "You want to fake—"

"The thing I've got is a fake. I just want to make another fake with a few differences. Then I want to feed it back into play and watch where the alarms sound."

Dolly turned away and walked across the alcove to the picture window behind them. She considered the view as precious seconds ticked by. "I look out this window, eighty floors above the streets of Chicago, but what I see is the Rauta Shèràa Consulate courtyard. I can feel the summer's raw heat through the glass. I expect to see Laumrau skimmers float into view, and watch the Laumrau walk and gesture again. Hear their loopy voices." She pressed her palms against the pane. "All because you show up in rough clothes with a bag on your shoulder and a wild story about Nema. You look different, yet the same, and anyone who doubted your identity would know you as soon as you opened your mouth. Always scamming. Always feeding back. Always looking for alarms." She turned. Her face held sadness and frustration. "That war is over, and this one, if this is indeed one, is none of your business."

Jani hoisted her duffel onto her lap. It dragged like lead. "I need your help."

"This is Registry. We're supposed to *stop* what you want to do."

"I only have a few hours."

"You're not listening."

"*Neither are you.* I want to replace what I believe to be a fake with another fake. A double-reverse. Registry investigators do it all the time when they suspect documents fraud and they want to traceback."

"You have no jurisdiction."

Jani tried to stand. Her head rocked. "Maybe Carson will help me. You said he's down the street at NUVA-SCAN?" She tried to grab the chair arms for balance, missed, and fell back.

Dolly's hands flew to her face. "You never grew up, did you? You just got older!" She cut around furniture and hurried to her side. "What is the matter with you!"

Jani struggled to a half-crouch, then slowly rose. "I need a vacuumbox, tools, a copier, and access to supplies. I came here because I knew that you'd have it all at the ready."

Dolly grabbed her arm to help support her. "You're in no condition—"

Jani pressed a hand to her stomach, and felt as well as heard the grumble. "Get me food. Chili. Curry. Something spicy. No milk or cheese. Bread—bread is good, but no butter. And coffee." She looked into her old schoolmate's eyes, and saw the anger and the aggravation. *"Dolly. Please."* She tried to get the sense of the sailracer, to find the wedge that would win her the opening she needed. "One thing you must admit, Dorothea Aryton, grubby, raving thing that I was—"

"I never said grubby or—"

"—is that on those hot summer days at the Rauta Shèràa Consulate, the one thing I never did was waste your time."

Something flickered in Dolly's eyes. Not a softening—never that, not between them. A touch of memory, maybe. Of jobs done well, and more importantly, of those left undone. She gripped Jani's arm more firmly, positioning herself so that they could walk side-by-side. "The Registry cannot support you if this backfires."

Jani almost sagged with relief, but stopped herself. Dolly wouldn't be a sure sale until the job was done, and she couldn't allow her any excuse to back out. "Of course not."

They started down the hall toward the workrooms. As they passed a sealed door, Jani caught the sulfurous rank of the nutrient tanks, where the new scanpack brains grew and developed. Her empty stomach turned.

With moves practiced on sailboards throughout the Commonwealth, Dolly countered her sag and struggled to hold her steady. "I'm taking you to the hospital."

"Fine. But not until I'm done."

Jani braced her feet on her lab chair crossbar and balanced her plate on her knees. The curried chicken with peanut sauce had cleared her head marvelously. She sopped up the remains of the sauce with bread, then washed it down with coffee that rivaled John Shroud's for punch and depth. She looked down to the far end of the lab bench, where Dolly leaned in skeptical examination, and raised her cup. "My compliments to your kitchen."

"Thank you." Dolly straightened as the door opened and two techs entered pushing laden skimcarts. "Put them here." She led them to benches on the opposite side of the large laboratory, and helped them unload the cart contents onto the benchtops.

Jani set her plate aside and eased off the seat. Her internal choppy seas had calmed—no more lightheadedness, and she felt stronger. She picked up her duffel and walked across the lab to where Dolly oversaw the unloading. "Got anything that can scan idomeni paper?"

Dolly shrugged halfheartedly. "We have some prototypes, but nothing I'd stake my rating on. Every document we get from them self-destructs when we try to crack it." She gave Jani a look of calculated disinterest. "We've begun to work with Neoclona to develop a scanpack that can read both types of chips. John's been very helpful."

"Has he?"

"Yes. We talk about you on occasion. I'm surprised you have trouble with him—I've always found him quite easy to work with."

He doesn't perceive you as a professional threat and he doesn't love you. Congrats—you've got the best of both worlds. Jani dropped her duffel onto a benchtop and opened it. She removed The Nema Letter, but left it in its slipcase as the techs unloaded the last of the equipment, killing time by leafing through the other documents Roni had given her in the hope they might prove interesting. Unfortunately, they turned out to be face pages and forewords from unrelated reports, dross and decoy only.

After the techs departed, she slid the heavy parchment out of the protective cover and lay it on the counter. "Some factions in Service and the government think Nema composed this document, which warns us against allowing the Haárin to continue to infiltrate the colonies. They take it as a sign that he'd like to serve as our agent."

"I gather I should keep this information to myself?" Dolly removed an elegant pair of wire-rimmed magnispecs from the pocket of her wrapshirt and put them on. "I don't believe it. Nema couldn't keep his mouth shut long enough to pull off a subterfuge like that." She picked up the document by the barest edges and eyed it from all angles. "Humans did this."

"Agreed. I'm worried, though, that if Shai and Cèel learn this letter exists, they'll use it as an excuse to recall Nema whether they think he compiled it or not. If they choose to regard it as a Laum–Knevçet Shèràa-scale treachery, they may take a more drastic step than mere recall. They may just kill him and be done with it." Jani removed the letter from Dolly's grasp, then moved down the bench toward a large rectangular instrument that looked like a handscanner with a lid. "So this is the devil's device?"

"The latest iteration." Dolly pushed her magnispecs atop her head, then slid aside the copier lid and pondered her reflection in the black glass surface. "Officially, it doesn't exist. Unofficially, we don't talk about it." She cast Jani a hard look. "And you treat it like just another tool in the tray."

"That's because it is." Jani nudged Dolly aside and laid the letter ink-side down on the copier surface. "How long does the duplication take?"

"Anywhere from fifteen minutes to five hours, depending on the complexity of the document." Dolly lowered the lid, then touched the side panel. Slivers of white light shone through hairline gaps in the seal. "First pass, it types the paper strata. Then it moves to inks, then foils. Those are easy—five minutes, tops."

"Then comes the fun." Jani watched as the color and intensity of the light slivers changed. Blazing blue. Dark red. An almost invisible green. "Reading the types of imbedded chips and identifying their settings."

"Assuming they'll let themselves be read." Dolly dragged over a lab chair and sat. "Proprietary paper locks this thing up like a dream. It knows a chip is there, but it can't read it, and it pitches a fit. Buzzes. Jams. Lights start blinkin'." She smoothed a well-manicured hand over the sleeve of her shirt. "I christened it 'Jani' some time ago."

"Thanks." Jani pulled over a chair, positioning it so she could watch the copier's every flash and flutter. "What would you say if I told you that the chips embedded in this document contain seventeen separate discrepancies, all of which make scanpacks scream aloud?"

"This copier is capable of error analysis. It should be able to untangle the snarl and define the problem when all a scanpack can do is tell you you're outside variance. What that implies to me is that whoever constructed this document never believed it would see the inside of Registry, which I find interesting considering the magnitude of the matter." Dolly plucked a pair of pinch-grips from the tool tray, and regarded them thoughtfully. "If you were out . . . in the field, how long would it take you to manufacture a copy like this?"

Euphemisms, euphemisms. "The class of criminal I worked with—" Jani stopped as Sasha's face formed in her mind. *You were never better than you had to be, Kilian—never forget that.* "I wouldn't have been able to. I couldn't access gear like this. I didn't work at the organized crime level. An exact copy of even a simple deed could take me weeks. Exact placement of chips and inserts is a bitch without a 3-D field array marking the positions. I'd have to do my best with my scanpack and a handheld measuring device. That's why low-level scams involve altering existing paper. Building a document from scratch is hard enough. Making an identical copy is beyond the capacity of most forgers unless they have access to something like this copier."

"Interesting." Dolly still concentrated her attention on the pinch-grips. "Carson mentioned to me just last week that your varied experiences made you a valuable resource. He asked that if I ran into you first, I should tell you that there's a position at NUVA-SCAN with your name on it."

Jani tried to visualize herself in a staid corporate conference room, surrounded by Family types. "Hmm."

"Here, too."

That brought Jani up short. She turned to Dolly to find her still enraptured by the pinch-grips. "Really?"

"We here at Registry nurse a fondness for the criminal mind. Saves training." Dolly looked up as the colored lights dimmed and a length of tissue-thin fiche spun out of the copier. "Well, that was fast. It's already time for the second act." She picked up the fiche and studied it. "Colony-sourced paper." She glanced at Jani. "Does Acadia tie into this at all?"

The home of L'araignée. "It might." She joined Dolly benchside. "Commercial or government-class?"

"Commercial. Fairly recent dating—early summer." Dolly walked across the lab to one of the wall-spanning cabinets, fiche in hand, and opened it to reveal shelf upon shelf filled with niche after niche of virgin paperstock. She pulled down her magnispecs so she could read the printed labels on the topmost shelves, then reached up and removed a single piece of parchment from one of the niches. "I doubt it would be government. Even if a Ministry is behind this, you wouldn't expect them to play quite so obvious a hand as to use their own paper, would you?"

"I would have expected them to cut to the chase and use idomeni paper. Nema would have used idomeni paper. Whoever planned this tried to be too clever." Jani stood up to watch as Dolly fed the sheet into a slot on the copier's side.

"The chips and foils are stored inside—saves on oxidative wear and tear." Dolly watched the paper disappear into the slot. Then she handed Jani the fiche with the air of a stern teacher returning a below-average grade. "In a few minutes, you will have an exact copy of your not-very-complicated letter." Her voice dropped an accusing half-tone. "Then it will be your turn, to do whatever it is that you do."

Jani perused the discrepancies the copier had listed. "Looks like Jani Junior had problems with the initiator chip, just like my scan-pack did. Can't define the error, though. Same with the others."

Dolly leaned back against her seat and folded her arms. "If those *are* idomeni chips loaded in that paper, then Jani Junior won't be able to read them. It will know that something is awry with the coding, but because of the differences between the idomeni proteins and ours, it won't be able to define the differences. I have no idomeni standards to load into Junior—I can't give it anything to compare to."

"That's been the problem with this all along." Jani picked through the UV styli scattered throughout the assorted trays. "The only way to prove this is indeed an idomeni document is to have an idomeni documents examiner scan it, and no one I've been working with wants that to happen because they don't want Shèrá to know what's going on."

"Convenient, that. You can construct as loopy a document as you want because no one who knows which end is up is ever going to get their hands on it to check it out." Dolly shifted restlessly. "So what are you going to do?"

"It shouldn't take long." Jani held the styli in her fist like a child gripping her coloring pens, and waited for the freshly imprinted document to emerge from the copier. "A shot here. A shot there." She let the paper slide onto her open palm, then walked down the bench to the vacuumbox. "The time-date stamp is still untouched. So's the counter chip that records the number of scans." Jani glanced at Dolly. "Would it count the copy as a scan?"

Dolly nodded. "Possibly."

"Then it fries." Jani slipped the document into the vacuumbox slot, tucked the styli in the box's access drawer, then stuck her hands in the gloves that would allow her to manipulate the materials in the vacuum. "And I bake the Environmental Variant."

Dolly's eyes slowly widened. "You're going to make the discrepancies look like a Brandenburg Progession."

"Yup." Jani positioned the document in the center of the vacuumbox platform, then looked through the lens array so she could visualize both the chips she needed to hit and the beams of UV light she needed to hit them with. "A prionic mutation that's initiated by broad-spectrum UV damage and eventually spreads throughout the document, rendering it unscanable."

"Those are extremely rare." Dolly closed in beside her. "And the mutation proceeds at a well-defined rate, hence the name."

"How many dexxies have seen one, do you think?" Jani chose one of the styli and activated it. "A real Progression, not the idealized deterioration they teach in school." She directed the thread-thin beam at the time-date chip. *Light . . . hit!* "After this gets out, you may get a few panicked calls. Professional reputations at stake, and all that." She activated the second stylus and directed it at the counter chip. *Light . . . hit!*

"I can stall, I suppose." Dolly's voice held a dubious edge.

"They'll fall all over themselves for a few days in the excitement of it all, before one of them cottons on that they may have been had." Jani zeroed in on the environmental chip. *Light . . . hit!* "And a few days should be more time than I need."

"For?"

"For 'Gotcha.' " Jani pulled out of the vacuumbox, then removed the styli and documents from the transfer drawers. "That special moment that we who have never grown up enjoy so much." She slid the faked Nema Letter into the smooth Exterior slipcase with the other documents and tucked the slipcase into her duffel. She felt wonderfully vigorous and alive now, in a way that seemed improbable only a half-hour before.

Then she turned to Dolly, found that grave countenance regarding her sadly, and felt the joy crack.

"I think I should keep this. It'll give me a chance to run some of the hybrid prototypes through their paces." Dolly slid the original letter into a Registry slipcase. The silvery surface caught the room light and flashed back stars. "Unless I find something, we won't be able to prove beyond doubt that those chips are not idomeni in origin. Nema may have worked out something like this to make sure all roads led back to him—are you willing to bet your 'pack that he isn't involved?"

Jani shouldered her bag. "I think . . ." The new letter felt as heavy as the old—she imagined Roni's growing panic weighing it down. "I think that if Nema realized how Shai and Cèel are working to cut him off, he would try something like this. And he'd fail. And he'd be executed by year's end." She checked her timepiece—she needed to go. But an explanation was owed, and she needed to provide it. "He suspects something is wrong. That's one reason I'm working so fast. I've made him promise to behave until I tell him it's all clear, but you remember how he was."

"Yes." Dolly fingered the edge of the slipcase. "I never liked him."

"I know." Jani turned to leave. "Therein the insurmountable difference between thee and me."

Jani deflected Dolly's insistence that she go to hospital with vague noises about an appointment to see John. Dolly threatened to follow up with a call of her own to her new work partner. Jani knew she'd be well away before her lie was discovered, so she responded with a cheery "go ahead."

She traveled home via the usual assortment of Ls and peoplemovers. She had overshot her self-allotted few hours, and knew Roni must be feeling the brunt of all Lescaux could bring to bear. *Whatever that is.* She didn't like him and that alone made her wary of him, since she seldom disliked a person without reason. *Even if that reason is that he's Lucien's twin, seen through a distorted mirror?* She clucked her tongue. *My, aren't we the philosophical one?*

She disembarked the last 'mover two blocks from home because her thigh muscles had cramped and she knew exercise would loosen them. She kept a brisk pace, and turned onto Armour Place to the loud pops of fastener guns and the hum of machinery as the construction crew within the renovation continued their labors.

She spotted Roni McGaw near the renovation entry, standing apart from the small crowd that had gathered to watch workers unload metal framework from a flatbed skimmer. As soon as Roni saw Jani, she turned in the opposite direction and walked, a slow, relaxed pace. She proceeded for half a block, then entered a small bookstore, successfully resisting any urge she may have felt to look behind to see if Jani followed.

By the time Jani entered the bookstore, Roni had already settled in front of a rack of audio wafers. Jani fingered through a bin of new releases until she found a collection of pop songs. She added a holozine so that they would be forced to give her a large sack to carry them in, and headed for the checkout.

Roni got in line behind her. She held an audio wafer as well, supplemented with another holozine the same size as Jani's.

Jani paid for her purchases with a nontrace chit. As she walked through the store to the exit, she picked through the outer pockets of her duffel as though she searched for something. Finally, she crouched on the floor and opened her duffel, picking through the folders. She tucked the sack in amid the folders, sliding the slipcase containing the faked Nema letter deftly between the pages of the holozine. Then she pulled the sack out again, as though she'd changed her mind.

As she straightened, she felt an elbow impact her shoulder. She dropped her duffel and bag to the floor.

"Oh Christ!" Roni didn't even look her in the face as she bustled about picking up bags. Jani barely caught the switch, so deftly did Roni obscure matters with the flaps of her jacket and general dithering. Then she was gone, out the door, the bag with the faked letter clutched to her chest, leaving Jani with a holozine about birds and, she was pleased to see, a copy of the Mussorgska she'd been meaning to buy for weeks.

Jani felt the adrenaline ebb for the third time that day as she trudged back to her building. She recovered her deliveries from Hodge, and scanned everything in the hall before opening her door. Even the parcel from Roni. Even the soles of her shoes.

She yawned as she entered her flat. She set everything aside but the Mussorgska, which she inserted into her audio system. Then she stretched out on the floor beside her desk, and shoved her duffel under her head to serve as a pillow. A nap before dinner with Steve and Angevin was a necessity if she wanted to avoid pitching face-forward onto her plate. As the strings swelled around her, she closed her eyes and pondered Roni's surprising competence, and the possibilities of alarms.

CHAPTER 11

Tsecha walked the embassy grounds, in the hope that exercise would soothe him. He felt disquiet when he remained in the embassy, a sense that things went on of which he did not know. So many humanish whom he had never before seen. So many meetings that he heard of *after* they had taken place.

It was one thing to refuse to go to the damned meetings. It was another to know you were not wanted.

But my Jani wishes me to wait. For what? *Until it is safe.* And what did that mean? *She does not trust me to tell me.* No one trusted him anymore, so it seemed, and truly.

"I am Égri niRau Tsecha. Representative of the Shèrá worldskein and Chief Propitiator of the Vynshàrau." So he spoke to the grass and the trees, which paid him as much attention as did any in the embassy. Even his Sànalàn had not wished him a glorious day, as she had each morning since her investiture.

He strode past the main building, the annexes, the row upon row of greenhouses and food storage facilities. Gradually, his step quickened and his stride widened, as though he could outdistance his worries if he tried. The pound of his feet striking the ground jarred along his spine and shook him to the teeth. His old joints protested the abuse, but he denied their plea, and picked up his pace even more.

Across the brilliant blue-green hybrid ground cover. Past the utilities huts. Through the barrier parks that sheltered the embassy property from the view of the neighboring Interior Ministry.

Tsecha broke through the last line of trees and stopped atop the rise to recover his breath. Below him lay the boundary area just inside the perimeter security stations that served as the dividing line between Vynshàrau and humanish. He surveyed the scattering of lowform structures that dotted the sequestration. *Our own place between the lines.* The compound where the Vynshàrau Haárin lived.

Tsecha took a step forward, then hesitated as a male emerged from one of the houses carrying a large bucket.

It is Sànalàn's tormenting tilemaster. Dathim Naré had removed his head cover. He had also exchanged his dull work uniform for a shirt that blazed blue as clear sky and trousers as green as humanish lawns, colors of the sky and sea more common to the southland-dwelling Pathen than the desert Vynshàrau. In spite of the chill, he wore no overrobe. He had rolled up his shirtsleeves and turned down the cuffs of his black boots—perspiration darkened his clothes as though he had run through a rainstorm.

Tsecha watched him upturn the bucket into a debris barrel. Shards of white tile clattered into the bin, flashing sunlight like the teeth of demons.

Dathim banged the bucket against the rim of the barrel—the clang of metal on metal filled the air as white dust clouded about him like smoke. He did not see Tsecha until he turned to walk back to the house. When he did, he stopped in mid-stride, the empty bucket dangling at his side.

"Glor-ries of the day to you, Tsechar-rau!" he shouted in trilled English, as though his Chief Propitiator's appearance was a common thing, worthy of the informality.

"Glories of the day to you, ní Dathim." Tsecha strolled down the rise toward him. "A cold day, and truly. How can you tolerate such?"

The male looked down at his bare forearms. His *à lérine* scars shone dark gold-brown and waled, as though parasites burrowed beneath his skin. "Today I retile a laving room, nìRau." He reached for his belt and took an ax-tail hammer from his tool-holster. "Removing the old is hard work. Hard work warms the blood." He swung the tool through the air—the sharply pointed hammer cut the air with a whistle, while the polished blade-end slivered white light into rainbow glisten.

Tsecha watched the back and forth of the hammer with tense fascination. As the Laumrau–Vynshà civil war had neared its bloody conclusion and weapons had grown scarce, the traditional tool had helped the forces of Morden nìRau Cèel capture the dominant city of Rauta Shèràa. They had, of course, not been used during the final battle, when the Vynshà had confirmed their ascendancy to "rau" and order had again been restored to the Shèrá worldskein. The Night of the Blade had been reserved for classical swords and knives, masterpieces of godly workmanship.

But there had been other nights. . . .

"You are on patrol, nìRau?" Dathim cocked his head in the direction of the Interior Ministry as he returned the ax-hammer to his holster. "The Interiors patrol many times a day. Four, five, six times or more. They watch us as the Laum did. I think myself in the High Sands when they pass in their skimmers."

High Sands. As much as he enjoyed his English, Tsecha did not like the postureless, gestureless translation of Rauta Shèràa. It left out so much. The prayers and the blood and the pain. "You are of the Shèràa, ní Dathim?"

"Yes, nìRau." Dathim tipped his bucket and clapped the bottom, forcing out the last puff of tile dust. "We lived in the city since my body-father's body-mother's outcast. Her Haárin name was Par Tenvin. My body-father's name was Naré Par." He reattached the bucket handle, which had loosened at one end because of his pounding. "And you know who I am."

Tsecha basked in the Haárin's arrogance. After the collected silence of the embassy, it felt as the warm winds of home. "Three generations? That is not so long."

"It is for Haárin. So many have gone to the colonies that three generations is a very long time indeed." Dathim bared his teeth. "No longer three, since I am here now. In She-ca-gho."

Tsecha studied Dathim—something about his appearance bothered him, but he could not say what. Then it struck him. Dathim wore his brown hair in neither the tight napeknot of an unbred or the braided fringe of a breeder. Instead, he had sheared it as short as some humanish males, his golden scalp bare above his ears and visible beneath the spiky, brush-like growth. A stunning thing, and truly. Tsecha had heard that some colonial Haárin had taken to shearing their hair, but he never expected to find such rebellion in the embassy itself. "You like Chicago, ní Dathim?"

"Like?" Dathim offered a perfect imitation of Jani's infuriatingly vague shrug. "It is a place like any other. Humanish are strange. But where humanish are is a good place for Haárin. To them, we are as born-sect. We are all we need to be." He bared his teeth again, though not so broadly. "Unless we are not careful, and take too much of their money. Then they will find a reason to hate us. I have read of humanish, so this I know, and truly."

As they spoke, they walked down the narrow stone path that led to Dathim's house. Like the other structures in the sequestration, the smooth-sided whitestone dwelling had been built along godly lines. All the doors and windows faced the tree barrier so that no inadvertent glimpse of humanish could be seen. The yellow polywood door had been polished to smooth glossiness, the only decoration a line of cursive carved across the top. A prayer to Shiou, the goddess of order.

As Dathim pushed the door aside, Tsecha noticed a walled-off area set along the lake-facing side of the house. "You have rebuilt your veranda, ní Dathim?" He walked around the side of the house and fingered the edge of the wall. The allowed paints transported from Rauta Shèràa had been formulated for desert climates—constant exposure to the lake-tinged air caused them to mottle. Dathim's once-white wall had already stained streaky grey, but as Tsecha recalled, it took a season or more for the discoloration to form. "You rebuilt it some time ago, from the look of it, and truly."

"Yes, nìRau Tsecha." Dathim's amber eyes focused above Tsecha's head, as was seemly.

"I only gave permission for the verandas to reopen for meditation last month."

"The humanish had deeded us the Lake Michigan Strip months ago, nìRau." Dathim gestured toward the water. "All ours, lake below and sky above, from here to the eastern Michigan province. They have not been able to transport foodstuffs across that area since they made their pledge. The place became clean as soon as they made their promise."

Tsecha gestured in emphasis. "Yes, but the final purifications were only completed during the last days of the blessed heat. Oligarch Cèel decreed the verandas could not be reopened until I pronounced those closing prayers." He raised his gaze until he could see into Dathim's eyes, and savored the hard light he saw there. Different than humanish. Most easy to read.

"Oligarch Cèel is overcautious, as always," Dathim replied. "We felt it safe to rebuild." His speech had slowed so every word sounded crisp and sharp.

"We?"

Dathim pointed to the other houses, one by one. "We." His gaze dropped until he looked Tsecha in the face.

The thrill of rebellion warred with the need for order in Tsecha's soul. He pressed his hand to his stomach to quell the battle. "Someone in the embassy must have known of this. So strange, and truly, that they did not tell me."

"Shai's suborn came here. We spoke." Dathim shrugged again. "But what can they do? What can you do? We are already outcast. We have lied and stolen, behaved in ways ungodly, seen more of humanish than you ever will, and for such have already paid with our souls."

"There are other punishments, ní Dathim."

"Yes, nìRau. You can send us back to the worldskein. But if you do, you will need to find more English-speakers who can mend the plumbing and tend the lawns and go out into ungodly Chicago when poison is needed to kill Earth insects or solder is needed to bind our godly but most leaky metal conduits. No matter how much you ship and how well you think you prepare, there will always be needs to go out into this city, and that is what we are for."

Tsecha crossed his open hands, palms up, in strong affirmation. "Such has always been the contract between Vynshàrau and Haárin. As when we were of Vynshà. As it has always been."

Dathim smiled with his mouth closed, an oversubtle expression that, combined with his haircut, made him look eerily humanish. "Yes, as it has always been. In whatever life you choose, in war and in peace, we are your glove, your mask, your shield. By doing that which we do, we allow you to be what you are. Such is our cost. But in exchange for having us do what we do, you must allow us to be as we are. Such is yours."

Tsecha's shoulders rounded as his enjoyment of Dathim's insubordination gave way to irritation. No Vynshàrau knew better than he of the defiant nature of Haárin, but he had done nothing to merit this outburst. "*I* have always known this, ní Dathim. Such is no surprise to *me*."

"No," said Dathim, his shoulders rounding in response. "No surprise to you. Avrèl nìRau Nema always knew how to use his Haárin well."

Tsecha slumped more, until he had to twist his neck to the side to look up at the taller male. He should have dropped his gaze, should have stared at the center of Dathim's chest. Such was much more seemly, but such, he sensed, would not meet Dathim's challenge. And Dathim challenged him, most assuredly. *But he has no right! He has no reason!* No, yet he did so. "That name has no place between us." Tsecha's voice emerged as a low rumble. "I did not give you leave to use it."

"No." The light in Dathim's eyes brightened. "Such is for your favored humanish and those in Council and Temple who have declared themselves against you. For all else, you are called by your Sìah Haárin name. Tsecha. Fool. But you do not live as a Haárin fool." He gestured toward the tree line. "You live a most godly life on the other side."

"I am still Chief Propitiator of the Vynshàrau. As such, I live where I must."

"Convenient, is it not, and truly?" Dathim straightened his shoulders and walked to his doorway. "I am unworthy to stand before you, nìRau Tsecha. Still, I beg you to enter this place and witness my labors." He looked back. "To bless them and remove all traces of ungodliness."

Tsecha watched the tilt of Dathim's head, his open-handed gesturing. He could detect no outward sign of disrespect—the male had learned to reserve such for his speech. *How humanish of him.* "I will bless your home, ní Dathim." He followed his refractory host into the house. *Whether the gods acknowledge the request is their decision.*

As he passed through the short entry hall, Dathim touched his left hand first to a small, black-stained wooden box that hung at eye-level on the wall, then to his stomach.

A reliquary? Dathim did not seem the type. Tsecha raised his hand to mimic his host's actions, but stopped just before his fingers contacted the box's surface. The front of the device held only a single decoration, but it was most distinctive. A clenched fist, gnarled and bony, the crumbled remains of some object barely visible between the fingers.

Caith. The goddess of annihilation. The least or the most of the Vynshàrau's eight dominant deities, depending on your point of view.

"It is a most blessed relic." Dathim stood in the center of the small main room and watched Tsecha with still regard. "It is from the crater at the Sands of Light's Weeping. At the site where the asteroid impacted so long ago, the heat melted the sand to glass. That reliquary contains a shard of the glass."

"Sands of Light's Weeping." Tsecha could barely force out the English words. "Knevçet Shèràa."

"Yes, nìRau. A blessed place, and truly."

"You worship Shiou on your doorway and Caith in your home. Such opposing views are most unusual. So unusual that it is a question whether one can trust them."

"All the doors here are the same. It would make more sense to say the builder of these houses worships Shiou." Dathim thumped a fist against his stomach. "The reliquary is mine."

And this is supposed to mean what *to me!* Tsecha pressed a hand to his own stomach, not to soothe his soul but to quell the growing ache. "You vex me, Dathim."

"I do what I do, nìRau." Dathim walked to his tree-facing window and swept the curtain aside, but the northern light did little to brighten the room. "As she did what she did. Your humanish. Twenty-six

Laumrau died at the Sands of Light's Weeping. Twenty-six Laumrau with no Haárin to guard them—your Kièrshia shot them as they took sacrament in their tents."

"She did so to save her suborns. The Laumrau would have killed them if she had not acted."

"But yet they died, as well. Her suborns." Dathim tilted his head in enquiry. "We have heard that van Reuter killed them. The Family member who is now much as Haárin, outcast among his own. Do you believe such was the case?" He shrugged again when Tsecha remained silent. "Sands of Light's Weeping. The Laumrau had attained many triumphs over the Vynshà until that point. After the slaughter, the tide of the war, as the humanish say, turned." Dathim stood still and silent by the window. Then he brushed his hands across the front of his shirt as though to clean them. "Come with me, nìRau. See what I labor upon."

Tsecha trudged forward, taking care to keep his eyes focused on Dathim's back so he would not see something he should not. He had never lived in such a house, where rooms and screened barriers served the same function as entire wings did in the embassy. He had no wish to look into Dathim's kitchen. It pained him to think what he might find there.

After only a few steps, he found himself a reluctant occupant of the laving room doorway. He allowed himself a small relief as he bore witness only to cloth-covered flooring, expanses of stripped wall, and stacks of colored tile.

Then he looked at the wall behind the small sink, and stared.

The sand dunes rolled across the space as they did in his memories of home. The colors warmed him by their very presence—the pale gold of the sand, the red-brown of the shadowed troughs between the dunes, the ivory of the peaks where the relentless sun drove all color away. All manner of tile shape, from square to circle to splinter, combined to form the scene, resolving into a whole as he drew away, then fracturing into discrete scenes as he drew close. Here, a scatter of stones. There, the curve of a bird in flight.

"I will replace the glaring white of the walls with this." Dathim picked up a square of lightest sand and held it out for inspection. "And I will edge near the ceiling and the floor with the red-brown of the shadows."

As when he first saw the cava shell in the embassy, Tsecha found himself groping for words to describe the beauty of the scene. "You do not reuse the tile you broke?" he finally asked, because he did not want Dathim to know how the magnificence of his work affected him.

Dathim shook his head. “That tile was inferior. It would not take a break well—it shattered into irregular pieces. And the color was too stark. I could not make it blend with the rest. And to blend is a good thing, is it not, nìRau?”

Tsecha picked up one of the sand squares and turned it over. “There is no purity mark.” He pointed to the blank surface. “No cursive signatory of the maker. This tile is not of idomeni.”

“No, nìRau. It is humanish. I purchase it in this city.”

“How ungodly.” Tsecha spoke as to himself. “You go into the city often?”

“Yes, nìRau. After I finish my work at the embassy. I do work for others here”—he gestured in the direction of the other houses—“repairs and alterations.”

Tsecha set down the tile, his gaze drifting again to the desert scene. “It is a creation of great beauty, and truly. One who conceives such deserves the blessing of the gods.”

“To serve well is its own blessing, nìRau.” Dathim picked up an abrading cloth and wiped it across an area of the wall still rough with old grout. “I serve this task as I do my others. Every morning, before the sunrise, I join my skein-sharers in the common room behind the central utilities array.” White powder spilled at his feet, greying his trousers and coating his black boots. “It is a good place. Quiet. Not a place where born-sects deign to gather, but I am still grateful for the small shelf where I store my tools and the section of bench where I can sit.”

Damn you, Haárin! Tsecha grappled with the urge to kick at the stacks of tile and send them clattering across the room. How Dathim could beckon and repel with the same words. Offer, and then take back. *But offer what?* He did not understand. *It is the way Dathim speaks.* Yes, that was the reason for his confusion, and truly. “How did you learn your English, ní Dathim?”

“I learn by listening, nìRau.” Dathim continued to abrade the wall as he turned and looked Tsecha in the face. “I am a most accomplished listener, and truly.” The words hung in the air, then filtered down as the dust. “You call your Kièrshia ‘nìaRauta Haárin.’ ”

Tsecha sighed. “Yes.”

“It is said that she is hybridizing, changing into a not-quite-idomeni, not-quite-humanish.” The soft rasp of the cloth filled the tiny room. The stone smelled of the powder. “You have said you believe we will all be as she is, that the worlds will command us to change, that our bodies will listen to the order of the worlds, and all will be the same."

Tsecha thought of his Jani. Their discussion in the garden. The way she moved and the strangeness of her eyes. "The commands have sounded in some colonies. They take different forms. In some worlds, a sickness in the bones, in others, an ache in the soul or an inability to eat blessed foods. But our physician-priests deny the will of the gods. They name it 'environmentally induced chimerization.' They attack it as illness and drive it away."

"Environmentally induced chimerization," Dathim repeated. "The annihilation of that which is." He removed the ax-hammer from his belt. "So often have I seen you walk this place, as fast as if demons chased you, pondering your 'that which is.' " He tapped the pointed hammer end sharply against a remaining expanse of white tile. "The Elyan Haárin will no longer be allowed to do business with humanish. So says my facilities dominant." The tile cracked like thin ice—Dathim pried it from the wall with the edge of the ax-blade, and the pieces tumbled to the canvas. "But that is not what you would have, is it, nìRau? You wish that this business continue. You would even allow it to grow, would you not? You would allow us to trade freely with humanish."

Tsecha watched Dathim work, and pondered their strange conversation. The Haárin's unwarranted challenges. The way he changed subjects, which made his words as difficult to follow as Jani's at her most obscure.

Only three generations as Haárin—I would have thought many more, if this one's attitude is as that of his forebears—

Tsecha's memory opened. Dathim's words served as key. The emotions of disputation. The smell of the dust. The beauty of the sand dunes. Together, they took him back to Rauta Shèràa, and the time when he answered to his born name, and many were the Haárin who came to him.

Memories. They revealed to him how to rework Dathim's words into the old patterns, the old vows.

I, Dathim Naré, outcast by way of Naré Par, who was outcast by way of Par Tenvin, offer myself in service to you, Avrèl nìRau Nema. I am skilled in tilecraft. I know facilities, and the ways of the embassy. I can go out into the city unimpeded, because such is my purpose and my way.

I know how to speak between lines.

I know your beliefs. I, too, await the annihilation of the old ways. Cèel and Shai are of the old ways, and I owe no loyalty to them.

I know you have walked this way many times. I have seen you. I planned to call out to you, boldly and openly, the next time you walked. And so I did.

I have been waiting for you.

Tsecha felt aspects of himself that he lately set aside, rejoin. Unlike the shards on the floor, never to be mended, his own fragments reshaped, his hope, fear, and anger. His pride. The glue that held them was the awareness that he had not felt for so long. That he was Vynshàrau of Shèràa, and that a Haárin who wished to serve well had offered him his aid. "Yes, ní Dathim, I would allow you to trade freely."

"As you say, nìRau." Dathim tapped and pulled. More tile tumbled to the covered floor. "Tomorrow is my first visit to the Exterior Ministry. I must study the room in person, assess the light and the space, and decide which scene will suit Her Excellency best."

Once more, Tsecha felt the cold of the air and heard the silence of the trees. "Shai agreed to allow you to work in the Ministry?"

"Yes, nìRau. Did she not tell you?" Dathim continued to work, his back to Tsecha, his sheared head silvered in the light. "Most unseemly, that she did not inform you of such. Of course, she did not wish to let me go. But nìaRauta Ulanova can be most persuasive." More tapping. More pulling. "You would have me deliver any message, nìRau?" The soft thud of shards hitting the cloth floor cover. "You would have me do anything?"

Tsecha again struggled with the inability to think clearly. *They have shut me out.* He pushed back one sleeve, and ran a finger along his many scars. *I should challenge Shai.* In Rauta Shèràa, there would be no question that he should offer *à lérine.* But if he did so here, would she accept? Would she even reply? Would Cèel consider such behavior unseemly, and recall them both? *No. He will not recall Shai.* Jani's truth struck him as a blow. *He will recall me.* Not openly, with challenge and argument and directness of idomeni, but quietly, for reasons other, as the humanish did. *Cèel and Shai have watched. They have learned.* To say one thing and mean another. To use their blades in his back. "I will decide later, ní Dathim." He took one last look at the rolling dunes. "Glories of the day to you."

Tsecha left the house to find the stone-paved street no longer empty. Other Haárin now walked, or talked in doorways. As he passed, the elders straightened in respectful greeting. Youngish stared after him more boldly, small hands clutching the overrobe hems of their house-parents. He gestured blessings to all of them, lifted his chin in gratitude at the offered thanks.

When he reached the treeline, he looked back to find Dathim standing in his doorway, ax-hammer in hand, watching him. Tsecha paused to offer a blessing, but before he could, the Haárin turned his back and disappeared into the darkness of his house.

CHAPTER 12

Jani passed the tables of an award-winning holoVee actor, the prima ballerina of the Capital Ballet, and the team captain of Gruppo Helvetica as she followed the maitre'd through Gaetan's mirrored main dining room. The ballerina, a favorite of Niall's, wore something wispy in black that was held together by thin silver straps and prayer.

Jani tugged at the snug bodice of her own gown. According to Gaetan's unwritten code, long dresses were *de rigueur* for women, which meant that one of John's gifts would at last see candlelight. At least the silver-green holosilk didn't pose any sartorial challenge—it was long-sleeved and floor-length all the way around, and lacked any slits or plunges that could have proved embarrassing if she moved like a normal human. *Unlike that copper thing.* The next time she saw John, she would have to ask him what the hell he'd been thinking when he bought *that.*

Her mood lifted when she caught sight of two familiar heads visible above the leather bolster of a corner booth. Auburn and carrot, straight and curly. Carrot-curly saw her first.

"Jani!" Angevin Wyle scooted out of her seat and circled around the table, handling her taupe satin with enviable ease. "You won me my bet!"

"Glad to hear it." Jani bent down to accept a neck-wrenching hug. "What was it?"

"Didn't think you'd wear a dress." Steven Forell stood, ever-present nicstick dangling from his lips. His hair and black dinner jacket had absorbed the clove-scented smoke—Jani stifled a film-threatening sneeze as he pulled her close. "You let me down, gel," he said as he released her. "Ange is gonna ride me 'bout this for a week."

"Two." Angevin looked Jani up and down, her pert face alight with approval. "I like it."

"Posh," Steve added. "Guess the fancy consulting life agrees with you."

They returned to the table—Steve grinned as he watched the maitre'd help Jani with her chair and spread the linen napkin across her lap. "World's not ready for this," he said after the man left. "You've gone all civilized."

"I've done a turn or two through society in my dim and distant past." Jani tucked her flowing skirts around her legs. "You make me sound barbaric."

"Nah. Streamlined, more like." Steve beckoned for the wine steward and waiter, who stood off to the side. "Like it were beneath your notice." He announced his own surrender to the status quo by extinguishing his 'stick before ordering the wine.

Glasses were filled and orders taken. Jani sipped iced water with lemon and nodded as Steve waxed rhapsodic about the Interior posting from which he and Angevin had just returned.

Angevin, however, refused to cooperate—for every bit of praise Steve tried to heap on his homeworld, she responded with a leveling aside. "I blame selective amnesia," she said as she extracted a steamed mussel from its shell. "Yes, Guernsey's pretty—"

"Gorgeous," Steve muttered.

"—and I got along with his family—"

"They fookin' adored you."

"—and yes, on paper, going there was a good career move." She regarded the sea-born morsel doubtfully before popping it in her mouth. "But nothing gets *done* out there. It takes weeks to process transactions that can be handled here in days. I thought Interior Main was bad—Helier Annex made them look like a Misty relay station."

"Colonies are more *relaxed,* Ange." Steve tore grilled shrimp from a skewer. "They don't take life rush-rush."

"Oh, belt it! You'd chewed your nails down to the second knuckle by the time we pulled out. The project teams we were assigned to missed *five* deadlines because paperwork we submitted for approvals disappeared down a rat-hole." Angevin attacked her butter-sauced fingers with a scented dispo. "Two of those were equipment requisitions for construction projects. The crews are sitting around waiting to work and nothing's been shipped in for them to work *with.* Those were Steve's—you can imagine how well those little mix-ups went over with his department head."

"Thanks for the reminder, love," Steve grumbled around a piece of green pepper.

"Paperwork probably got through all right. The equipment just got resold to a higher bidder." Jani stirred her soup. Beef consommé, protein-based and bland, the culinary equivalent of hot water.

"Folks been complainin' for a while." Steve's voice emerged small and slow, like a young boy confessing he'd stolen cookies. "When I send things home, gifts and suchlike, I use an Haárin courier service that has its own docks and staff." He frowned. "Except they're getting squeezed by the crooks."

Jani shivered and rubbed her upper arms. Either the dining room was set to "freeze" or her own thermostat misbehaved again. "Did your folks mention when the squeeze started?"

"Life's always been a free-for-all in Helier, but me folks said things started getting really bad early this year." Steve chewed on the deshrimped skewer. Like Niall, he needed something in his mouth when the going got bumpy.

About the time L'araignée *formed.* Jani stirred her soup. "Helier government doing anything?"

Steve snorted. "Yeah. Sitting about with their fingers up their bums."

"Wait a second." Angevin looked at him. "You knew about this, and you didn't bother to tell me what we'd be in for?"

Jani pushed her still-full soupbowl away. "When he left Helier, the problem hadn't grown to the extent that it affected the Cabinet annexes. No one ever dared tamper with them before. Times have changed."

"Tell me." Steve took the wooden skewer from his mouth and snapped it in half. "Lost a friend while we were there. Barry went to Oxbridge Combined, same as me. We both started at Interior right off—he left after the van Reuter dustup. Nabbed a job with Commerce, doing dock audits out of the Helier Annex." He fell silent—it seemed to take a lot for him to start talking again. "He called me one morning. He were auditing one of the bigger receiving companies. Whole box of scanpack chips gone missing. He thought he'd found an erase and reentry in the incoming log—he asked me questions about loading and unloading procedures 'cause I worked my way through Oxbridge on the docks." He frowned at the broken sticks in his hand, and tossed them on the table. "Security found his body that afternoon. He'd been stuffed in a supply closet, covered with a drop cloth."

Jani felt a twist of nausea at the thought of her parents. Of Niall. "Was it a professional killing?"

"Might've been." Steve tapped the back of his neck. "Snapped. Could've been a pro or just someone strong. Last I heard, ComPol were still investigating. Doubt they'll find anyone. It's been six months and they've come up with nothing."

The three of them sat in moody silence as the waiters removed, replaced, and refilled.

"Jan?" Steve's voice, gone soft again. "What's going on?"

"Later." Jani forced herself to eat. "At my flat."

"The concept of furniture!" Angevin had consumed most of the wine Steve had ordered. The alcohol lifted her mood and liberated her sense of drama—she strutted the center of Jani's main room, gesturing broadly. "Chairs! Couches!"

"Streamlined." Steve nodded his approval. "I, for one, am not surprised."

"I'm appalled." Angevin walked to one of the windows. "Views could be better, but parties are still a possibility."

Jani strolled to her side and looked out at the rainbow-lit park beyond. "I don't have time to throw parties."

"Don't think you should, with all this crap you got goin'." Steve picked through one of the piles on her desk. "Guess business is poppin'." He looked at her, eyes sharp with question.

Jani stepped away from the window and walked a tight circle. "How much have you heard?" She glanced at Angevin in time to see the guilty flinch.

"Trash report floatin' round with your name on it. Stolen equipment. Altered paperwork." Steve plucked a half-smoked 'stick from his jacket pocket and chewed it. "Bitty stuff, Jan—that's what we're hearin'. Earn you a slap on the hand from your ol' schoolie Aryton at the Reg, maybe." He tossed the old stick in the 'zap and ignited a fresh one. "Anything else goin' on that we should know about?" He walked back around the desk and perched on the corner. "Safety in numbers, an' all that."

"There are . . . problems with the idomeni."

"Oh, that's news. What else?"

"It's better if I don't say."

"Don't you trust us?"

"It's safer for you if I don't say. In fact, it would be in your best interest to leave here now."

"If I recall correctly, you invited us."

"That was a mistake. I'm sorry."

Steve regarded Jani steadily, then beckoned to Angevin. She

walked to him, her step steady, her wine euphoria vanished. He pulled her close; she nestled against him as he rested his chin atop her head. "Jani Kilian, I'll say it once and then no more. You believed I were innocent when no one else did. However much trouble you got, it'll never be enough to drive us away."

Jani fidgeted beneath two worried stares. *They're so young.* And yet, older than she had been at Knevçet Shèràa. *They can handle this.* Indeed, they might not have a choice. Despite the cover of night and the care she took in bringing them in through a side entrance, odds were good that someone had seen them. "If nothing else, my bad reputation could rub off on your blossoming careers."

Steve blew smoke. "Well, that's a load of tripe, innit?" He released Angevin, who began her own root through the paper on Jani's desk.

"Not to change the subject." She waved one of Jani's client logs in the air. "You have a report due tomorrow and all you've done is tabulated the data."

"I was going to finish it after you left." Jani hurried desk-side before Angevin uncovered any more half-completed work. "I just need to write a conclusion."

"It's an easy one." Angevin hiked her skirt and boosted atop the desk chair. "Just your standard summation. 'Here's your list of numbers, fool—if you'd had half as much sense as money, you could have done it yourself in ten minutes.' "

"Looks like you could use some help here, Jan, seein' as you'll be otherwise occupied salvaging yer tarnished reputation and all." Steve removed his dinner jacket, then wandered the room looking for a place to hang it. "We've got a few days before we clap on the Interior irons again. We'd be glad to help you out—right, Ange?" He opened the closet door with a grunt of triumph and stashed the jacket within, then resumed his ramble.

Angevin looked up from her summation. "We need to get typed into your workstation."

Jani stood back from the desk, hands on hips. "Do I have any say in this?"

Angevin shook her head. "No. And I hope you have a credit line in place," she added darkly, "because first thing in the morning, I'm leasing you some furniture."

"She's got plenty of furniture in here! And a few other things, besides." Steve stormed out of Jani's bedroom carrying a pair of Lucien's shoes. "So who do these belong to, then?" He waved one of the trainers in a threatening manner. "You think we're going to let some cad swank in and outta here without a thorough vettin', you got another thing comin'."

Oh, damn. Jani hadn't personally witnessed any confrontation, but according to what she had heard from her Dr. Montoya, Steve and Lucien had despised one another on sight. "You're not going to like it."

"I don't like it already." Steve continued to wave the shoe. "I'm standin' in for your dad, I am, and if you think—" The sound of the door mech cut him off, and he smirked. "Now, we'll get this business straightened out."

Lucien entered, attired in dress blue-greys, brimmed lid tucked under his arm. "Jan, we've got twenty minutes to get to the idomeni embassy. I've got a skim parked—" He slid to a stop and surveyed the scene. "Hello." He smiled warmly at Angevin, who grinned back in silly rapture.

Steve was much less impressed. "What the fook are you doing here?"

"Those are Lucien's shoes you're holding, Steve." Jani fielded his glare and threw it back. "He lives here when he visits the city."

"Twenty minutes." Lucien eyed Jani's dress. "I'll brief you while you change." He grabbed her elbow and steered her toward the bedroom. "What the hell are they doing here?"

"They're working for me for the next few days."

"What!" Lucien forced the door closed, then activated the lock. "Was it something I said?"

"I could use the help." Jani stopped in front of the dresser mirror to check her hair and makeup. "You said yourself that I've taken on too much."

"That's what employment services are for." Lucien moved in behind her and finger-combed his hair. "If you weren't so damned picky, you could have had someone here months ago."

"Thanks for the personnel advice."

"You're welcome."

"They're friends. I like them. They're staying." Jani walked to the closet to hunt for embassy-suitable clothes. She looked over a black trouser outfit from John, but vetoed it because of its plunging neckline and pushed it aside.

"Mind if I ask a question?"

Jani sensed Lucien standing behind her. She riffled through the hangers once, then again. "If you must."

"Why don't you ever look at yourself in the mirror?"

Jani forced herself to turn to him. "I don't know what you mean."

"You'll check your face for two seconds. Three, tops. Just to make sure you haven't smeared colorstick on your chin or something. Most women catch themselves in any reflective surface they can, but never you." Lucien leaned against the entry. "Don't you like what you see?"

You bastard. He could spot a weakness the way a carnivore scented prey. "I try not to get too wrapped up in what I look like." Jani studied a dark blue trouser suit, and voted it suitably somber. "That way, when I change, I won't know what I missed." She yanked at the gown's shoulder fasteners, but they remained stubbornly fixed in place.

"Is this one of John's gifts?" Lucien stepped closer. "I think I know how it operates." He tugged lightly at the places Jani had pulled without success. The seaming released with a sigh—the silk slid down Jani's body and puddled to the floor. His fingers followed close behind, down her arms, cupping her breasts, roaming over her stomach.

"What's happening at the embassy?" Jani could hear the hoarseness in her voice, and damned her weakness.

"SOS." Lucien nuzzled her neck, then gripped her shoulders and turned her around to face him. "Same old same old. . . ." He pulled her close and kissed her.

Jani savored his taste, pressed her naked skin against rough polywool. Shocks spread across her body as though the cloth held static. Her weak knee sagged as Lucien backed her against the closet wall—the sight of the blue trouser suit shook the sense back into her. "Twenty minutes," she gasped in his ear.

Lucien released her abruptly. He walked out of the closet and straight to the dresser. He braced his hands on the edge, his breathing irregular.

Jani resumed dressing eventually. When she walked to the mirror to check her face for smeared makeup, she ignored Lucien's pointed stare. "So what's the story?"

Lucien paced by the bed, lid in hand. "There are issues with Ani's tile. Believe it or not, some of the materials used in the manufacture could be classified as edible, and Shai's trying to use that as an excuse to can the project. Colonel Derringer ordered you called in."

"Derringer's going to be there?" Jani hefted her duffel. "That will be the highlight of my evening."

Steve and Angevin sat side-by-side at the desk, their heads bent together over an open file. They looked up as one when Jani and Lucien entered. Angevin smiled. Steve didn't.

"The idomeni embassy." He slipped off the chair. "That's the only place you're goin'?"

"Yes," Jani answered, because she knew Lucien wouldn't.

"Take some time, ya think? Couple hours?"

"Probably."

"He's drivin'?" Steve followed them into the hall.

"Yes, Daddy."

"We'll be waiting here for ya, Jan." Steve trailed them down the hallway and watched them until the lift doors closed.

Lucien watched him in return. *"Âne-recolteur—"*

Ass-picker. "Be quiet." Jani watched the floor indicator move. "Stop speaking French as though I don't understand."

"I hate that little bastard."

"Well, he hates you, too, so wallow in it."

Except for the assistant desk, the lobby proved empty at that late hour, the street devoid of traffic.

"I'm parked in the garage."

"I have trouble walking up and down that ramp."

"The battery was low—I needed to charge it."

"You just did this afternoon."

"I drove a lot today, ran it down." Lucien strode ahead of her at first. Then his step slowed until she caught him up. He slipped his arm around her shoulders and pulled her close.

What the—? Jani tried to shake off the unfamiliar embrace, without success. "What's with the bear hug?"

"Just trying something different," Lucien said sourly as he pulled his arm away. "No one else seems to mind." He stepped aside and let her precede him into the garage. "You know, the last time you received a summons like this, we were at the embassy for two days."

"Don't remind me." Jani edged down the steep ramp, her knee sagging with every stride. She felt Lucien's hand on her shoulder again, then her knee buckle. "Will you—!"

"I'm just trying to help—!"

A flash seared from the bottom of the ramp. A crack like a whip. Jani hit the ground and rolled behind a pillar. Tossed the bag aside. Reached for the shooter she hadn't carried for months, and cursed her empty hand.

I'm here for you, augie told her. He spoke to her with the slowing of her pounding heart, the quenching of the sour taste of fear. *You'll never die as long as I'm around.*

Jani heard the clatter of running, into the depths of the garage.

There they go, augie cried. *Get them!*

She rose to give chase—

"Jani!"

—but the outer voice stopped her. She turned, and saw Lucien struggle to sit upright, his tunic smoking.

He reached out to her. "It's not a graze—it's a full-front hit." He tried to bend his legs so he could rise, but they shot from beneath him as though he sat on wet ice.

Jani scooted to his side, her attention torn between assessing his wound and the dark interior of the garage. She reached inside of his tunic, and felt the tingle of residual charge as she dug out his hand-com and flicked the emergency call. "I can't tell if it's dead or not—the display is fried." She tossed it to one side and pushed down on Lucien's shoulders as he tried to rise. "Lay back! Stop fighting!"

"Why don't my legs work!"

"Nerve disruption. You just got hit by a bolt of lightning." She had to push with all her strength to keep him down—augie had him by the throat and the pain had yet to break through.

She pulled away his belt, the metal buckle still hot enough to sting. The shooter holster cracked in her hands, the weapon within burned like a live coal. She tossed the belt and holster aside and tucked the shooter in her pocket. She could feel its heat through her clothes as she continued to work.

The smoking polywool came next. Jani searched Lucien's disintegrating trousers, removing a charred wallet, vend tokens, and a mini-stylus and pocketing them as well. The stink of burnt fabric burned her throat and made her eyes tear. She pulled away fragments of shirt. Underwear. "Oh—"

"What!" Lucien tried to raise himself on his elbows to look.

"Get down." Jani pushed him back. "You're burned. It's bad. Stop moving around." She swallowed hard as the odor of charred flesh filled her nose. The burn covered the lower quarter of Lucien's abdomen—his right, her left—a sprawling oval of red-white blistering centered with charred, leathery black. Second- and third-degree burns, compounded by whatever internal damage the impact of the pulse packet caused and aggravated by Lucien's moving around.

"Jan?"

"Yeah."

"Am I still there?"

Jani glanced beneath the remains of Lucien's underwear. "Yup. The burn didn't spread that far."

Lucien laughed. "Probably not a jealous spouse then." The happy expression froze as sweat bloomed on his face. "It's starting to hurt."

"Stop moving around."

"Is that me that I smell? Medium or well-done?"

Jani rolled her duffel into a pillow and tucked it beneath Lucien's head. "Quiet."

Lucien stilled. Then the pain broke through in earnest. He gasped and stiffened. *"Ça ne fait mal!"*

"I know it hurts. I know. *Je le sais."*

"Ça ne—!"

"Paix, paix." Hush, hush. Jani pushed his damp hair off his forehead, whispering thanks when she heard the wail of an ambulance siren. She checked her timepiece. Only a few minutes had passed. Seemed like hours. Then she heard running. Instinct compelled her to reach for the shooter.

"Where are you!" A woman's voice.

"Down here!" Jani waited until she saw the skimgurney and Medibox before slipping the shooter back in her pocket.

The woman knelt beside Lucien as two other techs readied the gurney. She took in his uniform, then looked at Jani. "Augment?"

"Yes."

"Ab-scan," the woman said to one of the other techs. She probed Lucien's abdomen—he moaned and tried to push her away. "He's not rigid, but we could have shooter belly." A male tech knelt at Lucien's other side—together, the two of them adjusted a portable scanner over Lucien's stomach while the second man applied restraints to his hands.

Jani walked down to the end of the ramp, to the spot where she'd seen the flash. In the background, the techs talked in their own language. *Cardio-scan. Fluid replacement. Percent BSA. Debride.*

She found the shooter in the shadow of a pillar. A late-model Grenoble, dull blue and ugly, but powerful from mid-range on in. *The ID tags will be etched away. The markers embedded in the metal will point to a middleman-broker who went out of business five years ago.* And the professional who had pressed the charge-through would be halfway to O'Hare by now.

In the distance, she heard the nasal sing-song of a ComPol siren.

CHAPTER 13

"NìRau? NìRau?"

Tsecha's eyes snapped open. He blinked into the dark. At first, he thought the Laumrau had begun bombing again, that Aeri had awakened him so they could flee to the shelter of the Temple cellars. His heart skipped. He gripped the sides of his bed and braced for the blast.

But the face that bent over him was not Aeri's. Similar in shape but finer-boned, and much, much younger. Tsecha tried to look into its eyes, but it turned away.

What are you? Where is Aeri?

Then he remembered. That Aeri was dead. That the Laumrau were no more. That the war had ended long ago, and that he had not slept in his Temple rooms in Rauta Shèràa for a long time.

"NìRau, you must come to the meeting room." Sànalàn, Aeri's body-daughter, addressed Tsecha's footboard to prevent any more unseemly eye contact. "Suborn Oligarch Shai bids you attend."

"Nìa—?"

"There has been a shooting. Any more, nìaRauta Shai has forbidden me to say."

Tsecha rose too quickly for his old bones, and dressed as though he indeed heard the shatterboxes singing outside his window. Fear drove him. That, and the triumph he heard in Sànalàn's voice.

Tsecha edged about in his low seat and leafed through the scant few pages that lay in front of him. When he leaned forward to study the words more closely, the table's pointed edge caught him in his stomach, forcing him to sit back.

He looked one by one at the others who sat on either side of him, along the table's two arms. Suborn Oligarch Shai sat in the slightly higher seat to his left, as she had the previous day; Sànalàn's seat placed opposite hers on the right arm. The two lowest ranks in the room, Diplomatic Suborn Inèa and Communications Suborn Lonen, occupied the tallest seats at the ends of the arms.

Tsecha found the upward slant of the table disquieting. He felt dazed, as he had the night when the bombs fell and Aeri had not come for him. The night when he learned that Aeri would never come again.

He pushed thoughts of his dead suborn from his mind, and studied the others again. They had dressed hurriedly, as he had, their hair disarrayed, their overrobes bunched and creased. *As though they, too, flee the bombs.* He looked down at the paper once more. His soul ached from tension, but he dared not let it show. "This is all we know?"

"The Service has thwarted our attempts at message interception, nìRau." Lonen held on to the arms of her elevated chair as Tsecha had the sides of his bed. "They use cryptowave, and change the cipher with each word."

"Cryptowave for standard communication is most unseemly." Shai's roughened voice and harsh gestures defined her impatience. "This Pascal is known to us—we are entitled to be told of his condition, not to have to grab it from the air."

Tsecha reread the few words Lonen had been able to decrypt. *Jani Kilian . . . Lieutenant Pascal . . . shot upon entering . . . burned . . . other injuries.* "Has any formal explanation yet arrived?"

"No, nìRau." Diplomatic Suborn Inèa sat easily on her high seat. A perfect posture, of the sort Hansen had always called *angel on a pin.* "We have contacted Prime Minister Cao's offices for information. All they say is that"—she slipped into English—"*the situation is beneath control.*"

"*Under* control, nìa." Tsecha suppressed a gesture of berating. He reread Lonen's report once more, in the hope that what he did not see was there to be found, and that he could avoid the question that he knew the others waited for him to ask. But such, he decided as he turned the final page, was not to be. "Nìa Kilian was not hurt?" He heard Shai grumble in Low Vynshàrau and shift in her seat.

"We could not learn if she was, nìRau," Lonen replied with a hand curve of bewilderment. "We could not learn if she was not."

"This secrecy for no reason is repellant. This repellency defines the difference between humanish and idomeni more than any other thing." Shai elevated the language from formal Middle to formal

High Vynshàrau, so that her every feeling would be clearly revealed. "Our forthrightness in the midst of this secrecy leaves us at a disadvantage. If we request openly, we will only be told what Li Cao wishes us to know. Our interest will be taken as further reason to withhold—this I know from studying humanish, and truly."

Tsecha could see the tension in the posture of Diplomatic Suborn Inèa, much more so than in Lonen's or Sànalàn's. As if she knew what Shai would say next. *So, it happens.* He remained silent, and waited for what he knew must come.

"Much of our behavior leaves us at a disadvantage in dealing with humanish. We speak as we feel. We act in honesty. We offer everything. Humanish take all of it, and return nothing." Shai sat back in her chair and stretched her right arm out before her on the table, palm up. A gesture of pleading. "And so in the end are we left with nothing."

Tsecha toyed with the ends of his overrobe cuffs, rearranging them so as to expose the very edges of his many scars.

Shai understood the challenging nature of the gesture—her hesitancy before she spoke indicated such. Yet still she spoke. "We do not deserve *nothing.* We deserve to know all that the humanish wish to withhold from us." She turned her palm facedown, a sign of an unpleasant decision having been reached. "Morden nìRau Cèel sent us here because of our strength, because he knew that we would nurture and protect all that was as idomeni in the middle of this chill unholiness. In doing so, we have sacrificed much, including that which we sought most to protect. Our sovereignty." She drew her hands together, one atop the other, again palm down. The decision confirmed.

"I have consulted with Cèel these past weeks, and with our xenolinguists, and our behaviorists. Our conclusions concur. The humanish think us weak when we act as our way demands. They see our open disputation as disunity, our godly challenges as discord. They do not think us strong, and because of this, they feel right to hold back information from us, to break agreements and disregard contracts."

"But you wished breakage of the Elyan Haárin contract, Shai, and truly," Tsecha muttered without gesture, so low that only Shai could hear him.

Shai responded by raising the pitch of her voice, as in prayer. "Thus will we act strong as the humanish understand strong. Thus will we withhold our opinions, and keep our arguments amongst ourselves. Thus will we behave as one before them, as they behave as one before us."

Lonen crossed her left arm in front of her chest in supplication. "NìaRauta Shai, we will damn our souls if we behave as false."

"Then we will petition Caith to protect us, nìa Lonen, for only in this annihilation will we remain whole." Shai bared her teeth for an instant only, a truncated expression that signified as much as a humanish shrug. Or as little. "We are the stones that form the Way. Although we are as nothing, other Vynshàrau will tread on us, and thus make their way along the Bridge to the Star."

Tsecha remained quiet as the last tones of Shai's speech drifted through the air and settled, like Dathim's tile dust. He looked from figure to figure, searching for the subtle changes that would signal their agreement with the Suborn Oligarch. The elevation as they sat up straighter, to show their respect. The lifted curve of their left hands, to show their certainty of agreement. He saw them in Lonen, and of course, in Sànalàn, and in Inèa. He kept his own hands clasped before him on the table. He had reached his own difficult decision many years before—this night saw only the laying of another stone in his own long Way.

"Humanish secrecy defines itself not by what it does but by that which it leaves behind." Tsecha heard his own voice, low and measured. He petitioned no one with his words. "Trails of blood, and humiliation. Former Interior Minister van Reuter would attest to this, I believe." He bared his teeth wide, in the truest idomeni fashion. "I have read of the humanish writer Sandoval, who wrote that secrets bind with their own weight, that to carry many secrets is to wrap oneself in a chain of one's own making." He rounded his shoulders and slumped in his chair, a most obvious display of his displeasure. "You have bid us don our chains, at a time when we must move as free. You damn us, Shai."

Shai tossed her head and fluttered her right hand once, a gesture of the greatest disregard. "I seek to save us, Tsecha. It is you who will damn us with your beliefs and your false predictions. You announce them before the humanish, and thus give them reason to fear and mock us. You claim to speak for the gods, and in the gods' names you will dilute and dishonor us!"

Tsecha sensed the mood of the room, the acceptance of Shai's words in the postures of the others. "You speak as you do, Shai, because nìa Lonen and nìa Inèa and nìa Sànalàn give you leave with their every movement. In this room, at this time, you know how each of us regards you, and use such as a basis to decide how you will next act. No indecision. No uncertainty. Yet you will take that away from us all and call it strength, and you dare to accuse me of dishonor!"

"It is settled, Tsecha!"

"It was settled days ago. Before yesterday's meeting, when Anais commended the idomeni for their forthrightness, you already knew of this plan. You have studied the hiding lesson well, have you not, Shai? We both know that there is more to this than contracts." Tsecha tilted his head to the left until his ear touched his shoulder, and let the anger wash over him like the cold season air to come. "Say her name, Shai! In the name of annihilation, say the name of the one whom you will keep from this place, in the name of your new-found secrecy!"

Shai's voice lowered in menace. "Until we have received sufficient information regarding the condition of Lieutenant Pascal and the reason for the attack on him, we cannot allow your Kilian within these walls. Nor can we allow you to leave the embassy compound. It is a precaution—"

"It is cowardice!" Tsecha shouted now, his voice reverberating off the polished stone walls. "Wanton disregard of the truth you have denied since we lived at Temple. And now you will take this new truth that only you and your behaviorists see and use it as a way to separate me from my Kièrshia!"

Shai tensed, then raised her hands in argument. "Your Kilian—"

"My Kilian, my Jani, my Captain. My Eyes and Ears. My student. My teacher. *Mine.*" Tsecha forced himself silent. His heart pounded; his face burned. So unseemly, to rage in such an uncontrolled way. "You have learned well, Shai. In a few months, you have become as Anais or Li Cao. You will shut me up in this place, for my *safety.* You will keep me from my Jani and my Jani from me, for my own good. When has protection ever destroyed so utterly that which it was supposed to defend? Tell me, Shai, and damn your soul if you lie of this!"

Shai sat still. Then she rested her arms as Tsecha did. As a secular, her sleeves lacked the red banding that complemented *à lérine* scars so well. Her pale scars seemed to fade into the sameness of her skin.

Tsecha studied Shai's exposed arms for the ragged red of fresher lacerations, but could see none, not even the self-inflicted hack to the forearm that signaled the end of a bout. *It has been a long while since your last challenge.* He looked down at his own arms, and the spare scattering of red. *It has been a long time since mine.* How they would slash and stab at one another, the smooth parries of youth replaced by the deceptions and strategems of age. *I await your challenge, nìa.* It would no doubt prove an interesting encounter.

"You may well pronounce my soul damned, nìRau ti nìRau. You are my Chief Propitiator, my intercessor with the gods, and such is most assuredly your right. In the ways of the gods, no Vynshàrau is your dominant." Shai pushed away from the table, whatever challenge she felt to make put aside for another time. "But when you act as ambassador, you become a secular, and all seculars in this place answer to me. I have ordered that you will not leave this place. You will, therefore, not leave this place until I lift the order. For your safety." She stood, her overrobe falling in wrinkled folds to the floor. "Glories of this too-late night to you, Tsecha." She swept out the door behind Lonen and Inèa, and finally, his Sànalàn.

Tsecha gestured in easy agreement as the door closed. "Yes, nìa." He thought again of his Hansen. How he would pace and rail at times like these, when the Laumrau or the humanish Consulate had acted in some stupid manner and he knew nothing could be done to stop them. Tsecha tried to recall the comment Hansen used in those situations, which twinned so well the one he found himself in now. *Pissing into the wind.* Yes, that was it, and truly.

Tsecha tried to sleep, and failed. Tried to pray, and failed again.

He dressed. He walked. Throughout the embassy, and the altar room where he would soon pass his days, much to Shai's rejoicing. Out on the lake-facing verandas, where even in the dim of night, Vynshàrau contemplated, wrote, discussed.

Across the lawns. Past the buildings. He knew where he went, though what good it would do, he could not say. He wondered if Shai now had him watched, or if she felt her confinement order eliminated the need.

He had just reached the treeline when he heard the sound. He paused to listen to it, such a contrast to the rustle of leaves and crunch of undergrowth. The high-pitched *sweep sweep* of stone against metal. Odd to hear it in this place, at this time. It was a sound of the quarries, the weapons forges, and during the time of war, the hallowed courtyards of Temple. The steady hasp and scrape of a Vynshà sharpening a blade.

Tsecha followed the sound to a small clearing. Why did it not surprise him to find the crop-headed figure seated on a stump, stone in one hand, ax-hammer in the other? "You work so early, ní Dathim?"

"As do you, nìRau." Dathim did not look up. He had hung a lampstick by a cord around his neck; the yellow light illuminated the work of his hands. "Did the noise awaken you, as well?"

Tsecha lowered to the ground beside the stump. He looked up at Dathim's face and tried to discern his feeling, but all was obscured by the odd shadows cast by the lampstick. "I heard no noise in the embassy. My suborn awakened me." He debated telling Dathim of his house arrest. The Haárin had declared himself to him, and for that reason alone he had a right to know Tsecha's status.

But Tsecha decided against doing so. *I must fight secrets with secrets.* Dathim would find out from the guards or the embassy staff soon enough, and he would understand the reason for silence. If Shai discovered that the Chief Propitiator discussed such matters with an Haárin, confinement to the embassy for one could become confinement to rooms for both. "What noise did you hear, ní Dathim?"

"The ComPol sirens. Other sirens as well, for the skimmers that transport humanish sick and injured. But then, one hears those every night." Dathim set the stone aside, and held the ax-hammer blade close to his face. "Tonight has been most different." He tilted the blade end back and forth, then ran a finger along the edge. "Interior Security has been most active tonight, nìRau, and truly. Constant passes up and down our borders. Along the lakeshore, as nearly as they could approach. Overhead, in demiskimmers." Something about the blade made him frown. He lowered it and once more ministered to it with the stone. "I saw all this. Then I saw the embassy lights, and the activity of our guards."

Tsecha looked through the trees, and watched the green and blue lights of Vynshàrau and Interior lakeskimmers shimmer and reflect over the water. "My Lucien was shot."

"He is the youngish, the pale-haired soldier?" Dathim nodded in the humanish way, which signified that his head moved up and down. "I have seen him walk with you. I have seen him walk alone, in the public areas. Even though he stays within the allowed boundaries, the guards follow him most closely. He watches as someone who remembers what he sees. Not always a wise thing, for humanish." He lowered the stone to his lap and pointed to another tight formation of lakeskimmers that flitted on the Interior side of the Michigan Strip boundary. "The last time I saw this much activity was in the winter, when they took the dominant van Reuter away. For the entire season afterwards, when I traveled into the city, I heard the talk about that night. And now I see it again, for one humanish lieutenant who walks where he is allowed and remembers what he sees."

Tsecha thought back to the night of van Reuter's arrest. The incomprehensible cold. His Jani's rescue from Interior, which he had planned with Lucien. The pursuit. The fleeing. "My Jani was with Lucien. Any more than that, no one knows."

"Did she shoot him?" Dathim lifted his hand in question. "She shoots, nìRau. Such is her way."

"She would not shoot *him*!" Tsecha heard his own voice raised too loud, and berated himself. Such a shout, an avalanche of sharpening stones could not have drowned out. "They are friends," he added, much more quietly.

"As you say, nìRau." Dathim turned the stone over. The surface changed from rough to shiny, from honing to polishing. "But friends often turn on friends. This I know from reading humanish history."

"I, too, have read humanish history, ní Dathim."

"Have you, nìRau?" Another sweep of the stone. "No wonder you walk the night."

Tsecha clenched his hands at the Haárin's assured tone. "You vex me, ní Dathim."

"I am unworthy to sit in your presence, nìRau." Unworthy though he was, Dathim made no move to rise. Instead, he set the ax-hammer and stone on a nearby log and looked out once more toward the water. "I must return to sleep. Tomorrow, I visit the Exterior Ministry for the first time, to examine the space which Anais Ulanova wishes me to tile." The dimness played tricks with the bones of his face, filling in hollows with seeming substance, combining with his hair to make him appear even more humanish. "They will show me, among other places, a *lobby,* and a *conference room.* I am to look over each location very carefully, and pick the one that will highlight my stunning work the best—this was I told, and truly." Ready as he claimed to be to leave, Dathim made no attempt to gather his tools. "I am to look. And look." Instead, he sat slightly forward, hands on knees, perched to stand, yet waiting . . . waiting. . . .

Tsecha waited, as well, for the most seemly offer he knew to be forthcoming.

"Is there anything in particular you would have me look *for,* nìRau?"

Tsecha felt his heart catch, as it had all those times in Rauta Shèràa when his Hansen had made the same request. How Dathim had come to know of the behavior of spies, he did not think it wise to ask. Better to simply accept, and quickly. "Anything of this shooting, ní Dathim. Anything you see of my Jani." He picked up a twig and used it to poke beneath some fallen leaves. "Although I do not know how you will remove it from Exterior grounds."

"I know of facilities, nìRau. So I told you." Dathim grew still as an idomeni demiskimmer skirted the shore. "You should believe your fellow Haárin when they tell you of matters, and trust them to do as they say."

"Fellow—?" Tsecha's shoulders sagged as fatigue suddenly

overtook him—he could muster no anger at Dathim's impertinence "You claim to share skein and station with me, ní Dathim? You claim me as equal?"

"No, nìRau." Dathim stood slowly, long limbs unwinding. "I am able to leave this place, and you are not. You are a prisoner, and I am free. In such an instance, we are most unequal, would you not say?"

Tsecha twisted his head so quickly, his neck bones cracked like dried leaves. "You know of that? So soon?" Even the darkness could not obscure his shock—that he knew, though little did he care.

Dathim looked down on Tsecha from his great height. "Yes, nìRau—I know of your restriction. Thus did I hear from an embassy Haárin, who overheard a conversation between your suborn and Diplomatic Suborn Inèa. After your meeting, when you were informed of your imprisonment in the interest of your safety." He bent to pick up his tools. "Such listening is the way of Earth, nìRau. The way of humanish. Of your Eyes and Ears. It shocks me that you have not learned it better." He strode off, sharpening stone clenched in one hand, ax-hammer in the other, leaving Tsecha alone in the dark and the leaves.

CHAPTER 14

"Look at the light, Jani."

Jani glanced out the corner of her eye at the red illumination that fluttered just beyond arms' reach.

"You know better than that." Calvin Montoya stepped out from behind the lightbox. "I need to assess the activity level of your augmentation so I know how to treat you."

"*I'm* not injured. *I* wasn't shot."

"Look at the light."

Jani kept her eyes fixed on a point above the lightbox. Then, slowly, she dropped her gaze until she stared at the red head-on. "See? I told you I was fi—"

Suddenly, the light twinned. Once, then again and again. The pinpoints skittered across the source surface and throbbed in programmed patterns.

The examination room spun—Jani had to grip the edge of the scanbed to keep from toppling to the floor.

"That's what I thought," Montoya said smugly. "On the downward slope, but still firing. Augie had enough of a jolt to initiate normally—I think we can let you settle on your own without a takedown." He shut off the source, and the red dots faded to black. "Show me an augie that doesn't kick in when its owner's shot at, and I'll show one worthless bundle of brain cells."

Jani struggled to maintain her equilibrium. The walls of the examining room billowed out, then in, as though the room breathed. "I can show you another worthless—"

"*Testy,* aren't we?" Montoya pushed the lightbox to the far corner of the examination room. "Lieutenant Pascal will be all right."

"He didn't look all right in the ambulance." Jani watched Montoya fuss with a tray of instruments. He still wore the trimmed beard she recalled from the winter; his band-collar dinner jacket mirrored its rich black color. Together, they made him look like a cleric in a historical drama. *Bless me, Father, for I don't know what the hell's going on.* "How much longer will he be in Surgery?"

"They've only had him for half an hour." Montoya's voice still chided, but more gently. "He suffered serious injuries in addition to the burn. A shooter blast is like a kick in the gut—you know that as well as I do. Along with internal bleeding, add a ruptured peritoneum and a bruised kidney." He pulled a stool in front of the scanbed and sat. "He's young, strong, and augmented—he'll heal quickly, but he'll still need to *heal.*" He fingered the scuffed knee of Jani's trousers. "Now, you said you fell after the shot blitzed out."

"My right knee gave out when I walked down the ramp." Jani massaged the injured joint. It had begun to ache soon after she arrived at the hospital—now that her augie had backed down, it hurt every time she flexed it.

"Let's see what we have here." Montoya braced her foot atop his thigh and pushed up her trouser leg. "Oh, my." He probed the egg-sized bruise below the patella. "You've got some nice soft-tissue damage there. Augie quelled the worst of it, but I'll still fit it with a chillpack to ease the swelling."

Jani cupped her hand over her knee so Montoya couldn't probe it anymore. She could feel the heat radiate from the injury like a localized fever. "Can't you inject it with something so it heals faster?"

"No." He glanced up at her and smiled his regrets. "If I give you anything while augie is still active, your healing cascades will go into overdrive. A month from now, we'd have to remove tissue and bone growths, or worst case, have to rebuild the joint entirely." He pulled open a drawer in the base of the scanbed and removed a packet of gauze and an aerosol canister. "And there are just some risks we can't afford to take with you right now."

Jani leaned her head back and stared at the ceiling. "Meaning?" As if she didn't know. As if she hadn't heard the same excuses from a multitude of medical faces over the last few months.

"Meaning that you could react adversely to one of the accelerant proteins. If you did go into anaphylaxis, the only thing we could treat you with is adrenosol and your therapeutic index and toxic threshold overlap. In other words, a dose sufficient to help you could just as easily kill you." He pulled her hand away from her knee, sprayed her bruise, and wiped the freezing foam with the gauze. "We need to develop desensitizing proteins specific to you. We're close, but we're not there yet." He continued to spray the cooling, cleansing foam, then dab it away. "On the other hand, there's a chance you won't need them. If your response to past injury is any indication, your body is a healing accelerant factory on its own."

Jani looked at the *à lérine* wounds on her right arm, and compared them to the faint scars on her animandroid left. The real had caught up with the counterfeit—the wounds had already healed to silvered threads, as though she'd had them for years, not months. The residual weakness in her right knee served as the sole reminder of her most recent health disasters. According to every physician she spoke with, both Neoclona and Service, anyone else who had gone through the myriad adversities she had would be bedridden. Or dead.

John tells me I'll outlive everyone I know. All she'd lost in exchange was the right to call herself a human being. *I am a hybrid. A race of one.* The idea hadn't bothered her so much when she lived on the run—when all that matters is getting through today, who thinks about tomorrow?

But as her body continued to change and the inevitability of the process dawned, she'd come to resent every aspect of the transformation. That her life had become the eggshell walk of the chronically ill. That she couldn't put anything in her mouth without wondering whether it would sicken her. That she couldn't think an odd thought without worrying whether it was just a passing weirdness or the sign of a brain that didn't process things the same way anymore.

Add to that the reactions from others—the orderly who switched duties whenever she came in for a check-up because he thought hybridization contagious. The nurse who crossed herself when Jani looked her in the eye. The doctors who called her names when they thought she couldn't hear. Goldie. Pussy cat. *John would kill them if he knew.* But to what purpose, when others would take their place who felt the same. Even the kindest remarks, from Niall and Dolly, aggravated and worried her. She changed, and everyone could see that she changed. She couldn't hide it anymore.

She looked down at Montoya, who had finished with the foam and gauze, and now adjusted a padded coldpack around her knee. "Calvin?"

"Yes?"

"I'm tired of being a medical miracle."

His hands stalled. He didn't look up. "I'm sorry, Jani."

Jani studied the top of his head. The first traces of a bald spot had formed on his crown, a thumbnail-sized imperfection in his thick cap of straight black. *I spit in the eye of the inevitable,* he had told her when she asked him why he didn't correct it. His refusal to tweak his own little defect colored his judgment regarding hers. He was one of the few white coats who treated her like a woman named Jani, not a cross between a freak and the publication opportunity of a lifetime.

Jani tapped Montoya's bald spot to get his attention, then pointed to his jacket. "Where were you when you got the call?"

He grinned at her and sat up straighter. "My parents' fortieth wedding anniversary. Brothers, sisters, children, grandchildren." The grin wavered. "The party had just started to wind down. The call came at just the right time—I didn't have to help with the clean-up." He looked down again, but not soon enough to keep Jani from spotting the longing in his eyes.

"Guess it's my turn to say I'm sorry."

His head shot up. "Did you plan this?" He waited for her to shake her head. "Then don't apologize." He looked down again and fiddled with the coldpack. "So, I heard buzz that it was a robbery attempt."

"More than likely." Jani had no intention of discussing her certainty as to the professional nature of the attack. She placed a hand over her left shoulder, on the spot that Lucien had touched just before the shot. *Touched.* She winced as she pressed her fingers into the area. Make that *grabbed.* She'd find a bruise there in a few hours, augie or no.

"What's wrong?" Montoya stood up and kicked the stool back into its niche beneath a bench, then pushed back her T-shirt and probed her shoulder with the same uncomfortable thoroughness with which he'd examined her knee. "A robbery, huh? I've lived in this city awhile, you know? Robberies in garages happen. Not in the Parkway area, though. Too many Family members. Too much high-priced security." He took a scanner from the top of a nearby table and pressed it to her shoulder. "Bit of a wrench," he said as he read the display. "I don't need to reseat the arm, but it will be sore for a few days."

"Is this another 'augie will provide'?" Jani got down off the scanbed and tested her knee. Thanks to her internal factory, the sharp pain had already receded to a dull ache. Unfortunately, the motion aggravated her Montoya-induced vertigo—she had to keep one hand planted on the bed frame as she adjusted her trouser leg. "Why wouldn't criminals come to the Parkway? That's where the money is."

Montoya eyed her with professional scrutiny as she walked across the room. "A Chicago robber would not attempt to kill his victims. Bad for business. His colleagues would nail him before the ComPol did." He walked to her side. "Speaking of the ComPol, they're here. A detective inspector and a detective captain. John deposited them in a lounge down the hall."

"Really?" Jani recalled the green-and-white skimmer that had dogged the ambulance. She waved away Montoya's offer to help with her jacket, since he'd have detected the small but weighty presence of Lucien's shooter and personal effects in her side pocket.

"I wouldn't advise talking to them for at least two days. Not until we're sure augie has settled down." Montoya blocked her way to the door. "You're not yourself. That feeling of invincibility isn't the thing to take with you when you deal with authority."

Jani patted his shoulder. "Calvin, I was dealing with the ComPol back when you still had a full head of hair."

"That's cold."

"I'll be fine." She stepped around him and out the door.

The Outpatient wing was deserted at that late night hour. That made it easier to hear the raised voices emerging from the lounge where the ComPol awaited. Three voices—two women and a man.

"Ms. Kilian has nothing to say!" the man shouted. His voice was cultured Michigan provincial flavored with Earthbound Hispanic.

"Why don't we let Ms. Kilian tell us that!" one of the women countered.

"No!" the man responded. "Absolutely not. She is on bioemotional restriction and cannot be questioned at this time!"

Jani sneaked into the lounge entry so that she could gauge the combatants before stepping into the fray. The women appeared to be her age, and wore the professionally dour dark green of ComPol detectives. The man was older, a brown-skinned walking wire dressed in casual trousers and an expensive pullover. He spotted her first, and turned his back on the women's verbal barrage.

"Jani." He hurried over to her, his expression at once tranquil and alert, the way Val looked when he felt he needed to calm her down. "You shouldn't walk around." His face was shallow-boned and dominated by an aquiline nose, his hair a grizzled cap.

Jani took a step back. "Who the hell are you?"

"Joaquin Loiaza." He pulled up short and bowed from the waist. "John has asked me to represent you in this matter."

"You're a *lawyer*?" All the reply that elicited was a slow affirmative blink. "What the hell do I need a lawyer for!"

"That's our question too, Jani," one of the detectives piped.

"Did you see anything?" the other asked. "The garage's monitoring system was knocked out by the construction—you're our only witness."

Loiaza turned on them. *"Ms. Kilian has nothing—!"*

"Jani?"

Silence fell as everyone looked to the voice, a rumbling bass that made any word sound like a command from on high.

John Shroud stood in the hallway. He looked a study in ice: bone-white hair, milk-pale ascetic's face, an evening suit of palest blue. "Should you be walking about?" He turned his attention to Loiaza, who stiffened. "I asked you to see to this, Joaquin." As usual, John had filmed his eyes to match his clothing—the crystal blue glare moved from the lawyer to fix again on the reluctant client. "I'll see you back to your room." He walked toward Jani as though one quick move would dislodge his head. Spine straight, stride long and smooth. A weighty step, but fluid, like mercury.

Jani tried to dodge, but two ice-blue arms snaked around her and held her fast.

"You will come quietly." John spoke in her ear, sounding like Death come to collect his due.

"I don't need your lawyers, or your goddamned help!" Jani gripped the arms of the visitor's chair, supporting all her weight on her hands as she struggled to sit without bending her knee. The furniture in John's office was all ebon wood instead of battered metal, the floor covered with Persian carpets instead of cheap lyno. Yet still she sat, and still she argued, as she had so many times before in the basement of the Rauta Shèràa enclave hospital. "I could have found out what they knew. Who they suspected. Right now, I have *nothing!*"

"Any information they have, Joaquin will obtain through proper channels." John fell into his chair. The ergoworks screeched in protest. "Now are you going to tell me what happened tonight, or are you going to make me guess?" He slumped forward and worked his hands through his hair.

Jani counted slowly in an effort to quell her ire, using her throbbing knee as a metronome. "A robbery attempt." She watched John's hair catch the light like finely drawn platinum. She could still feel the pressure of his arms where he'd held her. "How long have you had that headache?" She imagined pressing her fingers into his nape and massaging the tension from the knotted muscle.

"I got it right about the time some misinformed idiot told me you'd been shot." John lifted his head. His melanin-deficient skin showed every crease and shadow of fatigue. "A robbery attempt." He sat back in his chair. "Well, time's passage has taught you consistency—that jibes with what Calvin said you told him. He and I managed to exchange a few words before I found you wandering the halls looking for trouble." He sounded all-business now, which meant his bullshit detector was activated and calibrated. "We agreed that it was utter garbage, of course, and that you're hiding something. So, what are you working on that could have precipitated this attack?"

"I push paper." Jani heard her voice rise, and tried to lower it. Her hand went to her left shoulder again. "I write reports. Those are not shooting offenses, even in this town."

"How do you expect me to lie for you if I don't know what the truth is?"

"Who's asking you to lie? This is Chicago. Things like this happen all the time."

"A robbery attempt gone awry? Jani Moragh, who do you think you're talking to?"

Jani flexed her knee. It scarcely hurt at all now. Either her little factory ran full-tilt or she was too angry to feel the pain. She rose shakily. "You started this interrogation right off the bat. Back in Rauta Shèràa, you'd at least offer me coffee first." She limped to the door. "Good night." She checked her timepiece. "Make that good morning."

"Wait a minute!" John hurried after her. "One of those detectives asked me whether Pascal carried a weapon in the course of his duties and if he still had it when he arrived in Triage. I told her I had it locked away in my office, and I know damned well she's going to show up inside the hour with a Request to Cooperate warrant and demand that I produce it."

Jani leaned against the doorway. Her stomach rumbled. She felt lightheaded. "I can hold it for him just as easily as you can." She dug Lucien's shooter out of her jacket pocket, taking care to leave his wallet and other things behind.

John plucked the shooter from her hand and walked to a large armoire that loomed like a monolith in the far corner of the room. "The bioemotional restriction on your MedRec prohibits you from carrying a dischargeable weapon." He opened a door and activated a touchlock. A small panel slid aside, and he inserted the shooter in the niche. "If you behave, it can be lifted by year's end. If you're caught carrying, it's an automatic two-year extension, and there's not a thing I can do about it."

"Who's asking you to do anything about it!" The shout rang in Jani's ears. The room spun. She slid down the wall, gasping each time her heel grabbed on the thick carpet and forced her to bend her knee.

John hurried to her side and knelt in front of her. He checked her eyes and pulse, then removed a sensor stylus from his pocket and pressed it against the tip of her right index finger. "Your blood sugar's in the basement," he said as he checked the readout. "When did you last eat?"

"Dinner." Jani rested her head against the doorjamb. The sharp wooden ridge dug into her scalp, but she didn't have the strength to move. "I met some friends at Gaetan's."

"Oh?" John loosened her jacket collar, then straightened out her leg. "Who?"

"Steve Forell and Angevin Wyle." Jani felt her mouth move, but the words sounded hollow, as though they came from another room. She hugged herself as a wave of the shivers overtook her.

John rose with a rumbling sigh. "Just sit quietly." He walked to the wall and slid aside a floor-to-ceiling panel, revealing an inset kitchenette. "Don't move," he warned as he disappeared within. Water ran. Something ground and gurgled. Soon, the weighty aroma of brewing coffee filled the air.

"What did you wear?" John's voice growled above the sputter of the brewer.

Jani took one deep breath, then another. Her head cleared. She didn't think caffeine could diffuse through the air, but this was *John's* coffee. "The green thing."

"The mermaid dress." John emerged bearing a tray, looking like heaven's headwaiter. "It's very pretty, but I rather wish you'd have tried one of the others." He handed her a cup. "The copper column is nice, I think. Off the shoulder—"

"Everybody's been out on the town tonight." Jani gestured toward John's suit, slamming the door on any further discussion of her shoulders. "Where were you?"

John eyed her in injury as he set the tray on the floor, then worked into a cross-legged position beside it. "A chamber music recital at the Capitoline. Calvin was—"

"His parents' fortieth. I know." She sipped her coffee. Make that *tried* to sip her coffee. She stared into her cup at the few centimeters of dark foam that filled the bottom.

"I want you to leave here in a relatively alert frame of mind, not in orbit." John handed her what looked like a brightly wrapped chocolate bar. "And not under arrest. Or under sanction, observation, or any other of the legion of oversights possible in this town. Removing Pascal's weapon from the scene was remarkably stupid—you should have handed it to one of the emergency techs immediately."

"It felt good to carry again." Jani examined the bar skeptically. "I hadn't been without for over twenty years."

"I find that a sad commentary on your life." John drew one knee up to his chest and draped his hand over it. His spine remained straight, though, his manner formal. Even after all these years, he still hadn't gotten the hang of *casual*, and the fact that he tried to pull it off under such tense circumstances raised warning alarms. "You don't need to live like a fugitive anymore. You have freedom, and with freedom comes alternatives." His voice dropped until it sounded like a whisper from inside her head. "There's no need for you to live here just because it's the only place on Earth that you know."

Jani nodded vaguely as she tore away the bar's purple and green wrapping. Her mouth watered as she inhaled the scents of chocolate and caramel. "What is this?"

"A meal bar," John snapped. "Now, as I was saying, there's no need for you to stay in Chicago. You could live anywhere."

"I have lived anywhere. Anywhere and everywhere. It's nice being able to stay in one place for a change." Jani broke off one end of the bar, catching the filling on her finger just before it dripped down the front of her jacket. She touched her finger to the tip of her tongue, and tasted the buttery gold of the richest confectionery. "S'-good." She popped the piece in her mouth.

"It's a calorie bomb. The way your post-trauma metabolism seems to be kicking along, you should eat two or three of those a day for the next week. That's in addition to your regular meals, *not* in place of." John set his cup on the tray with a clatter. "Are you going to stop changing the subject?"

Jani pulled off another piece of the bar. "I like it here. The work's interesting. And I have *friends*." It sounded strange to say that, considering she'd spent half her life fleeing any sort of connection. Strange, but nice. "There's Frances Hals and her husband. Steve and Angevin. And let's not forget Nema."

"Oh, let's, please." John picked up his cup, but instead of drinking he stared into it. "Work and friends can be found in every city. Seattle, for example, is filled with friendly people."

Most of whom are on your payroll. "I doubt they're any friendlier than they are here."

"I can guarantee no one would shoot at you." He looked up, filmed eyes glittering. "Jani, what hap—?" The entry buzzer interrupted him. *"Yes?"*

The door slid aside and Valentin Parini, John's partner in bleeding-edge science, entered. "It's only me." He looked down at John, then at Jani. “Somebody steal all the chairs?” His evening suit was dark brown, a color that complemented his ash brown hair and hazel eyes perfectly. He had strong bones and a brushed-back hairstyle that accented a widow’s peak—devilish handsome described him well.

“Where were you when you heard the good news?” John asked sourly.

“Dinner with the latest love of my life.” Val winked at Jani and touched the tip of his chin. “You’re dripping caramel.”

“We’ve just been working through a bout of the stubborns.” John handed Jani a dispo napkin, then rose to his feet. “If I ever decide to switch to Pediatrics, the behavioral courses should be a snap.” He picked up the tray and headed back to the kitchenette.

Jani stuck out her tongue at his receding back, then dabbed caramel from her chin. She swallowed the last bite of meal bar and washed it down with the scant remainder of the coffee. “How’s Lucien?” From out the corner of her eye, she saw John step to the kitchenette opening and stand still, listening.

Val saw him too. “He’s out of surgery.” He walked across the room and seated himself on the edge of John’s desk, within full view of his partner in crime.

Jani watched as an unreadable look passed between the two men. *Ah, this brings back memories.* It was a given that they kept something from her. Her job was to find out what it was. “Can I see him?”

Val shook his head. “Not until later today. A crew from Intelligence showed up—they’ve got him surrounded. Besides, we had to take him down before we could prep him, and between that and the post-anesthesia, he’s not discharging on all battery cells. Better to leave him alone for now.” He glanced at John, who nodded once and slipped out of sight.

“I’ll stop by this afternoon, then.” Jani rolled onto her left knee, waving off Val’s offer of help as she struggled to her feet. “I need to wash my hands.” She tested her right knee as she walked to the kitchenette, first by putting all her weight on it, then by flexing it as she stood in front of the sink. Both times, she elicited only the barest twinge. She dried her hands, then reached under her trouser leg and removed the coldpack.

John emerged from a walk-in pantry holding a plastic sack full of meal bars. “You should leave that on until you get home.”

Jani tossed the gel-filled pack into the sink. “My knee’s numb. It feels a lot better.” She accepted the bag of bars, taking care to avoid his eye. He’d start making suggestions if she didn’t move quickly. Dinner, with another gown thrown in as an inducement. A chamber music recital or two. The rest of their lives. "I had a duffel when I arrived here—where is it?"

"The Triage desk." John stepped in front of her, blocking her path. "I'd feel better if you told me you'd visit Seattle sometime soon. As in immediately."

"I'm sure you would." Jani dodged him easily. "How's your headache?"

"It had eased up, but now it's back. I'm worried about you."

"I'm sure you are." She brushed past a doleful Val, who had taken up sentry duty at the kitchenette entry.

"Seattle's a very nice city," he chimed in support.

"I'm sure it is." Jani stuffed the sack under her arm and darted into the solitary freedom of the hallway.

CHAPTER 15

Jani picked up her duffel in Triage, and refused the desk's offer to arrange a ride home. She walked out into the darkness, mindful that she wouldn't remain alone for long, that John would send a team of his Security officers after her to make sure she arrived home intact.

Sure enough, when she glanced back into the lobby, she saw the aide talking to her comport display, the rigid expression on her face announcing to all that she spoke to A Superior. Jani slipped out of sight and circled around the less-inviting region of the complex. Past the busy receiving docks, the medical waste treatment facility, the utilities outbuildings, all those places where someone in dark clothes carrying a bag and plastic food sack would blend.

She crossed State Street, and continued to veer south and east in the hope that John's Security would assume she had headed north toward the Parkway. Her left shoulder ached enough that she had to sling her duffel over her right; that in turn aggravated her iffy balance and hampered her stride. Her knee griped with every step, the shock of impact zinging down her shin. The damp chill seeped through her jacket. She walked in the shadows, avoiding the light of the streetlamps, all but invisible to the other pedestrians who trudged the early morning hours. Workers on mealbreak, on their way back to third shift jobs. Nightowls, prowling the twenty-four-hour clubs and shops.

Hired killers, hoping to finish what they started.

John's coffee and the meal bar worked magic on Jani's fatigued mental processes. Images that hadn't touched her at the time returned *en force*. The flash of the shooter. Lucien's pained rictus as the agony of the burn clamped down. The fear-driven quickness of John's actions as he aided her after her collapse. His urgings to leave Chicago.

Jani hopped a 'mover as soon as she reached the Boul. She nestled in a rear seat, her eyes on the few haggard faces that shared the ride. No one looked like a hired shooter. No one paid much attention to her. The men looked at her face, then gave her body a quick once-over. The women looked at her clothes and manner and relaxed, counting her another member of the working wounded and therefore safe to ignore.

She disembarked two blocks south and east of her building and approached it so she could see the front and side entrances. Skimmers drifted past—she edged away from the curb to discourage interested parties from offering her a lift.

She cut down a wide, well-kept alley and entered the garage through the entry opposite the one she and Lucien had used. From there, she surveyed the entire tableau. The ramp she'd walked down. The pillar from which shadow the shot had emerged. She studied the area for several minutes, imprinting its layout on her brain. Then she cut across the scancrete floor, her steps echoing in the empty space, and revisited the scene.

Scant remnants of ComPol presence littered the area. A few scraps of barrier tape. A skid mark from a holocam tripod. Jani touched the floor where Lucien had lain, situating in her mind the location of his wound.

She walked to the top of the ramp and switched her duffel to her left shoulder, wincing as the weight settled over the bruise. She stuffed the sack of meal bars into the bag so her hands would be free, as they had been at the time. She then walked down the too-steep incline, matching step for step where she had walked before, her knee complaining with every impact.

She stopped at the place where she had fallen.

Fallen.

I fell. She touched her left shoulder, probed the perimeter of the contusion. *I slipped. Lucien grabbed for me as I fell, to help me up.*

Standing upright, she faced the spot from where the shot had come. Imagining Lucien still behind her, she reached around and marked in the air the place where his right hip had been.

I fell . . . he tried to help me up.

His right—her left. Contorting her arms, she marked the place on her back that lined up with Lucien's wound. The place the shot would have hit if she hadn't fallen. She then drew an imaginary line through her body, marked the point where it emerged with her hand, and looked down—

He tried to help me up.

—to find she had placed her hand over her heart.

"Looks like you reached the same conclusion I did."

Jani wheeled, nerves keening as augie pricked up his ears.

"I was in my office when the word came." Niall emerged from the shadows. "Half of Intelligence is parked at Neoclona. Shroud must be having a fit." He wore dress blue-greys—the entry light splashed over him, highlighting his packed shooter holster. He strolled down the ramp, his knees taking the impacts with enviable ease. "How's Pretty Boy?"

"Groggy from takedown and anesthesia. They wouldn't let me see him, but I'm told he'll recover completely." Jani stepped down the ramp to the comfort of the level floor. She wandered to the column where she'd found the Grenoble, and saw only a yellow ComPol marker where the weapon had lain. "It is possible that he was the intended target."

"You willing to bet your 'pack on that?" Niall wandered a circle at the foot of the ramp, eyes locked on the scancrete floor. "You willing to bet that whoever wanted you dead knows they missed, and are blowing the dust off their back-up plan?"

Jani leaned against the column to take the weight off her right knee. "You would have to bring that up."

Niall dug into his tunic; a nicstick soon saw the light. He eyed Jani with weary patience. "What did you do?"

Jani pushed off the column and gravitated toward the rear of the expanse. "Nothing."

Niall hurried after her. "This was a messy attempt. Somebody is spooked about something, and they didn't have time to plan. What happened in the past twenty-four hours?"

Jani opened the door that led to the garage stairwell. "I found out my parents were on their way here. I ticked off Anais Ulanova." *I faked a document*—She paused in mid-climb, then sped up before Niall noticed. *I faked a document, and waited for the lids to pop.* "Something popped, all right."

"What did you say?"

"My knee popped. I fell on it during the attack."

Niall unholstered his shooter and moved to one side so that Jani no longer stood in his line of fire. He drew even with her on the stair, then waved her back as they approached the landing. "Stay behind me, and keep your head down." He pushed the door open and went in low, arms extended, shooter gripped in both hands.

Jani scooted around him and ducked behind a waist-high trashzap. "I don't see anything out of the ordinary." She sprawled flat on her stomach and searched for unusual shadows beneath the scattering of skimmers that populated the space.

Niall had darted behind a column. "I'm scanning, and I don't sense anybody." His rough whisper emerged from shadow. "We're alone." He stepped into the light and pocketed his small box-like scanner. He also reholstered his shooter, but took care to leave the clasp undone. "Is this just an attack of nerves, or did you see something?"

"Nerves." Jani walked around the level, glancing through skimmer windows and placing her hand on battery casings, feeling for the residual warmth that indicated a recent trip. "You think *L'araignée*'s behind this."

"You don't want to know what I think." Niall checked the download time on a charge unit. "Where were you two going?"

"Idomeni embassy. An ongoing project had blown up, and they needed my input."

"Did you call to confirm?"

"No. It was a common occurrence." Jani crouched low to explore the shadows beneath a skimmer. Her knee griped accordingly. "You're heading somewhere with this. Spit it out." She straightened to find Niall standing beside her. He made as if to say something, hesitated, then took a deep breath.

"My Guernsey buddy—he has connections in the Channel commercial sector, which is how he found out about *L'araignée*. He couldn't find out many member names, but one of the ones that he heard a lot was Le Blond."

"You think that refers to Lucien? Le Blond happens to be a very common surname in the Channel."

"Le Blond helped organize *L'araignée*, Jani. He was one of the driving forces. He used his Family connections to arrange sweetheart vendor and maintenance contracts for some of the less cultivated members. Now I don't think Pascal is half the genius he thinks himself, but he's no dummy, he has Family connections, and he was in the area during the time in question." Niall's voice had turned cold, hard, like his facts. "He set you up. *L'araignée* knows you promote Haárin business interests in the colonies and they see you as a threat. They yanked his string, and he complied. Only you fell. Pretty Boy tried to pull you back into the line of fire, but he got hit instead."

Jani kicked at the bare floor, then strode to the wall opposite. She felt better when she walked, even when she had nowhere to go.

Niall fell in behind her. "Jan, if it fit any better, you could wear it to Gaetan's."

Jani examined the wall, standing so the beam from a safety light fell over her shoulder and highlighted the area. "Does this surface look right to you?"

"That's my Jani. When in doubt, change the subject." Niall moved in behind her and sighted down. "No." He stepped around her and brushed his hand over the wall surface. "There's an area that looks dull. The rest of the wall is shiny coated scancrete. But there's an area that doesn't reflect."

Jani stepped in front of the dull portion and examined the boundary. "It's a sharp line." She scratched the matte surface with a fingernail. Fine grey powder fluffed—she backed away to avoid inhaling it and risk a film-splitting sneeze.

"Probably just a patch." Niall leaned against a scancrete portion of the wall and folded his arms. "Maybe there used to be a passage between the renovation and the garage."

Jani dropped her bag to the floor at her feet, placed both hands against the matte panel, and pushed. Lightly first, then harder as the squeaking of shifting polyfill sounded.

Niall grumbled as he moved in beside her and set his hands against the panel. "On three. One . . . two . . . *three*!"

The panel gave with the screech of a startled rodent, then toppled backward into the blackness with a soft, floaty *thuk*. Jani stepped to the side and the shelter of the solid wall, then looked across to Niall to find he had done the same *and* pulled his shooter. "I don't think it's that serious."

"No?" Niall glared across the open space. "You know that just by looking, do you?"

"Hodge said that the construction crew figured out a way to circumvent their parking ban." Jani stepped into the space, taking care not to trip over the narrow gap where the two buildings met. "They're supposed to park their skimmers in the trade lots three blocks away, but they don't find that amenable."

"So they park here and use their ready-made door? So much for high-priced Family security." Niall's voice held aggravated wonder as he followed Jani through the gap. "Holy—!"

They entered a vast skeletal coliseum. No trace remained of the living areas and office space that had filled the former manse. The ten-story interior had been carefully demolished—all the flooring and interior walls had been removed, leaving only the structural supports and the exterior walls with their historic marbles and sculpture. Rings of scaffolding marked every floor, joined by hoists and rack ladders and the occasional portable lift.

"They're supposed to finish this by Thanksgiving." Jani reached out and touched a scaffold support. "Does this look anywhere close to done to you?"

"It looks like a goddamned shooting gallery." Niall stood hands on hips and surveyed the space. "Anybody coming through this opening is a clear target for anybody hunkered down on one of those levels."

"You look at the world differently than the average person, Niall." Jani climbed partway up a ladder, then shook it to test its solidity.

"This is true." Niall sauntered over to a workbench, brushed off dust with the flat of his hand, and sat. "You going to talk to me, or are you going to keep ducking the issue?"

Jani jumped down from the ladder, taking care to land on her left foot. "I don't know what you mean."

"The hell you don't." Niall eyed her impatiently. "Pascal's going to be in the hospital for a while?" He waited for Jani's affirmative nod. "Leave him there." He looked around the desolate interior again, and grimaced. "This place gives me the jim-jams. Let's go."

"In a second." Jani rummaged through an equipment bin until she freed an aerosol dispenser of lubricant. "Heard anything about my folks?"

"Nothing new to report. Everything proceeding as planned." Niall watched her activate the dispenser. "What the hell are you doing now?"

"When you find a door, first thing you do is see where it goes. Then you fix what needs fixing and remember where it is, because you never know when you may need it." Jani sprayed the lubricant over the sides of the polyfill panel, then returned the dispenser to the tool bin.

Niall helped her drag the now-silent panel back into place. "You look at the world differently than the average person, Jani."

Jani shrugged, catching herself as her left shoulder bit. "This is true."

Niall accompanied Jani to her building entry, offering a not-so-subtle recommendation that she avoid further explorations for the balance of the night. Then a Service sedan drifted out of the darkness and up to the curb.

The passenger-side gullwing popped up; Lt. Pullman bent low to look through the breach. "Good morning, ma'am. Glad to see you're OK." He stopped just long enough for Niall to climb in, then swung the vehicle around and disappeared into the dark.

Jani entered the lobby to find the night desk waiting for her. The ComPol had been by . . . several times . . . they had left messages . . . this was highly irregular. . . .

So's being shot at. Jani left the agitated woman behind for the quiet of the lift. On the way up, she uncased a meal bar. Chocolate-caramel wasn't her first choice for an early morning snack, but she felt light-headed again and the last thing she needed was another trip to Neoclona to hear John rumble "I told you so."

She keyed into her flat, and slipped through the open door and into the path of a redheaded hurricane.

"Where the hell have you been!" Angevin had returned to her own flat in the interim—she had exchanged her eveningwear for a pullover and trousers in a lived-in shade of yellow. "We've been waiting for *hours*! Don't you know what a comport is!"

"How much do you know?" Jani extracted her arm from Angevin's grasp and headed for the kitchen to find something to wash the taste of meal bar from her mouth.

"Not a fookin' thing." Steve emerged from the kitchen, soft drink dispo in hand, wearing a darker version of Angevin's outfit. "Fifteen minutes after you leave, we hear sirens. Run down to the lobby just in time to see you tumble into the ambulance after Blondie. Then before you can say Bob's yer uncle, we're up the spout with fookin' ComPol."

"We tried to tap friends for news, but nobody knew anything and there was a comlock on calls going in and out of the Ministries." Angevin wedged herself between Jani and Steve. "Are you all right? How's Lucien?"

"I'm fine." Jani tried to circle around the pair, but they moved as one to block her. "Lucien took a shooter blast in the stomach. He suffered burns and impact injuries. He had just come out of Surgery when I left Neoclona. They wouldn't let me see him, though—he was too woozy. But he'll be fine."

"So everyone's *fine.*" Steve raised the dispo like a toast. "So all's bright and sunny and we kin go home, then?" He pushed Angevin aside as gently as his temper would allow and stepped up to Jani. She stood taller than he, but that didn't seem to faze him. "What. Happened?"

Jani squirted past him and darted into the kitchen. "Robbery attempt. Idiot fired before we could give him what he wanted." She yanked open the cooler and scrabbled for a dispo of lemon tonic. She cracked the seal and drank half the container, then turned to find Steve standing in the entry, choirboy face clawed by fatigue.

"I told Ange yer shook and I sent her to bed." He stepped inside and let the door close. "We're sleepin' here, in one of the spares. Brought bedrolls from our flat, until we can order proper furniture. We're movin' in—we're not leavin' you alone."

"That's not necessary."

"Bullshit."

"You could be leaving yourselves open to some sort of retaliation."

"So it warn't no fookin' robbery, were it? It's like what happened to Barry."

"It—it's possible."

The unsureness of Jani's response touched Steve. His anger softened to aggravation—he patted her arm and backed off. "Get some sleep. You look all-in." He took a final swig of his drink and poured the remainder down the sink.

Jani trudged to her bedroom. Undressed. Showered. The egg beneath her right knee had shrunk to a marble, and the joint itself didn't hurt at all when the spray hit it. Her shoulder did, however—if she twisted her neck just so, she could just glimpse the tender, purple-red swelling.

She carried her trouser suit to her closet to hang it up; as she did, she caught sight of the green holosilk. She felt the release of the seams, the slide of the material down her skin. She stood in the middle of the closet, clutching the trouser suit. Then she hangered it and closed the door.

She pulled a pair of sleep shorts and a T-shirt out of her dresser. In her effort to avoid the mirror, she found herself looking at the painting of the costumed couple. It proved a more complicated scene than she had initially thought. The gowned woman stood in the center of the ballroom, amid a swirl of dancing couples. She looked toward the veranda where the young officer, clad in brilliant white, stood, but her expression held more worry than welcome. She may have planned a tryst with him for later that evening, but someone had gotten his signals crossed.

"Is that what happened, Lucien?" She sketched an outline around the young officer with her finger. "Niall thinks you tried to set me up. John and Val think something's up, too. They sure don't want me talking to you." She flicked her finger against his painted brim, as if to knock it off.

Then, for the first time, Jani noted the man with whom the woman had been dancing before the officer made his appearance. A dour, older sort in a staid evening suit, he watched the woman with the same intensity with which she studied the officer. "What do you know that I don't, John?" Jani asked the figure. "Hard fact? Rumor? Or just jealousy?"

She piled into bed. Sleep came eventually. At one point, she dreamed a shooter crack. The imagined sound shook her awake—she opened her eyes to find herself clutching her T-shirt over her pounding heart. She managed to fall asleep again, but it took time. Her head ached, and she flinched at every sound.

CHAPTER 16

"And the plan fer the day is what, then?" Steve sat opposite Jani on the sitting room floor near the window, the remains of a makeshift breakfast scattered between them—tea, bread and jam for Steve, coffee and a meal bar for her. "Talk to the ComPol, get them off yer back?"

Jani braced against the wall and struggled to her feet. "I need to go to Sheridan." She picked a fleck of chocolate from the sleeve of her dark brown trouser suit and massaged away the miniscule smear. "Besides, I have a lawyer. His name is Joaquin Loiaza—let him talk to the ComPol."

"Ah, yeah?" Steve locked his hands around his knee and rocked back. "This is what you want me to tell the green-and-whites when they call for the eighty-seventh time, or better yet, stop by in person?"

"I'll talk to them." Angevin sat at Jani's desk and screened through comport listings for furniture companies. "I know exactly what to say."

"You know exactly what to say to get us all arrested." Steve expelled a healthy billow of smoke. "Ange and I will get started on your paper mail," he said to Jani as he rose, "just to kill time before the ComPol rounds us all up."

"I'm ordering furniture first." Angevin hit the comport pad. "If I have to sit in this chair for one more hour, I'm going to get a nosebleed."

"You found any catalogs?" Steve planted himself in front of the desk. "So's we know what we're orderin'? So's we don't wind up with three purple couches?"

"I know how to furnish a flat."

"Oh yeah? Well, *I* remember—"

"Have fun, kids." Jani pulled her duffel from beneath the desk and waved good-bye as she slipped out the door.

"Foreign Transactions, please." Jani held out her Fort Sheridan ID to the front gate check-in desk.

"Yes, ma'am. Wait here please." The desk corporal disappeared with the ID into the communications alcove.

Jani wandered the tiny lobby. Outside the front window, the main archway of the Shenandoah Gate glistened in the morning sun, its whitestone surface etched with the names of those killed in the Greatest War, the conflict that defined the Commonwealth and her colonies generations before. Tens of thousands of Earthbound names.

Along with a few colonial. Her ever-remembered dead, inscribed in the only memorial they would ever have. *Borgie. Yolan. Felicio. Stanleigh.* Eleven others. Their names didn't belong in the Gate—Jani reentered them by means various after the Gate monitors excised them during their weekly checks. It was a losing battle on her part, she knew—sooner or later, implacability and cryptography would triumph over guile and bloody-mindedness. *But until it does, I'll keep plugging them in.* All the dead merited remembrance, especially those everyone wished forgotten.

"Ma'am?"

Jani turned.

"Colonel Hals is expecting you." The corporal held out Jani's ID, along with a day pass to clip to her jacket. "She says you know the way."

"Lt. Ischi, of course, knew almost immediately it happened. That young man has connections from Base Command to the vehicle pool. He called me at home. 'I hope you don't mind, ma'am,' he said." Frances Hals turned away from her office window and frowned at Jani. She looked prim and collected in her fallweights, wavy brown hair tucked into a tight french roll. "I'm disappointed that you didn't call me yourself."

"I didn't have the time." Jani had settled into her regular place in the visitor's chair near Frances's desk. "I spent most of the night at Neoclona. When I finally got back to my place, it was all I could do to fall into bed."

"Hmm." Frances walked slowly back to her desk. "All our regularly scheduled dealings with the idomeni embassy have been cancelled until further notice." She lowered into her chair. "Looks like

Shai's using this little misfortune as an excuse to reel in Tsecha's lead."

"That doesn't surprise me." Jani crossed her legs with care. Her right knee no longer hurt, and she wanted to keep it that way. "I think she wants to shut him out completely."

"Are they allowed to do that?"

"I think they've started listening to their xenobehaviorists too. I also think the term 'loose shooter' has been explained to them *ad nauseum.*"

"Hmm." Frances's round face turned a study in downward curves. She didn't appear as eager to discuss Nema and his quirks as she normally was. "So." She sat forward, cupping her chin in her hands. "What happened?"

"Everybody keeps asking me that."

"You were shot at! Lucien was gravely wounded. Heaven forbid we should care."

Jani picked at the thin band of upholstery covering the chair arm. "I don't know for sure. I think it was a blown robbery attempt, but I just don't know." She held back a "damn it!" One thing she missed about her former life was that she had never let anyone get close enough to ask questions she didn't want to answer. The fact that she lacked a complete answer to this particular question aggravated her even more.

"You'll tell us when you know?"

"Yes."

"All right." Frances held up her hands in surrender, then toyed with the edge of her leather desk pad. "I hate to admit this, but I do have a selfish reason for bugging you." She gave the pad a last, irritated shove. "We've become quite involved with the doings at the embassy since your discharge. In just a few short months, Foreign Transactions has gone from being a glorified colonial shipping office to playing a major role in the determination of Commonwealth–Shèrá policy."

Jani nodded. "You put your bird on the line to make that happen. It was a gutsy move, and you pulled it off."

"You helped." Frances's brown eyes flared a "don't give me that" warning. "The problem is, now that we're perceived as an arm of Diplomatic, we no longer handle the sort of work we performed during your short but eventful stay here. In other words, without the idomeni, we don't have anything to do. And you know what happens when the Service finds out some of its own don't have anything to do?"

Jani tugged her duffel onto her lap. "Reassignment."

"It's not a given, but it has crossed my mind." Frances smiled knowingly. "So, given that I know how much you dislike having people fuss after you, consider my inquiry into your affairs completely self-serving."

Jani let her head drop back against the headrest. "I appreciate it, really."

"No, you don't—you hate it. You're a born lone operator. You prefer that people disappear until you need them."

Jani lifted her head and stared into a quietly attractive face softened with weary humor. She enjoyed Frances's spot-on character assessments . . . except when they were directed at her. "You're the second person to tell me that in the past two days."

"Who was the other one?"

"Dolly Aryton. I went to see her yesterday about some . . . stuff."

Frances had paused to take a sip of tea. She held a hand over her mouth as she grabbed for her napkin. "Dorothea—?" She coughed, then tried again. "The Registry Inspector General?"

"I went to school with her."

"I know that." Frances dabbed at her shirtfront. "Which one was she again?"

"Five of Six. Earthly Might. Family connections." Jani eyed her timepiece as surreptitiously as she could. "Mind if I ask a question?"

"Oh, for heaven's sakes, Jani." Frances's face tightened with aggravation.

Why do I seem to possess such talent in that regard? "Do you think I'm immature?"

"Immature? My word, what did Aryton say to you?" Frances folded the napkin into a neat square and set it next to her cup. "If it makes you feel better, no. My take on the Kilian psyche is that you don't have much use for the social details other people think are important. No one's going to get a 'Good morning, and how are the kids?' from you—you just jump right into the business and that tends to ruffle folks. You're also intensely private, and when someone probes, the walls fly up. Sometimes, that knocks people off-guard, and sometimes it makes them angry." She shrugged. "And sometimes they find it attractive." She studied the folded napkin, her lips pursing. "Like your fine Lt. Pascal. I can't think of another man of my acquaintance who has less interest in the everyday, and he follows you like a moth follows a flame."

But Niall would tell you that he had his reasons. Jani heard a mild bumping against the office entry, like someone moving furniture.

Frances sighed. "That's Ischi's latest version of a ten-minute warning. He thinks it's less rude. I wish he'd use the intercom like everyone else." She tapped her workstation touchboard and checked her calendar. "And I do have a meeting in twenty minutes at North Lakeside, so I had better get my tail in gear." She gathered some files from a slotted rack. "Did you come here for a reason, or was this an actual social call?"

"I felt restless." Jani forced a smile in an effort to practice one of those disregarded details. "I just wanted to talk." She fingered the day pass, which would allow her to walk unimpeded anywhere in the South Central area of the base. Not that a visit to her former CO had been an onerous price to pay to obtain it. She liked Frances, and enjoyed her company. She called her a friend. That made it OK. No harm, no foul.

South Central Bachelor Officers' Quarters were situated atop the highest in the series of rises that served as an informal boundary between the business side of the base region and the sports facilities that took up most of the West Central area. Twelve floors of white cement, unadorned and sparsely landscaped, it seemed designed with the intent to persuade its tenants to either marry or move out as soon as possible. An interim place for the newly commissioned, it contained nothing to recommend it as a long-term domicile.

Lucien's lived here for four years. Jani entered the empty lobby. *Officially.* In reality, he had spent most of the time on Anais Ulanova's Security team, and had lived where her orders demanded. A good part of that time, he had offered during one pillow confession, had been spent running down rumors of Jani's existence. And Jani had believed him. That's how they had met, after all, when Lucien served undercover on the Interior ship that ferried her to Earth for the first time.

But did he spend all his time looking for me? Or had he worked double-duty laying the groundwork for *L'araignée? Are you Monsieur Le Blond, Lucien?*

She darted past the open entry of the rec room, from which the raucous sounds of a Cup match emanated. Up the stairs to the mezzanine. Down the hall to the lift.

Fifth floor, Number 5W1. Jani watched the floor indicator flick upward. She had obtained the address months before from the Base Directory. She had never visited Lucien's rooms, though—he had never invited her and she felt that there were some things about him she didn't want to know.

My mistake. She disembarked the lift. Turned left. Right. Left. Stopped before the middle door in the short hallway.

L. Pascal. The name had been etched on a rectangle of unpolished metal, the sort of seat-of-the-pants doorplate meant to be disposed of in a few months. Jani gave the door a sharp rap, because no one ever heard loud sounds, only quiet ones. Hit the entry buzzer twice. Knocked again.

Then she dug into her duffel for Lucien's wallet and picked the meager contents, looking for a key card. *Although God knows what good it will do.* The lockmech consisted of a handpad as well as a card reader, and since Jani had never visited, Lucien had never had a chance to key in her print. She dug out the key card and ran it through the reader anyway, then touched her hand to the plate with a sigh of acknowledged defeat. *I should have asked Niall to crib me access, but then he'd know I suspect Lucien of something and he'd take that ball and run with it—*

She froze as she heard the *whirr* of the lock. The slide of a bolt. The whisper of polywood surfaces sliding over one another as the door swept aside.

Jani stared dumbly at the opened door, hopped over the threshold as the sound of approaching footsteps startled her, then damned herself for her stupidity as the door slid closed behind her.

He's trapped me. He had rigged a system that let people in, but didn't let them out. Base Security was no doubt bearing down on her location at that very moment.

Then I had better get a move on, hadn't I?

Jani looked around. The sitting room contained a couch along the near wall, a table with two chairs along the windowed far wall. A narrow desk stood in the near corner by the door, its work surface filled by a comport and a stylus holder.

Jani walked to the desk. The comport's incoming message indicator showed still and dark. She hit the command pad anyway, in case it malfunctioned, but the device remained silent.

She gave one of the drawer pulls a ginger yank—like the entry, it opened to her touch. *I know how he did it.* An Intelligence gadget expert like him would have had no trouble obtaining her scan from her ServRec and coding it into his room network.

She checked the drawer's bare interior, feeling along the top and the underside in case he had stuck anything in the runners. *A* L'araignée *expense chit. A nameplate reading "Le Blond."* She closed the drawer and opened another, riffled through the blank parchment pads, picked through the small dish containing salvaged parts from old styli. Examined the last drawer to find it empty.

As she gave the bare white walls a visual once-over, Jani dug into her briefbag for her own devices. The bugscan to check for monitoring appliances, the sniff to nose out whatever toys Lucien had stashed away for later use. She examined the couch cushions, the furniture frames, the baseboards, the lighting fixtures. She even peeled up a corner of the thin carpet to check for a floor cache. The flooring, however, proved to be solid poly, a material that prevented such a hiding place.

Jani moved on to the bathroom, which, like the sitting room, contained very little of its occupant. The shelf above the sink held only a stack of dispo cups and a toiletry kit. She unclasped the kit and rummaged through the compartments. *Shaver . . . soaps . . . hairwash . . . toothbrush . . .*

She probed the innermost pocket, flinching as her fingernail struck something hard. She pushed further, looping her finger around the small, stone-like object and pulling it out into the light.

Red and blue painted clothes reflected as though still wet. A tiny face, its eyes closed in sleep. The missing piece from the matryoshka. The innermost one.

The baby. Jani examined the tiny figure, on distracted lookout for any grooves or pinholes into which a bug could have been inserted. She skirted around any thoughts as to what the presence of the doll in Lucien's kit *meant*—that was the sort of question to toss at Dolly or Frances. *He put it here for me to find.* She held that thought close as she stuffed the doll back in its recess and set the bag back on the shelf, then scanned the bathroom as she had the sitting room.

The bedroom, to Jani's complete lack of surprise, was the one place where Lucien let his personality show. Instead of standard issue white polycottons, he'd made his bed with silk-like linens in the same rich, chocolate shade as his eyes. His pillows were overlarge and encased in paisley-patterned covers of burgundy, brown, and dark blue. Jani scanned them, then commenced a hand-search. She probed under one pillow, then inside the case itself. Her hand closed around something silky.

"What the hell . . . ?" She pulled out a favorite bandbra that she had given up for lost a month before. It had been laundered and carefully folded, and exuded the peppery aroma of an expensive cologne. She stared at it, her mind stalling as it did over the doll. *He . . . wanted me to find this.* It was the only reason that made sense. She tucked the bra back where she found it, then continued her exploration. She found nothing else of note, except for a few long strands of red hair.

She scanned the closet with its neat row of uniforms, the walls and fixtures. She then moved on to the dresser, which proved as sparsely decorated as the desk. Sparse, yes, but oh so tasteful. A brush-comb set in heavy sterling silver. A catch-all dish of antique china. A head and shoulders portrait of a young boy, framed in silver and leaning against the mirror.

Jani picked up the sketch. The boy appeared in his early teens, androgynous beauty just beginning to segue into masculine handsomeness. He wore an open-necked white shirt. His silver-blond hair fluttered in the artist's breeze.

"Portrait of the lieutenant as a young man." Jani pondered the familiar line of jaw and chin, then set the picture down and turned her attention to the drawers. There were three of them—she tugged open the top one.

Uh . . . huh. She lifted out a weighty silk scarf adorned with the bold scrollery popular with the Family women she had seen in her building. *I'll bet my 'pack this once belonged to Anais.* Several more bandbras and a couple of men's T-shirts, all laundered and scented.

Jani sorted and counted. Eight items in all, belonging to six women and two men. She wondered absently whether the redhead rated a souvenir, or if she hadn't yet worked her way into that special category. *And then there's me.* She wondered what she had done to rate the pillowcase of honor.

The next drawer contained a more mundane assortment—Lucien's underwear, socks, and gymwear.

Jani pulled at the bottom drawer, then pulled again. Repositioned her hands and yanked hard, without success. She set down her briefbag, crossed her legs at the ankle, and lowered to the floor. Tried to remove the drawer above to see if she could go in over the top, and found that one fastened to the runners in such a way that she'd need a metal saw to hack it out.

"This drawer, you lock. Why?" A snatch of childhood story surfaced in her memory. In it, the husband told his new bride, "You may open every door in the house but this one."

"And we know what she did, don't we?" Jani dragged her bag onto her lap. She pulled on a pair of dispo gloves, the sort she wore to keep skin oils from contacting delicate paper. She didn't care that she had left hair, skin, and fingerprints throughout the suite. She and Lucien had been seen together around Sheridan, and it would be his word against hers that she had never before visited his rooms. However, she hadn't yet left anything in a place no one would expect, and while her hair and skin cells could waft about and wind up anywhere, her prints would stay where they were put.

Gloves in place, she searched through her miscellaneous tools for a suitable pry, and uncovered a knife that she used to open particularly stubborn envelopes. "Yes, Lucien, I'm playing into your hands. I'm doing just what you want me to do. Well, you can needle me about it later." She stood, pulled the dresser away from the wall, and wedged the blade into the paper-thin gap where the dresser's back panel met the frame. Trying to lockpick or pry open the drawer from the front would have taken hours and tools and devices she didn't have. Besides, the drawer fronts were too thick and well protected, while the rear panel usually proved, as in this case, to be only a thin sheet of poly. *They never expect you to go through the back.* That lapse of judgment on the part of the furniture manufacturers of the Commonwealth had served her well for many years.

It took her thirty-two minutes to pry the side of the panel away from the frame to the point that she could fit her hand through the gap. She walked around to the front of the dresser, pulled out the drawer above the locked drawer as far as it could go, then returned to the rear. As it turned out, the drawers were separated by more thin layers of poly. An inconvenience, but not an insurmountable one. Jani wedged her knife into a corner and pried some more—after a few minutes, she had freed the edge sufficiently that with the help of a stylus-light, she could see into the locked drawer's interior.

She had to lie on her stomach and prop herself up on her elbows to see into the tight space. Her lower back cramped as she boosted her torso; the points of her elbows ached from supporting her weight. She flicked the light beam between tight and wide angle—tight was brighter, but wide illuminated a larger space. She had no idea what to expect. More valuable gifts? A long shooter, broken down into easily stored sections? Sex toys bizarre enough for even Lucien to hide?

Instead of any of those, she found . . . an arrangement. Neat rows of folded cloths, either napkins or scarfs, lined the bottom of the drawer. Centered atop most of the squares were small objects: a shot glass, a marker disc of the type handed out by casinos, a stylus, a small hairclip, and other items, their only commonality their small size and their ordinariness.

Jani counted. Lucien had folded twenty-four small squares, of which fifteen held objects. She tried to push her hand into the small breach so she could reach the casino marker, the closest object in the strange collection. Failing that, she crawled around the front for her bag and mined for the long-blade forceps she used to pick up delicate documents.

It was an easy pickup. She'd had practice at that sort of thing.

Jani stood up. Uncricked her back. Pocketed the marker. Smoothed the poly separator back into place and straightened the rear panel until only a minor bend at the corner betrayed her invasion.

He'll know. But that had been the point of the entire game, hadn't it? He'd know she looked, and he'd know she knew. *That he keeps souvenirs.* Of his special sexual conquests. *And other . . . events in his life.* Whatever they were.

Jani pushed the dresser back against the wall. Gathered her bag. Did one final sweep to make sure things looked as they had when she entered.

The front door opened for her, releasing her into the quiet of the hallway, negating her concern about reverse alarms. Three halls, three turns. The lift down to the mezzanine. The lobby, and the sounds of football matches. Outside, and the bright sun, cool breeze, and the bump and jostle of normal life.

Her nerves nipped at her—she braved the long hike to the Shenandoah Gate to dull their edge. She felt the casino marker in her pocket, weightless yet leaden, filled with information that she had always known existed, but hadn't needed until now.

CHAPTER 17

Tsecha leafed through the latest Council reports transmitted from Shèrá, combing through the phrases for his name. He did not see it, of course. Unless his workstation search of the machine versions of the documents had faltered badly, he did not expect to. *But I look anyway.* Because he had nothing else to do. Because he felt well on the Way to madness, and the turning of pages calmed his disjointed mind.

After he finished reading exactly three pages, he looked up to the timeform on his work table and counted backward, converting to humanish chronography as he did so. *Five hours since the sunrise.* Five hours since Dathim had departed for the Exterior Ministry to search for the most propitious place to lay his tile. Among other things.

Tsecha once more forced his gaze upon the Council report. After three more pages, he would look at the timeform again, count backward again, convert time again. He felt this pattern served him best. If he looked at the timeform more often, it appeared as though no interval had passed at all, as though all was *now* and nothing had happened. If he checked it less often . . . well, he could not check it less often. *Then I would go mad, and truly.*

He pressed his sleeve to his mouth to stifle an unseemly yawn. He had not slept. His encounter with Dathim had agitated and thrilled him. He had passed the night staring at his ceiling and remembering Rauta Shèràa during that final Laumrau season. The nights, long and sleepless as the one he had just spent, when he and his Hansen plotted and planned and searched the humanish enclave for his missing Jani.

Unfortunately, we did not find her. But they had battled John Shroud, for whom lies and deceit were as speaking and breathing, and to win that bout would have been most difficult. He and Hansen had no assistance, no information—the Consulate preferred to believe his Jani dead, therefore dead she was.

It seemed as though I fought only humanish then. His own Vynshàrau, he had not counted as adversary until the war's end. *Then when our time came, I fought them as they were meant to be fought.* Openly, with well-tuned argument and honorable disputation, not with the stealing of documents, the plundering of offices and laboratories, the treachery, and the lies. He and his many esteemed enemies would all have preferred to be slaughtered in the streets as the Laum had been rather than to stoop to such behavior in the sacred halls of Temple.

Now it appeared the time had changed, and with that change came confusion and difficulty in believing what had happened. *It was much easier to do this subterfuge when I was the only one who knew how.* Now everyone possessed such knowledge, from the Oligarch to the Haárin. *And I am left behind.*

Three more pages. Another evaluation of the timeform.

Tsecha leaned back in his chair. He felt the frame stab him in the usual places, the sole constancy in his life over the last days. *What do you do now, Dathim?* Which room did he stand in? Whose desk did he search? *Where did you learn such things?* Who had served as his Hansen, his teacher?

Three more pages. After he assessed time's passage, he paused to watch the shadows commence their meander across his wall. A worthless exercise, and truly. Most appropriate to his new station at the embassy.

"NìRau?"

Tsecha twisted in his chair, gouging himself in the side.

Sànalàn stood in the entry. She wore an informal overshirt and floor-length skirt in the color of wet sand, which meant she had been about the business of the altar room.

"The altar cloths should be changed. I have brought these for your approval." She stepped into the workroom and extended her arm, over which she'd draped several folded oblongs of brown and dull green. The cloths had been freshly laundered, the hems newly rolled. Hem-rolling was a tedious duty, and as such allowed for contemplation.

Ah. Tsecha took the top cloth from the pile and pretended to examine it as he awaited the outcome of Sànalàn's meditation. She offered no formal indication that she wished to discuss something with him. But she had been his assumptive daughter and suborn since

Aeri's death, and he had long ago learned to recognize her informal signs. "These are most sound, nìa, and truly." He handed the cloth back to her, and waited.

Sànalàn took the cloth and slapped it atop the pile. She then stood as though captured in place, as though a serpent crawled past her and she dared not move until it had passed.

Tsecha glanced back at his timeform. Dathim would no doubt spend most of the day at Exterior. Perhaps until sunset, or even beyond. This meant that Tsecha could offer Sànalàn as much time as she needed to discuss her meditations.

"We must speak, nìRau."

And so it began.

Tsecha closed the cover of the Council report. "Yes, nìa." He stood and walked to his window, which looked out over the embassy grounds, landscaped with the grasses and shrubs of Shèrá. "Say what you will." He fixed his gaze on what little of his homeworld that he recognized, and waited.

"You have stated repeatedly before idomeni and humanish that I am not to succeed you." Sànalàn's voice emerged level, with none of the elevated tones or inflections of supplication. "I have spoken of this with nìaRauta Shai. She tells me I should not be concerned, that I am your suborn by ordination of Temple and Council, and that more than your word is needed to remove me from this station."

Tsecha turned his hands palms-up and raised them to waist level, a gesture of profound agreement. "Such is true, nìa." He rounded his shoulders, but only by the smallest deviation from vertical. A hint of displeasure to come, rather than a warning of existing anger. "But you should consider that a suborn requires the complete confidence of her dominant in order to train effectively. You should also consider that, after the events of these last days, such confidence no longer exists."

"Did it ever?"

Tsecha turned to find Sànalàn standing beside his work table, one hand gripping the edge as though she needed support to stand. "For as long as I remember, you searched for her. From the time I first studied the scrolls and laved the altar stones, I listened to you talk of her to friends and enemies alike as though she served you and not me. I wondered for so long who this Kilian was, this strange humanish that you felt merited your place. Then I learned." She released her hold on the table, standing still and silent as though she needed to regain her balance. Then she pulled the cloths one by one from her arm and stacked them atop one another on the table.

After she finishes, she will pick them up, one by one, and place them again across her arm. Such actions, Tsecha knew as he knew his robes and his rings. "You learned only what Cèel and Shai wished you to know, nìa, that my Jani slaughtered the Laumrau as they took sacrament. They left it to me to tell you of the betrayal of our Way by the Laumrau, and the treachery of Rikart Neumann. By then, it was too late. Cèel's half-truths suited your ambitions better, thus you preferred them."

"My *ambitions*?" Sànalàn's voice deepened as her shoulders rounded. "I did not choose to serve as your suborn, nìRau, I was chosen. As was my body-father. As were you. As are all who serve the gods. We are given no choice." She clenched the topmost cloth she held, crumpling it as paper. "The gods marked me, nìRau, by birth and examination. Are you maintaining that they did not know what they did? Are you saying that you know better than they who should serve them?"

Tsecha turned away so that he could not see Sànalàn's posture. Only if he ignored her form and concentrated on her words could he divorce her from his memories of her youth, when she argued with him over lessons and made him laugh. When she spoke in ways that brought back her body-father. When he had esteemed her. *You have come here to betray me, nìa, to make me utter blasphemies that you can report to Shai.*

"You must provide me an answer, nìRau." The voice, stripped of respectful inflection, goaded him. "I am deserving of one, and truly."

The ground cover outside Tsecha's window captured the sunlight and returned a blaze of blue. *My Jani warned us all of the Sìah, and your love of rules. Now you will punish me for breaking rules by causing me to break more.* "You would perform adequately as Chief Propitiator if times were as normal, nìa. I have no doubts in that regard." Tsecha remained focused on the view out his window. "But as we change, as the times become not normal, adequacy will not serve. We will need the strength of one who knows how to fight, who knows death, who knows . . . loyalty." He heard a roaring in his head, as he had on the night Aeri died. The Laumrau had bombed the Temple, and all Vynshà knew that the next battles would attain a level unlike any ever fought by idomeni. "Even as she acts as toxin, even as she brings pain and change, my Jani protects those she calls her own." He offered silent prayer, and turned to face his traitor. *You may deny your truth in order to save it. I am Vynshàrau, and I would sooner die than corrupt it so.* "I predict great change, and with it, great pain. Those who claim my Jani as their dominant will need the protection that only she can give."

Sànalàn had once more gripped the edge of the work table, but whether she did so out of anger or fear for the steps she took, she did not make clear by her posture or gesture. "You deny the will of the gods?"

"I interpret what I believe their will to be. Cèel and Shai deny my interpretation because it does not suit their beliefs. They defer to me as propitiator, yet deny me the right to act as is my duty. So humanish are they in their conflict between words and actions, it is as though they have already hybridized." Tsecha savored the anger that leached into his words, and rounded his shoulders fully in gratifying announcement of the emotion. He wished his Jani in the room, so he could hear her yell at him to wait until it is safe. *It will never be safe, nìa. It will only . . . be.*

"You dishonor the Oligarch and his suborn with your words. You spread disorder as the winds strew sand." Sànalàn's own posture bowed to match his. "I should challenge you."

"Yes, nìa. You should." Tsecha fought back the impulse to shout aloud in joy. Only a little while before, he sat at his work table contemplating shadows. *And now I have this glorious declaration!* "But before you do so, consider the certain result. Consider that never in the history of the Vynshà Temple have declared enemies served as chief and suborn propitiator. Chained by tradition as Cèel is, do you believe and truly that he would allow such a thing?"

"Cèel is not so chained, nìRau." Sànalàn straightened in respect as she uttered the Oligarch's name. "He is the one who commands us to act as walls before the humanish—it is *you* who seek to shackle us by your interpretations of tradition. To scare us with your talk of hybridization, when we all know the blending will never be!" She bowed her shoulders again, in a hunch only possible in one so young. "You are disorderly! You are unseemly! I do challenge you!"

Tsecha could hear Hansen's voice in his head. *You get them where you want them, and then "Gotcha!"* Hansen spoke of the Consulate humanish, of course, but if idomeni were determined to behave as such, let them learn what it meant. "You must petition your dominant for the right to offer challenge." He slumped in grave dignity. "Do you petition me, nìa?"

Sànalàn's spine wavered as a young tree in the wind. "Yes, nìRau, I do petition you." Her voice lilted with uncertainty as the gravity of her action bore upon her.

Tsecha nodded in humanish nothingness. "Petition is conveyed. Right is granted. Challenge is accepted. Which of us will inform Suborn Oligarch Shai, nìa?"

The joy of challenge left Sànalàn's posture. Her left arm crossed over her soul in dismay. *"NìRau?"*

"Yes, nìa?" Tsecha bared his teeth.

"NìaRauta Shai will take no joy in this!"

"You are quite correct in that, nìa, and truly." He tried to imagine his Jani's reaction when she heard of what had transpired and felt his own soul clench, for his Jani scared him more than Shai ever did. "You have taken steps against me that no other suborn has ever taken against their dominant. In your fear of change, you have changed beyond belief."

Sànalàn's arm dropped to her side as her anger revived. "It is your Kilian's fault! I do this because of her!"

My toxin. "Yes, nìa. So you do." He jerked his shoulders in a maddening humanish shrug. "So do I." He turned away from his newest enemy toward the blue lawns of home. "So do we all."

"This is a desecration and a denigration! This is anathema!" Shai paced before her work table, a humanish trait that she had acquired during the War. "This cannot be!"

"Challenge cannot be retracted after it is accepted by the challenged, Shai." Tsecha stood in solitary censure in the middle of the Suborn Oligarch's private workroom. Sànalàn had long since been escorted to her rooms by Diplomatic Suborn Inèa, who had pledged to serve as her support, much to Shai's consternation.

"You knew this would happen, Tsecha." Shai lapsed into the short sentences and truncated gestures of Low Vynshàrau, as was her habit when angered. "She is as youngish, and your constant public declarations of Kilian have dishonored her. She sought to discuss the matter with you, and you lured her into the worst show of disunity that we have ever displayed!"

"You sent her to trap me into blasphemy. Your attempt failed. See the price of failure when you play as humanish?" Tsecha pressed a hand to the point where his left leg met his hip, and winced. "I am sitting down, Shai." He limped to a low seat set against the wall opposite Shai's desk.

Shai stopped in midstride. "You are not . . . ?"

"No, I am not *ill,* Shai." Tsecha stressed the word for sickness because he knew Shai disliked such things discussed openly. "I am only tired."

Shai swept her right hand across her face as though she brushed away one of Jani's wasps, a gesture of profound displeasure. "I did not send your own suborn to trap you."

"Do you think me stupid, Shai—of course you did."

"Do you call me a liar?"

"Does that shock you? I have called you worse." Tsecha maneuvered a cushion so that it padded a particularly sharp metal prong. "Have you learned anything of my Jani?"

Shai hesitated. "You will be most happy to hear that she is apparently most well. She roams the city. Lt. Pascal remains in the Neoclona facility. He is to leave soon, I understand. His injuries were not insignificant, but humanish augmentation precipitates rapid healing." She gestured in confusion. "How openly they speak of their illnesses. It stuns me continuously."

Tsecha sat so his left leg stuck straight out. A bizarre posture, complicated by the unfamiliar irritations of Shai's furniture. "It is wise to get past an enemy's ability to stun before imitating them in everything they do." He lapsed into Low Vynshàrau as well—the roughened language complimented his physical discomfort. "One of our soldiers would have explained such to you if you had asked."

"You are arrogant, Tsecha."

"I am arrogance itself, Shai. So I have been told many times." Tsecha felt the pain ease in his hip, a muscle cramp only. "When will the challenge be allowed to take place?"

"There will be no challenge." Shai walked again, this time to the far end of the long room and back. She had arranged all her furniture against the walls so nothing impeded her loping stride. "I will return you to Shèrá before I allow such."

"But you plan to do such anyway, Shai." Tsecha bared his teeth. "This is the excuse for which you have searched! Most excellent, Shai, and worthy of the most deceitful humanish."

"This challenge would devastate us. It will not be allowed to take place."

"As I am the challenged, it is for me to relinquish the right, and such I will never do."

"I will tell Cèel of this."

"Yes, Shai, you will tell. Such is your way." Tsecha rose and walked to the door, holding onto the heavy wood of the entry before pushing himself away and into the hall.

The news of Sànalàn's challenge had already traveled into every corner of the embassy with the air and the light. The greetings Tsecha received were delivered with gestures of perplexity and question, surprise and anger. He looked forward with thankfulness to the solitude of his rooms. Now, the prospect of turning pages held the promise of rest, which he needed most surely.

His step quickened as he approached his door. He did not notice the shadow across the hallway until it stepped forward into his path.

"You will walk with me, nìRau." Dathim wore the drab colors of a crafts worker, a dark green cloth wrapped around his shorn head. He spoke in statement, not in question, as though the possibility of refusal did not exist.

Tsecha again pressed a hand to his hip. The ache had returned, dull but persistent. Idomeni philosophers made much of the mind-focusing abilities of pain, but he had lost patience with such, and truly. *I must sleep.* And take sacrament—it had been seasons since he recalled a true longing in his soul for such.

Then he caught sight of the weighty sling pouch hanging from Dathim's shoulder, of the sort used by craftsworkers to carry their tools. "Yes, ní Dathim." He took a step forward and suppressed a groan as pain shot down his leg. "I will walk with you."

"The Exterior Ministry is a most strange place." Dathim's stride covered ground as rapidly as a skimmer. His speech came too quickly for his gestures to keep up—his posture altered so quickly he appeared in spasm. "Storage rooms next door to work rooms instead of in separate wings. Humanish sitting at work tables out in the open, in the middle of hallways!"

"They are called *receptionists*, ní Dathim." Tsecha struggled to match the Haárin's stride, but finally surrendered to pain and fatigue. "Or sometimes, they are just called *desks,* like the furniture at which they sit." He limped to the first bench he saw, and sank gratefully onto the sun-warmed surface. The radiant heat warmed him through his robes, a gift from the gods, and truly.

"Remarkable!" Dathim circled the bench, head down, like a youngish inscribing a games boundary. "NìaRauta Atar advised me to seek you out, nìRau Tsecha, for absolution. Such were the things we saw that she felt it necessary." He stopped in place and glanced at Tsecha. "This is why we speak here, nìRau. Because I seek absolution."

"Wise, ní Dathim."

"In case we are asked why we speak so frequently. It is because my soul is troubled by so much contact with humanish."

"I understand, ní Dathim."

Dathim turned full-face. His gold eyes altered to molten yellow in the bright sunlight. "You are not well, nìRau." Again, he spoke in statement, not in question.

"I am tired, ní Dathim." Tsecha shivered as a lake breeze brushed him. "I have not slept since we spoke amid the trees."

"I slept most well." Dathim sat, legs splayed in the sprawl of a humanish male. "It is wise to do so at times such as these." He lowered the sling pouch to the tiles at his feet and freed the closures. "Humanish are strange."

"Reading of and hearing of does not prepare one for the reality, ní Dathim." Tsecha paused to untangle one of his side braids, which a gust of breeze caused to entangle in an earring. "At times, the disorder is enlivening. Other times, it is most vexing, and tru—" His words expired to nothing as Dathim opened the sling pouch, and he saw what lay inside.

"They have no idea, nìRau." Dathim reached into the pouch and lifted out a documents slipcase. Beneath it lay more slipcases, folders, and wafer envelopes. "None."

"*Dathim.*" Tsecha leaned forward and ran a finger over the slipcase.

"They meet us outside, the humanish. Minister Ulanova is one of them. She laughs too loudly. Her hands flutter as a youngish. I do not like her." Dathim sat back, hands in tense rest atop his thighs, yellow eyes watching the water. "They lead us inside. Me. NìaRauta Atar, who does not belong but she is my facilities dominant, so I cannot argue. Ní Fa, who is suborn to me. The young pale-haired one, who looks as the lieutenant who was shot—?"

Tsecha visualized an angry red face. "Lescaux."

Dathim nodded. "Lescaux. He takes over. He precedes us, which is odd, considering his station. He should walk behind, and let one of his suborns lead, but such are humanish." He nudged the sling pouch with his booted toe, so that the gaping opening closed. "He is despised."

"Despised?"

"Beddy-Boy, they call him when he cannot hear." Dathim raised a hand and let it drop, a gesture that meant nothing. "Ulanova has elevated him. She touches him when she thinks they are alone, the way humanish do. Why do the others laugh?"

Tsecha flicked his right hand in puzzlement. "Humanish make mockery of such, I have learned. The difference in age and station bothers them. It makes no sense. Such elevations are most seemly. Most orderly."

"Maybe humanish get it wrong. Like Lescaux leading us. I have noticed that humanish often get it wrong." Dathim sat in silence, his gaze still on the water. "They show us the lobby first. It is an open space with many windows. Most appropriate for a wall mural or a floor work. Not *both*. NìaRauta Ulanova wants *both*." He reached up and tugged the cloth from his head, exposing his sheared scalp. "A smaller space, I tell them. Otherwise, it is too much. So they take me upstairs, to the conference room."

Tsecha grew aware that he held his breath, and forced himself to inhale.

"The room they show me is in the same wing with the dominants' rooms. The *offices*. I watch the humanish walk from one to the other as if what belongs to one belongs to all. No hand readers. No ear scans. They label the doors with the names of the residents. It is as walking into my workroom and taking a tool from its hook!" Dathim's breathing rasped, as though he ran. "They take me to the conference room. It is beside Ulanova's office, connected by an inner door."

Tsecha closed his eyes.

"They take me inside the conference room. It is large, with a window. I say I can tile the wall opposite the window. Ulanova says she wants the floor, as well. I say, too much. She says, what of the short wall? Perpendicular to the wall I will tile. Opposite the wall with the inner door." Dathim's breathing slowed. "I needed to sight. Several times. I say I need room to do such. Lescaux opens the inner door. I sight. Several times. The first time, I walk by Ulanova's desk. I look at what is there. I cannot tell what concerns your Kilian. The second time, I take a file from the middle of a stack, and put it in my pouch. The third time, another file from the top of a stack. Four, five, six times I sight. Each time, I take a file from a different place, except for the last time, when I take the wafers from a holder beside Ulanova's comport."

"But you do not know what you took?"

"It is on a dominant's work table. It must therefore be important."

"Yes." Tsecha opened his eyes, then squinted as the glare of the sun off a lakeswell pained him. "Ní Dathim?"

"Yes, nìRau?" Dathim sat forward in another humanish posture, elbows on knees, legs still open, hands hanging inward.

"When humanish steal, they follow certain protocols. Either they ensure that the thing they take will not be missed, or not be missed until they are well away." Hansen's rules played through Tsecha's memory, in his Tongue's mellow, musical voice. "It is best that the thief not be around to be linked to the thievery. Nìa Ulanova will realize quite soon that these files you have taken are no longer in her office. It may not take her long to determine that you took them, and you and I will still be here in this damned cold place when she does so."

Dathim held up his hands, then let them drop, yet another variation on the ubiquitous humanish shrug. "They would not think a Vynshàrau could do such things, nìRau."

"You are Vynshàrau *Haárin*, ní Dathim."

"How well do the humanish know the difference, nìRau?"

"They will soon learn." Tsecha rose slowly and trod the short path that led from the bench to a stand of shrubs. His hip no longer ached, but his head pounded.

"I did as you asked, nìRau." Dathim's voice pitched low in anger.

"I asked you to look for documents about my Jani."

"I did not have time to read, nìRau, only to take!"

"Yes, and now you must get rid of that which you took quite soon, and truly."

"How?"

"If I admit I have them . . . the humanish call such an *incident,* ní Dathim. Humanish do not like incidents." Tsecha turned and walked back to the bench, kicking at the pouch with his booted foot as he passed it.

"An incident?" Dathim's voice held a tension beyond anger. "As your suborn challenging you—that is an incident, also?"

"So, you have been listening to conversations in hallways again. Yes, ní Dathim, that is also an incident. I am quite good at them, and truly." Tsecha kicked at the pouch again. "I can think of only one way to get rid of these."

Dathim passed a hand over his clipped head. "Tell me, nìRau."

Tsecha told him.

CHAPTER 18

Jani returned to her flat to find a great deal less open space than when she left.

"Now this is more like it." Steve sprawled across one end of the room's new centerpiece, a large couch upholstered in ivory polycanvas. "And there's a table in the dining room now. With chairs yet. One can actually sit and eat and not have to chow over the kitchen sink—*that's* a concept I can live with."

"You've gone soft in your old age is your problem." Jani sat at the opposite end of the couch, picking through the leafy innards of her Neoclona vegetable sandwich as she surveyed her new furnishings. A pair of off-white chairs now sat in the far corner. Adding to the new decor were a few strategically placed birch tables, brushed steel floor lamps, and a huge oval rug in shades of sapphire, cream, and tan.

Jani popped the last bite of lunch into her mouth, then thumped the cushion on which she sat—it was thick and firm and buffered her back marvelously. "I'm going to miss that wide-open feel."

"Blow yer wide-open feel. Every time I talked, I heard an echo." Steve stuck an unignited 'stick in his mouth, and chewed reflectively. "So, what'd ya do at Sheridan?"

Jani plucked at the cushion edge. "Visited Frances Hals. I figured she'd heard about the shooting, and I knew she'd worry until I checked in."

"Could have called her. Saved a trip."

"Some things should be handled in person."

"Jan the Goodwill Ambassador. Will wonders never cease?" Steve lay back his head and stared at the ceiling. "I figured you'd have stopped by Intelligence, asked a few questions about Blondie.

Found out whether that embassy thing he came to take you to were a load or not."

It was. Jani reached into her jacket pocket and felt for the casino marker.

"Did ya hear me, Jan?"

"I heard you." She slipped out the plastic disc and examined it under the light of one of her new lamps. It was a hard, bright green, like a cheap gemstone. Three centimeters in diameter, smooth surfaces trimmed with a ridged rim.

"Gone gamblin', did ya?" Steve's brows arched. "Must've felt lucky—greens run five to ten thousand Comdollars, depending on the casino."

Jani held the marker directly up to the light source, squinting as she tried to see through it. "These things come loaded."

"With what? A chip?" Steve scooted down the couch, his clothes hissing against the polycanvas. "Might, since it's a big denomination. Casino might register them."

"They do." Jani lifted her duffel onto her lap. "Plastic this thick can be hard to scan."

"I can scan plastic. I used to have to log in equipment in Helier, so I had my 'pack source boosted." Angevin rounded the couch and sat on the floor at Jani's feet—she held a juice dispo in one hand and her scanpack in the other. "So how do you like my decorating?"

"Nice." Jani handed her the casino marker.

"She misses the wide-open feel," Steve added helpfully.

"Blow." Angevin worked through her 'pack start-up checks, then held out her hand for the marker. She passed her scanpack reading surface over one side, then the other. Once. Twice. Again. "It's colony. Beyond that, I can't tell anything."

"Too thick?" Jani took the marker from her and again held it under the lamplight.

"I don't think so." Angevin glowered at the disc with the suspicious eye of a thwarted dexxie. "Could be the dye in the plastic. Some of them emit at wavelengths that interfere with scanmechs. I'd need a sheath that filters at just the right hairline of the spectrum in order to read further."

"Could be sending blocking signals, too." Steve reached for the marker, but Jani batted his hand away.

"Blocking dyes and signals are controlled out of Registry." She held the marker by the edges and tried to flex it. "Legal casinos can't use them and the illegal ones don't bother. The only problem with this thing is it's too thick." She felt it bend, very slightly, and eased off. "It's a marker—they're never meant to leave the casino." She held it up to the light again to see if she could spot the whitened stress cracks. "Bets are tracked by other means. All this should contain is the name of the casino and the pit registry code." She gripped the edges again and flicked her wrists down. The marker snapped like an overbaked cookie.

"What the hell ya do that for!" Steve pulled the nicstick out of his mouth—it had suddenly developed a distinct bend in the mouthpiece. "You just—*gah*!" His hand flew to his mouth. He ran into the kitchen.

"Bit right through to the scent core." Angevin watched her lover's flight with a distinct lack of anxiety. "With his temper, he does that about once a week. Stings like hell for a few seconds, then his tongue goes numb. You'd think that would teach him not to smoke those damned clove things, but he's got a memory like a stalk of celery."

Jani dug tweezers out of her tool kit and probed one of the marker's newly exposed inside edges. "You don't seem concerned."

"Shuts him up for hours. Sometimes I appreciate the peace and quiet." Angevin grinned and hunched her shoulders as though she'd said something naughty. "But sometimes I ask him questions that he can't answer with a yes or no, just to see that Guernsey glower." She moved into a kneeling position and studied the marker half that Jani examined. "I hope you didn't screw up the chip."

Jani used the sharp points of the tweezers to work a groove into the broken edge. "In a casino, you pay for everything with markers. Officially, purchases and bets are tracked with handprints, but as part of the tradition, you go through the motions of paying with markers. They're made breakable so you can get change back. Because of that, the chips are offset in one of the quadrants, well away from the break-axes." She eased up on the pressure as she poked into a miniscule open space. "Get that antistat out of my bag."

Angevin pulled out the square of charge-dissipating black cloth that sat atop the muddle and spread it across Jani's knee. "Those chips don't self-destruct like doc insets, I gather?"

"No." Jani removed the chip from its home and placed it on the cloth. "They can, in fact, be reused. Like I said, all they contain is the casino and the reg number." She pulled her scanpack from her bag and activated it.

"Why do you need to know where it comes from?" Angevin managed an expression of disinterest, but her hands betrayed her, fingers curled and clenching.

"Just a data point." Jani held her scanpack over the chip, and watched the information scroll across her display. "Andalusia. That's a high-end club in Felix Majora, Felix's largest city."

"You're speaking from experience?" Angevin tried to smile, but the corners of her mouth twitched.

"I made a few business calls. Peeked through the trade entrance a couple of times." Jani recalled the black and yellow uniformed waitstaff, the vast expanses of spotless stainless steel in the kitchen. Andalusia was the sort of place that ran a credit check before letting a customer in the door. "Steve would call it posh and full of nobbies."

"He wouldn't call it much of anything at the moment." Angevin uncurled to her feet and gazed down at Jani. Her skin was clear cream, untouched by worry and a stress-shortened night spent in a bedroll in a strange flat. Only her eyes, mossy green and large, held the dull light of concern. "You're not going to tell us why you think this marker is important, are you?"

"It's just my curiosity." Jani tucked the chip back into its slotted home, then enfolded the two marker halves in the antistat and tucked the bundle into her duffel.

"You're a real good liar," Angevin snapped. "You're as good as Evan van Reuter. Around Interior Doc Control, we used to say that he could sell a potluck dinner to the idomeni."

Jani's head shot up. *"Don't ever compare me with him."*

Angevin took a step backward. "I'm—I'm sorry, I—"

"Just *don't.*"

"All right." Angevin glanced over Jani's head, and did a game job of wiping the upset from her face. "How are you feeling, darling?"

"Mmph." Steve circled around the couch and flopped back in his old seat. The skin around his mouth was reddened from scrubbing, the front of his pullover splattered with water.

"Well, I should get going." Jani stood and hoisted her duffel to her shoulder.

"But you just got here!" Angevin threw her hands in the air. "You haven't even seen the rest of the flat!"

Jani made a show of checking her timepiece. "I need to get to Neoclona. Val told me I could visit Lucien this afternoon."

"Nrrm." Steve got up just as Jani walked past him, bumping into her in the process.

Jani felt his hand slip in her jacket pocket. She maintained her path to the door without breaking stride, and exited into the hallway two steps ahead of Angevin.

"We need to go through your paper mail," Angevin called after her, "and you've got fifteen comport messages and you're going to miss a deadline on—"

Jani stopped short and turned around. "Angevin, someone shot at me last night. Now whether they meant to hit Lucien, or me, I don't know and I don't care. Pulse packets discharged in my vicinity make me edgy, and I mean to find out who fired that particular one and why."

Angevin planted in the middle of the hall. "I have spent half the morning taking calls from people asking where you are, and what happened last night, and are you under suspicion of anything. One son of a bitch had the nerve to ask if your past had caught up with you."

"Devinham, probably. His report is sitting atop the far right-hand stack. Call NUVA-SCAN Courier and tell them to come pick it up." Jani walked back to Angevin and placed a hand on her shoulder. "I'm caught up on my most pressing projects. I need to do some work tonight, which I will. And if any clients bail on me because they're afraid my grubby little past will rub off on them, I will deal with it." She walked backward toward the lift. "Right now, though, I'm going to visit someone who had half the skin of his lower abdomen seared off, and who feels like a elephant stepped on his lower back. OK?"

Angevin cringed at the description of Lucien's injuries. "Tell him I said hello."

"I will."

"Steve doesn't like him a bit."

"I am aware of that."

"I'll do what I can with the rest of your calendar."

"Thank you. I mean that." Jani stepped aboard the lift; just as the door closed, she caught a glimpse of Steve in the entry, hands buried in his pockets, angry stare focused on her.

Jani reached into her pocket and removed what Steve had stuffed there. It proved to be a folded piece of dispo towel. She opened it and read the hurried printing, made blurred by the way the stylus fluid bled through the cottony material.

Why are you protecting that bastard when he tried to set you up?

Jani touched her left shoulder, still bruised and tender from Lucien's grip. It seemed to be taking a longer than normal time to heal. As though the damage was worse than she thought. As though it believed she needed a reminder.

* * *

The main branch of the Capital Library loomed over its neighbor buildings like an overbearing professor, its stern stone and metal lines and forbidding entry inviting the information seeker while promising them a difficult search. Jani didn't know whether the stacks really were as daunting as their shelter made them appear—she had acquired a membership in order to access the free workstations reserved by the Library for the use of its patrons.

She entered the lift. Since she was the only occupant, she hit the pad for all twelve floors and got off at the fourth. She stalked the aisles until she found an unused carrel, and fed her rental card into the entry reader. An anonymous card, paid for with an anonymous vend token. What she lost in a business expense tax deduction, she gained in privacy.

She locked the carrel door and activated the privacy shading in the doorside window. Then she opened her duffel and removed all the things she needed to initiate a proper search. Notepad. Stylus. Dispo of lemon tonic. Anti-trace jig. She activated the palm-sized jig and attached to the workstation core, so that no one would be able to monitor her search.

Jani sat at the desk. She ratcheted the touchboard into a more comfortable position, then hesitated just as she made ready to initiate systems. "Would I feel better if I didn't know?" Maybe. "Would I feel safer?" There was only one answer to that question—she gave it by activating the station and wading through the Library's arcane search driver to the vast reaches of Colonial Archives.

Casinos—Felix Majora.

The Felicianos had a well-earned reputation for enjoying life. Felix Majora contained forty-seven casinos within its metro limits, with Andalusia topping the alphabetical list. Jani, however, didn't zone in on that target immediately. Instead, she keyed into the archives of the Vox Nacional, Felix Colony's most popular newssheet. She pondered the keyword request, entered *death* and *accident*, set the time limits to the months Lucien spent in the colonies earlier that year, and initiated the search.

She sipped her tonic as the display faded and the device went about its business. After a few seconds, it brightened to active blue, then darkened to the deep gold background and red arabesques of the Vox Nacional screens. A flicker, then a flood of print as a formidable list filled the display.

Five hundred eighty-seven names. Jani didn't know whether that number was high or low, incorrect or skewed by her search terms.

She entered various and sundry codes and passwords she had acquired by means fair and foul during her years living "out." Then she entered the reg code she had gleaned from Andalusia's chip and initiated a cross-sort of credit checks requested by Andalusia against the names of the deceased.

Within minutes, she had sifted out fourteen names. She whittled it by more than two-thirds after she discarded net worths below one hundred fifty thousand. No casino manager wanted to gut a new customer on the first go-round, therefore they never approved a credit line greater than ten percent of the customer's net worth. Steve had guessed low—green markers in Felix Majora signified a fifteen thousand Comdollar investment, therefore everyone worth less than one hundred fifty thousand fell by the wayside.

And then there were four . . .

Four names. Jani discarded that of the woman who choked on a sandwich at her family reunion. She also tossed out the man in his twenties who had decided to raid the Fort Constanza ordnance depot for Dia Felicia fireworks and fried himself on the security fence that ringed the Service base's outer perimeter.

And then there were two . . .

After a little more thought, she rejected the ninety-four-year-old man who had fallen in his bathroom and struck his head with killing force against the corner of his marble bath. He had been a cornerstone of the Majoran import-export cartel, which made his exclusion difficult. But it was the wrong sort of death. The wrong manner, wrong method.

And then there was one . . .

Etienne Palia. Killed when the racing-class skimmer he drove veered off Felix Majora's infamous Camino Loco and slammed into a scancrete abutment. Massive systems failure, according to the onsite investigator. A rare occurrence with that particular model skimmer, but not unheard of. Accidents did, after all, happen.

"The article says Palia was a businessman." No particular business mentioned, not even something vague like import-export. *A businessman.* Well, they all were, weren't they? No one ever admitted to an inquiring reporter, yes, I am a high-level soldier in a brand-new Commonwealth-spanning criminal organization. It was always, *I am a businessman,* said with a cool smile as unblinking eyes gazed directly into the holocam.

"Palia—member of *L'araignée*?" Jani doodled a looping question mark on the top page of the notepad. That's what she kept the writing materials for—any pertinent facts she would store in her head and her head only. She backed out of the search driver and powered down the workstation. Disengaged the anti-trace jig and tucked it away, along with the pad and stylus. Tossed back the last swallow of tonic, consigned the dispo to the sparky maw of the trashzap, and departed the carrel. Her stomach growled as she hit the walkway. She dug a meal bar out of her bag and consumed it in a few untasted bites.

Massive systems failure. The right sort of death. An assassination that a professional adept at gadgetry might pull off.

CHAPTER 19

As Jani negotiated the final turn leading to Lucien's hospital room, the sounds of a familiar voice raised in anger reached her. She opened the door slowly, poised to back away and flee around the nearest corner if the occasion demanded. Val Parini didn't often lose his temper. When he did, it paid to be elsewhere.

Unfortunately for Jani, Val also possessed the hearing of a nervous cat—he turned as soon as he heard the door mech. *"Damn it, Jan—you talk to him!"* He stood at the foot of Lucien's bed, recording board in one hand, stylus in the other. The stylus performed double-duty as a weapon—Val used it to stab the air with malice aforethought. "Only a certifiable idiot would sign himself out of here in the condition he's in!"

"I'm fine, really." Lucien stood bedside, looking as far from fine as Jani had ever seen him. He wore winter base casuals—grey pull-on pants and a loose blue pullover that hung untucked. His faded tan looked sallow, the overhead illumination highlighting the sheen of sweat that coated his forehead. He packed a plastic sack with the few items of clothing that had come through the shooting unscathed—his lid, his tietops, and socks. He moved in slow motion, turning with his whole body to avoid bending or flexing at the waist.

Jani saw him wince as he leaned forward to insert a sock into the bag. "Lucien, I think you should listen to Val."

"Damned right he should listen to Val. Now get back into bed before you pass out." Val circled to Lucien's side of the bed and reached for the sack, but Lucien stuck his arm straight out to the side to stop him.

"I've signed myself out. I'm not your problem anymore." He

lowered his arm, then resumed folding his other sock with a slowness that was maddening to watch. "Leave me alone."

Jani edged closer. "Do your superiors know you've done this?"

Lucien smiled as she approached, but exhaustion damped the usual four-alarm blaze to a dying ember. "It's easier to obtain forgiveness than permission." He closed the bag, tried to lift it, then gasped and let it drop back to the bed.

"This is *bullshit*!" Val headed for the door, open medcoat flapping. He stopped long enough to make a hurried entry into the board. "I'm countermanding that release right now." He pointed the stylus at Jani. "Don't you dare take him out of this room. I'm getting John. Maybe he can talk some sense into him." The stylus swung around toward Lucien. "Then I'm calling your CO."

Lucien waited for the door to close before speaking. "Jani, please get me out of here."

Jani hesitated. Then she walked around the bed to his side because she knew he expected her to come close and he'd wonder why if she didn't. "You can't even stand." As soon as she drew near, he leaned toward her and tried to kiss her, but she ducked him easily and grabbed his arm so she could steer him back to the bed. "And you sure as hell can't do *that,* so lie down."

"I love it when you order me around." Lucien slipped his arm around her waist and lay his head on her shoulder. Then he groaned. His weight shifted.

Jani widened her stance for stability and helped him lower onto the bed. She hoisted his legs, then supported his shoulders as he lay back, felt the sweat soak through the thin pullover knit as she held him. His face had paled to chalky ochre. "Asking if it hurts is a dumb question, isn't it?"

Lucien shook his head. "They implanted a pain med diffuser. I just feel pressure. Weight. Like I've got a cannonball lodged against my hip. But I'm so goddamned *weak*!" He gripped her wrist as soon as she let go of him. "I have to get out of here. Shroud does *not* like me."

Jani tried to ease out of Lucien's grasp, but as soon as she pulled one wrist away, he grabbed the other. "He won't allow his personal feelings to affect his treatment of you."

"Oh yeah? Are these the same personal feelings that didn't affect your treatment?" Blood rose in Lucien's cheeks, warming his pallor.

"You're just another patient—I'm the incredible ongoing experiment." Jani worked her wrist free, but she had to bend close to Lucien in order to do so, which gave him a chance to grab the hem of her jacket. "Damn it—will you knock it off!"

"I've missed you." Weak as he was, Lucien still pulled with enough force to drag her down beside him on the bed.

"Let me go!" Jani tried to work his fingers loose, but he outmaneuvered her once more by releasing the jacket and capturing both her wrists in a surprisingly strong grip. "I thought you were ready to faint."

"See? You're here five minutes, and I'm already feeling better." He slid his hands up her arms until he caught hold just above her elbows. "Take me home with you, and I'll be back to full strength in a week." He pulled her down to him. Because of the angle, his lips found her throat first, leaving a tracery of fire behind as they moved over the underside of her jaw and her chin, then settled over her mouth.

And then there was one . . . Jani tried to pull away, but Lucien's grip tightened. She'd have to wrench free and retreat to the middle of the room to ensure that he couldn't grab anything else, and that would make him wonder why she didn't want him to touch her. Then he'd start asking questions, like why hadn't she tried to visit him sooner, and what had she been doing since the shooting?

He let loose her arms. One hand moved to the back of her neck to guide her closer, while the other slid over the front of her jacket and settled over her breast, massaging it with a light, experienced touch.

Damn it! Jani's body reacted in fits and starts, warming to Lucien's taste and feel and her own arousal, then chilling as the memories intruded. Of the bottom drawer of a dresser, and fifteen objects nestled in their displays.

And then there was one . . . She braced her hands on either side of Lucien's head and tried to push away. But her hands wouldn't listen to her thinking brain—instead they worked through his hair, then under his head, embracing him, holding him closer—

"My apologies for the interruption."

Jani broke away from Lucien and twisted around to find John looming in the doorway, his long face a stern blank. Val peered from behind him, eyes widened in a *what the hell do you think you're doing* glare.

"I disagree with your assessment, Val. It appears Mr. Pascal may be fit for release after all." John closed in on the side of the bed. His eyes, filmed tiger's eye brown to match the day's tan shirt and trousers, never left Lucien's face. "How are you feeling today, Mr. Pascal, aside from the obvious?"

"John." Jani worked Lucien's distraction to her advantage, easing off the bed and into the nearby visitor's chair.

"Sorry." John didn't look apologetic. He didn't look at Jani, either, instead alternating his gaze between Lucien and the recording board that Val had shoved into his hands. "And the impediment to discharge is what?"

"Well, for one thing, the doctors and nurses are all *here,* not on Armour Place." Val shot Jani another aggravated look. "He suffered renal trauma. He's showing blood in his urine—"

"His hematuria's microscopic. The trauma proved relatively minor—the point of impact was too low to cause much damage." John glowered toward the bed. "That being said, Mr. Pascal, I really would *not* move around any more than absolutely necessary if I were you."

Lucien, who at that point had been trying to sit up, sank back against his pillows like a deflating balloon.

John returned to studying the board display. "He is receiving regular standard monitoring. Dressing changes—they're not as necessary as you think, Val. With his augmentation helping to speed things along, his wound has undergone a week's worth of healing in a day. He won't even need a dressing by the day after tomorrow—enough new skin cells will have bonded to the support to make it unnecessary."

"But John, his peritoneum—"

"The rupture was small—Osgood sealed it completely—"

Jani sat quietly, ignoring Lucien's attempts to catch her eye. *I don't want him in my flat.* But if she came right out and said that, Lucien would know she didn't want him near her, that she suspected him of something.

On the other hand . . . keeping Lucien in plain sight had its advantages. *Think of this professionally, not personally.* As the object of both Angevin's admiration and Steve's animosity, he would be carefully watched. In hospital, or as an outpatient at Sheridan, he could get up to anything. In her flat, his activities would be limited.

What did I tell Derringer . . . keep your friends close and your enemies closer. It only remained to be determined on which side of the line Lucien belonged.

"John, he's not one hundred percent ours to discharge." Val had wandered to the opposite side of the room and hoisted himself atop the lowboy dresser. "Service Medical has a say in when he leaves and where he spends his post-discharge recovery."

"So cart him out to Sheridan and get their buy-in. He can't be approved for active duty yet—he may as well stay in the city for a few days." Before Val could argue out from under, John pulled a stylus from his medcoat pocket and impressed his scrawl onto the board input. "Have Liu arrange an ambulance to Sheridan. While they've got him, Croydon and the set-up team can install all the necessary equipment at Armour Place. He can be settled in a couple of hours."

Val dismounted the dresser. "I don't think it's a good idea. I—" He glanced at Lucien, whose look at him had grown more focused, and fell silent.

"It's done. In the works." John walked to the door, handing off the recording board to Val on the way. "You wanted him so badly, you've got him. He's all yours."

It took Jani a few seconds to realize that John had directed the comment at her.

"This is the most ridiculous bloody thing I ever heard." Steve had fully recovered from his nicstick mishap and had been making up for lost talk time ever since Jani had returned to her flat to break the news. "He belongs at Sheridan—let them haul his freight till he's cleared fer active."

Jani peeked around the open doorway into the newly furnished spare bedroom, where "Croydon, Outpatient Services" and her team outfitted the French Quarter-style bed with detachable rails and a mattress that folded up like a chair or flattened at the touch of a pad. Rails had also been added to various points in the adjoining bath, attached with specialty bondings that would dissolve when exposed to ultra-high frequency vibration, leaving the walls "as clean as you please, ma'am." They had also installed a comport that patched through directly to Neoclona by touch or voice, and a small cooler stocked with nutritionals.

"It's possible that once Service Medical gets their hands on him, they won't let him leave." Jani stepped to one side as Croydon and crew bustled out of the bedroom, skimdolly of tools and equipment in tow. "I doubt he's been debriefed yet, and I'm sure Service Investigational has initiated their own inquiry into the shooting."

"Live in hope." Steve shoved an unactivated 'stick in his mouth and fell in behind the installers.

Die in despair. Jamira Shah Kilian used to pluck that saying out of the air at the damnedest times. Her daughter Jani hadn't liked it any better back then than she did now.

She entered the main room to find Angevin standing by the desk, holding a recording board.

"More calls. First, Colonel Derringer."

Jani stopped in the middle of the floor and covered her face with her hands. *You sent the skimmer for me this morning, and I wasn't here. Now you're going to get me.* "Shit."

"That's what I thought. What a creep. He said sorry that he missed your appointment this morning, but all hell had broken loose at Diplo because of the shooting. He wants to meet tomorrow. He said the idomeni embassy's locked Tsecha down, again because of the shooting. Says you and he need to 'rethink,' whatever that means."

The relief of reprieve evaporated. "They've pulled Nema out of the public eye?" Jani walked to her desk and sat heavily. "Did Derringer say for how long?"

"He didn't say much of anything. He said he'd prefer not to deal with *staff*. I almost told him what he could do with his *staff,* and his gold eagle, but I didn't want to get you into trouble."

Oh, you couldn't make matters any worse, trust me. Jani wondered if Derringer had heard any interesting news about The Nema Letter, or whether she'd have to prompt him herself to rescan it. *Oh look! The pattern's changed. It's not an idomeni document—it's just deteriorating.* She would have given a great deal to receive a call like that. A great deal.

"Jani?"

"Hmm?"

"Devinham said thanks for the report but that it wasn't what he wanted and he won't pay the delivery half of his bill." Angevin looked up from her board and crossed her eyes.

"It's exactly what he asked for and I have the comport recordings to prove it." Jani ran a hand over the curiously uncluttered surface of her desk, the result of Angevin's organizing. "But I knew he'd be trouble. That's why I charged him double my usual rate and made him pay half upfront."

"So you aren't going to file a complaint against him with Registry?"

"No. I'll just spread his name around. Within a month, not even the deregistered dexxies will take his business."

"Good." Angevin nodded agreement as she continued down her list. "Niall Pierce called to say he would have been by today, but he couldn't get away from Sheridan. He said you'd understand."

"I do." Jani checked her timepiece and wondered where her parents were. Still in transit from Mars? Docked at Luna, and checking their timepieces as well?

"He also asked me how you were. I told him you had just squirted out from under and were out and about, so you must be OK. That made him laugh." Angevin studied the display a little too carefully. "He seems nice."

Jani crumpled a sheet of notepaper and slow-motioned a throw at Angevin's head. "He has a girlfriend."

"Hmm." Another tickmark on the board input. "Kern Standish from Treasury. Allow me to quote. 'I heard what happened. If you think you're going to get away from me that easily, think again.' " Angevin glanced up. "Is he serious?"

"Yes and no." Jani grinned. "That's just his way of letting me know I'm still clean and green as far as he's concerned."

"As if you wouldn't be." Angevin frowned at the display. "You did have two cancellations, both from AgMin."

"If I recall, they're looking into negotiating food transport rights through newly leased idomeni GateWays. If they don't need me now, they sure as hell will later."

"Confidence. I like it." Angevin hoisted her stylus in an "up theirs" gesture. "Last and definitely least, Roni—"

Jani felt a jolt. "She called?"

"You know her?" Angevin shrugged. "She wasn't real talkative. She said she mispunched, that she had been trying to reach a bookstore down the street, that the code's only one character off."

"Did she say anything else?"

"She just started nattering, like she sometimes does. Said she had to get to the bookstore tonight before it closed at seven. Then she cut off." Angevin made another entry into the board, then shut it down. "That's it."

Jani directed her splintered attention to her desktop. "I have two analyses due tomorrow."

Steve chose that moment to emerge from the kitchen, half-eaten sandwich in one hand, juice dispo in the other. "I done a draft fer one of them. Since it were about Guernsey doc protocols, I figured I were qualified." He took an extra-large bite in answer to Jani's look of surprise. "Well, I had to do something today, didn't I? 'Sides furnishing the place fer visitors who belong *elsewhere*." He grimaced around a mouthful of 'cress and chutney. "Don't get yer hopes up. I left you the other one to do all by yerself. Wouldn't try to analyze Pathen Haárin contract practices on the best day I ever had."

Jani slipped off the seat and walked across the room to the window. She could see the bookstore from there. *One character off—does that mean six o'clock instead of seven, Roni, or does it mean eight?*

A soft jostle of her elbow made Jani flinch. She turned to find

Angevin gazing up at her with the look of worry that had become her baseline expression over the last twenty-four hours.

"I pulled all the pertinent data together. If you want to get started . . . ?"

"Is that really what Roni said? One character *off*?"

Angevin's eyes narrowed. "What is it with her?"

"I just want to know what she said. *Exactly* what she said."

"Why—?" Angevin pressed a hand to her forehead. "She said the code was one character off—one character off—one—*high*!" The hand dropped. "High. Like I wish I was right now." She grabbed Jani by the arm. "Now let's do some work before you lose all your clients and I have to send all my beautiful furniture back."

It felt good to work. Afterward, Jani even took the time to make herself her first hot meal since Gaetan's. She knew she strove to stay busy in order to keep her mind off all the things rattling around in her head. Her parents. Nema. Lucien. Her eight-up meeting with Roni. The ploy even worked to an extent. Unfortunately, it couldn't work forever.

"Jan?" Steve stuck his head in the kitchen door. "He's here." No need to say who "he" was.

Lucien made his entry in a skimchair pushed by Val Parini, who was in turn backed up by two Neoclona orderlies. "I'm here through the weekend. Then I have to report back, and they may decide to keep me."

"Live in hope," Steve muttered again. Jani wanted to ask him if he knew the rest of the damned saying.

As Val crossed the floor, his brow arched higher and higher. "And furniture finds Armour Place. Which room?"

"Down the hall, second right." Jani took note of Val's careful eyeballing. Full report to be submitted to John, she felt sure, along with the singular item that Lucien had been put up in his own room, not hers.

The skimchair wouldn't fit through the narrow doorway, so the orderlies took over. They hoisted Lucien as though he was a small boy and not a grown man and deposited him on the bed. They then checked the Outpatient installations while Val evaluated the patient's condition and made notes in a handheld.

Surrounded by medical bustle, the patient himself looked worn and a little bewildered. Lucien had exchanged his cast-off casuals for Main Hospital-issue pajamas and robe—he sat in bed looking like the heir apparent who had just been awakened and told *the King is dead, long live the King*. His eyes met Jani's, and he smiled warmly.

Le Blond. Jani forced herself to smile back.

Then Val tucked away his handheld and herded everyone out. "The patient needs his rest." He put his arm around Jani and steered her toward the door. "Let me give you the rundown." He prodded her into the hallway ahead of him, then grabbed her arm to stop her as she tried to follow the orderlies to the lift. "We can talk over here." He directed her to the window at the hallway's end, and pulled her down next to him as he took a seat on the sill.

"He can walk around a little, starting tomorrow. This place has a roof garden—he could putter around up there. His appetite's going to be voracious due to the rate at which he's healing. His temper may be short, too, because of the fatigue and assorted chemical imbalances." Val grinned at her, and shook his head. "I don't know why I'm telling you this—when it comes to augie cascades, you wrote the book."

Jani took his hand and squeezed it. "Thanks, Val." She flinched when he squeezed back hard enough to hurt.

"Be careful." The humor left his face—he looked nervy, his temper bubbling just beneath the surface. "And if you need anything, and I mean *anything,* just call."

Jani laughed, partly from stress and partly from the surprise at having a firmly held conviction blown out of the water. "Funny. I always thought you liked Lucien."

"Like?" Val chewed his lower lip. "He floors me. I could watch him forever. I'm not dead, Jan. Neither are you, apparently. That's some face to wake up next to."

"But?"

"But I've been *the* Valentin Parini for almost twenty years, and I've been dodging stuff like him since I banked my first million." Val's chiseled face took on a sad cast. "They tell you everything you want to hear, and they know how to show you the face you want to see. Even when you know in your bones that you can't trust them, you still try, because you can't accept the fact that they can't feel and that there's nothing, *nothing,* that they won't do to insure their survival. All I ever had at stake was some money, and maybe my heart." His eyes clouded as some buried memory surfaced. "But never my life." He raised her hand to his cheek. "If I thought I could convince you to move in with me for a few days . . . ?"

Jani freed her hand, then brushed a finger under Val's chin. "And leave Steve and Angevin alone with him?"

"He might torture them a little, like the cat he is. But they're not what he wants." Val sighed and scrubbed a hand through his hair. "John is so eaten up with jealousy right now that he can't see straight.

Otherwise, he'd tell you what I'm telling you. We're just a call away. We can do everything the big boys do, but in the end, we're not as . . . accountable."

Jani sat back against the window bracket and regarded her old friend through a new filter. "Val? I always thought you were the nice one."

Val stood. "If anything ever happened to you, John would tear this city apart." He looked down on her with a fondness that had developed improbably and withstood separation and medical disasters and the passage of time. "But he'd have to beat me to it." He bent over and kissed her, then turned and walked with a heavy step toward the lift.

Jani waved good-bye. Watched the lift door close and the numbers flicker as the car descended. Enjoyed the silence. It didn't surprise her to see the car start to ascend almost immediately. She knew she lived in a busy building, despite the façade of calm.

Then the car stopped at her floor. She sat up.

The lift door opened, and Niall Pierce stepped out. Instead of a Service uniform, he wore civvies—a dark blue shirt and black trousers. It struck Jani that while he roughened the edges of any uniform he wore, he lent a strange grace to civilian clothes. A sense of mystery. In either garb, he looked the hatchet man, but in civvies, you couldn't tell whose hatchet he swung.

He spotted her and stopped in the middle of the hallway, hands patting his pockets without diving in because the Spacer in him despised the sloppiness. "Jani?"

He didn't say anything else. He didn't have to.

CHAPTER 20

"Nervous?"

Jani look at Niall. He appeared at first glance to sit easily at the skimmer controls, but closer examination revealed the whitened knuckles, the tension along the jaw. "About as much as you are." She grinned when he glared at her. "Maybe a little more." But the smirk soon died, leaving her with the twisty gut and tripping heart. This wasn't augie's sort of strain. He had crawled off to recover his strength, leaving her to manage this emotional assault on her own.

"Shocked the hell out of me when Pull called to say they'd be hitting O'Hare in an hour. Lots of balls got dropped on this one—if it takes me a month to nail all the hides to the wall, I'll do it." Niall steered down a tree-lined Bluffs side street, then another, before veering onto the ramp leading to a Boul artery. He had driven with evasion in mind since they left Armour Place, but he changed directions and speeds so smoothly that for scattered moments Jani felt herself on a private guided tour of the capital and the Bluffs.

"How are they?" She almost coughed the words. Her throat had taken to tightening intermittently, with a pain that felt as though someone attempted her slow strangulation. She'd known someone who died that way, and the memory of being one of the first to find the body piled atop the rest of her jumbled emotions. She could feel the pressure build inside her head, making her feel one raw thought away from exploding.

"They seem fine. Exhausted, like the rest of us." Niall emphasized the point with a yawn. "Lots of questions about you. How you were. When you'd be visiting." The corner of his mouth curved. "Your mom talks more than your dad. Asks a lot of questions."

"Your point?"

"Just making an observation." He settled back in his seat, smiling quietly.

Jani let the silence carry them for a few kilometers, but as they continued north on the Boul, her nerves nagged again. "Where is this place?"

"I told you before. On the base."

Jani looked out the window at the homes they passed. Nice, anonymous homes with easy access to the Boul and the lake. "Why not a safe house in the Bluffs?"

"Not secure enough." Niall's voice tightened. "At Sheridan, they're shoulder-deep in steel blue. No one is going to get to them there."

What about the ones that are already there, Niall? Like the ones who dropped the ball on forwarding you the news that my folks arrived ahead of schedule. Jani sat forward, hands on knees, and willed the skimmer faster.

Dusk had settled by the time they reached Fort Sheridan. The western skies had colored with streaks of pink and purple, backed by the last light of the setting sun. To the east, the darker sky served as backdrop for the base sprawl, the single and multi-story buildings that stretched in street-split clusters to the horizon and beyond.

Instead of entering the base via the well-peopled Shenandoah Gate, Niall drove farther north and entered through an unmanned control point reserved for emergency vehicles. Once inside, he ignored signs and skimways, gliding over lawns and around buildings and trees at speeds that had Jani muttering a proxy version of the Pedestrian's Prayer and hoping the Grounds crews had been diligent in pruning low-hanging branches.

They settled to a stop in front of a nondescript two-story white-stone box. Only one other skimmer sat parked nearby—the place had the deserted look of an office annex in the middle of second shift meal break.

Niall popped both gullwings; they slid out of the vehicle and hurried up the short flight of steps.

The lobby consisted of a chip-sized entry, with barely enough room for the solemn Spacer who snapped to attention as soon as she saw Niall.

"Anyone else come here?"

"No, sir. You're the first, sir."

Jani felt her legs grow heavy as they entered the lift. She hugged herself as the shivers hit.

"What's wrong?" Niall took a step toward her.

"I'm fine. It's nerves, I think." Then her stomach growled. "Damn it!"

"I heard that from here." Niall leaned against the cabin wall as his alert stage dropped from red to orange. "Want me to get you something?"

"Yeah. If I'm going to be here for a while, I'll need it." The door opened and she stepped into a short hallway consisting of bare white walls and a floor of speckled grey lyno. "God, this is grim."

"Don't worry—what we saved on the hall, we spent on the rooms." Niall took a step back when Jani turned on him. "That was a *joke.*" He rummaged in his shirt pocket and pulled out his nicstick case. "Steady on, Jan, you're rubbing off." He shook out a 'stick, bit the bulb, and watched the smoke curl. "Third door on the left. Do you want me to come with?"

"No."

"You're fine. You look fine. You'll do fine."

"Yeah." Jani tugged at her jacket as she walked to the door. Why did she wear brown? *Maman hates brown.* She should have made Niall wait while she changed clothes. The sari would have been ridiculously inappropriate, but she had a wine red suit that she didn't wear often because she never knew when she'd get a call to the idomeni embassy and under the right light, it looked *almost* bright—

She stopped in front of the door, then looked back at Niall, who offered a grin and a thumbs-up. She pressed her hand to the entry pad. The doormech hissed and the bolts slid. The panel moved aside, and she stepped into the breach.

Niall had been partly correct about the rooms. The walls were still white, but the bareness had been cut with some unimaginative but pleasant landscapes. The depressing lyno had been covered with a green carpet patterned to look like leafy groundcover. The garden motif carried over to the couch and chairs that furnished the sitting room, with their frames of light brown woodweave and cushions awash with red and yellow flowers.

Declan and Jamira Kilian sat close together on the couch, a magazine spread across their knees. They had looked up as one as the door opened, and stared at Jani as she stepped into the room.

Jani stared back. Her mother's napeknot, as ever the poor containment for a thick waistfall of hair, had come undone and now hung over one shoulder in a stream of grey-tipped black. Jamira Shah neared seventy, yet her bold face looked little different from that of the woman whom Jani had last seen almost twenty years before. As always, she wore clothes designed to fight back the storm and wind of the north central islands. Today, bright yellow trousers and a patterned shirt in yellow, white, and orange that carried with them the warmth of a motherland she had never seen and the light of a sun she had felt for the first time that day.

"Jani-girl?"

Jani looked to her father, who studied her like a puzzling schematic. Declan the fixer. Kilian, who never met a system he couldn't crack. His was the seven-decade version of the impish face Dolly remembered, the face Jani had once shared. Upturned nose and apple cheeks ruddied by wind, framed by jet hair, cut by green sea eyes. He wore Channel colors, dark green and darker blue. Like his wife, he showed little of twenty years' passage. It took a special endurance to live on the islands, and more than time to age her natives.

Jani waited for her father to say more, for her mother to say anything. *Do I look that strange to you? Did the Misty distort my image—is that why you don't recognize me? Or is it because you don't think I look like I could be your daughter? Or anyone's daughter.*

Is it because you don't think I look human?

Jamira raised a hand to her mouth. Let it fall. Then she shoved the magazine onto her husband's lap. Rising quick and smooth, she legged across the fake greenery floor, strides growing shorter as she picked up speed. *"Ma petite fille!"* She knocked Jani back a step as she collided with her, wrapping her arms around her waist and pressing her face against her chest.

"Oui, Maman. It's me." Jani's throat clamped down hard, her voice emerging high and thin like a little girl's. She gripped the rope of hair, held it fast. Smelled jasmine perfume and makeup and the barest hint of incense from a distant shrine.

A heavier step approached. Stronger arms embraced. Sharp herb soap and hair like wire and a face rough with new beard. "Jani-girl."

"Papa." Jani heard the roar in her ears and called it the wind and tasted the salt on her face and called it the sea.

Felt a rent in her heart heal, and called it home.

"—and then Shamus returns from the stores and tells us that a man is looking for us." Jamira lifted her spoon from her cup and raised it like a question. " 'What man?' I asked. 'No one knows we are at Faeroe.' "

Jani sat back in her flower chair and watched her mother resume stirring her tea. "No. No one. Only Tante Smruti so she knows to keep an eye on things, and Cheecho so he knows to take care of the birds, and Jones the Grocery so she should stop the deliveries, and then all the people you asked to keep an eye on those three to make sure they do their jobs."

"Tell Smruti anything, may as well tell ChanNet." Declan frowned into his coffee, ignoring his wife's glower. "So, Shamus being Shamus, he raised his tail and pelted home. Just as he's gasping the details, I look out and see a skimmer in the circle. Dull green two-seater. Old. Sort of model you see around Faeroe. And out comes the man. Also the sort you see around Faeroe, at least these days. The kind that looks like he's just waiting for you to turn your back."

"He said he had a message from you, Janila. That you needed us and we had to come to Chicago." Jamira lifted a sandwich from the tray on the table in front of her and took a small, examining bite. "He gave us billets, and money for expenses, and a note in your handwriting. The note read just like you—to the point, with no explanation."

Jani looked across the room, where Niall perched atop a low cabinet. "They got hold of samples of my writing and knew enough about me to copy my style."

Niall nodded. He took a pull on his 'stick, then held his breath to leech the last molecule of nicotine from the smoke. "My Guernsey friend thinks *L'araignée* planned to waylay them at Helier Transfer Station. Busy place like that—who'd notice if two travelers disappeared? But the white paper had made the rounds out there, and the name Kilian was on everybody's mind. When it showed up on the passenger manifest of an Acadian cruiser, it was a footrace to see who'd get to the station first. We won."

"White paper?" Declan peered over the rim of his cup at Jani. "Did someone write you up, Jani-girl?"

"I work for the government, Papa. Someone decided to investigate me." Jani picked at the makeshift supper Niall had scrounged for her. Slices of kettle chicken soaked with Chinois hot sauce. Lemon wedges and a cup of red pepper for dredging. "When I was in hiding, I did what I had to. I helped smugglers. Tampered with documents. Some people think that makes me a security risk."

"Then there are those of us who think that makes her a consultant." Niall paused to blow a perfect smoke ring. "The white paper is a smear attempt. Your daughter is an important player in our dealings with the idomeni. Because of that, some very powerful economic forces who want to destabilize our relations with Shèrá would like to see her discredited."

Declan nodded. "I've tried to work with some of those forces. Make that *in spite* of them." The lines of his puckish face drew down.

As always, sadness made him look angry. "Those people tell you, 'We want this and this and that.' And if you don't give it to them, well . . ." He drew a shaky breath. "I've buried four good friends in the past months. They died because they wouldn't give up what they'd spent their lives building, because they wouldn't hand over this and this and that."

"Who?" Jani's hand tightened on the arm of her chair as she braced for the answer.

"Jani?" Niall leaned forward, voice and posture tense.

"People seldom leave Ville Acadie," Jani replied to his implicit concern. "I probably knew them."

Declan blinked as he spoke, as though he couldn't believe what he said. "Simone. The Fuel Cells, not the Butcher. Echevar and Samvoy, the cousins in construction, not their parents whom you knew." A pause. "Labat."

"Labat?" Jani looked again at Niall. "He ran the off-track near our house. He took bets that I wouldn't make it through OCS."

"He didn't count on your stubbornness, Jani-girl. He didn't always think things through, and he paid the big price." Declan's weak grin subsided. "The day after Labat's funeral, I shuttered my business and left my home, took my wife away from her family. I fled because I install and rework systems and they look for people like that. I knew one day, the shop door would open and I would look up and see two or three well-dressed, soft-spoken people standing there, and I would know the questions before they uttered them." His voice grew small. "And I'd think of four dead friends, and the answers I would give . . . would not be worthy of them."

Jamira reached out to him. When he didn't respond, she gripped his hand and laced her fingers through his. "They have always been in Ville Acadie, but they kept themselves to themselves. Now, they dine in the best clubs, build the largest homes. Send their children here to university. There are no brakes, no walls. Nothing stops them."

"Why didn't you tell me?" Jani watched her parents hold on to one another, and felt her freshly closed wounds ache anew. "I asked you why you left home, why you went to Faeroe. Why didn't you tell me!"

"We didn't want you to worry, Janila. We thought we would come here in the spring to visit, and not go back." Her mother forced a smile. "But spring came early."

"Doesn't the Acadian government do anything?" Niall didn't sound angry, only tired, as if he already knew the answer.

Declan snorted. "Oh, it does *something*. Takes its cut and turns its back." A gloomy silence settled, hanging over them until the room entry buzzer offered respite.

Niall pushed off the lowboy and opened the door. When he saw who stood in the hall, he beckoned to Jani. "We need to discuss logistics."

Jani rose awkwardly, hampered by her knee. Before she joined Niall, she leaned over the table and touched her father's shoulder. "You are worthy of every friend you ever had. The fact that you left La Ville means nothing. Everyone pulls back. Regroups. That doesn't make you a coward and it doesn't mean you're a sell-out. You don't belong to them."

"Yet." Declan made no move to touch her, no effort to meet her gaze. "That's what they do to you, Jani-girl. They plant that 'yet' in the back of your mind, and it grows until it eats you alive."

Jani waited for her father to look at her. When he didn't, she turned her attention to her mother. Jamira sat as her husband did, her shoulders rounding, her eyes focused on the floor. They both seemed drained of energy. Beaten. Old.

"I'll be in the hall with Niall," Jani said quietly. She watched the carpet as she made her traverse to the door, and found that she could pick out each individual leaf, discern every shade of green. She could thank augie for the heightened senses—it detected her growing rage and responded accordingly.

She walked out into the hall to find Niall surrounded by a circle of uniforms. Lt. Pullman was the only one she recognized—he smiled weakly at her, then returned his attention to the heating discussion.

"This is no time to be arguing jurisdiction, Major." Niall stood within a handbreadth of a red-faced woman in rumpled fallweights. "Your team lost them at MarsPort, and didn't pick them up again until they had almost boarded the wrong ship!"

"They were out of our sensor range for a grand total of ten seconds, and out of our physical sight for less than thirty." The major closed the distance to two fingers. "That does not, sir, in my estimation, qualify as lost!"

"I've seen people disappear in the time it took to turn a corner." Jani wedged in between a lieutenant in fallweights and a captain in dress blue-greys. "The time it took to turn around. Glance at a timepiece. Blink." She stepped inside the circle, shouldering Niall to one side and taking over his position in the major's face. "Ten seconds is enough time to hustle two people into a lift, or out a side door, or through an airlock." She saw the uncertainty in the woman's blood-shot eyes, and rode it. "Who lost them? I want names."

"I can't give you the—"

"Those were my parents they almost lost. You will give me their names."

"She will be reprimanded—"

"She?" Jani heard Niall groan. "Let me get this straight. You had one operative with a handheld sensor escort two people through one of the busiest transfer stations in the Commonwealth by *herself*!"

The woman rocked from foot to foot, then edged back a half-step. "It's . . . standard practice. Ma'am."

Jani closed the distance the major tried to open. If she left too much space, she'd have room to use her hands; that wasn't a risk she wanted to take with augie worrying his bit.

Then a glint of gold on the major's collar caught her eye. Augie liked flashes of light, and the overhead illumination playing off the woman's rank designators drew his attention. Bursts of gold from the oak leaves, and from the twin letter I's. "Intelligence?" Jani heard her voice like a shout, but no one flinched so she knew she couldn't have spoken that loudly. "When did you horn in on this?"

The major drew up as tall as she could, which meant that she hit Jani at shoulder height. The disadvantage seemed to bother her. She reversed another half-step and bumped into Pullman, who looked like he wanted to toss her back. "Since the case involves intersystem flight of colonials, it's standard practice for us to be included."

"No, it's not." Jani put a handlock on Niall's elbow and pulled him out of the circle and partway down the hall. "Why were they doing the tracking? You said your people were handling it."

"That's one of the things I'm trying to find out." Niall's face reddened with anger, embarrassment, or a combination of both.

Jani glanced back at the major, who was engaged in intense conversation with the dressy captain. "I'm taking them out of here. My folks. I'm taking them out."

"What?" Niall circled in front of her, blocking her view. "What are you talking about?"

"You said Intelligence helped compile the information in the white paper. That means they delineated the corruption in the Channel Worlds, then and now. They knew what the conditions were on Acadia. They knew better than any of you the risks my parents faced, and still they almost lost them at MarsPort." Jani stepped out to the side so she could watch the major, and found the major watching her as well. "Now you expect me to leave my parents here under their care?"

"Not under *their* care." Niall bent close. "I'm in charge."

"You may be in charge, Niall, but you're not in control. For every door you slam shut, they'll find two more."

"Are you saying you don't trust me? Is that what you're saying!"

"I trust you, Niall, but you're not the entire Service. You and Pull can't oversee everything. You can't vet everything. You can't see inside their heads."

"What?" Niall's brow drew down. "You think Intelligence screwed up on *purpose*?"

"They give *L'araignée* my folks now, *L'araignée* gives them something later. A crooked colonial governor. A bent general." A thought lasered through Jani's augie-cleared mind, like the reflection off the major's designators. "Your Guernsey buddy wouldn't happen to be Intelligence, would he?"

Niall grew still, his breathing irregular. He believed in his Service—its discipline and rigor had helped him pull himself from the Victorian gutter. He believed in his friends, too. "That's *coincidence.* Corin's different—I've known him for twenty years."

"I'm hearing that, from you of all people. There's no such thing as coincidence, Niall. You start believing in coincidence, you're *dead*!" Jani headed back down the hall toward the group, which had fractured into Pullman and the lieutenant on one side and the major and the captain on the other. She beckoned to Pullman, who hurried to her side. "I need a skimmer from the vehicle pool. A four-seater. Not the one they want to give you, but one you pick out yourself. Have it at the far-northwest automatic entry in fifteen minutes."

"Ma'am?" Pullman looked at Niall, who had dogged Jani's steps. "Sir, I thought—"

"Do it, Pull." Niall spoke with Declan Kilian's voice, drained and old.

Jani waited for Pullman to leave before speaking. "I'm sorry, Niall. But sometimes it's hardest to see what's closest to you." She turned her back so she wouldn't have to look at his face, and palmed into her parents' room.

"Papa? Maman?" She looked to the couch, and found it empty. The chairs. The bench seat by the shielded window. "Papa!" She stalked a quick circuit of the room, looking for an entry she had somehow missed the first time. Her heart slowed, then tripped, then slowed again. "Maman! *Pap*—!"

"Why you be shouting, Jani-girl?" Declan stuck his head through a gap between two panels in the far wall. "We're in the lave. Your mother tried to eat some of your chicken."

"Oh, shit!" Jani dodged around furniture and into the tiny bath to find Jamira bent over the sink, cupping water repeatedly over her mouth and chin. "Maman, I told you in all the Mistys that I eat strange food!"

"You did not say that you ate fire, Janila." Her mother straightened slowly. Her eyes teared as though she wept. Her nose and mouth had reddened and swelled. "Is that what Dr. Shroud did to you?"

Jani felt the strength of her mother's eyes, even through their mirrored reflection. "He did the best he could."

"Did he?" Jamira coughed, then tore a dispo towel from the sinkside dispenser and dried her mouth.

Declan looked from his wife to his daughter, as he had so often in the house on Rue D'Aubergine when he felt the drag of the undercurrent but couldn't decide which way the harbor. "You were calling us, Jani-girl?"

"*Oui,* Papa." Jani tore away from the sharp brown examination. "We're leaving."

"But we've just arrived."

"I have another place in mind. Where's your luggage?"

"The young major took charge of it at O'Hare, Janila." Jamira's eyes had stopped running, but she had to keep pausing to cough and blow her nose. "She said it would be brought to us after our talk with you."

"You have to leave that stuff here. Anything you need, I'll buy you."

"I packed equipment, Jani-girl." Declan nodded toward Jamira. "Your mother brought family things. And your dowry."

"You lugged fifteen kilos of jewelry?" Jani pressed her fingers to her tightening scalp. "It will be safe here. I just want Niall to check everything first." She waited for them to leave the bath ahead of her. Her father walked out right away, but her mother stopped to pull a handful of dispos from the dispenser and tuck them up her sleeves.

"Where are you taking us?" she asked, concentrating on her tissues.

Jani hesitated. "To—to someone I trust."

"To someone you trust. You do not trust Fort Sheridan, or the whole of the Service, or your scarred colonel. Yet there is *someone*." Jamira Shah tugged down her sleeves and walked to the door. "I must meet this person, Janila." She swept out, leaving behind a trail of softest scent.

By the time Jani returned to the hallway, all the uniforms had departed. Niall stood against the wall, unlit 'stick cupped in his hand. His eyes softened when he looked at her parents. Unfortunately, they chilled when they focused on her.

"Pull went to get the skimmer. Are you going to tell me where we're going, or do I have to guess?"

Jani told him.

And when he turned red and threatened to stop her, she told him again.

CHAPTER 21

Pullman proved his worth and wit by obtaining a skimmer equipped with an ultra-secured comline. Jani made one carefully worded call as the night scenery whipped past and offered the occasional bracing smile to her parents, who sat in hand-holding silence in the rear.

Niall didn't speak much, either. The efforts Jani made to draw him out by asking specific questions about timing and transfers elicited terse replies spoken around one nicstick after the other. By the time they reached Chicago, the skimmer cabin looked as though a smoke bomb had detonated. Jani hunted down the ventilator switch, but even though the influx of fresh air soon cleared the space, the damage had been done. Her eyes stung. Her films felt tight. *Don't let them break now.* That wasn't how she wanted her folks to find out how far down the hybridization path John Shroud had taken her. Judging from her mother's still-inflamed mouth and focused glare, the encounter with Jani's version of pleasantly spicy had been telling enough.

Niall turned off the Boul and steered them up and down midtown side streets before turning onto a short alley that was blocked at the end by a five-meter-high fence. The skimmer headlamps illuminated the security guard that opened the gate and waved them through, along with the trademark name that studded the top of the gate in letters half a meter high.

"Neoclona, Janila?" Her mother touched her shoulder. "Why did you bring us here?"

Jani ignored Niall's grumble. "They're private, Maman. Outside official channels." Val's words returned to her. "They're not as accountable, so they can do as I ask without needing to explain to anyone."

They turned sharply, then drove down the same wide utility road that Jani had walked the previous night. The road was as deserted now as it had been then, except for the lone figure standing in front of the water treatment station, his silver sport skimmer hovering alongside.

Niall slowed to a stop, reset the vehicle charge-through to "standby," and popped the gullwings. He alit from the skimmer and scanned the roofs of buildings, the sky overhead, on the lookout for holes in Neoclona security.

Before Jani could get out, Val hurried to her side and offered his arm. "Excuse the attire." He tugged at the neck of his stretched-out pullover. "I was having a quiet night at home when Security forwarded your call."

"So they're the only ones who know you're here?" Niall called out as he scanned an adjoining alley. "I trust they know how to keep their mouths shut."

"Yes, Colonel." Val looked at Jani, brows arched.

"Cautious." Jani let him help her out. Her back ached in earnest and a knifeprick of pain stabbed behind her right kneecap every time she flexed it. "I decided to take you up on your offer."

"I'm glad you did." Val slipped behind her and slid the seat forward. "Sir. Ma'am." He helped Declan and Jamira alight, then stood back, an over-wide smile frozen in place.

Well, well. Jani bit her lip to keep from grinning. Like Val angry, Val nervous was a rare event, worthy of note. "Maman. Papa. This is Dr. Valentin Parini. You received messages from him this summer, when I was sick. You'll be staying with him for the next few days."

Val and Declan muttered greetings and shook hands, then broke apart in that trailing way of men who had nothing to say to one another besides "Hello." The Parini charm worked a little better on Jamira, who lost some of her tension in the shelter of his quiet concern.

"I live in a building near the lake. I've got the entire top floor—you'll have your own wing." Val nodded toward Jani. "Jan said you had to leave your things behind at the base—some of the best shops in the city are within walking distance—"

"They can't leave the flat, Val," Jani broke in. "Not until Niall or I give a personal OK."

"Then I will send someone to get you anything you need." Val smiled gamely. "Clothes. Books. Anything."

Jani groaned quietly as the word *books* rang the memory bell. Had Roni McGaw given up on her yet, or did she still wait for her in front of the bookstore? Her mind spun in tight conspiracy circles—

did Roni know Niall would be coming for her? Did she have any knowledge of Service Intelligence's double-dealing? Had she contacted her in order to warn her, or to get her out of the way?

"Heads up."

Jani turned to find Niall standing next to their skimmer, his attention focused up the road.

Jani followed his gaze, and saw the growing headlamps of a rapidly approaching skimmer. *It's not going to be able to stop.* Judging from the rate at which the headlamps increased in size, the only thing that would bring it to a halt would be the side of a building. Or their skimmer.

"Get into that doorway!" Niall shouted. *"Now!"*

"No!" Val knew enough to approach Niall around the back. "I think I know who that is!"

"Thinking's not good enough, Parini." Niall reached to his belt and came up with his shooter. "You said no one knew you were here!"

Jani grabbed her mother's arm and herded her toward the doorway of the treatment plant. Jamira reached for Declan, and they daisy-chained into the sheltering dark.

"Janila, what is happening!"

"I don't know, Maman!" Jani swore under her breath, her hand aching for a weapon. She watched in helpless rage as the skimmer kept coming. Closer. Closer. *"Niall!"*

Niall ignored her. He raised his weapon.

Sighted down.

Fired.

The pulse packet impacted the driver's-side bumper, forcing the skimmer offcourse. Proximity alarms screamed. The vehicle spun halfway around in one direction, then another, as the driver and the balance arrays fought to keep it from careening into a building. The whine of reversing directionals joined the alarms in a night-splitting howl as the skimmer shuddered to a halt a scant few meters from Niall, who closed in, weapon raised. *"Get out of the vehicle! Now! Hands above your head!"*

"It's John, goddamn it!" Val circled to Niall's side, reached for his arm, and barely ducked his fist. *"Put that goddamned thing down!"*

Lights flashed around the corner. Emergency vehicles. Guards on foot, weapons drawn.

Jani shook off her mother's restraining grip and ran into the road, her knee threatening to buckle with every stride. *"Niall, stand down!"*

The driver's side gullwing of the damaged skimmer swept up. The telltale white head emerged.

"That was really stupid, John!" Val waved back the Neoclona guards. They obeyed grudgingly, glaring at Niall as though they wanted to toss him in the back of a security van and drop him on his head a few times on the way.

Niall slowly lowered his weapon. "I disagree with your friend, Dr. Shroud. Stupid doesn't even get it started!"

John struggled out of the skimmer. *"What the hell are you trying to do!"* He looked from his blistered bumper to the guards, then to Niall. His face slackened as the realization of what might have happened punched through his anger. He raised a hand to his mouth, and stared at the charred bumper.

"Janila?" Jani's mother came up behind her and tugged on her jacket. "Is that *your* Dr. Shroud?"

"Maman, how many other one-nine albinos do you think are out there?"

John grew still as the sight of Jani broke through his angry daze. Then he saw Jamira, and his hand dropped to his side. "*Val.* You should have called me directly."

Val aimed the same look at John that the guards had toward Niall. "I left a message," he said flatly. "You told me specifically that you didn't want to hear any more about Ja—"

"You should have called me directly." John undid the closure of his evening suit jacket and slid a hand in his pocket. In the next breath, he removed his hand from his pocket and refastened the closure. He'd chosen one of his more striking outfits, dark ivory and rigorously tailored.

Wonder what color he filmed his eyes? Jani ran down the list she had compiled over the summer. Light brown wouldn't raise any eyebrows. Gold or pearl would earn her the parental fish-eye she'd won as a youngster whenever she brought a particularly unsuitable friend home to visit. "Dr. John Shroud." She reached behind her and beckoned. "My parents, Declan Kilian and Jamira Shah."

John had recovered his composure by the time Jani finished her introduction, and stepped forward with the easy assurance of a man who walked on his own land. The light from a safety illumin fell across his face, highlighting amber-brown eyefilming that looked distinctive but not bizarre.

"Père Kilian. Mère Kilian." The polite Acadian titles and throaty French R's flowed, as though he'd been practicing. "I am at your service." He shook Declan's hand, then drew a collective gasp of surprise by bending over Jamira's and applying a haute formal not-quite-kiss on her knuckles.

"Dr. Shroud." Jamira reclaimed her hand with a cool smile. "So much kindness after such a raucous welcome."

"It's not kindness, Mère Kilian. It's a joy."

"Is it? Well, then, I should take advantage while I can, should I not?"

John's eyes sparked. He could reek charisma under the right circumstances, and the opportunity to bestow brought out the gallant in him. "You could never take advantage, Mère Kilian. Anything I have is yours." His deep bass flowed like warmed molasses. "You have but to ask."

"Really?" Jamira's brow arched. "Any*thing*?"

Jani leaned against the treatment facility wall and pressed fingertips to forehead. Twenty years had passed since she'd heard that questioning flick at the end of a word. Like the approaching skimmer headlamps, she realized what was happening, but knew she risked a good bashing if she tried to step in and stop it. She glanced at her father, who widened his eyes and looked at the ground.

"Anything, Mère Kilian." John's sugar synthesizer was running at full capacity now. "Name it."

Jamira patted her palms together in almost-silent clapping, her "decisions, decisions" gesture. Then it stopped, and her face lit. "I should like Luna, Dr. Shroud. Your moon. In a gift box. With a large red bow."

"Then you shall have it, Mère Kilian." John crossed his arm over his chest and bowed deeply, then straightened and spread his arm wide.

"So readily you promise me the moon, Dr. Shroud. Like a god." The lightness had left Jamira's voice. She looked pointedly at Jani, then back to John. "Who made you a god, Doctor? Who allowed you the right to promise what isn't yours to give?"

John froze in mid-flourish, his self-satisfied smile ebbing. Val mouthed an "ouch." Niall grinned for the first time since they left Sheridan.

Jamira brushed past John, eyes averted, and walked up the road toward Val's silver skimmer.

"We need to get going, folks. Our little noise and fireworks display must have attracted attention." Niall sauntered over to Val. "Is your in-vehicle comline secure?"

Val nodded, his attention focused on his business partner. John stood where Jamira had left him. He avoided everyone's gaze, and seemed preoccupied with the state of his jacket lining.

"We split them up," Niall continued, "and take separate routes. Do you have access to a private lift in your building?"

"Of course," Val said, eyes still on John.

"Well, don't use it. From here on in, it's the service lift only." Niall pulled Val to one side so they could continue their discussion.

Jani gave John a wide berth and rejoined her parents, who stood in huddled argument beside Val's skimmer.

"—need his help!" Declan's cheeks flared as though he'd been struck. "Couldn't you wait?"

"Non! Why should I?" Jamira's voice rasped. Her eyes brimmed. "That *bâtard* turned my daughter into an *anormal,* a mutant!"

The words stopped Jani in her tracks. A sudden ache flared in her gut and spread to her chest. "Is that what you think I am?" Her jaw felt wooden. "You thought I needed you, and you came. If you felt that way, why did you bother?"

Jamira's face paled to clay. "Janila, it is not to you that I say this."

Jani raised a hand to her eyes. She wanted to rip off the films, reveal the truth behind the lie, let her parents see. Let Niall see. "But who else could you say it to? *I'm* the freak, Maman. The abnormal." She tried to lift the right film away, but she couldn't slide her thumbnail underneath it far enough to get a good grip. "Before you left Acadia, you should have had one of the priests fashion you a charm to protect yourself from me." She dug the sliver of carved-away film from under her nail and flicked it away.

Jamira pressed a hand to her cheek, then took a step toward Jani and reached out. "Janila?"

"Time to go, folks." Niall stepped into the breach unseeing, jaunty grin still in place. "Jan, which skim' are you riding in?"

"I think it's better if I don't go with you." Jani turned her back on her mother's outstretched hand. "You never know." She saw the comprehension dawn in Niall's eyes, and turned away from that as well. "You just never know." She started to walk, although she had no idea where she should go.

"Janila!"

Jani's feet dragged to a halt as her mother's shout filled her ears, even as her will tried to propel her forward. She gasped as Jamira's arms snaked around her waist and squeezed until her ribs ached from the pressure, yet she couldn't bring herself to touch her hands. Heard her sobs, yet felt no urge to comfort her. *Freak.* Yes. Only a monster could remain untouched by such a firestorm of emotion. Only a wretch could be so cold. She pried her mother's arms loose. "You have to go. I'll visit . . . when I can." She forced herself to turn around, to stand still as Jamira again embraced her and whispered her name over and over, begging her forgiveness. "Go with Niall, Maman." She patted her mother's shoulder, then prodded her toward a shaken Niall. She watched them get into the Service skimmer, watched the skimmer bank and glide and disappear around the corner.

It took Jani some time to realize that she was being watched, as well. She looked around to find her father still standing beside Val's skimmer. He massaged his knuckles one at a time, a tic he took down from the shelf whenever his emotions threatened to get the better of him.

"Your mother loves you more than her own life, Jani-girl." Declan's voice emerged dead calm, as it did when he was the most angry. "You always fire at the wrong target. When you were mad at Cheecho, you took it out on his sister. When you were mad at your schoolwork, you took it out on your games, and I took the calls from the parents with the bruised children. When you were mad at van Reuter, you took it out on everyone but him." He walked around the skimmer to the passenger side and popped the gullwing. "Wrong target." He lowered inside the low-slung cabin and yanked the door closed, sitting in stiff-faced rage as a visibly distressed Val hurried over and inserted himself into the driver's seat.

Then Declan said something, and Val's head bobbed up and down in overwrought agreement. Declan opened his gullwing, struggled out of the skimmer, and strode back to Jani.

"Man his age driving that ridiculous thing. Looks a twit." He pulled Jani to him. "Be careful."

Jani hugged him hard, wishing part of the embrace travel to wherever Niall's skimmer was. "*Oui,* Papa."

"Don't stay away for days. She doesn't deserve that."

"I know, Papa."

"She loves you. I love you. You're our girl."

"I love you, too."

Declan released Jani and returned to the skimmer. The vehicle sped away—just as it cornered, Jani caught sight of her father's furiously waving hand. She raised her own in response, even though it was too late for him to see. Then she let it fall, and felt the numbness settle as she turned to walk up the road toward Neoclona Main.

"Where do you need to go?"

Jani wheeled to find John leaning against the treatment facility wall, jacket once more unfastened, hands shoved in trouser pockets. As distinctive as he was, he had a talent for fading into the background that she always found unsettling. "I don't know. Back home, I guess."

John pushed off the wall and ambled toward her. "I'll take you."

"You don't have to."

"Jani, just get in the goddamned skimmer."

As Jani opened her mouth to argue, her right knee started to ache, a low-level twinge that promised to become a higher-pitched misery if she kept walking. She limped after John, stood aside as he opened her gullwing for her, fell into her seat, and sat with hands folded in her lap as he closed her in.

John sat heavily himself, and punched the charge-through four times before it engaged. They maneuvered down the street and through the same gate Jani had entered seeming days ago.

The streets contained more people than they had earlier now that Chicago's night had begun in earnest. Jani glanced at John's dapper suit, and added two and two. "I blew another evening for you, didn't I?"

John was either too beaten or too angry to deny the obvious. "Dinner. With a very close friend."

"If she was that close, you shouldn't have left her."

"First I get the forward from Security with the notation that you'd called Val from a military line, then I get Val's message. What the hell did you expect me to do, waltz back to the sorbet!" John swerved too close to the skimmer in the next lane. Proximity alarms blared, and he jerked the wheel to return to his track. "I never said my friend was a *she*."

Jani watched the passing scenery, and thought of all the famous females she'd seen over the summer in the *Tribune-Times* or on the 'Vee. John's "very close friends" tended to fall into very specific categories. "Anybody I've heard of?"

John hesitated, then shrugged. "She sings at the Lyric occasionally."

"Hmm." Jani yawned. "Niall could probably recite her every role."

John struck an uneven beat on the steering wheel. "You really don't care, do you?"

"I abrogated the right to care the night I fled Rauta Shèràa. You asked me to stay. I said no. End of story."

"No. It never ends. We keep writing new chapters." The skimmer windows filtered the city light. The resulting semidark of the cabin offered the perfect backdrop for John's voice. "I love you."

"I love you, too." Jani answered automatically, but some truths were easier to admit than others. "Not that I had much choice. You were the first thing I saw when I came out of the coma, and you always did make a strong initial impression."

"Funny how some things never change. You used the same excuse back then." John wore the glower of a statue that had found a crack in its pedestal. "Maybe there's something to it. You were the first thing I saw when I opened my eyes, too. Figuratively speaking. I didn't have much . . . experience with women before you came along."

Didn't I know it. "You bury me with your regard, John, until I can neither move nor breathe. To save me the trouble of making choices, you make them for me. I can't live like that."

John snorted lightly, but didn't speak. The traffic jam that ensued as skimmers maneuvered around a double-parked people-mover gave him something to concentrate on for a time. "I really got off on the wrong foot with your mother," he said as the squeeze cleared. "Mind telling me what happened?"

"Niall got me some food while we were at Sheridan. Maman tried it, and the pepper almost did her in." Jani blinked away the ache as the image of her mother bent over the bathroom sink returned. *Anormal. Mutant.* "Your folks used to call you a freak, didn't they?"

"No, they had the Christian Fallback Council of Elders declare me Marked by God. Amounted to the same thing, though." John's lip curled. He had never offered more than the occasional remark concerning his youth. That reticence alone told one all they needed to know. "How would my life have changed if they had approved my *in utero* genetic adjustment? Would I have grown into the man I am? Built Neoclona? Would I even have studied medicine? I don't know. But as I told you back in the basement, by the time I was old enough to request adjustment on my own, I didn't want it. Being unique has its advantages." He glanced at Jani, and raised a hand in grudging admission. "It has its disadvantages, too, but overall the good outweighs the bad.

The skimmer turned onto Armour Place, and Jani leaned forward to stretch her back in preparation for the trudge across the lobby. "At least you could make a choice. Refer to my previous comment on the matter."

John edged the skimmer curbside, then waved away the doorman who hurried toward them. "Well," he said after a time, "that was an interesting interlude."

"Niall reacted to a perceived threat—"

"I'm not blaming him. If I'd seen a skimmer bearing down on you, I'd have shot at it myself." He focused his broody attention on his fingernails. "I wish you'd called me personally."

Jani shook her head. "Not after this afternoon."

John made as if to speak, but made do with a shaky exhale. The silence stretched. "Get some sleep," he finally said. "*Eat* first. Be careful, like your father said." He looked at Jani. His eyes were too dark for his sepulchre face, which seemed to glow in contrast. "Everybody's shooting at me tonight. I'm the right target he thinks you should hit, aren't I?"

Jani nodded. "I think so."

"That means I made a sterling impression on him, too. I'm . . . sorry, for what resulted." John groaned. "Val will speak up for me. They seem to like Val. But then, *everybody* likes Val. Hell, *Nema* likes Val."

"You need to get back to your singer. She likes you."

John shook his head. He had found a new scab to pick and refused to leave it alone. "She'd like Val if he'd have her."

"Don't underestimate yourself. You always did." Jani smiled as a few of the better memories resurfaced. "You have your moments."

"Oh yeah?" John perked. "I've got half a mind to press the accelerator to the floor. We could be in Seattle in two days." He sagged back in his seat. "Only problem is, the first time I slowed below forty, you'd bail out the window."

"I would—not—I—" Jani tried to formulate a lucid protest. But the fatigue and the emotional upheavals of the last few hours caved in on her, and she laughed instead. John gaped at her for a few moments, then joined in. They began quietly, then grew louder as various scenarios played through their minds.

The merriment fizzled. Jani wiped her eyes with care. She knew she had damaged her right film, and she no longer felt compelled to reveal herself to the world. "You don't want me, John. I'd make you as crazy as you'd make me. Go back to your singer. There's absolutely no reason for you to be alone."

John's grin died. "I've been alone since you left. The fact that another woman occasionally occupies your space doesn't make any difference." He unlatched Jani's gullwing, remaining silent as she disembarked, ignoring her good night and vanishing into the dark before she reached the building entry.

Jani stopped and stared at the place where the skimmer had parked, then to the dark into which it had disappeared. It had felt so warm inside. So quiet. So comforting. *If I just said the word, I could have that forever.* John would raise the walls and affix the locks, and nothing would ever reach her again.

Nothing.

Poor John. She yawned as she limped across the lobby. If she could beg any good luck from her Lord Ganesha, she would find

Steve, Angevin, and Lucien asleep. Particularly Lucien. She wouldn't possess the energy to deal with him unless she slept through the night and into the following day.

Pondering Lucien deflected her attention from her surroundings. She didn't see the figure dart in from the sitting area until it intercepted her.

"Where the hell have you been!" Angevin grabbed her hand and pulled her toward the lift bank. "We have been calling everybody and everywhere! Lucien even woke up his CO trying to track you down."

Jani flashed on the possibility of taking John up on his Seattle offer. If he was on his way back to his singer, Val could forward him Jani's message. They could leave inside the hour. "Angevin, I know I left some things undone, but I'll get to them first thing tomorrow, I prom—"

"Oh, you think it's that simple!" Angevin's eyes gleamed green fire. "*You just wait.*"

CHAPTER 22

"Angevin, what's going on? Angevin?" Jani hurried down the hall after the diminutive figure, who broke into a run as they neared the flat entry. *"Angevin!"*

"Did you know that the rear service entrance to this building isn't as well secured as it should be?" Angevin stopped in front of the door, then began to pace. Now that she'd made her goal, she couldn't follow through. "Did you? I sure as hell didn't. Heard the entry buzzer and assumed it was the front desk. Opened the door. *Guess what!"*

Jani looked from the door to Angevin's stricken face, then back again. "Who's in there? Are Steve and Lucien all right?"

"They're fine." Angevin took a step toward the door, then backed away again. "Maybe you should go in first."

"Oh, for—" Jani keyed in and gave a panel a good push to help it along. She strode through the entry, and saw Steve sitting at her desk, twisting an unlit 'stick between his fingers. "What's going on?"

Steve opened his mouth, then closed it. He held out his hand to Angevin, who had scuttled in behind Jani. Together, they pointed toward the sitting area.

Jani turned to find a robe-wrapped Lucien sitting in a chair that had been pushed in front of the couch. The couch itself was occupied by a formidably tall man, his head and shoulders towering above the seat back.

Man . . . Jani's senses gave her a swift kick, pointing out the dark gold tinge of the skin and the rigid posture. The jewel-rich green of the shirt, and the liquid-like way the material flowed over the broad back.

Then the head slowly turned, and she saw the eyes. Cracked gold glass, catching the light like gilt. “Ná Kièrshia.” The Haárin tilemaster rose to his feet. “I am Dathim Naré. NìRau Tsecha trusts you are most as uninjured, and bids me offer you the glories of the evening.” He spoke in English, flavored with the trilled R’s and biting consonants of Vynshàrau Haárin.

Ná? Jani detected the shortened vowels and altered accent of the Haárin feminine title. Well, that made sense. Or at least as much sense as everything else had that evening. “Ní Dathim. I am uninjured, yes.” She felt spun around, disoriented, like she’d just emerged from a pitch-dark Veedrome into the blaze of day. *What the hell time is it?* Too late at night to deal with an Haárin who sheared his head as humanish and felt no compunction about visiting his people’s Toxin in her downtown Chicago flat, surely. “My home is not clean. Your soul is in danger.” She had slipped from English into Vynshàrau Haárin without conscious thought, her straight back and anxious hand flicks defining her distress. “You should not be here.”

“I go where my dominant bids me go, regardless of the threat to my soul. I have declared myself to him. Such is my duty.” Dathim’s arms hung at his sides as he continued his half of the conversation in English. “He has bid me come here to witness your condition, and to bring you something that you must take care of.”

“Nema gave you something to give to me?” Jani groaned inwardly. Then again, judging by the odd looks she received from the assembled, maybe it wasn’t so inward. She walked to the sitting area. She had a choice of perching on the arm of Lucien’s chair or joining Dathim on the couch. Considering how she currently felt about Lucien and how her right knee and back felt about her, her choice proved no choice. She stepped past the chair without giving its occupant a look and sagged into a cross-legged slump on the couch, a respectful bodylength away from the Haárin.

Dathim sat as well. However, instead of pressing against the couch back, he shifted so that he nestled in the corner and faced Jani. That meant he couldn’t plant his booted feet side by side on the floor in the knees-together seat of a typical idomeni. Instead, he lifted his left leg and crossed it over his right leg, ankle to knee. Then he placed his left hand on the bent knee and stretched his right arm atop the arm of the couch in the classic “this is my space” sprawl of a human male.

Jani glanced at Lucien, who stared at the Haárin, his lips parted ever so slightly. If she didn’t know better, she’d have thought he had a crush on him. If she didn’t know better—

John, take me to Seattle! No, the last thing she needed was John and Seattle in any combination. *I'm tired, hungry, and in pain. Someone tried to kill me and my lover may have arranged it. My mother called me mutant tonight. Now Nema has a job for me.* Maybe she should call him and tell him it was safe, so that he could leave the embassy grounds and do whatever the hell it was himself. *Except he's been locked down. He can't leave. He's in trouble. Wake up!* She buried her face in her hands on the off chance that augie had gone south and she hallucinated. *When I look up, the far end of the couch will be empty.* Lucien will be gone, too. *He'll have been transferred to Whalen's Planet.* Steve and Angevin will have moved out. *I'll be alone, and it will be quiet, and I can sleep.*

She looked up to find Dathim studying her full-face, auric eyes shining. When she'd lived in the colonies and dealt with Haárin merchants on a daily basis, she had grown used to their efforts to adopt humanish appearance and the habit of direct eye contact. *Make that "somewhat used."* Idomeni appearance could be startling—to that, Dathim Naré had added his own spin. His was the long, bony face of his Vynshàrau forebears—his shorn hair accentuated the hard lines even more. He wore no overrobe atop his open-necked shirt and belted trousers. He wore no earrings. Not even his *à lérine* scars, the elongated welts ragged and brown against his dark gold skin, hinted at his alien nature. They could have been caused by an accident. He could have been a human male suffering from genetic disorders of the bone and liver, an inhabitant of one of the colonial outposts that had slipped beneath Neoclona's detection limit.

"You are unwell, Kièrshia? You do not act as bold as I have seen you at the embassy." Dathim's appearance seemed to alter his voice, making it sound merely foreign rather than alien. Deep. Rich. Not quite the twin of John's inestimable bass, but definitely a sibling.

"I've had a very long day, ní Dathim." Jani broke contact with the probing stare. *And you're making it longer.* "You said you had something to give me, from Nema." She reverted to English, since sitting cross-legged on a couch didn't lend itself to proper Vynshàrau Haárin language postures. "Could you give it to me, please?"

"Yes." Dathim twisted around, reached over the side of the couch, and came up holding a large idomeni-style briefbag. "NìRau Tsecha said that you will know what to do with these." He dropped the bag in the empty expanse between him and Jani. "I know what to do with them as well, but nìRau Tsecha does not trust my judgment. This is most unfortunate—I must ponder ways to earn his trust, and truly."

Jani watched Dathim as he unclasped the bag's complicated

fasteners. *Did I just hear an Haárin employ sarcasm?* He appeared perfectly serious, but Jani seldom met an idomeni who didn't. Nema bared his teeth more than most of his race and took pride in the fact that he had a sense of humor and knew how to use it, but he was an exception to every idomeni rule. *And now there's Dathim Naré.* The fact that he and Nema had found one another made her head ache. "Most as your dominant, ní Dathim, you possess a capacity to surprise."

"Surprise is a good thing, is it not, Kièrshia? A good thing for gaining humanish attention, and truly." Dathim undid the last fastener and pushed back the flap. "Surprise!"

Jani looked into the bag, and saw files and data wafers inserted in an array of upright pleated pockets. Files in burgundy folders. Files in white folders with burgundy trim. One file in a black folder. She tried to speak, but couldn't think of anything to say that Dathim would understand, even taking into account his expertise in sarcasm.

"Oh shit, Jan." Steve had wandered over to the couch. "Those are bloody Exterior Ministry Exec files."

The words "Exterior Ministry" brought Lucien out of his chair. He lifted one of the files out of its pocket, looked at the information tab that ran across the top, and shoved it back into place as though the paper stung to the touch. "I don't know about the rest of those files, but that one is classified 'For Ministers' Eyes Only.' At this moment, we're all facing at least twenty years in prison for violating the Commonwealth Secrets Act."

Jani looked at Dathim, who had resumed his cross-legged sprawl and looked extremely pleased with himself. "How did you steal these documents? More importantly, *why* did you steal these documents?"

"I took them out of Anais Ulanova's office. NìRau Tsecha wanted to learn more of your shooting, and believed that Anais Ulanova would possess information." He still watched Jani with interest, studying her reactions to his every revelation. "I was taken there to look at places to lay my tile. I examined the lobby, but the tilework that nìaRauta Ulanova wanted there was not suitable, so they took me to look at the conference room that was connected by a door to her office. She had many stacks of files on her desk. I took something from each stack."

Lucien slumped back into his chair. "I told her for years to seal that damned door."

Dathim finally used an Haárin gesture, a brush of his open right hand across his shirtfront that indicated relief. "I am most glad she did not listen to you, Lieutenant Pascal, and truly."

A glimmer of liveliness returned to Lucien's face. Oh yes, the fact that Dathim recognized him definitely pleased him. "You know me?"

"I have seen you at the embassy, with nìRau Tsecha. And alone. The lieutenant who remembers what he sees." Dathim regarded Lucien less intently than he did Jani. If he noticed Lucien's fascination with him, he gave no indication. But then, odds were overwhelming that he had no experience with human sexuality or any idea what that captivation implied.

"When Anais figures out that you rifled her office, and she will, Commonwealth–Shèrá relations are going to get interesting. I think the term 'major diplomatic incident' is applicable here." Jani fingered through the files. "And nìRau Nema expects me to do what with these? Return them?"

"Yes." Dathim gave a human-style shrug. "He said that you would see to them. He called this an 'incident,' too. He said that he is quite good at them."

"Oh, yeah." Jani glanced up at Steve, who looked sick to his stomach.

"We could turn them over to someone in my department." Lucien spoke to Jani, but he looked at Dathim. "Certain people owe me favors. It would be a no-questions-asked return. The best way to go about this, in my opinion."

Jani pretended to consider Lucien's offer, then shook her head. "If Service Intelligence turns them in, Exterior is going to think they took them in the first place. Service and Exterior are just starting to get along again—I don't think we want to risk scuttling any tenuous truces over this." In truth, she didn't want Intelligence sticking their nose in. Not after the way they bobbled her parents' transfer. *This needs to be handled by someone I trust.* Someone she could . . . persuade. She knew where she needed to go—she just needed to get there without tipping off Lucien.

"One of the ministry Doc Controls?" Angevin had joined Steve, placing herself in such a way that he hid her from Dathim's view. "Stuff happens. 'So-and-so left her briefbag behind after a meeting' is the standard excuse. The Ministries exchange unauthorized acquisitions all the time."

But the Ministries won't let me analyze these files before I give them back. Jani closed the bag flap and dragged the strap over her shoulder. "I'll think of something." She stood, not quite as shakily as Lucien, and limped across the room toward the kitchen. "Steve, run interference for ní Dathim while he leaves." She pushed past the sliding door, then leaned against the counter until she could dredge up the strength to walk to the cooler. "I just need some juice." And one of John's meal bars. That would provide enough energy to get her through the next few hours. "Hours." She yawned as she cracked the seal of a dispo of lemon tonic.

Jani had leaned her head back to drink when she heard the kitchen door open. She didn't bother to turn around. If it was Angevin or Steve, the melodious howls of shock and dismay would soon fill the air, and if it was Lucien. . . . She felt her body tighten in anticipation of his touch, and gave herself a mental swift kick.

"You are not as you should be."

Jani's throat stopped in mid-swallow. Her head came down, luckily over the sink. She spewed, coughed, and sneezed tonic—the bubbly astringency filled her nostrils and burned her sinuses. Her eyes teared as though she wept—she felt the damaged right film split. *"Damn—!"* She grabbed for the sinkside dispenser, yanked napkin after napkin, blew her nose and wiped her face. Then she turned, taking care to cover her exposed eye.

Dathim stood just inside the doorway. The prospect of entering a humanish kitchen seemed to have tempered his boldness. He touched the edge of a counter, the handle of a cupboard door. "I surprised you again." Then he drew his hand back and examined his fingertips, as though he expected the contact to leave a mark. "You surprise easily, and truly."

Jani watched in amazement as Dathim opened a drawer and removed a serving fork. "Is there nothing you fear, ní Dathim?" She spoke in Vynshàrau Haárin, so that her words would better express her shock at his actions.

"I am already damned, according to the Oligarch. What difference?" Dathim turned the fork over, then returned it to its holder and slid the drawer closed. "This kitchen is cleaner than I expected. We are told that humanish leave their food on the counter for the insects and the parasites to season."

"We sometimes leave out food, but it's covered. The production is tightly controlled and the food itself is treated, so there are no parasites." Jani gestured around her. "Do you see any insects?"

Dathim shrugged. "The Oligarch would say that the insects come out later. For each question, he has a ready answer." He looked at Jani. "You limp. You were hurt in the shooting?"

"I fell on my knee. It is as nothing."

"Lieutenant Pascal was hurt."

"Yes. He was shot in the lower abdomen. As you saw, he is weak, but he will recover."

"He stares at me."

Jani racked her brain for the right words. "He has never seen an Haárin with short hair."

"Ah." Dathim brushed his hand over his stubble. "You have damaged your eye?"

"Yes." Jani probed behind the dispo to wipe away a film fragment that had slithered down her cheek.

"Then you must be in pain."

"No."

"Eyes hurt when they are damaged."

"I'm all right."

Dathim's lips curved in a disturbingly human-like smile. "You have eyes like mine, but you do not want me to see them. You are my dominant according to nìRau Tsecha, but it shames you to look as I do. Just like nìRau Tsecha. He takes an Haárin name, but he lives as born-sect, because to live as I do would shame him."

Jani shifted her footing to take the weight off her aching knee. "Shame has nothing to do with it, ní Dathim." She waited for her knee to stop throbbing before she risked speaking again—the pain made her voice shake. "I am not your dominant. I am a humanish female who had an accident. The way my doctor chose to repair me resulted in genetic changes that have led to my looking a little like you. That's all."

"NìRau Tsecha chose you before you had your accident. He believed you could lead us through difficult times. Those are his words. I have never led, so I must submit to his experience in such things." Dathim took one step farther into the kitchen, then another. He opened the cooler, removed a dispo of grapefruit juice, and studied the label.

Sarcasm. Jani hoisted her lemon tonic to brave another sip—

"You look most odd standing there with one hand over your eye."

—and brought it back down just as quickly. *"Ní Dathim—"*

Before Jani could finish, Dathim strode across the narrow kitchen, grabbed her wrist, and yanked down.

"You—!" Jani threw the dispo into the sink and let the bag slide to the floor, then used her freed hand to try to loosen the Haárin's brutal grip. She wanted to use her legs and teeth as well, but she didn't want the sounds of a fight to reach the sitting room.

Then she looked up into Dathim's face, saw his bared teeth, and stopped struggling. "Let. Me. Go."

"Green. Not a common color for Vynshàrau, except near the north where our lands border those of the Oà. Many Oà have green eyes." Dathim pushed up Jani's sleeve, revealing her healed *à lérine* scars. Then he released her and took a step back. His air of self-satisfaction dissipated. *"Which eye is the fake, Kièrshia?"* He lapsed into his language. The pitch of his voice turned guttural. His shoulders rounded. *"Decide, or leave the Haárin be. Leave nìRau Tsecha be. He fights his suborn because of you. He fights everyone because of you."*

"Sànalàn? He's fighting Sànalàn?" Jani massaged her right wrist, which bore the imprint of Dathim's fingers. "It's because of what he said at the meeting, isn't it? I knew she'd be angry, but I didn't think she'd challenge him."

"It is another incident." Dathim resumed both his English and his examination of the kitchen appliances, opening the door to the oven and looking inside. "In truth, Shai will not approve this fight, but nìRau Tsecha will not retract his acceptance." He ran a finger along the inside of the oven, like a chef performing inspection. "He does this for you. What do you do for him?"

"I never asked him to do this for me. I never asked him to do anything. He never asked me, either. He just told me, 'This is what you will be!' " Jani heard her voice fill the small room, knew it carried to three pairs of ears beyond, and didn't care. "I am unfit to lead. I have no skill in government. I have a past that makes me dangerous to know. I want to be left alone."

"You want to be left alone." Dathim opened another cupboard and removed a prepack dinner from the shelf. "Yet when nìRau Tsecha gives you documents and says, 'Dispose of them,' I do not hear you say no. Such causes me to think that you do not wish to be so alone, no matter what you say. Such humanish confusion—it is not sound. You need to decide, Kièrshia." He stood quietly and read the back of the package, as if he had no interest in Jani's reply.

Jani watched him study the container, return it to its place, and remove another. "What do you want, ní Dathim?" Her fatigued brain traveled in loops and whorls, driven by anger and confusion. "Why are you doing this?"

Dathim closed the cupboard and turned to face her. Over the past minutes, he had performed acts that would have earned him expulsion from his enclave, yet he seemed as relaxed as if he had just arranged his tools or worked some tile. "I tire of sneaking off the embassy grounds in the night. I want to visit this damned cold place in the day. I want to sell my tilemastery here. I want to live here. Many of us wish the same."

"You want to leave the embassy grounds?" Jani watched as Dathim nodded. "Cèel will never allow you to establish an enclave in Chicago, and neither will my government."

"What Cèel wants is of no consequence. And if the things we offer please humanish enough, they will let us come, because they want what pleases them. But if they hesitate, you will persuade them, Kièrshia, that such is the proper thing to do. They will listen to you, because your past makes you dangerous to know, and because they smell the blood of Knevçet Shèràa when you speak." Dathim offered another close-lipped smile. "It is past our time to establish an enclave here. Even when humanish lived outside Rauta Shèràa before the war, they did not extend us an invitation to live here. And many of us wanted to come." He looked around the kitchen as though it were land he wished to purchase, then at Jani, his smug attitude returned. "Surprise, ná Kièrshia. You will soon not be alone."

CHAPTER 23

Dathim left quietly, a reluctant Steve at his back. Angevin, rattled unto silence, adjourned to Jani's desk and poked through the dwindling stacks. Lucien remained in his chair, gaze moving briefly to Jani before settling with eerie concentration toward the door.

Jani sought refuge in her bedroom. She refilmed her eye, then focused on the mechanical task of transferring the Exterior documents from the idomeni briefbag to her duffel. When Dathim's parting words threatened to punch through her thought barrier, she dropped a file or fussed with a clasp to ward them off. The ploy even worked the first few times she tried it—

You will soon not be alone.

—but it couldn't work forever.

She sat on the edge of the bed and pushed up her right sleeve. Her scars caught the light like silken threads. She could imagine the skin reddened where Dathim had grabbed her, even though the impress of his fingers had long since faded.

Which eye is the fake, Kièrshia?

Jani blinked slowly, mindful of the fresh filming. "They both are, strictly speaking." She tugged the sleeve back into place, then dragged her duffel onto her lap and closed the fasteners. "That's what happens when your doctor builds you from whatever he finds in his basement." She tried to smile, but Dathim's words persisted in her head.

They will listen to you . . . because they smell the blood of Knevçet Shèràa when you speak.

Jani sat quietly. Then she pushed her duffel back onto the bed, rose, and walked to her closet.

Her knee griped as she stood on her toes to reach the toiletry case, which taunted her from its resting place in the rear of the shelf. She tested the hanger bar for strength, then braced her left foot against the wall and pulled herself up, a move to which both her lower back and sore shoulder took vigorous exception.

She opened the bag slowly, as though she expected the contents to leap out at her. She put on the redstone ring—it slid easily on the third finger of her right hand, as it had for months. The soulcloth, she looped around her left wrist like a bracelet in the manner of a Vynshàrau soldier reclaiming his soul after a battle. Her long-dried blood had stiffened the fabric, making the tying difficult. She finally settled for winding the loose ends around the length and tucking them.

She stood and regarded her changed hands. John had switched out her left arm several times that summer, for reasons he had refused to make clear at the time. But now she could see—he had needed to play catch-up with the rapid changes her real arm had undergone. The longer, thinner fingers. The narrowed palms. The brown skin tinged with gold, as though she suffered from liver disease.

Jani held her left wrist up to her nose and sniffed the bracelet. The cloth smelled old, musty. Cold, if an odor could be classified that way. "The blood lost its smell long ago." She pulled the cloth from her wrist and the ring from her finger and thrust them back in the bag. Then she shoved the bag as far as she could into a dark corner of the shelf.

The night had grown cold and crisp; the dry air pulled the moisture from her eyefilms. Jani tugged up the field jacket collar, wishing she'd thought to stuff a pair of gloves in the pockets. Her stomach grumbled, and she rummaged through her duffel for one of John's meal bars. The fact that she had crammed the Exterior files into the bag complicated the search, already made difficult by the dark and her fatigue-dulled attention span. She pulled up beside a chrysanthemum-filled planter to search more easily.

She didn't catch the movement at first. A passing skimmer obscured matters, followed by the rowdy procession of some Family progeny out on a prowl. But as Jani returned her attention to her duffel, she caught the shadow flicker in the doorway across the street. The fidget of someone who thought themselves better hidden than they actually were.

Jani freed a meal bar from the morass with a flourish and removed the wrapper. Bit into it with apparent relish and continued her saunter down the street. She had traveled two blocks south of Armour

Place. Her original destination had been a people-mover stop that she didn't often use. Now, however, she veered west toward an area of commercial buildings.

The quality of the safety lighting deteriorated quickly. Soon Jani could only track her stalker by the occasional distant footfall. Whoever it was remained on the other side of the street, well back and out of sight. During daylight, Jani conceded, they could have tracked her for blocks without her knowledge, since they seemed to possess a decent grasp of basic shadowing. But night had proved their enemy rather than friend, as their step echoed along the deserted street.

Jani continued to wend deeper into the commercial pocket until follower and followed were the only two people to be seen. When she encountered a narrow alley between two shuttered buildings, she slipped down it. Once she reached the end, she nestled into the shadows, and waited.

For a time, all was silence but for her breathing and the beat of her heart. Then Jani heard the staccato scrape of leather sole on scancrete; the sound stopped at the mouth of the alley, then began again, drawing closer and growing louder as her follower approached. She reached into her duffel for her parchment opener, then let the bag slide to the ground. Her hand tightened around the blade's handle. She waited.

The steps quickened as they approached the end of the alley. Stopped as the stalker surveyed the darkness. Then they resumed, slowly, one long, low crunch after another, drawing nearer.

Jani waited until the sounds drew alongside. Slightly ahead. She tensed to spring—

"Jani? Are you back here?"

—and pulled the knife back just in time as she barreled into Roni and they tumbled onto the hard, cold scancrete. "You *jackass*!" She rolled away from her and swore again as she banged her right knee against the sharp corner of the building. "Why the hell didn't you announce yourself!"

Roni lay flat on her back. "I trusted you." She tried to lift her head and shoulders, groaned, and sagged back down. "I let you have a look at the idomeni ambassador's letter, and you fed me back a fake. I want the real letter back."

"I don't know what you're talking about."

"Bull." Roni struggled to a semi-sitting position and pressed a hand to the back of her head. "To add to my joy—I've spent most of the day in an emergency meeting—concerning some missing documents."

Jani braced against the building and worked to her feet. "Are you all right?"

"Don't change the subject." Roni looked dazed; her hair stuck straight up in places. "I waited for you by the bookstore for over three hours. When you didn't show, I hung around. I saw the Haárin tile-master enter your building carrying a bag. I saw him leave without it. I know you have those documents. Where are you taking them? I'm not too thrilled with you right now, so I suggest you give a straight answer."

Jani freed her duffel from its hiding place and hoisted it to her shoulder. The blade, she slipped into her jacket pocket for easier access—she had never seen the glittery look in Roni's eyes before, and she didn't want any surprises. "Like I said before, I don't know what you're—"

"Jani." Roni produced the female vocal version of Declan Kilian when he had had enough. "You and Tsecha are being set up. Now do you want to get to the bottom of this, or don't you?" She handcombed her hair, to little effect. "Look, you show me what you have, and I won't flag down the first green-and-white I see and have you arrested for possessing stolen property. Favor for favor—what do you say?"

"I just want to find out what the hell is going on." Roni lurched in her seat as the people-mover pulled away from the curb. "The Exterior Exec Wing has shut me out for weeks. I can't raise Ulanova on the 'port. And forget Beddy-Boy Lescaux. He's much too important to deal with the likes of me."

Jani looked up from her examination of her duffel. Her self-appointed partner had suffered a good scuffing from her tumble in the alley—cheek scratched and reddened, chin coated with a smear of blood. She'd cracked the back of her head against the scancrete, as well—a tuft of blood-matted hair marked the site of a scalp injury. "I still think you should stop by Neoclona to get your head checked out."

"Will you stop changing the subject?"

"Are you seeing double?"

"I can see you as clear as day." Roni glared at her sidelong. "Why did you duplicate that letter?"

Jani looked out her window in time to see a ComPol skimmer pull alongside. "I wanted to flush out whoever wrote it."

"Well, you sure flushed something, didn't you?" Roni probed the back of her head, and winced. "You know what was the main comment I heard around the offices today? That it was a shame that the wrong person got shot."

"I didn't realize Lucien was that well liked."

"He isn't."

The ComPol skimmer dogged the people-mover for half a block before speeding up. Jani watched it flit ahead of the lumbering vehicle and accelerate, warning lights flashing. "Like you said, someone is trying to set up Nema. I wanted to take the heat off him—whether people thought he'd actually composed the precis or not, they'd still use it as they saw fit. I thought the faked Brandenburg Progression would work, at least for a week or so, until I could figure out who was going after him." The ComPol lights disappeared into the distance, and she relaxed. "I took the chance that you wouldn't scan it as soon as you got your hands on it again."

"I scan that damned thing daily. It's become a hobby." Roni yawned. She wore a burgundy band-collared shirt beneath her charcoal trouser suit—the vivid colors accentuated her wounds. "I mean, it was a great idea. Take a Commonwealth document and twist it just enough to make it look as though an idomeni tried to fake it. Folks get so excited about catching an idomeni forgery that they don't stop to think whether the information in the document is worth a damn." She glanced at Jani a little less angrily. "What tipped you off?"

"I don't believe Nema would bother to sneak that sort of information. He'd tell us outright, and blow the consequences." Jani twitched a shoulder. "You?"

"I think he'd have done a better job. Any idomeni would have—they sure as hell wouldn't have tripped up on the damned initiator chip." Roni lifted one of her feet so she could study her shoes. "You even scanned the soles. You really are paranoid, aren't you?"

The Registry tower loomed ahead. Jani gathered her duffel and stood carefully. She had sustained less obvious injuries than Roni—a battering to her sore knee and a bruised elbow—but they combined to make her every movement a pleasure. "We're getting off at this stop."

Roni caught the view out the window, and shot Jani another hard look.

Jani shouldered her duffel as defiantly as she could with an elbow that delivered sparks along the length of her arm every time she moved. "I'm completely within my rights as an investigator-at-large."

"Oh, I'm sure you have an explanation for everything." Roni stood, and dabbed at her chin. "How do I look?"

"Like you just got rolled in a darkened alley."

"Gosh, I wonder why."

* * *

"Do you have an appointment?"

Jani looked around the waiting area that served the private side of Registry, which was empty but for her, Roni, and the bright young face that asked the question. "No." She forced a smile, and gazed down at the receptionist with as much benevolence as she could muster, considering. "But as a member of Registry, I am entitled to use the labs whenever I wish."

"Oh, I'm not questioning that, Ms. Kilian!" The young woman offered more of the wide-eyed Registry homage that Jani had not yet gotten used to. "But you've been through so much with the shooting and all and our lab staff is on meal break now and I'm sure one of the supervisors would be happy—"

"Jani?"

Jani restrained the urge to lay her head down on the desk as the familiar drawl wafted through the air. Instead, she turned and did her best to look wide-awake. "Dolly."

"We've heard all kinds of awful things. Glad to see none of them are true." Dolly walked toward them from the direction of the lift bank. "That being said, what *are* you doin' here?"

Jani glanced at the wall clock. "I could ask you the same question."

"I'm on-call this week. Resident expert to all and sundry at any time of the day or night." Dolly looked a little rousted herself. She wore another flowing outfit, crystal blue silk that matched her eyes. Not what Jani would classify as stay-at-home clothes—somewhere in Chicago, an expensive dinner grew cold on its plate. "I saw your names come up on the entry board and realized you're just the people to help me with my own little dilemma." She held her hand out to Roni, her gaze flicking over her roughed-up visage and disheveled clothes. "Hello, Ms. McGaw. You're the Exterior Chief."

"Yes, ma'am," Roni bubbled. "It's a pleasure to meet you at last." She grinned in starstruck rapture, then winced as her damaged face complained.

"Well, Doll, you tell us your dilemma and we'll tell you ours." Jani laughed, a single short hack. "Dolly's Dilemma. Dolly's Dreadful Dilemma. Dolly's Dastardly Dreadful Dilemma."

If Dolly felt any trace of good humor, she kept it to herself. "I remember a few times in Rauta Shèràa when you pushed yourself until the exhaustion made you silly. That never boded well for anybody." She turned and headed for the lift. "Let's adjourn to my office, shall we?"

* * *

"I was in the middle of a lovely supper when I received a call from Registry Security. The bottom has apparently dropped out at Exterior. They're missing some paper." Dolly walked to her sideboard and took a decanter from the liquor service. "The most interesting thing they had to say was that you were involved." She turned to look at Jani. "You and a staffer at the idomeni embassy." She poured a generous serving of gin, then dropped in a slice of lime and a few cubes of ice. "Does this have anything to do with that other matter you came to see me about?"

"Madame Aryton, I am also involved in that *other* matter." Roni glared at Jani, but turned professionally serious by the time Dolly returned to her desk. "Independent of Ms. Kilian, I have been trying to determine whether the alleged idomeni letter has any relation to certain other Exterior documents. Unfortunately, my experience with idomeni documents protocols isn't as extensive as it should be."

Madame? Jani stared at the scratched side of Roni's face, but was pointedly ignored. Therefore, she concentrated on picking up the thread Roni held out to her and weaving her part of the tale. "Ms. McGaw is consulting with me concerning these protocols. I'm comparing them to a wide range of humanish documents as a means of instruction."

Dolly sipped her drink, then set it down on the desk. She crossed her hands in her lap, every centimeter the dignified Family Lady. But her mind worked in circles—her acceptance into the Academy had depended on that ability, as had her survival in Chicago. "In other words, these documents that Exterior Security believes were taken by the idomeni—"

"—are right here in my possession." Roni hoisted Jani's duffel and patted it proprietarily.

Roni's revelation would have stopped a less-nimble mind, but it didn't even cause Dolly to tap the decelerator. "But why didn't you sign them out, Ms. McGaw? Exterior Security has no record of you doing so."

"According to Exterior policy, I'm exempt from that requirement. I have to remind Security of this on a regular basis, since it's not a policy of which they approve." Roni grimaced as she lowered the duffel back to the floor—apparently, not all her injuries were cosmetic, after all. "The built-in assumption is that I am cleared to see any piece of paper in the place."

"But is Jani cleared as well?" Dolly shot Jani a skeptical look.

"My understanding from Exterior Security was that she would have to make several jumps in esteem to qualify as *persona non grata.*"

"Roni only shows me what I'm cleared to see." Jani watched Dolly's posture, the way she held her hands. *All directions at once.* She knew the barrage was coming, she just wished she knew Dolly's mind well enough to know where she'd strike first. "I have Yellow clearance at Treasury and Orange at Commerce, so I'm not completely off-the-street."

Dolly paused to take another sip of her drink. "Roni? May I call you Roni?" She swirled her glass and smiled as Roni nodded and sat up expectantly. "What happened to your face?"

Jani sat back as easily as she could and watched Roni's jaw and neck tense.

"I'm not the most graceful thing on two feet, Madame." Roni grinned sheepishly and brushed a smudge of dirt from her sleeve. "I missed a step leaving a restaurant this evening, the results of which you can see."

Dolly's clear eyes never left Roni's face. "Did you fall on top of Jani? She appears a little bedraggled herself."

Jani shrugged. "I always look bedraggled, Dolly."

"No, you do not. You're a single word in a Commonwealth of paragraphs and one thing you have never been, Jani Kilian, is sloppy." Dolly set her glass down so that the ice clinked and liquor splashed. "I'm only going to say this once. You're dexxies who suspect documents fraud, and you're acting accordingly. A ticklish situation all around, but based on my experiences with my old school tie"—she nodded toward Jani—"I'm inclined to stand back and let you proceed. But you must let me know what is goin' on because one thing I most assuredly do *not* like—apart from having to excuse myself from an anniversary dinner with my spouse—is being surprised."

Jani knocked her fist against her forehead. Her timing with regards to other peoples' evenings just kept getting better and better. "You and Cairn."

"Twenty-six years today. We count from the day in prep school when she gave me her late great-grandmother's wedding ring and told me I was the one." Dolly offered the barest hint of a smile before the veil fell. "But enough about me and mine. I want to hear about you and yours, and I want to hear it fast, and I want to hear it now."

Jani looked at Roni. She eventually looked back. They communicated in the same way they worked, via mindreading supplemented by the occasional eyebrow twitch.

Jani opened the negotiations. "Can we talk while we work? Time may be getting short."

CHAPTER 24

They adjourned to another laboratory in a different part of the building. This time, Dolly assembled the equipment herself, eliminating the need for documents technicians with prying eyes.

The three of them worked to activate and calibrate the readers and interpreters, hands flicking over touchpads, speech reduced to the occasional short question or comment. Soon, all the start-up beeps and clicks silenced and indicator lights showed green.

Roni hauled Jani's duffel up on a desk in the middle of the room and cracked the closures, only to have Dolly encircle her wrist in a racing-hardened grip. "I'm waiting for that explanation."

Jani dug into one of the duffel's side pockets and snatched another meal bar. "A colonial business consortium called *L'araignée* may be the driving force behind this idomeni forgery. They may have also helped Service Intelligence compile information about my past for a white paper that's been coursing up and down Cabinet Row for the past few weeks." She pulled the wrapper from the bar and bit grudgingly. She'd grown sick of chocolate and caramel, but the sensation of a hollow pit where her stomach used to be convinced her that what she wanted had very little to do with what her body needed.

"I heard about that." Dolly released Roni's wrist with a small smile and left her to examine it, which Roni did with a pained frown. "Well, more than that, actually. I read it. So did Carson." She leaned against a counter and folded her arms. "After the news of the shooting made the rounds, he called to tell me that he'd double the salary-benefits package if you came to work for him. But then, Carson always did have a wild side." She looked at Jani. "You feel that the white paper and this idomeni letter are connected."

Jani bit, chewed, nodded. "I think some commercial factions are combining in an effort to destabilize human-idomeni relations in order to force the Haárin to end their business dealings with the colonies. The financial losses that humanish businesses are sustaining because of the Haárin influx are starting to mount. *L'araignée* is the name adopted by a Channel World business consortium that formed to fight the influx. It contains, unfortunately, both legitimate and criminal members, and the legit factions don't yet realize that they've made a deal with the devil. By the time they do, several colonial governments will be bankrupted and their business structures irreversibly damaged."

Roni had wandered from desk to counter. "*L'araignée*? Sounds like some of the outfits I had to deal with during my colonial stint." She examined her face in a cabinet's reflective surface, then stepped to the sink. "They'd be more than happy to help panicky Earthbound bureaucrats force out Haárin merchants, while they skim the cream off every transport payload that leaves a colonial dock." She ran the water and tried to scrub the dried blood off her chin. "That way, they can destabilize the Commonwealth system and make money off of it at the same time, which to them is the best of both worlds." She mouthed an "ouch" as her overzealous washing reopened the wound, and held a lab wipe over it to staunch the blood flow.

Dolly walked across the lab and plucked her glass from atop a reader case. She had exhausted the gin, and contented herself with crunching ice. "This all seems to boil down to money, and that conflicts with what I know of the idomeni. I lived in Rauta Shèràa for seven years. I schooled with them. Worked alongside them. Human business models do not apply. Their status has nothing to do with what they possess, but with what they are."

"You know born-sect, Dolly. The Haárin are different. They've developed a regard for the respect and freedom that doing sound business can earn them." Jani finished her meal bar and immediately sought another. "In the vast rambling construct of humanish commercialism, they have found a haven. A place where they can live and ply their trades without the interference from born-sect dominants. A place where the threats of born-sect unrest no longer touch them. They don't want to uproot their lives because two propitiators can't decide which spice should be used to flavor meats in the morning and which at night. They don't care about that anymore. Some of them are so far removed from their native culture that they've adopted humanish mannerisms and habits." Visions of Dathim Naré danced in her head. "I met an Haárin recently who wouldn't return to the worldskein if Cèel shoved a long shooter up his backside and threatened to press the charge-through." She comprehended the silence, and looked up to see both Dolly and Roni regarding her with their hands over their mouths.

Dolly spoke first. "Jani. What an image."

Jani pulled the black-covered file out of her duffel and walked to the reader. "You know what I mean."

"Yes." Dolly's eyes widened when she saw what Jani held. "Now that we've gotten the xenopolitical discussion out of the way, perhaps you could tell me what point of human documents protocol you needed to illustrate using a 'Ministers' Eyes Only' file?"

"I'll take that." Roni rushed to Jani's side. A subdued tug-of-war ensued until Dolly's intervention-with-arched-eyebrows gave the advantage to Roni, who plucked the top sheet from the file with an air of triumph and inserted the page in the reader slot.

Dolly cracked a cube between her teeth as she inserted herself between Jani and the reader, blocking Jani's view of the display. She removed the sheet from the reader slot and read it. "Roni, is this really germane to the discussion?"

Roni looked over her shoulder. Her eyes goggled. She took the paper from Dolly and tucked it back in the file.

Jani walked to the sink to wash her hands, and tried to catch a glimpse of the file along the way. "What is it?"

"Details of a Minister's personal life, which will no doubt be used to sway a vote or two in some future Council session." Dolly's voice had taken on a roughened velvet quality that, like Jamira Shah's questioning lilt, Jani remembered all too well. "Just how did you go about choosing these files, Roni?"

"We were in a hurry, Dolly. Roni became confused." Jani returned to the desk and pulled all the files out of the duffel. "OK, we're looking for Channel World references. Guernsey. Man. Jersey. Acadia. We're looking for my name. Service C-numbers. Haárin or idomeni references. For damned near anything we can find."

Dolly walked up to the desk and braced her hands on the edge. "Jani, what did I tell you in my office? Do you remember that far back?"

Jani held a sheaf of files out to her. "And what did I ask you two days ago? Do you remember that far back?"

"Jani—"

"Do I need to repeat it?"

"Wait a damned minute—"

"Do you think I'm wasting your time? If you say yes, we'll turn these documents over to you right now. You can return them to Exterior, and tell them they magically appeared on the Registry front step. Tell them anything you like." Jani pushed the files into Dolly's hands. "But here's something to keep in mind as you cover your Registry backside. Someone tried to kill me. They tried to kidnap my parents. They're trying to destroy Nema. I'm trying to find out who they are. At this particular moment, I don't have much patience with proper form or peoples' feelings. At this particular moment, you're either with me or against me, and either way, I'll remember till the day I die."

"Ja—?" Dolly looked from Jani, to the files in her hand, then back to Jani. Started to speak. Stopped. Then she turned and walked to an open stretch of counter top, spread out the files, opened one, and began to read.

"And my assignment is?" Roni stepped up to the desk and held out her hand.

Whether the strong emotion that flushed Roni's face and tightened her voice was anger or embarrassment, Jani didn't know or care. She handed Roni her share of the paper, then watched her pull a lab chair up to a bench, sit down, and open a file. Only then did she sit down herself and open the topmost of those that remained.

"I think I found something."

Jani looked up to find Roni hurrying across the lab toward the reader, and rose to join her. "What is it?"

"Meeting notes. Stuck off by themselves in a file. Guernsey watermark. They're encoded, but the reader should be able to decrypt." She pounded a beat on the reader to shake it out of standby. "Why do people take notes? Don't they know that once they write it down, they're mine for life?" Roni inserted the sheet of parchment in the reader, then stood back, rocking from one foot to the other as the paper disappeared into the slot. "On the other hand, this could be another false alarm."

Jani flexed her stiff back, her eyes on the instrument display. "Let's see what it says before we write it off."

"Write what off?" Dolly entered the lab juggling three dispos of vend alcove coffee.

"Roni's found meeting notes." Jani took one of the cups from Dolly and sniffed the steam. It held a sharp, burning odor, which meant the brew was old, which in turn meant that it would taste like fuel to her hybrid tastebuds. She didn't want to ask Dolly if the Hands of Might could lay hold of some pepper to kill the taste, however—judging from the look on Dolly's face, those Hands wouldn't be averse to boxing an Ear. Instead, Jani drank, swallowed, and kept her grimace to herself.

Roni took her own cup with the look of a drowning woman who had just been thrown a float. "The whole damned thing's encrypted," she said between sips. "Why would someone encrypt meeting notes? If the topic was so touchy, why write it down in the first place?"

"Sounds as through someone wanted to cover themselves." Dolly tossed a couple of tablets in her mouth, then washed them down. "But that doesn't mean the matter has anything to do with what we're investigating here. Nothing in this melange has even come close to whatever it is Jani's looking for—we've found everything from personnel profiles to construction plans for colonial buildings." She pressed her fingers to the bridge of her nose. "This will turn out to be someone's shopping list."

Behind them, the reader beeped. The original document emerged from the slot, followed a few seconds later by a decrypted fiche.

Roni grabbed them both, then handed off the original to Jani as she plundered the copy. "It's a note to Anais Ulanova," she muttered after a few seconds. "Bet that's why they wrote it down. Probably kept copies in lockboxes, too. What the hell does this mean? 'Met with Le Blond—' "

"Let me see it." Jani plucked the fiche from her hands and read it. "Met with Le Blond today. He will be at Exterior Main in three weeks. He says there are no problems. Service is set." She glanced up. "I don't know whether that's service as in served or *the* Service." She continued to read. "Contracts are set. Are—?" She cleared her throat. "Are you sure we must use him? He kills with his eyes. He is so cold—I do not trust him."

"Jani?" Dolly leaned toward her, headache-narrowed eyes lit with question. "What's wrong? You look like you've seen a ghost."

"No. I've seen those before." Jani beckoned to Roni. "Can you recall whether Anais would have been at Exterior Main in time to meet with Le Blond?"

Roni glanced at the date. "I'd have to check her calendar history."

Dolly gestured toward the lab comport. "You can do that from here."

Roni shook her head. "Not tonight, Madame. Exterior Security disconnected the Annex from CabNet when they filed the missing doc report. We're in lockdown until further notice—I'd have to go back to my office to check this."

* * *

"I don't know how the hell you talked us out of there." Roni fell into the people-mover seat, then leaned forward and rested her forehead against the seat in front of her. "Dolly wanted to kill you. She wanted to string you up by your heels over boiling oil. She wanted—"

"She wants to find out what's going on more." Jani watched the dead-of-night city drift past the 'mover window. "If Dathim could recall in which pile he found those notes, I'd send him back to steal the whole stack. It would all be there. The meetings. The payoffs. The plans. Everything pertaining to *L'araignée*'s birth. I bet the trail would lead right to whoever composed The Nema Letter and spearheaded the white paper."

"Let's not give Dathim Naré any more espionage practice, OK?" Roni sat back slowly. "Like I said back there, I'd dealt with outfits like them before. If you'd leveled with me from the beginning, *I* could have searched Anais's desk and uncovered the whole damned story."

"No." Jani shook her head, stopping when the rocking seemed to intensify. "*L'araignée*'s been leaving a trail of bodies. Ignorance is survival."

"Is it?" Roni rocked her head from shoulder to shoulder until the bones in her neck cracked. "That little bit Dathim stumbled upon is all we're going to get, unfortunately. My guess is that everything on Anais's desk has been locked up by Security, to be released into her hands only." She poked the plastic sack in her lap, into which Jani had transferred all the Exterior files except for The Nema Letter. Dolly had insisted on holding on to that "for safety's sake." Whether she meant the document's safety or their collective security, she didn't make clear. Considering her tense mood, Roni and Jani thought it wiser not to push for clarification.

"You're going to have a hell of a time burying those." Jani unbent her knee as far as she could without hitting the seat in front of her. The sharp pain had damped to a dull ache, but every step between the 'mover stop and her flat still promised agony. "What will you tell Lescaux?"

"I don't know. I'll think of something." Roni yawned and sagged further into her seat. " 'Le Blond.' You paled when you read that fiche." Her breathing slowed, as though she neared sleep. "You think it's Lucien, don't you?"

Jani yawned in response, wide enough for her jaw to crack. "I don't know."

"Don't give me that, all right—I've had a bad night." Roni scowled and touched her sore cheek. "I've been roughed up in an alley, I've made the Registry Inspector General's 'watch this one' list, and I've probably done myself out of a job." She pressed her hand to her face, bleary eyes locked in the middle distance. "When Lucien still worked at Exterior, I used to study him. Much as I hated him, I had to admire the way he just cut through the place. Peter looks like him—the hair, the eyes, but he really can't hold a candle. Lucien maneuvered people like pieces on a gameboard. Even Anais, although she didn't realize it until it was too late." She looked at Jani. "He threw her over for you. Did you ever wonder why?"

"Access to the idomeni, like I told you in your office." Jani thought back to Lucien's rapt studying of Dathim. "He finds them fascinating."

"Well, folks say you're part idomeni. Perhaps he thinks you're fascinating, too." Roni yawned again. "So, speaking of close but not quite, who was this person I remind you of?"

Jani turned her attention to the darkened buildings. "Yolan Cray. She was a corporal with the Twelfth Rover Corps. She died during the first bombing raid at Knevçet Shèràa."

"She was your friend?"

"Inasmuch as we could be, considering she was enlisted and I was an officer in the same outfit. We reported to an asshole—that promoted the sense of solidarity."

"Yeah, that'll do it." Roni nodded in the loose-necked way of the terminally punchy, then looked at Jani with bloodshot eyes. "You blame yourself for her death."

Jani started. "No, I don't—"

"Yes, you do. You think you're responsible for everybody. Nema, Tsecha, whatever you call him. Everybody, and everything." She fell silent. Her chin sagged to her chest. Jani had to nudge her awake when they arrived at their stop.

Roni hailed a 'taxi to take her to Exterior; Jani didn't hire one to take her to her building, out of habit. By the time she arrived, she had slipped into the auto-drive of the truly exhausted, barely lifting her feet above the ground, taking care not to stop for fear of never getting started again.

She entered her flat to find it darkened and quiet. As she passed her desk, she spotted a note attached to the back of her workstation so that she could see it on the way in. Angevin's handwriting. *You have some explaining to do.*

Jani crumpled the note and tossed it in the trashzap. Trudged into her bedroom, tossed her duffel bedside, and fell onto her stomach into bed, fully clothed.

She had just drifted off when the sound of footfalls jarred her awake. The heavy breathing unique to a body in discomfort. The sag of the mattress as Lucien got into bed beside her.

Silence. Then the voice that touched her where none ever had. "I've been waiting for you. Steve and Angevin gave up hours ago, but I waited. I was on the couch—I heard you come in. You walked right past me." Silence again, as though he waited for her to speak. "Thinking about Dathim Naré helped keep me awake. I've never seen an Haárin like him before."

Jani recalled his rapt look as he drank in Dathim's every move. "I noticed."

"Jealous?" A short expulsion of breath, as though he laughed. "Why do you think he cut his hair? Do you think the braids got in his way, or what?"

"I don't know. Why don't you ask him?"

"Maybe I will." Silence again, flavored with peevishness. Then Lucien cleared his throat. "Angevin said you went to Sheridan this morning. Make that yesterday morning."

Morning. It seemed like a year ago. "Yes. I needed to talk to Frances." Jani edged her hand in her pocket and felt for the antistat containing the broken marker.

"If I'd known, I'd have asked you to stop by my room and pick up a few things." The mattress flexed as Lucien shifted position. "I keyed it to you. Months ago. You were still on-base at the time. I waited for you to visit, but you never did."

Jani closed her fingers around the hard, sharp plastic of the broken marker half, and massaged the rough edge.

"Your parents are here. I found that out tonight, when I called I-Com to try and track you down." Another sigh. "Everything I know about you, I have to find out from other people."

Jani turned her head. "There wasn't time to tell you."

The dark form beside her reached out and touched her hair. "If you gave a damn about me, you'd make time." The hand moved lower, caressing her cheek. "But you don't, do you?" Lower, moving down her neck. "Where did you take the docs?"

Jani shifted her arm to block Lucien's hand so he couldn't work it lower. She wanted him to, in spite of everything, which was why she made sure to stop him. "I'm tired. We'll talk later."

Lucien pulled his hand away. "There's later, and then there's too late. Did you ever think of that?"

Jani didn't answer. She forced herself to remain awake until she heard Lucien's breathing slow and deepen in sleep. Then she struggled out of bed, her back aching, her knee popping with every step.

Her footsteps barely sounded as she walked across the sitting room, muffled as they were by Angevin's rented rugs. She opened the door to the entryway closet and hunted through the bags and boxes that had been delivered from the stores. She barely glanced at her beautiful sari, digging until she uncovered her Ganesha with its pedestal.

She set up the shrine in the corner of the room nearest her desk. After she set the figurine on its base and placed the brass bowl before it, she knelt, leaning forward and touching her forehead to the floor three times in rapid succession. *Help me, Lord,* she prayed to the embodiment of wisdom before her, to the remover of obstacles. *Help me find the answers I seek, even if they pain me.* She leaned forward again, this time keeping her forehead pressed to the floor.

I told Niall that there's no such thing as coincidence, that it's hardest to see that which is closest to you. Have I failed to heed my own warnings, Lord? Her knee throbbed from the press of her weight. *I have never obeyed my body instead of my brain—is this what I'm doing now?*

She remained on her knees on the hardwood floor and offered her pain as sacrifice, imagining it as gold coins that she tossed into the bowl. Only when her eyes teared and she bit her lip to suppress a cry did she struggle to her feet, store the empty boxes in the closet, and return to bed.

CHAPTER 25

Tsecha sat on the veranda of Dathim Naré's house and watched the lights of a Vynshàrau patrol skimmer flicker off the water. The activity had lessened considerably compared to earlier in the night. Then, the lake skimmers had traversed in pairs and triples, while demis swooped and glided above as seabirds chivying watercraft.

What do you look for, Shai? Tsecha watched the skimmer until it turned along the invisible border dividing idomeni waters from those of the Interior Ministry, then flitted toward the dim horizon. *What is out on the lake that you find so interesting? Do you search for documents, too?* He bared his teeth at the thought, but his humor quickly dissipated. He wished he had brought the timeform from his work table—the mental exercise of converting idomeni time to humanish would have occupied him, prevented his thoughts from wandering as the skimmers did over the water.

Where are you, ní Dathim? He focused his hearing in the still dark, straining for the distant wail of ComPol sirens. He had heard them now and again since the start of his vigil, their cry like the keen of the Rauta Shèràa alarms that had declaimed the arrival of the Laumrau bombs.

Ní Dathim?

Tsecha shifted in his strangely comfortable Haárin chair. Nowhere did the framing stab him. Not once did the angle of the seat threaten to tumble him onto the stones. He looked at the other dwellings—the enclave seemed as deserted in the darkness. No lights showed through windows. No Haárin sat outside and contemplated the water, or walked the stone-paved lane. So different than the born-sect who lived in the embassy, who discussed points of philosophy upon the veranda throughout the night, or sat in the archives and studied . . .

. . . or waited in the Haárin sequestration for their suborn to return. Tsecha fussed with the cuffs of his overrobe, tugging them low over the sleeves of the coldsuit that he wore beneath. Blessedly warm though he felt, he shivered as a breeze wafted off the lake, bringing with it the promise of the hellish winter to come, and the chill of more immediate concerns.

Ní Dathim . . . where are you?

He heard the distant crunch of footsteps upon the lane, and felt the clench in his soul. *I will not call out.* What if it was a guard, who had followed him from the embassy? Or Sànalàn, who seemed to beg his forgiveness each time she saw him, even as she challenged his every thought and action. Or Shai, come in person to demand an explanation for his visits to the sequestration.

This is my place, Shai—am I not Haárin, as declared by Temple and Council? Is not my name of Sìah Haárin? Tsecha. "Fool." Have I not been as outcast since the war? Even more so since you removed me from my station and ordered me to remain on the grounds of this waterbound place?

The footfalls grew nearer. Stopped before the door of the house. Then, slowly, turned and circled toward the veranda.

Tsecha rose to his feet as the footsteps rounded the corner, heart tripping as the figure darkened the veranda entry, then slowing as he recognized the strange, sheared head. "Ní Dathim. You could announce yourself."

"That would sound foolish, nìRau. Why would I announce myself to an empty house?" Dathim picked up a weighty metalframe seat and placed it beside Tsecha's. He sat heavily, in the humanish sprawl that he preferred, and rubbed a hand over his face. His chair matched Tsecha's in the height of its seat, so that he sat at the same level instead of a higher, more respectful one.

But such are Haárin—all the same within themselves. Such chairs as these had not been designed with the idea that Chief Propitiators would sit in them. "So, ní Dathim?" Tsecha sat down as well, then leaned forward so he could see the Haárin's eyes. For such purposes, sitting at the same level proved an advantage. "Where were you so long? Did you have trouble in the city?"

"No, nìRau, I had no trouble. I have been back for some time. I sat in the skimmer and thought . . . about many things." Dathim stared at the ground at his feet. "Humanish are strange."

"I know you think that, ní Dathim. You have said it before."

Tsecha waited for Dathim to say more, but the Haárin's face held the grim cast of one not inclined to speak. He thought to wave his hand in front of him, as he had once seen Lucien do to Jani when he had asked her a question and she did not answer. But before he could make his attempt, Dathim raised his head and looked at him.

"So. I saw her. Your Kilian."

"My Jani! She is unhurt?"

"She limps. She said that she fell during the shooting, and hurt her knee. It is not serious." Dathim looked out over the water. "The lieutenant is with her. Pascal."

"And he is well?"

"He was shot here. A grave wound, he told me, and truly." Dathim placed a hand beneath his soul, near his right hip. "He walks. Slowly, but he walks. He is pale, and tired. But still he watches, as he did here. Nothing escapes him." Dathim shifted in his seat. "He watched me, every move I made."

"My Lucien watches, Dathim, as you said. Such is his way."

"Kilian said it was because he had never before seen an Haárin with short hair." Dathim sat forward and let his hands dangle between his knees. "You would say Pascal is her suborn?"

Tsecha gestured in strong affirmation. "Yes, ní Dathim, I would, and truly. In the way that humanish can be true dominant and suborn, they are. My Lucien provides my Jani protection. She provides him status. It is a most reasonable arrangement, as far as I can see."

"Then she must know him well, and I must defer to that knowledge." Dathim turned his attention to his hands, and picked at his nails. "I gave the documents to her."

"Did she seem as angry?"

"I could not tell, nìRau. She is most as a wall. Even now."

"*Now,* ní Dathim?"

"Now that she is as Haárin." Dathim turned his head—the incident light reflected off his broad, bare brow. "She is as Haárin, nìRau, and truly. She does not move as humanish. Her gestures are too smooth. Her hands and wrists—too long and thin. She walks as idomeni, as well. Even though she limps, her stride is long and smooth." He looked back at his hands. "I saw one of her true eyes."

Tsecha felt the shocks of the past days redoubled. "How did you do such?"

Dathim gestured in the humanish manner, as though such startling details held little import. "It is not yet as mine. The center is still too small, the sclera too pale." He gestured in disappointment. "And they are *green*, like Oà. Why did her doctors make them green, instead of gold as Vynshàrau?"

"That was their color before, Dathim." Tsecha tried to imagine Jani's eyes, tried to extrapolate the hints and shadings he had seen revealed in the bright sunlight days earlier. "John Shroud had tried to leave her a little of what she was before. He thought it important."

"Hmph." Dathim did not sound impressed by that which John Shroud thought important. He turned back to the water, his great head stilling like an animal's on alert as the patrol skimmer made another traverse. "She denies she is your heir."

Tsecha gestured reluctant acceptance. "Humanish deny, ní Dathim, until that which they deny buries them. Such is their way, and truly."

"She does not want to be as Haárin. She is ashamed." Dathim's tense posture eased as the patrol skimmer darted away from them. "Her eyefilm broke. When it broke, she sought to hide her eye with her hand. When I forced her to show it to me, she grew so angry. She would have struck me, nìRau, but she restrained herself. Even though she is smaller than me, she would have injured me, and truly."

Tsecha slipped into Low Vynshàrau to convey the bluntness of his feeling. "My nìa does not like to be coerced, ní Dathim."

Dathim sat back with such force that his chair legs scraped along the stone. "And as we shelter your *nìa* who does not like to be coerced, who speaks to the Elyan Haárin and their broken contracts?" He spoke in English, blunter and more forceful still, a barrage of hard and sharp sounds that hammered the ears as bombs. "Who promotes the final order you so desire, nìRau? The harmony of Shiou that follows the upheaval of Caith? Is it nìaRauta Shai, who speaks for the Oligarch without thought as to what the words mean? Who wishes us back to the worldskein, to serve only our dominants as we did before the war? Is it the humanish ministers, who think only of the money they lose if they allow Haárin to live among them? Who speaks? You cannot—you have been silenced. I cannot—I am as nothing. But your nìaRauta Haárin knows Haárin and humanish, life as it is and as it must become. But where is she now, as the Haárin converge upon this cold city and Shai prepares to hammer them with Cèel's words? In her rooms, asleep, with her strange lieutenant who watches and the humanish tricks that cover that which she is!" Dathim fell silent, his breathing labored as though he ran a great distance.

As Dathim's words echoed in his mind, Tsecha again felt the wind brush in from off the water. This breeze, however, he did not find as chilling, but as a warm gust that riffled the flowing sleeves of his overrobe, pushing them up his arms.

He brushed down the soft material, then fingered the red banding that edged the sleeves. So long had he served as ambassador, as teacher, as irritant to his enemies, that he at times forgot his place as priest. But he still understood signs, the hints of order and disorder by which the gods informed him of their will. Thus did he know that he felt Caith in the strange warm wind, as he had felt her many times over the past days. Her ever-present whispers, in the hallways of the embassy, in the wind itself, unveiled his old disorder and reminded him of that which he once had been. Warrior. Killer. Walker in the Night. "My Jani. You would have her here to meet the Haárin, ní Dathim?"

Dathim gave a humanish nod. "If she came here, the born-sects would not dare to keep her out. Shai would admit to your power if she did so, a power she claims you no longer possess."

"The humanish Ministers would fight her presence. Anais Ulanova would lead them."

"The humanish Ministers, I have learned, have to answer to their *reporters,* who batter them as ax-hammers and carry news of their actions to all. These reporters would ask them why they do not permit your Jani to see the Elyan Haárin, and how would Anais answer? Would she speak the truth, that the Haárin are better at humanish business than humanish, and she must therefore work to keep them away from her poor merchants because they cannot compete? Away from the many other humanish who would buy from Haárin if they could?"

"No, ní Dathim—my Anais is more intelligent than that." Tsecha stood just as another gust of rebellious wind whipped at his sleeves. He walked to the veranda entry, clasping his hands behind his back as he did so to keep his cuffs fixed in place, and hidden from Caith's laughter. "She would say my nìa is unfit because of the crimes she has committed. She will talk of Knevçet Shèràa, and the death of Rikart Neumann. She will make my nìa appear most unseemly, and truly."

Dathim rose and stepped to Tsecha's side. He made no attempt to edge even a small step to the front of his propitiator, as would have been seemly. "Then let your Jani answer. She has met challenge before, nìRau—she wears the scars. She knows how to fight, and will continue to fight even as she bleeds." He held out his own arms and rolled back the sleeves, first one, then the other. Even in the darkness his scars showed, the ragged fissuring dark as ebon ink. "If I brought her here, she would see how it is for us, and she would fight for us. You say she fights for her own, nìRau. Who are more her own than we?"

Tsecha stepped off of the veranda and onto the lane. Past the dark, silent houses, then over the short stretch of dune toward the beach. He struggled to maintain his footing as his boot soles slid on the loose sand.

"You forced her yourself, nìRau." Dathim's voice sounded from behind, like the call of a tracking beast. "In the summer, you forced her to accept her first challenge, to fight nìaRauta Hantìa in her first *à lérine*. You did not think it such a bad thing then, when you used her *against* Cèel. But now I say we should use her *for* Haárin, and you hesitate. Why, nìRau? Is the chance to anger Cèel not great enough? Is the shock to the humanish when they see your Jani as she really is not great enough? Or are the Haárin not important enough?"

Tsecha wheeled, the sand dragging at his feet like undercurrent. "I warn you, Dathim! You vex—!" His words stopped as he watched Dathim mount the dune and stand astride it as a humanish statue—

—and as another Haárin mounted the dune and took her place beside him—

—and as the other Haárin scaled the short summit and took their places on either side, until the entire ridge filled. Shoulder to shoulder they stood, thirty or more, in their trousers and shirts and boots. Their overrobes, they had left behind. Their looping braids and nape knots, the males had sheared as Dathim had, while the females had undone theirs, or bound them in long tails in the manner of humanish females.

"Are we not important enough, nìRau!" Dathim stood with his arms hanging low, his hands curled in front of him, palms facing up. Not a gesture of idomeni, but of humanish question. "We who go out into this damned cold city so you can be as you are!"

Tsecha took a step back. Another. The Haárin made no move toward him, yet still he felt them push him back. "The battles will be fought in the embassy, ní Dathim! Against those who refuse to accept the truth as I know it will be!" Behind him, he heard the rumble of the lake, the dash of the low waves. The Haárin beach was not smooth sand as was the embassy's, but rock-strewn and rutted. He felt the water-slick rocks beneath his boots, and battled for balance on the uneven ground.

"Your truth, born-sect! The truth as you see it!" Dathim advanced a single stride down the dune, arms held out to his sides for balance. "But we have our truth, as well. Our truth is that we want to live here, in this damned cold place. As the Elyan Haárin do on Elyas. As the NorthPort Haárin do on Whalen's Planet. And the Phillipan, and the Serran. This is our colony, *here*! We will choose an enclave, *here*!"

"The humanish will not let you. Not *here*!" Tsecha tried to take an advancing step, but the strange warm wind swirled from his back to his front, stopping him in his tracks. He felt it rush up his sleeves, and damned Caith for her disorder. "They are not as us. They cannot leave alone. They will not allow you to live as you wish—you scare them!"

"Then they will scare. And your Jani will show them how not to fear."

"But they will fear her most of all!" Tsecha raised his arms above his head—a pleading stance. "It must be done my way, Dathim. First the embassy, and the meeting rooms. First, the Ministers, and the generals. *Then* the city. The city cannot come before. Humanish will not understand!"

Dathim had grown still upon the slope. He maintained his balance without laboring, as though he had always stood in such a way and could do so forever. The Haárin on either side of him remained in their places, silent, watching as he spoke their words, said that which they wished to be said.

"We are here," Dathim said from his slope. "We will stay. I have asked your Jani to help us in this, and I will ask again. It is your decision, nìRau, if you join us or not. You of the Haárin name and the priestly life. Your decision." He backed up the incline and disappeared over the other side. The other Haárin followed him, in ones and twos, until the ridge showed clear.

Tsecha listened to the rustle of the grasses, the rumble of the lake. He pulled down one skewed sleeve, then let his hand drop away, and heard Caith's laughter in the wind.

CHAPTER 26

Tsecha walked back to the embassy the same way he had come. Through the trees, across the lawns, toward the veranda.

He entered the sheltered haven with the timorous step of someone who now felt unsure whether he belonged, and looked around. Since her challenge, Sànalàn had taken to spending great stretches of the day and night in meditation, or in conversation with nìaRauta Inèa. Her accidental meetings with him had been frequent; Tsecha did not esteem these encounters, but now he anticipated them even less. With Caith's presence infused in the very air, who knew what disorder could ensue?

But the air felt cooler on the veranda than it had outside. He hoped it meant that Caith had been warned off, that Shiou and the other six gods had forced her back to her domain, a distant land of storm and upheaval. *Much as this place.* Tsecha turned, and looked out the entry toward the lake. *Storm and upheaval and shifting rocks beneath my feet.*

Tsecha looked around the veranda's main enclosure, and found it emptier than usual. He chose to take that as a favorable sign as well, and tucked into a darkened corner furnished with a pillow-seat and a low reading table. From there, he could observe the rest of the area as well as the entry from the embassy. If Shai or Sànalàn appeared, he could contract into his space like a cava into its shell and remain unobserved.

He lowered carefully. His hip no longer complained, but he must have twisted his right knee during his flight down the beach away from Dathim. The joint ached when he walked, and burned when he bent it. He took some time finding a comfortable position, and finally sat with his leg straightened before him. The mind-focusing ability of pain held no power for him now. He felt old and tired and discomfited, out of place in this most odd city that he had come to think of as his own.

You would live in Chicago, Dathim? Somewhere out in the storm and upheaval, amid the sirens and the shootings and Caith's strange winds. *The humanish are different here—this is their homeworld.* Tsecha rested his head against the stone wall that enclosed him, damning himself for his caution but unable to quell his apprehension. He who had gone out into the city so many times, in disguise and as himself, felt the raw stab of fear at the thought of Dathim Naré doing the same.

Dathim does not hide. The tilemaster displayed his work freely, and went about his business as though he lived in a worldskein colony. *He showed his cava shell tilework to Anais Ulanova, then walked into her office and stole documents.* Then he took them into the city as though such was something he did each day. Granted, his visit to Jani's home had upset him, but his was not the discomfort of an idomeni exposed to the ungodliness of a humanish house. He did not ask for absolution, or worry after his soul. *He wanted to convince her, persuade her.* Or, most likely, *order* her to assist him in his plans for the enclave. *And my Jani does not take orders.* Both idomeni and humanish had been forced to that conclusion long ago.

Tsecha felt his eyes grow heavy. It had become most late, and now that Dathim had returned safely from the city, he felt tired. He lay back in a half-recline, his head abutting cold stone, his sore leg braced against the hard edge of the table, suffering just enough discomfort to keep awake. *Dathim's chairs felt most comfortable.* Short hair, easeful furniture, no fear of humanish rooms—how readily Dathim Naré had adjusted to change. *More quickly even than I.* Tsecha felt a twinge in his soul, as though the pain in his knee had altered in location. *More quickly . . .*

He longed for the seclusion of his rooms, the quiet, the warmth that emerged from the output of a facilities array, not the laughing breath of a mocking goddess.

I am Haárin.

But who considered him such? Cèel and Shai, most certainly. They felt him most disordered, a traitor to his skein and sect. The only thing that saved him from the full vent of their wrath was the security of his station. He was their Chief Propitiator. In secular matters, he owed them obedience. In religious matters, which held greater import for any born-sect, they owed him their souls.

I am Haárin . . . by name.

He had earned the name Égri nìRau Tsecha, and truly. Over twenty-five humanish years ago, he had fought in Council and in Temple to allow humanish to form an enclave outside Rauta Shèràa. Then, he fought even more to allow them to study at the Academy. He had engaged and attacked both with words and with blades. There had been days when his enemies stood in line to declare themselves, when he fought *à lérine* with a weapon still bloody from the previous bout, when he could barely raise his arms for the number and pain of his wounds.

The hum of conversation snapped Tsecha out of his grim remembrance. He tensed as he waited for the speakers to walk into view, relaxing when he saw them to be Communications dominants whom he did not know well. He watched them disappear into another of the enclosures, gesturing in animated discussion. Then he tugged in irritation at the tight sleeves of the coldsuit. He felt hot here in the enclosure. Constricted. He had donned the suit in anticipation of the chill of the Haárin enclave—he did not need such protection in the shelter of the embassy.

Shelter . . .

Dathim believes me sheltered. Unaware of the desires of Haárin. *But I know them now.* As his Jani must, as well. Such would explain her stubborn denials of her hybridization, and her anger as she did so. She did not like to be tricked, and Dathim Naré the Tilemaster had tricked them all. He had not journeyed into the godless humanish city to deliver stolen papers into the safety of one who could dispose of them. He had done so to confront his leader, to tell her the time had come for her to lead them to their place in this damned cold city.

But she had denied him.

And now he met with his enclave, in a crowded room in one of the tiny houses beyond the trees, to discuss what to do next.

Tsecha imagined the Suborn Oligarch standing before him now, glaring down at him from her imposing height, shoulders rounded and hands twitching in displeasure. He imagined telling her words that she had no desire to hear.

The embassy Haárin no longer wish to serve us, Shai. Their wish now is to serve themselves. The machinations of the meeting room meant nothing to them anymore, now that they knew the freedom of the humanish colonial enclave. The complexities and formalities of born-sect challenge, upon which their futures once depended, now angered rather than distressed them. *They no longer care what we do, Shai. We bother them. We interfere with them.* Even he, who chose the name Égri nìRau Tsecha to symbolize his expulsion from Vynshàrau, mean nothing to Dathim and the others who populated the embassy sequestration. *They needed me to bring them Jani, and I could not do so. To them, I am worthless, Haárin by name and name only.*

"Name only." Tsecha spoke aloud in French, so that any who overheard him would not understand. *"I, who shed the blood of my enemies on the Temple floor."* He tried to move his right leg to a more easeful position, but his knee griped and the top of his head ached from pressing against the stone. *I, Avrèl nìRau Nema, have become as nothing.* Passed over by those he had once led. Cast aside by those who had once served him. Denied participation in reaching the goal toward which he had strove for half his life.

Do you think to deny me, Dathim? Is this what you wish, and truly?

He stared out at the empty veranda, filled only by the occasional murmur of voices or passing footfall.

As my Hansen used to say, "Think again."

He rose slowly. He walked until the needling in his right leg forced him to stop, then leaned against a pillar until the pain and numbness left him. Then he stepped off the veranda and headed for the trees, his stride growing longer and surer with every slow, strong beat of his heart.

Tsecha pressed the entry buzzer of the first house on the stone-paved path. The second. The third. He did so for a sense of completeness, of orderly progression, and to allow himself time to prepare. He also did it as a warning—the alarms echoed within the empty houses, sounding through the walls and along the deserted lane. A barely detectable alert, like the distant wail of the ComPol sirens.

When he finally reached Dathim Naré's house, he stood in front of the door for some time before daring to touch the entry pad. He sensed an ending here, as well as a beginning. As his walk down the lane had consisted of the conclusion of one step and the initiation of the following, so did his action here presage the end of one stage in his life and the start of the next. Not as one to be left behind, no, nor as one to be shunted aside. Such a fate was not meant for him, this he knew, and truly. Chief Propitiator of the Vynshàrau he was and would be until his death. Haárin he had been made, and would be until his death, as well.

Intercessor between his Jani and her people, he would become, even if the steps he took this night hastened that death.

He offered a whispered prayer as homage to Caith, then touched the pad. This buzzer seemed to sound more loudly than had the others. But then, such was to be expected. He heard no footsteps or voices just prior to the door opening, which meant someone had stood there and waited for him to request entry. Again, to be expected.

That the someone turned out to be Dathim Naré was the most expected thing of all.

"Ní Tsecha Égri." Dathim offered his odd humanish smile and stood aside to allow Tsecha entry.

Tsecha stepped inside, making sure to touch Caith's reliquary along the way. Behind him, he heard a harsh expulsion of breath, but whether that breath resulted from Dathim's surprise or his laughter, he did not bother to confirm.

Dathim's followers sat crowded in the center of the main room floor; they had arranged themselves in a tight circle as though to shelter themselves from nonexistent wind and cold. Not all the Haárin who had stood atop the ridge had gathered here. Tsecha recognized the female who had taken the place beside Dathim on the ridge, and several of the others who had stood closest to him. Eleven, he counted—the most wary, the most humanish-appearing, and thus the most outcast of all.

Dathim stepped around in front of him, gesturing to the others as he did so. "We have been waiting for you, ní Tsecha." He smiled again, as though saying the true Haárin version of Tsecha's name gave him pleasure.

"We have, and truly," Dathim's female said. She wore her brown hair unbraided and gathered in a loose stream that hung halfway down her back. From such, she gave no sign whether she was bred or unbred, whether any of the youngish who had stood watching Tsecha during his daylight visit had been birthed by her or not. "I am Beyva Kelohim, ní Tsecha. I speak for those who have awaited you but cannot be here to witness your arrival—glories of the day to come."

"Glories of the day to come," intoned the rest of the Haárin in one voice, a voice that held a wide range of accents, from crisp and clear to rolling and smooth.

"Glor-ries of the day to come." Dathim ended the round of greetings, his voice like the cold stone against which Tsecha had rested his head. He then joined his followers in the circle; Beyva edged aside, leaving a space for him beside her on the floor.

"How will we know if ná Kièrshia has succeeded in returning the documents, ní Tsecha?" Her voice sounded as Jani's, low for a female, and quiet.

And for my Jani, I know the voice means as opposite of that which she is. Tsecha drew close to the circle, and regarded Beyva most openly. She did the same, looking him in the face with no evidence of hesitation. She possessed the gold eyes of Vynshàrau; her particular variation darkened by brown flecks. Like Dathim, she wore trousers and a shirt of Pathen coloring. Bright orange topped with sea blue, a most startling combination, and truly.

"I have heard nothing. At times such as this, to hear nothing from humanish is a good thing." As Tsecha stepped up to the circle, two of the Haárin slid apart to make room for him. He lowered gently to the floor, his knee complaining with every incremental movement. "If Anais Ulanova had complained to us concerning these documents, I would have heard news of such from Suborn Oligarch Shai. The importance of the documents was such that she would most certainly have contacted us. Since she has not, I must assume that my Kièrshia has indeed managed to return them." He looked at the faces surrounding him—even Dathim regarded him with an air of solemn acceptance. All understood him to be the absolute authority in any matter regarding his Toxin. If he said something was so, than it was so. Knowing his Jani as he did, this unquestioning faith caused a clench in Tsecha's soul. Not that she would ever disgrace or betray him—of that he felt most sure. *But they expect that I know her mind. What she will do and when she will do it.* They expected him to know that which no *humanish* had ever divined. That terrified him.

"Ní Tsecha?"

Tsecha looked up to find Dathim's smile had returned.

"Should we remain here on the embassy grounds, or choose an enclave outside this city?" Dathim gestured toward the bare tile in the center of the circle, as though it contained a two-dimensional map or a three-dimensional relief. "Up to the north, in one of the lakeside preserves? Or out to the west, in the midst of Chicago's garden domes and kettle factories?" He watched the reactions of his followers. "In the midst of humanish food."

"Even the humanish would not subject us to such. Of this, I feel most sure." An Haárin who Tsecha recognized as one of the garden workers spoke with hesitance, his English an odd swirl. "They would send us further north, in the hope that the cold would freeze us into leaving."

"And they would not put us amid their food for fear of sabotage," Tsecha added. "Remember how they think. You cannot hope to live among them if you do not know how they think." He pointed to a nonexistent place on the imaginary map. "As I said before, this is the capital, home to the Earthbound humanish. The colony humanish tolerate us because we provide them with supplies that they cannot obtain from their own merchants, but in this city, all can get what they wish. They do not need us here, and humanish dispose of that which they do not need."

"You try to scare us, Tsecha?" Dathim's voice sounded again as the stone.

"I speak only truth, Dathim. Because you do not agree with it, you will not hear it. Allow me to honor you—you have become most as humanish already." Tsecha waved a dismissive hand as the Haárin's shoulders rounded. "And this will proceed how? Will you visit Shai in her rooms and demand the right to petition the humanish for permission to live here? Can you imagine what her reply will be, she who would send you back into the worldskein with the next sunrise? Or perhaps you will go to the humanish directly? I can tell you what they will answer, Dathim, and you will not like that, as well. Your shoulders will round and you will argue and dispute, but they will not hear you anymore. They will know what you wish, and they will refuse it. To confront directly as with idomeni is not the way to deal with humanish!" Tsecha waited for the sound of his words to die in his ears before flexing his back, first one way, then the other. Even the painful support of one of Shai's chairs would have been preferable to this free-sitting agony. But even with that being the case, he knew that he dared not leave. Intercession had become his duty, as it had with his late Hansen. *My Hansen, who died in the explosion of an Haárin bomb.* Tsecha imagined the smoke and rubble of the long-forgotten scene, and felt the frigid air once more through his coldsuit.

"Then what do we do, ní Tsecha?" Beyva tilted her head and lifted a cupped hand in a most Vynshàrau display of question.

"If I could speak with my Kièrshia, we could together determine something. If I could speak—"

Dathim again expelled breath. "If? Is not the question when? Where? How? You are bound to this land, Tsecha. You are under arrest."

Tsecha gestured agreement with a truncated Low Vynshàrau hand flick. "But you leave this land quite easily, Dathim. Any time you wish, so it appears, and truly." He stared at the blank center of their circle, and considered his next words. So easily had they formed in his mind that he knew they had been put there by a god. Whether that god be Shiou or Caith did not matter. He felt their divinity. Therefore, he was fated to speak them, and take the consequences as they came. "You will take me to her."

Dathim stared him in the face as the rest of the Haárin grew most still. "You are bound to this land, Tsecha, by Shai's decree."

"Yes." Tsecha again gestured strong affirmation, adding a humanish head nod for emphasis. "I am ambassador to this damned cold city. I am charged with representing my people to the humanish. Tell me, ní Dathim, if I am not to act as ambassador at this time, when am I? If not to prevent you from enraging the humanish so that they expel us all, when should I?"

"If not to prevent them from killing us all." The garden Haárin spoke once more, his voice as dead. "If not to prevent another Knevçet Shèràa."

Tsecha flicked his left hand in strongest disagreement. "Only my Kièrshia could enact another Knevçet Shèràa, and she would not do so in this case. She might yell, and question most loudly, but that is not the same as killing us all, and you are most stupid to say so!" He slumped with fatigue as his aged back surrendered its efforts to maintain its straightness. "If we persuade her of the worth of our argument, she will help us. She helps when she can. Such is her way, just as it is Shai's to press the old customs upon us all and Dathim's to trick and enrage." His knee ached again. He shivered, and longed for the soft and warmth of his bed.

Dathim smiled once more. "You are so sure of her, ní Tsecha. You are so sure of us all. I must indeed take you to this meeting." He looked to the timeform that sat within a niche on the other side of the room. "It is too late to go now—the darkness will soon be gone, and we still need darkness to travel in this city. But this next night we will go, and I will learn much of the ways of humanish from your discussions."

Beyva gestured in strong affirmation. "I will go, as well, to witness this discussion."

"And I will go," said the gardener. "I have never seen ná Kièrshia."

"And I will go—"

"And I—"

"I, as well."

"We will all go, and truly."

Tsecha looked at the faces around him. Some appeared cool and questioning as Dathim's. Others, as Beyva's, held youngish enthusiasm. None held confusion. Such had been left for him, so it seemed, to hold in his soul. *I will disobey Shai.* Such, she would not forgive. *Perhaps she will challenge me.* After fighting her, he would be most as outcast, and truly. He worked his hand beneath the short braids that fringed his forehead, and massaged the tightening bands that encircled his skull.

"If you go out in this city looking as you do, Tsecha, all who see you will know you as idomeni."

Tsecha looked up to see Dathim brush his hand over his own sheared head. "I have gone out into this city before, Dathim. My hair fits under a tight wig most well."

"A wig is trickery, is it not, Tsecha? But I am the trickster, and I see no need for such." Dathim lowered his chin in challenge. "You are our ambassador to humanish ways. So you said. So you said." He rose to his feet and walked across the room, disappearing through the front entry and into the night. One by one, the others followed him, the gardener and the rest, until Tsecha sat alone with Beyva.

He watched the door close. "Ní Dathim is most vexing." Once more, he pushed his forehead fringe aside to rub his scalp.

"Such is his way." Beyva lifted her right hand, open palm facing down. A gesture of acceptance. "He wishes to live as he will, where he will. Such is what we all wish."

Tsecha nodded in such a humanish manner that even he did not understand what he meant. He tugged at one of his braids, felt something give, then pulled back his hand to look at the short length of unfurled silver cord that he held between his fingers.

"You must retie it before you leave, ní Tsecha." Beyva rose. "The loose hair hangs before your eyes."

"Yes." Tsecha rolled the lock between his thumb and forefinger, then released it and instead tied the hair cord into a knot. He heard Beyva's footsteps, but did not look up to see where she walked or what she did. When he heard her approach from behind, he did not turn back to look at her.

He flinched when he felt her hands work through his braids. Then he felt the steady pull as she gathered the twirled lengths of hair in one hand, followed by the gradual loosening as she applied the cutter to the root of each one in turn and snipped it through.

"You will have to wear a covering out of doors, ní Tsecha," Beyva said as she cut. "You are not used to the cold."

Tsecha listened to the soft grassy sighs as his hair fell to the tile. Felt the slackening over his scalp as Beyva hacked away the tight braiding, and the pain in his head ease. It took so little time, to turn away from that which he had been. It took such simple acts, to become as outcast.

He sensed Beyva step back from him, and knew that she had finished. He rose, his knee cracking as it unbent. She held out the cloth to protect his head; he gave his answer by walking out the door and into the chill night, uncovered.

None saw him as he crossed through the trees, the lawns, the veranda. He entered the embassy and walked to the residence wing, up and down the halls to his rooms, seeing no one until the last corner when he turned and found himself face-to-face with Shai.

"Tsecha." The Suborn Oligarch stared at the top of his head, then turned from him, her shoulders hunched and rounding.

Tsecha said nothing in reply; Shai said no more. Humanish often said that there were times when no words were necessary. This was one of those times.

CHAPTER 27

She stood in a hallway, or an alley. Dim light seemed to come not from a single point but from all about her, as though the surfaces themselves served as the source of illumination. But even though she could see, she couldn't tell exactly where she was. The light wasn't bright enough to define any doors or openings that could identify the space. She could only sense that she stood in a walled place, long and narrow.

Her breathing came quick and hard. She could feel her heart pound, the pulse in her throat. Her right knee ached. She knew she had been running, but she couldn't remember why.

She touched the nearest wall. Green, it seemed to be—she couldn't see the color, but green made sense for some reason. The wall felt smooth as glass. Cold. The surface possessed a strange translucence, like a leaf coated with ice.

"Jani!"

She wheeled toward the shout. She recognized the voice, knew the name it called was hers. Strange name. She hadn't used it in a long time.

"Where the hell are you!"

A man's voice. Young. Angry.

I'm running from him. She remembered now.

"They're waiting for us at Gaetan's." Lucien appeared in the distance. He wore drop-dead whites, the formal Service uniform; he looked like the officer in his painting. "Your parents are there. They're worried about you. Your mother asked me why you ran away. I told her they needed you at the embassy—I didn't know what the hell else to say."

Jani remained silent, watching him. He looked far away, but she knew that was illusion. He had always been closer than she thought.

"Jani?" Lucien stepped down the narrow space toward her. What little light there was reflected off the white cloth, the badges and the gold braid on his shoulders. His silver-blond hair. How he glowed, like a platinum column. "They're waiting. Niall. Nema. John. Everyone." He removed his brimmed lid, the same gold-trimmed white as his uniform, and tucked it under his arm. "We can take the long way back, if that would make you feel better." He smiled as he held his hand out to her. His face seemed as translucent as the walls, as though it possessed layers, as well. "Let's go."

She backed away. One step. Another. Then turned and ran—

"Jani!"

—and collided with Sasha. Blood streamed down the side of his face. Jani reached out to touch the blood—just as she did, the light exploded through the coated walls. The force of the blast drove shards of ice into her body. She collapsed, heard Lucien close in from behind as her blood poured from gaping wounds and spread across the floor—

"Jani! Damn it, come on!"

She felt a hand close over her sore left shoulder, and struck out with all her remaining strength—

"Shit!"

The voice jarred Jani awake. Her heart stumbled and her chest tightened as she pushed herself into a sitting position, her hands scrabbling for purchase on the soft pillows. She comprehended the familiar around her—the armoire, the dresser, the windows, and walls.

"Jesus, gel! Steady on." Steve backed away from the bed, his arm crossed over his stomach. "Tryin' ta knock the wind outta me, or what?"

"I told you to just keep calling from a safe distance until she opened her eyes." Angevin stood at the foot of the bed, arms folded. "The last time I tried to wake her up by shaking her, she almost broke my wrist."

"No I dint—" Jani coughed the dryness from her throat. Then she licked her teeth, which felt unpleasantly coated. She looked down at herself. She recalled falling into bed fully clothed; sometime during the night, someone had removed her trouser suit and replaced it with a T-shirt and shorts. She hoped it was Angevin, but given the young woman's reluctance to approach her as she slept . . .

"We just wanted to see if you planned to wake up before the end of the year." Angevin remained by the footboard. "You've been sleeping for almost fifteen hours. Even Lucien's starting to worry."

"How is he?" Jani looked toward the door to make sure that *he* wasn't standing there, listening.

"He's fine." Steve's lips barely moved, as though two words concerning Lucien took more effort than he wanted to expend.

"You've had calls." Angevin frowned. "We wouldn't bother you otherwise."

Jani dropped her legs over the side, and let the momentum pull her to her feet. "What calls?"

"—and something stinks!" Derringer's reddened face filled the comport display. "Nobody questions this letter for weeks. Then you get involved and two days later, every dexxie in the city is backpedaling!" His eyes looked dull despite his anger, the skin beneath smudged with fatigue. Jani could imagine the late night meetings with Callum Burkett that led to his current exhausted state.

"I don't know what you did, you meddling pain in the ass bitch." Derringer paused to yawn, striking his desktop with his fist as it went on and on. "But I will find out and when I do, you can kiss any reversal of your bioemotional restriction good-bye."

Jani watched his face still, then shard like the ice walls in her nightmare. "What was the time stamp on this?"

"Oh-five twelve this morning. Judging from the look of him, he'd had a long day and a damned short night." Steve tipped back in his chair, his feet braced against the edge of Jani's desk. "I don't believe he let himself be recorded making a threat."

"He's panicked. He sees his quest for a star going down in flames, and every time he makes a move to cover himself, there's Callum Burkett asking him for a full and complete report." Jani stifled her own yawn. She still felt tired, even after her more than full night's sleep. "I'm not too worried. I think that by this point, he's screwed himself enough that Cal might be willing to listen to my side of the story."

Steve nodded, his fingers drumming a beat on his knees. "Not going to tell us what letter he's talking about, are you?"

"It's better if you don't know."

"You know, working with you is like punching through a GateWay without knowing if you'll make it out the other side. You just says yer prayers and takes yer chances."

"Sorry," Jani said, without feeling very sorry at all. The less you said, the less you needed to lie. The less you lied, the less you needed to remember.

"Well," Steve finally said, when it became obvious Jani wasn't going to say any more. "Then there's this cryptic masterpiece." He leaned forward and hit the comport pad.

Roni McGaw looked as though she'd gotten even less sleep than Derringer. "I left my stuff in your skimmer. Eight files, next to a big, empty box." The hollow-eyed face stilled, then fragmented.

"See what I mean?" Steve turned to Jani before Roni's image had dissolved completely. "You don't have a skimmer."

Jani suppressed a sigh as she watched the display dim. What had Roni found out? Had she been able to check Ulanova's calendar in Exterior systems? Had Security taken the next step and shut down the ministry entirely?

Steve crumpled a piece of notepaper and tossed it at the display. "She didn't even tell you what time she were bloody stopping by."

Yes, she did—oh-eight tonight. But she wanted to meet Jani in the garage instead of their favorite bookstore.

"Roni's good. She's been Exterior Doc Chief for three years." Angevin had dragged one of the dining room chairs beside the desk, and sat heavily. "At least she lends an air of legitimacy to all this muck."

"And what is *that* supposed to mean?" Jani started to rise, but Steve's hand on her arm compelled her to stay seated.

"There's one more." He picked up his nicstick case from its resting place atop a stack of files, and shook out a gold-and-white striped cylinder. "This was the kicker. Took us both aback, me and Ange." He hit the pad and sat back, smoking 'stick fixed between his teeth.

Jani groaned as this face formed.

"Janila?" Her mother looked back and forth, then up and down, as if she could look into Jani's flat if she tried hard enough. "Are you all right? Dr. Parini says that you are, but he has not seen you, so how would he know?" She leaned forward and dropped her voice. "He said I should not call you, but why not? His comport is secure, is it not? And yours, surely—" Her eyes widened as something off-screen captured her attention.

"Mère Kilian? Who are you talking to?" John's bass resounded in sharp question. "Val asked you not to contact anyone."

"I am just playing, Dr. Shroud. I am bored and I am playing." Jamira's hands moved toward the disconnect, but not quickly enough. A white hand shot in from the side and caught her wrist. A white face followed.

"*Damn.*" John's cheeks pinked as he comprehended the code on Val's display. He wore a jacket in Neoclona lilac, and had filmed his eyes the same startling shade. The purple accents heightened his flush so that he looked enraged. "You shouldn't have done this, Mère Kilian."

"No! No! Do not touch me, you—!" Jamira pulled back from John, but not in time—he caught her two thin wrists in one hand with a grip Jani prayed was more gentle then it looked. "Let me go!" Jamira tried to twist away, but John held on to her with brutal ease as he reached for the comport pad. "Janila, I am so sorry! I love you! Please come—"

Jani watched as the scene of her mother struggling in John's grasp faded. She hit the comport pad's reply button to try to reconnect to Val's flat, and felt only a little reassured to find the code had been blocked to all calls. Then she sat forward and buried her head in her hands.

"Jan?" Steve spoke. "Is that yer mum?"

Jani nodded. "My father's with her. They're"—she couldn't force herself to say the words—"at Val's flat," even though it didn't matter, even though every security force in the city knew where her parents were by now. "They're in a safe place." What had been a safe place. She wondered if John felt spooked enough to move them to one of the numerous Neoclona buildings located throughout the city. "Someone tried to set them up to be kidnapped, but we found out in time."

"You're sure about that?"

Jani's head shot up. Beside her, Steve muttered a not-so-soft "Shit."

Lucien sat on the edge of the couch back. He had exchanged his pajamas and robe for winter base casuals. Thanks to a combination of augmentation and a twenty-six-year-old body, he had lost the haze of pain and weakness; he looked merely tired now, rather than debilitated. "Neoclona's security force has always been overrated, in my opinion."

"Has it?" Jani rose, waving off Angevin's murmur of concern. "I disagree. Considering some of the things that had to be done, we didn't need an Office of Professional Standards getting in the way."

"Any security officer who answers to an OPS would have made sure the comports were blocked for outgoing. Failing that, they sure as hell would have canceled the transmission of that call." Lucien stood. "That's the problem when you use an actual home for a safe house—the people who live there tend to still treat it like a home." He waited for her to circle the desk, then walked to her. His step was still slow, but steady, unhampered by his injury. "I would have thought your good friend Niall would be involved in this, but no Service safe house that I know of lets their guests call out. Where are they, with John or Val?"

Jani brushed past him, her pace quickening as she neared her room. In the opening to the hallway, however, she stopped and turned back. Steve and Angevin regarded her as she expected them to, with a mixture of anger and hurt. She'd seen the look before, had accepted it as an inevitable and necessary part of her life. She would have worried if the faces around her looked too happy all the time. "I consider you my friends." She took care not to look at Lucien as she spoke. "But I've known people to die because they told their friends too much. I've known the friends to die, as well. The people Steve talked about at dinner, the ones who kill over a crateful of chips, those are the people we're dealing with here."

"We understand that," Angevin piped. "But—"

"But what?" Jani took a step back into the room. "But you wouldn't have said anything? But you'd have promised not to talk? How long would that promise last if someone held a shooter to your head? To Steve's head? How long would it last against an injector full of Sera? That was *my* mother's face on the display, not yours. If anything happened, you'd lose a few nights' sleep. But you'd get over it, because you'd have saved what meant most to you. Well, looking after what means most to me is how I've lived for the last twenty years, and I'm too goddamned old to change. You're both sweet kids, but if absolute push came to bottom line shove and you had to choose between each other and my mother, who would you pick?" She turned and headed for her room before they felt compelled to answer. Some things could never be spoken of between people who called themselves friends, or they wouldn't remain friends for long.

The memory of her mother struggling in John's grasp replayed in Jani's mind, and she struck the doorway with the flat of her hand on the way through. She already had her T-shirt up over her head when she heard the door open again. She pulled it off anyway, because she had slept the day away and had only a few hours before her meeting with Roni. Because she needed to shake off the last of her languor, shower and change clothes and brush the coating out of her mouth. Because she needed to contact John and find out if he had moved her parents, contact Niall and find out where the hell he was. "I don't have time for company."

"This isn't a social call." Lucien sat on the edge of the bed. His eyes fixed on her bare breasts, but only out of generalized interest. "Drives you crazy to be out of the loop, doesn't it? To not know what's going on. Well, triple it and you'll know how I feel."

"I didn't know that you felt at all." Jani sought the refuge of her closet, riffling through the hangers for her favorite Service surplus gear. She chose a muddy blue mechanic's coverall she'd swiped from a recycle bin, and added a black pullover to wear underneath in deference to the cold.

"Who are you meeting? John? McGaw? Going to go pound the last fastener in Derringer's career coffin?"

Jani turned to find Lucien standing in the closet entry. Even though he gripped the sides of the doorway, blocking her in, she didn't feel threatened. He wasn't yet back to full strength. If he did get out of hand, she'd just punch him in his burn. "Who said I'm meeting anybody?"

"Come on—I heard those messages!" Lucien's hair caught the light as it did in her nightmare. His show of anger weakened him—the way he sagged against the doorway implied that he needed the support. "You're going out there alone, with no idea who's waiting for you, unarmed, with no back-up. Is that what you call taking care of what means most to you?"

"Do you know something I don't?" Jani bundled her clothes in front of her bare chest and turned to Lucien. "That's nothing new, is it?" After a few seconds of warring stares he stepped aside with a huff and she retreated to the sanctuary of the bathroom.

CHAPTER 28

When Jani emerged from the bathroom, she found Lucien standing in front of the dresser, studying the painting of the lovers' triangle.

"This is about the shooting, isn't it? You think I set you up." His voice held the matter-of-fact tone he always used when discussing matters of life and death. "That's why you've shut me out. You don't trust me."

Jani tossed her clothes and towels in the cleaner. "I never trusted you."

"You did for some things. For things that mattered to both of us." He had managed something akin to a sad expression, which meant he felt as upset about someone else's feelings as he ever could. "I'll bet that's why you let me stay here. You wanted to keep an eye on me."

Jani turned her back on him and activated the cleaner. When the goal was to keep the lies to a minimum, you learned fast which things just weren't worth lying about.

"Do you think I'd have missed?" The injury in Lucien's voice had been replaced by chill pride. "If I had tried to kill you or had set you up to be killed, do you think I'd have failed?"

Jani walked to the dresser, working her fingers through her damp hair. "There's a first time for everything." She stepped around Lucien to collect her comb, and stopped in mid-grab when she saw the two halves of the casino marker lying atop the mirrored tray.

"Angevin tried to wake you to undress, but you'd turned to dead weight by that time. She didn't want to touch you—you strike out in your sleep, it seems. So she asked me to help." Lucien leaned close, until he spoke directly in Jani's ear. "Did you go in through the front of the dresser, or the back?"

"The back." Jani looked at him. His eyes had gone brown stone, which meant that whatever anger he felt hadn't claimed him completely. What she needed to watch for was the truly dead light, when he looked at her the way he did at everyone else. That would signal the true point of no return, the end of the arm's length discussions and tense treaties. That would mean only one of them would emerge alive. "Drawers are too difficult to break into quickly. The back is always faster."

Lucien nodded. Knowing him, he'd filed the knowledge away for future reference, if he didn't know it already. "Did you leave a mess?"

"The rear panel is a little bent. Somebody with a protein scanner would know I was in the room, but they'd have expected that since you keyed your door to me." Jani picked up one of the marker halves. "You killed him. Etienne Palia."

"As if you didn't know." Lucien shrugged. He tried to insert his hands in his pockets, but the pull of the cloth over his wound made him wince, forcing him to settle for a one-handed lean against the dresser. "You were living in Majora at the time—I considered tracking you down."

"Don't change the subject!" Jani struggled to keep her voice level. "Who ordered Palia's death? I realize that neither the Service nor the government are above arranging the occasional convenient demise, but was Palia powerful enough to merit their attention? Or did you hire yourself out to *L'araignée*, help them rid themselves of an officer who had gotten out of line? Or was it a more private killing? An angry husband? A gambling debt?"

"You would have hated him if you'd met him." Lucien smiled with a distinct lack of humor. "His behavior definitely ran counter to your personal code of ethics."

"Which ethics are those, the ones you helped research for my white paper?" Jani watched Lucien's face, alert for any flicker or shadow, any sign that she'd struck what passed for his nerve. "You were the busy boy, weren't you? Between contract killings for whoever paid your freight and digging the dirt on me, it's a wonder you had time to file your official Intelligence Updates."

Lucien slowly raised his hand. "I'd like to bring up two points, if I could?" He extended his thumb. "One—you're not dead. I'm fifteen for fifteen, and you're not dead."

Jani shook her head. "First time for—"

"*Two.*" Lucien extended his index finger, then pointed the mock weapon at her. "After you read that white paper, and I assume you did or Niall isn't half the ferret I think he is, did you stop to ponder the two interesting items that seemed to have been left out? The copying of the deed. The murder of that Family agent." He cocked his thumb back and forth, as though he activated a charge-through. "Of course, you had your reasons at the time. But they're the sorts of reasons that make sense to someone like me or Niall, not to people like Steve, or Angevin, or your good friends at Registry."

Jani felt her anger freeze into something more controllable, less human. "Are you threatening me?"

"No, I'd never threaten you. I know you too well." Lucien sighed. "A lot better, apparently, than you know me. I covered for you. I kept the really damning crap from getting into that white paper. No matter how much you try to deny it, you need me. I have always done you more good than harm. In every way." He took a step toward her, but stopped when she backed away. "You're unarmed. You're stupid to go out there."

"What good would you be? The ComPol turned your shooter over to your CO."

"You think that's the only one I've got! After all this, you think that's the only—" Lucien laughed, harder than Jani had ever seen him. He walked to the wall so he could brace against it as his shoulders shook, clasping his arms across his stomach and groaning as his wound complained. The pain calmed him—he wiped a hand over his face and looked at her, the animal ache dulling his eyes. "Do you really think that's the only one I've got?"

"No." Jani turned back to the mirror and focused on the periphery of her face. The part of her that she couldn't control worried after Lucien's pain and tried to think of a way to salve it, wondered why the implanted analgesic pump didn't do a better job. Yet again, she damned her weakness. "I don't need your help. Go to sleep. Go away. Go to hell." She pushed the comb through her hair and fought to keep from looking at herself too closely. So intent was she on avoiding her own gaze that she didn't sense Lucien's approach until she saw him in the mirror behind her.

He reached around her and picked up the two halves of the marker, one in each hand. "See these?" He held up one half to within a handspan of her nose. "This is you." Then he held up the other. "And this is me." He pressed the two halves together, broken edge to broken edge, until the plastic round looked whole again. "And this is us. Or it could be, only *you* won't admit it."

Jani bumped his stomach with the point of her elbow. The marker halves flew apart as he gasped and backpedaled; she barely kept from cringing, knowing his surprise and his pain. "Take that thing and get out."

"Why?" Lucien straightened slowly, his breathing irregular, the sweat beading on his forehead. "What are you afraid of? Is it that you need me? Or is it that you love me?"

"Don't flatter yourself." Jani resumed raking the comb through her hair. "I know what love is—you could never make that cut."

"Oh, I forgot. You love John." Lucien closed in again, this time grabbing her wrists so she couldn't elbow him. "Your creator." He wrapped his arms around her and rubbed his chin against the side of her neck. "Or maybe fellow freak is a better term these days."

Jani grew still. No, it was more than that. It was as though her blood ceased flowing and her heart stopped, as though her very cells suspended their function. She watched Lucien in the mirror as he nuzzled her neck, a neck that had lengthened over the past months. *My mother called me mutant . . .*

"I mean, compared to you, even *he* looks normal." Lucien rested his chin atop Jani's achy shoulder and regarded their reflection. "At least that's what I overheard at Neoclona. They talk about you constantly—you're their favorite pastime. It's the eyes that clinch it, according to the general opinion. Not that I have any basis for comparison. You've tied yourself in knots hiding them from me." He pressed close to her ear. "Here, kitty, kitty, kitty." He laughed as she struggled to break his grip. "Boy, they must be some sight. Creature from the GateWay. It Came from the Lost Colony. What did your parents say when they first saw you? 'Who are you and what did you do to our daughter?' Or did they just scream and run like hell?"

Jani stilled again, and watched Lucien's eyes in the mirror. His human eyes, which some would call beautiful, that obscured a hollow of a heart and a dried husk of a soul. *We are two halves of the same whole, aren't we? Both monsters, only you hide it so well.* She shook his hands from her wrists. Still captured by his arms, she turned to look him in the face. His smile brightened as their eyes met, like a bully who knew he'd hit his target.

Jani raised her hands to her eyes, slipped her thumbnails beneath the edges of the films, flicked out and down. The hydropolymer membranes came away with audible *pops*—they hung intact from her fingers, the green irises glittering, the white sclera milky and human and clean. She flipped them atop the dresser to desiccate.

Lucien's eyes widened. His smile faded. His mouth opened, but the words wouldn't emerge, even though his jaw worked, even though he tried to speak. His arms fell away. He stepped back, mouth agape.

"What's the matter, bully boy? Cat got your tongue?" Jani laughed in spite of her shame. Lucien stunned speechless was a sight to behold. An event to treasure, no matter the circumstances. *No matter* . . . If she told herself that long enough, maybe she'd believe it.

Then Lucien reached out. A tentative move, as though he feared rebuff. He brushed his fingers down her cheek, along the curve of her jaw. Then he gripped her by the shoulders and spun her so that she faced the mirror. *"Look."* When Jani tried to twist away, he flung one arm around her shoulders to hold her fast, then seized her jaw so she couldn't move her head. "I said *look,* damn it!"

Jani tried to look at the ceiling, the wall, the carved wood frame of the mirror. But Lucien held her so firmly that all she could move were her eyes—her head ached from the strain of trying not to look straight ahead. She surrendered, finally, and did as he demanded, bracing herself for his sly insults as she stared into the overlarge irises, the glass-green sclera.

"See." Lucien relaxed his grip on her jaw, until it became a caress. "They're beautiful. Like veined jade." He released her jaw and ran his hand over her breasts, down her stomach. "Gorgeous." He gripped her hip and pulled her closer, pressing himself against her.

Jani felt her nerves flare and her stomach tighten as Lucien's erection ground against her. She looked again at his reflection, and saw the same parted lips and focused dreaminess that he had displayed during Dathim Naré's visit. "Now who's the freak?" She heard the deepening catch in her voice, and hated herself just a little more.

"You're what we're all going to be someday, according to Nema. I'm just getting a head start." Lucien gripped her waist and turned her slowly, pressing against her as he did so their bodies never broke contact. It seemed to take forever. A single second. By the time she faced him, Jani's breathing had gone as raspy as his.

"This is ridiculous." She tried to squirm away, but her legs wouldn't listen. "You're in no condition."

"Never felt better." Lucien smiled lazily and reached for the top fastener of Jani's coverall.

"No!" She thrust her arms up and out, breaking his hold and driving him back. "You want to fuck the bizarre so damned bad, go cruise South Wabash and leave me the hell alone!"

Lucien blinked in unfocused confusion before shaking his head. “You’re not bizarre. You’re a beautiful woman.”

“Damn you for a liar!” Jani’s voice caught again. *Anormal . . . mutant.* Her throat ached and her warped eyes stung and passion had nothing whatsoever to do with it. “I’m not—a *woman* anymore.”

Lucien hesitated. “I know.” He held out his hand. “Please?” When she didn’t answer, he stepped closer and reached once more for the neck of her coverall. He opened one fastener, the next, slid the coverall off her shoulders, then knelt in front of her.

Jani leaned against the dresser and closed her eyes.

“No!” Lucien grabbed the front of her pullover and yanked, forcing her to look down. “Watch every move I make.” He undid the rest of the fasteners, then pulled the coverall down. Off one leg, then the other. Tossed it aside. “Look at me.” He peeled Jani’s pullover over her head and flung it atop the coverall. Then he slid her band-bra and underwear down her body, leaving a line of kisses in their wake.

Jani braced her hands on the edge of the dresser as her knees sagged and her body ached and warmed. A human ache. Blessedly human warmth.

“The idomeni don’t get as wrapped up in this as we do, do they?” Lucien’s eyes shone.

“No.” Jani reached down and pushed her hand through his hair. “They think we overcomplicate it.”

“I guess they don’t know everything.” Lucien massaged her inner thighs, then looked up to make sure she still watched. “It’s like gold. Warm gold.” He kissed the softest, warmest place, then stood up and undressed. He pulled his shirt over his head, pausing when he saw Jani stare at his burn. “It doesn’t hurt as long as I’m careful.”

“It looks like hell.” She stepped close and placed both her hands over the shiny pink expanse of flesh, then ran a finger over the whispery-thin grid lines of the grafting support. “And I know it hurts—you wince every time you move too fast. You can’t—”

“Yes, I can.” He pushed down his trousers, kicked off his trainers and socks and stood before her, naked and beautiful, but changed. Uncertain, faltering, as if he expected her to turn him down, even now.

Jani pressed close and kissed him, savoring his human taste, his human hands caressing her breasts and moving down her body. The sweet human agony that radiated from between her legs and the human moan that rose in her throat. She held him as he maneuvered her backward and braced her against the dresser. "This isn't going to work," she whispered into his hair. She felt his hands slip inside her and then she felt him inside her, slowly at first and then faster and faster, matched his every rhythm, and realized it worked just fine. She wrapped her legs around him to steady herself. Moved her hands over his back and chest, avoiding the burn. Heard him call to her and answered back. Watched his every response as he watched hers. Accepted him to her strange home and felt him embrace—embrace—what she didn't want and beg for—what she hated—and ask—and ask—

"Look at me."

—and ask—

"Look at me."

—until his human eyes finally closed and his back arched and his body stiffened and he cried out as he had on the floor of the garage after she fell and the shot took him instead.

Lucien sagged against her, his breathing slowing, his hands easing their bruising grip, his head cradled against her neck. Jani held him because she had no choice, because her body had frozen and she didn't know what else to do. "Let me go."

"No, not yet—"

"Let me go."

"No, not yet. Why—?"

But she had pushed him away and gathered up her clothes and fled to the bathroom before he made her answer the question.

Jani showered quickly. Dressed slowly. Refilmed her eyes carefully. If she could have drilled a hole in the wall so she could leave without having to walk through her bedroom, she would have. But she couldn't, so she gathered her frayed wits and faced what needed to be faced.

She found Lucien dressed, sitting on the edge of the bed, socks in hand. He seemed to know her thoughts—he barely looked up when she walked in the room.

Jani leaned against the armoire; the carved scrollwork of the doors dug into her back. "As soon as people heard about the shooting, they assumed you had something to do with it."

"Yes, they did, didn't they?" He shrugged. "Lucky you fell when you did." He draped one sock across his knee, then worked his fingers through the other. "Lucky I was there."

"What are you telling me, that you shoved me out of the way?"

Jani pushed off the armoire and paced. "You expect me to believe that you took my shot on purpose? *You?"*

Lucien didn't answer. He didn't look at her, but kept his human eyes fixed on his bundled sock.

Jani waited for him to argue, to try to charm her with a smile, to lie. When he didn't, she knew that he realized that it would do no good. That told her all she needed to know. "I want you to leave," she heard herself say, her voice hollow and distant. "Now. I'll have your gear sent to Sheridan tomorrow."

"This—" Lucien stopped. The cast of his face had turned tentative, as it had been such a short time before. As though he walked unfamiliar ground, and hated the sensation. "This *arrangement* of ours, as Nema calls it—it's not what I had in mind, either. I mean, it's just been one damned thing after another with you ever since we met!" He raised his thumb to his mouth and nipped at the nail. "What aggravates me the most is that you never stop to think about where you could go in this city if you could keep your mouth shut for five minutes at a stretch! You'll beat your head against the wall when there's a perfectly good door just around the corner." He yanked the sock straight, then bundled it again.

"I do not—love you. I have never—loved anybody. I can't, and I wouldn't want to if I could." Lucien's fingers slowed, stopped. "But according to all the testing I've had over the years, I am capable of remembering . . . what it may have been like once. If I try. Like when you catch a whiff of something, a flower, or something baking, and the memories come back." His uncertain expression combined with stray shadow to soften his face so he looked as he did in his teenaged portrait. "I've always been loyal to you. Always."

Jani watched the light play over Lucien's hair as once more, Val's words came back to her. *He's always shown me the face he knows I want to see. That's all he is—shadow and reflection. That's all he's ever been. Why can't I accept it?* "You don't know the meaning of the word."

"I beg to differ," Lucien replied. "When loyalty is your profession, you learn what it means and you do not dare forget."

"Don't you? I'd think after the first half-dozen deals, the lines would start to blur." Jani slumped against the armoire. She knew she sounded petulant, childish, but she didn't care. She knew he had betrayed her and tried to hate him. Knew she couldn't and that she probably never would, and hated herself instead. "Service. Exterior. *L'araignée*. The occasional freelance." She heard her voice scale upward, and struggled to bring it under control. "What term best describes you? Double agent? Triple agent? Dodecahedral agent?"

"You always knew what I was. What I am. Are you saying you only realized it now—who are you kidding?" Lucien pulled on the bundled sock, then the other. "If anyone ever compiled a white paper on me, I daresay it would hold your attention. I have a talent for deceit, and I've made it pay. But I also have a talent for picking the winning horse, and I've made that pay, too." He pushed his feet into his trainers and adjusted the fasteners. "Along the way I've had many masters, and I've served them all very well." He stood slowly, one hand resting over the shooter burn. "But I served you best." He walked to the door without looking at her, his step silent, the only sound that of the panel opening, then closing.

Jani waited before walking out to the main room. She didn't want to see Lucien leave, in case the sight of him compelled her to change her mind and ask him to stay. She concentrated instead on what she'd tell Val when he asked the whereabouts of his patient, and on how she'd remove the outpatient gear from the spare bedroom. She thought of everything but Lucien. Everything but . . .

. . . and found that that ploy didn't work for long either.

She found Steve and Angevin sprawled on the couch. "Right ho, Jan!" Steve said as he stuck a celebratory 'stick in his mouth.

Before he could ignite it, Jani pulled him to his feet and dragged him after her to the door. "We'll be right back," she called to Angevin, who stared after them in bewilderment.

"Where we goin'?" Steve tried to squirm out of her grip as they hustled toward the lift.

Jani pushed him into the car and thumped her fist against the pad until the doors closed. "I want you to help me with something."

Hodge called to them as they crossed the lobby. Jani offered a quick wave, but kept moving. Out the door. Across the street to the garage.

"Jan?" Steve sounded edgy now. "What we doin'?"

"A demonstration, to ease both our troubled minds." Jani pushed Steve ahead of her down the entry ramp, then pulled him to a stop when they reached the place where Lucien had fallen. "Stand behind me."

"'K."

"Closer."

"Right."

"Off to the left, half a meter, *stop*."

"'K."

Jani pointed to the left and down. "The shot is going to come from there. I'm in position for it now, but I'm falling." She bent over and to the right, a slow-motion version of her head-first tumble. "You want me to get hit—what do you do?"

"I—" Steve reached out and grabbed her around the upper arm. "Hard to get a bloody grip. Nothing else to hold on to if I want to pull—" His hand fell away. "Jan, what the hell—?"

Jani turned on him. "If Lucien wanted to drag me back into the line of fire, he'd have grabbed my arm and pulled, like you did. But he pushed, down and away. Hard. He almost dislocated my shoulder—it still hurts."

"So?" Steve took a step back. Another. "He pushed you down on the ground so you'd be a sitting duck for the shooter. So you couldn't run."

"The pulse was aimed *here,* Steve." Jani held her arm straight out, her fist marking the spot where the shot impacted Lucien. "This was a quick 'n' dirty attempt. The shooter only had time to fire once. The set-up was supposed to do the work. Lucien botched the set-up." She turned, and saw Angevin standing at the top of the ramp, her hands over her mouth. "He found out about the hit on me. Not soon enough to stop it, but soon enough to screw it up." He couldn't afford to stop it. He owed a certain amount of loyalty to someone in *L'araignée*, and Lucien always took care to cultivate his loyalties. No one ever questioned you when you took care to appear unquestionable.

"You can't say you believe that!" Steve hurried after Jani as she mounted the ramp and fled the garage. "You can't say he's got you believin' that!" He picked up his pace as they burst onto the sidewalk, which was lit by late afternoon sun and clear of pedestrians. "He's a bloody damned liar, Jan—he's been one all his life!" He shouted after her as Angevin grabbed his arm and tried to drag him across the street and into the quiet, calm lobby. "Jan! *Jan!*"

But Jani didn't answer him. She walked down the street, toward an office building that contained a bank of public comports. She concentrated on the call she needed to make to John, on the wording she'd use, so that no one who happened to overhear would think she talked about her parents. So no one would think her questionable, or wonder at her loyalties. She didn't think about anything else. Or anyone. Or so she told herself. She'd had lots of practice in telling herself things, just as she'd had practice in avoiding them. Things she didn't want to hear, didn't want to know. Didn't believe, despite the evidence to the contrary. Of damning testimony that disappeared. Of a sore shoulder that wouldn't heal, and a shooter pulse that cracked half a meter up and to the side. Stood to reason. She could be a bloody damned liar herself when she needed to be. So she knew a lie when she heard it, and knew the truth when she heard it too.

CHAPTER 29

A harried-looking Neoclona staffer answered Jani's call. No, Dr. Shroud was not available. No, Ms. Kilian, he didn't leave a message for you. Yes, Ms. Kilian, I will tell him that you called.

Jani tried the code to Val's flat, and found it still blocked. That bothered her. Blocking was a viable method for silencing talkative mothers for the short term, but it lacked elegance when employed for too long. In other words, it blared to one and all the fact that something highly unusual had occurred at Chez Parini. *Maybe Val just forgot to lift it.* She hoped that didn't mean that her parents still remained with him. She hoped John had the presence of mind to move them, or that Niall had overstepped the boundaries she had imposed on him and stuck his nose where it needed to be stuck.

Jani sat forward, elbows on knees, and thumped her head against the wall of the comport booth. "John, you're not an idiot—couldn't you have left me *something*?" When this was all over, she'd have to ask Roni McGaw to give him lessons in veiled communication.

Roni McGaw. Jani checked her timepiece. She still had an hour to wait before she met with Roni. *Did you check Anais's calendar? What did you find?* Proof that she had met with Lucien on Amsun during the time *L'araignée* formed? That she had approved plans, authorized expenses, requested assassinations?

Jani called Niall's flat, received no answer, left no message. She struggled to slow her racing mind, to keep the crazy thoughts from leaping to the fore. That Niall had been waylaid on the way back to Sheridan, and now lay trussed and drugged in a shielded room in an anonymous house somewhere in Chicago. Or that he had taken her distrust of the Service and turned it into distrust of him, and instead lay in a bed in the Sheridan Main Hospital, turning ever more inward as the psychotherapeuticians labored yet again to bring him back.

Jani thumped her head against the wall again, as though she could pound the thoughts from her head via brute force. *An overactive imagination is a terrible thing.* The OCS instructor who had given voice to that gem had referred to excessive overstrategizing, but he could have been referring to the fix in which she found herself now. Out of the loop, dependent on others' skills to protect what meant most to her, with only her own questioning mind for company. *Drives you crazy, doesn't it . . . ?* If Lucien had appeared before her now, she would have struck him.

Her stomach interrupted with a grumble, and she debated returning to her flat to get something to eat. But she didn't want to face more of Steve's protests, his arguments delineating Lucien's guilt. Instead, she dug into her pockets and collected all the vend tokens she could find. Somewhere in the building there was a vend alcove, and somewhere in that alcove's coolers and hot boxes was something she could eat. Then she'd find a quiet corner, a place where she could close her eyes and clear her head. And wait.

The clip of Jani's bootheels on the scancrete echoed along the alleys she cut through, sounded more softly within the wider brick canyon of Armour Place. She passed few people on the way to the garage during this dividing time between day and night. She recognized some of the faces, and watched them just as warily as the ones she didn't. When she finally reached the garage, she kept walking, circling around the renovation and down the next street so that she could enter the garage from the rear.

Jani surveyed the space as she had on the night of the shooting, on the lookout this time not for returning assassins, but for Roni, or for her skimmer, if she had used one.

She paced, suddenly self-conscious and wary of being seen. She knew she could pass for an employee from a nearby shop waiting for her ride, for an impatient girlfriend waiting for her date. She wished Niall could have shadowed her. She wished augie would show up to calm her nerves. She—

A *thud* sounded as something heavy hit the floor above. Jani patted her coverall pocket for the shooter that wasn't there, and headed for the stairwell she and Niall had used to gain access to the garage's upper level. As she approached the door, she looked down and saw a metal wedge lying on the floor nearby. She picked it up, hefted it, then swung it by the narrow end. A doorstop, hollow-forged and badly dented. It was barely heavy enough to serve as a suitable weapon, but it would have to do.

She crept up the stairs, her eyes on the door above. She heard another sound as she neared the landing, the scrape of a sole against the smooth scancrete. Whoever it was, they made no effort to hide their presence. *It's probably just someone come to collect their skimmer. This* is *a garage.* Her hand tightened around the doorstop anyway.

She stopped in front of the door and debated how to go in. Slowly wouldn't work. The safety lighting in the stairwell couldn't be quenched—she'd be perfectly backlit as soon as she cracked open the door.

Jani crouched low. In one smooth motion, she pushed open the door and drop-rolled into the shadow of the same column she had hidden behind during her foray with Niall. She hugged the base and scanned the area, staying low so she could look beneath the skimmers. Row after row hovered silently in the half-light, the hum and click of the charge units the only sounds Jani heard but for her breathing. *Someone must be throwing a party tonight.* That would explain the number of skimmers. She felt like a child trying to see around a roomful of furniture.

She heard the running steps before she saw motion off to her right, partially hidden by broken rows of skimmers. She darted after the sound, because the innocent didn't run, because a chase gave her something on which to focus her twangy nerves. She kept her head low, gaze flicking above and below the vehicles, and caught the shadowy reflection of someone on the enameled surfaces.

There were three exits, not counting the do-it-yourself doorway that the construction crew had made—the door Jani had used, another door at the far end of the space, and the ramp used by the vehicles. The shape headed for the far door, but it had a great many skimmers to dodge around to get there. Jani heard the slide of shoes on scancrete, another *thud* as her quarry tripped and fell, a gasp of pained surprise. She rounded and cut in an intercept pattern, so she could head them off before they made the door.

As she drew closer, she heard the slide of cloth over smooth floor. One of the skimmers trembled, a four-door sedan that covered a lot of floor space.

She circled back behind the skimmer, in the hope that whoever had crawled beneath would still be looking toward the door, and that if they'd been armed, they'd have shot at her by now. When she reached the rear of the vehicle, she ducked down, tossed the doorstop aside, reached out, and grabbed. Her hands closed around two thin ankles. *Kids!* She dragged the squirming, struggling form into the light as she squelched the urge to howl. *Kids playing—!*

Then the garish clothes struck her—sapphire and glaring orange—the liquid flow of the cloth—long brown hair bound in a horsetail, but something wasn't right—*damn, this is a tall kid!*

Her quarry twisted around and goggled at her, cracked amber eyes catching the dim light and holding it fast.

Jani let loose the Haárin's ankles and stumbled backward, falling against a late-model sports skimmer. The vehicle's proximity alarm emitted a warning chirp—she fell to her hands and knees and scooted across the floor to get out of range before the tiny sound erupted into a blare. Something in her right knee shifted as it impacted the scancrete—she fell onto her side and clasped her hands around the throbbing joint.

The Haárin boosted herself into a crouch, ready to dart away. Then she eased back on her heels and looked Jani in the face, openly and boldly. "You are—ná Kièrshia?" Her English sounded crisp, as though she'd spoken it for a long time.

"Yes." Jani tried to straighten her knee, stopping in mid-flex when she heard the near door open and a jumble of footsteps pad toward them. She looked up, and almost gave voice to her howl as eight more Haárin heads regarded her over the top of the sedan.

Then the door opened again. More footsteps. Two more heads, the sight of which stopped the howl in Jani's throat. Dathim Naré, and next to him, Nema. "NìRau?" She boosted to her feet and limped toward him. "What's going on?"

"Ní Tsecha," Dathim interrupted, giving the title the long "a" twist of the Haárin. "He is nìRau no more. He has joined us now, and truly."

"NìRau," Jani repeated with feeling as she ignored Dathim and confronted her silent teacher. "Why have you left the embassy? Did Shai lift your restriction?"

Dathim tossed a Low Vynshàrau hand twitch of dismissal. "He does not answer to nìaRauta Shai anym—"

Jani swung around to face him. "I am *not* talking to you!" Her knee complained at the rapid movement, and she turned back to Nema more slowly. "NìRau? Did Shai give you permission to leave the grounds?"

"No, nìa." Nema looked down at her, his expression so somber that she feared him ill. He didn't wear the marks of the sickbed, however, the black-trimmed overrobe or the single hoop earring in his right ear. In fact, he wore no overrobe at all, only his usual off-white shirt and trousers, topped by a brown knee-length coat made from the idomeni equivalent of wool. He wore no earrings, either—the multiple holes dotted his lobes, more glaring in their emptiness than the most complex goldwire helix. Strange that Jani could see his ears—he must have bound his braids in the brown scarf he had twisted about his head in imitation of Dathim—

Jani raised her hands to the sides of Nema's head and pushed back the scarf. The pale brown stubble that covered his scalp shone in the soft light of the garage. She brushed her hand over it as her breath caught. She felt the tears course down her cheeks, and made no effort to wipe them away. "Did you do this?" She spun toward Dathim, and used the pain in her knee to stoke her anger. "Did you!"

"Are you talking to me *now*, ná Kièrshia?" Dathim bent low to look her in the face. "No, I did not cut ní Tsecha's hair."

"I did it." The female whom Jani had pulled from beneath the skimmer stepped forward. "He bade me, and I did as he bade. He chose his own way, ná Kièrshia, and truly."

"Ná Beyva speaks the truth, nìa." Nema gripped Jani's chin between his thumb and forefinger. "I have chosen to declare myself as Haárin, to declare my faith in the future as I know it must be." He tilted her head to one side, then the other, his eyes searching hers. "We have come here to request that you do the same, that you appear at the conclave as a supporter of the Elyan Haárin, that you show your faith in the future as well."

Jani tried to pull back. "I begged you to wait. The problem I told you about—I took care of it. Another day or two, and all the fuss over the shooting would have dissipated. Shai would have had no choice but to release you to attend the conclave." She knew Nema attempted to discern her eyes through their filming. Dathim must have told him about the incident in the kitchen, and the glimpse he had managed to steal. *If he could see them for himself, he would be so happy.* But she had no film with her to cover them again. What if one of the partygoers chose that moment to return to their skimmer? But, but, but . . . She tried to concentrate on policy, to veer away from the personal. "NìRau, it is much more important that you participate in the conclave rather than me. You're the Haárin's religious dominant, as well as Cèel's." She touched the side of his shorn head. How old he looked, without his braids and his jewelry. "Have you stopped to think how the Elyan Haárin might react to this?"

"They will rejoice to see it. The Elyan now cut their hair as well." Dathim stepped to Nema's side, an action that made him look for one surreal moment like a Cabinet press aide intercepting an inappropriate question. His chill attempt at a humanish smile only served to reinforce the image. "Ah. My apologies, ná Kièrshia. You did not ask me."

"NìRau." Jani took Nema by the elbow and steered him away from the hovering Dathim. "Cèel and Shai have begun to act as humanish leaders. They have chosen to treat your attempts at open disputation as an affront, a threat to idomeni solidarity. The fact that your suborn had challenged you must have infuriated them. How do you think they will treat your adopting the appearance of their most rebellious Haárin?"

A lick of the old fire flared in Nema's eyes—he bared his teeth. "They will be most as outraged."

"They may recall you to Shèrá."

"Yes, nìa."

"They may execute you."

Nema paused. Then he pulled the scarf from its tenuous perch on his head and regarded it thoughtfully. "It occurred to me that when the gods informed me of the future, they did not also guarantee my presence in it." He turned the scarf over in his hands. "But you will live, I think, nìa. John Shroud would split the universe in half rather than allow you to die. And you will ensure that the future develops as it must."

Jani glanced at her timepiece, and swallowed a curse. "I must meet with someone. It is important that I see her. What we discuss will affect what happens at the conclave." She looked up at Nema's face, and blinked as her eyes filled. "I wish you would have discussed this with me. I wish you would have waited."

"The time for waiting is past, nìa." Nema unknotted his scarf and wrapped it around his head. "You must attend the conclave."

"Yes, you must." Dathim again stepped up to Nema's side. "Even though you are not talking to me, I am bound to question you on this matter." He had allowed the barest hint of supplication into his voice, which up until then had emerged a most idomeni low-pitched growl. "Will you speak for us?"

Jani sneaked another look at her timepiece. Roni must be awaiting her in the garage's lower level, pacing and muttering to herself. It struck Jani that she might be the searching type, and that if she was, she could burst through one of the doors at any moment. *And wouldn't she get an eyeful.* She had to get Nema and his band out of sight and out of reach. Now. "If I do, will you take nìRau Nema back to the embassy?"

"No. I will not return nìRau Nema." Dathim stood with his hands behind his back and his head cocked to the side. He hadn't learned to match the humanish gestures and postures he had learned with his attitudes—his pose of innocent question warred with the challenge in his voice. "But I will take back ní Tsecha."

Nema watched the interplay with an expression of contentment. "He is most vexing, is he not, nìa?"

"Most." Jani took Nema by the arm and steered him toward the same door through which he had entered, herding the rest of the Haárin ahead of them as she did.

"I assume you came here in one of the embassy vehicles?" An image flashed of eleven idomeni crammed into a sedan, arms and legs jutting through open windows, like teenagers on a spree. "Where did you hide it?" she asked as she pressed her fingertips against her tightening brow.

"In plain sight," Nema replied, "something I have learned during my time in Chicago."

"Define 'plain sight.'"

"On the street next to this one, with some other skimmers." Nema looked at Jani, head tilted in question. "Are you unwell, nìa?"

"I'm just fine, nìRau." *And I'll feel even better when I know you're on your way back to the embassy.* She felt the pressure of the other Haárin's stares. Ná Beyva, she noticed, watched her particularly, her horsetail whipping back and forth as she tried to keep from trodding on the heels of the Haárin ahead of her.

"You are short," she finally said, hesitating in the doorway.

"Most humanish are short compared to Vynshàrau, ná Beyva." Jani raised her right hand in a gesture of submission, an acceptance of fate.

"But as you change, you will grow taller?"

Jani's gesture altered to something less submissive. "I have grown already."

Beyva bared her teeth. "Such is a great thing, ná Kièrshia, and truly!"

Jani watched as Beyva brushed a large smudge of dirt from the front of her shirt. "Did you hurt yourself?"

Beyva looked at her. "Hurt? You did not hurt me, Kièrshia. You only pulled me."

"Not then. Before, when you fell."

"I did not fall, Kièrshia. I heard someone fall, but it was not me!" Beyva bounded down the stairs two at a time, hair flouncing, and disappeared around the bend before Jani could question her further.

"I can no longer step down stairs in such a way." Nema disengaged himself from Jani's grasp and walked out onto the landing. "My poor bones would shatter, and truly." He pulled his coat more tightly about him. "It would not be so sad a thing, to leave this damned cold place."

"I thought you liked Chicago." Jani's voice shook, although she tried to stop it.

"In the summer." He started down the steps. "But this cold makes my bones ache, and gives me strange dreams." He maintained his measured pace, his eyes focused on the downward trek. "Glories of the night to you, nìa." He didn't look back at her. His steady plod echoed within the stairwell as he descended out of sight.

"He is afraid."

Jani spun around, her breath hissing through her teeth as her knee twisted. "What the hell are you still doing here!"

"I want to see what you look for. What makes you fear, as ní Tsecha fears." Dathim leaned against the stairwell doorway in a slump-shouldered pose that would have made Lucien groan in his sleep. "Although his fears are as different, I believe. He fears that Cèel may indeed kill him. Cèel has his own fears. He fears the Oà, who have never ruled over idomeni. But now the Oà grow strong on Shèrá as the Vynshàrau spread themselves throughout the worldskein. He also fears Anais Ulanova, who lies." He pushed off the entry and walked toward her. "But mostly he fears you, because he knows that if he kills Tsecha, you will do to him what you did to the Laumrau."

Jani started down the stairs. "You should catch up with the others, or they will leave you behind." If she had met Dathim on a colony, she would have admired his rebellious attitude, but this was Earth and his defiance threatened someone she cared for and at this moment she despised him.

"I can find my way back without them. I have walked the night city before." Dathim quickened his step so he edged up beside her. "You have covered your eyes again."

"Yes."

"You are still ashamed."

"Humanish do not like those who look too different. If I am to work in this city, if I am to help you, I must blend in as well as possible."

"That is what ní Tsecha gave as his reasons for living in the embassy, for calling himself Haárin in name only. Work. Blending. Fear of upsetting. All excuses, to deny that which he was." Dathim looked at her. "You do not like these words, ná Kièrshia. And because I speak them, you do not like me." His voice sounded full and strong, as though he enjoyed the prospect.

"You have risked my teacher's life," Jani replied in High Vynshàrau, because she knew Dathim would understand both the words and the formality behind them, and that the decorum would irritate him. *"Such is a concern to me, and truly."* She blew through the stairwell door and down the walkway behind the garage, looking for a skimmer that hadn't been there when she had walked the place before, and not finding one. "Damn it!"

"You wait for your lieutenant?" Exhibitionist though he was, Dathim had sense enough to duck into a shadowed doorway.

"No." Jani walked to the corner and looked around. No agitated Exterior Ministry Documents Chiefs to be seen, unfortunately. *Someone fell and fell hard, and Beyva saw nothing.* She rejoined Dathim, who still stood in the doorway. "I'm worried. The one I wait for is never late, and I don't see her." She eyed the doorways across the street and waited for Roni to stride out of one of them and berate her for being late. And waited. . . .

Someone fell . . .

Jani backed away from the skimmer and rejoined Dathim on the sidewalk. He had taken a seat on a bench in front of a shuttered shop. Wise move on his part, whether he realized it or not. He looked much less distinctive sitting down.

"You have found nothing?" His voice held the barest hint of uncertainty.

Jani sat down beside him. "Nothing."

Dathim leaned back and crossed his legs. "You will return to your home."

"No." *Someone fell . . . on the second level, damn it!* Jani bounded to her feet. "I need to go into the construction next door."

Dathim made as though to rise. "I will go with you—"

"No." Jani watched a couple walking hand-in-hand down the opposite sidewalk. They looked in her and Dathim's direction, then turned to one another and fell into whispered argument. Jani could fill in the words without hearing them. *Did you see—! Yes, I saw—! Do you think—? No, it can't be. Yes, it can. No, it can't!*

Jani watched them disappear around the corner, still arguing and looking over their shoulders. "You've been spotted. You need to get out of here." She stood. "How will you get back to the embassy?"

"There is a plumber near this place—the embassy purchases from her. She will take me."

"Ask her to make a call for you." Jani scrabbled through her pockets for a stylus and a scrap of paper, and wrote down Niall's code. "She should say, 'Come to the shooting gallery.'"

"Come. To. The. Shooting. Gallery." Dathim nodded after each word. "And this humanish will come?" He studied Niall's code before stashing it in his trouser pocket.

"I hope so." Jani walked to the garage entry and searched the dark corners near the walls. "Ah-ha." She bent and picked up another metal wedge. This one was larger, heavier, like a chock used to brace a wheeled vehicle. She hefted it, trying to gauge its balance. So intent was she on it that she didn't notice Dathim had rejoined her until he took it from her hands.

"What is this?" he asked as he examined it.

Jani reached for the stop, but Dathim held it just beyond her grasp. "Damn it, give it to me!"

"Is it a charm?"

"No. It's a weapon." Jani tried once more to grab it, but Dathim backed away from her.

"This is not a weapon." He wrinkled his nose. "A shooter is a weapon."

"I can't carry a shooter!"

"Why not?"

"Because I'm crazy, now give me back my chock!"

Dathim's hand lowered slowly. "Crazy?"

Jani tapped the side of her head. "Most ill. In the head. If I'm caught carrying a weapon, I will have to live in a hospital until someone decides to let me out."

"House arrest, like ní Tsecha." Dathim looked at the chock again, then reached beneath his coat and unlatched something from his belt. "Here." He pulled out an ax-hammer, and held it out to her handle-first. "This is not a weapon either, so even a crazy humanish can carry it."

Jani hesitated, then gripped the ruthlessly elegant tool. So perfectly balanced was it that it felt weightless, even though it weighed several kilos. She swung it, and watched the hammerhead catch the light. "You carry this everywhere you go?"

Dathim nodded. "As I did during the war, when things that were not weapons were the only weapons to be had." He looked up the quiet street, then down. "May you find she who you are meeting. May there not be blood. If there is, may it not be yours." He trotted across the street, disappearing down an alley just as the curious couple reappeared around the corner, a friend in tow.

Jani backed into the darkness of the garage entry and watched the trio point down the now-deserted street and argue. Then she slipped the ax-hammer through a belt loop and reentered the garage.

CHAPTER 30

A cluster of couples entered the garage as Jani crossed the floor, their laughter as rich as their clothing. They paid her no mind. She looked like staff in her coverall and boots, and their sort never paid attention to staff.

Jani slipped into the stairwell as the cluster stopped before the lift that would take them to the second floor. She ran up the stairs, her knee singing, and hurried along the wall toward the foamfill. She pushed against the foam as the chime from the ascending lift sounded from the adjacent wall. Enough spraylube remained to quench the surface-surface rubbing to a mouse-like squeak. She slipped behind the barrier and pushed it back into place just as she heard the lift doors open and the laughing voices sound.

She turned slowly, giving her eyes time to adjust to the dark. She exhaled through her mouth and watched her breath puff. The cold, half-lit garage was a haven compared to this clammy, dim place.

—goddamned shooting gallery—

Jani crept toward the vast interior. As she approached the entry, she looked up at the tier upon tier of scaffolds strung with safety illumins, like the balconies in a skeletal theater. She looked down at the floor, checking the dust for the ribbon trails that two heels would leave if the body they belonged to had been dragged. She stilled, straining for any sound.

I can stand right here until Niall shows up. Assuming he showed up at all. Even if he did, it wouldn't change whatever had already happened to Roni, and it sure as hell wouldn't prevent what could still happen in the next few minutes.

Jani removed the ax-hammer from her belt and held it against her leg so the safety illumins wouldn't reflect off the metal and highlight her position. Then she stepped out into the dim, trying as best she could to hide behind the tool trolley.

"Jani."

A voice Jani knew. A voice she hadn't expected until she heard it. She wondered if Roni had felt the same. "Is that you, Peter?"

"Step out to the middle of the floor. I can't see you very well."

Jani slipped the ax-hammer behind her back to her left hand and plucked a short length of pipe from the top of the trolley with her right. "I'm coming." She paced carefully, one foot in front of the other, a stride she knew made her look unsteady, tentative. "What are you doing here?"

"I could ask you the same question." Peter Lescaux looked down on her from the second floor scaffold. He rested only his left hand on the rail, which meant he held a shooter in the right. Construction dust lightened his black evening suit to grey.

"I had a surprise encounter with some idomeni." Jani smiled. Odds were good that he had seen Beyva when he subdued Roni and dragged her through the opening, so it would do no good to lie about it. "I've become a tourist attraction, someone they want to meet. I just saw a group of them off."

"I saw you with one of them, looking at skimmers." Lescaux pointed across the space, toward the tarpaulin-covered windows. "Through there. You looked worried, as if you waited for someone and they didn't show." He tugged at his jacket. "That was my problem. I should learn never to believe a lady when she says she'll be right along."

Jani kicked at the floor, raising a cloud of construction dust. "Messy place for an assignation, don't you think?"

"Oh, I've used worse." Lescaux shrugged. "Ani has informers staking out every mattress in the city. Pascal warned me she was the jealous type, but in the interest of career advancement, one does what one must."

Jani felt augie dig his heels into her sides to prod her. Lescaux was trying to delay her, and augie whispered that she couldn't afford to be delayed. "This is ridiculous, us talking like this. Why don't you come down here?" She started across the floor. "Better yet, why don't I come up there?"

"No!" Lescaux shifted from one foot to the other, still taking care to hide his right hand behind him. "You'll get as dirty as I am."

"What's a little dirt?" Jani tossed the pipe aside so that it banged and rolled across the floor, so that Lescaux would think she was no longer armed. She scrambled up the ladder, taking advantage of the dark at the top to switch the ax-hammer back to her right hand. Her knee didn't hurt at all now.

She legged over the safety rail and onto the scaffold platform. She had only taken a couple of steps when she saw Roni's crumpled body laying near a smaller version of the main floor's massive tool trolley. She could see the back of her head, the drying blood that matted and blackened her hair.

"I told you you'd get dirty." Lescaux withdrew his right arm from behind his back. He indeed held a shooter.

Jani took a step toward Roni. "Is she still alive?"

"Not for much longer." Lescaux raised the shooter to eye-level and sighted down. "I knew it was a mistake to show you that letter. But Derringer was so damned hot to turn you into his agent and grind you under his heel. He laughed about it on the way to pick you up. But I knew. I knew."

Jani shifted her weight and edged another half-step forward. "You know a lot, Peter, I'm sure."

"Stick your flattery up your ass!"

Jani shifted her weight again. A quarter-step, this time. "Lucien visited Guernsey. Lucien visited Anais. Whenever we read the name Le Blond, we thought of him."

"Your mistake." Lescaux grinned. "The one time I didn't mind my predecessor getting the credit." His hand tightened around the shooter, but not enough. If Lucien had stood in his place, he'd have shot her by now. *"Stop."*

Jani halted in mid-step. "Roni must have made the leap, figured out that since you were on colonial assignment, you could have been Le Blond." She hesitated, then made a leap of her own. "Did you plan my parents' kidnapping?"

"Yes. Tried to. Damn that split-lipped bastard anyway." Lescaux's look chilled, but with his weak chin, it just made him look petulant.

Jani glanced at Roni, looking for any movement of the back or shoulder to indicate she breathed. As long as she breathed, however poorly, they had time. If she stopped, they had four minutes.

Roni lay still. So still.

Jani felt the head of the ax-hammer nudge her leg. She had to play this her way. Lescaux held a shooter, yes, but having the better weapon didn't always confer the advantage. Lescaux needed the experience to go with it, and judging from the wild look in his eye, he didn't have it. Niall, yes. Lucien, definitely. *Me . . . yes.* It took a certain brand of nerve to keep killing after the first blow had been struck, and Lescaux had already expended his initial burst on Roni. Now, he'd had time to think of all the complications, feel his mouth go dry as he watched them multiply beyond belief. How would he get rid of Roni's body? Jani's body? How would he clean up the trace evidence and could he do it before the morning construction crew arrived in a few hours and who could he use as an alibi and had anyone seen him enter the garage . . . ?

My way. My speed. My call. Force his hand. Make him act. He was a changeling, not the real thing, and changelings always gave themselves away.

She took another step forward.

"I told you to stop!" Lescaux sighted down again. His hand shook just enough.

Jani brought the ax-hammer around and hurtled forward. The shooter cracked—the pulse packet struck her left side and sent her spinning into the trolley. The edge of the upended lid caught her alongside the head. A corner of the case punched her square in her left ribs. She tumbled to the scaffold floor as tool trays flipped into the air, fell across her body, her head. Tools clattered and rolled, tumbling over the side to the main floor two stories below.

Jani lay atop a pile of fasteners and cutter blades. The edges and points razored through her coverall into the skin beneath. Her limbs twitched and her heart skipped beats as the energy from the shot dissipated throughout her body.

Then augie placed his hand over her heart. Her scattered thoughts collected. The pain in her ribs faded. She lay still, still as death. A cold metal tray had fallen across her head and pressed atop the side of her face. The ax-hammer remained looped to her right wrist—she tried to close her fingers around the handle, but they refused to obey. Once more she squeezed. One finger tightened. Another.

The footsteps approached, as Jani knew they would. Stopped at her feet. She lay twisted, her chest facing the floor, her head close to the wall, covered by metal. If Lescaux just wanted to make sure she was dead, he could administer the coup de grace to the heart. If he wanted to eliminate all hope of revival, he would have to shoot her in the head.

If he wants to shoot me in the heart, he'll have to turn me over. If he wants to shoot me in the head, he'll have to move the tray. If Lescaux decided on the heart shot, he'd have to touch her. *He won't. He can't.* She held her breath as he stepped closer to the wall to push away the tray and take the head shot. *Lucien would use a stick to move the tray. He wouldn't risk getting too close.* But Lescaux wasn't Lucien.

Just as Jani felt the pressure of the tray lessen, she pushed up and twisted around, swinging the ax-hammer in an upward arc. The blade end caught Lescaux in the jaw—blood sprayed as he stumbled back.

Jani struggled to her feet. Her ribs squeezed her left side with every breath. Her left leg shuddered, and she stumbled. She tried to raise her left arm for balance, but it seemed glued to her side.

Lescaux raised his shooter once more. Jani thought he smiled, at first, until she saw that her blow had hacked and torn his lower lip and chin so that the skin hung down, revealing his bottom teeth. His jaw looked skewed. Blood spattered his crooked face and soaked the front of his dinner jacket. He stood in front of the railing, placed his free hand on it to steady himself, and sighted.

Jani slipped the strap from her wrist and hurled the ax-hammer. It hit Lescaux high in the chest—his shooter arm jerked up, the momentum curving him backward. He cried out as he tumbled over the railing.

Jani sagged to one knee, then down on her side. The room tilted, spun, darkened around the edges. She could see the ax-hammer from where she lay. It had fallen near the edge of the scaffold, the handle and part of the head coated with Lescaux's blood. What bare metal remained reflected the light from a safety illumin. The shine drew Jani's tunneling stare, fading and flaring as a tremor shook her body and her eyes closed.

She heard. Hearing was the hardiest sense, and she heard. The squeak and flex of the ladder. Footsteps approaching, the scaffold floor shuddering beneath their weight. She tried to get up, to move away. It was Lescaux. Had to be. He had survived the fall and come to kill her—come to make sure—

She opened her eyes when she felt the hands. Gold-skinned and long-fingered, they ran along her body from her head down, probing shooter-burned tissue and dislocated joints and cracked bone with the sure touch of a medic.

Then the probing ceased. The hands disappeared from Jani's view, then returned to pick up the ax-hammer. The last thing she saw before she blacked out were the hands bundling the weapon in a length of patterned brown cloth.

"Look at the light."

Jani raised her grudging gaze. "Didn't we just go through this a couple of days ago?"

Calvin Montoya glared at her over the top of the lightbox. "Humor me."

Jani stared into the blackness that hid the rest of Montoya's body from view. She gripped the edge of the bed as the first red lights flickered, then weaved from side to side as the progression continued.

"Oh, you're tailing quite nicely on your own. No takedown for you." Montoya shut down the lightbox and rolled it to the far side of the examining room. "Although I really wish you would reconsider this takedown-avoidance method of yours. Being attacked twice in three days is a bit much, don't you think?" He wore casual trousers and a pullover instead of eveningwear. A quiet night at home with his girlfriend was all Jani had disrupted this time.

Jani stared down at her stockinged feet, flexing her toes and knocking her heels together. The orderly who had prepped her had confiscated her blood-spattered boots, but had let her keep her socks. He had also made her exchange her bloodstained coverall for a set of bright purple Neoclona work clothes. She looked like a walking bruise, and judging from the stabs and aches that radiated up and down her left side, she'd feel like one in a few hours. *But at least I can sit upright and bitch about the fact.* She glanced up at Montoya, who downloaded data from the lightbox into his recording board. "How's—Roni McGaw?"

Montoya didn't look up. "I don't know."

"So why don't you find out?"

"Because *you* are my concern right now. After I take care of you, I will visit Neuro and find out what I can about Ms. McGaw." Montoya looked up and sighed. "All right?"

Before Jani could respond that, no, it really wasn't all right, the door swept aside and Val blew in like a lake breeze. He wore dark blue trousers and a green and blue patterned sweater and looked like he had been somewhere spreading charm. "'Lo." He sidestepped over to Montoya and peeked over his shoulder at Jani's chart. "How is she?"

Jani waved at him. "She's sitting right here and can answer for herself, thanks."

Val stuck out his tongue at her, then turned back to Montoya. "So?"

"She brained herself on the edge of that tool trolley. Scan's negative. I closed the gash with glue before anything important leaked out. I'd label that the least of her injuries." Montoya answered Jani's glower with one of his own. "Fractured clavicle—I injected bone sealer and reseated the arm. Minor burns in the same area caused by the shooter pulse. First degree—I applied that new salve the Pharma group developed, and it took the reddening and pain right out. Three cracked ribs, all on the left side. I taped them. We can leave the rest to augie. Had to refill the carrier in her left leg and close up forty-seven assorted hacks and gashes—according to Niall Pierce, she fell on a pile of building fasteners after she was shot."

Jani perked up. "Niall's here?"

"Oh yes." Montoya gazed up at the ceiling, begging respite. "They're lined up waiting to see you. Mainline colonels and attorneys and parents—"

"My folks are here!" Jani slid off the scanbed, but as soon as she tried to stand, the room tilted and wobbled. She grabbed the edge of the bed to keep from falling, swallowing hard as the acid bubbled up her throat.

"Yes! Now sit down before you fall down!" Montoya pushed Jani's chart into Val's hands and hurried to her side. "They're in the VIP suite in the penthouse, receiving the royal treatment." He helped her climb atop the scanbed and held her while she steadied. Only when he felt sure that she wouldn't tumble to the floor did he return to his chart entries.

"We had to flee to the North Bay compound after . . . you know." Val shuffled guiltily to her bedside. "But as soon as we got the call that you had been brought in, we piled into skimmers and made the trek back down, breaking all existing speed limits along the way." He eyed Jani sharply. "We made the assumption that the danger is probably passed at this point."

Jani shrugged, and regretted it immediately. "Probably."

"Good, because I don't think those poor people can take much more of this." Val leaned against the bed. The vivacity vanished—he yawned and rubbed his eyes. "Hell, *I* can't take much more of this." He boosted upright. "We stopped by your flat on the way in, just to check things. Steve and Angevin were there, going not-so-quietly mad. Lively pair, those two." His bleary gaze sharpened. "They told me you threw out Lucien."

Jani examined her hands. An abrasion encircled her right wrist, courtesy of the ax-hammer strap. "I did, but I think I made a mistake."

Val shook his head. "No, you didn't. Not even close."

Jani watched him grow still and dull. "Can you tell me how Roni McGaw is?"

Val looked back at Montoya, who nodded. By the time he turned back to Jani, his shiny air had tarnished completely. "She was dying when the ambulance brought her in. We had to install a DeVries shunt to halt the brain damage caused by the prolonged reduction in blood flow. Right now she's in induced coma while we try to fix what broke. We won't know how she is until we drain the regen solutions and test functional levels."

Val's every word struck Jani, one blow after another. It never changed—she never changed. She was slow. Stupid. She didn't think. Delays, and more delays. Her past dictating her future, defining it, predicting it. Yolan died because of her slowness. Borgi. The other Rovers. And all she could do to honor their memories was steal them a place on someone else's monument. "I should have gone in there as soon as I felt something was wrong, but I waited too long. *Again.* I wait—"

Val's face flushed. "You stepped in front of a shooter to get her here. If that shot had been a little lower and to the left, you'd be lying in the room next to her and that's only if you'd been damned lucky. So I don't want to hear about how this is all your bloody fault, do you understand!"

Jani looked away from Val and stared at the blank wall until her eyes stopped swimming. "Can I see her?"

Val and Montoya shook their heads and answered as one. "No, your parents want to see you—Niall—calls from Registry—Dolly—John—Loiaza has some questions—"

Jani raised her hand, and the babble ceased. "I want to see her."

Montoya wouldn't let Jani attempt the long walk to the Neuro wing on her own, so Val volunteered to play skimchair navigator. He pushed her slowly, and made a few wrong turns along the way. Jani knew he wanted to tire her out in the hope that she'd change her mind and postpone her visit. One would think that after all they'd been through together, he'd have known better.

As they turned down Neuro's hushed main corridor, Jani eyed the nurses' stations and looked into every open door. "Who's guarding her?"

"Ours." Val looked cowed as Jani twisted around to stare at him. "They've been briefed by Niall. You don't need to worry about them."

They pulled up in front of a door bracketed by a man and woman wearing street clothes and packed holsters. Jani took a deep breath, then nodded to Val. He edged the skimchair forward, and the door swept aside.

The room was lit with soft background illumination. Silent, but for the soft murmurs of the assorted instruments that surrounded the bed.

Roni McGaw didn't take up much space. Her bedclothes barely seemed to rise above the level of the mattress—Jani had to squint in the half-light to assure herself that a person really lay there.

Then she looked more carefully, and her breath caught. Roni looked mummy-like, her head swaddled in a white wrap that shielded her eyes and left only her nose and mouth visible. Her head and upper body lay slightly elevated on a wedge-shaped pillow. Her hands rested on her stomach. Tubes everywhere—nasogastric, catheter, IV. The apparatus for the DeVries shunt filled the wall behind the bed like a vast and complex headboard, a multicolored array of blinking indicators and scrolling displays.

"That was you last summer." Val pushed Jani close to the bed. "Eamon installed some improvements when he visited last month, as well. The shunt inlet and outlet are fixed inside the pillow assembly. Roni's head is immobilized within a light restraint cage that's attached to the pillow. The last thing we want is for any of that plumbing to shift."

Jani reached up and touched the back of her neck, just above the hairline. She could barely feel the thread-fine scars that marked the sites of her own shunt jacks. "Did you shave her head, too?"

"Yes. We have no choice, what with all the relays and monitors we attach. But hey, your hair grew back. Hers will, too." He grasped one of Jani's curls and gave it a tug. "I'm going to check in with John, give your folks an update. I'll stop back in, say, fifteen minutes?"

Jani nodded. She felt Val's hand on her good shoulder, the increase in pressure as he squeezed. Then it was gone. She heard the muffled tread of his shoes on the lyno, the hush and whisper of the door.

She sat, silent. She'd never possessed the gift for knowing the right words, but what could one say at a time like this? *I'm sorry I missed the cues . . . I'm sorry I lost sight of your back.* How many people over the years did she have reason to say that to? Yolan. Betha. Sasha. You'd think the words would come easily to her—she'd needed them often enough.

"I had the same thing you've got now." Jani paused to clear her throat. "A DeVries shunt. Eamon DeVries is a creep of the first press, but he designed a good shunt." She fingered the crease of her grape-colored trousers, feeling like an inkblot amid the light-colored surroundings. "You'll have a headache after they bring you out of coma. It lasts for a few days—you think your brain is going to burst out your ears every time you move your head. But you get over it." She looked to the wall opposite. No window, not even a nature holograph. It irked her that they would assume Roni wouldn't need any diversions. Jani recalled many details of her own hospital room, things she confirmed after she regained consciousness. She made a mental note to discuss the matter with John.

"Did it catch you by surprise when you realized Lescaux had spearheaded the letter? It did me; I never thought he had it in him. And he didn't, really, he only wished he did. That made him doubly dangerous." She recalled the Lescaux she had seen at the idomeni embassy, his barely suppressed rage when he caught Anais gazing longingly at Lucien. The jealousy had shown itself then—she should have known it would matter. "I'm sorry. I should have realized." She switched her attention from the still figure in the bed to the blinking illumins above, on the alert for any signs of trouble.

"After you get out of this. . . ." She dug a thumbnail into the arm of her chair and waited for her throat to loosen. "If you're going to continue in this line of work, you need to learn a few rules. Laws of survival. They're simple, but they're not always intuitive. One, remember that trust is earned, not bestowed. Two, travel light and travel armed. Three, don't write anything down—sheer hell telling a dexxie something like that, I know, but it's better for you in the long run. We wouldn't have had a thing on Lescaux if that idiot in Helier hadn't written down the details of that meeting. Up until then, all signs pointed to Lucien." Thoughts of Lucien intruded, and she quieted until they went away.

"Back to the commandments. Use public whenever possible. That applies to comports and transportation. Lescaux must have had a snoop on your office line—that's how he knew you were meeting me somewhere tonight. All he had to do was get into his skimmer and follow you. If you'd stuck to the L's and people-movers, you and I could be sitting right now in my flat setting up our case against him and he'd be stuck on a train to Minneapolis wondering what the hell happened." She smiled at the thought, but it faded quickly.

"I'm sorry I didn't get to you sooner. But Nema came out of nowhere and Cèel will execute him if he gets any sort of chance. I had to make sure he got back to the embassy. Then Dathim wouldn't leave me alone." She thought of long-fingered gold hands evaluating her wounds, reclaiming the ax-hammer, and wondered if she had hallucinated them. "But then, if he hadn't given me the ax-hammer, I wouldn't be sitting here jabbering at you now." She relaxed, a little, as the truth of the statement settled over her. "That chock wouldn't have had the same effect, no matter how hard I threw it. And I could only have thrown it once. I would have saved so much time if I had a shooter. This bioemotional restriction is a pain in the ass. They'll probably pin one on you, too, until you show them to their satisfaction that you haven't gone over the side." She slumped in her chair. Her entire body ached.

"You're too nice for this sort of work. You need to be a bit of the bastard. Like Niall. Like me. I'm not saying that you have to . . . stop caring—do that, and you become a monster. I think we both know a few names we could plug into that category." She thought of Lucien again, and paused for a time before speaking. "But caring too much freezes you, hangs you with targets that everyone one else can see. It makes you vulnerable, and you can't afford that. Not in this city. It's a delicate balance. Difficult to achieve. I can't quite seem to get the hang of it myself." Her voice dropped in volume, dwindled to nothing. She felt useless and stupid talking to the air.

"Get well, Roni, please." She fell silent, her eyes on the door, and listened to the soft clicks and hisses of the shunt pumps and the faint hum of the monitors.

CHAPTER 31

"And the worry, Janila. When we could not speak with you. When Dr. Parini told us we had to flee Chicago, but that we could not take you with us." Jamira Kilian broke off a piece of breakfast cake and dipped it in her side dish of maple syrup. "Then we get the call that you had been in a fight, that you had been hurt." She grimaced at the sodden tidbit and set it down on her plate. "Your Dr. Shroud drove us back. The speed! I wondered if we would make it back here alive."

Jani stirred the dregs of her soup. Chickpeas and rice in a tomato sauce spicy enough to make *her* eyes water—not her usual morning fare, but someone must have thought she needed an olfactory kick in the pants. "He's not *my* Dr. Shroud, Maman."

"Hmph." Declan Kilian eyed her over the rim of his coffee cup. "Remember that white tiger they kept at the park preserve when you were little? The one that spent all his time pacing the grounds and standing on the highest points, watching everyone? The one where you felt better knowing that a very wide moat separated the two of you? Shroud reminded me of him. I would not like to be the person who makes him angry."

Jani pushed her bowl aside, then tried to appreciate the view as she avoided her parents' probing looks. They sat in the dining room of the Neoclona VIP suite, seventy-five stories above Chicago. Tinted windows formed the exterior walls, allowing well-filtered views of the sunrise over Lake Michigan, the Commerce Ministry compound, and the skyscraper jungle of the deepest downtown. *Tiger John's stalking grounds.* She looked at her mother. "I thought you didn't like him."

"I do not. Not really. He did not think things through where you were concerned. Now he spends all his time trying to play catch-up, and it is you who pay the price." Jamira held out her hand, her eyes shining. "*Ma petite fille,* it was not you that I yelled at that night."

Jani brushed her fingers with her own. "I know, Maman."

Jamira chuffed and fussed with the napkin on her lap. "No, you don't know. But you won't talk about it, either, so we are left where we were." She exhaled with a frustrated gust. "I want you to be happy, and healthy, and live without pain. Ridiculous things for a mother to ask for her child, I know." She sat back, a cup of jasmine tea cradled in her hands. "Two things I can say in Dr. Shroud's favor. He never left us alone, even when we wanted him to. He made sure we were safe. And he worried about you so—I could tell." She inhaled the fragrant steam that rose from her cup. "And as your father said, better a man like him as a friend than as an enemy. In this day, the way things are, it is good to have friends."

Jani pushed back her chair and walked to the window. The grandness of the dining room made her restless. So had the plush gold and white bedroom where she had spent what little had remained of the night, and the eerie way that the staff seemed to know what she wanted before she asked for it. *I was not born to the purple, royalty's or Neoclona's.* She longed for her flat, her piled desk. Her own bedroom. *I must be feeling better.* She could already raise her left arm level with her shoulder, and scarcely felt any twinges in her ribs when she breathed. *All the little factories must be running full-tilt.*

"What are we doing today, Janila?" Her mother had adjourned to a couch by the lake-facing window, tea and the day's *Tribune-Times* in hand. "Dr. Parini made lists for me of things to do in Chicago—sheets and sheets. Parks and museums and shops. If I stay here until I am one hundred, I will not be able to do all he suggested."

Declan joined his wife, plucking pages from the newssheet after she finished perusing them. "The Commerce Ministry is giving a party next week in honor of the Commonwealth Cup Final Four. Dr. Shroud said that we are all invited." His eyes lit in anticipation. "All of the United will be there. Desjarlais, even. And Heinrich and Zaentz, from Gruppo."

Jani perched on the far end of the couch. Replace the posh surroundings with a crowded eating area that vied for space with the overflow from her father's workroom and her mother's collection of glass figurines, and it was a replay of her childhood mornings—breakfast, newssheets, plans for the day.

I have plans for the day. The Elyan Haárin had arrived with the dawn, and she had already received a formal request from Cal Burkett to attend the afternoon's conclave. After that, she received an identical invitation from the Commerce Ministry. Then one from the Treasury Ministry. No word from Nema, however. Not that she expected Shai to allow him to contact her.

Jani picked at her sleeves. She still wore the purple outfit the orderly had scrounged for her the night before. John had, of course, offered her access to every shop in Chicago, but she planned to use the need to change clothes as an excuse to return to her flat. She had not yet decided whether to attend the conclave. Even thinking about the need to think about it made her nervous. But when she made the decision, it would be on her own turf, and in her own good time. And in the meantime, she had time. *Free* time, the first she'd had in weeks.

"Hand me the Government page, please." She took the newssheet section from her father, then walked back to the table to get another cup of coffee.

Jani left her parents a few hours later with the pledge to return that night. She departed Neoclona with every intention of making the northward trek via her usual system of L's and people-movers. It didn't disappoint her, however, to find Niall waiting for her in the building entry circle, wearing dress blue-greys and a smug expression.

"I'm your new best friend, by special request of General Burkett." He led her to a dark blue Service-issue two-door, popped the gullwing for her, and shut her in, his eyes on the teeming morning traffic.

Unlike the sleek Lucien, Niall *looked* like a walking sidearm. Jani waited for him to close himself in and merge into traffic before speaking. He had a job to do, and her new job was to let him do it. "Who else is out there?" she asked, after a slight easing in Niall's level of alert let her know it was OK to talk.

"Five vehicles behind, five ahead, and checkpoints all along the way." Niall grinned. "Nowhere near the level of the PM. More a Deputy Minister."

"You trying to tell me my days of hopping the L are over?"

"You got it." He reached into his tunic and pulled out his nicstick case. "Burkett wants you to have it. Burkett called in all kinds of markers to get it. Pledged a few, too, from what I heard. That attack last night sure lit a fire under his brass." As if to illustrate his point, Niall shook out a 'stick and bit the bulb end. The tip flared orange; the smoke streamed.

Jani recalled Derringer's last message, his sleep-starved face. "When did you talk to Burkett?"

Niall nodded through the haze. "At about 0300. He looked pissed as hell. Not that he doesn't always look like that, but this held a special edge."

"You talk to him in person?"

"Yeah."

"Derringer with him?"

"Nah. Didn't see him."

Jani smiled. *Looks like your career plans hit a snag, Eugene.* She wondered how long it would be before he turned up again at the embassy, if ever.

Then the thought occurred that Derringer could face something more drastic than mere reassignment. *Lie down with dogs, get up with fleas.* That didn't bother her, either. She settled back in her seat and watched the city float past. "Montoya mentioned that you had been at the hospital. I looked for you later, but I couldn't find you."

"I rode point for your ambulance. Then I spent the rest of the night running from pillar to post trying to find out what the hell happened." Niall looked at her. "Care to compare notes?"

"Who else was at the scene?"

"No, none of this answering questions with questions. I've watched you tie other people in knots doing that, and I'm not going to let you do it with me." Niall blew smoke as he turned onto Armour Place a little more sharply than necessary. "I was on the way back from North Bay when I got your message."

Jani smiled at him. "You helped move my folks. Thanks."

"You're welcome and don't change the subject." Niall slowed to a stop in front of her building. "I wonder how long it's going to take these people to realize that you're the reason their nice, quiet neighborhood has hosted three attempted murders and one accidental death in the last three days."

"Lescaux wasn't an accident."

"Well, rumor has it." Niall tossed another, colder grin at her as he waved the doorman away and popped his own door. "I say we let rumor keep it."

Steve and Angevin reacted predictably to Jani's return, giving loud and persistent voice to the fact that while they were thrilled that she lived, they'd kill her themselves if she ever put them through "hell like this" again.

"Calls. Let's talk about calls." Angevin fell onto the couch next to Jani, recording board in hand. "*Trib-Times,* chief Cabinet correspondent. PM's office. Commerce office. Treasury. AgMin. Hodge, begging our pardon but asking if you were all right."

Jani looked across the room at Steve, who sat next to Niall on the window seat and smoked. "What did you tell him?"

"We lied. Said you were fine. Like we knew what the fook were goin' on." Steve punctuated his displeasure with a smoke ring.

"General Burkett," Angevin continued the litany of calls. "Frances Hals. Aunt Dolly."

Jani waggled her eyebrows. "*Aunt* Dolly?"

"Swank," Steve muttered.

"And the list repeats." Angevin dropped the recording board on the seat and slumped dramatically. "There are a lot of deputy ministers mixed in here too, all asking whether you'll be attending the conclave at the embassy this afternoon."

"Can't be bothered with the names of mere deputies—just too fookin' many to count." Steve walked to the couch, planting himself in front of Jani. "Gel, I'm enraptured that you're all right, but I can't live like this. It's aging me prematurely."

Jani turned to Angevin. "I'm sorry. Really."

Angevin shrugged. "We lived. Kept busy. Your projects are caught up—I've learned a whole lot about many subjects of which I knew nothing two days ago." She yawned. "And a few of your clients asked that their stuff be put on hold until after the conclave. That saved us some grief." She blinked. Yawned again. Her eyes watered. "So, are you going to the conclave?"

Jani looked down at her clothes. The brilliant purple held a magenta cast in the morning light. She hated magenta.

"I need to get out of these clothes. I'll be back." She had darted into her room and locked the door behind her before anyone had a chance to stop her.

She perched on the windowsill overlooking the alley and watched the occasional lunchtime trespassers cut through on their way back to work. She wanted to stop them, ask them questions. About their lives. Their thoughts.

Did anyone ever hate you enough to try to kill you? Did anyone ever think you dangerous enough to kill? Did you wonder how the hell you got in that position in the first place? Was it something you did, or was it simply the fact that you were?

She tried to transmit her questions to a young woman who scurried down the alley, a sheaf of papers flapping in her hand.

Have you ever killed anyone? Did you ever put a friend in the hospital because of a mistake you made? Did a friend ever die because of a mistake you made?

She pulled her right knee up to her chin. It didn't hurt much now, and last night she could barely walk on it.

If someone asked you to be the point man for a new world order, would you say yes? If you knew saying yes would separate you from work you enjoyed, people you loved, would you agree?

If you knew that saying yes meant never being able to call yourself human again, would you still think it a good idea?

She rolled her left shoulder, and felt the mildest of twinges. *Four hours to go.* She shifted position so she couldn't see the clock atop the armoire.

She tried to ignore the knock at her door. Neither Steve nor Angevin were the most patient of souls—they'd give up and leave, eventually.

But this knock went on, and on, and on.

"Wait a minute!" Jani struggled to her feet, shaking the life back into her right leg as she limped to the door and deactivated the lock. "I just wanted a little bit of downtime—is that too much to ask—?" Her complaint fizzled when she found Niall standing in the hall, hand clenched in the mail fist salute of someone who would knock as long as he had to.

"We the hapless bystanders wondered if you planned to come out sometime this year." He lowered his arm and took a step back, his manner suddenly tentative.

Jani stepped aside. When Niall still held back, she grabbed his sleeve and pulled him into her room. "This isn't the sanctum sanctorum—come on in."

"I didn't say it was." He hurried toward the window, shooting his cuffs along the way. "You're going to need to move to a higher floor—this won't do."

"It's cheap."

"And for good reason." Niall fiddled with the privacy setting on the windowside touchpad; the glass darkened to black. "I'll talk to the building manager—what's his name—Hodge—and find out what else is available. If I don't like anything here, be prepared to move." He turned to her, the hard-edged Spec Service officer once more. "Is this something I should plan to do this afternoon, or will you need me to drive you someplace?"

"Is this your way of asking me if I'm going to the conclave?" Jani crossed one foot over the other and lowered to the floor. "I've still got two hours to make up my mind."

"One, if you take preliminaries into account." Niall wandered over and sat on the floor across from her. Like John, he didn't relax well—he braced straight-backed against the bedframe, and even though he tugged at his tunic's banded collar, he made no move to loosen it. "So?"

Jani had no trouble defining the question contained in that single word. "I'm not political. I'm not the least bit skilled in that area."

Niall shrugged. "So much the better. Politicians got us into this mess in the first place."

"No. Greed got us into this mess. For money, power, career advancement. Simple, dull, boring greed." Jani tried to pull both knees to her chest, but her cracked ribs objected, forcing her to sit with her left leg straight in front of her. "And say what you will, but we are going to need politically skilled people to get us out of this mess. The ability to deal is necessary. To compromise. To not take everything personally. I don't possess that mind-set, and it's not something I can learn. I could butcher these negotiations and set back human-idomeni relations twenty years."

Niall rested his head against the footboard. His scar skewed his quizzical frown into a scowl. "What do you think should happen?"

Jani groaned. Her head had started to ache. "I think we should purchase the microbial filter from the Elyan Haárin until we can build a new Karistos treatment plant. We need to set up a timetable for the construction, and stick to it so that the unaligned Elyan merchants see that we mean it when we say that we won't tolerate any bullshit. Any businesses affiliated with *L'araignée* shouldn't be allowed to bid for the job, but I doubt that will happen. So, if any of them win, they'll need to be watched."

Niall nodded. "Accounts to be paid on a milestone basis. Have their work inspected every step of the way." He paused. His hand went to his tunic collar, as though it felt tighter.

Jani grinned humorlessly at his discomfort. "Yep. They'll scream, and the Elyan government will scream, and the Elyan Haárin will scream. We're probably going to have to drag the Service in to act as a silent threat, so someone from Intelligence will scream that we're blowing their deals with *L'araignée*. It will be a mess however it's handled, but the important thing is that we're left with a working water treatment plant. Once the Elyans have one thing that works, they're going to want more things that work. If they know they'll have the government watching their back as they obtain those things, they can begin to rebuild their broken system. Something like *L'araignée* needs to be excised one tendril at a time. You do that by making their method of doing business uneconomical, and vigilance backed by a strong Service threat equals uneconomical. That's my solution, and if you think it will be as easy as I make it sound, your collar really is too tight."

Niall pulled his hand away from his neck, his face reddening. "I think what you've said sounds quite reasonable."

"Once I proposed it in open session, I'd give it five minutes before Ulanova's team tears it to shreds." Jani straightened her right leg and lay back. Everything hurt now—her shoulder, her ribs, her back. "Does what I want to do have any bearing on this? Does the fact that I do not want to spend the rest of my life grappling with the Anais Ulanovas of the Commonwealth come into play at all?"

"How often does what you want have anything to do with anything?" Niall regarded her with an odd admixture of impatience and kindness. "You and I came up from the same place. A hardscrabble colony youth leaves wounds that never heal." His honey eyes darkened. "One thing you learn is that what you *want* to do doesn't always matter. It's what you *can* do. What you have to do. What you must do."

"Duty?" Jani cocked an eyebrow. "I was never the best soldier in the Service, Niall, or didn't you notice?"

"Obedience isn't your strong suit, no." Niall's lip twitched, but the smile soon faded. "But I will say without reservation that you're one of the most dutiful people I've ever known." He fixed his gaze on the opposite wall. "I'd follow you into hell, because I know you'd bring me out, or stay behind and burn with me. What you'd never do is leave me behind to burn by myself. That's not a bad quality for a future Chief Propitiator to have, I should think." He boosted to his feet. "I can't tell you what to do. I wouldn't try—not with a decision like this. But I've never seen you give less than everything, no matter who you angered, and regardless of the cost to you. That has to count for something, even in this lousy city." He nodded sharply to her, his manner turned formal, distant, as though he felt he'd revealed too much and needed to shut down fast. "I'll be in the other room."

Jani listened to the door close, the fading echo of Niall's footsteps. "Dutiful." She stared at the ceiling. "I don't want to be dutiful. I want to be left alone." The armoire clock chimed the half-hour. "They'd eat me alive, Niall. I'm not political. I'm . . . what I am." Derringer's "meddling bitch." Frances's "lone operator."

She sat up by rolling onto her right side and pushing herself to her knees. Then she went to her closet and hunted down the lightest-color suit she owned, a tan tunic and trouser combination. She tossed it on the bed, then retired to the bathroom to shower. Her left side had indeed turned into a relief map of bruises and gashes. She stood sideways in the water stream, and counted down the minutes.

Dutiful. The suit fit her, even though she had bought it months before. Shoes had become as big a problem as clothes, since her feet had grown longer and narrower, but she managed to uncover a pair of brown boots that didn't feel too tight.

She studied herself in the mirror as she arranged her hair. The suit, spare and utilitarian, looked like a uniform of sorts. It lacked medals and badges because she hadn't yet earned any in this particular war, and it lacked rank designators because thus far, she didn't need any. *I belong to an army of one.* She laughed at her own pomposity; the sound died as she continued to stare in the mirror, and thought of sheared heads and horsetails, and gold hands closing around the handle of an ax-hammer.

Not alone. Not really. Not anymore. Others followed her, which meant she needed to lead.

She peeled off the eyefilms one at a time, then returned to the bathroom to wash them down the sink. As she walked back into the bedroom, she watched herself in the mirror to observe the effect.

Her eyes caught the light in strange ways, shades of green from forest to lightest sea. *They're not . . . beautiful.* But they defined her somehow, as her filmed eyes never did. Not human anymore, but not idomeni, either. *In-between.* She tried to see what Lucien saw, even though she knew that she never would. *Not beautiful.* But what she was, now. Point man.

She headed for the door, then stopped and detoured to her closet. Given the state of her ribs, stretching proved impossible—she had to drag the clothes cleaner into the space to serve as a stepstool so she could reach the back of the shelf.

She slid on the redstone ring, then wrapped the soulcloth round her wrist. The single knot stayed tied and the ends remained tucked. She took that as a favorable omen.

The armoire clock chimed the hour as Jani walked out into the main room. Steve and Niall stood by the window smoking and talking while Angevin sat on the couch and leafed through a magazine.

Angevin saw her first—she tossed the magazine aside and bounded to her feet. "Hey, there she—!" She stopped. Stared. Squinted. Then she emitted a tiny yelp and slapped her hand over her mouth.

Steve and Niall had fallen silent. Steve took one step closer, then another. "Bloody hell, Jan." He stuck his half-spent 'stick in his mouth, and worked it from side to side.

Niall extinguished his own 'stick and brushed off his tunic.

Then he stepped around Steve and walked to Jani's side. "Are you sure?"

Jani tried to smile, then shook her head. "No. But I doubt if I ever will be." She walked to the desk and gathered up her duffel. "Let's go."

CHAPTER 32

The ride down to the lobby proceeded without incident, if only because they didn't encounter anyone. The traverse of the lobby itself drew no notice until Hodge negotiated an intercept route from the front desk, meeting them just before they reached the entry.

"Mistress Kilian, I'm so glad to find—" Trained in the art of ignoring Family foibles, he cropped his start before it turned into a stare and barely missed a beat. "—that you are all right." He took a step closer, and dropped his voice. "I'm so sorry about that young lady. So lucky that you found her before that awful young man—" His lips pressed in a thin white line as he dealt with yet another blow to his gentle neighborhood. "Well. As I said. So glad. Mistress. Sir." He nodded, then returned to the refuge of his desk.

"Mistress? What year is this, anyway?" Niall waved off the doorman who stood beside the skimmer they had arrived in. At the same time, another sedan, a dark green four-door, lumbered curbside. The gullwing popped up and Lieutenant Pullman emerged, wearing dress blue-greys and an anxious smile.

"Check that one over"—Niall pointed to the dark blue two-door—"then rotate it out."

"Sir." Pullman saluted, then turned to Jani. "Ma'am, I hope"—his eyes widened, but he clamped down as quickly as Hodge—"hope that you and your folks are OK."

"Yes, we are." Jani lifted her chin and smiled broadly. The idea of an idomeni teeth-baring crossed her mind, but she liked Pull. Better to save that surprise for someone she didn't. "Thanks."

"My job. Ma'am." Pullman led her around to the passenger side and closed her in.

"A different skimmer for every trip?" Jani watched Pullman recede in her side mirror. "What did you do, requisition the entire Sheridan vehicle pool?"

Niall shrugged. "Just standard precautions."

"You're enjoying this, aren't you?"

"Frankly? No." He expression sombered. "The courtly Mr. Hodge isn't the only one disgusted by the actions of his fellow man."

"He seemed to have a good idea of what happened. What are they saying? I checked the *Trib-Times* from cover to cover. Couldn't find a thing."

"I hit the garage just as the clean-up was winding down. Family security everywhere, tidying up for the ComPol. The official story is that you stumbled upon Lescaux attacking Roni, and were injured trying to intervene. Lescaux fell to his death trying to get away." Niall steered onto the Boul access road that skirted the idomeni property. "I'm guessing that's close enough to what actually happened to pass ComPol muster?"

"I haven't talked to them yet. With Joaquin Loiaza around, I may never."

"I met him once, you know. He was van Reuter's attorney. Sold him out but good."

"Niall, that doesn't make me feel better."

"Oh, you've got nothing to worry about. You're the sort of client he likes—on your way *up* the food chain." Niall slowed through the first unstaffed idomeni checkpoint. "So, feel any different?"

Jani's stomach clenched as they passed beneath the silvery arch. "Except for assorted hospital stays, this is the longest I've ever gone without filming since Rauta Shèràa." She widened her eyes, closed them, then opened them. "I got used to them always feeling a little tight, and now that feeling's gone." She looked out her window and watched the landscape drift past. Blue-tinged grasses. Stunted yellow and green-leafed shrubs. "It's strange."

Niall slowed the skimmer. "If you want to go back—"

"No." Jani held an image in her mind now, of a shorn head and a look of quiet acceptance. *It occurred to me that when the gods informed me of the future, they did not also guarantee my presence in it.* "I owe someone this."

"What?" Niall looked alarmed. "Are you sure you don't—"

"I'm sure." Jani watched the first of the staffed checkpoints appeared in the distance. "I'm sure."

* * *

Vehicles filled the stone-paved courtyard. Jani recognized Callum Burkett's steel blue triple-length, along with the color-coded entries belonging to the various Ministries: green for Commerce, gold for Treasury, black for Interior. She recognized Anais Ulanova's triple-length, as well, its burgundy color damped by a spray-on filter to the color of coffee beans.

Niall steered them to an opening beside Burkett's vehicle, lowered the power to standby, and waited. "You've gone quiet," he said after a time.

Jani leaned back her head so she could check her eyes in the side mirror. "Be honest—what do I look like?"

Niall fingered the steering wheel. His mien altered from professional vigilance to the sort of introspection he saved for his off-hours. "I met a lady in the meads, full beautiful, a faery's child. Her hair was long, her foot was light, and her eyes were wild." He smiled softly. "Keats. *La belle dame sans merci.*"

"The beautiful woman without mercy." Kind of Niall to say. Not that Jani believed it. She tugged at one of her curls. "Not long. Rather short, in fact."

"Ah, well. So much for that." Niall popped his gullwing and exited the skimmer.

"So my eyes look wild, huh?" Jani asked as she followed suit. "That should go over big." She hoisted her duffel to her right shoulder and watched the faces that turned toward her, bracing for the reactions. The courtyard air was still and cool. She shivered, and blamed the temperature.

"Kilian!" Callum Burkett broke away from a Minister-cluster and crossed the courtyard toward her. Dressed in desertweights, his expression grim, he resembled Derringer enough to have fathered him. "We should talk before this thing sta—" He froze in mid-stride, his front foot in the air, looking as though he'd caught himself before he stepped in something embarrassing. Then the foot lowered. So did his voice. "Is this some kind of joke?"

"Not by any means, General." Jani felt the heat flood her cheeks. "This is what I really look like." She glanced past him in time to see more heads turn in their direction.

Burkett directed his stone-grey glare at Niall. "Did you know about this, Colonel?"

"Do you mean, sir, have I noticed that Ms. Kilian's eyes look different?" Niall regarded Jani with a look of studious examination, the duck-and-dodge in full force. "Yes, sir. Rather striking, I think—"

"I mean, did you help plan—"

"No! He did not. He did, in fact, ask me several times if I wished to reconsider." Jani wedged herself between Niall and an Article 13. "My eyes. My call. I have my reasons, which will reveal themselves presently."

Burkett's face reddened. His arms hung at his sides, hands slowly clenching.

Oh, Cal, you hate surprises, I know, and you've had a couple of zingers over the past few days, haven't you? Jani made a show of scanning the crowd. "Where's Eugene? I don't see him."

Burkett's eyes narrowed. "He's . . . been reassigned."

Jani nodded. "Thank you for the security."

"You're . . . welcome. I trust you're . . . all right?"

"Yes. Thanks. You're going to take care of my bioemotional restriction, aren't you?"

A pause. "Yes."

"I know what I'm doing."

"I hope so." Burkett dropped his gaze, then tensed. "That's a soulcloth."

Jani followed the angle of his stare and pulled down the red braid, which had been half-hidden by her tunic cuff. "Yes."

Burkett started to speak. Stopped. He looked at Jani, his expression altered to hangdog uncertainty. "Well." He nodded to her, then turned on his heel and clipped toward a concerned-looking major who had emerged from one of the groups.

"Poor Cal. Every time he thinks he's got you sussed, you throw him another curve." Niall veered close. "Do you know what you're doing?"

Jani nodded. "The idomeni have an idea what I look like. So do most of the people I work with. It's . . . time."

"Well, I'll be out here with the rest of the chauffeurs if you need me." Niall tried to look encouraging, but he could only manage tense. He scanned the assorted faces one last time, then moved off to the far side of the yard.

Jani caught sight of the brown-clad diplomatic suborn emerging through the beaten bronze door, and made her way to the center of the courtyard to take her place in the rank line. As she walked, she grew conscious of an invisible barrier growing around her, formed from unease and the pressure of scrutiny. She would have expected it even if she hadn't chosen to reveal herself—word of Lescaux's death had had almost a day to percolate through the Ministries; the true story that the Family security officers had pieced together had no doubt whipped around, as well.

She heard a few gasps, followed by low muttering, as she took her place. Some stared openly, others, furtively. *Look at it this way—it could be worse.* For example, she'd yet to negotiate a Chicago city street.

Jani realized that the voices behind her had receded to nothing. She turned, and found herself looking into Anais Ulanova's red-rimmed eyes.

The woman wore black. No jewelry. She seemed oblivious to the change in Jani's appearance—the emotion in her pained brown stare originated in a deep place, slicing past the physical into Jani's own inner dwelling. For an uncounted time, no one moved. No one breathed.

Then the suborn broke the silence with her call. *"Time!"* People hurried to their places in line, jostling and muttering.

Jani turned to face front as the bronze doors swung wide, conscious with every forward step she took of the danger bearing down from behind.

They trooped the halls in single-file, like prep schoolers returning from recess. Jani looked down each bare-walled hallway they passed, through each open door, on the watch for the faces from the night before. Beyva's. Dathim's.

Nema's.

Her anxiety ramped as they entered the meeting room. Under normal conditions, Nema would have met the delegations by now, moving down the line shaking hands and commenting loudly about the weather.

But conditions aren't normal, are they? Jani wended through the banked rows toward her usual place behind Burkett, then remained standing as those of higher rank filed in.

Burkett fractured a few minor rules of protocol by dodging around assorted deputies to reach his seat ahead of them. His eyes still had that slitted look, which meant a headache had settled in for the duration. A thin film of sweat coated his brow, as well.

Jani touched her own forehead. *Still dry.* She felt quite comfortable now that she thought about it, which meant that the Vynshàrau had cranked up the temperature to the upper limit of humanish comfort.

"Someday we're going to have one of these get-togethers in my neck of the woods and so help me God, it will be payback time." Burkett tugged at his trousers as he sat.

Jani took her seat. This allowed her an unrestricted view of the back of Burkett's tan shirt, through which the first faint splotches of sweat had bloomed. "Lieutenant Ischi once suggested the Arctic test facility."

Burkett's stiff posture unwound ever so slightly. "The ATF?" A ghost of a smile had crossed his face by the time he turned to face front.

Most of the humanish had settled into their seats when the doors opened again and the lower-ranked born-sect idomeni filed in. Clothed in shades of sand and dun, hair bound in napeknots or arranged in fringed braids, earrings flashing in the chandelier light. Documents and communications suborns, charged with recording the minutes. Shai's clerks and researchers. Dominants from various departments. Religious Suborn Sànalàn, looking worn and subdued.

Then came a blue-clothed figure, like a fault in a pale stone. The lowest-ranking of the Elyan Haárin. Female, her waist-length light brown hair bound in a single braid. Then came a male, clad in orange and yellow, brown hair sheared so closely that the room light flashed off golden patches of exposed scalp. They seated themselves on the highseats at the far end of the V-shaped table and busied themselves pulling documents from the briefbags they wore slung across their shoulders.

Another shear-headed male followed. He wore black trousers and shirt, topped with a leopard-print jacket cut like a humanish male's daysuit coat. Around his neck, he had knotted a long strip of orange cloth that was without question the Elyan Haárin version of a humanish neckpiece. He carried his briefbag using a handstrap. Jani harbored the sense that he didn't want to rumple his jacket.

Burkett twisted around in his seat. "Did you know about this?"

Jani shook her head. "It doesn't surprise me, though."

"That makes one of us." He pressed his fingers to his temple as he turned back to the entry procession.

Two more Haárin had entered—a male and a female. The male wore more traditional garb, a pale green shirt and trousers topped with an overrobe the color of dried grass. He wore his brown hair in an odd hybrid style, a humanish pageboy that he had braided into a skull-defining cap. The female, the group's dominant, leaned toward a taut humanish look—grey tunic and trousers, her grey-streaked brown hair bound in a loose horsetail. She and the male took their seats on the same arm of the V, and leafed through files that had been laid out for them by their three suborns.

The room's atmosphere had altered with the successive appearance of each Haárin. Jani likened it to walking out on a sheet of ice and feeling that subtle shift beneath one's feet, hearing the faintest of squeals as the first cracks formed and radiated, then tensing for whatever came next.

After the Haárin dominant seated herself, the first wave of Vynshàrau diplomats entered. Speaker to Colonies Daès and his suborn, followed by Suborn Oligarch Shai's suborn, and finally, Shai herself. With them came the return to sartorial sanity, born-sect-style, sands and off-whites and hair arranged in fringed braids.

Anais Ulanova then entered, partnered with a young woman who had the look of the hurriedly briefed about her. Prime Minister Li Cao's chief aide, followed by the PM herself. Arrangements at table, murmured greetings in High Vynshàrau and English, the scrape of seats. Only one seat remained empty at the table now, the lowest seat at the head of the V.

Jani looked to the door, and prayed. To Ganesha. To whichever god cared to listen. She wondered if she could dash to the door before Burkett could stop her, mount a search through the winding halls of the embassy until she found whom she sought. Until she made sure Nema still lived.

Then Sànalàn rose, crossed her right arm over her chest until she grasped her shoulder, and spoke, flowing syllables uttered in a high keen. The official opening of the conclave, a prayer to Shiou to instill order, that had once been Nema's duty to perform.

Jani watched the figures seated at the table. All sat with their heads high, their eyes closed, the standard idomeni position of invocation. Not a word had they said about Nema's absence. *How humanish of them.* Yet somehow, the determined ignorance of the situation imbued the empty chair at the head of the table with a strange power, like the gap in a demiskimmer formation left to commemorate a missing pilot.

Anais broke this particular formation only once, looking out toward the crowd until she saw Jani. The cold light of triumph shimmered in her eyes as she turned back to the table.

It took some time for the sound to cut through Sànalàn's pitched voice. By the time Jani heard it, she had the impression it had gone on for some time. The muffled sounds of argument, audible through the panel. Faces turned toward the door.

Then the panel flew aside and Nema swept in, a guard at his heels. Jani didn't recognize him at first—his sheared head looked even more startling in the bright light of the room. He wore his off-white shirt and trousers, his red-cuffed overrobe and rings. His earrings glittered in garish array, fully exposed as they now were to the light. He looked traditional in every way, but for the hair.

He scanned the rows of banked seats. Jani knew he searched for her—she raised a hand to gain his attention.

"Nìa." Nema's face seemed to split as he bared his teeth. "You are most well, in spite of your battle!"

"Inshah." Jani was dimly aware of Burkett leaning forward to cradle his head in his hands. "Yes, I am well."

"I had heard you had been *shot.*"

"Grazed, inshah." Jani felt the tension suffuse the air around her. She watched Ulanova at the table, her face averted, her back straight.

"Grazed." Nema seemed to ponder the word. "My Anais's Lescaux tried to kill you."

"Tsecha." Shai's shoulders rounded in threat. "You have been removed from these proceedings. You have received warnings to not interfere. You have disobeyed."

"You removed Égri nìRau Tsecha from the proceedings, Shai. The ambassador of the Shèrá worldskein. I am not here as such." He ignored the guard who stood at his shoulder, which seemed a safe thing to do—her reluctance to lay hands upon her Chief Propitiator was evident in her posture. Instead, he directed his attention toward the Elyan Haárin dominant. "I come here as Tsecha Égri, dominant of the Earth Haárin, sect-sharer with the Elyan Haárin. It is they I ask for the privilege to sit at this table. It is their right to extend or deny."

The Elyan Haárin dominant looked at her suborn, who responded with a truncated hand flip that Jani couldn't interpret. Then they leaned close to one another and took turns speaking in each other's ears, a profoundly humanish conduct that caused Shai to round her shoulders even more and set the human half of the room abuzz.

"Ná Feyó?" Shai barked after the conversation had gone on for some time. "Do you agree to ní Tsecha's request?" Her tone implied that any agreement would be looked on with disfavor. Murmurs filled the air again when the assembled realized that she had called Tsecha by his true Haárin title, not the dressed-up "Rau" version.

Feyó lifted her head. "I do with gratitude, and truly, nìaRauta." Her English rang mellow and slightly drawled. She reminded Jani of Dolly Aryton at her most formal, and like the Hands of Might, she radiated calm. "He should sit next to me." She indicated the space between her and her suborn.

The assembled grew restive as a guard was dispatched to find a chair of the proper height. Burkett took the opportunity to lean back. "What the hell is going on, Kilian?"

Jani grinned down at him. "I think it's the new order asserting itself, General."

"*New* order? I haven't gotten used to the old one yet." He dug into the briefbag that the major had handed off to him during the seating, and pulled out a recording board to take notes.

Nema, meanwhile, walked to his seat beside Feyó, letting his hand trail along the back of his former seat at the point of the V. "I have right of suborn, ná Feyó?" he asked as he sat.

"Yes, nìR—" Feyó stopped herself. The new order had apparently caught her by surprise, as well. "Yes, ní Tsecha."

"Nìa?" Nema held out his hand toward Jani. "Come."

Jani hesitated as every face in the room, humanish and idomeni, turned toward her. Then she rose and stepped out onto the floor. Nema bared his teeth when he spotted the ring; the look sombered when he caught sight of the braided soulcloth. "So the soldier has at last reclaimed her soul." He took her hand and squeezed it in most humanish reassurance.

Jani's aches had receded in the background, supplanted by a soft roaring that filled her head. *Welcome to the way it is.* She took her place at the meeting table, in a hastily acquired highseat next to Feyó's suborn. She looked across the V, and found herself the focus of distressed examination by PM Cao and her aide. Jani bared her teeth wide, which only seemed to alarm them more.

The blue-clad Elyan Haárin clerk set a folder before Nema, then walked downtable and handed one to Jani. Their eyes met. The Haárin's widened. Then she bared her teeth. "*Hah!* Ná Kièrshia! I rejoice that Lescaux did not kill you, so I could laugh at your eyes!" Her sharp laugh cut through the room, an open acknowledgment of everything the humanish avoided, passed over, or studied with sidelong glances.

The renewed conversational buzz settled eventually. "Now." Shai lifted her right hand upward in supplication. "*Now,* we begin."

"—not possible." Ulanova's aide shook her head. "Our position has not changed from that of early this week. The Haárin components cannot be readily retrofitted to the existing plant, and the time it would take to develop the necessary adaptive technology would be better spent designing and building a new facility."

"Your Elyan governor signed a contract with us," Feyó said softly, "through his Department of Utilities suborn."

"Suborns make mistakes, Nìa Feyó." PM Cao closed her left hand into a fist and held it up to chest height, palm-side facing up.

"Their dominants cannot always be held responsible for what they do." She smiled, but the expression soon froze when she heard Shai's suborn laugh and saw the increasing curvature of Shai's shoulders.

Jani bit her lip and avoided Nema's stare, which was at that moment burning a hole in the side of her face. *I will not laugh at my Prime Minister.* Not even when she calls a made-sect Haárin by a born-sect title and compounds the offense by gesturing in High Vynshàrau that said Haárin is acting like a brat, thus insulting the Suborn Oligarch in the process.

"I am not born-sect, Your Excellency." Feyó kept her voice level and her hands folded on the table. "And I do not believe that I am acting as foolish."

Cao's golden face darkened. "I meant no offense, nì—" The apology fizzled as she tried to figure out exactly what her offense had been.

"No, I know you did not, Your Excellency." Shai uncurved her shoulders, but only a little. "Humanish never do. They make mistakes, because their suborns do not instruct them properly, and they cannot be expected to know such, because they are not responsible."

Cao's eyes widened in surprise. She looked at Nema, who gestured in commiseration, but didn't speak.

Well, you wanted him out and you got your wish. Now you get to deal with Shai, who doesn't like you and won't cut you any slack when you garble her languages. Jani flipped the file folder open, then shut it. "We cannot allow insults, unintentional or otherwise, to obscure the matter we are assembled here to discuss. Karistos city engineers have stated that the soonest the new treatment plant can be constructed and qualified for use is eighteen months from the day of groundbreaking. This means a new plant is at least two years away. The current facility is already functioning at maximum and the feeling is that service cut-offs will need to be instituted in order to meet demand for the coming summer. These same engineers have also stated, in writing, that the Haárin microbial filter array being offered for retrofit can be in-line within sixty Common days and if put in place will alleviate the need for any type of service slowdown." She looked across the table to find a bank of humanish faces regarding her as the enemy. "Will someone tell me what the problem is!"

Ulanova spoke slowly, grudgingly, as if any word spoken to Jani was one word too many. "My engineers disagree."

And so it went. Two hours passed before Cao requested a recess, which Shai reluctantly granted.

* * *

"She'll just keep pitting her experts against Elyas's experts, and she'll win because she's here and they're there." Kern Standish kicked at the ground and shoved his hands in his pockets.

"Why aren't the Elyan engineers here?" Jani leaned against a tree to straighten her back. She had left Nema to the Elyan Haárin and Burkett to his major, and had adjourned to the allowed gardens with Kern and the other Cabinet aides she had worked with over the months. She had steeled herself against their reactions to her appearance, but thus far had fielded no more than a few pointed stares. "If they'd left Elyas the same time as the Haárin, they'd have been here."

"They were supposed to be," a young woman from AgMin piped. "All hell broke loose just before they were scheduled to leave. A shuttleport nav rig blitzed out—nothing could leave the ground for four days."

Jani looked at the averted faces around her. "Sabotage?" She received a mime's chorus of shrugs and headshakes in reply. "Did anyone see where Ulanova went after we adjourned?"

"The public veranda, like usual," replied the AgMin aide.

"I'll see you inside." Jani set off in that direction.

"Gonna give her the evil eye?" One of the Treasury aides, who had been silent up until then, shot Jani a guilty glance, then turned his back.

Kern bristled. "Damn it, Maurier, you really are as stupid as you look, aren't you?"

"Well, it's one more idea than we have at the moment." Jani forced a smile and received a few in return, which under the circumstances was probably the best she could hope for.

She cut around the outer perimeter wall of the public veranda. As she neared the entry that led out to the gardens, she heard voices, Cao's and Ulanova's.

"—smoothing things with Shai will be difficult, Ani."

"We'll think of something."

"I suppose we'll have to pay attention during our language lessons from now on." Cao's voice held a bite she never let her public hear. "Do you think they'll send Tsecha home?"

There was a weighty pause before Ulanova replied. "It is to be hoped."

"Do you think so?" Cao sounded doubtful. "I would miss him. Even when he aggravated the hell out of me, I felt no malice in him."

"He only hides it better than the rest."

"Hmm." Now it was Cao's turn to ponder. "I think this revelation puts a new spin on things, no matter what you say."

"We all knew she was a medical freak, Li. Shroud's pet experiment. If she thinks this qualifies her as some sort of emissary, it is up to us to let her know that she is mistaken. We will have to wait until after Tsecha is recalled, of course—she is his favorite. But we shouldn't have to put up with either of them for much longer."

"As you say." The high-pitched click of heels on tile sounded. "I have to talk to the moderates before we reconvene, make sure they understand our point of view." The steps silenced. "Will you be all right, Ani?"

"Of course." Ulanova's voice sounded smooth and strong. "I'll meet you inside."

Jani waited until she heard the door to the embassy close. Then she stepped through the opening and onto the veranda.

Ulanova stood before a column-like fountain. She held one hand under the gentle stream and let it trickle over her fingers. She appeared thoughtful, calmer than she had in the courtyard, but still not relaxed.

Jani took another step, making sure that her shoes scraped against the tile. "Have you visited your Doc Chief in hospital, Your Excellency?"

Ulanova spun around. Water sprayed from her fingers, splashing over her tunic and arcing through the air.

"She was dying when they brought her in." Jani tried to clasp her hands behind her back, but her cracked collarbone balked and she had to settle for sliding them in her pockets. "They've jacked a DeVries shunt into her brain. It will be some time before they know if she'll recover, and to what extent." As Jani circled, Ulanova kept turning ever so slowly so that she faced her at all times.

Jani kept talking. Idomeni meeting breaks were short, and she knew she didn't have much time. "She and I found paper linking Peter to the Helier meetings during which *L'araignée* was formed. That paper also shows that he met with you during your trips to Exterior Main on Amsun. His meetings with you followed his trips to Helier. Coincidence, I'm sure you'll say."

"I have *nothing* to say to you." Ulanova's voice emerged as a hiss; she turned and walked toward the door.

"Then you brought Peter home with you," Jani called after her. "He lacked the skill and experience to act as a Cabinet-level Chief of Staff and it showed, but people laughed it off. Just a case of Anais's glands getting the better of her, silly woman. But that wasn't his purpose for being here. As *L'araignée*'s point man, he needed access to the people the Chief of Staff job would bring him in contact with. He needed to feel out the Merchants' Associations, the other Ministries. Mark the dangers with red flags and arrange their removal." Jani watched Ulanova slow to stillness as she spoke. She knew she was right, but she appreciated the reassurance. "Nema was one of the dangers—he promoted Haárin business interests, and some of our trade groups were listening. So Peter tried to set him up as a traitor to his people."

Ulanova laughed, a dry, old sound. "My poor Peter did that, did he?" She turned to face Jani, dark eyes shiny with hate. "My poor Peter, whom you killed."

"Have you visited your Doc Chief in hospital, Your Excellency? Your poor Peter stove in the back of her head." Jani pressed a hand to her aching ribs. "When he had a chance to plan, he did all right. With a few tweaks, The Nema Letter would have worked a charm. But when he had to think on his feet he fell back on the tried and true methods of his kind, and that's where he stumbled. When he realized that I had figured out that The Nema Letter was a fake, he abandoned his attempts to ruin my reputation with the white paper and just tried to have me killed outright."

"Your *reputation*!" Ulanova paused to gain control of herself—her face had reddened alarmingly. "You stole documents, you and my Documents Chief. You forged, you deceived—"

"With Registry support. We were dealing with suspected fraud, and Dolly Aryton and I do go back a ways." Jani checked her timepiece. She didn't have more than a few minutes left. "Funny thing—throughout all this, I found allies I didn't know I had. After the white paper came out, after the shooting, even after last night, the calls never stopped. Family members asked me to attend this meeting. They've asked my advice for months: how to work with the Haárin, how to deal with Cèel, how to function in a Commonwealth that's starting to blur around the edges. It's as if I've become the ad hoc Exterior Minister. They're coming to me for this information because they either know they won't get it from you, or they know they can't believe what they get. Your old friends don't trust you anymore."

The first quiet ripple broke Ulanova's still surface. A barely perceptible twitch around the eyes. "No, but they fear me, and fear is much the stronger."

"Is it?" Jani leaned against the wall as her back tightened. "If I advise them that your actions pose a threat to the Commonwealth and that they need to shut you down, they may balk at first, but in time the idea will appeal to them. They're afraid of you, yes, but they fear for themselves more. The pie is shrinking, and it will occur to them that if they cut you out, there will be more for them. So if you keep to your present course, you won't be fighting me. You'll be fighting Li and Jorge and Yvette and Gisela and all those other old friends. All I'll have to do is show them where to slip the knife. What happened to Evan van Reuter could happen to you. Death by gutted home and confiscated fortune and no one answering your calls. And what will *L'araignée* do when they realize you're no longer the power they thought you were?"

The door leading into the embassy flung open. A diplomatic suborn stuck out his head, called *"Time,"* and slipped back inside, leaving Ulanova standing with her hand to her throat.

"It won't be simple, slipping out of the arrangements you've made. This water treatment plant fiasco, for example—awarding the short-term contract to the Elyan Haárin will cause you problems. You may have to up your security—I know someone who can advise you in that regard." Jani walked to the veranda's garden exit, then paused and turned back. "I'd suggest mending fences with Nema, too. If he takes his place as full Haárin, the colonial Haárin will look to him for guidance. If he broaches the subject of an Haárin enclave, I'd listen to him." She looked at her right hand—her ring flashed in the sunlight. "You might also let Dathim Naré follow through on that tile project at your Annex."

Anais's face flared anew. "That—he *stole* from my office!"

"Did he?" Jani stared at Anais until the woman broke contact. "I'll see you back at table, Your Excellency."

CHAPTER 33

Tsecha followed ná Feyó back into the meeting room. He could sense many sorts of emotions in the humanish he passed in the hallways. Discomfort. Surprise. Confusion. He understood their reactions. *They believe I have shown disloyalty to Shai and through her, to Cèel.* Some, such as Li Cao and Anais, rejoiced in this since they believed his behavior would lead to his recall to Shèrá. Others such as his Jani despaired, for the same reason.

And so it may be. Shai, now grown so mindful of humanish opinion, would retaliate, of that he felt most sure. *In the name of the worldskein,* she would entone as she condemned him. *In defense of order.* And so would Cèel support her in her decision, because he hated him so.

Tsecha lowered into his chair and looked about the room. Odd, to sit in this higher seat—he could see the tops of heads for the first time since his youth, before his ascension to Chief Propitiator. *Daès has a bald spot.* He bared his teeth at the discovery, but his enjoyment soon abated as less amusing thoughts intruded.

I should have challenged you before the war, Cèel. At least their animosity would have been well and truly declared. As it was now it felt an unfinished thing, like Dathim's half-formed shell. And so it would remain, if the fate his Jani feared came to pass. *Will Cèel kill me outright?* Or would he let Tsecha live in a death of his own devising, a sequestered existence spent knowing that the future that the gods had foretold would never come to pass?

"I looked for you, nìRau. I thought we should at least confer before this starts up again, seeing as I am your suborn."

Tsecha turned to find his Jani standing beside him. He looked into her eyes and joy filled his soul, expelling the despair. "Green as Oà—just as Dathim said!"

"Not dark enough yet. I have seen Oà, you know." She looked about the room, her posture tense, as though she watched for something. "I thought ní Dathim might attempt to attend this."

"He would not be allowed, nìa. He is not government Haárin." Tsecha gripped Jani's chin, turning her head so that he could again look into her eyes. Even the fact that they were colored the same as Cèel's could not diminish his delight. "You should not have hidden them for as long as you did."

"I may be sorry I didn't hide them longer." She winced and pulled his hand away. "Ouch."

"Ouch?" Tsecha slumped more formally. "Ah. Your graze gives you pain. Your inconsequential injury, which is as nothing and may thus be ignored."

"I never said it didn't hurt." Jani turned her neck one way, then the other, until bones cracked.

"Young Lescaux died trying to kill you. That is what ní Dathim told me." Tsecha looked toward Anais's still-empty chair. The call to return had been given some time ago—why had she not yet come? "If she did not hate you before, she most assuredly hates you now."

"Such is of no consequence."

Tsecha again regarded his Jani. Her voice sounded odd, as it had during their talk in the garden, days before. Devoid of inflection. Stripped of emotion. The sound of words struck on stone. "Nìa, what have you done?"

"No more than was necessary." She looked down at him. "And no less." She had bent over the table, her hands braced on the edge as though she needed the support. The posture caused the sleeves of her jacket to ride up her arms.

Tsecha touched the soulcloth encircling Jani's left wrist. The material felt stiff. "No more. And no less."

Jani lifted her hands from the table so that her sleeves slipped down. "Did you and the Elyan Haárin discuss any strategies to try to sway Shai's opinion away from isolationism?"

"How you change the subject, nìa, whenever you do not want to answer the question."

"At the moment, the answer to *my* question is more important."

Tsecha swept his right hand across the table. Not strictly a negative gesture, but not one that allowed for much hope either. "Shai does not wish the Haárin to trade with humanish, especially materials as sensitive as those that treat water. It is more blending than she can bear, and truly."

"It is a vast step." Feyó leaned forward so she could speak to them both. "Since we ourselves will not be drinking this water or attempting to reclaim the filter assemblies, we do not feel there is a violation of our dietary protocols. But nìaRauta Shai is born-sect, and as such is conservative in the extreme. We are at a loss, and truly, as to how to convince her to reconsider." She looked up at Jani and held out her hand. "Ná Kièrshia. It is a pleasure to meet you at last."

Jani hesitated before shaking hands. "Glories of the day to you, ná Feyó." She seemed to be trying not to smile, but since Feyó smiled at her, what difference could it make? "May your gods and mine allow for a seemly outcome to this muddle."

Then Anais Ulanova reentered the room, followed closely by Li Cao, and brought an end to all smiles. Cao held her hands in front of her, as would a youngish who reached for her parent. She appeared as surprised, even angry. Tsecha had seen her look as such before, but never had her good friend Anais been the cause for her alarm.

Tsecha watched the women take their seats, then he looked up the table at his Jani. She had already sat down, her balance easy and sure. *Angel on a pin.* She watched the women, as well, her face as stripped of feeling as her voice had been when she told Tsecha what she had done. *No more than was necessary.* Whatever that was.

Then Anais lifted her gaze. She and Jani looked at one another in that intense humanish way that said something had occurred between them. Tsecha tried to analyze the look, define it as his handheld defined words, but the challenge of spoken humanish language was as nothing compared to this, their language between the lines.

His pondering was interrupted when Daès returned, followed by Shai. The Suborn Oligarch offered him her own intensity, a subtle rounding of her shoulders that foretold the tone of their next encounter.

Papers shuffled. Shai's suborn raised her head to speak, a sign that decisions had been made and this meeting neared its end. "It is considered that the contract signed between the representatives of the Elyan Haárin enclave and they of the Commonwealth colony should be set—should be—" The suborn's voice faltered. The murmurs from the banked seats rose once more as Anais Ulanova raised her hand.

She did not sit straight and tall as she spoke, as she had before. Her words did not emerge strong, but came softly, almost as a whisper. Several times, the swell of sound from the other humanish overwhelmed her, compelling her to repeat herself. ". . . reconsidered the

Exterior position," she said as Cao watched her, her own confusion displaying itself in the constant working of her fingers. ". . . safety of the Karistos water supply is of paramount importance . . . needs of the citizenry. . . ."

Tsecha looked out at Burkett, who sat with his hand to his face, finger curled over his upper lip, his eyes on Jani. The other Cabinet suborns watched her as well, Standish from Treasury and all the others who found her during every recess or questioned her in the hallways. They did not appear triumphant, though. They did not seem pleased. Surprised, yes, as Shai appeared surprised, shoulders straightening in puzzlement as her suborn took notes, flowing script coursing across the surface of her recording board. For while it was Anais Ulanova who spoke as herself, it was Jani Kilian's words that she uttered, the same words heard in this room only a few days before. Words that Anais herself had denied as foolish and without merit.

Anais completed her mouthing of Jani's words. Then came the scratch of styli, the rustle of documents, the occasional swallowed cough.

The waiting.

Tsecha watched Shai. He had known her since their youngish days, when he lived at Temple and she schooled there. They had despised one another from their first meeting. But it had been a dull, simple dislike, not the pitched battle of wills and ideologies that would have led to an offer of challenge. Until now. *If you challenge my Jani, I will challenge you.* He watched her page through her documents using only her thumb and forefinger, as though she picked petals from a thorny bloom. *You even fear paper, Shai. How do you think to govern Haárin?*

"I am surprised, Your Excellency, at your most sudden change of mind," Shai finally said, after she had plucked the last of her pages. "I have known since my arrival of your distrust of idomeni, and I felt most sure of your decision in this."

Tsecha felt the clench in his soul as his shoulders rounded. "You hoped for her to take action so you would not have to take it yourself. You wished her distrust of idomeni to obscure your distrust of humanish and of your own Haárin. You are dishonest, Shai."

No murmurs followed Tsecha's words. No sound of any type, or movement, either. He could sense Jani's stare from downtable. But he knew that if he turned to her, she would try to compel him to silence, and now was not the time for such. She had already done what she felt was necessary, and bent Anais to her will. Now, it was his turn to bend Shai to his.

Shai's fingers shook as she reached for a piece of paper that she did not need. Such had been her way at Temple school, when she nursed her angers until they caused her stylus to shake and blot her writing. "Your opinion has no place here, Tsecha." Her voice shook as well, as it had always done. "Your right to speak for Vynshàrau is no more."

Tsecha gestured insignificance. Next to him, he could sense Feyó's surprise, the sudden spark of tension. "I have said already that I do not speak as ambassador."

"Then you will speak not."

"As Tsecha Égri, I will speak as Haárin. The Elyan Haárin traveled here to speak for themselves, therefore Haárin are allowed to speak!"

Shai's shoulders curved in extreme upset—if she had been humanish, one would think her violently ill. "You cannot speak as one, then the other, Tsecha—such is as ridiculous!"

Thank you, Shai—in your clumsiness, you provide me the opening I require. "But Vynshàrau and Haárin have always worked together, Shai. Haárin served us most well during the war of our ascendancy. Many of our military strategists have stated that without their assistance, we would not have won. That without their actions during the Night of the Blade, we would not have maintained that victory."

"Vynshàrau have always acknowledged the acts of Haárin, Tsecha. You are not the only one in this room who remembers the war. Godly though it was, it changed us all." Shai looked in Jani's direction, but so far had she come down the damned path of discretion that she did not mention Knevçet Shèràa. "We who honor our traditions wish to mend all that fractured during that time, and to reaffirm the pact between Vynshàrau and Haárin."

"Tradition." Tsecha tugged at his red-trimmed sleeves, as he had at every meeting. His own tradition—he took comfort in it now. "In our born-sect tradition of dominant and suborn, we offer respect for respect, protection for honor. Even as a dominant compels obedience, so must their domination be as godly, as seemly. We do not misuse our suborns as humanish have at times misused those who served them." That comment drew a rise of discontent from the banked seats, but such did not bother Tsecha. He liked humanish a great deal, but he had read their histories and he knew their faults. "We reserve that misuse for our Haárin. We send them to fight when it suits us. To kill. To die. We send them into this city, demand that they forfeit their souls so that our utilities function and our gardens

remain alive. And then when they take one action to help themselves maintain the life they have, we demand that they cease, because we suddenly fear them when they do what they do."

"To live with humanish!" Shai's humanish restraint shattered. She bowed her back and twisted her neck in an extreme exclamation of outrage as Tsecha had not seen since Temple. "To sell them the mechanisms of our food and water!" She flicked her hand in disgust at the Elyan Haárin. "To dress as they do, talk and act as they do! To behave in godless ways and then come here and demand our benediction as they do so!"

As one, Feyó and the other Elyan Haárin slumped into postures of extreme defense. "Such have we always done!" cried the male in black and orange.

Tsecha raised a hand, gesturing for the male to restrain himself. "Indeed. Such have they always done. The Haárin serve as our blade, and a blade does no good in its sheath. It only serves when it cuts, even when it cuts the one who wields it. Such is as it is—it knows no other way!" He sagged back in his chair—the act of blessed disputation drained so. "To live as idomeni is to live in balance. Within our skeins, our sects, our worldskein, all must be as symmetrical. Cooperation occurs, even between the most opposite. Differences are acknowledged, but they do not eliminate collaboration. Or as the humanish say, give and take." He bared his teeth at the phrase, since it reminded him of Hansen.

"Our gods do so," he continued. "Give and take. Shiou and Caith have walked together on the Way since the birth of the First Star. They battle, yes. Such is their way. But for one to live without the other? Such desolation! How could one define themselves if the other did not exist?" He held his hands out to Shai in entreaty. *Think! As you have not done since Temple, think!* "How does the order of Vynshàrau define itself if the chaos of Haárin does not exist? And if you compel Haárin to draw back into the worldskein, to cease to function as our blade, where is our balance?" His hands dropped. So quickly he had lost the will to argue, but how long could he posit that air was to be inhaled with one who insisted upon holding her breath? "So speaks the priest, which I will be for not much longer, if Cèel has his way. Yet so I speak, regardless. Order must be maintained, and if the Haárin are not allowed to do as they must, then so ends order. Will you end order here, Shai? In this room, now, will you cause it to cease to be?"

Shai had gradually straightened as Tsecha spoke. Not, he knew, because his words did not anger her, but because her bones were old and she could not maintain the true posture of rage. "You have had your life to practice twisting words as rope around your adversary's neck, Tsecha. One who has not studied as you have suffers a disadvantage." She fingered the edge of a document, tapped the end of her stylus on the table, delayed as humanish delayed when the last thing they wanted to do was decide. "If these filters are provided to the Karistos humanish, they will be gone from us. It will be as though they never existed."

Feyó's back unbent gradually. "Indeed, nìaRauta, such is so. The assemblies will be turned over to the humanish engineers to reconstruct as they will—we will never see them again."

Shai sat in silence, until humanish fidgeted and sneaked glances at their timepieces. But in the end, she acceded to the will of the gods, because she was a most orderly Vynshàrau, and as such, it was the only thing she could do.

They stood outside the meeting room afterward, in the huddled groups that humanish always formed after such occasions. Tsecha watched them gather, break apart, then gather once more. *Like mist into droplets,* Hansen had used to say. *Just watch out for the flood.*

"I still don't believe they gave the OK. Shai was one baby-step away from adjourning the meeting." Standish pushed a hand through his hair, which had grown more curly and unruly in the heat of the embassy.

"She really didn't have a choice. Neither of them did." Jani leaned against the wall. Her eyes had dulled. She looked as tired, as pained. "The citizens of one of the largest colonial capitals go without potable water because a Family sweetheart deal prevents them from implementing the quick-fix? That's a kick in the head to every pro-colonial claim the government has made since the spring, and they can't afford to act that way anymore."

"They saw the light?" Burkett wiped a cloth over his face, which shone with sweat. His hair looked as though he had walked in rain. "*Somebody* saw *something*, and it sure as hell wasn't the light. I can't carry tales of smoke-filled rooms back to Mako, Kilian—I need to know what the hell is going on."

Jani's wearied manner did not alter as she regarded the angry general. She had seen him enraged so many times—perhaps she had grown used to such. "What would any intelligent being consider to be the desired outcome of this?" She waited for Burkett to respond, even though she must have known that he would not. "A working water treatment facility for Karistos, right? Well, we'll have it if we keep on top of it, and I gave nothing away. That's goal in this game, by any measure." She pushed off the wall and walked to Tsecha, her step slow. "If you'll excuse us." She took his arm and pulled him down the hall. "Let's see—how much trouble are you in now?" she asked when they had walked far enough away to not be overheard.

Tsecha looked back at their group, which had already re-coalesced. Other droplets formed nearby, with members moving from one to another quite freely. *The flood begins . . .* "My theology is quite sound, nìa."

"Yes, I'm sure it is. Shai has probably already Misty'd a recording to the Temple scholars with an order to come up with a rebuttal immediately." She turned to watch Anais and PM Cao leave the meeting room; neither looked back at her. "The Elyan Haárin seemed quite pleased."

Tsecha bared his teeth. "We are to meet after early evening sacrament to discuss their situation."

"Their situation?" Jani smiled. "Congratulations, nìRau, you've become a lobbyist." She looked at him. Her true eyes had shown for but a short time, yet it seemed as if they had always been such. "You're lucky that Cèel can't afford trouble with the Haárin—their support may save your life. That life, however, may be very different from the one you have now."

Tsecha hesitated, then hunched his shoulders in a humanish shrug. "It is the life I am to have. The life on the edge of the blade." His soul ached as he pondered the quiet of the embassy, a quiet in which he took comfort, but that he had most assuredly sacrificed. "I will not be alone, nìa, of that I am most sure. You will be there, I believe, if only to anger General Burkett."

"That's a full-time job." Jani looked down at the floor. Some time passed before she spoke. "You still call me nìa. That's wrong—you should call me ná, in proper Haárin fashion."

"I shall call you as I wish, *nìa.*"

Her eyes brightened. Her idomeni eyes. "Does that mean I can still call you Nema?"

Tsecha gripped her chin and tilted her head upward. Gently this time, in deference to her pain. "That is not my name."

Jani's eyes filled, mist into droplets. "You know how to reach me, just in case." She lifted his hand away, squeezing it just before she let it go. "Be careful, ní Tsecha."

Tsecha watched her walk away. Her strange colonel waited in the entry for her. Pierce, who seemed so much as Dathim. *We each have our blade, and truly.* He wondered whether he would soon have need of his.

* * *

Tsecha met with the Elyan Haárin several times over the next days. He greatly esteemed ná Feyó. She was first-generation Haárin, an agronomist who had been expelled from the Academy before the war. They discussed her theories from sunrise to sunset and beyond. How the idomeni insistence on grown food played a major role in holding back their colonial expansion, how synthesized foods as those humanish used offered the best solution to this problem. Such discourse thrilled him, terrified him, and told him how much he needed to learn to consider himself true Haárin.

The morning the Elyan Haárin departed, Tsecha rose to bid them well. He stood out on the beach in the cold damp as their demiskimmer took to the air and veered toward HollandPort, watching it until it vanished in the glare of the rising sun. When he turned back to the embassy, he did not feel surprise to see Shai's suborn waiting for him atop the grassy rise. He only wondered why Shai delayed as long as she had.

"Seat yourself, Tsecha." Shai sat at her work table, the latest delivery of Council documents stacked in piles around her. "So, your Haárin have departed."

"They are not my Haárin, Shai."

"Are they not?" She looked at him, her posture still as clenched as it had been days before. "Whose are they, then? Not mine. That I know, and truly." She paged through one file, then another, as though what she sought was so unimportant that she had lost it. Tsecha had often seen Anais Ulanova do the same—he wondered if Shai had stolen the strategy from her.

Shai finally found what she searched for at the bottom of a high stack of files. She must have worked quite hard, to lose the fate of her Chief Propitiator so completely. "Cèel is most angry with you."

Tsecha squirmed against the seat back. The discomfort of Shai's seat aggravated him, for he had grown used to the comfort of Haárin chairs over the past days. "Such does not surprise me."

"So angry is he that he did not record his own pronouncement of your fate. He had his documents suborn write it out, and sent it to me to read."

Tsecha laughed. "He thinks he can mislead the gods by obscuring his trail! How humanish he becomes!" His laughter grew even more as Shai's back hunched. "Pronounce my fate, Shai. In Cèel's words, which he denies before they are even uttered."

Shai hesitated before she spoke. When the words sounded at last, they came quickly, as Vynshàrau, showing that Cèel had not yet lost himself completely. "Haárin you say you are. Therefore Haárin you will be, from this time forth." She closed the file, and pushed it away as though the contents repelled her. "You bring disorder upon us, Tsecha. Chaos. Never has a Chief Propitiator been expelled from office. The humanish will believe us mad."

"The humanish can match us, madness for madness. Some may even wonder why Cèel waited so long." Tsecha regarded his red-trimmed cuffs for the last time. "NìaRauta Sànalàn is not ready."

"Lecturers from Temple will arrive as soon as their absences can be arranged. They will see to her instruction."

"And you will continue here as ambassador?"

"Until Cèel chooses a replacement, yes."

Tsecha took one breath, then another. Haárin breath, inhaled by an outcast. He stood, slipped off the overrobe of his office, and draped it across Shai's desk. "I look forward to sitting at table with you in many meetings to come, Shai. You will wish you had killed me, and truly." Then he left before she could pronounce more of Cèel's anger, and returned to his rooms to claim the few objects he wished to keep.

He crossed the veranda for the last time as the humanish sun ascended to prime. Walked across the lawns. Disappeared into the trees. He had packed his few possessions in a carryall that he wore slung across his shoulders, in imitation of Feyó's suborns. He had changed his clothes, trading his crisp off-white for dark and worn. Black shirt. Brown trousers. Black boots. He would obtain colors as soon as he could, dress in blues and greens and oranges. But for now, he walked as shadow.

They awaited him in the lane, Beyva and the rest, welcoming him with smiles and greetings and laughter. They herded around him and pushed him onward, as the sea pushed the wave, toward the house in which they had gathered a seeming age of evenings ago. Dathim stood in the entry, brightly clothed, ax-hammer gripped in his hand.

"We have been waiting for you, Tsecha. We, the embassy's blade!" Dathim stepped aside and gestured for him to step forward. "Your house has been waiting for you."

Tsecha stopped short. "*Your* house, ní Dathim."

"No, this is not my house, ní Tsecha. Mine is that one." Dathim pointed to a smaller dwelling at the far end of the lane, near the base of the grassy rise. "This house"—he patted the side of the entry—"this house has been empty for some time. I have labored to prepare it for he who would live here."

Tsecha took a step forward. Another. He touched the entry stonework, and pondered what he knew of this place. A place blessed by annihilation and adorned with the dunes of Knevçet Shèràa. A place of meeting, and rebellion, and change.

"It is a good house, and truly." He touched the reliquary, muttered a prayer, and walked inside.

CHAPTER 34

"Do you know who's going to be at this thing, besides the Commonwealth Cup semifinalists? Everybody. Absolutely *everybody*!" Angevin dug through the pile of gowns on Jani's bed, flinging about expensive fabrics like used dispos.

"I already know what I'm going to wear. Bought it last week. Fits perfectly." Jani sat on the floor in front of the dresser, well out of range of flying dresses. "You've had a week to prep for this. I kept telling you, 'Go shopping.' "

"*When?* This place has been a zoo ever since the conclave." Angevin stretched out a gold column gown on the bed and eyed it skeptically. "First, the move." She gestured vaguely around the larger bedroom, with its tenth-floor cityscape view. "Security in and out all week, installing things. Then the workload. You get any more two-hundred-page Cabinet contracts, you're going to have to charter someone to close out your books at the end of the year."

"I planned on doing that anyway." Jani walked to her closet and took out her own choice for the evening. "Dolly recommended a firm that Registry uses. They cost a mint, and they're reputed to be real pains in the ass. Chances are good that they're as honest as you'll get in Chicago and no one could persuade them to set me up on an embezzlement charge."

"You're worried about that?" Angevin dragged her gown to one side so Jani would have room to set out her own outfit.

"Worried, no. Ever mindful, yes." Jani took her clothes from their wrappings and laid them out. "The old-fashioned frame-up seems to be the standard way of doing business in this city, and I'll be damned if I'm going to make it easy for somebody." She swept the sea-blue sari across the silvery pants and top. "What do you think?"

"I could cry." Angevin whimpered as she stroked the turquoise silk. "How are you going to wear your eyes?"

Jani grinned. The question had become a point of fun between them, as well as a way to help everyone, herself included, adjust to the change. "Clothed, I think. It's not an official government function and I don't feel like being gawped at. Not that I may not be anyway, but why ask for it?" She walked to the dresser and picked through the multitude of packages her mother had brought her from Acadia. "I need to decide on jewelry," she said as she liberated a huge padded bag from the collection.

Angevin gasped as Jani unfastened the bag's flaps and opened it like a book, revealing row after row of gems and metal. Platinum earrings and rings. Gold bracelets. "My God!" She held up a necklace of hammered gold discs. "When are you supposed to wear all this?"

"My wedding day. All in one shot." Jani chuckled at Angevin's shocked look. "You never heard the term 'more metal than an Acadian wedding'? A bride was supposed to wear her dowry on her back. You should see the daughters from wealthy families—they can barely move for the gold. I remember when I was little, seeing holos of a bride who had to be floated up to the altar on a skimdolly." She examined a pair of aquamarine teardrop earrings. "Course, this stuff isn't worth near as much now as it was when the tradition began. But it's bright and shiny and custom dictates that it matters."

They both started as the comport buzzer blatted; Angevin glowered at the extension unit on Jani's end table. "Let Steve get it. If I never again see another begging, pleading face on a display, I'll survive quite happily." She hefted a gold-link bracelet and mouthed a *wow*. "Isn't it bad luck to wear this stuff before your wedding or something?"

"Oh, I think all bets are off where that's concerned. When your folks turn it over to you, it becomes yours to do with as you please." Jani perused her nuptial stockpile with a hand pressed to her forehead. "I think I'm going to make do with about five percent of this, so Maman can ask me why I'm not wearing anything." She set aside the aquamarine earrings, the huge stones set in platinum, and the matching collar-like necklace. Then she added an array of gold and platinum bracelets because she liked how the wide bands covered the *à lérine* scars on her forearms.

"You're going to look *so* exotic, and I'm going to look like I should be parking skimmers." Angevin glared at the door as a knock sounded. She bundled her dress over her arm and hurried to answer it.

"Hey, don't leave this stuff—!" Jani stopped in mid-sentence when she saw Steve standing in the doorway, an anxious-looking Lt. Pullman at his back.

"That was Val on the com." Steve grinned. "You need to get to Neoclona right away."

"We started picking up the increased neuronal activity as soon as we flushed out the regen solutions and unjacked the shunt." Dr. Wismuth, one of the many neurologists Jani had come to know, was short and round and bobbed like a happy balloon down the hall ahead of her. "Then we began what we call our systems checks—somatic, visual, auditory, etc. . . ." She pushed the door to the room aside before it had a chance to open completely, ignoring the warning buzzer. "We've noted some issues with visual acuity that may or may not repair themselves. Her speech is slurred. She remembers nothing that happened the day of the assault"—Wismuth's bubbling ebbed—"which isn't entirely bad." She beckoned for Jani to follow her into the darkened room. "Her head is still restrained, and will be for a few more days. She's still swaddled. We don't normally allow visitors other than immediate family at this stage, but I know you've been here every day since she arrived, and Val insisted that you had a right to know." She stepped aside, allowing Jani a clear path to the bed.

The headboard blinked and fluttered less now that the shunt had been removed and Roni had regained some level of consciousness. Her hands moved constantly, fingers first flexing, then bending, then straightening as though she pointed. The part of her face that was visible held a tense, knitted expression, as though she suffered a severe headache. Considering what Jani recalled of her own post-shunt return to consciousness, she probably did.

Then Roni's eyes, mere slits due to the swelling caused by the shunt, opened. She moved her mouth like an infant trying to vocalize. The rate of her hand movements increased. The psychotropic headboard blinked and fluttered more rapidly. Jani hung back, her heart in her throat and her hands clenched in her pockets, until Dr. Wismuth pushed her forward. "You need to move up—all you are is a blur from this distance."

"Sorry." Jani stepped closer to the bed, and hoped Wismuth couldn't see the tears running down her cheeks. *Sorry. Sorry. Sorry.*

"Jah—" Roni's agitated movements slowed. A corner of her mouth twitched. " 'lo."

"Hello." Jani coughed to loosen her tightening chest. "I won't ask how you feel. I know how you feel."

Roni blew out a very weak snort. "Yah. Head hur'. Stup' shunt." Her mouth curved a little more. "Mom here. Da. Helluva way to ge' a vis-it." Her hand movements increased again. "Thinkin'. Some'en wron'. Luu-sheen. Peeth-aah. Bot' blon.' Col' eyes." Then the motion slowed again. Her face relaxed as though she slept.

Wismuth tugged on Jani's sleeve. "Does that mean something? She's been repeating it for hours."

Jani nodded. "It concerns the matter we were working on the day of the assault. We were trying to determine an identity with a very sparse physical description."

"Oh, this is good, yes!" Wismuth bustled toward the door, barely avoiding a collision with Val in the entry.

"Wiz is wearing her note-taking face." Val sauntered up to Jani and wrapped his arms around her. He wore a green plaid shirt—he pressed her face to his shoulder and patted the back of her head. "It's absorbent—go ahead."

Jani hugged him back. "If I had—"

"I don't want to hear any ifs out of you, remember?" Val pushed her back so he could look her in the face. "She can hear us. If you're going to beat yourself up, we need to go someplace else." He glanced at the bed. "We should leave anyway—that woman needs her rest."

They walked into the hall, arms around each other's waists. Jani blinked as the bright lights struck her and she felt the old familiar tightening of her eyefilms. "What's the prognosis?"

"At this stage, a hell of a lot better than average." Val hugged her again. "I won't go into gory details, but judging from the severity of that blow she suffered, she's lucky she stayed alive long enough to get here."

"Lucky I finally found her, you mean."

"Jan, we still know very little about what happened that night, and until we do, I wish you'd stick the guilt back in the box." Val slowed to a stop, gripped Jani by the shoulders, and turned her to face him. "She's alive. She's lucid. The vast majority of her responses to stimuli fall within normal variation. She suffered less serious cerebral damage than you did. You were out for almost five weeks, not five days, and look how you turned out. Given time, she stands a great chance of making a full and complete recovery."

Jani exhaled with a shudder. "Her personality—"

"Initial signs look good, but we won't know the fine detail for weeks." Val shook her gently, in deference to her mending collarbone.

"Let's discuss some items that we do know. You saved her life. You could have died in the process. The two things that saved you both are that she's a very lucky young woman and you're a medical wonder." His green-brown eyes shone with a hard light. "Give yourself a break, for once in your damned life. Not everything that happens to everyone you know is your fault." He hugged her again, and they continued walking. "You going to the party tonight?"

Jani shrugged. "I guess."

Val nodded with medical finality. "You better. You should have a great time, a wonderful time." He led her to the lift that would take her down to the garages. "Then tomorrow morning, you should come back here and tell Roni all about it. It'll do you both good." He shoved her gently into the open cabin, in which Pullman already stood waiting. "Now go."

Pullman escorted her to the VIP level. He looked the gentle giant in his dress blue-greys; it was hard to believe he carried enough firepower on his person to flatten a fair-sized building. "Good news, ma'am?" He popped the rear gullwing of Jani's latest conveyance, a dark red four-door.

"Yes. Good news." Jani slipped into the backseat, and smiled up at Pullman as he closed her in. *She's alive . . . she's lucid . . . we talked a little. I'll tell her all about the party in the morning.* Yes, she would. Oh yes, she would.

"Janila, look at all this food!" Jamira held her plate in front of her like a barrier. Then she edged closer to Jani and dropped her voice. "Can you eat any of it?"

"Some of it, Maman." Jani looked over the banked tables, a stationary feast moored by goldware and crystal and candlesticks the size of Pullman's forearms. "I just don't know where to start."

"Allow me." John Shroud took the plate from Jani's hands and filled it. He wore a smart evening suit in pearl grey and had filmed his eyes to match; the tempered light of the ballroom softened his spectral edge. "Good evening, Mère Kilian," he rumbled with a host's smile. "Are you having a good time?"

"Yes, Dr. Shroud." Jamira's smile stayed true, her truce with John still in place. "How Declan and I danced. Such wonderful music, waltzes and à deux. Now he is in the other room, watching football holos and stuttering like a young boy in the presence of Le Vieux Rouge."

John looked back at Jani, near-invisible eyebrows arched in question.

"The Old Red. Acadia Central United's nickname." Jani took the plate from him and stared at the numerous tiny servings of meats, breads, and hors d'oeuvres. "You expect me to eat this tonight?"

"It's just a little of everything."

"I think *everything* is the key word." Jani used a two-pronged fork to skewer a shrimp the size of her finger as she surveyed the huge ballroom. "I saw the PM a little while ago."

"She made one pass through the room and left. Anais sent her regrets this morning. The people I spoke with who asked about you seemed eager to talk to you. The usual Ministers, along with business leaders anxious about the Haárin influx. So in answer to your unasked question, no, I don't believe there's anyone here you need to avoid." John looked down at her and smiled. "See, I can be useful."

"I never said you couldn't." Jani stuffed the shrimp in her mouth to forestall further conversation, then turned as a familiar babble of voices sounded from behind.

"My dear, you look lovely!" Jamira handed Steve her plate so she could offer silent applause for Angevin's golden gown.

"Oh, so do you!" Angevin touched the gold-trimmed edge of Jamira's fuchsia sari, which flowed over trousers and top of muted gold. Behind her, Steve stood in his basic black evening suit and juggled his and Jamira's plates. He glanced at Jani and rolled his eyes as Angevin and Jamira fell into animated conversation.

Jani felt a hand touch her shoulder, and turned to find John beckoning for her to follow him. They walked to a small pedestal table near the dividing line between the dining and the dancing. Couples in rainbow eveningwear swirled past as the music swelled, forcing them to bend close together so they could hear one another.

John had gotten a drink, something caramel-colored and potent-looking, like the bourbon Evan van Reuter used to imbibe incessantly. "I assume your folks are staying?"

"Do they have a choice?" Jani looked out over the Commerce Ministry ballroom, an immense space with high tiered ceilings, chandeliers, and walls of french doors leading out to terraces and gardens. "They can't go back to Acadia. I think they realized that the day they bugged out. Maman brought my dowry jewelry and all her family holos and mementoes. Papa brought most of his tools and handheld instruments. Niall has them in his sights—they've got round-the-clock protection although I don't think they realize what that means." She studied the milling diners and dancers, on the lookout for the waiter who strayed near, the gowned woman who asked for the time. Watchers all, guardians all, shadows all, courtesy of Niall Pierce, who currently resided in a command center in a nether part of the building and rode herd over a score of Cabinet and Family security forces. "I never thanked you for taking care of them."

"No need." John bent closer, until their arms touched. "You ask—I comply. Or haven't you figured that out yet?" His voice seemed to emerge from the very air surrounding them. "That's all you have to do. Just ask. It's very simple."

"No, it isn't."

"Of course it is. All it takes is practice. 'John, do this. John, attend.' "

John, take over my life. Jani kept that thought to herself. John was better at that sort of argument than she. The only sure way to fend him off would be to say something cutting, and she didn't want to spoil the evening that way. The music, the lights, and the color combined to make a storybook setting and she wanted to enjoy it, if only as a spectator.

She let her gaze drift over the heads of the dancers, to the view through the french doors. The night air chilled, but assorted weather barriers had made the terrace a haven for those in search of respite from the noise and glitter. At first, she ignored the distant glimmer of white as it drew near the windows, taking it for a guest returning from a wander among the trees. Then the figure walked into the full blaze of light that flooded the terrace, and her heart skipped.

Lucien stepped up to the doors and scanned the interior scene. He wore drop-dead whites, the gold shoulder boards and looped braids snagging the light and slicing it into metallic rainbows. He stiffened like a hunting dog on point when he spotted her, but instead of entering the ballroom immediately, he held back. One hand on the door catch, eyes on her, like the soldier in her painting, he stood still and straight and awaited his mistress's pleasure.

After a moment that seemed like nothing and like forever, Jani smiled. Only then did Lucien open the door. He strode the perimeter of the ballroom, chased by stares, the light of the chandeliers shimmering off his silvery head.

John's voice sounded like distant thunder. "What the hell is he doing here?"

"Good evening." Lucien set his brimmed lid atop the table, and immediately nabbed a glass of juice from a passing waiter. "My God, I haven't seen a scrum like this since Cao's granddaughter's wedding last year."

John didn't appear impressed with that social credential. "I don't recall your name on this invitation list, Pascal."

"I'm a late addition, sir. To Colonel Pierce's security team."

Lucien raised his non-alcoholic glass. "I'm on duty." He looked from John to Jani, added two and two, and nailed four. Eyes flashing cold, he set down his drink and held out his hand to Jani. "Care to dance, ma'am?"

Jani pretended to ponder, until she saw the hand waver and uncertainty flicker in those chill eyes. Only then did she take Lucien's hand and let him lead her out on the floor. "Are you really a member of Niall's security?" she asked after they had picked up the step to the à deux that the orchestra played.

"He signed me up because I used to work for Ani. I think he was concerned she might try to pull something. Or maybe he was concerned I might try to pull something."

"Is dancing with me on the duty list? I didn't check."

"We're all supposed to keep an eye on you. What better way?" Lucien stepped back and gave her a lengthy head to toe examination. "You look beautiful."

"Thank you." Jani drank in that inestimable face. "So do you."

"Hmm." Lucien pulled her close. "You covered your eyes."

Jani tried to ignore the press of his body against hers, a feat she didn't quite manage. "Niall and I worked out a protocol. Official government functions where I'm acting in some sort of intermediary capacity for the idomeni, the films come off. Purely social stuff, like this, they stay on."

"How about if the person you're with simply prefers you without them?"

Jani felt the blush rise. She hoped Lucien wasn't close enough to feel it, too. She looked toward the table, where John watched them, drink in hand, and steered until she had turned her back to him.

Lucien hugged Jani closer. "How—are you?" For the first time, his voice sounded stilted, rehearsed, as though it was a question he had never asked before. Her beautiful, fractured prince.

This princess isn't so intact herself. Jani rested her cheek on his shoulder. The polywool felt pleasantly rough. "Fine." The orchestra played Eduard, and she savored the rise and fall of the strings. "Usual aches and pains."

"Umm." Lucien sounded like he knew the feeling. "I assume you heard about Tsecha."

"Yes. Considering all Cèel could have done, he got off easy. But he wanted it. I think he decided that becoming true Haárin was the best way for him to work toward his new order."

"Well, like everything he does, his new order means more work for everybody. They've signed me up for another class. Haárin Language Protocols—what a surprise." Lucien paused. "It's next week."

Jani grinned. "Is it?"

"Yeah." Lucien sighed. "I guess I'll have to get to know our friendly in-city BOQ."

"I guess you will."

"Heard you moved upstairs to a bigger flat."

"Yes."

"Hmm." Lucien tried another angle of approach. "Is dinner out of the question?"

Jani counted to ten before answering. "Dinner's fine."

"Then that will have to do, I guess." He pulled her closer. "For now." His fingers fluttered along the seam of her fitted top. "This opens up along the side."

They finished that dance, and the next, and the next. The monster prince and his changeling princess, in a world where survival was a happy ending and you took your magic where you found it. By the time they returned to the table for Lucien's lid, John had departed, the only signs of his presence three glasses depleted of their contents and a linen napkin crumpled into a tight ball.

After being introduced to Jamira and impressing her mightily, Lucien took his leave to return to the command center. Jani made rounds, talked with the people who had been anxious to meet her, and kept a daughterly eye on her parents, who appeared ready to waltz, eat, and talk until the last candle guttered to extinction.

She finally broke away, taking refuge in a secluded hallway that was far enough away from the ballroom to discourage casual visitation. She found a narrow windowseat, wedged into it, and watched the activity on the terrace.

"How are you holding up?"

Jani turned to find Niall standing in a doorway. Since his job kept him behind the scenes, he had opted for dress blue-greys rather than the more formal whites. He looked as tired as she felt. A half-smoked 'stick dangled from his lips. "I would have to say, Colonel, that I have just about reached my limit."

Niall took the 'stick from his mouth and studied it. "I know just what you need." He pulled a handcom from his pocket and barked a few terse orders. "Follow me, please, ma'am," he said as he repocketed the device.

They exited through a side door. Pullman waited for them with the skimmer of the day, a black two-door. They closed themselves in, and Niall steered into the early morning quiet.

"If you want to change . . . ?" He reached behind his seat and pulled out a small duffel. "I've got a set of casuals. You'll swim in them, but they might be more comfortable than that get-up." He glanced at her sidelong and grinned in bemusement. "Never saw so much damned metal in my life."

"You should see all the stuff I didn't wear." Jani piled into the backseat and unclasped earrings and bracelets, then paused as she unpinned her sari. "You know, if an enterprising reporter gets holos of this, I'll entertain Chicago for at least a month." That kept them both laughing until they left the city behind.

They drove through Bluffs neighborhoods that Jani recognized, then down darker streets that she didn't, finally ending up on a dirt trail that led down to a secluded stretch of beach.

"Belongs to a friend." Niall popped both gullwings and walked out onto the sand, unclasping the neck of his tunic along the way. As he activated an underground fuel vent, Jani gathered wood and leaves and heaped them around the outlet. After she finished, Niall activated a 'stick and tossed it on the pile. The fire sputtered, then caught when he increased the fuel flow. He and Jani lowered to the seat offered by a convenient log, and watched the flames.

"Haven't seen you much these past few days." Niall braced his ti-etops against the fire containment ring. "How are you?"

"Fine." Jani uncovered a stick that had been buried in the sand and poked at the fire.

Niall picked up a pinecone and tossed it from hand to hand. "When my love swears that she is made of truth, I do believe her, though I know she lies."

Jani racked her brain for the titles of all the books Niall had lent her that she'd never read. "More Keats?"

He mimed throwing the pinecone at her head. "Shakespeare. Sonnet 138. I keep meaning—"

"—to lend me the sonnets." Jani scooted nearer the fire and rubbed her cold hands. "There was one thing of his that you lent me that I read, and it stuck with me." She raised one finger like an instructor's pointer. "Exit, pursued by a bear."

"That's from *The Winter's Tale.*" Niall emitted a bear-like growl himself. "That's not what I had in mind."

"No, but it is remarkably descriptive of my life thus far." Jani stared into the flames, the heat pulling the moisture from her films. "It just might remain so."

Niall made as though to speak, but before he could, something in his tunic beeped. "Excuse me." He pulled out his handcom and listened, then muttered an "Out" and stashed it away again. "We're going to have company."

Jani let her head drop between her knees. "You want to hear me whine like Angevin, don't you?"

Niall smiled. "Oh, somehow I don't think you'll mind." He rose and walked toward the water.

The lights began as pinpoints far to the south. As they neared, Jani picked up the blue sidelights, as well. Lakeskimmer lights. She rose to join Niall. "You called him?"

Niall turned around and tossed the pinecone in the fire, where it sizzled and flared. "I thought you could use some cheering up."

The lakeskimmer drew close and slowed to a hover. Tsecha stood up in his seat while next to him, Dathim worked to hold the craft level. *"Nìa! It is pretty damned cold out here!"*

"It's warm by the fire!" Jani swatted her head of security when he burst out laughing. They stepped out to the water's edge to grab hold of the skimmer and guide it ashore. As Jani walked around to the pilot's side, she looked up at Dathim. He stared back, the arrogant cast of their first meeting absent. Then he nodded, once, a motion so slight as to be almost undetectable.

"I have not sat at a fire such as this since I schooled at Temple." Tsecha clambered over the side of the skimmer and strode along the sand. "We would sit and tell one another of our homes, and the cities from where we had come." He wore a shirt that matched the blue sidelights in color and brightness, dark green trousers, and covered it all with the same brown coat he had worn during his first city expedition with Dathim. He had wrapped his head, as well, with a length of green cloth. "We shall do that," he said as he dragged another log seat closer to the fire. "We shall talk of the cities from where we came, then we will talk of the cities to which we will go."

And so they did, until the rising sun backlit the lake horizon. Every so often, sparks shot up from the fire and spread across the sky, like new stars looking for a home.

Appendix

Transcript of conversation appended to Patient File S-1.
Participant key: JS-John Shroud; ED-
Eamon DeVries; VP-Valentin Parini
<start conversation>

JS: Eamon, have you sent your comments on Jani's prostheses to her file? Staff meeting's in an hour—I want to evaluate your findings before we sit.

ED: You'll be evaluating *my* findings? Since when? You handle the genetics muck, I play with the gadgets and flashing lights, remember?

JS: Just send me the updates.

ED: <pause> Fine—see attached. As you can no doubt conclude from the stress and balance scans—adept as you are at your new-found specialty—she needs a new left arm and leg.

JS: <pause> We just switched out limbs a few months ago.

ED: <laughter> Yes, well, she's a growing gel, John. No matter what your experts do to try and slow her down, she brushes it off and continues on her merry hybrid way.

JS: We can discuss that at the meeting—I have a few ideas—

ED: Filled to the brim with ideas, aren't you, Johnny? Just like the first day we met. Ah, will I ever forget it? Me pushing through the crowds at the Rauta Shèràa shuttleport, on the lookout for that white head of yours and not finding it. Then just when I figured you'd stood me up, you emerged from the shadows. Somber as a judge pronouncing sentence, you were, with your hellbound pup at your heels.

VP: Thanks, Eamon.

ED: Ah, Valentin. I wondered when you'd speak up. But you always did wait to gauge your master's mood before opening your mouth.

VP: Bit of a son of a bitch yourself, aren't you? You came soon enough when John called, just like you did twenty years ago. "For the thrill and the hell of it." Isn't that what you said in Rauta Shèràa? "For the joy of sticking it to Morden nìRau Cèel."

JS: I think we've all grown beyond that, Val.

VP: No, we haven't. We've been battling Cèel ever since he tried to convince the Laumrau to reject our applications to work at the Rauta Shèràa consulate.

JS: Cèel tried to convince the Laumrau to block every application. He didn't trust any human who wanted to come to Shèrá. He's from the warrior skein—distrust is his job.

VP: Can the charitable assessment. Cèel knew why you wanted to work there, just like he knew why Eamon and I came when you called us. Nema's rumblings about a new universal order had just escaped Temple confines and made it out into the Commonwealth. You heard the stories at Oxbridge, same as I did at Harvard, and Eamon at Lyon. A hybrid race—the idea grabbed us by the collective throat and didn't let go until we banded together and made our own hash of it!

JS: Val? <pause> Why the nerves? What's bothering you?

ED: His conscience is gripping him, like it did in the basement. I always told him to leave it beneath the nearest lamppost where it belonged, but he never listened to me.

VP: It—it's just that now that I can see Jani every day . . . I see what she has to go through and I wonder if we did the right thing.

JS: Val, if we hadn't, she wouldn't be here today.

VP: I know, but—

ED: It's too late for regrets, boyo. Ten years ago you'd have been able to put the genie back in the bottle, but now any attempt to change Kilian back to fully human would kill her. She is what she is. John's labor of misplaced love, tumbled from her pedestal straight into the scrum of Commonwealth-idomeni politics. If you're looking for something to be sorry for, be sorry for that!

<end of conversation>

Kristine Smith is the author of *Rules of Conflict* and *Code of Conduct*. She works as a process development scientist for a large pharmaceutical manufacturer and lives in northern Illinois. Visit her website at *www.sff.net/people/ksmith.*